SIR WALTER SCOTT CLASSICS COLLECTION

Ivanhoe, The Lady of the Lake, Rob Roy

WALTER SCOTT

This work is a product of its time and place and may include values, images, events, and language that are offensive to modern sensibilities. Reader discretion is advised.

Ivanhoe: Originally published in 1819, this work by Sir Walter Scott (1771-1832) is in the public domain in the United States, United Kingdom, and other jurisdictions.

The Lady of the Lake: Originally published in 1809-10, this work by Sir Walter Scott (1771-1832) is in the public domain in the United States, United Kingdom, and other jurisdictions.

Rob Roy: Originally published in 1817, this work by Sir Walter Scott (1771-1832) is in the public domain in the United States, United Kingdom, and other jurisdictions.

No copyright claim is made with respect to public domain works.

This work reflects minor editorial revisions to the original texts.

Cover art features "Sir Walter Scott," 1830, by August Edouart (French, 1789-1861), courtesy of the Metropolitan Institute of Art, Open Access Public Domain.

CONTENTS

IVANHOE 1
THE LADY OF THE LAKE 311
ROB ROY 437

IVANHOE
A ROMANCE

IVANHOE

A ROMANCE

I.

> Thus communed these; while to their lowly dome,
> The full-fed swine return'd with evening home;
> Compell'd, reluctant, to the several sties,
> With din obstreperous, and ungrateful cries.
>
> — POPE'S ODYSSEY

In that pleasant district of merry England which is watered by the river Don, there extended in ancient times a large forest, covering the greater part of the beautiful hills and valleys which lie between Sheffield and the pleasant town of Doncaster. The remains of this extensive wood are still to be seen at the noble seats of Wentworth, of Warncliffe Park, and around Rotherham. Here haunted of yore the fabulous Dragon of Wantley; here were fought many of the most desperate battles during the Civil Wars of the Roses; and here also flourished in ancient times those bands of gallant outlaws, whose deeds have been rendered so popular in English song.

Such being our chief scene, the date of our story refers to a period towards the end of the reign of Richard I., when his return from his long captivity had become an event rather wished than hoped for by his despairing subjects, who were in the meantime subjected to every species of subordinate oppression. The nobles, whose power had become exorbitant during the reign of Stephen, and whom the prudence of Henry the Second had scarce reduced to some degree of subjection to the crown, had now resumed their ancient license in its utmost extent; despising the feeble interference of the English Council of State, fortifying their castles, increasing the number of their dependants, reducing all around them to a state of vassalage, and striving by every means in their power, to place themselves each at the head of such forces as might enable him to make a figure in the national convulsions which appeared to be impending.

The situation of the inferior gentry, or Franklins, as they were called, who, by the law and spirit of the English constitution, were entitled to hold themselves independent of feudal tyranny, became now unusually precarious. If, as was most generally the case, they placed themselves under the protection of any of the petty kings in their vicinity, accepted of feudal offices in his household, or bound themselves by mutual treaties of alliance and protection, to support him in his enterprises, they might indeed purchase temporary repose; but it must be with the sacrifice of that independence which was so dear to every English bosom, and at the certain hazard of being involved as a party in whatever rash expedition the ambition of their protector might lead him to undertake. On the other hand, such and so multiplied were the means of vexation and oppression possessed by the great Barons, that they never wanted the pretext, and seldom the will, to harass and pursue, even to the very edge of destruction, any of their less powerful neighbours, who attempted to separate themselves from their authority, and to trust for their protection, during the dangers of the times, to their own inoffensive conduct, and to the laws of the land.

A circumstance which greatly tended to enhance the tyranny of the nobility, and the sufferings of the inferior classes, arose from the consequences of the Conquest by Duke William of Normandy. Four generations had not sufficed to blend the hostile blood of the Normans and Anglo-Saxons, or to unite, by common language and mutual interests, two hostile races, one of which still felt the elation of triumph, while the other groaned under all the consequences of defeat. The power had been completely placed in the hands of the Norman nobility, by the event of the battle of Hastings, and it had been used, as our histories assure us, with no moderate hand. The whole race of Saxon princes and nobles had been extirpated or disinherited, with few or no exceptions; nor were the numbers great who possessed land in the country of their fathers, even as proprietors of the second, or of yet inferior classes. The royal policy had long been to weaken, by every means, legal or illegal, the strength of a part of the population which was justly considered as nourishing the most inveterate antipathy to their victor. All the monarchs of the Norman race had shown the most marked predilection for their Norman subjects; the laws of the chase, and many others equally unknown to the milder and more free spirit of the Saxon constitution, had been fixed upon the necks of the subjugated inhabitants, to add weight, as it were, to the feudal chains with which they were loaded. At court, and in the castles of the great nobles, where the pomp and state of a court was emulated, Norman-French was the only language employed; in courts of law, the pleadings and judgments were delivered in the same tongue. In short, French was the language of honour, of chivalry, and even of justice, while the far more manly and expressive Anglo-Saxon was abandoned to the use of rustics and hinds, who knew no other. Still, however, the necessary intercourse between the lords of the soil, and those oppressed inferior beings by whom that soil was cultivated, occasioned the gradual formation of a dialect, compounded betwixt the French and the Anglo-Saxon, in which they could render themselves mutually intelligible to each other; and from this necessity arose by degrees the structure of our present English language, in which the speech of the victors and the vanquished have been so happily blended together; and which has since been so richly improved by importations from the classical languages, and from those spoken by the southern nations of Europe.

This state of things I have thought it necessary to premise for the information of the general reader, who might be apt to forget, that, although no great historical events, such as war or insurrection, mark the existence of the Anglo-Saxons as a separate people subsequent to the reign of William the Second; yet the great national distinctions betwixt them and their conquerors, the recollection of what they had formerly been, and to what they were now reduced, continued down to the reign of Edward the Third, to keep open the wounds which the Conquest had inflicted, and to maintain a line of separation betwixt the descendants of the victor Normans and the vanquished Saxons.

The sun was setting upon one of the rich grassy glades of that forest, which we have mentioned in the beginning of the chapter. Hundreds of broad-headed, short-stemmed, wide-branched oaks, which had witnessed perhaps the stately march of the Roman soldiery, flung their gnarled arms over a thick carpet of the most delicious green sward; in some places they were intermingled with beeches, hollies, and copsewood of various descriptions, so closely as totally to intercept the level beams of the sinking sun; in others they receded from each other, forming those long sweeping vistas, in the intricacy of which the eye delights to lose itself, while imagination considers them as the paths to yet wilder scenes of silvan solitude. Here the red rays of the sun shot a broken and discoloured light, that partially hung upon the shattered boughs and mossy trunks of the trees, and there they illuminated in brilliant patches the portions of turf to which they made their way. A considerable open space, in the midst of this glade, seemed formerly to have been dedicated to the rites of Druidical superstition; for, on the summit of a hillock, so regular as to seem artificial, there still remained part of a circle of rough unhewn stones, of large dimensions. Seven stood upright; the rest had been dislodged from their places, probably by the zeal of some convert to Christianity, and lay, some prostrate near their former site, and others on the side of the hill. One large stone only had found its way to the bottom, and in stopping the course of a small brook, which glided smoothly round the foot of the eminence, gave, by its opposition, a feeble voice of murmur to the placid and elsewhere silent streamlet.

The human figures which completed this landscape, were in number two, partaking, in their dress and appearance, of that wild and rustic character, which belonged to the woodlands of the West-Riding of Yorkshire at that early period. The eldest of these men had a stern, savage, and wild aspect. His garment was of the simplest form imaginable, being a close jacket with sleeves, composed of the tanned skin of some animal, on which the hair had been originally left, but which had been worn off in so many places, that it would have been difficult to distinguish from the patches that remained, to what creature the fur had belonged. This primeval vestment reached from the throat to the knees, and served at once all the usual purposes of body-clothing; there was no wider opening at the collar, than was necessary to admit the passage of the head, from which it may be inferred, that it was put on by slipping it over the head and shoulders, in the manner of a modern shirt, or ancient hauberk. Sandals, bound with thongs made of boars' hide, protected the feet, and a roll of thin leather was twined artificially round the legs, and, ascending above the calf, left the knees bare, like those of a Scottish Highlander. To make the jacket sit yet more close to the body, it was gathered at the middle by a broad leathern belt, secured by a brass buckle; to one side of which was attached a sort of scrip, and to the other a ram's horn, accoutred with a mouthpiece, for the purpose of blowing. In the same belt was stuck one of those long, broad, sharp-pointed, and two-edged knives, with a buck's-horn handle, which were fabricated in the neighbourhood, and bore even at this early period the name of a Sheffield whittle. The man had no covering upon his head, which was only defended by his own thick hair, matted and twisted together, and scorched by the influence of the sun into a rusty dark-red colour, forming a contrast with the overgrown beard upon his cheeks, which was rather of a yellow or amber hue. One part of his dress only remains, but it is too remarkable to be suppressed; it was a brass ring, resembling a dog's collar, but without any opening, and soldered fast round his neck, so loose as to form no impediment to his breathing, yet so tight as to be incapable of being removed, excepting by the use of the file. On this singular gorget was engraved, in Saxon characters, an inscription of the following purport:—"Gurth, the son of Beowulph, is the born thrall of Cedric of Rotherwood."

Beside the swine-herd, for such was Gurth's occupation, was seated, upon one of the fallen Druidical monuments, a person about ten years younger in appearance, and whose dress, though resembling his companion's in form, was of better materials, and of a more fantastic appearance. His jacket had been stained of a bright purple hue, upon which there had been some attempt to paint grotesque ornaments in different colours. To the jacket he added a short cloak, which scarcely reached half way down his thigh; it was of crimson cloth, though a good deal soiled, lined with bright yellow; and as he could transfer it from one shoulder to the other, or at his pleasure draw it all around him, its width, contrasted with its want of longitude, formed a fantastic piece of drapery. He had thin silver bracelets upon his arms, and on his neck a collar of the same metal bearing the inscription, "Wamba, the son of Witless, is the thrall of Cedric of Rotherwood." This personage had the same sort of sandals with his companion, but instead of the roll of leather thong, his legs were cased in a sort of gaiters, of which one was red and the other yellow. He was provided also with a cap, having around it more than one bell, about the size of those attached to hawks, which jingled as he turned his head to one side or other; and as he seldom remained a minute in the same posture, the sound might be considered as incessant. Around the edge of this cap was a stiff bandeau of leather, cut at the top into open work, resembling a coronet, while a prolonged bag arose from within it, and fell down on one shoulder like an old-fashioned nightcap, or a jelly-bag, or the head-gear of a modern hussar. It was to this part of the cap that the bells were attached; which circumstance, as well as the shape of his head-dress, and his own half-crazed, half-cunning expression of countenance, sufficiently pointed him out as belonging to the race of domestic clowns or jesters, maintained in the houses of the wealthy, to help away the tedium of those lingering hours which they were obliged to spend within doors. He bore, like his companion, a scrip, attached to his belt, but had neither horn nor knife, being probably considered as belonging to a class whom it is esteemed dangerous to intrust with edge-tools. In place of these, he was equipped with a sword of lath, resembling that with which Harlequin operates his wonders upon the modern stage.

The outward appearance of these two men formed scarce a stronger contrast than their look and demeanour. That of the serf, or bondsman, was sad and sullen; his aspect was bent on the ground with an appearance of deep dejection, which might be almost construed into apathy, had not the fire which occasionally sparkled in his red eye manifested that there slumbered, under the appearance of sullen despondency, a sense of oppression, and a disposition to resistance. The looks of Wamba, on the other hand, indicated, as usual with his class, a sort of vacant curiosity, and fidgetty impatience of any posture of repose, together with the utmost self-satisfaction respecting his own situation, and the appearance which he made. The dialogue which they maintained between them, was carried on in Anglo-Saxon, which, as we said before, was universally spoken by the inferior classes, excepting the Norman soldiers, and the immediate personal dependants of the great feudal nobles. But to give their conversation in the original would convey but little information to the modern reader, for whose benefit we beg to offer the following translation:

"The curse of St Withold upon these infernal porkers!" said the swine-herd, after blowing his horn obstreperously, to collect together the scattered herd of swine, which, answering his call with notes equally melodious, made, however, no haste to remove themselves from the luxurious banquet of beech-mast and acorns on which they had fattened, or to forsake the marshy banks of the rivulet, where several of them, half plunged in mud, lay stretched at their ease, altogether regardless of the voice of their keeper. "The curse of St Withold upon them and upon me!" said Gurth; "if the two-legged wolf snap not up some of them ere nightfall, I am no true man. Here, Fangs! Fangs!" he ejaculated at the top of his voice to a ragged wolfish-looking dog, a sort of lurcher, half mastiff, half greyhound, which ran limping about as if with the purpose of seconding his master in collecting the refractory grunters; but which, in fact, from misapprehension of the swine-herd's signals, ignorance of his own duty, or malice prepense, only drove them hither and thither, and increased the evil which he seemed to design to remedy. "A devil draw the teeth of him," said Gurth, "and the mother of mischief confound the Ranger of the forest, that cuts the foreclaws off our dogs, and makes them unfit for their trade! Wamba, up and help me an thou be'st a man; take a turn round the back o' the hill to gain the wind on them; and when thous't got the weather-gage, thou mayst drive them before thee as gently as so many innocent lambs."

"Truly," said Wamba, without stirring from the spot, "I have consulted my legs upon this matter, and they are altogether of opinion, that to carry my gay garments through these sloughs, would be an act of unfriendship to my sovereign person and royal wardrobe; wherefore, Gurth, I advise thee to call off Fangs, and leave the herd to their destiny, which, whether they meet with bands of travelling soldiers, or of outlaws, or of wandering pilgrims, can be little else than to be converted into Normans before morning, to thy no small ease and comfort."

"The swine turned Normans to my comfort!" quoth Gurth; "expound that to me, Wamba, for my brain is too dull, and my mind too vexed, to read riddles."

"Why, how call you those grunting brutes running about on their four legs?" demanded Wamba.

"Swine, fool, swine," said the herd, "every fool knows that."

"And swine is good Saxon," said the Jester; "but how call you the sow when she is flayed, and drawn, and quartered, and hung up by the heels, like a traitor?"

"Pork," answered the swine-herd.

"I am very glad every fool knows that too," said Wamba, "and pork, I think, is good Norman-French; and so when the brute lives, and is in the charge of a Saxon slave, she goes by her Saxon name; but becomes a Norman, and is called pork, when she is carried to the Castle-hall to feast among the nobles; what dost thou think of this, friend Gurth, ha?"

"It is but too true doctrine, friend Wamba, however it got into thy fool's pate."

"Nay, I can tell you more," said Wamba, in the same tone; "there is old Alderman Ox continues to hold his Saxon epithet, while he is under the charge of serfs and bondsmen such as thou, but becomes Beef, a fiery French gallant, when he arrives before the worshipful jaws that are destined to consume him. Mynheer Calf, too, becomes Monsieur de Veau in the like manner; he is Saxon when he requires tendance, and takes a Norman name when he becomes matter of enjoyment."

"By St Dunstan," answered Gurth, "thou speakest but sad truths; little is left to us but the air we breathe, and that appears to have been reserved with much hesitation, solely for the purpose of enabling us to endure the tasks they lay upon our shoulders. The finest and the fattest is for their board; the loveliest is for their couch; the best and bravest supply their foreign masters with soldiers, and whiten distant lands with their bones, leaving few here who have either will or the power to protect the unfortunate Saxon. God's blessing on our master Cedric, he hath done the work of a man in standing in the gap; but Reginald Front-de-Boeuf is coming down to this country in person, and we shall soon see how little Cedric's trouble will avail him.—Here, here," he exclaimed again, raising his voice, "So ho! so ho! well done, Fangs! thou hast them all before thee now, and bring'st them on bravely, lad."

"Gurth," said the Jester, "I know thou thinkest me a fool, or thou wouldst not be so rash in putting thy head into my mouth. One word to Reginald Front-de-Boeuf, or Philip de Malvoisin, that thou hast spoken treason against the Norman,—and thou art but a cast-away swineherd,—thou wouldst waver on one of these trees as a terror to all evil speakers against dignities."

"Dog, thou wouldst not betray me," said Gurth, "after having led me on to speak so much at disadvantage?"

"Betray thee!" answered the Jester; "no, that were the trick of a wise man; a fool cannot half so well help himself—but soft, whom have we here?" he said, listening to the trampling of several horses which became then audible.

"Never mind whom," answered Gurth, who had now got his herd before him, and, with the aid of Fangs, was driving them down one of the long dim vistas which we have endeavoured to describe.

"Nay, but I must see the riders," answered Wamba; "perhaps they are come from Fairy-land with a message from King Oberon."

"A murrain take thee," rejoined the swine-herd; "wilt thou talk of such things, while a terrible storm of thunder and lightning is raging within a few miles of us? Hark, how the thunder rumbles! and for summer rain, I never saw such broad downright flat drops fall out of the clouds; the oaks, too, notwithstanding the calm weather, sob and creak with their great boughs as if announcing a tempest. Thou canst play the rational if thou wilt; credit me for once, and let us home ere the storm begins to rage, for the night will be fearful."

Wamba seemed to feel the force of this appeal, and accompanied his companion, who began his journey after catching up a long quarter-staff which lay upon the grass beside him. This second Eumaeus strode hastily down the forest glade, driving before him, with the assistance of Fangs, the whole herd of his inharmonious charge.

II.

> A Monk there was, a fayre for the maistrie,
> An outrider that loved venerie;
> A manly man, to be an Abbot able,
> Full many a daintie horse had he in stable:
> And whan he rode, men might his bridle hear
> Gingeling in a whistling wind as clear,
> And eke as loud, as doth the chapell bell,
> There as this lord was keeper of the cell.
>
> — CHAUCER

Notwithstanding the occasional exhortation and chiding of his companion, the noise of the horsemen's feet continuing to approach, Wamba could not be prevented from lingering occasionally on the road, upon every pretence which occurred; now catching from the hazel a cluster of half-ripe nuts, and now turning his head to leer after a cottage maiden who crossed their path. The horsemen, therefore, soon overtook them on the road.

Their numbers amounted to ten men, of whom the two who rode foremost seemed to be persons of considerable importance, and the others their attendants. It was not difficult to ascertain the condition and character of one of these personages. He was obviously an ecclesiastic of high rank; his dress was that of a Cistercian Monk, but composed of materials much finer than those which the rule of that order admitted. His mantle and hood were of the best Flanders cloth, and fell in ample, and not ungraceful folds, around a handsome, though somewhat corpulent person. His countenance bore as little the marks of self-denial, as his habit indicated contempt of worldly splendour. His features might have been called good, had there not lurked under the pent-house of his eye, that sly epicurean twinkle which indicates the cautious voluptuary. In other respects, his profession and situation had taught him a ready command over his countenance, which he could contract at pleasure into solemnity, although its natural expression was that of good-humoured social indulgence. In defiance of conventual rules, and the edicts of popes and councils, the sleeves of this dignitary were lined and turned up with rich furs, his mantle secured at the throat with a golden clasp, and the whole dress proper to his order as much refined upon and ornamented, as that of a quaker beauty of the present day, who, while she retains the garb and costume of her sect continues to give to its simplicity, by the choice of materials and the mode of disposing them, a certain air of coquettish attraction, savouring but too much of the vanities of the world.

This worthy churchman rode upon a well-fed ambling mule, whose furniture was highly decorated, and whose bridle, according to the fashion of the day, was ornamented with silver bells. In his seat he had nothing of the awkwardness of the convent, but displayed the easy and habitual grace of a well-trained horseman. Indeed, it seemed that so humble a conveyance as a mule, in however good case, and however well broken to a pleasant and accommodating amble, was only used by the gallant monk for travelling on the road. A lay brother, one of those who followed in the train, had, for his use on other occasions, one of the most handsome Spanish jennets ever bred at Andalusia, which merchants used at that time to import, with great trouble and risk, for the use of persons of wealth and distinction. The saddle and housings of this superb palfrey were covered by a long foot-cloth, which reached nearly to the ground, and on which were richly embroidered, mitres, crosses, and other ecclesiastical emblems. Another lay brother led a sumpter mule, loaded probably with his superior's baggage; and two monks of his own order, of inferior station, rode together in the rear, laughing and conversing with each other, without taking much notice of the other members of the cavalcade.

The companion of the church dignitary was a man past forty, thin, strong, tall, and muscular; an athletic figure, which long fatigue and constant exercise seemed to have left none of the softer part of the human form, having reduced the whole to brawn, bones, and sinews, which had sustained a thousand toils, and were ready to dare a thousand more. His head was covered with a scarlet cap, faced with fur—of that kind which the French call "mortier", from its resemblance to the shape of an inverted mortar. His countenance was therefore fully displayed, and its expression was calculated to impress a degree of awe, if not of fear, upon strangers. High features, naturally strong and powerfully expressive, had been burnt almost into Negro blackness by constant exposure to the tropical sun, and might, in their ordinary state, be said to slumber after the storm of passion had passed away; but the projection of the veins of the forehead, the readiness with which the upper lip and its thick black moustaches quivered upon the slightest emotion, plainly intimated that the tempest might be again and easily awakened. His keen, piercing, dark eyes, told in every glance a history of difficulties subdued, and dangers dared, and seemed to challenge opposition to his wishes, for the pleasure of sweeping it from his road by a determined exertion of courage and of will; a deep scar on his brow gave additional sternness to his countenance, and a sinister expression to one of his eyes, which had been slightly injured on the same occasion, and of which the vision, though perfect, was in a slight and partial degree distorted.

The upper dress of this personage resembled that of his companion in shape, being a long monastic mantle; but the colour, being scarlet, showed that he did not belong to any of the four regular orders of monks. On the right shoulder of the mantle there was cut, in white cloth, a cross of a peculiar form. This upper robe concealed what at first view seemed rather inconsistent with its form, a shirt, namely, of linked mail, with sleeves and gloves of the same, curiously plaited and interwoven, as flexible to the body as those which are now wrought in the stocking-loom, out of less obdurate materials. The fore-part of his thighs, where the folds of his mantle permitted them to be seen, were also covered with linked mail; the knees and feet were defended by splints, or thin plates of steel, ingeniously jointed upon each other; and mail hose, reaching from the ankle to the knee, effectually protected the legs, and completed the rider's defensive armour. In his girdle he wore a long and double-edged dagger, which was the only offensive weapon about his person.

He rode, not a mule, like his companion, but a strong hackney for the road, to save his gallant war-horse, which a squire led behind, fully accoutred for battle, with a chamfron or plaited head-piece upon his head, having a short spike projecting from the front. On one side of the saddle hung a short battle-axe, richly inlaid with Damascene carving; on the other the rider's plumed head-piece and hood of mail, with a long two-handed sword, used by the chivalry of the period. A second squire held aloft his master's lance, from the extremity of which fluttered a small banderole, or streamer, bearing a cross of the same form with that embroidered upon his cloak. He also carried his small triangular shield, broad enough at the top to protect the breast, and from thence diminishing to a point. It was covered with a scarlet cloth, which prevented the device from being seen.

These two squires were followed by two attendants, whose dark visages, white turbans, and the Oriental form of their garments, showed them to be natives of some distant Eastern country.

The whole appearance of this warrior and his retinue was wild and outlandish; the dress of his squires was gorgeous, and his Eastern attendants wore silver collars round their throats, and bracelets of the same metal upon their swarthy arms and legs, of which the former were naked from the elbow, and the latter from mid-leg to ankle. Silk and embroidery distinguished their dresses, and marked the wealth and importance of their master; forming, at the same time, a striking contrast with the martial simplicity of his own attire. They were armed with crooked sabres, having the hilt and baldric inlaid with gold, and matched with Turkish daggers of yet more costly workmanship. Each of them bore at his saddle-bow a bundle of darts or javelins, about four feet in length, having sharp steel heads, a weapon much in use among the Saracens, and of which the memory is yet preserved in the martial exercise called "El Jerrid", still practised in the Eastern countries.

The steeds of these attendants were in appearance as foreign as their riders. They were of Saracen origin, and consequently of Arabian descent; and their fine slender limbs, small fetlocks, thin manes, and easy springy motion, formed a marked contrast with the large-jointed, heavy horses, of which the race was cultivated in Flanders and in Normandy, for mounting the men-at-arms of the period in all the panoply of plate and mail; and which, placed by the side of those Eastern coursers, might have passed for a personification of substance and of shadow.

The singular appearance of this cavalcade not only attracted the curiosity of Wamba, but excited even that of his less volatile companion. The monk he instantly knew to be the Prior of Jorvaulx Abbey, well known for many miles around as a lover of the chase, of the banquet, and, if fame did him not wrong, of other worldly pleasures still more inconsistent with his monastic vows.

Yet so loose were the ideas of the times respecting the conduct of the clergy, whether secular or regular, that the Prior Aymer maintained a fair character in the neighbourhood of his abbey. His free and jovial temper, and the readiness with which he granted absolution from all ordinary delinquencies, rendered him a favourite among the nobility and principal gentry, to several of whom he was allied by birth, being of a distinguished Norman family. The ladies, in particular, were not disposed to scan too nicely the morals of a man who was a professed admirer of their sex, and who possessed many means of dispelling the ennui which was too apt to intrude upon the halls and bowers of an ancient feudal castle. The Prior mingled in the sports of the field with more than due eagerness, and was allowed to possess the best-trained hawks, and the fleetest greyhounds in the North Riding; circumstances which strongly recommended him to the youthful gentry. With the old, he had another part to play, which, when needful, he could sustain with great decorum. His knowledge of books, however superficial, was sufficient to impress upon their ignorance respect for his supposed learning; and the gravity of his deportment and language, with the high tone which he exerted in setting forth the authority of the church and of the priesthood, impressed them no less with an opinion of his sanctity. Even the common people, the severest critics of the conduct of their betters, had commiseration with the follies of Prior Aymer. He was generous; and charity, as it is well known, covereth a multitude of sins, in another sense than that in which it is said to do so in Scripture. The revenues of the monastery, of which a large part was at his disposal, while they gave him the means of supplying his own very considerable expenses, afforded also those largesses which he bestowed among the peasantry, and with which he frequently relieved the distresses of the oppressed. If Prior Aymer rode hard in the chase, or remained long at the banquet,—if Prior Aymer was seen, at the early peep of dawn, to enter the postern of the abbey, as he glided home from some rendezvous which had occupied the hours of darkness, men only shrugged up their shoulders, and reconciled themselves to his irregularities, by recollecting that the same were practised by many of his brethren who had no redeeming qualities whatsoever to atone for them. Prior Aymer, therefore, and his character, were well known to our Saxon serfs, who made their rude obeisance, and received his "benedicite, mes filz," in return.

But the singular appearance of his companion and his attendants, arrested their attention and excited their wonder, and they could scarcely attend to the Prior of Jorvaulx' question, when he demanded if they knew of any place of harbourage in the vicinity; so much were they surprised at the half monastic, half military appearance of the swarthy stranger, and at the uncouth dress and arms of his Eastern attendants. It is probable, too, that the language in which the benediction was conferred, and the information asked, sounded ungracious, though not probably unintelligible, in the ears of the Saxon peasants.

"I asked you, my children," said the Prior, raising his voice, and using the lingua Franca, or mixed language, in which the Norman and Saxon races conversed with each other, "if there be in this neighbourhood any good man, who, for the love of God, and devotion to Mother Church, will give two of her humblest servants, with their train, a night's hospitality and refreshment?"

This he spoke with a tone of conscious importance, which formed a strong contrast to the modest terms which he thought it proper to employ.

"Two of the humblest servants of Mother Church!" repeated Wamba to himself,—

but, fool as he was, taking care not to make his observation audible; "I should like to see her seneschals, her chief butlers, and other principal domestics!"

After this internal commentary on the Prior's speech, he raised his eyes, and replied to the question which had been put.

"If the reverend fathers," he said, "loved good cheer and soft lodging, few miles of riding would carry them to the Priory of Brinxworth, where their quality could not but secure them the most honourable reception; or if they preferred spending a penitential evening, they might turn down yonder wild glade, which would bring them to the hermitage of Copmanhurst, where a pious anchoret would make them sharers for the night of the shelter of his roof and the benefit of his prayers."

The Prior shook his head at both proposals.

"Mine honest friend," said he, "if the jangling of thy bells had not dizzied thine understanding, thou mightst know "Clericus clericum non decimat"; that is to say, we churchmen do not exhaust each other's hospitality, but rather require that of the laity, giving them thus an opportunity to serve God in honouring and relieving his appointed servants."

"It is true," replied Wamba, "that I, being but an ass, am, nevertheless, honoured to hear the bells as well as your reverence's mule; notwithstanding, I did conceive that the charity of Mother Church and her servants might be said, with other charity, to begin at home."

"A truce to thine insolence, fellow," said the armed rider, breaking in on his prattle with a high and stern voice, "and tell us, if thou canst, the road to—How call'd you your Franklin, Prior Aymer?"

"Cedric," answered the Prior; "Cedric the Saxon.—Tell me, good fellow, are we near his dwelling, and can you show us the road?"

"The road will be uneasy to find," answered Gurth, who broke silence for the first time, "and the family of Cedric retire early to rest."

"Tush, tell not me, fellow," said the military rider; "'tis easy for them to arise and supply the wants of travellers such as we are, who will not stoop to beg the hospitality which we have a right to command."

"I know not," said Gurth, sullenly, "if I should show the way to my master's house, to those who demand as a right, the shelter which most are fain to ask as a favour."

"Do you dispute with me, slave!" said the soldier; and, setting spurs to his horse, he caused him make a demivolte across the path, raising at the same time the riding rod which he held in his hand, with a purpose of chastising what he considered as the insolence of the peasant.

Gurth darted at him a savage and revengeful scowl, and with a fierce, yet hesitating motion, laid his hand on the haft of his knife; but the interference of Prior Aymer, who pushed his mule betwixt his companion and the swineherd, prevented the meditated violence.

"Nay, by St Mary, brother Brian, you must not think you are now in Palestine, predominating over heathen Turks and infidel Saracens; we islanders love not blows, save those of holy Church, who chasteneth whom she loveth.—Tell me, good fellow," said he to Wamba, and seconded his speech by a small piece of silver coin, "the way to Cedric the Saxon's; you cannot be ignorant of it, and it is your duty to direct the wanderer even when his character is less sanctified than ours."

"In truth, venerable father," answered the Jester, "the Saracen head of your right reverend companion has frightened out of mine the way home—I am not sure I shall get there to-night myself."

"Tush," said the Abbot, "thou canst tell us if thou wilt. This reverend brother has been all his life engaged in fighting among the Saracens for the recovery of the Holy Sepulchre; he is of the order of Knights Templars, whom you may have heard of; he is half a monk, half a soldier."

"If he is but half a monk," said the Jester, "he should not be wholly unreasonable with those whom he meets upon the road, even if they should be in no hurry to answer questions that no way concern them."

"I forgive thy wit," replied the Abbot, "on condition thou wilt show me the way to Cedric's mansion."

"Well, then," answered Wamba, "your reverences must hold on this path till you come to a sunken cross, of which scarce a cubit's length remains above ground; then take the path to the left, for there are four which meet at Sunken Cross, and I trust your reverences will obtain shelter before the storm comes on."

The Abbot thanked his sage adviser; and the cavalcade, setting spurs to their horses, rode on as men do who wish to reach their inn before the bursting of a night-storm. As their horses' hoofs died away, Gurth said to his companion, "If they follow thy wise direction, the reverend fathers will hardly reach Rotherwood this night."

"No," said the Jester, grinning, "but they may reach Sheffield if they have good luck, and that is as fit a place for them. I am not so bad a woodsman as to show the dog where the deer lies, if I have no mind he should chase him."

"Thou art right," said Gurth; "it were ill that Aymer saw the Lady Rowena; and it were worse, it may be, for Cedric to quarrel, as is most likely he would, with this military monk. But, like good servants let us hear and see, and say nothing."

We return to the riders, who had soon left the bondsmen far behind them, and who maintained the following conversation in the Norman-French language, usually employed by the superior classes, with the exception of the few who were still inclined to boast their Saxon descent.

"What mean these fellows by their capricious insolence?" said the Templar to the Benedictine, "and why did you prevent me from chastising it?"

"Marry, brother Brian," replied the Prior, "touching the one of them, it were hard for me to render a reason for a fool speaking according to his folly; and the other churl is of that savage, fierce, intractable race, some of whom, as I have often told you, are still to be found among the descendants of the conquered Saxons, and whose supreme pleasure it is to testify, by all means in their power, their aversion to their conquerors."

"I would soon have beat him into courtesy," observed Brian; "I am accustomed to deal with such spirits: Our Turkish captives are as fierce and intractable as Odin himself could have been; yet two months in my household, under the management of my master of the slaves, has made them humble, submissive, serviceable, and observant of your will. Marry, sir, you must be aware of the poison and the dagger; for they use either with free will when you give them the slightest opportunity."

"Ay, but," answered Prior Aymer, "every land has its own manners and fashions; and, besides that beating this fellow could procure us no information respecting the road to Cedric's house, it would have been sure to have established a quarrel betwixt you and him had we found our way thither. Remember what I told you: this wealthy franklin is proud, fierce, jealous, and irritable, a withstander of the nobility, and even of his neighbors, Reginald Front-de-Boeuf and Philip Malvoisin, who are no babies to strive with. He stands up sternly for the privileges of his race, and is so proud of his uninterrupted descend from Hereward, a renowned champion of the Heptarchy, that he is universally called Cedric the Saxon; and makes a boast of his belonging to a people from whom many others endeaver to hide their descent, lest they should encounter a share of the 'vae victis,' or severities imposed upon the vanquished."

"Prior Aymer," said the Templar, "you are a man of gallantry, learned in the study of beauty, and as expert as a troubadour in all matters concerning the 'arrets' of love; but I shall expect much beauty in this celebrated Rowena to counterbalance the self-denial and forbearance which I must exert if I am to court the favor of such a seditious churl as you have described her father Cedric."

"Cedric is not her father," replied the Prior, "and is but of remote relation: she is descended from higher blood than even he pretends to, and is but distantly connected with him by birth. Her guardian, however, he is, self-constituted as I believe; but his ward is as dear to him as if she were his own child. Of her beauty you shall soon be judge; and if the purity of her complexion, and the majestic, yet soft expression of a mild blue eye, do not chase from your memory the black-tressed girls of Palestine, ay, or the houris of old Mahound's paradise, I am an infidel, and no true son of the church."

"Should your boasted beauty," said the Templar, "be weighed in the balance and found wanting, you know our wager?"

"My gold collar," answered the Prior, "against ten butts of Chian wine;—they are mine as securely as if they were already in the convent vaults, under the key of old Dennis the cellarer."

"And I am myself to be judge," said the Templar, "and am only to be convicted on my own admission, that I have seen no maiden so beautiful since Pentecost was a twelvemonth. Ran it not so?—Prior, your collar is in danger; I will wear it over my gorget in the lists of Ashby-de-la-Zouche."

"Win it fairly," said the Prior, "and wear it as ye will; I will trust your giving true response, on your word as a knight and as a churchman. Yet, brother, take my advice, and file your tongue to a little more courtesy than your habits of predominating over infidel captives and Eastern bondsmen have accustomed you. Cedric the Saxon, if offended,—and he is noway slack in taking offence,—is a man who, without respect to your knighthood, my high office, or the sanctity of either, would clear his house of us, and send us to lodge with the larks, though the hour were midnight. And be careful how you look on Rowena, whom he cherishes with the most jealous care; an he take the least alarm in that quarter we are but lost men. It is said he banished his only son from his family for lifting his eyes in the way of affection towards this beauty, who may be worshipped, it seems, at a distance, but is not to be approached with other thoughts than such as we bring to the shrine of the Blessed Virgin."

"Well, you have said enough," answered the Templar; "I will for a night put on the needful restraint, and deport me as meekly as a maiden; but as for the fear of his expelling us by violence, myself and squires, with Hamet and Abdalla, will warrant you against that disgrace. Doubt not that we shall be strong enough to make good our quarters."

"We must not let it come so far," answered the Prior; "but here is the clown's sunken cross, and the night is so dark that we can hardly see which of the roads we are to follow. He bid us turn, I think to the left."

"To the right," said Brian, "to the best of my remembrance."

"To the left, certainly, the left; I remember his pointing with his wooden sword."

"Ay, but he held his sword in his left hand, and so pointed across his body with it," said the Templar.

Each maintained his opinion with sufficient obstinacy, as is usual in all such cases; the attendants were appealed to, but they had not been near enough to hear Wamba's directions. At length Brian remarked, what had at first escaped him in the twilight; "Here is some one either asleep, or lying dead at the foot of this cross—Hugo, stir him with the butt-end of thy lance."

This was no sooner done than the figure arose, exclaiming in good French, "Whosoever thou art, it is discourteous in you to disturb my thoughts."

"We did but wish to ask you," said the Prior, "the road to Rotherwood, the abode of Cedric the Saxon."

"I myself am bound thither," replied the stranger; "and if I had a horse, I would be your guide, for the way is somewhat intricate, though perfectly well known to me."

"Thou shalt have both thanks and reward, my friend," said the Prior, "if thou wilt bring us to Cedric's in safety."

And he caused one of his attendants to mount his own led horse, and give that upon which he had hitherto ridden to the stranger, who was to serve for a guide.

Their conductor pursued an opposite road from that which Wamba had recommended, for the purpose of misleading them. The path soon led deeper into the woodland, and crossed more than one brook, the approach to which was rendered perilous by the marshes through which it flowed; but the stranger seemed to know, as if by instinct, the soundest ground and the safest points of passage; and by dint of caution and attention, brought the party safely into a wilder avenue than any they had yet seen; and, pointing to a large low irregular building at the upper extremity, he said to the Prior, "Yonder is Rotherwood, the dwelling of Cedric the Saxon."

This was a joyful intimation to Aymer, whose nerves were none of the strongest, and who had suffered such agitation and alarm in the course of passing through the dangerous bogs, that he had not yet had the curiosity to ask his guide a single question. Finding himself now at his ease and near shelter, his curiosity began to awake, and he demanded of the guide who and what he was.

"A Palmer, just returned from the Holy Land," was the answer.

"You had better have tarried there to fight for the recovery of the Holy Sepulchre," said the Templar.

"True, Reverend Sir Knight," answered the Palmer, to whom the appearance of the Templar seemed perfectly familiar; "but when those who are under oath to recover the holy city, are found travelling at such a distance from the scene of their duties, can you wonder that a peaceful peasant like me should decline the task which they have abandoned?"

The Templar would have made an angry reply, but was interrupted by the Prior, who again expressed his astonishment, that their guide, after such long absence, should be so perfectly acquainted with the passes of the forest.

"I was born a native of these parts," answered their guide, and as he made the reply they stood before the mansion of Cedric;—a low irregular building, containing several court-yards or enclosures, extending over a considerable space of ground, and which, though its size argued the inhabitant to be a person of wealth, differed entirely from the tall, turretted, and castellated buildings in which the Norman nobility resided, and which had become the universal style of architecture throughout England.

Rotherwood was not, however, without defences; no habitation, in that disturbed period, could have been so, without the risk of being plundered and burnt before the next morning. A deep fosse, or ditch, was drawn round the whole building, and filled with water from a neighbouring stream. A double stockade, or palisade, composed of pointed beams, which the adjacent forest supplied, defended the outer and inner bank of the trench. There was an entrance from the west through the outer stockade, which communicated by a drawbridge, with a similar opening in the interior defences. Some precautions had been taken to place those entrances under the protection of projecting angles, by which they might be flanked in case of need by archers or slingers.

Before this entrance the Templar wound his horn loudly; for the rain, which had long threatened, began now to descend with great violence.

III.

> Then (sad relief!) from the bleak coast that hears
> The German Ocean roar, deep-blooming, strong,
> And yellow hair'd, the blue-eyed Saxon came.
>
> — THOMSON'S LIBERTY

In a hall, the height of which was greatly disproportioned to its extreme length and width, a long oaken table, formed of planks rough-hewn from the forest, and which had scarcely received any polish, stood ready prepared for the evening meal of Cedric the Saxon. The roof, composed of beams and rafters, had nothing to divide the apartment from the sky excepting the planking and thatch; there was a huge fireplace at either end of the hall, but as the chimneys were constructed in a very clumsy manner, at least as much of the smoke found its way into the apartment as escaped by the proper vent. The constant vapour which this occasioned, had polished the rafters and beams of the low-browed hall, by encrusting them with a black varnish of soot. On the sides of the apartment hung implements of war and of the chase, and there were at each corner folding doors, which gave access to other parts of the extensive building.

The other appointments of the mansion partook of the rude simplicity of the Saxon period, which Cedric piqued himself upon maintaining. The floor was composed of earth mixed with lime, trodden into a hard substance, such as is often employed in flooring our modern barns. For about one quarter of the length of the apartment, the floor was raised by a step, and this space, which was called the dais, was occupied only by the principal members of the family, and visitors of distinction. For this purpose, a table richly covered with scarlet cloth was placed transversely across the platform, from the middle of which ran the longer and lower board, at which the domestics and inferior persons fed, down towards the bottom of the hall. The whole resembled the form of the letter T, or some of those ancient dinner-tables, which, arranged on the same principles, may be still seen in the antique Colleges of Oxford or Cambridge. Massive chairs and settles of carved oak were placed upon the dais, and over these seats and the more elevated table was fastened a canopy of cloth, which served in some degree to protect the dignitaries who occupied that distinguished station from the weather, and especially from the rain, which in some places found its way through the ill-constructed roof.

The walls of this upper end of the hall, as far as the dais extended, were covered with hangings or curtains, and upon the floor there was a carpet, both of which were adorned with some attempts at tapestry, or embroidery, executed with brilliant or rather gaudy colouring. Over the lower range of table, the roof, as we have noticed, had no covering; the rough plastered walls were left bare, and the rude earthen floor was uncarpeted; the board was uncovered by a cloth, and rude massive benches supplied the place of chairs.

In the centre of the upper table, were placed two chairs more elevated than the rest, for the master and mistress of the family, who presided over the scene of hospitality, and from doing so derived their Saxon title of honour, which signifies "the Dividers of Bread."

To each of these chairs was added a footstool, curiously carved and inlaid with ivory, which mark of distinction was peculiar to them. One of these seats was at present occupied by Cedric the Saxon, who, though but in rank a thane, or, as the Normans called him, a Franklin, felt, at the delay of his evening meal, an irritable impatience, which might have become an alderman, whether of ancient or of modern times.

It appeared, indeed, from the countenance of this proprietor, that he was of a frank, but hasty and choleric temper. He was not above the middle stature, but broad-shouldered, long-armed, and powerfully made, like one accustomed to endure the fatigue of war or of the chase; his face was broad, with large blue eyes, open and frank features, fine teeth, and a well formed head, altogether expressive of that sort of good-humour which often lodges with a sudden and hasty temper. Pride and jealousy there was in his eye, for his life had been spent in asserting rights which were constantly liable to invasion; and the prompt, fiery, and resolute disposition of the man, had been kept constantly upon the alert by the circumstances of his situation. His long yellow hair was equally divided on the top of his head and upon his brow, and combed down on each side to the length of his shoulders; it had but little tendency to grey, although Cedric was approaching to his sixtieth year.

His dress was a tunic of forest green, furred at the throat and cuffs with what was called minever; a kind of fur inferior in quality to ermine, and formed, it is believed, of the skin of the grey squirrel. This doublet hung unbuttoned over a close dress of scarlet which sat tight to his body; he had breeches of the same, but they did not reach below the lower part of the thigh, leaving the knee exposed. His feet had sandals of the same fashion with the peasants, but of finer materials, and secured in the front with golden clasps. He had bracelets of gold upon his arms, and a broad collar of the same precious metal around his neck. About his waist he wore a richly-studded belt, in which was stuck a short straight two-edged sword, with a sharp point, so disposed as to hang almost perpendicularly by his side. Behind his seat was hung a scarlet cloth cloak lined with fur, and a cap of the same materials richly embroidered, which completed the dress of the opulent landholder when he chose to go forth. A short boar-spear, with a broad and bright steel head, also reclined against the back of his chair, which served him, when he walked abroad, for the purposes of a staff or of a weapon, as chance might require.

Several domestics, whose dress held various proportions betwixt the richness of their master's, and the coarse and simple attire of Gurth the swine-herd, watched the looks and waited the commands of the Saxon dignitary. Two or three servants of a superior order stood behind their master upon the dais; the rest occupied the lower part of the hall. Other attendants there were of a different description; two or three large and shaggy greyhounds, such as were then employed in hunting the stag and wolf; as many slow-hounds of a large bony breed, with thick necks, large heads, and long ears; and one or two of the smaller dogs, now called terriers, which waited with impatience the arrival of the supper; but, with the sagacious knowledge of physiognomy peculiar to their race, forbore to intrude upon the moody silence of their master, apprehensive probably of a small white truncheon which lay by Cedric's trencher, for the purpose of repelling the advances of his four-legged dependants. One grisly old wolf-dog alone, with the liberty of an indulged favourite, had planted himself close by the chair of state, and occasionally ventured to solicit notice by putting his large hairy head upon his master's knee, or pushing his nose into his hand. Even he was repelled by the stern command, "Down, Balder, down! I am not in the humour for foolery."

In fact, Cedric, as we have observed, was in no very placid state of mind. The Lady Rowena, who had been absent to attend an evening mass at a distant church, had but just returned, and was changing her garments, which had been wetted by the storm. There were as yet no tidings of Gurth and his charge, which should long since have been driven home from the forest and such was the insecurity of the period, as to render it probable that the delay might be explained by some depreciation of the outlaws, with whom the adjacent forest abounded, or by the violence of some neighbouring baron, whose consciousness of strength made him equally negligent of the laws of property. The matter was of consequence, for great part of the domestic wealth of the Saxon proprietors consisted in numerous herds of swine, especially in forest-land, where those animals easily found their food.

Besides these subjects of anxiety, the Saxon thane was impatient for the presence of his favourite clown Wamba, whose jests, such as they were, served for a sort of seasoning to his evening meal, and to the deep draughts of ale and wine with which he was in the habit of accompanying it. Add to all this, Cedric had fasted since noon, and his usual supper hour was long past, a cause of irritation common to country squires, both in ancient and modern times. His displeasure was expressed in broken sentences, partly muttered to himself, partly addressed to the domestics who stood around; and particularly to his cupbearer, who offered him from time to time, as a sedative, a silver goblet filled with wine—"Why tarries the Lady Rowena?"

"She is but changing her head-gear," replied a female attendant, with as much confidence as the favourite lady's-maid usually answers the master of a modern family; "you would not wish her to sit down to the banquet in her hood and kirtle? and no lady within the shire can be quicker in arraying herself than my mistress."

This undeniable argument produced a sort of acquiescent umph! on the part of the Saxon, with the addition, "I wish her devotion may choose fair weather for the next visit to St John's Kirk;—but what, in the name of ten devils," continued he, turning to the cupbearer, and raising his voice as if happy to have found a channel into which he might divert his indignation without fear or control—"what, in the name of ten devils, keeps Gurth so long afield? I suppose we shall have an evil account of the herd; he was wont to be a faithful and cautious drudge, and I had destined him for something better; perchance I might even have made him one of my warders."

Oswald the cupbearer modestly suggested, "that it was scarce an hour since the tolling of the curfew;" an ill-chosen apology, since it turned upon a topic so harsh to Saxon ears.

"The foul fiend," exclaimed Cedric, "take the curfew-bell, and the tyrannical bastard by whom it was devised, and the heartless slave who names it with a Saxon tongue to a Saxon ear! The curfew!" he added, pausing, "ay, the curfew; which compels true men to extinguish their lights, that thieves and robbers may work their deeds in darkness!—Ay, the curfew;—Reginald Front-de-Boeuf and Philip de Malvoisin know the use of the curfew as well as William the Bastard himself, or e'er a Norman adventurer that fought at Hastings. I shall hear, I guess, that my property has been swept off to save from starving the hungry banditti, whom they cannot support but by theft and robbery. My faithful slave is murdered, and my goods are taken for a prey—and Wamba—where is Wamba? Said not some one he had gone forth with Gurth?"

Oswald replied in the affirmative.

"Ay? why this is better and better! he is carried off too, the Saxon fool, to serve the Norman lord. Fools are we all indeed that serve them, and fitter subjects for their scorn and laughter, than if we were born with but half our wits. But I will be avenged," he added, starting from his chair in impatience at the supposed injury, and catching hold of his boar-spear; "I will go with my complaint to the great council; I have friends, I have followers—man to man will I appeal the Norman to the lists; let him come in his plate and his mail, and all that can render cowardice bold; I have sent such a javelin as this through a stronger fence than three of their war shields!—Haply they think me old; but they shall find, alone and childless as I am, the blood of Hereward is in the veins of Cedric.—Ah, Wilfred, Wilfred!" he exclaimed in a lower tone, "couldst thou have ruled thine unreasonable passion, thy father had not been left in his age like the solitary oak that throws out its shattered and unprotected branches against the full sweep of the tempest!" The reflection seemed to conjure into sadness his irritated feelings. Replacing his javelin, he

IVANHOE

resumed his seat, bent his looks downward, and appeared to be absorbed in melancholy reflection.

From his musing, Cedric was suddenly awakened by the blast of a horn, which was replied to by the clamorous yells and barking of all the dogs in the hall, and some twenty or thirty which were quartered in other parts of the building. It cost some exercise of the white truncheon, well seconded by the exertions of the domestics, to silence this canine clamour.

"To the gate, knaves!" said the Saxon, hastily, as soon as the tumult was so much appeased that the dependants could hear his voice. "See what tidings that horn tells us of—to announce, I ween, some hership and robbery which has been done upon my lands."

Returning in less than three minutes, a warder announced "that the Prior Aymer of Jorvaulx, and the good knight Brian de Bois-Guilbert, commander of the valiant and venerable order of Knights Templars, with a small retinue, requested hospitality and lodging for the night, being on their way to a tournament which was to be held not far from Ashby-de-la-Zouche, on the second day from the present."

"Aymer, the Prior Aymer? Brian de Bois-Guilbert?"—muttered Cedric; "Normans both;—but Norman or Saxon, the hospitality of Rotherwood must not be impeached; they are welcome, since they have chosen to halt—more welcome would they have been to have ridden further on their way—But it were unworthy to murmur for a night's lodging and a night's food; in the quality of guests, at least, even Normans must suppress their insolence.—Go, Hundebert," he added, to a sort of major-domo who stood behind him with a white wand; "take six of the attendants, and introduce the strangers to the guests' lodging. Look after their horses and mules, and see their train lack nothing. Let them have change of vestments if they require it, and fire, and water to wash, and wine and ale; and bid the cooks add what they hastily can to our evening meal; and let it be put on the board when those strangers are ready to share it. Say to them, Hundebert, that Cedric would himself bid them welcome, but he is under a vow never to step more than three steps from the dais of his own hall to meet any who shares not the blood of Saxon royalty. Begone! see them carefully tended; let them not say in their pride, the Saxon churl has shown at once his poverty and his avarice."

The major-domo departed with several attendants, to execute his master's commands.

"The Prior Aymer!" repeated Cedric, looking to Oswald, "the brother, if I mistake not, of Giles de Mauleverer, now lord of Middleham?"

Oswald made a respectful sign of assent. "His brother sits in the seat, and usurps the patrimony, of a better race, the race of Ulfgar of Middleham; but what Norman lord doth not the same? This Prior is, they say, a free and jovial priest, who loves the wine-cup and the bugle-horn better than bell and book: Good; let him come, he shall be welcome. How named ye the Templar?"

"Brian de Bois-Guilbert."

"Bois-Guilbert," said Cedric, still in the musing, half-arguing tone, which the habit of living among dependants had accustomed him to employ, and which resembled a man who talks to himself rather than to those around him—"Bois-Guilbert? that name has been spread wide both for good and evil. They say he is valiant as the bravest of his order; but stained with their usual vices, pride, arrogance, cruelty, and voluptuousness; a hard-hearted man, who knows neither fear of earth, nor awe of heaven. So say the few warriors who have returned from Palestine.—Well; it is but for one night; he shall be welcome too.—Oswald, broach the oldest wine-cask; place the best mead, the mightiest ale, the richest morat, the most sparkling cider, the most odoriferous pigments, upon the board; fill the largest horns —Templars and Abbots love good wines and good measure.—Elgitha, let thy Lady Rowena, know we shall not this night expect her in the hall, unless such be her especial pleasure."

"But it will be her especial pleasure," answered Elgitha, with great readiness, "for she is ever desirous to hear the latest news from Palestine."

Cedric darted at the forward damsel a glance of hasty resentment; but Rowena, and whatever belonged to her, were privileged and secure from his anger. He only replied, "Silence, maiden; thy tongue outruns thy discretion. Say my message to thy mistress, and let her do her pleasure. Here, at least, the descendant of Alfred still reigns a princess." Elgitha left the apartment.

"Palestine!" repeated the Saxon; "Palestine! how many ears are turned to the tales which dissolute crusaders, or hypocritical pilgrims, bring from that fatal land! I too might ask—I too might enquire—I too might listen with a beating heart to fables which the wily strollers devise to cheat us into hospitality—but no—The son who has disobeyed me is no longer mine; nor will I concern myself more for his fate than for that of the most worthless among the millions that ever shaped the cross on their shoulder, rushed into excess and blood-guiltiness, and called it an accomplishment of the will of God."

He knit his brows, and fixed his eyes for an instant on the ground; as he raised them, the folding doors at the bottom of the hall were cast wide, and, preceded by the major-domo with his wand, and four domestics bearing blazing torches, the guests of the evening entered the apartment.

IV.

> With sheep and shaggy goats the porkers bled,
> And the proud steer was on the marble spread;
> With fire prepared, they deal the morsels round,
> Wine rosy bright the brimming goblets crown'd.
>
> Disposed apart, Ulysses shares the treat;
> A trivet table and ignobler seat,
> The Prince assigns—
>
> — ODYSSEY, BOOK XXI

The Prior Aymer had taken the opportunity afforded him, of changing his riding robe for one of yet more costly materials, over which he wore a cope curiously embroidered. Besides the massive golden signet ring, which marked his ecclesiastical dignity, his fingers, though contrary to the canon, were loaded with precious gems;

his sandals were of the finest leather which was imported from Spain; his beard trimmed to as small dimensions as his order would possibly permit, and his shaven crown concealed by a scarlet cap richly embroidered.

The appearance of the Knight Templar was also changed; and, though less studiously bedecked with ornament, his dress was as rich, and his appearance far more commanding, than that of his companion. He had exchanged his shirt of mail for an under tunic of dark purple silk, garnished with furs, over which flowed his long robe of spotless white, in ample folds. The eight-pointed cross of his order was cut on the shoulder of his mantle in black velvet. The high cap no longer invested his brows, which were only shaded by short and thick curled hair of a raven blackness, corresponding to his unusually swart complexion. Nothing could be more gracefully majestic than his step and manner, had they not been marked by a predominant air of haughtiness, easily acquired by the exercise of unresisted authority.

These two dignified persons were followed by their respective attendants, and at a more humble distance by their guide, whose figure had nothing more remarkable than it derived from the usual weeds of a pilgrim. A cloak or mantle of coarse black serge, enveloped his whole body. It was in shape something like the cloak of a modern hussar, having similar flaps for covering the arms, and was called a "Sclaveyn", or "Sclavonian". Coarse sandals, bound with thongs, on his bare feet; a broad and shadowy hat, with cockle-shells stitched on its brim, and a long staff shod with iron, to the upper end of which was attached a branch of palm, completed the palmer's attire. He followed modestly the last of the train which entered the hall, and, observing that the lower table scarce afforded room sufficient for the domestics of Cedric and the retinue of his guests, he withdrew to a settle placed beside and almost under one of the large chimneys, and seemed to employ himself in drying his garments, until the retreat of some one should make room at the board, or the hospitality of the steward should supply him with refreshments in the place he had chosen apart.

Cedric rose to receive his guests with an air of dignified hospitality, and, descending from the dais, or elevated part of his hall, made three steps towards them, and then awaited their approach.

"I grieve," he said, "reverend Prior, that my vow binds me to advance no farther upon this floor of my fathers, even to receive such guests as you, and this valiant Knight of the Holy Temple. But my steward has expounded to you the cause of my seeming discourtesy. Let me also pray, that you will excuse my speaking to you in my native language, and that you will reply in the same if your knowledge of it permits; if not, I sufficiently understand Norman to follow your meaning."

"Vows," said the Abbot, "must be unloosed, worthy Franklin, or permit me rather to say, worthy Thane, though the title is antiquated. Vows are the knots which tie us to Heaven—they are the cords which bind the sacrifice to the horns of the altar,—and are therefore,—as I said before,—to be unloosened and discharged, unless our holy Mother Church shall pronounce the contrary. And respecting language, I willingly hold communication in that spoken by my respected grandmother, Hilda of Middleham, who died in odour of sanctity, little short, if we may presume to say so, of her glorious namesake, the blessed Saint Hilda of Whitby, God be gracious to her soul!"

When the Prior had ceased what he meant as a conciliatory harangue, his companion said briefly and emphatically, "I speak ever French, the language of King Richard and his nobles; but I understand English sufficiently to communicate with the natives of the country."

Cedric darted at the speaker one of those hasty and impatient glances, which comparisons between the two rival nations seldom failed to call forth; but, recollecting the duties of hospitality, he suppressed further show of resentment, and, motioning with his hand, caused his guests to assume two seats a little lower than his own, but placed close beside him, and gave a signal that the evening meal should be placed upon the board.

While the attendants hastened to obey Cedric's commands, his eye distinguished Gurth the swineherd, who, with his companion Wamba, had just entered the hall. "Send these loitering knaves up hither," said the Saxon, impatiently. And when the culprits came before the dais,—"How comes it, villains! that you have loitered abroad so late as this? Hast thou brought home thy charge, sirrah Gurth, or hast thou left them to robbers and marauders?"

"The herd is safe, so please ye," said Gurth.

"But it does not please me, thou knave," said Cedric, "that I should be made to suppose otherwise for two hours, and sit here devising vengeance against my neighbours for wrongs they have not done me. I tell thee, shackles and the prison-house shall punish the next offence of this kind."

Gurth, knowing his master's irritable temper, attempted no exculpation; but the Jester, who could presume upon Cedric's tolerance, by virtue of his privileges as a fool, replied for them both; "In troth, uncle Cedric, you are neither wise nor reasonable to-night."

"'How, sir?" said his master; "you shall to the porter's lodge, and taste of the discipline there, if you give your foolery such license."

"First let your wisdom tell me," said Wamba, "is it just and reasonable to punish one person for the fault of another?"

"Certainly not, fool," answered Cedric.

"Then why should you shackle poor Gurth, uncle, for the fault of his dog Fangs? for I dare be sworn we lost not a minute by the way, when we had got our herd together, which Fangs did not manage until we heard the vesper-bell."

"Then hang up Fangs," said Cedric, turning hastily towards the swineherd, "if the fault is his, and get thee another dog."

"Under favour, uncle," said the Jester, "that were still somewhat on the bow-hand of fair justice; for it was no fault of Fangs that he was lame and could not gather the herd, but the fault of those that struck off two of his fore-claws, an operation for which, if the poor fellow had been consulted, he would scarce have given his voice."

"And who dared to lame an animal which belonged to my bondsman?" said the Saxon, kindling in wrath.

"Marry, that did old Hubert," said Wamba, "Sir Philip de Malvoisin's keeper of the chase. He caught Fangs strolling in the forest, and said he chased the deer contrary to his master's right, as warden of the walk."

"The foul fiend take Malvoisin," answered the Saxon, "and his keeper both! I will teach them that the wood was disforested in terms of the great Forest Charter. But enough of this. Go to, knave, go to thy place—and thou, Gurth, get thee another dog, and should the keeper dare to touch it, I will mar his archery; the curse of a coward on my head, if I strike not off the forefinger of his right hand!—he shall draw bowstring no more.—I crave your pardon, my worthy guests. I am beset here with neighbours that match your infidels, Sir Knight, in Holy Land. But your homely fare is before you; feed, and let welcome make amends for hard fare."

The feast, however, which was spread upon the board, needed no apologies from the lord of the mansion. Swine's flesh, dressed in several modes, appeared on the lower part of the board, as also that of fowls, deer, goats, and hares, and various kinds of fish, together with huge loaves and cakes of bread, and sundry confections made of fruits and honey. The smaller sorts of wild-fowl, of which there was abundance, were not served up in platters, but brought in upon small wooden spits or broaches, and offered by the pages and domestics who bore them, to each guest in succession, who cut from them such a portion as he pleased. Beside each person of rank was placed a goblet of silver; the lower board was accommodated with large drinking horns.

When the repast was about to commence, the major-domo, or steward, suddenly raising his wand, said aloud,—"Forbear!—Place for the Lady Rowena."

A side-door at the upper end of the hall now opened behind the banquet table, and Rowena, followed by four female attendants, entered the apartment. Cedric, though surprised, and perhaps not altogether agreeably so, at his ward appearing in public on this occasion, hastened to meet her, and to conduct her, with respectful ceremony, to the elevated seat at his own right hand, appropriated to the lady of the mansion. All stood up to receive her; and, replying to their courtesy by a mute gesture of salutation, she moved gracefully forward to assume her place at the board. Ere she had time to do so, the Templar whispered to the Prior, "I shall wear no collar of gold of yours at the tournament. The Chian wine is your own."

"Said I not so?" answered the Prior; "but check your raptures, the Franklin observes you."

Unheeding this remonstrance, and accustomed only to act upon the immediate impulse of his own wishes, Brian de Bois-Guilbert kept his eyes riveted on the Saxon beauty, more striking perhaps to his imagination, because differing widely from those of the Eastern sultanas.

Formed in the best proportions of her sex, Rowena was tall in stature, yet not so much so as to attract observation on account of superior height. Her complexion was exquisitely fair, but the noble cast of her head and features prevented the insipidity which sometimes attaches to fair beauties. Her clear blue eye, which sat enshrined beneath a graceful eyebrow of brown sufficiently marked to give expression to the forehead, seemed capable to kindle as well as melt, to command as well as to beseech. If mildness were the more natural expression of such a combination of features, it was plain, that in the present instance, the exercise of habitual superiority, and the reception of general homage, had given to the Saxon lady a loftier character, which mingled with and qualified that bestowed by nature. Her profuse hair, of a colour betwixt brown and flaxen, was arranged in a fanciful and graceful manner in numerous ringlets, to form which art had probably aided nature. These locks were braided with gems, and, being worn at full length, intimated the noble birth and freeborn condition of the maiden. A golden chain, to which was attached a small reliquary of the same metal, hung round her neck. She wore bracelets on her arms, which were bare. Her dress was an under-gown and kirtle of pale sea-green silk, over which hung a long loose robe, which reached to the ground, having very wide sleeves, which came down, however, very little below the elbow. This robe was crimson, and manufactured out of the very finest wool. A veil of silk, interwoven with gold, was attached to the upper part of it, which could be, at the wearer's pleasure, either drawn over the face and bosom after the Spanish fashion, or disposed as a sort of drapery round the shoulders.

When Rowena perceived the Knight Templar's eyes bent on her with an ardour, that, compared with the dark caverns under which they moved, gave them the effect of lighted charcoal, she drew with dignity the veil around her face, as an intimation that the determined freedom of his glance was disagreeable. Cedric saw the motion and its cause. "Sir Templar," said he, "the cheeks of our Saxon maidens have seen too little of the sun to enable them to bear the fixed glance of a crusader."

"If I have offended," replied Sir Brian, "I crave your pardon,—that is, I crave the Lady Rowena's pardon,—for my humility will carry me no lower."

"The Lady Rowena," said the Prior, "has punished us all, in chastising the boldness of my friend. Let me hope she will be less cruel to the splendid train which are to meet at the tournament."

"Our going thither," said Cedric, "is uncertain. I love not these vanities, which were unknown to my fathers when England was free."

"Let us hope, nevertheless," said the Prior, "our company may determine you to travel thitherward; when the roads are so unsafe, the escort of Sir Brian de Bois-Guilbert is not to be despised."

"Sir Prior," answered the Saxon, "wheresoever I have travelled in this land, I have hitherto found myself, with the assistance of my good sword and faithful followers, in no respect needful of other aid. At present, if we indeed journey to Ashby-de-la-Zouche, we do so with my noble neighbour and countryman Athelstane of Coningsburgh, and with such a train as would set outlaws and feudal enemies at defiance.—I drink to you, Sir Prior, in this cup of wine, which I trust your taste will approve, and I thank you for your courtesy. Should you be so rigid in adhering to monastic rule," he added, "as to prefer your acid preparation of milk, I hope you will not strain courtesy to do me reason."

"Nay," said the Priest, laughing, "it is only in our abbey that we confine ourselves to the 'lac dulce' or the 'lac acidum' either. Conversing with, the world, we use the world's fashions, and therefore I answer your pledge in this honest wine, and leave the weaker liquor to my lay-brother."

"And I," said the Templar, filling his goblet, "drink wassail to the fair Rowena; for since her namesake introduced the word into England, has never been one more worthy of such a tribute. By my faith, I could pardon the unhappy Vortigern, had he half the cause that we now witness, for making shipwreck of his honour and his kingdom."

"I will spare your courtesy, Sir Knight," said Rowena with dignity, and without unveiling herself; "or rather I will tax it so far as to require of you the latest news from Palestine, a theme more agreeable to our English ears than the compliments which your French breeding teaches."

"I have little of importance to say, lady," answered Sir Brian de Bois-Guilbert, "excepting the confirmed tidings of a truce with Saladin."

He was interrupted by Wamba, who had taken his appropriated seat upon a chair, the back of which was decorated with two ass's ears, and which was placed about two steps behind that of his master, who, from time to time, supplied him with victuals from his own trencher; a favour, however, which the Jester shared with the favourite dogs, of whom, as we have already noticed, there were several in attendance. Here sat Wamba, with a small table before him, his heels tucked up against the bar of the chair, his cheeks sucked up so as to make his jaws resemble a pair of nutcrackers, and his eyes half-shut, yet watching with alertness every opportunity to exercise his licensed foolery.

"These truces with the infidels," he exclaimed, without caring how suddenly he interrupted the stately Templar, "make an old man of me!"

"Go to, knave, how so?" said Cedric, his features prepared to receive favourably the expected jest.

"Because," answered Wamba, "I remember three of them in my day, each of which was to endure for the course of fifty years; so that, by computation, I must be at least a hundred and fifty years old."

"I will warrant you against dying of old age, however," said the Templar, who now recognised his friend of the forest; "I will assure you from all deaths but a violent one, if you give such directions to wayfarers, as you did this night to the Prior and me."

"How, sirrah!" said Cedric, "misdirect travellers? We must have you whipt; you are at least as much rogue as fool."

"I pray thee, uncle," answered the Jester, "let my folly, for once, protect my roguery. I did but make a mistake between my right hand and my left; and he might have pardoned a greater, who took a fool for his counsellor and guide."

Conversation was here interrupted by the entrance of the porter's page, who announced that there was a stranger at the gate, imploring admittance and hospitality.

"Admit him," said Cedric, "be he who or what he may;—a night like that which roars without, compels even wild animals to herd with tame, and to seek the protection of man, their mortal foe, rather than perish by the elements. Let his wants be ministered to with all care—look to it, Oswald."

And the steward left the banqueting hall to see the commands of his patron obeyed.

V.

> Hath not a Jew eyes? Hath not a Jew hands, organs, dimensions,
> senses, affections, passions? Fed with the same food, hurt with
> the same weapons, subject to the same diseases, healed by the
> same means, warmed and cooled by the same winter and summer, as
> a Christian is?
>
> — MERCHANT OF VENICE

Oswald, returning, whispered into the ear of his master, "It is a Jew, who calls himself Isaac of York; is it fit I should marshall him into the hall?"

"Let Gurth do thine office, Oswald," said Wamba with his usual effrontery; "the swineherd will be a fit usher to the Jew."

"St Mary," said the Abbot, crossing himself, "an unbelieving Jew, and admitted into this presence!"

"A dog Jew," echoed the Templar, "to approach a defender of the Holy Sepulchre?"

"By my faith," said Wamba, "it would seem the Templars love the Jews' inheritance better than they do their company."

"Peace, my worthy guests," said Cedric; "my hospitality must not be bounded by your dislikes. If Heaven bore with the whole nation of stiff-necked unbelievers for more years than a layman can number, we may endure the presence of one Jew for a few hours. But I constrain no man to converse or to feed with him.—Let him have a board and a morsel apart,—unless," he said smiling, "these turban'd strangers will admit his society."

"Sir Franklin," answered the Templar, "my Saracen slaves are true Moslems, and scorn as much as any Christian to hold intercourse with a Jew."

"Now, in faith," said Wamba, "I cannot see that the worshippers of Mahound and Termagaunt have so greatly the advantage over the people once chosen of Heaven."

"He shall sit with thee, Wamba," said Cedric; "the fool and the knave will be well met."

"The fool," answered Wamba, raising the relics of a gammon of bacon, "will take care to erect a bulwark against the knave."

"Hush," said Cedric, "for here he comes."

Introduced with little ceremony, and advancing with fear and hesitation, and many a bow of deep humility, a tall thin old man, who, however, had lost by the habit of stooping much of his actual height, approached the lower end of the board. His features, keen and regular, with an aquiline nose, and piercing black eyes; his high and wrinkled forehead, and long grey hair and beard, would have been considered as handsome, had they not been the marks of a physiognomy peculiar to a race, which, during those dark ages, was alike detested by the credulous and prejudiced vulgar, and persecuted by the greedy and rapacious nobility, and who, perhaps, owing to that very hatred and persecution, had adopted a national character, in which there was much, to say the least, mean and unamiable.

The Jew's dress, which appeared to have suffered considerably from the storm, was a plain russet cloak of many folds, covering a dark purple tunic. He had large boots lined with fur, and a belt around his waist, which sustained a small knife, together with a case for writing materials, but no weapon. He wore a high square yellow cap of a peculiar fashion, assigned to his nation to distinguish them from Christians, and which he doffed with great humility at the door of the hall.

The reception of this person in the hall of Cedric the Saxon, was such as might have satisfied the most prejudiced enemy of the tribes of Israel. Cedric himself coldly nodded in answer to the Jew's repeated salutations, and signed to him to take place at the lower end of the table, where, however, no one offered to make room for him. On the contrary, as he passed along the file, casting a timid supplicating glance, and turning towards each of those who occupied the lower end of the board, the Saxon domestics squared their shoulders, and continued to devour their supper with great perseverance, paying not the least attention to the wants of the new guest. The attendants of the Abbot crossed themselves, with looks of pious horror, and the very heathen Saracens, as Isaac drew near them, curled up their whiskers with indignation, and laid their hands on their poniards, as if ready to rid themselves by the most desperate means from the apprehended contamination of his nearer approach.

Probably the same motives which induced Cedric to open his hall to this son of a rejected people, would have made him insist on his attendants receiving Isaac with more courtesy. But the Abbot had, at this moment, engaged him in a most interesting discussion on the breed and character of his favourite hounds, which he would not have interrupted for matters of much greater importance than that of a Jew going to bed supperless. While Isaac thus stood an outcast in the present society, like his people among the nations, looking in vain for welcome or resting place, the pilgrim who sat by the chimney took compassion upon him, and resigned his seat, saying briefly, "Old man, my garments are dried, my hunger is appeased, thou art both wet and fasting." So saying, he gathered together, and brought to a flame, the decaying brands which lay scattered on the ample hearth; took from the larger board a mess of pottage and seethed kid, placed it upon the small table at which he had himself supped, and, without waiting the Jew's thanks, went to the other side of the hall;— whether from unwillingness to hold more close communication with the object of his benevolence, or from a wish to draw near to the upper end of the table, seemed uncertain.

Had there been painters in those days capable to execute such a subject, the Jew, as he bent his withered form, and expanded his chilled and trembling hands over the fire, would have formed no bad emblematical personification of the Winter season. Having dispelled the cold, he turned eagerly to the smoking mess which was placed before him, and ate with a haste and an apparent relish, that seemed to betoken long abstinence from food.

Meanwhile the Abbot and Cedric continued their discourse upon hunting; the Lady Rowena seemed engaged in conversation with one of her attendant females; and the haughty Templar, whose eye wandered from the Jew to the Saxon beauty, revolved in his mind thoughts which appeared deeply to interest him.

"I marvel, worthy Cedric," said the Abbot, as their discourse proceeded, "that, great as your predilection is for your own manly language, you do not receive the Norman-French into your favour, so far at least as the mystery of wood-craft and hunting is concerned. Surely no tongue is so rich in the various phrases which the field-sports demand, or furnishes means to the experienced woodman so well to express his jovial art."

"Good Father Aymer," said the Saxon, "be it known to you, I care not for those over-sea refinements, without which I can well enough take my pleasure in the woods. I can wind my horn, though I call not the blast either a 'recheate' or a 'morte'—I can cheer my dogs on the prey, and I can flay and quarter the animal when it is brought down, without using the newfangled jargon of 'curee, arbor, nombles', and all the babble of the fabulous Sir Tristrem."

"The French," said the Templar, raising his voice with the presumptuous and authoritative tone which he used upon all occasions, "is not only the natural language of the chase, but that of love and of war, in which ladies should be won and enemies defied."

"Pledge me in a cup of wine, Sir Templar," said Cedric, "and fill another to the Abbot, while I look back some thirty years to tell you another tale. As Cedric the Saxon then was, his plain English tale needed no garnish from French troubadours, when it was told in the ear of beauty; and the field of Northallerton, upon the day of the Holy Standard, could tell whether the Saxon war-cry was not heard as far within the ranks of the Scottish host as the 'cri de guerre' of the boldest Norman baron. To the memory of the brave who fought there!—Pledge me, my guests." He drank deep, and went on with increasing warmth. "Ay, that was a day of cleaving of shields, when a hundred banners were bent forwards over the heads of the valiant, and blood flowed round like water, and death was held better than flight. A Saxon bard had called it a feast of the swords—a gathering of the eagles to the prey—the clashing of bills upon shield and helmet, the shouting of battle more joyful than the clamour of a bridal. But our bards are no more," he said; "our deeds are lost in those of another race—our language—our very name—is hastening to decay, and none mourns for it save one solitary old man—Cupbearer! knave, fill the goblets—To the strong in arms, Sir Templar, be their race or language what it will, who now bear them best in Palestine among the champions of the Cross!"

"It becomes not one wearing this badge to answer," said Sir Brian de Bois-Guilbert; "yet to whom, besides the sworn Champions of the Holy Sepulchre, can the palm be assigned among the champions of the Cross?"

"To the Knights Hospitallers," said the Abbot; "I have a brother of their order."

"I impeach not their fame," said the Templar; "nevertheless—"

"I think, friend Cedric," said Wamba, interfering, "that had Richard of the Lion's Heart been wise enough to have taken a fool's advice, he might have staid at home with his merry Englishmen, and left the recovery of Jerusalem to those same Knights who had most to do with the loss of it."

"Were there, then, none in the English army," said the Lady Rowena, "whose names are worthy to be mentioned with the Knights of the Temple, and of St John?"

"Forgive me, lady," replied De Bois-Guilbert; "the English monarch did, indeed, bring to Palestine a host of gallant warriors, second only to those whose breasts have been the unceasing bulwark of that blessed land."

"Second to NONE," said the Pilgrim, who had stood near enough to hear, and had listened to this conversation with marked impatience. All turned toward the spot from whence this unexpected asseveration was heard.

"I say," repeated the Pilgrim in a firm and strong voice, "that the English chivalry were second to NONE who ever drew sword in defence of the Holy Land. I say besides, for I saw it, that King Richard himself, and five of his knights, held a tournament after the taking of St John-de-Acre, as challengers against all comers. I say that, on that day, each knight ran three courses, and cast to the ground three antagonists. I add, that seven of these assailants were Knights of the Temple—and Sir Brian de Bois-Guilbert well knows the truth of what I tell you."

It is impossible for language to describe the bitter scowl of rage which rendered yet darker the swarthy countenance of the Templar. In the extremity of his resentment and confusion, his quivering fingers griped towards the handle of his sword, and perhaps only withdrew, from the consciousness that no act of violence could be safely executed in that place and presence. Cedric, whose feelings were all of a right onward and simple kind, and were seldom occupied by more than one object at once, omitted, in the joyous glee with which he heard of the glory of his countrymen, to remark the angry confusion of his guest; "I would give thee this golden bracelet, Pilgrim," he said, "couldst thou tell me the names of those knights who upheld so gallantly the renown of merry England."

"That will I do blithely," replied the Pilgrim, "and without guerdon; my oath, for a time, prohibits me from touching gold."

"I will wear the bracelet for you, if you will, friend Palmer," said Wamba.

"The first in honour as in arms, in renown as in place," said the Pilgrim, "was the brave Richard, King of England."

"I forgive him," said Cedric; "I forgive him his descent from the tyrant Duke William."

"The Earl of Leicester was the second," continued the Pilgrim; "Sir Thomas Multon of Gilsland was the third."

"Of Saxon descent, he at least," said Cedric, with exultation.

"Sir Foulk Doilly the fourth," proceeded the Pilgrim.

"Saxon also, at least by the mother's side," continued Cedric, who listened with the utmost eagerness, and forgot, in part at least, his hatred to the Normans, in the common triumph of the King of England and his islanders. "And who was the fifth?" he demanded.

"The fifth was Sir Edwin Turneham."

"Genuine Saxon, by the soul of Hengist!" shouted Cedric—"And the sixth?" he continued with eagerness—"how name you the sixth?"

"The sixth," said the Palmer, after a pause, in which he seemed to recollect himself, "was a young knight of lesser renown and lower rank, assumed into that honourable company, less to aid their enterprise than to make up their number—his name dwells not in my memory."

"Sir Palmer," said Sir Brian de Bois-Guilbert scornfully, "this assumed forgetfulness, after so much has been remembered, comes too late to serve your purpose. I will myself tell the name of the knight before whose lance fortune and my horse's fault occasioned my falling—it was the Knight of Ivanhoe; nor was there one of the six that, for his years, had more renown in arms.—Yet this will I say, and loudly—that were he in England, and durst repeat, in this week's tournament, the challenge of St John-de-Acre, I, mounted and armed as I now am, would give him every advantage of weapons, and abide the result."

"Your challenge would soon be answered," replied the Palmer, "were your antagonist near you. As the matter is, disturb not the peaceful hall with vaunts of the issue of the conflict, which you well know cannot take place. If Ivanhoe ever returns from Palestine, I will be his surety that he meets you."

"A goodly security!" said the Knight Templar; "and what do you proffer as a pledge?"

"This reliquary," said the Palmer, taking a small ivory box from his bosom, and crossing himself, "containing a portion of the true cross, brought from the Monastery of Mount Carmel."

The Prior of Jorvaulx crossed himself and repeated a pater noster, in which all devoutly joined, excepting the Jew, the Mahomedans, and the Templar; the latter of whom, without vailing his bonnet, or testifying any reverence for the alleged sanctity of the relic, took from his neck a gold chain, which he flung on the board, saying— "Let Prior Aymer hold my pledge and that of this nameless vagrant, in token that when the Knight of Ivanhoe comes within the four seas of Britain, he underlies the challenge of Brian de Bois-Guilbert, which, if he answer not, I will proclaim him as a coward on the walls of every Temple Court in Europe."

"It will not need," said the Lady Rowena, breaking silence; "My voice shall be heard, if no other in this hall is raised in behalf of the absent Ivanhoe. I affirm he will meet fairly every honourable challenge. Could my weak warrant add security to the inestimable pledge of this holy pilgrim, I would pledge name and fame that Ivanhoe gives this proud knight the meeting he desires."

A crowd of conflicting emotions seemed to have occupied Cedric, and kept him silent during this discussion. Gratified pride, resentment, embarrassment, chased each other over his broad and open brow, like the shadow of clouds drifting over a harvest-field; while his attendants, on whom the name of the sixth knight seemed to produce an effect almost electrical, hung in suspense upon their master's looks. But when Rowena spoke, the sound of her voice seemed to startle him from his silence.

"Lady," said Cedric, "this beseems not; were further pledge necessary, I myself, offended, and justly offended, as I am, would yet gage my honour for the honour of Ivanhoe. But the wager of battle is complete, even according to the fantastic fashions of Norman chivalry—Is it not, Father Aymer?"

"It is," replied the Prior; "and the blessed relic and rich chain will I bestow safely in the treasury of our convent, until the decision of this warlike challenge."

Having thus spoken, he crossed himself again and again, and after many genuflections and muttered prayers, he delivered the reliquary to Brother Ambrose, his attendant monk, while he himself swept up with less ceremony, but perhaps with no less internal satisfaction, the golden chain, and bestowed it in a pouch lined with perfumed leather, which opened under his arm. "And now, Sir Cedric," he said, "my ears are chiming vespers with the strength of your good wine—permit us another pledge to the welfare of the Lady Rowena, and indulge us with liberty to pass to our repose."

"By the rood of Bromholme," said the Saxon, "you do but small credit to your fame, Sir Prior! Report speaks you a bonny monk, that would hear the matin chime ere he quitted his bowl; and, old as I am, I feared to have shame in encountering you. But, by my faith, a Saxon boy of twelve, in my time, would not so soon have relinquished his goblet."

The Prior had his own reasons, however, for persevering in the course of temperance which he had adopted. He was not only a professional peacemaker, but from practice a hater of all feuds and brawls. It was not altogether from a love to his neighbour, or to himself, or from a mixture of both. On the present occasion, he had an instinctive apprehension of the fiery temper of the Saxon, and saw the danger that the reckless and presumptuous spirit, of which his companion had already given so many proofs, might at length produce some disagreeable explosion. He therefore gently insinuated the incapacity of the native of any other country to engage in the genial conflict of the bowl with the hardy and strong-headed Saxons; something he mentioned, but slightly, about his own holy character, and ended by pressing his proposal to depart to repose.

The grace-cup was accordingly served round, and the guests, after making deep obeisance to their landlord and to the Lady Rowena, arose and mingled in the hall, while the heads of the family, by separate doors, retired with their attendants.

"Unbelieving dog," said the Templar to Isaac the Jew, as he passed him in the throng, "dost thou bend thy course to the tournament?"

"I do so propose," replied Isaac, bowing in all humility, "if it please your reverend valour."

"Ay," said the Knight, "to gnaw the bowels of our nobles with usury, and to gull women and boys with gauds and toys—I warrant thee store of shekels in thy Jewish scrip."

"Not a shekel, not a silver penny, not a halfling—so help me the God of Abraham!" said the Jew, clasping his hands; "I go but to seek the assistance of some brethren of my tribe to aid me to pay the fine which the Exchequer of the Jews have imposed upon me—Father Jacob be my speed! I am an impoverished wretch—the very gaberdine I wear is borrowed from Reuben of Tadcaster."

The Templar smiled sourly as he replied, "Beshrew thee for a false-hearted liar!" and passing onward, as if disdaining farther conference, he communed with his Moslem slaves in a language unknown to the bystanders. The poor Israelite seemed so staggered by the address of the military monk, that the Templar had passed on to the extremity of the hall ere he raised his head from the humble posture which he had assumed, so far as to be sensible of his departure. And when he did look around, it was with the astonished air of one at whose feet a thunderbolt has just burst, and who hears still the astounding report ringing in his ears.

The Templar and Prior were shortly after marshalled to their sleeping apartments by the steward and the cupbearer, each attended by two torchbearers and two servants carrying refreshments, while servants of inferior condition indicated to their retinue and to the other guests their respective places of repose.

VI.

> To buy his favour I extend this friendship:
> If he will take it, so; if not, adieu;
> And, for my love, I pray you wrong me not.
>
> — MERCHANT OF VENICE

As the Palmer, lighted by a domestic with a torch, passed through the intricate combination of apartments of this large and irregular mansion, the cupbearer coming behind him whispered in his ear, that if he had no objection to a cup of good mead in his apartment, there were many domestics in that family who would gladly hear the news he had brought from the Holy Land, and particularly that which concerned the Knight of Ivanhoe. Wamba presently appeared to urge the same request, observing that a cup after midnight was worth three after curfew. Without disputing a maxim urged by such grave authority, the Palmer thanked them for their courtesy, but observed that he had included in his religious vow, an obligation never to speak in the kitchen on matters which were prohibited in the hall. "That vow," said Wamba to the cupbearer, "would scarce suit a serving-man."

The cupbearer shrugged up his shoulders in displeasure. "I thought to have lodged him in the solere chamber," said he; "but since he is so unsocial to Christians, e'en let him take the next stall to Isaac the Jew's.—Anwold," said he to the torch-bearer, "carry the Pilgrim to the southern cell.—I give you good-night," he added, "Sir Palmer, with small thanks for short courtesy."

"Good-night, and Our Lady's benison," said the Palmer, with composure; and his guide moved forward.

In a small antechamber, into which several doors opened, and which was lighted by a small iron lamp, they met a second interruption from the waiting-maid of Rowena, who, saying in a tone of authority, that her mistress desired to speak with the Palmer, took the torch from the hand of Anwold, and, bidding him await her return, made a sign to the Palmer to follow. Apparently he did not think it proper to decline this invitation as he had done the former; for, though his gesture indicated some surprise at the summons, he obeyed it without answer or remonstrance.

A short passage, and an ascent of seven steps, each of which was composed of a solid beam of oak, led him to the apartment of the Lady Rowena, the rude magnificence of which corresponded to the respect which was paid to her by the lord of the mansion. The walls were covered with embroidered hangings, on which different-coloured silks, interwoven with gold and silver threads, had been employed with all the art of which the age was capable, to represent the sports of hunting and hawking. The bed was adorned with the same rich tapestry, and surrounded with curtains dyed with purple. The seats had also their stained coverings, and one, which was higher than the rest, was accommodated with a footstool of ivory, curiously carved.

No fewer than four silver candelabras, holding great waxen torches, served to illuminate this apartment. Yet let not modern beauty envy the magnificence of a Saxon princess. The walls of the apartment were so ill finished and so full of crevices, that the rich hangings shook in the night blast, and, in despite of a sort of screen intended to protect them from the wind, the flame of the torches streamed sideways into the air, like the unfurled pennon of a chieftain. Magnificence there was, with some rude attempt at taste; but of comfort there was little, and, being unknown, it was unmissed.

The Lady Rowena, with three of her attendants standing at her back, and arranging her hair ere she lay down to rest, was seated in the sort of throne already mentioned, and looked as if born to exact general homage. The Pilgrim acknowledged her claim to it by a low genuflection.

"Rise, Palmer," said she graciously. "The defender of the absent has a right to favourable reception from all who value truth, and honour manhood." She then said to her train, "Retire, excepting only Elgitha; I would speak with this holy Pilgrim."

The maidens, without leaving the apartment, retired to its further extremity, and sat down on a small bench against the wall, where they remained mute as statues, though at such a distance that their whispers could not have interrupted the conversation of their mistress.

"Pilgrim," said the lady, after a moment's pause, during which she seemed uncertain how to address him, "you this night mentioned a name—I mean," she said, with a degree of effort, "the name of Ivanhoe, in the halls where by nature and kindred it should have sounded most acceptably; and yet, such is the perverse course of fate, that of many whose hearts must have throbbed at the sound, I, only, dare ask you where, and in what condition, you left him of whom you spoke?—We heard, that, having remained in Palestine, on account of his impaired health, after the departure of the English army, he had experienced the persecution of the French faction, to whom the Templars are known to be attached."

"I know little of the Knight of Ivanhoe," answered the Palmer, with a troubled voice. "I would I knew him better, since you, lady, are interested in his fate. He hath, I believe, surmounted the persecution of his enemies in Palestine, and is on the eve of returning to England, where you, lady, must know better than I, what is his chance of happiness."

The Lady Rowena sighed deeply, and asked more particularly when the Knight of Ivanhoe might be expected in his native country, and whether he would not be exposed to great dangers by the road. On the first point, the Palmer professed ignorance; on the second, he said that the voyage might be safely made by the way of Venice and Genoa, and from thence through France to England. "Ivanhoe," he said, "was so well acquainted with the language and manners of the French, that there was no fear of his incurring any hazard during that part of his travels."

"Would to God," said the Lady Rowena, "he were here safely arrived, and able to bear arms in the approaching tourney, in which the chivalry of this land are expected to display their address and valour. Should Athelstane of Coningsburgh obtain the prize, Ivanhoe is like to hear evil tidings when he reaches England.—How looked he, stranger, when you last saw him? Had disease laid her hand heavy upon his strength and comeliness?"

"He was darker," said the Palmer, "and thinner, than when he came from Cyprus in the train of Coeur-de-Lion, and care seemed to sit heavy on his brow; but I approached not his presence, because he is unknown to me."

"He will," said the lady, "I fear, find little in his native land to clear those clouds from his countenance. Thanks, good Pilgrim, for your information concerning the companion of my childhood.—Maidens," she said, "draw near—offer the sleeping cup to this holy man, whom I will no longer detain from repose."

One of the maidens presented a silver cup, containing a rich mixture of wine and spice, which Rowena barely put to her lips. It was then offered to the Palmer, who, after a low obeisance, tasted a few drops.

"Accept this alms, friend," continued the lady, offering a piece of gold, "in acknowledgment of thy painful travail, and of the shrines thou hast visited."

The Palmer received the boon with another low reverence, and followed Edwina out of the apartment.

In the anteroom he found his attendant Anwold, who, taking the torch from the hand of the waiting-maid, conducted him with more haste than ceremony to an exterior and ignoble part of the building, where a number of small apartments, or rather cells, served for sleeping places to the lower order of domestics, and to strangers of mean degree.

"In which of these sleeps the Jew?" said the Pilgrim.

"The unbelieving dog," answered Anwold, "kennels in the cell next your holiness. —St Dunstan, how it must be scraped and cleansed ere it be again fit for a Christian!"

"And where sleeps Gurth the swineherd?" said the stranger.

"Gurth," replied the bondsman, "sleeps in the cell on your right, as the Jew on that to your left; you serve to keep the child of circumcision separate from the abomination of his tribe. You might have occupied a more honourable place had you accepted of Oswald's invitation."

"It is as well as it is," said the Palmer; "the company, even of a Jew, can hardly spread contamination through an oaken partition."

So saying, he entered the cabin allotted to him, and taking the torch from the domestic's hand, thanked him, and wished him good-night. Having shut the door of his cell, he placed the torch in a candlestick made of wood, and looked around his sleeping apartment, the furniture of which was of the most simple kind. It consisted of a rude wooden stool, and still ruder hutch or bed-frame, stuffed with clean straw, and accommodated with two or three sheepskins by way of bed-clothes.

The Palmer, having extinguished his torch, threw himself, without taking off any part of his clothes, on this rude couch, and slept, or at least retained his recumbent posture, till the earliest sunbeams found their way through the little grated window, which served at once to admit both air and light to his uncomfortable cell. He then started up, and after repeating his matins, and adjusting his dress, he left it, and entered that of Isaac the Jew, lifting the latch as gently as he could.

The inmate was lying in troubled slumber upon a couch similar to that on which the Palmer himself had passed the night. Such parts of his dress as the Jew had laid aside on the preceding evening, were disposed carefully around his person, as if to prevent the hazard of their being carried off during his slumbers. There was a trouble on his brow amounting almost to agony. His hands and arms moved convulsively, as if struggling with the nightmare; and besides several ejaculations in Hebrew, the following were distinctly heard in the Norman-English, or mixed language of the country: "For the sake of the God of Abraham, spare an unhappy old man! I am poor, I am penniless—should your irons wrench my limbs asunder, I could not gratify you!"

The Palmer awaited not the end of the Jew's vision, but stirred him with his pilgrim's staff. The touch probably associated, as is usual, with some of the apprehensions excited by his dream; for the old man started up, his grey hair standing almost erect upon his head, and huddling some part of his garments about him, while he held the detached pieces with the tenacious grasp of a falcon, he fixed upon the Palmer his keen black eyes, expressive of wild surprise and of bodily apprehension.

"Fear nothing from me, Isaac," said the Palmer, "I come as your friend."

"The God of Israel requite you," said the Jew, greatly relieved; "I dreamed—But Father Abraham be praised, it was but a dream." Then, collecting himself, he added in his usual tone, "And what may it be your pleasure to want at so early an hour with the poor Jew?"

"It is to tell you," said the Palmer, "that if you leave not this mansion instantly, and travel not with some haste, your journey may prove a dangerous one."

"Holy father!" said the Jew, "whom could it interest to endanger so poor a wretch as I am?"

"The purpose you can best guess," said the Pilgrim; "but rely on this, that when the Templar crossed the hall yesternight, he spoke to his Mussulman slaves in the Saracen language, which I well understand, and charged them this morning to watch the journey of the Jew, to seize upon him when at a convenient distance from the mansion, and to conduct him to the castle of Philip de Malvoisin, or to that of Reginald Front-de-Boeuf."

It is impossible to describe the extremity of terror which seized upon the Jew at this information, and seemed at once to overpower his whole faculties. His arms fell down to his sides, and his head drooped on his breast, his knees bent under his weight, every nerve and muscle of his frame seemed to collapse and lose its energy, and he sunk at the foot of the Palmer, not in the fashion of one who intentionally stoops, kneels, or prostrates himself to excite compassion, but like a man borne down on all sides by the pressure of some invisible force, which crushes him to the earth without the power of resistance.

"Holy God of Abraham!" was his first exclamation, folding and elevating his wrinkled hands, but without raising his grey head from the pavement; "Oh, holy Moses! O, blessed Aaron! the dream is not dreamed for nought, and the vision cometh not in vain! I feel their irons already tear my sinews! I feel the rack pass over my body like the saws, and harrows, and axes of iron over the men of Rabbah, and of the cities of the children of Ammon!"

"Stand up, Isaac, and hearken to me," said the Palmer, who viewed the extremity of his distress with a compassion in which contempt was largely mingled; "you have cause for your terror, considering how your brethren have been used, in order to extort from them their hoards, both by princes and nobles; but stand up, I say, and I will point out to you the means of escape. Leave this mansion instantly, while its inmates sleep sound after the last night's revel. I will guide you by the secret paths of the forest, known as well to me as to any forester that ranges it, and I will not leave you till you are under safe conduct of some chief or baron going to the tournament, whose good-will you have probably the means of securing."

As the ears of Isaac received the hopes of escape which this speech intimated, he began gradually, and inch by inch, as it were, to raise himself up from the ground, until he fairly rested upon his knees, throwing back his long grey hair and beard, and fixing his keen black eyes upon the Palmer's face, with a look expressive at once of hope and fear, not unmingled with suspicion. But when he heard the concluding part of the sentence, his original terror appeared to revive in full force, and he dropt once more on his face, exclaiming, "'I' possess the means of securing good-will! alas! there is but one road to the favour of a Christian, and how can the poor Jew find it, whom extortions have already reduced to the misery of Lazarus?" Then, as if suspicion had overpowered his other feelings, he suddenly exclaimed, "For the love of God, young man, betray me not—for the sake of the Great Father who made us all, Jew as well as Gentile, Israelite and Ishmaelite—do me no treason! I have not means to secure the good-will of a Christian beggar, were he rating it at a single penny." As he spoke these last words, he raised himself, and grasped the Palmer's mantle with a look of the most earnest entreaty. The pilgrim extricated himself, as if there were contamination in the touch.

"Wert thou loaded with all the wealth of thy tribe," he said, "what interest have I to injure thee?—In this dress I am vowed to poverty, nor do I change it for aught save a horse and a coat of mail. Yet think not that I care for thy company, or propose myself advantage by it; remain here if thou wilt—Cedric the Saxon may protect thee."

"Alas!" said the Jew, "he will not let me travel in his train—Saxon or Norman will be equally ashamed of the poor Israelite; and to travel by myself through the domains of Philip de Malvoisin and Reginald Front-de-Boeuf—Good youth, I will go with you! —Let us haste—let us gird up our loins—let us flee!—Here is thy staff, why wilt thou tarry?"

"I tarry not," said the Pilgrim, giving way to the urgency of his companion; "but I must secure the means of leaving this place—follow me."

He led the way to the adjoining cell, which, as the reader is apprised, was occupied by Gurth the swineherd.—"Arise, Gurth," said the Pilgrim, "arise quickly. Undo the postern gate, and let out the Jew and me."

Gurth, whose occupation, though now held so mean, gave him as much consequence in Saxon England as that of Eumaeus in Ithaca, was offended at the familiar and commanding tone assumed by the Palmer. "The Jew leaving Rotherwood," said he, raising himself on his elbow, and looking superciliously at him without quitting his pallet, "and travelling in company with the Palmer to boot—"

"I should as soon have dreamt," said Wamba, who entered the apartment at the instant, "of his stealing away with a gammon of bacon."

"Nevertheless," said Gurth, again laying down his head on the wooden log which served him for a pillow, "both Jew and Gentile must be content to abide the opening of the great gate—we suffer no visitors to depart by stealth at these unseasonable hours."

"Nevertheless," said the Pilgrim, in a commanding tone, "you will not, I think, refuse me that favour."

So saying, he stooped over the bed of the recumbent swineherd, and whispered something in his ear in Saxon. Gurth started up as if electrified. The Pilgrim, raising his finger in an attitude as if to express caution, added, "Gurth, beware—thou are wont to be prudent. I say, undo the postern—thou shalt know more anon."

With hasty alacrity Gurth obeyed him, while Wamba and the Jew followed, both wondering at the sudden change in the swineherd's demeanour. "My mule, my mule!" said the Jew, as soon as they stood without the postern.

"Fetch him his mule," said the Pilgrim; "and, hearest thou,—let me have another, that I may bear him company till he is beyond these parts—I will return it safely to some of Cedric's train at Ashby. And do thou"—he whispered the rest in Gurth's ear.

"Willingly, most willingly shall it be done," said Gurth, and instantly departed to execute the commission.

"I wish I knew," said Wamba, when his comrade's back was turned, "what you Palmers learn in the Holy Land."

"To say our orisons, fool," answered the Pilgrim, "to repent our sins, and to mortify ourselves with fastings, vigils, and long prayers."

"Something more potent than that," answered the Jester; "for when would repentance or prayer make Gurth do a courtesy, or fasting or vigil persuade him to lend you a mule?—I trow you might as well have told his favourite black boar of thy vigils and penance, and wouldst have gotten as civil an answer."

"Go to," said the Pilgrim, "thou art but a Saxon fool."

"Thou sayst well," said the Jester; "had I been born a Norman, as I think thou art, I would have had luck on my side, and been next door to a wise man."

At this moment Gurth appeared on the opposite side of the moat with the mules. The travellers crossed the ditch upon a drawbridge of only two planks breadth, the narrowness of which was matched with the straitness of the postern, and with a little wicket in the exterior palisade, which gave access to the forest. No sooner had they reached the mules, than the Jew, with hasty and trembling hands, secured behind the saddle a small bag of blue buckram, which he took from under his cloak, containing, as he muttered, "a change of raiment—only a change of raiment." Then getting upon the animal with more alacrity and haste than could have been anticipated from his years, he lost no time in so disposing of the skirts of his gabardine as to conceal completely from observation the burden which he had thus deposited "en croupe".

The Pilgrim mounted with more deliberation, reaching, as he departed, his hand to Gurth, who kissed it with the utmost possible veneration. The swineherd stood gazing after the travellers until they were lost under the boughs of the forest path, when he was disturbed from his reverie by the voice of Wamba.

"Knowest thou," said the Jester, "my good friend Gurth, that thou art strangely courteous and most unwontedly pious on this summer morning? I would I were a black Prior or a barefoot Palmer, to avail myself of thy unwonted zeal and courtesy—certes, I would make more out of it than a kiss of the hand."

"Thou art no fool thus far, Wamba," answered Gurth, "though thou arguest from appearances, and the wisest of us can do no more—But it is time to look after my charge."

So saying, he turned back to the mansion, attended by the Jester.

Meanwhile the travellers continued to press on their journey with a dispatch which argued the extremity of the Jew's fears, since persons at his age are seldom fond of rapid motion. The Palmer, to whom every path and outlet in the wood appeared to be familiar, led the way through the most devious paths, and more than once excited anew the suspicion of the Israelite, that he intended to betray him into some ambuscade of his enemies.

His doubts might have been indeed pardoned; for, except perhaps the flying fish, there was no race existing on the earth, in the air, or the waters, who were the object of such an unintermitting, general, and relentless persecution as the Jews of this period. Upon the slightest and most unreasonable pretences, as well as upon accusations the most absurd and groundless, their persons and property were exposed to every turn of popular fury; for Norman, Saxon, Dane, and Briton, however adverse these races were to each other, contended which should look with greatest detestation upon a people, whom it was accounted a point of religion to hate, to revile, to despise, to plunder, and to persecute. The kings of the Norman race, and the independent nobles, who followed their example in all acts of tyranny, maintained against this devoted people a persecution of a more regular, calculated, and self-interested kind. It is a well-known story of King John, that he confined a wealthy Jew in one of the royal castles, and daily caused one of his teeth to be torn out, until, when the jaw of the unhappy Israelite was half disfurnished, he consented to pay a large sum, which it was the tyrant's object to extort from him. The little ready money which was in the country was chiefly in possession of this persecuted people, and the nobility hesitated not to follow the example of their sovereign, in wringing it from them by every species of oppression, and even personal torture. Yet the passive courage inspired by the love of gain, induced the Jews to dare the various evils to which they were subjected, in consideration of the immense profits which they were enabled to realize in a country naturally so wealthy as England. In spite of every kind of discouragement, and even of the special court of taxations already mentioned, called the Jews' Exchequer, erected for the very purpose of despoiling and distressing them, the Jews increased, multiplied, and accumulated huge sums, which they transferred from one hand to another by means of bills of exchange—an invention for which commerce is said to be indebted to them, and which enabled them to transfer their wealth from land to land, that when threatened with oppression in one country, their treasure might be secured in another.

The obstinacy and avarice of the Jews being thus in a measure placed in opposition to the fanaticism that tyranny of those under whom they lived, seemed to increase in proportion to the persecution with which they were visited; and the immense wealth they usually acquired in commerce, while it frequently placed them in danger, was at other times used to extend their influence, and to secure to them a certain degree of protection. On these terms they lived; and their character, influenced accordingly, was watchful, suspicious, and timid—yet obstinate, uncomplying, and skilful in evading the dangers to which they were exposed.

When the travellers had pushed on at a rapid rate through many devious paths, the Palmer at length broke silence.

"That large decayed oak," he said, "marks the boundaries over which Front-de-Boeuf claims authority—we are long since far from those of Malvoisin. There is now no fear of pursuit."

"May the wheels of their chariots be taken off," said the Jew, "like those of the host of Pharaoh, that they may drive heavily!—But leave me not, good Pilgrim—Think but of that fierce and savage Templar, with his Saracen slaves—they will regard neither territory, nor manor, nor lordship."

"Our road," said the Palmer, "should here separate; for it beseems not men of my character and thine to travel together longer than needs must be. Besides, what succour couldst thou have from me, a peaceful Pilgrim, against two armed heathens?"

"O good youth," answered the Jew, "thou canst defend me, and I know thou wouldst. Poor as I am, I will requite it—not with money, for money, so help me my Father Abraham, I have none—but—"

"Money and recompense," said the Palmer, interrupting him, "I have already said I require not of thee. Guide thee I can; and, it may be, even in some sort defend thee; since to protect a Jew against a Saracen, can scarce be accounted unworthy of a Christian. Therefore, Jew, I will see thee safe under some fitting escort. We are now not far from the town of Sheffield, where thou mayest easily find many of thy tribe with whom to take refuge."

"The blessing of Jacob be upon thee, good youth!" said the Jew; "in Sheffield I can harbour with my kinsman Zareth, and find some means of travelling forth with safety."

"Be it so," said the Palmer; "at Sheffield then we part, and half-an-hour's riding will bring us in sight of that town."

The half hour was spent in perfect silence on both parts; the Pilgrim perhaps disdaining to address the Jew, except in case of absolute necessity, and the Jew not presuming to force a conversation with a person whose journey to the Holy Sepulchre gave a sort of sanctity to his character. They paused on the top of a gently rising bank, and the Pilgrim, pointing to the town of Sheffield, which lay beneath them, repeated the words, "Here, then, we part."

"Not till you have had the poor Jew's thanks," said Isaac; "for I presume not to ask you to go with me to my kinsman Zareth's, who might aid me with some means of repaying your good offices."

"I have already said," answered the Pilgrim, "that I desire no recompense. If among the huge list of thy debtors, thou wilt, for my sake, spare the gyves and the dungeon to some unhappy Christian who stands in thy danger, I shall hold this morning's service to thee well bestowed."

"Stay, stay," said the Jew, laying hold of his garment; "something would I do more than this, something for thyself.—God knows the Jew is poor—yes, Isaac is the beggar of his tribe—but forgive me should I guess what thou most lackest at this moment."

"If thou wert to guess truly," said the Palmer, "it is what thou canst not supply, wert thou as wealthy as thou sayst thou art poor."

"As I say?" echoed the Jew; "O! believe it, I say but the truth; I am a plundered, indebted, distressed man. Hard hands have wrung from me my goods, my money, my ships, and all that I possessed—Yet I can tell thee what thou lackest, and, it may be, supply it too. Thy wish even now is for a horse and armour."

The Palmer started, and turned suddenly towards the Jew:—"What fiend prompted that guess?" said he, hastily.

"No matter," said the Jew, smiling, "so that it be a true one—and, as I can guess thy want, so I can supply it."

"But consider," said the Palmer, "my character, my dress, my vow."

"I know you Christians," replied the Jew, "and that the noblest of you will take the staff and sandal in superstitious penance, and walk afoot to visit the graves of dead men."

"Blaspheme not, Jew," said the Pilgrim, sternly.

"Forgive me," said the Jew; "I spoke rashly. But there dropt words from you last night and this morning, that, like sparks from flint, showed the metal within; and in the bosom of that Palmer's gown, is hidden a knight's chain and spurs of gold. They glanced as you stooped over my bed in the morning."

The Pilgrim could not forbear smiling. "Were thy garments searched by as curious an eye, Isaac," said he, "what discoveries might not be made?"

"No more of that," said the Jew, changing colour; and drawing forth his writing materials in haste, as if to stop the conversation, he began to write upon a piece of paper which he supported on the top of his yellow cap, without dismounting from his mule. When he had finished, he delivered the scroll, which was in the Hebrew character, to the Pilgrim, saying, "In the town of Leicester all men know the rich Jew, Kirjath Jairam of Lombardy; give him this scroll—he hath on sale six Milan harnesses, the worst would suit a crowned head—ten goodly steeds, the worst might mount a king, were he to do battle for his throne. Of these he will give thee thy choice, with every thing else that can furnish thee forth for the tournament: when it is over, thou wilt return them safely—unless thou shouldst have wherewith to pay their value to the owner."

"But, Isaac," said the Pilgrim, smiling, "dost thou know that in these sports, the arms and steed of the knight who is unhorsed are forfeit to his victor? Now I may be unfortunate, and so lose what I cannot replace or repay."

The Jew looked somewhat astounded at this possibility; but collecting his courage, he replied hastily. "No—no—no—It is impossible—I will not think so. The blessing of Our Father will be upon thee. Thy lance will be powerful as the rod of Moses."

So saying, he was turning his mule's head away, when the Palmer, in his turn, took hold of his gaberdine. "Nay, but Isaac, thou knowest not all the risk. The steed may be slain, the armour injured—for I will spare neither horse nor man. Besides, those of thy tribe give nothing for nothing; something there must be paid for their use."

The Jew twisted himself in the saddle, like a man in a fit of the colic; but his better feelings predominated over those which were most familiar to him. "I care not," he said, "I care not—let me go. If there is damage, it will cost you nothing—if there is usage money, Kirjath Jairam will forgive it for the sake of his kinsman Isaac. Fare thee well!—Yet hark thee, good youth," said he, turning about, "thrust thyself not too forward into this vain hurly-burly—I speak not for endangering the steed, and coat of armour, but for the sake of thine own life and limbs."

"Gramercy for thy caution," said the Palmer, again smiling; "I will use thy courtesy frankly, and it will go hard with me but I will requite it."

They parted, and took different roads for the town of Sheffield.

VII.

> Knights, with a long retinue of their squires,
> In gaudy liveries march and quaint attires;
> One laced the helm, another held the lance,
> A third the shining buckler did advance.
> The courser paw'd the ground with restless feet,
> And snorting foam'd and champ'd the golden bit.
> The smiths and armourers on palfreys ride,
> Files in their hands, and hammers at their side;
> And nails for loosen'd spears, and thongs for shields provide.
> The yeomen guard the streets in seemly bands;
> And clowns come crowding on, with cudgels in their hands.

IVANHOE

— PALAMON AND ARCITE

The condition of the English nation was at this time sufficiently miserable. King Richard was absent a prisoner, and in the power of the perfidious and cruel Duke of Austria. Even the very place of his captivity was uncertain, and his fate but very imperfectly known to the generality of his subjects, who were, in the meantime, a prey to every species of subaltern oppression.

Prince John, in league with Philip of France, Coeur-de-Lion's mortal enemy, was using every species of influence with the Duke of Austria, to prolong the captivity of his brother Richard, to whom he stood indebted for so many favours. In the meantime, he was strengthening his own faction in the kingdom, of which he proposed to dispute the succession, in case of the King's death, with the legitimate heir, Arthur Duke of Brittany, son of Geoffrey Plantagenet, the elder brother of John. This usurpation, it is well known, he afterwards effected. His own character being light, profligate, and perfidious, John easily attached to his person and faction, not only all who had reason to dread the resentment of Richard for criminal proceedings during his absence, but also the numerous class of "lawless resolutes," whom the crusades had turned back on their country, accomplished in the vices of the East, impoverished in substance, and hardened in character, and who placed their hopes of harvest in civil commotion. To these causes of public distress and apprehension, must be added, the multitude of outlaws, who, driven to despair by the oppression of the feudal nobility, and the severe exercise of the forest laws, banded together in large gangs, and, keeping possession of the forests and the wastes, set at defiance the justice and magistracy of the country. The nobles themselves, each fortified within his own castle, and playing the petty sovereign over his own dominions, were the leaders of bands scarce less lawless and oppressive than those of the avowed depredators. To maintain these retainers, and to support the extravagance and magnificence which their pride induced them to affect, the nobility borrowed sums of money from the Jews at the most usurious interest, which gnawed into their estates like consuming cankers, scarce to be cured unless when circumstances gave them an opportunity of getting free, by exercising upon their creditors some act of unprincipled violence.

Under the various burdens imposed by this unhappy state of affairs, the people of England suffered deeply for the present, and had yet more dreadful cause to fear for the future. To augment their misery, a contagious disorder of a dangerous nature spread through the land; and, rendered more virulent by the uncleanness, the indifferent food, and the wretched lodging of the lower classes, swept off many whose fate the survivors were tempted to envy, as exempting them from the evils which were to come.

Yet amid these accumulated distresses, the poor as well as the rich, the vulgar as well as the noble, in the event of a tournament, which was the grand spectacle of that age, felt as much interested as the half-starved citizen of Madrid, who has not a real left to buy provisions for his family, feels in the issue of a bull-feast. Neither duty nor infirmity could keep youth or age from such exhibitions. The Passage of Arms, as it was called, which was to take place at Ashby, in the county of Leicester, as champions of the first renown were to take the field in the presence of Prince John himself, who was expected to grace the lists, had attracted universal attention, and an immense confluence of persons of all ranks hastened upon the appointed morning to the place of combat.

The scene was singularly romantic. On the verge of a wood, which approached to within a mile of the town of Ashby, was an extensive meadow, of the finest and most beautiful green turf, surrounded on one side by the forest, and fringed on the other by straggling oak-trees, some of which had grown to an immense size. The ground, as if fashioned on purpose for the martial display which was intended, sloped gradually down on all sides to a level bottom, which was enclosed for the lists with strong palisades, forming a space of a quarter of a mile in length, and about half as broad. The form of the enclosure was an oblong square, save that the corners were considerably rounded off, in order to afford more convenience for the spectators. The openings for the entry of the combatants were at the northern and southern extremities of the lists, accessible by strong wooden gates, each wide enough to admit two horsemen riding abreast. At each of these portals were stationed two heralds, attended by six trumpets, as many pursuivants, and a strong body of men-at-arms for maintaining order, and ascertaining the quality of the knights who proposed to engage in this martial game.

On a platform beyond the southern entrance, formed by a natural elevation of the ground, were pitched five magnificent pavilions, adorned with pennons of russet and black, the chosen colours of the five knights challengers. The cords of the tents were of the same colour. Before each pavilion was suspended the shield of the knight by whom it was occupied, and beside it stood his squire, quaintly disguised as a salvage or silvan man, or in some other fantastic dress, according to the taste of his master, and the character he was pleased to assume during the game.

The central pavilion, as the place of honour, had been assigned to Brian be Bois-Guilbert, whose renown in all games of chivalry, no less than his connexions with the knights who had undertaken this Passage of Arms, had occasioned him to be eagerly received into the company of the challengers, and even adopted as their chief and leader, though he had so recently joined them. On one side of his tent were pitched those of Reginald Front-de-Boeuf and Richard de Malvoisin, and on the other was the pavilion of Hugh de Grantmesnil, a noble baron in the vicinity, whose ancestor had been Lord High Steward of England in the time of the Conqueror, and his son William Rufus. Ralph de Vipont, a knight of St John of Jerusalem, who had some ancient possessions at a place called Heather, near Ashby-de-la-Zouche, occupied the fifth pavilion. From the entrance into the lists, a gently sloping passage, ten yards in breadth, led up to the platform on which the tents were pitched. It was strongly secured by a palisade on each side, as was the esplanade in front of the pavilions, and the whole was guarded by men-at-arms.

The northern access to the lists terminated in a similar entrance of thirty feet in breadth, at the extremity of which was a large enclosed space for such knights as might be disposed to enter the lists with the challengers, behind which were placed tents containing refreshments of every kind for their accommodation, with armourers, tarriers, and other attendants, in readiness to give their services wherever they might be necessary.

The exterior of the lists was in part occupied by temporary galleries, spread with tapestry and carpets, and accommodated with cushions for the convenience of those ladies and nobles who were expected to attend the tournament. A narrow space, betwixt these galleries and the lists, gave accommodation for yeomanry and spectators of a better degree than the mere vulgar, and might be compared to the pit of a theatre. The promiscuous multitude arranged themselves upon large banks of turf prepared for the purpose, which, aided by the natural elevation of the ground, enabled them to overlook the galleries, and obtain a fair view into the lists. Besides the accommodation which these stations afforded, many hundreds had perched themselves on the branches of the trees which surrounded the meadow; and even the steeple of a country church, at some distance, was crowded with spectators.

It only remains to notice respecting the general arrangement, that one gallery in the very centre of the eastern side of the lists, and consequently exactly opposite to the spot where the shock of the combat was to take place, was raised higher than the others, more richly decorated, and graced by a sort of throne and canopy, on which the royal arms were emblazoned. Squires, pages, and yeomen in rich liveries, waited around this place of honour, which was designed for Prince John and his attendants. Opposite to this royal gallery was another, elevated to the same height, on the western side of the lists; and more gaily, if less sumptuously decorated, than that destined for the Prince himself. A train of pages and of young maidens, the most beautiful who could be selected, gaily dressed in fancy habits of green and pink, surrounded a throne decorated in the same colours. Among pennons and flags bearing wounded hearts, burning hearts, bleeding hearts, bows and quivers, and all the commonplace emblems of the triumphs of Cupid, a blazoned inscription informed the spectators, that this seat of honour was designed for "La Royne de las Beaulte et des Amours". But who was to represent the Queen of Beauty and of Love on the present occasion no one was prepared to guess.

Meanwhile, spectators of every description thronged forward to occupy their respective stations, and not without many quarrels concerning those which they were entitled to hold. Some of these were settled by the men-at-arms with brief ceremony; the shafts of their battle-axes, and pummels of their swords, being readily employed as arguments to convince the more refractory. Others, which involved the rival claims of more elevated persons, were determined by the heralds, or by the two marshals of the field, William de Wyvil, and Stephen de Martival, who, armed at all points, rode up and down the lists to enforce and preserve good order among the spectators.

Gradually the galleries became filled with knights and nobles, in their robes of peace, whose long and rich-tinted mantles were contrasted with the gayer and more splendid habits of the ladies, who, in a greater proportion than even the men themselves, thronged to witness a sport, which one would have thought too bloody and dangerous to afford their sex much pleasure. The lower and interior space was soon filled by substantial yeomen and burghers, and such of the lesser gentry, as, from modesty, poverty, or dubious title, durst not assume any higher place. It was of course amongst these that the most frequent disputes for precedence occurred.

"Dog of an unbeliever," said an old man, whose threadbare tunic bore witness to his poverty, as his sword, and dagger, and golden chain intimated his pretensions to rank,—"whelp of a she-wolf! darest thou press upon a Christian, and a Norman gentleman of the blood of Montdidier?"

This rough expostulation was addressed to no other than our acquaintance Isaac, who, richly and even magnificently dressed in a gaberdine ornamented with lace and lined with fur, was endeavouring to make place in the foremost row beneath the gallery for his daughter, the beautiful Rebecca, who had joined him at Ashby, and who was now hanging on her father's arm, not a little terrified by the popular displeasure which seemed generally excited by her parent's presumption. But Isaac, though we have seen him sufficiently timid on other occasions, knew well that at present he had nothing to fear. It was not in places of general resort, or where their equals were assembled, that any avaricious or malevolent noble durst offer him injury. At such meetings the Jews were under the protection of the general law; and if that proved a weak assurance, it usually happened that there were among the persons assembled some barons, who, for their own interested motives, were ready to act as their protectors. On the present occasion, Isaac felt more than usually confident, being aware that Prince John was even then in the very act of negotiating a large loan from the Jews of York, to be secured upon certain jewels and lands. Isaac's own share in this transaction was considerable, and he well knew that the Prince's eager desire to bring it to a conclusion would ensure him his protection in the dilemma in which he stood.

Emboldened by these considerations, the Jew pursued his point, and jostled the Norman Christian, without respect either to his descent, quality, or religion. The complaints of the old man, however, excited the indignation of the bystanders. One of these, a stout well-set yeoman, arrayed in Lincoln green, having twelve arrows stuck in his belt, with a baldric and badge of silver, and a bow of six feet length in his hand, turned short round, and while his countenance, which his constant exposure to weather had rendered brown as a hazel nut, grew darker with anger, he advised the Jew to remember that all the wealth he had acquired by sucking the blood of his miserable victims had but swelled him like a bloated spider, which might be overlooked while he kept in a corner, but would be crushed if it ventured into the light. This intimation, delivered in Norman-English with a firm voice and a stern aspect, made the Jew shrink back; and he would have probably withdrawn himself altogether from a vicinity so dangerous, had not the attention of every one been called to the sudden entrance of Prince John, who at that moment entered the lists, attended by a numerous and gay train, consisting partly of laymen, partly of churchmen, as light in their dress, and as gay in their demeanour, as their companions. Among the latter was the Prior of Jorvaulx, in the most gallant trim which a dignitary of the church could venture to exhibit. Fur and gold were not spared in his garments; and the points of his boots, out-heroding the preposterous fashion of the time, turned up so very far, as to be attached, not to his knees merely, but to his very girdle, and effectually prevented him from putting his foot into the stirrup. This, however, was a slight inconvenience to the gallant Abbot, who, perhaps, even rejoicing in the opportunity to display his accomplished horsemanship before so many spectators, especially of the fair sex, dispensed with the use of these supports to a timid rider. The rest of Prince John's retinue consisted of the favourite leaders of his mercenary troops, some marauding barons and profligate attendants upon the court, with several Knights Templars and Knights of St John.

It may be here remarked, that the knights of these two orders were accounted hostile to King Richard, having adopted the side of Philip of France in the long train of disputes which took place in Palestine betwixt that monarch and the lion-hearted King of England. It was the well-known consequence of this discord that Richard's repeated victories had been rendered fruitless, his romantic attempts to besiege Jerusalem disappointed, and the fruit of all the glory which he had acquired had dwindled into an uncertain truce with the Sultan Saladin. With the same policy which had dictated the conduct of their brethren in the Holy Land, the Templars and Hospitallers in England and Normandy attached themselves to the faction of Prince John, having little reason to desire the return of Richard to England, or the succession of Arthur, his legitimate heir. For the opposite reason, Prince John hated and contemned the few Saxon families of consequence which subsisted in England, and omitted no opportunity of mortifying and affronting them; being conscious that his person and pretensions were disliked by them, as well as by the greater part of the English commons, who feared farther innovation upon their rights and liberties, from a sovereign of John's licentious and tyrannical disposition.

Attended by this gallant equipage, himself well mounted, and splendidly dressed in crimson and in gold, bearing upon his hand a falcon, and having his head covered by a rich fur bonnet, adorned with a circle of precious stones, from which his long curled hair escaped and overspread his shoulders, Prince John, upon a grey and high-mettled palfrey, caracoled within the lists at the head of his jovial party, laughing loud with his train, and eyeing with all the boldness of royal criticism the beauties who adorned the lofty galleries.

Those who remarked in the physiognomy of the Prince a dissolute audacity, mingled with extreme haughtiness and indifference to the feelings of others could not yet deny to his countenance that sort of comeliness which belongs to an open set of features, well formed by nature, modelled by art to the usual rules of courtesy, yet so far frank and honest, that they seemed as if they disclaimed to conceal the natural workings of the soul. Such an expression is often mistaken for manly frankness, when in truth it arises from the reckless indifference of a libertine disposition, conscious of superiority of birth, of wealth, or of some other adventitious advantage, totally unconnected with personal merit. To those who did not think so deeply, and they were the greater number by a hundred to one, the splendour of Prince John's "rheno", (i.e. fur tippet,) the richness of his cloak, lined with the most costly sables, his maroquin boots and golden spurs, together with the grace with which he managed his palfrey, were sufficient to merit clamorous applause.

In his joyous caracole round the lists, the attention of the Prince was called by the commotion, not yet subsided, which had attended the ambitious movement of Isaac towards the higher places of the assembly. The quick eye of Prince John instantly recognised the Jew, but was much more agreeably attracted by the beautiful daughter of Zion, who, terrified by the tumult, clung close to the arm of her aged father.

The figure of Rebecca might indeed have compared with the proudest beauties of England, even though it had been judged by as shrewd a connoisseur as Prince John. Her form was exquisitely symmetrical, and was shown to advantage by a sort of Eastern dress, which she wore according to the fashion of the females of her nation. Her turban of yellow silk suited well with the darkness of her complexion. The brilliancy of her eyes, the superb arch of her eyebrows, her well-formed aquiline nose, her teeth as white as pearl, and the profusion of her sable tresses, which, each arranged in its own little spiral of twisted curls, fell down upon as much of a lovely neck and bosom as a simarre of the richest Persian silk, exhibiting flowers in their natural colours embossed upon a purple ground, permitted to be visible—all these constituted a combination of loveliness, which yielded not to the most beautiful of the maidens who surrounded her. It is true, that of the golden and pearl-studded clasps, which closed her vest from the throat to the waist, the three uppermost were left unfastened on account of the heat, which somewhat enlarged the prospect to which we allude. A diamond necklace, with pendants of inestimable value, were by this means also made more conspicuous. The feather of an ostrich, fastened in her turban by an agraffe set with brilliants, was another distinction of the beautiful Jewess, scoffed and sneered at by the proud dames who sat above her, but secretly envied by those who affected to deride them.

"By the bald scalp of Abraham," said Prince John, "yonder Jewess must be the very model of that perfection, whose charms drove frantic the wisest king that ever lived! What sayest thou, Prior Aymer?—By the Temple of that wise king, which our wiser brother Richard proved unable to recover, she is the very Bride of the Canticles!"

"The Rose of Sharon and the Lily of the Valley,"—answered the Prior, in a sort of snuffling tone; "but your Grace must remember she is still but a Jewess."

"Ay!" added Prince John, without heeding him, "and there is my Mammon of unrighteousness too—the Marquis of Marks, the Baron of Byzants, contesting for place with penniless dogs, whose threadbare cloaks have not a single cross in their pouches to keep the devil from dancing there. By the body of St Mark, my prince of supplies, with his lovely Jewess, shall have a place in the gallery!—What is she, Isaac? Thy wife or thy daughter, that Eastern houri that thou lockest under thy arm as thou wouldst thy treasure-casket?"

"My daughter Rebecca, so please your Grace," answered Isaac, with a low congee, nothing embarrassed by the Prince's salutation, in which, however, there was at least as much mockery as courtesy.

"The wiser man thou," said John, with a peal of laughter, in which his gay followers obsequiously joined. "But, daughter or wife, she should be preferred according to her beauty and thy merits.—Who sits above there?" he continued, bending his eye on the gallery. "Saxon churls, lolling at their lazy length!—out upon them!—let them sit close, and make room for my prince of usurers and his lovely daughter. I'll make the hinds know they must share the high places of the synagogue with those whom the synagogue properly belongs to."

Those who occupied the gallery to whom this injurious and unpolite speech was addressed, were the family of Cedric the Saxon, with that of his ally and kinsman, Athelstane of Coningsburgh, a personage, who, on account of his descent from the last Saxon monarchs of England, was held in the highest respect by all the Saxon natives of the north of England. But with the blood of this ancient royal race, many of their infirmities had descended to Athelstane. He was comely in countenance, bulky and strong in person, and in the flower of his age—yet inanimate in expression, dull-eyed, heavy-browed, inactive and sluggish in all his motions, and so slow in resolution, that the soubriquet of one of his ancestors was conferred upon him, and he was very generally called Athelstane the Unready. His friends, and he had many, who, as well as Cedric, were passionately attached to him, contended that this sluggish temper arose not from want of courage, but from mere want of decision; others alleged that his hereditary vice of drunkenness had obscured his faculties, never of a very acute order, and that the passive courage and meek good-nature which remained behind, were merely the dregs of a character that might have been deserving of praise, but of which all the valuable parts had flown off in the progress of a long course of brutal debauchery.

It was to this person, such as we have described him, that the Prince addressed his imperious command to make place for Isaac and Rebecca. Athelstane, utterly confounded at an order which the manners and feelings of the times rendered so injuriously insulting, unwilling to obey, yet undetermined how to resist, opposed only the "vis inertiae" to the will of John; and, without stirring or making any motion whatever of obedience, opened his large grey eyes, and stared at the Prince with an astonishment which had in it something extremely ludicrous. But the impatient John regarded it in no such light.

"The Saxon porker," he said, "is either asleep or minds me not—Prick him with your lance, De Bracy," speaking to a knight who rode near him, the leader of a band of Free Companions, or Condottieri; that is, of mercenaries belonging to no particular nation, but attached for the time to any prince by whom they were paid. There was a murmur even among the attendants of Prince John; but De Bracy, whose profession freed him from all scruples, extended his long lance over the space which separated the gallery from the lists, and would have executed the commands of the Prince before Athelstane the Unready had recovered presence of mind sufficient even to draw back his person from the weapon, had not Cedric, as prompt as his companion was tardy, unsheathed, with the speed of lightning, the short sword which he wore, and at a single blow severed the point of the lance from the handle. The blood rushed into the countenance of Prince John. He swore one of his deepest oaths, and was about to utter some threat corresponding in violence, when he was diverted from his purpose, partly by his own attendants, who gathered around him conjuring him to be patient, partly by a general exclamation of the crowd, uttered in loud applause of the spirited conduct of Cedric. The Prince rolled his eyes in indignation, as if to collect some safe and easy victim; and chancing to encounter the firm glance of the same archer whom we have already noticed, and who seemed to persist in his gesture of applause, in spite of the frowning aspect which the Prince bent upon him, he demanded his reason for clamouring thus.

"I always add my hollo," said the yeoman, "when I see a good shot, or a gallant blow."

"Sayst thou?" answered the Prince; "then thou canst hit the white thyself, I'll warrant."

"A woodsman's mark, and at woodsman's distance, I can hit," answered the yeoman.

"And Wat Tyrrel's mark, at a hundred yards," said a voice from behind, but by whom uttered could not be discerned.

This allusion to the fate of William Rufus, his Relative, at once incensed and alarmed Prince John. He satisfied himself, however, with commanding the men-at-arms, who surrounded the lists, to keep an eye on the braggart, pointing to the yeoman.

"By St Grizzel," he added, "we will try his own skill, who is so ready to give his voice to the feats of others!"

"I shall not fly the trial," said the yeoman, with the composure which marked his whole deportment.

"Meanwhile, stand up, ye Saxon churls," said the fiery Prince; "for, by the light of Heaven, since I have said it, the Jew shall have his seat amongst ye!"

"By no means, an it please your Grace!—it is not fit for such as we to sit with the rulers of the land," said the Jew; whose ambition for precedence though it had led him to dispute Place with the extenuated and impoverished descendant of the line of Montdidier, by no means stimulated him to an intrusion upon the privileges of the wealthy Saxons.

"Up, infidel dog when I command you," said Prince John, "or I will have thy swarthy hide stript off, and tanned for horse-furniture."

Thus urged, the Jew began to ascend the steep and narrow steps which led up to the gallery.

"Let me see," said the Prince, "who dare stop him," fixing his eye on Cedric, whose attitude intimated his intention to hurl the Jew down headlong.

The catastrophe was prevented by the clown Wamba, who, springing betwixt his master and Isaac, and exclaiming, in answer to the Prince's defiance, "Marry, that will I!" opposed to the beard of the Jew a shield of brawn, which he plucked from beneath his cloak, and with which, doubtless, he had furnished himself, lest the tournament should have proved longer than his appetite could endure abstinence. Finding the abomination of his tribe opposed to his very nose, while the Jester, at the same time, flourished his wooden sword above his head, the Jew recoiled, missed his footing, and rolled down the steps,—an excellent jest to the spectators, who set up a loud laughter, in which Prince John and his attendants heartily joined.

"Deal me the prize, cousin Prince," said Wamba; "I have vanquished my foe in fair fight with sword and shield," he added, brandishing the brawn in one hand and the wooden sword in the other.

"Who, and what art thou, noble champion?" said Prince John, still laughing.

"A fool by right of descent," answered the Jester; "I am Wamba, the son of Witless, who was the son of Weatherbrain, who was the son of an Alderman."

"Make room for the Jew in front of the lower ring," said Prince John, not unwilling perhaps to, seize an apology to desist from his original purpose; "to place the vanquished beside the victor were false heraldry."

"Knave upon fool were worse," answered the Jester, "and Jew upon bacon worst of all."

"Gramercy! good fellow," cried Prince John, "thou pleasest me—Here, Isaac, lend me a handful of byzants."

As the Jew, stunned by the request, afraid to refuse, and unwilling to comply, fumbled in the furred bag which hung by his girdle, and was perhaps endeavouring to ascertain how few coins might pass for a handful, the Prince stooped from his jennet and settled Isaac's doubts by snatching the pouch itself from his side; and flinging to

Wamba a couple of the gold pieces which it contained, he pursued his career round the lists, leaving the Jew to the derision of those around him, and himself receiving as much applause from the spectators as if he had done some honest and honourable action.

VIII.

> At this the challenger with fierce defy
> His trumpet sounds; the challenged makes reply:
> With clangour rings the field, resounds the vaulted sky.
> Their visors closed, their lances in the rest,
> Or at the helmet pointed or the crest,
> They vanish from the barrier, speed the race,
> And spurring see decrease the middle space.
>
> — PALAMON AND ARCITE

In the midst of Prince John's cavalcade, he suddenly stopt, and appealing to the Prior of Jorvaulx, declared the principal business of the day had been forgotten.

"By my halidom," said he, "we have forgotten, Sir Prior, to name the fair Sovereign of Love and of Beauty, by whose white hand the palm is to be distributed. For my part, I am liberal in my ideas, and I care not if I give my vote for the black-eyed Rebecca."

"Holy Virgin," answered the Prior, turning up his eyes in horror, "a Jewess!—We should deserve to be stoned out of the lists; and I am not yet old enough to be a martyr. Besides, I swear by my patron saint, that she is far inferior to the lovely Saxon, Rowena."

"Saxon or Jew," answered the Prince, "Saxon or Jew, dog or hog, what matters it? I say, name Rebecca, were it only to mortify the Saxon churls."

A murmur arose even among his own immediate attendants.

"This passes a jest, my lord," said De Bracy; "no knight here will lay lance in rest if such an insult is attempted."

"It is the mere wantonness of insult," said one of the oldest and most important of Prince John's followers, Waldemar Fitzurse, "and if your Grace attempt it, cannot but prove ruinous to your projects."

"I entertained you, sir," said John, reining up his palfrey haughtily, "for my follower, but not for my counsellor."

"Those who follow your Grace in the paths which you tread," said Waldemar, but speaking in a low voice, "acquire the right of counsellors; for your interest and safety are not more deeply gaged than their own."

From the tone in which this was spoken, John saw the necessity of acquiescence "I did but jest," he said; "and you turn upon me like so many adders! Name whom you will, in the fiend's name, and please yourselves."

"Nay, nay," said De Bracy, "let the fair sovereign's throne remain unoccupied, until the conqueror shall be named, and then let him choose the lady by whom it shall be filled. It will add another grace to his triumph, and teach fair ladies to prize the love of valiant knights, who can exalt them to such distinction."

"If Brian de Bois-Guilbert gain the prize," said the Prior, "I will gage my rosary that I name the Sovereign of Love and Beauty."

"Bois-Guilbert," answered De Bracy, "is a good lance; but there are others around these lists, Sir Prior, who will not fear to encounter him."

"Silence, sirs," said Waldemar, "and let the Prince assume his seat. The knights and spectators are alike impatient, the time advances, and highly fit it is that the sports should commence."

Prince John, though not yet a monarch, had in Waldemar Fitzurse all the inconveniences of a favourite minister, who, in serving his sovereign, must always do so in his own way. The Prince acquiesced, however, although his disposition was precisely of that kind which is apt to be obstinate upon trifles, and, assuming his throne, and being surrounded by his followers, gave signal to the heralds to proclaim the laws of the tournament, which were briefly as follows:

First, the five challengers were to undertake all comers.

Secondly, any knight proposing to combat, might, if he pleased, select a special antagonist from among the challengers, by touching his shield. If he did so with the reverse of his lance, the trial of skill was made with what were called the arms of courtesy, that is, with lances at whose extremity a piece of round flat board was fixed, so that no danger was encountered, save from the shock of the horses and riders. But if the shield was touched with the sharp end of the lance, the combat was understood to be at "outrance", that is, the knights were to fight with sharp weapons, as in actual battle.

Thirdly, when the knights present had accomplished their vow, by each of them breaking five lances, the Prince was to declare the victor in the first day's tourney, who should receive as prize a warhorse of exquisite beauty and matchless strength; and in addition to this reward of valour, it was now declared, he should have the peculiar honour of naming the Queen of Love and Beauty, by whom the prize should be given on the ensuing day.

Fourthly, it was announced, that, on the second day, there should be a general tournament, in which all the knights present, who were desirous to win praise, might take part; and being divided into two bands of equal numbers, might fight it out manfully, until the signal was given by Prince John to cease the combat. The elected Queen of Love and Beauty was then to crown the knight whom the Prince should adjudge to have borne himself best in this second day, with a coronet composed of thin gold plate, cut into the shape of a laurel crown. On this second day the knightly games ceased. But on that which was to follow, feats of archery, of bull-baiting, and other popular amusements, were to be practised, for the more immediate amusement of the populace. In this manner did Prince John endeavour to lay the foundation of a popularity, which he was perpetually throwing down by some inconsiderate act of wanton aggression upon the feelings and prejudices of the people.

The lists now presented a most splendid spectacle. The sloping galleries were crowded with all that was noble, great, wealthy, and beautiful in the northern and midland parts of England; and the contrast of the various dresses of these dignified spectators, rendered the view as gay as it was rich, while the interior and lower space, filled with the substantial burgesses and yeomen of merry England, formed, in their more plain attire, a dark fringe, or border, around this circle of brilliant embroidery, relieving, and, at the same time, setting off its splendour.

The heralds finished their proclamation with their usual cry of "Largesse, largesse, gallant knights!" and gold and silver pieces were showered on them from the galleries, it being a high point of chivalry to exhibit liberality towards those whom the age accounted at once the secretaries and the historians of honour. The bounty of the spectators was acknowledged by the customary shouts of "Love of Ladies—Death of Champions—Honour to the Generous—Glory to the Brave!" To which the more humble spectators added their acclamations, and a numerous band of trumpeters the flourish of their martial instruments. When these sounds had ceased, the heralds withdrew from the lists in gay and glittering procession, and none remained within them save the marshals of the field, who, armed cap-a-pie, sat on horseback, motionless as statues, at the opposite ends of the lists. Meantime, the enclosed space at the northern extremity of the lists, large as it was, was now completely crowded with knights desirous to prove their skill against the challengers, and, when viewed from the galleries, presented the appearance of a sea of waving plumage, intermixed with glistening helmets, and tall lances, to the extremities of which were, in many cases, attached small pennons of about a span's breadth, which, fluttering in the air as the breeze caught them, joined with the restless motion of the feathers to add liveliness to the scene.

At length the barriers were opened, and five knights, chosen by lot, advanced slowly into the area; a single champion riding in front, and the other four following in pairs. All were splendidly armed, and my Saxon authority (in the Wardour Manuscript) records at great length their devices, their colours, and the embroidery of their horse trappings. It is unnecessary to be particular on these subjects. To borrow lines from a contemporary poet, who has written but too little:

"The knights are dust,
And their good swords are rust,
Their souls are with the saints, we trust."

Their escutcheons have long mouldered from the walls of their castles. Their castles themselves are but green mounds and shattered ruins—the place that once knew them, knows them no more—nay, many a race since theirs has died out and been forgotten in the very land which they occupied, with all the authority of feudal proprietors and feudal lords. What, then, would it avail the reader to know their names, or the evanescent symbols of their martial rank!

Now, however, no whit anticipating the oblivion which awaited their names and feats, the champions advanced through the lists, restraining their fiery steeds, and compelling them to move slowly, while, at the same time, they exhibited their paces, together with the grace and dexterity of the riders. As the procession entered the lists, the sound of a wild Barbaric music was heard from behind the tents of the challengers, where the performers were concealed. It was of Eastern origin, having been brought from the Holy Land; and the mixture of the cymbals and bells seemed to bid welcome at once, and defiance, to the knights as they advanced. With the eyes of an immense concourse of spectators fixed upon them, the five knights advanced up the platform upon which the tents of the challengers stood, and there separating themselves, each touched slightly, and with the reverse of his lance, the shield of the antagonist to whom he wished to oppose himself. The lower orders of spectators in general —nay, many of the higher class, and it is even said several of the ladies, were rather disappointed at the champions choosing the arms of courtesy. For the same sort of persons, who, in the present day, applaud most highly the deepest tragedies, were then interested in a tournament exactly in proportion to the danger incurred by the champions engaged.

Having intimated their more pacific purpose, the champions retreated to the extremity of the lists, where they remained drawn up in a line; while the challengers, sallying each from his pavilion, mounted their horses, and, headed by Brian de Bois-Guilbert, descended from the platform, and opposed themselves individually to the knights who had touched their respective shields.

At the flourish of clarions and trumpets, they started out against each other at full gallop; and such was the superior dexterity or good fortune of the challengers, that those opposed to Bois-Guilbert, Malvoisin, and Front-de-Boeuf, rolled on the ground. The antagonist of Grantmesnil, instead of bearing his lance-point fair against the crest or the shield of his enemy, swerved so much from the direct line as to break the weapon athwart the person of his opponent—a circumstance which was accounted more disgraceful than that of being actually unhorsed; because the latter might happen from accident, whereas the former evinced awkwardness and want of management of the weapon and of the horse. The fifth knight alone maintained the honour of his party, and parted fairly with the Knight of St John, both splintering their lances without advantage on either side.

The shouts of the multitude, together with the acclamations of the heralds, and the clangour of the trumpets, announced the triumph of the victors and the defeat of the vanquished. The former retreated to their pavilions, and the latter, gathering themselves up as they could, withdrew from the lists in disgrace and dejection, to agree with their victors concerning the redemption of their arms and their horses, which, according to the laws of the tournament, they had forfeited. The fifth of their number alone tarried in the lists long enough to be greeted by the applauses of the spectators, amongst whom he retreated, to the aggravation, doubtless, of his companions' mortification.

A second and a third party of knights took the field; and although they had various success, yet, upon the whole, the advantage decidedly remained with the challengers, not one of whom lost his seat or swerved from his charge—misfortunes which befell one or two of their antagonists in each encounter. The spirits, therefore, of those opposed to them, seemed to be considerably damped by their continued success. Three knights only appeared on the fourth entry, who, avoiding the shields of Bois-Guilbert and Front-de-Boeuf, contented themselves with touching those of the three other knights, who had not altogether manifested the same strength and dexterity. This politic selection did not alter the fortune of the field, the challengers were still successful: one of their antagonists was overthrown, and both the others failed in the "attaint", that is, in striking the helmet and shield of their antagonist firmly and strongly, with the lance held in a direct line, so that the weapon might break unless the champion was overthrown.

After this fourth encounter, there was a considerable pause; nor did it appear that any one was very desirous of renewing the contest. The spectators murmured among themselves; for, among the challengers, Malvoisin and Front-de-Boeuf were unpopular from their characters, and the others, except Grantmesnil, were disliked as strangers and foreigners.

But none shared the general feeling of dissatisfaction so keenly as Cedric the Saxon, who saw, in each advantage gained by the Norman challengers, a repeated triumph over the honour of England. His own education had taught him no skill in the games of chivalry, although, with the arms of his Saxon ancestors, he had manifested himself, on many occasions, a brave and determined soldier. He looked anxiously to Athelstane, who had learned the accomplishments of the age, as if desiring that he should make some personal effort to recover the victory which was passing into the hands of the Templar and his associates. But, though both stout of heart, and strong of person, Athelstane had a disposition too inert and unambitious to make the exertions which Cedric seemed to expect from him.

"The day is against England, my lord," said Cedric, in a marked tone; "are you not tempted to take the lance?"

"I shall tilt to-morrow" answered Athelstane, "in the 'melee'; it is not worth while for me to arm myself to-day."

Two things displeased Cedric in this speech. It contained the Norman word "melee", (to express the general conflict,) and it evinced some indifference to the honour of the country; but it was spoken by Athelstane, whom he held in such profound respect, that he would not trust himself to canvass his motives or his foibles. Moreover, he had no time to make any remark, for Wamba thrust in his word, observing, "It was better, though scarce easier, to be the best man among a hundred, than the best man of two."

Athelstane took the observation as a serious compliment; but Cedric, who better understood the Jester's meaning, darted at him a severe and menacing look; and lucky it was for Wamba, perhaps, that the time and place prevented his receiving, notwithstanding his place and service, more sensible marks of his master's resentment.

The pause in the tournament was still uninterrupted, excepting by the voices of the heralds exclaiming—"Love of ladies, splintering of lances! stand forth gallant knights, fair eyes look upon your deeds!"

The music also of the challengers breathed from time to time wild bursts expressive of triumph or defiance, while the clowns grudged a holiday which seemed to pass away in inactivity; and old knights and nobles lamented in whispers the decay of martial spirit, spoke of the triumphs of their younger days, but agreed that the land did not now supply dames of such transcendent beauty as had animated the jousts of former times. Prince John began to talk to his attendants about making ready the banquet, and the necessity of adjudging the prize to Brian de Bois-Guilbert, who had, with a single spear, overthrown two knights, and foiled a third.

At length, as the Saracenic music of the challengers concluded one of those long and high flourishes with which they had broken the silence of the lists, it was answered by a solitary trumpet, which breathed a note of defiance from the northern extremity. All eyes were turned to see the new champion which these sounds announced, and no sooner were the barriers opened than he paced into the lists. As far as could be judged of a man sheathed in armour, the new adventurer did not greatly exceed the middle size, and seemed to be rather slender than strongly made. His suit of armour was formed of steel, richly inlaid with gold, and the device on his shield was a young oak-tree pulled up by the roots, with the Spanish word Desdichado, signifying Disinherited. He was mounted on a gallant black horse, and as he passed through the lists he gracefully saluted the Prince and the ladies by lowering his lance. The dexterity with which he managed his steed, and something of youthful grace which he displayed in his manner, won him the favour of the multitude, which some of the lower classes expressed by calling out, "Touch Ralph de Vipont's shield—touch the Hospitallers shield; he has the least sure seat, he is your cheapest bargain."

The champion, moving onward amid these well-meant hints, ascended the platform by the sloping alley which led to it from the lists, and, to the astonishment of all present, riding straight up to the central pavilion, struck with the sharp end of his spear the shield of Brian de Bois-Guilbert until it rung again. All stood astonished at his presumption, but none more than the redoubted Knight whom he had thus defied to mortal combat, and who, little expecting so rude a challenge, was standing carelessly at the door of the pavilion.

"Have you confessed yourself, brother," said the Templar, "and have you heard mass this morning, that you peril your life so frankly?"

"I am fitter to meet death than thou art" answered the Disinherited Knight; for by this name the stranger had recorded himself in the books of the tourney.

"Then take your place in the lists," said Bois-Guilbert, "and look your last upon the sun; for this night thou shalt sleep in paradise."

"Gramercy for thy courtesy," replied the Disinherited Knight, "and to requite it, I advise thee to take a fresh horse and a new lance, for by my honour you will need both."

Having expressed himself thus confidently, he reined his horse backward down the slope which he had ascended, and compelled him in the same manner to move backward through the lists, till he reached the northern extremity, where he remained stationary, in expectation of his antagonist. This feat of horsemanship again attracted the applause of the multitude.

However incensed at his adversary for the precautions which he recommended, Brian de Bois-Guilbert did not neglect his advice; for his honour was too nearly concerned, to permit his neglecting any means which might ensure victory over his presumptuous opponent. He changed his horse for a proved and fresh one of great strength and spirit. He chose a new and a tough spear, lest the wood of the former might have been strained in the previous encounters he had sustained. Lastly, he laid aside his shield, which had received some little damage, and received another from his squires. His first had only borne the general device of his rider, representing two knights riding upon one horse, an emblem expressive of the original humility and poverty of the Templars, qualities which they had since exchanged for the arrogance and wealth that finally occasioned their suppression. Bois-Guilbert's new shield bore a raven in full flight, holding in its claws a skull, and bearing the motto, "Gare le Corbeau".

When the two champions stood opposed to each other at the two extremities of the lists, the public expectation was strained to the highest pitch. Few augured the possibility that the encounter could terminate well for the Disinherited Knight, yet his courage and gallantry secured the general good wishes of the spectators.

The trumpets had no sooner given the signal, than the champions vanished from their posts with the speed of lightning, and closed in the centre of the lists with the shock of a thunderbolt. The lances burst into shivers up to the very grasp, and it seemed at the moment that both knights had fallen, for the shock had made each horse recoil backwards upon its haunches. The address of the riders recovered their steeds by use of the bridle and spur; and having glared on each other for an instant with eyes which seemed to flash fire through the bars of their visors, each made a demi-volte, and, retiring to the extremity of the lists, received a fresh lance from the attendants.

A loud shout from the spectators, waving of scarfs and handkerchiefs, and general acclamations, attested the interest taken by the spectators in this encounter; the most equal, as well as the best performed, which had graced the day. But no sooner had the knights resumed their station, than the clamour of applause was hushed into a silence, so deep and so dead, that it seemed the multitude were afraid even to breathe.

A few minutes pause having been allowed, that the combatants and their horses might recover breath, Prince John with his truncheon signed to the trumpets to sound the onset. The champions a second time sprung from their stations, and closed in the centre of the lists, with the same speed, the same dexterity, the same violence, but not the same equal fortune as before.

In this second encounter, the Templar aimed at the centre of his antagonist's shield, and struck it so fair and forcibly, that his spear went to shivers, and the Disinherited Knight reeled in his saddle. On the other hand, that champion had, in the beginning of his career, directed the point of his lance towards Bois-Guilbert's shield, but, changing his aim almost in the moment of encounter, he addressed it to the helmet, a mark more difficult to hit, but which, if attained, rendered the shock more irresistible. Fair and true he hit the Norman on the visor, where his lance's point kept hold of the bars. Yet, even at this disadvantage, the Templar sustained his high reputation; and had not the girths of his saddle burst, he might not have been unhorsed. As it chanced, however, saddle, horse, and man, rolled on the ground under a cloud of dust.

To extricate himself from the stirrups and fallen steed, was to the Templar scarce the work of a moment; and, stung with madness, both at his disgrace and at the acclamations with which it was hailed by the spectators, he drew his sword and waved it in defiance of his conqueror. The Disinherited Knight sprung from his steed, and also unsheathed his sword. The marshals of the field, however, spurred their horses between them, and reminded them, that the laws of the tournament did not, on the present occasion, permit this species of encounter.

"We shall meet again, I trust," said the Templar, casting a resentful glance at his antagonist; "and where there are none to separate us."

"If we do not," said the Disinherited Knight, "the fault shall not be mine. On foot or horseback, with spear, with axe, or with sword, I am alike ready to encounter thee."

More and angrier words would have been exchanged, but the marshals, crossing their lances betwixt them, compelled them to separate. The Disinherited Knight returned to his first station, and Bois-Guilbert to his tent, where he remained for the rest of the day in an agony of despair.

Without alighting from his horse, the conqueror called for a bowl of wine, and opening the beaver, or lower part of his helmet, announced that he quaffed it, "To all true English hearts, and to the confusion of foreign tyrants." He then commanded his trumpet to sound a defiance to the challengers, and desired a herald to announce to them, that he should make no election, but was willing to encounter them in the order in which they pleased to advance against him.

The gigantic Front-de-Boeuf, armed in sable armour, was the first who took the field. He bore on a white shield a black bull's head, half defaced by the numerous encounters which he had undergone, and bearing the arrogant motto, "Cave, Adsum". Over this champion the Disinherited Knight obtained a slight but decisive advantage. Both Knights broke their lances fairly, but Front-de-Boeuf, who lost a stirrup in the encounter, was adjudged to have the disadvantage.

In the stranger's third encounter with Sir Philip Malvoisin, he was equally successful; striking that baron so forcibly on the casque, that the laces of the helmet broke, and Malvoisin, only saved from falling by being unhelmeted, was declared vanquished like his companions.

In his fourth combat with De Grantmesnil, the Disinherited Knight showed as much courtesy as he had hitherto evinced courage and dexterity. De Grantmesnil's horse, which was young and violent, reared and plunged in the course of the career so as to disturb the rider's aim, and the stranger, declining to take the advantage which this accident afforded him, raised his lance, and passing his antagonist without touching him, wheeled his horse and rode back again to his own end of the lists, offering his antagonist, by a herald, the chance of a second encounter. This De Grantmesnil declined, avowing himself vanquished as much by the courtesy as by the address of his opponent.

Ralph de Vipont summed up the list of the stranger's triumphs, being hurled to the ground with such force, that the blood gushed from his nose and his mouth, and he was borne senseless from the lists.

The acclamations of thousands applauded the unanimous award of the Prince and marshals, announcing that day's honours to the Disinherited Knight.

IX.

> ——In the midst was seen
> A lady of a more majestic mien,
> By stature and by beauty mark'd their sovereign Queen.
>
> And as in beauty she surpass'd the choir,

So nobler than the rest was her attire;
A crown of ruddy gold enclosed her brow,
Plain without pomp, and rich without a show;
A branch of Agnus Castus in her hand,
She bore aloft her symbol of command.

— THE FLOWER AND THE LEAF

William de Wyvil and Stephen de Martival, the marshals of the field, were the first to offer their congratulations to the victor, praying him, at the same time, to suffer his helmet to be unlaced, or, at least, that he would raise his visor ere they conducted him to receive the prize of the day's tourney from the hands of Prince John. The Disinherited Knight, with all knightly courtesy, declined their request, alleging, that he could not at this time suffer his face to be seen, for reasons which he had assigned to the heralds when he entered the lists. The marshals were perfectly satisfied by this reply; for amidst the frequent and capricious vows by which knights were accustomed to bind themselves in the days of chivalry, there were none more common than those by which they engaged to remain incognito for a certain space, or until some particular adventure was achieved. The marshals, therefore, pressed no farther into the mystery of the Disinherited Knight, but, announcing to Prince John the conqueror's desire to remain unknown, they requested permission to bring him before his Grace, in order that he might receive the reward of his valour.

John's curiosity was excited by the mystery observed by the stranger; and, being already displeased with the issue of the tournament, in which the challengers whom he favoured had been successively defeated by one knight, he answered haughtily to the marshals, "By the light of Our Lady's brow, this same knight hath been disinherited as well of his courtesy as of his lands, since he desires to appear before us without uncovering his face.—Wot ye, my lords," he said, turning round to his train, "who this gallant can be, that bears himself thus proudly?"

"I cannot guess," answered De Bracy, "nor did I think there had been within the four seas that girth Britain a champion that could bear down these five knights in one day's jousting. By my faith, I shall never forget the force with which he shocked De Vipont. The poor Hospitaller was hurled from his saddle like a stone from a sling."

"Boast not of that," said a Knight of St John, who was present; "your Temple champion had no better luck. I saw your brave lance, Bois-Guilbert, roll thrice over, grasping his hands full of sand at every turn."

De Bracy, being attached to the Templars, would have replied, but was prevented by Prince John. "Silence, sirs!" he said; "what unprofitable debate have we here?"

"The victor," said De Wyvil, "still waits the pleasure of your highness."

"It is our pleasure," answered John, "that he do so wait until we learn whether there is not some one who can at least guess at his name and quality. Should he remain there till night-fall, he has had work enough to keep him warm."

"Your Grace," said Waldemar Fitzurse, "will do less than due honour to the victor, if you compel him to wait till we tell your highness that which we cannot know; at least I can form no guess—unless he be one of the good lances who accompanied

King Richard to Palestine, and who are now straggling homeward from the Holy Land."

"It may be the Earl of Salisbury," said De Bracy; "he is about the same pitch."

"Sir Thomas de Multon, the Knight of Gilsland, rather," said Fitzurse; "Salisbury is bigger in the bones." A whisper arose among the train, but by whom first suggested could not be ascertained. "It might be the King—it might be Richard Coeur-de-Lion himself!"

"Over God's forbode!" said Prince John, involuntarily turning at the same time as pale as death, and shrinking as if blighted by a flash of lightning; "Waldemar!—De Bracy! brave knights and gentlemen, remember your promises, and stand truly by me!"

"Here is no danger impending," said Waldemar Fitzurse; "are you so little acquainted with the gigantic limbs of your father's son, as to think they can be held within the circumference of yonder suit of armour?—De Wyvil and Martival, you will best serve the Prince by bringing forward the victor to the throne, and ending an error that has conjured all the blood from his cheeks.—Look at him more closely," he continued, "your highness will see that he wants three inches of King Richard's height, and twice as much of his shoulder-breadth. The very horse he backs, could not have carried the ponderous weight of King Richard through a single course."

While he was yet speaking, the marshals brought forward the Disinherited Knight to the foot of a wooden flight of steps, which formed the ascent from the lists to Prince John's throne. Still discomposed with the idea that his brother, so much injured, and to whom he was so much indebted, had suddenly arrived in his native kingdom, even the distinctions pointed out by Fitzurse did not altogether remove the Prince's apprehensions; and while, with a short and embarrassed eulogy upon his valour, he caused to be delivered to him the war-horse assigned as the prize, he trembled lest from the barred visor of the mailed form before him, an answer might be returned, in the deep and awful accents of Richard the Lion-hearted.

But the Disinherited Knight spoke not a word in reply to the compliment of the Prince, which he only acknowledged with a profound obeisance.

The horse was led into the lists by two grooms richly dressed, the animal itself being fully accoutred with the richest war-furniture; which, however, scarcely added to the value of the noble creature in the eyes of those who were judges. Laying one hand upon the pommel of the saddle, the Disinherited Knight vaulted at once upon the back of the steed without making use of the stirrup, and, brandishing aloft his lance, rode twice around the lists, exhibiting the points and paces of the horse with the skill of a perfect horseman.

The appearance of vanity, which might otherwise have been attributed to this display, was removed by the propriety shown in exhibiting to the best advantage the princely reward with which he had been just honoured, and the Knight was again greeted by the acclamations of all present.

In the meanwhile, the bustling Prior of Jorvaulx had reminded Prince John, in a whisper, that the victor must now display his good judgment, instead of his valour, by selecting from among the beauties who graced the galleries a lady, who should fill the throne of the Queen of Beauty and of Love, and deliver the prize of the tourney upon the ensuing day. The Prince accordingly made a sign with his truncheon, as the Knight passed him in his second career around the lists. The Knight turned towards the throne, and, sinking his lance, until the point was within a foot of the ground, remained motionless, as if expecting John's commands; while all admired the sudden dexterity with which he instantly reduced his fiery steed from a state of violent emotion and high excitation to the stillness of an equestrian statue.

"Sir Disinherited Knight," said Prince John, "since that is the only title by which we can address you, it is now your duty, as well as privilege, to name the fair lady, who, as Queen of Honour and of Love, is to preside over next day's festival. If, as a stranger in our land, you should require the aid of other judgment to guide your own, we can only say that Alicia, the daughter of our gallant knight Waldemar Fitzurse, has at our court been long held the first in beauty as in place. Nevertheless, it is your undoubted prerogative to confer on whom you please this crown, by the delivery of which to the lady of your choice, the election of to-morrow's Queen will be formal and complete.—Raise your lance."

The Knight obeyed; and Prince John placed upon its point a coronet of green satin, having around its edge a circlet of gold, the upper edge of which was relieved by arrow-points and hearts placed interchangeably, like the strawberry leaves and balls upon a ducal crown.

In the broad hint which he dropped respecting the daughter of Waldemar Fitzurse, John had more than one motive, each the offspring of a mind, which was a strange mixture of carelessness and presumption with low artifice and cunning. He wished to banish from the minds of the chivalry around him his own indecent and unacceptable jest respecting the Jewess Rebecca; he was desirous of conciliating Alicia's father Waldemar, of whom he stood in awe, and who had more than once shown himself dissatisfied during the course of the day's proceedings. He had also a wish to establish himself in the good graces of the lady; for John was at least as licentious in his pleasures as profligate in his ambition. But besides all these reasons, he was desirous to raise up against the Disinherited Knight (towards whom he already entertained a strong dislike) a powerful enemy in the person of Waldemar Fitzurse, who was likely, he thought, highly to resent the injury done to his daughter, in case, as was not unlikely, the victor should make another choice.

And so indeed it proved. For the Disinherited Knight passed the gallery close to that of the Prince, in which the Lady Alicia was seated in the full pride of triumphant beauty, and, pacing forwards as slowly as he had hitherto rode swiftly around the lists, he seemed to exercise his right of examining the numerous fair faces which adorned that splendid circle.

It was worth while to see the different conduct of the beauties who underwent this examination, during the time it was proceeding. Some blushed, some assumed an air of pride and dignity, some looked straight forward, and essayed to seem utterly unconscious of what was going on, some drew back in alarm, which was perhaps affected, some endeavoured to forbear smiling, and there were two or three who laughed outright. There were also some who dropped their veils over their charms; but, as the Wardour Manuscript says these were fair ones of ten years standing, it may be supposed that, having had their full share of such vanities, they were willing to withdraw their claim, in order to give a fair chance to the rising beauties of the age.

At length the champion paused beneath the balcony in which the Lady Rowena was placed, and the expectation of the spectators was excited to the utmost.

It must be owned, that if an interest displayed in his success could have bribed the Disinherited Knight, the part of the lists before which he paused had merited his predilection. Cedric the Saxon, overjoyed at the discomfiture of the Templar, and still more so at the miscarriage of his two malevolent neighbours, Front-de-Boeuf and Malvoisin, had, with his body half stretched over the balcony, accompanied the victor in each course, not with his eyes only, but with his whole heart and soul. The Lady Rowena had watched the progress of the day with equal attention, though without openly betraying the same intense interest. Even the unmoved Athelstane had shown symptoms of shaking off his apathy, when, calling for a huge goblet of muscadine, he quaffed it to the health of the Disinherited Knight. Another group, stationed under the gallery occupied by the Saxons, had shown no less interest in the fate of the day.

"Father Abraham!" said Isaac of York, when the first course was run betwixt the Templar and the Disinherited Knight, "how fiercely that Gentile rides! Ah, the good horse that was brought all the long way from Barbary, he takes no more care of him than if he were a wild ass's colt—and the noble armour, that was worth so many zecchins to Joseph Pareira, the armourer of Milan, besides seventy in the hundred of profits, he cares for it as little as if he had found it in the highways!"

"If he risks his own person and limbs, father," said Rebecca, "in doing such a dreadful battle, he can scarce be expected to spare his horse and armour."

"Child!" replied Isaac, somewhat heated, "thou knowest not what thou speakest— His neck and limbs are his own, but his horse and armour belong to—Holy Jacob! what was I about to say!—Nevertheless, it is a good youth—See, Rebecca! see, he is again about to go up to battle against the Philistine—Pray, child—pray for the safety of the good youth,—and of the speedy horse, and the rich armour.—God of my fathers!" he again exclaimed, "he hath conquered, and the uncircumcised Philistine hath fallen before his lance,—even as Og the King of Bashan, and Sihon, King of the Amorites, fell before the sword of our fathers!—Surely he shall take their gold and their silver, and their war-horses, and their armour of brass and of steel, for a prey and for a spoil."

The same anxiety did the worthy Jew display during every course that was run, seldom failing to hazard a hasty calculation concerning the value of the horse and armour which was forfeited to the champion upon each new success. There had been therefore no small interest taken in the success of the Disinherited Knight, by those who occupied the part of the lists before which he now paused.

Whether from indecision, or some other motive of hesitation, the champion of the day remained stationary for more than a minute, while the eyes of the silent audience were riveted upon his motions; and then, gradually and gracefully sinking the point of his lance, he deposited the coronet which it supported at the feet of the fair Rowena. The trumpets instantly sounded, while the heralds proclaimed the Lady Rowena the Queen of Beauty and of Love for the ensuing day, menacing with suitable penalties those who should be disobedient to her authority. They then repeated their cry of Largesse, to which Cedric, in the height of his joy, replied by an ample donative, and to which Athelstane, though less promptly, added one equally large.

There was some murmuring among the damsels of Norman descent, who were as much unused to see the preference given to a Saxon beauty, as the Norman nobles were to sustain defeat in the games of chivalry which they themselves had introduced. But these sounds of disaffection were drowned by the popular shout of "Long live the Lady Rowena, the chosen and lawful Queen of Love and of Beauty!" To which many in the lower area added, "Long live the Saxon Princess! long live the race of the immortal Alfred!"

However unacceptable these sounds might be to Prince John, and to those around him, he saw himself nevertheless obliged to confirm the nomination of the victor, and accordingly calling to horse, he left his throne; and mounting his jennet, accompanied by his train, he again entered the lists. The Prince paused a moment beneath the gallery of the Lady Alicia, to whom he paid his compliments, observing, at the same time, to those around him—"By my halidome, sirs! if the Knight's feats in arms have shown that he hath limbs and sinews, his choice hath no less proved that his eyes are none of the clearest."

It was on this occasion, as during his whole life, John's misfortune, not perfectly to understand the characters of those whom he wished to conciliate. Waldemar Fitzurse was rather offended than pleased at the Prince stating thus broadly an opinion, that his daughter had been slighted.

"I know no right of chivalry," he said, "more precious or inalienable than that of each free knight to choose his lady-love by his own judgment. My daughter courts distinction from no one; and in her own character, and in her own sphere, will never fail to receive the full proportion of that which is her due."

Prince John replied not; but, spurring his horse, as if to give vent to his vexation, he made the animal bound forward to the gallery where Rowena was seated, with the crown still at her feet.

"Assume," he said, "fair lady, the mark of your sovereignty, to which none vows homage more sincerely than ourself, John of Anjou; and if it please you to-day, with your noble sire and friends, to grace our banquet in the Castle of Ashby, we shall learn to know the empress to whose service we devote to-morrow."

Rowena remained silent, and Cedric answered for her in his native Saxon.

"The Lady Rowena," he said, "possesses not the language in which to reply to your courtesy, or to sustain her part in your festival. I also, and the noble Athelstane of Coningsburgh, speak only the language, and practise only the manners, of our fathers. We therefore decline with thanks your Highness's courteous invitation to the banquet. To-morrow, the Lady Rowena will take upon her the state to which she has been called by the free election of the victor Knight, confirmed by the acclamations of the people."

So saying, he lifted the coronet, and placed it upon Rowena's head, in token of her acceptance of the temporary authority assigned to her.

"What says he?" said Prince John, affecting not to understand the Saxon language, in which, however, he was well skilled. The purport of Cedric's speech was repeated to him in French. "It is well," he said; "to-morrow we will ourself conduct this mute sovereign to her seat of dignity.—You, at least, Sir Knight," he added, turning to the victor, who had remained near the gallery, "will this day share our banquet?"

The Knight, speaking for the first time, in a low and hurried voice, excused himself by pleading fatigue, and the necessity of preparing for to-morrow's encounter.

"It is well," said Prince John, haughtily; "although unused to such refusals, we will endeavour to digest our banquet as we may, though ungraced by the most successful in arms, and his elected Queen of Beauty."

So saying, he prepared to leave the lists with his glittering train, and his turning his steed for that purpose, was the signal for the breaking up and dispersion of the spectators.

Yet, with the vindictive memory proper to offended pride, especially when combined with conscious want of desert, John had hardly proceeded three paces, ere again, turning around, he fixed an eye of stern resentment upon the yeoman who had displeased him in the early part of the day, and issued his commands to the men-at-arms who stood near—"On your life, suffer not that fellow to escape."

The yeoman stood the angry glance of the Prince with the same unvaried steadiness which had marked his former deportment, saying, with a smile, "I have no intention to leave Ashby until the day after to-morrow—I must see how Staffordshire and Leicestershire can draw their bows—the forests of Needwood and Charnwood must rear good archers."

"I," said Prince John to his attendants, but not in direct reply,—"I will see how he can draw his own; and woe betide him unless his skill should prove some apology for his insolence!"

"It is full time," said De Bracy, "that the 'outrecuidance' of these peasants should be restrained by some striking example."

Waldemar Fitzurse, who probably thought his patron was not taking the readiest road to popularity, shrugged up his shoulders and was silent. Prince John resumed his retreat from the lists, and the dispersion of the multitude became general.

In various routes, according to the different quarters from which they came, and in groups of various numbers, the spectators were seen retiring over the plain. By far the most numerous part streamed towards the town of Ashby, where many of the distinguished persons were lodged in the castle, and where others found accommodation in the town itself. Among these were most of the knights who had already appeared in the tournament, or who proposed to fight there the ensuing day, and who, as they rode slowly along, talking over the events of the day, were greeted with loud shouts by the populace. The same acclamations were bestowed upon Prince John, although he was indebted for them rather to the splendour of his appearance and train, than to the popularity of his character.

A more sincere and more general, as well as a better-merited acclamation, attended the victor of the day, until, anxious to withdraw himself from popular notice, he accepted the accommodation of one of those pavilions pitched at the extremities of the lists, the use of which was courteously tendered him by the marshals of the field. On his retiring to his tent, many who had lingered in the lists, to look upon and form conjectures concerning him, also dispersed.

The signs and sounds of a tumultuous concourse of men lately crowded together in one place, and agitated by the same passing events, were now exchanged for the distant hum of voices of different groups retreating in all directions, and these speedily died away in silence. No other sounds were heard save the voices of the menials who stripped the galleries of their cushions and tapestry, in order to put them in safety for the night, and wrangled among themselves for the half-used bottles of wine and relics of the refreshment which had been served round to the spectators.

Beyond the precincts of the lists more than one forge was erected; and these now began to glimmer through the twilight, announcing the toil of the armourers, which was to continue through the whole night, in order to repair or alter the suits of armour to be used again on the morrow.

A strong guard of men-at-arms, renewed at intervals, from two hours to two hours, surrounded the lists, and kept watch during the night.

X.

> Thus, like the sad presaging raven, that tolls
> The sick man's passport in her hollow beak,
> And in the shadow of the silent night
> Doth shake contagion from her sable wings;
> Vex'd and tormented, runs poor Barrabas,
> With fatal curses towards these Christians.
>
> — JEW OF MALTA

The Disinherited Knight had no sooner reached his pavilion, than squires and pages in abundance tendered their services to disarm him, to bring fresh attire, and to offer him the refreshment of the bath. Their zeal on this occasion was perhaps sharpened by curiosity, since every one desired to know who the knight was that had gained so many laurels, yet had refused, even at the command of Prince John, to lift his visor or to name his name. But their officious inquisitiveness was not gratified. The Disinherited Knight refused all other assistance save that of his own squire, or rather yeoman —a clownish-looking man, who, wrapt in a cloak of dark-coloured felt, and having his head and face half-buried in a Norman bonnet made of black fur, seemed to affect the incognito as much as his master. All others being excluded from the tent, this attendant relieved his master from the more burdensome parts of his armour, and placed food and wine before him, which the exertions of the day rendered very acceptable.

The Knight had scarcely finished a hasty meal, ere his menial announced to him that five men, each leading a barbed steed, desired to speak with him. The Disinherited Knight had exchanged his armour for the long robe usually worn by those of his condition, which, being furnished with a hood, concealed the features, when such was the pleasure of the wearer, almost as completely as the visor of the helmet itself, but the twilight, which was now fast darkening, would of itself have rendered a disguise unnecessary, unless to persons to whom the face of an individual chanced to be particularly well known.

The Disinherited Knight, therefore, stept boldly forth to the front of his tent, and found in attendance the squires of the challengers, whom he easily knew by their russet and black dresses, each of whom led his master's charger, loaded with the armour in which he had that day fought.

"According to the laws of chivalry," said the foremost of these men, "I, Baldwin de Oyley, squire to the redoubted Knight Brian de Bois-Guilbert, make offer to you, styling yourself, for the present, the Disinherited Knight, of the horse and armour used by the said Brian de Bois-Guilbert in this day's Passage of Arms, leaving it with your nobleness to retain or to ransom the same, according to your pleasure; for such is the law of arms."

The other squires repeated nearly the same formula, and then stood to await the decision of the Disinherited Knight.

"To you four, sirs," replied the Knight, addressing those who had last spoken, "and to your honourable and valiant masters, I have one common reply. Commend me to the noble knights, your masters, and say, I should do ill to deprive them of steeds and arms which can never be used by braver cavaliers.—I would I could here end my message to these gallant knights; but being, as I term myself, in truth and earnest, the Disinherited, I must be thus far bound to your masters, that they will, of their courtesy, be pleased to ransom their steeds and armour, since that which I wear I can hardly term mine own."

"We stand commissioned, each of us," answered the squire of Reginald Front-de-Boeuf, "to offer a hundred zecchins in ransom of these horses and suits of armour."

"It is sufficient," said the Disinherited Knight. "Half the sum my present necessities compel me to accept; of the remaining half, distribute one moiety among yourselves, sir squires, and divide the other half betwixt the heralds and the pursuivants, and minstrels, and attendants."

The squires, with cap in hand, and low reverences, expressed their deep sense of a courtesy and generosity not often practised, at least upon a scale so extensive. The Disinherited Knight then addressed his discourse to Baldwin, the squire of Brian de Bois-Guilbert. "From your master," said he, "I will accept neither arms nor ransom. Say to him in my name, that our strife is not ended—no, not till we have fought as well with swords as with lances—as well on foot as on horseback. To this mortal quarrel he has himself defied me, and I shall not forget the challenge.—Meantime, let him be assured, that I hold him not as one of his companions, with whom I can with pleasure exchange courtesies; but rather as one with whom I stand upon terms of mortal defiance."

"My master," answered Baldwin, "knows how to requite scorn with scorn, and blows with blows, as well as courtesy with courtesy. Since you disdain to accept from him any share of the ransom at which you have rated the arms of the other knights, I must leave his armour and his horse here, being well assured that he will never deign to mount the one nor wear the other."

"You have spoken well, good squire," said the Disinherited Knight, "well and boldly, as it beseemeth him to speak who answers for an absent master. Leave not, however, the horse and armour here. Restore them to thy master; or, if he scorns to accept them, retain them, good friend, for thine own use. So far as they are mine, I bestow them upon you freely."

Baldwin made a deep obeisance, and retired with his companions; and the Disinherited Knight entered the pavilion.

"Thus far, Gurth," said he, addressing his attendant, "the reputation of English chivalry hath not suffered in my hands."

"And I," said Gurth, "for a Saxon swineherd, have not ill played the personage of a Norman squire-at-arms."

"Yea, but," answered the Disinherited Knight, "thou hast ever kept me in anxiety lest thy clownish bearing should discover thee."

"Tush!" said Gurth, "I fear discovery from none, saving my playfellow, Wamba the Jester, of whom I could never discover whether he were most knave or fool. Yet I could scarce choose but laugh, when my old master passed so near to me, dreaming all the while that Gurth was keeping his porkers many a mile off, in the thickets and swamps of Rotherwood. If I am discovered——"

"Enough," said the Disinherited Knight, "thou knowest my promise."

"Nay, for that matter," said Gurth, "I will never fail my friend for fear of my skin-cutting. I have a tough hide, that will bear knife or scourge as well as any boar's hide in my herd."

"Trust me, I will requite the risk you run for my love, Gurth," said the Knight. "Meanwhile, I pray you to accept these ten pieces of gold."

"I am richer," said Gurth, putting them into his pouch, "than ever was swineherd or bondsman."

"Take this bag of gold to Ashby," continued his master, "and find out Isaac the Jew of York, and let him pay himself for the horse and arms with which his credit supplied me."

"Nay, by St Dunstan," replied Gurth, "that I will not do."

"How, knave," replied his master, "wilt thou not obey my commands?"

"So they be honest, reasonable, and Christian commands," replied Gurth; "but this is none of these. To suffer the Jew to pay himself would be dishonest, for it would be cheating my master; and unreasonable, for it were the part of a fool; and unchristian, since it would be plundering a believer to enrich an infidel."

"See him contented, however, thou stubborn varlet," said the Disinherited Knight.

"I will do so," said Gurth, taking the bag under his cloak, and leaving the apartment; "and it will go hard," he muttered, "but I content him with one-half of his own asking." So saying, he departed, and left the Disinherited Knight to his own perplexed ruminations; which, upon more accounts than it is now possible to communicate to the reader, were of a nature peculiarly agitating and painful.

We must now change the scene to the village of Ashby, or rather to a country house in its vicinity belonging to a wealthy Israelite, with whom Isaac, his daughter, and retinue, had taken up their quarters; the Jews, it is well known, being as liberal in exercising the duties of hospitality and charity among their own people, as they were alleged to be reluctant and churlish in extending them to those whom they termed Gentiles, and whose treatment of them certainly merited little hospitality at their hand.

In an apartment, small indeed, but richly furnished with decorations of an Oriental taste, Rebecca was seated on a heap of embroidered cushions, which, piled along a low platform that surrounded the chamber, served, like the estrada of the Spaniards, instead of chairs and stools. She was watching the motions of her father with a look of anxious and filial affection, while he paced the apartment with a dejected mien and disordered step; sometimes clasping his hands together—sometimes casting his eyes to the roof of the apartment, as one who laboured under great mental tribulation. "O, Jacob!" he exclaimed—"O, all ye twelve Holy Fathers of our tribe! what a losing venture is this for one who hath duly kept every jot and tittle of the law of Moses—Fifty zecchins wrenched from me at one clutch, and by the talons of a tyrant!"

"But, father," said Rebecca, "you seemed to give the gold to Prince John willingly."

"Willingly? the blotch of Egypt upon him!—Willingly, saidst thou?—Ay, as willingly as when, in the Gulf of Lyons, I flung over my merchandise to lighten the ship, while she laboured in the tempest—robed the seething billows in my choice silks—perfumed their briny foam with myrrh and aloes—enriched their caverns with gold and silver work! And was not that an hour of unutterable misery, though my own hands made the sacrifice?"

"But it was a sacrifice which Heaven exacted to save our lives," answered Rebecca, "and the God of our fathers has since blessed your store and your gettings."

"Ay," answered Isaac, "but if the tyrant lays hold on them as he did to-day, and compels me to smile while he is robbing me?—O, daughter, disinherited and wandering as we are, the worst evil which befalls our race is, that when we are wronged and plundered, all the world laughs around, and we are compelled to suppress our sense of injury, and to smile tamely, when we would revenge bravely."

"Think not thus of it, my father," said Rebecca; "we also have advantages. These Gentiles, cruel and oppressive as they are, are in some sort dependent on the dispersed children of Zion, whom they despise and persecute. Without the aid of our wealth, they could neither furnish forth their hosts in war, nor their triumphs in peace, and the gold which we lend them returns with increase to our coffers. We are like the herb which flourisheth most when it is most trampled on. Even this day's pageant had not proceeded without the consent of the despised Jew, who furnished the means."

"Daughter," said Isaac, "thou hast harped upon another string of sorrow. The goodly steed and the rich armour, equal to the full profit of my adventure with our Kirjath Jairam of Leicester—there is a dead loss too—ay, a loss which swallows up the gains of a week; ay, of the space between two Sabbaths—and yet it may end better than I now think, for 'tis a good youth."

"Assuredly," said Rebecca, "you shall not repent you of requiting the good deed received of the stranger knight."

"I trust so, daughter," said Isaac, "and I trust too in the rebuilding of Zion; but as well do I hope with my own bodily eyes to see the walls and battlements of the new Temple, as to see a Christian, yea, the very best of Christians, repay a debt to a Jew, unless under the awe of the judge and jailor."

So saying, he resumed his discontented walk through the apartment; and Rebecca, perceiving that her attempts at consolation only served to awaken new subjects of complaint, wisely desisted from her unavailing efforts—a prudential line of conduct, and we recommend to all who set up for comforters and advisers, to follow it in the like circumstances.

The evening was now becoming dark, when a Jewish servant entered the apartment, and placed upon the table two silver lamps, fed with perfumed oil; the richest wines, and the most delicate refreshments, were at the same time displayed by another Israelitish domestic on a small ebony table, inlaid with silver; for, in the interior of their houses, the Jews refused themselves no expensive indulgences. At the same time the servant informed Isaac, that a Nazarene (so they termed Christians, while conversing among themselves) desired to speak with him. He that would live by traffic, must hold himself at the disposal of every one claiming business with him. Isaac at once replaced on the table the untasted glass of Greek wine which he had just raised to his lips, and saying hastily to his daughter, "Rebecca, veil thyself," commanded the stranger to be admitted.

Just as Rebecca had dropped over her fine features a screen of silver gauze which reached to her feet, the door opened, and Gurth entered, wrapt in the ample folds of his Norman mantle. His appearance was rather suspicious than prepossessing, especially as, instead of doffing his bonnet, he pulled it still deeper over his rugged brow.

"Art thou Isaac the Jew of York?" said Gurth, in Saxon.

"I am," replied Isaac, in the same language, (for his traffic had rendered every tongue spoken in Britain familiar to him)—"and who art thou?"

"That is not to the purpose," answered Gurth.

"As much as my name is to thee," replied Isaac; "for without knowing thine, how can I hold intercourse with thee?"

"Easily," answered Gurth; "I, being to pay money, must know that I deliver it to the right person; thou, who are to receive it, will not, I think, care very greatly by whose hands it is delivered."

"O," said the Jew, "you are come to pay moneys?—Holy Father Abraham! that altereth our relation to each other. And from whom dost thou bring it?"

"From the Disinherited Knight," said Gurth, "victor in this day's tournament. It is the price of the armour supplied to him by Kirjath Jairam of Leicester, on thy recommendation. The steed is restored to thy stable. I desire to know the amount of the sum which I am to pay for the armour."

"I said he was a good youth!" exclaimed Isaac with joyful exultation. "A cup of wine will do thee no harm," he added, filling and handing to the swineherd a richer drought than Gurth had ever before tasted. "And how much money," continued Isaac, "has thou brought with thee?"

"Holy Virgin!" said Gurth, setting down the cup, "what nectar these unbelieving dogs drink, while true Christians are fain to quaff ale as muddy and thick as the draff we give to hogs!—What money have I brought with me?" continued the Saxon, when he had finished this uncivil ejaculation, "even but a small sum; something in hand the whilst. What, Isaac! thou must bear a conscience, though it be a Jewish one."

"Nay, but," said Isaac, "thy master has won goodly steeds and rich armours with the strength of his lance, and of his right hand—but 'tis a good youth—the Jew will take these in present payment, and render him back the surplus."

"My master has disposed of them already," said Gurth.

"Ah! that was wrong," said the Jew, "that was the part of a fool. No Christians here could buy so many horses and armour—no Jew except myself would give him half the values. But thou hast a hundred zecchins with thee in that bag," said Isaac, prying under Gurth's cloak, "it is a heavy one."

"I have heads for cross-bow bolts in it," said Gurth, readily.

"Well, then"—said Isaac, panting and hesitating between habitual love of gain and a new-born desire to be liberal in the present instance, "if I should say that I would take eighty zecchins for the good steed and the rich armour, which leaves me not a guilder's profit, have you money to pay me?"

"Barely," said Gurth, though the sum demanded was more reasonable than he expected, "and it will leave my master nigh penniless. Nevertheless, if such be your least offer, I must be content."

"Fill thyself another goblet of wine," said the Jew. "Ah! eighty zecchins is too little. It leaveth no profit for the usages of the moneys; and, besides, the good horse may have suffered wrong in this day's encounter. O, it was a hard and a dangerous meeting! man and steed rushing on each other like wild bulls of Bashan! The horse cannot but have had wrong."

"And I say," replied Gurth, "he is sound, wind and limb; and you may see him now, in your stable. And I say, over and above, that seventy zecchins is enough for the armour, and I hope a Christian's word is as good as a Jew's. If you will not take seventy, I will carry this bag" (and he shook it till the contents jingled) "back to my master."

"Nay, nay!" said Isaac; "lay down the talents—the shekels—the eighty zecchins, and thou shalt see I will consider thee liberally."

Gurth at length complied; and telling out eighty zecchins upon the table, the Jew delivered out to him an acquittance for the horse and suit of armour. The Jew's hand trembled for joy as he wrapped up the first seventy pieces of gold. The last ten he told over with much deliberation, pausing, and saying something as he took each piece from the table, and dropt it into his purse. It seemed as if his avarice were struggling with his better nature, and compelling him to pouch zecchin after zecchin while his generosity urged him to restore some part at least to his benefactor, or as a donation to his agent. His whole speech ran nearly thus:

"Seventy-one—seventy-two; thy master is a good youth—seventy-three, an excellent youth—seventy-four—that piece hath been clipt within the ring—seventy-five—and that looketh light of weight—seventy-six—when thy master wants money, let him come to Isaac of York—seventy-seven—that is, with reasonable security." Here he made a considerable pause, and Gurth had good hope that the last three pieces might escape the fate of their comrades; but the enumeration proceeded.—"Seventy-eight—thou art a good fellow—seventy-nine—and deservest something for thyself—"

Here the Jew paused again, and looked at the last zecchin, intending, doubtless, to bestow it upon Gurth. He weighed it upon the tip of his finger, and made it ring by dropping it upon the table. Had it rung too flat, or had it felt a hair's breadth too light, generosity had carried the day; but, unhappily for Gurth, the chime was full and true, the zecchin plump, newly coined, and a grain above weight. Isaac could not find in his heart to part with it, so dropt it into his purse as if in absence of mind, with the words, "Eighty completes the tale, and I trust thy master will reward thee handsomely.—Surely," he added, looking earnestly at the bag, "thou hast more coins in that pouch?"

Gurth grinned, which was his nearest approach to a laugh, as he replied, "About the same quantity which thou hast just told over so carefully." He then folded the quittance, and put it under his cap, adding,—"Peril of thy beard, Jew, see that this be full and ample!" He filled himself unbidden, a third goblet of wine, and left the apartment without ceremony.

"Rebecca," said the Jew, "that Ishmaelite hath gone somewhat beyond me. Nevertheless his master is a good youth—ay, and I am well pleased that he hath gained shekels of gold and shekels of silver, even by the speed of his horse and by the strength of his lance, which, like that of Goliath the Philistine, might vie with a weaver's beam."

As he turned to receive Rebecca's answer, he observed, that during his chattering with Gurth, she had left the apartment unperceived.

In the meanwhile, Gurth had descended the stair, and, having reached the dark antechamber or hall, was puzzling about to discover the entrance, when a figure in white, shown by a small silver lamp which she held in her hand, beckoned him into a side apartment. Gurth had some reluctance to obey the summons. Rough and impetuous as a wild boar, where only earthly force was to be apprehended, he had all the characteristic terrors of a Saxon respecting fawns, forest-fiends, white women, and the whole of the superstitions which his ancestors had brought with them from the wilds of Germany. He remembered, moreover, that he was in the house of a Jew, a people who, besides the other unamiable qualities which popular report ascribed to them, were supposed to be profound necromancers and cabalists. Nevertheless, after a moment's pause, he obeyed the beckoning summons of the apparition, and followed her into the apartment which she indicated, where he found to his joyful surprise that his fair guide was the beautiful Jewess whom he had seen at the tournament, and a short time in her father's apartment.

She asked him the particulars of his transaction with Isaac, which he detailed accurately.

"My father did but jest with thee, good fellow," said Rebecca; "he owes thy master deeper kindness than these arms and steed could pay, were their value tenfold. What sum didst thou pay my father even now?"

"Eighty zecchins," said Gurth, surprised at the question.

"In this purse," said Rebecca, "thou wilt find a hundred. Restore to thy master that which is his due, and enrich thyself with the remainder. Haste—begone—stay not to render thanks! and beware how you pass through this crowded town, where thou mayst easily lose both thy burden and thy life.—Reuben," she added, clapping her hands together, "light forth this stranger, and fail not to draw lock and bar behind him." Reuben, a dark-brow'd and black-bearded Israelite, obeyed her summons, with a torch in his hand; undid the outward door of the house, and conducting Gurth across a paved court, let him out through a wicket in the entrance-gate, which he closed behind him with such bolts and chains as would well have become that of a prison.

"By St Dunstan," said Gurth, as he stumbled up the dark avenue, "this is no Jewess, but an angel from heaven! Ten zecchins from my brave young master—twenty from this pearl of Zion—Oh, happy day!—Such another, Gurth, will redeem thy bondage, and make thee a brother as free of thy guild as the best. And then do I lay down my swineherd's horn and staff, and take the freeman's sword and buckler, and follow my young master to the death, without hiding either my face or my name."

XI.

>   1st Outlaw: Stand, sir, and throw us that you have about you;
>   If not, we'll make you sit, and rifle you.
>   Speed: Sir, we are undone! these are the villains
>   That all the travellers do fear so much.
>   Val: My friends,—
>   1st Out: That's not so, sir, we are your enemies.
>   2d Out: Peace! we'll hear him.
>   3d Out: Ay, by my beard, will we;
>   For he's a proper man.
>
>   — TWO GENTLEMEN OF VERONA

The nocturnal adventures of Gurth were not yet concluded; indeed he himself became partly of that mind, when, after passing one or two straggling houses which stood in the outskirts of the village, he found himself in a deep lane, running between two banks overgrown with hazel and holly, while here and there a dwarf oak flung its arms altogether across the path. The lane was moreover much rutted and broken up by the carriages which had recently transported articles of various kinds to the tournament; and it was dark, for the banks and bushes intercepted the light of the harvest moon.

From the village were heard the distant sounds of revelry, mixed occasionally with loud laughter, sometimes broken by screams, and sometimes by wild strains of distant music. All these sounds, intimating the disorderly state of the town, crowded with military nobles and their dissolute attendants, gave Gurth some uneasiness. "The Jewess was right," he said to himself. "By heaven and St Dunstan, I would I were safe at my journey's end with all this treasure! Here are such numbers, I will not say of arrant thieves, but of errant knights and errant squires, errant monks and errant minstrels, errant jugglers and errant jesters, that a man with a single merk would be in danger, much more a poor swineherd with a whole bagful of zecchins. Would I were out of the shade of these infernal bushes, that I might at least see any of St Nicholas's clerks before they spring on my shoulders."

Gurth accordingly hastened his pace, in order to gain the open common to which the lane led, but was not so fortunate as to accomplish his object. Just as he had attained the upper end of the lane, where the underwood was thickest, four men sprung upon him, even as his fears anticipated, two from each side of the road, and seized him so fast, that resistance, if at first practicable, would have been now too late.—"Surrender your charge," said one of them; "we are the deliverers of the commonwealth, who ease every man of his burden."

"You should not ease me of mine so lightly," muttered Gurth, whose surly honesty could not be tamed even by the pressure of immediate violence,—"had I it but in my power to give three strokes in its defence."

"We shall see that presently," said the robber; and, speaking to his companions, he added, "bring along the knave. I see he would have his head broken, as well as his purse cut, and so be let blood in two veins at once."

Gurth was hurried along agreeably to this mandate, and having been dragged somewhat roughly over the bank, on the left-hand side of the lane, found himself in a straggling thicket, which lay betwixt it and the open common. He was compelled to follow his rough conductors into the very depth of this cover, where they stopt unexpectedly in an irregular open space, free in a great measure from trees, and on which, therefore, the beams of the moon fell without much interruption from boughs and leaves. Here his captors were joined by two other persons, apparently belonging to the gang. They had short swords by their sides, and quarter-staves in their hands, and Gurth could now observe that all six wore visors, which rendered their occupation a matter of no question, even had their former proceedings left it in doubt.

"What money hast thou, churl?" said one of the thieves.

"Thirty zecchins of my own property," answered Gurth, doggedly.

"A forfeit—a forfeit," shouted the robbers; "a Saxon hath thirty zecchins, and returns sober from a village! An undeniable and unredeemable forfeit of all he hath about him."

"I hoarded it to purchase my freedom," said Gurth.

"Thou art an ass," replied one of the thieves "three quarts of double ale had rendered thee as free as thy master, ay, and freer too, if he be a Saxon like thyself."

"A sad truth," replied Gurth; "but if these same thirty zecchins will buy my freedom from you, unloose my hands, and I will pay them to you."

"Hold," said one who seemed to exercise some authority over the others; "this bag which thou bearest, as I can feel through thy cloak, contains more coin than thou hast told us of."

"It is the good knight my master's," answered Gurth, "of which, assuredly, I would not have spoken a word, had you been satisfied with working your will upon mine own property."

"Thou art an honest fellow," replied the robber, "I warrant thee; and we worship not St Nicholas so devoutly but what thy thirty zecchins may yet escape, if thou deal uprightly with us. Meantime render up thy trust for a time." So saying, he took from Gurth's breast the large leathern pouch, in which the purse given him by Rebecca was enclosed, as well as the rest of the zecchins, and then continued his interrogation.—"Who is thy master?"

"The Disinherited Knight," said Gurth.

"Whose good lance," replied the robber, "won the prize in to-day's tourney? What is his name and lineage?"

"It is his pleasure," answered Gurth, "that they be concealed; and from me, assuredly, you will learn nought of them."

"What is thine own name and lineage?"

"To tell that," said Gurth, "might reveal my master's."

"Thou art a saucy groom," said the robber, "but of that anon. How comes thy master by this gold? is it of his inheritance, or by what means hath it accrued to him?"

"By his good lance," answered Gurth.—"These bags contain the ransom of four good horses, and four good suits of armour."

"How much is there?" demanded the robber.

"Two hundred zecchins."

"Only two hundred zecchins!" said the bandit; "your master hath dealt liberally by the vanquished, and put them to a cheap ransom. Name those who paid the gold."

Gurth did so.

"The armour and horse of the Templar Brian de Bois-Guilbert, at what ransom were they held?—Thou seest thou canst not deceive me."

"My master," replied Gurth, "will take nought from the Templar save his life's-blood. They are on terms of mortal defiance, and cannot hold courteous intercourse together."

"Indeed!"—repeated the robber, and paused after he had said the word. "And what wert thou now doing at Ashby with such a charge in thy custody?"

"I went thither to render to Isaac the Jew of York," replied Gurth, "the price of a suit of armour with which he fitted my master for this tournament."

"And how much didst thou pay to Isaac?—Methinks, to judge by weight, there is still two hundred zecchins in this pouch."

"I paid to Isaac," said the Saxon, "eighty zecchins, and he restored me a hundred in lieu thereof."

"How! what!" exclaimed all the robbers at once; "darest thou trifle with us, that thou tellest such improbable lies?"

"What I tell you," said Gurth, "is as true as the moon is in heaven. You will find the just sum in a silken purse within the leathern pouch, and separate from the rest of the gold."

"Bethink thee, man," said the Captain, "thou speakest of a Jew—of an Israelite,—as unapt to restore gold, as the dry sand of his deserts to return the cup of water which the pilgrim spills upon them."

"There is no more mercy in them," said another of the banditti, "than in an unbribed sheriffs officer."

"It is, however, as I say," said Gurth.

"Strike a light instantly," said the Captain; "I will examine this said purse; and if it be as this fellow says, the Jew's bounty is little less miraculous than the stream which relieved his fathers in the wilderness."

A light was procured accordingly, and the robber proceeded to examine the purse. The others crowded around him, and even two who had hold of Gurth relaxed their grasp while they stretched their necks to see the issue of the search. Availing himself of their negligence, by a sudden exertion of strength and activity, Gurth shook himself free of their hold, and might have escaped, could he have resolved to leave his master's property behind him. But such was no part of his intention. He wrenched a quarter-staff from one of the fellows, struck down the Captain, who was altogether unaware of his purpose, and had well-nigh repossessed himself of the pouch and treasure. The thieves, however, were too nimble for him, and again secured both the bag and the trusty Gurth.

"Knave!" said the Captain, getting up, "thou hast broken my head; and with other men of our sort thou wouldst fare the worse for thy insolence. But thou shalt know thy fate instantly. First let us speak of thy master; the knight's matters must go before the squire's, according to the due order of chivalry. Stand thou fast in the meantime—if thou stir again, thou shalt have that will make thee quiet for thy life—Comrades!" he then said, addressing his gang, "this purse is embroidered with Hebrew characters, and I well believe the yeoman's tale is true. The errant knight, his master, must needs pass us toll-free. He is too like ourselves for us to make booty of him, since dogs should not worry dogs where wolves and foxes are to be found in abundance."

"Like us?" answered one of the gang; "I should like to hear how that is made good."

"Why, thou fool," answered the Captain, "is he not poor and disinherited as we are?—Doth he not win his substance at the sword's point as we do?—Hath he not beaten Front-de-Boeuf and Malvoisin, even as we would beat them if we could? Is he not the enemy to life and death of Brian de Bois-Guilbert, whom we have so much reason to fear? And were all this otherwise, wouldst thou have us show a worse conscience than an unbeliever, a Hebrew Jew?"

"Nay, that were a shame," muttered the other fellow; "and yet, when I served in the band of stout old Gandelyn, we had no such scruples of conscience. And this insolent peasant,—he too, I warrant me, is to be dismissed scatheless?"

"Not if THOU canst scathe him," replied the Captain.—"Here, fellow," continued he, addressing Gurth, "canst thou use the staff, that thou starts to it so readily?"

"I think," said Gurth, "thou shouldst be best able to reply to that question."

"Nay, by my troth, thou gavest me a round knock," replied the Captain; "do as much for this fellow, and thou shalt pass scot-free; and if thou dost not—why, by my faith, as thou art such a sturdy knave, I think I must pay thy ransom myself.—Take thy staff, Miller," he added, "and keep thy head; and do you others let the fellow go, and give him a staff—there is light enough to lay on load by."

The two champions being alike armed with quarter-staves, stepped forward into the centre of the open space, in order to have the full benefit of the moonlight; the thieves in the meantime laughing, and crying to their comrade, "Miller! beware thy toll-dish." The Miller, on the other hand, holding his quarter-staff by the middle, and making it flourish round his head after the fashion which the French call "faire le moulinet", exclaimed boastfully, "Come on, churl, an thou darest: thou shalt feel the strength of a miller's thumb!"

"If thou be'st a miller," answered Gurth, undauntedly, making his weapon play around his head with equal dexterity, "thou art doubly a thief, and I, as a true man, bid thee defiance."

So saying, the two champions closed together, and for a few minutes they displayed great equality in strength, courage, and skill, intercepting and returning the blows of their adversary with the most rapid dexterity, while, from the continued clatter of their weapons, a person at a distance might have supposed that there were at least six persons engaged on each side. Less obstinate, and even less dangerous combats, have been described in good heroic verse; but that of Gurth and the Miller must remain unsung, for want of a sacred poet to do justice to its eventful progress. Yet, though quarter-staff play be out of date, what we can in prose we will do for these bold champions.

Long they fought equally, until the Miller began to lose temper at finding himself so stoutly opposed, and at hearing the laughter of his companions, who, as usual in such cases, enjoyed his vexation. This was not a state of mind favourable to the noble game of quarter-staff, in which, as in ordinary cudgel-playing, the utmost coolness is requisite; and it gave Gurth, whose temper was steady, though surly, the opportunity of acquiring a decided advantage, in availing himself of which he displayed great mastery.

The Miller pressed furiously forward, dealing blows with either end of his weapon alternately, and striving to come to half-staff distance, while Gurth defended himself against the attack, keeping his hands about a yard asunder, and covering himself by shifting his weapon with great celerity, so as to protect his head and body. Thus did he maintain the defensive, making his eye, foot, and hand keep true time, until, observing his antagonist to lose wind, he darted the staff at his face with his left hand; and, as the Miller endeavoured to parry the thrust, he slid his right hand down to his left, and with the full swing of the weapon struck his opponent on the left side of the head, who instantly measured his length upon the green sward.

"Well and yeomanly done!" shouted the robbers; "fair play and Old England for ever! The Saxon hath saved both his purse and his hide, and the Miller has met his match."

"Thou mayst go thy ways, my friend," said the Captain, addressing Gurth, in special confirmation of the general voice, "and I will cause two of my comrades to guide thee by the best way to thy master's pavilion, and to guard thee from night-walkers that might have less tender consciences than ours; for there is many one of them upon the amble in such a night as this. Take heed, however," he added sternly; "remember thou hast refused to tell thy name—ask not after ours, nor endeavour to discover who or what we are; for, if thou makest such an attempt, thou wilt come by worse fortune than has yet befallen thee."

Gurth thanked the Captain for his courtesy, and promised to attend to his recommendation. Two of the outlaws, taking up their quarter-staves, and desiring Gurth to follow close in the rear, walked roundly forward along a by-path, which traversed the thicket and the broken ground adjacent to it. On the very verge of the thicket two men spoke to his conductors, and receiving an answer in a whisper, withdrew into the wood, and suffered them to pass unmolested. This circumstance induced Gurth to believe both that the gang was strong in numbers, and that they kept regular guards around their place of rendezvous.

When they arrived on the open heath, where Gurth might have had some trouble in finding his road, the thieves guided him straight forward to the top of a little eminence, whence he could see, spread beneath him in the moonlight, the palisades of the lists, the glimmering pavilions pitched at either end, with the pennons which adorned them fluttering in the moonbeams, and from which could be heard the hum of the song with which the sentinels were beguiling their night-watch.

Here the thieves stopt.

"We go with you no farther," said they; "it were not safe that we should do so.—Remember the warning you have received—keep secret what has this night befallen you, and you will have no room to repent it—neglect what is now told you, and the Tower of London shall not protect you against our revenge."

"Good night to you, kind sirs," said Gurth; "I shall remember your orders, and trust that there is no offence in wishing you a safer and an honester trade."

Thus they parted, the outlaws returning in the direction from whence they had come, and Gurth proceeding to the tent of his master, to whom, notwithstanding the injunction he had received, he communicated the whole adventures of the evening.

The Disinherited Knight was filled with astonishment, no less at the generosity of Rebecca, by which, however, he resolved he would not profit, than that of the robbers, to whose profession such a quality seemed totally foreign. His course of reflections upon these singular circumstances was, however, interrupted by the necessity for taking repose, which the fatigue of the preceding day, and the propriety of refreshing himself for the morrow's encounter, rendered alike indispensable.

The knight, therefore, stretched himself for repose upon a rich couch with which the tent was provided; and the faithful Gurth, extending his hardy limbs upon a bear-skin which formed a sort of carpet to the pavilion, laid himself across the opening of the tent, so that no one could enter without awakening him.

XII.

> The heralds left their pricking up and down,
> Now ringen trumpets loud and clarion.
> There is no more to say, but east and west,
> In go the speares sadly in the rest,
> In goth the sharp spur into the side,
> There see men who can just and who can ride;
> There shiver shaftes upon shieldes thick,
> He feeleth through the heart-spone the prick;
> Up springen speares, twenty feet in height,
> Out go the swordes to the silver bright;
> The helms they to-hewn and to-shred;
> Out burst the blood with stern streames red.
>
> — CHAUCER

Morning arose in unclouded splendour, and ere the sun was much above the horizon, the idlest or the most eager of the spectators appeared on the common, moving to the lists as to a general centre, in order to secure a favourable situation for viewing the continuation of the expected games.

The marshals and their attendants appeared next on the field, together with the heralds, for the purpose of receiving the names of the knights who intended to joust, with the side which each chose to espouse. This was a necessary precaution, in order to secure equality betwixt the two bodies who should be opposed to each other.

According to due formality, the Disinherited Knight was to be considered as leader of the one body, while Brian de Bois-Guilbert, who had been rated as having done second-best in the preceding day, was named first champion of the other band. Those who had concurred in the challenge adhered to his party of course, excepting only Ralph de Vipont, whom his fall had rendered unfit so soon to put on his armour. There was no want of distinguished and noble candidates to fill up the ranks on either side.

In fact, although the general tournament, in which all knights fought at once, was more dangerous than single encounters, they were, nevertheless, more frequented and practised by the chivalry of the age. Many knights, who had not sufficient confidence in their own skill to defy a single adversary of high reputation, were, nevertheless, desirous of displaying their valour in the general combat, where they might meet others with whom they were more upon an equality. On the present occasion, about fifty knights were inscribed as desirous of combating upon each side, when the marshals declared that no more could be admitted, to the disappointment of several who were too late in preferring their claim to be included.

About the hour of ten o'clock, the whole plain was crowded with horsemen, horsewomen, and foot-passengers, hastening to the tournament; and shortly after, a grand flourish of trumpets announced Prince John and his retinue, attended by many of those knights who meant to take share in the game, as well as others who had no such intention.

About the same time arrived Cedric the Saxon, with the Lady Rowena, unattended, however, by Athelstane. This Saxon lord had arrayed his tall and strong person in armour, in order to take his place among the combatants; and, considerably to the surprise of Cedric, had chosen to enlist himself on the part of the Knight Templar. The Saxon, indeed, had remonstrated strongly with his friend upon the injudicious choice he had made of his party; but he had only received that sort of answer usually given by those who are more obstinate in following their own course, than strong in justifying it.

His best, if not his only reason, for adhering to the party of Brian de Bois-Guilbert, Athelstane had the prudence to keep to himself. Though his apathy of disposition prevented his taking any means to recommend himself to the Lady Rowena, he was, nevertheless, by no means insensible to her charms, and considered his union with her as a matter already fixed beyond doubt, by the assent of Cedric and her other friends. It had therefore been with smothered displeasure that the proud though indolent Lord of Coningsburgh beheld the victor of the preceding day select Rowena as the object of that honour which it became his privilege to confer. In order to punish him for a preference which seemed to interfere with his own suit, Athelstane, confident of his strength, and to whom his flatterers, at least, ascribed great skill in arms, had determined not only to deprive the Disinherited Knight of his powerful succour, but, if an opportunity should occur, to make him feel the weight of his battle-axe.

De Bracy, and other knights attached to Prince John, in obedience to a hint from him, had joined the party of the challengers, John being desirous to secure, if possible, the victory to that side. On the other hand, many other knights, both English and Norman, natives and strangers, took part against the challengers, the more readily that the opposite band was to be led by so distinguished a champion as the Disinherited Knight had approved himself.

As soon as Prince John observed that the destined Queen of the day had arrived upon the field, assuming that air of courtesy which sat well upon him when he was pleased to exhibit it, he rode forward to meet her, doffed his bonnet, and, alighting from his horse, assisted the Lady Rowena from her saddle, while his followers uncovered at the same time, and one of the most distinguished dismounted to hold her palfrey.

"It is thus," said Prince John, "that we set the dutiful example of loyalty to the Queen of Love and Beauty, and are ourselves her guide to the throne which she must this day occupy.—Ladies," he said, "attend your Queen, as you wish in your turn to be distinguished by like honours."

So saying, the Prince marshalled Rowena to the seat of honour opposite his own, while the fairest and most distinguished ladies present crowded after her to obtain places as near as possible to their temporary sovereign.

No sooner was Rowena seated, than a burst of music, half-drowned by the shouts of the multitude, greeted her new dignity. Meantime, the sun shone fierce and bright upon the polished arms of the knights of either side, who crowded the opposite extremities of the lists, and held eager conference together concerning the best mode of arranging their line of battle, and supporting the conflict.

The heralds then proclaimed silence until the laws of the tourney should be rehearsed. These were calculated in some degree to abate the dangers of the day; a precaution the more necessary, as the conflict was to be maintained with sharp swords and pointed lances.

The champions were therefore prohibited to thrust with the sword, and were confined to striking. A knight, it was announced, might use a mace or battle-axe at pleasure, but the dagger was a prohibited weapon. A knight unhorsed might renew the fight on foot with any other on the opposite side in the same predicament; but mounted horsemen were in that case forbidden to assail him. When any knight could force his antagonist to the extremity of the lists, so as to touch the palisade with his person or arms, such opponent was obliged to yield himself vanquished, and his armour and horse were placed at the disposal of the conqueror. A knight thus overcome was not permitted to take farther share in the combat. If any combatant was struck down, and unable to recover his feet, his squire or page might enter the lists, and drag his master out of the press; but in that case the knight was adjudged vanquished, and his arms and horse declared forfeited. The combat was to cease as soon as Prince John should throw down his leading staff, or truncheon; another precaution usually taken to prevent the unnecessary effusion of blood by the too long endurance of a sport so desperate. Any knight breaking the rules of the tournament, or otherwise transgressing the rules of honourable chivalry, was liable to be stript of his arms, and, having his shield reversed to be placed in that posture astride upon the bars of the palisade, and exposed to public derision, in punishment of his unknightly conduct. Having announced these precautions, the heralds concluded with an exhortation to each good knight to do his duty, and to merit favour from the Queen of Beauty and of Love.

This proclamation having been made, the heralds withdrew to their stations. The knights, entering at either end of the lists in long procession, arranged themselves in a double file, precisely opposite to each other, the leader of each party being in the centre of the foremost rank, a post which he did not occupy until each had carefully marshalled the ranks of his party, and stationed every one in his place.

It was a goodly, and at the same time an anxious, sight, to behold so many gallant champions, mounted bravely, and armed richly, stand ready prepared for an encounter so formidable, seated on their war-saddles like so many pillars of iron, and awaiting the signal of encounter with the same ardour as their generous steeds, which, by neighing and pawing the ground, gave signal of their impatience.

As yet the knights held their long lances upright, their bright points glancing to the sun, and the streamers with which they were decorated fluttering over the plumage of the helmets. Thus they remained while the marshals of the field surveyed their ranks with the utmost exactness, lest either party had more or fewer than the appointed number. The tale was found exactly complete. The marshals then withdrew from the lists, and William de Wyvil, with a voice of thunder, pronounced the signal words—"Laissez aller!" The trumpets sounded as he spoke—the spears of the champions were at once lowered and placed in the rests—the spurs were dashed into the flanks of the horses, and the two foremost ranks of either party rushed upon each other in full gallop, and met in the middle of the lists with a shock, the sound of which was heard at a mile's distance. The rear rank of each party advanced at a slower pace to sustain the defeated, and follow up the success of the victors of their party.

The consequences of the encounter were not instantly seen, for the dust raised by the trampling of so many steeds darkened the air, and it was a minute ere the anxious spectator could see the fate of the encounter. When the fight became visible, half the knights on each side were dismounted, some by the dexterity of their adversary's lance,—some by the superior weight and strength of opponents, which had borne down both horse and man,—some lay stretched on earth as if never more to rise,—some had already gained their feet, and were closing hand to hand with those of their antagonists who were in the same predicament,—and several on both sides, who had received wounds by which they were disabled, were stopping their blood by their scarfs, and endeavouring to extricate themselves from the tumult. The mounted knights, whose lances had been almost all broken by the fury of the encounter, were now closely engaged with their swords, shouting their war-cries, and exchanging buffets, as if honour and life depended on the issue of the combat.

The tumult was presently increased by the advance of the second rank on either side, which, acting as a reserve, now rushed on to aid their companions. The followers of Brian de Bois-Guilbert shouted—"Ha! Beau-seant! Beau-seant!

"—For the Temple—For the Temple!" The opposite party shouted in answer—"Desdichado! Desdichado!"—which watch-word they took from the motto upon their leader's shield.

The champions thus encountering each other with the utmost fury, and with alternate success, the tide of battle seemed to flow now toward the southern, now toward the northern extremity of the lists, as the one or the other party prevailed. Meantime the clang of the blows, and the shouts of the combatants, mixed fearfully with the sound of the trumpets, and drowned the groans of those who fell, and lay rolling defenceless beneath the feet of the horses. The splendid armour of the combatants was now defaced with dust and blood, and gave way at every stroke of the sword and battle-axe. The gay plumage, shorn from the crests, drifted upon the breeze like snow-flakes. All that was beautiful and graceful in the martial array had disappeared, and what was now visible was only calculated to awake terror or compassion.

Yet such is the force of habit, that not only the vulgar spectators, who are naturally attracted by sights of horror, but even the ladies of distinction who crowded the galleries, saw the conflict with a thrilling interest certainly, but without a wish to withdraw their eyes from a sight so terrible. Here and there, indeed, a fair cheek might turn pale, or a faint scream might be heard, as a lover, a brother, or a husband, was struck from his horse. But, in general, the ladies around encouraged the combatants, not only by clapping their hands and waving their veils and kerchiefs, but even by exclaiming, "Brave lance! Good sword!" when any successful thrust or blow took place under their observation.

Such being the interest taken by the fair sex in this bloody game, that of the men is the more easily understood. It showed itself in loud acclamations upon every change of fortune, while all eyes were so riveted on the lists, that the spectators seemed as if they themselves had dealt and received the blows which were there so freely bestowed. And between every pause was heard the voice of the heralds, exclaiming, "Fight on, brave knights! Man dies, but glory lives!—Fight on—death is better than defeat!—Fight on, brave knights!—for bright eyes behold your deeds!"

Amid the varied fortunes of the combat, the eyes of all endeavoured to discover the leaders of each band, who, mingling in the thick of the fight, encouraged their companions both by voice and example. Both displayed great feats of gallantry, nor did either Bois-Guilbert or the Disinherited Knight find in the ranks opposed to them a champion who could be termed their unquestioned match. They repeatedly endeavoured to single out each other, spurred by mutual animosity, and aware that the fall of either leader might be considered as decisive of victory. Such, however, was the crowd and confusion, that, during the earlier part of the conflict, their efforts to meet were unavailing, and they were repeatedly separated by the eagerness of their followers, each of whom was anxious to win honour, by measuring his strength against the leader of the opposite party.

But when the field became thin by the numbers on either side who had yielded themselves vanquished, had been compelled to the extremity of the lists, or been otherwise rendered incapable of continuing the strife, the Templar and the Disinherited Knight at length encountered hand to hand, with all the fury that mortal animosity, joined to rivalry of honour, could inspire. Such was the address of each in parrying and striking, that the spectators broke forth into a unanimous and involuntary shout, expressive of their delight and admiration.

But at this moment the party of the Disinherited Knight had the worst; the gigantic arm of Front-de-Boeuf on the one flank, and the ponderous strength of Athelstane on the other, bearing down and dispersing those immediately exposed to them. Finding themselves freed from their immediate antagonists, it seems to have occurred to both these knights at the same instant, that they would render the most decisive advantage to their party, by aiding the Templar in his contest with his rival. Turning their horses, therefore, at the same moment, the Norman spurred against the Disinherited Knight on the one side, and the Saxon on the other. It was utterly impossible that the object of this unequal and unexpected assault could have sustained it, had he not been warned by a general cry from the spectators, who could not but take interest in one exposed to such disadvantage.

"Beware! beware! Sir Disinherited!" was shouted so universally, that the knight became aware of his danger; and, striking a full blow at the Templar, he reined back his steed in the same moment, so as to escape the charge of Athelstane and Front-de-Boeuf. These knights, therefore, their aim being thus eluded, rushed from opposite sides betwixt the object of their attack and the Templar, almost running their horses against each other ere they could stop their career. Recovering their horses however, and wheeling them round, the whole three pursued their united purpose of bearing to the earth the Disinherited Knight.

Nothing could have saved him, except the remarkable strength and activity of the noble horse which he had won on the preceding day.

This stood him in the more stead, as the horse of Bois-Guilbert was wounded, and those of Front-de-Boeuf and Athelstane were both tired with the weight of their gigantic masters, clad in complete armour, and with the preceding exertions of the day. The masterly horsemanship of the Disinherited Knight, and the activity of the noble animal which he mounted, enabled him for a few minutes to keep at sword's point his three antagonists, turning and wheeling with the agility of a hawk upon the wing, keeping his enemies as far separate as he could, and rushing now against the one, now against the other, dealing sweeping blows with his sword, without waiting to receive those which were aimed at him in return.

But although the lists rang with the applauses of his dexterity, it was evident that he must at last be overpowered; and the nobles around Prince John implored him with one voice to throw down his warder, and to save so brave a knight from the disgrace of being overcome by odds.

"Not I, by the light of Heaven!" answered Prince John; "this same springald, who conceals his name, and despises our proffered hospitality, hath already gained one prize, and may now afford to let others have their turn." As he spoke thus, an unexpected incident changed the fortune of the day.

There was among the ranks of the Disinherited Knight a champion in black armour, mounted on a black horse, large of size, tall, and to all appearance powerful and strong, like the rider by whom he was mounted. This knight, who bore on his shield no device of any kind, had hitherto evinced very little interest in the event of the fight, beating off with seeming ease those combatants who attacked him, but neither pursuing his advantages, nor himself assailing any one. In short, he had hitherto acted the part rather of a spectator than of a party in the tournament, a circumstance which procured him among the spectators the name of "Le Noir Faineant", or the Black Sluggard.

At once this knight seemed to throw aside his apathy, when he discovered the leader of his party so hard bestead; for, setting spurs to his horse, which was quite fresh, he came to his assistance like a thunderbolt, exclaiming, in a voice like a trumpet-call, "Desdichado, to the rescue!" It was high time; for, while the Disinherited Knight was pressing upon the Templar, Front-de-Boeuf had got nigh to him with his uplifted sword; but ere the blow could descend, the Sable Knight dealt a stroke on his head, which, glancing from the polished helmet, lighted with violence scarcely abated on the "chamfron" of the steed, and Front-de-Boeuf rolled on the ground, both horse and man equally stunned by the fury of the blow. "Le Noir Faineant" then turned his horse upon Athelstane of Coningsburgh; and his own sword having been broken in his encounter with Front-de-Boeuf, he wrenched from the hand of the bulky Saxon the battle-axe which he wielded, and, like one familiar with the use of the weapon, bestowed him such a blow upon the crest, that Athelstane also lay senseless on the field. Having achieved this double feat, for which he was the more highly applauded that it was totally unexpected from him, the knight seemed to resume the sluggishness of his character, returning calmly to the northern extremity of the lists, leaving his leader to cope as he best could with Brian de Bois-Guilbert. This was no longer matter of so much difficulty as formerly. The Templars horse had bled much, and gave way under the shock of the Disinherited Knight's charge. Brian de Bois-Guilbert rolled on the field, encumbered with the stirrup, from which he was unable to draw his foot. His antagonist sprung from horseback, waved his fatal sword over the head of his adversary, and commanded him to yield himself; when Prince John, more moved by the Templars dangerous situation than he had been by that of his rival, saved him the mortification of confessing himself vanquished, by casting down his warder, and putting an end to the conflict.

It was, indeed, only the relics and embers of the fight which continued to burn; for of the few knights who still continued in the lists, the greater part had, by tacit consent, forborne the conflict for some time, leaving it to be determined by the strife of the leaders.

The squires, who had found it a matter of danger and difficulty to attend their masters during the engagement, now thronged into the lists to pay their dutiful attendance to the wounded, who were removed with the utmost care and attention to the neighbouring pavilions, or to the quarters prepared for them in the adjoining village.

Thus ended the memorable field of Ashby-de-la-Zouche, one of the most gallantly contested tournaments of that age; for although only four knights, including one who was smothered by the heat of his armour, had died upon the field, yet upwards of thirty were desperately wounded, four or five of whom never recovered. Several more were disabled for life; and those who escaped best carried the marks of the conflict to the grave with them. Hence it is always mentioned in the old records, as the Gentle and Joyous Passage of Arms of Ashby.

It being now the duty of Prince John to name the knight who had done best, he determined that the honour of the day remained with the knight whom the popular voice had termed "Le Noir Faineant." It was pointed out to the Prince, in impeachment of this decree, that the victory had been in fact won by the Disinherited Knight, who, in the course of the day, had overcome six champions with his own hand, and who had finally unhorsed and struck down the leader of the opposite party. But Prince John adhered to his own opinion, on the ground that the Disinherited Knight and his party had lost the day, but for the powerful assistance of the Knight of the Black Armour, to whom, therefore, he persisted in awarding the prize.

To the surprise of all present, however, the knight thus preferred was nowhere to be found. He had left the lists immediately when the conflict ceased, and had been observed by some spectators to move down one of the forest glades with the same slow pace and listless and indifferent manner which had procured him the epithet of the Black Sluggard. After he had been summoned twice by sound of trumpet, and proclamation of the heralds, it became necessary to name another to receive the honours which had been assigned to him. Prince John had now no further excuse for resisting the claim of the Disinherited Knight, whom, therefore, he named the champion of the day.

Through a field slippery with blood, and encumbered with broken armour and the bodies of slain and wounded horses, the marshals of the lists again conducted the victor to the foot of Prince John's throne.

"Disinherited Knight," said Prince John, "since by that title only you will consent to be known to us, we a second time award to you the honours of this tournament, and announce to you your right to claim and receive from the hands of the Queen of Love and Beauty, the Chaplet of Honour which your valour has justly deserved." The Knight bowed low and gracefully, but returned no answer.

While the trumpets sounded, while the heralds strained their voices in proclaiming honour to the brave and glory to the victor—while ladies waved their silken kerchiefs and embroidered veils, and while all ranks joined in a clamorous shout of exultation, the marshals conducted the Disinherited Knight across the lists to the foot of that throne of honour which was occupied by the Lady Rowena.

On the lower step of this throne the champion was made to kneel down. Indeed his whole action since the fight had ended, seemed rather to have been upon the impulse of those around him than from his own free will; and it was observed that he tottered as they guided him the second time across the lists. Rowena, descending from her station with a graceful and dignified step, was about to place the chaplet which she held in her hand upon the helmet of the champion, when the marshals exclaimed with one voice, "It must not be thus—his head must be bare." The knight muttered faintly a few words, which were lost in the hollow of his helmet, but their purport seemed to be a desire that his casque might not be removed.

Whether from love of form, or from curiosity, the marshals paid no attention to his expressions of reluctance, but unhelmed him by cutting the laces of his casque, and undoing the fastening of his gorget. When the helmet was removed, the well-formed, yet sun-burnt features of a young man of twenty-five were seen, amidst a profusion of short fair hair. His countenance was as pale as death, and marked in one or two places with streaks of blood.

Rowena had no sooner beheld him than she uttered a faint shriek; but at once summoning up the energy of her disposition, and compelling herself, as it were, to proceed, while her frame yet trembled with the violence of sudden emotion, she placed upon the drooping head of the victor the splendid chaplet which was the destined reward of the day, and pronounced, in a clear and distinct tone, these words: "I bestow on thee this chaplet, Sir Knight, as the meed of valour assigned to this day's victor:" Here she paused a moment, and then firmly added, "And upon brows more worthy could a wreath of chivalry never be placed!"

The knight stooped his head, and kissed the hand of the lovely Sovereign by whom his valour had been rewarded; and then, sinking yet farther forward, lay prostrate at her feet.

There was a general consternation. Cedric, who had been struck mute by the sudden appearance of his banished son, now rushed forward, as if to separate him from Rowena. But this had been already accomplished by the marshals of the field, who, guessing the cause of Ivanhoe's swoon, had hastened to undo his armour, and found that the head of a lance had penetrated his breastplate, and inflicted a wound in his side.

XIII.

> "Heroes, approach!" Atrides thus aloud,
> "Stand forth distinguish'd from the circling crowd,
> Ye who by skill or manly force may claim,
> Your rivals to surpass and merit fame.
> This cow, worth twenty oxen, is decreed,
> For him who farthest sends the winged reed."
>
> — ILIAD

The name of Ivanhoe was no sooner pronounced than it flew from mouth to mouth, with all the celerity with which eagerness could convey and curiosity receive it. It was not long ere it reached the circle of the Prince, whose brow darkened as he heard the news. Looking around him, however, with an air of scorn, "My Lords," said he, "and especially you, Sir Prior, what think ye of the doctrine the learned tell us, concerning innate attractions and antipathies? Methinks that I felt the presence of my brother's minion, even when I least guessed whom yonder suit of armour enclosed."

"Front-de-Boeuf must prepare to restore his fief of Ivanhoe," said De Bracy, who, having discharged his part honourably in the tournament, had laid his shield and helmet aside, and again mingled with the Prince's retinue.

"Ay," answered Waldemar Fitzurse, "this gallant is likely to reclaim the castle and manor which Richard assigned to him, and which your Highness's generosity has since given to Front-de-Boeuf."

"Front-de-Boeuf," replied John, "is a man more willing to swallow three manors such as Ivanhoe, than to disgorge one of them. For the rest, sirs, I hope none here will deny my right to confer the fiefs of the crown upon the faithful followers who are around me, and ready to perform the usual military service, in the room of those who have wandered to foreign Countries, and can neither render homage nor service when called upon."

The audience were too much interested in the question not to pronounce the Prince's assumed right altogether indubitable. "A generous Prince!—a most noble Lord, who thus takes upon himself the task of rewarding his faithful followers!"

Such were the words which burst from the train, expectants all of them of similar grants at the expense of King Richard's followers and favourites, if indeed they had not as yet received such. Prior Aymer also assented to the general proposition, observing, however, "That the blessed Jerusalem could not indeed be termed a foreign country. She was 'communis mater'—the mother of all Christians. But he saw not," he declared, "how the Knight of Ivanhoe could plead any advantage from this, since he" (the Prior) "was assured that the crusaders, under Richard, had never proceeded much farther than Askalon, which, as all the world knew, was a town of the Philistines, and entitled to none of the privileges of the Holy City."

Waldemar, whose curiosity had led him towards the place where Ivanhoe had fallen to the ground, now returned. "The gallant," said he, "is likely to give your Highness little disturbance, and to leave Front-de-Boeuf in the quiet possession of his gains—he is severely wounded."

"Whatever becomes of him," said Prince John, "he is victor of the day; and were he tenfold our enemy, or the devoted friend of our brother, which is perhaps the same, his wounds must be looked to—our own physician shall attend him."

A stern smile curled the Prince's lip as he spoke. Waldemar Fitzurse hastened to reply, that Ivanhoe was already removed from the lists, and in the custody of his friends.

"I was somewhat afflicted," he said, "to see the grief of the Queen of Love and Beauty, whose sovereignty of a day this event has changed into mourning. I am not a man to be moved by a woman's lament for her lover, but this same Lady Rowena suppressed her sorrow with such dignity of manner, that it could only be discovered by her folded hands, and her tearless eye, which trembled as it remained fixed on the lifeless form before her."

"Who is this Lady Rowena," said Prince John, "of whom we have heard so much?"

"A Saxon heiress of large possessions," replied the Prior Aymer; "a rose of loveliness, and a jewel of wealth; the fairest among a thousand, a bundle of myrrh, and a cluster of camphire."

"We shall cheer her sorrows," said Prince John, "and amend her blood, by wedding her to a Norman. She seems a minor, and must therefore be at our royal disposal in marriage.—How sayst thou, De Bracy? What thinkst thou of gaining fair lands and livings, by wedding a Saxon, after the fashion of the followers of the Conqueror?"

"If the lands are to my liking, my lord," answered De Bracy, "it will be hard to displease me with a bride; and deeply will I hold myself bound to your highness for a good deed, which will fulfil all promises made in favour of your servant and vassal."

"We will not forget it," said Prince John; "and that we may instantly go to work, command our seneschal presently to order the attendance of the Lady Rowena and her company—that is, the rude churl her guardian, and the Saxon ox whom the Black Knight struck down in the tournament, upon this evening's banquet.—De Bigot," he added to his seneschal, "thou wilt word this our second summons so courteously, as to gratify the pride of these Saxons, and make it impossible for them again to refuse; although, by the bones of Becket, courtesy to them is casting pearls before swine."

Prince John had proceeded thus far, and was about to give the signal for retiring from the lists, when a small billet was put into his hand.

"From whence?" said Prince John, looking at the person by whom it was delivered.

"From foreign parts, my lord, but from whence I know not" replied his attendant. "A Frenchman brought it hither, who said, he had ridden night and day to put it into the hands of your highness."

The Prince looked narrowly at the superscription, and then at the seal, placed so as to secure the flex-silk with which the billet was surrounded, and which bore the impression of three fleurs-de-lis. John then opened the billet with apparent agitation, which visibly and greatly increased when he had perused the contents, which were expressed in these words:

"Take heed to yourself for the Devil is unchained!"

The Prince turned as pale as death, looked first on the earth, and then up to heaven, like a man who has received news that sentence of execution has been passed upon him. Recovering from the first effects of his surprise, he took Waldemar Fitzurse and De Bracy aside, and put the billet into their hands successively. "It means," he added, in a faltering voice, "that my brother Richard has obtained his freedom."

"This may be a false alarm, or a forged letter," said De Bracy.

"It is France's own hand and seal," replied Prince John.

"It is time, then," said Fitzurse, "to draw our party to a head, either at York, or some other centrical place. A few days later, and it will be indeed too late. Your highness must break short this present mummery."

"The yeomen and commons," said De Bracy, "must not be dismissed discontented, for lack of their share in the sports."

"The day," said Waldemar, "is not yet very far spent—let the archers shoot a few rounds at the target, and the prize be adjudged. This will be an abundant fulfilment of the Prince's promises, so far as this herd of Saxon serfs is concerned."

"I thank thee, Waldemar," said the Prince; "thou remindest me, too, that I have a debt to pay to that insolent peasant who yesterday insulted our person. Our banquet also shall go forward to-night as we proposed. Were this my last hour of power, it should be an hour sacred to revenge and to pleasure—let new cares come with to-morrow's new day."

The sound of the trumpets soon recalled those spectators who had already begun to leave the field; and proclamation was made that Prince John, suddenly called by high and peremptory public duties, held himself obliged to discontinue the entertainments of to-morrow's festival: Nevertheless, that, unwilling so many good yeoman should depart without a trial of skill, he was pleased to appoint them, before leaving the ground, presently to execute the competition of archery intended for the morrow. To the best archer a prize was to be awarded, being a bugle-horn, mounted with silver, and a silken baldric richly ornamented with a medallion of St Hubert, the patron of silvan sport.

More than thirty yeomen at first presented themselves as competitors, several of whom were rangers and under-keepers in the royal forests of Needwood and Charnwood. When, however, the archers understood with whom they were to be matched, upwards of twenty withdrew themselves from the contest, unwilling to encounter the dishonour of almost certain defeat. For in those days the skill of each celebrated marksman was as well known for many miles round him, as the qualities of a horse trained at Newmarket are familiar to those who frequent that well-known meeting.

The diminished list of competitors for silvan fame still amounted to eight. Prince John stepped from his royal seat to view more nearly the persons of these chosen yeomen, several of whom wore the royal livery. Having satisfied his curiosity by this investigation, he looked for the object of his resentment, whom he observed standing on the same spot, and with the same composed countenance which he had exhibited upon the preceding day.

"Fellow," said Prince John, "I guessed by thy insolent babble that thou wert no true lover of the longbow, and I see thou darest not adventure thy skill among such merry-men as stand yonder."

"Under favour, sir," replied the yeoman, "I have another reason for refraining to shoot, besides the fearing discomfiture and disgrace."

"And what is thy other reason?" said Prince John, who, for some cause which perhaps he could not himself have explained, felt a painful curiosity respecting this individual.

"Because," replied the woodsman, "I know not if these yeomen and I are used to shoot at the same marks; and because, moreover, I know not how your Grace might relish the winning of a third prize by one who has unwittingly fallen under your displeasure."

Prince John coloured as he put the question, "What is thy name, yeoman?"

"Locksley," answered the yeoman.

"Then, Locksley," said Prince John, "thou shalt shoot in thy turn, when these yeomen have displayed their skill. If thou carriest the prize, I will add to it twenty nobles; but if thou losest it, thou shalt be stript of thy Lincoln green, and scourged out of the lists with bowstrings, for a wordy and insolent braggart."

"And how if I refuse to shoot on such a wager?" said the yeoman.—"Your Grace's power, supported, as it is, by so many men-at-arms, may indeed easily strip and scourge me, but cannot compel me to bend or to draw my bow."

"If thou refusest my fair proffer," said the Prince, "the Provost of the lists shall cut thy bowstring, break thy bow and arrows, and expel thee from the presence as a faint-hearted craven."

"This is no fair chance you put on me, proud Prince," said the yeoman, "to compel me to peril myself against the best archers of Leicester And Staffordshire, under the penalty of infamy if they should overshoot me. Nevertheless, I will obey your pleasure."

"Look to him close, men-at-arms," said Prince John, "his heart is sinking; I am jealous lest he attempt to escape the trial.—And do you, good fellows, shoot boldly round; a buck and a butt of wine are ready for your refreshment in yonder tent, when the prize is won."

A target was placed at the upper end of the southern avenue which led to the lists. The contending archers took their station in turn, at the bottom of the southern access, the distance between that station and the mark allowing full distance for what was called a shot at rovers. The archers, having previously determined by lot their order of precedence, were to shoot each three shafts in succession. The sports were regulated by an officer of inferior rank, termed the Provost of the Games; for the high rank of the marshals of the lists would have been held degraded, had they condescended to superintend the sports of the yeomanry.

One by one the archers, stepping forward, delivered their shafts yeomanlike and bravely. Of twenty-four arrows, shot in succession, ten were fixed in the target, and the others ranged so near it, that, considering the distance of the mark, it was accounted good archery. Of the ten shafts which hit the target, two within the inner ring were shot by Hubert, a forester in the service of Malvoisin, who was accordingly pronounced victorious.

"Now, Locksley," said Prince John to the bold yeoman, with a bitter smile, "wilt thou try conclusions with Hubert, or wilt thou yield up bow, baldric, and quiver, to the Provost of the sports?"

"Sith it be no better," said Locksley, "I am content to try my fortune; on condition that when I have shot two shafts at yonder mark of Hubert's, he shall be bound to shoot one at that which I shall propose."

"That is but fair," answered Prince John, "and it shall not be refused thee.—If thou dost beat this braggart, Hubert, I will fill the bugle with silver-pennies for thee."

"A man can do but his best," answered Hubert; "but my grandsire drew a good long bow at Hastings, and I trust not to dishonour his memory."

The former target was now removed, and a fresh one of the same size placed in its room. Hubert, who, as victor in the first trial of skill, had the right to shoot first, took his aim with great deliberation, long measuring the distance with his eye, while he held in his hand his bended bow, with the arrow placed on the string. At length he made a step forward, and raising the bow at the full stretch of his left arm, till the centre or grasping-place was nigh level with his face, he drew his bowstring to his ear. The arrow whistled through the air, and lighted within the inner ring of the target, but not exactly in the centre.

"You have not allowed for the wind, Hubert," said his antagonist, bending his bow, "or that had been a better shot."

So saying, and without showing the least anxiety to pause upon his aim, Locksley stept to the appointed station, and shot his arrow as carelessly in appearance as if he had not even looked at the mark. He was speaking almost at the instant that the shaft left the bowstring, yet it alighted in the target two inches nearer to the white spot which marked the centre than that of Hubert.

"By the light of heaven!" said Prince John to Hubert, "an thou suffer that runagate knave to overcome thee, thou art worthy of the gallows!"

Hubert had but one set speech for all occasions. "An your highness were to hang me," he said, "a man can but do his best. Nevertheless, my grandsire drew a good bow—"

"The foul fiend on thy grandsire and all his generation!" interrupted John, "shoot, knave, and shoot thy best, or it shall be the worse for thee!"

Thus exhorted, Hubert resumed his place, and not neglecting the caution which he had received from his adversary, he made the necessary allowance for a very light air of wind, which had just arisen, and shot so successfully that his arrow alighted in the very centre of the target.

"A Hubert! a Hubert!" shouted the populace, more interested in a known person than in a stranger. "In the clout!—in the clout!—a Hubert for ever!"

"Thou canst not mend that shot, Locksley," said the Prince, with an insulting smile.

"I will notch his shaft for him, however," replied Locksley.

And letting fly his arrow with a little more precaution than before, it lighted right upon that of his competitor, which it split to shivers. The people who stood around were so astonished at his wonderful dexterity, that they could not even give vent to their surprise in their usual clamour. "This must be the devil, and no man of flesh and blood," whispered the yeomen to each other; "such archery was never seen since a bow was first bent in Britain."

"And now," said Locksley, "I will crave your Grace's permission to plant such a mark as is used in the North Country; and welcome every brave yeoman who shall try a shot at it to win a smile from the bonny lass he loves best."

He then turned to leave the lists. "Let your guards attend me," he said, "if you please—I go but to cut a rod from the next willow-bush."

Prince John made a signal that some attendants should follow him in case of his escape: but the cry of "Shame! shame!" which burst from the multitude, induced him to alter his ungenerous purpose.

Locksley returned almost instantly with a willow wand about six feet in length, perfectly straight, and rather thicker than a man's thumb. He began to peel this with great composure, observing at the same time, that to ask a good woodsman to shoot at a target so broad as had hitherto been used, was to put shame upon his skill. "For his own part," he said, "and in the land where he was bred, men would as soon take for their mark King Arthur's round-table, which held sixty knights around it. A child of seven years old," he said, "might hit yonder target with a headless shaft; but," added he, walking deliberately to the other end of the lists, and sticking the willow wand upright in the ground, "he that hits that rod at five-score yards, I call him an archer fit to bear both bow and quiver before a king, an it were the stout King Richard himself."

"My grandsire," said Hubert, "drew a good bow at the battle of Hastings, and never shot at such a mark in his life—and neither will I. If this yeoman can cleave that rod, I give him the bucklers—or rather, I yield to the devil that is in his jerkin, and not to any human skill; a man can but do his best, and I will not shoot where I am sure to miss. I might as well shoot at the edge of our parson's whittle, or at a wheat straw, or at a sunbeam, as at a twinkling white streak which I can hardly see."

"Cowardly dog!" said Prince John.—"Sirrah Locksley, do thou shoot; but, if thou hittest such a mark, I will say thou art the first man ever did so. However it be, thou shalt not crow over us with a mere show of superior skill."

"I will do my best, as Hubert says," answered Locksley; "no man can do more."

So saying, he again bent his bow, but on the present occasion looked with attention to his weapon, and changed the string, which he thought was no longer truly round, having been a little frayed by the two former shots. He then took his aim with some deliberation, and the multitude awaited the event in breathless silence. The archer vindicated their opinion of his skill: his arrow split the willow rod against which it was aimed. A jubilee of acclamations followed; and even Prince John, in admiration of Locksley's skill, lost for an instant his dislike to his person. "These twenty nobles," he said, "which, with the bugle, thou hast fairly won, are thine own; we will make them fifty, if thou wilt take livery and service with us as a yeoman of our body guard, and be near to our person. For never did so strong a hand bend a bow, or so true an eye direct a shaft."

"Pardon me, noble Prince," said Locksley; "but I have vowed, that if ever I take service, it should be with your royal brother King Richard. These twenty nobles I leave to Hubert, who has this day drawn as brave a bow as his grandsire did at Hastings. Had his modesty not refused the trial, he would have hit the wand as well I."

Hubert shook his head as he received with reluctance the bounty of the stranger, and Locksley, anxious to escape further observation, mixed with the crowd, and was seen no more.

The victorious archer would not perhaps have escaped John's attention so easily, had not that Prince had other subjects of anxious and more important meditation pressing upon his mind at that instant. He called upon his chamberlain as he gave the signal for retiring from the lists, and commanded him instantly to gallop to Ashby, and seek out Isaac the Jew. "Tell the dog," he said, "to send me, before sun-down, two thousand crowns. He knows the security; but thou mayst show him this ring for a token. The rest of the money must be paid at York within six days. If he neglects, I will have the unbelieving villain's head. Look that thou pass him not on the way; for the circumcised slave was displaying his stolen finery amongst us."

So saying, the Prince resumed his horse, and returned to Ashby, the whole crowd breaking up and dispersing upon his retreat.

XIV.

> In rough magnificence array'd,
> When ancient Chivalry display'd
> The pomp of her heroic games,
> And crested chiefs and tissued dames
> Assembled, at the clarion's call,
> In some proud castle's high arch'd hall.
>
> — WARTON

Prince John held his high festival in the Castle of Ashby. This was not the same building of which the stately ruins still interest the traveller, and which was erected at a later period by the Lord Hastings, High Chamberlain of England, one of the first victims of the tyranny of Richard the Third, and yet better known as one of Shakspeare's characters than by his historical fame. The castle and town of Ashby, at this time, belonged to Roger de Quincy, Earl of Winchester, who, during the period of our history, was absent in the Holy Land. Prince John, in the meanwhile, occupied his castle, and disposed of his domains without scruple; and seeking at present to dazzle men's eyes by his hospitality and magnificence, had given orders for great preparations, in order to render the banquet as splendid as possible.

The purveyors of the Prince, who exercised on this and other occasions the full authority of royalty, had swept the country of all that could be collected which was esteemed fit for their master's table. Guests also were invited in great numbers; and in the necessity in which he then found himself of courting popularity, Prince John had extended his invitation to a few distinguished Saxon and Danish families, as well as to the Norman nobility and gentry of the neighbourhood. However despised and degraded on ordinary occasions, the great numbers of the Anglo-Saxons must necessarily render them formidable in the civil commotions which seemed approaching, and it was an obvious point of policy to secure popularity with their leaders.

It was accordingly the Prince's intention, which he for some time maintained, to treat these unwonted guests with a courtesy to which they had been little accustomed. But although no man with less scruple made his ordinary habits and feelings bend to his interest, it was the misfortune of this Prince, that his levity and petulance were perpetually breaking out, and undoing all that had been gained by his previous dissimulation.

Of this fickle temper he gave a memorable example in Ireland, when sent thither by his father, Henry the Second, with the purpose of buying golden opinions of the inhabitants of that new and important acquisition to the English crown. Upon this occasion the Irish chieftains contended which should first offer to the young Prince their loyal homage and the kiss of peace. But, instead of receiving their salutations with courtesy, John and his petulant attendants could not resist the temptation of pulling the long beards of the Irish chieftains; a conduct which, as might have been expected, was highly resented by these insulted dignitaries, and produced fatal consequences to the English domination in Ireland. It is necessary to keep these inconsistencies of John's character in view, that the reader may understand his conduct during the present evening.

In execution of the resolution which he had formed during his cooler moments, Prince John received Cedric and Athelstane with distinguished courtesy, and expressed his disappointment, without resentment, when the indisposition of Rowena was alleged by the former as a reason for her not attending upon his gracious summons. Cedric and Athelstane were both dressed in the ancient Saxon garb, which, although not unhandsome in itself, and in the present instance composed of costly materials, was so remote in shape and appearance from that of the other guests, that Prince John took great credit to himself with Waldemar Fitzurse for refraining from laughter at a sight which the fashion of the day rendered ridiculous. Yet, in the eye of sober judgment, the short close tunic and long mantle of the Saxons was a more graceful, as well as a more convenient dress, than the garb of the Normans, whose under garment was a long doublet, so loose as to resemble a shirt or waggoner's frock, covered by a cloak of scanty dimensions, neither fit to defend the wearer from cold or from rain, and the only purpose of which appeared to be to display as much fur, embroidery, and jewellery work, as the ingenuity of the tailor could contrive to lay upon it. The Emperor Charlemagne, in whose reign they were first introduced, seems to have been very sensible of the inconveniences arising from the fashion of this garment. "In Heaven's name," said he, "to what purpose serve these abridged cloaks? If we are in bed they are no cover, on horseback they are no protection from the wind and rain, and when seated, they do not guard our legs from the damp or the frost."

Nevertheless, spite of this imperial objurgation, the short cloaks continued in fashion down to the time of which we treat, and particularly among the princes of the House of Anjou. They were therefore in universal use among Prince John's courtiers; and the long mantle, which formed the upper garment of the Saxons, was held in proportional derision.

The guests were seated at a table which groaned under the quantity of good cheer. The numerous cooks who attended on the Prince's progress, having exerted all their art in varying the forms in which the ordinary provisions were served up, had succeeded almost as well as the modern professors of the culinary art in rendering them perfectly unlike their natural appearance. Besides these dishes of domestic origin, there were various delicacies brought from foreign parts, and a quantity of rich pastry, as well as of the simnel-bread and wastle cakes, which were only used at the tables of the highest nobility. The banquet was crowned with the richest wines, both foreign and domestic.

But, though luxurious, the Norman nobles were not generally speaking an intemperate race. While indulging themselves in the pleasures of the table, they aimed at delicacy, but avoided excess, and were apt to attribute gluttony and drunkenness to the vanquished Saxons, as vices peculiar to their inferior station. Prince John, indeed, and those who courted his pleasure by imitating his foibles, were apt to indulge to excess in the pleasures of the trencher and the goblet; and indeed it is well known that his death was occasioned by a surfeit upon peaches and new ale. His conduct, however, was an exception to the general manners of his countrymen.

With sly gravity, interrupted only by private signs to each other, the Norman knights and nobles beheld the ruder demeanour of Athelstane and Cedric at a banquet, to the form and fashion of which they were unaccustomed. And while their manners were thus the subject of sarcastic observation, the untaught Saxons unwittingly transgressed several of the arbitrary rules established for the regulation of society. Now, it is well known, that a man may with more impunity be guilty of an actual breach either of real good breeding or of good morals, than appear ignorant of the most minute point of fashionable etiquette. Thus Cedric, who dried his hands with a towel, instead of suffering the moisture to exhale by waving them gracefully in the air, incurred more ridicule than his companion Athelstane, when he swallowed to his own single share the whole of a large pasty composed of the most exquisite foreign delicacies, and termed at that time a "Karum-Pie". When, however, it was discovered, by a serious cross-examination, that the Thane of Coningsburgh (or Franklin, as the Normans termed him) had no idea what he had been devouring, and that he had taken the contents of the Karum-pie for larks and pigeons, whereas they were in fact beccaficoes and nightingales, his ignorance brought him in for an ample share of the ridicule which would have been more justly bestowed on his gluttony.

The long feast had at length its end; and, while the goblet circulated freely, men talked of the feats of the preceding tournament,—of the unknown victor in the archery games, of the Black Knight, whose self-denial had induced him to withdraw from the honours he had won,—and of the gallant Ivanhoe, who had so dearly bought the honours of the day. The topics were treated with military frankness, and the jest and laugh went round the hall. The brow of Prince John alone was overclouded during these discussions; some overpowering care seemed agitating his mind, and it was only when he received occasional hints from his attendants, that he seemed to take interest in what was passing around him. On such occasions he would start up, quaff a cup of wine as if to raise his spirits, and then mingle in the conversation by some observation made abruptly or at random.

"We drink this beaker," said he, "to the health of Wilfred of Ivanhoe, champion of this Passage of Arms, and grieve that his wound renders him absent from our board —Let all fill to the pledge, and especially Cedric of Rotherwood, the worthy father of a son so promising."

"No, my lord," replied Cedric, standing up, and placing on the table his untasted cup, "I yield not the name of son to the disobedient youth, who at once despises my commands, and relinquishes the manners and customs of his fathers."

"'Tis impossible," cried Prince John, with well-feigned astonishment, "that so gallant a knight should be an unworthy or disobedient son!"

"Yet, my lord," answered Cedric, "so it is with this Wilfred. He left my homely dwelling to mingle with the gay nobility of your brother's court, where he learned to do those tricks of horsemanship which you prize so highly. He left it contrary to my wish and command; and in the days of Alfred that would have been termed disobedience—ay, and a crime severely punishable."

"Alas!" replied Prince John, with a deep sigh of affected sympathy, "since your son was a follower of my unhappy brother, it need not be enquired where or from whom he learned the lesson of filial disobedience."

Thus spake Prince John, wilfully forgetting, that of all the sons of Henry the Second, though no one was free from the charge, he himself had been most distinguished for rebellion and ingratitude to his father.

"I think," said he, after a moment's pause, "that my brother proposed to confer upon his favourite the rich manor of Ivanhoe."

"He did endow him with it," answered Cedric; "nor is it my least quarrel with my son, that he stooped to hold, as a feudal vassal, the very domains which his fathers possessed in free and independent right."

"We shall then have your willing sanction, good Cedric," said Prince John, "to confer this fief upon a person whose dignity will not be diminished by holding land of the British crown.—Sir Reginald Front-de-Boeuf," he said, turning towards that Baron, "I trust you will so keep the goodly Barony of Ivanhoe, that Sir Wilfred shall not incur his father's farther displeasure by again entering upon that fief."

"By St Anthony!" answered the black-brow'd giant, "I will consent that your highness shall hold me a Saxon, if either Cedric or Wilfred, or the best that ever bore English blood, shall wrench from me the gift with which your highness has graced me."

"Whoever shall call thee Saxon, Sir Baron," replied Cedric, offended at a mode of expression by which the Normans frequently expressed their habitual contempt of the English, "will do thee an honour as great as it is undeserved."

Front-de-Boeuf would have replied, but Prince John's petulance and levity got the start.

"Assuredly," said be, "my lords, the noble Cedric speaks truth; and his race may claim precedence over us as much in the length of their pedigrees as in the longitude of their cloaks."

"They go before us indeed in the field—as deer before dogs," said Malvoisin.

"And with good right may they go before us—forget not," said the Prior Aymer, "the superior decency and decorum of their manners."

"Their singular abstemiousness and temperance," said De Bracy, forgetting the plan which promised him a Saxon bride.

"Together with the courage and conduct," said Brian de Bois-Guilbert, "by which they distinguished themselves at Hastings and elsewhere."

While, with smooth and smiling cheek, the courtiers, each in turn, followed their Prince's example, and aimed a shaft of ridicule at Cedric, the face of the Saxon became inflamed with passion, and he glanced his eyes fiercely from one to another, as if the quick succession of so many injuries had prevented his replying to them in turn; or, like a baited bull, who, surrounded by his tormentors, is at a loss to choose from among them the immediate object of his revenge. At length he spoke, in a voice half choked with passion; and, addressing himself to Prince John as the head and front of the offence which he had received, "Whatever," he said, "have been the follies and vices of our race, a Saxon would have been held 'nidering'," (the most emphatic term for abject worthlessness,) "who should in his own hall, and while his own wine-cup passed, have treated, or suffered to be treated, an unoffending guest as your highness has this day beheld me used; and whatever was the misfortune of our fathers on the field of Hastings, those may at least be silent," here he looked at Front-de-Boeuf and the Templar, "who have within these few hours once and again lost saddle and stirrup before the lance of a Saxon."

"By my faith, a biting jest!" said Prince John. "How like you it, sirs?—Our Saxon subjects rise in spirit and courage; become shrewd in wit, and bold in bearing, in these unsettled times—What say ye, my lords?—By this good light, I hold it best to take our galleys, and return to Normandy in time."

"For fear of the Saxons?" said De Bracy, laughing; "we should need no weapon but our hunting spears to bring these boars to bay."

"A truce with your raillery, Sir Knights," said Fitzurse;—"and it were well," he added, addressing the Prince, "that your highness should assure the worthy Cedric there is no insult intended him by jests, which must sound but harshly in the ear of a stranger."

"Insult?" answered Prince John, resuming his courtesy of demeanour; "I trust it will not be thought that I could mean, or permit any, to be offered in my presence. Here! I fill my cup to Cedric himself, since he refuses to pledge his son's health."

The cup went round amid the well-dissembled applause of the courtiers, which, however, failed to make the impression on the mind of the Saxon that had been designed. He was not naturally acute of perception, but those too much undervalued his understanding who deemed that this flattering compliment would obliterate the sense of the prior insult. He was silent, however, when the royal pledge again passed round, "To Sir Athelstane of Coningsburgh."

The knight made his obeisance, and showed his sense of the honour by draining a huge goblet in answer to it.

"And now, sirs," said Prince John, who began to be warmed with the wine which he had drank, "having done justice to our Saxon guests, we will pray of them some requital to our courtesy.—Worthy Thane," he continued, addressing Cedric, "may we pray you to name to us some Norman whose mention may least sully your mouth, and to wash down with a goblet of wine all bitterness which the sound may leave behind it?"

Fitzurse arose while Prince John spoke, and gliding behind the seat of the Saxon, whispered to him not to omit the opportunity of putting an end to unkindness betwixt the two races, by naming Prince John. The Saxon replied not to this politic insinuation, but, rising up, and filling his cup to the brim, he addressed Prince John in these words: "Your highness has required that I should name a Norman deserving to be remembered at our banquet. This, perchance, is a hard task, since it calls on the slave to sing the praises of the master—upon the vanquished, while pressed by all the evils of conquest, to sing the praises of the conqueror. Yet I will name a Norman—the first in arms and in place—the best and the noblest of his race. And the lips that shall refuse to pledge me to his well-earned fame, I term false and dishonoured, and will so maintain them with my life.—I quaff this goblet to the health of Richard the Lionhearted!"

Prince John, who had expected that his own name would have closed the Saxon's speech, started when that of his injured brother was so unexpectedly introduced. He raised mechanically the wine-cup to his lips, then instantly set it down, to view the demeanour of the company at this unexpected proposal, which many of them felt it as unsafe to oppose as to comply with. Some of them, ancient and experienced courtiers, closely imitated the example of the Prince himself, raising the goblet to their lips, and again replacing it before them. There were many who, with a more generous feeling, exclaimed, "Long live King Richard! and may he be speedily restored to us!" And some few, among whom were Front-de-Boeuf and the Templar, in sullen disdain suffered their goblets to stand untasted before them. But no man ventured directly to gainsay a pledge filled to the health of the reigning monarch.

Having enjoyed his triumph for about a minute, Cedric said to his companion, "Up, noble Athelstane! we have remained here long enough, since we have requited the hospitable courtesy of Prince John's banquet. Those who wish to know further of our rude Saxon manners must henceforth seek us in the homes of our fathers, since we have seen enough of royal banquets, and enough of Norman courtesy."

So saying, he arose and left the banqueting room, followed by Athelstane, and by several other guests, who, partaking of the Saxon lineage, held themselves insulted by the sarcasms of Prince John and his courtiers.

"By the bones of St Thomas," said Prince John, as they retreated, "the Saxon churls have borne off the best of the day, and have retreated with triumph!"

"'Conclamatum est, poculatum est'," said Prior Aymer; "we have drunk and we have shouted,—it were time we left our wine flagons."

"The monk hath some fair penitent to shrive to-night, that he is in such a hurry to depart," said De Bracy.

"Not so, Sir Knight," replied the Abbot; "but I must move several miles forward this evening upon my homeward journey."

"They are breaking up," said the Prince in a whisper to Fitzurse; "their fears anticipate the event, and this coward Prior is the first to shrink from me."

"Fear not, my lord," said Waldemar; "I will show him such reasons as shall induce him to join us when we hold our meeting at York.—Sir Prior," he said, "I must speak with you in private, before you mount your palfrey."

The other guests were now fast dispersing, with the exception of those immediately attached to Prince John's faction, and his retinue.

"This, then, is the result of your advice," said the Prince, turning an angry countenance upon Fitzurse; "that I should be bearded at my own board by a drunken Saxon churl, and that, on the mere sound of my brother's name, men should fall off from me as if I had the leprosy?"

"Have patience, sir," replied his counsellor; "I might retort your accusation, and blame the inconsiderate levity which foiled my design, and misled your own better judgment. But this is no time for recrimination. De Bracy and I will instantly go among these shuffling cowards, and convince them they have gone too far to recede."

"It will be in vain," said Prince John, pacing the apartment with disordered steps, and expressing himself with an agitation to which the wine he had drank partly contributed—"It will be in vain—they have seen the handwriting on the wall—they have marked the paw of the lion in the sand—they have heard his approaching roar shake the wood—nothing will reanimate their courage."

"Would to God," said Fitzurse to De Bracy, "that aught could reanimate his own! His brother's very name is an ague to him. Unhappy are the counsellors of a Prince, who wants fortitude and perseverance alike in good and in evil!"

XV.

> And yet he thinks,—ha, ha, ha, ha,—he thinks
> I am the tool and servant of his will.
> Well, let it be; through all the maze of trouble
> His plots and base oppression must create,
> I'll shape myself a way to higher things,
> And who will say 'tis wrong?
>
> — BASIL, A TRAGEDY

No spider ever took more pains to repair the shattered meshes of his web, than did Waldemar Fitzurse to reunite and combine the scattered members of Prince John's cabal. Few of these were attached to him from inclination, and none from personal regard. It was therefore necessary, that Fitzurse should open to them new prospects of advantage, and remind them of those which they at present enjoyed. To the young and wild nobles, he held out the prospect of unpunished license and uncontrolled revelry; to the ambitious, that of power, and to the covetous, that of increased wealth and extended domains. The leaders of the mercenaries received a donation in gold; an argument the most persuasive to their minds, and without which all others would have proved in vain. Promises were still more liberally distributed than money by this active agent; and, in fine, nothing was left undone that could determine the wavering, or animate the disheartened. The return of King Richard he spoke of as an event altogether beyond the reach of probability; yet, when he observed, from the doubtful looks and uncertain answers which he received, that this was the apprehension by which the minds of his accomplices were most haunted, he boldly treated that event, should it really take place, as one which ought not to alter their political calculations.

"If Richard returns," said Fitzurse, "he returns to enrich his needy and impoverished crusaders at the expense of those who did not follow him to the Holy Land. He returns to call to a fearful reckoning, those who, during his absence, have done aught that can be construed offence or encroachment upon either the laws of the land or the privileges of the crown. He returns to avenge upon the Orders of the Temple and the Hospital, the preference which they showed to Philip of France during the wars in the Holy Land. He returns, in fine, to punish as a rebel every adherent of his brother Prince John. Are ye afraid of his power?" continued the artful confident of that Prince, "we acknowledge him a strong and valiant knight; but these are not the days of King Arthur, when a champion could encounter an army. If Richard indeed comes back, it must be alone,—unfollowed—unfriended. The bones of his gallant army have whitened the sands of Palestine. The few of his followers who have returned have straggled hither like this Wilfred of Ivanhoe, beggared and broken men.—And what talk ye of Richard's right of birth?" he proceeded, in answer to those who objected scruples on that head. "Is Richard's title of primogeniture more decidedly certain than that of Duke Robert of Normandy, the Conqueror's eldest son? And yet William the Red, and Henry, his second and third brothers, were successively preferred to him by the voice of the nation, Robert had every merit which can be pleaded for Richard; he was a bold knight, a good leader, generous to his friends and to the church, and, to crown the whole, a crusader and a conqueror of the Holy Sepulchre; and yet he died a blind and miserable prisoner in the Castle of Cardiff, because he opposed himself to the will of the people, who chose that he should not rule over them. It is our right," he said, "to choose from the blood royal the prince who is best qualified to hold the supreme power—that is," said he, correcting himself, "him whose election will best promote the interests of the nobility. In personal qualifications," he added, "it was possible that Prince John might be inferior to his brother Richard; but when it was considered that the latter returned with the sword of vengeance in his hand, while the former held out rewards, immunities, privileges, wealth, and honours, it could not be doubted which was the king whom in wisdom the nobility were called on to support."

These, and many more arguments, some adapted to the peculiar circumstances of those whom he addressed, had the expected weight with the nobles of Prince John's faction. Most of them consented to attend the proposed meeting at York, for the purpose of making general arrangements for placing the crown upon the head of Prince John.

It was late at night, when, worn out and exhausted with his various exertions, however gratified with the result, Fitzurse, returning to the Castle of Ashby, met with De Bracy, who had exchanged his banqueting garments for a short green kirtle, with hose of the same cloth and colour, a leathern cap or head-piece, a short sword, a horn slung over his shoulder, a long bow in his hand, and a bundle of arrows stuck in his belt. Had Fitzurse met this figure in an outer apartment, he would have passed him without notice, as one of the yeomen of the guard; but finding him in the inner hall, he looked at him with more attention, and recognised the Norman knight in the dress of an English yeoman.

"What mummery is this, De Bracy?" said Fitzurse, somewhat angrily; "is this a time for Christmas gambols and quaint maskings, when the fate of our master, Prince John, is on the very verge of decision? Why hast thou not been, like me, among these heartless cravens, whom the very name of King Richard terrifies, as it is said to do the children of the Saracens?"

"I have been attending to mine own business," answered De Bracy calmly, "as you, Fitzurse, have been minding yours."

"I minding mine own business!" echoed Waldemar; "I have been engaged in that of Prince John, our joint patron."

"As if thou hadst any other reason for that, Waldemar," said De Bracy, "than the promotion of thine own individual interest? Come, Fitzurse, we know each other—ambition is thy pursuit, pleasure is mine, and they become our different ages. Of Prince John thou thinkest as I do; that he is too weak to be a determined monarch, too tyrannical to be an easy monarch, too insolent and presumptuous to be a popular monarch, and too fickle and timid to be long a monarch of any kind. But he is a monarch by whom Fitzurse and De Bracy hope to rise and thrive; and therefore you aid him with your policy, and I with the lances of my Free Companions."

"A hopeful auxiliary," said Fitzurse impatiently; "playing the fool in the very moment of utter necessity.—What on earth dost thou purpose by this absurd disguise at a moment so urgent?"

"To get me a wife," answered De Bracy coolly, "after the manner of the tribe of Benjamin."

"The tribe of Benjamin?" said Fitzurse; "I comprehend thee not."

"Wert thou not in presence yester-even," said De Bracy, "when we heard the Prior Aymer tell us a tale in reply to the romance which was sung by the Minstrel?—He told how, long since in Palestine, a deadly feud arose between the tribe of Benjamin and the rest of the Israelitish nation; and how they cut to pieces well-nigh all the chivalry of that tribe; and how they swore by our blessed Lady, that they would not permit those who remained to marry in their lineage; and how they became grieved for their vow, and sent to consult his holiness the Pope how they might be absolved from it; and how, by the advice of the Holy Father, the youth of the tribe of Benjamin carried off from a superb tournament all the ladies who were there present, and thus won them wives without the consent either of their brides or their brides' families."

"I have heard the story," said Fitzurse, "though either the Prior or thou has made some singular alterations in date and circumstances."

"I tell thee," said De Bracy, "that I mean to purvey me a wife after the fashion of the tribe of Benjamin; which is as much as to say, that in this same equipment I will fall upon that herd of Saxon bullocks, who have this night left the castle, and carry off from them the lovely Rowena."

"Art thou mad, De Bracy?" said Fitzurse. "Bethink thee that, though the men be Saxons, they are rich and powerful, and regarded with the more respect by their countrymen, that wealth and honour are but the lot of few of Saxon descent."

"And should belong to none," said De Bracy; "the work of the Conquest should be completed."

"This is no time for it at least," said Fitzurse "the approaching crisis renders the favour of the multitude indispensable, and Prince John cannot refuse justice to any one who injures their favourites."

"Let him grant it, if he dare," said De Bracy; "he will soon see the difference betwixt the support of such a lusty lot of spears as mine, and that of a heartless mob of Saxon churls. Yet I mean no immediate discovery of myself. Seem I not in this garb as bold a forester as ever blew horn? The blame of the violence shall rest with the outlaws of the Yorkshire forests. I have sure spies on the Saxon's motions—To-night they sleep in the convent of Saint Wittol, or Withold, or whatever they call that churl of a Saxon Saint at Burton-on-Trent. Next day's march brings them within our reach, and, falcon-ways, we swoop on them at once. Presently after I will appear in mine own shape, play the courteous knight, rescue the unfortunate and afflicted fair one from the hands of the rude ravishers, conduct her to Front-de-Boeuf's Castle, or to Normandy, if it should be necessary, and produce her not again to her kindred until she be the bride and dame of Maurice de Bracy."

"A marvellously sage plan," said Fitzurse, "and, as I think, not entirely of thine own device.—Come, be frank, De Bracy, who aided thee in the invention? and who is to assist in the execution? for, as I think, thine own band lies as far off as York."

"Marry, if thou must needs know," said De Bracy, "it was the Templar Brian de Bois-Guilbert that shaped out the enterprise, which the adventure of the men of Benjamin suggested to me. He is to aid me in the onslaught, and he and his followers will personate the outlaws, from whom my valorous arm is, after changing my garb, to rescue the lady."

"By my halidome," said Fitzurse, "the plan was worthy of your united wisdom! and thy prudence, De Bracy, is most especially manifested in the project of leaving the lady in the hands of thy worthy confederate. Thou mayst, I think, succeed in taking her from her Saxon friends, but how thou wilt rescue her afterwards from the clutches of Bois-Guilbert seems considerably more doubtful—He is a falcon well accustomed to pounce on a partridge, and to hold his prey fast."

"He is a Templar," said De Bracy, "and cannot therefore rival me in my plan of wedding this heiress;—and to attempt aught dishonourable against the intended bride of De Bracy—By Heaven! were he a whole Chapter of his Order in his single person, he dared not do me such an injury!"

"Then since nought that I can say," said Fitzurse, "will put this folly from thy imagination, (for well I know the obstinacy of thy disposition,) at least waste as little time as possible—let not thy folly be lasting as well as untimely."

"I tell thee," answered De Bracy, "that it will be the work of a few hours, and I shall be at York—at the head of my daring and valorous fellows, as ready to support any bold design as thy policy can be to form one.—But I hear my comrades assembling, and the steeds stamping and neighing in the outer court.—Farewell.—I go, like a true knight, to win the smiles of beauty."

"Like a true knight?" repeated Fitzurse, looking after him; "like a fool, I should say, or like a child, who will leave the most serious and needful occupation, to chase the down of the thistle that drives past him.—But it is with such tools that I must work;—and for whose advantage?—For that of a Prince as unwise as he is profligate, and as likely to be an ungrateful master as he has already proved a rebellious son and an unnatural brother.—But he—he, too, is but one of the tools with which I labour; and, proud as he is, should he presume to separate his interest from mine, this is a secret which he shall soon learn."

The meditations of the statesman were here interrupted by the voice of the Prince from an interior apartment, calling out, "Noble Waldemar Fitzurse!" and, with bonnet doffed, the future Chancellor (for to such high preferment did the wily Norman aspire) hastened to receive the orders of the future sovereign.

XVI.

> Far in a wild, unknown to public view,
> From youth to age a reverend hermit grew;
> The moss his bed, the cave his humble cell,
> His food the fruits, his drink the crystal well
> Remote from man, with God he pass'd his days,
> Prayer all his business—all his pleasure praise.
>
> — PARNELL

The reader cannot have forgotten that the event of the tournament was decided by the exertions of an unknown knight, whom, on account of the passive and indifferent conduct which he had manifested on the former part of the day, the spectators had entitled, "Le Noir Faineant". This knight had left the field abruptly when the victory was achieved; and when he was called upon to receive the reward of his valour, he was nowhere to be found. In the meantime, while summoned by heralds and by trumpets, the knight was holding his course northward, avoiding all frequented paths, and taking the shortest road through the woodlands. He paused for the night at a small hostelry lying out of the ordinary route, where, however, he obtained from a wandering minstrel news of the event of the tourney.

On the next morning the knight departed early, with the intention of making a long journey; the condition of his horse, which he had carefully spared during the preceding morning, being such as enabled him to travel far without the necessity of much repose. Yet his purpose was baffled by the devious paths through which he rode, so that when evening closed upon him, he only found himself on the frontiers of the West Riding of Yorkshire. By this time both horse and man required refreshment, and it became necessary, moreover, to look out for some place in which they might spend the night, which was now fast approaching.

The place where the traveller found himself seemed unpropitious for obtaining either shelter or refreshment, and he was likely to be reduced to the usual expedient of knights-errant, who, on such occasions, turned their horses to graze, and laid themselves down to meditate on their lady-mistress, with an oak-tree for a canopy. But the Black Knight either had no mistress to meditate upon, or, being as indifferent in love as he seemed to be in war, was not sufficiently occupied by passionate reflections upon her beauty and cruelty, to be able to parry the effects of fatigue and hunger, and suffer love to act as a substitute for the solid comforts of a bed and supper. He felt dissatisfied, therefore, when, looking around, he found himself deeply involved in woods, through which indeed there were many open glades, and some paths, but such as seemed only formed by the numerous herds of cattle which grazed in the forest, or by the animals of chase, and the hunters who made prey of them.

The sun, by which the knight had chiefly directed his course, had now sunk behind the Derbyshire hills on his left, and every effort which he might make to pursue his journey was as likely to lead him out of his road as to advance him on his route. After having in vain endeavoured to select the most beaten path, in hopes it might lead to the cottage of some herdsman, or the silvan lodge of a forester, and having repeatedly found himself totally unable to determine on a choice, the knight resolved to trust to the sagacity of his horse; experience having, on former occasions, made him acquainted with the wonderful talent possessed by these animals for extricating themselves and their riders on such emergencies.

The good steed, grievously fatigued with so long a day's journey under a rider cased in mail, had no sooner found, by the slackened reins, that he was abandoned to his own guidance, than he seemed to assume new strength and spirit; and whereas, formerly he had scarce replied to the spur, otherwise than by a groan, he now, as if proud of the confidence reposed in him, pricked up his ears, and assumed, of his own accord, a more lively motion. The path which the animal adopted rather turned off from the course pursued by the knight during the day; but as the horse seemed confident in his choice, the rider abandoned himself to his discretion.

He was justified by the event; for the footpath soon after appeared a little wider and more worn, and the tinkle of a small bell gave the knight to understand that he was in the vicinity of some chapel or hermitage.

Accordingly, he soon reached an open plat of turf, on the opposite side of which, a rock, rising abruptly from a gently sloping plain, offered its grey and weatherbeaten front to the traveller. Ivy mantled its sides in some places, and in others oaks and holly bushes, whose roots found nourishment in the cliffs of the crag, waved over the precipices below, like the plumage of the warrior over his steel helmet, giving grace to that whose chief expression was terror. At the bottom of the rock, and leaning, as it were, against it, was constructed a rude hut, built chiefly of the trunks of trees felled in the neighbouring forest, and secured against the weather by having its crevices stuffed with moss mingled with clay. The stem of a young fir-tree lopped of its branches, with a piece of wood tied across near the top, was planted upright by the door, as a rude emblem of the holy cross. At a little distance on the right hand, a fountain of the purest water trickled out of the rock, and was received in a hollow stone, which labour had formed into a rustic basin. Escaping from thence, the stream murmured down the descent by a channel which its course had long worn, and so wandered through the little plain to lose itself in the neighbouring wood.

Beside this fountain were the ruins of a very small chapel, of which the roof had partly fallen in. The building, when entire, had never been above sixteen feet long by twelve feet in breadth, and the roof, low in proportion, rested upon four concentric arches which sprung from the four corners of the building, each supported upon a short and heavy pillar. The ribs of two of these arches remained, though the roof had fallen down betwixt them; over the others it remained entire. The entrance to this ancient place of devotion was under a very low round arch, ornamented by several courses of that zig-zag moulding, resembling shark's teeth, which appears so often in the more ancient Saxon architecture. A belfry rose above the porch on four small pillars, within which hung the green and weatherbeaten bell, the feeble sounds of which had been some time before heard by the Black Knight.

The whole peaceful and quiet scene lay glimmering in twilight before the eyes of the traveller, giving him good assurance of lodging for the night; since it was a special duty of those hermits who dwelt in the woods, to exercise hospitality towards benighted or bewildered passengers.

Accordingly, the knight took no time to consider minutely the particulars which we have detailed, but thanking Saint Julian (the patron of travellers) who had sent him good harbourage, he leaped from his horse and assailed the door of the hermitage with the butt of his lance, in order to arouse attention and gain admittance.

It was some time before he obtained any answer, and the reply, when made, was unpropitious.

"Pass on, whosoever thou art," was the answer given by a deep hoarse voice from within the hut, "and disturb not the servant of God and St Dunstan in his evening devotions."

"Worthy father," answered the knight, "here is a poor wanderer bewildered in these woods, who gives thee the opportunity of exercising thy charity and hospitality."

"Good brother," replied the inhabitant of the hermitage, "it has pleased Our Lady and St Dunstan to destine me for the object of those virtues, instead of the exercise thereof. I have no provisions here which even a dog would share with me, and a horse of any tenderness of nurture would despise my couch—pass therefore on thy way, and God speed thee."

"But how," replied the knight, "is it possible for me to find my way through such a wood as this, when darkness is coming on? I pray you, reverend father as you are a Christian, to undo your door, and at least point out to me my road."

"And I pray you, good Christian brother," replied the anchorite, "to disturb me no more. You have already interrupted one 'pater', two 'aves', and a 'credo', which I, miserable sinner that I am, should, according to my vow, have said before moonrise."

"The road—the road!" vociferated the knight, "give me directions for the road, if I am to expect no more from thee."

"The road," replied the hermit, "is easy to hit. The path from the wood leads to a morass, and from thence to a ford, which, as the rains have abated, may now be passable. When thou hast crossed the ford, thou wilt take care of thy footing up the left bank, as it is somewhat precipitous; and the path, which hangs over the river, has lately, as I learn, (for I seldom leave the duties of my chapel,) given way in sundry places. Thou wilt then keep straight forward—"

"A broken path—a precipice—a ford, and a morass!" said the knight interrupting him,—"Sir Hermit, if you were the holiest that ever wore beard or told bead, you shall scarce prevail on me to hold this road to-night. I tell thee, that thou, who livest by the charity of the country—ill deserved, as I doubt it is—hast no right to refuse shelter to the wayfarer when in distress. Either open the door quickly, or, by the rood, I will beat it down and make entry for myself."

"Friend wayfarer," replied the hermit, "be not importunate; if thou puttest me to use the carnal weapon in mine own defence, it will be e'en the worse for you."

At this moment a distant noise of barking and growling, which the traveller had for some time heard, became extremely loud and furious, and made the knight suppose that the hermit, alarmed by his threat of making forcible entry, had called the dogs who made this clamour to aid him in his defence, out of some inner recess in which they had been kennelled. Incensed at this preparation on the hermit's part for making good his inhospitable purpose, the knight struck the door so furiously with his foot, that posts as well as staples shook with violence.

The anchorite, not caring again to expose his door to a similar shock, now called out aloud, "Patience, patience—spare thy strength, good traveller, and I will presently undo the door, though, it may be, my doing so will be little to thy pleasure."

The door accordingly was opened; and the hermit, a large, strong-built man, in his sackcloth gown and hood, girt with a rope of rushes, stood before the knight. He had in one hand a lighted torch, or link, and in the other a baton of crab-tree, so thick and heavy, that it might well be termed a club. Two large shaggy dogs, half greyhound half mastiff, stood ready to rush upon the traveller as soon as the door should be opened. But when the torch glanced upon the lofty crest and golden spurs of the knight, who stood without, the hermit, altering probably his original intentions, repressed the rage of his auxiliaries, and, changing his tone to a sort of churlish courtesy, invited the knight to enter his hut, making excuse for his unwillingness to open his lodge after sunset, by alleging the multitude of robbers and outlaws who were abroad, and who gave no honour to Our Lady or St Dunstan, nor to those holy men who spent life in their service.

"The poverty of your cell, good father," said the knight, looking around him, and seeing nothing but a bed of leaves, a crucifix rudely carved in oak, a missal, with a rough-hewn table and two stools, and one or two clumsy articles of furniture—"the poverty of your cell should seem a sufficient defence against any risk of thieves, not to mention the aid of two trusty dogs, large and strong enough, I think, to pull down a stag, and of course, to match with most men."

"The good keeper of the forest," said the hermit, "hath allowed me the use of these animals, to protect my solitude until the times shall mend."

Having said this, he fixed his torch in a twisted branch of iron which served for a candlestick; and, placing the oaken trivet before the embers of the fire, which he refreshed with some dry wood, he placed a stool upon one side of the table, and beckoned to the knight to do the same upon the other.

They sat down, and gazed with great gravity at each other, each thinking in his heart that he had seldom seen a stronger or more athletic figure than was placed opposite to him.

"Reverend hermit," said the knight, after looking long and fixedly at his host, "were it not to interrupt your devout meditations, I would pray to know three things of your holiness; first, where I am to put my horse?—secondly, what I can have for supper?—thirdly, where I am to take up my couch for the night?"

"I will reply to you," said the hermit, "with my finger, it being against my rule to speak by words where signs can answer the purpose." So saying, he pointed successively to two corners of the hut. "Your stable," said he, "is there—your bed there; and," reaching down a platter with two handfuls of parched pease upon it from the neighbouring shelf, and placing it upon the table, he added, "your supper is here."

The knight shrugged his shoulders, and leaving the hut, brought in his horse, (which in the interim he had fastened to a tree,) unsaddled him with much attention, and spread upon the steed's weary back his own mantle.

The hermit was apparently somewhat moved to compassion by the anxiety as well as address which the stranger displayed in tending his horse; for, muttering something about provender left for the keeper's palfrey, he dragged out of a recess a bundle of forage, which he spread before the knight's charger, and immediately afterwards shook down a quantity of dried fern in the corner which he had assigned for the rider's couch. The knight returned him thanks for his courtesy; and, this duty done, both resumed their seats by the table, whereon stood the trencher of pease placed between them. The hermit, after a long grace, which had once been Latin, but of which original language few traces remained, excepting here and there the long rolling termination of some word or phrase, set example to his guest, by modestly putting into a very large mouth, furnished with teeth which might have ranked with those of a boar both in sharpness and whiteness, some three or four dried pease, a miserable grist as it seemed for so large and able a mill.

The knight, in order to follow so laudable an example, laid aside his helmet, his corslet, and the greater part of his armour, and showed to the hermit a head thick-curled with yellow hair, high features, blue eyes, remarkably bright and sparkling, a mouth well formed, having an upper lip clothed with mustachoes darker than his hair, and bearing altogether the look of a bold, daring, and enterprising man, with which his strong form well corresponded.

The hermit, as if wishing to answer to the confidence of his guest, threw back his cowl, and showed a round bullet head belonging to a man in the prime of life. His close-shaven crown, surrounded by a circle of stiff curled black hair, had something the appearance of a parish pinfold begirt by its high hedge. The features expressed nothing of monastic austerity, or of ascetic privations; on the contrary, it was a bold bluff countenance, with broad black eyebrows, a well-turned forehead, and cheeks as round and vermilion as those of a trumpeter, from which descended a long and curly black beard. Such a visage, joined to the brawny form of the holy man, spoke rather of sirloins and haunches, than of pease and pulse. This incongruity did not escape the guest. After he had with great difficulty accomplished the mastication of a mouthful of the dried pease, he found it absolutely necessary to request his pious entertainer to furnish him with some liquor; who replied to his request by placing before him a large can of the purest water from the fountain.

"It is from the well of St Dunstan," said he, "in which, betwixt sun and sun, he baptized five hundred heathen Danes and Britons—blessed be his name!" And applying his black beard to the pitcher, he took a draught much more moderate in quantity than his encomium seemed to warrant.

"It seems to me, reverend father," said the knight, "that the small morsels which you eat, together with this holy, but somewhat thin beverage, have thriven with you marvellously. You appear a man more fit to win the ram at a wrestling match, or the ring at a bout at quarter-staff, or the bucklers at a sword-play, than to linger out your time in this desolate wilderness, saying masses, and living upon parched pease and cold water."

"Sir Knight," answered the hermit, "your thoughts, like those of the ignorant laity, are according to the flesh. It has pleased Our Lady and my patron saint to bless the pittance to which I restrain myself, even as the pulse and water was blessed to the children Shadrach, Meshech, and Abednego, who drank the same rather than defile themselves with the wine and meats which were appointed them by the King of the Saracens."

"Holy father," said the knight, "upon whose countenance it hath pleased Heaven to work such a miracle, permit a sinful layman to crave thy name?"

"Thou mayst call me," answered the hermit, "the Clerk of Copmanhurst, for so I am termed in these parts—They add, it is true, the epithet holy, but I stand not upon that, as being unworthy of such addition.—And now, valiant knight, may I pray ye for the name of my honourable guest?"

"Truly," said the knight, "Holy Clerk of Copmanhurst, men call me in these parts the Black Knight,—many, sir, add to it the epithet of Sluggard, whereby I am no way ambitious to be distinguished."

The hermit could scarcely forbear from smiling at his guest's reply.

"I see," said he, "Sir Sluggish Knight, that thou art a man of prudence and of counsel; and moreover, I see that my poor monastic fare likes thee not, accustomed, perhaps, as thou hast been, to the license of courts and of camps, and the luxuries of cities; and now I bethink me, Sir Sluggard, that when the charitable keeper of this forest-walk left those dogs for my protection, and also those bundles of forage, he left me also some food, which, being unfit for my use, the very recollection of it had escaped me amid my more weighty meditations."

"I dare be sworn he did so," said the knight; "I was convinced that there was better food in the cell, Holy Clerk, since you first doffed your cowl.—Your keeper is ever a jovial fellow; and none who beheld thy grinders contending with these pease, and thy throat flooded with this ungenial element, could see thee doomed to such horse-provender and horse-beverage," (pointing to the provisions upon the table,) "and refrain from mending thy cheer. Let us see the keeper's bounty, therefore, without delay."

The hermit cast a wistful look upon the knight, in which there was a sort of comic expression of hesitation, as if uncertain how far he should act prudently in trusting his guest. There was, however, as much of bold frankness in the knight's countenance as was possible to be expressed by features. His smile, too, had something in it irresistibly comic, and gave an assurance of faith and loyalty, with which his host could not refrain from sympathizing.

After exchanging a mute glance or two, the hermit went to the further side of the hut, and opened a hutch, which was concealed with great care and some ingenuity. Out of the recesses of a dark closet, into which this aperture gave admittance, he brought a large pasty, baked in a pewter platter of unusual dimensions. This mighty dish he placed before his guest, who, using his poniard to cut it open, lost no time in making himself acquainted with its contents.

"How long is it since the good keeper has been here?" said the knight to his host, after having swallowed several hasty morsels of this reinforcement to the hermit's good cheer.

"About two months," answered the father hastily.

"By the true Lord," answered the knight, "every thing in your hermitage is miraculous, Holy Clerk! for I would have been sworn that the fat buck which furnished this venison had been running on foot within the week."

The hermit was somewhat discountenanced by this observation; and, moreover, he made but a poor figure while gazing on the diminution of the pasty, on which his guest was making desperate inroads; a warfare in which his previous profession of abstinence left him no pretext for joining.

"I have been in Palestine, Sir Clerk," said the knight, stopping short of a sudden, "and I bethink me it is a custom there that every host who entertains a guest shall assure him of the wholesomeness of his food, by partaking of it along with him. Far be it from me to suspect so holy a man of aught inhospitable; nevertheless I will be highly bound to you would you comply with this Eastern custom."

"To ease your unnecessary scruples, Sir Knight, I will for once depart from my rule," replied the hermit. And as there were no forks in those days, his clutches were instantly in the bowels of the pasty.

The ice of ceremony being once broken, it seemed matter of rivalry between the guest and the entertainer which should display the best appetite; and although the former had probably fasted longest, yet the hermit fairly surpassed him.

"Holy Clerk," said the knight, when his hunger was appeased, "I would gage my good horse yonder against a zecchin, that that same honest keeper to whom we are obliged for the venison has left thee a stoup of wine, or a runlet of canary, or some such trifle, by way of ally to this noble pasty. This would be a circumstance, doubtless, totally unworthy to dwell in the memory of so rigid an anchorite; yet, I think, were you to search yonder crypt once more, you would find that I am right in my conjecture."

The hermit only replied by a grin; and returning to the hutch, he produced a leathern bottle, which might contain about four quarts. He also brought forth two large drinking cups, made out of the horn of the urus, and hooped with silver. Having made this goodly provision for washing down the supper, he seemed to think no farther ceremonious scruple necessary on his part; but filling both cups, and saying, in the Saxon fashion, "'Waes hael', Sir Sluggish Knight!" he emptied his own at a draught.

"'Drink hael', Holy Clerk of Copmanhurst!" answered the warrior, and did his host reason in a similar brimmer.

"Holy Clerk," said the stranger, after the first cup was thus swallowed, "I cannot but marvel that a man possessed of such thews and sinews as thine, and who therewithal shows the talent of so goodly a trencher-man, should think of abiding by himself in this wilderness. In my judgment, you are fitter to keep a castle or a fort, eating of the fat and drinking of the strong, than to live here upon pulse and water, or even upon the charity of the keeper. At least, were I as thou, I should find myself both disport and plenty out of the king's deer. There is many a goodly herd in these forests, and a buck will never be missed that goes to the use of Saint Dunstan's chaplain."

"Sir Sluggish Knight," replied the Clerk, "these are dangerous words, and I pray you to forbear them. I am true hermit to the king and law, and were I to spoil my liege's game, I should be sure of the prison, and, an my gown saved me not, were in some peril of hanging."

"Nevertheless, were I as thou," said the knight, "I would take my walk by moonlight, when foresters and keepers were warm in bed, and ever and anon,—as I pattered my prayers,—I would let fly a shaft among the herds of dun deer that feed in the glades—Resolve me, Holy Clerk, hast thou never practised such a pastime?"

"Friend Sluggard," answered the hermit, "thou hast seen all that can concern thee of my housekeeping, and something more than he deserves who takes up his quarters by violence. Credit me, it is better to enjoy the good which God sends thee, than to be impertinently curious how it comes. Fill thy cup, and welcome; and do not, I pray thee, by further impertinent enquiries, put me to show that thou couldst hardly have made good thy lodging had I been earnest to oppose thee."

"By my faith," said the knight, "thou makest me more curious than ever! Thou art the most mysterious hermit I ever met; and I will know more of thee ere we part. As for thy threats, know, holy man, thou speakest to one whose trade it is to find out danger wherever it is to be met with."

"Sir Sluggish Knight, I drink to thee," said the hermit; "respecting thy valour much, but deeming wondrous slightly of thy discretion. If thou wilt take equal arms with me, I will give thee, in all friendship and brotherly love, such sufficing penance and complete absolution, that thou shalt not for the next twelve months sin the sin of excess of curiosity."

The knight pledged him, and desired him to name his weapons.

"There is none," replied the hermit, "from the scissors of Delilah, and the tenpenny nail of Jael, to the scimitar of Goliath, at which I am not a match for thee—But, if I am to make the election, what sayst thou, good friend, to these trinkets?"

Thus speaking, he opened another hutch, and took out from it a couple of broadswords and bucklers, such as were used by the yeomanry of the period. The knight, who watched his motions, observed that this second place of concealment was furnished with two or three good long-bows, a cross-bow, a bundle of bolts for the latter, and half-a-dozen sheaves of arrows for the former. A harp, and other matters of a very uncanonical appearance, were also visible when this dark recess was opened.

"I promise thee, brother Clerk," said he, "I will ask thee no more offensive questions. The contents of that cupboard are an answer to all my enquiries; and I see a weapon there" (here he stooped and took out the harp) "on which I would more gladly prove my skill with thee, than at the sword and buckler."

"I hope, Sir Knight," said the hermit, "thou hast given no good reason for thy surname of the Sluggard. I do promise thee I suspect thee grievously. Nevertheless, thou art my guest, and I will not put thy manhood to the proof without thine own free will. Sit thee down, then, and fill thy cup; let us drink, sing, and be merry. If thou knowest ever a good lay, thou shalt be welcome to a nook of pasty at Copmanhurst so long as I serve the chapel of St Dunstan, which, please God, shall be till I change my grey covering for one of green turf. But come, fill a flagon, for it will crave some time to tune the harp; and nought pitches the voice and sharpens the ear like a cup of wine. For my part, I love to feel the grape at my very finger-ends before they make the harp-strings tinkle."

XVII.

> At eve, within yon studious nook,
> I ope my brass-embossed book,
> Portray'd with many a holy deed
> Of martyrs crown'd with heavenly meed;
> Then, as my taper waxes dim,

Chant, ere I sleep, my measured hymn.

Who but would cast his pomp away,
To take my staff and amice grey,
And to the world's tumultuous stage,
Prefer the peaceful Hermitage?

— WARTON

Notwithstanding the prescription of the genial hermit, with which his guest willingly complied, he found it no easy matter to bring the harp to harmony.

"Methinks, holy father," said he, "the instrument wants one string, and the rest have been somewhat misused."

"Ay, mark'st thou that?" replied the hermit; "that shows thee a master of the craft. Wine and wassail," he added, gravely casting up his eyes—"all the fault of wine and wassail!—I told Allan-a-Dale, the northern minstrel, that he would damage the harp if he touched it after the seventh cup, but he would not be controlled—Friend, I drink to thy successful performance."

So saying, he took off his cup with much gravity, at the same time shaking his head at the intemperance of the Scottish harper.

The knight in the meantime, had brought the strings into some order, and after a short prelude, asked his host whether he would choose a "sirvente" in the language of "oc", or a "lai" in the language of "oui", or a "virelai", or a ballad in the vulgar English.

"A ballad, a ballad," said the hermit, "against all the 'ocs' and 'ouis' of France. Downright English am I, Sir Knight, and downright English was my patron St Dunstan, and scorned 'oc' and 'oui', as he would have scorned the parings of the devil's hoof—downright English alone shall be sung in this cell."

"I will assay, then," said the knight, "a ballad composed by a Saxon glee-man, whom I knew in Holy Land."

It speedily appeared, that if the knight was not a complete master of the minstrel art, his taste for it had at least been cultivated under the best instructors. Art had taught him to soften the faults of a voice which had little compass, and was naturally rough rather than mellow, and, in short, had done all that culture can do in supplying natural deficiencies. His performance, therefore, might have been termed very respectable by abler judges than the hermit, especially as the knight threw into the notes now a degree of spirit, and now of plaintive enthusiasm, which gave force and energy to the verses which he sung.

THE CRUSADER'S RETURN.
1.
High deeds achieved of knightly fame,
From Palestine the champion came;
The cross upon his shoulders borne,
Battle and blast had dimm'd and torn.
Each dint upon his batter'd shield

Was token of a foughten field;
And thus, beneath his lady's bower,
He sung as fell the twilight hour:—
2.
"Joy to the fair!—thy knight behold,
Return'd from yonder land of gold;
No wealth he brings, nor wealth can need,
Save his good arms and battle-steed
His spurs, to dash against a foe,
His lance and sword to lay him low;
Such all the trophies of his toil,
Such—and the hope of Tekla's smile!
3.
"Joy to the fair! whose constant knight
Her favour fired to feats of might;
Unnoted shall she not remain,
Where meet the bright and noble train;
Minstrel shall sing and herald tell—
'Mark yonder maid of beauty well,
'Tis she for whose bright eyes were won
The listed field at Askalon!
4.
"'Note well her smile!—it edged the blade
Which fifty wives to widows made,
When, vain his strength and Mahound's spell,
Iconium's turban'd Soldan fell.
Seest thou her locks, whose sunny glow
Half shows, half shades, her neck of snow?
Twines not of them one golden thread,
But for its sake a Paynim bled.'
5.
"Joy to the fair!—my name unknown,
Each deed, and all its praise thine own
Then, oh! unbar this churlish gate,
The night dew falls, the hour is late.
Inured to Syria's glowing breath,
I feel the north breeze chill as death;
Let grateful love quell maiden shame,
And grant him bliss who brings thee fame."

During this performance, the hermit demeaned himself much like a first-rate critic of the present day at a new opera. He reclined back upon his seat, with his eyes half shut; now, folding his hands and twisting his thumbs, he seemed absorbed in attention, and anon, balancing his expanded palms, he gently flourished them in time to the music. At one or two favourite cadences, he threw in a little assistance of his own, where the knight's voice seemed unable to carry the air so high as his worshipful

IVANHOE

taste approved. When the song was ended, the anchorite emphatically declared it a good one, and well sung.

"And yet," said he, "I think my Saxon countrymen had herded long enough with the Normans, to fall into the tone of their melancholy ditties. What took the honest knight from home? or what could he expect but to find his mistress agreeably engaged with a rival on his return, and his serenade, as they call it, as little regarded as the caterwauling of a cat in the gutter? Nevertheless, Sir Knight, I drink this cup to thee, to the success of all true lovers—I fear you are none," he added, on observing that the knight (whose brain began to be heated with these repeated draughts) qualified his flagon from the water pitcher.

"Why," said the knight, "did you not tell me that this water was from the well of your blessed patron, St Dunstan?"

"Ay, truly," said the hermit, "and many a hundred of pagans did he baptize there, but I never heard that he drank any of it. Every thing should be put to its proper use in this world. St Dunstan knew, as well as any one, the prerogatives of a jovial friar."

And so saying, he reached the harp, and entertained his guest with the following characteristic song, to a sort of derry-down chorus, appropriate to an old English ditty.

THE BAREFOOTED FRIAR.
1.
I'll give thee, good fellow, a twelvemonth or twain,
To search Europe through, from Byzantium to Spain;
But ne'er shall you find, should you search till you tire,
So happy a man as the Barefooted Friar.
2.
Your knight for his lady pricks forth in career,
And is brought home at even-song prick'd through with a spear;
I confess him in haste—for his lady desires
No comfort on earth save the Barefooted Friar's.
3.
Your monarch?—Pshaw! many a prince has been known
To barter his robes for our cowl and our gown,
But which of us e'er felt the idle desire
To exchange for a crown the grey hood of a Friar!
4.
The Friar has walk'd out, and where'er he has gone,
The land and its fatness is mark'd for his own;
He can roam where he lists, he can stop when he tires,
For every man's house is the Barefooted Friar's.
5.
He's expected at noon, and no wight till he comes
May profane the great chair, or the porridge of plums
For the best of the cheer, and the seat by the fire,
Is the undenied right of the Barefooted Friar.
6.

>   He's expected at night, and the pasty's made hot,
>   They broach the brown ale, and they fill the black pot,
>   And the goodwife would wish the goodman in the mire,
>   Ere he lack'd a soft pillow, the Barefooted Friar.
>   7.
>   Long flourish the sandal, the cord, and the cope,
>   The dread of the devil and trust of the Pope;
>   For to gather life's roses, unscathed by the briar,
>   Is granted alone to the Barefooted Friar.

"By my troth," said the knight, "thou hast sung well and lustily, and in high praise of thine order. And, talking of the devil, Holy Clerk, are you not afraid that he may pay you a visit during some of your uncanonical pastimes?"

"I uncanonical!" answered the hermit; "I scorn the charge—I scorn it with my heels!—I serve the duty of my chapel duly and truly—Two masses daily, morning and evening, primes, noons, and vespers, 'aves, credos, paters'—"

"Excepting moonlight nights, when the venison is in season," said his guest.

"'Exceptis excipiendis'" replied the hermit, "as our old abbot taught me to say, when impertinent laymen should ask me if I kept every punctilio of mine order."

"True, holy father," said the knight; "but the devil is apt to keep an eye on such exceptions; he goes about, thou knowest, like a roaring lion."

"Let him roar here if he dares," said the friar; "a touch of my cord will make him roar as loud as the tongs of St Dunstan himself did. I never feared man, and I as little fear the devil and his imps. Saint Dunstan, Saint Dubric, Saint Winibald, Saint Winifred, Saint Swibert, Saint Willick, not forgetting Saint Thomas a Kent, and my own poor merits to speed, I defy every devil of them, come cut and long tail.—But to let you into a secret, I never speak upon such subjects, my friend, until after morning vespers."

He changed the conversation; fast and furious grew the mirth of the parties, and many a song was exchanged betwixt them, when their revels were interrupted by a loud knocking at the door of the hermitage.

The occasion of this interruption we can only explain by resuming the adventures of another set of our characters; for, like old Ariosto, we do not pique ourselves upon continuing uniformly to keep company with any one personage of our drama.

XVIII.

>   Away! our journey lies through dell and dingle,
>   Where the blithe fawn trips by its timid mother,
>   Where the broad oak, with intercepting boughs,
>   Chequers the sunbeam in the green-sward alley—
>   Up and away!—for lovely paths are these
>   To tread, when the glad Sun is on his throne
>   Less pleasant, and less safe, when Cynthia's lamp
>   With doubtful glimmer lights the dreary forest.

When Cedric the Saxon saw his son drop down senseless in the lists at Ashby, his first impulse was to order him into the custody and care of his own attendants, but the words choked in his throat. He could not bring himself to acknowledge, in presence of such an assembly, the son whom he had renounced and disinherited. He ordered, however, Oswald to keep an eye upon him; and directed that officer, with two of his serfs, to convey Ivanhoe to Ashby as soon as the crowd had dispersed. Oswald, however, was anticipated in this good office. The crowd dispersed, indeed, but the knight was nowhere to be seen.

It was in vain that Cedric's cupbearer looked around for his young master—he saw the bloody spot on which he had lately sunk down, but himself he saw no longer; it seemed as if the fairies had conveyed him from the spot. Perhaps Oswald (for the Saxons were very superstitious) might have adopted some such hypothesis, to account for Ivanhoe's disappearance, had he not suddenly cast his eye upon a person attired like a squire, in whom he recognised the features of his fellow-servant Gurth. Anxious concerning his master's fate, and in despair at his sudden disappearance, the translated swineherd was searching for him everywhere, and had neglected, in doing so, the concealment on which his own safety depended. Oswald deemed it his duty to secure Gurth, as a fugitive of whose fate his master was to judge.

Renewing his enquiries concerning the fate of Ivanhoe, the only information which the cupbearer could collect from the bystanders was, that the knight had been raised with care by certain well-attired grooms, and placed in a litter belonging to a lady among the spectators, which had immediately transported him out of the press. Oswald, on receiving this intelligence, resolved to return to his master for farther instructions, carrying along with him Gurth, whom he considered in some sort as a deserter from the service of Cedric.

The Saxon had been under very intense and agonizing apprehensions concerning his son; for Nature had asserted her rights, in spite of the patriotic stoicism which laboured to disown her. But no sooner was he informed that Ivanhoe was in careful, and probably in friendly hands, than the paternal anxiety which had been excited by the dubiety of his fate, gave way anew to the feeling of injured pride and resentment, at what he termed Wilfred's filial disobedience.

"Let him wander his way," said he—"let those leech his wounds for whose sake he encountered them. He is fitter to do the juggling tricks of the Norman chivalry than to maintain the fame and honour of his English ancestry with the glaive and brown-bill, the good old weapons of his country."

"If to maintain the honour of ancestry," said Rowena, who was present, "it is sufficient to be wise in council and brave in execution—to be boldest among the bold, and gentlest among the gentle, I know no voice, save his father's—"

"Be silent, Lady Rowena!—on this subject only I hear you not. Prepare yourself for the Prince's festival: we have been summoned thither with unwonted circumstance of honour and of courtesy, such as the haughty Normans have rarely used to our race since the fatal day of Hastings. Thither will I go, were it only to show these proud

Normans how little the fate of a son, who could defeat their bravest, can affect a Saxon."

"Thither," said Rowena, "do I NOT go; and I pray you to beware, lest what you mean for courage and constancy, shall be accounted hardness of heart."

"Remain at home, then, ungrateful lady," answered Cedric; "thine is the hard heart, which can sacrifice the weal of an oppressed people to an idle and unauthorized attachment. I seek the noble Athelstane, and with him attend the banquet of John of Anjou."

He went accordingly to the banquet, of which we have already mentioned the principal events. Immediately upon retiring from the castle, the Saxon thanes, with their attendants, took horse; and it was during the bustle which attended their doing so, that Cedric, for the first time, cast his eyes upon the deserter Gurth. The noble Saxon had returned from the banquet, as we have seen, in no very placid humour, and wanted but a pretext for wreaking his anger upon some one.

"The gyves!" he said, "the gyves!—Oswald—Hundibert!—Dogs and villains!—why leave ye the knave unfettered?"

Without daring to remonstrate, the companions of Gurth bound him with a halter, as the readiest cord which occurred. He submitted to the operation without remonstrance, except that, darting a reproachful look at his master, he said, "This comes of loving your flesh and blood better than mine own."

"To horse, and forward!" said Cedric.

"It is indeed full time," said the noble Athelstane; "for, if we ride not the faster, the worthy Abbot Waltheoff's preparations for a rere-supper will be altogether spoiled."

The travellers, however, used such speed as to reach the convent of St Withold's before the apprehended evil took place. The Abbot, himself of ancient Saxon descent, received the noble Saxons with the profuse and exuberant hospitality of their nation, wherein they indulged to a late, or rather an early hour; nor did they take leave of their reverend host the next morning until they had shared with him a sumptuous refection.

As the cavalcade left the court of the monastery, an incident happened somewhat alarming to the Saxons, who, of all people of Europe, were most addicted to a superstitious observance of omens, and to whose opinions can be traced most of those notions upon such subjects, still to be found among our popular antiquities. For the Normans being a mixed race, and better informed according to the information of the times, had lost most of the superstitious prejudices which their ancestors had brought from Scandinavia, and piqued themselves upon thinking freely on such topics.

In the present instance, the apprehension of impending evil was inspired by no less respectable a prophet than a large lean black dog, which, sitting upright, howled most piteously as the foremost riders left the gate, and presently afterwards, barking wildly, and jumping to and fro, seemed bent upon attaching itself to the party.

"I like not that music, father Cedric," said Athelstane; for by this title of respect he was accustomed to address him.

"Nor I either, uncle," said Wamba; "I greatly fear we shall have to pay the piper."

"In my mind," said Athelstane, upon whose memory the Abbot's good ale (for Burton was already famous for that genial liquor) had made a favourable impression,—"in my mind we had better turn back, and abide with the Abbot until the afternoon. It is unlucky to travel where your path is crossed by a monk, a hare, or a howling dog, until you have eaten your next meal."

"Away!" said Cedric, impatiently; "the day is already too short for our journey. For the dog, I know it to be the cur of the runaway slave Gurth, a useless fugitive like its master."

So saying, and rising at the same time in his stirrups, impatient at the interruption of his journey, he launched his javelin at poor Fangs—for Fangs it was, who, having traced his master thus far upon his stolen expedition, had here lost him, and was now, in his uncouth way, rejoicing at his reappearance. The javelin inflicted a wound upon the animal's shoulder, and narrowly missed pinning him to the earth; and Fangs fled howling from the presence of the enraged thane. Gurth's heart swelled within him; for he felt this meditated slaughter of his faithful adherent in a degree much deeper than the harsh treatment he had himself received. Having in vain attempted to raise his hand to his eyes, he said to Wamba, who, seeing his master's ill humour had prudently retreated to the rear, "I pray thee, do me the kindness to wipe my eyes with the skirt of thy mantle; the dust offends me, and these bonds will not let me help myself one way or another."

Wamba did him the service he required, and they rode side by side for some time, during which Gurth maintained a moody silence. At length he could repress his feelings no longer.

"Friend Wamba," said he, "of all those who are fools enough to serve Cedric, thou alone hast dexterity enough to make thy folly acceptable to him. Go to him, therefore, and tell him that neither for love nor fear will Gurth serve him longer. He may strike the head from me—he may scourge me—he may load me with irons—but henceforth he shall never compel me either to love or to obey him. Go to him, then, and tell him that Gurth the son of Beowulph renounces his service."

"Assuredly," said Wamba, "fool as I am, I shall not do your fool's errand. Cedric hath another javelin stuck into his girdle, and thou knowest he does not always miss his mark."

"I care not," replied Gurth, "how soon he makes a mark of me. Yesterday he left Wilfred, my young master, in his blood. To-day he has striven to kill before my face the only other living creature that ever showed me kindness. By St Edmund, St Dunstan, St Withold, St Edward the Confessor, and every other Saxon saint in the calendar," (for Cedric never swore by any that was not of Saxon lineage, and all his household had the same limited devotion,) "I will never forgive him!"

"To my thinking now," said the Jester, who was frequently wont to act as peacemaker in the family, "our master did not propose to hurt Fangs, but only to affright him. For, if you observed, he rose in his stirrups, as thereby meaning to overcast the mark; and so he would have done, but Fangs happening to bound up at the very moment, received a scratch, which I will be bound to heal with a penny's breadth of tar."

"If I thought so," said Gurth—"if I could but think so—but no—I saw the javelin was well aimed—I heard it whizz through the air with all the wrathful malevolence of him who cast it, and it quivered after it had pitched in the ground, as if with regret for having missed its mark. By the hog dear to St Anthony, I renounce him!"

And the indignant swineherd resumed his sullen silence, which no efforts of the Jester could again induce him to break.

Meanwhile Cedric and Athelstane, the leaders of the troop, conversed together on the state of the land, on the dissensions of the royal family, on the feuds and quarrels among the Norman nobles, and on the chance which there was that the oppressed Saxons might be able to free themselves from the yoke of the Normans, or at least to elevate themselves into national consequence and independence, during the civil convulsions which were likely to ensue. On this subject Cedric was all animation. The restoration of the independence of his race was the idol of his heart, to which he had willingly sacrificed domestic happiness and the interests of his own son. But, in order to achieve this great revolution in favour of the native English, it was necessary that they should be united among themselves, and act under an acknowledged head. The necessity of choosing their chief from the Saxon blood-royal was not only evident in itself, but had been made a solemn condition by those whom Cedric had intrusted with his secret plans and hopes. Athelstane had this quality at least; and though he had few mental accomplishments or talents to recommend him as a leader, he had still a goodly person, was no coward, had been accustomed to martial exercises, and seemed willing to defer to the advice of counsellors more wise than himself. Above all, he was known to be liberal and hospitable, and believed to be good-natured. But whatever pretensions Athelstane had to be considered as head of the Saxon confederacy, many of that nation were disposed to prefer to the title of the Lady Rowena, who drew her descent from Alfred, and whose father having been a chief renowned for wisdom, courage, and generosity, his memory was highly honoured by his oppressed countrymen.

It would have been no difficult thing for Cedric, had he been so disposed, to have placed himself at the head of a third party, as formidable at least as any of the others. To counterbalance their royal descent, he had courage, activity, energy, and, above all, that devoted attachment to the cause which had procured him the epithet of The Saxon, and his birth was inferior to none, excepting only that of Athelstane and his ward. These qualities, however, were unalloyed by the slightest shade of selfishness; and, instead of dividing yet farther his weakened nation by forming a faction of his own, it was a leading part of Cedric's plan to extinguish that which already existed, by promoting a marriage betwixt Rowena and Athelstane. An obstacle occurred to this his favourite project, in the mutual attachment of his ward and his son and hence the original cause of the banishment of Wilfred from the house of his father.

This stern measure Cedric had adopted, in hopes that, during Wilfred's absence, Rowena might relinquish her preference, but in this hope he was disappointed; a disappointment which might be attributed in part to the mode in which his ward had been educated. Cedric, to whom the name of Alfred was as that of a deity, had treated the sole remaining scion of that great monarch with a degree of observance, such as, perhaps, was in those days scarce paid to an acknowledged princess. Rowena's will had been in almost all cases a law to his household; and Cedric himself, as if determined that her sovereignty should be fully acknowledged within that little circle at least, seemed to take a pride in acting as the first of her subjects. Thus trained in the exercise not only of free will, but despotic authority, Rowena was, by her previous education, disposed both to resist and to resent any attempt to control her affections, or dispose of her hand contrary to her inclinations, and to assert her independence in a case in which even those females who have been trained up to obedience and subjection, are not infrequently apt to dispute the authority of guardians and parents. The opinions which she felt strongly, she avowed boldly; and Cedric, who could not free himself from his habitual deference to her opinions, felt totally at a loss how to enforce his authority of guardian.

It was in vain that he attempted to dazzle her with the prospect of a visionary throne. Rowena, who possessed strong sense, neither considered his plan as practicable, nor as desirable, so far as she was concerned, could it have been achieved. Without attempting to conceal her avowed preference of Wilfred of Ivanhoe, she declared that, were that favoured knight out of question, she would rather take refuge in a convent, than share a throne with Athelstane, whom, having always despised, she now began, on account of the trouble she received on his account, thoroughly to detest.

Nevertheless, Cedric, whose opinions of women's constancy was far from strong, persisted in using every means in his power to bring about the proposed match, in which he conceived he was rendering an important service to the Saxon cause. The sudden and romantic appearance of his son in the lists at Ashby, he had justly regarded as almost a death's blow to his hopes. His paternal affection, it is true, had for an instant gained the victory over pride and patriotism; but both had returned in full force, and under their joint operation, he was now bent upon making a determined effort for the union of Athelstane and Rowena, together with expediting those other measures which seemed necessary to forward the restoration of Saxon independence.

On this last subject, he was now labouring with Athelstane, not without having reason, every now and then, to lament, like Hotspur, that he should have moved such a dish of skimmed milk to so honourable an action. Athelstane, it is true, was vain enough, and loved to have his ears tickled with tales of his high descent, and of his right by inheritance to homage and sovereignty. But his petty vanity was sufficiently gratified by receiving this homage at the hands of his immediate attendants, and of the Saxons who approached him. If he had the courage to encounter danger, he at least hated the trouble of going to seek it; and while he agreed in the general principles laid down by Cedric concerning the claim of the Saxons to independence, and was still more easily convinced of his own title to reign over them when that independence should be attained, yet when the means of asserting these rights came to be discussed, he was still "Athelstane the Unready," slow, irresolute, procrastinating, and unenterprising. The warm and impassioned exhortations of Cedric had as little effect upon his impassive temper, as red-hot balls alighting in the water, which produce a little sound and smoke, and are instantly extinguished.

If, leaving this task, which might be compared to spurring a tired jade, or to hammering upon cold iron, Cedric fell back to his ward Rowena, he received little more satisfaction from conferring with her. For, as his presence interrupted the discourse between the lady and her favourite attendant upon the gallantry and fate of Wilfred, Elgitha failed not to revenge both her mistress and herself, by recurring to the overthrow of Athelstane in the lists, the most disagreeable subject which could greet the ears of Cedric. To this sturdy Saxon, therefore, the day's journey was fraught with all manner of displeasure and discomfort; so that he more than once internally cursed the tournament, and him who had proclaimed it, together with his own folly in ever thinking of going thither.

At noon, upon the motion of Athelstane, the travellers paused in a woodland shade by a fountain, to repose their horses and partake of some provisions, with which the hospitable Abbot had loaded a sumpter mule. Their repast was a pretty long one; and these several interruptions rendered it impossible for them to hope to reach Rotherwood without travelling all night, a conviction which induced them to proceed on their way at a more hasty pace than they had hitherto used.

XIX.

> A train of armed men, some noble dame
> Escorting, (so their scatter'd words discover'd,
> As unperceived I hung upon their rear,)
> Are close at hand, and mean to pass the night
> Within the castle.
>
> — ORRA, A TRAGEDY

The travellers had now reached the verge of the wooded country, and were about to plunge into its recesses, held dangerous at that time from the number of outlaws whom oppression and poverty had driven to despair, and who occupied the forests in such large bands as could easily bid defiance to the feeble police of the period. From these rovers, however, notwithstanding the lateness of the hour Cedric and Athelstane accounted themselves secure, as they had in attendance ten servants, besides Wamba and Gurth, whose aid could not be counted upon, the one being a jester and the other a captive. It may be added, that in travelling thus late through the forest, Cedric and Athelstane relied on their descent and character, as well as their courage. The outlaws, whom the severity of the forest laws had reduced to this roving and desperate mode of life, were chiefly peasants and yeomen of Saxon descent, and were generally supposed to respect the persons and property of their countrymen.

As the travellers journeyed on their way, they were alarmed by repeated cries for assistance; and when they rode up to the place from whence they came, they were surprised to find a horse-litter placed upon the ground, beside which sat a young woman, richly dressed in the Jewish fashion, while an old man, whose yellow cap proclaimed him to belong to the same nation, walked up and down with gestures expressive of the deepest despair, and wrung his hands, as if affected by some strange disaster.

To the enquiries of Athelstane and Cedric, the old Jew could for some time only answer by invoking the protection of all the patriarchs of the Old Testament successively against the sons of Ishmael, who were coming to smite them, hip and thigh, with the edge of the sword. When he began to come to himself out of this agony of terror, Isaac of York (for it was our old friend) was at length able to explain, that he had hired a body-guard of six men at Ashby, together with mules for carrying the litter of a sick friend. This party had undertaken to escort him as far as Doncaster. They had come thus far in safety; but having received information from a woodcutter that there was a strong band of outlaws lying in wait in the woods before them, Isaac's mercenaries had not only taken flight, but had carried off with them the horses which bore the litter and left the Jew and his daughter without the means either of defence or of retreat, to be plundered, and probably murdered, by the banditti, who they expected every moment would bring down upon them. "Would it but please your valours," added Isaac, in a tone of deep humiliation, "to permit the poor Jews to travel under your safeguard, I swear by the tables of our law, that never has favour been conferred upon a child of Israel since the days of our captivity, which shall be more gratefully acknowledged."

"Dog of a Jew!" said Athelstane, whose memory was of that petty kind which stores up trifles of all kinds, but particularly trifling offences, "dost not remember how thou didst beard us in the gallery at the tilt-yard? Fight or flee, or compound with the outlaws as thou dost list, ask neither aid nor company from us; and if they rob only such as thee, who rob all the world, I, for mine own share, shall hold them right honest folk."

Cedric did not assent to the severe proposal of his companion. "We shall do better," said he, "to leave them two of our attendants and two horses to convey them back to the next village. It will diminish our strength but little; and with your good sword, noble Athelstane, and the aid of those who remain, it will be light work for us to face twenty of those runagates."

Rowena, somewhat alarmed by the mention of outlaws in force, and so near them, strongly seconded the proposal of her guardian. But Rebecca suddenly quitting her dejected posture, and making her way through the attendants to the palfrey of the Saxon lady, knelt down, and, after the Oriental fashion in addressing superiors, kissed the hem of Rowena's garment. Then rising, and throwing back her veil, she implored her in the great name of the God whom they both worshipped, and by that revelation of the Law upon Mount Sinai, in which they both believed, that she would have compassion upon them, and suffer them to go forward under their safeguard. "It is not for myself that I pray this favour," said Rebecca; "nor is it even for that poor old man. I know that to wrong and to spoil our nation is a light fault, if not a merit, with the Christians; and what is it to us whether it be done in the city, in the desert, or in the field? But it is in the name of one dear to many, and dear even to you, that I beseech you to let this sick person be transported with care and tenderness under your protection. For, if evil chance him, the last moment of your life would be embittered with regret for denying that which I ask of you."

The noble and solemn air with which Rebecca made this appeal, gave it double weight with the fair Saxon.

"The man is old and feeble," she said to her guardian, "the maiden young and beautiful, their friend sick and in peril of his life—Jews though they be, we cannot as Christians leave them in this extremity. Let them unload two of the sumpter-mules, and put the baggage behind two of the serfs. The mules may transport the litter, and we have led horses for the old man and his daughter."

Cedric readily assented to what she proposed, and Athelstane only added the condition, "that they should travel in the rear of the whole party, where Wamba," he said, "might attend them with his shield of boar's brawn."

"I have left my shield in the tilt-yard," answered the Jester, "as has been the fate of many a better knight than myself."

Athelstane coloured deeply, for such had been his own fate on the last day of the tournament; while Rowena, who was pleased in the same proportion, as if to make amends for the brutal jest of her unfeeling suitor, requested Rebecca to ride by her side.

"It were not fit I should do so," answered Rebecca, with proud humility, "where my society might be held a disgrace to my protectress."

By this time the change of baggage was hastily achieved; for the single word "outlaws" rendered every one sufficiently alert, and the approach of twilight made the sound yet more impressive. Amid the bustle, Gurth was taken from horseback, in the course of which removal he prevailed upon the Jester to slack the cord with which his arms were bound. It was so negligently refastened, perhaps intentionally, on the part of Wamba, that Gurth found no difficulty in freeing his arms altogether from bondage, and then, gliding into the thicket, he made his escape from the party.

The bustle had been considerable, and it was some time before Gurth was missed; for, as he was to be placed for the rest of the journey behind a servant, every one supposed that some other of his companions had him under his custody, and when it began to be whispered among them that Gurth had actually disappeared, they were under such immediate expectation of an attack from the outlaws, that it was not held convenient to pay much attention to the circumstance.

The path upon which the party travelled was now so narrow, as not to admit, with any sort of convenience, above two riders abreast, and began to descend into a dingle, traversed by a brook whose banks were broken, swampy, and overgrown with dwarf willows. Cedric and Athelstane, who were at the head of their retinue, saw the risk of being attacked at this pass; but neither of them having had much practice in war, no better mode of preventing the danger occurred to them than that they should hasten through the defile as fast as possible. Advancing, therefore, without much order, they had just crossed the brook with a part of their followers, when they were assailed in front, flank, and rear at once, with an impetuosity to which, in their confused and ill-prepared condition, it was impossible to offer effectual resistance. The shout of "A white dragon!—a white dragon!—Saint George for merry England!" war-cries adopted by the assailants, as belonging to their assumed character of Saxon outlaws, was heard on every side, and on every side enemies appeared with a rapidity of advance and attack which seemed to multiply their numbers.

Both the Saxon chiefs were made prisoners at the same moment, and each under circumstances expressive of his character. Cedric, the instant that an enemy appeared, launched at him his remaining javelin, which, taking better effect than that which he had hurled at Fangs, nailed the man against an oak-tree that happened to be close behind him. Thus far successful, Cedric spurred his horse against a second, drawing his sword at the same time, and striking with such inconsiderate fury, that his weapon encountered a thick branch which hung over him, and he was disarmed by the violence of his own blow. He was instantly made prisoner, and pulled from his horse by two or three of the banditti who crowded around him. Athelstane shared his captivity, his bridle having been seized, and he himself forcibly dismounted, long before he could draw his weapon, or assume any posture of effectual defence.

The attendants, embarrassed with baggage, surprised and terrified at the fate of their masters, fell an easy prey to the assailants; while the Lady Rowena, in the centre of the cavalcade, and the Jew and his daughter in the rear, experienced the same misfortune.

Of all the train none escaped except Wamba, who showed upon the occasion much more courage than those who pretended to greater sense. He possessed himself of a sword belonging to one of the domestics, who was just drawing it with a tardy and irresolute hand, laid it about him like a lion, drove back several who approached him, and made a brave though ineffectual attempt to succour his master. Finding himself overpowered, the Jester at length threw himself from his horse, plunged into the thicket, and, favoured by the general confusion, escaped from the scene of action. Yet the valiant Jester, as soon as he found himself safe, hesitated more than once whether he should not turn back and share the captivity of a master to whom he was sincerely attached.

"I have heard men talk of the blessings of freedom," he said to himself, "but I wish any wise man would teach me what use to make of it now that I have it."

As he pronounced these words aloud, a voice very near him called out in a low and cautious tone, "Wamba!" and, at the same time, a dog, which he recognised to be Fangs, jumped up and fawned upon him. "Gurth!" answered Wamba, with the same caution, and the swineherd immediately stood before him.

"What is the matter?" said he eagerly; "what mean these cries, and that clashing of swords?"

"Only a trick of the times," said Wamba; "they are all prisoners."

"Who are prisoners?" exclaimed Gurth, impatiently.

"My lord, and my lady, and Athelstane, and Hundibert, and Oswald."

"In the name of God!" said Gurth, "how came they prisoners?—and to whom?"

"Our master was too ready to fight," said the Jester; "and Athelstane was not ready enough, and no other person was ready at all. And they are prisoners to green cassocks, and black visors. And they lie all tumbled about on the green, like the crab-apples that you shake down to your swine. And I would laugh at it," said the honest Jester, "if I could for weeping." And he shed tears of unfeigned sorrow.

Gurth's countenance kindled—"Wamba," he said, "thou hast a weapon, and thy heart was ever stronger than thy brain,—we are only two—but a sudden attack from men of resolution will do much—follow me!"

"Whither?—and for what purpose?" said the Jester.

"To rescue Cedric."

"But you have renounced his service but now," said Wamba.

"That," said Gurth, "was but while he was fortunate—follow me!"

As the Jester was about to obey, a third person suddenly made his appearance, and commanded them both to halt. From his dress and arms, Wamba would have conjectured him to be one of those outlaws who had just assailed his master; but, besides that he wore no mask, the glittering baldric across his shoulder, with the rich bugle-horn which it supported, as well as the calm and commanding expression of his voice and manner, made him, notwithstanding the twilight, recognise Locksley the yeoman, who had been victorious, under such disadvantageous circumstances, in the contest for the prize of archery.

"What is the meaning of all this," said he, "or who is it that rifle, and ransom, and make prisoners, in these forests?"

"You may look at their cassocks close by," said Wamba, "and see whether they be thy children's coats or no—for they are as like thine own, as one green pea-cod is to another."

"I will learn that presently," answered Locksley; "and I charge ye, on peril of your lives, not to stir from the place where ye stand, until I have returned. Obey me, and it shall be the better for you and your masters.—Yet stay, I must render myself as like these men as possible."

So saying he unbuckled his baldric with the bugle, took a feather from his cap, and gave them to Wamba; then drew a vizard from his pouch, and, repeating his charges to them to stand fast, went to execute his purposes of reconnoitring.

"Shall we stand fast, Gurth?" said Wamba; "or shall we e'en give him leg-bail? In my foolish mind, he had all the equipage of a thief too much in readiness, to be himself a true man."

"Let him be the devil," said Gurth, "an he will. We can be no worse of waiting his return. If he belong to that party, he must already have given them the alarm, and it will avail nothing either to fight or fly. Besides, I have late experience, that errant thieves are not the worst men in the world to have to deal with."

The yeoman returned in the course of a few minutes.

"Friend Gurth," he said, "I have mingled among yon men, and have learnt to whom they belong, and whither they are bound. There is, I think, no chance that they will proceed to any actual violence against their prisoners. For three men to attempt them at this moment, were little else than madness; for they are good men of war, and have, as such, placed sentinels to give the alarm when any one approaches. But I trust soon to gather such a force, as may act in defiance of all their precautions; you are both servants, and, as I think, faithful servants, of Cedric the Saxon, the friend of the rights of Englishmen. He shall not want English hands to help him in this extremity. Come then with me, until I gather more aid."

So saying, he walked through the wood at a great pace, followed by the jester and the swineherd. It was not consistent with Wamba's humour to travel long in silence.

"I think," said he, looking at the baldric and bugle which he still carried, "that I saw the arrow shot which won this gay prize, and that not so long since as Christmas."

"And I," said Gurth, "could take it on my halidome, that I have heard the voice of the good yeoman who won it, by night as well as by day, and that the moon is not three days older since I did so."

"Mine honest friends," replied the yeoman, "who, or what I am, is little to the present purpose; should I free your master, you will have reason to think me the best friend you have ever had in your lives. And whether I am known by one name or another—or whether I can draw a bow as well or better than a cow-keeper, or whether it is my pleasure to walk in sunshine or by moonlight, are matters, which, as they do not concern you, so neither need ye busy yourselves respecting them."

"Our heads are in the lion's mouth," said Wamba, in a whisper to Gurth, "get them out how we can."

"Hush—be silent," said Gurth. "Offend him not by thy folly, and I trust sincerely that all will go well."

XX.

> When autumn nights were long and drear,
> And forest walks were dark and dim,
> How sweetly on the pilgrim's ear
> Was wont to steal the hermit's hymn
>
> Devotion borrows Music's tone,
> And Music took Devotion's wing;
> And, like the bird that hails the sun,
> They soar to heaven, and soaring sing.
>
> — THE HERMIT OF ST CLEMENT'S WELL

It was after three hours' good walking that the servants of Cedric, with their mysterious guide, arrived at a small opening in the forest, in the centre of which grew an oak-tree of enormous magnitude, throwing its twisted branches in every direction. Beneath this tree four or five yeomen lay stretched on the ground, while another, as sentinel, walked to and fro in the moonlight shade.

Upon hearing the sound of feet approaching, the watch instantly gave the alarm, and the sleepers as suddenly started up and bent their bows. Six arrows placed on the string were pointed towards the quarter from which the travellers approached, when their guide, being recognised, was welcomed with every token of respect and attachment, and all signs and fears of a rough reception at once subsided.

"Where is the Miller?" was his first question.

"On the road towards Rotherham."

"With how many?" demanded the leader, for such he seemed to be.

"With six men, and good hope of booty, if it please St Nicholas."

"Devoutly spoken," said Locksley; "and where is Allan-a-Dale?"

"Walked up towards the Watling-street, to watch for the Prior of Jorvaulx."

"That is well thought on also," replied the Captain;—"and where is the Friar?"

"In his cell."

"Thither will I go," said Locksley. "Disperse and seek your companions. Collect what force you can, for there's game afoot that must be hunted hard, and will turn to bay. Meet me here by daybreak.—And stay," he added, "I have forgotten what is most necessary of the whole—Two of you take the road quickly towards Torquilstone, the Castle of Front-de-Boeuf. A set of gallants, who have been masquerading in such guise as our own, are carrying a band of prisoners thither—Watch them closely, for even if they reach the castle before we collect our force, our honour is concerned to punish them, and we will find means to do so. Keep a close watch on them therefore;

and dispatch one of your comrades, the lightest of foot, to bring the news of the yeomen thereabout."

They promised implicit obedience, and departed with alacrity on their different errands. In the meanwhile, their leader and his two companions, who now looked upon him with great respect, as well as some fear, pursued their way to the Chapel of Copmanhurst.

When they had reached the little moonlight glade, having in front the reverend, though ruinous chapel, and the rude hermitage, so well suited to ascetic devotion, Wamba whispered to Gurth, "If this be the habitation of a thief, it makes good the old proverb, The nearer the church the farther from God.—And by my coxcomb," he added, "I think it be even so—Hearken but to the black sanctus which they are singing in the hermitage!"

In fact the anchorite and his guest were performing, at the full extent of their very powerful lungs, an old drinking song, of which this was the burden:—

"Come, trowl the brown bowl to me,
Bully boy, bully boy,
Come, trowl the brown bowl to me:
Ho! jolly Jenkin, I spy a knave in drinking,
Come, trowl the brown bowl to me."

"Now, that is not ill sung," said Wamba, who had thrown in a few of his own flourishes to help out the chorus. "But who, in the saint's name, ever expected to have heard such a jolly chant come from out a hermit's cell at midnight!"

"Marry, that should I," said Gurth, "for the jolly Clerk of Copmanhurst is a known man, and kills half the deer that are stolen in this walk. Men say that the keeper has complained to his official, and that he will be stripped of his cowl and cope altogether, if he keeps not better order."

While they were thus speaking, Locksley's loud and repeated knocks had at length disturbed the anchorite and his guest. "By my beads," said the hermit, stopping short in a grand flourish, "here come more benighted guests. I would not for my cowl that they found us in this goodly exercise. All men have their enemies, good Sir Sluggard; and there be those malignant enough to construe the hospitable refreshment which I have been offering to you, a weary traveller, for the matter of three short hours, into sheer drunkenness and debauchery, vices alike alien to my profession and my disposition."

"Base calumniators!" replied the knight; "I would I had the chastising of them. Nevertheless, Holy Clerk, it is true that all have their enemies; and there be those in this very land whom I would rather speak to through the bars of my helmet than barefaced."

"Get thine iron pot on thy head then, friend Sluggard, as quickly as thy nature will permit," said the hermit, "while I remove these pewter flagons, whose late contents run strangely in mine own pate; and to drown the clatter—for, in faith, I feel somewhat unsteady—strike into the tune which thou hearest me sing; it is no matter for the words—I scarce know them myself."

So saying, he struck up a thundering "De profundis clamavi", under cover of which he removed the apparatus of their banquet: while the knight, laughing heartily, and arming himself all the while, assisted his host with his voice from time to time as his mirth permitted.

"What devil's matins are you after at this hour?" said a voice from without.

"Heaven forgive you, Sir Traveller!" said the hermit, whose own noise, and perhaps his nocturnal potations, prevented from recognising accents which were tolerably familiar to him—"Wend on your way, in the name of God and Saint Dunstan, and disturb not the devotions of me and my holy brother."

"Mad priest," answered the voice from without, "open to Locksley!"

"All's safe—all's right," said the hermit to his companion.

"But who is he?" said the Black Knight; "it imports me much to know."

"Who is he?" answered the hermit; "I tell thee he is a friend."

"But what friend?" answered the knight; "for he may be friend to thee and none of mine?"

"What friend?" replied the hermit; "that, now, is one of the questions that is more easily asked than answered. What friend?—why, he is, now that I bethink me a little, the very same honest keeper I told thee of a while since."

"Ay, as honest a keeper as thou art a pious hermit," replied the knight, "I doubt it not. But undo the door to him before he beat it from its hinges."

The dogs, in the meantime, which had made a dreadful baying at the commencement of the disturbance, seemed now to recognise the voice of him who stood without; for, totally changing their manner, they scratched and whined at the door, as if interceding for his admission. The hermit speedily unbolted his portal, and admitted Locksley, with his two companions.

"Why, hermit," was the yeoman's first question as soon as he beheld the knight, "what boon companion hast thou here?"

"A brother of our order," replied the friar, shaking his head; "we have been at our orisons all night."

"He is a monk of the church militant, I think," answered Locksley; "and there be more of them abroad. I tell thee, friar, thou must lay down the rosary and take up the quarter-staff; we shall need every one of our merry men, whether clerk or layman.—But," he added, taking him a step aside, "art thou mad? to give admittance to a knight thou dost not know? Hast thou forgot our articles?"

"Not know him!" replied the friar, boldly, "I know him as well as the beggar knows his dish."

"And what is his name, then?" demanded Locksley.

"His name," said the hermit—"his name is Sir Anthony of Scrabelstone—as if I would drink with a man, and did not know his name!"

"Thou hast been drinking more than enough, friar," said the woodsman, "and, I fear, prating more than enough too."

"Good yeoman," said the knight, coming forward, "be not wroth with my merry host. He did but afford me the hospitality which I would have compelled from him if he had refused it."

"Thou compel!" said the friar; "wait but till have changed this grey gown for a green cassock, and if I make not a quarter-staff ring twelve upon thy pate, I am neither true clerk nor good woodsman."

While he spoke thus, he stript off his gown, and appeared in a close black buckram doublet and drawers, over which he speedily did on a cassock of green, and hose of the same colour. "I pray thee truss my points," said he to Wamba, "and thou shalt have a cup of sack for thy labour."

"Gramercy for thy sack," said Wamba; "but think'st thou it is lawful for me to aid you to transmew thyself from a holy hermit into a sinful forester?"

"Never fear," said the hermit; "I will but confess the sins of my green cloak to my greyfriar's frock, and all shall be well again."

"Amen!" answered the Jester; "a broadcloth penitent should have a sackcloth confessor, and your frock may absolve my motley doublet into the bargain."

So saying, he accommodated the friar with his assistance in tying the endless number of points, as the laces which attached the hose to the doublet were then termed.

While they were thus employed, Locksley led the knight a little apart, and addressed him thus:—"Deny it not, Sir Knight—you are he who decided the victory to the advantage of the English against the strangers on the second day of the tournament at Ashby."

"And what follows if you guess truly, good yeoman?" replied the knight.

"I should in that case hold you," replied the yeoman, "a friend to the weaker party."

"Such is the duty of a true knight at least," replied the Black Champion; "and I would not willingly that there were reason to think otherwise of me."

"But for my purpose," said the yeoman, "thou shouldst be as well a good Englishman as a good knight; for that, which I have to speak of, concerns, indeed, the duty of every honest man, but is more especially that of a true-born native of England."

"You can speak to no one," replied the knight, "to whom England, and the life of every Englishman, can be dearer than to me."

"I would willingly believe so," said the woodsman, "for never had this country such need to be supported by those who love her. Hear me, and I will tell thee of an enterprise, in which, if thou be'st really that which thou seemest, thou mayst take an honourable part. A band of villains, in the disguise of better men than themselves, have made themselves master of the person of a noble Englishman, called Cedric the Saxon, together with his ward, and his friend Athelstane of Coningsburgh, and have transported them to a castle in this forest, called Torquilstone. I ask of thee, as a good knight and a good Englishman, wilt thou aid in their rescue?"

"I am bound by my vow to do so," replied the knight; "but I would willingly know who you are, who request my assistance in their behalf?"

"I am," said the forester, "a nameless man; but I am the friend of my country, and of my country's friends—With this account of me you must for the present remain satisfied, the more especially since you yourself desire to continue unknown. Believe, however, that my word, when pledged, is as inviolate as if I wore golden spurs."

"I willingly believe it," said the knight; "I have been accustomed to study men's countenances, and I can read in thine honesty and resolution. I will, therefore, ask thee no further questions, but aid thee in setting at freedom these oppressed captives;

which done, I trust we shall part better acquainted, and well satisfied with each other."

"So," said Wamba to Gurth,—for the friar being now fully equipped, the Jester, having approached to the other side of the hut, had heard the conclusion of the conversation,—"So we have got a new ally?—I trust the valour of the knight will be truer metal than the religion of the hermit, or the honesty of the yeoman; for this Locksley looks like a born deer-stealer, and the priest like a lusty hypocrite."

"Hold thy peace, Wamba," said Gurth; "it may all be as thou dost guess; but were the horned devil to rise and proffer me his assistance to set at liberty Cedric and the Lady Rowena, I fear I should hardly have religion enough to refuse the foul fiend's offer, and bid him get behind me."

The friar was now completely accoutred as a yeoman, with sword and buckler, bow, and quiver, and a strong partisan over his shoulder. He left his cell at the head of the party, and, having carefully locked the door, deposited the key under the threshold.

"Art thou in condition to do good service, friar," said Locksley, "or does the brown bowl still run in thy head?"

"Not more than a drought of St Dunstan's fountain will allay," answered the priest; "something there is of a whizzing in my brain, and of instability in my legs, but you shall presently see both pass away."

So saying, he stepped to the stone basin, in which the waters of the fountain as they fell formed bubbles which danced in the white moonlight, and took so long a drought as if he had meant to exhaust the spring.

"When didst thou drink as deep a drought of water before, Holy Clerk of Copmanhurst?" said the Black Knight.

"Never since my wine-butt leaked, and let out its liquor by an illegal vent," replied the friar, "and so left me nothing to drink but my patron's bounty here."

Then plunging his hands and head into the fountain, he washed from them all marks of the midnight revel.

Thus refreshed and sobered, the jolly priest twirled his heavy partisan round his head with three fingers, as if he had been balancing a reed, exclaiming at the same time, "Where be those false ravishers, who carry off wenches against their will? May the foul fiend fly off with me, if I am not man enough for a dozen of them."

"Swearest thou, Holy Clerk?" said the Black Knight.

"Clerk me no Clerks," replied the transformed priest; "by Saint George and the Dragon, I am no longer a shaveling than while my frock is on my back—When I am cased in my green cassock, I will drink, swear, and woo a lass, with any blithe forester in the West Riding."

"Come on, Jack Priest," said Locksley, "and be silent; thou art as noisy as a whole convent on a holy eve, when the Father Abbot has gone to bed.—Come on you, too, my masters, tarry not to talk of it—I say, come on, we must collect all our forces, and few enough we shall have, if we are to storm the Castle of Reginald Front-de-Boeuf."

"What! is it Front-de-Boeuf," said the Black Knight, "who has stopt on the king's highway the king's liege subjects?—Is he turned thief and oppressor?"

"Oppressor he ever was," said Locksley.

"And for thief," said the priest, "I doubt if ever he were even half so honest a man as many a thief of my acquaintance."

"Move on, priest, and be silent," said the yeoman; "it were better you led the way to the place of rendezvous, than say what should be left unsaid, both in decency and prudence."

XXI.

> Alas, how many hours and years have past,
> Since human forms have round this table sate,
> Or lamp, or taper, on its surface gleam'd!
> Methinks, I hear the sound of time long pass'd
> Still murmuring o'er us, in the lofty void
> Of these dark arches, like the ling'ring voices
> Of those who long within their graves have slept.
>
> — ORRA, A TRAGEDY

While these measures were taking in behalf of Cedric and his companions, the armed men by whom the latter had been seized, hurried their captives along towards the place of security, where they intended to imprison them. But darkness came on fast, and the paths of the wood seemed but imperfectly known to the marauders. They were compelled to make several long halts, and once or twice to return on their road to resume the direction which they wished to pursue. The summer morn had dawned upon them ere they could travel in full assurance that they held the right path. But confidence returned with light, and the cavalcade now moved rapidly forward. Meanwhile, the following dialogue took place between the two leaders of the banditti.

"It is time thou shouldst leave us, Sir Maurice," said the Templar to De Bracy, "in order to prepare the second part of thy mystery. Thou art next, thou knowest, to act the Knight Deliverer."

"I have thought better of it," said De Bracy; "I will not leave thee till the prize is fairly deposited in Front-de-Boeuf's castle. There will I appear before the Lady Rowena in mine own shape, and trust that she will set down to the vehemence of my passion the violence of which I have been guilty."

"And what has made thee change thy plan, De Bracy?" replied the Knight Templar.

"That concerns thee nothing," answered his companion.

"I would hope, however, Sir Knight," said the Templar, "that this alteration of measures arises from no suspicion of my honourable meaning, such as Fitzurse endeavoured to instil into thee?"

"My thoughts are my own," answered De Bracy; "the fiend laughs, they say, when one thief robs another; and we know, that were he to spit fire and brimstone instead, it would never prevent a Templar from following his bent."

"Or the leader of a Free Company," answered the Templar, "from dreading at the hands of a comrade and friend, the injustice he does to all mankind."

"This is unprofitable and perilous recrimination," answered De Bracy; "suffice it to say, I know the morals of the Temple-Order, and I will not give thee the power of cheating me out of the fair prey for which I have run such risks."

"Psha," replied the Templar, "what hast thou to fear?—Thou knowest the vows of our order."

"Right well," said De Bracy, "and also how they are kept. Come, Sir Templar, the laws of gallantry have a liberal interpretation in Palestine, and this is a case in which I will trust nothing to your conscience."

"Hear the truth, then," said the Templar; "I care not for your blue-eyed beauty. There is in that train one who will make me a better mate."

"What! wouldst thou stoop to the waiting damsel?" said De Bracy.

"No, Sir Knight," said the Templar, haughtily. "To the waiting-woman will I not stoop. I have a prize among the captives as lovely as thine own."

"By the mass, thou meanest the fair Jewess!" said De Bracy.

"And if I do," said Bois-Guilbert, "who shall gainsay me?"

"No one that I know," said De Bracy, "unless it be your vow of celibacy, or a check of conscience for an intrigue with a Jewess."

"For my vow," said the Templar, "our Grand Master hath granted me a dispensation. And for my conscience, a man that has slain three hundred Saracens, need not reckon up every little failing, like a village girl at her first confession upon Good Friday eve."

"Thou knowest best thine own privileges," said De Bracy. "Yet, I would have sworn thy thought had been more on the old usurer's money bags, than on the black eyes of the daughter."

"I can admire both," answered the Templar; "besides, the old Jew is but half-prize. I must share his spoils with Front-de-Boeuf, who will not lend us the use of his castle for nothing. I must have something that I can term exclusively my own by this foray of ours, and I have fixed on the lovely Jewess as my peculiar prize. But, now thou knowest my drift, thou wilt resume thine own original plan, wilt thou not?—Thou hast nothing, thou seest, to fear from my interference."

"No," replied De Bracy, "I will remain beside my prize. What thou sayst is passing true, but I like not the privileges acquired by the dispensation of the Grand Master, and the merit acquired by the slaughter of three hundred Saracens. You have too good a right to a free pardon, to render you very scrupulous about peccadilloes."

While this dialogue was proceeding, Cedric was endeavouring to wring out of those who guarded him an avowal of their character and purpose. "You should be Englishmen," said he; "and yet, sacred Heaven! you prey upon your countrymen as if you were very Normans. You should be my neighbours, and, if so, my friends; for which of my English neighbours have reason to be otherwise? I tell ye, yeomen, that even those among ye who have been branded with outlawry have had from me protection; for I have pitied their miseries, and curst the oppression of their tyrannic nobles. What, then, would you have of me? or in what can this violence serve ye?—Ye are worse than brute beasts in your actions, and will you imitate them in their very dumbness?"

It was in vain that Cedric expostulated with his guards, who had too many good reasons for their silence to be induced to break it either by his wrath or his expostulations. They continued to hurry him along, travelling at a very rapid rate, until, at the end of an avenue of huge trees, arose Torquilstone, now the hoary and ancient castle of Reginald Front-de-Boeuf. It was a fortress of no great size, consisting of a donjon, or large and high square tower, surrounded by buildings of inferior height, which were encircled by an inner court-yard. Around the exterior wall was a deep moat, supplied with water from a neighbouring rivulet. Front-de-Boeuf, whose character placed him often at feud with his enemies, had made considerable additions to the strength of his castle, by building towers upon the outward wall, so as to flank it at every angle. The access, as usual in castles of the period, lay through an arched barbican, or outwork, which was terminated and defended by a small turret at each corner.

Cedric no sooner saw the turrets of Front-de-Boeuf's castle raise their grey and moss-grown battlements, glimmering in the morning sun above the wood by which they were surrounded, than he instantly augured more truly concerning the cause of his misfortune.

"I did injustice," he said, "to the thieves and outlaws of these woods, when I supposed such banditti to belong to their bands; I might as justly have confounded the foxes of these brakes with the ravening wolves of France. Tell me, dogs—is it my life or my wealth that your master aims at? Is it too much that two Saxons, myself and the noble Athelstane, should hold land in the country which was once the patrimony of our race?—Put us then to death, and complete your tyranny by taking our lives, as you began with our liberties. If the Saxon Cedric cannot rescue England, he is willing to die for her. Tell your tyrannical master, I do only beseech him to dismiss the Lady Rowena in honour and safety. She is a woman, and he need not dread her; and with us will die all who dare fight in her cause."

The attendants remained as mute to this address as to the former, and they now stood before the gate of the castle. De Bracy winded his horn three times, and the archers and cross-bow men, who had manned the wall upon seeing their approach, hastened to lower the drawbridge, and admit them. The prisoners were compelled by their guards to alight, and were conducted to an apartment where a hasty repast was offered them, of which none but Athelstane felt any inclination to partake. Neither had the descendant of the Confessor much time to do justice to the good cheer placed before them, for their guards gave him and Cedric to understand that they were to be imprisoned in a chamber apart from Rowena. Resistance was vain; and they were compelled to follow to a large room, which, rising on clumsy Saxon pillars, resembled those refectories and chapter-houses which may be still seen in the most ancient parts of our most ancient monasteries.

The Lady Rowena was next separated from her train, and conducted, with courtesy, indeed, but still without consulting her inclination, to a distant apartment. The same alarming distinction was conferred on Rebecca, in spite of her father's entreaties, who offered even money, in this extremity of distress, that she might be permitted to abide with him. "Base unbeliever," answered one of his guards, "when thou hast seen thy lair, thou wilt not wish thy daughter to partake it." And, without farther discussion, the old Jew was forcibly dragged off in a different direction from the other prisoners. The domestics, after being carefully searched and disarmed, were confined in another part of the castle; and Rowena was refused even the comfort she might have derived from the attendance of her handmaiden Elgitha.

The apartment in which the Saxon chiefs were confined, for to them we turn our first attention, although at present used as a sort of guard-room, had formerly been the great hall of the castle. It was now abandoned to meaner purposes, because the present lord, among other additions to the convenience, security, and beauty of his baronial residence, had erected a new and noble hall, whose vaulted roof was supported by lighter and more elegant pillars, and fitted up with that higher degree of ornament, which the Normans had already introduced into architecture.

Cedric paced the apartment, filled with indignant reflections on the past and on the present, while the apathy of his companion served, instead of patience and philosophy, to defend him against every thing save the inconvenience of the present moment; and so little did he feel even this last, that he was only from time to time roused to a reply by Cedric's animated and impassioned appeal to him.

"Yes," said Cedric, half speaking to himself, and half addressing himself to Athelstane, "it was in this very hall that my father feasted with Torquil Wolfganger, when he entertained the valiant and unfortunate Harold, then advancing against the Norwegians, who had united themselves to the rebel Tosti. It was in this hall that Harold returned the magnanimous answer to the ambassador of his rebel brother. Oft have I heard my father kindle as he told the tale. The envoy of Tosti was admitted, when this ample room could scarce contain the crowd of noble Saxon leaders, who were quaffing the blood-red wine around their monarch."

"I hope," said Athelstane, somewhat moved by this part of his friend's discourse, "they will not forget to send us some wine and refactions at noon—we had scarce a breathing-space allowed to break our fast, and I never have the benefit of my food when I eat immediately after dismounting from horseback, though the leeches recommend that practice."

Cedric went on with his story without noticing this interjectional observation of his friend.

"The envoy of Tosti," he said, "moved up the hall, undismayed by the frowning countenances of all around him, until he made his obeisance before the throne of King Harold.

"'What terms,' he said, 'Lord King, hath thy brother Tosti to hope, if he should lay down his arms, and crave peace at thy hands?'

"'A brother's love,' cried the generous Harold, 'and the fair earldom of Northumberland.'

"'But should Tosti accept these terms,' continued the envoy, 'what lands shall be assigned to his faithful ally, Hardrada, King of Norway?'

"'Seven feet of English ground,' answered Harold, fiercely, 'or, as Hardrada is said to be a giant, perhaps we may allow him twelve inches more.'

"The hall rung with acclamations, and cup and horn was filled to the Norwegian, who should be speedily in possession of his English territory."

"I could have pledged him with all my soul," said Athelstane, "for my tongue cleaves to my palate."

"The baffled envoy," continued Cedric, pursuing with animation his tale, though it interested not the listener, "retreated, to carry to Tosti and his ally the ominous answer of his injured brother. It was then that the distant towers of York, and the bloody streams of the Derwent, beheld that direful conflict, in which, after displaying the most undaunted valour, the King of Norway, and Tosti, both fell, with ten thousand of their bravest followers. Who would have thought that upon the proud day when this battle was won, the very gale which waved the Saxon banners in triumph, was filling the Norman sails, and impelling them to the fatal shores of Sussex?—Who would have thought that Harold, within a few brief days, would himself possess no more of his kingdom, than the share which he allotted in his wrath to the Norwegian invader?—Who would have thought that you, noble Athelstane—that you, descended of Harold's blood, and that I, whose father was not the worst defender of the Saxon crown, should be prisoners to a vile Norman, in the very hall in which our ancestors held such high festival?"

"It is sad enough," replied Athelstane; "but I trust they will hold us to a moderate ransom—At any rate it cannot be their purpose to starve us outright; and yet, although it is high noon, I see no preparations for serving dinner. Look up at the window, noble Cedric, and judge by the sunbeams if it is not on the verge of noon."

"It may be so," answered Cedric; "but I cannot look on that stained lattice without its awakening other reflections than those which concern the passing moment, or its privations. When that window was wrought, my noble friend, our hardy fathers knew not the art of making glass, or of staining it—The pride of Wolfganger's father brought an artist from Normandy to adorn his hall with this new species of emblazonment, that breaks the golden light of God's blessed day into so many fantastic hues. The foreigner came here poor, beggarly, cringing, and subservient, ready to doff his cap to the meanest native of the household. He returned pampered and proud, to tell his rapacious countrymen of the wealth and the simplicity of the Saxon nobles—a folly, oh, Athelstane, foreboded of old, as well as foreseen, by those descendants of Hengist and his hardy tribes, who retained the simplicity of their manners. We made these strangers our bosom friends, our confidential servants; we borrowed their artists and their arts, and despised the honest simplicity and hardihood with which our brave ancestors supported themselves, and we became enervated by Norman arts long ere we fell under Norman arms. Far better was our homely diet, eaten in peace and liberty, than the luxurious dainties, the love of which hath delivered us as bondsmen to the foreign conqueror!"

"I should," replied Athelstane, "hold very humble diet a luxury at present; and it astonishes me, noble Cedric, that you can bear so truly in mind the memory of past deeds, when it appeareth you forget the very hour of dinner."

"It is time lost," muttered Cedric apart and impatiently, "to speak to him of aught else but that which concerns his appetite! The soul of Hardicanute hath taken possession of him, and he hath no pleasure save to fill, to swill, and to call for more.—Alas!" said he, looking at Athelstane with compassion, "that so dull a spirit should be lodged in so goodly a form! Alas! that such an enterprise as the regeneration of England should turn on a hinge so imperfect! Wedded to Rowena, indeed, her nobler and more generous soul may yet awake the better nature which is torpid within him. Yet how should this be, while Rowena, Athelstane, and I myself, remain the prisoners of this brutal marauder and have been made so perhaps from a sense of the dangers which our liberty might bring to the usurped power of his nation?"

While the Saxon was plunged in these painful reflections, the door of their prison opened, and gave entrance to a sewer, holding his white rod of office. This important person advanced into the chamber with a grave pace, followed by four attendants, bearing in a table covered with dishes, the sight and smell of which seemed to be an instant compensation to Athelstane for all the inconvenience he had undergone. The persons who attended on the feast were masked and cloaked.

"What mummery is this?" said Cedric; "think you that we are ignorant whose prisoners we are, when we are in the castle of your master? Tell him," he continued, willing to use this opportunity to open a negotiation for his freedom,—"Tell your master, Reginald Front-de-Boeuf, that we know no reason he can have for withholding our liberty, excepting his unlawful desire to enrich himself at our expense. Tell him that we yield to his rapacity, as in similar circumstances we should do to that of a literal robber. Let him name the ransom at which he rates our liberty, and it shall be paid, providing the exaction is suited to our means." The sewer made no answer, but bowed his head.

"And tell Sir Reginald Front-de-Boeuf," said Athelstane, "that I send him my mortal defiance, and challenge him to combat with me, on foot or horseback, at any secure place, within eight days after our liberation; which, if he be a true knight, he will not, under these circumstances, venture to refuse or to delay."

"I shall deliver to the knight your defiance," answered the sewer; "meanwhile I leave you to your food."

The challenge of Athelstane was delivered with no good grace; for a large mouthful, which required the exercise of both jaws at once, added to a natural hesitation, considerably damped the effect of the bold defiance it contained. Still, however, his speech was hailed by Cedric as an incontestible token of reviving spirit in his companion, whose previous indifference had begun, notwithstanding his respect for Athelstane's descent, to wear out his patience. But he now cordially shook hands with him in token of his approbation, and was somewhat grieved when Athelstane observed, "that he would fight a dozen such men as Front-de-Boeuf, if, by so doing, he could hasten his departure from a dungeon where they put so much garlic into their pottage." Notwithstanding this intimation of a relapse into the apathy of sensuality, Cedric placed himself opposite to Athelstane, and soon showed, that if the distresses of his country could banish the recollection of food while the table was uncovered, yet no sooner were the victuals put there, than he proved that the appetite of his Saxon ancestors had descended to him along with their other qualities.

The captives had not long enjoyed their refreshment, however, ere their attention was disturbed even from this most serious occupation by the blast of a horn winded before the gate. It was repeated three times, with as much violence as if it had been blown before an enchanted castle by the destined knight, at whose summons halls and towers, barbican and battlement, were to roll off like a morning vapour. The Saxons started from the table, and hastened to the window. But their curiosity was disappointed; for these outlets only looked upon the court of the castle, and the sound came from beyond its precincts. The summons, however, seemed of importance, for a considerable degree of bustle instantly took place in the castle.

XXII.

> My daughter—O my ducats—O my daughter!
> ———O my Christian ducats!
> Justice—the Law—my ducats, and my daughter!

— MERCHANT OF VENICE

Leaving the Saxon chiefs to return to their banquet as soon as their ungratified curiosity should permit them to attend to the calls of their half-satiated appetite, we have to look in upon the yet more severe imprisonment of Isaac of York. The poor Jew had been hastily thrust into a dungeon-vault of the castle, the floor of which was deep beneath the level of the ground, and very damp, being lower than even the moat itself. The only light was received through one or two loop-holes far above the reach of the captive's hand. These apertures admitted, even at mid-day, only a dim and uncertain light, which was changed for utter darkness long before the rest of the castle had lost the blessing of day. Chains and shackles, which had been the portion of former captives, from whom active exertions to escape had been apprehended, hung rusted and empty on the walls of the prison, and in the rings of one of those sets of fetters there remained two mouldering bones, which seemed to have been once those of the human leg, as if some prisoner had been left not only to perish there, but to be consumed to a skeleton.

At one end of this ghastly apartment was a large fire-grate, over the top of which were stretched some transverse iron bars, half devoured with rust.

The whole appearance of the dungeon might have appalled a stouter heart than that of Isaac, who, nevertheless, was more composed under the imminent pressure of danger, than he had seemed to be while affected by terrors, of which the cause was as yet remote and contingent. The lovers of the chase say that the hare feels more agony during the pursuit of the greyhounds, than when she is struggling in their fangs.

And thus it is probable, that the Jews, by the very frequency of their fear on all occasions, had their minds in some degree prepared for every effort of tyranny which could be practised upon them; so that no aggression, when it had taken place, could bring with it that surprise which is the most disabling quality of terror. Neither was it the first time that Isaac had been placed in circumstances so dangerous. He had therefore experience to guide him, as well as hope, that he might again, as formerly, be delivered as a prey from the fowler. Above all, he had upon his side the unyielding obstinacy of his nation, and that unbending resolution, with which Israelites have been frequently known to submit to the uttermost evils which power and violence can inflict upon them, rather than gratify their oppressors by granting their demands.

In this humour of passive resistance, and with his garment collected beneath him to keep his limbs from the wet pavement, Isaac sat in a corner of his dungeon, where his folded hands, his dishevelled hair and beard, his furred cloak and high cap, seen by the wiry and broken light, would have afforded a study for Rembrandt, had that celebrated painter existed at the period. The Jew remained, without altering his position, for nearly three hours, at the expiry of which steps were heard on the dungeon stair. The bolts screamed as they were withdrawn—the hinges creaked as the wicket opened, and Reginald Front-de-Boeuf, followed by the two Saracen slaves of the Templar, entered the prison.

Front-de-Boeuf, a tall and strong man, whose life had been spent in public war or in private feuds and broils, and who had hesitated at no means of extending his feudal power, had features corresponding to his character, and which strongly expressed the fiercer and more malignant passions of the mind. The scars with which his visage was seamed, would, on features of a different cast, have excited the sympathy and veneration due to the marks of honourable valour; but, in the peculiar case of Front-de-Boeuf, they only added to the ferocity of his countenance, and to the dread which his presence inspired. This formidable baron was clad in a leathern doublet, fitted close to his body, which was frayed and soiled with the stains of his armour. He had no weapon, excepting a poniard at his belt, which served to counter-balance the weight of the bunch of rusty keys that hung at his right side.

The black slaves who attended Front-de-Boeuf were stripped of their gorgeous apparel, and attired in jerkins and trowsers of coarse linen, their sleeves being tucked up above the elbow, like those of butchers when about to exercise their function in the slaughter-house. Each had in his hand a small pannier; and, when they entered the dungeon, they stopt at the door until Front-de-Boeuf himself carefully locked and double-locked it. Having taken this precaution, he advanced slowly up the apartment towards the Jew, upon whom he kept his eye fixed, as if he wished to paralyze him with his glance, as some animals are said to fascinate their prey. It seemed indeed as if the sullen and malignant eye of Front-de-Boeuf possessed some portion of that supposed power over his unfortunate prisoner. The Jew sat with his mouth agape, and his eyes fixed on the savage baron with such earnestness of terror, that his frame seemed literally to shrink together, and to diminish in size while encountering the fierce Norman's fixed and baleful gaze. The unhappy Isaac was deprived not only of the power of rising to make the obeisance which his terror dictated, but he could not even doff his cap, or utter any word of supplication; so strongly was he agitated by the conviction that tortures and death were impending over him.

On the other hand, the stately form of the Norman appeared to dilate in magnitude, like that of the eagle, which ruffles up its plumage when about to pounce on its defenceless prey. He paused within three steps of the corner in which the unfortunate Jew had now, as it were, coiled himself up into the smallest possible space, and made a sign for one of the slaves to approach. The black satellite came forward accordingly, and, producing from his basket a large pair of scales and several weights, he laid them at the feet of Front-de-Boeuf, and again retired to the respectful distance, at which his companion had already taken his station.

The motions of these men were slow and solemn, as if there impended over their souls some preconception of horror and of cruelty. Front-de-Boeuf himself opened the scene by thus addressing his ill-fated captive.

"Most accursed dog of an accursed race," he said, awaking with his deep and sullen voice the sullen echoes of his dungeon vault, "seest thou these scales?"

The unhappy Jew returned a feeble affirmative.

"In these very scales shalt thou weigh me out," said the relentless Baron, "a thousand silver pounds, after the just measure and weight of the Tower of London."

"Holy Abraham!" returned the Jew, finding voice through the very extremity of his danger, "heard man ever such a demand?—Who ever heard, even in a minstrel's tale, of such a sum as a thousand pounds of silver?—What human sight was ever blessed with the vision of such a mass of treasure?—Not within the walls of York, ransack my house and that of all my tribe, wilt thou find the tithe of that huge sum of silver that thou speakest of."

"I am reasonable," answered Front-de-Boeuf, "and if silver be scant, I refuse not gold. At the rate of a mark of gold for each six pounds of silver, thou shalt free thy unbelieving carcass from such punishment as thy heart has never even conceived."

"Have mercy on me, noble knight!" exclaimed Isaac; "I am old, and poor, and helpless. It were unworthy to triumph over me—It is a poor deed to crush a worm."

"Old thou mayst be," replied the knight; "more shame to their folly who have suffered thee to grow grey in usury and knavery—Feeble thou mayst be, for when had a Jew either heart or hand—But rich it is well known thou art."

"I swear to you, noble knight," said the Jew "by all which I believe, and by all which we believe in common——"

"Perjure not thyself," said the Norman, interrupting him, "and let not thine obstinacy seal thy doom, until thou hast seen and well considered the fate that awaits thee. Think not I speak to thee only to excite thy terror, and practise on the base cowardice thou hast derived from thy tribe. I swear to thee by that which thou dost NOT believe, by the gospel which our church teaches, and by the keys which are given her to bind and to loose, that my purpose is deep and peremptory. This dungeon is no place for trifling. Prisoners ten thousand times more distinguished than thou have died within these walls, and their fate hath never been known! But for thee is reserved a long and lingering death, to which theirs were luxury."

He again made a signal for the slaves to approach, and spoke to them apart, in their own language; for he also had been in Palestine, where perhaps, he had learnt his lesson of cruelty. The Saracens produced from their baskets a quantity of charcoal, a pair of bellows, and a flask of oil. While the one struck a light with a flint and steel, the other disposed the charcoal in the large rusty grate which we have already mentioned, and exercised the bellows until the fuel came to a red glow.

"Seest thou, Isaac," said Front-de-Boeuf, "the range of iron bars above the glowing charcoal?— on that warm couch thou shalt lie, stripped of thy clothes as if thou wert to rest on a bed of down. One of these slaves shall maintain the fire beneath thee, while the other shall anoint thy wretched limbs with oil, lest the roast should burn.—Now, choose betwixt such a scorching bed and the payment of a thousand pounds of silver; for, by the head of my father, thou hast no other option."

"It is impossible," exclaimed the miserable Jew—"it is impossible that your purpose can be real! The good God of nature never made a heart capable of exercising such cruelty!"

"Trust not to that, Isaac," said Front-de-Boeuf, "it were a fatal error. Dost thou think that I, who have seen a town sacked, in which thousands of my Christian countrymen perished by sword, by flood, and by fire, will blench from my purpose for the outcries or screams of one single wretched Jew?—or thinkest thou that these swarthy slaves, who have neither law, country, nor conscience, but their master's will—who use the poison, or the stake, or the poniard, or the cord, at his slightest wink—

thinkest thou that THEY will have mercy, who do not even understand the language in which it is asked?—Be wise, old man; discharge thyself of a portion of thy superfluous wealth; repay to the hands of a Christian a part of what thou hast acquired by the usury thou hast practised on those of his religion. Thy cunning may soon swell out once more thy shrivelled purse, but neither leech nor medicine can restore thy scorched hide and flesh wert thou once stretched on these bars. Tell down thy ransom, I say, and rejoice that at such rate thou canst redeem thee from a dungeon, the secrets of which few have returned to tell. I waste no more words with thee—choose between thy dross and thy flesh and blood, and as thou choosest, so shall it be."

"So may Abraham, Jacob, and all the fathers of our people assist me," said Isaac, "I cannot make the choice, because I have not the means of satisfying your exorbitant demand!"

"Seize him and strip him, slaves," said the knight, "and let the fathers of his race assist him if they can."

The assistants, taking their directions more from the Baron's eye and his hand than his tongue, once more stepped forward, laid hands on the unfortunate Isaac, plucked him up from the ground, and, holding him between them, waited the hardhearted Baron's farther signal. The unhappy Jew eyed their countenances and that of Front-de-Boeuf, in hope of discovering some symptoms of relenting; but that of the Baron exhibited the same cold, half-sullen, half-sarcastic smile which had been the prelude to his cruelty; and the savage eyes of the Saracens, rolling gloomily under their dark brows, acquiring a yet more sinister expression by the whiteness of the circle which surrounds the pupil, evinced rather the secret pleasure which they expected from the approaching scene, than any reluctance to be its directors or agents. The Jew then looked at the glowing furnace, over which he was presently to be stretched, and seeing no chance of his tormentor's relenting, his resolution gave way.

"I will pay," he said, "the thousand pounds of silver—That is," he added, after a moment's pause, "I will pay it with the help of my brethren; for I must beg as a mendicant at the door of our synagogue ere I make up so unheard-of a sum.—When and where must it be delivered?"

"Here," replied Front-de-Boeuf, "here it must be delivered—weighed it must be—weighed and told down on this very dungeon floor.—Thinkest thou I will part with thee until thy ransom is secure?"

"And what is to be my surety," said the Jew, "that I shall be at liberty after this ransom is paid?"

"The word of a Norman noble, thou pawn-broking slave," answered Front-de-Boeuf; "the faith of a Norman nobleman, more pure than the gold and silver of thee and all thy tribe."

"I crave pardon, noble lord," said Isaac timidly, "but wherefore should I rely wholly on the word of one who will trust nothing to mine?"

"Because thou canst not help it, Jew," said the knight, sternly. "Wert thou now in thy treasure-chamber at York, and were I craving a loan of thy shekels, it would be thine to dictate the time of payment, and the pledge of security. This is MY treasure-chamber. Here I have thee at advantage, nor will I again deign to repeat the terms on which I grant thee liberty."

The Jew groaned deeply.—"Grant me," he said, "at least with my own liberty, that of the companions with whom I travel. They scorned me as a Jew, yet they pitied my desolation, and because they tarried to aid me by the way, a share of my evil hath come upon them; moreover, they may contribute in some sort to my ransom."

"If thou meanest yonder Saxon churls," said Front-de-Boeuf, "their ransom will depend upon other terms than thine. Mind thine own concerns, Jew, I warn thee, and meddle not with those of others."

"I am, then," said Isaac, "only to be set at liberty, together with mine wounded friend?"

"Shall I twice recommend it," said Front-de-Boeuf, "to a son of Israel, to meddle with his own concerns, and leave those of others alone?—Since thou hast made thy choice, it remains but that thou payest down thy ransom, and that at a short day."

"Yet hear me," said the Jew—"for the sake of that very wealth which thou wouldst obtain at the expense of thy——" Here he stopt short, afraid of irritating the savage Norman. But Front-de-Boeuf only laughed, and himself filled up the blank at which the Jew had hesitated.

"At the expense of my conscience, thou wouldst say, Isaac; speak it out—I tell thee, I am reasonable. I can bear the reproaches of a loser, even when that loser is a Jew. Thou wert not so patient, Isaac, when thou didst invoke justice against Jacques Fitzdotterel, for calling thee a usurious blood-sucker, when thy exactions had devoured his patrimony."

"I swear by the Talmud," said the Jew, "that your valour has been misled in that matter. Fitzdotterel drew his poniard upon me in mine own chamber, because I craved him for mine own silver. The term of payment was due at the Passover."

"I care not what he did," said Front-de-Boeuf; "the question is, when shall I have mine own?—when shall I have the shekels, Isaac?"

"Let my daughter Rebecca go forth to York," answered Isaac, "with your safe conduct, noble knight, and so soon as man and horse can return, the treasure——" Here he groaned deeply, but added, after the pause of a few seconds,—"The treasure shall be told down on this very floor."

"Thy daughter!" said Front-de-Boeuf, as if surprised,—"By heavens, Isaac, I would I had known of this. I deemed that yonder black-browed girl had been thy concubine, and I gave her to be a handmaiden to Sir Brian de Bois-Guilbert, after the fashion of patriarchs and heroes of the days of old, who set us in these matters a wholesome example."

The yell which Isaac raised at this unfeeling communication made the very vault to ring, and astounded the two Saracens so much that they let go their hold of the Jew. He availed himself of his enlargement to throw himself on the pavement, and clasp the knees of Front-de-Boeuf.

"Take all that you have asked," said he, "Sir Knight—take ten times more—reduce me to ruin and to beggary, if thou wilt,—nay, pierce me with thy poniard, broil me on that furnace, but spare my daughter, deliver her in safety and honour!—As thou art born of woman, spare the honour of a helpless maiden—She is the image of my deceased Rachel, she is the last of six pledges of her love—Will you deprive a widowed husband of his sole remaining comfort?—Will you reduce a father to wish that his only living child were laid beside her dead mother, in the tomb of our fathers?"

"I would," said the Norman, somewhat relenting, "that I had known of this before. I thought your race had loved nothing save their moneybags."

"Think not so vilely of us, Jews though we be," said Isaac, eager to improve the moment of apparent sympathy; "the hunted fox, the tortured wildcat loves its young—the despised and persecuted race of Abraham love their children!"

"Be it so," said Front-de-Boeuf; "I will believe it in future, Isaac, for thy very sake—but it aids us not now, I cannot help what has happened, or what is to follow; my word is passed to my comrade in arms, nor would I break it for ten Jews and Jewesses to boot. Besides, why shouldst thou think evil is to come to the girl, even if she became Bois-Guilbert's booty?"

"There will, there must!" exclaimed Isaac, wringing his hands in agony; "when did Templars breathe aught but cruelty to men, and dishonour to women!"

"Dog of an infidel," said Front-de-Boeuf, with sparkling eyes, and not sorry, perhaps, to seize a pretext for working himself into a passion, "blaspheme not the Holy Order of the Temple of Zion, but take thought instead to pay me the ransom thou hast promised, or woe betide thy Jewish throat!"

"Robber and villain!" said the Jew, retorting the insults of his oppressor with passion, which, however impotent, he now found it impossible to bridle, "I will pay thee nothing—not one silver penny will I pay thee, unless my daughter is delivered to me in safety and honour!"

"Art thou in thy senses, Israelite?" said the Norman, sternly—"has thy flesh and blood a charm against heated iron and scalding oil?"

"I care not!" said the Jew, rendered desperate by paternal affection; "do thy worst. My daughter is my flesh and blood, dearer to me a thousand times than those limbs which thy cruelty threatens. No silver will I give thee, unless I were to pour it molten down thy avaricious throat—no, not a silver penny will I give thee, Nazarene, were it to save thee from the deep damnation thy whole life has merited! Take my life if thou wilt, and say, the Jew, amidst his tortures, knew how to disappoint the Christian."

"We shall see that," said Front-de-Boeuf; "for by the blessed rood, which is the abomination of thy accursed tribe, thou shalt feel the extremities of fire and steel!—Strip him, slaves, and chain him down upon the bars."

In spite of the feeble struggles of the old man, the Saracens had already torn from him his upper garment, and were proceeding totally to disrobe him, when the sound of a bugle, twice winded without the castle, penetrated even to the recesses of the dungeon, and immediately after loud voices were heard calling for Sir Reginald Front-de-Boeuf. Unwilling to be found engaged in his hellish occupation, the savage Baron gave the slaves a signal to restore Isaac's garment, and, quitting the dungeon with his attendants, he left the Jew to thank God for his own deliverance, or to lament over his daughter's captivity, and probable fate, as his personal or parental feelings might prove strongest.

XXIII.

> Nay, if the gentle spirit of moving words
> Can no way change you to a milder form,
> I'll woo you, like a soldier, at arms' end,
> And love you 'gainst the nature of love, force you.
>
> — TWO GENTLEMEN OF VERONA

The apartment to which the Lady Rowena had been introduced was fitted up with some rude attempts at ornament and magnificence, and her being placed there might be considered as a peculiar mark of respect not offered to the other prisoners. But the wife of Front-de-Boeuf, for whom it had been originally furnished, was long dead, and decay and neglect had impaired the few ornaments with which her taste had adorned it. The tapestry hung down from the walls in many places, and in others was tarnished and faded under the effects of the sun, or tattered and decayed by age. Desolate, however, as it was, this was the apartment of the castle which had been judged most fitting for the accommodation of the Saxon heiress; and here she was left to meditate upon her fate, until the actors in this nefarious drama had arranged the several parts which each of them was to perform. This had been settled in a council held by Front-de-Boeuf, De Bracy, and the Templar, in which, after a long and warm debate concerning the several advantages which each insisted upon deriving from his peculiar share in this audacious enterprise, they had at length determined the fate of their unhappy prisoners.

It was about the hour of noon, therefore, when De Bracy, for whose advantage the expedition had been first planned, appeared to prosecute his views upon the hand and possessions of the Lady Rowena.

The interval had not entirely been bestowed in holding council with his confederates, for De Bracy had found leisure to decorate his person with all the foppery of the times. His green cassock and vizard were now flung aside. His long luxuriant hair was trained to flow in quaint tresses down his richly furred cloak. His beard was closely shaved, his doublet reached to the middle of his leg, and the girdle which secured it, and at the same time supported his ponderous sword, was embroidered and embossed with gold work. We have already noticed the extravagant fashion of the shoes at this period, and the points of Maurice de Bracy's might have challenged the prize of extravagance with the gayest, being turned up and twisted like the horns of a ram. Such was the dress of a gallant of the period; and, in the present instance, that effect was aided by the handsome person and good demeanour of the wearer, whose manners partook alike of the grace of a courtier, and the frankness of a soldier.

He saluted Rowena by doffing his velvet bonnet, garnished with a golden broach, representing St Michael trampling down the Prince of Evil. With this, he gently motioned the lady to a seat; and, as she still retained her standing posture, the knight ungloved his right hand, and motioned to conduct her thither. But Rowena declined, by her gesture, the proffered compliment, and replied, "If I be in the presence of my jailor, Sir Knight—nor will circumstances allow me to think otherwise—it best becomes his prisoner to remain standing till she learns her doom."

"Alas! fair Rowena," returned De Bracy, "you are in presence of your captive, not your jailor; and it is from your fair eyes that De Bracy must receive that doom which you fondly expect from him."

"I know you not, sir," said the lady, drawing herself up with all the pride of offended rank and beauty; "I know you not—and the insolent familiarity with which you apply to me the jargon of a troubadour, forms no apology for the violence of a robber."

"To thyself, fair maid," answered De Bracy, in his former tone—"to thine own charms be ascribed whate'er I have done which passed the respect due to her, whom I have chosen queen of my heart, and lodestar of my eyes."

"I repeat to you, Sir Knight, that I know you not, and that no man wearing chain and spurs ought thus to intrude himself upon the presence of an unprotected lady."

"That I am unknown to you," said De Bracy, "is indeed my misfortune; yet let me hope that De Bracy's name has not been always unspoken, when minstrels or heralds have praised deeds of chivalry, whether in the lists or in the battle-field."

"To heralds and to minstrels, then, leave thy praise, Sir Knight," replied Rowena, "more suiting for their mouths than for thine own; and tell me which of them shall record in song, or in book of tourney, the memorable conquest of this night, a conquest obtained over an old man, followed by a few timid hinds; and its booty, an unfortunate maiden, transported against her will to the castle of a robber?"

"You are unjust, Lady Rowena," said the knight, biting his lips in some confusion, and speaking in a tone more natural to him than that of affected gallantry, which he had at first adopted; "yourself free from passion, you can allow no excuse for the frenzy of another, although caused by your own beauty."

"I pray you, Sir Knight," said Rowena, "to cease a language so commonly used by strolling minstrels, that it becomes not the mouth of knights or nobles. Certes, you constrain me to sit down, since you enter upon such commonplace terms, of which each vile crowder hath a stock that might last from hence to Christmas."

"Proud damsel," said De Bracy, incensed at finding his gallant style procured him nothing but contempt—"proud damsel, thou shalt be as proudly encountered. Know then, that I have supported my pretensions to your hand in the way that best suited thy character. It is meeter for thy humour to be wooed with bow and bill, than in set terms, and in courtly language."

"Courtesy of tongue," said Rowena, "when it is used to veil churlishness of deed, is but a knight's girdle around the breast of a base clown. I wonder not that the restraint appears to gall you—more it were for your honour to have retained the dress and language of an outlaw, than to veil the deeds of one under an affectation of gentle language and demeanour."

"You counsel well, lady," said the Norman; "and in the bold language which best justifies bold action I tell thee, thou shalt never leave this castle, or thou shalt leave it as Maurice de Bracy's wife. I am not wont to be baffled in my enterprises, nor needs a Norman noble scrupulously to vindicate his conduct to the Saxon maiden whom he distinguishes by the offer of his hand. Thou art proud, Rowena, and thou art the fitter to be my wife. By what other means couldst thou be raised to high honour and to princely place, saving by my alliance? How else wouldst thou escape from the mean precincts of a country grange, where Saxons herd with the swine which form their wealth, to take thy seat, honoured as thou shouldst be, and shalt be, amid all in England that is distinguished by beauty, or dignified by power?"

"Sir Knight," replied Rowena, "the grange which you contemn hath been my shelter from infancy; and, trust me, when I leave it—should that day ever arrive—it shall be with one who has not learnt to despise the dwelling and manners in which I have been brought up."

"I guess your meaning, lady," said De Bracy, "though you may think it lies too obscure for my apprehension. But dream not, that Richard Coeur de Lion will ever resume his throne, far less that Wilfred of Ivanhoe, his minion, will ever lead thee to his footstool, to be there welcomed as the bride of a favourite. Another suitor might feel jealousy while he touched this string; but my firm purpose cannot be changed by a passion so childish and so hopeless. Know, lady, that this rival is in my power, and that it rests but with me to betray the secret of his being within the castle to Front-de-Boeuf, whose jealousy will be more fatal than mine."

"Wilfred here?" said Rowena, in disdain; "that is as true as that Front-de-Boeuf is his rival."

De Bracy looked at her steadily for an instant.

"Wert thou really ignorant of this?" said he; "didst thou not know that Wilfred of Ivanhoe travelled in the litter of the Jew?—a meet conveyance for the crusader, whose doughty arm was to reconquer the Holy Sepulchre!" And he laughed scornfully.

"And if he is here," said Rowena, compelling herself to a tone of indifference, though trembling with an agony of apprehension which she could not suppress, "in what is he the rival of Front-de-Boeuf? or what has he to fear beyond a short imprisonment, and an honourable ransom, according to the use of chivalry?"

"Rowena," said De Bracy, "art thou, too, deceived by the common error of thy sex, who think there can be no rivalry but that respecting their own charms? Knowest thou not there is a jealousy of ambition and of wealth, as well as of love; and that this our host, Front-de-Boeuf, will push from his road him who opposes his claim to the fair barony of Ivanhoe, as readily, eagerly, and unscrupulously, as if he were preferred to him by some blue-eyed damsel? But smile on my suit, lady, and the wounded champion shall have nothing to fear from Front-de-Boeuf, whom else thou mayst mourn for, as in the hands of one who has never shown compassion."

"Save him, for the love of Heaven!" said Rowena, her firmness giving way under terror for her lover's impending fate.

"I can—I will—it is my purpose," said De Bracy; "for, when Rowena consents to be the bride of De Bracy, who is it shall dare to put forth a violent hand upon her kinsman—the son of her guardian—the companion of her youth? But it is thy love must buy his protection. I am not romantic fool enough to further the fortune, or avert the fate, of one who is likely to be a successful obstacle between me and my wishes. Use thine influence with me in his behalf, and he is safe,—refuse to employ it, Wilfred dies, and thou thyself art not the nearer to freedom."

"Thy language," answered Rowena, "hath in its indifferent bluntness something which cannot be reconciled with the horrors it seems to express. I believe not that thy purpose is so wicked, or thy power so great."

"Flatter thyself, then, with that belief," said De Bracy, "until time shall prove it false. Thy lover lies wounded in this castle—thy preferred lover. He is a bar betwixt Front-de-Boeuf and that which Front-de-Boeuf loves better than either ambition or beauty. What will it cost beyond the blow of a poniard, or the thrust of a javelin, to silence his opposition for ever? Nay, were Front-de-Boeuf afraid to justify a deed so open, let the leech but give his patient a wrong draught—let the chamberlain, or the nurse who tends him, but pluck the pillow from his head, and Wilfred in his present condition, is sped without the effusion of blood. Cedric also—"

"And Cedric also," said Rowena, repeating his words; "my noble—my generous guardian! I deserved the evil I have encountered, for forgetting his fate even in that of his son!"

"Cedric's fate also depends upon thy determination," said De Bracy; "and I leave thee to form it."

Hitherto, Rowena had sustained her part in this trying scene with undismayed courage, but it was because she had not considered the danger as serious and imminent. Her disposition was naturally that which physiognomists consider as proper to fair complexions, mild, timid, and gentle; but it had been tempered, and, as it were, hardened, by the circumstances of her education. Accustomed to see the will of all, even of Cedric himself, (sufficiently arbitrary with others,) give way before her wishes, she had acquired that sort of courage and self-confidence which arises from the habitual and constant deference of the circle in which we move. She could scarce conceive the possibility of her will being opposed, far less that of its being treated with total disregard.

Her haughtiness and habit of domination was, therefore, a fictitious character, induced over that which was natural to her, and it deserted her when her eyes were opened to the extent of her own danger, as well as that of her lover and her guardian; and when she found her will, the slightest expression of which was wont to command respect and attention, now placed in opposition to that of a man of a strong, fierce, and determined mind, who possessed the advantage over her, and was resolved to use it, she quailed before him.

After casting her eyes around, as if to look for the aid which was nowhere to be found, and after a few broken interjections, she raised her hands to heaven, and burst into a passion of uncontrolled vexation and sorrow. It was impossible to see so beautiful a creature in such extremity without feeling for her, and De Bracy was not unmoved, though he was yet more embarrassed than touched. He had, in truth, gone too far to recede; and yet, in Rowena's present condition, she could not be acted on either by argument or threats. He paced the apartment to and fro, now vainly exhorting the terrified maiden to compose herself, now hesitating concerning his own line of conduct.

If, thought he, I should be moved by the tears and sorrow of this disconsolate damsel, what should I reap but the loss of these fair hopes for which I have encountered so much risk, and the ridicule of Prince John and his jovial comrades? "And yet," he said to himself, "I feel myself ill framed for the part which I am playing. I cannot look on so fair a face while it is disturbed with agony, or on those eyes when they are drowned in tears. I would she had retained her original haughtiness of disposition, or that I had a larger share of Front-de-Boeuf's thrice-tempered hardness of heart!"

Agitated by these thoughts, he could only bid the unfortunate Rowena be comforted, and assure her, that as yet she had no reason for the excess of despair to which she was now giving way. But in this task of consolation De Bracy was interrupted by the horn, "hoarse-winded blowing far and keen," which had at the same time alarmed the other inmates of the castle, and interrupted their several plans of avarice and of license. Of them all, perhaps, De Bracy least regretted the interruption; for his conference with the Lady Rowena had arrived at a point, where he found it equally difficult to prosecute or to resign his enterprise.

And here we cannot but think it necessary to offer some better proof than the incidents of an idle tale, to vindicate the melancholy representation of manners which has been just laid before the reader. It is grievous to think that those valiant barons, to whose stand against the crown the liberties of England were indebted for their existence, should themselves have been such dreadful oppressors, and capable of excesses contrary not only to the laws of England, but to those of nature and humanity. But, alas! we have only to extract from the industrious Henry one of those numerous passages which he has collected from contemporary historians, to prove that fiction itself can hardly reach the dark reality of the horrors of the period.

The description given by the author of the Saxon Chronicle of the cruelties exercised in the reign of King Stephen by the great barons and lords of castles, who were all Normans, affords a strong proof of the excesses of which they were capable when their passions were inflamed. "They grievously oppressed the poor people by building castles; and when they were built, they filled them with wicked men, or rather devils, who seized both men and women who they imagined had any money, threw them into prison, and put them to more cruel tortures than the martyrs ever endured. They suffocated some in mud, and suspended others by the feet, or the head, or the thumbs, kindling fires below them. They squeezed the heads of some with knotted cords till they pierced their brains, while they threw others into dungeons swarming with serpents, snakes, and toads." But it would be cruel to put the reader to the pain of perusing the remainder of this description.

As another instance of these bitter fruits of conquest, and perhaps the strongest that can be quoted, we may mention, that the Princess Matilda, though a daughter of the King of Scotland, and afterwards both Queen of England, niece to Edgar Atheling, and mother to the Empress of Germany, the daughter, the wife, and the mother of monarchs, was obliged, during her early residence for education in England, to assume the veil of a nun, as the only means of escaping the licentious pursuit of the Norman nobles. This excuse she stated before a great council of the clergy of England, as the sole reason for her having taken the religious habit. The assembled clergy admitted the validity of the plea, and the notoriety of the circumstances upon which it was founded; giving thus an indubitable and most remarkable testimony to the existence of that disgraceful license by which that age was stained. It was a matter of public knowledge, they said, that after the conquest of King William, his Norman followers, elated by so great a victory, acknowledged no law but their own wicked pleasure, and not only despoiled the conquered Saxons of their lands and their goods, but invaded the honour of their wives and of their daughters with the most unbridled license; and hence it was then common for matrons and maidens of noble families to assume the veil, and take shelter in convents, not as called thither by the vocation of God, but solely to preserve their honour from the unbridled wickedness of man.

Such and so licentious were the times, as announced by the public declaration of the assembled clergy, recorded by Eadmer; and we need add nothing more to vindicate the probability of the scenes which we have detailed, and are about to detail, upon the more apocryphal authority of the Wardour MS.

XXIV.

I'll woo her as the lion woos his bride.

— DOUGLAS

While the scenes we have described were passing in other parts of the castle, the Jewess Rebecca awaited her fate in a distant and sequestered turret. Hither she had been led by two of her disguised ravishers, and on being thrust into the little cell, she found herself in the presence of an old sibyl, who kept murmuring to herself a Saxon rhyme, as if to beat time to the revolving dance which her spindle was performing upon the floor. The hag raised her head as Rebecca entered, and scowled at the fair Jewess with the malignant envy with which old age and ugliness, when united with evil conditions, are apt to look upon youth and beauty.

"Thou must up and away, old house-cricket," said one of the men; "our noble master commands it—Thou must e'en leave this chamber to a fairer guest."

"Ay," grumbled the hag, "even thus is service requited. I have known when my bare word would have cast the best man-at-arms among ye out of saddle and out of service; and now must I up and away at the command of every groom such as thou."

"Good Dame Urfried," said the other man, "stand not to reason on it, but up and away. Lords' hests must be listened to with a quick ear. Thou hast had thy day, old dame, but thy sun has long been set. Thou art now the very emblem of an old warhorse turned out on the barren heath—thou hast had thy paces in thy time, but now a broken amble is the best of them—Come, amble off with thee."

"Ill omens dog ye both!" said the old woman; "and a kennel be your buryingplace! May the evil demon Zernebock tear me limb from limb, if I leave my own cell ere I have spun out the hemp on my distaff!"

"Answer it to our lord, then, old housefiend," said the man, and retired; leaving Rebecca in company with the old woman, upon whose presence she had been thus unwillingly forced.

"What devil's deed have they now in the wind?" said the old hag, murmuring to herself, yet from time to time casting a sidelong and malignant glance at Rebecca; "but it is easy to guess—Bright eyes, black locks, and a skin like paper, ere the priest stains it with his black unguent—Ay, it is easy to guess why they send her to this lone turret, whence a shriek could no more be heard than at the depth of five hundred fathoms beneath the earth.—Thou wilt have owls for thy neighbours, fair one; and their screams will be heard as far, and as much regarded, as thine own. Outlandish, too," she said, marking the dress and turban of Rebecca—"What country art thou of? —a Saracen? or an Egyptian?—Why dost not answer?—thou canst weep, canst thou not speak?"

"Be not angry, good mother," said Rebecca.

"Thou needst say no more," replied Urfried "men know a fox by the train, and a Jewess by her tongue."

"For the sake of mercy," said Rebecca, "tell me what I am to expect as the conclusion of the violence which hath dragged me hither! Is it my life they seek, to atone for my religion? I will lay it down cheerfully."

"Thy life, minion?" answered the sibyl; "what would taking thy life pleasure them?—Trust me, thy life is in no peril. Such usage shalt thou have as was once thought good enough for a noble Saxon maiden. And shall a Jewess, like thee, repine because she hath no better? Look at me—I was as young and twice as fair as thou, when Front-de-Boeuf, father of this Reginald, and his Normans, stormed this castle. My father and his seven sons defended their inheritance from story to story, from chamber to chamber—There was not a room, not a step of the stair, that was not slippery with their blood. They died—they died every man; and ere their bodies were cold, and ere their blood was dried, I had become the prey and the scorn of the conqueror!"

"Is there no help?—Are there no means of escape?" said Rebecca—"Richly, richly would I requite thine aid."

"Think not of it," said the hag; "from hence there is no escape but through the gates of death; and it is late, late," she added, shaking her grey head, "ere these open to us—Yet it is comfort to think that we leave behind us on earth those who shall be wretched as ourselves. Fare thee well, Jewess!—Jew or Gentile, thy fate would be the same; for thou hast to do with them that have neither scruple nor pity. Fare thee well, I say. My thread is spun out—thy task is yet to begin."

"Stay! stay! for Heaven's sake!" said Rebecca; "stay, though it be to curse and to revile me—thy presence is yet some protection."

"The presence of the mother of God were no protection," answered the old woman. "There she stands," pointing to a rude image of the Virgin Mary, "see if she can avert the fate that awaits thee."

She left the room as she spoke, her features writhed into a sort of sneering laugh, which made them seem even more hideous than their habitual frown. She locked the door behind her, and Rebecca might hear her curse every step for its steepness, as slowly and with difficulty she descended the turret-stair.

Rebecca was now to expect a fate even more dreadful than that of Rowena; for what probability was there that either softness or ceremony would be used towards one of her oppressed race, whatever shadow of these might be preserved towards a Saxon heiress? Yet had the Jewess this advantage, that she was better prepared by habits of thought, and by natural strength of mind, to encounter the dangers to which she was exposed. Of a strong and observing character, even from her earliest years, the pomp and wealth which her father displayed within his walls, or which she witnessed in the houses of other wealthy Hebrews, had not been able to blind her to the precarious circumstances under which they were enjoyed. Like Damocles at his celebrated banquet, Rebecca perpetually beheld, amid that gorgeous display, the sword which was suspended over the heads of her people by a single hair. These reflections had tamed and brought down to a pitch of sounder judgment a temper, which, under other circumstances, might have waxed haughty, supercilious, and obstinate.

From her father's example and injunctions, Rebecca had learnt to bear herself courteously towards all who approached her. She could not indeed imitate his excess of subservience, because she was a stranger to the meanness of mind, and to the constant state of timid apprehension, by which it was dictated; but she bore herself with a proud humility, as if submitting to the evil circumstances in which she was placed as the daughter of a despised race, while she felt in her mind the consciousness that she was entitled to hold a higher rank from her merit, than the arbitrary despotism of religious prejudice permitted her to aspire to.

Thus prepared to expect adverse circumstances, she had acquired the firmness necessary for acting under them. Her present situation required all her presence of mind, and she summoned it up accordingly.

Her first care was to inspect the apartment; but it afforded few hopes either of escape or protection. It contained neither secret passage nor trap-door, and unless where the door by which she had entered joined the main building, seemed to be circumscribed by the round exterior wall of the turret. The door had no inside bolt or bar. The single window opened upon an embattled space surmounting the turret, which gave Rebecca, at first sight, some hopes of escaping; but she soon found it had no communication with any other part of the battlements, being an isolated bartisan, or balcony, secured, as usual, by a parapet, with embrasures, at which a few archers might be stationed for defending the turret, and flanking with their shot the wall of the castle on that side.

There was therefore no hope but in passive fortitude, and in that strong reliance on Heaven natural to great and generous characters. Rebecca, however erroneously taught to interpret the promises of Scripture to the chosen people of Heaven, did not err in supposing the present to be their hour of trial, or in trusting that the children of Zion would be one day called in with the fulness of the Gentiles. In the meanwhile, all around her showed that their present state was that of punishment and probation, and that it was their especial duty to suffer without sinning. Thus prepared to consider herself as the victim of misfortune, Rebecca had early reflected upon her own state, and schooled her mind to meet the dangers which she had probably to encounter.

The prisoner trembled, however, and changed colour, when a step was heard on the stair, and the door of the turret-chamber slowly opened, and a tall man, dressed as one of those banditti to whom they owed their misfortune, slowly entered, and shut the door behind him; his cap, pulled down upon his brows, concealed the upper part of his face, and he held his mantle in such a manner as to muffle the rest. In this guise, as if prepared for the execution of some deed, at the thought of which he was himself ashamed, he stood before the affrighted prisoner; yet, ruffian as his dress bespoke him, he seemed at a loss to express what purpose had brought him thither, so that Rebecca, making an effort upon herself, had time to anticipate his explanation. She had already unclasped two costly bracelets and a collar, which she hastened to proffer to the supposed outlaw, concluding naturally that to gratify his avarice was to bespeak his favour.

"Take these," she said, "good friend, and for God's sake be merciful to me and my aged father! These ornaments are of value, yet are they trifling to what he would bestow to obtain our dismissal from this castle, free and uninjured."

"Fair flower of Palestine," replied the outlaw, "these pearls are orient, but they yield in whiteness to your teeth; the diamonds are brilliant, but they cannot match your eyes; and ever since I have taken up this wild trade, I have made a vow to prefer beauty to wealth."

"Do not do yourself such wrong," said Rebecca; "take ransom, and have mercy!—Gold will purchase you pleasure,—to misuse us, could only bring thee remorse. My father will willingly satiate thy utmost wishes; and if thou wilt act wisely, thou mayst purchase with our spoils thy restoration to civil society—mayst obtain pardon for past errors, and be placed beyond the necessity of committing more."

"It is well spoken," replied the outlaw in French, finding it difficult probably to sustain, in Saxon, a conversation which Rebecca had opened in that language; "but know, bright lily of the vale of Baca! that thy father is already in the hands of a powerful alchemist, who knows how to convert into gold and silver even the rusty bars of a dungeon grate. The venerable Isaac is subjected to an alembic, which will distil from him all he holds dear, without any assistance from my requests or thy entreaty. The ransom must be paid by love and beauty, and in no other coin will I accept it."

"Thou art no outlaw," said Rebecca, in the same language in which he addressed her; "no outlaw had refused such offers. No outlaw in this land uses the dialect in which thou hast spoken. Thou art no outlaw, but a Norman—a Norman, noble perhaps in birth—O, be so in thy actions, and cast off this fearful mask of outrage and violence!"

"And thou, who canst guess so truly," said Brian de Bois-Guilbert, dropping the mantle from his face, "art no true daughter of Israel, but in all, save youth and beauty, a very witch of Endor. I am not an outlaw, then, fair rose of Sharon. And I am one who will be more prompt to hang thy neck and arms with pearls and diamonds, which so well become them, than to deprive thee of these ornaments."

"What wouldst thou have of me," said Rebecca, "if not my wealth?—We can have nought in common between us—you are a Christian—I am a Jewess.—Our union were contrary to the laws, alike of the church and the synagogue."

"It were so, indeed," replied the Templar, laughing; "wed with a Jewess? 'Despardieux!'—Not if she were the Queen of Sheba! And know, besides, sweet daughter of Zion, that were the most Christian king to offer me his most Christian daughter, with Languedoc for a dowery, I could not wed her. It is against my vow to love any maiden, otherwise than 'par amours', as I will love thee. I am a Templar. Behold the cross of my Holy Order."

"Darest thou appeal to it," said Rebecca, "on an occasion like the present?"

"And if I do so," said the Templar, "it concerns not thee, who art no believer in the blessed sign of our salvation."

"I believe as my fathers taught," said Rebecca; "and may God forgive my belief if erroneous! But you, Sir Knight, what is yours, when you appeal without scruple to that which you deem most holy, even while you are about to transgress the most solemn of your vows as a knight, and as a man of religion?"

"It is gravely and well preached, O daughter of Sirach!" answered the Templar; "but, gentle Ecclesiastics, thy narrow Jewish prejudices make thee blind to our high privilege. Marriage were an enduring crime on the part of a Templar; but what lesser folly I may practise, I shall speedily be absolved from at the next Preceptory of our Order. Not the wisest of monarchs, not his father, whose examples you must needs allow are weighty, claimed wider privileges than we poor soldiers of the Temple of Zion have won by our zeal in its defence. The protectors of Solomon's Temple may claim license by the example of Solomon."

"If thou readest the Scripture," said the Jewess, "and the lives of the saints, only to justify thine own license and profligacy, thy crime is like that of him who extracts poison from the most healthful and necessary herbs."

The eyes of the Templar flashed fire at this reproof—"Hearken," he said, "Rebecca; I have hitherto spoken mildly to thee, but now my language shall be that of a conqueror. Thou art the captive of my bow and spear—subject to my will by the laws of all nations; nor will I abate an inch of my right, or abstain from taking by violence what thou refusest to entreaty or necessity."

"Stand back," said Rebecca—"stand back, and hear me ere thou offerest to commit a sin so deadly! My strength thou mayst indeed overpower for God made women weak, and trusted their defence to man's generosity. But I will proclaim thy villainy, Templar, from one end of Europe to the other. I will owe to the superstition of thy brethren what their compassion might refuse me, Each Preceptory—each Chapter of thy Order, shall learn, that, like a heretic, thou hast sinned with a Jewess. Those who tremble not at thy crime, will hold thee accursed for having so far dishonoured the cross thou wearest, as to follow a daughter of my people."

"Thou art keen-witted, Jewess," replied the Templar, well aware of the truth of what she spoke, and that the rules of his Order condemned in the most positive manner, and under high penalties, such intrigues as he now prosecuted, and that, in some instances, even degradation had followed upon it—"thou art sharp-witted," he said; "but loud must be thy voice of complaint, if it is heard beyond the iron walls of this castle; within these, murmurs, laments, appeals to justice, and screams for help, die alike silent away. One thing only can save thee, Rebecca. Submit to thy fate—embrace our religion, and thou shalt go forth in such state, that many a Norman lady shall yield as well in pomp as in beauty to the favourite of the best lance among the defenders of the Temple."

"Submit to my fate!" said Rebecca—"and, sacred Heaven! to what fate?—embrace thy religion! and what religion can it be that harbours such a villain?—THOU the best lance of the Templars!—Craven knight!—forsworn priest! I spit at thee, and I defy thee.—The God of Abraham's promise hath opened an escape to his daughter—even from this abyss of infamy!"

As she spoke, she threw open the latticed window which led to the bartisan, and in an instant after, stood on the very verge of the parapet, with not the slightest screen between her and the tremendous depth below. Unprepared for such a desperate effort, for she had hitherto stood perfectly motionless, Bois-Guilbert had neither time to intercept nor to stop her. As he offered to advance, she exclaimed, "Remain where thou art, proud Templar, or at thy choice advance!—one foot nearer, and I plunge myself from the precipice; my body shall be crushed out of the very form of humanity upon the stones of that court-yard, ere it become the victim of thy brutality!"

As she spoke this, she clasped her hands and extended them towards heaven, as if imploring mercy on her soul before she made the final plunge. The Templar hesitated, and a resolution which had never yielded to pity or distress, gave way to his admiration of her fortitude. "Come down," he said, "rash girl!—I swear by earth, and sea, and sky, I will offer thee no offence."

"I will not trust thee, Templar," said Rebecca; "thou hast taught me better how to estimate the virtues of thine Order. The next Preceptory would grant thee absolution for an oath, the keeping of which concerned nought but the honour or the dishonour of a miserable Jewish maiden."

"You do me injustice," exclaimed the Templar fervently; "I swear to you by the name which I bear—by the cross on my bosom—by the sword on my side—by the ancient crest of my fathers do I swear, I will do thee no injury whatsoever! If not for thyself, yet for thy father's sake forbear! I will be his friend, and in this castle he will need a powerful one."

"Alas!" said Rebecca, "I know it but too well—dare I trust thee?"

"May my arms be reversed, and my name dishonoured," said Brian de Bois-Guilbert, "if thou shalt have reason to complain of me! Many a law, many a commandment have I broken, but my word never."

"I will then trust thee," said Rebecca, "thus far;" and she descended from the verge of the battlement, but remained standing close by one of the embrasures, or "machicolles", as they were then called.—"Here," she said, "I take my stand. Remain where thou art, and if thou shalt attempt to diminish by one step the distance now between us, thou shalt see that the Jewish maiden will rather trust her soul with God, than her honour to the Templar!"

While Rebecca spoke thus, her high and firm resolve, which corresponded so well with the expressive beauty of her countenance, gave to her looks, air, and manner, a dignity that seemed more than mortal. Her glance quailed not, her cheek blanched not, for the fear of a fate so instant and so horrible; on the contrary, the thought that she had her fate at her command, and could escape at will from infamy to death, gave a yet deeper colour of carnation to her complexion, and a yet more brilliant fire to her eye. Bois-Guilbert, proud himself and high-spirited, thought he had never beheld beauty so animated and so commanding.

"Let there be peace between us, Rebecca," he said.

"Peace, if thou wilt," answered Rebecca—"Peace—but with this space between."

"Thou needst no longer fear me," said Bois-Guilbert.

"I fear thee not," replied she; "thanks to him that reared this dizzy tower so high, that nought could fall from it and live—thanks to him, and to the God of Israel!—I fear thee not."

"Thou dost me injustice," said the Templar; "by earth, sea, and sky, thou dost me injustice! I am not naturally that which you have seen me, hard, selfish, and relentless. It was woman that taught me cruelty, and on woman therefore I have exercised it; but not upon such as thou. Hear me, Rebecca—Never did knight take lance in his hand with a heart more devoted to the lady of his love than Brian de Bois-Guilbert. She, the daughter of a petty baron, who boasted for all his domains but a ruinous tower, and an unproductive vineyard, and some few leagues of the barren Landes of Bourdeaux, her name was known wherever deeds of arms were done, known wider than that of many a lady's that had a county for a dowery.—Yes," he continued, pacing up and down the little platform, with an animation in which he seemed to lose all consciousness of Rebecca's presence—"Yes, my deeds, my danger, my blood, made the name of Adelaide de Montemare known from the court of Castile to that of Byzantium. And how was I requited?—When I returned with my dear-bought honours, purchased by toil and blood, I found her wedded to a Gascon squire, whose name was never heard beyond the limits of his own paltry domain! Truly did I love her, and bitterly did I revenge me of her broken faith! But my vengeance has recoiled on myself. Since that day I have separated myself from life and its ties—My manhood must know no domestic home—must be soothed by no affectionate wife—My age must know no kindly hearth—My grave must be solitary, and no offspring must outlive me, to bear the ancient name of Bois-Guilbert. At the feet of my Superior I have laid down the right of self-action—the privilege of independence. The Templar, a serf in all but the name, can possess neither lands nor goods, and lives, moves, and breathes, but at the will and pleasure of another."

"Alas!" said Rebecca, "what advantages could compensate for such an absolute sacrifice?"

"The power of vengeance, Rebecca," replied the Templar, "and the prospects of ambition."

"An evil recompense," said Rebecca, "for the surrender of the rights which are dearest to humanity."

"Say not so, maiden," answered the Templar; "revenge is a feast for the gods! And if they have reserved it, as priests tell us, to themselves, it is because they hold it an enjoyment too precious for the possession of mere mortals.—And ambition? it is a temptation which could disturb even the bliss of heaven itself."—He paused a moment, and then added, "Rebecca! she who could prefer death to dishonour, must have a proud and a powerful soul. Mine thou must be!—Nay, start not," he added, "it must be with thine own consent, and on thine own terms. Thou must consent to share with me hopes more extended than can be viewed from the throne of a monarch!—Hear me ere you answer and judge ere you refuse.—The Templar loses, as thou hast said, his social rights, his power of free agency, but he becomes a member and a limb of a mighty body, before which thrones already tremble,—even as the single drop of rain which mixes with the sea becomes an individual part of that resistless ocean, which undermines rocks and ingulfs royal armadas. Such a swelling flood is that powerful league. Of this mighty Order I am no mean member, but already one of the Chief Commanders, and may well aspire one day to hold the baton of Grand Master. The poor soldiers of the Temple will not alone place their foot upon the necks of kings —a hemp-sandall'd monk can do that. Our mailed step shall ascend their throne— our gauntlet shall wrench the sceptre from their gripe. Not the reign of your vainly-expected Messiah offers such power to your dispersed tribes as my ambition may aim at. I have sought but a kindred spirit to share it, and I have found such in thee."

"Sayest thou this to one of my people?" answered Rebecca. "Bethink thee—"

"Answer me not," said the Templar, "by urging the difference of our creeds; within our secret conclaves we hold these nursery tales in derision. Think not we long remained blind to the idiotical folly of our founders, who forswore every delight of life for the pleasure of dying martyrs by hunger, by thirst, and by pestilence, and by the swords of savages, while they vainly strove to defend a barren desert, valuable only in the eyes of superstition. Our Order soon adopted bolder and wider views, and found out a better indemnification for our sacrifices. Our immense possessions in every kingdom of Europe, our high military fame, which brings within our circle the flower of chivalry from every Christian clime—these are dedicated to ends of which our pious founders little dreamed, and which are equally concealed from such weak spirits as embrace our Order on the ancient principles, and whose superstition makes them our passive tools. But I will not further withdraw the veil of our mysteries. That bugle-sound announces something which may require my presence. Think on what I have said.—Farewell!—I do not say forgive me the violence I have threatened, for it was necessary to the display of thy character. Gold can be only known by the application of the touchstone. I will soon return, and hold further conference with thee."

He re-entered the turret-chamber, and descended the stair, leaving Rebecca scarcely more terrified at the prospect of the death to which she had been so lately exposed, than at the furious ambition of the bold bad man in whose power she found herself so unhappily placed. When she entered the turret-chamber, her first duty was to return thanks to the God of Jacob for the protection which he had afforded her, and to implore its continuance for her and for her father. Another name glided into her petition—it was that of the wounded Christian, whom fate had placed in the hands of bloodthirsty men, his avowed enemies. Her heart indeed checked her, as if, even in communing with the Deity in prayer, she mingled in her devotions the recollection of one with whose fate hers could have no alliance—a Nazarene, and an enemy to her faith. But the petition was already breathed, nor could all the narrow prejudices of her sect induce Rebecca to wish it recalled.

XXV.

A damn'd cramp piece of penmanship as ever I saw in my life!

— SHE STOOPS TO CONQUER

When the Templar reached the hall of the castle, he found De Bracy already there. "Your love-suit," said De Bracy, "hath, I suppose, been disturbed, like mine, by this obstreperous summons. But you have come later and more reluctantly, and therefore I presume your interview has proved more agreeable than mine."

"Has your suit, then, been unsuccessfully paid to the Saxon heiress?" said the Templar.

"By the bones of Thomas a Becket," answered De Bracy, "the Lady Rowena must have heard that I cannot endure the sight of women's tears."

"Away!" said the Templar; "thou a leader of a Free Company, and regard a woman's tears! A few drops sprinkled on the torch of love, make the flame blaze the brighter."

"Gramercy for the few drops of thy sprinkling," replied De Bracy; "but this damsel hath wept enough to extinguish a beacon-light. Never was such wringing of hands and such overflowing of eyes, since the days of St Niobe, of whom Prior Aymer told us. A water-fiend hath possessed the fair Saxon."

"A legion of fiends have occupied the bosom of the Jewess," replied the Templar; "for, I think no single one, not even Apollyon himself, could have inspired such indomitable pride and resolution.—But where is Front-de-Boeuf? That horn is sounded more and more clamorously."

"He is negotiating with the Jew, I suppose," replied De Bracy, coolly; "probably the howls of Isaac have drowned the blast of the bugle. Thou mayst know, by experience, Sir Brian, that a Jew parting with his treasures on such terms as our friend Front-de-Boeuf is like to offer, will raise a clamour loud enough to be heard over twenty horns and trumpets to boot. But we will make the vassals call him."

They were soon after joined by Front-de-Boeuf, who had been disturbed in his tyrannic cruelty in the manner with which the reader is acquainted, and had only tarried to give some necessary directions.

"Let us see the cause of this cursed clamour," said Front-de-Boeuf—"here is a letter, and, if I mistake not, it is in Saxon."

He looked at it, turning it round and round as if he had had really some hopes of coming at the meaning by inverting the position of the paper, and then handed it to De Bracy.

"It may be magic spells for aught I know," said De Bracy, who possessed his full proportion of the ignorance which characterised the chivalry of the period. "Our chaplain attempted to teach me to write," he said, "but all my letters were formed like spear-heads and sword-blades, and so the old shaveling gave up the task."

"Give it me," said the Templar. "We have that of the priestly character, that we have some knowledge to enlighten our valour."

"Let us profit by your most reverend knowledge, then," said De Bracy; "what says the scroll?"

"It is a formal letter of defiance," answered the Templar; "but, by our Lady of Bethlehem, if it be not a foolish jest, it is the most extraordinary cartel that ever was sent across the drawbridge of a baronial castle."

"Jest!" said Front-de-Boeuf, "I would gladly know who dares jest with me in such a matter!—Read it, Sir Brian."

The Templar accordingly read it as follows:—"I, Wamba, the son of Witless, Jester to a noble and free-born man, Cedric of Rotherwood, called the Saxon,—And I, Gurth, the son of Beowulph, the swineherd——"

"Thou art mad," said Front-de-Boeuf, interrupting the reader.

"By St Luke, it is so set down," answered the Templar. Then resuming his task, he went on,—"I, Gurth, the son of Beowulph, swineherd unto the said Cedric, with the assistance of our allies and confederates, who make common cause with us in this our feud, namely, the good knight, called for the present 'Le Noir Faineant', and the stout yeoman, Robert Locksley, called Cleave-the-Wand. Do you, Reginald Front de-Boeuf, and your allies and accomplices whomsoever, to wit, that whereas you have, without cause given or feud declared, wrongfully and by mastery seized upon the person of our lord and master the said Cedric; also upon the person of a noble and freeborn damsel, the Lady Rowena of Hargottstandstede; also upon the person of a noble and freeborn man, Athelstane of Coningsburgh; also upon the persons of certain freeborn men, their 'cnichts'; also upon certain serfs, their born bondsmen; also upon a certain Jew, named Isaac of York, together with his daughter, a Jewess, and certain horses and mules: Which noble persons, with their 'cnichts' and slaves, and also with the horses and mules, Jew and Jewess beforesaid, were all in peace with his majesty, and travelling as liege subjects upon the king's highway; therefore we require and demand that the said noble persons, namely, Cedric of Rotherwood, Rowena of Hargottstandstede, Athelstane of Coningsburgh, with their servants, 'cnichts', and followers, also the horses and mules, Jew and Jewess aforesaid, together with all goods and chattels to them pertaining, be, within an hour after the delivery hereof, delivered to us, or to those whom we shall appoint to receive the same, and that untouched and unharmed in body and goods. Failing of which, we do pronounce to you, that we hold ye as robbers and traitors, and will wager our bodies against ye in battle, siege, or otherwise, and do our utmost to your annoyance and destruction. Wherefore may God have you in his keeping.—Signed by us upon the eve of St Withold's day, under the great trysting oak in the Hart-hill Walk, the above being written by a holy man, Clerk to God, our Lady, and St Dunstan, in the Chapel of Copmanhurst."

At the bottom of this document was scrawled, in the first place, a rude sketch of a cock's head and comb, with a legend expressing this hieroglyphic to be the sign-manual of Wamba, son of Witless. Under this respectable emblem stood a cross, stated to be the mark of Gurth, the son of Beowulph. Then was written, in rough bold characters, the words, "Le Noir Faineant". And, to conclude the whole, an arrow, neatly enough drawn, was described as the mark of the yeoman Locksley.

The knights heard this uncommon document read from end to end, and then gazed upon each other in silent amazement, as being utterly at a loss to know what it could portend. De Bracy was the first to break silence by an uncontrollable fit of laughter, wherein he was joined, though with more moderation, by the Templar. Front-de-Boeuf, on the contrary, seemed impatient of their ill-timed jocularity.

"I give you plain warning," he said, "fair sirs, that you had better consult how to bear yourselves under these circumstances, than give way to such misplaced merriment."

"Front-de-Boeuf has not recovered his temper since his late overthrow," said De Bracy to the Templar; "he is cowed at the very idea of a cartel, though it come but from a fool and a swineherd."

"By St Michael," answered Front-de-Boeuf, "I would thou couldst stand the whole brunt of this adventure thyself, De Bracy. These fellows dared not have acted with such inconceivable impudence, had they not been supported by some strong bands. There are enough of outlaws in this forest to resent my protecting the deer. I did but tie one fellow, who was taken redhanded and in the fact, to the horns of a wild stag, which gored him to death in five minutes, and I had as many arrows shot at me as there were launched against yonder target at Ashby.—Here, fellow," he added, to one of his attendants, "hast thou sent out to see by what force this precious challenge is to be supported?"

"There are at least two hundred men assembled in the woods," answered a squire who was in attendance.

"Here is a proper matter!" said Front-de-Boeuf, "this comes of lending you the use of my castle, that cannot manage your undertaking quietly, but you must bring this nest of hornets about my ears!"

"Of hornets?" said De Bracy; "of stingless drones rather; a band of lazy knaves, who take to the wood, and destroy the venison rather than labour for their maintenance."

"Stingless!" replied Front-de-Boeuf; "fork-headed shafts of a cloth-yard in length, and these shot within the breadth of a French crown, are sting enough."

"For shame, Sir Knight!" said the Templar. "Let us summon our people, and sally forth upon them. One knight—ay, one man-at-arms, were enough for twenty such peasants."

"Enough, and too much," said De Bracy; "I should only be ashamed to couch lance against them."

"True," answered Front-de-Boeuf; "were they black Turks or Moors, Sir Templar, or the craven peasants of France, most valiant De Bracy; but these are English yeomen, over whom we shall have no advantage, save what we may derive from our arms and horses, which will avail us little in the glades of the forest. Sally, saidst thou? we have scarce men enough to defend the castle. The best of mine are at York; so is all your band, De Bracy; and we have scarcely twenty, besides the handful that were engaged in this mad business."

"Thou dost not fear," said the Templar, "that they can assemble in force sufficient to attempt the castle?"

"Not so, Sir Brian," answered Front-de-Boeuf. "These outlaws have indeed a daring captain; but without machines, scaling ladders, and experienced leaders, my castle may defy them."

"Send to thy neighbours," said the Templar, "let them assemble their people, and come to the rescue of three knights, besieged by a jester and a swineherd in the baronial castle of Reginald Front-de-Boeuf!"

"You jest, Sir Knight," answered the baron; "but to whom should I send?—Malvoisin is by this time at York with his retainers, and so are my other allies; and so should I have been, but for this infernal enterprise."

"Then send to York, and recall our people," said De Bracy. "If they abide the shaking of my standard, or the sight of my Free Companions, I will give them credit for the boldest outlaws ever bent bow in green-wood."

"And who shall bear such a message?" said Front-de-Boeuf; "they will beset every path, and rip the errand out of his bosom.—I have it," he added, after pausing for a moment—"Sir Templar, thou canst write as well as read, and if we can but find the writing materials of my chaplain, who died a twelvemonth since in the midst of his Christmas carousals—"

"So please ye," said the squire, who was still in attendance, "I think old Urfried has them somewhere in keeping, for love of the confessor. He was the last man, I have heard her tell, who ever said aught to her, which man ought in courtesy to address to maid or matron."

"Go, search them out, Engelred," said Front-de-Boeuf; "and then, Sir Templar, thou shalt return an answer to this bold challenge."

"I would rather do it at the sword's point than at that of the pen," said Bois-Guilbert; "but be it as you will."

He sat down accordingly, and indited, in the French language, an epistle of the following tenor:—"Sir Reginald Front-de-Boeuf, with his noble and knightly allies and confederates, receive no defiances at the hands of slaves, bondsmen, or fugitives. If the person calling himself the Black Knight have indeed a claim to the honours of chivalry, he ought to know that he stands degraded by his present association, and has no right to ask reckoning at the hands of good men of noble blood. Touching the prisoners we have made, we do in Christian charity require you to send a man of religion, to receive their confession, and reconcile them with God; since it is our fixed intention to execute them this morning before noon, so that their heads being placed on the battlements, shall show to all men how lightly we esteem those who have bestirred themselves in their rescue. Wherefore, as above, we require you to send a priest to reconcile them to God, in doing which you shall render them the last earthly service."

This letter being folded, was delivered to the squire, and by him to the messenger who waited without, as the answer to that which he had brought.

The yeoman having thus accomplished his mission, returned to the head-quarters of the allies, which were for the present established under a venerable oak-tree, about three arrow-flights distant from the castle. Here Wamba and Gurth, with their allies the Black Knight and Locksley, and the jovial hermit, awaited with impatience an answer to their summons. Around, and at a distance from them, were seen many a bold yeoman, whose silvan dress and weatherbeaten countenances showed the ordinary nature of their occupation. More than two hundred had already assembled, and others were fast coming in. Those whom they obeyed as leaders were only distinguished from the others by a feather in the cap, their dress, arms, and equipments being in all other respects the same.

Besides these bands, a less orderly and a worse armed force, consisting of the Saxon inhabitants of the neighbouring township, as well as many bondsmen and servants from Cedric's extensive estate, had already arrived, for the purpose of assisting in his rescue. Few of these were armed otherwise than with such rustic weapons as necessity sometimes converts to military purposes. Boar-spears, scythes, flails, and the like, were their chief arms; for the Normans, with the usual policy of conquerors, were jealous of permitting to the vanquished Saxons the possession or the use of swords and spears. These circumstances rendered the assistance of the Saxons far from being so formidable to the besieged, as the strength of the men themselves, their superior numbers, and the animation inspired by a just cause, might otherwise well have made them. It was to the leaders of this motley army that the letter of the Templar was now delivered.

Reference was at first made to the chaplain for an exposition of its contents.

"By the crook of St Dunstan," said that worthy ecclesiastic, "which hath brought more sheep within the sheepfold than the crook of e'er another saint in Paradise, I swear that I cannot expound unto you this jargon, which, whether it be French or Arabic, is beyond my guess."

He then gave the letter to Gurth, who shook his head gruffly, and passed it to Wamba. The Jester looked at each of the four corners of the paper with such a grin of affected intelligence as a monkey is apt to assume upon similar occasions, then cut a caper, and gave the letter to Locksley.

"If the long letters were bows, and the short letters broad arrows, I might know something of the matter," said the brave yeoman; "but as the matter stands, the meaning is as safe, for me, as the stag that's at twelve miles distance."

"I must be clerk, then," said the Black Knight; and taking the letter from Locksley, he first read it over to himself, and then explained the meaning in Saxon to his confederates.

"Execute the noble Cedric!" exclaimed Wamba; "by the rood, thou must be mistaken, Sir Knight."

"Not I, my worthy friend," replied the knight, "I have explained the words as they are here set down."

"Then, by St Thomas of Canterbury," replied Gurth, "we will have the castle, should we tear it down with our hands!"

"We have nothing else to tear it with," replied Wamba; "but mine are scarce fit to make mammocks of freestone and mortar."

"'Tis but a contrivance to gain time," said Locksley; "they dare not do a deed for which I could exact a fearful penalty."

"I would," said the Black Knight, "there were some one among us who could obtain admission into the castle, and discover how the case stands with the besieged. Methinks, as they require a confessor to be sent, this holy hermit might at once exercise his pious vocation, and procure us the information we desire."

"A plague on thee, and thy advice!" said the pious hermit; "I tell thee, Sir Slothful Knight, that when I doff my friar's frock, my priesthood, my sanctity, my very Latin, are put off along with it; and when in my green jerkin, I can better kill twenty deer than confess one Christian."

"I fear," said the Black Knight, "I fear greatly, there is no one here that is qualified to take upon him, for the nonce, this same character of father confessor?"

All looked on each other, and were silent.

"I see," said Wamba, after a short pause, "that the fool must be still the fool, and put his neck in the venture which wise men shrink from. You must know, my dear cousins and countrymen, that I wore russet before I wore motley, and was bred to be a friar, until a brain-fever came upon me and left me just wit enough to be a fool. I trust, with the assistance of the good hermit's frock, together with the priesthood, sanctity, and learning which are stitched into the cowl of it, I shall be found qualified to administer both worldly and ghostly comfort to our worthy master Cedric, and his companions in adversity."

"Hath he sense enough, thinkst thou?" said the Black Knight, addressing Gurth.

"I know not," said Gurth; "but if he hath not, it will be the first time he hath wanted wit to turn his folly to account."

"On with the frock, then, good fellow," quoth the Knight, "and let thy master send us an account of their situation within the castle. Their numbers must be few, and it is five to one they may be accessible by a sudden and bold attack. Time wears—away with thee."

"And, in the meantime," said Locksley, "we will beset the place so closely, that not so much as a fly shall carry news from thence. So that, my good friend," he continued, addressing Wamba, "thou mayst assure these tyrants, that whatever violence they exercise on the persons of their prisoners, shall be most severely repaid upon their own."

"Pax vobiscum," said Wamba, who was now muffled in his religious disguise.

And so saying he imitated the solemn and stately deportment of a friar, and departed to execute his mission.

XXVI.

> The hottest horse will oft be cool,
> The dullest will show fire;
> The friar will often play the fool,
> The fool will play the friar.
>
> — OLD SONG

When the Jester, arrayed in the cowl and frock of the hermit, and having his knotted cord twisted round his middle, stood before the portal of the castle of Front-de-Boeuf, the warder demanded of him his name and errand.

"Pax vobiscum," answered the Jester, "I am a poor brother of the Order of St Francis, who come hither to do my office to certain unhappy prisoners now secured within this castle."

"Thou art a bold friar," said the warder, "to come hither, where, saving our own drunken confessor, a cock of thy feather hath not crowed these twenty years."

"Yet I pray thee, do mine errand to the lord of the castle," answered the pretended friar; "trust me it will find good acceptance with him, and the cock shall crow, that the whole castle shall hear him."

"Gramercy," said the warder; "but if I come to shame for leaving my post upon thine errand, I will try whether a friar's grey gown be proof against a grey-goose shaft."

With this threat he left his turret, and carried to the hall of the castle his unwonted intelligence, that a holy friar stood before the gate and demanded instant admission. With no small wonder he received his master's commands to admit the holy man immediately; and, having previously manned the entrance to guard against surprise, he obeyed, without further scruple, the commands which he had received. The harebrained self-conceit which had emboldened Wamba to undertake this dangerous office, was scarce sufficient to support him when he found himself in the presence of a man so dreadful, and so much dreaded, as Reginald Front-de-Boeuf, and he brought out his "pax vobiscum", to which he, in a good measure, trusted for supporting his character, with more anxiety and hesitation than had hitherto accompanied it. But Front-de-Boeuf was accustomed to see men of all ranks tremble in his presence, so that the timidity of the supposed father did not give him any cause of suspicion.

"Who and whence art thou, priest?" said he.

"'Pax vobiscum'," reiterated the Jester, "I am a poor servant of St Francis, who, travelling through this wilderness, have fallen among thieves, (as Scripture hath it,) 'quidam viator incidit in latrones', which thieves have sent me unto this castle in order to do my ghostly office on two persons condemned by your honourable justice."

"Ay, right," answered Front-de-Boeuf; "and canst thou tell me, holy father, the number of those banditti?"

"Gallant sir," answered the Jester, "'nomen illis legio', their name is legion."

"Tell me in plain terms what numbers there are, or, priest, thy cloak and cord will ill protect thee."

"Alas!" said the supposed friar, "'cor meum eructavit', that is to say, I was like to burst with fear! but I conceive they may be—what of yeomen—what of commons, at least five hundred men."

"What!" said the Templar, who came into the hall that moment, "muster the wasps so thick here? it is time to stifle such a mischievous brood." Then taking Front-de-Boeuf aside "Knowest thou the priest?"

"He is a stranger from a distant convent," said Front-de-Boeuf; "I know him not."

"Then trust him not with thy purpose in words," answered the Templar. "Let him carry a written order to De Bracy's company of Free Companions, to repair instantly to their master's aid. In the meantime, and that the shaveling may suspect nothing, permit him to go freely about his task of preparing these Saxon hogs for the slaughter-house."

"It shall be so," said Front-de-Boeuf. And he forthwith appointed a domestic to conduct Wamba to the apartment where Cedric and Athelstane were confined.

The impatience of Cedric had been rather enhanced than diminished by his confinement. He walked from one end of the hall to the other, with the attitude of one who advances to charge an enemy, or to storm the breach of a beleaguered place, sometimes ejaculating to himself, sometimes addressing Athelstane, who stoutly and stoically awaited the issue of the adventure, digesting, in the meantime, with great composure, the liberal meal which he had made at noon, and not greatly interesting himself about the duration of his captivity, which he concluded, would, like all earthly evils, find an end in Heaven's good time.

"'Pax vobiscum'," said the Jester, entering the apartment; "the blessing of St Dunstan, St Dennis, St Duthoc, and all other saints whatsoever, be upon ye and about ye."

"Enter freely," answered Cedric to the supposed friar; "with what intent art thou come hither?"

"To bid you prepare yourselves for death," answered the Jester.

"It is impossible!" replied Cedric, starting. "Fearless and wicked as they are, they dare not attempt such open and gratuitous cruelty!"

"Alas!" said the Jester, "to restrain them by their sense of humanity, is the same as to stop a runaway horse with a bridle of silk thread. Bethink thee, therefore, noble Cedric, and you also, gallant Athelstane, what crimes you have committed in the flesh; for this very day will ye be called to answer at a higher tribunal."

"Hearest thou this, Athelstane?" said Cedric; "we must rouse up our hearts to this last action, since better it is we should die like men, than live like slaves."

"I am ready," answered Athelstane, "to stand the worst of their malice, and shall walk to my death with as much composure as ever I did to my dinner."

"Let us then unto our holy gear, father," said Cedric.

"Wait yet a moment, good uncle," said the Jester, in his natural tone; "better look long before you leap in the dark."

"By my faith," said Cedric, "I should know that voice!"

"It is that of your trusty slave and jester," answered Wamba, throwing back his cowl. "Had you taken a fool's advice formerly, you would not have been here at all. Take a fool's advice now, and you will not be here long."

"How mean'st thou, knave?" answered the Saxon.

"Even thus," replied Wamba; "take thou this frock and cord, which are all the orders I ever had, and march quietly out of the castle, leaving me your cloak and girdle to take the long leap in thy stead."

"Leave thee in my stead!" said Cedric, astonished at the proposal; "why, they would hang thee, my poor knave."

"E'en let them do as they are permitted," said Wamba; "I trust—no disparagement to your birth—that the son of Witless may hang in a chain with as much gravity as the chain hung upon his ancestor the alderman."

"Well, Wamba," answered Cedric, "for one thing will I grant thy request. And that is, if thou wilt make the exchange of garments with Lord Athelstane instead of me."

"No, by St Dunstan," answered Wamba; "there were little reason in that. Good right there is, that the son of Witless should suffer to save the son of Hereward; but little wisdom there were in his dying for the benefit of one whose fathers were strangers to his."

"Villain," said Cedric, "the fathers of Athelstane were monarchs of England!"

"They might be whomsoever they pleased," replied Wamba; "but my neck stands too straight upon my shoulders to have it twisted for their sake. Wherefore, good my master, either take my proffer yourself, or suffer me to leave this dungeon as free as I entered."

"Let the old tree wither," continued Cedric, "so the stately hope of the forest be preserved. Save the noble Athelstane, my trusty Wamba! it is the duty of each who has Saxon blood in his veins. Thou and I will abide together the utmost rage of our injurious oppressors, while he, free and safe, shall arouse the awakened spirits of our countrymen to avenge us."

"Not so, father Cedric," said Athelstane, grasping his hand,—for, when roused to think or act, his deeds and sentiments were not unbecoming his high race—"Not so," he continued; "I would rather remain in this hall a week without food save the prisoner's stinted loaf, or drink save the prisoner's measure of water, than embrace the opportunity to escape which the slave's untaught kindness has purveyed for his master."

"You are called wise men, sirs," said the Jester, "and I a crazed fool; but, uncle Cedric, and cousin Athelstane, the fool shall decide this controversy for ye, and save ye the trouble of straining courtesies any farther. I am like John-a-Duck's mare, that will let no man mount her but John-a-Duck. I came to save my master, and if he will not consent—basta—I can but go away home again. Kind service cannot be chucked from hand to hand like a shuttlecock or stool-ball. I'll hang for no man but my own born master."

"Go, then, noble Cedric," said Athelstane, "neglect not this opportunity. Your presence without may encourage friends to our rescue—your remaining here would ruin us all."

"And is there any prospect, then, of rescue from without?" said Cedric, looking to the Jester.

"Prospect, indeed!" echoed Wamba; "let me tell you, when you fill my cloak, you are wrapped in a general's cassock. Five hundred men are there without, and I was this morning one of the chief leaders. My fool's cap was a casque, and my bauble a truncheon. Well, we shall see what good they will make by exchanging a fool for a wise man. Truly, I fear they will lose in valour what they may gain in discretion. And so farewell, master, and be kind to poor Gurth and his dog Fangs; and let my cockscomb hang in the hall at Rotherwood, in memory that I flung away my life for my master, like a faithful—fool."

The last word came out with a sort of double expression, betwixt jest and earnest. The tears stood in Cedric's eyes.

"Thy memory shall be preserved," he said, "while fidelity and affection have honour upon earth! But that I trust I shall find the means of saving Rowena, and thee, Athelstane, and thee, also, my poor Wamba, thou shouldst not overbear me in this matter."

The exchange of dress was now accomplished, when a sudden doubt struck Cedric.

"I know no language," he said, "but my own, and a few words of their mincing Norman. How shall I bear myself like a reverend brother?"

"The spell lies in two words," replied Wamba—"'Pax vobiscum' will answer all queries. If you go or come, eat or drink, bless or ban, 'Pax vobiscum' carries you through it all. It is as useful to a friar as a broomstick to a witch, or a wand to a conjurer. Speak it but thus, in a deep grave tone,—'Pax vobiscum!'—it is irresistible—Watch and ward, knight and squire, foot and horse, it acts as a charm upon them all. I think, if they bring me out to be hanged to-morrow, as is much to be doubted they may, I will try its weight upon the finisher of the sentence."

"If such prove the case," said the master, "my religious orders are soon taken—'Pax vobiscum'. I trust I shall remember the pass-word.—Noble Athelstane, farewell; and farewell, my poor boy, whose heart might make amends for a weaker head—I will save you, or return and die with you. The royal blood of our Saxon kings shall not be spilt while mine beats in my veins; nor shall one hair fall from the head of the kind knave who risked himself for his master, if Cedric's peril can prevent it.—Farewell."

"Farewell, noble Cedric," said Athelstane; "remember it is the true part of a friar to accept refreshment, if you are offered any."

"Farewell, uncle," added Wamba; "and remember 'Pax vobiscum'."

Thus exhorted, Cedric sallied forth upon his expedition; and it was not long ere he had occasion to try the force of that spell which his Jester had recommended as omnipotent. In a low-arched and dusky passage, by which he endeavoured to work his way to the hall of the castle, he was interrupted by a female form.

"'Pax vobiscum!'" said the pseudo friar, and was endeavouring to hurry past, when a soft voice replied, "'Et vobis—quaso, domine reverendissime, pro misericordia vestra'."

"I am somewhat deaf," replied Cedric, in good Saxon, and at the same time muttered to himself, "A curse on the fool and his 'Pax vobiscum!' I have lost my javelin at the first cast."

It was, however, no unusual thing for a priest of those days to be deaf of his Latin ear, and this the person who now addressed Cedric knew full well.

"I pray you of dear love, reverend father," she replied in his own language, "that you will deign to visit with your ghostly comfort a wounded prisoner of this castle, and have such compassion upon him and us as thy holy office teaches—Never shall good deed so highly advantage thy convent."

"Daughter," answered Cedric, much embarrassed, "my time in this castle will not permit me to exercise the duties of mine office—I must presently forth—there is life and death upon my speed."

"Yet, father, let me entreat you by the vow you have taken on you," replied the suppliant, "not to leave the oppressed and endangered without counsel or succour."

"May the fiend fly away with me, and leave me in Ifrin with the souls of Odin and of Thor!" answered Cedric impatiently, and would probably have proceeded in the same tone of total departure from his spiritual character, when the colloquy was interrupted by the harsh voice of Urfried, the old crone of the turret.

"How, minion," said she to the female speaker, "is this the manner in which you requite the kindness which permitted thee to leave thy prison-cell yonder?—Puttest thou the reverend man to use ungracious language to free himself from the importunities of a Jewess?"

"A Jewess!" said Cedric, availing himself of the information to get clear of their interruption,—"Let me pass, woman! stop me not at your peril. I am fresh from my holy office, and would avoid pollution."

"Come this way, father," said the old hag, "thou art a stranger in this castle, and canst not leave it without a guide. Come hither, for I would speak with thee.—And you, daughter of an accursed race, go to the sick man's chamber, and tend him until my return; and woe betide you if you again quit it without my permission!"

Rebecca retreated. Her importunities had prevailed upon Urfried to suffer her to quit the turret, and Urfried had employed her services where she herself would most gladly have paid them, by the bedside of the wounded Ivanhoe. With an understanding awake to their dangerous situation, and prompt to avail herself of each means of safety which occurred, Rebecca had hoped something from the presence of a man of religion, who, she learned from Urfried, had penetrated into this godless castle. She watched the return of the supposed ecclesiastic, with the purpose of addressing him, and interesting him in favour of the prisoners; with what imperfect success the reader has been just acquainted.

XXVII.

> Fond wretch! and what canst thou relate,
> But deeds of sorrow, shame, and sin?

Thy deeds are proved—thou know'st thy fate;
But come, thy tale—begin—begin.

But I have griefs of other kind,
Troubles and sorrows more severe;
Give me to ease my tortured mind,
Lend to my woes a patient ear;
And let me, if I may not find
A friend to help—find one to hear.

— CRABBE'S HALL OF JUSTICE

When Urfried had with clamours and menaces driven Rebecca back to the apartment from which she had sallied, she proceeded to conduct the unwilling Cedric into a small apartment, the door of which she heedfully secured. Then fetching from a cupboard a stoup of wine and two flagons, she placed them on the table, and said in a tone rather asserting a fact than asking a question, "Thou art Saxon, father—Deny it not," she continued, observing that Cedric hastened not to reply; "the sounds of my native language are sweet to mine ears, though seldom heard save from the tongues of the wretched and degraded serfs on whom the proud Normans impose the meanest drudgery of this dwelling. Thou art a Saxon, father—a Saxon, and, save as thou art a servant of God, a freeman.—Thine accents are sweet in mine ear."

"Do not Saxon priests visit this castle, then?" replied Cedric; "it were, methinks, their duty to comfort the outcast and oppressed children of the soil."

"They come not—or if they come, they better love to revel at the boards of their conquerors," answered Urfried, "than to hear the groans of their countrymen—so, at least, report speaks of them—of myself I can say little. This castle, for ten years, has opened to no priest save the debauched Norman chaplain who partook the nightly revels of Front-de-Boeuf, and he has been long gone to render an account of his stewardship.—But thou art a Saxon—a Saxon priest, and I have one question to ask of thee."

"I am a Saxon," answered Cedric, "but unworthy, surely, of the name of priest. Let me begone on my way—I swear I will return, or send one of our fathers more worthy to hear your confession."

"Stay yet a while," said Urfried; "the accents of the voice which thou hearest now will soon be choked with the cold earth, and I would not descend to it like the beast I have lived. But wine must give me strength to tell the horrors of my tale." She poured out a cup, and drank it with a frightful avidity, which seemed desirous of draining the last drop in the goblet. "It stupifies," she said, looking upwards as she finished her drought, "but it cannot cheer—Partake it, father, if you would hear my tale without sinking down upon the pavement." Cedric would have avoided pledging her in this ominous conviviality, but the sign which she made to him expressed impatience and despair. He complied with her request, and answered her challenge in a large wine-cup; she then proceeded with her story, as if appeased by his complaisance.

"I was not born," she said, "father, the wretch that thou now seest me. I was free, was happy, was honoured, loved, and was beloved. I am now a slave, miserable and degraded—the sport of my masters' passions while I had yet beauty—the object of their contempt, scorn, and hatred, since it has passed away. Dost thou wonder, father, that I should hate mankind, and, above all, the race that has wrought this change in me? Can the wrinkled decrepit hag before thee, whose wrath must vent itself in impotent curses, forget she was once the daughter of the noble Thane of Torquilstone, before whose frown a thousand vassals trembled?"

"Thou the daughter of Torquil Wolfganger!" said Cedric, receding as he spoke; "thou—thou—the daughter of that noble Saxon, my father's friend and companion in arms!"

"Thy father's friend!" echoed Urfried; "then Cedric called the Saxon stands before me, for the noble Hereward of Rotherwood had but one son, whose name is well known among his countrymen. But if thou art Cedric of Rotherwood, why this religious dress?—hast thou too despaired of saving thy country, and sought refuge from oppression in the shade of the convent?"

"It matters not who I am," said Cedric; "proceed, unhappy woman, with thy tale of horror and guilt!—Guilt there must be—there is guilt even in thy living to tell it."

"There is—there is," answered the wretched woman, "deep, black, damning guilt, —guilt, that lies like a load at my breast—guilt, that all the penitential fires of hereafter cannot cleanse.—Yes, in these halls, stained with the noble and pure blood of my father and my brethren—in these very halls, to have lived the paramour of their murderer, the slave at once and the partaker of his pleasures, was to render every breath which I drew of vital air, a crime and a curse."

"Wretched woman!" exclaimed Cedric. "And while the friends of thy father— while each true Saxon heart, as it breathed a requiem for his soul, and those of his valiant sons, forgot not in their prayers the murdered Ulrica—while all mourned and honoured the dead, thou hast lived to merit our hate and execration—lived to unite thyself with the vile tyrant who murdered thy nearest and dearest—who shed the blood of infancy, rather than a male of the noble house of Torquil Wolfganger should survive—with him hast thou lived to unite thyself, and in the hands of lawless love!"

"In lawless hands, indeed, but not in those of love!" answered the hag; "love will sooner visit the regions of eternal doom, than those unhallowed vaults.—No, with that at least I cannot reproach myself—hatred to Front-de-Boeuf and his race governed my soul most deeply, even in the hour of his guilty endearments."

"You hated him, and yet you lived," replied Cedric; "wretch! was there no poniard —no knife—no bodkin!—Well was it for thee, since thou didst prize such an existence, that the secrets of a Norman castle are like those of the grave. For had I but dreamed of the daughter of Torquil living in foul communion with the murderer of her father, the sword of a true Saxon had found thee out even in the arms of thy paramour!"

"Wouldst thou indeed have done this justice to the name of Torquil?" said Ulrica, for we may now lay aside her assumed name of Urfried; "thou art then the true Saxon report speaks thee! for even within these accursed walls, where, as thou well sayest, guilt shrouds itself in inscrutable mystery, even there has the name of Cedric been sounded—and I, wretched and degraded, have rejoiced to think that there yet breathed an avenger of our unhappy nation.—I also have had my hours of vengeance—I have fomented the quarrels of our foes, and heated drunken revelry into murderous broil—I have seen their blood flow—I have heard their dying groans!—Look on me, Cedric—are there not still left on this foul and faded face some traces of the features of Torquil?"

"Ask me not of them, Ulrica," replied Cedric, in a tone of grief mixed with abhorrence; "these traces form such a resemblance as arises from the graves of the dead, when a fiend has animated the lifeless corpse."

"Be it so," answered Ulrica; "yet wore these fiendish features the mask of a spirit of light when they were able to set at variance the elder Front-de-Boeuf and his son Reginald! The darkness of hell should hide what followed, but revenge must lift the veil, and darkly intimate what it would raise the dead to speak aloud. Long had the smouldering fire of discord glowed between the tyrant father and his savage son—long had I nursed, in secret, the unnatural hatred—it blazed forth in an hour of drunken wassail, and at his own board fell my oppressor by the hand of his own son—such are the secrets these vaults conceal!—Rend asunder, ye accursed arches," she added, looking up towards the roof, "and bury in your fall all who are conscious of the hideous mystery!"

"And thou, creature of guilt and misery," said Cedric, "what became thy lot on the death of thy ravisher?"

"Guess it, but ask it not.—Here—here I dwelt, till age, premature age, has stamped its ghastly features on my countenance—scorned and insulted where I was once obeyed, and compelled to bound the revenge which had once such ample scope, to the efforts of petty malice of a discontented menial, or the vain or unheeded curses of an impotent hag—condemned to hear from my lonely turret the sounds of revelry in which I once partook, or the shrieks and groans of new victims of oppression."

"Ulrica," said Cedric, "with a heart which still, I fear, regrets the lost reward of thy crimes, as much as the deeds by which thou didst acquire that meed, how didst thou dare to address thee to one who wears this robe? Consider, unhappy woman, what could the sainted Edward himself do for thee, were he here in bodily presence? The royal Confessor was endowed by heaven with power to cleanse the ulcers of the body, but only God himself can cure the leprosy of the soul."

"Yet, turn not from me, stern prophet of wrath," she exclaimed, "but tell me, if thou canst, in what shall terminate these new and awful feelings that burst on my solitude—Why do deeds, long since done, rise before me in new and irresistible horrors? What fate is prepared beyond the grave for her, to whom God has assigned on earth a lot of such unspeakable wretchedness? Better had I turn to Woden, Hertha, and Zernebock—to Mista, and to Skogula, the gods of our yet unbaptized ancestors, than endure the dreadful anticipations which have of late haunted my waking and my sleeping hours!"

"I am no priest," said Cedric, turning with disgust from this miserable picture of guilt, wretchedness, and despair; "I am no priest, though I wear a priest's garment."

"Priest or layman," answered Ulrica, "thou art the first I have seen for twenty years, by whom God was feared or man regarded; and dost thou bid me despair?"

"I bid thee repent," said Cedric. "Seek to prayer and penance, and mayest thou find acceptance! But I cannot, I will not, longer abide with thee."

"Stay yet a moment!" said Ulrica; "leave me not now, son of my father's friend, lest the demon who has governed my life should tempt me to avenge myself of thy hard-hearted scorn—Thinkest thou, if Front-de-Boeuf found Cedric the Saxon in his castle, in such a disguise, that thy life would be a long one?—Already his eye has been upon thee like a falcon on his prey."

"And be it so," said Cedric; "and let him tear me with beak and talons, ere my tongue say one word which my heart doth not warrant. I will die a Saxon—true in word, open in deed—I bid thee avaunt!—touch me not, stay me not!—The sight of Front-de-Boeuf himself is less odious to me than thou, degraded and degenerate as thou art."

"Be it so," said Ulrica, no longer interrupting him; "go thy way, and forget, in the insolence of thy superority, that the wretch before thee is the daughter of thy father's friend.—Go thy way—if I am separated from mankind by my sufferings—separated from those whose aid I might most justly expect—not less will I be separated from them in my revenge!—No man shall aid me, but the ears of all men shall tingle to hear of the deed which I shall dare to do!—Farewell!—thy scorn has burst the last tie which seemed yet to unite me to my kind—a thought that my woes might claim the compassion of my people."

"Ulrica," said Cedric, softened by this appeal, "hast thou borne up and endured to live through so much guilt and so much misery, and wilt thou now yield to despair when thine eyes are opened to thy crimes, and when repentance were thy fitter occupation?"

"Cedric," answered Ulrica, "thou little knowest the human heart. To act as I have acted, to think as I have thought, requires the maddening love of pleasure, mingled with the keen appetite of revenge, the proud consciousness of power; droughts too intoxicating for the human heart to bear, and yet retain the power to prevent. Their force has long passed away—Age has no pleasures, wrinkles have no influence, revenge itself dies away in impotent curses. Then comes remorse, with all its vipers, mixed with vain regrets for the past, and despair for the future!—Then, when all other strong impulses have ceased, we become like the fiends in hell, who may feel remorse, but never repentance.—But thy words have awakened a new soul within me—Well hast thou said, all is possible for those who dare to die!—Thou hast shown me the means of revenge, and be assured I will embrace them. It has hitherto shared this wasted bosom with other and with rival passions—henceforward it shall possess me wholly, and thou thyself shalt say, that, whatever was the life of Ulrica, her death well became the daughter of the noble Torquil. There is a force without beleaguering this accursed castle—hasten to lead them to the attack, and when thou shalt see a red flag wave from the turret on the eastern angle of the donjon, press the Normans hard—they will then have enough to do within, and you may win the wall in spite both of bow and mangonel.—Begone, I pray thee—follow thine own fate, and leave me to mine."

Cedric would have enquired farther into the purpose which she thus darkly announced, but the stern voice of Front-de-Boeuf was heard, exclaiming, "Where tarries this loitering priest? By the scallop-shell of Compostella, I will make a martyr of him, if he loiters here to hatch treason among my domestics!"

"What a true prophet," said Ulrica, "is an evil conscience! But heed him not—out and to thy people—Cry your Saxon onslaught, and let them sing their war-song of Rollo, if they will; vengeance shall bear a burden to it."

As she thus spoke, she vanished through a private door, and Reginald Front-de-Boeuf entered the apartment. Cedric, with some difficulty, compelled himself to make obeisance to the haughty Baron, who returned his courtesy with a slight inclination of the head.

"Thy penitents, father, have made a long shrift—it is the better for them, since it is the last they shall ever make. Hast thou prepared them for death?"

"I found them," said Cedric, in such French as he could command, "expecting the worst, from the moment they knew into whose power they had fallen."

"How now, Sir Friar," replied Front-de-Boeuf, "thy speech, methinks, smacks of a Saxon tongue?"

"I was bred in the convent of St Withold of Burton," answered Cedric.

"Ay?" said the Baron; "it had been better for thee to have been a Norman, and better for my purpose too; but need has no choice of messengers. That St Withold's of Burton is an owlet's nest worth the harrying. The day will soon come that the frock shall protect the Saxon as little as the mail-coat."

"God's will be done," said Cedric, in a voice tremulous with passion, which Front-de-Boeuf imputed to fear.

"I see," said he, "thou dreamest already that our men-at-arms are in thy refectory and thy ale-vaults. But do me one cast of thy holy office, and, come what list of others, thou shalt sleep as safe in thy cell as a snail within his shell of proof."

"Speak your commands," said Cedric, with suppressed emotion.

"Follow me through this passage, then, that I may dismiss thee by the postern."

And as he strode on his way before the supposed friar, Front-de-Boeuf thus schooled him in the part which he desired he should act.

"Thou seest, Sir Friar, yon herd of Saxon swine, who have dared to environ this castle of Torquilstone—Tell them whatever thou hast a mind of the weakness of this fortalice, or aught else that can detain them before it for twenty-four hours. Meantime bear thou this scroll—But soft—canst read, Sir Priest?"

"Not a jot I," answered Cedric, "save on my breviary; and then I know the characters, because I have the holy service by heart, praised be Our Lady and St Withold!"

"The fitter messenger for my purpose.—Carry thou this scroll to the castle of Philip de Malvoisin; say it cometh from me, and is written by the Templar Brian de Bois-Guilbert, and that I pray him to send it to York with all the speed man and horse can make. Meanwhile, tell him to doubt nothing, he shall find us whole and sound behind our battlement—Shame on it, that we should be compelled to hide thus by a pack of runagates, who are wont to fly even at the flash of our pennons and the tramp of our horses! I say to thee, priest, contrive some cast of thine art to keep the knaves where they are, until our friends bring up their lances. My vengeance is awake, and she is a falcon that slumbers not till she has been gorged."

"By my patron saint," said Cedric, with deeper energy than became his character, "and by every saint who has lived and died in England, your commands shall be obeyed! Not a Saxon shall stir from before these walls, if I have art and influence to detain them there."

"Ha!" said Front-de-Boeuf, "thou changest thy tone, Sir Priest, and speakest brief and bold, as if thy heart were in the slaughter of the Saxon herd; and yet thou art thyself of kindred to the swine?"

Cedric was no ready practiser of the art of dissimulation, and would at this moment have been much the better of a hint from Wamba's more fertile brain. But necessity, according to the ancient proverb, sharpens invention, and he muttered something under his cowl concerning the men in question being excommunicated outlaws both to church and to kingdom.

"'Despardieux'," answered Front-de-Boeuf, "thou hast spoken the very truth—I forgot that the knaves can strip a fat abbot, as well as if they had been born south of yonder salt channel. Was it not he of St Ives whom they tied to an oak-tree, and compelled to sing a mass while they were rifling his mails and his wallets?—No, by our Lady—that jest was played by Gualtier of Middleton, one of our own companions-at-arms. But they were Saxons who robbed the chapel at St Bees of cup, candlestick and chalice, were they not?"

"They were godless men," answered Cedric.

"Ay, and they drank out all the good wine and ale that lay in store for many a secret carousal, when ye pretend ye are but busied with vigils and primes!—Priest, thou art bound to revenge such sacrilege."

"I am indeed bound to vengeance," murmured Cedric; "Saint Withold knows my heart."

Front-de-Boeuf, in the meanwhile, led the way to a postern, where, passing the moat on a single plank, they reached a small barbican, or exterior defence, which communicated with the open field by a well-fortified sallyport.

"Begone, then; and if thou wilt do mine errand, and if thou return hither when it is done, thou shalt see Saxon flesh cheap as ever was hog's in the shambles of Sheffield. And, hark thee, thou seemest to be a jolly confessor—come hither after the onslaught, and thou shalt have as much Malvoisie as would drench thy whole convent."

"Assuredly we shall meet again," answered Cedric.

"Something in hand the whilst," continued the Norman; and, as they parted at the postern door, he thrust into Cedric's reluctant hand a gold byzant, adding, "Remember, I will fly off both cowl and skin, if thou failest in thy purpose."

"And full leave will I give thee to do both," answered Cedric, leaving the postern, and striding forth over the free field with a joyful step, "if, when we meet next, I deserve not better at thine hand."—Turning then back towards the castle, he threw the piece of gold towards the donor, exclaiming at the same time, "False Norman, thy money perish with thee!"

Front-de-Boeuf heard the words imperfectly, but the action was suspicious— "Archers," he called to the warders on the outward battlements, "send me an arrow through yon monk's frock!—yet stay," he said, as his retainers were bending their bows, "it avails not—we must thus far trust him since we have no better shift. I think he dares not betray me—at the worst I can but treat with these Saxon dogs whom I have safe in kennel.—Ho! Giles jailor, let them bring Cedric of Rotherwood before me, and the other churl, his companion—him I mean of Coningsburgh—Athelstane there, or what call they him? Their very names are an encumbrance to a Norman knight's mouth, and have, as it were, a flavour of bacon—Give me a stoup of wine, as jolly Prince John said, that I may wash away the relish—place it in the armoury, and thither lead the prisoners."

His commands were obeyed; and, upon entering that Gothic apartment, hung with many spoils won by his own valour and that of his father, he found a flagon of wine on the massive oaken table, and the two Saxon captives under the guard of four of his dependants. Front-de-Boeuf took a long drought of wine, and then addressed his prisoners;—for the manner in which Wamba drew the cap over his face, the change of dress, the gloomy and broken light, and the Baron's imperfect acquaintance with the features of Cedric, (who avoided his Norman neighbours, and seldom stirred beyond his own domains,) prevented him from discovering that the most important of his captives had made his escape.

"Gallants of England," said Front-de-Boeuf, "how relish ye your entertainment at Torquilstone?—Are ye yet aware what your 'surquedy' and 'outrecuidance' merit, for scoffing at the entertainment of a prince of the House of Anjou?—Have ye forgotten how ye requited the unmerited hospitality of the royal John? By God and St Dennis, an ye pay not the richer ransom, I will hang ye up by the feet from the iron bars of these windows, till the kites and hooded crows have made skeletons of you!—Speak out, ye Saxon dogs—what bid ye for your worthless lives?—How say you, you of Rotherwood?"

"Not a doit I," answered poor Wamba—"and for hanging up by the feet, my brain has been topsy-turvy, they say, ever since the biggin was bound first round my head; so turning me upside down may peradventure restore it again."

"Saint Genevieve!" said Front-de-Boeuf, "what have we got here?"

And with the back of his hand he struck Cedric's cap from the head of the Jester, and throwing open his collar, discovered the fatal badge of servitude, the silver collar round his neck.

"Giles—Clement—dogs and varlets!" exclaimed the furious Norman, "what have you brought me here?"

"I think I can tell you," said De Bracy, who just entered the apartment. "This is Cedric's clown, who fought so manful a skirmish with Isaac of York about a question of precedence."

"I shall settle it for them both," replied Front-de-Boeuf; "they shall hang on the same gallows, unless his master and this boar of Coningsburgh will pay well for their lives. Their wealth is the least they can surrender; they must also carry off with them the swarms that are besetting the castle, subscribe a surrender of their pretended immunities, and live under us as serfs and vassals; too happy if, in the new world that is about to begin, we leave them the breath of their nostrils.—Go," said he to two of his attendants, "fetch me the right Cedric hither, and I pardon your error for once; the rather that you but mistook a fool for a Saxon franklin."

"Ay, but," said Wamba, "your chivalrous excellency will find there are more fools than franklins among us."

"What means the knave?" said Front-de-Boeuf, looking towards his followers, who, lingering and loath, faltered forth their belief, that if this were not Cedric who was there in presence, they knew not what was become of him.

"Saints of Heaven!" exclaimed De Bracy, "he must have escaped in the monk's garments!"

"Fiends of hell!" echoed Front-de-Boeuf, "it was then the boar of Rotherwood whom I ushered to the postern, and dismissed with my own hands!—And thou," he said to Wamba, "whose folly could overreach the wisdom of idiots yet more gross than thyself—I will give thee holy orders—I will shave thy crown for thee!—Here, let them tear the scalp from his head, and then pitch him headlong from the battlements—Thy trade is to jest, canst thou jest now?"

"You deal with me better than your word, noble knight," whimpered forth poor Wamba, whose habits of buffoonery were not to be overcome even by the immediate prospect of death; "if you give me the red cap you propose, out of a simple monk you will make a cardinal."

"The poor wretch," said De Bracy, "is resolved to die in his vocation.—Front-de-Boeuf, you shall not slay him. Give him to me to make sport for my Free Companions.—How sayst thou, knave? Wilt thou take heart of grace, and go to the wars with me?"

"Ay, with my master's leave," said Wamba; "for, look you, I must not slip collar" (and he touched that which he wore) "without his permission."

"Oh, a Norman saw will soon cut a Saxon collar." said De Bracy.

"Ay, noble sir," said Wamba, "and thence goes the proverb—

'Norman saw on English oak,
On English neck a Norman yoke;
Norman spoon in English dish,
And England ruled as Normans wish;
Blithe world to England never will be more,
Till England's rid of all the four.'"

"Thou dost well, De Bracy," said Front-de-Boeuf, "to stand there listening to a fool's jargon, when destruction is gaping for us! Seest thou not we are overreached, and that our proposed mode of communicating with our friends without has been disconcerted by this same motley gentleman thou art so fond to brother? What views have we to expect but instant storm?"

"To the battlements then," said De Bracy; "when didst thou ever see me the graver for the thoughts of battle? Call the Templar yonder, and let him fight but half so well for his life as he has done for his Order—Make thou to the walls thyself with thy huge body—Let me do my poor endeavour in my own way, and I tell thee the Saxon outlaws may as well attempt to scale the clouds, as the castle of Torquilstone; or, if you will treat with the banditti, why not employ the mediation of this worthy franklin, who seems in such deep contemplation of the wine-flagon?—Here, Saxon," he continued, addressing Athelstane, and handing the cup to him, "rinse thy throat with that noble liquor, and rouse up thy soul to say what thou wilt do for thy liberty."

"What a man of mould may," answered Athelstane, "providing it be what a man of manhood ought.—Dismiss me free, with my companions, and I will pay a ransom of a thousand marks."

"And wilt moreover assure us the retreat of that scum of mankind who are swarming around the castle, contrary to God's peace and the king's?" said Front-de-Boeuf.

"In so far as I can," answered Athelstane, "I will withdraw them; and I fear not but that my father Cedric will do his best to assist me."

"We are agreed then," said Front-de-Boeuf—"thou and they are to be set at freedom, and peace is to be on both sides, for payment of a thousand marks. It is a trifling ransom, Saxon, and thou wilt owe gratitude to the moderation which accepts of it in exchange of your persons. But mark, this extends not to the Jew Isaac."

"Nor to the Jew Isaac's daughter," said the Templar, who had now joined them.

"Neither," said Front-de-Boeuf, "belong to this Saxon's company."

"I were unworthy to be called Christian, if they did," replied Athelstane: "deal with the unbelievers as ye list."

"Neither does the ransom include the Lady Rowena," said De Bracy. "It shall never be said I was scared out of a fair prize without striking a blow for it."

"Neither," said Front-de-Boeuf, "does our treaty refer to this wretched Jester, whom I retain, that I may make him an example to every knave who turns jest into earnest."

"The Lady Rowena," answered Athelstane, with the most steady countenance, "is my affianced bride. I will be drawn by wild horses before I consent to part with her. The slave Wamba has this day saved the life of my father Cedric—I will lose mine ere a hair of his head be injured."

"Thy affianced bride?—The Lady Rowena the affianced bride of a vassal like thee?" said De Bracy; "Saxon, thou dreamest that the days of thy seven kingdoms are returned again. I tell thee, the Princes of the House of Anjou confer not their wards on men of such lineage as thine."

"My lineage, proud Norman," replied Athelstane, "is drawn from a source more pure and ancient than that of a beggarly Frenchman, whose living is won by selling the blood of the thieves whom he assembles under his paltry standard. Kings were my ancestors, strong in war and wise in council, who every day feasted in their hall more hundreds than thou canst number individual followers; whose names have been sung by minstrels, and their laws recorded by Wittenagemotes; whose bones were interred amid the prayers of saints, and over whose tombs minsters have been builded."

"Thou hast it, De Bracy," said Front-de-Boeuf, well pleased with the rebuff which his companion had received; "the Saxon hath hit thee fairly."

"As fairly as a captive can strike," said De Bracy, with apparent carelessness; "for he whose hands are tied should have his tongue at freedom.—But thy glibness of reply, comrade," rejoined he, speaking to Athelstane, "will not win the freedom of the Lady Rowena."

To this Athelstane, who had already made a longer speech than was his custom to do on any topic, however interesting, returned no answer. The conversation was interrupted by the arrival of a menial, who announced that a monk demanded admittance at the postern gate.

"In the name of Saint Bennet, the prince of these bull-beggars," said Front-de-Boeuf, "have we a real monk this time, or another impostor? Search him, slaves—for an ye suffer a second impostor to be palmed upon you, I will have your eyes torn out, and hot coals put into the sockets."

"Let me endure the extremity of your anger, my lord," said Giles, "if this be not a real shaveling. Your squire Jocelyn knows him well, and will vouch him to be brother Ambrose, a monk in attendance upon the Prior of Jorvaulx."

"Admit him," said Front-de-Boeuf; "most likely he brings us news from his jovial master. Surely the devil keeps holiday, and the priests are relieved from duty, that they are strolling thus wildly through the country. Remove these prisoners; and, Saxon, think on what thou hast heard."

"I claim," said Athelstane, "an honourable imprisonment, with due care of my board and of my couch, as becomes my rank, and as is due to one who is in treaty for ransom. Moreover, I hold him that deems himself the best of you, bound to answer to me with his body for this aggression on my freedom. This defiance hath already been sent to thee by thy sewer; thou underliest it, and art bound to answer me—There lies my glove."

"I answer not the challenge of my prisoner," said Front-de-Boeuf; "nor shalt thou, Maurice de Bracy.—Giles," he continued, "hang the franklin's glove upon the tine of yonder branched antlers: there shall it remain until he is a free man. Should he then presume to demand it, or to affirm he was unlawfully made my prisoner, by the belt of Saint Christopher, he will speak to one who hath never refused to meet a foe on foot or on horseback, alone or with his vassals at his back!"

The Saxon prisoners were accordingly removed, just as they introduced the monk Ambrose, who appeared to be in great perturbation.

"This is the real 'Deus vobiscum'," said Wamba, as he passed the reverend brother; "the others were but counterfeits."

"Holy Mother," said the monk, as he addressed the assembled knights, "I am at last safe and in Christian keeping!"

"Safe thou art," replied De Bracy; "and for Christianity, here is the stout Baron Reginald Front-de-Boeuf, whose utter abomination is a Jew; and the good Knight Templar, Brian de Bois-Guilbert, whose trade is to slay Saracens—If these are not good marks of Christianity, I know no other which they bear about them."

"Ye are friends and allies of our reverend father in God, Aymer, Prior of Jorvaulx," said the monk, without noticing the tone of De Bracy's reply; "ye owe him aid both by knightly faith and holy charity; for what saith the blessed Saint Augustin, in his treatise 'De Civitate Dei'——"

"What saith the devil!" interrupted Front-de-Boeuf; "or rather what dost thou say, Sir Priest? We have little time to hear texts from the holy fathers."

"'Sancta Maria!'" ejaculated Father Ambrose, "how prompt to ire are these unhallowed laymen!—But be it known to you, brave knights, that certain murderous caitiffs, casting behind them fear of God, and reverence of his church, and not regarding the bull of the holy see, 'Si quis, suadende Diabolo'——"

"Brother priest," said the Templar, "all this we know or guess at—tell us plainly, is thy master, the Prior, made prisoner, and to whom?"

"Surely," said Ambrose, "he is in the hands of the men of Belial, infesters of these woods, and contemners of the holy text, 'Touch not mine anointed, and do my prophets naught of evil.'"

"Here is a new argument for our swords, sirs," said Front-de-Boeuf, turning to his companions; "and so, instead of reaching us any assistance, the Prior of Jorvaulx requests aid at our hands? a man is well helped of these lazy churchmen when he hath most to do!—But speak out, priest, and say at once, what doth thy master expect from us?"

"So please you," said Ambrose, "violent hands having been imposed on my reverend superior, contrary to the holy ordinance which I did already quote, and the men of Belial having rifled his mails and budgets, and stripped him of two hundred marks of pure refined gold, they do yet demand of him a large sum beside, ere they will suffer him to depart from their uncircumcised hands. Wherefore the reverend father in God prays you, as his dear friends, to rescue him, either by paying down the ransom at which they hold him, or by force of arms, at your best discretion."

"The foul fiend quell the Prior!" said Front-de-Boeuf; "his morning's drought has been a deep one. When did thy master hear of a Norman baron unbuckling his purse to relieve a churchman, whose bags are ten times as weighty as ours?—And how can we do aught by valour to free him, that are cooped up here by ten times our number, and expect an assault every moment?"

"And that was what I was about to tell you," said the monk, "had your hastiness allowed me time. But, God help me, I am old, and these foul onslaughts distract an aged man's brain. Nevertheless, it is of verity that they assemble a camp, and raise a bank against the walls of this castle."

"To the battlements!" cried De Bracy, "and let us mark what these knaves do without;" and so saying, he opened a latticed window which led to a sort of bartisan or projecting balcony, and immediately called from thence to those in the apartment—"Saint Dennis, but the old monk hath brought true tidings!—They bring forward mantelets and pavisses, and the archers muster on the skirts of the wood like a dark cloud before a hailstorm."

Reginald Front-de-Boeuf also looked out upon the field, and immediately snatched his bugle; and, after winding a long and loud blast, commanded his men to their posts on the walls.

"De Bracy, look to the eastern side, where the walls are lowest—Noble Bois-Guilbert, thy trade hath well taught thee how to attack and defend, look thou to the western side—I myself will take post at the barbican. Yet, do not confine your exertions to any one spot, noble friends!—we must this day be everywhere, and multiply ourselves, were it possible, so as to carry by our presence succour and relief wherever the attack is hottest. Our numbers are few, but activity and courage may supply that defect, since we have only to do with rascal clowns."

"But, noble knights," exclaimed Father Ambrose, amidst the bustle and confusion occasioned by the preparations for defence, "will none of ye hear the message of the reverend father in God Aymer, Prior of Jorvaulx?—I beseech thee to hear me, noble Sir Reginald!"

"Go patter thy petitions to heaven," said the fierce Norman, "for we on earth have no time to listen to them.—Ho! there, Anselm I see that seething pitch and oil are ready to pour on the heads of these audacious traitors—Look that the cross-bowmen lack not bolts. —Fling abroad my banner with the old bull's head—the knaves shall soon find with whom they have to do this day!"

"But, noble sir," continued the monk, persevering in his endeavours to draw attention, "consider my vow of obedience, and let me discharge myself of my Superior's errand."

"Away with this prating dotard," said Front-de Boeuf, "lock him up in the chapel, to tell his beads till the broil be over. It will be a new thing to the saints in Torquilstone to hear aves and paters; they have not been so honoured, I trow, since they were cut out of stone."

"Blaspheme not the holy saints, Sir Reginald," said De Bracy, "we shall have need of their aid to-day before yon rascal rout disband."

"I expect little aid from their hand," said Front-de-Boeuf, "unless we were to hurl them from the battlements on the heads of the villains. There is a huge lumbering Saint Christopher yonder, sufficient to bear a whole company to the earth."

The Templar had in the meantime been looking out on the proceedings of the besiegers, with rather more attention than the brutal Front-de-Boeuf or his giddy companion.

"By the faith of mine order," he said, "these men approach with more touch of discipline than could have been judged, however they come by it. See ye how dexterously they avail themselves of every cover which a tree or bush affords, and shun exposing themselves to the shot of our cross-bows? I spy neither banner nor pennon among them, and yet will I gage my golden chain, that they are led on by some noble knight or gentleman, skilful in the practice of wars."

"I espy him," said De Bracy; "I see the waving of a knight's crest, and the gleam of his armour. See yon tall man in the black mail, who is busied marshalling the farther troop of the rascaille yeomen—by Saint Dennis, I hold him to be the same whom we called 'Le Noir Faineant', who overthrew thee, Front-de-Boeuf, in the lists at Ashby."

"So much the better," said Front-de-Boeuf, "that he comes here to give me my revenge. Some hilding fellow he must be, who dared not stay to assert his claim to the tourney prize which chance had assigned him. I should in vain have sought for him where knights and nobles seek their foes, and right glad am I he hath here shown himself among yon villain yeomanry."

The demonstrations of the enemy's immediate approach cut off all farther discourse. Each knight repaired to his post, and at the head of the few followers whom they were able to muster, and who were in numbers inadequate to defend the whole extent of the walls, they awaited with calm determination the threatened assault.

XXVIII.

> This wandering race, sever'd from other men,
> Boast yet their intercourse with human arts;
> The seas, the woods, the deserts, which they haunt,
> Find them acquainted with their secret treasures:
> And unregarded herbs, and flowers, and blossoms,
> Display undreamt-of powers when gather'd by them.
>
> — THE JEW

Our history must needs retrograde for the space of a few pages, to inform the reader of certain passages material to his understanding the rest of this important narrative. His own intelligence may indeed have easily anticipated that, when Ivanhoe sunk down, and seemed abandoned by all the world, it was the importunity of Rebecca which prevailed on her father to have the gallant young warrior transported from the lists to the house which for the time the Jews inhabited in the suburbs of Ashby.

It would not have been difficult to have persuaded Isaac to this step in any other circumstances, for his disposition was kind and grateful. But he had also the prejudices and scrupulous timidity of his persecuted people, and those were to be conquered.

"Holy Abraham!" he exclaimed, "he is a good youth, and my heart bleeds to see the gore trickle down his rich embroidered hacqueton, and his corslet of goodly price —but to carry him to our house!—damsel, hast thou well considered?—he is a Christian, and by our law we may not deal with the stranger and Gentile, save for the advantage of our commerce."

"Speak not so, my dear father," replied Rebecca; "we may not indeed mix with them in banquet and in jollity; but in wounds and in misery, the Gentile becometh the Jew's brother."

"I would I knew what the Rabbi Jacob Ben Tudela would opine on it," replied Isaac;—"nevertheless, the good youth must not bleed to death. Let Seth and Reuben bear him to Ashby."

"Nay, let them place him in my litter," said Rebecca; "I will mount one of the palfreys."

"That were to expose thee to the gaze of those dogs of Ishmael and of Edom," whispered Isaac, with a suspicious glance towards the crowd of knights and squires. But Rebecca was already busied in carrying her charitable purpose into effect, and listed not what he said, until Isaac, seizing the sleeve of her mantle, again exclaimed, in a hurried voice—"Beard of Aaron!—what if the youth perish!—if he die in our custody, shall we not be held guilty of his blood, and be torn to pieces by the multitude?"

"He will not die, my father," said Rebecca, gently extricating herself from the grasp of Isaac "he will not die unless we abandon him; and if so, we are indeed answerable for his blood to God and to man."

"Nay," said Isaac, releasing his hold, "it grieveth me as much to see the drops of his blood, as if they were so many golden byzants from mine own purse; and I well know, that the lessons of Miriam, daughter of the Rabbi Manasses of Byzantium whose soul is in Paradise, have made thee skilful in the art of healing, and that thou knowest the craft of herbs, and the force of elixirs. Therefore, do as thy mind giveth thee—thou art a good damsel, a blessing, and a crown, and a song of rejoicing unto me and unto my house, and unto the people of my fathers."

The apprehensions of Isaac, however, were not ill founded; and the generous and grateful benevolence of his daughter exposed her, on her return to Ashby, to the unhallowed gaze of Brian de Bois-Guilbert. The Templar twice passed and repassed them on the road, fixing his bold and ardent look on the beautiful Jewess; and we have already seen the consequences of the admiration which her charms excited when accident threw her into the power of that unprincipled voluptuary.

Rebecca lost no time in causing the patient to be transported to their temporary dwelling, and proceeded with her own hands to examine and to bind up his wounds. The youngest reader of romances and romantic ballads, must recollect how often the females, during the dark ages, as they are called, were initiated into the mysteries of surgery, and how frequently the gallant knight submitted the wounds of his person to her cure, whose eyes had yet more deeply penetrated his heart.

But the Jews, both male and female, possessed and practised the medical science in all its branches, and the monarchs and powerful barons of the time frequently committed themselves to the charge of some experienced sage among this despised people, when wounded or in sickness. The aid of the Jewish physicians was not the less eagerly sought after, though a general belief prevailed among the Christians, that the Jewish Rabbins were deeply acquainted with the occult sciences, and particularly with the cabalistical art, which had its name and origin in the studies of the sages of Israel. Neither did the Rabbins disown such acquaintance with supernatural arts, which added nothing (for what could add aught?) to the hatred with which their nation was regarded, while it diminished the contempt with which that malevolence was mingled. A Jewish magician might be the subject of equal abhorrence with a Jewish usurer, but he could not be equally despised. It is besides probable, considering the wonderful cures they are said to have performed, that the Jews possessed some secrets of the healing art peculiar to themselves, and which, with the exclusive spirit arising out of their condition, they took great care to conceal from the Christians amongst whom they dwelt.

The beautiful Rebecca had been heedfully brought up in all the knowledge proper to her nation, which her apt and powerful mind had retained, arranged, and enlarged, in the course of a progress beyond her years, her sex, and even the age in which she lived. Her knowledge of medicine and of the healing art had been acquired under an aged Jewess, the daughter of one of their most celebrated doctors, who loved Rebecca as her own child, and was believed to have communicated to her secrets, which had been left to herself by her sage father at the same time, and under the same circumstances. The fate of Miriam had indeed been to fall a sacrifice to the fanaticism of the times; but her secrets had survived in her apt pupil.

Rebecca, thus endowed with knowledge as with beauty, was universally revered and admired by her own tribe, who almost regarded her as one of those gifted women mentioned in the sacred history. Her father himself, out of reverence for her talents, which involuntarily mingled itself with his unbounded affection, permitted the maiden a greater liberty than was usually indulged to those of her sex by the habits of her people, and was, as we have just seen, frequently guided by her opinion, even in preference to his own.

When Ivanhoe reached the habitation of Isaac, he was still in a state of unconsciousness, owing to the profuse loss of blood which had taken place during his exertions in the lists. Rebecca examined the wound, and having applied to it such vulnerary remedies as her art prescribed, informed her father that if fever could be averted, of which the great bleeding rendered her little apprehensive, and if the healing balsam of Miriam retained its virtue, there was nothing to fear for his guest's life, and that he might with safety travel to York with them on the ensuing day. Isaac looked a little blank at this annunciation. His charity would willingly have stopped short at Ashby, or at most would have left the wounded Christian to be tended in the house where he was residing at present, with an assurance to the Hebrew to whom it belonged, that all expenses should be duly discharged. To this, however, Rebecca opposed many reasons, of which we shall only mention two that had peculiar weight with Isaac. The one was, that she would on no account put the phial of precious balsam into the hands of another physician even of her own tribe, lest that valuable mystery should be discovered; the other, that this wounded knight, Wilfred of Ivanhoe, was an intimate favourite of Richard Coeur-de-Lion, and that, in case the monarch should return, Isaac, who had supplied his brother John with treasure to prosecute his rebellious purposes, would stand in no small need of a powerful protector who enjoyed Richard's favour.

"Thou art speaking but sooth, Rebecca," said Isaac, giving way to these weighty arguments—"it were an offending of Heaven to betray the secrets of the blessed Miriam; for the good which Heaven giveth, is not rashly to be squandered upon others, whether it be talents of gold and shekels of silver, or whether it be the secret mysteries of a wise physician—assuredly they should be preserved to those to whom Providence hath vouchsafed them. And him whom the Nazarenes of England call the Lion's Heart, assuredly it were better for me to fall into the hands of a strong lion of Idumea than into his, if he shall have got assurance of my dealing with his brother. Wherefore I will lend ear to thy counsel, and this youth shall journey with us unto York, and our house shall be as a home to him until his wounds shall be healed. And if he of the Lion Heart shall return to the land, as is now noised abroad, then shall this Wilfred of Ivanhoe be unto me as a wall of defence, when the king's displeasure shall burn high against thy father. And if he doth not return, this Wilfred may natheless repay us our charges when he shall gain treasure by the strength of his spear and of his sword, even as he did yesterday and this day also. For the youth is a good youth, and keepeth the day which he appointeth, and restoreth that which he borroweth, and succoureth the Israelite, even the child of my father's house, when he is encompassed by strong thieves and sons of Belial."

It was not until evening was nearly closed that Ivanhoe was restored to consciousness of his situation. He awoke from a broken slumber, under the confused impressions which are naturally attendant on the recovery from a state of insensibility. He was unable for some time to recall exactly to memory the circumstances which had preceded his fall in the lists, or to make out any connected chain of the events in which he had been engaged upon the yesterday. A sense of wounds and injury, joined to great weakness and exhaustion, was mingled with the recollection of blows dealt and received, of steeds rushing upon each other, overthrowing and overthrown—of shouts and clashing of arms, and all the heady tumult of a confused fight. An effort to draw aside the curtain of his couch was in some degree successful, although rendered difficult by the pain of his wound.

To his great surprise he found himself in a room magnificently furnished, but having cushions instead of chairs to rest upon, and in other respects partaking so much of Oriental costume, that he began to doubt whether he had not, during his sleep, been transported back again to the land of Palestine. The impression was increased, when, the tapestry being drawn aside, a female form, dressed in a rich habit, which partook more of the Eastern taste than that of Europe, glided through the door which it concealed, and was followed by a swarthy domestic.

As the wounded knight was about to address this fair apparition, she imposed silence by placing her slender finger upon her ruby lips, while the attendant, approaching him, proceeded to uncover Ivanhoe's side, and the lovely Jewess satisfied herself that the bandage was in its place, and the wound doing well. She performed her task with a graceful and dignified simplicity and modesty, which might, even in more civilized days, have served to redeem it from whatever might seem repugnant to female delicacy. The idea of so young and beautiful a person engaged in attendance on a sick-bed, or in dressing the wound of one of a different sex, was melted away and lost in that of a beneficent being contributing her effectual aid to relieve pain, and to avert the stroke of death. Rebecca's few and brief directions were given in the Hebrew language to the old domestic; and he, who had been frequently her assistant in similar cases, obeyed them without reply.

The accents of an unknown tongue, however harsh they might have sounded when uttered by another, had, coming from the beautiful Rebecca, the romantic and pleasing effect which fancy ascribes to the charms pronounced by some beneficent fairy, unintelligible, indeed, to the ear, but, from the sweetness of utterance, and benignity of aspect, which accompanied them, touching and affecting to the heart. Without making an attempt at further question, Ivanhoe suffered them in silence to take the measures they thought most proper for his recovery; and it was not until those were completed, and this kind physician about to retire, that his curiosity could no longer be suppressed.—"Gentle maiden," he began in the Arabian tongue, with which his Eastern travels had rendered him familiar, and which he thought most likely to be understood by the turban'd and caftan'd damsel who stood before him—"I pray you, gentle maiden, of your courtesy—"

But here he was interrupted by his fair physician, a smile which she could scarce suppress dimpling for an instant a face, whose general expression was that of contemplative melancholy. "I am of England, Sir Knight, and speak the English tongue, although my dress and my lineage belong to another climate."

"Noble damsel,"—again the Knight of Ivanhoe began; and again Rebecca hastened to interrupt him.

"Bestow not on me, Sir Knight," she said, "the epithet of noble. It is well you should speedily know that your handmaiden is a poor Jewess, the daughter of that Isaac of York, to whom you were so lately a good and kind lord. It well becomes him, and those of his household, to render to you such careful tendance as your present state necessarily demands."

I know not whether the fair Rowena would have been altogether satisfied with the species of emotion with which her devoted knight had hitherto gazed on the beautiful features, and fair form, and lustrous eyes, of the lovely Rebecca; eyes whose brilliancy was shaded, and, as it were, mellowed, by the fringe of her long silken eyelashes, and which a minstrel would have compared to the evening star darting its rays through a bower of jessamine. But Ivanhoe was too good a Catholic to retain the same class of feelings towards a Jewess. This Rebecca had foreseen, and for this very purpose she had hastened to mention her father's name and lineage; yet—for the fair and wise daughter of Isaac was not without a touch of female weakness—she could not but sigh internally when the glance of respectful admiration, not altogether unmixed with tenderness, with which Ivanhoe had hitherto regarded his unknown benefactress, was exchanged at once for a manner cold, composed, and collected, and fraught with no deeper feeling than that which expressed a grateful sense of courtesy received from an unexpected quarter, and from one of an inferior race. It was not that Ivanhoe's former carriage expressed more than that general devotional homage which youth always pays to beauty; yet it was mortifying that one word should operate as a spell to remove poor Rebecca, who could not be supposed altogether ignorant of her title to such homage, into a degraded class, to whom it could not be honourably rendered.

But the gentleness and candour of Rebecca's nature imputed no fault to Ivanhoe for sharing in the universal prejudices of his age and religion. On the contrary the fair Jewess, though sensible her patient now regarded her as one of a race of reprobation, with whom it was disgraceful to hold any beyond the most necessary intercourse, ceased not to pay the same patient and devoted attention to his safety and convalescence. She informed him of the necessity they were under of removing to York, and of her father's resolution to transport him thither, and tend him in his own house until his health should be restored. Ivanhoe expressed great repugnance to this plan, which he grounded on unwillingness to give farther trouble to his benefactors.

"Was there not," he said, "in Ashby, or near it, some Saxon franklin, or even some wealthy peasant, who would endure the burden of a wounded countryman's residence with him until he should be again able to bear his armour?—Was there no convent of Saxon endowment, where he could be received?—Or could he not be transported as far as Burton, where he was sure to find hospitality with Waltheoff, the Abbot of St Withold's, to whom he was related?"

"Any, the worst of these harbourages," said Rebecca, with a melancholy smile, "would unquestionably be more fitting for your residence than the abode of a despised Jew; yet, Sir Knight, unless you would dismiss your physician, you cannot change your lodging. Our nation, as you well know, can cure wounds, though we deal not in inflicting them; and in our own family, in particular, are secrets which have been handed down since the days of Solomon, and of which you have already experienced the advantages. No Nazarene—I crave your forgiveness, Sir Knight—no Christian leech, within the four seas of Britain, could enable you to bear your corslet within a month."

"And how soon wilt THOU enable me to brook it?" said Ivanhoe, impatiently.

"Within eight days, if thou wilt be patient and conformable to my directions," replied Rebecca.

"By Our Blessed Lady," said Wilfred, "if it be not a sin to name her here, it is no time for me or any true knight to be bedridden; and if thou accomplish thy promise, maiden, I will pay thee with my casque full of crowns, come by them as I may."

"I will accomplish my promise," said Rebecca, "and thou shalt bear thine armour on the eighth day from hence, if thou will grant me but one boon in the stead of the silver thou dost promise me."

"If it be within my power, and such as a true Christian knight may yield to one of thy people," replied Ivanhoe, "I will grant thy boon blithely and thankfully."

"Nay," answered Rebecca, "I will but pray of thee to believe henceforward that a

Jew may do good service to a Christian, without desiring other guerdon than the blessing of the Great Father who made both Jew and Gentile."

"It were sin to doubt it, maiden," replied Ivanhoe; "and I repose myself on thy skill without further scruple or question, well trusting you will enable me to bear my corslet on the eighth day. And now, my kind leech, let me enquire of the news abroad. What of the noble Saxon Cedric and his household?—what of the lovely Lady—" He stopt, as if unwilling to speak Rowena's name in the house of a Jew—"Of her, I mean, who was named Queen of the tournament?"

"And who was selected by you, Sir Knight, to hold that dignity, with judgment which was admired as much as your valour," replied Rebecca.

The blood which Ivanhoe had lost did not prevent a flush from crossing his cheek, feeling that he had incautiously betrayed a deep interest in Rowena by the awkward attempt he had made to conceal it.

"It was less of her I would speak," said he, "than of Prince John; and I would fain know somewhat of a faithful squire, and why he now attends me not?"

"Let me use my authority as a leech," answered Rebecca, "and enjoin you to keep silence, and avoid agitating reflections, whilst I apprize you of what you desire to know. Prince John hath broken off the tournament, and set forward in all haste towards York, with the nobles, knights, and churchmen of his party, after collecting such sums as they could wring, by fair means or foul, from those who are esteemed the wealthy of the land. It is said he designs to assume his brother's crown."

"Not without a blow struck in its defence," said Ivanhoe, raising himself upon the couch, "if there were but one true subject in England I will fight for Richard's title with the best of them—ay, one or two, in his just quarrel!"

"But that you may be able to do so," said Rebecca touching his shoulder with her hand, "you must now observe my directions, and remain quiet."

"True, maiden," said Ivanhoe, "as quiet as these disquieted times will permit—And of Cedric and his household?"

"His steward came but brief while since," said the Jewess, "panting with haste, to ask my father for certain monies, the price of wool the growth of Cedric's flocks, and from him I learned that Cedric and Athelstane of Coningsburgh had left Prince John's lodging in high displeasure, and were about to set forth on their return homeward."

"Went any lady with them to the banquet?" said Wilfred.

"The Lady Rowena," said Rebecca, answering the question with more precision than it had been asked—"The Lady Rowena went not to the Prince's feast, and, as the steward reported to us, she is now on her journey back to Rotherwood, with her guardian Cedric. And touching your faithful squire Gurth——"

"Ha!" exclaimed the knight, "knowest thou his name?—But thou dost," he immediately added, "and well thou mayst, for it was from thy hand, and, as I am now convinced, from thine own generosity of spirit, that he received but yesterday a hundred zecchins."

"Speak not of that," said Rebecca, blushing deeply; "I see how easy it is for the tongue to betray what the heart would gladly conceal."

"But this sum of gold," said Ivanhoe, gravely, "my honour is concerned in repaying it to your father."

"Let it be as thou wilt," said Rebecca, "when eight days have passed away; but think not, and speak not now, of aught that may retard thy recovery."

"Be it so, kind maiden," said Ivanhoe; "I were most ungrateful to dispute thy commands. But one word of the fate of poor Gurth, and I have done with questioning thee."

"I grieve to tell thee, Sir Knight," answered the Jewess, "that he is in custody by the order of Cedric."—And then observing the distress which her communication gave to Wilfred, she instantly added, "But the steward Oswald said, that if nothing occurred to renew his master's displeasure against him, he was sure that Cedric would pardon Gurth, a faithful serf, and one who stood high in favour, and who had but committed this error out of the love which he bore to Cedric's son. And he said, moreover, that he and his comrades, and especially Wamba the Jester, were resolved to warn Gurth to make his escape by the way, in case Cedric's ire against him could not be mitigated."

"Would to God they may keep their purpose!" said Ivanhoe; "but it seems as if I were destined to bring ruin on whomsoever hath shown kindness to me. My king, by whom I was honoured and distinguished, thou seest that the brother most indebted to him is raising his arms to grasp his crown;—my regard hath brought restraint and trouble on the fairest of her sex;—and now my father in his mood may slay this poor bondsman but for his love and loyal service to me!—Thou seest, maiden, what an ill-fated wretch thou dost labour to assist; be wise, and let me go, ere the misfortunes which track my footsteps like slot-hounds, shall involve thee also in their pursuit."

"Nay," said Rebecca, "thy weakness and thy grief, Sir Knight, make thee miscalculate the purposes of Heaven. Thou hast been restored to thy country when it most needed the assistance of a strong hand and a true heart, and thou hast humbled the pride of thine enemies and those of thy king, when their horn was most highly exalted, and for the evil which thou hast sustained, seest thou not that Heaven has raised thee a helper and a physician, even among the most despised of the land?—Therefore, be of good courage, and trust that thou art preserved for some marvel which thine arm shall work before this people. Adieu—and having taken the medicine which I shall send thee by the hand of Reuben, compose thyself again to rest, that thou mayest be the more able to endure the journey on the succeeding day."

Ivanhoe was convinced by the reasoning, and obeyed the directions, of Rebecca. The drought which Reuben administered was of a sedative and narcotic quality, and secured the patient sound and undisturbed slumbers. In the morning his kind physician found him entirely free from feverish symptoms, and fit to undergo the fatigue of a journey.

He was deposited in the horse-litter which had brought him from the lists, and every precaution taken for his travelling with ease. In one circumstance only even the entreaties of Rebecca were unable to secure sufficient attention to the accommodation of the wounded knight. Isaac, like the enriched traveller of Juvenal's tenth satire, had ever the fear of robbery before his eyes, conscious that he would be alike accounted fair game by the marauding Norman noble, and by the Saxon outlaw. He therefore journeyed at a great rate, and made short halts, and shorter repasts, so that he passed by Cedric and Athelstane who had several hours the start of him, but who had been delayed by their protracted feasting at the convent of Saint Withold's. Yet such was the virtue of Miriam's balsam, or such the strength of Ivanhoe's constitution, that he did not sustain from the hurried journey that inconvenience which his kind physician had apprehended.

In another point of view, however, the Jew's haste proved somewhat more than good speed. The rapidity with which he insisted on travelling, bred several disputes between him and the party whom he had hired to attend him as a guard. These men were Saxons, and not free by any means from the national love of ease and good living which the Normans stigmatized as laziness and gluttony. Reversing Shylock's position, they had accepted the employment in hopes of feeding upon the wealthy Jew, and were very much displeased when they found themselves disappointed, by the rapidity with which he insisted on their proceeding. They remonstrated also upon the risk of damage to their horses by these forced marches. Finally, there arose betwixt Isaac and his satellites a deadly feud, concerning the quantity of wine and ale to be allowed for consumption at each meal. And thus it happened, that when the alarm of danger approached, and that which Isaac feared was likely to come upon him, he was deserted by the discontented mercenaries on whose protection he had relied, without using the means necessary to secure their attachment.

In this deplorable condition the Jew, with his daughter and her wounded patient, were found by Cedric, as has already been noticed, and soon afterwards fell into the power of De Bracy and his confederates. Little notice was at first taken of the horse-litter, and it might have remained behind but for the curiosity of De Bracy, who looked into it under the impression that it might contain the object of his enterprise, for Rowena had not unveiled herself. But De Bracy's astonishment was considerable, when he discovered that the litter contained a wounded man, who, conceiving himself to have fallen into the power of Saxon outlaws, with whom his name might be a protection for himself and his friends, frankly avowed himself to be Wilfred of Ivanhoe.

The ideas of chivalrous honour, which, amidst his wildness and levity, never utterly abandoned De Bracy, prohibited him from doing the knight any injury in his defenceless condition, and equally interdicted his betraying him to Front-de-Boeuf, who would have had no scruples to put to death, under any circumstances, the rival claimant of the fief of Ivanhoe. On the other hand, to liberate a suitor preferred by the Lady Rowena, as the events of the tournament, and indeed Wilfred's previous banishment from his father's house, had made matter of notoriety, was a pitch far above the flight of De Bracy's generosity. A middle course betwixt good and evil was all which he found himself capable of adopting, and he commanded two of his own squires to keep close by the litter, and to suffer no one to approach it. If questioned, they were directed by their master to say, that the empty litter of the Lady Rowena was employed to transport one of their comrades who had been wounded in the scuffle. On arriving at Torquilstone, while the Knight Templar and the lord of that castle were each intent upon their own schemes, the one on the Jew's treasure, and the other on his daughter, De Bracy's squires conveyed Ivanhoe, still under the name of a wounded comrade, to a distant apartment. This explanation was accordingly returned by these men to Front-de-Boeuf, when he questioned them why they did not make for the battlements upon the alarm.

"A wounded companion!" he replied in great wrath and astonishment. "No wonder that churls and yeomen wax so presumptuous as even to lay leaguer before castles, and that clowns and swineherds send defiances to nobles, since men-at-arms have turned sick men's nurses, and Free Companions are grown keepers of dying folk's curtains, when the castle is about to be assailed.—To the battlements, ye loitering villains!" he exclaimed, raising his stentorian voice till the arches around rung again, "to the battlements, or I will splinter your bones with this truncheon!"

The men sulkily replied, "that they desired nothing better than to go to the battlements, providing Front-de-Boeuf would bear them out with their master, who had commanded them to tend the dying man."

"The dying man, knaves!" rejoined the Baron; "I promise thee we shall all be dying men an we stand not to it the more stoutly. But I will relieve the guard upon this caitiff companion of yours.—Here, Urfried—hag—fiend of a Saxon witch—hearest me not?—tend me this bedridden fellow since he must needs be tended, whilst these knaves use their weapons.—Here be two arblasts, comrades, with windlaces and quarrels —to the barbican with you, and see you drive each bolt through a Saxon brain."

The men, who, like most of their description, were fond of enterprise and detested inaction, went joyfully to the scene of danger as they were commanded, and thus the charge of Ivanhoe was transferred to Urfried, or Ulrica. But she, whose brain was burning with remembrance of injuries and with hopes of vengeance, was readily induced to devolve upon Rebecca the care of her patient.

XXIX.

Ascend the watch-tower yonder, valiant soldier,
Look on the field, and say how goes the battle.

— SCHILLER'S *MAID OF ORLEANS*

A moment of peril is often also a moment of open-hearted kindness and affection. We are thrown off our guard by the general agitation of our feelings, and betray the intensity of those, which, at more tranquil periods, our prudence at least conceals, if it cannot altogether suppress them. In finding herself once more by the side of Ivanhoe, Rebecca was astonished at the keen sensation of pleasure which she experienced, even at a time when all around them both was danger, if not despair. As she felt his pulse, and enquired after his health, there was a softness in her touch and in her accents implying a kinder interest than she would herself have been pleased to have voluntarily expressed. Her voice faltered and her hand trembled, and it was only the cold question of Ivanhoe, "Is it you, gentle maiden?" which recalled her to herself, and reminded her the sensations which she felt were not and could not be mutual. A sigh escaped, but it was scarce audible; and the questions which she asked the knight concerning his state of health were put in the tone of calm friendship. Ivanhoe answered her hastily that he was, in point of health, as well, and better than he could have expected—"Thanks," he said, "dear Rebecca, to thy helpful skill."

"He calls me DEAR Rebecca," said the maiden to herself, "but it is in the cold and careless tone which ill suits the word. His war-horse—his hunting hound, are dearer to him than the despised Jewess!"

"My mind, gentle maiden," continued Ivanhoe, "is more disturbed by anxiety, than my body with pain. From the speeches of those men who were my warders just now, I learn that I am a prisoner, and, if I judge aright of the loud hoarse voice which even now dispatched them hence on some military duty, I am in the castle of Front-de-Boeuf—If so, how will this end, or how can I protect Rowena and my father?"

"He names not the Jew or Jewess," said Rebecca internally; "yet what is our portion in him, and how justly am I punished by Heaven for letting my thoughts dwell upon him!" She hastened after this brief self-accusation to give Ivanhoe what information she could; but it amounted only to this, that the Templar Bois-Guilbert, and the Baron Front-de-Boeuf, were commanders within the castle; that it was beleaguered from without, but by whom she knew not. She added, that there was a Christian priest within the castle who might be possessed of more information.

"A Christian priest!" said the knight, joyfully; "fetch him hither, Rebecca, if thou canst—say a sick man desires his ghostly counsel—say what thou wilt, but bring him—something I must do or attempt, but how can I determine until I know how matters stand without?"

Rebecca in compliance with the wishes of Ivanhoe, made that attempt to bring Cedric into the wounded Knight's chamber, which was defeated as we have already seen by the interference of Urfried, who had also been on the watch to intercept the supposed monk. Rebecca retired to communicate to Ivanhoe the result of her errand.

They had not much leisure to regret the failure of this source of intelligence, or to contrive by what means it might be supplied; for the noise within the castle, occasioned by the defensive preparations which had been considerable for some time, now increased into tenfold bustle and clamour. The heavy, yet hasty step of the men-at-arms, traversed the battlements or resounded on the narrow and winding passages and stairs which led to the various bartisans and points of defence. The voices of the knights were heard, animating their followers, or directing means of defence, while their commands were often drowned in the clashing of armour, or the clamorous shouts of those whom they addressed. Tremendous as these sounds were, and yet more terrible from the awful event which they presaged, there was a sublimity mixed with them, which Rebecca's high-toned mind could feel even in that moment of terror. Her eye kindled, although the blood fled from her cheeks; and there was a strong mixture of fear, and of a thrilling sense of the sublime, as she repeated, half whispering to herself, half speaking to her companion, the sacred text,—"The quiver rattleth—the glittering spear and the shield—the noise of the captains and the shouting!"

But Ivanhoe was like the war-horse of that sublime passage, glowing with impatience at his inactivity, and with his ardent desire to mingle in the affray of which these sounds were the introduction. "If I could but drag myself," he said, "to yonder window, that I might see how this brave game is like to go—If I had but bow to shoot a shaft, or battle-axe to strike were it but a single blow for our deliverance!—It is in vain—it is in vain—I am alike nerveless and weaponless!"

"Fret not thyself, noble knight," answered Rebecca, "the sounds have ceased of a sudden—it may be they join not battle."

"Thou knowest nought of it," said Wilfred, impatiently; "this dead pause only shows that the men are at their posts on the walls, and expecting an instant attack; what we have heard was but the instant muttering of the storm—it will burst anon in all its fury.—Could I but reach yonder window!"

"Thou wilt but injure thyself by the attempt, noble knight," replied his attendant. Observing his extreme solicitude, she firmly added, "I myself will stand at the lattice, and describe to you as I can what passes without."

"You must not—you shall not!" exclaimed Ivanhoe; "each lattice, each aperture, will be soon a mark for the archers; some random shaft—"

"It shall be welcome!" murmured Rebecca, as with firm pace she ascended two or three steps, which led to the window of which they spoke.

"Rebecca, dear Rebecca!" exclaimed Ivanhoe, "this is no maiden's pastime—do not expose thyself to wounds and death, and render me for ever miserable for having given the occasion; at least, cover thyself with yonder ancient buckler, and show as little of your person at the lattice as may be."

Following with wonderful promptitude the directions of Ivanhoe, and availing herself of the protection of the large ancient shield, which she placed against the lower part of the window, Rebecca, with tolerable security to herself, could witness part of what was passing without the castle, and report to Ivanhoe the preparations which the assailants were making for the storm. Indeed the situation which she thus obtained was peculiarly favourable for this purpose, because, being placed on an angle of the main building, Rebecca could not only see what passed beyond the precincts of the castle, but also commanded a view of the outwork likely to be the first object of the meditated assault. It was an exterior fortification of no great height or strength, intended to protect the postern-gate, through which Cedric had been recently dismissed by Front-de-Boeuf. The castle moat divided this species of barbican from the rest of the fortress, so that, in case of its being taken, it was easy to cut off the communication with the main building, by withdrawing the temporary bridge. In the outwork was a sallyport corresponding to the postern of the castle, and the whole was surrounded by a strong palisade. Rebecca could observe, from the number of men placed for the defence of this post, that the besieged entertained apprehensions for its safety; and from the mustering of the assailants in a direction nearly opposite to the outwork, it seemed no less plain that it had been selected as a vulnerable point of attack.

These appearances she hastily communicated to Ivanhoe, and added, "The skirts of the wood seem lined with archers, although only a few are advanced from its dark shadow."

"Under what banner?" asked Ivanhoe.

"Under no ensign of war which I can observe," answered Rebecca.

"A singular novelty," muttered the knight, "to advance to storm such a castle without pennon or banner displayed!—Seest thou who they be that act as leaders?"

"A knight, clad in sable armour, is the most conspicuous," said the Jewess; "he alone is armed from head to heel, and seems to assume the direction of all around him."

"What device does he bear on his shield?" replied Ivanhoe.

"Something resembling a bar of iron, and a padlock painted blue on the black shield."

"A fetterlock and shacklebolt azure," said Ivanhoe; "I know not who may bear the device, but well I ween it might now be mine own. Canst thou not see the motto?"

"Scarce the device itself at this distance," replied Rebecca; "but when the sun glances fair upon his shield, it shows as I tell you."

"Seem there no other leaders?" exclaimed the anxious enquirer.

"None of mark and distinction that I can behold from this station," said Rebecca; "but, doubtless, the other side of the castle is also assailed. They appear even now preparing to advance—God of Zion, protect us!—What a dreadful sight!—Those who advance first bear huge shields and defences made of plank; the others follow, bending their bows as they come on.—They raise their bows!—God of Moses, forgive the creatures thou hast made!"

Her description was here suddenly interrupted by the signal for assault, which was given by the blast of a shrill bugle, and at once answered by a flourish of the Norman trumpets from the battlements, which, mingled with the deep and hollow clang of the nakers, (a species of kettle-drum,) retorted in notes of defiance the challenge of the enemy. The shouts of both parties augmented the fearful din, the assailants crying, "Saint George for merry England!" and the Normans answering them with loud cries of "En avant De Bracy!—Beau-seant! Beau-seant!—Front-de-Boeuf a la rescousse!" according to the war-cries of their different commanders.

It was not, however, by clamour that the contest was to be decided, and the desperate efforts of the assailants were met by an equally vigorous defence on the part of the besieged. The archers, trained by their woodland pastimes to the most effective use of the long-bow, shot, to use the appropriate phrase of the time, so "wholly together," that no point at which a defender could show the least part of his person, escaped their cloth-yard shafts. By this heavy discharge, which continued as thick and sharp as hail, while, notwithstanding, every arrow had its individual aim, and flew by scores together against each embrasure and opening in the parapets, as well as at every window where a defender either occasionally had post, or might be suspected to be stationed,—by this sustained discharge, two or three of the garrison were slain, and several others wounded. But, confident in their armour of proof, and in the cover which their situation afforded, the followers of Front-de-Boeuf, and his allies, showed an obstinacy in defence proportioned to the fury of the attack and replied with the discharge of their large cross-bows, as well as with their long-bows, slings, and other missile weapons, to the close and continued shower of arrows; and, as the assailants were necessarily but indifferently protected, did considerably more damage than they received at their hand. The whizzing of shafts and of missiles, on both sides, was only interrupted by the shouts which arose when either side inflicted or sustained some notable loss.

"And I must lie here like a bedridden monk," exclaimed Ivanhoe, "while the game that gives me freedom or death is played out by the hand of others!—Look from the window once again, kind maiden, but beware that you are not marked by the archers beneath—Look out once more, and tell me if they yet advance to the storm."

With patient courage, strengthened by the interval which she had employed in mental devotion, Rebecca again took post at the lattice, sheltering herself, however, so as not to be visible from beneath.

"What dost thou see, Rebecca?" again demanded the wounded knight.

"Nothing but the cloud of arrows flying so thick as to dazzle mine eyes, and to hide the bowmen who shoot them."

"That cannot endure," said Ivanhoe; "if they press not right on to carry the castle by pure force of arms, the archery may avail but little against stone walls and bulwarks. Look for the Knight of the Fetterlock, fair Rebecca, and see how he bears himself; for as the leader is, so will his followers be."

"I see him not," said Rebecca.

"Foul craven!" exclaimed Ivanhoe; "does he blench from the helm when the wind blows highest?"

"He blenches not! he blenches not!" said Rebecca, "I see him now; he leads a body of men close under the outer barrier of the barbican. —They pull down the piles and palisades; they hew down the barriers with axes.—His high black plume floats abroad over the throng, like a raven over the field of the slain.—They have made a breach in the barriers—they rush in—they are thrust back!—Front-de-Boeuf heads the defenders; I see his gigantic form above the press. They throng again to the breach, and the pass is disputed hand to hand, and man to man. God of Jacob! it is the meeting of two fierce tides—the conflict of two oceans moved by adverse winds!"

She turned her head from the lattice, as if unable longer to endure a sight so terrible.

"Look forth again, Rebecca," said Ivanhoe, mistaking the cause of her retiring; "the archery must in some degree have ceased, since they are now fighting hand to hand.—Look again, there is now less danger."

Rebecca again looked forth, and almost immediately exclaimed, "Holy prophets of the law! Front-de-Boeuf and the Black Knight fight hand to hand on the breach, amid the roar of their followers, who watch the progress of the strife—Heaven strike with the cause of the oppressed and of the captive!" She then uttered a loud shriek, and exclaimed, "He is down!—he is down!"

"Who is down?" cried Ivanhoe; "for our dear Lady's sake, tell me which has fallen?"

"The Black Knight," answered Rebecca, faintly; then instantly again shouted with joyful eagerness—"But no—but no!—the name of the Lord of Hosts be blessed!—he is on foot again, and fights as if there were twenty men's strength in his single arm—His sword is broken—he snatches an axe from a yeoman—he presses Front-de-Boeuf with blow on blow—The giant stoops and totters like an oak under the steel of the woodman—he falls—he falls!"

"Front-de-Boeuf?" exclaimed Ivanhoe.

"Front-de-Boeuf!" answered the Jewess; "his men rush to the rescue, headed by the haughty Templar—their united force compels the champion to pause—They drag Front-de-Boeuf within the walls."

"The assailants have won the barriers, have they not?" said Ivanhoe.

"They have—they have!" exclaimed Rebecca—"and they press the besieged hard upon the outer wall; some plant ladders, some swarm like bees, and endeavour to ascend upon the shoulders of each other—down go stones, beams, and trunks of trees upon their heads, and as fast as they bear the wounded to the rear, fresh men supply their places in the assault—Great God! hast thou given men thine own image, that it should be thus cruelly defaced by the hands of their brethren!"

"Think not of that," said Ivanhoe; "this is no time for such thoughts—Who yield? —who push their way?"

"The ladders are thrown down," replied Rebecca, shuddering; "the soldiers lie grovelling under them like crushed reptiles—The besieged have the better."

"Saint George strike for us!" exclaimed the knight; "do the false yeomen give way?"

"No!" exclaimed Rebecca, "they bear themselves right yeomanly—the Black Knight approaches the postern with his huge axe—the thundering blows which he deals, you may hear them above all the din and shouts of the battle—Stones and beams are hailed down on the bold champion—he regards them no more than if they were thistle-down or feathers!"

"By Saint John of Acre," said Ivanhoe, raising himself joyfully on his couch, "methought there was but one man in England that might do such a deed!"

"The postern gate shakes," continued Rebecca; "it crashes—it is splintered by his blows—they rush in—the outwork is won—Oh, God!—they hurl the defenders from the battlements—they throw them into the moat—O men, if ye be indeed men, spare them that can resist no longer!"

"The bridge—the bridge which communicates with the castle—have they won that pass?" exclaimed Ivanhoe.

"No," replied Rebecca, "The Templar has destroyed the plank on which they crossed—few of the defenders escaped with him into the castle—the shrieks and cries which you hear tell the fate of the others—Alas!—I see it is still more difficult to look upon victory than upon battle."

"What do they now, maiden?" said Ivanhoe; "look forth yet again—this is no time to faint at bloodshed."

"It is over for the time," answered Rebecca; "our friends strengthen themselves within the outwork which they have mastered, and it affords them so good a shelter from the foemen's shot, that the garrison only bestow a few bolts on it from interval to interval, as if rather to disquiet than effectually to injure them."

"Our friends," said Wilfred, "will surely not abandon an enterprise so gloriously begun and so happily attained.—O no! I will put my faith in the good knight whose axe hath rent heart-of-oak and bars of iron.—Singular," he again muttered to himself, "if there be two who can do a deed of such derring-do! —a fetterlock, and a shackle-bolt on a field sable—what may that mean?—seest thou nought else, Rebecca, by which the Black Knight may be distinguished?"

"Nothing," said the Jewess; "all about him is black as the wing of the night raven. Nothing can I spy that can mark him further—but having once seen him put forth his strength in battle, methinks I could know him again among a thousand warriors. He rushes to the fray as if he were summoned to a banquet. There is more than mere strength, there seems as if the whole soul and spirit of the champion were given to every blow which he deals upon his enemies. God assoilize him of the sin of bloodshed!—it is fearful, yet magnificent, to behold how the arm and heart of one man can triumph over hundreds."

"Rebecca," said Ivanhoe, "thou hast painted a hero; surely they rest but to refresh their force, or to provide the means of crossing the moat—Under such a leader as thou hast spoken this knight to be, there are no craven fears, no cold-blooded delays, no yielding up a gallant emprize; since the difficulties which render it arduous render it also glorious. I swear by the honour of my house—I vow by the name of my bright lady-love, I would endure ten years' captivity to fight one day by that good knight's side in such a quarrel as this!"

"Alas," said Rebecca, leaving her station at the window, and approaching the couch of the wounded knight, "this impatient yearning after action—this struggling with and repining at your present weakness, will not fail to injure your returning health—How couldst thou hope to inflict wounds on others, ere that be healed which thou thyself hast received?"

"Rebecca," he replied, "thou knowest not how impossible it is for one trained to actions of chivalry to remain passive as a priest, or a woman, when they are acting deeds of honour around him. The love of battle is the food upon which we live—the dust of the 'melee' is the breath of our nostrils! We live not—we wish not to live—longer than while we are victorious and renowned—Such, maiden, are the laws of chivalry to which we are sworn, and to which we offer all that we hold dear."

"Alas!" said the fair Jewess, "and what is it, valiant knight, save an offering of sacrifice to a demon of vain glory, and a passing through the fire to Moloch?—What remains to you as the prize of all the blood you have spilled—of all the travail and pain you have endured—of all the tears which your deeds have caused, when death hath broken the strong man's spear, and overtaken the speed of his war-horse?"

"What remains?" cried Ivanhoe; "Glory, maiden, glory! which gilds our sepulchre and embalms our name."

"Glory?" continued Rebecca; "alas, is the rusted mail which hangs as a hatchment over the champion's dim and mouldering tomb—is the defaced sculpture of the inscription which the ignorant monk can hardly read to the enquiring pilgrim—are these sufficient rewards for the sacrifice of every kindly affection, for a life spent miserably that ye may make others miserable? Or is there such virtue in the rude rhymes of a wandering bard, that domestic love, kindly affection, peace and happiness, are so wildly bartered, to become the hero of those ballads which vagabond minstrels sing to drunken churls over their evening ale?"

"By the soul of Hereward!" replied the knight impatiently, "thou speakest, maiden, of thou knowest not what. Thou wouldst quench the pure light of chivalry, which alone distinguishes the noble from the base, the gentle knight from the churl and the savage; which rates our life far, far beneath the pitch of our honour; raises us victorious over pain, toil, and suffering, and teaches us to fear no evil but disgrace. Thou art no Christian, Rebecca; and to thee are unknown those high feelings which swell the bosom of a noble maiden when her lover hath done some deed of emprize which sanctions his flame. Chivalry!—why, maiden, she is the nurse of pure and high affection—the stay of the oppressed, the redresser of grievances, the curb of the power of the tyrant—Nobility were but an empty name without her, and liberty finds the best protection in her lance and her sword."

"I am, indeed," said Rebecca, "sprung from a race whose courage was distinguished in the defence of their own land, but who warred not, even while yet a nation, save at the command of the Deity, or in defending their country from oppression. The sound of the trumpet wakes Judah no longer, and her despised children are now but the unresisting victims of hostile and military oppression. Well hast thou spoken, Sir Knight,—until the God of Jacob shall raise up for his chosen people a second Gideon, or a new Maccabeus, it ill beseemeth the Jewish damsel to speak of battle or of war."

The high-minded maiden concluded the argument in a tone of sorrow, which deeply expressed her sense of the degradation of her people, embittered perhaps by the idea that Ivanhoe considered her as one not entitled to interfere in a case of honour, and incapable of entertaining or expressing sentiments of honour and generosity.

"How little he knows this bosom," she said, "to imagine that cowardice or meanness of soul must needs be its guests, because I have censured the fantastic chivalry of the Nazarenes! Would to heaven that the shedding of mine own blood, drop by drop, could redeem the captivity of Judah! Nay, would to God it could avail to set free my father, and this his benefactor, from the chains of the oppressor! The proud Christian should then see whether the daughter of God's chosen people dared not to die as bravely as the vainest Nazarene maiden, that boasts her descent from some petty chieftain of the rude and frozen north!"

She then looked towards the couch of the wounded knight.

"He sleeps," she said; "nature exhausted by sufferance and the waste of spirits, his wearied frame embraces the first moment of temporary relaxation to sink into slumber. Alas! is it a crime that I should look upon him, when it may be for the last time? —When yet but a short space, and those fair features will be no longer animated by the bold and buoyant spirit which forsakes them not even in sleep!—When the nostril shall be distended, the mouth agape, the eyes fixed and bloodshot; and when the proud and noble knight may be trodden on by the lowest caitiff of this accursed castle, yet stir not when the heel is lifted up against him!—And my father!—oh, my father! evil is it with his daughter, when his grey hairs are not remembered because of the golden locks of youth!—What know I but that these evils are the messengers of Jehovah's wrath to the unnatural child, who thinks of a stranger's captivity before a parent's? who forgets the desolation of Judah, and looks upon the comeliness of a Gentile and a stranger?—But I will tear this folly from my heart, though every fibre bleed as I rend it away!"

She wrapped herself closely in her veil, and sat down at a distance from the couch of the wounded knight, with her back turned towards it, fortifying, or endeavouring to fortify her mind, not only against the impending evils from without, but also against those treacherous feelings which assailed her from within.

XXX.

> Approach the chamber, look upon his bed.
> His is the passing of no peaceful ghost,
> Which, as the lark arises to the sky,

'Mid morning's sweetest breeze and softest dew,
Is wing'd to heaven by good men's sighs and tears!—
Anselm parts otherwise.

— OLD PLAY

During the interval of quiet which followed the first success of the besiegers, while the one party was preparing to pursue their advantage, and the other to strengthen their means of defence, the Templar and De Bracy held brief council together in the hall of the castle.

"Where is Front-de-Boeuf?" said the latter, who had superintended the defence of the fortress on the other side; "men say he hath been slain."

"He lives," said the Templar, coolly, "lives as yet; but had he worn the bull's head of which he bears the name, and ten plates of iron to fence it withal, he must have gone down before yonder fatal axe. Yet a few hours, and Front-de-Boeuf is with his fathers—a powerful limb lopped off Prince John's enterprise."

"And a brave addition to the kingdom of Satan," said De Bracy; "this comes of reviling saints and angels, and ordering images of holy things and holy men to be flung down on the heads of these rascaille yeomen."

"Go to—thou art a fool," said the Templar; "thy superstition is upon a level with Front-de-Boeuf's want of faith; neither of you can render a reason for your belief or unbelief."

"Benedicite, Sir Templar," replied De Bracy, "pray you to keep better rule with your tongue when I am the theme of it. By the Mother of Heaven, I am a better Christian man than thou and thy fellowship; for the 'bruit' goeth shrewdly out, that the most holy Order of the Temple of Zion nurseth not a few heretics within its bosom, and that Sir Brian de Bois-Guilbert is of the number."

"Care not thou for such reports," said the Templar; "but let us think of making good the castle.—How fought these villain yeomen on thy side?"

"Like fiends incarnate," said De Bracy. "They swarmed close up to the walls, headed, as I think, by the knave who won the prize at the archery, for I knew his horn and baldric. And this is old Fitzurse's boasted policy, encouraging these malapert knaves to rebel against us! Had I not been armed in proof, the villain had marked me down seven times with as little remorse as if I had been a buck in season. He told every rivet on my armour with a cloth-yard shaft, that rapped against my ribs with as little compunction as if my bones had been of iron—But that I wore a shirt of Spanish mail under my plate-coat, I had been fairly sped."

"But you maintained your post?" said the Templar. "We lost the outwork on our part."

"That is a shrewd loss," said De Bracy; "the knaves will find cover there to assault the castle more closely, and may, if not well watched, gain some unguarded corner of a tower, or some forgotten window, and so break in upon us. Our numbers are too few for the defence of every point, and the men complain that they can nowhere show themselves, but they are the mark for as many arrows as a parish-butt on a holyday even. Front-de-Boeuf is dying too, so we shall receive no more aid from his bull's head and brutal strength. How think you, Sir Brian, were we not better make a virtue of necessity, and compound with the rogues by delivering up our prisoners?"

"How?" exclaimed the Templar; "deliver up our prisoners, and stand an object alike of ridicule and execration, as the doughty warriors who dared by a night-attack to possess themselves of the persons of a party of defenceless travellers, yet could not make good a strong castle against a vagabond troop of outlaws, led by swineherds, jesters, and the very refuse of mankind?—Shame on thy counsel, Maurice de Bracy!—The ruins of this castle shall bury both my body and my shame, ere I consent to such base and dishonourable composition."

"Let us to the walls, then," said De Bracy, carelessly; "that man never breathed, be he Turk or Templar, who held life at lighter rate than I do. But I trust there is no dishonour in wishing I had here some two scores of my gallant troop of Free Companions?—Oh, my brave lances! if ye knew but how hard your captain were this day bested, how soon should I see my banner at the head of your clump of spears! And how short while would these rabble villains stand to endure your encounter!"

"Wish for whom thou wilt," said the Templar, "but let us make what defence we can with the soldiers who remain—They are chiefly Front-de-Boeuf's followers, hated by the English for a thousand acts of insolence and oppression."

"The better," said De Bracy; "the rugged slaves will defend themselves to the last drop of their blood, ere they encounter the revenge of the peasants without. Let us up and be doing, then, Brian de Bois-Guilbert; and, live or die, thou shalt see Maurice de Bracy bear himself this day as a gentleman of blood and lineage."

"To the walls!" answered the Templar; and they both ascended the battlements to do all that skill could dictate, and manhood accomplish, in defence of the place. They readily agreed that the point of greatest danger was that opposite to the outwork of which the assailants had possessed themselves. The castle, indeed, was divided from that barbican by the moat, and it was impossible that the besiegers could assail the postern-door, with which the outwork corresponded, without surmounting that obstacle; but it was the opinion both of the Templar and De Bracy, that the besiegers, if governed by the same policy their leader had already displayed, would endeavour, by a formidable assault, to draw the chief part of the defenders' observation to this point, and take measures to avail themselves of every negligence which might take place in the defence elsewhere. To guard against such an evil, their numbers only permitted the knights to place sentinels from space to space along the walls in communication with each other, who might give the alarm whenever danger was threatened. Meanwhile, they agreed that De Bracy should command the defence at the postern, and the Templar should keep with him a score of men or thereabouts as a body of reserve, ready to hasten to any other point which might be suddenly threatened. The loss of the barbican had also this unfortunate effect, that, notwithstanding the superior height of the castle walls, the besieged could not see from them, with the same precision as before, the operations of the enemy; for some straggling underwood approached so near the sallyport of the outwork, that the assailants might introduce into it whatever force they thought proper, not only under cover, but even without the knowledge of the defenders. Utterly uncertain, therefore, upon what point the storm was to burst, De Bracy and his companion were under the necessity of providing against every possible contingency, and their followers, however brave, experienced the anxious dejection of mind incident to men enclosed by enemies, who possessed the power of choosing their time and mode of attack.

Meanwhile, the lord of the beleaguered and endangered castle lay upon a bed of bodily pain and mental agony. He had not the usual resource of bigots in that superstitious period, most of whom were wont to atone for the crimes they were guilty of by liberality to the church, stupefying by this means their terrors by the idea of atonement and forgiveness; and although the refuge which success thus purchased, was no more like to the peace of mind which follows on sincere repentance, than the turbid stupefaction procured by opium resembles healthy and natural slumbers, it was still a state of mind preferable to the agonies of awakened remorse. But among the vices of Front-de-Boeuf, a hard and griping man, avarice was predominant; and he preferred setting church and churchmen at defiance, to purchasing from them pardon and absolution at the price of treasure and of manors. Nor did the Templar, an infidel of another stamp, justly characterise his associate, when he said Front-de-Boeuf could assign no cause for his unbelief and contempt for the established faith; for the Baron would have alleged that the Church sold her wares too dear, that the spiritual freedom which she put up to sale was only to be bought like that of the chief captain of Jerusalem, "with a great sum," and Front-de-Boeuf preferred denying the virtue of the medicine, to paying the expense of the physician.

But the moment had now arrived when earth and all his treasures were gliding from before his eyes, and when the savage Baron's heart, though hard as a nether millstone, became appalled as he gazed forward into the waste darkness of futurity. The fever of his body aided the impatience and agony of his mind, and his death-bed exhibited a mixture of the newly awakened feelings of horror, combating with the fixed and inveterate obstinacy of his disposition;—a fearful state of mind, only to be equalled in those tremendous regions, where there are complaints without hope, remorse without repentance, a dreadful sense of present agony, and a presentiment that it cannot cease or be diminished!

"Where be these dog-priests now," growled the Baron, "who set such price on their ghostly mummery?—where be all those unshod Carmelites, for whom old Front-de-Boeuf founded the convent of St Anne, robbing his heir of many a fair rood of meadow, and many a fat field and close—where be the greedy hounds now?—Swilling, I warrant me, at the ale, or playing their juggling tricks at the bedside of some miserly churl.—Me, the heir of their founder—me, whom their foundation binds them to pray for—me—ungrateful villains as they are!—they suffer to die like the houseless dog on yonder common, unshriven and unhouseled!—Tell the Templar to come hither—he is a priest, and may do something—But no!—as well confess myself to the devil as to Brian de Bois-Guilbert, who recks neither of heaven nor of hell.—I have heard old men talk of prayer—prayer by their own voice—Such need not to court or to bribe the false priest—But I—I dare not!"

"Lives Reginald Front-de-Boeuf," said a broken and shrill voice close by his bedside, "to say there is that which he dares not!"

The evil conscience and the shaken nerves of Front-de-Boeuf heard, in this strange interruption to his soliloquy, the voice of one of those demons, who, as the superstition of the times believed, beset the beds of dying men to distract their thoughts, and turn them from the meditations which concerned their eternal welfare. He shuddered and drew himself together; but, instantly summoning up his wonted resolution, he exclaimed, "Who is there?—what art thou, that darest to echo my words in a tone like that of the night-raven?—Come before my couch that I may see thee."

"I am thine evil angel, Reginald Front-de-Boeuf," replied the voice.

"Let me behold thee then in thy bodily shape, if thou be'st indeed a fiend," replied the dying knight; "think not that I will blench from thee.—By the eternal dungeon, could I but grapple with these horrors that hover round me, as I have done with mortal dangers, heaven or hell should never say that I shrunk from the conflict!"

"Think on thy sins, Reginald Front-de-Boeuf," said the almost unearthly voice, "on rebellion, on rapine, on murder!—Who stirred up the licentious John to war against his grey-headed father—against his generous brother?"

"Be thou fiend, priest, or devil," replied Front-de-Boeuf, "thou liest in thy throat! —Not I stirred John to rebellion—not I alone—there were fifty knights and barons, the flower of the midland counties—better men never laid lance in rest—And must I answer for the fault done by fifty?—False fiend, I defy thee! Depart, and haunt my couch no more—let me die in peace if thou be mortal—if thou be a demon, thy time is not yet come."

"In peace thou shalt NOT die," repeated the voice; "even in death shalt thou think on thy murders—on the groans which this castle has echoed—on the blood that is engrained in its floors!"

"Thou canst not shake me by thy petty malice," answered Front-de-Boeuf, with a ghastly and constrained laugh. "The infidel Jew—it was merit with heaven to deal with him as I did, else wherefore are men canonized who dip their hands in the blood of Saracens?—The Saxon porkers, whom I have slain, they were the foes of my country, and of my lineage, and of my liege lord.—Ho! ho! thou seest there is no crevice in my coat of plate—Art thou fled?—art thou silenced?"

"No, foul parricide!" replied the voice; "think of thy father!—think of his death!— think of his banquet-room flooded with his gore, and that poured forth by the hand of a son!"

"Ha!" answered the Baron, after a long pause, "an thou knowest that, thou art indeed the author of evil, and as omniscient as the monks call thee!—That secret I deemed locked in my own breast, and in that of one besides—the temptress, the partaker of my guilt.—Go, leave me, fiend! and seek the Saxon witch Ulrica, who alone could tell thee what she and I alone witnessed.—Go, I say, to her, who washed the wounds, and straighted the corpse, and gave to the slain man the outward show of one parted in time and in the course of nature—Go to her, she was my temptress, the foul provoker, the more foul rewarder, of the deed—let her, as well as I, taste of the tortures which anticipate hell!"

"She already tastes them," said Ulrica, stepping before the couch of Front-de-Boeuf; "she hath long drunken of this cup, and its bitterness is now sweetened to see that thou dost partake it.—Grind not thy teeth, Front-de-Boeuf—roll not thine eyes— clench not thine hand, nor shake it at me with that gesture of menace!—The hand which, like that of thy renowned ancestor who gained thy name, could have broken with one stroke the skull of a mountain-bull, is now unnerved and powerless as mine own!"

"Vile murderous hag!" replied Front-de-Boeuf; "detestable screech-owl! it is then thou who art come to exult over the ruins thou hast assisted to lay low?"

"Ay, Reginald Front-de-Boeuf," answered she, "it is Ulrica!—it is the daughter of the murdered Torquil Wolfganger!—it is the sister of his slaughtered sons!—it is she who demands of thee, and of thy father's house, father and kindred, name and fame —all that she has lost by the name of Front-de-Boeuf!—Think of my wrongs, Front-de-Boeuf, and answer me if I speak not truth. Thou hast been my evil angel, and I will be thine—I will dog thee till the very instant of dissolution!"

"Detestable fury!" exclaimed Front-de-Boeuf, "that moment shalt thou never witness—Ho! Giles, Clement, and Eustace! Saint Maur, and Stephen! seize this damned witch, and hurl her from the battlements headlong—she has betrayed us to the Saxon!—Ho! Saint Maur! Clement! false-hearted, knaves, where tarry ye?"

"Call on them again, valiant Baron," said the hag, with a smile of grisly mockery; "summon thy vassals around thee, doom them that loiter to the scourge and the dungeon—But know, mighty chief," she continued, suddenly changing her tone, "thou shalt have neither answer, nor aid, nor obedience at their hands.—Listen to these horrid sounds," for the din of the recommenced assault and defence now rung fearfully loud from the battlements of the castle; "in that war-cry is the downfall of thy house—The blood-cemented fabric of Front-de-Boeuf's power totters to the foundation, and before the foes he most despised!—The Saxon, Reginald!—the scorned Saxon assails thy walls!—Why liest thou here, like a worn-out hind, when the Saxon storms thy place of strength?"

"Gods and fiends!" exclaimed the wounded knight; "O, for one moment's strength, to drag myself to the 'melee', and perish as becomes my name!"

"Think not of it, valiant warrior!" replied she; "thou shalt die no soldier's death, but perish like the fox in his den, when the peasants have set fire to the cover around it."

"Hateful hag! thou liest!" exclaimed Front-de-Boeuf; "my followers bear them bravely—my walls are strong and high—my comrades in arms fear not a whole host of Saxons, were they headed by Hengist and Horsa!—The war-cry of the Templar and of the Free Companions rises high over the conflict! And by mine honour, when we kindle the blazing beacon, for joy of our defence, it shall consume thee, body and bones; and I shall live to hear thou art gone from earthly fires to those of that hell, which never sent forth an incarnate fiend more utterly diabolical!"

"Hold thy belief," replied Ulrica, "till the proof reach thee—But, no!" she said, interrupting herself, "thou shalt know, even now, the doom, which all thy power, strength, and courage, is unable to avoid, though it is prepared for thee by this feeble band. Markest thou the smouldering and suffocating vapour which already eddies in sable folds through the chamber?—Didst thou think it was but the darkening of thy bursting eyes—the difficulty of thy cumbered breathing?—No! Front-de-Boeuf, there is another cause—Rememberest thou the magazine of fuel that is stored beneath these apartments?"

"Woman!" he exclaimed with fury, "thou hast not set fire to it?—By heaven, thou hast, and the castle is in flames!"

"They are fast rising at least," said Ulrica, with frightful composure; "and a signal shall soon wave to warn the besiegers to press hard upon those who would extinguish them.—Farewell, Front-de-Boeuf!—May Mista, Skogula, and Zernebock, gods of the ancient Saxons—fiends, as the priests now call them—supply the place of comforters at your dying bed, which Ulrica now relinquishes!—But know, if it will give thee comfort to know it, that Ulrica is bound to the same dark coast with thyself, the companion of thy punishment as the companion of thy guilt.—And now, parricide, farewell for ever!—May each stone of this vaulted roof find a tongue to echo that title into thine ear!"

So saying, she left the apartment; and Front-de-Boeuf could hear the crash of the ponderous key, as she locked and double-locked the door behind her, thus cutting off the most slender chance of escape. In the extremity of agony he shouted upon his servants and allies—"Stephen and Saint Maur!—Clement and Giles!—I burn here unaided!—To the rescue—to the rescue, brave Bois-Guilbert, valiant De Bracy!—It is Front-de-Boeuf who calls!—It is your master, ye traitor squires!—Your ally—your brother in arms, ye perjured and faithless knights!—all the curses due to traitors upon your recreant heads, do you abandon me to perish thus miserably!—They hear me not—they cannot hear me—my voice is lost in the din of battle.—The smoke rolls thicker and thicker—the fire has caught upon the floor below—O, for one drought of the air of heaven, were it to be purchased by instant annihilation!" And in the mad frenzy of despair, the wretch now shouted with the shouts of the fighters, now muttered curses on himself, on mankind, and on Heaven itself.—"The red fire flashes through the thick smoke!" he exclaimed; "the demon marches against me under the banner of his own element—Foul spirit, avoid!—I go not with thee without my comrades—all, all are thine, that garrison these walls—Thinkest thou Front-de-Boeuf will be singled out to go alone?—No—the infidel Templar—the licentious De Bracy—Ulrica, the foul murdering strumpet—the men who aided my enterprises—the dog Saxons and accursed Jews, who are my prisoners—all, all shall attend me—a goodly fellowship as ever took the downward road—Ha, ha, ha!" and he laughed in his frenzy till the vaulted roof rang again. "Who laughed there?" exclaimed Front-de-Boeuf, in altered mood, for the noise of the conflict did not prevent the echoes of his own mad laughter from returning upon his ear—"who laughed there?—Ulrica, was it thou?—Speak, witch, and I forgive thee—for, only thou or the fiend of hell himself could have laughed at such a moment. Avaunt—avaunt!—"

But it were impious to trace any farther the picture of the blasphemer and parricide's deathbed.

XXXI.

> Once more unto the breach, dear friends, once more,
> Or, close the wall up with our English dead.
> ———And you, good yeomen,
> Whose limbs were made in England, show us here
> The mettle of your pasture—let us swear
> That you are worth your breeding.
>
> — KING HENRY V

Cedric, although not greatly confident in Ulrica's message, omitted not to communicate her promise to the Black Knight and Locksley. They were well pleased to find they had a friend within the place, who might, in the moment of need, be able to facilitate their entrance, and readily agreed with the Saxon that a storm, under whatever disadvantages, ought to be attempted, as the only means of liberating the prisoners now in the hands of the cruel Front-de-Boeuf.

"The royal blood of Alfred is endangered," said Cedric.

"The honour of a noble lady is in peril," said the Black Knight.

"And, by the Saint Christopher at my baldric," said the good yeoman, "were there no other cause than the safety of that poor faithful knave, Wamba, I would jeopard a joint ere a hair of his head were hurt."

"And so would I," said the Friar; "what, sirs! I trust well that a fool—I mean, d'ye see me, sirs, a fool that is free of his guild and master of his craft, and can give as much relish and flavour to a cup of wine as ever a flitch of bacon can—I say, brethren, such a fool shall never want a wise clerk to pray for or fight for him at a strait, while I can say a mass or flourish a partisan." And with that he made his heavy halberd to play around his head as a shepherd boy flourishes his light crook.

"True, Holy Clerk," said the Black Knight, "true as if Saint Dunstan himself had said it.—And now, good Locksley, were it not well that noble Cedric should assume the direction of this assault?"

"Not a jot I," returned Cedric; "I have never been wont to study either how to take or how to hold out those abodes of tyrannic power, which the Normans have erected in this groaning land. I will fight among the foremost; but my honest neighbours well know I am not a trained soldier in the discipline of wars, or the attack of strongholds."

"Since it stands thus with noble Cedric," said Locksley, "I am most willing to take on me the direction of the archery; and ye shall hang me up on my own Trysting-tree, an the defenders be permitted to show themselves over the walls without being stuck with as many shafts as there are cloves in a gammon of bacon at Christmas."

"Well said, stout yeoman," answered the Black Knight; "and if I be thought worthy to have a charge in these matters, and can find among these brave men as many as are willing to follow a true English knight, for so I may surely call myself, I am ready, with such skill as my experience has taught me, to lead them to the attack of these walls."

The parts being thus distributed to the leaders, they commenced the first assault, of which the reader has already heard the issue.

When the barbican was carried, the Sable Knight sent notice of the happy event to Locksley, requesting him at the same time, to keep such a strict observation on the castle as might prevent the defenders from combining their force for a sudden sally, and recovering the outwork which they had lost. This the knight was chiefly desirous of avoiding, conscious that the men whom he led, being hasty and untrained volunteers, imperfectly armed and unaccustomed to discipline, must, upon any sudden attack, fight at great disadvantage with the veteran soldiers of the Norman knights, who were well provided with arms both defensive and offensive; and who, to match the zeal and high spirit of the besiegers, had all the confidence which arises from perfect discipline and the habitual use of weapons.

The knight employed the interval in causing to be constructed a sort of floating bridge, or long raft, by means of which he hoped to cross the moat in despite of the resistance of the enemy. This was a work of some time, which the leaders the less regretted, as it gave Ulrica leisure to execute her plan of diversion in their favour, whatever that might be.

When the raft was completed, the Black Knight addressed the besiegers:—"It avails not waiting here longer, my friends; the sun is descending to the west—and I have that upon my hands which will not permit me to tarry with you another day. Besides, it will be a marvel if the horsemen come not upon us from York, unless we speedily accomplish our purpose. Wherefore, one of ye go to Locksley, and bid him commence a discharge of arrows on the opposite side of the castle, and move forward as if about to assault it; and you, true English hearts, stand by me, and be ready to thrust the raft endlong over the moat whenever the postern on our side is thrown open. Follow me boldly across, and aid me to burst yon sallyport in the main wall of the castle. As many of you as like not this service, or are but ill armed to meet it, do you man the top of the outwork, draw your bow-strings to your ears, and mind you quell with your shot whatever shall appear to man the rampart—Noble Cedric, wilt thou take the direction of those which remain?"

"Not so, by the soul of Hereward!" said the Saxon; "lead I cannot; but may posterity curse me in my grave, if I follow not with the foremost wherever thou shalt point the way—The quarrel is mine, and well it becomes me to be in the van of the battle."

"Yet, bethink thee, noble Saxon," said the knight, "thou hast neither hauberk, nor corslet, nor aught but that light helmet, target, and sword."

"The better!" answered Cedric; "I shall be the lighter to climb these walls. And,—forgive the boast, Sir Knight,—thou shalt this day see the naked breast of a Saxon as boldly presented to the battle as ever ye beheld the steel corslet of a Norman."

"In the name of God, then," said the knight, "fling open the door, and launch the floating bridge."

The portal, which led from the inner-wall of the barbican to the moat, and which corresponded with a sallyport in the main wall of the castle, was now suddenly opened; the temporary bridge was then thrust forward, and soon flashed in the waters, extending its length between the castle and outwork, and forming a slippery and precarious passage for two men abreast to cross the moat. Well aware of the importance of taking the foe by surprise, the Black Knight, closely followed by Cedric, threw himself upon the bridge, and reached the opposite side. Here he began to thunder with his axe upon the gate of the castle, protected in part from the shot and stones cast by the defenders by the ruins of the former drawbridge, which the Templar had demolished in his retreat from the barbican, leaving the counterpoise still attached to the upper part of the portal. The followers of the knight had no such shelter; two were instantly shot with cross-bow bolts, and two more fell into the moat; the others retreated back into the barbican.

The situation of Cedric and of the Black Knight was now truly dangerous, and would have been still more so, but for the constancy of the archers in the barbican, who ceased not to shower their arrows upon the battlements, distracting the attention of those by whom they were manned, and thus affording a respite to their two chiefs from the storm of missiles which must otherwise have overwhelmed them. But their situation was eminently perilous, and was becoming more so with every moment.

"Shame on ye all!" cried De Bracy to the soldiers around him; "do ye call yourselves cross-bowmen, and let these two dogs keep their station under the walls of the castle?—Heave over the coping stones from the battlements, an better may not be—Get pick-axe and levers, and down with that huge pinnacle!" pointing to a heavy piece of stone carved-work that projected from the parapet.

At this moment the besiegers caught sight of the red flag upon the angle of the tower which Ulrica had described to Cedric. The stout yeoman Locksley was the first who was aware of it, as he was hasting to the outwork, impatient to see the progress of the assault.

"Saint George!" he cried, "Merry Saint George for England!—To the charge, bold yeomen!—why leave ye the good knight and noble Cedric to storm the pass alone?—make in, mad priest, show thou canst fight for thy rosary,—make in, brave yeomen!—the castle is ours, we have friends within—See yonder flag, it is the appointed signal—Torquilstone is ours!—Think of honour, think of spoil—One effort, and the place is ours!"

With that he bent his good bow, and sent a shaft right through the breast of one of the men-at-arms, who, under De Bracy's direction, was loosening a fragment from one of the battlements to precipitate on the heads of Cedric and the Black Knight. A second soldier caught from the hands of the dying man the iron crow, with which he heaved at and had loosened the stone pinnacle, when, receiving an arrow through his head-piece, he dropped from the battlements into the moat a dead man. The men-at-arms were daunted, for no armour seemed proof against the shot of this tremendous archer.

"Do you give ground, base knaves!" said De Bracy; "'Mount joye Saint Dennis!'—Give me the lever!"

And, snatching it up, he again assailed the loosened pinnacle, which was of weight enough, if thrown down, not only to have destroyed the remnant of the drawbridge, which sheltered the two foremost assailants, but also to have sunk the rude float of planks over which they had crossed. All saw the danger, and the boldest, even the stout Friar himself, avoided setting foot on the raft. Thrice did Locksley bend his shaft against De Bracy, and thrice did his arrow bound back from the knight's armour of proof.

"Curse on thy Spanish steel-coat!" said Locksley, "had English smith forged it, these arrows had gone through, an as if it had been silk or sendal." He then began to call out, "Comrades! friends! noble Cedric! bear back, and let the ruin fall."

His warning voice was unheard, for the din which the knight himself occasioned by his strokes upon the postern would have drowned twenty war-trumpets. The faithful Gurth indeed sprung forward on the planked bridge, to warn Cedric of his impending fate, or to share it with him. But his warning would have come too late; the massive pinnacle already tottered, and De Bracy, who still heaved at his task, would have accomplished it, had not the voice of the Templar sounded close in his ears:—

"All is lost, De Bracy, the castle burns."

"Thou art mad to say so!" replied the knight.

"It is all in a light flame on the western side. I have striven in vain to extinguish it."

With the stern coolness which formed the basis of his character, Brian de Bois-Guilbert communicated this hideous intelligence, which was not so calmly received by his astonished comrade.

"Saints of Paradise!" said De Bracy; "what is to be done? I vow to Saint Nicholas of Limoges a candlestick of pure gold—"

"Spare thy vow," said the Templar, "and mark me. Lead thy men down, as if to a sally; throw the postern-gate open—There are but two men who occupy the float, fling them into the moat, and push across for the barbican. I will charge from the main gate, and attack the barbican on the outside; and if we can regain that post, be assured we shall defend ourselves until we are relieved, or at least till they grant us fair quarter."

"It is well thought upon," said De Bracy; "I will play my part—Templar, thou wilt not fail me?"

"Hand and glove, I will not!" said Bois-Guilbert. "But haste thee, in the name of God!"

De Bracy hastily drew his men together, and rushed down to the postern-gate, which he caused instantly to be thrown open. But scarce was this done ere the portentous strength of the Black Knight forced his way inward in despite of De Bracy and his followers. Two of the foremost instantly fell, and the rest gave way notwithstanding all their leader's efforts to stop them.

"Dogs!" said De Bracy, "will ye let TWO men win our only pass for safety?"

"He is the devil!" said a veteran man-at-arms, bearing back from the blows of their sable antagonist.

"And if he be the devil," replied De Bracy, "would you fly from him into the mouth of hell?—the castle burns behind us, villains!—let despair give you courage, or let me forward! I will cope with this champion myself."

And well and chivalrous did De Bracy that day maintain the fame he had acquired in the civil wars of that dreadful period. The vaulted passage to which the postern gave entrance, and in which these two redoubted champions were now fighting hand to hand, rung with the furious blows which they dealt each other, De Bracy with his sword, the Black Knight with his ponderous axe. At length the Norman received a blow, which, though its force was partly parried by his shield, for otherwise never more would De Bracy have again moved limb, descended yet with such violence on his crest, that he measured his length on the paved floor.

"Yield thee, De Bracy," said the Black Champion, stooping over him, and holding against the bars of his helmet the fatal poniard with which the knights dispatched their enemies, (and which was called the dagger of mercy,)—"yield thee, Maurice de Bracy, rescue or no rescue, or thou art but a dead man."

"I will not yield," replied De Bracy faintly, "to an unknown conqueror. Tell me thy name, or work thy pleasure on me—it shall never be said that Maurice de Bracy was prisoner to a nameless churl."

The Black Knight whispered something into the ear of the vanquished.

"I yield me to be true prisoner, rescue or no rescue," answered the Norman, exchanging his tone of stern and determined obstinacy for one of deep though sullen submission.

"Go to the barbican," said the victor, in a tone of authority, "and there wait my further orders."

"Yet first, let me say," said De Bracy, "what it imports thee to know. Wilfred of Ivanhoe is wounded and a prisoner, and will perish in the burning castle without present help."

"Wilfred of Ivanhoe!" exclaimed the Black Knight—"prisoner, and perish!—The life of every man in the castle shall answer it if a hair of his head be singed—Show me his chamber!"

"Ascend yonder winding stair," said De Bracy; "it leads to his apartment—Wilt thou not accept my guidance?" he added, in a submissive voice.

"No. To the barbican, and there wait my orders. I trust thee not, De Bracy."

During this combat and the brief conversation which ensued, Cedric, at the head of a body of men, among whom the Friar was conspicuous, had pushed across the bridge as soon as they saw the postern open, and drove back the dispirited and despairing followers of De Bracy, of whom some asked quarter, some offered vain resistance, and the greater part fled towards the court-yard. De Bracy himself arose from the ground, and cast a sorrowful glance after his conqueror. "He trusts me not!" he repeated; "but have I deserved his trust?" He then lifted his sword from the floor, took off his helmet in token of submission, and, going to the barbican, gave up his sword to Locksley, whom he met by the way.

As the fire augmented, symptoms of it became soon apparent in the chamber, where Ivanhoe was watched and tended by the Jewess Rebecca. He had been awakened from his brief slumber by the noise of the battle; and his attendant, who had, at his anxious desire, again placed herself at the window to watch and report to him the fate of the attack, was for some time prevented from observing either, by the increase of the smouldering and stifling vapour. At length the volumes of smoke which rolled into the apartment—the cries for water, which were heard even above the din of the battle made them sensible of the progress of this new danger.

"The castle burns," said Rebecca; "it burns!—What can we do to save ourselves?"

"Fly, Rebecca, and save thine own life," said Ivanhoe, "for no human aid can avail me."

"I will not fly," answered Rebecca; "we will be saved or perish together—And yet, great God!—my father, my father—what will be his fate!"

At this moment the door of the apartment flew open, and the Templar presented himself,—a ghastly figure, for his gilded armour was broken and bloody, and the plume was partly shorn away, partly burnt from his casque. "I have found thee," said he to Rebecca; "thou shalt prove I will keep my word to share weal and woe with thee—There is but one path to safety, I have cut my way through fifty dangers to point it to thee—up, and instantly follow me!"

"Alone," answered Rebecca, "I will not follow thee. If thou wert born of woman—if thou hast but a touch of human charity in thee—if thy heart be not hard as thy breastplate—save my aged father—save this wounded knight!"

"A knight," answered the Templar, with his characteristic calmness, "a knight, Rebecca, must encounter his fate, whether it meet him in the shape of sword or flame—and who recks how or where a Jew meets with his?"

"Savage warrior," said Rebecca, "rather will I perish in the flames than accept safety from thee!"

"Thou shalt not choose, Rebecca—once didst thou foil me, but never mortal did so twice."

So saying, he seized on the terrified maiden, who filled the air with her shrieks, and bore her out of the room in his arms in spite of her cries, and without regarding the menaces and defiance which Ivanhoe thundered against him. "Hound of the Temple—stain to thine Order—set free the damsel! Traitor of Bois-Guilbert, it is Ivanhoe commands thee!—Villain, I will have thy heart's blood!"

"I had not found thee, Wilfred," said the Black Knight, who at that instant entered the apartment, "but for thy shouts."

"If thou be'st true knight," said Wilfred, "think not of me—pursue yon ravisher—save the Lady Rowena—look to the noble Cedric!"

"In their turn," answered he of the Fetterlock, "but thine is first."

And seizing upon Ivanhoe, he bore him off with as much ease as the Templar had carried off Rebecca, rushed with him to the postern, and having there delivered his burden to the care of two yeomen, he again entered the castle to assist in the rescue of the other prisoners.

One turret was now in bright flames, which flashed out furiously from window and shot-hole. But in other parts, the great thickness of the walls and the vaulted roofs of the apartments, resisted the progress of the flames, and there the rage of man still triumphed, as the scarce more dreadful element held mastery elsewhere; for the besiegers pursued the defenders of the castle from chamber to chamber, and satiated in their blood the vengeance which had long animated them against the soldiers of the tyrant Front-de-Boeuf. Most of the garrison resisted to the uttermost—few of them asked quarter—none received it. The air was filled with groans and clashing of arms—the floors were slippery with the blood of despairing and expiring wretches.

Through this scene of confusion, Cedric rushed in quest of Rowena, while the faithful Gurth, following him closely through the "melee", neglected his own safety while he strove to avert the blows that were aimed at his master. The noble Saxon was so fortunate as to reach his ward's apartment just as she had abandoned all hope of safety, and, with a crucifix clasped in agony to her bosom, sat in expectation of instant death. He committed her to the charge of Gurth, to be conducted in safety to the barbican, the road to which was now cleared of the enemy, and not yet interrupted by the flames. This accomplished, the loyal Cedric hastened in quest of his friend Athelstane, determined, at every risk to himself, to save that last scion of Saxon royalty. But ere Cedric penetrated as far as the old hall in which he had himself been a prisoner, the inventive genius of Wamba had procured liberation for himself and his companion in adversity.

When the noise of the conflict announced that it was at the hottest, the Jester began to shout, with the utmost power of his lungs, "Saint George and the dragon!—Bonny Saint George for merry England!—The castle is won!" And these sounds he rendered yet more fearful, by banging against each other two or three pieces of rusty armour which lay scattered around the hall.

A guard, which had been stationed in the outer, or anteroom, and whose spirits were already in a state of alarm, took fright at Wamba's clamour, and, leaving the door open behind them, ran to tell the Templar that foemen had entered the old hall. Meantime the prisoners found no difficulty in making their escape into the anteroom, and from thence into the court of the castle, which was now the last scene of contest. Here sat the fierce Templar, mounted on horseback, surrounded by several of the garrison both on horse and foot, who had united their strength to that of this renowned leader, in order to secure the last chance of safety and retreat which remained to them. The drawbridge had been lowered by his orders, but the passage was beset; for the archers, who had hitherto only annoyed the castle on that side by their missiles, no sooner saw the flames breaking out, and the bridge lowered, than they thronged to the entrance, as well to prevent the escape of the garrison, as to secure their own share of booty ere the castle should be burnt down. On the other hand, a party of the besiegers who had entered by the postern were now issuing out into the court-yard, and attacking with fury the remnant of the defenders who were thus assaulted on both sides at once.

Animated, however, by despair, and supported by the example of their indomitable leader, the remaining soldiers of the castle fought with the utmost valour; and, being well-armed, succeeded more than once in driving back the assailants, though much inferior in numbers. Rebecca, placed on horseback before one of the Templar's Saracen slaves, was in the midst of the little party; and Bois-Guilbert, notwithstanding the confusion of the bloody fray, showed every attention to her safety. Repeatedly he was by her side, and, neglecting his own defence, held before her the fence of his triangular steel-plated shield; and anon starting from his position by her, he cried his war-cry, dashed forward, struck to earth the most forward of the assailants, and was on the same instant once more at her bridle rein.

Athelstane, who, as the reader knows, was slothful, but not cowardly, beheld the female form whom the Templar protected thus sedulously, and doubted not that it was Rowena whom the knight was carrying off, in despite of all resistance which could be offered.

"By the soul of Saint Edward," he said, "I will rescue her from yonder over-proud knight, and he shall die by my hand!"

"Think what you do!" cried Wamba; "hasty hand catches frog for fish—by my bauble, yonder is none of my Lady Rowena—see but her long dark locks!—Nay, an ye will not know black from white, ye may be leader, but I will be no follower—no bones of mine shall be broken unless I know for whom.—And you without armour too!—Bethink you, silk bonnet never kept out steel blade.—Nay, then, if wilful will to water, wilful must drench.—'Deus vobiscum', most doughty Athelstane!"—he concluded, loosening the hold which he had hitherto kept upon the Saxon's tunic.

To snatch a mace from the pavement, on which it lay beside one whose dying grasp had just relinquished it—to rush on the Templar's band, and to strike in quick succession to the right and left, levelling a warrior at each blow, was, for Athelstane's great strength, now animated with unusual fury, but the work of a single moment; he was soon within two yards of Bois-Guilbert, whom he defied in his loudest tone.

"Turn, false-hearted Templar! let go her whom thou art unworthy to touch—turn, limb of a hand of murdering and hypocritical robbers!"

"Dog!" said the Templar, grinding his teeth, "I will teach thee to blaspheme the holy Order of the Temple of Zion;" and with these words, half-wheeling his steed, he made a demi-courbette towards the Saxon, and rising in the stirrups, so as to take full advantage of the descent of the horse, he discharged a fearful blow upon the head of Athelstane.

Well said Wamba, that silken bonnet keeps out no steel blade. So trenchant was the Templar's weapon, that it shore asunder, as it had been a willow twig, the tough and plaited handle of the mace, which the ill-fated Saxon reared to parry the blow, and, descending on his head, levelled him with the earth.

"'Ha! Beau-seant!'" exclaimed Bois-Guilbert, "thus be it to the maligners of the Temple-knights!" Taking advantage of the dismay which was spread by the fall of Athelstane, and calling aloud, "Those who would save themselves, follow me!" he pushed across the drawbridge, dispersing the archers who would have intercepted them. He was followed by his Saracens, and some five or six men-at-arms, who had mounted their horses. The Templar's retreat was rendered perilous by the numbers of arrows shot off at him and his party; but this did not prevent him from galloping round to the barbican, of which, according to his previous plan, he supposed it possible De Bracy might have been in possession.

"De Bracy! De Bracy!" he shouted, "art thou there?"

"I am here," replied De Bracy, "but I am a prisoner."

"Can I rescue thee?" cried Bois-Guilbert.

"No," replied De Bracy; "I have rendered me, rescue or no rescue. I will be true prisoner. Save thyself—there are hawks abroad—put the seas betwixt you and England—I dare not say more."

"Well," answered the Templar, "an thou wilt tarry there, remember I have redeemed word and glove. Be the hawks where they will, methinks the walls of the Preceptory of Templestowe will be cover sufficient, and thither will I, like heron to her haunt."

Having thus spoken, he galloped off with his followers.

Those of the castle who had not gotten to horse, still continued to fight desperately with the besiegers, after the departure of the Templar, but rather in despair of quarter than that they entertained any hope of escape. The fire was spreading rapidly through all parts of the castle, when Ulrica, who had first kindled it, appeared on a turret, in the guise of one of the ancient furies, yelling forth a war-song, such as was of yore raised on the field of battle by the scalds of the yet heathen Saxons. Her long dishevelled grey hair flew back from her uncovered head; the inebriating delight of gratified vengeance contended in her eyes with the fire of insanity; and she brandished the distaff which she held in her hand, as if she had been one of the Fatal Sisters, who spin and abridge the thread of human life. Tradition has preserved some wild strophes of the barbarous hymn which she chanted wildly amid that scene of fire and of slaughter:—

IVANHOE

1.
Whet the bright steel,
Sons of the White Dragon!
Kindle the torch,
Daughter of Hengist!
The steel glimmers not for the carving of the banquet,
It is hard, broad, and sharply pointed;
The torch goeth not to the bridal chamber,
It steams and glitters blue with sulphur.
Whet the steel, the raven croaks!
Light the torch, Zernebock is yelling!
Whet the steel, sons of the Dragon!
Kindle the torch, daughter of Hengist!

2.
The black cloud is low over the thane's castle
The eagle screams—he rides on its bosom.
Scream not, grey rider of the sable cloud,
Thy banquet is prepared!
The maidens of Valhalla look forth,
The race of Hengist will send them guests.
Shake your black tresses, maidens of Valhalla!
And strike your loud timbrels for joy!
Many a haughty step bends to your halls,
Many a helmed head.

3.
Dark sits the evening upon the thanes castle,
The black clouds gather round;
Soon shall they be red as the blood of the valiant!
The destroyer of forests shall shake his red crest against them.
He, the bright consumer of palaces,
Broad waves he his blazing banner,
Red, wide and dusky,
Over the strife of the valiant:
His joy is in the clashing swords and broken bucklers;
He loves to lick the hissing blood as it bursts warm from the wound!

4.
All must perish!
The sword cleaveth the helmet;
The strong armour is pierced by the lance;
Fire devoureth the dwelling of princes,
Engines break down the fences of the battle.

> All must perish!
> The race of Hengist is gone—
> The name of Horsa is no more!
> Shrink not then from your doom, sons of the sword!
> Let your blades drink blood like wine;
> Feast ye in the banquet of slaughter,
> By the light of the blazing halls!
> Strong be your swords while your blood is warm,
> And spare neither for pity nor fear,
> For vengeance hath but an hour;
> Strong hate itself shall expire
> I also must perish!

The towering flames had now surmounted every obstruction, and rose to the evening skies one huge and burning beacon, seen far and wide through the adjacent country. Tower after tower crashed down, with blazing roof and rafter; and the combatants were driven from the court-yard. The vanquished, of whom very few remained, scattered and escaped into the neighbouring wood. The victors, assembling in large bands, gazed with wonder, not unmixed with fear, upon the flames, in which their own ranks and arms glanced dusky red. The maniac figure of the Saxon Ulrica was for a long time visible on the lofty stand she had chosen, tossing her arms abroad with wild exultation, as if she reined empress of the conflagration which she had raised. At length, with a terrific crash, the whole turret gave way, and she perished in the flames which had consumed her tyrant. An awful pause of horror silenced each murmur of the armed spectators, who, for the space of several minutes, stirred not a finger, save to sign the cross. The voice of Locksley was then heard, "Shout, yeomen! —the den of tyrants is no more! Let each bring his spoil to our chosen place of rendezvous at the Trysting-tree in the Harthill-walk; for there at break of day will we make just partition among our own bands, together with our worthy allies in this great deed of vengeance."

XXXII.

> Trust me each state must have its policies:
> Kingdoms have edicts, cities have their charters;
> Even the wild outlaw, in his forest-walk,
> Keeps yet some touch of civil discipline;
> For not since Adam wore his verdant apron,
> Hath man with man in social union dwelt,
> But laws were made to draw that union closer.
>
> — OLD PLAY

The daylight had dawned upon the glades of the oak forest. The green boughs glittered with all their pearls of dew. The hind led her fawn from the covert of high fern to the more open walks of the greenwood, and no huntsman was there to watch or intercept the stately hart, as he paced at the head of the antler'd herd.

The outlaws were all assembled around the Trysting-tree in the Harthill-walk, where they had spent the night in refreshing themselves after the fatigues of the siege, some with wine, some with slumber, many with hearing and recounting the events of the day, and computing the heaps of plunder which their success had placed at the disposal of their Chief.

The spoils were indeed very large; for, notwithstanding that much was consumed, a great deal of plate, rich armour, and splendid clothing, had been secured by the exertions of the dauntless outlaws, who could be appalled by no danger when such rewards were in view. Yet so strict were the laws of their society, that no one ventured to appropriate any part of the booty, which was brought into one common mass, to be at the disposal of their leader.

The place of rendezvous was an aged oak; not however the same to which Locksley had conducted Gurth and Wamba in the earlier part of the story, but one which was the centre of a silvan amphitheatre, within half a mile of the demolished castle of Torquilstone. Here Locksley assumed his seat—a throne of turf erected under the twisted branches of the huge oak, and the silvan followers were gathered around him. He assigned to the Black Knight a seat at his right hand, and to Cedric a place upon his left.

"Pardon my freedom, noble sirs," he said, "but in these glades I am monarch—they are my kingdom; and these my wild subjects would reck but little of my power, were I, within my own dominions, to yield place to mortal man.—Now, sirs, who hath seen our chaplain? where is our curtal Friar? A mass amongst Christian men best begins a busy morning."—No one had seen the Clerk of Copmanhurst. "Over gods forbode!" said the outlaw chief, "I trust the jolly priest hath but abidden by the wine-pot a thought too late. Who saw him since the castle was ta'en?"

"I," quoth the Miller, "marked him busy about the door of a cellar, swearing by each saint in the calendar he would taste the smack of Front-de-Boeuf's Gascoigne wine."

"Now, the saints, as many as there be of them," said the Captain, "forefend, lest he has drunk too deep of the wine-butts, and perished by the fall of the castle!—Away, Miller!—take with you enow of men, seek the place where you last saw him—throw water from the moat on the scorching ruins—I will have them removed stone by stone ere I lose my curtal Friar."

The numbers who hastened to execute this duty, considering that an interesting division of spoil was about to take place, showed how much the troop had at heart the safety of their spiritual father.

"Meanwhile, let us proceed," said Locksley; "for when this bold deed shall be sounded abroad, the bands of De Bracy, of Malvoisin, and other allies of Front-de-Boeuf, will be in motion against us, and it were well for our safety that we retreat from the vicinity.—Noble Cedric," he said, turning to the Saxon, "that spoil is divided into two portions; do thou make choice of that which best suits thee, to recompense thy people who were partakers with us in this adventure."

"Good yeoman," said Cedric, "my heart is oppressed with sadness. The noble Athelstane of Coningsburgh is no more—the last sprout of the sainted Confessor!

Hopes have perished with him which can never return!—A sparkle hath been quenched by his blood, which no human breath can again rekindle! My people, save the few who are now with me, do but tarry my presence to transport his honoured remains to their last mansion. The Lady Rowena is desirous to return to Rotherwood, and must be escorted by a sufficient force. I should, therefore, ere now, have left this place; and I waited—not to share the booty, for, so help me God and Saint Withold! as neither I nor any of mine will touch the value of a liard,—I waited but to render my thanks to thee and to thy bold yeomen, for the life and honour ye have saved."

"Nay, but," said the chief Outlaw, "we did but half the work at most—take of the spoil what may reward your own neighbours and followers."

"I am rich enough to reward them from mine own wealth," answered Cedric.

"And some," said Wamba, "have been wise enough to reward themselves; they do not march off empty-handed altogether. We do not all wear motley."

"They are welcome," said Locksley; "our laws bind none but ourselves."

"But, thou, my poor knave," said Cedric, turning about and embracing his Jester, "how shall I reward thee, who feared not to give thy body to chains and death instead of mine!—All forsook me, when the poor fool was faithful!"

A tear stood in the eye of the rough Thane as he spoke—a mark of feeling which even the death of Athelstane had not extracted; but there was something in the half-instinctive attachment of his clown, that waked his nature more keenly than even grief itself.

"Nay," said the Jester, extricating himself from master's caress, "if you pay my service with the water of your eye, the Jester must weep for company, and then what becomes of his vocation?—But, uncle, if you would indeed pleasure me, I pray you to pardon my playfellow Gurth, who stole a week from your service to bestow it on your son."

"Pardon him!" exclaimed Cedric; "I will both pardon and reward him.—Kneel down, Gurth."—The swineherd was in an instant at his master's feet—"THEOW and ESNE art thou no longer," said Cedric touching him with a wand; "FOLKFREE and SACLESS art thou in town and from town, in the forest as in the field. A hide of land I give to thee in my steads of Walbrugham, from me and mine to thee and thine aye and for ever; and God's malison on his head who this gainsays!"

No longer a serf, but a freeman and a landholder, Gurth sprung upon his feet, and twice bounded aloft to almost his own height from the ground. "A smith and a file," he cried, "to do away the collar from the neck of a freeman!—Noble master! doubled is my strength by your gift, and doubly will I fight for you!—There is a free spirit in my breast—I am a man changed to myself and all around.—Ha, Fangs!" he continued,—for that faithful cur, seeing his master thus transported, began to jump upon him, to express his sympathy,—"knowest thou thy master still?"

"Ay," said Wamba, "Fangs and I still know thee, Gurth, though we must needs abide by the collar; it is only thou art likely to forget both us and thyself."

"I shall forget myself indeed ere I forget thee, true comrade," said Gurth; "and were freedom fit for thee, Wamba, the master would not let thee want it."

"Nay," said Wamba, "never think I envy thee, brother Gurth; the serf sits by the hall-fire when the freeman must forth to the field of battle—And what saith Oldhelm of Malmsbury—Better a fool at a feast than a wise man at a fray."

The tramp of horses was now heard, and the Lady Rowena appeared, surrounded by several riders, and a much stronger party of footmen, who joyfully shook their pikes and clashed their brown-bills for joy of her freedom. She herself, richly attired, and mounted on a dark chestnut palfrey, had recovered all the dignity of her manner, and only an unwonted degree of paleness showed the sufferings she had undergone. Her lovely brow, though sorrowful, bore on it a cast of reviving hope for the future, as well as of grateful thankfulness for the past deliverance—She knew that Ivanhoe was safe, and she knew that Athelstane was dead. The former assurance filled her with the most sincere delight; and if she did not absolutely rejoice at the latter, she might be pardoned for feeling the full advantage of being freed from further persecution on the only subject in which she had ever been contradicted by her guardian Cedric.

As Rowena bent her steed towards Locksley's seat, that bold yeoman, with all his followers, rose to receive her, as if by a general instinct of courtesy. The blood rose to her cheeks, as, courteously waving her hand, and bending so low that her beautiful and loose tresses were for an instant mixed with the flowing mane of her palfrey, she expressed in few but apt words her obligations and her gratitude to Locksley and her other deliverers.—"God bless you, brave men," she concluded, "God and Our Lady bless you and requite you for gallantly perilling yourselves in the cause of the oppressed!—If any of you should hunger, remember Rowena has food—if you should thirst, she has many a butt of wine and brown ale—and if the Normans drive ye from these walks, Rowena has forests of her own, where her gallant deliverers may range at full freedom, and never ranger ask whose arrow hath struck down the deer."

"Thanks, gentle lady," said Locksley; "thanks from my company and myself. But, to have saved you requites itself. We who walk the greenwood do many a wild deed, and the Lady Rowena's deliverance may be received as an atonement."

Again bowing from her palfrey, Rowena turned to depart; but pausing a moment, while Cedric, who was to attend her, was also taking his leave, she found herself unexpectedly close by the prisoner De Bracy. He stood under a tree in deep meditation, his arms crossed upon his breast, and Rowena was in hopes she might pass him unobserved. He looked up, however, and, when aware of her presence, a deep flush of shame suffused his handsome countenance. He stood a moment most irresolute; then, stepping forward, took her palfrey by the rein, and bent his knee before her.

"Will the Lady Rowena deign to cast an eye—on a captive knight—on a dishonoured soldier?"

"Sir Knight," answered Rowena, "in enterprises such as yours, the real dishonour lies not in failure, but in success."

"Conquest, lady, should soften the heart," answered De Bracy; "let me but know that the Lady Rowena forgives the violence occasioned by an ill-fated passion, and she shall soon learn that De Bracy knows how to serve her in nobler ways."

"I forgive you, Sir Knight," said Rowena, "as a Christian."

"That means," said Wamba, "that she does not forgive him at all."

"But I can never forgive the misery and desolation your madness has occasioned," continued Rowena.

"Unloose your hold on the lady's rein," said Cedric, coming up. "By the bright sun above us, but it were shame, I would pin thee to the earth with my javelin—but be well assured, thou shalt smart, Maurice de Bracy, for thy share in this foul deed."

"He threatens safely who threatens a prisoner," said De Bracy; "but when had a Saxon any touch of courtesy?"

Then retiring two steps backward, he permitted the lady to move on.

Cedric, ere they departed, expressed his peculiar gratitude to the Black Champion, and earnestly entreated him to accompany him to Rotherwood.

"I know," he said, "that ye errant knights desire to carry your fortunes on the point of your lance, and reck not of land or goods; but war is a changeful mistress, and a home is sometimes desirable even to the champion whose trade is wandering. Thou hast earned one in the halls of Rotherwood, noble knight. Cedric has wealth enough to repair the injuries of fortune, and all he has is his deliverer's—Come, therefore, to Rotherwood, not as a guest, but as a son or brother."

"Cedric has already made me rich," said the Knight,—"he has taught me the value of Saxon virtue. To Rotherwood will I come, brave Saxon, and that speedily; but, as now, pressing matters of moment detain me from your halls. Peradventure when I come hither, I will ask such a boon as will put even thy generosity to the test."

"It is granted ere spoken out," said Cedric, striking his ready hand into the gauntleted palm of the Black Knight,—"it is granted already, were it to affect half my fortune."

"Gage not thy promise so lightly," said the Knight of the Fetterlock; "yet well I hope to gain the boon I shall ask. Meanwhile, adieu."

"I have but to say," added the Saxon, "that, during the funeral rites of the noble Athelstane, I shall be an inhabitant of the halls of his castle of Coningsburgh—They will be open to all who choose to partake of the funeral banqueting; and, I speak in name of the noble Edith, mother of the fallen prince, they will never be shut against him who laboured so bravely, though unsuccessfully, to save Athelstane from Norman chains and Norman steel."

"Ay, ay," said Wamba, who had resumed his attendance on his master, "rare feeding there will be—pity that the noble Athelstane cannot banquet at his own funeral.—But he," continued the Jester, lifting up his eyes gravely, "is supping in Paradise, and doubtless does honour to the cheer."

"Peace, and move on," said Cedric, his anger at this untimely jest being checked by the recollection of Wamba's recent services. Rowena waved a graceful adieu to him of the Fetterlock—the Saxon bade God speed him, and on they moved through a wide glade of the forest.

They had scarce departed, ere a sudden procession moved from under the greenwood branches, swept slowly round the silvan amphitheatre, and took the same direction with Rowena and her followers. The priests of a neighbouring convent, in expectation of the ample donation, or "soul-scat", which Cedric had propined, attended upon the car in which the body of Athelstane was laid, and sang hymns as it was sadly and slowly borne on the shoulders of his vassals to his castle of Coningsburgh, to be there deposited in the grave of Hengist, from whom the deceased derived his long descent. Many of his vassals had assembled at the news of his death, and followed the bier with all the external marks, at least, of dejection and sorrow. Again the outlaws arose, and paid the same rude and spontaneous homage to death, which they had so lately rendered to beauty—the slow chant and mournful step of the priests brought back to their remembrance such of their comrades as had fallen in the yesterday's array. But such recollections dwell not long with those who lead a life of danger and enterprise, and ere the sound of the death-hymn had died on the wind, the outlaws were again busied in the distribution of their spoil.

"Valiant knight," said Locksley to the Black Champion, "without whose good heart and mighty arm our enterprise must altogether have failed, will it please you to take from that mass of spoil whatever may best serve to pleasure you, and to remind you of this my Trysting-tree?"

"I accept the offer," said the Knight, "as frankly as it is given; and I ask permission to dispose of Sir Maurice de Bracy at my own pleasure."

"He is thine already," said Locksley, "and well for him! else the tyrant had graced the highest bough of this oak, with as many of his Free-Companions as we could gather, hanging thick as acorns around him.—But he is thy prisoner, and he is safe, though he had slain my father."

"De Bracy," said the Knight, "thou art free—depart. He whose prisoner thou art scorns to take mean revenge for what is past. But beware of the future, lest a worse thing befall thee.—Maurice de Bracy, I say BEWARE!"

De Bracy bowed low and in silence, and was about to withdraw, when the yeomen burst at once into a shout of execration and derision. The proud knight instantly stopped, turned back, folded his arms, drew up his form to its full height, and exclaimed, "Peace, ye yelping curs! who open upon a cry which ye followed not when the stag was at bay—De Bracy scorns your censure as he would disdain your applause. To your brakes and caves, ye outlawed thieves! and be silent when aught knightly or noble is but spoken within a league of your fox-earths."

This ill-timed defiance might have procured for De Bracy a volley of arrows, but for the hasty and imperative interference of the outlaw Chief. Meanwhile the knight caught a horse by the rein, for several which had been taken in the stables of Front-de-Boeuf stood accoutred around, and were a valuable part of the booty. He threw himself upon the saddle, and galloped off through the wood.

When the bustle occasioned by this incident was somewhat composed, the chief Outlaw took from his neck the rich horn and baldric which he had recently gained at the strife of archery near Ashby.

"Noble knight." he said to him of the Fetterlock, "if you disdain not to grace by your acceptance a bugle which an English yeoman has once worn, this I will pray you to keep as a memorial of your gallant bearing—and if ye have aught to do, and, as happeneth oft to a gallant knight, ye chance to be hard bested in any forest between Trent and Tees, wind three mots upon the horn thus, 'Wa-sa-hoa!' and it may well chance ye shall find helpers and rescue."

He then gave breath to the bugle, and winded once and again the call which he described, until the knight had caught the notes.

"Gramercy for the gift, bold yeoman," said the Knight; "and better help than thine and thy rangers would I never seek, were it at my utmost need." And then in his turn he winded the call till all the greenwood rang.

"Well blown and clearly," said the yeoman; "beshrew me an thou knowest not as much of woodcraft as of war!—thou hast been a striker of deer in thy day, I warrant. —Comrades, mark these three mots—it is the call of the Knight of the Fetterlock; and he who hears it, and hastens not to serve him at his need, I will have him scourged out of our band with his own bowstring."

"Long live our leader!" shouted the yeomen, "and long live the Black Knight of the Fetterlock!—May he soon use our service, to prove how readily it will be paid."

Locksley now proceeded to the distribution of the spoil, which he performed with the most laudable impartiality. A tenth part of the whole was set apart for the church, and for pious uses; a portion was next allotted to a sort of public treasury; a part was assigned to the widows and children of those who had fallen, or to be expended in masses for the souls of such as had left no surviving family. The rest was divided amongst the outlaws, according to their rank and merit, and the judgment of the Chief, on all such doubtful questions as occurred, was delivered with great shrewdness, and received with absolute submission. The Black Knight was not a little surprised to find that men, in a state so lawless, were nevertheless among themselves so regularly and equitably governed, and all that he observed added to his opinion of the justice and judgment of their leader.

When each had taken his own proportion of the booty, and while the treasurer, accompanied by four tall yeomen, was transporting that belonging to the state to some place of concealment or of security, the portion devoted to the church still remained unappropriated.

"I would," said the leader, "we could hear tidings of our joyous chaplain—he was never wont to be absent when meat was to be blessed, or spoil to be parted; and it is his duty to take care of these the tithes of our successful enterprise. It may be the office has helped to cover some of his canonical irregularities. Also, I have a holy brother of his a prisoner at no great distance, and I would fain have the Friar to help me to deal with him in due sort—I greatly misdoubt the safety of the bluff priest."

"I were right sorry for that," said the Knight of the Fetterlock, "for I stand indebted to him for the joyous hospitality of a merry night in his cell. Let us to the ruins of the castle; it may be we shall there learn some tidings of him."

While they thus spoke, a loud shout among the yeomen announced the arrival of him for whom they feared, as they learned from the stentorian voice of the Friar himself, long before they saw his burly person.

"Make room, my merry-men!" he exclaimed; "room for your godly father and his prisoner—Cry welcome once more.—I come, noble leader, like an eagle with my prey in my clutch."—And making his way through the ring, amidst the laughter of all around, he appeared in majestic triumph, his huge partisan in one hand, and in the other a halter, one end of which was fastened to the neck of the unfortunate Isaac of York, who, bent down by sorrow and terror, was dragged on by the victorious priest, who shouted aloud, "Where is Allan-a-Dale, to chronicle me in a ballad, or if it were but a lay?—By Saint Hermangild, the jingling crowder is ever out of the way where there is an apt theme for exalting valour!"

"Curtal Priest," said the Captain, "thou hast been at a wet mass this morning, as early as it is. In the name of Saint Nicholas, whom hast thou got here?"

"A captive to my sword and to my lance, noble Captain," replied the Clerk of Copmanhurst; "to my bow and to my halberd, I should rather say; and yet I have redeemed him by my divinity from a worse captivity. Speak, Jew—have I not ransomed thee from Sathanas?—have I not taught thee thy 'credo', thy 'pater', and thine 'Ave Maria'?—Did I not spend the whole night in drinking to thee, and in expounding of mysteries?"

"For the love of God!" ejaculated the poor Jew, "will no one take me out of the keeping of this mad—I mean this holy man?"

"How's this, Jew?" said the Friar, with a menacing aspect; "dost thou recant, Jew? —Bethink thee, if thou dost relapse into thine infidelity, though thou are not so tender as a suckling pig—I would I had one to break my fast upon—thou art not too tough to be roasted! Be conformable, Isaac, and repeat the words after me. 'Ave Maria'!—"

"Nay, we will have no profanation, mad Priest," said Locksley; "let us rather hear where you found this prisoner of thine."

"By Saint Dunstan," said the Friar, "I found him where I sought for better ware! I did step into the cellarage to see what might be rescued there; for though a cup of burnt wine, with spice, be an evening's drought for an emperor, it were waste, methought, to let so much good liquor be mulled at once; and I had caught up one runlet of sack, and was coming to call more aid among these lazy knaves, who are ever to seek when a good deed is to be done, when I was avised of a strong door— Aha! thought I, here is the choicest juice of all in this secret crypt; and the knave butler, being disturbed in his vocation, hath left the key in the door—In therefore I went, and found just nought besides a commodity of rusted chains and this dog of a Jew, who presently rendered himself my prisoner, rescue or no rescue. I did but refresh myself after the fatigue of the action, with the unbeliever, with one humming cup of sack, and was proceeding to lead forth my captive, when, crash after crash, as with wild thunder-dint and levin-fire, down toppled the masonry of an outer tower, (marry beshrew their hands that built it not the firmer!) and blocked up the passage. The roar of one falling tower followed another—I gave up thought of life; and deeming it a dishonour to one of my profession to pass out of this world in company with a Jew, I heaved up my halberd to beat his brains out; but I took pity on his grey hairs, and judged it better to lay down the partisan, and take up my spiritual weapon for his conversion. And truly, by the blessing of Saint Dunstan, the seed has been sown in good soil; only that, with speaking to him of mysteries through the whole night, and being in a manner fasting, (for the few droughts of sack which I sharpened my wits with were not worth marking,) my head is well-nigh dizzied, I trow.—But I was clean exhausted.—Gilbert and Wibbald know in what state they found me— quite and clean exhausted."

"We can bear witness," said Gilbert; "for when we had cleared away the ruin, and by Saint Dunstan's help lighted upon the dungeon stair, we found the runlet of sack half empty, the Jew half dead, and the Friar more than half—exhausted, as he calls it."

"Ye be knaves! ye lie!" retorted the offended Friar; "it was you and your gormandizing companions that drank up the sack, and called it your morning draught—I am a pagan, an I kept it not for the Captain's own throat. But what recks it? The Jew is converted, and understands all I have told him, very nearly, if not altogether, as well as myself."

"Jew," said the Captain, "is this true? hast thou renounced thine unbelief?"

"May I so find mercy in your eyes," said the Jew, "as I know not one word which the reverend prelate spake to me all this fearful night. Alas! I was so distraught with agony, and fear, and grief, that had our holy father Abraham come to preach to me, he had found but a deaf listener."

"Thou liest, Jew, and thou knowest thou dost." said the Friar; "I will remind thee of but one word of our conference—thou didst promise to give all thy substance to our holy Order."

"So help me the Promise, fair sirs," said Isaac, even more alarmed than before, "as no such sounds ever crossed my lips! Alas! I am an aged beggar'd man—I fear me a childless—have ruth on me, and let me go!"

"Nay," said the Friar, "if thou dost retract vows made in favour of holy Church, thou must do penance."

Accordingly, he raised his halberd, and would have laid the staff of it lustily on the Jew's shoulders, had not the Black Knight stopped the blow, and thereby transferred the Holy Clerk's resentment to himself.

"By Saint Thomas of Kent," said he, "an I buckle to my gear, I will teach thee, sir lazy lover, to mell with thine own matters, maugre thine iron case there!"

"Nay, be not wroth with me," said the Knight; "thou knowest I am thy sworn friend and comrade."

"I know no such thing," answered the Friar; "and defy thee for a meddling coxcomb!"

"Nay, but," said the Knight, who seemed to take a pleasure in provoking his quondam host, "hast thou forgotten how, that for my sake (for I say nothing of the temptation of the flagon and the pasty) thou didst break thy vow of fast and vigil?"

"Truly, friend," said the Friar, clenching his huge fist, "I will bestow a buffet on thee."

"I accept of no such presents," said the Knight; "I am content to take thy cuff as a loan, but I will repay thee with usury as deep as ever thy prisoner there exacted in his traffic."

"I will prove that presently," said the Friar.

"Hola!" cried the Captain, "what art thou after, mad Friar? brawling beneath our Trysting-tree?"

"No brawling," said the Knight, "it is but a friendly interchange of courtesy.—Friar, strike an thou darest—I will stand thy blow, if thou wilt stand mine."

"Thou hast the advantage with that iron pot on thy head," said the churchman; "but have at thee—Down thou goest, an thou wert Goliath of Gath in his brazen helmet."

The Friar bared his brawny arm up to the elbow, and putting his full strength to the blow, gave the Knight a buffet that might have felled an ox. But his adversary stood firm as a rock. A loud shout was uttered by all the yeomen around; for the Clerk's cuff was proverbial amongst them, and there were few who, in jest or earnest, had not had the occasion to know its vigour.

"Now, Priest," said, the Knight, pulling off his gauntlet, "if I had vantage on my head, I will have none on my hand—stand fast as a true man."

"'Genam meam dedi vapulatori'—I have given my cheek to the smiter," said the

Priest; "an thou canst stir me from the spot, fellow, I will freely bestow on thee the Jew's ransom."

So spoke the burly Priest, assuming, on his part, high defiance. But who may resist his fate? The buffet of the Knight was given with such strength and good-will, that the Friar rolled head over heels upon the plain, to the great amazement of all the spectators. But he arose neither angry nor crestfallen.

"Brother," said he to the Knight, "thou shouldst have used thy strength with more discretion. I had mumbled but a lame mass an thou hadst broken my jaw, for the piper plays ill that wants the nether chops. Nevertheless, there is my hand, in friendly witness, that I will exchange no more cuffs with thee, having been a loser by the barter. End now all unkindness. Let us put the Jew to ransom, since the leopard will not change his spots, and a Jew he will continue to be."

"The Priest," said Clement, "is not half so confident of the Jew's conversion, since he received that buffet on the ear."

"Go to, knave, what pratest thou of conversions?—what, is there no respect?—all masters and no men?—I tell thee, fellow, I was somewhat totty when I received the good knight's blow, or I had kept my ground under it. But an thou gibest more of it, thou shalt learn I can give as well as take."

"Peace all!" said the Captain. "And thou, Jew, think of thy ransom; thou needest not to be told that thy race are held to be accursed in all Christian communities, and trust me that we cannot endure thy presence among us. Think, therefore, of an offer, while I examine a prisoner of another cast."

"Were many of Front-de-Boeuf's men taken?" demanded the Black Knight.

"None of note enough to be put to ransom," answered the Captain; "a set of hilding fellows there were, whom we dismissed to find them a new master—enough had been done for revenge and profit; the bunch of them were not worth a cardecu. The prisoner I speak of is better booty—a jolly monk riding to visit his leman, an I may judge by his horse-gear and wearing apparel.—Here cometh the worthy prelate, as pert as a pyet." And, between two yeomen, was brought before the silvan throne of the outlaw Chief, our old friend, Prior Aymer of Jorvaulx.

XXXIII.

>—Flower of warriors,
>How is't with Titus Lartius?
>MARCIUS.—As with a man busied about decrees,
>Condemning some to death and some to exile,
>Ransoming him or pitying, threatening the other.
>
>— CORIOLANUS

The captive Abbot's features and manners exhibited a whimsical mixture of offended pride, and deranged foppery and bodily terror.

"Why, how now, my masters?" said he, with a voice in which all three emotions were blended. "What order is this among ye? Be ye Turks or Christians, that handle a churchman?—Know ye what it is, 'manus imponere in servos Domini'? Ye have plundered my mails—torn my cope of curious cut lace, which might have served a cardinal!—Another in my place would have been at his 'excommunicabo vos'; but I am placible, and if ye order forth my palfreys, release my brethren, and restore my mails, tell down with all speed an hundred crowns to be expended in masses at the high altar of Jorvaulx Abbey, and make your vow to eat no venison until next Pentecost, it may be you shall hear little more of this mad frolic."

"Holy Father," said the chief Outlaw, "it grieves me to think that you have met with such usage from any of my followers, as calls for your fatherly reprehension."

"Usage!" echoed the priest, encouraged by the mild tone of the silvan leader; "it were usage fit for no hound of good race—much less for a Christian—far less for a priest—and least of all for the Prior of the holy community of Jorvaulx. Here is a profane and drunken minstrel, called Allan-a-Dale—'nebulo quidam'—who has menaced me with corporal punishment—nay, with death itself, an I pay not down four hundred crowns of ransom, to the boot of all the treasure he hath already robbed me of—gold chains and gymmal rings to an unknown value; besides what is broken and spoiled among their rude hands, such as my pouncer-box and silver crisping-tongs."

"It is impossible that Allan-a-Dale can have thus treated a man of your reverend bearing," replied the Captain.

"It is true as the gospel of Saint Nicodemus," said the Prior; "he swore, with many a cruel north-country oath, that he would hang me up on the highest tree in the greenwood."

"Did he so in very deed? Nay, then, reverend father, I think you had better comply with his demands—for Allan-a-Dale is the very man to abide by his word when he has so pledged it."

"You do but jest with me," said the astounded Prior, with a forced laugh; "and I love a good jest with all my heart. But, ha! ha! ha! when the mirth has lasted the livelong night, it is time to be grave in the morning."

"And I am as grave as a father confessor," replied the Outlaw; "you must pay a round ransom, Sir Prior, or your convent is likely to be called to a new election; for your place will know you no more."

"Are ye Christians," said the Prior, "and hold this language to a churchman?"

"Christians! ay, marry are we, and have divinity among us to boot," answered the Outlaw. "Let our buxom chaplain stand forth, and expound to this reverend father the texts which concern this matter."

The Friar, half-drunk, half-sober, had huddled a friar's frock over his green cassock, and now summoning together whatever scraps of learning he had acquired by rote in former days, "Holy father," said he, "'Deus faciat salvam benignitatem vestram'—You are welcome to the greenwood."

"What profane mummery is this?" said the Prior. "Friend, if thou be'st indeed of the church, it were a better deed to show me how I may escape from these men's hands, than to stand ducking and grinning here like a morris-dancer."

"Truly, reverend father," said the Friar, "I know but one mode in which thou mayst escape. This is Saint Andrew's day with us, we are taking our tithes."

"But not of the church, then, I trust, my good brother?" said the Prior.

"Of church and lay," said the Friar; "and therefore, Sir Prior 'facite vobis amicos de Mammone iniquitatis'—make yourselves friends of the Mammon of unrighteousness, for no other friendship is like to serve your turn."

"I love a jolly woodsman at heart," said the Prior, softening his tone; "come, ye must not deal too hard with me—I can well of woodcraft, and can wind a horn clear and lustily, and hollo till every oak rings again—Come, ye must not deal too hard with me."

"Give him a horn," said the Outlaw; "we will prove the skill he boasts of."

The Prior Aymer winded a blast accordingly. The Captain shook his head.

"Sir Prior," he said, "thou blowest a merry note, but it may not ransom thee—we cannot afford, as the legend on a good knight's shield hath it, to set thee free for a blast. Moreover, I have found thee—thou art one of those, who, with new French graces and Tra-li-ras, disturb the ancient English bugle notes.—Prior, that last flourish on the recheat hath added fifty crowns to thy ransom, for corrupting the true old manly blasts of venerie."

"Well, friend," said the Abbot, peevishly, "thou art ill to please with thy woodcraft. I pray thee be more conformable in this matter of my ransom. At a word—since I must needs, for once, hold a candle to the devil—what ransom am I to pay for walking on Watling-street, without having fifty men at my back?"

"Were it not well," said the Lieutenant of the gang apart to the Captain, "that the Prior should name the Jew's ransom, and the Jew name the Prior's?"

"Thou art a mad knave," said the Captain, "but thy plan transcends!—Here, Jew, step forth—Look at that holy Father Aymer, Prior of the rich Abbey of Jorvaulx, and tell us at what ransom we should hold him?—Thou knowest the income of his convent, I warrant thee."

"O, assuredly," said Isaac. "I have trafficked with the good fathers, and bought wheat and barley, and fruits of the earth, and also much wool. O, it is a rich abbey-stede, and they do live upon the fat, and drink the sweet wines upon the lees, these good fathers of Jorvaulx. Ah, if an outcast like me had such a home to go to, and such incomings by the year and by the month, I would pay much gold and silver to redeem my captivity."

"Hound of a Jew!" exclaimed the Prior, "no one knows better than thy own cursed self, that our holy house of God is indebted for the finishing of our chancel—"

"And for the storing of your cellars in the last season with the due allowance of Gascon wine," interrupted the Jew; "but that—that is small matters."

"Hear the infidel dog!" said the churchman; "he jangles as if our holy community did come under debts for the wines we have a license to drink, 'propter necessitatem, et ad frigus depellendum'. The circumcised villain blasphemeth the holy church, and Christian men listen and rebuke him not!"

"All this helps nothing," said the leader.—"Isaac, pronounce what he may pay, without flaying both hide and hair."

"An six hundred crowns," said Isaac, "the good Prior might well pay to your honoured valours, and never sit less soft in his stall."

"Six hundred crowns," said the leader, gravely; "I am contented—thou hast well spoken, Isaac—six hundred crowns.—It is a sentence, Sir Prior."

"A sentence!—a sentence!" exclaimed the band; "Solomon had not done it better."

"Thou hearest thy doom, Prior," said the leader.

"Ye are mad, my masters," said the Prior; "where am I to find such a sum? If I sell the very pyx and candlesticks on the altar at Jorvaulx, I shall scarce raise the half; and it will be necessary for that purpose that I go to Jorvaulx myself; ye may retain as borrows my two priests."

"That will be but blind trust," said the Outlaw; "we will retain thee, Prior, and send them to fetch thy ransom. Thou shalt not want a cup of wine and a collop of venison the while; and if thou lovest woodcraft, thou shalt see such as your north country never witnessed."

"Or, if so please you," said Isaac, willing to curry favour with the outlaws, "I can send to York for the six hundred crowns, out of certain monies in my hands, if so be that the most reverend Prior present will grant me a quittance."

"He shall grant thee whatever thou dost list, Isaac," said the Captain; "and thou shalt lay down the redemption money for Prior Aymer as well as for thyself."

"For myself! ah, courageous sirs," said the Jew, "I am a broken and impoverished man; a beggar's staff must be my portion through life, supposing I were to pay you fifty crowns."

"The Prior shall judge of that matter," replied the Captain.—"How say you, Father Aymer? Can the Jew afford a good ransom?"

"Can he afford a ransom?" answered the Prior "Is he not Isaac of York, rich enough to redeem the captivity of the ten tribes of Israel, who were led into Assyrian bondage?—I have seen but little of him myself, but our cellarer and treasurer have dealt largely with him, and report says that his house at York is so full of gold and silver as is a shame in any Christian land. Marvel it is to all living Christian hearts that such gnawing adders should be suffered to eat into the bowels of the state, and even of the holy church herself, with foul usuries and extortions."

"Hold, father," said the Jew, "mitigate and assuage your choler. I pray of your reverence to remember that I force my monies upon no one. But when churchman and layman, prince and prior, knight and priest, come knocking to Isaac's door, they borrow not his shekels with these uncivil terms. It is then, Friend Isaac, will you pleasure us in this matter, and our day shall be truly kept, so God sa' me?—and Kind Isaac, if ever you served man, show yourself a friend in this need! And when the day comes, and I ask my own, then what hear I but Damned Jew, and The curse of Egypt on your tribe, and all that may stir up the rude and uncivil populace against poor strangers!"

"Prior," said the Captain, "Jew though he be, he hath in this spoken well. Do thou, therefore, name his ransom, as he named thine, without farther rude terms."

"None but 'latro famosus'—the interpretation whereof," said the Prior, "will I give at some other time and tide—would place a Christian prelate and an unbaptized Jew upon the same bench. But since ye require me to put a price upon this caitiff, I tell you openly that ye will wrong yourselves if you take from him a penny under a thousand crowns."

"A sentence!—a sentence!" exclaimed the chief Outlaw.

"A sentence!—a sentence!" shouted his assessors; "the Christian has shown his good nurture, and dealt with us more generously than the Jew."

"The God of my fathers help me!" said the Jew; "will ye bear to the ground an impoverished creature?—I am this day childless, and will ye deprive me of the means of livelihood?"

"Thou wilt have the less to provide for, Jew, if thou art childless," said Aymer.

"Alas! my lord," said Isaac, "your law permits you not to know how the child of our bosom is entwined with the strings of our heart—O Rebecca! laughter of my beloved Rachel! were each leaf on that tree a zecchin, and each zecchin mine own, all that mass of wealth would I give to know whether thou art alive, and escaped the hands of the Nazarene!"

"Was not thy daughter dark-haired?" said one of the outlaws; "and wore she not a veil of twisted sendal, broidered with silver?"

"She did!—she did!" said the old man, trembling with eagerness, as formerly with fear. "The blessing of Jacob be upon thee! canst thou tell me aught of her safety?"

"It was she, then," said the yeoman, "who was carried off by the proud Templar, when he broke through our ranks on yester-even. I had drawn my bow to send a shaft after him, but spared him even for the sake of the damsel, who I feared might take harm from the arrow."

"Oh!" answered the Jew, "I would to God thou hadst shot, though the arrow had pierced her bosom!—Better the tomb of her fathers than the dishonourable couch of the licentious and savage Templar. Ichabod! Ichabod! the glory hath departed from my house!"

"Friends," said the Chief, looking round, "the old man is but a Jew, natheless his grief touches me.—Deal uprightly with us, Isaac—will paying this ransom of a thousand crowns leave thee altogether penniless?"

Isaac, recalled to think of his worldly goods, the love of which, by dint of inveterate habit, contended even with his parental affection, grew pale, stammered, and could not deny there might be some small surplus.

"Well—go to—what though there be," said the Outlaw, "we will not reckon with thee too closely. Without treasure thou mayst as well hope to redeem thy child from the clutches of Sir Brian de Bois-Guilbert, as to shoot a stag-royal with a headless shaft. —We will take thee at the same ransom with Prior Aymer, or rather at one hundred crowns lower, which hundred crowns shall be mine own peculiar loss, and not light upon this worshipful community; and so we shall avoid the heinous offence of rating a Jew merchant as high as a Christian prelate, and thou wilt have six hundred crowns remaining to treat for thy daughter's ransom. Templars love the glitter of silver shekels as well as the sparkle of black eyes.—Hasten to make thy crowns chink in the ear of De Bois-Guilbert, ere worse comes of it. Thou wilt find him, as our scouts have brought notice, at the next Preceptory house of his Order.—Said I well, my merry mates?"

The yeomen expressed their wonted acquiescence in their leader's opinion; and Isaac, relieved of one half of his apprehensions, by learning that his daughter lived, and might possibly be ransomed, threw himself at the feet of the generous Outlaw, and, rubbing his beard against his buskins, sought to kiss the hem of his green cassock. The Captain drew himself back, and extricated himself from the Jew's grasp, not without some marks of contempt.

"Nay, beshrew thee, man, up with thee! I am English born, and love no such Eastern prostrations—Kneel to God, and not to a poor sinner, like me."

"Ay, Jew," said Prior Aymer; "kneel to God, as represented in the servant of his altar, and who knows, with thy sincere repentance and due gifts to the shrine of Saint Robert, what grace thou mayst acquire for thyself and thy daughter Rebecca? I grieve for the maiden, for she is of fair and comely countenance,—I beheld her in the lists of Ashby. Also Brian de Bois-Guilbert is one with whom I may do much—bethink thee how thou mayst deserve my good word with him."

"Alas! alas!" said the Jew, "on every hand the spoilers arise against me—I am given as a prey unto the Assyrian, and a prey unto him of Egypt."

"And what else should be the lot of thy accursed race?" answered the Prior; "for what saith holy writ, 'verbum Domini projecerunt, et sapientia est nulla in eis'—they have cast forth the word of the Lord, and there is no wisdom in them; 'propterea dabo mulieres eorum exteris'—I will give their women to strangers, that is to the Templar, as in the present matter; 'et thesauros eorum haeredibus alienis', and their treasures to others—as in the present case to these honest gentlemen."

Isaac groaned deeply, and began to wring his hands, and to relapse into his state of desolation and despair. But the leader of the yeomen led him aside.

"Advise thee well, Isaac," said Locksley, "what thou wilt do in this matter; my counsel to thee is to make a friend of this churchman. He is vain, Isaac, and he is covetous; at least he needs money to supply his profusion. Thou canst easily gratify his greed; for think not that I am blinded by thy pretexts of poverty. I am intimately acquainted, Isaac, with the very iron chest in which thou dost keep thy money-bags—What! know I not the great stone beneath the apple-tree, that leads into the vaulted chamber under thy garden at York?" The Jew grew as pale as death—"But fear nothing from me," continued the yeoman, "for we are of old acquainted. Dost thou not remember the sick yeoman whom thy fair daughter Rebecca redeemed from the gyves at York, and kept him in thy house till his health was restored, when thou didst dismiss him recovered, and with a piece of money?—Usurer as thou art, thou didst never place coin at better interest than that poor silver mark, for it has this day saved thee five hundred crowns."

"And thou art he whom we called Diccon Bend-the-Bow?" said Isaac; "I thought ever I knew the accent of thy voice."

"I am Bend-the-Bow," said the Captain, "and Locksley, and have a good name besides all these."

"But thou art mistaken, good Bend-the-Bow, concerning that same vaulted apartment. So help me Heaven, as there is nought in it but some merchandises which I will gladly part with to you—one hundred yards of Lincoln green to make doublets to thy men, and a hundred staves of Spanish yew to make bows, and a hundred silken bowstrings, tough, round, and sound—these will I send thee for thy good-will, honest Diccon, an thou wilt keep silence about the vault, my good Diccon."

"Silent as a dormouse," said the Outlaw; "and never trust me but I am grieved for thy daughter. But I may not help it—The Templars lances are too strong for my archery in the open field—they would scatter us like dust. Had I but known it was Rebecca when she was borne off, something might have been done; but now thou must needs proceed by policy. Come, shall I treat for thee with the Prior?"

"In God's name, Diccon, an thou canst, aid me to recover the child of my bosom!"

"Do not thou interrupt me with thine ill-timed avarice," said the Outlaw, "and I will deal with him in thy behalf."

He then turned from the Jew, who followed him, however, as closely as his shadow.

"Prior Aymer," said the Captain, "come apart with me under this tree. Men say thou dost love wine, and a lady's smile, better than beseems thy Order, Sir Priest; but with that I have nought to do. I have heard, too, thou dost love a brace of good dogs and a fleet horse, and it may well be that, loving things which are costly to come by, thou hatest not a purse of gold. But I have never heard that thou didst love oppression or cruelty.—Now, here is Isaac willing to give thee the means of pleasure and pastime in a bag containing one hundred marks of silver, if thy intercession with thine ally the Templar shall avail to procure the freedom of his daughter."

"In safety and honour, as when taken from me," said the Jew, "otherwise it is no bargain."

"Peace, Isaac," said the Outlaw, "or I give up thine interest.—What say you to this my purpose, Prior Aymer?"

"The matter," quoth the Prior, "is of a mixed condition; for, if I do a good deal on the one hand, yet, on the other, it goeth to the vantage of a Jew, and in so much is against my conscience. Yet, if the Israelite will advantage the Church by giving me somewhat over to the building of our dortour, I will take it on my conscience to aid him in the matter of his daughter."

"For a score of marks to the dortour," said the Outlaw,—"Be still, I say, Isaac!—or for a brace of silver candlesticks to the altar, we will not stand with you."

"Nay, but, good Diccon Bend-the-Bow"—said Isaac, endeavouring to interpose.

"Good Jew—good beast—good earthworm!" said the yeoman, losing patience; "an thou dost go on to put thy filthy lucre in the balance with thy daughter's life and honour, by Heaven, I will strip thee of every maravedi thou hast in the world, before three days are out!"

Isaac shrunk together, and was silent.

"And what pledge am I to have for all this?" said the Prior.

"When Isaac returns successful through your mediation," said the Outlaw, "I swear by Saint Hubert, I will see that he pays thee the money in good silver, or I will reckon with him for it in such sort, he had better have paid twenty such sums."

"Well then, Jew," said Aymer, "since I must needs meddle in this matter, let me have the use of thy writing-tablets—though, hold—rather than use thy pen, I would fast for twenty-four hours, and where shall I find one?"

"If your holy scruples can dispense with using the Jew's tablets, for the pen I can find a remedy," said the yeoman; and, bending his bow, he aimed his shaft at a wild-goose which was soaring over their heads, the advanced-guard of a phalanx of his tribe, which were winging their way to the distant and solitary fens of Holderness. The bird came fluttering down, transfixed with the arrow.

"There, Prior," said the Captain, "are quills enow to supply all the monks of Jorvaulx for the next hundred years, an they take not to writing chronicles."

The Prior sat down, and at great leisure indited an epistle to Brian de Bois-Guilbert, and having carefully sealed up the tablets, delivered them to the Jew, saying, "This will be thy safe-conduct to the Preceptory of Templestowe, and, as I think, is most likely to accomplish the delivery of thy daughter, if it be well backed with proffers of advantage and commodity at thine own hand; for, trust me well, the good Knight Bois-Guilbert is of their confraternity that do nought for nought."

"Well, Prior," said the Outlaw, "I will detain thee no longer here than to give the Jew a quittance for the six hundred crowns at which thy ransom is fixed—I accept of him for my pay-master; and if I hear that ye boggle at allowing him in his accompts the sum so paid by him, Saint Mary refuse me, an I burn not the abbey over thine head, though I hang ten years the sooner!"

With a much worse grace than that wherewith he had penned the letter to Bois-Guilbert, the Prior wrote an acquittance, discharging Isaac of York of six hundred crowns, advanced to him in his need for acquittal of his ransom, and faithfully promising to hold true compt with him for that sum.

"And now," said Prior Aymer, "I will pray you of restitution of my mules and palfreys, and the freedom of the reverend brethren attending upon me, and also of the gymmal rings, jewels, and fair vestures, of which I have been despoiled, having now satisfied you for my ransom as a true prisoner."

"Touching your brethren, Sir Prior," said Locksley, "they shall have present freedom, it were unjust to detain them; touching your horses and mules, they shall also be restored, with such spending-money as may enable you to reach York, for it were cruel to deprive you of the means of journeying.—But as concerning rings, jewels, chains, and what else, you must understand that we are men of tender consciences, and will not yield to a venerable man like yourself, who should be dead to the vanities of this life, the strong temptation to break the rule of his foundation, by wearing rings, chains, or other vain gauds."

"Think what you do, my masters," said the Prior, "ere you put your hand on the Church's patrimony—These things are 'inter res sacras', and I wot not what judgment might ensue were they to be handled by laical hands."

"I will take care of that, reverend Prior," said the Hermit of Copmanhurst; "for I will wear them myself."

"Friend, or brother," said the Prior, in answer to this solution of his doubts, "if thou hast really taken religious orders, I pray thee to look how thou wilt answer to thine official for the share thou hast taken in this day's work."

"Friend Prior," returned the Hermit, "you are to know that I belong to a little diocese, where I am my own diocesan, and care as little for the Bishop of York as I do for the Abbot of Jorvaulx, the Prior, and all the convent."

"Thou art utterly irregular," said the Prior; "one of those disorderly men, who, taking on them the sacred character without due cause, profane the holy rites, and endanger the souls of those who take counsel at their hands; 'lapides pro pane condonantes iis', giving them stones instead of bread as the Vulgate hath it."

"Nay," said the Friar, "an my brain-pan could have been broken by Latin, it had not held so long together.—I say, that easing a world of such misproud priests as thou art of their jewels and their gimcracks, is a lawful spoiling of the Egyptians."

"Thou be'st a hedge-priest," said the Prior, in great wrath, "'excommunicabo vos'."

"Thou be'st thyself more like a thief and a heretic," said the Friar, equally indignant; "I will pouch up no such affront before my parishioners, as thou thinkest it not shame to put upon me, although I be a reverend brother to thee. 'Ossa ejus perfringam', I will break your bones, as the Vulgate hath it."

"Hola!" cried the Captain, "come the reverend brethren to such terms?—Keep thine assurance of peace, Friar.—Prior, an thou hast not made thy peace perfect with God, provoke the Friar no further.—Hermit, let the reverend father depart in peace, as a ransomed man."

The yeomen separated the incensed priests, who continued to raise their voices, vituperating each other in bad Latin, which the Prior delivered the more fluently, and the Hermit with the greater vehemence. The Prior at length recollected himself sufficiently to be aware that he was compromising his dignity, by squabbling with such a hedge-priest as the Outlaw's chaplain, and being joined by his attendants, rode off with considerably less pomp, and in a much more apostolical condition, so far as worldly matters were concerned, than he had exhibited before this rencounter.

It remained that the Jew should produce some security for the ransom which he was to pay on the Prior's account, as well as upon his own. He gave, accordingly, an order sealed with his signet, to a brother of his tribe at York, requiring him to pay to the bearer the sum of a thousand crowns, and to deliver certain merchandises specified in the note.

"My brother Sheva," he said, groaning deeply, "hath the key of my warehouses."

"And of the vaulted chamber," whispered Locksley.

"No, no—may Heaven forefend!" said Isaac; "evil is the hour that let any one whomsoever into that secret!"

"It is safe with me," said the Outlaw, "so be that this thy scroll produce the sum therein nominated and set down.—But what now, Isaac? art dead? art stupefied? hath the payment of a thousand crowns put thy daughter's peril out of thy mind?"

The Jew started to his feet—"No, Diccon, no—I will presently set forth.—Farewell, thou whom I may not call good, and dare not and will not call evil."

Yet ere Isaac departed, the Outlaw Chief bestowed on him this parting advice:—"Be liberal of thine offers, Isaac, and spare not thy purse for thy daughter's safety. Credit me, that the gold thou shalt spare in her cause, will hereafter give thee as much agony as if it were poured molten down thy throat."

Isaac acquiesced with a deep groan, and set forth on his journey, accompanied by two tall foresters, who were to be his guides, and at the same time his guards, through the wood.

The Black Knight, who had seen with no small interest these various proceedings, now took his leave of the Outlaw in turn; nor could he avoid expressing his surprise at having witnessed so much of civil policy amongst persons cast out from all the ordinary protection and influence of the laws.

"Good fruit, Sir Knight," said the yeoman, "will sometimes grow on a sorry tree; and evil times are not always productive of evil alone and unmixed. Amongst those who are drawn into this lawless state, there are, doubtless, numbers who wish to exercise its license with some moderation, and some who regret, it may be, that they are obliged to follow such a trade at all."

"And to one of those," said the Knight, "I am now, I presume, speaking?"

"Sir Knight," said the Outlaw, "we have each our secret. You are welcome to form your judgment of me, and I may use my conjectures touching you, though neither of our shafts may hit the mark they are shot at. But as I do not pray to be admitted into your mystery, be not offended that I preserve my own."

"I crave pardon, brave Outlaw," said the Knight, "your reproof is just. But it may be we shall meet hereafter with less of concealment on either side.—Meanwhile we part friends, do we not?"

"There is my hand upon it," said Locksley; "and I will call it the hand of a true Englishman, though an outlaw for the present."

"And there is mine in return," said the Knight, "and I hold it honoured by being clasped with yours. For he that does good, having the unlimited power to do evil, deserves praise not only for the good which he performs, but for the evil which he forbears. Fare thee well, gallant Outlaw!" Thus parted that fair fellowship; and He of the Fetterlock, mounting upon his strong war-horse, rode off through the forest.

XXXIV.

KING JOHN.—I'll tell thee what, my friend,
He is a very serpent in my way;
And wheresoe'er this foot of mine doth tread,
He lies before me.—Dost thou understand me?

— KING JOHN

There was brave feasting in the Castle of York, to which Prince John had invited those nobles, prelates, and leaders, by whose assistance he hoped to carry through his ambitious projects upon his brother's throne. Waldemar Fitzurse, his able and politic agent, was at secret work among them, tempering all to that pitch of courage which was necessary in making an open declaration of their purpose. But their enterprise was delayed by the absence of more than one main limb of the confederacy. The stubborn and daring, though brutal courage of Front-de-Boeuf; the buoyant spirits and bold bearing of De Bracy; the sagacity, martial experience, and renowned valour of Brian de Bois-Guilbert, were important to the success of their conspiracy; and, while cursing in secret their unnecessary and unmeaning absence, neither John nor his adviser dared to proceed without them. Isaac the Jew also seemed to have vanished, and with him the hope of certain sums of money, making up the subsidy for which Prince John had contracted with that Israelite and his brethren. This deficiency was likely to prove perilous in an emergency so critical.

It was on the morning after the fall of Torquilstone, that a confused report began to spread abroad in the city of York, that De Bracy and Bois-Guilbert, with their confederate Front-de-Boeuf, had been taken or slain. Waldemar brought the rumour to Prince John, announcing, that he feared its truth the more that they had set out with a small attendance, for the purpose of committing an assault on the Saxon Cedric and his attendants. At another time the Prince would have treated this deed of violence as a good jest; but now, that it interfered with and impeded his own plans, he exclaimed against the perpetrators, and spoke of the broken laws, and the infringement of public order and of private property, in a tone which might have become King Alfred.

"The unprincipled marauders," he said—"were I ever to become monarch of England, I would hang such transgressors over the drawbridges of their own castles."

"But to become monarch of England," said his Ahithophel coolly, "it is necessary not only that your Grace should endure the transgressions of these unprincipled marauders, but that you should afford them your protection, notwithstanding your laudable zeal for the laws they are in the habit of infringing. We shall be finely helped, if the churl Saxons should have realized your Grace's vision, of converting feudal drawbridges into gibbets; and yonder bold-spirited Cedric seemeth one to whom such an imagination might occur. Your Grace is well aware, it will be dangerous to stir without Front-de-Boeuf, De Bracy, and the Templar; and yet we have gone too far to recede with safety."

Prince John struck his forehead with impatience, and then began to stride up and down the apartment.

"The villains," he said, "the base treacherous villains, to desert me at this pinch!"

"Nay, say rather the feather-pated giddy madmen," said Waldemar, "who must be toying with follies when such business was in hand."

"What is to be done?" said the Prince, stopping short before Waldemar.

"I know nothing which can be done," answered his counsellor, "save that which I have already taken order for.—I came not to bewail this evil chance with your Grace, until I had done my best to remedy it."

"Thou art ever my better angel, Waldemar," said the Prince; "and when I have such a chancellor to advise withal, the reign of John will be renowned in our annals. —What hast thou commanded?"

"I have ordered Louis Winkelbrand, De Bracy's lieutenant, to cause his trumpet sound to horse, and to display his banner, and to set presently forth towards the castle of Front-de-Boeuf, to do what yet may be done for the succour of our friends."

Prince John's face flushed with the pride of a spoilt child, who has undergone what it conceives to be an insult. "By the face of God!" he said, "Waldemar Fitzurse, much hast thou taken upon thee! and over malapert thou wert to cause trumpet to blow, or banner to be raised, in a town where ourselves were in presence, without our express command."

"I crave your Grace's pardon," said Fitzurse, internally cursing the idle vanity of his patron; "but when time pressed, and even the loss of minutes might be fatal, I judged it best to take this much burden upon me, in a matter of such importance to your Grace's interest."

"Thou art pardoned, Fitzurse," said the prince, gravely; "thy purpose hath atoned for thy hasty rashness.—But whom have we here?—De Bracy himself, by the rood!— and in strange guise doth he come before us."

It was indeed De Bracy—"bloody with spurring, fiery red with speed." His armour bore all the marks of the late obstinate fray, being broken, defaced, and stained with blood in many places, and covered with clay and dust from the crest to the spur. Undoing his helmet, he placed it on the table, and stood a moment as if to collect himself before he told his news.

"De Bracy," said Prince John, "what means this?—Speak, I charge thee!—Are the

Saxons in rebellion?"

"Speak, De Bracy," said Fitzurse, almost in the same moment with his master, "thou wert wont to be a man—Where is the Templar?—where Front-de-Boeuf?"

"The Templar is fled," said De Bracy; "Front-de-Boeuf you will never see more. He has found a red grave among the blazing rafters of his own castle and I alone am escaped to tell you."

"Cold news," said Waldemar, "to us, though you speak of fire and conflagration."

"The worst news is not yet said," answered De Bracy; and, coming up to Prince John, he uttered in a low and emphatic tone—"Richard is in England—I have seen and spoken with him."

Prince John turned pale, tottered, and caught at the back of an oaken bench to support himself—much like to a man who receives an arrow in his bosom.

"Thou ravest, De Bracy," said Fitzurse, "it cannot be."

"It is as true as truth itself," said De Bracy; "I was his prisoner, and spoke with him."

"With Richard Plantagenet, sayest thou?" continued Fitzurse.

"With Richard Plantagenet," replied De Bracy, "with Richard Coeur-de-Lion—with Richard of England."

"And thou wert his prisoner?" said Waldemar; "he is then at the head of a power?"

"No—only a few outlawed yeomen were around him, and to these his person is unknown. I heard him say he was about to depart from them. He joined them only to assist at the storming of Torquilstone."

"Ay," said Fitzurse, "such is indeed the fashion of Richard—a true knight-errant he, and will wander in wild adventure, trusting the prowess of his single arm, like any Sir Guy or Sir Bevis, while the weighty affairs of his kingdom slumber, and his own safety is endangered.—What dost thou propose to do De Bracy?"

"I?—I offered Richard the service of my Free Lances, and he refused them—I will lead them to Hull, seize on shipping, and embark for Flanders; thanks to the bustling times, a man of action will always find employment. And thou, Waldemar, wilt thou take lance and shield, and lay down thy policies, and wend along with me, and share the fate which God sends us?"

"I am too old, Maurice, and I have a daughter," answered Waldemar.

"Give her to me, Fitzurse, and I will maintain her as fits her rank, with the help of lance and stirrup," said De Bracy.

"Not so," answered Fitzurse; "I will take sanctuary in this church of Saint Peter—the Archbishop is my sworn brother."

During this discourse, Prince John had gradually awakened from the stupor into which he had been thrown by the unexpected intelligence, and had been attentive to the conversation which passed betwixt his followers. "They fall off from me," he said to himself, "they hold no more by me than a withered leaf by the bough when a breeze blows on it!—Hell and fiends! can I shape no means for myself when I am deserted by these cravens?"—He paused, and there was an expression of diabolical passion in the constrained laugh with which he at length broke in on their conversation.

"Ha, ha, ha! my good lords, by the light of Our Lady's brow, I held ye sage men, bold men, ready-witted men; yet ye throw down wealth, honour, pleasure, all that our noble game promised you, at the moment it might be won by one bold cast!"

"I understand you not," said De Bracy. "As soon as Richard's return is blown abroad, he will be at the head of an army, and all is then over with us. I would counsel you, my lord, either to fly to France or take the protection of the Queen Mother."

"I seek no safety for myself," said Prince John, haughtily; "that I could secure by a word spoken to my brother. But although you, De Bracy, and you, Waldemar Fitzurse, are so ready to abandon me, I should not greatly delight to see your heads blackening on Clifford's gate yonder. Thinkest thou, Waldemar, that the wily Archbishop will not suffer thee to be taken from the very horns of the altar, would it make his peace with King Richard? And forgettest thou, De Bracy, that Robert Estoteville lies betwixt thee and Hull with all his forces, and that the Earl of Essex is gathering his followers? If we had reason to fear these levies even before Richard's return, trowest thou there is any doubt now which party their leaders will take? Trust me, Estoteville alone has strength enough to drive all thy Free Lances into the Humber."—Waldemar Fitzurse and De Bracy looked in each other's faces with blank dismay.—"There is but one road to safety," continued the Prince, and his brow grew black as midnight; "this object of our terror journeys alone—He must be met withal."

"Not by me," said De Bracy, hastily; "I was his prisoner, and he took me to mercy. I will not harm a feather in his crest."

"Who spoke of harming him?" said Prince John, with a hardened laugh; "the knave will say next that I meant he should slay him!—No—a prison were better; and whether in Britain or Austria, what matters it?—Things will be but as they were when we commenced our enterprise—It was founded on the hope that Richard would remain a captive in Germany—Our uncle Robert lived and died in the castle of Cardiffe."

"Ay, but," said Waldemar, "your sire Henry sate more firm in his seat than your Grace can. I say the best prison is that which is made by the sexton—no dungeon like a church-vault! I have said my say."

"Prison or tomb," said De Bracy, "I wash my hands of the whole matter."

"Villain!" said Prince John, "thou wouldst not bewray our counsel?"

"Counsel was never bewrayed by me," said De Bracy, haughtily, "nor must the name of villain be coupled with mine!"

"Peace, Sir Knight!" said Waldemar; "and you, good my lord, forgive the scruples of valiant De Bracy; I trust I shall soon remove them."

"That passes your eloquence, Fitzurse," replied the Knight.

"Why, good Sir Maurice," rejoined the wily politician, "start not aside like a scared steed, without, at least, considering the object of your terror.—This Richard—but a day since, and it would have been thy dearest wish to have met him hand to hand in the ranks of battle—a hundred times I have heard thee wish it."

"Ay," said De Bracy, "but that was as thou sayest, hand to hand, and in the ranks of battle! Thou never heardest me breathe a thought of assaulting him alone, and in a forest."

"Thou art no good knight if thou dost scruple at it," said Waldemar. "Was it in battle that Lancelot de Lac and Sir Tristram won renown? or was it not by encountering gigantic knights under the shade of deep and unknown forests?"

"Ay, but I promise you," said De Bracy, "that neither Tristram nor Lancelot would have been match, hand to hand, for Richard Plantagenet, and I think it was not their wont to take odds against a single man."

"Thou art mad, De Bracy—what is it we propose to thee, a hired and retained captain of Free Companions, whose swords are purchased for Prince John's service? Thou art apprized of our enemy, and then thou scruplest, though thy patron's fortunes, those of thy comrades, thine own, and the life and honour of every one amongst us, be at stake!"

"I tell you," said De Bracy, sullenly, "that he gave me my life. True, he sent me from his presence, and refused my homage—so far I owe him neither favour nor allegiance—but I will not lift hand against him."

"It needs not—send Louis Winkelbrand and a score of thy lances."

"Ye have sufficient ruffians of your own," said De Bracy; "not one of mine shall budge on such an errand."

"Art thou so obstinate, De Bracy?" said Prince John; "and wilt thou forsake me, after so many protestations of zeal for my service?"

"I mean it not," said De Bracy; "I will abide by you in aught that becomes a knight, whether in the lists or in the camp; but this highway practice comes not within my vow."

"Come hither, Waldemar," said Prince John. "An unhappy prince am I. My father, King Henry, had faithful servants—He had but to say that he was plagued with a factious priest, and the blood of Thomas-a-Becket, saint though he was, stained the steps of his own altar.—Tracy, Morville, Brito loyal and daring subjects, your names, your spirit, are extinct! and although Reginald Fitzurse hath left a son, he hath fallen off from his father's fidelity and courage."

"He has fallen off from neither," said Waldemar Fitzurse; "and since it may not better be, I will take on me the conduct of this perilous enterprise. Dearly, however, did my father purchase the praise of a zealous friend; and yet did his proof of loyalty to Henry fall far short of what I am about to afford; for rather would I assail a whole calendar of saints, than put spear in rest against Coeur-de-Lion.—De Bracy, to thee I must trust to keep up the spirits of the doubtful, and to guard Prince John's person. If you receive such news as I trust to send you, our enterprise will no longer wear a doubtful aspect.—Page," he said, "hie to my lodgings, and tell my armourer to be there in readiness; and bid Stephen Wetheral, Broad Thoresby, and the Three Spears of Spyinghow, come to me instantly; and let the scout-master, Hugh Bardon, attend me also.—Adieu, my Prince, till better times." Thus speaking, he left the apartment. "He goes to make my brother prisoner," said Prince John to De Bracy, "with as little touch of compunction, as if it but concerned the liberty of a Saxon franklin. I trust he will observe our orders, and use our dear Richard's person with all due respect."

De Bracy only answered by a smile.

"By the light of Our Lady's brow," said Prince John, "our orders to him were most precise—though it may be you heard them not, as we stood together in the oriel window—Most clear and positive was our charge that Richard's safety should be cared for, and woe to Waldemar's head if he transgress it!"

"I had better pass to his lodgings," said De Bracy, "and make him fully aware of your Grace's pleasure; for, as it quite escaped my ear, it may not perchance have reached that of Waldemar."

"Nay, nay," said Prince John, impatiently, "I promise thee he heard me; and, besides, I have farther occupation for thee. Maurice, come hither; let me lean on thy shoulder."

They walked a turn through the hall in this familiar posture, and Prince John, with an air of the most confidential intimacy, proceeded to say, "What thinkest thou of this Waldemar Fitzurse, my De Bracy?—He trusts to be our Chancellor. Surely we will pause ere we give an office so high to one who shows evidently how little he reverences our blood, by his so readily undertaking this enterprise against Richard. Thou dost think, I warrant, that thou hast lost somewhat of our regard, by thy boldly declining this unpleasing task—But no, Maurice! I rather honour thee for thy virtuous constancy. There are things most necessary to be done, the perpetrator of which we neither love nor honour; and there may be refusals to serve us, which shall rather exalt in our estimation those who deny our request. The arrest of my unfortunate brother forms no such good title to the high office of Chancellor, as thy chivalrous and courageous denial establishes in thee to the truncheon of High Marshal. Think of this, De Bracy, and begone to thy charge."

"Fickle tyrant!" muttered De Bracy, as he left the presence of the Prince; "evil luck have they who trust thee. Thy Chancellor, indeed!—He who hath the keeping of thy conscience shall have an easy charge, I trow. But High Marshal of England! that," he said, extending his arm, as if to grasp the baton of office, and assuming a loftier stride along the antechamber, "that is indeed a prize worth playing for!"

De Bracy had no sooner left the apartment than Prince John summoned an attendant.

"Bid Hugh Bardon, our scout-master, come hither, as soon as he shall have spoken with Waldemar Fitzurse."

The scout-master arrived after a brief delay, during which John traversed the apartment with, unequal and disordered steps.

"Bardon," said he, "what did Waldemar desire of thee?"

"Two resolute men, well acquainted with these northern wilds, and skilful in tracking the tread of man and horse."

"And thou hast fitted him?"

"Let your grace never trust me else," answered the master of the spies. "One is from Hexamshire; he is wont to trace the Tynedale and Teviotdale thieves, as a bloodhound follows the slot of a hurt deer. The other is Yorkshire bred, and has twanged his bowstring right oft in merry Sherwood; he knows each glade and dingle, copse and high-wood, betwixt this and Richmond."

"'Tis well," said the Prince.—"Goes Waldemar forth with them?"

"Instantly," said Bardon.

"With what attendance?" asked John, carelessly.

"Broad Thoresby goes with him, and Wetheral, whom they call, for his cruelty, Stephen Steel-heart; and three northern men-at-arms that belonged to Ralph Middleton's gang—they are called the Spears of Spyinghow."

"'Tis well," said Prince John; then added, after a moment's pause, "Bardon, it imports our service that thou keep a strict watch on Maurice De Bracy—so that he shall not observe it, however—And let us know of his motions from time to time—with whom he converses, what he proposeth. Fail not in this, as thou wilt be answerable."

Hugh Bardon bowed, and retired.

"If Maurice betrays me," said Prince John—"if he betrays me, as his bearing leads me to fear, I will have his head, were Richard thundering at the gates of York."

XXXV.

> Arouse the tiger of Hyrcanian deserts,
> Strive with the half-starved lion for his prey;
> Lesser the risk, than rouse the slumbering fire
> Of wild Fanaticism.
>
> *— ANONYMOUS*

Our tale now returns to Isaac of York.—Mounted upon a mule, the gift of the Outlaw, with two tall yeomen to act as his guard and guides, the Jew had set out for the Preceptory of Templestowe, for the purpose of negotiating his daughter's redemption. The Preceptory was but a day's journey from the demolished castle of Torquilstone, and the Jew had hoped to reach it before nightfall; accordingly, having dismissed his guides at the verge of the forest, and rewarded them with a piece of silver, he began to press on with such speed as his weariness permitted him to exert. But his strength failed him totally ere he had reached within four miles of the Temple-Court; racking pains shot along his back and through his limbs, and the excessive anguish which he felt at heart being now augmented by bodily suffering, he was rendered altogether incapable of proceeding farther than a small market-town, were dwelt a Jewish Rabbi of his tribe, eminent in the medical profession, and to whom Isaac was well known. Nathan Ben Israel received his suffering countryman with that kindness which the law prescribed, and which the Jews practised to each other. He insisted on his betaking himself to repose, and used such remedies as were then in most repute to check the progress of the fever, which terror, fatigue, ill usage, and sorrow, had brought upon the poor old Jew.

On the morrow, when Isaac proposed to arise and pursue his journey, Nathan remonstrated against his purpose, both as his host and as his physician. It might cost him, he said, his life. But Isaac replied, that more than life and death depended upon his going that morning to Templestowe.

"To Templestowe!" said his host with surprise again felt his pulse, and then muttered to himself, "His fever is abated, yet seems his mind somewhat alienated and disturbed."

"And why not to Templestowe?" answered his patient. "I grant thee, Nathan, that it is a dwelling of those to whom the despised Children of the Promise are a stumbling-block and an abomination; yet thou knowest that pressing affairs of traffic sometimes carry us among these bloodthirsty Nazarene soldiers, and that we visit the

Preceptories of the Templars, as well as the Commanderies of the Knights Hospitallers, as they are called."

"I know it well," said Nathan; "but wottest thou that Lucas de Beaumanoir, the chief of their Order, and whom they term Grand Master, is now himself at Templestowe?"

"I know it not," said Isaac; "our last letters from our brethren at Paris advised us that he was at that city, beseeching Philip for aid against the Sultan Saladine."

"He hath since come to England, unexpected by his brethren," said Ben Israel; "and he cometh among them with a strong and outstretched arm to correct and to punish. His countenance is kindled in anger against those who have departed from the vow which they have made, and great is the fear of those sons of Belial. Thou must have heard of his name?"

"It is well known unto me," said Isaac; "the Gentiles deliver this Lucas Beaumanoir as a man zealous to slaying for every point of the Nazarene law; and our brethren have termed him a fierce destroyer of the Saracens, and a cruel tyrant to the Children of the Promise."

"And truly have they termed him," said Nathan the physician. "Other Templars may be moved from the purpose of their heart by pleasure, or bribed by promise of gold and silver; but Beaumanoir is of a different stamp—hating sensuality, despising treasure, and pressing forward to that which they call the crown of martyrdom—The God of Jacob speedily send it unto him, and unto them all! Specially hath this proud man extended his glove over the children of Judah, as holy David over Edom, holding the murder of a Jew to be an offering of as sweet savour as the death of a Saracen. Impious and false things has he said even of the virtues of our medicines, as if they were the devices of Satan—The Lord rebuke him!"

"Nevertheless," said Isaac, "I must present myself at Templestowe, though he hath made his face like unto a fiery furnace seven times heated."

He then explained to Nathan the pressing cause of his journey. The Rabbi listened with interest, and testified his sympathy after the fashion of his people, rending his clothes, and saying, "Ah, my daughter!—ah, my daughter!—Alas! for the beauty of Zion!—Alas! for the captivity of Israel!"

"Thou seest," said Isaac, "how it stands with me, and that I may not tarry. Peradventure, the presence of this Lucas Beaumanoir, being the chief man over them, may turn Brian de Bois-Guilbert from the ill which he doth meditate, and that he may deliver to me my beloved daughter Rebecca."

"Go thou," said Nathan Ben Israel, "and be wise, for wisdom availed Daniel in the den of lions into which he was cast; and may it go well with thee, even as thine heart wisheth. Yet, if thou canst, keep thee from the presence of the Grand Master, for to do foul scorn to our people is his morning and evening delight. It may be if thou couldst speak with Bois-Guilbert in private, thou shalt the better prevail with him; for men say that these accursed Nazarenes are not of one mind in the Preceptory—May their counsels be confounded and brought to shame! But do thou, brother, return to me as if it were to the house of thy father, and bring me word how it has sped with thee; and well do I hope thou wilt bring with thee Rebecca, even the scholar of the wise Miriam, whose cures the Gentiles slandered as if they had been wrought by necromancy."

Isaac accordingly bade his friend farewell, and about an hour's riding brought him before the Preceptory of Templestowe.

This establishment of the Templars was seated amidst fair meadows and pastures, which the devotion of the former Preceptor had bestowed upon their Order. It was strong and well fortified, a point never neglected by these knights, and which the disordered state of England rendered peculiarly necessary. Two halberdiers, clad in black, guarded the drawbridge, and others, in the same sad livery, glided to and fro upon the walls with a funereal pace, resembling spectres more than soldiers. The inferior officers of the Order were thus dressed, ever since their use of white garments, similar to those of the knights and esquires, had given rise to a combination of certain false brethren in the mountains of Palestine, terming themselves Templars, and bringing great dishonour on the Order. A knight was now and then seen to cross the court in his long white cloak, his head depressed on his breast, and his arms folded. They passed each other, if they chanced to meet, with a slow, solemn, and mute greeting; for such was the rule of their Order, quoting thereupon the holy texts, "In many words thou shalt not avoid sin," and "Life and death are in the power of the tongue." In a word, the stern ascetic rigour of the Temple discipline, which had been so long exchanged for prodigal and licentious indulgence, seemed at once to have revived at Templestowe under the severe eye of Lucas Beaumanoir.

Isaac paused at the gate, to consider how he might seek entrance in the manner most likely to bespeak favour; for he was well aware, that to his unhappy race the reviving fanaticism of the Order was not less dangerous than their unprincipled licentiousness; and that his religion would be the object of hate and persecution in the one case, as his wealth would have exposed him in the other to the extortions of unrelenting oppression.

Meantime Lucas Beaumanoir walked in a small garden belonging to the Preceptory, included within the precincts of its exterior fortification, and held sad and confidential communication with a brother of his Order, who had come in his company from Palestine.

The Grand Master was a man advanced in age, as was testified by his long grey beard, and the shaggy grey eyebrows overhanging eyes, of which, however, years had been unable to quench the fire. A formidable warrior, his thin and severe features retained the soldier's fierceness of expression; an ascetic bigot, they were no less marked by the emaciation of abstinence, and the spiritual pride of the self-satisfied devotee. Yet with these severer traits of physiognomy, there was mixed somewhat striking and noble, arising, doubtless, from the great part which his high office called upon him to act among monarchs and princes, and from the habitual exercise of supreme authority over the valiant and high-born knights, who were united by the rules of the Order. His stature was tall, and his gait, undepressed by age and toil, was erect and stately. His white mantle was shaped with severe regularity, according to the rule of Saint Bernard himself, being composed of what was then called Burrel cloth, exactly fitted to the size of the wearer, and bearing on the left shoulder the octangular cross peculiar to the Order, formed of red cloth. No vair or ermine decked this garment; but in respect of his age, the Grand Master, as permitted by the rules, wore his doublet lined and trimmed with the softest lambskin, dressed with the wool outwards, which was the nearest approach he could regularly make to the use of fur, then the greatest luxury of dress. In his hand he bore that singular "abacus", or staff of office, with which Templars are usually represented, having at the upper end a round plate, on which was engraved the cross of the Order, inscribed within a circle or orle, as heralds term it. His companion, who attended on this great personage, had nearly the same dress in all respects, but his extreme deference towards his Superior showed that no other equality subsisted between them. The Preceptor, for such he was in rank, walked not in a line with the Grand Master, but just so far behind that Beaumanoir could speak to him without turning round his head.

"Conrade," said the Grand Master, "dear companion of my battles and my toils, to thy faithful bosom alone I can confide my sorrows. To thee alone can I tell how oft, since I came to this kingdom, I have desired to be dissolved and to be with the just. Not one object in England hath met mine eye which it could rest upon with pleasure, save the tombs of our brethren, beneath the massive roof of our Temple Church in yonder proud capital. O, valiant Robert de Ros! did I exclaim internally, as I gazed upon these good soldiers of the cross, where they lie sculptured on their sepulchres,— O, worthy William de Mareschal! open your marble cells, and take to your repose a weary brother, who would rather strive with a hundred thousand pagans than witness the decay of our Holy Order!"

"It is but true," answered Conrade Mont-Fitchet; "it is but too true; and the irregularities of our brethren in England are even more gross than those in France."

"Because they are more wealthy," answered the Grand Master. "Bear with me, brother, although I should something vaunt myself. Thou knowest the life I have led, keeping each point of my Order, striving with devils embodied and disembodied, striking down the roaring lion, who goeth about seeking whom he may devour, like a good knight and devout priest, wheresoever I met with him—even as blessed Saint Bernard hath prescribed to us in the forty-fifth capital of our rule, 'Ut Leo semper feriatur'.

"But by the Holy Temple! the zeal which hath devoured my substance and my life, yea, the very nerves and marrow of my bones; by that very Holy Temple I swear to thee, that save thyself and some few that still retain the ancient severity of our Order, I look upon no brethren whom I can bring my soul to embrace under that holy name. What say our statutes, and how do our brethren observe them? They should wear no vain or worldly ornament, no crest upon their helmet, no gold upon stirrup or bridle-bit; yet who now go pranked out so proudly and so gaily as the poor soldiers of the Temple? They are forbidden by our statutes to take one bird by means of another, to shoot beasts with bow or arblast, to halloo to a hunting-horn, or to spur the horse after game. But now, at hunting and hawking, and each idle sport of wood and river, who so prompt as the Templars in all these fond vanities? They are forbidden to read, save what their Superior permitted, or listen to what is read, save such holy things as may be recited aloud during the hours of refaction; but lo! their ears are at the command of idle minstrels, and their eyes study empty romaunts. They were commanded to extirpate magic and heresy. Lo! they are charged with studying the accursed cabalistical secrets of the Jews, and the magic of the Paynim Saracens. Simpleness of diet was prescribed to them, roots, pottage, gruels, eating flesh but thrice a-week, because the accustomed feeding on flesh is a dishonourable corruption of the body; and behold, their tables groan under delicate fare! Their drink was to be water, and now, to drink like a Templar, is the boast of each jolly boon companion! This very garden, filled as it is with curious herbs and trees sent from the Eastern climes, better becomes the harem of an unbelieving Emir, than the plot which Christian Monks should devote to raise their homely pot-herbs.—And O, Conrade! well it were that the relaxation of discipline stopped even here!—Well thou knowest that we were forbidden to receive those devout women, who at the beginning were associated as sisters of our Order, because, saith the forty-sixth chapter, the Ancient Enemy hath, by female society, withdrawn many from the right path to paradise. Nay, in the last capital, being, as it were, the cope-stone which our blessed founder placed on the pure and undefiled doctrine which he had enjoined, we are prohibited from offering, even to our sisters and our mothers, the kiss of affection— 'ut omnium mulierum fugiantur oscula'.—I shame to speak—I shame to think—of the corruptions which have rushed in upon us even like a flood. The souls of our pure founders, the spirits of Hugh de Payen and Godfrey de Saint Omer, and of the blessed Seven who first joined in dedicating their lives to the service of the Temple, are disturbed even in the enjoyment of paradise itself. I have seen them, Conrade, in the visions of the night—their sainted eyes shed tears for the sins and follies of their brethren, and for the foul and shameful luxury in which they wallow. Beaumanoir, they say, thou slumberest—awake! There is a stain in the fabric of the Temple, deep and foul as that left by the streaks of leprosy on the walls of the infected houses of old.

"The soldiers of the Cross, who should shun the glance of a woman as the eye of a basilisk, live in open sin, not with the females of their own race only, but with the daughters of the accursed heathen, and more accursed Jew. Beaumanoir, thou sleepest; up, and avenge our cause!—Slay the sinners, male and female!—Take to thee the brand of Phineas!—The vision fled, Conrade, but as I awaked I could still hear the clank of their mail, and see the waving of their white mantles.—And I will do according to their word, I WILL purify the fabric of the Temple! and the unclean stones in which the plague is, I will remove and cast out of the building."

"Yet bethink thee, reverend father," said Mont-Fitchet, "the stain hath become engrained by time and consuetude; let thy reformation be cautious, as it is just and wise."

"No, Mont-Fitchet," answered the stern old man—"it must be sharp and sudden—the Order is on the crisis of its fate. The sobriety, self-devotion, and piety of our predecessors, made us powerful friends—our presumption, our wealth, our luxury, have raised up against us mighty enemies.—We must cast away these riches, which are a temptation to princes—we must lay down that presumption, which is an offence to them—we must reform that license of manners, which is a scandal to the whole Christian world! Or—mark my words—the Order of the Temple will be utterly demolished—and the Place thereof shall no more be known among the nations."

"Now may God avert such a calamity!" said the Preceptor.

"Amen," said the Grand Master, with solemnity, "but we must deserve his aid. I tell thee, Conrade, that neither the powers in Heaven, nor the powers on earth, will longer endure the wickedness of this generation—My intelligence is sure—the ground on which our fabric is reared is already undermined, and each addition we make to the structure of our greatness will only sink it the sooner in the abyss. We must retrace our steps, and show ourselves the faithful Champions of the Cross, sacrificing to our calling, not alone our blood and our lives—not alone our lusts and our vices—but our ease, our comforts, and our natural affections, and act as men convinced that many a pleasure which may be lawful to others, is forbidden to the vowed soldier of the Temple."

At this moment a squire, clothed in a threadbare vestment, (for the aspirants after this holy Order wore during their noviciate the cast-off garments of the knights,) entered the garden, and, bowing profoundly before the Grand Master, stood silent, awaiting his permission ere he presumed to tell his errand.

"Is it not more seemly," said the Grand Master, "to see this Damian, clothed in the garments of Christian humility, thus appear with reverend silence before his Superior, than but two days since, when the fond fool was decked in a painted coat, and jangling as pert and as proud as any popinjay?—Speak, Damian, we permit thee—What is thine errand?"

"A Jew stands without the gate, noble and reverend father," said the Squire, "who prays to speak with brother Brian de Bois-Guilbert."

"Thou wert right to give me knowledge of it," said the Grand Master; "in our presence a Preceptor is but as a common compeer of our Order, who may not walk according to his own will, but to that of his Master—even according to the text, 'In the hearing of the ear he hath obeyed me.'—It imports us especially to know of this Bois-Guilbert's proceedings," said he, turning to his companion.

"Report speaks him brave and valiant," said Conrade.

"And truly is he so spoken of," said the Grand Master; "in our valour only we are not degenerated from our predecessors, the heroes of the Cross. But brother Brian came into our Order a moody and disappointed man, stirred, I doubt me, to take our vows and to renounce the world, not in sincerity of soul, but as one whom some touch of light discontent had driven into penitence. Since then, he hath become an active and earnest agitator, a murmurer, and a machinator, and a leader amongst those who impugn our authority; not considering that the rule is given to the Master even by the symbol of the staff and the rod—the staff to support the infirmities of the weak—the rod to correct the faults of delinquents.—Damian," he continued, "lead the Jew to our presence."

The squire departed with a profound reverence, and in a few minutes returned, marshalling in Isaac of York. No naked slave, ushered into the presence of some mighty prince, could approach his judgment-seat with more profound reverence and terror than that with which the Jew drew near to the presence of the Grand Master. When he had approached within the distance of three yards, Beaumanoir made a sign with his staff that he should come no farther. The Jew kneeled down on the earth which he kissed in token of reverence; then rising, stood before the Templars, his hands folded on his bosom, his head bowed on his breast, in all the submission of Oriental slavery.

"Damian," said the Grand Master, "retire, and have a guard ready to await our sudden call; and suffer no one to enter the garden until we shall leave it."—The squire bowed and retreated.—"Jew," continued the haughty old man, "mark me. It suits not our condition to hold with thee long communication, nor do we waste words or time upon any one. Wherefore be brief in thy answers to what questions I shall ask thee, and let thy words be of truth; for if thy tongue doubles with me, I will have it torn from thy misbelieving jaws."

The Jew was about to reply, but the Grand Master went on.

"Peace, unbeliever!—not a word in our presence, save in answer to our questions. —What is thy business with our brother Brian de Bois-Guilbert?"

Isaac gasped with terror and uncertainty. To tell his tale might be interpreted into scandalizing the Order; yet, unless he told it, what hope could he have of achieving his daughter's deliverance? Beaumanoir saw his mortal apprehension, and condescended to give him some assurance.

"Fear nothing," he said, "for thy wretched person, Jew, so thou dealest uprightly in this matter. I demand again to know from thee thy business with Brian de Bois-Guilbert?"

"I am bearer of a letter," stammered out the Jew, "so please your reverend valour, to that good knight, from Prior Aymer of the Abbey of Jorvaulx."

"Said I not these were evil times, Conrade?" said the Master. "A Cistertian Prior sends a letter to a soldier of the Temple, and can find no more fitting messenger than an unbelieving Jew.—Give me the letter."

The Jew, with trembling hands, undid the folds of his Armenian cap, in which he had deposited the Prior's tablets for the greater security, and was about to approach, with hand extended and body crouched, to place it within the reach of his grim interrogator.

"Back, dog!" said the Grand Master; "I touch not misbelievers, save with the sword.—Conrade, take thou the letter from the Jew, and give it to me."

Beaumanoir, being thus possessed of the tablets, inspected the outside carefully, and then proceeded to undo the packthread which secured its folds. "Reverend father," said Conrade, interposing, though with much deference, "wilt thou break the seal?"

"And will I not?" said Beaumanoir, with a frown. "Is it not written in the forty-second capital, 'De Lectione Literarum' that a Templar shall not receive a letter, no not from his father, without communicating the same to the Grand Master, and reading it in his presence?"

He then perused the letter in haste, with an expression of surprise and horror; read it over again more slowly; then holding it out to Conrade with one hand, and slightly striking it with the other, exclaimed—"Here is goodly stuff for one Christian man to write to another, and both members, and no inconsiderable members, of religious professions! When," said he solemnly, and looking upward, "wilt thou come with thy fanners to purge the thrashing-floor?"

Mont-Fitchet took the letter from his Superior, and was about to peruse it.

"Read it aloud, Conrade," said the Grand Master,—"and do thou" (to Isaac) "attend to the purport of it, for we will question thee concerning it."

Conrade read the letter, which was in these words: "Aymer, by divine grace, Prior of the Cistertian house of Saint Mary's of Jorvaulx, to Sir Brian de Bois-Guilbert, a Knight of the holy Order of the Temple, wisheth health, with the bounties of King Bacchus and of my Lady Venus. Touching our present condition, dear Brother, we are a captive in the hands of certain lawless and godless men, who have not feared to detain our person, and put us to ransom; whereby we have also learned of Front-de-Boeuf's misfortune, and that thou hast escaped with that fair Jewish sorceress, whose black eyes have bewitched thee. We are heartily rejoiced of thy safety; nevertheless, we pray thee to be on thy guard in the matter of this second Witch of Endor; for we are privately assured that your Great Master, who careth not a bean for cherry cheeks and black eyes, comes from Normandy to diminish your mirth, and amend your misdoings. Wherefore we pray you heartily to beware, and to be found watching, even as the Holy Text hath it, 'Invenientur vigilantes'. And the wealthy Jew her father, Isaac of York, having prayed of me letters in his behalf, I gave him these, earnestly advising, and in a sort entreating, that you do hold the damsel to ransom, seeing he will pay you from his bags as much as may find fifty damsels upon safer terms, whereof I trust to have my part when we make merry together, as true brothers, not forgetting the wine-cup. For what saith the text, 'Vinum laetificat cor hominis'; and again, 'Rex delectabitur pulchritudine tua'.

"Till which merry meeting, we wish you farewell. Given from this den of thieves, about the hour of matins,

"Aymer Pr. S. M. Jorvolciencis.

"'Postscriptum.' Truly your golden chain hath not long abidden with me, and will now sustain, around the neck of an outlaw deer-stealer, the whistle wherewith he calleth on his hounds."

"What sayest thou to this, Conrade?" said the Grand Master—"Den of thieves! and a fit residence is a den of thieves for such a Prior. No wonder that the hand of God is upon us, and that in the Holy Land we lose place by place, foot by foot, before the infidels, when we have such churchmen as this Aymer.—And what meaneth he, I trow, by this second Witch of Endor?" said he to his confident, something apart. Conrade was better acquainted (perhaps by practice) with the jargon of gallantry, than was his Superior; and he expounded the passage which embarrassed the Grand Master, to be a sort of language used by worldly men towards those whom they loved 'par amours'; but the explanation did not satisfy the bigoted Beaumanoir.

"There is more in it than thou dost guess, Conrade; thy simplicity is no match for this deep abyss of wickedness. This Rebecca of York was a pupil of that Miriam of whom thou hast heard. Thou shalt hear the Jew own it even now." Then turning to Isaac, he said aloud, "Thy daughter, then, is prisoner with Brian de Bois-Guilbert?"

"Ay, reverend valorous sir," stammered poor Isaac, "and whatsoever ransom a poor man may pay for her deliverance——"

"Peace!" said the Grand Master. "This thy daughter hath practised the art of healing, hath she not?"

"Ay, gracious sir," answered the Jew, with more confidence; "and knight and yeoman, squire and vassal, may bless the goodly gift which Heaven hath assigned to her. Many a one can testify that she hath recovered them by her art, when every other human aid hath proved vain; but the blessing of the God of Jacob was upon her."

Beaumanoir turned to Mont-Fitchet with a grim smile. "See, brother," he said, "the deceptions of the devouring Enemy! Behold the baits with which he fishes for souls, giving a poor space of earthly life in exchange for eternal happiness hereafter. Well said our blessed rule, 'Semper percutiatur leo vorans'.—Up on the lion! Down with the destroyer!" said he, shaking aloft his mystic abacus, as if in defiance of the powers of darkness—"Thy daughter worketh the cures, I doubt not," thus he went on to address the Jew, "by words and sighs, and periapts, and other cabalistical mysteries."

"Nay, reverend and brave Knight," answered Isaac, "but in chief measure by a balsam of marvellous virtue."

"Where had she that secret?" said Beaumanoir.

"It was delivered to her," answered Isaac, reluctantly, "by Miriam, a sage matron of our tribe."

"Ah, false Jew!" said the Grand Master; "was it not from that same witch Miriam, the abomination of whose enchantments have been heard of throughout every Christian land?" exclaimed the Grand Master, crossing himself. "Her body was burnt at a stake, and her ashes were scattered to the four winds; and so be it with me and mine Order, if I do not as much to her pupil, and more also! I will teach her to throw spell and incantation over the soldiers of the blessed Temple.—There, Damian, spurn this Jew from the gate—shoot him dead if he oppose or turn again. With his daughter we will deal as the Christian law and our own high office warrant."

Poor Isaac was hurried off accordingly, and expelled from the preceptory; all his entreaties, and even his offers, unheard and disregarded. He could do not better than return to the house of the Rabbi, and endeavour, through his means, to learn how his daughter was to be disposed of. He had hitherto feared for her honour, he was now to tremble for her life. Meanwhile, the Grand Master ordered to his presence the Preceptor of Templestowe.

XXXVI.

> Say not my art is fraud—all live by seeming.
> The beggar begs with it, and the gay courtier
> Gains land and title, rank and rule, by seeming;
> The clergy scorn it not, and the bold soldier
> Will eke with it his service.—All admit it,
> All practise it; and he who is content
> With showing what he is, shall have small credit
> In church, or camp, or state—So wags the world.
>
> — OLD PLAY

Albert Malvoisin, President, or, in the language of the Order, Preceptor of the establishment of Templestowe, was brother to that Philip Malvoisin who has been already occasionally mentioned in this history, and was, like that baron, in close league with Brian de Bois-Guilbert.

Amongst dissolute and unprincipled men, of whom the Temple Order included but too many, Albert of Templestowe might be distinguished; but with this difference from the audacious Bois-Guilbert, that he knew how to throw over his vices and his ambition the veil of hypocrisy, and to assume in his exterior the fanaticism which he internally despised. Had not the arrival of the Grand Master been so unexpectedly sudden, he would have seen nothing at Templestowe which might have appeared to argue any relaxation of discipline. And, even although surprised, and, to a certain extent, detected, Albert Malvoisin listened with such respect and apparent contrition to the rebuke of his Superior, and made such haste to reform the particulars he censured,—succeeded, in fine, so well in giving an air of ascetic devotion to a family which had been lately devoted to license and pleasure, that Lucas Beaumanoir began to entertain a higher opinion of the Preceptor's morals, than the first appearance of the establishment had inclined him to adopt.

But these favourable sentiments on the part of the Grand Master were greatly shaken by the intelligence that Albert had received within a house of religion the Jewish captive, and, as was to be feared, the paramour of a brother of the Order; and when Albert appeared before him, he was regarded with unwonted sternness.

"There is in this mansion, dedicated to the purposes of the holy Order of the Temple," said the Grand Master, in a severe tone, "a Jewish woman, brought hither by a brother of religion, by your connivance, Sir Preceptor."

Albert Malvoisin was overwhelmed with confusion; for the unfortunate Rebecca had been confined in a remote and secret part of the building, and every precaution used to prevent her residence there from being known. He read in the looks of Beaumanoir ruin to Bois-Guilbert and to himself, unless he should be able to avert the impending storm.

"Why are you mute?" continued the Grand Master.

"Is it permitted to me to reply?" answered the Preceptor, in a tone of the deepest humility, although by the question he only meant to gain an instant's space for arranging his ideas.

"Speak, you are permitted," said the Grand Master—"speak, and say, knowest thou the capital of our holy rule,—'De commilitonibus Templi in sancta civitate, qui cum miserrimis mulieribus versantur, propter oblectationem carnis?'"

"Surely, most reverend father," answered the Preceptor, "I have not risen to this office in the Order, being ignorant of one of its most important prohibitions."

"How comes it, then, I demand of thee once more, that thou hast suffered a brother to bring a paramour, and that paramour a Jewish sorceress, into this holy place, to the stain and pollution thereof?"

"A Jewish sorceress!" echoed Albert Malvoisin; "good angels guard us!"

"Ay, brother, a Jewish sorceress!" said the Grand Master, sternly. "I have said it. Darest thou deny that this Rebecca, the daughter of that wretched usurer Isaac of York, and the pupil of the foul witch Miriam, is now—shame to be thought or spoken!—lodged within this thy Preceptory?"

"Your wisdom, reverend father," answered the Preceptor, "hath rolled away the darkness from my understanding. Much did I wonder that so good a knight as Brian de Bois-Guilbert seemed so fondly besotted on the charms of this female, whom I received into this house merely to place a bar betwixt their growing intimacy, which else might have been cemented at the expense of the fall of our valiant and religious brother."

"Hath nothing, then, as yet passed betwixt them in breach of his vow?" demanded the Grand Master.

"What! under this roof?" said the Preceptor, crossing himself; "Saint Magdalene and the ten thousand virgins forbid!—No! if I have sinned in receiving her here, it was in the erring thought that I might thus break off our brother's besotted devotion to this Jewess, which seemed to me so wild and unnatural, that I could not but ascribe it to some touch of insanity, more to be cured by pity than reproof. But since your reverend wisdom hath discovered this Jewish queen to be a sorceress, perchance it may account fully for his enamoured folly."

"It doth!—it doth!" said Beaumanoir. "See, brother Conrade, the peril of yielding to the first devices and blandishments of Satan! We look upon woman only to gratify the lust of the eye, and to take pleasure in what men call her beauty; and the Ancient Enemy, the devouring Lion, obtains power over us, to complete, by talisman and spell, a work which was begun by idleness and folly. It may be that our brother Bois-Guilbert does in this matter deserve rather pity than severe chastisement; rather the support of the staff, than the strokes of the rod; and that our admonitions and prayers may turn him from his folly, and restore him to his brethren."

"It were deep pity," said Conrade Mont-Fitchet, "to lose to the Order one of its best lances, when the Holy Community most requires the aid of its sons. Three hundred Saracens hath this Brian de Bois-Guilbert slain with his own hand."

"The blood of these accursed dogs," said the Grand Master, "shall be a sweet and acceptable offering to the saints and angels whom they despise and blaspheme; and with their aid will we counteract the spells and charms with which our brother is entwined as in a net. He shall burst the bands of this Delilah, as Sampson burst the two new cords with which the Philistines had bound him, and shall slaughter the infidels, even heaps upon heaps. But concerning this foul witch, who hath flung her enchantments over a brother of the Holy Temple, assuredly she shall die the death."

"But the laws of England,"—said the Preceptor, who, though delighted that the Grand Master's resentment, thus fortunately averted from himself and Bois-Guilbert, had taken another direction, began now to fear he was carrying it too far.

"The laws of England," interrupted Beaumanoir, "permit and enjoin each judge to execute justice within his own jurisdiction. The most petty baron may arrest, try, and condemn a witch found within his own domain. And shall that power be denied to the Grand Master of the Temple within a preceptory of his Order?—No!—we will judge and condemn. The witch shall be taken out of the land, and the wickedness thereof shall be forgiven. Prepare the Castle-hall for the trial of the sorceress."

Albert Malvoisin bowed and retired,—not to give directions for preparing the hall, but to seek out Brian de Bois-Guilbert, and communicate to him how matters were likely to terminate. It was not long ere he found him, foaming with indignation at a repulse he had anew sustained from the fair Jewess. "The unthinking," he said, "the ungrateful, to scorn him who, amidst blood and flames, would have saved her life at the risk of his own! By Heaven, Malvoisin! I abode until roof and rafters crackled and crashed around me. I was the butt of a hundred arrows; they rattled on mine armour like hailstones against a latticed casement, and the only use I made of my shield was for her protection. This did I endure for her; and now the self-willed girl upbraids me that I did not leave her to perish, and refuses me not only the slightest proof of gratitude, but even the most distant hope that ever she will be brought to grant any. The devil, that possessed her race with obstinacy, has concentrated its full force in her single person!"

"The devil," said the Preceptor, "I think, possessed you both. How oft have I preached to you caution, if not continence? Did I not tell you that there were enough willing Christian damsels to be met with, who would think it sin to refuse so brave a knight 'le don d'amoureux merci', and you must needs anchor your affection on a wilful, obstinate Jewess! By the mass, I think old Lucas Beaumanoir guesses right, when he maintains she hath cast a spell over you."

"Lucas Beaumanoir!"—said Bois-Guilbert reproachfully—"Are these your precautions, Malvoisin? Hast thou suffered the dotard to learn that Rebecca is in the Preceptory?"

"How could I help it?" said the Preceptor. "I neglected nothing that could keep secret your mystery; but it is betrayed, and whether by the devil or no, the devil only can tell. But I have turned the matter as I could; you are safe if you renounce Rebecca. You are pitied—the victim of magical delusion. She is a sorceress, and must suffer as such."

"She shall not, by Heaven!" said Bois-Guilbert.

"By Heaven, she must and will!" said Malvoisin. "Neither you nor any one else can save her. Lucas Beaumanoir hath settled that the death of a Jewess will be a sin-offering sufficient to atone for all the amorous indulgences of the Knights Templars; and thou knowest he hath both the power and will to execute so reasonable and pious a purpose."

"Will future ages believe that such stupid bigotry ever existed!" said Bois-Guilbert, striding up and down the apartment.

"What they may believe, I know not," said Malvoisin, calmly; "but I know well, that in this our day, clergy and laymen, take ninety-nine to the hundred, will cry 'amen' to the Grand Master's sentence."

"I have it," said Bois-Guilbert. "Albert, thou art my friend. Thou must connive at her escape, Malvoisin, and I will transport her to some place of greater security and secrecy."

"I cannot, if I would," replied the Preceptor; "the mansion is filled with the attendants of the Grand Master, and others who are devoted to him. And, to be frank with you, brother, I would not embark with you in this matter, even if I could hope to bring my bark to haven. I have risked enough already for your sake. I have no mind to encounter a sentence of degradation, or even to lose my Preceptory, for the sake of a painted piece of Jewish flesh and blood. And you, if you will be guided by my counsel, will give up this wild-goose chase, and fly your hawk at some other game. Think, Bois-Guilbert,—thy present rank, thy future honours, all depend on thy place in the Order. Shouldst thou adhere perversely to thy passion for this Rebecca, thou wilt give Beaumanoir the power of expelling thee, and he will not neglect it. He is jealous of the truncheon which he holds in his trembling gripe, and he knows thou stretchest thy bold hand towards it. Doubt not he will ruin thee, if thou affordest him a pretext so fair as thy protection of a Jewish sorceress. Give him his scope in this matter, for thou canst not control him. When the staff is in thine own firm grasp, thou mayest caress the daughters of Judah, or burn them, as may best suit thine own humour."

"Malvoisin," said Bois-Guilbert, "thou art a cold-blooded—"

"Friend," said the Preceptor, hastening to fill up the blank, in which Bois-Guilbert would probably have placed a worse word,—"a cold-blooded friend I am, and therefore more fit to give thee advice. I tell thee once more, that thou canst not save Rebecca. I tell thee once more, thou canst but perish with her. Go hie thee to the Grand Master—throw thyself at his feet and tell him—"

"Not at his feet, by Heaven! but to the dotard's very beard will I say—"

"Say to him, then, to his beard," continued Malvoisin, coolly, "that you love this captive Jewess to distraction; and the more thou dost enlarge on thy passion, the greater will be his haste to end it by the death of the fair enchantress; while thou, taken in flagrant delict by the avowal of a crime contrary to thine oath, canst hope no aid of thy brethren, and must exchange all thy brilliant visions of ambition and power, to lift perhaps a mercenary spear in some of the petty quarrels between Flanders and Burgundy."

"Thou speakest the truth, Malvoisin," said Brian de Bois-Guilbert, after a moment's reflection. "I will give the hoary bigot no advantage over me; and for Rebecca, she hath not merited at my hand that I should expose rank and honour for her sake. I will cast her off—yes, I will leave her to her fate, unless—"

"Qualify not thy wise and necessary resolution," said Malvoisin; "women are but the toys which amuse our lighter hours—ambition is the serious business of life. Perish a thousand such frail baubles as this Jewess, before thy manly step pause in the brilliant career that lies stretched before thee! For the present we part, nor must we be seen to hold close conversation—I must order the hall for his judgment-seat."

"What!" said Bois-Guilbert, "so soon?"

"Ay," replied the Preceptor, "trial moves rapidly on when the judge has determined the sentence beforehand."

"Rebecca," said Bois-Guilbert, when he was left alone, "thou art like to cost me dear—Why cannot I abandon thee to thy fate, as this calm hypocrite recommends?—One effort will I make to save thee—but beware of ingratitude! for if I am again repulsed, my vengeance shall equal my love. The life and honour of Bois-Guilbert must not be hazarded, where contempt and reproaches are his only reward."

The Preceptor had hardly given the necessary orders, when he was joined by Conrade Mont-Fitchet, who acquainted him with the Grand Master's resolution to bring the Jewess to instant trial for sorcery.

"It is surely a dream," said the Preceptor; "we have many Jewish physicians, and we call them not wizards though they work wonderful cures."

"The Grand Master thinks otherwise," said Mont-Fitchet; "and, Albert, I will be upright with thee—wizard or not, it were better that this miserable damsel die, than that Brian de Bois-Guilbert should be lost to the Order, or the Order divided by internal dissension. Thou knowest his high rank, his fame in arms—thou knowest the zeal with which many of our brethren regard him—but all this will not avail him with our Grand Master, should he consider Brian as the accomplice, not the victim, of this Jewess. Were the souls of the twelve tribes in her single body, it were better she suffered alone, than that Bois-Guilbert were partner in her destruction."

"I have been working him even now to abandon her," said Malvoisin; "but still, are there grounds enough to condemn this Rebecca for sorcery?—Will not the Grand Master change his mind when he sees that the proofs are so weak?"

"They must be strengthened, Albert," replied Mont-Fitchet, "they must be strengthened. Dost thou understand me?"

"I do," said the Preceptor, "nor do I scruple to do aught for advancement of the Order—but there is little time to find engines fitting."

"Malvoisin, they MUST be found," said Conrade; "well will it advantage both the

Order and thee. This Templestowe is a poor Preceptory—that of Maison-Dieu is worth double its value—thou knowest my interest with our old Chief—find those who can carry this matter through, and thou art Preceptor of Maison-Dieu in the fertile Kent—How sayst thou?"

"There is," replied Malvoisin, "among those who came hither with Bois-Guilbert, two fellows whom I well know; servants they were to my brother Philip de Malvoisin, and passed from his service to that of Front-de-Boeuf—It may be they know something of the witcheries of this woman."

"Away, seek them out instantly—and hark thee, if a byzant or two will sharpen their memory, let them not be wanting."

"They would swear the mother that bore them a sorceress for a zecchin," said the Preceptor.

"Away, then," said Mont-Fitchet; "at noon the affair will proceed. I have not seen our senior in such earnest preparation since he condemned to the stake Hamet Alfagi, a convert who relapsed to the Moslem faith."

The ponderous castle-bell had tolled the point of noon, when Rebecca heard a trampling of feet upon the private stair which led to her place of confinement. The noise announced the arrival of several persons, and the circumstance rather gave her joy; for she was more afraid of the solitary visits of the fierce and passionate Bois-Guilbert than of any evil that could befall her besides. The door of the chamber was unlocked, and Conrade and the Preceptor Malvoisin entered, attended by four warders clothed in black, and bearing halberds.

"Daughter of an accursed race!" said the Preceptor, "arise and follow us."

"Whither," said Rebecca, "and for what purpose?"

"Damsel," answered Conrade, "it is not for thee to question, but to obey. Nevertheless, be it known to thee, that thou art to be brought before the tribunal of the Grand Master of our holy Order, there to answer for thine offences."

"May the God of Abraham be praised!" said Rebecca, folding her hands devoutly; "the name of a judge, though an enemy to my people, is to me as the name of a protector. Most willingly do I follow thee—permit me only to wrap my veil around my head."

They descended the stair with slow and solemn step, traversed a long gallery, and, by a pair of folding doors placed at the end, entered the great hall in which the Grand Master had for the time established his court of justice.

The lower part of this ample apartment was filled with squires and yeomen, who made way not without some difficulty for Rebecca, attended by the Preceptor and Mont-Fitchet, and followed by the guard of halberdiers, to move forward to the seat appointed for her. As she passed through the crowd, her arms folded and her head depressed, a scrap of paper was thrust into her hand, which she received almost unconsciously, and continued to hold without examining its contents. The assurance that she possessed some friend in this awful assembly gave her courage to look around, and to mark into whose presence she had been conducted. She gazed, accordingly, upon the scene, which we shall endeavour to describe in the next chapter.

XXXVII.

Stern was the law which bade its vot'ries leave
At human woes with human hearts to grieve;
Stern was the law, which at the winning wile
Of frank and harmless mirth forbade to smile;
But sterner still, when high the iron-rod
Of tyrant power she shook, and call'd that power of God.

— THE MIDDLE AGES

The Tribunal, erected for the trial of the innocent and unhappy Rebecca, occupied the dais or elevated part of the upper end of the great hall—a platform, which we have already described as the place of honour, destined to be occupied by the most distinguished inhabitants or guests of an ancient mansion.

On an elevated seat, directly before the accused, sat the Grand Master of the Temple, in full and ample robes of flowing white, holding in his hand the mystic staff, which bore the symbol of the Order. At his feet was placed a table, occupied by two scribes, chaplains of the Order, whose duty it was to reduce to formal record the proceedings of the day. The black dresses, bare scalps, and demure looks of these church-men, formed a strong contrast to the warlike appearance of the knights who attended, either as residing in the Preceptory, or as come thither to attend upon their Grand Master. The Preceptors, of whom there were four present, occupied seats lower in height, and somewhat drawn back behind that of their superior; and the knights, who enjoyed no such rank in the Order, were placed on benches still lower, and preserving the same distance from the Preceptors as these from the Grand Master. Behind them, but still upon the dais or elevated portion of the hall, stood the esquires of the Order, in white dresses of an inferior quality.

The whole assembly wore an aspect of the most profound gravity; and in the faces of the knights might be perceived traces of military daring, united with the solemn carriage becoming men of a religious profession, and which, in the presence of their Grand Master, failed not to sit upon every brow.

The remaining and lower part of the hall was filled with guards, holding partisans, and with other attendants whom curiosity had drawn thither, to see at once a Grand Master and a Jewish sorceress. By far the greater part of those inferior persons were, in one rank or other, connected with the Order, and were accordingly distinguished by their black dresses. But peasants from the neighbouring country were not refused admittance; for it was the pride of Beaumanoir to render the edifying spectacle of the justice which he administered as public as possible. His large blue eyes seemed to expand as he gazed around the assembly, and his countenance appeared elated by the conscious dignity, and imaginary merit, of the part which he was about to perform. A psalm, which he himself accompanied with a deep mellow voice, which age had not deprived of its powers, commenced the proceedings of the day; and the solemn sounds, "Venite exultemus Domino", so often sung by the Templars before engaging with earthly adversaries, was judged by Lucas most appropriate to introduce the approaching triumph, for such he deemed it, over the powers of darkness. The deep prolonged notes, raised by a hundred masculine voices accustomed to combine in the choral chant, arose to the vaulted roof of the hall, and rolled on amongst its arches with the pleasing yet solemn sound of the rushing of mighty waters.

When the sounds ceased, the Grand Master glanced his eye slowly around the circle, and observed that the seat of one of the Preceptors was vacant. Brian de Bois-Guilbert, by whom it had been occupied, had left his place, and was now standing near the extreme corner of one of the benches occupied by the Knights Companions of the Temple, one hand extending his long mantle, so as in some degree to hide his face; while the other held his cross-handled sword, with the point of which, sheathed as it was, he was slowly drawing lines upon the oaken floor.

"Unhappy man!" said the Grand Master, after favouring him with a glance of compassion. "Thou seest, Conrade, how this holy work distresses him. To this can the light look of woman, aided by the Prince of the Powers of this world, bring a valiant and worthy knight!—Seest thou he cannot look upon us; he cannot look upon her; and who knows by what impulse from his tormentor his hand forms these cabalistic lines upon the floor?—It may be our life and safety are thus aimed at; but we spit at and defy the foul enemy. 'Semper Leo percutiatur!'"

This was communicated apart to his confidential follower, Conrade Mont-Fitchet. The Grand Master then raised his voice, and addressed the assembly.

"Reverend and valiant men, Knights, Preceptors, and Companions of this Holy Order, my brethren and my children!—you also, well-born and pious Esquires, who aspire to wear this holy Cross!—and you also, Christian brethren, of every degree!—Be it known to you, that it is not defect of power in us which hath occasioned the assembling of this congregation; for, however unworthy in our person, yet to us is committed, with this batoon, full power to judge and to try all that regards the weal of this our Holy Order. Holy Saint Bernard, in the rule of our knightly and religious profession, hath said, in the fifty-ninth capital, that he would not that brethren be called together in council, save at the will and command of the Master; leaving it free to us, as to those more worthy fathers who have preceded us in this our office, to judge, as well of the occasion as of the time and place in which a chapter of the whole Order, or of any part thereof, may be convoked. Also, in all such chapters, it is our duty to hear the advice of our brethren, and to proceed according to our own pleasure. But when the raging wolf hath made an inroad upon the flock, and carried off one member thereof, it is the duty of the kind shepherd to call his comrades together, that with bows and slings they may quell the invader, according to our well-known rule, that the lion is ever to be beaten down. We have therefore summoned to our presence a Jewish woman, by name Rebecca, daughter of Isaac of York—a woman infamous for sortileges and for witcheries; whereby she hath maddened the blood, and besotted the brain, not of a churl, but of a Knight—not of a secular Knight, but of one devoted to the service of the Holy Temple—not of a Knight Companion, but of a Preceptor of our Order, first in honour as in place. Our brother, Brian de Bois-Guilbert, is well known to ourselves, and to all degrees who now hear me, as a true and zealous champion of the Cross, by whose arm many deeds of valour have been wrought in the Holy Land, and the holy places purified from pollution by the blood of those infidels who defiled them. Neither have our brother's sagacity and prudence been less in repute among his brethren than his valour and discipline; in so much, that knights, both in eastern and western lands, have named De Bois-Guilbert as one who may well be put in nomination as successor to this batoon, when it shall please Heaven to release us from the toil of bearing it. If we were told that such a man, so honoured, and so honourable, suddenly casting away regard for his character, his vows, his brethren, and his prospects, had associated to himself a Jewish damsel, wandered in this lewd company, through solitary places, defended her person in preference to his own, and, finally, was so utterly blinded and besotted by his folly, as to bring her even to one of our own Preceptories, what should we say but that the noble knight was possessed by some evil demon, or influenced by some wicked spell?—If we could suppose it otherwise, think not rank, valour, high repute, or any earthly consideration, should prevent us from visiting him with punishment, that the evil thing might be removed, even according to the text, 'Auferte malum ex vobis'. For various and heinous are the acts of transgression against the rule of our blessed Order in this lamentable history.—1st, He hath walked according to his proper will, contrary to capital 33, 'Quod nullus juxta propriam voluntatem incedat'.—2d, He hath held communication with an excommunicated person, capital 57, 'Ut fratres non participent cum excommunicatis', and therefore hath a portion in 'Anathema Maranatha'.—3d, He hath conversed with strange women, contrary to the capital, 'Ut fratres non conversantur cum extraneis mulieribus'.—4th, He hath not avoided, nay, he hath, it is to be feared, solicited the kiss of woman; by which, saith the last rule of our renowned Order, 'Ut fugiantur oscula', the soldiers of the Cross are brought into a snare. For which heinous and multiplied guilt, Brian de Bois-Guilbert should be cut off and cast out from our congregation, were he the right hand and right eye thereof."

He paused. A low murmur went through the assembly. Some of the younger part, who had been inclined to smile at the statute 'De osculis fugiendis', became now grave enough, and anxiously waited what the Grand Master was next to propose.

"Such," he said, "and so great should indeed be the punishment of a Knight Templar, who wilfully offended against the rules of his Order in such weighty points. But if, by means of charms and of spells, Satan had obtained dominion over the Knight, perchance because he cast his eyes too lightly upon a damsel's beauty, we are then rather to lament than chastise his backsliding; and, imposing on him only such penance as may purify him from his iniquity, we are to turn the full edge of our indignation upon the accursed instrument, which had so well-nigh occasioned his utter falling away.—Stand forth, therefore, and bear witness, ye who have witnessed these unhappy doings, that we may judge of the sum and bearing thereof; and judge whether our justice may be satisfied with the punishment of this infidel woman, or if we must go on, with a bleeding heart, to the further proceeding against our brother."

Several witnesses were called upon to prove the risks to which Bois-Guilbert exposed himself in endeavouring to save Rebecca from the blazing castle, and his neglect of his personal defence in attending to her safety. The men gave these details with the exaggerations common to vulgar minds which have been strongly excited by any remarkable event, and their natural disposition to the marvellous was greatly increased by the satisfaction which their evidence seemed to afford to the eminent person for whose information it had been delivered. Thus the dangers which Bois-

Guilbert surmounted, in themselves sufficiently great, became portentous in their narrative. The devotion of the Knight to Rebecca's defence was exaggerated beyond the bounds, not only of discretion, but even of the most frantic excess of chivalrous zeal; and his deference to what she said, even although her language was often severe and upbraiding, was painted as carried to an excess, which, in a man of his haughty temper, seemed almost preternatural.

The Preceptor of Templestowe was then called on to describe the manner in which Bois-Guilbert and the Jewess arrived at the Preceptory. The evidence of Malvoisin was skilfully guarded. But while he apparently studied to spare the feelings of Bois-Guilbert, he threw in, from time to time, such hints, as seemed to infer that he laboured under some temporary alienation of mind, so deeply did he appear to be enamoured of the damsel whom he brought along with him. With sighs of penitence, the Preceptor avowed his own contrition for having admitted Rebecca and her lover within the walls of the Preceptory—"But my defence," he concluded, "has been made in my confession to our most reverend father the Grand Master; he knows my motives were not evil, though my conduct may have been irregular. Joyfully will I submit to any penance he shall assign me."

"Thou hast spoken well, Brother Albert," said Beaumanoir; "thy motives were good, since thou didst judge it right to arrest thine erring brother in his career of precipitate folly. But thy conduct was wrong; as he that would stop a runaway steed, and seizing by the stirrup instead of the bridle, receiveth injury himself, instead of accomplishing his purpose. Thirteen paternosters are assigned by our pious founder for matins, and nine for vespers; be those services doubled by thee. Thrice a-week are Templars permitted the use of flesh; but do thou keep fast for all the seven days. This do for six weeks to come, and thy penance is accomplished."

With a hypocritical look of the deepest submission, the Preceptor of Templestowe bowed to the ground before his Superior, and resumed his seat.

"Were it not well, brethren," said the Grand Master, "that we examine something into the former life and conversation of this woman, specially that we may discover whether she be one likely to use magical charms and spells, since the truths which we have heard may well incline us to suppose, that in this unhappy course our erring brother has been acted upon by some infernal enticement and delusion?"

Herman of Goodalricke was the Fourth Preceptor present; the other three were Conrade, Malvoisin, and Bois-Guilbert himself. Herman was an ancient warrior, whose face was marked with scars inflicted by the sabre of the Moslemah, and had great rank and consideration among his brethren. He arose and bowed to the Grand Master, who instantly granted him license of speech. "I would crave to know, most Reverend Father, of our valiant brother, Brian de Bois-Guilbert, what he says to these wondrous accusations, and with what eye he himself now regards his unhappy intercourse with this Jewish maiden?"

"Brian de Bois-Guilbert," said the Grand Master, "thou hearest the question which our Brother of Goodalricke desirest thou shouldst answer. I command thee to reply to him."

Bois-Guilbert turned his head towards the Grand Master when thus addressed, and remained silent.

"He is possessed by a dumb devil," said the Grand Master. "Avoid thee, Sathanus!

—Speak, Brian de Bois-Guilbert, I conjure thee, by this symbol of our Holy Order."

Bois-Guilbert made an effort to suppress his rising scorn and indignation, the expression of which, he was well aware, would have little availed him. "Brian de Bois-Guilbert," he answered, "replies not, most Reverend Father, to such wild and vague charges. If his honour be impeached, he will defend it with his body, and with that sword which has often fought for Christendom."

"We forgive thee, Brother Brian," said the Grand Master; "though that thou hast boasted thy warlike achievements before us, is a glorifying of thine own deeds, and cometh of the Enemy, who tempteth us to exalt our own worship. But thou hast our pardon, judging thou speakest less of thine own suggestion than from the impulse of him whom by Heaven's leave, we will quell and drive forth from our assembly." A glance of disdain flashed from the dark fierce eyes of Bois-Guilbert, but he made no reply.—"And now," pursued the Grand Master, "since our Brother of Goodalricke's question has been thus imperfectly answered, pursue we our quest, brethren, and with our patron's assistance, we will search to the bottom this mystery of iniquity.—Let those who have aught to witness of the life and conversation of this Jewish woman, stand forth before us." There was a bustle in the lower part of the hall, and when the Grand Master enquired the reason, it was replied, there was in the crowd a bedridden man, whom the prisoner had restored to the perfect use of his limbs, by a miraculous balsam.

The poor peasant, a Saxon by birth, was dragged forward to the bar, terrified at the penal consequences which he might have incurred by the guilt of having been cured of the palsy by a Jewish damsel. Perfectly cured he certainly was not, for he supported himself forward on crutches to give evidence. Most unwilling was his testimony, and given with many tears; but he admitted that two years since, when residing at York, he was suddenly afflicted with a sore disease, while labouring for Isaac the rich Jew, in his vocation of a joiner; that he had been unable to stir from his bed until the remedies applied by Rebecca's directions, and especially a warming and spicy-smelling balsam, had in some degree restored him to the use of his limbs. Moreover, he said, she had given him a pot of that precious ointment, and furnished him with a piece of money withal, to return to the house of his father, near to Templestowe. "And may it please your gracious Reverence," said the man, "I cannot think the damsel meant harm by me, though she hath the ill hap to be a Jewess; for even when I used her remedy, I said the Pater and the Creed, and it never operated a whit less kindly—"

"Peace, slave," said the Grand Master, "and begone! It well suits brutes like thee to be tampering and trinketing with hellish cures, and to be giving your labour to the sons of mischief. I tell thee, the fiend can impose diseases for the very purpose of removing them, in order to bring into credit some diabolical fashion of cure. Hast thou that unguent of which thou speakest?"

The peasant, fumbling in his bosom with a trembling hand, produced a small box, bearing some Hebrew characters on the lid, which was, with most of the audience, a sure proof that the devil had stood apothecary. Beaumanoir, after crossing himself, took the box into his hand, and, learned in most of the Eastern tongues, read with ease the motto on the lid,—"The Lion of the tribe of Judah hath conquered."

"Strange powers of Sathanas." said he, "which can convert Scripture into blasphemy, mingling poison with our necessary food!—Is there no leech here who can tell us the ingredients of this mystic unguent?"

Two mediciners, as they called themselves, the one a monk, the other a barber, appeared, and avouched they knew nothing of the materials, excepting that they savoured of myrrh and camphire, which they took to be Oriental herbs. But with the true professional hatred to a successful practitioner of their art, they insinuated that, since the medicine was beyond their own knowledge, it must necessarily have been compounded from an unlawful and magical pharmacopeia; since they themselves, though no conjurors, fully understood every branch of their art, so far as it might be exercised with the good faith of a Christian. When this medical research was ended, the Saxon peasant desired humbly to have back the medicine which he had found so salutary; but the Grand Master frowned severely at the request. "What is thy name, fellow?" said he to the cripple.

"Higg, the son of Snell," answered the peasant.

"Then Higg, son of Snell," said the Grand Master, "I tell thee it is better to be bedridden, than to accept the benefit of unbelievers' medicine that thou mayest arise and walk; better to despoil infidels of their treasure by the strong hand, than to accept of them benevolent gifts, or do them service for wages. Go thou, and do as I have said."

"Alack," said the peasant, "an it shall not displease your Reverence, the lesson comes too late for me, for I am but a maimed man; but I will tell my two brethren, who serve the rich Rabbi Nathan Ben Samuel, that your mastership says it is more lawful to rob him than to render him faithful service."

"Out with the prating villain!" said Beaumanoir, who was not prepared to refute this practical application of his general maxim.

Higg, the son of Snell, withdrew into the crowd, but, interested in the fate of his benefactress, lingered until he should learn her doom, even at the risk of again encountering the frown of that severe judge, the terror of which withered his very heart within him.

At this period of the trial, the Grand Master commanded Rebecca to unveil herself. Opening her lips for the first time, she replied patiently, but with dignity,—"That it was not the wont of the daughters of her people to uncover their faces when alone in an assembly of strangers." The sweet tones of her voice, and the softness of her reply, impressed on the audience a sentiment of pity and sympathy. But Beaumanoir, in whose mind the suppression of each feeling of humanity which could interfere with his imagined duty, was a virtue of itself, repeated his commands that his victim should be unveiled. The guards were about to remove her veil accordingly, when she stood up before the Grand Master and said, "Nay, but for the love of your own daughters—Alas," she said, recollecting herself, "ye have no daughters!—yet for the remembrance of your mothers—for the love of your sisters, and of female decency, let me not be thus handled in your presence; it suits not a maiden to be disrobed by such rude grooms. I will obey you," she added, with an expression of patient sorrow in her voice, which had almost melted the heart of Beaumanoir himself; "ye are elders among your people, and at your command I will show the features of an ill-fated maiden."

She withdrew her veil, and looked on them with a countenance in which bashfulness contended with dignity. Her exceeding beauty excited a murmur of surprise, and the younger knights told each other with their eyes, in silent correspondence, that Brian's best apology was in the power of her real charms, rather than of her imaginary witchcraft. But Higg, the son of Snell, felt most deeply the effect produced by the sight of the countenance of his benefactress.

"Let me go forth," he said to the warders at the door of the hall,—"let me go forth!—To look at her again will kill me, for I have had a share in murdering her."

"Peace, poor man," said Rebecca, when she heard his exclamation; "thou hast done me no harm by speaking the truth—thou canst not aid me by thy complaints or lamentations. Peace, I pray thee—go home and save thyself."

Higg was about to be thrust out by the compassion of the warders, who were apprehensive lest his clamorous grief should draw upon them reprehension, and upon himself punishment. But he promised to be silent, and was permitted to remain. The two men-at-arms, with whom Albert Malvoisin had not failed to communicate upon the import of their testimony, were now called forward. Though both were hardened and inflexible villains, the sight of the captive maiden, as well as her excelling beauty, at first appeared to stagger them; but an expressive glance from the Preceptor of Templestowe restored them to their dogged composure; and they delivered, with a precision which would have seemed suspicious to more impartial judges, circumstances either altogether fictitious or trivial, and natural in themselves, but rendered pregnant with suspicion by the exaggerated manner in which they were told, and the sinister commentary which the witnesses added to the facts. The circumstances of their evidence would have been, in modern days, divided into two classes—those which were immaterial, and those which were actually and physically impossible. But both were, in those ignorant and superstitions times, easily credited as proofs of guilt.—The first class set forth, that Rebecca was heard to mutter to herself in an unknown tongue—that the songs she sung by fits were of a strangely sweet sound, which made the ears of the hearer tingle, and his heart throb—that she spoke at times to herself, and seemed to look upward for a reply—that her garments were of a strange and mystic form, unlike those of women of good repute—that she had rings impressed with cabalistical devices, and that strange characters were broidered on her veil.

All these circumstances, so natural and so trivial, were gravely listened to as proofs, or, at least, as affording strong suspicions that Rebecca had unlawful correspondence with mystical powers.

But there was less equivocal testimony, which the credulity of the assembly, or of the greater part, greedily swallowed, however incredible. One of the soldiers had seen her work a cure upon a wounded man, brought with them to the castle of Torquilstone. She did, he said, make certain signs upon the wound, and repeated certain mysterious words, which he blessed God he understood not, when the iron head of a square cross-bow bolt disengaged itself from the wound, the bleeding was stanched, the wound was closed, and the dying man was, within a quarter of an hour, walking upon the ramparts, and assisting the witness in managing a mangonel, or machine for hurling stones. This legend was probably founded upon the fact, that Rebecca had attended on the wounded Ivanhoe when in the castle of Torquilstone.

But it was the more difficult to dispute the accuracy of the witness, as, in order to produce real evidence in support of his verbal testimony, he drew from his pouch the very bolt-head, which, according to his story, had been miraculously extracted from the wound; and as the iron weighed a full ounce, it completely confirmed the tale, however marvellous.

His comrade had been a witness from a neighbouring battlement of the scene betwixt Rebecca and Bois-Guilbert, when she was upon the point of precipitating herself from the top of the tower. Not to be behind his companion, this fellow stated, that he had seen Rebecca perch herself upon the parapet of the turret, and there take the form of a milk-white swan, under which appearance she flitted three times round the castle of Torquilstone; then again settle on the turret, and once more assume the female form.

Less than one half of this weighty evidence would have been sufficient to convict any old woman, poor and ugly, even though she had not been a Jewess. United with that fatal circumstance, the body of proof was too weighty for Rebecca's youth, though combined with the most exquisite beauty.

The Grand Master had collected the suffrages, and now in a solemn tone demanded of Rebecca what she had to say against the sentence of condemnation, which he was about to pronounce.

"To invoke your pity," said the lovely Jewess, with a voice somewhat tremulous with emotion, "would, I am aware, be as useless as I should hold it mean. To state that to relieve the sick and wounded of another religion, cannot be displeasing to the acknowledged Founder of both our faiths, were also unavailing; to plead that many things which these men (whom may Heaven pardon!) have spoken against me are impossible, would avail me but little, since you believe in their possibility; and still less would it advantage me to explain, that the peculiarities of my dress, language, and manners, are those of my people—I had well-nigh said of my country, but alas! we have no country. Nor will I even vindicate myself at the expense of my oppressor, who stands there listening to the fictions and surmises which seem to convert the tyrant into the victim.—God be judge between him and me! but rather would I submit to ten such deaths as your pleasure may denounce against me, than listen to the suit which that man of Belial has urged upon me—friendless, defenceless, and his prisoner. But he is of your own faith, and his lightest affirmance would weigh down the most solemn protestations of the distressed Jewess. I will not therefore return to himself the charge brought against me—but to himself—Yes, Brian de Bois-Guilbert, to thyself I appeal, whether these accusations are not false? as monstrous and calumnious as they are deadly?"

There was a pause; all eyes turned to Brain de Bois-Guilbert. He was silent.

"Speak," she said, "if thou art a man—if thou art a Christian, speak!—I conjure thee, by the habit which thou dost wear, by the name thou dost inherit—by the knighthood thou dost vaunt—by the honour of thy mother—by the tomb and the bones of thy father—I conjure thee to say, are these things true?"

"Answer her, brother," said the Grand Master, "if the Enemy with whom thou dost wrestle will give thee power."

In fact, Bois-Guilbert seemed agitated by contending passions, which almost convulsed his features, and it was with a constrained voice that at last he replied, looking to Rebecca,—"The scroll!—the scroll!"

"Ay," said Beaumanoir, "this is indeed testimony! The victim of her witcheries can only name the fatal scroll, the spell inscribed on which is, doubtless, the cause of his silence."

But Rebecca put another interpretation on the words extorted as it were from Bois-Guilbert, and glancing her eye upon the slip of parchment which she continued to hold in her hand, she read written thereupon in the Arabian character, "Demand a Champion!" The murmuring commentary which ran through the assembly at the strange reply of Bois-Guilbert, gave Rebecca leisure to examine and instantly to destroy the scroll unobserved. When the whisper had ceased, the Grand Master spoke.

"Rebecca, thou canst derive no benefit from the evidence of this unhappy knight, for whom, as we well perceive, the Enemy is yet too powerful. Hast thou aught else to say?"

"There is yet one chance of life left to me," said Rebecca, "even by your own fierce laws. Life has been miserable—miserable, at least, of late—but I will not cast away the gift of God, while he affords me the means of defending it. I deny this charge—I maintain my innocence, and I declare the falsehood of this accusation—I challenge the privilege of trial by combat, and will appear by my champion."

"And who, Rebecca," replied the Grand Master, "will lay lance in rest for a sorceress? who will be the champion of a Jewess?"

"God will raise me up a champion," said Rebecca—"It cannot be that in merry England—the hospitable, the generous, the free, where so many are ready to peril their lives for honour, there will not be found one to fight for justice. But it is enough that I challenge the trial by combat—there lies my gage."

She took her embroidered glove from her hand, and flung it down before the Grand Master with an air of mingled simplicity and dignity, which excited universal surprise and admiration.

XXXVIII.

—There I throw my gage,
To prove it on thee to the extremest point
Of martial daring.

— RICHARD II

Even Lucas Beaumanoir himself was affected by the mien and appearance of Rebecca. He was not originally a cruel or even a severe man; but with passions by nature cold, and with a high, though mistaken, sense of duty, his heart had been gradually hardened by the ascetic life which he pursued, the supreme power which he enjoyed, and the supposed necessity of subduing infidelity and eradicating heresy, which he conceived peculiarly incumbent on him. His features relaxed in their usual severity as he gazed upon the beautiful creature before him, alone, unfriended, and defending herself with so much spirit and courage. He crossed himself twice, as doubting whence arose the unwonted softening of a heart, which on such occasions used to resemble in hardness the steel of his sword. At length he spoke.

"Damsel," he said, "if the pity I feel for thee arise from any practice thine evil arts have made on me, great is thy guilt. But I rather judge it the kinder feelings of nature, which grieves that so goodly a form should be a vessel of perdition. Repent, my daughter—confess thy witchcrafts—turn thee from thine evil faith—embrace this holy emblem, and all shall yet be well with thee here and hereafter. In some sisterhood of the strictest order, shalt thou have time for prayer and fitting penance, and that repentance not to be repented of. This do and live—what has the law of Moses done for thee that thou shouldest die for it?"

"It was the law of my fathers," said Rebecca; "it was delivered in thunders and in storms upon the mountain of Sinai, in cloud and in fire. This, if ye are Christians, ye believe—it is, you say, recalled; but so my teachers have not taught me."

"Let our chaplain," said Beaumanoir, "stand forth, and tell this obstinate infidel—"

"Forgive the interruption," said Rebecca, meekly; "I am a maiden, unskilled to dispute for my religion, but I can die for it, if it be God's will.—Let me pray your answer to my demand of a champion."

"Give me her glove," said Beaumanoir. "This is indeed," he continued, as he looked at the flimsy texture and slender fingers, "a slight and frail gage for a purpose so deadly!—Seest thou, Rebecca, as this thin and light glove of thine is to one of our heavy steel gauntlets, so is thy cause to that of the Temple, for it is our Order which thou hast defied."

"Cast my innocence into the scale," answered Rebecca, "and the glove of silk shall outweigh the glove of iron."

"Then thou dost persist in thy refusal to confess thy guilt, and in that bold challenge which thou hast made?"

"I do persist, noble sir," answered Rebecca.

"So be it then, in the name of Heaven," said the Grand Master; "and may God show the right!"

"Amen," replied the Preceptors around him, and the word was deeply echoed by the whole assembly.

"Brethren," said Beaumanoir, "you are aware that we might well have refused to this woman the benefit of the trial by combat—but though a Jewess and an unbeliever, she is also a stranger and defenceless, and God forbid that she should ask the benefit of our mild laws, and that it should be refused to her. Moreover, we are knights and soldiers as well as men of religion, and shame it were to us upon any pretence, to refuse proffered combat. Thus, therefore, stands the case. Rebecca, the daughter of Isaac of York, is, by many frequent and suspicious circumstances, defamed of sorcery practised on the person of a noble knight of our holy Order, and hath challenged the combat in proof of her innocence. To whom, reverend brethren, is it your opinion that we should deliver the gage of battle, naming him, at the same time, to be our champion on the field?"

"To Brian de Bois-Guilbert, whom it chiefly concerns," said the Preceptor of Goodalricke, "and who, moreover, best knows how the truth stands in this matter."

"But if," said the Grand Master, "our brother Brian be under the influence of a charm or a spell—we speak but for the sake of precaution, for to the arm of none of our holy Order would we more willingly confide this or a more weighty cause."

"Reverend father," answered the Preceptor of Goodalricke, "no spell can effect the champion who comes forward to fight for the judgment of God."

"Thou sayest right, brother," said the Grand Master. "Albert Malvoisin, give this gage of battle to Brian de Bois-Guilbert.—It is our charge to thee, brother," he continued, addressing himself to Bois-Guilbert, "that thou do thy battle manfully, nothing doubting that the good cause shall triumph.—And do thou, Rebecca, attend, that we assign thee the third day from the present to find a champion."

"That is but brief space," answered Rebecca, "for a stranger, who is also of another faith, to find one who will do battle, wagering life and honour for her cause, against a knight who is called an approved soldier."

"We may not extend it," answered the Grand Master; "the field must be foughten in our own presence, and divers weighty causes call us on the fourth day from hence."

"God's will be done!" said Rebecca; "I put my trust in Him, to whom an instant is as effectual to save as a whole age."

"Thou hast spoken well, damsel," said the Grand Master; "but well know we who can array himself like an angel of light. It remains but to name a fitting place of combat, and, if it so hap, also of execution.—Where is the Preceptor of this house?"

Albert Malvoisin, still holding Rebecca's glove in his hand, was speaking to Bois-Guilbert very earnestly, but in a low voice.

"How!" said the Grand Master, "will he not receive the gage?"

"He will—he doth, most Reverend Father," said Malvoisin, slipping the glove under his own mantle. "And for the place of combat, I hold the fittest to be the lists of Saint George belonging to this Preceptory, and used by us for military exercise."

"It is well," said the Grand Master.—"Rebecca, in those lists shalt thou produce thy champion; and if thou failest to do so, or if thy champion shall be discomfited by the judgment of God, thou shalt then die the death of a sorceress, according to doom. —Let this our judgment be recorded, and the record read aloud, that no one may pretend ignorance."

One of the chaplains, who acted as clerks to the chapter, immediately engrossed the order in a huge volume, which contained the proceedings of the Templar Knights when solemnly assembled on such occasions; and when he had finished writing, the other read aloud the sentence of the Grand Master, which, when translated from the Norman-French in which it was couched, was expressed as follows.—

"Rebecca, a Jewess, daughter of Isaac of York, being attainted of sorcery, seduction, and other damnable practices, practised on a Knight of the most Holy Order of the Temple of Zion, doth deny the same; and saith, that the testimony delivered against her this day is false, wicked, and disloyal; and that by lawful 'essoine' of her body as being unable to combat in her own behalf, she doth offer, by a champion instead thereof, to avouch her case, he performing his loyal 'devoir' in all knightly sort, with such arms as to gage of battle do fully appertain, and that at her peril and cost. And therewith she proffered her gage. And the gage having been delivered to the noble Lord and Knight, Brian de Bois-Guilbert, of the Holy Order of the Temple of

Zion, he was appointed to do this battle, in behalf of his Order and himself, as injured and impaired by the practices of the appellant. Wherefore the most reverend Father and puissant Lord, Lucas Marquis of Beaumanoir, did allow of the said challenge, and of the said 'essoine' of the appellant's body, and assigned the third day for the said combat, the place being the enclosure called the lists of Saint George, near to the Preceptory of Templestowe. And the Grand Master appoints the appellant to appear there by her champion, on pain of doom, as a person convicted of sorcery or seduction; and also the defendant so to appear, under the penalty of being held and adjudged recreant in case of default; and the noble Lord and most reverend Father aforesaid appointed the battle to be done in his own presence, and according to all that is commendable and profitable in such a case. And may God aid the just cause!"

"Amen!" said the Grand Master; and the word was echoed by all around. Rebecca spoke not, but she looked up to heaven, and, folding her hands, remained for a minute without change of attitude. She then modestly reminded the Grand Master, that she ought to be permitted some opportunity of free communication with her friends, for the purpose of making her condition known to them, and procuring, if possible, some champion to fight in her behalf.

"It is just and lawful," said the Grand Master; "choose what messenger thou shalt trust, and he shall have free communication with thee in thy prison-chamber."

"Is there," said Rebecca, "any one here, who, either for love of a good cause, or for ample hire, will do the errand of a distressed being?"

All were silent; for none thought it safe, in the presence of the Grand Master, to avow any interest in the calumniated prisoner, lest he should be suspected of leaning towards Judaism. Not even the prospect of reward, far less any feelings of compassion alone, could surmount this apprehension.

Rebecca stood for a few moments in indescribable anxiety, and then exclaimed, "Is it really thus?—And, in English land, am I to be deprived of the poor chance of safety which remains to me, for want of an act of charity which would not be refused to the worst criminal?"

Higg, the son of Snell, at length replied, "I am but a maimed man, but that I can at all stir or move was owing to her charitable assistance.—I will do thine errand," he added, addressing Rebecca, "as well as a crippled object can, and happy were my limbs fleet enough to repair the mischief done by my tongue. Alas! when I boasted of thy charity, I little thought I was leading thee into danger!"

"God," said Rebecca, "is the disposer of all. He can turn back the captivity of Judah, even by the weakest instrument. To execute his message the snail is as sure a messenger as the falcon. Seek out Isaac of York—here is that will pay for horse and man—let him have this scroll.—I know not if it be of Heaven the spirit which inspires me, but most truly do I judge that I am not to die this death, and that a champion will be raised up for me. Farewell!—Life and death are in thy haste."

The peasant took the scroll, which contained only a few lines in Hebrew. Many of the crowd would have dissuaded him from touching a document so suspicious; but Higg was resolute in the service of his benefactress. She had saved his body, he said, and he was confident she did not mean to peril his soul.

"I will get me," he said, "my neighbour Buthan's good capul, and I will be at York within as brief space as man and beast may."

But as it fortuned, he had no occasion to go so far, for within a quarter of a mile from the gate of the Preceptory he met with two riders, whom, by their dress and their huge yellow caps, he knew to be Jews; and, on approaching more nearly, discovered that one of them was his ancient employer, Isaac of York. The other was the Rabbi Ben Samuel; and both had approached as near to the Preceptory as they dared, on hearing that the Grand Master had summoned a chapter for the trial of a sorceress.

"Brother Ben Samuel," said Isaac, "my soul is disquieted, and I wot not why. This charge of necromancy is right often used for cloaking evil practices on our people."

"Be of good comfort, brother," said the physician; "thou canst deal with the Nazarenes as one possessing the mammon of unrighteousness, and canst therefore purchase immunity at their hands—it rules the savage minds of those ungodly men, even as the signet of the mighty Solomon was said to command the evil genii.—But what poor wretch comes hither upon his crutches, desiring, as I think, some speech of me?—Friend," continued the physician, addressing Higg, the son of Snell, "I refuse thee not the aid of mine art, but I relieve not with one asper those who beg for alms upon the highway. Out upon thee!—Hast thou the palsy in thy legs? then let thy hands work for thy livelihood; for, albeit thou be'st unfit for a speedy post, or for a careful shepherd, or for the warfare, or for the service of a hasty master, yet there be occupations—How now, brother?" said he, interrupting his harangue to look towards Isaac, who had but glanced at the scroll which Higg offered, when, uttering a deep groan, he fell from his mule like a dying man, and lay for a minute insensible.

The Rabbi now dismounted in great alarm, and hastily applied the remedies which his art suggested for the recovery of his companion. He had even taken from his pocket a cupping apparatus, and was about to proceed to phlebotomy, when the object of his anxious solicitude suddenly revived; but it was to dash his cap from his head, and to throw dust on his grey hairs. The physician was at first inclined to ascribe this sudden and violent emotion to the effects of insanity; and, adhering to his original purpose, began once again to handle his implements. But Isaac soon convinced him of his error.

"Child of my sorrow," he said, "well shouldst thou be called Benoni, instead of Rebecca! Why should thy death bring down my grey hairs to the grave, till, in the bitterness of my heart, I curse God and die!"

"Brother," said the Rabbi, in great surprise, "art thou a father in Israel, and dost thou utter words like unto these?—I trust that the child of thy house yet liveth?"

"She liveth," answered Isaac; "but it is as Daniel, who was called Beltheshazzar, even when within the den of the lions. She is captive unto those men of Belial, and they will wreak their cruelty upon her, sparing neither for her youth nor her comely favour. O! she was as a crown of green palms to my grey locks; and she must wither in a night, like the gourd of Jonah!—Child of my love!—child of my old age!—oh, Rebecca, daughter of Rachel! the darkness of the shadow of death hath encompassed thee."

"Yet read the scroll," said the Rabbi; "peradventure it may be that we may yet find out a way of deliverance."

"Do thou read, brother," answered Isaac, "for mine eyes are as a fountain of water."

The physician read, but in their native language, the following words:—

"To Isaac, the son of Adonikam, whom the Gentiles call Isaac of York, peace and the blessing of the promise be multiplied unto thee!—My father, I am as one doomed to die for that which my soul knoweth not—even for the crime of witchcraft. My father, if a strong man can be found to do battle for my cause with sword and spear, according to the custom of the Nazarenes, and that within the lists of Templestowe, on the third day from this time, peradventure our fathers' God will give him strength to defend the innocent, and her who hath none to help her. But if this may not be, let the virgins of our people mourn for me as for one cast off, and for the hart that is stricken by the hunter, and for the flower which is cut down by the scythe of the mower. Wherefore look now what thou doest, and whether there be any rescue. One Nazarene warrior might indeed bear arms in my behalf, even Wilfred, son of Cedric, whom the Gentiles call Ivanhoe. But he may not yet endure the weight of his armour. Nevertheless, send the tidings unto him, my father; for he hath favour among the strong men of his people, and as he was our companion in the house of bondage, he may find some one to do battle for my sake. And say unto him, even unto him, even unto Wilfred, the son of Cedric, that if Rebecca live, or if Rebecca die, she liveth or dieth wholly free of the guilt she is charged withal. And if it be the will of God that thou shalt be deprived of thy daughter, do not thou tarry, old man, in this land of bloodshed and cruelty; but betake thyself to Cordova, where thy brother liveth in safety, under the shadow of the throne, even of the throne of Boabdil the Saracen; for less cruel are the cruelties of the Moors unto the race of Jacob, than the cruelties of the Nazarenes of England."

Isaac listened with tolerable composure while Ben Samuel read the letter, and then again resumed the gestures and exclamations of Oriental sorrow, tearing his garments, besprinkling his head with dust, and ejaculating, "My daughter! my daughter! flesh of my flesh, and bone of my bone!"

"Yet," said the Rabbi, "take courage, for this grief availeth nothing. Gird up thy loins, and seek out this Wilfred, the son of Cedric. It may be he will help thee with counsel or with strength; for the youth hath favour in the eyes of Richard, called of the Nazarenes Coeur-de-Lion, and the tidings that he hath returned are constant in the land. It may be that he may obtain his letter, and his signet, commanding these men of blood, who take their name from the Temple to the dishonour thereof, that they proceed not in their purposed wickedness."

"I will seek him out," said Isaac, "for he is a good youth, and hath compassion for the exile of Jacob. But he cannot bear his armour, and what other Christian shall do battle for the oppressed of Zion?"

"Nay, but," said the Rabbi, "thou speakest as one that knoweth not the Gentiles. With gold shalt thou buy their valour, even as with gold thou buyest thine own safety. Be of good courage, and do thou set forward to find out this Wilfred of Ivanhoe. I will also up and be doing, for great sin it were to leave thee in thy calamity. I will hie me to the city of York, where many warriors and strong men are assembled, and doubt not I will find among them some one who will do battle for thy daughter; for gold is their god, and for riches will they pawn their lives as well as their lands.—Thou wilt fulfil, my brother, such promise as I may make unto them in thy name?"

"Assuredly, brother," said Isaac, "and Heaven be praised that raised me up a comforter in my misery. Howbeit, grant them not their full demand at once, for thou shalt find it the quality of this accursed people that they will ask pounds, and peradventure accept of ounces—Nevertheless, be it as thou willest, for I am distracted in this thing, and what would my gold avail me if the child of my love should perish!"

"Farewell," said the physician, "and may it be to thee as thy heart desireth."

They embraced accordingly, and departed on their several roads. The crippled peasant remained for some time looking after them.

"These dog-Jews!" said he; "to take no more notice of a free guild-brother, than if I were a bond slave or a Turk, or a circumcised Hebrew like themselves! They might have flung me a mancus or two, however. I was not obliged to bring their unhallowed scrawls, and run the risk of being bewitched, as more folks than one told me. And what care I for the bit of gold that the wench gave me, if I am to come to harm from the priest next Easter at confession, and be obliged to give him twice as much to make it up with him, and be called the Jew's flying post all my life, as it may hap, into the bargain? I think I was bewitched in earnest when I was beside that girl!—But it was always so with Jew or Gentile, whosoever came near her—none could stay when she had an errand to go—and still, whenever I think of her, I would give shop and tools to save her life."

XXXIX.

> O maid, unrelenting and cold as thou art,
> My bosom is proud as thine own.
>
> — SEWARD

It was in the twilight of the day when her trial, if it could be called such, had taken place, that a low knock was heard at the door of Rebecca's prison-chamber. It disturbed not the inmate, who was then engaged in the evening prayer recommended by her religion, and which concluded with a hymn we have ventured thus to translate into English.

> When Israel, of the Lord beloved,
> Out of the land of bondage came,
> Her father's God before her moved,
> An awful guide, in smoke and flame.
> By day, along the astonish'd lands
> The cloudy pillar glided slow;
> By night, Arabia's crimson'd sands
> Return'd the fiery column's glow.
>
> There rose the choral hymn of praise,
> And trump and timbrel answer'd keen,
> And Zion's daughters pour'd their lays,
> With priest's and warrior's voice between.
> No portents now our foes amaze,

Forsaken Israel wanders lone;
Our fathers would not know THY ways,
And THOU hast left them to their own.

But, present still, though now unseen;
When brightly shines the prosperous day,
Be thoughts of THEE a cloudy screen
To temper the deceitful ray.
And oh, when stoops on Judah's path
In shade and storm the frequent night,
Be THOU, long-suffering, slow to wrath,
A burning, and a shining light!

Our harps we left by Babel's streams,
The tyrant's jest, the Gentile's scorn;
No censer round our altar beams,
And mute our timbrel, trump, and horn.
But THOU hast said, the blood of goat,
The flesh of rams, I will not prize;
A contrite heart, and humble thought,
Are mine accepted sacrifice.

When the sounds of Rebecca's devotional hymn had died away in silence, the low knock at the door was again renewed. "Enter," she said, "if thou art a friend; and if a foe, I have not the means of refusing thy entrance."

"I am," said Brian de Bois-Guilbert, entering the apartment, "friend or foe, Rebecca, as the event of this interview shall make me."

Alarmed at the sight of this man, whose licentious passion she considered as the root of her misfortunes, Rebecca drew backward with a cautious and alarmed, yet not a timorous demeanour, into the farthest corner of the apartment, as if determined to retreat as far as she could, but to stand her ground when retreat became no longer possible. She drew herself into an attitude not of defiance, but of resolution, as one that would avoid provoking assault, yet was resolute to repel it, being offered, to the utmost of her power.

"You have no reason to fear me, Rebecca," said the Templar; "or if I must so qualify my speech, you have at least NOW no reason to fear me."

"I fear you not, Sir Knight," replied Rebecca, although her short-drawn breath seemed to belie the heroism of her accents; "my trust is strong, and I fear thee not."

"You have no cause," answered Bois-Guilbert, gravely; "my former frantic attempts you have not now to dread. Within your call are guards, over whom I have no authority. They are designed to conduct you to death, Rebecca, yet would not suffer you to be insulted by any one, even by me, were my frenzy—for frenzy it is—to urge me so far."

"May Heaven be praised!" said the Jewess; "death is the least of my apprehensions in this den of evil."

"Ay," replied the Templar, "the idea of death is easily received by the courageous mind, when the road to it is sudden and open. A thrust with a lance, a stroke with a sword, were to me little—To you, a spring from a dizzy battlement, a stroke with a sharp poniard, has no terrors, compared with what either thinks disgrace. Mark me—I say this—perhaps mine own sentiments of honour are not less fantastic, Rebecca, than thine are; but we know alike how to die for them."

"Unhappy man," said the Jewess; "and art thou condemned to expose thy life for principles, of which thy sober judgment does not acknowledge the solidity? Surely this is a parting with your treasure for that which is not bread—but deem not so of me. Thy resolution may fluctuate on the wild and changeful billows of human opinion, but mine is anchored on the Rock of Ages."

"Silence, maiden," answered the Templar; "such discourse now avails but little. Thou art condemned to die not a sudden and easy death, such as misery chooses, and despair welcomes, but a slow, wretched, protracted course of torture, suited to what the diabolical bigotry of these men calls thy crime."

"And to whom—if such my fate—to whom do I owe this?" said Rebecca "surely only to him, who, for a most selfish and brutal cause, dragged me hither, and who now, for some unknown purpose of his own, strives to exaggerate the wretched fate to which he exposed me."

"Think not," said the Templar, "that I have so exposed thee; I would have bucklered thee against such danger with my own bosom, as freely as ever I exposed it to the shafts which had otherwise reached thy life."

"Had thy purpose been the honourable protection of the innocent," said Rebecca, "I had thanked thee for thy care—as it is, thou hast claimed merit for it so often, that I tell thee life is worth nothing to me, preserved at the price which thou wouldst exact for it."

"Truce with thine upbraidings, Rebecca," said the Templar; "I have my own cause of grief, and brook not that thy reproaches should add to it."

"What is thy purpose, then, Sir Knight?" said the Jewess; "speak it briefly.—If thou hast aught to do, save to witness the misery thou hast caused, let me know it; and then, if so it please you, leave me to myself—the step between time and eternity is short but terrible, and I have few moments to prepare for it."

"I perceive, Rebecca," said Bois-Guilbert, "that thou dost continue to burden me with the charge of distresses, which most fain would I have prevented."

"Sir Knight," said Rebecca, "I would avoid reproaches—But what is more certain than that I owe my death to thine unbridled passion?"

"You err—you err,"—said the Templar, hastily, "if you impute what I could neither foresee nor prevent to my purpose or agency.—Could I guess the unexpected arrival of yon dotard, whom some flashes of frantic valour, and the praises yielded by fools to the stupid self-torments of an ascetic, have raised for the present above his own merits, above common sense, above me, and above the hundreds of our Order, who think and feel as men free from such silly and fantastic prejudices as are the grounds of his opinions and actions?"

"Yet," said Rebecca, "you sate a judge upon me, innocent—most innocent—as you knew me to be—you concurred in my condemnation, and, if I aright understood, are yourself to appear in arms to assert my guilt, and assure my punishment."

"Thy patience, maiden," replied the Templar. "No race knows so well as thine own tribes how to submit to the time, and so to trim their bark as to make advantage even of an adverse wind."

"Lamented be the hour," said Rebecca, "that has taught such art to the House of Israel! but adversity bends the heart as fire bends the stubborn steel, and those who are no longer their own governors, and the denizens of their own free independent state, must crouch before strangers. It is our curse, Sir Knight, deserved, doubtless, by our own misdeeds and those of our fathers; but you—you who boast your freedom as your birthright, how much deeper is your disgrace when you stoop to soothe the prejudices of others, and that against your own conviction?"

"Your words are bitter, Rebecca," said Bois-Guilbert, pacing the apartment with impatience, "but I came not hither to bandy reproaches with you.—Know that Bois-Guilbert yields not to created man, although circumstances may for a time induce him to alter his plan. His will is the mountain stream, which may indeed be turned for a little space aside by the rock, but fails not to find its course to the ocean. That scroll which warned thee to demand a champion, from whom couldst thou think it came, if not from Bois-Guilbert? In whom else couldst thou have excited such interest?"

"A brief respite from instant death," said Rebecca, "which will little avail me—was this all thou couldst do for one, on whose head thou hast heaped sorrow, and whom thou hast brought near even to the verge of the tomb?"

"No maiden," said Bois-Guilbert, "this was NOT all that I purposed. Had it not been for the accursed interference of yon fanatical dotard, and the fool of Goodalricke, who, being a Templar, affects to think and judge according to the ordinary rules of humanity, the office of the Champion Defender had devolved, not on a Preceptor, but on a Companion of the Order. Then I myself—such was my purpose—had, on the sounding of the trumpet, appeared in the lists as thy champion, disguised indeed in the fashion of a roving knight, who seeks adventures to prove his shield and spear; and then, let Beaumanoir have chosen not one, but two or three of the brethren here assembled, I had not doubted to cast them out of the saddle with my single lance. Thus, Rebecca, should thine innocence have been avouched, and to thine own gratitude would I have trusted for the reward of my victory."

"This, Sir Knight," said Rebecca, "is but idle boasting—a brag of what you would have done had you not found it convenient to do otherwise. You received my glove, and my champion, if a creature so desolate can find one, must encounter your lance in the lists—yet you would assume the air of my friend and protector!"

"Thy friend and protector," said the Templar, gravely, "I will yet be—but mark at what risk, or rather at what certainty, of dishonour; and then blame me not if I make my stipulations, before I offer up all that I have hitherto held dear, to save the life of a Jewish maiden."

"Speak," said Rebecca; "I understand thee not."

"Well, then," said Bois-Guilbert, "I will speak as freely as ever did doting penitent to his ghostly father, when placed in the tricky confessional.—Rebecca, if I appear not in these lists I lose fame and rank—lose that which is the breath of my nostrils, the esteem, I mean, in which I am held by my brethren, and the hopes I have of succeeding to that mighty authority, which is now wielded by the bigoted dotard Lucas de Beaumanoir, but of which I should make a different use. Such is my certain doom, except I appear in arms against thy cause. Accursed be he of Goodalricke, who baited this trap for me! and doubly accursed Albert de Malvoisin, who withheld me from the resolution I had formed, of hurling back the glove at the face of the superstitious and superannuated fool, who listened to a charge so absurd, and against a creature so high in mind, and so lovely in form as thou art!"

"And what now avails rant or flattery?" answered Rebecca. "Thou hast made thy choice between causing to be shed the blood of an innocent woman, or of endangering thine own earthly state and earthly hopes—What avails it to reckon together?—thy choice is made."

"No, Rebecca," said the knight, in a softer tone, and drawing nearer towards her; "my choice is NOT made—nay, mark, it is thine to make the election. If I appear in the lists, I must maintain my name in arms; and if I do so, championed or unchampioned, thou diest by the stake and faggot, for there lives not the knight who hath coped with me in arms on equal issue, or on terms of vantage, save Richard Coeur-de-Lion, and his minion of Ivanhoe. Ivanhoe, as thou well knowest, is unable to bear his corslet, and Richard is in a foreign prison. If I appear, then thou diest, even although thy charms should instigate some hot-headed youth to enter the lists in thy defence."

"And what avails repeating this so often?" said Rebecca.

"Much," replied the Templar; "for thou must learn to look at thy fate on every side."

"Well, then, turn the tapestry," said the Jewess, "and let me see the other side."

"If I appear," said Bois-Guilbert, "in the fatal lists, thou diest by a slow and cruel death, in pain such as they say is destined to the guilty hereafter. But if I appear not, then am I a degraded and dishonoured knight, accused of witchcraft and of communion with infidels—the illustrious name which has grown yet more so under my wearing, becomes a hissing and a reproach. I lose fame, I lose honour, I lose the prospect of such greatness as scarce emperors attain to—I sacrifice mighty ambition, I destroy schemes built as high as the mountains with which heathens say their heaven was once nearly scaled—and yet, Rebecca," he added, throwing himself at her feet, "this greatness will I sacrifice, this fame will I renounce, this power will I forego, even now when it is half within my grasp, if thou wilt say, Bois-Guilbert, I receive thee for my lover."

"Think not of such foolishness, Sir Knight," answered Rebecca, "but hasten to the Regent, the Queen Mother, and to Prince John—they cannot, in honour to the English crown, allow of the proceedings of your Grand Master. So shall you give me protection without sacrifice on your part, or the pretext of requiring any requital from me."

"With these I deal not," he continued, holding the train of her robe—"it is thee only I address; and what can counterbalance thy choice? Bethink thee, were I a fiend, yet death is a worse, and it is death who is my rival."

"I weigh not these evils," said Rebecca, afraid to provoke the wild knight, yet equally determined neither to endure his passion, nor even feign to endure it. "Be a man, be a Christian! If indeed thy faith recommends that mercy which rather your tongues than your actions pretend, save me from this dreadful death, without seeking a requital which would change thy magnanimity into base barter."

"No, damsel!" said the proud Templar, springing up, "thou shalt not thus impose on me—if I renounce present fame and future ambition, I renounce it for thy sake, and we will escape in company. Listen to me, Rebecca," he said, again softening his tone; "England,—Europe,—is not the world. There are spheres in which we may act, ample enough even for my ambition. We will go to Palestine, where Conrade, Marquis of Montserrat, is my friend—a friend free as myself from the doting scruples which fetter our free-born reason—rather with Saladin will we league ourselves, than endure the scorn of the bigots whom we contemn.—I will form new paths to greatness," he continued, again traversing the room with hasty strides—"Europe shall hear the loud step of him she has driven from her sons!—Not the millions whom her crusaders send to slaughter, can do so much to defend Palestine—not the sabres of the thousands and ten thousands of Saracens can hew their way so deep into that land for which nations are striving, as the strength and policy of me and those brethren, who, in despite of yonder old bigot, will adhere to me in good and evil. Thou shalt be a queen, Rebecca—on Mount Carmel shall we pitch the throne which my valour will gain for you, and I will exchange my long-desired batoon for a sceptre!"

"A dream," said Rebecca; "an empty vision of the night, which, were it a waking reality, affects me not. Enough, that the power which thou mightest acquire, I will never share; nor hold I so light of country or religious faith, as to esteem him who is willing to barter these ties, and cast away the bonds of the Order of which he is a sworn member, in order to gratify an unruly passion for the daughter of another people.—Put not a price on my deliverance, Sir Knight—sell not a deed of generosity—protect the oppressed for the sake of charity, and not for a selfish advantage—Go to the throne of England; Richard will listen to my appeal from these cruel men."

"Never, Rebecca!" said the Templar, fiercely. "If I renounce my Order, for thee alone will I renounce it—Ambition shall remain mine, if thou refuse my love; I will not be fooled on all hands.—Stoop my crest to Richard?—ask a boon of that heart of pride?—Never, Rebecca, will I place the Order of the Temple at his feet in my person. I may forsake the Order, I never will degrade or betray it."

"Now God be gracious to me," said Rebecca, "for the succour of man is well-nigh hopeless!"

"It is indeed," said the Templar; "for, proud as thou art, thou hast in me found thy match. If I enter the lists with my spear in rest, think not any human consideration shall prevent my putting forth my strength; and think then upon thine own fate—to die the dreadful death of the worst of criminals—to be consumed upon a blazing pile —dispersed to the elements of which our strange forms are so mystically composed—not a relic left of that graceful frame, from which we could say this lived and moved! —Rebecca, it is not in woman to sustain this prospect—thou wilt yield to my suit."

"Bois-Guilbert," answered the Jewess, "thou knowest not the heart of woman, or hast only conversed with those who are lost to her best feelings. I tell thee, proud Templar, that not in thy fiercest battles hast thou displayed more of thy vaunted courage, than has been shown by woman when called upon to suffer by affection or duty. I am myself a woman, tenderly nurtured, naturally fearful of danger, and impatient of pain—yet, when we enter those fatal lists, thou to fight and I to suffer, I feel the strong assurance within me, that my courage shall mount higher than thine. Farewell—I waste no more words on thee; the time that remains on earth to the daughter of Jacob must be otherwise spent—she must seek the Comforter, who may hide his face from his people, but who ever opens his ear to the cry of those who seek him in sincerity and in truth."

"We part then thus?" said the Templar, after a short pause; "would to Heaven that we had never met, or that thou hadst been noble in birth and Christian in faith!—Nay, by Heaven! when I gaze on thee, and think when and how we are next to meet, I could even wish myself one of thine own degraded nation; my hand conversant with ingots and shekels, instead of spear and shield; my head bent down before each petty noble, and my look only terrible to the shivering and bankrupt debtor—this could I wish, Rebecca, to be near to thee in life, and to escape the fearful share I must have in thy death."

"Thou hast spoken the Jew," said Rebecca, "as the persecution of such as thou art has made him. Heaven in ire has driven him from his country, but industry has opened to him the only road to power and to influence, which oppression has left unbarred. Read the ancient history of the people of God, and tell me if those, by whom Jehovah wrought such marvels among the nations, were then a people of misers and of usurers!—And know, proud knight, we number names amongst us to which your boasted northern nobility is as the gourd compared with the cedar— names that ascend far back to those high times when the Divine Presence shook the mercy-seat between the cherubim, and which derive their splendour from no earthly prince, but from the awful Voice, which bade their fathers be nearest of the congregation to the Vision—Such were the princes of the House of Jacob."

Rebecca's colour rose as she boasted the ancient glories of her race, but faded as she added, with at sigh, "Such WERE the princes of Judah, now such no more!—They are trampled down like the shorn grass, and mixed with the mire of the ways. Yet are there those among them who shame not such high descent, and of such shall be the daughter of Isaac the son of Adonikam! Farewell!—I envy not thy blood-won honours—I envy not thy barbarous descent from northern heathens—I envy thee not thy faith, which is ever in thy mouth, but never in thy heart nor in thy practice."

"There is a spell on me, by Heaven!" said Bois-Guilbert. "I almost think yon besotted skeleton spoke truth, and that the reluctance with which I part from thee hath something in it more than is natural.—Fair creature!" he said, approaching near her, but with great respect,—"so young, so beautiful, so fearless of death! and yet doomed to die, and with infamy and agony. Who would not weep for thee?—The tear, that has been a stranger to these eyelids for twenty years, moistens them as I gaze on thee. But it must be—nothing may now save thy life. Thou and I are but the blind instruments of some irresistible fatality, that hurries us along, like goodly vessels driving before the storm, which are dashed against each other, and so perish. Forgive me, then, and let us part, at least, as friends part. I have assailed thy resolution in vain, and mine own is fixed as the adamantine decrees of fate."

"Thus," said Rebecca, "do men throw on fate the issue of their own wild passions. But I do forgive thee, Bois-Guilbert, though the author of my early death. There are noble things which cross over thy powerful mind; but it is the garden of the sluggard, and the weeds have rushed up, and conspired to choke the fair and wholesome blossom."

"Yes," said the Templar, "I am, Rebecca, as thou hast spoken me, untaught, untamed—and proud, that, amidst a shoal of empty fools and crafty bigots, I have retained the preeminent fortitude that places me above them. I have been a child of battle from my youth upward, high in my views, steady and inflexible in pursuing them. Such must I remain—proud, inflexible, and unchanging; and of this the world shall have proof.—But thou forgivest me, Rebecca?"

"As freely as ever victim forgave her executioner."

"Farewell, then," said the Templar, and left the apartment.

The Preceptor Albert waited impatiently in an adjacent chamber the return of Bois-Guilbert.

"Thou hast tarried long," he said; "I have been as if stretched on red-hot iron with very impatience. What if the Grand Master, or his spy Conrade, had come hither? I had paid dear for my complaisance.—But what ails thee, brother?—Thy step totters, thy brow is as black as night. Art thou well, Bois-Guilbert?"

"Ay," answered the Templar, "as well as the wretch who is doomed to die within an hour.—Nay, by the rood, not half so well—for there be those in such state, who can lay down life like a cast-off garment. By Heaven, Malvoisin, yonder girl hath well-nigh unmanned me. I am half resolved to go to the Grand Master, abjure the Order to his very teeth, and refuse to act the brutality which his tyranny has imposed on me."

"Thou art mad," answered Malvoisin; "thou mayst thus indeed utterly ruin thyself, but canst not even find a chance thereby to save the life of this Jewess, which seems so precious in thine eyes. Beaumanoir will name another of the Order to defend his judgment in thy place, and the accused will as assuredly perish as if thou hadst taken the duty imposed on thee."

"'Tis false—I will myself take arms in her behalf," answered the Templar, haughtily; "and, should I do so, I think, Malvoisin, that thou knowest not one of the Order, who will keep his saddle before the point of my lance."

"Ay, but thou forgettest," said the wily adviser, "thou wilt have neither leisure nor opportunity to execute this mad project. Go to Lucas Beaumanoir, and say thou hast renounced thy vow of obedience, and see how long the despotic old man will leave thee in personal freedom. The words shall scarce have left thy lips, ere thou wilt either be an hundred feet under ground, in the dungeon of the Preceptory, to abide trial as a recreant knight; or, if his opinion holds concerning thy possession, thou wilt be enjoying straw, darkness, and chains, in some distant convent cell, stunned with exorcisms, and drenched with holy water, to expel the foul fiend which hath obtained dominion over thee. Thou must to the lists, Brian, or thou art a lost and dishonoured man."

"I will break forth and fly," said Bois-Guilbert—"fly to some distant land, to which folly and fanaticism have not yet found their way. No drop of the blood of this most excellent creature shall be spilled by my sanction."

"Thou canst not fly," said the Preceptor; "thy ravings have excited suspicion, and thou wilt not be permitted to leave the Preceptory. Go and make the essay—present thyself before the gate, and command the bridge to be lowered, and mark what answer thou shalt receive.—Thou are surprised and offended; but is it not the better for thee? Wert thou to fly, what would ensue but the reversal of thy arms, the dishonour of thine ancestry, the degradation of thy rank?—Think on it. Where shall thine old companions in arms hide their heads when Brian de Bois-Guilbert, the best lance of the Templars, is proclaimed recreant, amid the hisses of the assembled people? What grief will be at the Court of France! With what joy will the haughty Richard hear the news, that the knight that set him hard in Palestine, and well-nigh darkened his renown, has lost fame and honour for a Jewish girl, whom he could not even save by so costly a sacrifice!"

"Malvoisin," said the Knight, "I thank thee—thou hast touched the string at which my heart most readily thrills!—Come of it what may, recreant shall never be added to the name of Bois-Guilbert. Would to God, Richard, or any of his vaunting minions of England, would appear in these lists! But they will be empty—no one will risk to break a lance for the innocent, the forlorn."

"The better for thee, if it prove so," said the Preceptor; "if no champion appears, it is not by thy means that this unlucky damsel shall die, but by the doom of the Grand Master, with whom rests all the blame, and who will count that blame for praise and commendation."

"True," said Bois-Guilbert; "if no champion appears, I am but a part of the pageant, sitting indeed on horseback in the lists, but having no part in what is to follow."

"None whatever," said Malvoisin; "no more than the armed image of Saint George when it makes part of a procession."

"Well, I will resume my resolution," replied the haughty Templar. "She has despised me—repulsed me—reviled me—And wherefore should I offer up for her whatever of estimation I have in the opinion of others? Malvoisin, I will appear in the lists."

He left the apartment hastily as he uttered these words, and the Preceptor followed, to watch and confirm him in his resolution; for in Bois-Guilbert's fame he had himself a strong interest, expecting much advantage from his being one day at the head of the Order, not to mention the preferment of which Mont-Fitchet had given him hopes, on condition he would forward the condemnation of the unfortunate Rebecca. Yet although, in combating his friend's better feelings, he possessed all the advantage which a wily, composed, selfish disposition has over a man agitated by strong and contending passions, it required all Malvoisin's art to keep Bois-Guilbert steady to the purpose he had prevailed on him to adopt. He was obliged to watch him closely to prevent his resuming his purpose of flight, to intercept his communication with the Grand Master, lest he should come to an open rupture with his Superior, and to renew, from time to time, the various arguments by which he endeavoured to show, that, in appearing as champion on this occasion, Bois-Guilbert, without either accelerating or ensuring the fate of Rebecca, would follow the only course by which he could save himself from degradation and disgrace.

XL.

Shadows avaunt!—Richard's himself again.

— RICHARD III

When the Black Knight—for it becomes necessary to resume the train of his adventures—left the Trysting-tree of the generous Outlaw, he held his way straight to a neighbouring religious house, of small extent and revenue, called the Priory of Saint Botolph, to which the wounded Ivanhoe had been removed when the castle was taken, under the guidance of the faithful Gurth, and the magnanimous Wamba. It is unnecessary at present to mention what took place in the interim betwixt Wilfred and his deliverer; suffice it to say, that after long and grave communication, messengers were dispatched by the Prior in several directions, and that on the succeeding morning the Black Knight was about to set forth on his journey, accompanied by the jester Wamba, who attended as his guide.

"We will meet," he said to Ivanhoe, "at Coningsburgh, the castle of the deceased Athelstane, since there thy father Cedric holds the funeral feast for his noble relation. I would see your Saxon kindred together, Sir Wilfred, and become better acquainted with them than heretofore. Thou also wilt meet me; and it shall be my task to reconcile thee to thy father."

So saying, he took an affectionate farewell of Ivanhoe, who expressed an anxious desire to attend upon his deliverer. But the Black Knight would not listen to the proposal.

"Rest this day; thou wilt have scarce strength enough to travel on the next. I will have no guide with me but honest Wamba, who can play priest or fool as I shall be most in the humour."

"And I," said Wamba, "will attend you with all my heart. I would fain see the feasting at the funeral of Athelstane; for, if it be not full and frequent, he will rise from the dead to rebuke cook, sewer, and cupbearer; and that were a sight worth seeing. Always, Sir Knight, I will trust your valour with making my excuse to my master Cedric, in case mine own wit should fail."

"And how should my poor valour succeed, Sir Jester, when thy light wit halts?—resolve me that."

"Wit, Sir Knight," replied the Jester, "may do much. He is a quick, apprehensive knave, who sees his neighbours blind side, and knows how to keep the lee-gage when his passions are blowing high. But valour is a sturdy fellow, that makes all split. He rows against both wind and tide, and makes way notwithstanding; and, therefore, good Sir Knight, while I take advantage of the fair weather in our noble master's temper, I will expect you to bestir yourself when it grows rough."

"Sir Knight of the Fetterlock, since it is your pleasure so to be distinguished," said Ivanhoe, "I fear me you have chosen a talkative and a troublesome fool to be your guide. But he knows every path and alley in the woods as well as e'er a hunter who frequents them; and the poor knave, as thou hast partly seen, is as faithful as steel."

"Nay," said the Knight, "an he have the gift of showing my road, I shall not grumble with him that he desires to make it pleasant.—Fare thee well, kind Wilfred—I charge thee not to attempt to travel till to-morrow at earliest."

So saying, he extended his hand to Ivanhoe, who pressed it to his lips, took leave of the Prior, mounted his horse, and departed, with Wamba for his companion. Ivanhoe followed them with his eyes, until they were lost in the shades of the surrounding forest, and then returned into the convent.

But shortly after matin-song, he requested to see the Prior. The old man came in haste, and enquired anxiously after the state of his health.

"It is better," he said, "than my fondest hope could have anticipated; either my wound has been slighter than the effusion of blood led me to suppose, or this balsam hath wrought a wonderful cure upon it. I feel already as if I could bear my corslet; and so much the better, for thoughts pass in my mind which render me unwilling to remain here longer in inactivity."

"Now, the saints forbid," said the Prior, "that the son of the Saxon Cedric should leave our convent ere his wounds were healed! It were shame to our profession were we to suffer it."

"Nor would I desire to leave your hospitable roof, venerable father," said Ivanhoe, "did I not feel myself able to endure the journey, and compelled to undertake it."

"And what can have urged you to so sudden a departure?" said the Prior.

"Have you never, holy father," answered the Knight, "felt an apprehension of approaching evil, for which you in vain attempted to assign a cause?—Have you never found your mind darkened, like the sunny landscape, by the sudden cloud, which augurs a coming tempest?—And thinkest thou not that such impulses are deserving of attention, as being the hints of our guardian spirits, that danger is impending?"

"I may not deny," said the Prior, crossing himself, "that such things have been, and have been of Heaven; but then such communications have had a visibly useful scope and tendency. But thou, wounded as thou art, what avails it thou shouldst follow the steps of him whom thou couldst not aid, were he to be assaulted?"

"Prior," said Ivanhoe, "thou dost mistake—I am stout enough to exchange buffets with any who will challenge me to such a traffic—But were it otherwise, may I not aid him were he in danger, by other means than by force of arms? It is but too well known that the Saxons love not the Norman race, and who knows what may be the issue, if he break in upon them when their hearts are irritated by the death of Athelstane, and their heads heated by the carousal in which they will indulge themselves? I hold his entrance among them at such a moment most perilous, and I am resolved to share or avert the danger; which, that I may the better do, I would crave of thee the use of some palfrey whose pace may be softer than that of my 'destrier'."

"Surely," said the worthy churchman; "you shall have mine own ambling jennet, and I would it ambled as easy for your sake as that of the Abbot of Saint Albans. Yet this will I say for Malkin, for so I call her, that unless you were to borrow a ride on the juggler's steed that paces a hornpipe amongst the eggs, you could not go a journey on a creature so gentle and smooth-paced. I have composed many a homily on her back, to the edification of my brethren of the convent, and many poor Christian souls."

"I pray you, reverend father," said Ivanhoe, "let Malkin be got ready instantly, and bid Gurth attend me with mine arms."

"Nay, but fair sir," said the Prior, "I pray you to remember that Malkin hath as little skill in arms as her master, and that I warrant not her enduring the sight or weight of your full panoply. O, Malkin, I promise you, is a beast of judgment, and will contend against any undue weight—I did but borrow the 'Fructus Temporum' from the priest of Saint Bees, and I promise you she would not stir from the gate until I had exchanged the huge volume for my little breviary."

"Trust me, holy father," said Ivanhoe, "I will not distress her with too much

IVANHOE

weight; and if she calls a combat with me, it is odds but she has the worst."

This reply was made while Gurth was buckling on the Knight's heels a pair of large gilded spurs, capable of convincing any restive horse that his best safety lay in being conformable to the will of his rider.

The deep and sharp rowels with which Ivanhoe's heels were now armed, began to make the worthy Prior repent of his courtesy, and ejaculate,—"Nay, but fair sir, now I bethink me, my Malkin abideth not the spur—Better it were that you tarry for the mare of our manciple down at the Grange, which may be had in little more than an hour, and cannot but be tractable, in respect that she draweth much of our winter firewood, and eateth no corn."

"I thank you, reverend father, but will abide by your first offer, as I see Malkin is already led forth to the gate. Gurth shall carry mine armour; and for the rest, rely on it, that as I will not overload Malkin's back, she shall not overcome my patience. And now, farewell!"

Ivanhoe now descended the stairs more hastily and easily than his wound promised, and threw himself upon the jennet, eager to escape the importunity of the Prior, who stuck as closely to his side as his age and fatness would permit, now singing the praises of Malkin, now recommending caution to the Knight in managing her.

"She is at the most dangerous period for maidens as well as mares," said the old man, laughing at his own jest, "being barely in her fifteenth year."

Ivanhoe, who had other web to weave than to stand canvassing a palfrey's paces with its owner, lent but a deaf ear to the Prior's grave advices and facetious jests, and having leapt on his mare, and commanded his squire (for such Gurth now called himself) to keep close by his side, he followed the track of the Black Knight into the forest, while the Prior stood at the gate of the convent looking after him, and ejaculating,—"Saint Mary! how prompt and fiery be these men of war! I would I had not trusted Malkin to his keeping, for, crippled as I am with the cold rheum, I am undone if aught but good befalls her. And yet," said he, recollecting himself, "as I would not spare my own old and disabled limbs in the good cause of Old England, so Malkin must e'en run her hazard on the same venture; and it may be they will think our poor house worthy of some munificent guerdon—or, it may be, they will send the old Prior a pacing nag. And if they do none of these, as great men will forget little men's service, truly I shall hold me well repaid in having done that which is right. And it is now well-nigh the fitting time to summon the brethren to breakfast in the refectory—Ah! I doubt they obey that call more cheerily than the bells for primes and matins."

So the Prior of Saint Botolph's hobbled back again into the refectory, to preside over the stockfish and ale, which was just serving out for the friars' breakfast. Busy and important, he sat him down at the table, and many a dark word he threw out, of benefits to be expected to the convent, and high deeds of service done by himself, which, at another season, would have attracted observation. But as the stockfish was highly salted, and the ale reasonably powerful, the jaws of the brethren were too anxiously employed to admit of their making much use of their ears; nor do we read of any of the fraternity, who was tempted to speculate upon the mysterious hints of their Superior, except Father Diggory, who was severely afflicted by the toothache, so that he could only eat on one side of his jaws.

In the meantime, the Black Champion and his guide were pacing at their leisure through the recesses of the forest; the good Knight whiles humming to himself the lay of some enamoured troubadour, sometimes encouraging by questions the prating disposition of his attendant, so that their dialogue formed a whimsical mixture of song and jest, of which we would fain give our readers some idea. You are then to imagine this Knight, such as we have already described him, strong of person, tall, broad-shouldered, and large of bone, mounted on his mighty black charger, which seemed made on purpose to bear his weight, so easily he paced forward under it, having the visor of his helmet raised, in order to admit freedom of breath, yet keeping the beaver, or under part, closed, so that his features could be but imperfectly distinguished. But his ruddy embrowned cheek-bones could be plainly seen, and the large and bright blue eyes, that flashed from under the dark shade of the raised visor; and the whole gesture and look of the champion expressed careless gaiety and fearless confidence—a mind which was unapt to apprehend danger, and prompt to defy it when most imminent—yet with whom danger was a familiar thought, as with one whose trade was war and adventure.

The Jester wore his usual fantastic habit, but late accidents had led him to adopt a good cutting falchion, instead of his wooden sword, with a targe to match it; of both which weapons he had, notwithstanding his profession, shown himself a skilful master during the storming of Torquilstone. Indeed, the infirmity of Wamba's brain consisted chiefly in a kind of impatient irritability, which suffered him not long to remain quiet in any posture, or adhere to any certain train of ideas, although he was for a few minutes alert enough in performing any immediate task, or in apprehending any immediate topic. On horseback, therefore, he was perpetually swinging himself backwards and forwards, now on the horse's ears, then anon on the very rump of the animal,—now hanging both his legs on one side, and now sitting with his face to the tail, moping, mowing, and making a thousand apish gestures, until his palfrey took his freaks so much to heart, as fairly to lay him at his length on the green grass—an incident which greatly amused the Knight, but compelled his companion to ride more steadily thereafter.

At the point of their journey at which we take them up, this joyous pair were engaged in singing a virelai, as it was called, in which the clown bore a mellow burden, to the better instructed Knight of the Fetterlock. And thus run the ditty:—

Anna-Marie, love, up is the sun,
Anna-Marie, love, morn is begun,
Mists are dispersing, love, birds singing free,
Up in the morning, love, Anna-Marie.
Anna-Marie, love, up in the morn,
The hunter is winding blithe sounds on his horn,
The echo rings merry from rock and from tree,
'Tis time to arouse thee, love, Anna-Marie.

Wamba.

O Tybalt, love, Tybalt, awake me not yet,

Around my soft pillow while softer dreams flit,
For what are the joys that in waking we prove,
Compared with these visions, O, Tybalt, my love?
Let the birds to the rise of the mist carol shrill,
Let the hunter blow out his loud horn on the hill,
Softer sounds, softer pleasures, in slumber I prove,—
But think not I dreamt of thee, Tybalt, my love.

"A dainty song," said Wamba, when they had finished their carol, "and I swear by my bauble, a pretty moral!—I used to sing it with Gurth, once my playfellow, and now, by the grace of God and his master, no less than a freemen; and we once came by the cudgel for being so entranced by the melody, that we lay in bed two hours after sunrise, singing the ditty betwixt sleeping and waking—my bones ache at thinking of the tune ever since. Nevertheless, I have played the part of Anna-Marie, to please you, fair sir."

The Jester next struck into another carol, a sort of comic ditty, to which the Knight, catching up the tune, replied in the like manner.

Knight and Wamba.

There came three merry men from south, west, and north,
Ever more sing the roundelay;
To win the Widow of Wycombe forth,
And where was the widow might say them nay?

The first was a knight, and from Tynedale he came,
Ever more sing the roundelay;
And his fathers, God save us, were men of great fame,
And where was the widow might say him nay?

Of his father the laird, of his uncle the squire,
He boasted in rhyme and in roundelay;
She bade him go bask by his sea-coal fire,
For she was the widow would say him nay.

Wamba.

The next that came forth, swore by blood and by nails,
Merrily sing the roundelay;
Hur's a gentleman, God wot, and hur's lineage was of Wales,
And where was the widow might say him nay?

Sir David ap Morgan ap Griffith ap Hugh
Ap Tudor ap Rhice, quoth his roundelay
She said that one widow for so many was too few,
And she bade the Welshman wend his way.

But then next came a yeoman, a yeoman of Kent,
Jollily singing his roundelay;
He spoke to the widow of living and rent,
And where was the widow could say him nay?

Both.

So the knight and the squire were both left in the mire,
There for to sing their roundelay;
For a yeoman of Kent, with his yearly rent,
There never was a widow could say him nay.

"I would, Wamba," said the knight, "that our host of the Trysting-tree, or the jolly Friar, his chaplain, heard this thy ditty in praise of our bluff yeoman."

"So would not I," said Wamba—"but for the horn that hangs at your baldric."

"Ay," said the Knight,—"this is a pledge of Locksley's goodwill, though I am not like to need it. Three mots on this bugle will, I am assured, bring round, at our need, a jolly band of yonder honest yeomen."

"I would say, Heaven forefend," said the Jester, "were it not that that fair gift is a pledge they would let us pass peaceably."

"Why, what meanest thou?" said the Knight; "thinkest thou that but for this pledge of fellowship they would assault us?"

"Nay, for me I say nothing," said Wamba; "for green trees have ears as well as stone walls. But canst thou construe me this, Sir Knight—When is thy wine-pitcher and thy purse better empty than full?"

"Why, never, I think," replied the Knight.

"Thou never deservest to have a full one in thy hand, for so simple an answer! Thou hadst best empty thy pitcher ere thou pass it to a Saxon, and leave thy money at home ere thou walk in the greenwood."

"You hold our friends for robbers, then?" said the Knight of the Fetterlock.

"You hear me not say so, fair sir," said Wamba; "it may relieve a man's steed to take of his mail when he hath a long journey to make; and, certes, it may do good to the rider's soul to ease him of that which is the root of evil; therefore will I give no hard names to those who do such services. Only I would wish my mail at home, and my purse in my chamber, when I meet with these good fellows, because it might save them some trouble."

"WE are bound to pray for them, my friend, notwithstanding the fair character thou dost afford them."

"Pray for them with all my heart," said Wamba; "but in the town, not in the greenwood, like the Abbot of Saint Bees, whom they caused to say mass with an old hollow oak-tree for his stall."

"Say as thou list, Wamba," replied the Knight, "these yeomen did thy master Cedric yeomanly service at Torquilstone."

"Ay, truly," answered Wamba; "but that was in the fashion of their trade with Heaven."

"Their trade, Wamba! how mean you by that?" replied his companion.

"Marry, thus," said the Jester. "They make up a balanced account with Heaven, as our old cellarer used to call his ciphering, as fair as Isaac the Jew keeps with his debtors, and, like him, give out a very little, and take large credit for doing so; reckoning, doubtless, on their own behalf the seven-fold usury which the blessed text hath promised to charitable loans."

"Give me an example of your meaning, Wamba,—I know nothing of ciphers or rates of usage," answered the Knight.

"Why," said Wamba, "an your valour be so dull, you will please to learn that those honest fellows balance a good deed with one not quite so laudable; as a crown given to a begging friar with an hundred byzants taken from a fat abbot, or a wench kissed in the greenwood with the relief of a poor widow."

"Which of these was the good deed, which was the felony?" interrupted the Knight.

"A good gibe! a good gibe!" said Wamba; "keeping witty company sharpeneth the apprehension. You said nothing so well, Sir Knight, I will be sworn, when you held drunken vespers with the bluff Hermit.—But to go on. The merry-men of the forest set off the building of a cottage with the burning of a castle,—the thatching of a choir against the robbing of a church,—the setting free a poor prisoner against the murder of a proud sheriff; or, to come nearer to our point, the deliverance of a Saxon franklin against the burning alive of a Norman baron. Gentle thieves they are, in short, and courteous robbers; but it is ever the luckiest to meet with them when they are at the worst."

"How so, Wamba?" said the Knight.

"Why, then they have some compunction, and are for making up matters with Heaven. But when they have struck an even balance, Heaven help them with whom they next open the account! The travellers who first met them after their good service at Torquilstone would have a woeful flaying.—And yet," said Wamba, coming close up to the Knight's side, "there be companions who are far more dangerous for travellers to meet than yonder outlaws."

"And who may they be, for you have neither bears nor wolves, I trow?" said the Knight.

"Marry, sir, but we have Malvoisin's men-at-arms," said Wamba; "and let me tell you, that, in time of civil war, a halfscore of these is worth a band of wolves at any time. They are now expecting their harvest, and are reinforced with the soldiers that escaped from Torquilstone. So that, should we meet with a band of them, we are like to pay for our feats of arms.—Now, I pray you, Sir Knight, what would you do if we met two of them?"

"Pin the villains to the earth with my lance, Wamba, if they offered us any impediment."

"But what if there were four of them?"

"They should drink of the same cup," answered the Knight.

"What if six," continued Wamba, "and we as we now are, barely two—would you not remember Locksley's horn?"

"What! sound for aid," exclaimed the Knight, "against a score of such 'rascaille' as these, whom one good knight could drive before him, as the wind drives the withered leaves?"

"Nay, then," said Wamba, "I will pray you for a close sight of that same horn that hath so powerful a breath."

The Knight undid the clasp of the baldric, and indulged his fellow-traveller, who immediately hung the bugle round his own neck.

"Tra-lira-la," said he, whistling the notes; "nay, I know my gamut as well as another."

"How mean you, knave?" said the Knight; "restore me the bugle."

"Content you, Sir Knight, it is in safe keeping. When Valour and Folly travel, Folly should bear the horn, because she can blow the best."

"Nay but, rogue," said the Black Knight, "this exceedeth thy license—Beware ye tamper not with my patience."

"Urge me not with violence, Sir Knight," said the Jester, keeping at a distance from the impatient champion, "or Folly will show a clean pair of heels, and leave Valour to find out his way through the wood as best he may."

"Nay, thou hast hit me there," said the Knight; "and, sooth to say, I have little time to jangle with thee. Keep the horn an thou wilt, but let us proceed on our journey."

"You will not harm me, then?" said Wamba.

"I tell thee no, thou knave!"

"Ay, but pledge me your knightly word for it," continued Wamba, as he approached with great caution.

"My knightly word I pledge; only come on with thy foolish self."

"Nay, then, Valour and Folly are once more boon companions," said the Jester, coming up frankly to the Knight's side; "but, in truth, I love not such buffets as that you bestowed on the burly Friar, when his holiness rolled on the green like a king of the nine-pins. And now that Folly wears the horn, let Valour rouse himself, and shake his mane; for, if I mistake not, there are company in yonder brake that are on the look-out for us."

"What makes thee judge so?" said the Knight.

"Because I have twice or thrice noticed the glance of a motion from amongst the green leaves. Had they been honest men, they had kept the path. But yonder thicket is a choice chapel for the Clerks of Saint Nicholas."

"By my faith," said the Knight, closing his visor, "I think thou be'st in the right on't."

And in good time did he close it, for three arrows, flew at the same instant from the suspected spot against his head and breast, one of which would have penetrated to the brain, had it not been turned aside by the steel visor. The other two were averted by the gorget, and by the shield which hung around his neck.

"Thanks, trusty armourers," said the Knight.—"Wamba, let us close with them," —and he rode straight to the thicket. He was met by six or seven men-at-arms, who ran against him with their lances at full career. Three of the weapons struck against him, and splintered with as little effect as if they had been driven against a tower of steel. The Black Knight's eyes seemed to flash fire even through the aperture of his visor. He raised himself in his stirrups with an air of inexpressible dignity, and exclaimed, "What means this, my masters!"—The men made no other reply than by drawing their swords and attacking him on every side, crying, "Die, tyrant!"

"Ha! Saint Edward! Ha! Saint George!" said the Black Knight, striking down a man at every invocation; "have we traitors here?"

His opponents, desperate as they were, bore back from an arm which carried death in every blow, and it seemed as if the terror of his single strength was about to gain the battle against such odds, when a knight, in blue armour, who had hitherto kept himself behind the other assailants, spurred forward with his lance, and taking aim, not at the rider but at the steed, wounded the noble animal mortally.

"That was a felon stroke!" exclaimed the Black Knight, as the steed fell to the earth, bearing his rider along with him.

And at this moment, Wamba winded the bugle, for the whole had passed so speedily, that he had not time to do so sooner. The sudden sound made the murderers bear back once more, and Wamba, though so imperfectly weaponed, did not hesitate to rush in and assist the Black Knight to rise.

"Shame on ye, false cowards!" exclaimed he in the blue harness, who seemed to lead the assailants, "do ye fly from the empty blast of a horn blown by a Jester?"

Animated by his words, they attacked the Black Knight anew, whose best refuge was now to place his back against an oak, and defend himself with his sword. The felon knight, who had taken another spear, watching the moment when his formidable antagonist was most closely pressed, galloped against him in hopes to nail him with his lance against the tree, when his purpose was again intercepted by Wamba. The Jester, making up by agility the want of strength, and little noticed by the men-at-arms, who were busied in their more important object, hovered on the skirts of the fight, and effectually checked the fatal career of the Blue Knight, by hamstringing his horse with a stroke of his sword. Horse and man went to the ground; yet the situation of the Knight of the Fetterlock continued very precarious, as he was pressed close by several men completely armed, and began to be fatigued by the violent exertions necessary to defend himself on so many points at nearly the same moment, when a grey-goose shaft suddenly stretched on the earth one of the most formidable of his assailants, and a band of yeomen broke forth from the glade, headed by Locksley and the jovial Friar, who, taking ready and effectual part in the fray, soon disposed of the ruffians, all of whom lay on the spot dead or mortally wounded. The Black Knight thanked his deliverers with a dignity they had not observed in his former bearing, which hitherto had seemed rather that of a blunt bold soldier, than of a person of exalted rank.

"It concerns me much," he said, "even before I express my full gratitude to my ready friends, to discover, if I may, who have been my unprovoked enemies.—Open the visor of that Blue Knight, Wamba, who seems the chief of these villains."

The Jester instantly made up to the leader of the assassins, who, bruised by his fall, and entangled under the wounded steed, lay incapable either of flight or resistance.

"Come, valiant sir," said Wamba, "I must be your armourer as well as your equerry—I have dismounted you, and now I will unhelm you."

So saying, with no very gentle hand he undid the helmet of the Blue Knight, which, rolling to a distance on the grass, displayed to the Knight of the Fetterlock grizzled locks, and a countenance he did not expect to have seen under such circumstances.

"Waldemar Fitzurse!" he said in astonishment; "what could urge one of thy rank and seeming worth to so foul an undertaking?"

"Richard," said the captive Knight, looking up to him, "thou knowest little of mankind, if thou knowest not to what ambition and revenge can lead every child of Adam."

"Revenge?" answered the Black Knight; "I never wronged thee—On me thou hast nought to revenge."

"My daughter, Richard, whose alliance thou didst scorn—was that no injury to a Norman, whose blood is noble as thine own?"

"Thy daughter?" replied the Black Knight; "a proper cause of enmity, and followed up to a bloody issue!—Stand back, my masters, I would speak to him alone.—And now, Waldemar Fitzurse, say me the truth—confess who set thee on this traitorous deed."

"Thy father's son," answered Waldemar, "who, in so doing, did but avenge on thee thy disobedience to thy father."

Richard's eyes sparkled with indignation, but his better nature overcame it. He pressed his hand against his brow, and remained an instant gazing on the face of the humbled baron, in whose features pride was contending with shame.

"Thou dost not ask thy life, Waldemar," said the King.

"He that is in the lion's clutch," answered Fitzurse, "knows it were needless."

"Take it, then, unasked," said Richard; "the lion preys not on prostrate carcasses.—Take thy life, but with this condition, that in three days thou shalt leave England, and go to hide thine infamy in thy Norman castle, and that thou wilt never mention the name of John of Anjou as connected with thy felony. If thou art found on English ground after the space I have allotted thee, thou diest—or if thou breathest aught that can attaint the honour of my house, by Saint George! not the altar itself shall be a sanctuary. I will hang thee out to feed the ravens, from the very pinnacle of thine own castle.—Let this knight have a steed, Locksley, for I see your yeomen have caught those which were running loose, and let him depart unharmed."

"But that I judge I listen to a voice whose behests must not be disputed," answered the yeoman, "I would send a shaft after the skulking villain that should spare him the labour of a long journey."

"Thou bearest an English heart, Locksley," said the Black Knight, "and well dost judge thou art the more bound to obey my behest—I am Richard of England!"

At these words, pronounced in a tone of majesty suited to the high rank, and no less distinguished character of Coeur-de-Lion, the yeomen at once kneeled down before him, and at the same time tendered their allegiance, and implored pardon for their offences.

"Rise, my friends," said Richard, in a gracious tone, looking on them with a countenance in which his habitual good-humour had already conquered the blaze of hasty resentment, and whose features retained no mark of the late desperate conflict, excepting the flush arising from exertion,—"Arise," he said, "my friends!—Your misdemeanours, whether in forest or field, have been atoned by the loyal services you rendered my distressed subjects before the walls of Torquilstone, and the rescue you have this day afforded to your sovereign. Arise, my liegemen, and be good subjects in future.—And thou, brave Locksley—"

"Call me no longer Locksley, my Liege, but know me under the name, which, I fear, fame hath blown too widely not to have reached even your royal ears—I am Robin Hood of Sherwood Forest."

"King of Outlaws, and Prince of good fellows!" said the King, "who hath not heard a name that has been borne as far as Palestine? But be assured, brave Outlaw, that no deed done in our absence, and in the turbulent times to which it hath given rise, shall be remembered to thy disadvantage."

"True says the proverb," said Wamba, interposing his word, but with some abatement of his usual petulance,—

"'When the cat is away, The mice will play.'"

"What, Wamba, art thou there?" said Richard; "I have been so long of hearing thy voice, I thought thou hadst taken flight."

"I take flight!" said Wamba; "when do you ever find Folly separated from Valour? There lies the trophy of my sword, that good grey gelding, whom I heartily wish upon his legs again, conditioning his master lay there houghed in his place. It is true, I gave a little ground at first, for a motley jacket does not brook lance-heads, as a steel doublet will. But if I fought not at sword's point, you will grant me that I sounded the onset."

"And to good purpose, honest Wamba," replied the King. "Thy good service shall not be forgotten."

"'Confiteor! Confiteor!'"—exclaimed, in a submissive tone, a voice near the King's side—"my Latin will carry me no farther—but I confess my deadly treason, and pray leave to have absolution before I am led to execution!"

Richard looked around, and beheld the jovial Friar on his knees, telling his rosary, while his quarter-staff, which had not been idle during the skirmish, lay on the grass beside him. His countenance was gathered so as he thought might best express the most profound contrition, his eyes being turned up, and the corners of his mouth drawn down, as Wamba expressed it, like the tassels at the mouth of a purse. Yet this demure affectation of extreme penitence was whimsically belied by a ludicrous meaning which lurked in his huge features, and seemed to pronounce his fear and repentance alike hypocritical.

"For what art thou cast down, mad Priest?" said Richard; "art thou afraid thy diocesan should learn how truly thou dost serve Our Lady and Saint Dunstan?—Tush, man! fear it not; Richard of England betrays no secrets that pass over the flagon."

"Nay, most gracious sovereign," answered the Hermit, (well known to the curious in penny-histories of Robin Hood, by the name of Friar Tuck,) "it is not the crosier I fear, but the sceptre.—Alas! that my sacrilegious fist should ever have been applied to the ear of the Lord's anointed!"

"Ha! ha!" said Richard, "sits the wind there?—In truth I had forgotten the buffet, though mine ear sung after it for a whole day. But if the cuff was fairly given, I will be judged by the good men around, if it was not as well repaid—or, if thou thinkest I still owe thee aught, and will stand forth for another counterbuff—"

"By no means," replied Friar Tuck, "I had mine own returned, and with usury—may your Majesty ever pay your debts as fully!"

"If I could do so with cuffs," said the King, "my creditors should have little reason to complain of an empty exchequer."

"And yet," said the Friar, resuming his demure hypocritical countenance, "I know not what penance I ought to perform for that most sacrilegious blow!—"

"Speak no more of it, brother," said the King; "after having stood so many cuffs from Paynims and misbelievers, I were void of reason to quarrel with the buffet of a clerk so holy as he of Copmanhurst. Yet, mine honest Friar, I think it would be best both for the church and thyself, that I should procure a license to unfrock thee, and retain thee as a yeoman of our guard, serving in care of our person, as formerly in attendance upon the altar of Saint Dunstan."

"My Liege," said the Friar, "I humbly crave your pardon; and you would readily grant my excuse, did you but know how the sin of laziness has beset me. Saint Dunstan—may he be gracious to us!—stands quiet in his niche, though I should forget my orisons in killing a fat buck—I stay out of my cell sometimes a night, doing I wot not what—Saint Dunstan never complains—a quiet master he is, and a peaceful, as ever was made of wood.—But to be a yeoman in attendance on my sovereign the King—the honour is great, doubtless—yet, if I were but to step aside to comfort a widow in one corner, or to kill a deer in another, it would be, 'where is the dog Priest?' says one. 'Who has seen the accursed Tuck?' says another. 'The unfrocked villain destroys more venison than half the country besides,' says one keeper; 'And is hunting after every shy doe in the country!' quoth a second.—In fine, good my Liege, I pray you to leave me as you found me; or, if in aught you desire to extend your benevolence to me, that I may be considered as the poor Clerk of Saint Dunstan's cell in Copmanhurst, to whom any small donation will be most thankfully acceptable."

"I understand thee," said the King, "and the Holy Clerk shall have a grant of vert and venison in my woods of Warncliffe. Mark, however, I will but assign thee three bucks every season; but if that do not prove an apology for thy slaying thirty, I am no Christian knight nor true king."

"Your Grace may be well assured," said the Friar, "that, with the grace of Saint Dunstan, I shall find the way of multiplying your most bounteous gift."

"I nothing doubt it, good brother," said the King; "and as venison is but dry food, our cellarer shall have orders to deliver to thee a butt of sack, a runlet of Malvoisie, and three hogsheads of ale of the first strike, yearly—If that will not quench thy thirst, thou must come to court, and become acquainted with my butler."

"But for Saint Dunstan?" said the Friar—

"A cope, a stole, and an altar-cloth shalt thou also have," continued the King, crossing himself—"But we may not turn our game into earnest, lest God punish us for thinking more on our follies than on his honour and worship."

"I will answer for my patron," said the Priest, joyously.

"Answer for thyself, Friar," said King Richard, something sternly; but immediately stretching out his hand to the Hermit, the latter, somewhat abashed, bent his knee, and saluted it. "Thou dost less honour to my extended palm than to my clenched fist," said the Monarch; "thou didst only kneel to the one, and to the other didst prostrate thyself."

But the Friar, afraid perhaps of again giving offence by continuing the conversation in too jocose a style—a false step to be particularly guarded against by those who converse with monarchs—bowed profoundly, and fell into the rear.

At the same time, two additional personages appeared on the scene.

XLI.

All hail to the lordlings of high degree,
Who live not more happy, though greater than we!
Our pastimes to see,
Under every green tree,
In all the gay woodland, right welcome ye be.

— MACDONALD

The new comers were Wilfred of Ivanhoe, on the Prior of Botolph's palfrey, and Gurth, who attended him, on the Knight's own war-horse. The astonishment of Ivanhoe was beyond bounds, when he saw his master besprinkled with blood, and six or seven dead bodies lying around in the little glade in which the battle had taken place. Nor was he less surprised to see Richard surrounded by so many silvan attendants, the outlaws, as they seemed to be, of the forest, and a perilous retinue therefore for a prince. He hesitated whether to address the King as the Black Knight-errant, or in what other manner to demean himself towards him. Richard saw his embarrassment.

"Fear not, Wilfred," he said, "to address Richard Plantagenet as himself, since thou seest him in the company of true English hearts, although it may be they have been urged a few steps aside by warm English blood."

"Sir Wilfred of Ivanhoe," said the gallant Outlaw, stepping forward, "my assurances can add nothing to those of our sovereign; yet, let me say somewhat proudly, that of men who have suffered much, he hath not truer subjects than those who now stand around him."

"I cannot doubt it, brave man," said Wilfred, "since thou art of the number—But what mean these marks of death and danger? these slain men, and the bloody armour of my Prince?"

"Treason hath been with us, Ivanhoe," said the King; "but, thanks to these brave men, treason hath met its meed—But, now I bethink me, thou too art a traitor," said Richard, smiling; "a most disobedient traitor; for were not our orders positive, that thou shouldst repose thyself at Saint Botolph's until thy wound was healed?"

"It is healed," said Ivanhoe; "it is not of more consequence than the scratch of a bodkin. But why, oh why, noble Prince, will you thus vex the hearts of your faithful servants, and expose your life by lonely journeys and rash adventures, as if it were of no more value than that of a mere knight-errant, who has no interest on earth but what lance and sword may procure him?"

"And Richard Plantagenet," said the King, "desires no more fame than his good lance and sword may acquire him—and Richard Plantagenet is prouder of achieving an adventure, with only his good sword, and his good arm to speed, than if he led to battle a host of an hundred thousand armed men."

"But your kingdom, my Liege," said Ivanhoe, "your kingdom is threatened with dissolution and civil war—your subjects menaced with every species of evil, if deprived of their sovereign in some of those dangers which it is your daily pleasure to incur, and from which you have but this moment narrowly escaped."

"Ho! ho! my kingdom and my subjects?" answered Richard, impatiently; "I tell thee, Sir Wilfred, the best of them are most willing to repay my follies in kind—For example, my very faithful servant, Wilfred of Ivanhoe, will not obey my positive commands, and yet reads his king a homily, because he does not walk exactly by his advice. Which of us has most reason to upbraid the other?—Yet forgive me, my faithful Wilfred. The time I have spent, and am yet to spend in concealment, is, as I explained to thee at Saint Botolph's, necessary to give my friends and faithful nobles time to assemble their forces, that when Richard's return is announced, he should be at the head of such a force as enemies shall tremble to face, and thus subdue the meditated treason, without even unsheathing a sword. Estoteville and Bohun will not be strong enough to move forward to York for twenty-four hours. I must have news of Salisbury from the south; and of Beauchamp, in Warwickshire; and of Multon and Percy in the north. The Chancellor must make sure of London. Too sudden an appearance would subject me to dangers, other than my lance and sword, though backed by the bow of bold Robin, or the quarter-staff of Friar Tuck, and the horn of the sage Wamba, may be able to rescue me from."

Wilfred bowed in submission, well knowing how vain it was to contend with the wild spirit of chivalry which so often impelled his master upon dangers which he might easily have avoided, or rather, which it was unpardonable in him to have sought out. The young knight sighed, therefore, and held his peace; while Richard, rejoiced at having silenced his counsellor, though his heart acknowledged the justice of the charge he had brought against him, went on in conversation with Robin Hood. —"King of Outlaws," he said, "have you no refreshment to offer to your brother sovereign? for these dead knaves have found me both in exercise and appetite."

"In troth," replied the Outlaw, "for I scorn to lie to your Grace, our larder is chiefly supplied with—" He stopped, and was somewhat embarrassed.

"With venison, I suppose?" said Richard, gaily; "better food at need there can be none—and truly, if a king will not remain at home and slay his own game, methinks he should not brawl too loud if he finds it killed to his hand."

"If your Grace, then," said Robin, "will again honour with your presence one of Robin Hood's places of rendezvous, the venison shall not be lacking; and a stoup of ale, and it may be a cup of reasonably good wine, to relish it withal."

The Outlaw accordingly led the way, followed by the buxom Monarch, more happy, probably, in this chance meeting with Robin Hood and his foresters, than he would have been in again assuming his royal state, and presiding over a splendid circle of peers and nobles. Novelty in society and adventure were the zest of life to Richard Coeur-de-Lion, and it had its highest relish when enhanced by dangers encountered and surmounted. In the lion-hearted King, the brilliant, but useless character, of a knight of romance, was in a great measure realized and revived; and the personal glory which he acquired by his own deeds of arms, was far more dear to his excited imagination, than that which a course of policy and wisdom would have spread around his government. Accordingly, his reign was like the course of a brilliant and rapid meteor, which shoots along the face of Heaven, shedding around an unnecessary and portentous light, which is instantly swallowed up by universal darkness; his feats of chivalry furnishing themes for bards and minstrels, but affording none of those solid benefits to his country on which history loves to pause, and hold up as an example to posterity. But in his present company Richard showed to the greatest imaginable advantage. He was gay, good-humoured, and fond of manhood in every rank of life.

Beneath a huge oak-tree the silvan repast was hastily prepared for the King of England, surrounded by men outlaws to his government, but who now formed his court and his guard. As the flagon went round, the rough foresters soon lost their awe for the presence of Majesty. The song and the jest were exchanged—the stories of former deeds were told with advantage; and at length, and while boasting of their successful infraction of the laws, no one recollected they were speaking in presence of their natural guardian. The merry King, nothing heeding his dignity any more than his company, laughed, quaffed, and jested among the jolly band. The natural and rough sense of Robin Hood led him to be desirous that the scene should be closed ere any thing should occur to disturb its harmony, the more especially that he observed Ivanhoe's brow clouded with anxiety. "We are honoured," he said to Ivanhoe, apart, "by the presence of our gallant Sovereign; yet I would not that he dallied with time, which the circumstances of his kingdom may render precious."

"It is well and wisely spoken, brave Robin Hood," said Wilfred, apart; "and know, moreover, that they who jest with Majesty even in its gayest mood are but toying with the lion's whelp, which, on slight provocation, uses both fangs and claws."

"You have touched the very cause of my fear," said the Outlaw; "my men are rough by practice and nature, the King is hasty as well as good-humoured; nor know I how soon cause of offence may arise, or how warmly it may be received—it is time this revel were broken off."

"It must be by your management then, gallant yeoman," said Ivanhoe; "for each hint I have essayed to give him serves only to induce him to prolong it."

"Must I so soon risk the pardon and favour of my Sovereign?" said Robin Hood, pausing for all instant; "but by Saint Christopher, it shall be so. I were undeserving his grace did I not peril it for his good.—Here, Scathlock, get thee behind yonder thicket, and wind me a Norman blast on thy bugle, and without an instant's delay on peril of your life."

Scathlock obeyed his captain, and in less than five minutes the revellers were startled by the sound of his horn.

"It is the bugle of Malvoisin," said the Miller, starting to his feet, and seizing his bow. The Friar dropped the flagon, and grasped his quarter-staff. Wamba stopt short in the midst of a jest, and betook himself to sword and target. All the others stood to their weapons.

Men of their precarious course of life change readily from the banquet to the battle; and, to Richard, the exchange seemed but a succession of pleasure. He called for his helmet and the most cumbrous parts of his armour, which he had laid aside; and while Gurth was putting them on, he laid his strict injunctions on Wilfred, under pain of his highest displeasure, not to engage in the skirmish which he supposed was approaching.

"Thou hast fought for me an hundred times, Wilfred,—and I have seen it. Thou shalt this day look on, and see how Richard will fight for his friend and liegeman."

In the meantime, Robin Hood had sent off several of his followers in different directions, as if to reconnoitre the enemy; and when he saw the company effectually broken up, he approached Richard, who was now completely armed, and, kneeling down on one knee, craved pardon of his Sovereign.

"For what, good yeoman?" said Richard, somewhat impatiently. "Have we not already granted thee a full pardon for all transgressions? Thinkest thou our word is a feather, to be blown backward and forward between us? Thou canst not have had time to commit any new offence since that time?"

"Ay, but I have though," answered the yeoman, "if it be an offence to deceive my prince for his own advantage. The bugle you have heard was none of Malvoisin's, but blown by my direction, to break off the banquet, lest it trenched upon hours of dearer import than to be thus dallied with."

He then rose from his knee, folded his arm on his bosom, and in a manner rather respectful than submissive, awaited the answer of the King,—like one who is conscious he may have given offence, yet is confident in the rectitude of his motive. The blood rushed in anger to the countenance of Richard; but it was the first transient emotion, and his sense of justice instantly subdued it.

"The King of Sherwood," he said, "grudges his venison and his wine-flask to the King of England? It is well, bold Robin!—but when you come to see me in merry London, I trust to be a less niggard host. Thou art right, however, good fellow. Let us therefore to horse and away—Wilfred has been impatient this hour. Tell me, bold Robin, hast thou never a friend in thy band, who, not content with advising, will needs direct thy motions, and look miserable when thou dost presume to act for thyself?"

"Such a one," said Robin, "is my Lieutenant, Little John, who is even now absent on an expedition as far as the borders of Scotland; and I will own to your Majesty, that I am sometimes displeased by the freedom of his councils—but, when I think twice, I cannot be long angry with one who can have no motive for his anxiety save zeal for his master's service."

"Thou art right, good yeoman," answered Richard; "and if I had Ivanhoe, on the one hand, to give grave advice, and recommend it by the sad gravity of his brow, and thee, on the other, to trick me into what thou thinkest my own good, I should have as little the freedom of mine own will as any king in Christendom or Heathenesse.—But come, sirs, let us merrily on to Coningsburgh, and think no more on't."

Robin Hood assured them that he had detached a party in the direction of the road they were to pass, who would not fail to discover and apprize them of any secret ambuscade; and that he had little doubt they would find the ways secure, or, if otherwise, would receive such timely notice of the danger as would enable them to fall back on a strong troop of archers, with which he himself proposed to follow on the same route.

The wise and attentive precautions adopted for his safety touched Richard's feelings, and removed any slight grudge which he might retain on account of the deception the Outlaw Captain had practised upon him. He once more extended his hand to Robin Hood, assured him of his full pardon and future favour, as well as his firm resolution to restrain the tyrannical exercise of the forest rights and other oppressive laws, by which so many English yeomen were driven into a state of rebellion. But Richard's good intentions towards the bold Outlaw were frustrated by the King's untimely death; and the Charter of the Forest was extorted from the unwilling hands of King John when he succeeded to his heroic brother. As for the rest of Robin Hood's career, as well as the tale of his treacherous death, they are to be found in those blackletter garlands, once sold at the low and easy rate of one halfpenny.

"Now cheaply purchased at their weight in gold."

The Outlaw's opinion proved true; and the King, attended by Ivanhoe, Gurth, and Wamba, arrived, without any interruption, within view of the Castle of Coningsburgh, while the sun was yet in the horizon.

There are few more beautiful or striking scenes in England, than are presented by the vicinity of this ancient Saxon fortress. The soft and gentle river Don sweeps through an amphitheatre, in which cultivation is richly blended with woodland, and on a mount, ascending from the river, well defended by walls and ditches, rises this ancient edifice, which, as its Saxon name implies, was, previous to the Conquest, a royal residence of the kings of England. The outer walls have probably been added by the Normans, but the inner keep bears token of very great antiquity. It is situated on a mount at one angle of the inner court, and forms a complete circle of perhaps twenty-five feet in diameter. The wall is of immense thickness, and is propped or defended by six huge external buttresses which project from the circle, and rise up against the sides of the tower as if to strengthen or to support it. These massive buttresses are solid when they arise from the foundation, and a good way higher up; but are hollowed out towards the top, and terminate in a sort of turrets communicating with the interior of the keep itself. The distant appearance of this huge building, with these singular accompaniments, is as interesting to the lovers of the picturesque, as the interior of the castle is to the eager antiquary, whose imagination it carries back to the days of the Heptarchy. A barrow, in the vicinity of the castle, is pointed out as the tomb of the memorable Hengist; and various monuments, of great antiquity and curiosity, are shown in the neighbouring churchyard.

When Coeur-de-Lion and his retinue approached this rude yet stately building, it was not, as at present, surrounded by external fortifications. The Saxon architect had exhausted his art in rendering the main keep defensible, and there was no other circumvallation than a rude barrier of palisades.

A huge black banner, which floated from the top of the tower, announced that the obsequies of the late owner were still in the act of being solemnized. It bore no emblem of the deceased's birth or quality, for armorial bearings were then a novelty among the Norman chivalry themselves and, were totally unknown to the Saxons. But above the gate was another banner, on which the figure of a white horse, rudely painted, indicated the nation and rank of the deceased, by the well-known symbol of Hengist and his Saxon warriors.

All around the castle was a scene of busy commotion; for such funeral banquets were times of general and profuse hospitality, which not only every one who could claim the most distant connexion with the deceased, but all passengers whatsoever, were invited to partake. The wealth and consequence of the deceased Athelstane, occasioned this custom to be observed in the fullest extent.

Numerous parties, therefore, were seen ascending and descending the hill on which the castle was situated; and when the King and his attendants entered the open and unguarded gates of the external barrier, the space within presented a scene not easily reconciled with the cause of the assemblage. In one place cooks were toiling to roast huge oxen, and fat sheep; in another, hogsheads of ale were set abroach, to be drained at the freedom of all comers. Groups of every description were to be seen devouring the food and swallowing the liquor thus abandoned to their discretion. The naked Saxon serf was drowning the sense of his half-year's hunger and thirst, in one day of gluttony and drunkenness—the more pampered burgess and guild-brother was eating his morsel with gust, or curiously criticising the quantity of the malt and the skill of the brewer. Some few of the poorer Norman gentry might also be seen, distinguished by their shaven chins and short cloaks, and not less so by their keeping together, and looking with great scorn on the whole solemnity, even while condescending to avail themselves of the good cheer which was so liberally supplied.

Mendicants were of course assembled by the score, together with strolling soldiers returned from Palestine, (according to their own account at least,) pedlars were displaying their wares, travelling mechanics were enquiring after employment, and wandering palmers, hedge-priests, Saxon minstrels, and Welsh bards, were muttering prayers, and extracting mistuned dirges from their harps, crowds, and rotes.

One sent forth the praises of Athelstane in a doleful panegyric; another, in a Saxon genealogical poem, rehearsed the uncouth and harsh names of his noble ancestry. Jesters and jugglers were not awanting, nor was the occasion of the assembly supposed to render the exercise of their profession indecorous or improper. Indeed the ideas of the Saxons on these occasions were as natural as they were rude. If sorrow was thirsty, there was drink—if hungry, there was food—if it sunk down upon and saddened the heart, here were the means supplied of mirth, or at least of amusement. Nor did the assistants scorn to avail themselves of those means of consolation, although, every now and then, as if suddenly recollecting the cause which had brought them together, the men groaned in unison, while the females, of whom many were present, raised up their voices and shrieked for very woe.

Such was the scene in the castle-yard at Coningsburgh when it was entered by Richard and his followers. The seneschal or steward deigned not to take notice of the groups of inferior guests who were perpetually entering and withdrawing, unless so far as was necessary to preserve order; nevertheless he was struck by the good mien of the Monarch and Ivanhoe, more especially as he imagined the features of the latter were familiar to him. Besides, the approach of two knights, for such their dress bespoke them, was a rare event at a Saxon solemnity, and could not but be regarded as a sort of honour to the deceased and his family. And in his sable dress, and holding in his hand his white wand of office, this important personage made way through the miscellaneous assemblage of guests, thus conducting Richard and Ivanhoe to the entrance of the tower. Gurth and Wamba speedily found acquaintances in the court-yard, nor presumed to intrude themselves any farther until their presence should be required.

XLII.

> I found them winding of Marcello's corpse.
> And there was such a solemn melody,
> 'Twixt doleful songs, tears, and sad elegies,—
> Such as old grandames, watching by the dead,
> Are wont to outwear the night with.
>
> — OLD PLAY

The mode of entering the great tower of Coningsburgh Castle is very peculiar, and partakes of the rude simplicity of the early times in which it was erected. A flight of steps, so deep and narrow as to be almost precipitous, leads up to a low portal in the south side of the tower, by which the adventurous antiquary may still, or at least could a few years since, gain access to a small stair within the thickness of the main wall of the tower, which leads up to the third story of the building,—the two lower being dungeons or vaults, which neither receive air nor light, save by a square hole in the third story, with which they seem to have communicated by a ladder. The access to the upper apartments in the tower which consist in all of four stories, is given by stairs which are carried up through the external buttresses.

By this difficult and complicated entrance, the good King Richard, followed by his faithful Ivanhoe, was ushered into the round apartment which occupies the whole of the third story from the ground. Wilfred, by the difficulties of the ascent, gained time to muffle his face in his mantle, as it had been held expedient that he should not present himself to his father until the King should give him the signal.

There were assembled in this apartment, around a large oaken table, about a dozen of the most distinguished representatives of the Saxon families in the adjacent counties. They were all old, or, at least, elderly men; for the younger race, to the great displeasure of the seniors, had, like Ivanhoe, broken down many of the barriers which separated for half a century the Norman victors from the vanquished Saxons. The downcast and sorrowful looks of these venerable men, their silence and their mournful posture, formed a strong contrast to the levity of the revellers on the outside of the castle. Their grey locks and long full beards, together with their antique tunics and loose black mantles, suited well with the singular and rude apartment in which they were seated, and gave the appearance of a band of ancient worshippers of Woden, recalled to life to mourn over the decay of their national glory.

Cedric, seated in equal rank among his countrymen, seemed yet, by common consent, to act as chief of the assembly. Upon the entrance of Richard (only known to him as the valorous Knight of the Fetterlock) he arose gravely, and gave him welcome by the ordinary salutation, "Waes hael", raising at the same time a goblet to his head. The King, no stranger to the customs of his English subjects, returned the greeting with the appropriate words, "Drinc hael", and partook of a cup which was handed to him by the sewer. The same courtesy was offered to Ivanhoe, who pledged his father in silence, supplying the usual speech by an inclination of his head, lest his voice should have been recognised.

When this introductory ceremony was performed, Cedric arose, and, extending his hand to Richard, conducted him into a small and very rude chapel, which was excavated, as it were, out of one of the external buttresses. As there was no opening, saving a little narrow loop-hole, the place would have been nearly quite dark but for two flambeaux or torches, which showed, by a red and smoky light, the arched roof and naked walls, the rude altar of stone, and the crucifix of the same material.

Before this altar was placed a bier, and on each side of this bier kneeled three priests, who told their beads, and muttered their prayers, with the greatest signs of external devotion. For this service a splendid "soul-scat" was paid to the convent of Saint Edmund's by the mother of the deceased; and, that it might be fully deserved, the whole brethren, saving the lame Sacristan, had transferred themselves to Coningsburgh, where, while six of their number were constantly on guard in the performance of divine rites by the bier of Athelstane, the others failed not to take their share of the refreshments and amusements which went on at the castle. In maintaining this pious watch and ward, the good monks were particularly careful not to interrupt their hymns for an instant, lest Zernebock, the ancient Saxon Apollyon, should lay his clutches on the departed Athelstane. Nor were they less careful to prevent any unhallowed layman from touching the pall, which, having been that used at the funeral of Saint Edmund, was liable to be desecrated, if handled by the profane. If, in truth, these attentions could be of any use to the deceased, he had some right to expect them at the hands of the brethren of Saint Edmund's, since, besides a hundred mancuses of gold paid down as the soul-ransom, the mother of Athelstane had announced her intention of endowing that foundation with the better part of the lands of the deceased, in order to maintain perpetual prayers for his soul, and that of her departed husband. Richard and Wilfred followed the Saxon Cedric into the apartment of death, where, as their guide pointed with solemn air to the untimely bier of Athelstane, they followed his example in devoutly crossing themselves, and muttering a brief prayer for the weal of the departed soul.

This act of pious charity performed, Cedric again motioned them to follow him, gliding over the stone floor with a noiseless tread; and, after ascending a few steps, opened with great caution the door of a small oratory, which adjoined to the chapel. It was about eight feet square, hollowed, like the chapel itself, out of the thickness of the wall; and the loop-hole, which enlightened it, being to the west, and widening considerably as it sloped inward, a beam of the setting sun found its way into its dark recess, and showed a female of a dignified mien, and whose countenance retained the marked remains of majestic beauty. Her long mourning robes and her flowing wimple of black cypress, enhanced the whiteness of her skin, and the beauty of her light-coloured and flowing tresses, which time had neither thinned nor mingled with silver. Her countenance expressed the deepest sorrow that is consistent with resignation. On the stone table before her stood a crucifix of ivory, beside which was laid a missal, having its pages richly illuminated, and its boards adorned with clasps of gold, and bosses of the same precious metal.

"Noble Edith," said Cedric, after having stood a moment silent, as if to give Richard and Wilfred time to look upon the lady of the mansion, "these are worthy strangers, come to take a part in thy sorrows. And this, in especial, is the valiant Knight who fought so bravely for the deliverance of him for whom we this day mourn."

"His bravery has my thanks," returned the lady; "although it be the will of Heaven that it should be displayed in vain. I thank, too, his courtesy, and that of his companion, which hath brought them hither to behold the widow of Adeling, the mother of Athelstane, in her deep hour of sorrow and lamentation. To your care, kind kinsman, I intrust them, satisfied that they will want no hospitality which these sad walls can yet afford."

The guests bowed deeply to the mourning parent, and withdrew from their hospitable guide.

Another winding stair conducted them to an apartment of the same size with that which they had first entered, occupying indeed the story immediately above. From this room, ere yet the door was opened, proceeded a low and melancholy strain of vocal music. When they entered, they found themselves in the presence of about twenty matrons and maidens of distinguished Saxon lineage. Four maidens, Rowena leading the choir, raised a hymn for the soul of the deceased, of which we have only been able to decipher two or three stanzas:—

Dust unto dust,
To this all must;
The tenant hath resign'd
The faded form
To waste and worm—
Corruption claims her kind.

Through paths unknown
Thy soul hath flown,
To seek the realms of woe,
Where fiery pain
Shall purge the stain
Of actions done below.

In that sad place,
By Mary's grace,
Brief may thy dwelling be
Till prayers and alms,
And holy psalms,
Shall set the captive free.

While this dirge was sung, in a low and melancholy tone, by the female choristers, the others were divided into two bands, of which one was engaged in bedecking, with such embroidery as their skill and taste could compass, a large silken pall, destined to cover the bier of Athelstane, while the others busied themselves in selecting, from baskets of flowers placed before them, garlands, which they intended for the same mournful purpose. The behaviour of the maidens was decorous, if not marked with deep affliction; but now and then a whisper or a smile called forth the rebuke of the severer matrons, and here and there might be seen a damsel more interested in endeavouring to find out how her mourning-robe became her, than in the dismal ceremony for which they were preparing. Neither was this propensity (if we must needs confess the truth) at all diminished by the appearance of two strange knights, which occasioned some looking up, peeping, and whispering. Rowena alone, too proud to be vain, paid her greeting to her deliverer with a graceful courtesy. Her demeanour was serious, but not dejected; and it may be doubted whether thoughts of Ivanhoe, and of the uncertainty of his fate, did not claim as great a share in her gravity as the death of her kinsman.

To Cedric, however, who, as we have observed, was not remarkably clear-sighted on such occasions, the sorrow of his ward seemed so much deeper than any of the other maidens, that he deemed it proper to whisper the explanation—"She was the affianced bride of the noble Athelstane."—It may be doubted whether this communication went a far way to increase Wilfred's disposition to sympathize with the mourners of Coningsburgh.

Having thus formally introduced the guests to the different chambers in which the obsequies of Athelstane were celebrated under different forms, Cedric conducted them into a small room, destined, as he informed them, for the exclusive accomodation of honourable guests, whose more slight connexion with the deceased might render them unwilling to join those who were immediately effected by the unhappy event. He assured them of every accommodation, and was about to withdraw when the Black Knight took his hand.

"I crave to remind you, noble Thane," he said, "that when we last parted, you promised, for the service I had the fortune to render you, to grant me a boon."

"It is granted ere named, noble Knight," said Cedric; "yet, at this sad moment——"

"Of that also," said the King, "I have bethought me—but my time is brief—neither does it seem to me unfit, that, when closing the grave on the noble Athelstane, we should deposit therein certain prejudices and hasty opinions."

"Sir Knight of the Fetterlock," said Cedric, colouring, and interrupting the King in his turn, "I trust your boon regards yourself and no other; for in that which concerns the honour of my house, it is scarce fitting that a stranger should mingle."

"Nor do I wish to mingle," said the King, mildly, "unless in so far as you will admit me to have an interest. As yet you have known me but as the Black Knight of the Fetterlock—Know me now as Richard Plantagenet."

"Richard of Anjou!" exclaimed Cedric, stepping backward with the utmost astonishment.

"No, noble Cedric—Richard of England!—whose deepest interest—whose deepest wish, is to see her sons united with each other.—And, how now, worthy Thane! hast thou no knee for thy prince?"

"To Norman blood," said Cedric, "it hath never bended."

"Reserve thine homage then," said the Monarch, "until I shall prove my right to it by my equal protection of Normans and English."

"Prince," answered Cedric, "I have ever done justice to thy bravery and thy worth —Nor am I ignorant of thy claim to the crown through thy descent from Matilda, niece to Edgar Atheling, and daughter to Malcolm of Scotland. But Matilda, though of the royal Saxon blood, was not the heir to the monarchy."

"I will not dispute my title with thee, noble Thane," said Richard, calmly; "but I will bid thee look around thee, and see where thou wilt find another to be put into the scale against it."

"And hast thou wandered hither, Prince, to tell me so?" said Cedric—"To upbraid me with the ruin of my race, ere the grave has closed o'er the last scion of Saxon royalty?"—His countenance darkened as he spoke.—"It was boldly—it was rashly done!"

"Not so, by the holy rood!" replied the King; "it was done in the frank confidence which one brave man may repose in another, without a shadow of danger."

"Thou sayest well, Sir King—for King I own thou art, and wilt be, despite of my feeble opposition.—I dare not take the only mode to prevent it, though thou hast placed the strong temptation within my reach!"

"And now to my boon," said the King, "which I ask not with one jot the less confidence, that thou hast refused to acknowledge my lawful sovereignty. I require of thee, as a man of thy word, on pain of being held faithless, man-sworn, and 'nidering', to forgive and receive to thy paternal affection the good knight, Wilfred of Ivanhoe. In this reconciliation thou wilt own I have an interest—the happiness of my friend, and the quelling of dissension among my faithful people."

"And this is Wilfred!" said Cedric, pointing to his son.

"My father!—my father!" said Ivanhoe, prostrating himself at Cedric's feet, "grant me thy forgiveness!"

"Thou hast it, my son," said Cedric, raising him up. "The son of Hereward knows how to keep his word, even when it has been passed to a Norman. But let me see thee use the dress and costume of thy English ancestry—no short cloaks, no gay bonnets, no fantastic plumage in my decent household. He that would be the son of Cedric, must show himself of English ancestry.—Thou art about to speak," he added, sternly, "and I guess the topic. The Lady Rowena must complete two years' mourning, as for a betrothed husband—all our Saxon ancestors would disown us were we to treat of a new union for her ere the grave of him she should have wedded—him, so much the most worthy of her hand by birth and ancestry—is yet closed. The ghost of Athelstane himself would burst his bloody cerements and stand before us to forbid such dishonour to his memory."

It seemed as if Cedric's words had raised a spectre; for, scarce had he uttered them ere the door flew open, and Athelstane, arrayed in the garments of the grave, stood before them, pale, haggard, and like something arisen from the dead!

The effect of this apparition on the persons present was utterly appalling. Cedric started back as far as the wall of the apartment would permit, and, leaning against it as one unable to support himself, gazed on the figure of his friend with eyes that seemed fixed, and a mouth which he appeared incapable of shutting. Ivanhoe crossed himself, repeating prayers in Saxon, Latin, or Norman-French, as they occurred to his memory, while Richard alternately said, "Benedicite", and swore, "Mort de ma vie!"

In the meantime, a horrible noise was heard below stairs, some crying, "Secure the treacherous monks!"—others, "Down with them into the dungeon!"—others, "Pitch them from the highest battlements!"

"In the name of God!" said Cedric, addressing what seemed the spectre of his departed friend, "if thou art mortal, speak!—if a departed spirit, say for what cause thou dost revisit us, or if I can do aught that can set thy spirit at repose.—Living or dead, noble Athelstane, speak to Cedric!"

"I will," said the spectre, very composedly, "when I have collected breath, and when you give me time—Alive, saidst thou?—I am as much alive as he can be who has fed on bread and water for three days, which seem three ages—Yes, bread and water, Father Cedric! By Heaven, and all saints in it, better food hath not passed my weasand for three livelong days, and by God's providence it is that I am now here to tell it."

"Why, noble Athelstane," said the Black Knight, "I myself saw you struck down by the fierce Templar towards the end of the storm at Torquilstone, and as I thought, and Wamba reported, your skull was cloven through the teeth."

"You thought amiss, Sir Knight," said Athelstane, "and Wamba lied. My teeth are in good order, and that my supper shall presently find—No thanks to the Templar though, whose sword turned in his hand, so that the blade struck me flatlings, being averted by the handle of the good mace with which I warded the blow; had my steel-cap been on, I had not valued it a rush, and had dealt him such a counter-buff as would have spoilt his retreat. But as it was, down I went, stunned, indeed, but unwounded. Others, of both sides, were beaten down and slaughtered above me, so that I never recovered my senses until I found myself in a coffin—(an open one, by good luck)—placed before the altar of the church of Saint Edmund's. I sneezed repeatedly—groaned—awakened and would have arisen, when the Sacristan and Abbot, full of terror, came running at the noise, surprised, doubtless, and no way pleased to find the man alive, whose heirs they had proposed themselves to be. I asked for wine—they gave me some, but it must have been highly medicated, for I slept yet more deeply than before, and wakened not for many hours. I found my arms swathed down—my feet tied so fast that mine ankles ache at the very remembrance—the place was utterly dark—the oubliette, as I suppose, of their accursed convent, and from the close, stifled, damp smell, I conceive it is also used for a place of sepulture. I had strange thoughts of what had befallen me, when the door of my dungeon creaked, and two villain monks entered. They would have persuaded me I was in purgatory, but I knew too well the pursy short-breathed voice of the Father Abbot.—Saint Jeremy! how different from that tone with which he used to ask me for another slice of the haunch!—the dog has feasted with me from Christmas to Twelfth-night."

"Have patience, noble Athelstane," said the King, "take breath—tell your story at leisure—beshrew me but such a tale is as well worth listening to as a romance."

"Ay but, by the rood of Bromeholm, there was no romance in the matter!" said Athelstane.—"A barley loaf and a pitcher of water—that THEY gave me, the niggardly traitors, whom my father, and I myself, had enriched, when their best resources were the flitches of bacon and measures of corn, out of which they wheedled poor serfs and bondsmen, in exchange for their prayers—the nest of foul ungrateful vipers—barley bread and ditch water to such a patron as I had been! I will smoke them out of their nest, though I be excommunicated!"

"But, in the name of Our Lady, noble Athelstane," said Cedric, grasping the hand of his friend, "how didst thou escape this imminent danger—did their hearts relent?"

"Did their hearts relent!" echoed Athelstane.—"Do rocks melt with the sun? I should have been there still, had not some stir in the Convent, which I find was their procession hitherward to eat my funeral feast, when they well knew how and where I had been buried alive, summoned the swarm out of their hive. I heard them droning out their death-psalms, little judging they were sung in respect for my soul by those who were thus famishing my body. They went, however, and I waited long for food—no wonder—the gouty Sacristan was even too busy with his own provender to mind mine. At length down he came, with an unstable step and a strong flavour of wine and spices about his person. Good cheer had opened his heart, for he left me a nook of pasty and a flask of wine, instead of my former fare. I ate, drank, and was invigorated; when, to add to my good luck, the Sacristan, too totty to discharge his duty of turnkey fitly, locked the door beside the staple, so that it fell ajar. The light, the food, the wine, set my invention to work. The staple to which my chains were fixed, was more rusted than I or the villain Abbot had supposed. Even iron could not remain without consuming in the damps of that infernal dungeon."

"Take breath, noble Athelstane," said Richard, "and partake of some refreshment, ere you proceed with a tale so dreadful."

"Partake!" quoth Athelstane; "I have been partaking five times to-day—and yet a morsel of that savoury ham were not altogether foreign to the matter; and I pray you, fair sir, to do me reason in a cup of wine."

The guests, though still agape with astonishment, pledged their resuscitated landlord, who thus proceeded in his story:—He had indeed now many more auditors than those to whom it was commenced, for Edith, having given certain necessary orders for arranging matters within the Castle, had followed the dead-alive up to the stranger's apartment attended by as many of the guests, male and female, as could squeeze into the small room, while others, crowding the staircase, caught up an erroneous edition of the story, and transmitted it still more inaccurately to those beneath, who again sent it forth to the vulgar without, in a fashion totally irreconcilable to the real fact. Athelstane, however, went on as follows, with the history of his escape:—

"Finding myself freed from the staple, I dragged myself up stairs as well as a man loaded with shackles, and emaciated with fasting, might; and after much groping about, I was at length directed, by the sound of a jolly roundelay, to the apartment where the worthy Sacristan, an it so please ye, was holding a devil's mass with a huge beetle-browed, broad-shouldered brother of the grey-frock and cowl, who looked much more like a thief than a clergyman. I burst in upon them, and the fashion of my grave-clothes, as well as the clanking of my chains, made me more resemble an inhabitant of the other world than of this. Both stood aghast; but when I knocked down the Sacristan with my fist, the other fellow, his pot-companion, fetched a blow at me with a huge quarter-staff."

"This must be our Friar Tuck, for a count's ransom," said Richard, looking at Ivanhoe.

"He may be the devil, an he will," said Athelstane. "Fortunately he missed the aim; and on my approaching to grapple with him, took to his heels and ran for it. I failed not to set my own heels at liberty by means of the fetter-key, which hung amongst others at the sexton's belt; and I had thoughts of beating out the knave's brains with the bunch of keys, but gratitude for the nook of pasty and the flask of wine which the rascal had imparted to my captivity, came over my heart; so, with a brace of hearty kicks, I left him on the floor, pouched some baked meat, and a leathern bottle of wine, with which the two venerable brethren had been regaling, went to the stable, and found in a private stall mine own best palfrey, which, doubtless, had been set apart for the holy Father Abbot's particular use. Hither I came with all the speed the beast could compass—man and mother's son flying before me wherever I came, taking me for a spectre, the more especially as, to prevent my being recognised, I drew the corpse-hood over my face. I had not gained admittance into my own castle, had I not been supposed to be the attendant of a juggler who is making the people in the castle-yard very merry, considering they are assembled to celebrate their lord's funeral—I say the sewer thought I was dressed to bear a part in the tregetour's mummery, and so I got admission, and did but disclose myself to my mother, and eat a hasty morsel, ere I came in quest of you, my noble friend."

"And you have found me," said Cedric, "ready to resume our brave projects of honour and liberty. I tell thee, never will dawn a morrow so auspicious as the next, for the deliverance of the noble Saxon race."

"Talk not to me of delivering any one," said Athelstane; "it is well I am delivered myself. I am more intent on punishing that villain Abbot. He shall hang on the top of this Castle of Coningsburgh, in his cope and stole; and if the stairs be too strait to admit his fat carcass, I will have him craned up from without."

"But, my son," said Edith, "consider his sacred office."

"Consider my three days' fast," replied Athelstane; "I will have their blood every one of them. Front-de-Boeuf was burnt alive for a less matter, for he kept a good table for his prisoners, only put too much garlic in his last dish of pottage. But these hypocritical, ungrateful slaves, so often the self-invited flatterers at my board, who gave me neither pottage nor garlic, more or less, they die, by the soul of Hengist!"

"But the Pope, my noble friend,"—said Cedric—

"But the devil, my noble friend,"—answered Athelstane; "they die, and no more of them. Were they the best monks upon earth, the world would go on without them."

"For shame, noble Athelstane," said Cedric; "forget such wretches in the career of glory which lies open before thee. Tell this Norman prince, Richard of Anjou, that, lion-hearted as he is, he shall not hold undisputed the throne of Alfred, while a male descendant of the Holy Confessor lives to dispute it."

"How!" said Athelstane, "is this the noble King Richard?"

"It is Richard Plantagenet himself," said Cedric; "yet I need not remind thee that, coming hither a guest of free-will, he may neither be injured nor detained prisoner—thou well knowest thy duty to him as his host."

"Ay, by my faith!" said Athelstane; "and my duty as a subject besides, for I here tender him my allegiance, heart and hand."

"My son," said Edith, "think on thy royal rights!"

"Think on the freedom of England, degenerate Prince!" said Cedric.

"Mother and friend," said Athelstane, "a truce to your upbraidings—bread and water and a dungeon are marvellous mortifiers of ambition, and I rise from the tomb a wiser man than I descended into it. One half of those vain follies were puffed into mine ear by that perfidious Abbot Wolfram, and you may now judge if he is a counsellor to be trusted. Since these plots were set in agitation, I have had nothing but hurried journeys, indigestions, blows and bruises, imprisonments and starvation; besides that they can only end in the murder of some thousands of quiet folk. I tell you, I will be king in my own domains, and nowhere else; and my first act of dominion shall be to hang the Abbot."

"And my ward Rowena," said Cedric—"I trust you intend not to desert her?"

"Father Cedric," said Athelstane, "be reasonable. The Lady Rowena cares not for me—she loves the little finger of my kinsman Wilfred's glove better than my whole person. There she stands to avouch it—Nay, blush not, kinswoman, there is no shame in loving a courtly knight better than a country franklin—and do not laugh neither, Rowena, for grave-clothes and a thin visage are, God knows, no matter of merriment —Nay, an thou wilt needs laugh, I will find thee a better jest—Give me thy hand, or rather lend it me, for I but ask it in the way of friendship.—Here, cousin Wilfred of Ivanhoe, in thy favour I renounce and abjure—-Hey! by Saint Dunstan, our cousin Wilfred hath vanished!—Yet, unless my eyes are still dazzled with the fasting I have undergone, I saw him stand there but even now."

All now looked around and enquired for Ivanhoe, but he had vanished. It was at length discovered that a Jew had been to seek him; and that, after very brief conference, he had called for Gurth and his armour, and had left the castle.

"Fair cousin," said Athelstane to Rowena, "could I think that this sudden disappearance of Ivanhoe was occasioned by other than the weightiest reason, I would myself resume—"

But he had no sooner let go her hand, on first observing that Ivanhoe had disappeared, than Rowena, who had found her situation extremely embarrassing, had taken the first opportunity to escape from the apartment.

"Certainly," quoth Athelstane, "women are the least to be trusted of all animals, monks and abbots excepted. I am an infidel, if I expected not thanks from her, and perhaps a kiss to boot—These cursed grave-clothes have surely a spell on them, every one flies from me.—To you I turn, noble King Richard, with the vows of allegiance, which, as a liege-subject—"

But King Richard was gone also, and no one knew whither. At length it was learned that he had hastened to the court-yard, summoned to his presence the Jew who had spoken with Ivanhoe, and after a moment's speech with him, had called vehemently to horse, thrown himself upon a steed, compelled the Jew to mount another, and set off at a rate, which, according to Wamba, rendered the old Jew's neck not worth a penny's purchase.

"By my halidome!" said Athelstane, "it is certain that Zernebock hath possessed himself of my castle in my absence. I return in my grave-clothes, a pledge restored from the very sepulchre, and every one I speak to vanishes as soon as they hear my voice!—But it skills not talking of it. Come, my friends—such of you as are left, follow me to the banquet-hall, lest any more of us disappear—it is, I trust, as yet tolerably furnished, as becomes the obsequies of an ancient Saxon noble; and should we tarry any longer, who knows but the devil may fly off with the supper?"

XLIII.

> Be Mowbray's sins so heavy in his bosom,
> That they may break his foaming courser's back,
> And throw the rider headlong in the lists,
> A caitiff recreant!
>
> — RICHARD II

Our scene now returns to the exterior of the Castle, or Preceptory, of Templestowe, about the hour when the bloody die was to be cast for the life or death of Rebecca. It was a scene of bustle and life, as if the whole vicinity had poured forth its inhabitants to a village wake, or rural feast. But the earnest desire to look on blood and death, is not peculiar to those dark ages; though in the gladiatorial exercise of single combat and general tourney, they were habituated to the bloody spectacle of brave men falling by each other's hands. Even in our own days, when morals are better understood, an execution, a bruising match, a riot, or a meeting of radical reformers, collects, at considerable hazard to themselves, immense crowds of spectators, otherwise little interested, except to see how matters are to be conducted, or whether the heroes of the day are, in the heroic language of insurgent tailors, flints or dunghills.

The eyes, therefore, of a very considerable multitude, were bent on the gate of the Preceptory of Templestowe, with the purpose of witnessing the procession; while still greater numbers had already surrounded the tiltyard belonging to that establishment. This enclosure was formed on a piece of level ground adjoining to the Preceptory, which had been levelled with care, for the exercise of military and chivalrous sports. It occupied the brow of a soft and gentle eminence, was carefully palisaded around, and, as the Templars willingly invited spectators to be witnesses of their skill in feats of chivalry, was amply supplied with galleries and benches for their use.

On the present occasion, a throne was erected for the Grand Master at the east end, surrounded with seats of distinction for the Preceptors and Knights of the Order. Over these floated the sacred standard, called "Le Beau-seant", which was the ensign, as its name was the battle-cry, of the Templars.

At the opposite end of the lists was a pile of faggots, so arranged around a stake, deeply fixed in the ground, as to leave a space for the victim whom they were destined to consume, to enter within the fatal circle, in order to be chained to the stake by the fetters which hung ready for that purpose. Beside this deadly apparatus stood four black slaves, whose colour and African features, then so little known in England, appalled the multitude, who gazed on them as on demons employed about their own diabolical exercises. These men stirred not, excepting now and then, under the direction of one who seemed their chief, to shift and replace the ready fuel. They looked not on the multitude. In fact, they seemed insensible of their presence, and of every thing save the discharge of their own horrible duty.

And when, in speech with each other, they expanded their blubber lips, and showed their white fangs, as if they grinned at the thoughts of the expected tragedy, the startled commons could scarcely help believing that they were actually the familiar spirits with whom the witch had communed, and who, her time being out, stood ready to assist in her dreadful punishment. They whispered to each other, and communicated all the feats which Satan had performed during that busy and unhappy period, not failing, of course, to give the devil rather more than his due.

"Have you not heard, Father Dennet," quoth one boor to another advanced in years, "that the devil has carried away bodily the great Saxon Thane, Athelstane of Coningsburgh?"

"Ay, but he brought him back though, by the blessing of God and Saint Dunstan."

"How's that?" said a brisk young fellow, dressed in a green cassock embroidered with gold, and having at his heels a stout lad bearing a harp upon his back, which betrayed his vocation. The Minstrel seemed of no vulgar rank; for, besides the splendour of his gaily braidered doublet, he wore around his neck a silver chain, by which hung the "wrest", or key, with which he tuned his harp. On his right arm was a silver plate, which, instead of bearing, as usual, the cognizance or badge of the baron to whose family he belonged, had barely the word SHERWOOD engraved upon it.— "How mean you by that?" said the gay Minstrel, mingling in the conversation of the peasants; "I came to seek one subject for my rhyme, and, by'r Lady, I were glad to find two."

"It is well avouched," said the elder peasant, "that after Athelstane of Coningsburgh had been dead four weeks—"

"That is impossible," said the Minstrel; "I saw him in life at the Passage of Arms at Ashby-de-la-Zouche."

"Dead, however, he was, or else translated," said the younger peasant; "for I heard the Monks of Saint Edmund's singing the death's hymn for him; and, moreover, there was a rich death-meal and dole at the Castle of Coningsburgh, as right was; and thither had I gone, but for Mabel Parkins, who—"

"Ay, dead was Athelstane," said the old man, shaking his head, "and the more pity it was, for the old Saxon blood—"

"But, your story, my masters—your story," said the Minstrel, somewhat impatiently.

"Ay, ay—construe us the story," said a burly Friar, who stood beside them, leaning on a pole that exhibited an appearance between a pilgrim's staff and a quarter-staff, and probably acted as either when occasion served,—"Your story," said the stalwart churchman; "burn not daylight about it—we have short time to spare."

"An please your reverence," said Dennet, "a drunken priest came to visit the Sacristan at Saint Edmund's—"

"It does not please my reverence," answered the churchman, "that there should be such an animal as a drunken priest, or, if there were, that a layman should so speak him. Be mannerly, my friend, and conclude the holy man only wrapt in meditation, which makes the head dizzy and foot unsteady, as if the stomach were filled with new wine—I have felt it myself."

"Well, then," answered Father Dennet, "a holy brother came to visit the Sacristan at Saint Edmund's—a sort of hedge-priest is the visitor, and kills half the deer that are stolen in the forest, who loves the tinkling of a pint-pot better than the sacring-bell, and deems a flitch of bacon worth ten of his breviary; for the rest, a good fellow and a merry, who will flourish a quarter-staff, draw a bow, and dance a Cheshire round, with e'er a man in Yorkshire."

"That last part of thy speech, Dennet," said the Minstrel, "has saved thee a rib or twain."

"Tush, man, I fear him not," said Dennet; "I am somewhat old and stiff, but when I fought for the bell and ram at Doncaster—"

"But the story—the story, my friend," again said the Minstrel.

"Why, the tale is but this—Athelstane of Coningsburgh was buried at Saint Edmund's."

"That's a lie, and a loud one," said the Friar, "for I saw him borne to his own Castle of Coningsburgh."

"Nay, then, e'en tell the story yourself, my masters," said Dennet, turning sulky at these repeated contradictions; and it was with some difficulty that the boor could be prevailed on, by the request of his comrade and the Minstrel, to renew his tale.—"These two 'sober' friars," said he at length, "since this reverend man will needs have them such, had continued drinking good ale, and wine, and what not, for the best part for a summer's day, when they were aroused by a deep groan, and a clanking of chains, and the figure of the deceased Athelstane entered the apartment, saying, 'Ye evil shep-herds!—'"

"It is false," said the Friar, hastily, "he never spoke a word."

"So ho! Friar Tuck," said the Minstrel, drawing him apart from the rustics; "we have started a new hare, I find."

"I tell thee, Allan-a-Dale," said the Hermit, "I saw Athelstane of Coningsburgh as much as bodily eyes ever saw a living man. He had his shroud on, and all about him smelt of the sepulchre—A butt of sack will not wash it out of my memory."

"Pshaw!" answered the Minstrel; "thou dost but jest with me!"

"Never believe me," said the Friar, "an I fetched not a knock at him with my quarter-staff that would have felled an ox, and it glided through his body as it might through a pillar of smoke!"

"By Saint Hubert," said the Minstrel, "but it is a wondrous tale, and fit to be put in metre to the ancient tune, 'Sorrow came to the old Friar.'"

"Laugh, if ye list," said Friar Tuck; "but an ye catch me singing on such a theme, may the next ghost or devil carry me off with him headlong! No, no—I instantly formed the purpose of assisting at some good work, such as the burning of a witch, a judicial combat, or the like matter of godly service, and therefore am I here."

As they thus conversed, the heavy bell of the church of Saint Michael of Templestowe, a venerable building, situated in a hamlet at some distance from the Preceptory, broke short their argument. One by one the sullen sounds fell successively on the ear, leaving but sufficient space for each to die away in distant echo, ere the air was again filled by repetition of the iron knell. These sounds, the signal of the approaching ceremony, chilled with awe the hearts of the assembled multitude, whose eyes were now turned to the Preceptory, expecting the approach of the Grand Master, the champion, and the criminal.

At length the drawbridge fell, the gates opened, and a knight, bearing the great standard of the Order, sallied from the castle, preceded by six trumpets, and followed by the Knights Preceptors, two and two, the Grand Master coming last, mounted on a stately horse, whose furniture was of the simplest kind. Behind him came Brian de Bois-Guilbert, armed cap-a-pie in bright armour, but without his lance, shield, and sword, which were borne by his two esquires behind him. His face, though partly hidden by a long plume which floated down from his barrel-cap, bore a strong and mingled expression of passion, in which pride seemed to contend with irresolution. He looked ghastly pale, as if he had not slept for several nights, yet reined his pawing war-horse with the habitual ease and grace proper to the best lance of the Order of the Temple. His general appearance was grand and commanding; but, looking at him with attention, men read that in his dark features, from which they willingly withdrew their eyes.

On either side rode Conrade of Mont-Fitchet, and Albert de Malvoisin, who acted as godfathers to the champion. They were in their robes of peace, the white dress of the Order. Behind them followed other Companions of the Temple, with a long train of esquires and pages clad in black, aspirants to the honour of being one day Knights of the Order. After these neophytes came a guard of warders on foot, in the same sable livery, amidst whose partisans might be seen the pale form of the accused, moving with a slow but undismayed step towards the scene of her fate. She was stript of all her ornaments, lest perchance there should be among them some of those amulets which Satan was supposed to bestow upon his victims, to deprive them of the power of confession even when under the torture. A coarse white dress, of the simplest form, had been substituted for her Oriental garments; yet there was such an exquisite mixture of courage and resignation in her look, that even in this garb, and with no other ornament than her long black tresses, each eye wept that looked upon her, and the most hardened bigot regretted the fate that had converted a creature so goodly into a vessel of wrath, and a waged slave of the devil.

A crowd of inferior personages belonging to the Preceptory followed the victim, all moving with the utmost order, with arms folded, and looks bent upon the ground.

This slow procession moved up the gentle eminence, on the summit of which was the tiltyard, and, entering the lists, marched once around them from right to left, and when they had completed the circle, made a halt. There was then a momentary bustle, while the Grand Master and all his attendants, excepting the champion and his godfathers, dismounted from their horses, which were immediately removed out of the lists by the esquires, who were in attendance for that purpose.

The unfortunate Rebecca was conducted to the black chair placed near the pile. On her first glance at the terrible spot where preparations were making for a death alike dismaying to the mind and painful to the body, she was observed to shudder and shut her eyes, praying internally doubtless, for her lips moved though no speech was heard. In the space of a minute she opened her eyes, looked fixedly on the pile as if to familiarize her mind with the object, and then slowly and naturally turned away her head.

Meanwhile, the Grand Master had assumed his seat; and when the chivalry of his order was placed around and behind him, each in his due rank, a loud and long flourish of the trumpets announced that the Court were seated for judgment. Malvoisin, then, acting as godfather of the champion, stepped forward, and laid the glove of the Jewess, which was the pledge of battle, at the feet of the Grand Master.

"Valorous Lord, and reverend Father," said he, "here standeth the good Knight,

Brian de Bois-Guilbert, Knight Preceptor of the Order of the Temple, who, by accepting the pledge of battle which I now lay at your reverence's feet, hath become bound to do his devoir in combat this day, to maintain that this Jewish maiden, by name Rebecca, hath justly deserved the doom passed upon her in a Chapter of this most Holy Order of the Temple of Zion, condemning her to die as a sorceress;—here, I say, he standeth, such battle to do, knightly and honourable, if such be your noble and sanctified pleasure."

"Hath he made oath," said the Grand Master, "that his quarrel is just and honourable? Bring forward the Crucifix and the 'Te igitur'."

"Sir, and most reverend father," answered Malvoisin, readily, "our brother here present hath already sworn to the truth of his accusation in the hand of the good Knight Conrade de Mont-Fitchet; and otherwise he ought not to be sworn, seeing that his adversary is an unbeliever, and may take no oath."

This explanation was satisfactory, to Albert's great joy; for the wily knight had foreseen the great difficulty, or rather impossibility, of prevailing upon Brian de Bois-Guilbert to take such an oath before the assembly, and had invented this excuse to escape the necessity of his doing so.

The Grand Master, having allowed the apology of Albert Malvoisin, commanded the herald to stand forth and do his devoir. The trumpets then again flourished, and a herald, stepping forward, proclaimed aloud,—"Oyez, oyez, oyez. —Here standeth the good Knight, Sir Brian de Bois-Guilbert, ready to do battle with any knight of free blood, who will sustain the quarrel allowed and allotted to the Jewess Rebecca, to try by champion, in respect of lawful essoine of her own body; and to such champion the reverend and valorous Grand Master here present allows a fair field, and equal partition of sun and wind, and whatever else appertains to a fair combat." The trumpets again sounded, and there was a dead pause of many minutes.

"No champion appears for the appellant," said the Grand Master. "Go, herald, and ask her whether she expects any one to do battle for her in this her cause." The herald went to the chair in which Rebecca was seated, and Bois-Guilbert suddenly turning his horse's head toward that end of the lists, in spite of hints on either side from Malvoisin and Mont-Fitchet, was by the side of Rebecca's chair as soon as the herald.

"Is this regular, and according to the law of combat?" said Malvoisin, looking to the Grand Master.

"Albert de Malvoisin, it is," answered Beaumanoir; "for in this appeal to the judgment of God, we may not prohibit parties from having that communication with each other, which may best tend to bring forth the truth of the quarrel."

In the meantime, the herald spoke to Rebecca in these terms:—"Damsel, the Honourable and Reverend the Grand Master demands of thee, if thou art prepared with a champion to do battle this day in thy behalf, or if thou dost yield thee as one justly condemned to a deserved doom?"

"Say to the Grand Master," replied Rebecca, "that I maintain my innocence, and do not yield me as justly condemned, lest I become guilty of mine own blood. Say to him, that I challenge such delay as his forms will permit, to see if God, whose opportunity is in man's extremity, will raise me up a deliverer; and when such uttermost space is passed, may His holy will be done!" The herald retired to carry this answer to the Grand Master.

"God forbid," said Lucas Beaumanoir, "that Jew or Pagan should impeach us of injustice!—Until the shadows be cast from the west to the eastward, will we wait to see if a champion shall appear for this unfortunate woman. When the day is so far passed, let her prepare for death."

The herald communicated the words of the Grand Master to Rebecca, who bowed her head submissively, folded her arms, and, looking up towards heaven, seemed to expect that aid from above which she could scarce promise herself from man. During this awful pause, the voice of Bois-Guilbert broke upon her ear—it was but a whisper, yet it startled her more than the summons of the herald had appeared to do.

"Rebecca," said the Templar, "dost thou hear me?"

"I have no portion in thee, cruel, hard-hearted man," said the unfortunate maiden.

"Ay, but dost thou understand my words?" said the Templar; "for the sound of my voice is frightful in mine own ears. I scarce know on what ground we stand, or for what purpose they have brought us hither.—This listed space—that chair—these faggots—I know their purpose, and yet it appears to me like something unreal—the fearful picture of a vision, which appals my sense with hideous fantasies, but convinces not my reason."

"My mind and senses keep touch and time," answered Rebecca, "and tell me alike that these faggots are destined to consume my earthly body, and open a painful but a brief passage to a better world."

"Dreams, Rebecca,—dreams," answered the Templar; "idle visions, rejected by the wisdom of your own wiser Sadducees. Hear me, Rebecca," he said, proceeding with animation; "a better chance hast thou for life and liberty than yonder knaves and dotard dream of. Mount thee behind me on my steed—on Zamor, the gallant horse that never failed his rider. I won him in single fight from the Soldan of Trebizond—mount, I say, behind me—in one short hour is pursuit and enquiry far behind—a new world of pleasure opens to thee—to me a new career of fame. Let them speak the doom which I despise, and erase the name of Bois-Guilbert from their list of monastic slaves! I will wash out with blood whatever blot they may dare to cast on my scutcheon."

"Tempter," said Rebecca, "begone!—Not in this last extremity canst thou move me one hair's-breadth from my resting place—surrounded as I am by foes, I hold thee as my worst and most deadly enemy—avoid thee, in the name of God!"

Albert Malvoisin, alarmed and impatient at the duration of their conference, now advanced to interrupt it.

"Hath the maiden acknowledged her guilt?" he demanded of Bois-Guilbert; "or is she resolute in her denial?"

"She is indeed resolute," said Bois-Guilbert.

"Then," said Malvoisin, "must thou, noble brother, resume thy place to attend the issue—The shades are changing on the circle of the dial—Come, brave Bois-Guilbert —come, thou hope of our holy Order, and soon to be its head."

As he spoke in this soothing tone, he laid his hand on the knight's bridle, as if to lead him back to his station.

"False villain! what meanest thou by thy hand on my rein?" said Sir Brian, angrily.

And shaking off his companion's grasp, he rode back to the upper end of the lists.

"There is yet spirit in him," said Malvoisin apart to Mont-Fitchet, "were it well directed—but, like the Greek fire, it burns whatever approaches it."

The Judges had now been two hours in the lists, awaiting in vain the appearance of a champion.

"And reason good," said Friar Tuck, "seeing she is a Jewess—and yet, by mine Order, it is hard that so young and beautiful a creature should perish without one blow being struck in her behalf! Were she ten times a witch, provided she were but the least bit of a Christian, my quarter-staff should ring noon on the steel cap of yonder fierce Templar, ere he carried the matter off thus."

It was, however, the general belief that no one could or would appear for a Jewess, accused of sorcery; and the knights, instigated by Malvoisin, whispered to each other, that it was time to declare the pledge of Rebecca forfeited. At this instant a knight, urging his horse to speed, appeared on the plain advancing towards the lists. A hundred voices exclaimed, "A champion! a champion!" And despite the prepossessions and prejudices of the multitude, they shouted unanimously as the knight rode into the tiltyard. The second glance, however, served to destroy the hope that his timely arrival had excited. His horse, urged for many miles to its utmost speed, appeared to reel from fatigue, and the rider, however undauntedly he presented himself in the lists, either from weakness, weariness, or both, seemed scarce able to support himself in the saddle.

To the summons of the herald, who demanded his rank, his name, and purpose, the stranger knight answered readily and boldly, "I am a good knight and noble, come hither to sustain with lance and sword the just and lawful quarrel of this damsel, Rebecca, daughter of Isaac of York; to uphold the doom pronounced against her to be false and truthless, and to defy Sir Brian de Bois-Guilbert, as a traitor, murderer, and liar; as I will prove in this field with my body against his, by the aid of God, of Our Lady, and of Monseigneur Saint George, the good knight."

"The stranger must first show," said Malvoisin, "that he is good knight, and of honourable lineage. The Temple sendeth not forth her champions against nameless men."

"My name," said the Knight, raising his helmet, "is better known, my lineage more pure, Malvoisin, than thine own. I am Wilfred of Ivanhoe."

"I will not fight with thee at present," said the Templar, in a changed and hollow voice. "Get thy wounds healed, purvey thee a better horse, and it may be I will hold it worth my while to scourge out of thee this boyish spirit of bravado."

"Ha! proud Templar," said Ivanhoe, "hast thou forgotten that twice didst thou fall before this lance? Remember the lists at Acre—remember the Passage of Arms at Ashby—remember thy proud vaunt in the halls of Rotherwood, and the gage of your gold chain against my reliquary, that thou wouldst do battle with Wilfred of Ivanhoe, and recover the honour thou hadst lost! By that reliquary and the holy relic it contains, I will proclaim thee, Templar, a coward in every court in Europe—in every Preceptory of thine Order—unless thou do battle without farther delay."

Bois-Guilbert turned his countenance irresolutely towards Rebecca, and then exclaimed, looking fiercely at Ivanhoe, "Dog of a Saxon! take thy lance, and prepare for the death thou hast drawn upon thee!"

"Does the Grand Master allow me the combat?" said Ivanhoe.

"I may not deny what thou hast challenged," said the Grand Master, "provided the maiden accepts thee as her champion. Yet I would thou wert in better plight to do battle. An enemy of our Order hast thou ever been, yet would I have thee honourably met with."

"Thus—thus as I am, and not otherwise," said Ivanhoe; "it is the judgment of God —to his keeping I commend myself.—Rebecca," said he, riding up to the fatal chair, "dost thou accept of me for thy champion?"

"I do," she said—"I do," fluttered by an emotion which the fear of death had been unable to produce, "I do accept thee as the champion whom Heaven hath sent me. Yet, no—no—thy wounds are uncured—Meet not that proud man—why shouldst thou perish also?"

But Ivanhoe was already at his post, and had closed his visor, and assumed his lance. Bois-Guilbert did the same; and his esquire remarked, as he clasped his visor, that his face, which had, notwithstanding the variety of emotions by which he had been agitated, continued during the whole morning of an ashy paleness, was now become suddenly very much flushed.

The herald, then, seeing each champion in his place, uplifted his voice, repeating thrice—"Faites vos devoirs, preux chevaliers!" After the third cry, he withdrew to one side of the lists, and again proclaimed, that none, on peril of instant death, should dare, by word, cry, or action, to interfere with or disturb this fair field of combat. The Grand Master, who held in his hand the gage of battle, Rebecca's glove, now threw it into the lists, and pronounced the fatal signal words, "Laissez aller".

The trumpets sounded, and the knights charged each other in full career. The wearied horse of Ivanhoe, and its no less exhausted rider, went down, as all had expected, before the well-aimed lance and vigorous steed of the Templar. This issue of the combat all had foreseen; but although the spear of Ivanhoe did but, in comparison, touch the shield of Bois-Guilbert, that champion, to the astonishment of all who beheld it reeled in his saddle, lost his stirrups, and fell in the lists.

Ivanhoe, extricating himself from his fallen horse, was soon on foot, hastening to mend his fortune with his sword; but his antagonist arose not. Wilfred, placing his foot on his breast, and the sword's point to his throat, commanded him to yield him, or die on the spot. Bois-Guilbert returned no answer.

"Slay him not, Sir Knight," cried the Grand Master, "unshriven and unabsolved— kill not body and soul! We allow him vanquished."

He descended into the lists, and commanded them to unhelm the conquered champion. His eyes were closed—the dark red flush was still on his brow. As they looked on him in astonishment, the eyes opened—but they were fixed and glazed. The flush passed from his brow, and gave way to the pallid hue of death. Unscathed by the lance of his enemy, he had died a victim to the violence of his own contending passions.

"This is indeed the judgment of God," said the Grand Master, looking upwards— "'Fiat voluntas tua!'"

XLIV.

So! now 'tis ended, like an old wife's story.

— WEBSTER

When the first moments of surprise were over, Wilfred of Ivanhoe demanded of the Grand Master, as judge of the field, if he had manfully and rightfully done his duty in the combat? "Manfully and rightfully hath it been done," said the Grand Master. "I pronounce the maiden free and guiltless—The arms and the body of the deceased knight are at the will of the victor."

"I will not despoil him of his weapons," said the Knight of Ivanhoe, "nor condemn his corpse to shame—he hath fought for Christendom—God's arm, no human hand, hath this day struck him down. But let his obsequies be private, as becomes those of a man who died in an unjust quarrel.—And for the maiden—"

He was interrupted by a clattering of horses' feet, advancing in such numbers, and so rapidly, as to shake the ground before them; and the Black Knight galloped into the lists. He was followed by a numerous band of men-at-arms, and several knights in complete armour.

"I am too late," he said, looking around him. "I had doomed Bois-Guilbert for mine own property.—Ivanhoe, was this well, to take on thee such a venture, and thou scarce able to keep thy saddle?"

"Heaven, my Liege," answered Ivanhoe, "hath taken this proud man for its victim. He was not to be honoured in dying as your will had designed."

"Peace be with him," said Richard, looking steadfastly on the corpse, "if it may be so—he was a gallant knight, and has died in his steel harness full knightly. But we must waste no time—Bohun, do thine office!"

A Knight stepped forward from the King's attendants, and, laying his hand on the shoulder of Albert de Malvoisin, said, "I arrest thee of High Treason."

The Grand Master had hitherto stood astonished at the appearance of so many warriors.—He now spoke.

"Who dares to arrest a Knight of the Temple of Zion, within the girth of his own Preceptory, and in the presence of the Grand Master? and by whose authority is this bold outrage offered?"

"I make the arrest," replied the Knight—"I, Henry Bohun, Earl of Essex, Lord High Constable of England."

"And he arrests Malvoisin," said the King, raising his visor, "by the order of Richard Plantagenet, here present.—Conrade Mont-Fitchet, it is well for thee thou art born no subject of mine.—But for thee, Malvoisin, thou diest with thy brother Philip, ere the world be a week older."

"I will resist thy doom," said the Grand Master.

"Proud Templar," said the King, "thou canst not—look up, and behold the Royal Standard of England floats over thy towers instead of thy Temple banner!—Be wise, Beaumanoir, and make no bootless opposition—Thy hand is in the lion's mouth."

"I will appeal to Rome against thee," said the Grand Master, "for usurpation on the immunities and privileges of our Order."

"Be it so," said the King; "but for thine own sake tax me not with usurpation now. Dissolve thy Chapter, and depart with thy followers to thy next Preceptory, (if thou canst find one), which has not been made the scene of treasonable conspiracy against the King of England—Or, if thou wilt, remain, to share our hospitality, and behold our justice."

"To be a guest in the house where I should command?" said the Templar; "never! —Chaplains, raise the Psalm, 'Quare fremuerunt Gentes?'—Knights, squires, and followers of the Holy Temple, prepare to follow the banner of 'Beau-seant!'"

The Grand Master spoke with a dignity which confronted even that of England's king himself, and inspired courage into his surprised and dismayed followers. They gathered around him like the sheep around the watch-dog, when they hear the baying of the wolf. But they evinced not the timidity of the scared flock—there were dark brows of defiance, and looks which menaced the hostility they dared not to proffer in words. They drew together in a dark line of spears, from which the white cloaks of the knights were visible among the dusky garments of their retainers, like the lighter-coloured edges of a sable cloud. The multitude, who had raised a clamorous shout of reprobation, paused and gazed in silence on the formidable and experienced body to which they had unwarily bade defiance, and shrunk back from their front.

The Earl of Essex, when he beheld them pause in their assembled force, dashed the rowels into his charger's sides, and galloped backwards and forwards to array his followers, in opposition to a band so formidable. Richard alone, as if he loved the danger his presence had provoked, rode slowly along the front of the Templars, calling aloud, "What, sirs! Among so many gallant knights, will none dare splinter a spear with Richard?—Sirs of the Temple! your ladies are but sun-burned, if they are not worth the shiver of a broken lance?"

"The Brethren of the Temple," said the Grand Master, riding forward in advance of their body, "fight not on such idle and profane quarrel—and not with thee, Richard of England, shall a Templar cross lance in my presence. The Pope and Princes of Europe shall judge our quarrel, and whether a Christian prince has done well in bucklering the cause which thou hast to-day adopted. If unassailed, we depart assailing no one. To thine honour we refer the armour and household goods of the Order which we leave behind us, and on thy conscience we lay the scandal and offence thou hast this day given to Christendom."

With these words, and without waiting a reply, the Grand Master gave the signal of departure. Their trumpets sounded a wild march, of an Oriental character, which formed the usual signal for the Templars to advance. They changed their array from a line to a column of march, and moved off as slowly as their horses could step, as if to show it was only the will of their Grand Master, and no fear of the opposing and superior force, which compelled them to withdraw.

"By the splendour of Our Lady's brow!" said King Richard, "it is pity of their lives that these Templars are not so trusty as they are disciplined and valiant."

The multitude, like a timid cur which waits to bark till the object of its challenge has turned his back, raised a feeble shout as the rear of the squadron left the ground.

During the tumult which attended the retreat of the Templars, Rebecca saw and heard nothing—she was locked in the arms of her aged father, giddy, and almost senseless, with the rapid change of circumstances around her. But one word from Isaac at length recalled her scattered feelings.

"Let us go," he said, "my dear daughter, my recovered treasure—let us go to throw ourselves at the feet of the good youth."

"Not so," said Rebecca, "O no—no—no—I must not at this moment dare to speak to him—Alas! I should say more than—No, my father, let us instantly leave this evil place."

"But, my daughter," said Isaac, "to leave him who hath come forth like a strong man with his spear and shield, holding his life as nothing, so he might redeem thy captivity; and thou, too, the daughter of a people strange unto him and his—this is service to be thankfully acknowledged."

"It is—it is—most thankfully—most devoutly acknowledged," said Rebecca—"it shall be still more so—but not now—for the sake of thy beloved Rachel, father, grant my request—not now!"

"Nay, but," said Isaac, insisting, "they will deem us more thankless than mere dogs!"

"But thou seest, my dear father, that King Richard is in presence, and that—"

"True, my best—my wisest Rebecca!—Let us hence—let us hence!—Money he will lack, for he has just returned from Palestine, and, as they say, from prison—and pretext for exacting it, should he need any, may arise out of my simple traffic with his brother John. Away, away, let us hence!"

And hurrying his daughter in his turn, he conducted her from the lists, and by means of conveyance which he had provided, transported her safely to the house of the Rabbi Nathan.

The Jewess, whose fortunes had formed the principal interest of the day, having now retired unobserved, the attention of the populace was transferred to the Black Knight. They now filled the air with "Long life to Richard with the Lion's Heart, and down with the usurping Templars!"

"Notwithstanding all this lip-loyalty," said Ivanhoe to the Earl of Essex, "it was well the King took the precaution to bring thee with him, noble Earl, and so many of thy trusty followers."

The Earl smiled and shook his head.

"Gallant Ivanhoe," said Essex, "dost thou know our Master so well, and yet suspect him of taking so wise a precaution! I was drawing towards York having heard that Prince John was making head there, when I met King Richard, like a true knight-errant, galloping hither to achieve in his own person this adventure of the Templar and the Jewess, with his own single arm. I accompanied him with my band, almost maugre his consent."

"And what news from York, brave Earl?" said Ivanhoe; "will the rebels bide us there?"

"No more than December's snow will bide July's sun," said the Earl; "they are dispersing; and who should come posting to bring us the news, but John himself!"

"The traitor! the ungrateful insolent traitor!" said Ivanhoe; "did not Richard order him into confinement?"

"O! he received him," answered the Earl, "as if they had met after a hunting party;

and, pointing to me and our men-at-arms, said, 'Thou seest, brother, I have some angry men with me—thou wert best go to our mother, carry her my duteous affection, and abide with her until men's minds are pacified.'"

"And this was all he said?" enquired Ivanhoe; "would not any one say that this Prince invites men to treason by his clemency?"

"Just," replied the Earl, "as the man may be said to invite death, who undertakes to fight a combat, having a dangerous wound unhealed."

"I forgive thee the jest, Lord Earl," said Ivanhoe; "but, remember, I hazarded but my own life—Richard, the welfare of his kingdom."

"Those," replied Essex, "who are specially careless of their own welfare, are seldom remarkably attentive to that of others—But let us haste to the castle, for Richard meditates punishing some of the subordinate members of the conspiracy, though he has pardoned their principal."

From the judicial investigations which followed on this occasion, and which are given at length in the Wardour Manuscript, it appears that Maurice de Bracy escaped beyond seas, and went into the service of Philip of France; while Philip de Malvoisin, and his brother Albert, the Preceptor of Templestowe, were executed, although Waldemar Fitzurse, the soul of the conspiracy, escaped with banishment; and Prince John, for whose behoof it was undertaken, was not even censured by his good-natured brother. No one, however, pitied the fate of the two Malvoisins, who only suffered the death which they had both well deserved, by many acts of falsehood, cruelty, and oppression.

Briefly after the judicial combat, Cedric the Saxon was summoned to the court of Richard, which, for the purpose of quieting the counties that had been disturbed by the ambition of his brother, was then held at York. Cedric tushed and pshawed more than once at the message—but he refused not obedience. In fact, the return of Richard had quenched every hope that he had entertained of restoring a Saxon dynasty in England; for, whatever head the Saxons might have made in the event of a civil war, it was plain that nothing could be done under the undisputed dominion of Richard, popular as he was by his personal good qualities and military fame, although his administration was wilfully careless, now too indulgent, and now allied to despotism.

But, moreover, it could not escape even Cedric's reluctant observation, that his project for an absolute union among the Saxons, by the marriage of Rowena and Athelstane, was now completely at an end, by the mutual dissent of both parties concerned. This was, indeed, an event which, in his ardour for the Saxon cause, he could not have anticipated, and even when the disinclination of both was broadly and plainly manifested, he could scarce bring himself to believe that two Saxons of royal descent should scruple, on personal grounds, at an alliance so necessary for the public weal of the nation. But it was not the less certain: Rowena had always expressed her repugnance to Athelstane, and now Athelstane was no less plain and positive in proclaiming his resolution never to pursue his addresses to the Lady Rowena. Even the natural obstinacy of Cedric sunk beneath these obstacles, where he, remaining on the point of junction, had the task of dragging a reluctant pair up to it, one with each hand. He made, however, a last vigorous attack on Athelstane, and he found that resuscitated sprout of Saxon royalty engaged, like country squires of our own day, in a furious war with the clergy.

It seems that, after all his deadly menaces against the Abbot of Saint Edmund's, Athelstane's spirit of revenge, what between the natural indolent kindness of his own disposition, what through the prayers of his mother Edith, attached, like most ladies, (of the period,) to the clerical order, had terminated in his keeping the Abbot and his monks in the dungeons of Coningsburgh for three days on a meagre diet. For this atrocity the Abbot menaced him with excommunication, and made out a dreadful list of complaints in the bowels and stomach, suffered by himself and his monks, in consequence of the tyrannical and unjust imprisonment they had sustained. With this controversy, and with the means he had adopted to counteract this clerical persecution, Cedric found the mind of his friend Athelstane so fully occupied, that it had no room for another idea. And when Rowena's name was mentioned the noble Athelstane prayed leave to quaff a full goblet to her health, and that she might soon be the bride of his kinsman Wilfred. It was a desperate case therefore. There was obviously no more to be made of Athelstane; or, as Wamba expressed it, in a phrase which has descended from Saxon times to ours, he was a cock that would not fight.

There remained betwixt Cedric and the determination which the lovers desired to come to, only two obstacles—his own obstinacy, and his dislike of the Norman dynasty. The former feeling gradually gave way before the endearments of his ward, and the pride which he could not help nourishing in the fame of his son. Besides, he was not insensible to the honour of allying his own line to that of Alfred, when the superior claims of the descendant of Edward the Confessor were abandoned for ever. Cedric's aversion to the Norman race of kings was also much undermined,—first, by consideration of the impossibility of ridding England of the new dynasty, a feeling which goes far to create loyalty in the subject to the king "de facto"; and, secondly, by the personal attention of King Richard, who delighted in the blunt humour of Cedric, and, to use the language of the Wardour Manuscript, so dealt with the noble Saxon, that, ere he had been a guest at court for seven days, he had given his consent to the marriage of his ward Rowena and his son Wilfred of Ivanhoe.

The nuptials of our hero, thus formally approved by his father, were celebrated in the most august of temples, the noble Minster of York. The King himself attended, and from the countenance which he afforded on this and other occasions to the distressed and hitherto degraded Saxons, gave them a safer and more certain prospect of attaining their just rights, than they could reasonably hope from the precarious chance of a civil war. The Church gave her full solemnities, graced with all the splendour which she of Rome knows how to apply with such brilliant effect.

Gurth, gallantly apparelled, attended as esquire upon his young master whom he had served so faithfully, and the magnanimous Wamba, decorated with a new cap and a most gorgeous set of silver bells. Sharers of Wilfred's dangers and adversity, they remained, as they had a right to expect, the partakers of his more prosperous career.

But besides this domestic retinue, these distinguished nuptials were celebrated by the attendance of the high-born Normans, as well as Saxons, joined with the universal jubilee of the lower orders, that marked the marriage of two individuals as a pledge of the future peace and harmony betwixt two races, which, since that period, have been so completely mingled, that the distinction has become wholly invisible. Cedric lived to see this union approximate towards its completion; for as the two nations mixed in society and formed intermarriages with each other, the Normans abated their scorn, and the Saxons were refined from their rusticity. But it was not until the reign of Edward the Third that the mixed language, now termed English, was spoken at the court of London, and that the hostile distinction of Norman and Saxon seems entirely to have disappeared.

It was upon the second morning after this happy bridal, that the Lady Rowena was made acquainted by her handmaid Elgitha, that a damsel desired admission to her presence, and solicited that their parley might be without witness. Rowena wondered, hesitated, became curious, and ended by commanding the damsel to be admitted, and her attendants to withdraw.

She entered—a noble and commanding figure, the long white veil, in which she was shrouded, overshadowing rather than concealing the elegance and majesty of her shape. Her demeanour was that of respect, unmingled by the least shade either of fear, or of a wish to propitiate favour. Rowena was ever ready to acknowledge the claims, and attend to the feelings, of others. She arose, and would have conducted her lovely visitor to a seat; but the stranger looked at Elgitha, and again intimated a wish to discourse with the Lady Rowena alone. Elgitha had no sooner retired with unwilling steps, than, to the surprise of the Lady of Ivanhoe, her fair visitant kneeled on one knee, pressed her hands to her forehead, and bending her head to the ground, in spite of Rowena's resistance, kissed the embroidered hem of her tunic.

"What means this, lady?" said the surprised bride; "or why do you offer to me a deference so unusual?"

"Because to you, Lady of Ivanhoe," said Rebecca, rising up and resuming the usual quiet dignity of her manner, "I may lawfully, and without rebuke, pay the debt of gratitude which I owe to Wilfred of Ivanhoe. I am—forgive the boldness which has offered to you the homage of my country—I am the unhappy Jewess, for whom your husband hazarded his life against such fearful odds in the tiltyard of Templestowe."

"Damsel," said Rowena, "Wilfred of Ivanhoe on that day rendered back but in slight measure your unceasing charity towards him in his wounds and misfortunes. Speak, is there aught remains in which he or I can serve thee?"

"Nothing," said Rebecca, calmly, "unless you will transmit to him my grateful farewell."

"You leave England then?" said Rowena, scarce recovering the surprise of this extraordinary visit.

"I leave it, lady, ere this moon again changes. My father had a brother high in favour with Mohammed Boabdil, King of Grenada—thither we go, secure of peace and protection, for the payment of such ransom as the Moslem exact from our people."

"And are you not then as well protected in England?" said Rowena. "My husband has favour with the King—the King himself is just and generous."

"Lady," said Rebecca, "I doubt it not—but the people of England are a fierce race, quarrelling ever with their neighbours or among themselves, and ready to plunge the sword into the bowels of each other. Such is no safe abode for the children of my people. Ephraim is an heartless dove—Issachar an over-laboured drudge, which stoops between two burdens. Not in a land of war and blood, surrounded by hostile neighbours, and distracted by internal factions, can Israel hope to rest during her wanderings."

"But you, maiden," said Rowena—"you surely can have nothing to fear. She who nursed the sick-bed of Ivanhoe," she continued, rising with enthusiasm—"she can have nothing to fear in England, where Saxon and Norman will contend who shall most do her honour."

"Thy speech is fair, lady," said Rebecca, "and thy purpose fairer; but it may not be—there is a gulf betwixt us. Our breeding, our faith, alike forbid either to pass over it. Farewell—yet, ere I go indulge me one request. The bridal-veil hangs over thy face; deign to raise it, and let me see the features of which fame speaks so highly."

"They are scarce worthy of being looked upon," said Rowena; "but, expecting the same from my visitant, I remove the veil."

She took it off accordingly; and, partly from the consciousness of beauty, partly from bashfulness, she blushed so intensely, that cheek, brow, neck, and bosom, were suffused with crimson. Rebecca blushed also, but it was a momentary feeling; and, mastered by higher emotions, past slowly from her features like the crimson cloud, which changes colour when the sun sinks beneath the horizon.

"Lady," she said, "the countenance you have deigned to show me will long dwell in my remembrance. There reigns in it gentleness and goodness; and if a tinge of the world's pride or vanities may mix with an expression so lovely, how should we chide that which is of earth for bearing some colour of its original? Long, long will I remember your features, and bless God that I leave my noble deliverer united with—"

She stopped short—her eyes filled with tears. She hastily wiped them, and answered to the anxious enquiries of Rowena—"I am well, lady—well. But my heart swells when I think of Torquilstone and the lists of Templestowe.—Farewell. One, the most trifling part of my duty, remains undischarged. Accept this casket—startle not at its contents."

Rowena opened the small silver-chased casket, and perceived a carcanet, or neck lace, with ear-jewels, of diamonds, which were obviously of immense value.

"It is impossible," she said, tendering back the casket. "I dare not accept a gift of such consequence."

"Yet keep it, lady," returned Rebecca.—"You have power, rank, command, influence; we have wealth, the source both of our strength and weakness; the value of these toys, ten times multiplied, would not influence half so much as your slightest wish. To you, therefore, the gift is of little value,—and to me, what I part with is of much less. Let me not think you deem so wretchedly ill of my nation as your commons believe. Think ye that I prize these sparkling fragments of stone above my liberty? or that my father values them in comparison to the honour of his only child? Accept them, lady—to me they are valueless. I will never wear jewels more."

"You are then unhappy!" said Rowena, struck with the manner in which Rebecca uttered the last words. "O, remain with us—the counsel of holy men will wean you from your erring law, and I will be a sister to you."

"No, lady," answered Rebecca, the same calm melancholy reigning in her soft voice and beautiful features—"that—may not be. I may not change the faith of my fathers like a garment unsuited to the climate in which I seek to dwell, and unhappy, lady, I will not be. He, to whom I dedicate my future life, will be my comforter, if I do His will."

"Have you then convents, to one of which you mean to retire?" asked Rowena.

"No, lady," said the Jewess; "but among our people, since the time of Abraham downwards, have been women who have devoted their thoughts to Heaven, and their actions to works of kindness to men, tending the sick, feeding the hungry, and relieving the distressed. Among these will Rebecca be numbered. Say this to thy lord, should he chance to enquire after the fate of her whose life he saved."

There was an involuntary tremour on Rebecca's voice, and a tenderness of accent, which perhaps betrayed more than she would willingly have expressed. She hastened to bid Rowena adieu.

"Farewell," she said. "May He, who made both Jew and Christian, shower down on you his choicest blessings! The bark that waits us hence will be under weigh ere we can reach the port."

She glided from the apartment, leaving Rowena surprised as if a vision had passed before her. The fair Saxon related the singular conference to her husband, on whose mind it made a deep impression. He lived long and happily with Rowena, for they were attached to each other by the bonds of early affection, and they loved each other the more, from the recollection of the obstacles which had impeded their union. Yet it would be enquiring too curiously to ask, whether the recollection of Rebecca's beauty and magnanimity did not recur to his mind more frequently than the fair descendant of Alfred might altogether have approved.

Ivanhoe distinguished himself in the service of Richard, and was graced with farther marks of the royal favour. He might have risen still higher, but for the premature death of the heroic Coeur-de-Lion, before the Castle of Chaluz, near Limoges. With the life of a generous, but rash and romantic monarch, perished all the projects which his ambition and his generosity had formed; to whom may be applied, with a slight alteration, the lines composed by Johnson for Charles of Sweden—

> His fate was destined to a foreign strand,
> A petty fortress and an "humble" hand;
> He left the name at which the world grew pale,
> To point a moral, or adorn a TALE.

THE LADY OF THE LAKE

THE LADY OF THE LAKE

CANTO FIRST. THE CHASE.

    Harp of the North! that mouldering long hast hung
    On the witch-elm that shades Saint Fillan's spring
    And down the fitful breeze thy numbers flung,
    Till envious ivy did around thee cling,
    Muffling with verdant ringlet every string,—
    O Minstrel Harp, still must thine accents sleep?
    Mid rustling leaves and fountains murmuring,
    Still must thy sweeter sounds their silence keep,
    Nor bid a warrior smile, nor teach a maid to weep?

    Not thus, in ancient days of Caledon,
    Was thy voice mute amid the festal crowd,
    When lay of hopeless love, or glory won,
    Aroused the fearful or subdued the proud.
    At each according pause was heard aloud
    Thine ardent symphony sublime and high!
    Fair dames and crested chiefs attention bowed;
    For still the burden of thy minstrelsy
    Was Knighthood's dauntless deed, and Beauty's matchless eye.

    O, wake once more! how rude soe'er the hand
    That ventures o'er thy magic maze to stray;
    O, wake once more! though scarce my skill command
    Some feeble echoing of thine earlier lay:

Though harsh and faint, and soon to die away,
And all unworthy of thy nobler strain,
Yet if one heart throb higher at its sway,
The wizard note has not been touched in vain.
Then silent be no more! Enchantress, wake again!

I.

The stag at eve had drunk his fill,
Where danced the moon on Monan's rill,
And deep his midnight lair had made
In lone Glenartney's hazel shade;
But when the sun his beacon red
Had kindled on Benvoirlich's head,
The deep-mouthed bloodhound's heavy bay
Resounded up the rocky way,
And faint, from farther distance borne,
Were heard the clanging hoof and horn.

II.

As Chief, who hears his warder call,
'To arms! the foemen storm the wall,'
The antlered monarch of the waste
Sprung from his heathery couch in haste.
But ere his fleet career he took,
The dew-drops from his flanks he shook;
Like crested leader proud and high
Tossed his beamed frontlet to the sky;
A moment gazed adown the dale,
A moment snuffed the tainted gale,
A moment listened to the cry,
That thickened as the chase drew nigh;
Then, as the headmost foes appeared,
With one brave bound the copse he cleared,
And, stretching forward free and far,
Sought the wild heaths of Uam-Var.

III.

Yelled on the view the opening pack;
Rock, glen, and cavern paid them back;
To many a mingled sound at once
The awakened mountain gave response.
A hundred dogs bayed deep and strong,
Clattered a hundred steeds along,

Their peal the merry horns rung out,
A hundred voices joined the shout;
With hark and whoop and wild halloo,
No rest Benvoirlich's echoes knew.
Far from the tumult fled the roe,
Close in her covert cowered the doe,
The falcon, from her cairn on high,
Cast on the rout a wondering eye,
Till far beyond her piercing ken
The hurricane had swept the glen.
Faint, and more faint, its failing din
Returned from cavern, cliff, and linn,
And silence settled, wide and still,
On the lone wood and mighty hill.

IV.

Less loud the sounds of sylvan war
Disturbed the heights of Uam-Var,
And roused the cavern where, 't is told,
A giant made his den of old;
For ere that steep ascent was won,
High in his pathway hung the sun,
And many a gallant, stayed perforce,
Was fain to breathe his faltering horse,
And of the trackers of the deer
Scarce half the lessening pack was near;
So shrewdly on the mountain-side
Had the bold burst their mettle tried.

V.

The noble stag was pausing now
Upon the mountain's southern brow,
Where broad extended, far beneath,
The varied realms of fair Menteith.
With anxious eye he wandered o'er
Mountain and meadow, moss and moor,
And pondered refuge from his toil,
By far Lochard or Aberfoyle.
But nearer was the copsewood gray
That waved and wept on Loch Achray,
And mingled with the pine-trees blue
On the bold cliffs of Benvenue.
Fresh vigor with the hope returned,
With flying foot the heath he spurned,

Held westward with unwearied race,
And left behind the panting chase.

VI.

'T were long to tell what steeds gave o'er,
As swept the hunt through Cambusmore;
What reins were tightened in despair,
When rose Benledi's ridge in air;
Who flagged upon Bochastle's heath,
Who shunned to stem the flooded Teith,—
For twice that day, from shore to shore,
The gallant stag swam stoutly o'er.
Few were the stragglers, following far,
That reached the lake of Vennachar;
And when the Brigg of Turk was won,
The headmost horseman rode alone.

VII.

Alone, but with unbated zeal,
That horseman plied the scourge and steel;
For jaded now, and spent with toil,
Embossed with foam, and dark with soil,
While every gasp with sobs he drew,
The laboring stag strained full in view.
Two dogs of black Saint Hubert's breed,
Unmatched for courage, breath, and speed,
Fast on his flying traces came,
And all but won that desperate game;
For, scarce a spear's length from his haunch,
Vindictive toiled the bloodhounds stanch;
Nor nearer might the dogs attain,
Nor farther might the quarry strain
Thus up the margin of the lake,
Between the precipice and brake,
O'er stock and rock their race they take.

VIII.

The Hunter marked that mountain high,
The lone lake's western boundary,
And deemed the stag must turn to bay,
Where that huge rampart barred the way;
Already glorying in the prize,
Measured his antlers with his eyes;

For the death-wound and death-halloo
Mustered his breath, his whinyard drew:—
But thundering as he came prepared,
With ready arm and weapon bared,
The wily quarry shunned the shock,
And turned him from the opposing rock;
Then, dashing down a darksome glen,
Soon lost to hound and Hunter's ken,
In the deep Trosachs' wildest nook
His solitary refuge took.
There, while close couched the thicket shed
Cold dews and wild flowers on his head,
He heard the baffled dogs in vain
Rave through the hollow pass amain,
Chiding the rocks that yelled again.

IX.

Close on the hounds the Hunter came,
To cheer them on the vanished game;
But, stumbling in the rugged dell,
The gallant horse exhausted fell.
The impatient rider strove in vain
To rouse him with the spur and rein,
For the good steed, his labors o'er,
Stretched his stiff limbs, to rise no more;
Then, touched with pity and remorse,
He sorrowed o'er the expiring horse.
'I little thought, when first thy rein
I slacked upon the banks of Seine,
That Highland eagle e'er should feed
On thy fleet limbs, my matchless steed!
Woe worth the chase, woe worth the day,
That costs thy life, my gallant gray!'

X.

Then through the dell his horn resounds,
From vain pursuit to call the hounds.
Back limped, with slow and crippled pace,
The sulky leaders of the chase;
Close to their master's side they pressed,
With drooping tail and humbled crest;
But still the dingle's hollow throat
Prolonged the swelling bugle-note.
The owlets started from their dream,

The eagles answered with their scream,
Round and around the sounds were cast,
Till echo seemed an answering blast;
And on the Hunter tried his way,
To join some comrades of the day,
Yet often paused, so strange the road,
So wondrous were the scenes it showed.

XI.

The western waves of ebbing day
Rolled o'er the glen their level way;
Each purple peak, each flinty spire,
Was bathed in floods of living fire.
But not a setting beam could glow
Within the dark ravines below,
Where twined the path in shadow hid,
Round many a rocky pyramid,
Shooting abruptly from the dell
Its thunder-splintered pinnacle;
Round many an insulated mass,
The native bulwarks of the pass,
Huge as the tower which builders vain
Presumptuous piled on Shinar's plain.
The rocky summits, split and rent,
Formed turret, dome, or battlement.
Or seemed fantastically set
With cupola or minaret,
Wild crests as pagod ever decked,
Or mosque of Eastern architect.
Nor were these earth-born castles bare,
Nor lacked they many a banner fair;
For, from their shivered brows displayed,
Far o'er the unfathomable glade,
All twinkling with the dewdrop sheen,
The briar-rose fell in streamers green,
kind creeping shrubs of thousand dyes
Waved in the west-wind's summer sighs.

XII.

Boon nature scattered, free and wild,
Each plant or flower, the mountain's child.
Here eglantine embalmed the air,
Hawthorn and hazel mingled there;
The primrose pale and violet flower

THE LADY OF THE LAKE

Found in each cliff a narrow bower;
Foxglove and nightshade, side by side,
Emblems of punishment and pride,
Grouped their dark hues with every stain
The weather-beaten crags retain.
With boughs that quaked at every breath,
Gray birch and aspen wept beneath;
Aloft, the ash and warrior oak
Cast anchor in the rifted rock;
And, higher yet, the pine-tree hung
His shattered trunk, and frequent flung,
Where seemed the cliffs to meet on high,
His boughs athwart the narrowed sky.
Highest of all, where white peaks glanced,
Where glistening streamers waved and danced,
The wanderer's eye could barely view
The summer heaven's delicious blue;
So wondrous wild, the whole might seem
The scenery of a fairy dream.

XIII.

Onward, amid the copse 'gan peep
A narrow inlet, still and deep,
Affording scarce such breadth of brim
As served the wild duck's brood to swim.
Lost for a space, through thickets veering,
But broader when again appearing,
Tall rocks and tufted knolls their face
Could on the dark-blue mirror trace;
And farther as the Hunter strayed,
Still broader sweep its channels made.
The shaggy mounds no longer stood,
Emerging from entangled wood,
But, wave-encircled, seemed to float,
Like castle girdled with its moat;
Yet broader floods extending still
Divide them from their parent hill,
Till each, retiring, claims to be
An islet in an inland sea.

XIV.

And now, to issue from the glen,
No pathway meets the wanderer's ken,
Unless he climb with footing nice

A far-projecting precipice.
The broom's tough roots his ladder made,
The hazel saplings lent their aid;
And thus an airy point he won,
Where, gleaming with the setting sun,
One burnished sheet of living gold,
Loch Katrine lay beneath him rolled,
In all her length far winding lay,
With promontory, creek, and bay,
And islands that, empurpled bright,
Floated amid the livelier light,
And mountains that like giants stand
To sentinel enchanted land.
High on the south, huge Benvenue
Down to the lake in masses threw
Crags, knolls, and mounds, confusedly hurled,
The fragments of an earlier world;
A wildering forest feathered o'er
His ruined sides and summit hoar,
While on the north, through middle air,
Ben-an heaved high his forehead bare.

XV.

From the steep promontory gazed
The stranger, raptured and amazed,
And, 'What a scene were here,' he cried,
'For princely pomp or churchman's pride!
On this bold brow, a lordly tower;
In that soft vale, a lady's bower;
On yonder meadow far away,
The turrets of a cloister gray;
How blithely might the bugle-horn
Chide on the lake the lingering morn!
How sweet at eve the lover's lute
Chime when the groves were still and mute!
And when the midnight moon should lave
Her forehead in the silver wave,
How solemn on the ear would come
The holy matins' distant hum,
While the deep peal's commanding tone
Should wake, in yonder islet lone,
A sainted hermit from his cell,
To drop a bead with every knell!
And bugle, lute, and bell, and all,
Should each bewildered stranger call

To friendly feast and lighted hall.

XVI.

'Blithe were it then to wander here!
But now—beshrew yon nimble deer—
Like that same hermit's, thin and spare,
The copse must give my evening fare;
Some mossy bank my couch must be,
Some rustling oak my canopy.
Yet pass we that; the war and chase
Give little choice of resting-place;—
A summer night in greenwood spent
Were but to-morrow's merriment:
But hosts may in these wilds abound,
Such as are better missed than found;
To meet with Highland plunderers here
Were worse than loss of steed or deer.—
I am alone;—my bugle-strain
May call some straggler of the train;
Or, fall the worst that may betide,
Ere now this falchion has been tried.'

XVII.

But scarce again his horn he wound,
When lo! forth starting at the sound,
From underneath an aged oak
That slanted from the islet rock,
A damsel guider of its way,
A little skiff shot to the bay,
That round the promontory steep
Led its deep line in graceful sweep,
Eddying, in almost viewless wave,
The weeping willow twig to rave,
And kiss, with whispering sound and slow,
The beach of pebbles bright as snow.
The boat had touched this silver strand
Just as the Hunter left his stand,
And stood concealed amid the brake,
To view this Lady of the Lake.
The maiden paused, as if again
She thought to catch the distant strain.
With head upraised, and look intent,
And eye and ear attentive bent,
And locks flung back, and lips apart,

Like monument of Grecian art,
In listening mood, she seemed to stand,
The guardian Naiad of the strand.

XVIII.

And ne'er did Grecian chisel trace
A Nymph, a Naiad, or a Grace,
Of finer form or lovelier face!
What though the sun, with ardent frown,
Had slightly tinged her cheek with brown,—
The sportive toil, which, short and light
Had dyed her glowing hue so bright,
Served too in hastier swell to show
Short glimpses of a breast of snow:
What though no rule of courtly grace
To measured mood had trained her pace,—
A foot more light, a step more true,
Ne'er from the heath-flower dashed the dew;
E'en the slight harebell raised its head,
Elastic from her airy tread:
What though upon her speech there hung
The accents of the mountain tongue,—
Those silver sounds, so soft, so dear,
The listener held his breath to hear!

XIX.

A chieftain's daughter seemed the maid;
Her satin snood, her silken plaid,
Her golden brooch, such birth betrayed.
And seldom was a snood amid
Such wild luxuriant ringlets hid,
Whose glossy black to shame might bring
The plumage of the raven's wing;
And seldom o'er a breast so fair
Mantled a plaid with modest care,
And never brooch the folds combined
Above a heart more good and kind.
Her kindness and her worth to spy,
You need but gaze on Ellen's eye;
Not Katrine in her mirror blue
Gives back the shaggy banks more true,
Than every free-born glance confessed
The guileless movements of her breast;
Whether joy danced in her dark eye,

Or woe or pity claimed a sigh,
Or filial love was glowing there,
Or meek devotion poured a prayer,
Or tale of injury called forth
The indignant spirit of the North.
One only passion unrevealed
With maiden pride the maid concealed,
Yet not less purely felt the flame;—
O, need I tell that passion's name?

XX.

Impatient of the silent horn,
Now on the gale her voice was borne:—
'Father!' she cried; the rocks around
Loved to prolong the gentle sound.
Awhile she paused, no answer came;—
'Malcolm, was thine the blast?' the name
Less resolutely uttered fell,
The echoes could not catch the swell.
'A stranger I,' the Huntsman said,
Advancing from the hazel shade.
The maid, alarmed, with hasty oar
Pushed her light shallop from the shore,
And when a space was gained between,
Closer she drew her bosom's screen;—
So forth the startled swan would swing,
So turn to prune his ruffled wing.
Then safe, though fluttered and amazed,
She paused, and on the stranger gazed.
Not his the form, nor his the eye,
That youthful maidens wont to fly.

XXI.

On his bold visage middle age
Had slightly pressed its signet sage,
Yet had not quenched the open truth
And fiery vehemence of youth;
Forward and frolic glee was there,
The will to do, the soul to dare,
The sparkling glance, soon blown to fire,
Of hasty love or headlong ire.
His limbs were cast in manly could
For hardy sports or contest bold;
And though in peaceful garb arrayed,

And weaponless except his blade,
His stately mien as well implied
A high-born heart, a martial pride,
As if a baron's crest he wore,
And sheathed in armor bode the shore.
Slighting the petty need he showed,
He told of his benighted road;
His ready speech flowed fair and free,
In phrase of gentlest courtesy,
Yet seemed that tone and gesture bland
Less used to sue than to command.

XXII.

Awhile the maid the stranger eyed,
And, reassured, at length replied,
That Highland halls were open still
To wildered wanderers of the hill.
'Nor think you unexpected come
To yon lone isle, our desert home;
Before the heath had lost the dew,
This morn, a couch was pulled for you;
On yonder mountain's purple head
Have ptarmigan and heath-cock bled,
And our broad nets have swept the mere,
To furnish forth your evening cheer.'—
'Now, by the rood, my lovely maid,
Your courtesy has erred,' he said;
'No right have I to claim, misplaced,
The welcome of expected guest.
A wanderer, here by fortune toss,
My way, my friends, my courser lost,
I ne'er before, believe me, fair,
Have ever drawn your mountain air,
Till on this lake's romantic strand
I found a fey in fairy land!'—

XXIII.

'I well believe,' the maid replied,
As her light skiff approached the side,—
'I well believe, that ne'er before
Your foot has trod Loch Katrine's shore
But yet, as far as yesternight,
Old Allan-bane foretold your plight,—
A gray-haired sire, whose eye intent

Was on the visioned future bent.
He saw your steed, a dappled gray,
Lie dead beneath the birchen way;
Painted exact your form and mien,
Your hunting-suit of Lincoln green,
That tasselled horn so gayly gilt,
That falchion's crooked blade and hilt,
That cap with heron plumage trim,
And yon two hounds so dark and grim.
He bade that all should ready be
To grace a guest of fair degree;
But light I held his prophecy,
And deemed it was my father's horn
Whose echoes o'er the lake were borne.'

XXIV.

The stranger smiled:—'Since to your home
A destined errant-knight I come,
Announced by prophet sooth and old,
Doomed, doubtless, for achievement bold,
I 'll lightly front each high emprise
For one kind glance of those bright eyes.
Permit me first the task to guide
Your fairy frigate o'er the tide.'
The maid, with smile suppressed and sly,
The toil unwonted saw him try;
For seldom, sure, if e'er before,
His noble hand had grasped an oar:
Yet with main strength his strokes he drew,
And o'er the lake the shallop flew;
With heads erect and whimpering cry,
The hounds behind their passage ply.
Nor frequent does the bright oar break
The darkening mirror of the lake,
Until the rocky isle they reach,
And moor their shallop on the beach.

XXV.

The stranger viewed the shore around;
'T was all so close with copsewood bound,
Nor track nor pathway might declare
That human foot frequented there,
Until the mountain maiden showed
A clambering unsuspected road,

That winded through the tangled screen,
And opened on a narrow green,
Where weeping birch and willow round
With their long fibres swept the ground.
Here, for retreat in dangerous hour,
Some chief had framed a rustic bower.

XXVI.

It was a lodge of ample size,
But strange of structure and device;
Of such materials as around
The workman's hand had readiest found.
Lopped of their boughs, their hoar trunks bared,
And by the hatchet rudely squared,
To give the walls their destined height,
The sturdy oak and ash unite;
While moss and clay and leaves combined
To fence each crevice from the wind.
The lighter pine-trees overhead
Their slender length for rafters spread,
And withered heath and rushes dry
Supplied a russet canopy.
Due westward, fronting to the green,
A rural portico was seen,
Aloft on native pillars borne,
Of mountain fir with bark unshorn
Where Ellen's hand had taught to twine
The ivy and Idaean vine,
The clematis, the favored flower
Which boasts the name of virgin-bower,
And every hardy plant could bear
Loch Katrine's keen and searching air.
An instant in this porch she stayed,
And gayly to the stranger said:
'On heaven and on thy lady call,
And enter the enchanted hall!'

XXVII.

'My hope, my heaven, my trust must be,
My gentle guide, in following thee!'—
He crossed the threshold,—and a clang
Of angry steel that instant rang.
To his bold brow his spirit rushed,
But soon for vain alarm he blushed

When on the floor he saw displayed,
Cause of the din, a naked blade
Dropped from the sheath, that careless flung
Upon a stag's huge antlers swung;
For all around, the walls to grace,
Hung trophies of the fight or chase:
A target there, a bugle here,
A battle-axe, a hunting-spear,
And broadswords, bows, and arrows store,
With the tusked trophies of the boar.
Here grins the wolf as when he died,
And there the wild-cat's brindled hide
The frontlet of the elk adorns,
Or mantles o'er the bison's horns;
Pennons and flags defaced and stained,
That blackening streaks of blood retained,
And deer-skins, dappled, dun, and white,
With otter's fur and seal's unite,
In rude and uncouth tapestry all,
To garnish forth the sylvan hall.

XXVIII.

The wondering stranger round him gazed,
And next the fallen weapon raised:—
Few were the arms whose sinewy strength
Sufficed to stretch it forth at length.
And as the brand he poised and swayed,
'I never knew but one,' he said,
'Whose stalwart arm might brook to wield
A blade like this in battle-field.'
She sighed, then smiled and took the word:
'You see the guardian champion's sword;
As light it trembles in his hand
As in my grasp a hazel wand:
My sire's tall form might grace the part
Of Ferragus or Ascabart,
But in the absent giant's hold
Are women now, and menials old.'

XXIX.

The mistress of the mansion came,
Mature of age, a graceful dame,
Whose easy step and stately port
Had well become a princely court,

To whom, though more than kindred knew,
Young Ellen gave a mother's due.
Meet welcome to her guest she made,
And every courteous rite was paid
That hospitality could claim,
Though all unasked his birth and name.
Such then the reverence to a guest,
That fellest foe might join the feast,
And from his deadliest foeman's door
Unquestioned turn the banquet o'er
At length his rank the stranger names,
'The Knight of Snowdoun, James Fitz-James;
Lord of a barren heritage,
Which his brave sires, from age to age,
By their good swords had held with toil;
His sire had fallen in such turmoil,
And he, God wot, was forced to stand
Oft for his right with blade in hand.
This morning with Lord Moray's train
He chased a stalwart stag in vain,
Outstripped his comrades, missed the deer,
Lost his good steed, and wandered here.'

XXX.

Fain would the Knight in turn require
The name and state of Ellen's sire.
Well showed the elder lady's mien
That courts and cities she had seen;
Ellen, though more her looks displayed
The simple grace of sylvan maid,
In speech and gesture, form and face,
Showed she was come of gentle race.
'T were strange in ruder rank to find
Such looks, such manners, and such mind.
Each hint the Knight of Snowdoun gave,
Dame Margaret heard with silence grave;
Or Ellen, innocently gay,
Turned all inquiry light away:—
'Weird women we! by dale and down
We dwell, afar from tower and town.
We stem the flood, we ride the blast,
On wandering knights our spells we cast;
While viewless minstrels touch the string,
'Tis thus our charmed rhymes we sing.'
She sung, and still a harp unseen

Filled up the symphony between.

XXXI.

Song.

Soldier, rest! thy warfare o'er,
    Sleep the sleep that knows not breaking;
Dream of battled fields no more,
    Days of danger, nights of waking.
In our isle's enchanted hall,
    Hands unseen thy couch are strewing,
Fairy strains of music fall,
    Every sense in slumber dewing.
Soldier, rest! thy warfare o'er,
Dream of fighting fields no more;
Sleep the sleep that knows not breaking,
Morn of toil, nor night of waking.

'No rude sound shall reach thine ear,
    Armor's clang or war-steed champing
Trump nor pibroch summon here
    Mustering clan or squadron tramping.
Yet the lark's shrill fife may come
    At the daybreak from the fallow,
And the bittern sound his drum
    Booming from the sedgy shallow.
Ruder sounds shall none be near,
Guards nor warders challenge here,
Here's no war-steed's neigh and champing,
Shouting clans or squadrons stamping.'

XXXII.

She paused,—then, blushing, led the lay,
To grace the stranger of the day.
Her mellow notes awhile prolong
The cadence of the flowing song,
Till to her lips in measured frame
The minstrel verse spontaneous came.

Song Continued.

'Huntsman, rest! thy chase is done;
    While our slumbrous spells assail ye,
Dream not, with the rising sun,

Bugles here shall sound reveille.
Sleep! the deer is in his den;
   Sleep! thy hounds are by thee lying;
Sleep! nor dream in yonder glen
How thy gallant steed lay dying.
Huntsman, rest! thy chase is done;
Think not of the rising sun,
For at dawning to assail ye
Here no bugles sound reveille.'

XXXIII.

The hall was cleared,—the stranger's bed,
Was there of mountain heather spread,
Where oft a hundred guests had lain,
And dreamed their forest sports again.
But vainly did the heath-flower shed
Its moorland fragrance round his head;
Not Ellen's spell had lulled to rest
The fever of his troubled breast.
In broken dreams the image rose
Of varied perils, pains, and woes:
His steed now flounders in the brake,
Now sinks his barge upon the lake;
Now leader of a broken host,
His standard falls, his honor's lost.
Then,—from my couch may heavenly might
Chase that worst phantom of the night!—
Again returned the scenes of youth,
Of confident, undoubting truth;
Again his soul he interchanged
With friends whose hearts were long estranged.
They come, in dim procession led,
The cold, the faithless, and the dead;
As warm each hand, each brow as gay,
As if they parted yesterday.
And doubt distracts him at the view,—
O were his senses false or true?
Dreamed he of death or broken vow,
Or is it all a vision now?

XXXIV.

At length, with Ellen in a grove
He seemed to walk and speak of love;
She listened with a blush and sigh,

His suit was warm, his hopes were high.
He sought her yielded hand to clasp,
And a cold gauntlet met his grasp:
The phantom's sex was changed and gone,
Upon its head a helmet shone;
Slowly enlarged to giant size,
With darkened cheek and threatening eyes,
The grisly visage, stern and hoar,
To Ellen still a likeness bore.—
He woke, and, panting with affright,
Recalled the vision of the night.
The hearth's decaying brands were red
And deep and dusky lustre shed,
Half showing, half concealing, all
The uncouth trophies of the hall.
Mid those the stranger fixed his eye
Where that huge falchion hung on high,
And thoughts on thoughts, a countless throng,
Rushed, chasing countless thoughts along,
Until, the giddy whirl to cure,
He rose and sought the moonshine pure.

XXXV.

The wild rose, eglantine, and broom
Wasted around their rich perfume;
The birch-trees wept in fragrant balm;
The aspens slept beneath the calm;
The silver light, with quivering glance,
Played on the water's still expanse,—
Wild were the heart whose passion's sway
Could rage beneath the sober ray!
He felt its calm, that warrior guest,
While thus he communed with his breast:—
'Why is it, at each turn I trace
Some memory of that exiled race?
Can I not mountain maiden spy,
But she must bear the Douglas eye?
Can I not view a Highland brand,
But it must match the Douglas hand?
Can I not frame a fevered dream,
But still the Douglas is the theme?
I'll dream no more,—by manly mind
Not even in sleep is will resigned.
My midnight orisons said o'er,
I'll turn to rest, and dream no more.'

His midnight orisons he told,
A prayer with every bead of gold,
Consigned to heaven his cares and woes,
And sunk in undisturbed repose,
Until the heath-cock shrilly crew,
And morning dawned on Benvenue.

CANTO SECOND. THE ISLAND

I.

At morn the black-cock trims his jetty wing,
    'T is morning prompts the linnet's blithest lay,
All Nature's children feel the matin spring
    Of life reviving, with reviving day;
And while yon little bark glides down the bay,
    Wafting the stranger on his way again,
Morn's genial influence roused a minstrel gray,
    And sweetly o'er the lake was heard thy strain,
Mixed with the sounding harp, O white-haired Allan-bane!

II.

Song.

'Not faster yonder rowers' might
    Flings from their oars the spray,
Not faster yonder rippling bright,
That tracks the shallop's course in light,
    Melts in the lake away,
Than men from memory erase
The benefits of former days;
Then, stranger, go! good speed the while,
Nor think again of the lonely isle.

'High place to thee in royal court,
    High place in battled line,
Good hawk and hound for sylvan sport!
Where beauty sees the brave resort,
    The honored meed be thine!
True be thy sword, thy friend sincere,
Thy lady constant, kind, and dear,
And lost in love's and friendship's smile
Be memory of the lonely isle!

III.

Song Continued.

'But if beneath yon southern sky
    A plaided stranger roam,
Whose drooping crest and stifled sigh,
And sunken cheek and heavy eye,
    Pine for his Highland home;
Then, warrior, then be thine to show
The care that soothes a wanderer's woe;
Remember then thy hap erewhile,
A stranger in the lonely isle.

'Or if on life's uncertain main
    Mishap shall mar thy sail;
If faithful, wise, and brave in vain,
Woe, want, and exile thou sustain
    Beneath the fickle gale;
Waste not a sigh on fortune changed,
On thankless courts, or friends estranged,
But come where kindred worth shall smile,
To greet thee in the lonely isle.'

IV.

As died the sounds upon the tide,
The shallop reached the mainland side,
And ere his onward way he took,
The stranger cast a lingering look,
Where easily his eye might reach
The Harper on the islet beach,
Reclined against a blighted tree,
As wasted, gray, and worn as he.
To minstrel meditation given,
His reverend brow was raised to heaven,
As from the rising sun to claim
A sparkle of inspiring flame.
His hand, reclined upon the wire,
Seemed watching the awakening fire;
So still he sat as those who wait
Till judgment speak the doom of fate;
So still, as if no breeze might dare
To lift one lock of hoary hair;
So still, as life itself were fled
In the last sound his harp had sped.

V.

Upon a rock with lichens wild,
Beside him Ellen sat and smiled.—
Smiled she to see the stately drake
Lead forth his fleet upon the lake,
While her vexed spaniel from the beach
Bayed at the prize beyond his reach?
Yet tell me, then, the maid who knows,
Why deepened on her cheek the rose?—
Forgive, forgive, Fidelity!
Perchance the maiden smiled to see
Yon parting lingerer wave adieu,
And stop and turn to wave anew;
And, lovely ladies, ere your ire
Condemn the heroine of my lyre,
Show me the fair would scorn to spy
And prize such conquest of her eye!

VI.

While yet he loitered on the spot,
It seemed as Ellen marked him not;
But when he turned him to the glade,
One courteous parting sign she made;
And after, oft the knight would say,
That not when prize of festal day
Was dealt him by the brightest fair
Who e'er wore jewel in her hair,
So highly did his bosom swell
As at that simple mute farewell.
Now with a trusty mountain-guide,
And his dark stag-hounds by his side,
He parts,—the maid, unconscious still,
Watched him wind slowly round the hill;
But when his stately form was hid,
The guardian in her bosom chid,—
'Thy Malcolm! vain and selfish maid!'
'T was thus upbraiding conscience said,—
'Not so had Malcolm idly hung
On the smooth phrase of Southern tongue;
Not so had Malcolm strained his eye
Another step than thine to spy.'—
'Wake, Allan-bane,' aloud she cried
To the old minstrel by her side,—
'Arouse thee from thy moody dream!

I 'll give thy harp heroic theme,
And warm thee with a noble name;
Pour forth the glory of the Graeme!'
Scarce from her lip the word had rushed,
When deep the conscious maiden blushed;
For of his clan, in hall and bower,
Young Malcolm Graeme was held the flower.

VII.

The minstrel waked his harp,—three times
Arose the well-known martial chimes,
And thrice their high heroic pride
In melancholy murmurs died.
'Vainly thou bidst, O noble maid,'
Clasping his withered hands, he said,
'Vainly thou bidst me wake the strain,
Though all unwont to bid in vain.
Alas! than mine a mightier hand
Has tuned my harp, my strings has spanned!
I touch the chords of joy, but low
And mournful answer notes of woe;
And the proud march which victors tread
Sinks in the wailing for the dead.
O, well for me, if mine alone
That dirge's deep prophetic tone!
If, as my tuneful fathers said,
This harp, which erst Saint Modan swayed,
Can thus its master's fate foretell,
Then welcome be the minstrel's knell.'

VIII.

'But ah! dear lady, thus it sighed,
The eve thy sainted mother died;
And such the sounds which, while I strove
To wake a lay of war or love,
Came marring all the festal mirth,
Appalling me who gave them birth,
And, disobedient to my call,
Wailed loud through Bothwell's bannered hall.
Ere Douglases, to ruin driven,
Were exiled from their native heaven.—
O! if yet worse mishap and woe
My master's house must undergo,
Or aught but weal to Ellen fair

Brood in these accents of despair,
No future bard, sad Harp! shall fling
Triumph or rapture from thy string;
One short, one final strain shall flow,
Fraught with unutterable woe,
Then shivered shall thy fragments lie,
Thy master cast him down and die!'

IX.

Soothing she answered him: 'Assuage,
Mine honored friend, the fears of age;
All melodies to thee are known
That harp has rung or pipe has blown,
In Lowland vale or Highland glen,
From Tweed to Spey—what marvel, then,
At times unbidden notes should rise,
Confusedly bound in memory's ties,
Entangling, as they rush along,
The war-march with the funeral song?—
Small ground is now for boding fear;
Obscure, but safe, we rest us here.
My sire, in native virtue great,
Resigning lordship, lands, and state,
Not then to fortune more resigned
Than yonder oak might give the wind;
The graceful foliage storms may reeve,
'Fine noble stem they cannot grieve.
For me'—she stooped, and, looking round,
Plucked a blue harebell from the ground,—
'For me, whose memory scarce conveys
An image of more splendid days,
This little flower that loves the lea
May well my simple emblem be;
It drinks heaven's dew as blithe as rose
That in the King's own garden grows;
And when I place it in my hair,
Allan, a bard is bound to swear
He ne'er saw coronet so fair.'
Then playfully the chaplet wild
She wreathed in her dark locks, and smiled.

X.

Her smile, her speech, with winning sway
Wiled the old Harper's mood away.

With such a look as hermits throw,
When angels stoop to soothe their woe
He gazed, till fond regret and pride
Thrilled to a tear, then thus replied:
'Loveliest and best! thou little know'st
The rank, the honors, thou hast lost!
O. might I live to see thee grace,
In Scotland's court, thy birthright place,
To see my favorite's step advance
The lightest in the courtly dance,
The cause of every gallant's sigh,
And leading star of every eye,
And theme of every minstrel's art,
The Lady of the Bleeding Heart!'

XI.

'Fair dreams are these,' the maiden cried,—
Light was her accent, yet she sighed,—
'Yet is this mossy rock to me
Worth splendid chair and canopy;
Nor would my footstep spring more gay
In courtly dance than blithe strathspey,
Nor half so pleased mine ear incline
To royal minstrel's lay as thine.
And then for suitors proud and high,
To bend before my conquering eye,—
Thou, flattering bard! thyself wilt say,
That grim Sir Roderick owns its sway.
The Saxon scourge, Clan-Alpine's pride,
The terror of Loch Lomond's side,
Would, at my suit, thou know'st, delay
A Lennox foray—for a day.'—

XII.

The ancient bard her glee repressed:
'Ill hast thou chosen theme for jest!
For who, through all this western wild,
Named Black Sir Roderick e'er, and smiled?
In Holy-Rood a knight he slew;
I saw, when back the dirk he drew,
Courtiers give place before the stride
Of the undaunted homicide;
And since, though outlawed, hath his hand
Full sternly kept his mountain land.

Who else dared give—ah! woe the day,
That I such hated truth should say!—
The Douglas, like a stricken deer,
Disowned by every noble peer,
Even the rude refuge we have here?
Alas, this wild marauding
Chief Alone might hazard our relief,
And now thy maiden charms expand,
Looks for his guerdon in thy hand;
Full soon may dispensation sought,
To back his suit, from Rome be brought.
Then, though an exile on the hill,
Thy father, as the Douglas, still
Be held in reverence and fear;
And though to Roderick thou'rt so dear
That thou mightst guide with silken thread.
Slave of thy will, this chieftain dread,
Yet, O loved maid, thy mirth refrain!
Thy hand is on a lion's mane.'—

XIII.

Minstrel,' the maid replied, and high
Her father's soul glanced from her eye,
'My debts to Roderick's house I know:
All that a mother could bestow
To Lady Margaret's care I owe,
Since first an orphan in the wild
She sorrowed o'er her sister's child;
To her brave chieftain son, from ire
Of Scotland's king who shrouds my sire,
A deeper, holier debt is owed;
And, could I pay it with my blood, Allan!
Sir Roderick should command
My blood, my life,—but not my hand.
Rather will Ellen Douglas dwell
A votaress in Maronnan's cell;
Rather through realms beyond the sea,
Seeking the world's cold charity
Where ne'er was spoke a Scottish word,
And ne'er the name of Douglas heard
An outcast pilgrim will she rove,
Than wed the man she cannot love.

XIV.

'Thou shak'st, good friend, thy tresses gray,—
That pleading look, what can it say
But what I own?—I grant him brave,
But wild as Bracklinn's thundering wave;
And generous,—save vindictive mood
Or jealous transport chafe his blood:
I grant him true to friendly band,
As his claymore is to his hand;
But O! that very blade of steel
More mercy for a foe would feel:
I grant him liberal, to fling
Among his clan the wealth they bring,
When back by lake and glen they wind,
And in the Lowland leave behind,
Where once some pleasant hamlet stood,
A mass of ashes slaked with blood.
The hand that for my father fought
I honor, as his daughter ought;
But can I clasp it reeking red
From peasants slaughtered in their shed?
No! wildly while his virtues gleam,
They make his passions darker seem,
And flash along his spirit high,
Like lightning o'er the midnight sky.
While yet a child,—and children know,
Instinctive taught, the friend and foe,—
I shuddered at his brow of gloom,
His shadowy plaid and sable plume;
A maiden grown, I ill could bear
His haughty mien and lordly air:
But, if thou join'st a suitor's claim,
In serious mood, to Roderick's name.
I thrill with anguish! or, if e'er
A Douglas knew the word, with fear.
To change such odious theme were best,—
What think'st thou of our stranger guest? '—

XV.

'What think I of him?—woe the while
That brought such wanderer to our isle!
Thy father's battle-brand, of yore
For Tine-man forged by fairy lore,
What time he leagued, no longer foes
His Border spears with Hotspur's bows,
Did, self-unscabbarded, foreshow

The footstep of a secret foe.
If courtly spy hath harbored here,
What may we for the Douglas fear?
What for this island, deemed of old
Clan-Alpine's last and surest hold?
If neither spy nor foe, I pray
What yet may jealous Roderick say?—
Nay, wave not thy disdainful head!
Bethink thee of the discord dread
That kindled when at Beltane game
Thou least the dance with Malcolm Graeme;
Still, though thy sire the peace renewed
Smoulders in Roderick's breast the feud:
Beware!—But hark! what sounds are these?
My dull ears catch no faltering breeze
No weeping birch nor aspens wake,
Nor breath is dimpling in the lake;
Still is the canna's hoary beard,
Yet, by my minstrel faith, I heard—
And hark again! some pipe of war
Sends the hold pibroch from afar.'

XVI.

Far up the lengthened lake were spied
Four darkening specks upon the tide,
That, slow enlarging on the view,
Four manned and massed barges grew,
And, bearing downwards from Glengyle,
Steered full upon the lonely isle;
The point of Brianchoil they passed,
And, to the windward as they cast,
Against the sun they gave to shine
The bold Sir Roderick's bannered Pine.
Nearer and nearer as they bear,
Spears, pikes, and axes flash in air.
Now might you see the tartars brave,
And plaids and plumage dance and wave:
Now see the bonnets sink and rise,
As his tough oar the rower plies;
See, flashing at each sturdy stroke,
The wave ascending into smoke;
See the proud pipers on the bow,
And mark the gaudy streamers flow
From their loud chanters down, and sweep
The furrowed bosom of the deep,

THE LADY OF THE LAKE

As, rushing through the lake amain,
They plied the ancient Highland strain.

XVII.

Ever, as on they bore, more loud
And louder rung the pibroch proud.
At first the sounds, by distance tame,
Mellowed along the waters came,
And, lingering long by cape and bay,
Wailed every harsher note away,
Then bursting bolder on the ear,
The clan's shrill Gathering they could hear,
Those thrilling sounds that call the might
Of old Clan-Alpine to the fight.
Thick beat the rapid notes, as when
The mustering hundreds shake the glen,
And hurrying at the signal dread,
'Fine battered earth returns their tread.
Then prelude light, of livelier tone,
Expressed their merry marching on,
Ere peal of closing battle rose,
With mingled outcry, shrieks, and blows;
And mimic din of stroke and ward,
As broadsword upon target jarred;
And groaning pause, ere yet again,
Condensed, the battle yelled amain:
The rapid charge, the rallying shout,
Retreat borne headlong into rout,
And bursts of triumph, to declare
Clan-Alpine's congest—all were there.
Nor ended thus the strain, but slow
Sunk in a moan prolonged and low,
And changed the conquering clarion swell
For wild lament o'er those that fell.

XVIII.

The war-pipes ceased, but lake and hill
Were busy with their echoes still;
And, when they slept, a vocal strain
Bade their hoarse chorus wake again,
While loud a hundred clansmen raise
Their voices in their Chieftain's praise.
Each boatman, bending to his oar,
With measured sweep the burden bore,

In such wild cadence as the breeze
Makes through December's leafless trees.
The chorus first could Allan know,
'Roderick Vich Alpine, ho! fro!'
And near, and nearer as they rowed,
Distinct the martial ditty flowed.

XIX.

Boat Song

Hail to the Chief who in triumph advances!
    Honored and blessed be the ever-green Pine!
Long may the tree, in his banner that glances,
    Flourish, the shelter and grace of our line!
    Heaven send it happy dew,
    Earth lend it sap anew,
    Gayly to bourgeon and broadly to grow,
    While every Highland glen
    Sends our shout back again,
'Roderigh Vich Alpine dhu, ho! ieroe!'

Ours is no sapling, chance-sown by the fountain,

    Blooming at Beltane, in winter to fade;
When the whirlwind has stripped every leaf on the mountain,
    The more shall Clan-Alpine exult in her shade.
    Moored in the rifted rock,
    Proof to the tempest's shock,
    Firmer he roots him the ruder it blow;
    Menteith and Breadalbane, then,
    Echo his praise again,
'Roderigh Vich Alpine dhu, ho! ieroe!'

XX.

Proudly our pibroch has thrilled in Glen Fruin,
    And Bannochar's groans to our slogan replied;
Glen Luss and Ross-dhu, they are smoking in ruin,
    And the best of Loch Lomond lie dead on her side.
    Widow and Saxon maid
    Long shall lament our raid,
    Think of Clan-Alpine with fear and with woe;
    Lennox and Leven-glen
    Shake when they hear again,
'Roderigh Vich Alpine dhu, ho! ieroe!'

Row, vassals, row, for the pride of the Highlands!
　　Stretch to your oars for the ever-green Pine!
O that the rosebud that graces yon islands
　　Were wreathed in a garland around him to twine!
　　　O that some seedling gem,
　　　Worthy such noble stem,
　　Honored and blessed in their shadow might grow!
　　　Loud should Clan-Alpine then
　　　Ring from her deepmost glen,
　　Roderigh Vich Alpine dhu, ho! ieroe!'

XXI.

With all her joyful female band
Had Lady Margaret sought the strand.
Loose on the breeze their tresses flew,
And high their snowy arms they threw,
As echoing back with shrill acclaim,
And chorus wild, the Chieftain's name;
While, prompt to please, with mother's art
The darling passion of his heart,
The Dame called Ellen to the strand,
To greet her kinsman ere he land:
'Come, loiterer, come! a Douglas thou,
And shun to wreathe a victor's brow?'
Reluctantly and slow, the maid
The unwelcome summoning obeyed,
And when a distant bugle rung,
In the mid-path aside she sprung:—
'List, Allan-bane! From mainland cast
I hear my father's signal blast.
Be ours,' she cried, 'the skiff to guide,
And waft him from the mountain-side.'
Then, like a sunbeam, swift and bright,
She darted to her shallop light,
And, eagerly while Roderick scanned,
For her dear form, his mother's band,
The islet far behind her lay,
And she had landed in the bay.

XXII.

Some feelings are to mortals given
With less of earth in them than heaven;
And if there be a human tear
From passion's dross refined and clear,

A tear so limpid and so meek
It would not stain an angel's cheek,
'Tis that which pious fathers shed
Upon a duteous daughter's head!
And as the Douglas to his breast
His darling Ellen closely pressed,
Such holy drops her tresses steeped,
Though 't was an hero's eye that weeped.
Nor while on Ellen's faltering tongue
Her filial welcomes crowded hung,
Marked she that fear—affection's proof—
Still held a graceful youth aloof;
No! not till Douglas named his name,
Although the youth was Malcolm Graeme.

XXIII.

Allan, with wistful look the while,
Marked Roderick landing on the isle;
His master piteously he eyed,
Then gazed upon the Chieftain's pride,
Then dashed with hasty hand away
From his dimmed eye the gathering spray;
And Douglas, as his hand he laid
On Malcolm's shoulder, kindly said:
'Canst thou, young friend, no meaning spy
In my poor follower's glistening eye?
I'll tell thee:—he recalls the day
When in my praise he led the lay
O'er the arched gate of Bothwell proud,
While many a minstrel answered loud,
When Percy's Norman pennon, won
In bloody field, before me shone,
And twice ten knights, the least a name
As mighty as yon Chief may claim,
Gracing my pomp, behind me came.
Yet trust me, Malcolm, not so proud
Was I of all that marshalled crowd,
Though the waned crescent owned my might,
And in my train trooped lord and knight,
Though Blantyre hymned her holiest lays,
And Bothwell's bards flung back my praise,
As when this old man's silent tear,
And this poor maid's affection dear,
A welcome give more kind and true
Than aught my better fortunes knew.

Forgive, my friend, a father's boast,—
O, it out-beggars all I lost!'

XXIV.

Delightful praise!—like summer rose,
That brighter in the dew-drop glows,
The bashful maiden's cheek appeared,
For Douglas spoke, and Malcolm heard.
The flush of shame-faced joy to hide,
The hounds, the hawk, her cares divide;
The loved caresses of the maid
The dogs with crouch and whimper paid;
And, at her whistle, on her hand
The falcon took his favorite stand,
Closed his dark wing, relaxed his eye,
Nor, though unhooded, sought to fly.
And, trust, while in such guise she stood,
Like fabled Goddess of the wood,
That if a father's partial thought
O'erweighed her worth and beauty aught,
Well might the lover's judgment fail
To balance with a juster scale;
For with each secret glance he stole,
The fond enthusiast sent his soul.

XXV.

Of stature fair, and slender frame,
But firmly knit, was Malcolm Graeme.
The belted plaid and tartan hose
Did ne'er more graceful limbs disclose;
His flaxen hair, of sunny hue,
Curled closely round his bonnet blue.
Trained to the chase, his eagle eye
The ptarmigan in snow could spy;
Each pass, by mountain, lake, and heath,
He knew, through Lennox and Menteith;
Vain was the bound of dark-brown doe
When Malcolm bent his sounding bow,
And scarce that doe, though winged with fear,
Outstripped in speed the mountaineer:
Right up Ben Lomond could he press,
And not a sob his toil confess.
His form accorded with a mind
Lively and ardent, frank and kind;

A blither heart, till Ellen came
Did never love nor sorrow tame;
It danced as lightsome in his breast
As played the feather on his crest.
Yet friends, who nearest knew the youth
His scorn of wrong, his zeal for truth
And bards, who saw his features bold
When kindled by the tales of old
Said, were that youth to manhood grown,
Not long should Roderick Dhu's renown
Be foremost voiced by mountain fame,
But quail to that of Malcolm Graeme.

XXVI.

Now back they wend their watery way,
And, 'O my sire!' did Ellen say,
'Why urge thy chase so far astray?
And why so late returned? And why '—
The rest was in her speaking eye.
'My child, the chase I follow far,
'Tis mimicry of noble war;
And with that gallant pastime reft
Were all of Douglas I have left.
I met young Malcolm as I strayed
Far eastward, in Glenfinlas' shade
Nor strayed I safe, for all around
Hunters and horsemen scoured the ground.
This youth, though still a royal ward,
Risked life and land to be my guard,
And through the passes of the wood
Guided my steps, not unpursued;
And Roderick shall his welcome make,
Despite old spleen, for Douglas' sake.
Then must he seek Strath-Endrick glen
Nor peril aught for me again.'

XXVII.

Sir Roderick, who to meet them came,
Reddened at sight of Malcolm Graeme,
Yet, not in action, word, or eye,
Failed aught in hospitality.
In talk and sport they whiled away
The morning of that summer day;
But at high noon a courier light

Held secret parley with the knight,
Whose moody aspect soon declared
That evil were the news he heard.
Deep thought seemed toiling in his head;
Yet was the evening banquet made
Ere he assembled round the flame
His mother, Douglas, and the Graeme,
And Ellen too; then cast around
His eyes, then fixed them on the ground,
As studying phrase that might avail
Best to convey unpleasant tale.
Long with his dagger's hilt he played,
Then raised his haughty brow, and said:—

XXVIII.

'Short be my speech;—nor time affords,
Nor my plain temper, glozing words.
Kinsman and father,—if such name
Douglas vouchsafe to Roderick's claim;
Mine honored mother;—Ellen,—why,
My cousin, turn away thine eye?—
And Graeme, in whom I hope to know
Full soon a noble friend or foe,
When age shall give thee thy command,
And leading in thy native land,—
List all!—The King's vindictive pride
Boasts to have tamed the Border-side,
Where chiefs, with hound and trawl; who came
To share their monarch's sylvan game,
Themselves in bloody toils were snared,
And when the banquet they prepared,
And wide their loyal portals flung,
O'er their own gateway struggling hung.
Loud cries their blood from Meggat's mead,
From Yarrow braes and banks of Tweed,
Where the lone streams of Ettrick glide,
And from the silver Teviot's side;
The dales, where martial clans did ride,
Are now one sheep-walk, waste and wide.
This tyrant of the Scottish throne,
So faithless and so ruthless known,
Now hither comes; his end the same,
The same pretext of sylvan game.
What grace for Highland Chiefs, judge ye
By fate of Border chivalry.

Yet more; amid Glenfinlas' green,
Douglas, thy stately form was seen.
This by espial sure I know:
Your counsel in the streight I show.'

XXIX.

Ellen and Margaret fearfully
Sought comfort in each other's eye,
Then turned their ghastly look, each one,
This to her sire, that to her son.
The hasty color went and came
In the bold cheek of Malcohm Graeme,
But from his glance it well appeared
'T was but for Ellen that he feared;
While, sorrowful, but undismayed,
The Douglas thus his counsel said:
'Brave Roderick, though the tempest roar,
It may but thunder and pass o'er;
Nor will I here remain an hour,
To draw the lightning on thy bower;
For well thou know'st, at this gray head
The royal bolt were fiercest sped.
For thee, who, at thy King's command,
Canst aid him with a gallant band,
Submission, homage, humbled pride,
Shall turn the Monarch's wrath aside.
Poor remnants of the Bleeding Heart,
Ellen and I will seek apart
The refuge of some forest cell,
There, like the hunted quarry, dwell,
Till on the mountain and the moor
The stern pursuit be passed and o'er,'—

XXX.

'No, by mine honor,' Roderick said,
'So help me Heaven, and my good blade!
No, never! Blasted be yon Pine,
My father's ancient crest and mine,
If from its shade in danger part
The lineage of the Bleeding Heart!
Hear my blunt speech: grant me this maid
To wife, thy counsel to mine aid;
To Douglas, leagued with Roderick Dhu,
Will friends and allies flock enow;

Like cause of doubt, distrust, and grief,
Will bind to us each Western Chief
When the loud pipes my bridal tell,
The Links of Forth shall hear the knell,
The guards shall start in Stirling's porch;
And when I light the nuptial torch,
A thousand villages in flames
Shall scare the slumbers of King James!—
Nay, Ellen, blench not thus away,
And, mother, cease these signs, I pray;
I meant not all my heat might say.—
Small need of inroad or of fight,
When the sage Douglas may unite
Each mountain clan in friendly band,
To guard the passes of their land,
Till the foiled King from pathless glen
Shall bootless turn him home again.'

XXXI.

There are who have, at midnight hour,
In slumber scaled a dizzy tower,
And, on the verge that beetled o'er
The ocean tide's incessant roar,
Dreamed calmly out their dangerous dream,
Till wakened by the morning beam;
When, dazzled by the eastern glow,
Such startler cast his glance below,
And saw unmeasured depth around,
And heard unintermitted sound,
And thought the battled fence so frail,
It waved like cobweb in the gale;
Amid his senses' giddy wheel,
Did he not desperate impulse feel,
Headlong to plunge himself below,
And meet the worst his fears foreshow?—
Thus Ellen, dizzy and astound,
As sudden ruin yawned around,
By crossing terrors wildly tossed,
Still for the Douglas fearing most,
Could scarce the desperate thought withstand,
To buy his safety with her hand.

XXXII.

Such purpose dread could Malcolm spy

In Ellen's quivering lip and eye,
And eager rose to speak,—but ere
His tongue could hurry forth his fear,
Had Douglas marked the hectic strife,
Where death seemed combating with life;
For to her cheek, in feverish flood,
One instant rushed the throbbing blood,
Then ebbing back, with sudden sway,
Left its domain as wan as clay.
'Roderick, enough! enough!' he cried,
'My daughter cannot be thy bride;
Not that the blush to wooer dear,
Nor paleness that of maiden fear.
It may not be,—forgive her,
Chief, Nor hazard aught for our relief.
Against his sovereign, Douglas ne'er
Will level a rebellious spear.
'T was I that taught his youthful hand
To rein a steed and wield a brand;
I see him yet, the princely boy!
Not Ellen more my pride and joy;
I love him still, despite my wrongs
By hasty wrath and slanderous tongues.
O. seek the grace you well may find,
Without a cause to mine combined!'

XXXIII.

Twice through the hall the Chieftain strode;
The waving of his tartars broad,
And darkened brow, where wounded pride
With ire and disappointment vied
Seemed, by the torch's gloomy light,
Like the ill Demon of the night,
Stooping his pinions' shadowy sway
Upon the righted pilgrim's way:
But, unrequited Love! thy dart
Plunged deepest its envenomed smart,
And Roderick, with thine anguish stung,
At length the hand of Douglas wrung,
While eyes that mocked at tears before
With bitter drops were running o'er.
The death-pangs of long-cherished hope
Scarce in that ample breast had scope
But, struggling with his spirit proud,
Convulsive heaved its checkered shroud,

THE LADY OF THE LAKE

While every sob—so mute were all
Was heard distinctly through the ball.
The son's despair, the mother's look,
Ill might the gentle Ellen brook;
She rose, and to her side there came,
To aid her parting steps, the Graeme.

XXXIV.

Then Roderick from the Douglas broke—
As flashes flame through sable smoke,
Kindling its wreaths, long, dark, and low,
To one broad blaze of ruddy glow,
So the deep anguish of despair
Burst, in fierce jealousy, to air.
With stalwart grasp his hand he laid
On Malcolm's breast and belted plaid:
'Back, beardless boy!' he sternly said,
'Back, minion! holdst thou thus at naught
The lesson I so lately taught?
This roof, the Douglas, and that maid,
Thank thou for punishment delayed.'
Eager as greyhound on his game,
Fiercely with Roderick grappled Graeme.
'Perish my name, if aught afford
Its Chieftain safety save his sword!'
Thus as they strove their desperate hand
Griped to the dagger or the brand,
And death had been—but Douglas rose,
And thrust between the struggling foes
His giant strength:—'Chieftains, forego!
I hold the first who strikes my foe.—
Madmen, forbear your frantic jar!
What! is the Douglas fallen so far,
His daughter's hand is deemed the spoil
Of such dishonorable broil?'
Sullen and slowly they unclasp,
As struck with shame, their desperate grasp,
And each upon his rival glared,
With foot advanced and blade half bared.

XXXV.

Ere yet the brands aloft were flung,
Margaret on Roderick's mantle hung,
And Malcolm heard his Ellen's scream,

As faltered through terrific dream.
Then Roderick plunged in sheath his sword,
And veiled his wrath in scornful word:'
Rest safe till morning; pity 't were
Such cheek should feel the midnight air!
Then mayst thou to James Stuart tell,
Roderick will keep the lake and fell,
Nor lackey with his freeborn clan
The pageant pomp of earthly man.
More would he of Clan-Alpine know,
Thou canst our strength and passes show.—
Malise, what ho!'—his henchman came:
'Give our safe-conduct to the Graeme.'
Young Malcolm answered, calm and bold:'
Fear nothing for thy favorite hold;
The spot an angel deigned to grace
Is blessed, though robbers haunt the place.
Thy churlish courtesy for those
Reserve, who fear to be thy foes.
As safe to me the mountain way
At midnight as in blaze of day,
Though with his boldest at his back
Even Roderick Dhu beset the track.—
Brave Douglas,—lovely Ellen,—nay,
Naught here of parting will I say.
Earth does not hold a lonesome glen
So secret but we meet again.—
Chieftain! we too shall find an hour,'—
He said, and left the sylvan bower.

XXXVI.

Old Allan followed to the strand—
Such was the Douglas's command—
And anxious told, how, on the morn,
The stern Sir Roderick deep had sworn,
The Fiery Cross should circle o'er
Dale, glen, and valley, down and moor
Much were the peril to the Graeme
From those who to the signal came;
Far up the lake 't were safest land,
Himself would row him to the strand.
He gave his counsel to the wind,
While Malcolm did, unheeding, bind,
Round dirk and pouch and broadsword rolled,
His ample plaid in tightened fold,

And stripped his limbs to such array
As best might suit the watery way,—

XXXVII.

Then spoke abrupt: 'Farewell to thee,
Pattern of old fidelity!'
The Minstrel's hand he kindly pressed,—
'O, could I point a place of rest!
My sovereign holds in ward my land,
My uncle leads my vassal band;
To tame his foes, his friends to aid,
Poor Malcolm has but heart and blade.
Yet, if there be one faithful Graeme
Who loves the chieftain of his name,
Not long shall honored Douglas dwell
Like hunted stag in mountain cell;
Nor, ere yon pride-swollen robber dare,—
I may not give the rest to air!
Tell Roderick Dhu I owed him naught,
Not tile poor service of a boat,
To waft me to yon mountain-side.'
Then plunged he in the flashing tide.
Bold o'er the flood his head he bore,
And stoutly steered him from the shore;
And Allan strained his anxious eye,
Far mid the lake his form to spy,
Darkening across each puny wave,
To which the moon her silver gave.
Fast as the cormorant could skim.
The swimmer plied each active limb;
Then landing in the moonlight dell,
Loud shouted of his weal to tell.
The Minstrel heard the far halloo,
And joyful from the shore withdrew.

CANTO THIRD. THE GATHERING.

I.

Time rolls his ceaseless course. The race of yore,
    Who danced our infancy upon their knee,
And told our marvelling boyhood legends store
    Of their strange ventures happed by land or sea,
How are they blotted from the things that be!

How few, all weak and withered of their force,
Wait on the verge of dark eternity,
   Like stranded wrecks, the tide returning hoarse,
To sweep them from out sight! Time rolls his ceaseless course.

Yet live there still who can remember well,
   How, when a mountain chief his bugle blew,
Both field and forest, dingle, cliff; and dell,
   And solitary heath, the signal knew;
And fast the faithful clan around him drew.
   What time the warning note was keenly wound,
What time aloft their kindred banner flew,
   While clamorous war-pipes yelled the gathering sound,
And while the Fiery Cross glanced like a meteor, round.

II.

The Summer dawn's reflected hue
To purple changed Loch Katrine blue;
Mildly and soft the western breeze
Just kissed the lake, just stirred the trees,
And the pleased lake, like maiden coy,
Trembled but dimpled not for joy
The mountain-shadows on her breast
Were neither broken nor at rest;
In bright uncertainty they lie,
Like future joys to Fancy's eye.
The water-lily to the light
Her chalice reared of silver bright;
The doe awoke, and to the lawn,
Begemmed with dew-drops, led her fawn;
The gray mist left the mountain-side,
The torrent showed its glistening pride;
Invisible in flecked sky The lark sent clown her revelry:
The blackbird and the speckled thrush
Good-morrow gave from brake and bush;
In answer cooed the cushat dove
Her notes of peace and rest and love.

III.

No thought of peace, no thought of rest,
Assuaged the storm in Roderick's breast.
With sheathed broadsword in his hand,
Abrupt he paced the islet strand,
And eyed the rising sun, and laid

His hand on his impatient blade.
Beneath a rock, his vassals' care
Was prompt the ritual to prepare,
With deep and deathful meaning fraught;
For such Antiquity had taught
Was preface meet, ere yet abroad
The Cross of Fire should take its road.
The shrinking band stood oft aghast
At the impatient glance he cast;—
Such glance the mountain eagle threw,
As, from the cliffs of Benvenue,
She spread her dark sails on the wind,
And, high in middle heaven reclined,
With her broad shadow on the lake,
Silenced the warblers of the brake.

IV.

A heap of withered boughs was piled,
Of juniper and rowan wild,
Mingled with shivers from the oak,
Rent by the lightning's recent stroke.
Brian the Hermit by it stood,
Barefooted, in his frock and hood.
His grizzled beard and matted hair
Obscured a visage of despair;
His naked arms and legs, seamed o'er,
The scars of frantic penance bore.
That monk, of savage form and face
The impending danger of his race
Had drawn from deepest solitude
Far in Benharrow's bosom rude.
Not his the mien of Christian priest,
But Druid's, from the grave released
Whose hardened heart and eye might brook
On human sacrifice to look;
And much, 't was said, of heathen lore
Mixed in the charms he muttered o'er.
The hallowed creed gave only worse
And deadlier emphasis of curse.
No peasant sought that Hermit's prayer
His cave the pilgrim shunned with care,
The eager huntsman knew his bound
And in mid chase called off his hound;'
Or if, in lonely glen or strath,
The desert-dweller met his path

He prayed, and signed the cross between,
While terror took devotion's mien.

V.

Of Brian's birth strange tales were told.
His mother watched a midnight fold,
Built deep within a dreary glen,
Where scattered lay the bones of men
In some forgotten battle slain,
And bleached by drifting wind and rain.
It might have tamed a warrior's heart
To view such mockery of his art!
The knot-grass fettered there the hand
Which once could burst an iron band;
Beneath the broad and ample bone,
That bucklered heart to fear unknown,
A feeble and a timorous guest,
The fieldfare framed her lowly nest;
There the slow blindworm left his slime
On the fleet limbs that mocked at time;
And there, too, lay the leader's skull
Still wreathed with chaplet, flushed and full,
For heath-bell with her purple bloom
Supplied the bonnet and the plume.
All night, in this sad glen the maid
Sat shrouded in her mantle's shade:
She said no shepherd sought her side,
No hunter's hand her snood untied.
Yet ne'er again to braid her hair
The virgin snood did Alive wear;
Gone was her maiden glee and sport,
Her maiden girdle all too short,
Nor sought she, from that fatal night,
Or holy church or blessed rite
But locked her secret in her breast,
And died in travail, unconfessed.

VI.

Alone, among his young compeers,
Was Brian from his infant years;
A moody and heart-broken boy,
Estranged from sympathy and joy
Bearing each taunt which careless tongue
On his mysterious lineage flung.

Whole nights he spent by moonlight pale
To wood and stream his teal, to wail,
Till, frantic, he as truth received
What of his birth the crowd believed,
And sought, in mist and meteor fire,
To meet and know his Phantom Sire!
In vain, to soothe his wayward fate,
The cloister oped her pitying gate;
In vain the learning of the age
Unclasped the sable-lettered page;
Even in its treasures he could find
Food for the fever of his mind.
Eager he read whatever tells
Of magic, cabala, and spells,
And every dark pursuit allied
To curious and presumptuous pride;
Till with fired brain and nerves o'erstrung,
And heart with mystic horrors wrung,
Desperate he sought Benharrow's den,
And hid him from the haunts of men.

VII.

The desert gave him visions wild,
Such as might suit the spectre's child.
Where with black cliffs the torrents toil,
He watched the wheeling eddies boil,
Jill from their foam his dazzled eyes
Beheld the River Demon rise:
The mountain mist took form and limb
Of noontide hag or goblin grim;
The midnight wind came wild and dread,
Swelled with the voices of the dead;
Far on the future battle-heath
His eye beheld the ranks of death:
Thus the lone Seer, from mankind hurled,
Shaped forth a disembodied world.
One lingering sympathy of mind
Still bound him to the mortal kind;
The only parent he could claim
Of ancient Alpine's lineage came.
Late had he heard, in prophet's dream,
The fatal Ben-Shie's boding scream;
Sounds, too, had come in midnight blast
Of charging steeds, careering fast
Along Benharrow's shingly side,

Where mortal horseman ne'er might ride;
The thunderbolt had split the pine,—
All augured ill to Alpine's line.
He girt his loins, and came to show
The signals of impending woe,
And now stood prompt to bless or ban,
As bade the Chieftain of his clan.

VIII.

'T was all prepared;—and from the rock
A goat, the patriarch of the flock,
Before the kindling pile was laid,
And pierced by Roderick's ready blade.
Patient the sickening victim eyed
The life-blood ebb in crimson tide
Down his clogged beard and shaggy limb,
Till darkness glazed his eyeballs dim.
The grisly priest, with murmuring prayer,
A slender crosslet framed with care,
A cubit's length in measure due;
The shaft and limbs were rods of yew,
Whose parents in Inch-Cailliach wave
Their shadows o'er Clan-Alpine's grave,
And, answering Lomond's breezes deep,
Soothe many a chieftain's endless sleep.
The Cross thus formed he held on high,
With wasted hand and haggard eye,
And strange and mingled feelings woke,
While his anathema he spoke:—

IX.

'Woe to the clansman who shall view
This symbol of sepulchral yew,
Forgetful that its branches grew
Where weep the heavens their holiest dew
   On Alpine's dwelling low!
Deserter of his Chieftain's trust,
He ne'er shall mingle with their dust,
But, from his sires and kindred thrust,
Each clansman's execration just
   Shall doom him wrath and woe.'
He paused;—the word the vassals took,
With forward step and fiery look,
On high their naked brands they shook,

Their clattering targets wildly strook;
    And first in murmur low,
Then like the billow in his course,
That far to seaward finds his source,
And flings to shore his mustered force,
Burst with loud roar their answer hoarse,
'Woe to the traitor, woe!'
Ben-an's gray scalp the accents knew,
The joyous wolf from covert drew,
The exulting eagle screamed afar,—
They knew the voice of Alpine's war.

X.

The shout was hushed on lake and fell,
The Monk resumed his muttered spell:
Dismal and low its accents came,
The while he scathed the Cross with flame;
And the few words that reached the air,
Although the holiest name was there,
Had more of blasphemy than prayer.
But when he shook above the crowd
Its kindled points, he spoke aloud:—
'Woe to the wretch who fails to rear
At this dread sign the ready spear!
For, as the flames this symbol sear,
His home, the refuge of his fear,
    A kindred fate shall know;
Far o'er its roof the volumed flame
Clan-Alpine's vengeance shall proclaim,
While maids and matrons on his name
Shall call down wretchedness and shame,
    And infamy and woe.'
Then rose the cry of females, shrill
As goshawk's whistle on the hill,
Denouncing misery and ill,
Mingled with childhood's babbling trill
    Of curses stammered slow;
Answering with imprecation dread,
'Sunk be his home in embers red!
And cursed be the meanest shed
That o'er shall hide the houseless head
    We doom to want and woe!'
A sharp and shrieking echo gave,
Coir-Uriskin, thy goblin cave!
And the gray pass where birches wave

WALTER SCOTT

    On Beala-nam-bo.

XI.

Then deeper paused the priest anew,
And hard his laboring breath he drew,
While, with set teeth and clenched hand,
And eyes that glowed like fiery brand,
He meditated curse more dread,
And deadlier, on the clansman's head
Who, summoned to his chieftain's aid,
The signal saw and disobeyed.
The crosslet's points of sparkling wood
He quenched among the bubbling blood.
And, as again the sign he reared,
Hollow and hoarse his voice was heard:
'When flits this Cross from man to man,
Vich-Alpine's summons to his clan,
Burst be the ear that fails to heed!
Palsied the foot that shuns to speed!
May ravens tear the careless eyes,
Wolves make the coward heart their prize!
As sinks that blood-stream in the earth,
So may his heart's-blood drench his hearth!
As dies in hissing gore the spark,
Quench thou his light, Destruction dark!
And be the grace to him denied,
Bought by this sign to all beside!
He ceased; no echo gave again
The murmur of the deep Amen.

XII.

Then Roderick with impatient look
From Brian's hand the symbol took:
'Speed, Malise, speed' he said, and gave
The crosslet to his henchman brave.
'The muster-place be Lanrick mead—
Instant the time—-speed, Malise, speed!'
Like heath-bird, when the hawks pursue,
A barge across Loch Katrine flew:
High stood the henchman on the prow;
So rapidly the barge-mall row,
The bubbles, where they launched the boat,
Were all unbroken and afloat,
Dancing in foam and ripple still,

THE LADY OF THE LAKE

When it had neared the mainland hill;
And from the silver beach's side
Still was the prow three fathom wide,
When lightly bounded to the land
The messenger of blood and brand.

XIII.

Speed, Malise, speed! the dun deer's hide
On fleeter foot was never tied.
Speed, Malise, speed! such cause of haste
Thine active sinews never braced.
Bend 'gainst the steepy hill thy breast,
Burst down like torrent from its crest;
With short and springing footstep pass
The trembling bog and false morass;
Across the brook like roebuck bound,
And thread the brake like questing hound;
The crag is high, the scaur is deep,
Yet shrink not from the desperate leap:
Parched are thy burning lips and brow,
Yet by the fountain pause not now;
Herald of battle, fate, and fear,
Stretch onward in thy fleet career!
The wounded hind thou track'st not now,
Pursuest not maid through greenwood bough,
Nor priest thou now thy flying pace
With rivals in the mountain race;
But danger, death, and warrior deed
Are in thy course—speed, Malise, speed!

XIV.

Fast as the fatal symbol flies,
In arms the huts and hamlets rise;
From winding glen, from upland brown,
They poured each hardy tenant down.
Nor slacked the messenger his pace;
He showed the sign, he named the place,
And, pressing forward like the wind,
Left clamor and surprise behind.
The fisherman forsook the strand,
The swarthy smith took dirk and brand;
With changed cheer, the mower blithe
Left in the half-cut swath his scythe;
The herds without a keeper strayed,

The plough was in mid-furrow staved,
The falconer tossed his hawk away,
The hunter left the stag at hay;
Prompt at the signal of alarms,
Each son of Alpine rushed to arms;
So swept the tumult and affray
Along the margin of Achray.
Alas, thou lovely lake! that e'er
Thy banks should echo sounds of fear!
The rocks, the bosky thickets, sleep
So stilly on thy bosom deep,
The lark's blithe carol from the cloud
Seems for the scene too gayly loud.

XV.

Speed, Malise, speed! The lake is past,
Duncraggan's huts appear at last,
And peep, like moss-grown rocks, half seen
Half hidden in the copse so green;
There mayst thou rest, thy labor done,
Their lord shall speed the signal on.—
As stoops the hawk upon his prey,
The henchman shot him down the way.
What woful accents load the gale?
The funeral yell, the female wail!
A gallant hunter's sport is o'er,
A valiant warrior fights no more.
Who, in the battle or the chase,
At Roderick's side shall fill his place!—
Within the hall, where torch's ray
Supplies the excluded beams of day,
Lies Duncan on his lowly bier,
And o'er him streams his widow's tear.
His stripling son stands mournful by,
His youngest weeps, but knows not why;
The village maids and matrons round
The dismal coronach resound.

XVI.

Coronach.

He is gone on the mountain,
   He is lost to the forest,
Like a summer-dried fountain,

When our need was the sorest.
The font, reappearing,
    From the rain-drops shall borrow,
But to us comes no cheering,
    To Duncan no morrow!

The hand of the reaper
    Takes the ears that are hoary,
But the voice of the weeper
    Wails manhood in glory.
The autumn winds rushing
    Waft the leaves that are searest,
But our flower was in flushing,
    When blighting was nearest.

Fleet foot on the correi,
    Sage counsel in cumber,
Red hand in the foray,
    How sound is thy slumber!
Like the dew on the mountain,
    Like the foam on the river,
Like the bubble on the fountain,
    Thou art gone, and forever!

XVII.

See Stumah, who, the bier beside
His master's corpse with wonder eyed,
Poor Stumah! whom his least halloo
Could send like lightning o'er the dew,
Bristles his crest, and points his ears,
As if some stranger step he hears.
'T is not a mourner's muffled tread,
Who comes to sorrow o'er the dead,
But headlong haste or deadly fear
Urge the precipitate career.
All stand aghast:—unheeding all,
The henchman bursts into the hall;
Before the dead man's bier he stood,
Held forth the Cross besmeared with blood;
'The muster-place is Lanrick mead;
Speed forth the signal! clansmen, speed!'

XVIII.

Angus, the heir of Duncan's line,

Sprung forth and seized the fatal sign.
In haste the stripling to his side
His father's dirk and broadsword tied;
But when he saw his mother's eye
Watch him in speechless agony,
Back to her opened arms he flew
Pressed on her lips a fond adieu,—
'Alas' she sobbed,—'and yet be gone,
And speed thee forth, like Duncan's son!'
One look he cast upon the bier,
Dashed from his eye the gathering tear,
Breathed deep to clear his laboring breast,
And tossed aloft his bonnet crest,
Then, like the high-bred colt when, freed,
First he essays his fire and speed,
He vanished, and o'er moor and moss
Sped forward with the Fiery Cross.
Suspended was the widow's tear
While yet his footsteps she could hear;
And when she marked the henchman's eye
Wet with unwonted sympathy,
'Kinsman,' she said, 'his race is run
That should have sped thine errand on.
The oak teas fallen?—the sapling bough Is all
Duncraggan's shelter now
Yet trust I well, his duty done,
The orphan's God will guard my son.—
And you, in many a danger true
At Duncan's hest your blades that drew,
To arms, and guard that orphan's head!
Let babes and women wail the dead.'
Then weapon-clang and martial call
Resounded through the funeral hall,
While from the walls the attendant band
Snatched sword and targe with hurried hand;
And short and flitting energy
Glanced from the mourner's sunken eye,
As if the sounds to warrior dear
Might rouse her Duncan from his bier.
But faded soon that borrowed force;
Grief claimed his right, and tears their course.

XIX.

Benledi saw the Cross of Fire,
It glanced like lightning up Strath-Ire.

THE LADY OF THE LAKE

O'er dale and hill the summons flew,
Nor rest nor pause young Angus knew;
The tear that gathered in his eye
He deft the mountain-breeze to dry;
Until, where Teith's young waters roll
Betwixt him and a wooded knoll
That graced the sable strath with green,
The chapel of Saint Bride was seen.
Swoln was the stream, remote the bridge,
But Angus paused not on the edge;
Though the clerk waves danced dizzily,
Though reeled his sympathetic eye,
He dashed amid the torrent's roar:
His right hand high the crosslet bore,
His left the pole-axe grasped, to guide
And stay his footing in the tide.
He stumbled twice,—the foam splashed high,
With hoarser swell the stream raced by;
And had he fallen,—forever there,
Farewell Duncraggan's orphan heir!
But still, as if in parting life,
Firmer he grasped the Cross of strife,
Until the opposing bank he gained,
And up the chapel pathway strained.
A blithesome rout that morning-tide
Had sought the chapel of Saint Bride.
Her troth Tombea's Mary gave
To Norman, heir of Armandave,
And, issuing from the Gothic arch,
The bridal now resumed their march.
In rude but glad procession came
Bonneted sire and coif-clad dame;
And plaided youth, with jest and jeer
Which snooded maiden would not hear:
And children, that, unwitting why,
Lent the gay shout their shrilly cry;
And minstrels, that in measures vied
Before the young and bonny bride,
Whose downcast eye and cheek disclose
The tear and blush of morning rose.
With virgin step and bashful hand
She held the kerchief's snowy band.
The gallant bridegroom by her side
Beheld his prize with victor's pride.
And the glad mother in her ear
Was closely whispering word of cheer.

XXI.

Who meets them at the churchyard gate?
The messenger of fear and fate!
Haste in his hurried accent lies,
And grief is swimming in his eyes.
All dripping from the recent flood,
Panting and travel-soiled he stood,
The fatal sign of fire and sword
Held forth, and spoke the appointed word:
'The muster-place is Lanrick mead;
Speed forth the signal! Norman, speed!'
And must he change so soon the hand
Just linked to his by holy band,
For the fell Cross of blood and brand?
And must the day so blithe that rose,
And promised rapture in the close,
Before its setting hour, divide
The bridegroom from the plighted bride?
O fatal doom'—it must! it must!
Clan-Alpine's cause, her Chieftain's trust,
Her summons dread, brook no delay;
Stretch to the race,—away! away!

XXII.

Yet slow he laid his plaid aside,
And lingering eyed his lovely bride,
Until he saw the starting tear
Speak woe he might not stop to cheer:
Then, trusting not a second look,
In haste he sped hind up the brook,
Nor backward glanced till on the heath
Where Lubnaig's lake supplies the Teith,—
What in the racer's bosom stirred?
The sickening pang of hope deferred,
And memory with a torturing train
Of all his morning visions vain.
Mingled with love's impatience, came
The manly thirst for martial fame;
The stormy joy of mountaineers
Ere yet they rush upon the spears;
And zeal for Clan and Chieftain burning,
And hope, from well-fought field returning,
With war's red honors on his crest,
To clasp his Mary to his breast.

Stung by such thoughts, o'er bank and brae,
Like fire from flint he glanced away,
While high resolve and feeling strong
Burst into voluntary song.

XXIII.

Song.

The heath this night must be my bed,
The bracken curtain for my head,
My lullaby the warder's tread,
    Far, far, from love and thee, Mary;
To-morrow eve, more stilly laid,
My couch may be my bloody plaid,
My vesper song thy wail, sweet maid!
    It will not waken me, Mary!

I may not, dare not, fancy now
The grief that clouds thy lovely brow,
I dare not think upon thy vow,
    And all it promised me, Mary.
No fond regret must Norman know;
When bursts Clan-Alpine on the foe,
His heart must be like bended bow,
    His foot like arrow free, Mary.

A time will come with feeling fraught,
For, if I fall in battle fought,
Thy hapless lover's dying thought
    Shall be a thought on thee, Mary.
And if returned from conquered foes,
How blithely will the evening close,
How sweet the linnet sing repose,
    To my young bride and me, Mary!

XXIV.

Not faster o'er thy heathery braes
Balquidder, speeds the midnight blaze,
Rushing in conflagration strong
Thy deep ravines and dells along,
Wrapping thy cliffs in purple glow,
And reddening the dark lakes below;
Nor faster speeds it, nor so far,
As o'er thy heaths the voice of war.

The signal roused to martial coil
The sullen margin of Loch Voil,
Waked still Loch Doine, and to the source
Alarmed, Balvaig, thy swampy course;
Thence southward turned its rapid road
Adown Strath-Gartney's valley broad
Till rose in arms each man might claim
A portion in Clan-Alpine's name,
From the gray sire, whose trembling hand
Could hardly buckle on his brand,
To the raw boy, whose shaft and bow
Were yet scarce terror to the crow.
Each valley, each sequestered glen,
Mustered its little horde of men
That met as torrents from the height
In Highland dales their streams unite
Still gathering, as they pour along,
A voice more loud, a tide more strong,
Till at the rendezvous they stood
By hundreds prompt for blows and blood,
Each trained to arms since life began,
Owning no tie but to his clan,
No oath but by his chieftain's hand,
No law but Roderick Dhu's command.

XXV.

That summer morn had Roderick Dhu
Surveyed the skirts of Benvenue,
And sent his scouts o'er hill and heath,
To view the frontiers of Menteith.
All backward came with news of truce;
Still lay each martial Graeme and Bruce,
In Rednock courts no horsemen wait,
No banner waved on Cardross gate,
On Duchray's towers no beacon shone,
Nor scared the herons from Loch Con;
All seemed at peace.—Now wot ye wily
The Chieftain with such anxious eye,
Ere to the muster he repair,
This western frontier scanned with care?—
In Benvenue's most darksome cleft,
A fair though cruel pledge was left;
For Douglas, to his promise true,
That morning from the isle withdrew,
And in a deep sequestered dell

Had sought a low and lonely cell.
By many a bard in Celtic tongue
Has Coir-nan-Uriskin been sung
A softer name the Saxons gave,
And called the grot the Goblin Cave.

XXVI.

It was a wild and strange retreat,
As e'er was trod by outlaw's feet.
The dell, upon the mountain's crest,
Yawned like a gash on warrior's breast;
Its trench had stayed full many a rock,
Hurled by primeval earthquake shock
From Benvenue's gray summit wild,
And here, in random ruin piled,
They frowned incumbent o'er the spot
And formed the rugged sylvan 'rot.
The oak and birch with mingled shade
At noontide there a twilight made,
Unless when short and sudden shone
Some straggling beam on cliff or stone,
With such a glimpse as prophet's eye
Gains on thy depth, Futurity.
No murmur waked the solemn still,
Save tinkling of a fountain rill;
But when the wind chafed with the lake,
A sullen sound would upward break,
With dashing hollow voice, that spoke
The incessant war of wave and rock.
Suspended cliffs with hideous sway
Seemed nodding o'er the cavern gray.
From such a den the wolf had sprung,
In such the wild-cat leaves her young;
Yet Douglas and his daughter fair
Sought for a space their safety there.
Gray Superstition's whisper dread
Debarred the spot to vulgar tread;
For there, she said, did fays resort,
And satyrs hold their sylvan court,
By moonlight tread their mystic maze,
And blast the rash beholder's gaze.

XXVII.

Now eve, with western shadows long,

Floated on Katrine bright and strong,
When Roderick with a chosen few
Repassed the heights of Benvenue.
Above the Goblin Cave they go,
Through the wild pass of Beal-nam-bo;
The prompt retainers speed before,
To launch the shallop from the shore,
For 'cross Loch Katrine lies his way
To view the passes of Achray,
And place his clansmen in array.
Yet lags the Chief in musing mind,
Unwonted sight, his men behind.
A single page, to bear his sword,
Alone attended on his lord;
The rest their way through thickets break,
And soon await him by the lake.
It was a fair and gallant sight
To view them from the neighboring height,
By the low-levelled sunbeam's light!
For strength and stature, from the clan
Each warrior was a chosen man,
As even afar might well be seen,
By their proud step and martial mien.
Their feathers dance, their tartars float,
Their targets gleam, as by the boat
A wild and warlike group they stand,
That well became such mountain-strand.

XXVIII.

Their Chief with step reluctant still
Was lingering on the craggy hill,
Hard by where turned apart the road
To Douglas's obscure abode.
It was but with that dawning morn
That Roderick Dhu had proudly sworn
To drown his love in war's wild roar,
Nor think of Ellen Douglas more;
But he who stems a stream with sand,
And fetters flame with flaxen band,
Has yet a harder task to prove,—
By firm resolve to conquer love!
Eve finds the Chief, like restless ghost,
Still hovering near his treasure lost;
For though his haughty heart deny
A parting meeting to his eye

Still fondly strains his anxious ear
The accents of her voice to hear,
And inly did he curse the breeze
That waked to sound the rustling trees.
But hark! what mingles in the strain?
It is the harp of Allan-bane,
That wakes its measure slow and high,
Attuned to sacred minstrelsy.
What melting voice attends the strings?
'Tis Ellen, or an angel, sings.

XXIX.

Hymn to the Virgin.

Ave. Maria! maiden mild!
   Listen to a maiden's prayer!
Thou canst hear though from the wild,
   Thou canst save amid despair.
Safe may we sleep beneath thy care,
   Though banished, outcast, and reviled—
Maiden! hear a maiden's prayer;
   Mother, hear a suppliant child!
     Ave Maria!

Ave Maria! undefiled!
   The flinty couch we now must share
Shall seem with down of eider piled,
   If thy protection hover there.
The murky cavern's heavy air
   Shall breathe of balm if thou hast smiled;
Then, Maiden! hear a maiden's prayer,
   Mother, list a suppliant child!
     Ave Maria!

Ave. Maria! stainless styled!
   Foul demons of the earth and air,
From this their wonted haunt exiled,
   Shall flee before thy presence fair.
We bow us to our lot of care,
   Beneath thy guidance reconciled:
Hear for a maid a maiden's prayer,
   And for a father hear a child!
     Ave Maria!

XXX.

Died on the harp the closing hymn,—
Unmoved in attitude and limb,
As listening still, Clan-Alpine's lord
Stood leaning on his heavy sword,
Until the page with humble sign
Twice pointed to the sun's decline.
Then while his plaid he round him cast,
'It is the last time— 'tis the last,'
He muttered thrice,—'the last time e'er
That angel-voice shall Roderick hear''
It was a goading thought,—his stride
Hied hastier down the mountain-side;
Sullen he flung him in the boat
An instant 'cross the lake it shot.
They landed in that silvery bay,
And eastward held their hasty way
Till, with the latest beams of light,
The band arrived on Lanrick height'
Where mustered in the vale below
Clan-Alpine's men in martial show.

XXXI.

A various scene the clansmen made:
Some sat, some stood, some slowly strayed:
But most, with mantles folded round,
Were couched to rest upon the ground,
Scarce to be known by curious eye
From the deep heather where they lie,
So well was matched the tartan screen
With heath-bell dark and brackens green;
Unless where, here and there, a blade
Or lance's point a glimmer made,
Like glow-worm twinkling through the shade.
But when, advancing through the gloom,
They saw the Chieftain's eagle plume,
Their shout of welcome, shrill and wide,
Shook the steep mountain's steady side.
Thrice it arose, and lake and fell
Three times returned the martial yell;
It died upon Bochastle's plain,
And Silence claimed her evening reign.

CANTO FOURTH. THE PROPHECY.

I.

The rose is fairest when 't is budding new,
And hope is brightest when it dawns from fears;
The rose is sweetest washed with morning dew
And love is loveliest when embalmed in tears.
O wilding rose, whom fancy thus endears,
I bid your blossoms in my bonnet wave,
Emblem of hope and love through future years!'
Thus spoke young Norman, heir of Armandave,
What time the sun arose on Vennachar's broad wave.

II.

Such fond conceit, half said, half sung,
Love prompted to the bridegroom's tongue.
All while he stripped the wild-rose spray,
His axe and bow beside him lay,
For on a pass 'twixt lake and wood
A wakeful sentinel he stood.
Hark!—on the rock a footstep rung,
And instant to his arms he sprung.
'Stand, or thou diest!—What, Malise?—soon
Art thou returned from Braes of Doune.
By thy keen step and glance I know,
Thou bring'st us tidings of the foe.'—
For while the Fiery Cross tried on,
On distant scout had Malise gone.—
'Where sleeps the Chief?' the henchman said.
'Apart, in yonder misty glade;
To his lone couch I'll be your guide.'—
Then called a slumberer by his side,
And stirred him with his slackened bow,—
'Up, up, Glentarkin! rouse thee, ho!
We seek the Chieftain; on the track
Keep eagle watch till I come back.'

III.

Together up the pass they sped:
'What of the foeman?' Norman said.—
'Varying reports from near and far;
This certain,—that a band of war

Has for two days been ready boune,
At prompt command to march from Doune;
King James the while, with princely powers,
Holds revelry in Stirling towers.
Soon will this dark and gathering cloud
Speak on our glens in thunder loud.
Inured to bide such bitter bout,
The warrior's plaid may bear it out;
But, Norman, how wilt thou provide
A shelter for thy bonny bride?"—
'What! know ye not that Roderick's care
To the lone isle hath caused repair
Each maid and matron of the clan,
And every child and aged man
Unfit for arms; and given his charge,
Nor skiff nor shallop, boat nor barge,
Upon these lakes shall float at large,
But all beside the islet moor,
That such dear pledge may rest secure?'—

IV.

"T is well advised,—the Chieftain's plan
Bespeaks the father of his clan.
But wherefore sleeps Sir Roderick Dhu
Apart from all his followers true?'
'It is because last evening-tide
Brian an augury hath tried,
Of that dread kind which must not be
Unless in dread extremity,
The Taghairm called; by which, afar,
Our sires foresaw the events of war.
Duncraggan's milk-white bull they slew,'—

Malise.

'Ah! well the gallant brute I knew!
The choicest of the prey we had
When swept our merrymen Gallangad.
His hide was snow, his horns were dark,
His red eye glowed like fiery spark;
So fierce, so tameless, and so fleet,
Sore did he cumber our retreat,
And kept our stoutest kerns in awe,
Even at the pass of Beal 'maha.
But steep and flinty was the road,

And sharp the hurrying pikeman's goad,
And when we came to Dennan's Row
A child might scathless stroke his brow.'

V.

Norman.

'That bull was slain; his reeking hide
They stretched the cataract beside,
Whose waters their wild tumult toss
Adown the black and craggy boss
Of that huge cliff whose ample verge
Tradition calls the Hero's Targe.
Couched on a shelf beneath its brink,
Close where the thundering torrents sink,
Rocking beneath their headlong sway,
And drizzled by the ceaseless spray,
Midst groan of rock and roar of stream,
The wizard waits prophetic dream.
Nor distant rests the Chief;—but hush!
See, gliding slow through mist and bush,
The hermit gains yon rock, and stands
To gaze upon our slumbering bands.
Seems he not, Malise, dike a ghost,
That hovers o'er a slaughtered host?
Or raven on the blasted oak,
That, watching while the deer is broke,
His morsel claims with sullen croak?'

Malise.

'Peace! peace! to other than to me
Thy words were evil augury;
But still I hold Sir Roderick's blade
Clan-Alpine's omen and her aid,
Not aught that, gleaned from heaven or hell,
Yon fiend-begotten Monk can tell.
The Chieftain joins him, see—and now
Together they descend the brow.'

VI.

And, as they came, with Alpine's Lord
The Hermit Monk held solemn word:—.
'Roderick! it is a fearful strife,

For man endowed with mortal life
Whose shroud of sentient clay can still
Feel feverish pang and fainting chill,
Whose eye can stare in stony trance
Whose hair can rouse like warrior's lance,
'Tis hard for such to view, unfurled,
The curtain of the future world.
Yet, witness every quaking limb,
My sunken pulse, mine eyeballs dim,
My soul with harrowing anguish torn,
This for my Chieftain have I borne!—
The shapes that sought my fearful couch
A human tongue may ne'er avouch;
No mortal man—save he, who, bred
Between the living and the dead,
Is gifted beyond nature's law
Had e'er survived to say he saw.
At length the fateful answer came
In characters of living flame!
Not spoke in word, nor blazed in scroll,
But borne and branded on my soul:—
WHICH SPILLS THE FOREMOST FOEMAN'S LIFE,
THAT PARTY CONQUERS IN THE STRIFE.'

VII.

'Thanks, Brian, for thy zeal and care!
Good is thine augury, and fair.
Clan-Alpine ne'er in battle stood
But first our broadswords tasted blood.
A surer victim still I know,
Self-offered to the auspicious blow:
A spy has sought my land this morn,—
No eve shall witness his return!
My followers guard each pass's mouth,
To east, to westward, and to south;
Red Murdoch, bribed to be his guide,
Has charge to lead his steps aside,
Till in deep path or dingle brown
He light on those shall bring him clown.
But see, who comes his news to show!
Malise! what tidings of the foe?'

VIII.

'At Doune, o'er many a spear and glaive

THE LADY OF THE LAKE

Two Barons proud their banners wave.
I saw the Moray's silver star,
And marked the sable pale of Mar.'
'By Alpine's soul, high tidings those!
I love to hear of worthy foes.
When move they on?' 'To-morrow's noon
Will see them here for battle boune.'
'Then shall it see a meeting stern!
But, for the place,—say, couldst thou learn
Nought of the friendly clans of Earn?
Strengthened by them, we well might bide
The battle on Benledi's side.
Thou couldst not?—well! Clan-Alpine's men
Shall man the Trosachs' shaggy glen;
Within Loch Katrine's gorge we'll fight,
All in our maids' and matrons' sight,
Each for his hearth and household fire,
Father for child, and son for sire Lover
for maid beloved!—But why
Is it the breeze affects mine eye?
Or dost thou come, ill-omened tear!
A messenger of doubt or fear?
No! sooner may the Saxon lance
Unfix Benledi from his stance,
Than doubt or terror can pierce through
The unyielding heart of Roderick Dhu!
'tis stubborn as his trusty targe.
Each to his post!—all know their charge.'
The pibroch sounds, the bands advance,
The broadswords gleam, the banners dance'
Obedient to the Chieftain's glance.—
I turn me from the martial roar
And seek Coir-Uriskin once more.

IX.

Where is the Douglas?—he is gone;
And Ellen sits on the gray stone
Fast by the cave, and makes her moan,
While vainly Allan's words of cheer
Are poured on her unheeding ear.
'He will return—dear lady, trust!—
With joy return;—he will—he must.
Well was it time to seek afar
Some refuge from impending war,
When e'en Clan-Alpine's rugged swarm

Are cowed by the approaching storm.
I saw their boats with many a light,
Floating the livelong yesternight,
Shifting like flashes darted forth
By the red streamers of the north;
I marked at morn how close they ride,
Thick moored by the lone islet's side,
Like wild ducks couching in the fen
When stoops the hawk upon the glen.
Since this rude race dare not abide
The peril on the mainland side,
Shall not thy noble father's care
Some safe retreat for thee prepare?'

X.

Ellen.

'No, Allan, no' Pretext so kind
My wakeful terrors could not blind.
When in such tender tone, yet grave,
Douglas a parting blessing gave,
The tear that glistened in his eye
Drowned not his purpose fixed and high.
My soul, though feminine and weak,
Can image his; e'en as the lake,
Itself disturbed by slightest stroke.
Reflects the invulnerable rock.
He hears report of battle rife,
He deems himself the cause of strife.
I saw him redden when the theme
Turned, Allan, on thine idle dream
Of Malcolm Graeme in fetters bound,
Which I, thou saidst, about him wound.
Think'st thou he bowed thine omen aught?
O no' 't was apprehensive thought
For the kind youth,—for Roderick too—
Let me be just—that friend so true;
In danger both, and in our cause!
Minstrel, the Douglas dare not pause.
Why else that solemn warning given,
'If not on earth, we meet in heaven!'
Why else, to Cambus-kenneth's fane,
If eve return him not again,
Am I to hie and make me known?
Alas! he goes to Scotland's throne,

THE LADY OF THE LAKE

Buys his friends' safety with his own;
He goes to do—what I had done,
Had Douglas' daughter been his son!'

XI.

'Nay, lovely Ellen!—dearest, nay!
If aught should his return delay,
He only named yon holy fane
As fitting place to meet again.
Be sure he's safe; and for the Graeme,—
Heaven's blessing on his gallant name!—
My visioned sight may yet prove true,
Nor bode of ill to him or you.
When did my gifted dream beguile?
Think of the stranger at the isle,
And think upon the harpings slow
That presaged this approaching woe!
Sooth was my prophecy of fear;
Believe it when it augurs cheer.
Would we had left this dismal spot!
Ill luck still haunts a fairy spot!
Of such a wondrous tale I know—
Dear lady, change that look of woe,
My harp was wont thy grief to cheer.'

Ellen.

'Well, be it as thou wilt;
I hear, But cannot stop the bursting tear.'
The Minstrel tried his simple art,
Rut distant far was Ellen's heart.

XII.

Ballad.

Alice Brand.

Merry it is in the good greenwood,
   When the mavis and merle are singing,
When the deer sweeps by, and the hounds are in cry,
   And the hunter's horn is ringing.

'O Alice Brand, my native land
   Is lost for love of you;

And we must hold by wood and word,
    As outlaws wont to do.

'O Alice, 't was all for thy locks so bright,
    And 't was all for thine eyes so blue,
That on the night of our luckless flight
    Thy brother bold I slew.

'Now must I teach to hew the beech
    The hand that held the glaive,
For leaves to spread our lowly bed,
    And stakes to fence our cave.

'And for vest of pall, thy fingers small,
    That wont on harp to stray,
A cloak must shear from the slaughtered deer,
    To keep the cold away.'

'O Richard! if my brother died,
    'T was but a fatal chance;
For darkling was the battle tried,
    And fortune sped the lance.

'If pall and vair no more I wear,
    Nor thou the crimson sheen
As warm, we'll say, is the russet gray,
    As gay the forest-green.

'And, Richard, if our lot be hard,
    And lost thy native land,
Still Alice has her own Richard,
    And he his Alice Brand.'

XIII.

Ballad Continued.

'tis merry, 'tis merry, in good greenwood;
    So blithe Lady Alice is singing;
On the beech's pride, and oak's brown side,
    Lord Richard's axe is ringing.

Up spoke the moody Elfin King,
    Who woned within the hill,—
Like wind in the porch of a ruined church,
    His voice was ghostly shrill.

THE LADY OF THE LAKE

'Why sounds yon stroke on beech and oak,
    Our moonlight circle's screen?
Or who comes here to chase the deer,
    Beloved of our Elfin Queen?
Or who may dare on wold to wear
    The fairies' fatal green?

'Up, Urgan, up! to yon mortal hie,
    For thou wert christened man;
For cross or sign thou wilt not fly,
    For muttered word or ban.

'Lay on him the curse of the withered heart,
    The curse of the sleepless eye;
Till he wish and pray that his life would part,
    Nor yet find leave to die.'

XIV.

Ballad Continued.

'Tis merry, 'tis merry, in good greenwood,
    Though the birds have stilled their singing;
The evening blaze cloth Alice raise,
    And Richard is fagots bringing.

Up Urgan starts, that hideous dwarf,
    Before Lord Richard stands,
And, as he crossed and blessed himself,
    'I fear not sign,' quoth the grisly elf,
    'That is made with bloody hands.'

But out then spoke she, Alice Brand,
    That woman void of fear,—
'And if there's blood upon his hand,
    'Tis but the blood of deer.'

'Now loud thou liest, thou bold of mood!
    It cleaves unto his hand,
The stain of thine own kindly blood,
    The blood of Ethert Brand.'

Then forward stepped she, Alice Brand,
    And made the holy sign,—
'And if there's blood on Richard's hand,
    A spotless hand is mine.

'And I conjure thee, demon elf,
  By Him whom demons fear,
To show us whence thou art thyself,
  And what thine errand here?'

XV.

Ballad Continued.

"Tis merry, 'tis merry, in Fairy-land,
  When fairy birds are singing,
When the court cloth ride by their monarch's side,
  With bit and bridle ringing:

'And gayly shines the Fairy-land—
  But all is glistening show,
Like the idle gleam that December's beam
  Can dart on ice and snow.

'And fading, like that varied gleam,
  Is our inconstant shape,
Who now like knight and lady seem,
  And now like dwarf and ape.

'It was between the night and day,
  When the Fairy King has power,
That I sunk down in a sinful fray,
And 'twixt life and death was snatched away
  To the joyless Elfin bower.

'But wist I of a woman bold,
  Who thrice my brow durst sign,
I might regain my mortal mould,
  As fair a form as thine.'

She crossed him once—she crossed him twice—
  That lady was so brave;
The fouler grew his goblin hue,
  The darker grew the cave.

She crossed him thrice, that lady bold;
  He rose beneath her hand
The fairest knight on Scottish mould,
  Her brother, Ethert Brand!

Merry it is in good greenwood,

    When the mavis and merle are singing,
But merrier were they in Dunfermline gray,
    When all the bells were ringing.
XVI.

Just as the minstrel sounds were stayed,
A stranger climbed the steepy glade;
His martial step, his stately mien,
His hunting-suit of Lincoln green,
His eagle glance, remembrance claims—
'Tis Snowdoun's Knight, 'tis James Fitz-James.
Ellen beheld as in a dream,
Then, starting, scarce suppressed a scream:
'O stranger! in such hour of fear
What evil hap has brought thee here?'
'An evil hap how can it be
That bids me look again on thee?
By promise bound, my former guide
Met me betimes this morning-tide,
And marshalled over bank and bourne
The happy path of my return.'
'The happy path!—what! said he naught
Of war, of battle to be fought,
Of guarded pass?' 'No, by my faith!
Nor saw I aught could augur scathe.'
'O haste thee, Allan, to the kern:
Yonder his tartars I discern;
Learn thou his purpose, and conjure
That he will guide the stranger sure!—
What prompted thee, unhappy man?
The meanest serf in Roderick's clan
Had not been bribed, by love or fear,
Unknown to him to guide thee here.'
XVII.

'Sweet Ellen, dear my life must be,
Since it is worthy care from thee;
Yet life I hold but idle breath
When love or honor's weighed with death.
Then let me profit by my chance,
And speak my purpose bold at once.
I come to bear thee from a wild
Where ne'er before such blossom smiled,
By this soft hand to lead thee far
From frantic scenes of feud and war.
Near Bochastle my horses wait;

They bear us soon to Stirling gate.
I'll place thee in a lovely bower,
I'll guard thee like a tender flower—'
'O hush, Sir Knight! 't were female art,
To say I do not read thy heart;
Too much, before, my selfish ear
Was idly soothed my praise to hear.
That fatal bait hath lured thee back,
In deathful hour, o'er dangerous track;
And how, O how, can I atone
The wreck my vanity brought on!—
One way remains—I'll tell him all—
Yes! struggling bosom, forth it shall!
Thou, whose light folly bears the blame,
Buy thine own pardon with thy shame!
But first—my father is a man
Outlawed and exiled, under ban;
The price of blood is on his head,
With me 't were infamy to wed.
Still wouldst thou speak?—then hear the truth!
Fitz-James, there is a noble youth—
If yet he is!—exposed for me
And mine to dread extremity—
Thou hast the secret of my bears;
Forgive, be generous, and depart!'
XVIII.

Fitz-James knew every wily train
A lady's fickle heart to gain,
But here he knew and felt them vain.
There shot no glance from Ellen's eye,
To give her steadfast speech the lie;
In maiden confidence she stood,
Though mantled in her cheek the blood
And told her love with such a sigh
Of deep and hopeless agony,
As death had sealed her Malcolm's doom
And she sat sorrowing on his tomb.
Hope vanished from Fitz-James's eye,
But not with hope fled sympathy.
He proffered to attend her side,
As brother would a sister guide.
'O little know'st thou Roderick's heart!
Safer for both we go apart.
O haste thee, and from Allan learn
If thou mayst trust yon wily kern.'

With hand upon his forehead laid,
The conflict of his mind to shade,
A parting step or two he made;
Then, as some thought had crossed his brain
He paused, and turned, and came again.
XIX.

'Hear, lady, yet a parting word!—
It chanced in fight that my poor sword
Preserved the life of Scotland's lord.
This ring the grateful Monarch gave,
And bade, when I had boon to crave,
To bring it back, and boldly claim
The recompense that I would name.
Ellen, I am no courtly lord,
But one who lives by lance and sword,
Whose castle is his helm and shield,
His lordship the embattled field.
What from a prince can I demand,
Who neither reck of state nor land?
Ellen, thy hand—the ring is thine;
Each guard and usher knows the sign.
Seek thou the King without delay;
This signet shall secure thy way:
And claim thy suit, whate'er it be,
As ransom of his pledge to me.'
He placed the golden circlet on,
Paused—kissed her hand—and then was gone.
The aged Minstrel stood aghast,
So hastily Fitz-James shot past.
He joined his guide, and wending down
The ridges of the mountain brown,
Across the stream they took their way
That joins Loch Katrine to Achray.

XX

All in the Trosachs' glen was still,
Noontide was sleeping on the hill:
Sudden his guide whooped loud and high—
'Murdoch! was that a signal cry?'—
He stammered forth, 'I shout to scare
Yon raven from his dainty fare.'
He looked—he knew the raven's prey,
His own brave steed: 'Ah! gallant gray!
For thee—for me, perchance—'t were well

We ne'er had seen the Trosachs' dell.—
Murdoch, move first—but silently;
Whistle or whoop, and thou shalt die!'
Jealous and sullen on they fared,
Each silent, each upon his guard.

XXI.

Now wound the path its dizzy ledge
Around a precipice's edge,
When lo! a wasted female form,
Blighted by wrath of sun and storm,
In tattered weeds and wild array,
Stood on a cliff beside the way,
And glancing round her restless eye,
Upon the wood, the rock, the sky,
Seemed naught to mark, yet all to spy.
Her brow was wreathed with gaudy broom;
With gesture wild she waved a plume
Of feathers, which the eagles fling
To crag and cliff from dusky wing;
Such spoils her desperate step had sought,
Where scarce was footing for the goat.
The tartan plaid she first descried,
And shrieked till all the rocks replied;
As loud she laughed when near they drew,
For then the Lowland garb she knew;
And then her hands she wildly wrung,
And then she wept, and then she sung—
She sung!—the voice, in better time,
Perchance to harp or lute might chime;
And now, though strained and roughened, still
Rung wildly sweet to dale and hill.

XXII.

Song.

They bid me sleep, they bid me pray,
    They say my brain is warped and wrung—
I cannot sleep on Highland brae,
    I cannot pray in Highland tongue.
But were I now where Allan glides,
Or heard my native Devan's tides,
So sweetly would I rest, and pray
That Heaven would close my wintry day!

THE LADY OF THE LAKE

'Twas thus my hair they bade me braid,
   They made me to the church repair;
It was my bridal morn they said,
   And my true love would meet me there.
But woe betide the cruel guile
That drowned in blood the morning smile!
And woe betide the fairy dream!
I only waked to sob and scream.

XXIII.

'Who is this maid? what means her lay?
She hovers o'er the hollow way,
And flutters wide her mantle gray,
As the lone heron spreads his wing,
By twilight, o'er a haunted spring.'
"Tis Blanche of Devan,' Murdoch said,
'A crazed and captive Lowland maid,
Ta'en on the morn she was a bride,
When Roderick forayed Devan-side.
The gay bridegroom resistance made,
And felt our Chief's unconquered blade.
I marvel she is now at large,
But oft she 'scapes from Maudlin's charge.—
Hence, brain-sick fool!'—He raised his bow:—
'Now, if thou strik'st her but one blow,
I'll pitch thee from the cliff as far
As ever peasant pitched a bar!'
'Thanks, champion, thanks' the Maniac cried,
And pressed her to Fitz-James's side.
'See the gray pennons I prepare,
To seek my true love through the air!
I will not lend that savage groom,
To break his fall, one downy plume!
No!—deep amid disjointed stones,
The wolves shall batten on his bones,
And then shall his detested plaid,
By bush and brier in mid-air stayed,
Wave forth a banner fail and free,
Meet signal for their revelry.'

XXIV

'Hush thee, poor maiden, and be still!'
'O! thou look'st kindly, and I will.
Mine eye has dried and wasted been,

But still it loves the Lincoln green;
And, though mine ear is all unstrung,
Still, still it loves the Lowland tongue.

'For O my sweet William was forester true,
    He stole poor Blanche's heart away!
His coat it was all of the greenwood hue,
    And so blithely he trilled the Lowland lay!

'It was not that I meant to tell...
But thou art wise and guessest well.'
Then, in a low and broken tone,
And hurried note, the song went on.
Still on the Clansman fearfully
She fixed her apprehensive eye,
Then turned it on the Knight, and then
Her look glanced wildly o'er the glen.

XXV.

'The toils are pitched, and the stakes are set,—
    Ever sing merrily, merrily;
The bows they bend, and the knives they whet,
    Hunters live so cheerily.

It was a stag, a stag of ten,
    Bearing its branches sturdily;
He came stately down the glen,—
    Ever sing hardily, hardily.

'It was there he met with a wounded doe,
    She was bleeding deathfully;
She warned him of the toils below,
    O. so faithfully, faithfully!

'He had an eye, and he could heed,—
    Ever sing warily, warily;
He had a foot, and he could speed,—
    Hunters watch so narrowly.'

XXVI.

Fitz-James's mind was passion-tossed,
When Ellen's hints and fears were lost;
But Murdoch's shout suspicion wrought,
And Blanche's song conviction brought.

THE LADY OF THE LAKE

Not like a stag that spies the snare,
But lion of the hunt aware,
He waved at once his blade on high,
'Disclose thy treachery, or die!'
Forth at hell speed the Clansman flew,
But in his race his bow he drew.
The shaft just grazed Fitz-James's crest,
And thrilled in Blanche's faded breast.—
Murdoch of Alpine! prove thy speed,
For ne'er had Alpine's son such need;
With heart of fire, and foot of wind,
The fierce avenger is behind!
Fate judges of the rapid strife—
The forfeit death—the prize is life;
Thy kindred ambush lies before,
Close couched upon the heathery moor;
Them couldst thou reach!—it may not be
Thine ambushed kin thou ne'er shalt see,
The fiery Saxon gains on thee!—
Resistless speeds the deadly thrust,
As lightning strikes the pine to dust;
With foot and hand Fitz-James must strain
Ere he can win his blade again.
Bent o'er the fallen with falcon eye,
He grimly smiled to see him die,
Then slower wended back his way,
Where the poor maiden bleeding lay.

XXVII.

She sat beneath the birchen tree,
Her elbow resting on her knee;
She had withdrawn the fatal shaft,
And gazed on it, and feebly laughed;
Her wreath of broom and feathers gray,
Daggled with blood, beside her lay.
The Knight to stanch the life-stream tried,—
'Stranger, it is in vain!' she cried.
'This hour of death has given me more
Of reason's power than years before;
For, as these ebbing veins decay,
My frenzied visions fade away.
A helpless injured wretch I die,
And something tells me in thine eye
That thou wert mine avenger born.
Seest thou this tress?—O. still I 've worn

This little tress of yellow hair,
Through danger, frenzy, and despair!
It once was bright and clear as thine,
But blood and tears have dimmed its shine.
I will not tell thee when 't was shred,
Nor from what guiltless victim's head,—
My brain would turn!—but it shall wave
Like plumage on thy helmet brave,
Till sun and wind shall bleach the stain,
And thou wilt bring it me again.
I waver still.—O God! more bright
Let reason beam her parting light!—
O. by thy knighthood's honored sign,
And for thy life preserved by mine,
When thou shalt see a darksome man,
Who boasts him Chief of Alpine's Clan,
With tartars broad and shadowy plume,
And hand of blood, and brow of gloom
Be thy heart bold, thy weapon strong,
And wreak poor Blanche of Devan's wrong!—
They watch for thee by pass and fell...
Avoid the path... O God!... farewell.'

XXVIII.

A kindly heart had brave Fitz-James;
Fast poured his eyes at pity's claims;
And now, with mingled grief and ire,
He saw the murdered maid expire.
'God, in my need, be my relief,
As I wreak this on yonder Chief!'
A lock from Blanche's tresses fair
He blended with her bridegroom's hair;
The mingled braid in blood he dyed,
And placed it on his bonnet-side:
'By Him whose word is truth, I swear,
No other favour will I wear,
Till this sad token I imbrue
In the best blood of Roderick Dhu!—
But hark! what means yon faint halloo?
The chase is up,—but they shall know,
The stag at bay 's a dangerous foe.'
Barred from the known but guarded way,
Through copse and cliffs Fitz-James must stray,
And oft must change his desperate track,
By stream and precipice turned back.

Heartless, fatigued, and faint, at length,
From lack of food and loss of strength
He couched him in a thicket hoar
And thought his toils and perils o'er:—
'Of all my rash adventures past,
This frantic feat must prove the last!
Who e'er so mad but might have guessed
That all this Highland hornet's nest
Would muster up in swarms so soon
As e'er they heard of bands at Doune?—
Like bloodhounds now they search me out,—
Hark, to the whistle and the shout!—
If farther through the wilds I go,
I only fall upon the foe:
I'll couch me here till evening gray,
Then darkling try my dangerous way.'

XXIX.

The shades of eve come slowly down,
The woods are wrapt in deeper brown,
The owl awakens from her dell,
The fox is heard upon the fell;
Enough remains of glimmering light
To guide the wanderer's steps aright,
Yet not enough from far to show
His figure to the watchful foe.
With cautious step and ear awake,
He climbs the crag and threads the brake;
And not the summer solstice there
Tempered the midnight mountain air,
But every breeze that swept the wold
Benumbed his drenched limbs with cold.
In dread, in danger, and alone,
Famished and chilled, through ways unknown,
Tangled and steep, he journeyed on;
Till, as a rock's huge point he turned,
A watch-fire close before him burned.

XXX.

Beside its embers red and clear
Basked in his plaid a mountaineer;
And up he sprung with sword in hand,—
'Thy name and purpose! Saxon, stand!'
'A stranger.' 'What dost thou require?'

'Rest and a guide, and food and fire
My life's beset, my path is lost,
The gale has chilled my limbs with frost.'
'Art thou a friend to Roderick?' 'No.'
'Thou dar'st not call thyself a foe?'
'I dare! to him and all the band
He brings to aid his murderous hand.'
'Bold words!—but, though the beast of game
The privilege of chase may claim,
Though space and law the stag we lend
Ere hound we slip or bow we bend
Who ever recked, where, how, or when,
The prowling fox was trapped or slain?
Thus treacherous scouts,—yet sure they lie
Who say thou cam'st a secret spy!'—
'They do, by heaven!—come Roderick Dhu
And of his clan the boldest two
And let me but till morning rest,
I write the falsehood on their crest.'
If by the blaze I mark aright
Thou bear'st the belt and spur of Knight.'
'Then by these tokens mayst thou know
Each proud oppressor's mortal foe.'
'Enough, enough; sit down and share
A soldier's couch, a soldier's fare.'

XXXI.

He gave him of his Highland cheer,
The hardened flesh of mountain deer;
Dry fuel on the fire he laid,
And bade the Saxon share his plaid.
He tended him like welcome guest,
Then thus his further speech addressed:—
'Stranger, I am to Roderick Dhu
A clansman born, a kinsman true;
Each word against his honour spoke
Demands of me avenging stroke;
Yet more,—upon thy fate, 'tis said,
A mighty augury is laid.
It rests with me to wind my horn,—
Thou art with numbers overborne;
It rests with me, here, brand to brand,
Worn as thou art, to bid thee stand:
But, not for clan, nor kindred's cause,
Will I depart from honour's laws;

To assail a wearied man were shame,
And stranger is a holy name;
Guidance and rest, and food and fire,
In vain he never must require.
Then rest thee here till dawn of day;
Myself will guide thee on the way,
O'er stock and stone, through watch and ward,
Till past Clan-Alpine's outmost guard,
As far as Coilantogle's ford;
From thence thy warrant is thy sword.'
'I take thy courtesy, by heaven,
As freely as 'tis nobly given!'
Well, rest thee; for the bittern's cry
Sings us the lake's wild lullaby.'
With that he shook the gathered heath,
And spread his plaid upon the wreath;
And the brave foemen, side by side,
Lay peaceful down like brothers tried,
And slept until the dawning beam
Purpled the mountain and the stream.

CANTO FIFTH. THE COMBAT.

I.

Fair as the earliest beam of eastern light,
   When first, by the bewildered pilgrim spied,
It smiles upon the dreary brow of night
   And silvers o'er the torrent's foaming tide
And lights the fearful path on mountain-side,—
   Fair as that beam, although the fairest far,
Giving to horror grace, to danger pride,
   Shine martial Faith, and Courtesy's bright star
Through all the wreckful storms that cloud the brow of War.

II.

That early beam, so fair and sheen,
Was twinkling through the hazel screen
When, rousing at its glimmer red,
The warriors left their lowly bed,
Looked out upon the dappled sky,
Muttered their soldier matins try,
And then awaked their fire, to steal,
As short and rude, their soldier meal.

That o'er, the Gael around him threw
His graceful plaid of varied hue,
And, true to promise, led the way,
By thicket green and mountain gray.
A wildering path!—they winded now
Along the precipice's brow,
Commanding the rich scenes beneath,
The windings of the Forth and Teith,
And all the vales between that lie.
Till Stirling's turrets melt in sky;
Then, sunk in copse, their farthest glance
Gained not the length of horseman's lance.
'Twas oft so steep, the foot was as fain
Assistance from the hand to gain;
So tangled oft that, bursting through,
Each hawthorn shed her showers of dew,—
That diamond dew, so pure and clear,
It rivals all but Beauty's tear!

III.

At length they came where, stern and steep,
The hill sinks down upon the deep.
Here Vennachar in silver flows,
There, ridge on ridge, Benledi rose;
Ever the hollow path twined on,
Beneath steep hank and threatening stone;
A hundred men might hold the post
With hardihood against a host.
The rugged mountain's scanty cloak
Was dwarfish shrubs of birch and oak
With shingles bare, and cliffs between
And patches bright of bracken green,
And heather black, that waved so high,
It held the copse in rivalry.
But where the lake slept deep and still
Dank osiers fringed the swamp and hill;
And oft both path and hill were torn
Where wintry torrent down had borne
And heaped upon the cumbered land
Its wreck of gravel, rocks, and sand.
So toilsome was the road to trace
The guide, abating of his pace,
Led slowly through the pass's jaws
And asked Fitz-James by what strange cause
He sought these wilds, traversed by few

Without a pass from Roderick Dhu.

IV.

'Brave Gael, my pass, in danger tried
Hangs in my belt and by my side
Yet, sooth to tell,' the Saxon said,
'I dreamt not now to claim its aid.
When here, but three days since,
I came Bewildered in pursuit of game,
All seemed as peaceful and as still
As the mist slumbering on yon hill;
Thy dangerous Chief was then afar,
Nor soon expected back from war.
Thus said, at least, my mountain-guide,
Though deep perchance the villain lied.'
'Yet why a second venture try?'
'A warrior thou, and ask me why!—
Moves our free course by such fixed cause
As gives the poor mechanic laws?
Enough, I sought to drive away
The lazy hours of peaceful day;
Slight cause will then suffice to guide
A Knight's free footsteps far and wide,—
A falcon flown, a greyhound strayed,
The merry glance of mountain maid;
Or, if a path be dangerous known,
The danger's self is lure alone.'

V.

'Thy secret keep, I urge thee not;—
Yet, ere again ye sought this spot,
Say, heard ye naught of Lowland war,
Against Clan-Alpine, raised by Mar?'
'No, by my word;—of bands prepared
To guard King James's sports I heard;
Nor doubt I aught, but, when they hear
This muster of the mountaineer,
Their pennons will abroad be flung,
Which else in Doune had peaceful hung.'
'Free be they flung! for we were loath
Their silken folds should feast the moth.
Free be they flung!—as free shall wave
Clan-Alpine's pine in banner brave.
But, stranger, peaceful since you came,

Bewildered in the mountain-game,
Whence the bold boast by which you show
Vich-Alpine's vowed and mortal foe?'
'Warrior, but yester-morn I knew
Naught of thy Chieftain, Roderick Dhu,
Save as an outlawed desperate man,
The chief of a rebellious clan,
Who, in the Regent's court and sight,
With ruffian dagger stabbed a knight;
Yet this alone might from his part
Sever each true and loyal heart.'

VI.

Wrathful at such arraignment foul,
Dark lowered the clansman's sable scowl.
A space he paused, then sternly said,
'And heardst thou why he drew his blade?
Heardst thou that shameful word and blow
Brought Roderick's vengeance on his foe?
What recked the Chieftain if he stood
On Highland heath or Holy-Rood?
He rights such wrong where it is given,
If it were in the court of heaven.'
'Still was it outrage;—yet, 'tis true,
Not then claimed sovereignty his due;
While Albany with feeble hand
Held borrowed truncheon of command,
The young King, mewed in Stirling tower,
Was stranger to respect and power.
But then, thy Chieftain's robber life!—
Winning mean prey by causeless strife,
Wrenching from ruined Lowland swain
His herds and harvest reared in vain,—
Methinks a soul like thine should scorn
The spoils from such foul foray borne.'

VII.

The Gael beheld him grim the while,
And answered with disdainful smile:
'Saxon, from yonder mountain high,
I marked thee send delighted eye
Far to the south and east, where lay,
Extended in succession gay,
Deep waving fields and pastures green,

THE LADY OF THE LAKE

With gentle slopes and groves between:—
These fertile plains, that softened vale,
Were once the birthright of the Gael;
The stranger came with iron hand,
And from our fathers reft the land.
Where dwell we now? See, rudely swell
Crag over crag, and fell o'er fell.
Ask we this savage hill we tread
For fattened steer or household bread,
Ask we for flocks these shingles dry,
And well the mountain might reply,—
"To you, as to your sires of yore,
Belong the target and claymore!
I give you shelter in my breast,
Your own good blades must win the rest."
Pent in this fortress of the North,
Think'st thou we will not sally forth,
To spoil the spoiler as we may,
And from the robber rend the prey?
Ay, by my soul!—While on yon plain
The Saxon rears one shock of grain,
While of ten thousand herds there strays
But one along yon river's maze,—
The Gael, of plain and river heir,
Shall with strong hand redeem his share.
Where live the mountain Chiefs who hold
That plundering Lowland field and fold
Is aught but retribution true?
Seek other cause 'gainst Roderick Dhu.'

VIII.

Answered Fitz-James: 'And, if I sought,
Think'st thou no other could be brought?
What deem ye of my path waylaid?
My life given o'er to ambuscade?'
'As of a meed to rashness due:
Hadst thou sent warning fair and true,—
I seek my hound or falcon strayed,
I seek, good faith, a Highland maid,—
Free hadst thou been to come and go;
But secret path marks secret foe.
Nor yet for this, even as a spy,
Hadst thou, unheard, been doomed to die,
Save to fulfil an augury.'
'Well, let it pass; nor will I now

Fresh cause of enmity avow
To chafe thy mood and cloud thy brow.
Enough, I am by promise tied
To match me with this man of pride:
Twice have I sought Clan-Alpine's glen
In peace; but when I come again,
I come with banner, brand, and bow,
As leader seeks his mortal foe.
For love-lore swain in lady's bower
Ne'er panted for the appointed hour
As I, until before me stand
This rebel Chieftain and his band!'

IX.

'Have then thy wish!'—He whistled shrill
And he was answered from the hill;
Wild as the scream of the curlew,
From crag to crag the signal flew.
Instant, through copse and heath, arose
Bonnets and spears and bended bows
On right, on left, above, below,
Sprung up at once the lurking foe;
From shingles gray their lances start,
The bracken bush sends forth the dart,
The rushes and the willow-wand
Are bristling into axe and brand,
And every tuft of broom gives life
'To plaided warrior armed for strife.
That whistle garrisoned the glen
At once with full five hundred men,
As if the yawning hill to heaven
A subterranean host had given.
Watching their leader's beck and will,
All silent there they stood and still.
Like the loose crags whose threatening mass
Lay tottering o'er the hollow pass,
As if an infant's touch could urge
Their headlong passage down the verge,
With step and weapon forward flung,
Upon the mountain-side they hung.
The Mountaineer cast glance of pride
Along Benledi's living side,
Then fixed his eye and sable brow
Full on Fitz-James: 'How say'st thou now?
These are Clan-Alpine's warriors true;

And, Saxon,—I am Roderick Dhu!'

X.

Fitz-James was brave:—though to his heart
The life-blood thrilled with sudden start,
He manned himself with dauntless air,
Returned the Chief his haughty stare,
His back against a rock he bore,
And firmly placed his foot before:—
'Come one, come all! this rock shall fly
From its firm base as soon as I.'
Sir Roderick marked,—and in his eyes
Respect was mingled with surprise,
And the stern joy which warriors feel
In foeman worthy of their steel.
Short space he stood—then waved his hand:
Down sunk the disappearing band;
Each warrior vanished where he stood,
In broom or bracken, heath or wood;
Sunk brand and spear and bended bow,
In osiers pale and copses low;
It seemed as if their mother Earth
Had swallowed up her warlike birth.
The wind's last breath had tossed in air
Pennon and plaid and plumage fair,—
The next but swept a lone hill-side
Where heath and fern were waving wide:
The sun's last glance was glinted back
From spear and glaive, from targe and jack,—
The next, all unreflected, shone
On bracken green and cold gray stone.

XI.

Fitz-James looked round,—yet scarce believed
The witness that his sight received;
Such apparition well might seem
Delusion of a dreadful dream.
Sir Roderick in suspense he eyed,
And to his look the Chief replied:
'Fear naught—nay, that I need not say
But—doubt not aught from mine array.
Thou art my guest;—I pledged my word
As far as Coilantogle ford:
Nor would I call a clansman's brand

For aid against one valiant hand,
Though on our strife lay every vale
Rent by the Saxon from the Gael.
So move we on;—I only meant
To show the reed on which you leant,
Deeming this path you might pursue
Without a pass from Roderick Dhu.'
They moved;—I said Fitz-James was brave
As ever knight that belted glaive,
Yet dare not say that now his blood
Kept on its wont and tempered flood,
As, following Roderick's stride, he drew
That seeming lonesome pathway through,
Which yet by fearful proof was rife
With lances, that, to take his life,
Waited but signal from a guide,
So late dishonored and defied.
Ever, by stealth, his eye sought round
The vanished guardians of the ground,
And stir'd from copse and heather deep
Fancy saw spear and broadsword peep,
And in the plover's shrilly strain
The signal whistle heard again.
Nor breathed he free till far behind
The pass was left; for then they wind
Along a wide and level green,
Where neither tree nor tuft was seen,
Nor rush nor bush of broom was near,
To hide a bonnet or a spear.

XII.

The Chief in silence strode before,
And reached that torrent's sounding shore,
Which, daughter of three mighty lakes,
From Vennachar in silver breaks,
Sweeps through the plain, and ceaseless mines
On Bochastle the mouldering lines,
Where Rome, the Empress of the world,
Of yore her eagle wings unfurled.
And here his course the Chieftain stayed,
Threw down his target and his plaid,
And to the Lowland warrior said:
'Bold Saxon! to his promise just,
Vich-Alpine has discharged his trust.
This murderous Chief, this ruthless man,

This head of a rebellious clan,
Hath led thee safe, through watch and ward,
Far past Clan-Alpine's outmost guard.
Now, man to man, and steel to steel,
A Chieftain's vengeance thou shalt feel.
See, here all vantageless I stand,
Armed like thyself with single brand;
For this is Coilantogle ford,
And thou must keep thee with thy sword.'

XIII.

The Saxon paused: 'I ne'er delayed,
When foeman bade me draw my blade;
Nay more, brave Chief, I vowed thy death;
Yet sure thy fair and generous faith,
And my deep debt for life preserved,
A better meed have well deserved:
Can naught but blood our feud atone?
Are there no means?'—'No, stranger, none!
And hear,—to fire thy flagging zeal,—
The Saxon cause rests on thy steel;
For thus spoke Fate by prophet bred
Between the living and the dead:"
Who spills the foremost foeman's life,
His party conquers in the strife."'
'Then, by my word,' the Saxon said,
"The riddle is already read.
Seek yonder brake beneath the cliff,—
There lies Red Murdoch, stark and stiff.
Thus Fate hath solved her prophecy;
Then yield to Fate, and not to me.
To James at Stirling let us go,
When, if thou wilt be still his foe,
Or if the King shall not agree
To grant thee grace and favor free,
I plight mine honor, oath, and word
That, to thy native strengths restored,
With each advantage shalt thou stand
That aids thee now to guard thy land.'

XIV.

Dark lightning flashed from Roderick's eye:
'Soars thy presumption, then, so high,
Because a wretched kern ye slew,

Homage to name to Roderick Dhu?
He yields not, he, to man nor Fate!
Thou add'st but fuel to my hate;—
My clansman's blood demands revenge.
Not yet prepared?—By heaven, I change
My thought, and hold thy valor light
As that of some vain carpet knight,
Who ill deserved my courteous care,
And whose best boast is but to wear
A braid of his fair lady's hair.' 'I thank thee,
Roderick, for the word!
It nerves my heart, it steels my sword;
For I have sworn this braid to stain
In the best blood that warms thy vein.
Now, truce, farewell! and, rush, begone!—
Yet think not that by thee alone,
Proud Chief! can courtesy be shown;
Though not from copse, or heath, or cairn,
Start at my whistle clansmen stern,
Of this small horn one feeble blast
Would fearful odds against thee cast.
But fear not—doubt not—which thou wilt—
We try this quarrel hilt to hilt.'
Then each at once his falchion drew,
Each on the ground his scabbard threw
Each looked to sun and stream and plain
As what they ne'er might see again;
Then foot and point and eye opposed,
In dubious strife they darkly closed.

XV.

Ill fared it then with Roderick Dhu,
That on the field his targe he threw,
Whose brazen studs and tough bull-hide
Had death so often dashed aside;
For, trained abroad his arms to wield
Fitz-James's blade was sword and shield.
He practised every pass and ward,
To thrust, to strike, to feint, to guard;
While less expert, though stronger far,
The Gael maintained unequal war.
Three times in closing strife they stood
And thrice the Saxon blade drank blood;
No stinted draught, no scanty tide,
The gushing flood the tartars dyed.

Fierce Roderick felt the fatal drain,
And showered his blows like wintry rain;
And, as firm rock or castle-roof
Against the winter shower is proof,
The foe, invulnerable still,
Foiled his wild rage by steady skill;
Till, at advantage ta'en, his brand
Forced Roderick's weapon from his hand,
And backward borne upon the lea,
Brought the proud Chieftain to his knee.

XVI.

Now yield thee, or by Him who made
The world, thy heart's blood dyes my blade!;
'Thy threats, thy mercy, I defy!
Let recreant yield, who fears to die.'
Like adder darting from his coil,
Like wolf that dashes through the toil,
Like mountain-cat who guards her young,
Full at Fitz-James's throat he sprung;
Received, but recked not of a wound,
And locked his arms his foeman round.
Now, gallant Saxon, hold thine own!
No maiden's hand is round thee thrown!
That desperate grasp thy frame might feel
Through bars of brass and triple steel!
They tug, they strain! down, down they go,
The Gael above, Fitz-James below.
The Chieftain's gripe his throat compressed,
His knee was planted on his breast;
His clotted locks he backward threw,
Across his brow his hand he drew,
From blood and mist to clear his sight,
Then gleamed aloft his dagger bright!
But hate and fury ill supplied
The stream of life's exhausted tide,
And all too late the advantage came,
To turn the odds of deadly game;
For, while the dagger gleamed on high,
Reeled soul and sense, reeled brain and eye.
Down came the blow! but in the heath
The erring blade found bloodless sheath.
The struggling foe may now unclasp
The fainting Chief's relaxing grasp;
Unwounded from the dreadful close,

But breathless all, Fitz-James arose.

XVII.

He faltered thanks to Heaven for life,
Redeemed, unhoped, from desperate strife;
Next on his foe his look he cast,
Whose every gasp appeared his last
In Roderick's gore he dipped the braid,—
'Poor Blanche! thy wrongs are dearly paid;
Yet with thy foe must die, or live,
The praise that faith and valor give.'
With that he blew a bugle note,
Undid the collar from his throat,
Unbonneted, and by the wave
Sat down his brow and hands to rave.
Then faint afar are heard the feet
Of rushing steeds in gallop fleet;
The sounds increase, and now are seen
Four mounted squires in Lincoln green;
Two who bear lance, and two who lead
By loosened rein a saddled steed;
Each onward held his headlong course,
And by Fitz-James reined up his horse,—
With wonder viewed the bloody spot,—
'Exclaim not, gallants' question not.—
You, Herbert and Luffness, alight
And bind the wounds of yonder knight;
Let the gray palfrey bear his weight,
We destined for a fairer freight,
And bring him on to Stirling straight;
I will before at better speed,
To seek fresh horse and fitting weed.
The sun rides high;—I must be boune
To see the archer-game at noon;
But lightly Bayard clears the lea.—
De Vaux and Herries, follow me.

XVIII.

'Stand, Bayard, stand!'—the steed obeyed,
With arching neck and bended head,
And glancing eye and quivering ear,
As if he loved his lord to hear.
No foot Fitz-James in stirrup stayed,
No grasp upon the saddle laid,

But wreathed his left hand in the mane,
And lightly bounded from the plain,
Turned on the horse his armed heel,
And stirred his courage with the steel.
Bounded the fiery steed in air,
The rider sat erect and fair,
Then like a bolt from steel crossbow
Forth launched, along the plain they go.
They dashed that rapid torrent through,
And up Carhonie's hill they flew;
Still at the gallop pricked the Knight,
His merrymen followed as they might.
Along thy banks, swift Teith! they ride,
And in the race they mock thy tide;
Torry and Lendrick now are past,
And Deanstown lies behind them cast;
They rise, the bannered towers of Doune,
They sink in distant woodland soon;
Blair-Drummond sees the hoofs strike fire,
They sweep like breeze through Ochtertyre;
They mark just glance and disappear
The lofty brow of ancient Kier;
They bathe their coursers' sweltering sides
Dark Forth! amid thy sluggish tides,
And on the opposing shore take ground
With plash, with scramble, and with bound.
Right-hand they leave thy cliffs, Craig-Forth!
And soon the bulwark of the North,
Gray Stirling, with her towers and town,
Upon their fleet career looked down.

XIX.

As up the flinty path they strained,
Sudden his steed the leader reined;
A signal to his squire he flung,
Who instant to his stirrup sprung:—
'Seest thou, De Vaux, yon woodsman gray,
Who townward holds the rocky way,
Of stature tall and poor array?
Mark'st thou the firm, yet active stride,
With which he scales the mountain-side?
Know'st thou from whence he comes, or whom?'
'No, by my word;—a burly groom
He seems, who in the field or chase
A baron's train would nobly grace—'

'Out, out, De Vaux! can fear supply,
And jealousy, no sharper eye?
Afar, ere to the hill he drew,
That stately form and step I knew;
Like form in Scotland is not seen,
Treads not such step on Scottish green.
'Tis James of Douglas, by Saint Serle!
The uncle of the banished Earl.
Away, away, to court, to show
The near approach of dreaded foe:
The King must stand upon his guard;
Douglas and he must meet prepared.'
Then right-hand wheeled their steeds, and straight
They won the Castle's postern gate.

XX.

The Douglas, who had bent his way
From Cambus-kenneth's abbey gray,
Now, as he climbed the rocky shelf,
Held sad communion with himself:—
'Yes! all is true my fears could frame;
A prisoner lies the noble Graeme,
And fiery Roderick soon will feel
The vengeance of the royal steel.
I, only I, can ward their fate,—
God grant the ransom come not late!
The Abbess hath her promise given,
My child shall be the bride of Heaven;—
Be pardoned one repining tear!
For He who gave her knows how dear,
How excellent!—but that is by,
And now my business is—to die.—
Ye towers! within whose circuit dread
A Douglas by his sovereign bled;
And thou, O sad and fatal mound!
That oft hast heard the death-axe sound.
As on the noblest of the land
Fell the stern headsmen's bloody hand,—
The dungeon, block, and nameless tomb
Prepare—for Douglas seeks his doom!
But hark! what blithe and jolly peal
Makes the Franciscan steeple reel?
And see! upon the crowded street,
In motley groups what masquers meet!
Banner and pageant, pipe and drum,

And merry morrice-dancers come.
I guess, by all this quaint array,
The burghers hold their sports to-day.
James will be there; he loves such show,
Where the good yeoman bends his bow,
And the tough wrestler foils his foe,
As well as where, in proud career,
The high-born filter shivers spear.
I'll follow to the Castle-park,
And play my prize;—King James shall mark
If age has tamed these sinews stark,
Whose force so oft in happier days
His boyish wonder loved to praise.'

XXI.

The Castle gates were open flung,
The quivering drawbridge rocked and rung,
And echoed loud the flinty street
Beneath the coursers' clattering feet,
As slowly down the steep descent
Fair Scotland's King and nobles went,
While all along the crowded way
Was jubilee and loud huzza.
And ever James was bending low
To his white jennet's saddle-bow,
Doffing his cap to city dame,
Who smiled and blushed for pride and shame.
And well the simperer might be vain,—
He chose the fairest of the train.
Gravely he greets each city sire,
Commends each pageant's quaint attire,
Gives to the dancers thanks aloud,
And smiles and nods upon the crowd,
Who rend the heavens with their acclaims,—
'Long live the Commons' King, King James!'
Behind the King thronged peer and knight,
And noble dame and damsel bright,
Whose fiery steeds ill brooked the stay
Of the steep street and crowded way.
But in the train you might discern
Dark lowering brow and visage stern;
There nobles mourned their pride restrained,
And the mean burgher's joys disdained;
And chiefs, who, hostage for their clan,
Were each from home a banished man,

There thought upon their own gray tower,
Their waving woods, their feudal power,
And deemed themselves a shameful part
Of pageant which they cursed in heart.

XXII.

Now, in the Castle-park, drew out
Their checkered bands the joyous rout.
There morricers, with bell at heel
And blade in hand, their mazes wheel;
But chief, beside the butts, there stand
Bold Robin Hood and all his band,—
Friar Tuck with quarterstaff and cowl,
Old Scathelocke with his surly scowl,
Maid Marian, fair as ivory bone,
Scarlet, and Mutch, and Little John;
Their bugles challenge all that will,
In archery to prove their skill.
The Douglas bent a bow of might,—
His first shaft centred in the white,
And when in turn he shot again,
His second split the first in twain.
From the King's hand must Douglas take
A silver dart, the archers' stake;
Fondly he watched, with watery eye,
Some answering glance of sympathy,—
No kind emotion made reply!
Indifferent as to archer wight,
The monarch gave the arrow bright.

XXIII.

Now, clear the ring! for, hand to hand,
The manly wrestlers take their stand.
Two o'er the rest superior rose,
And proud demanded mightier foes,—
Nor called in vain, for Douglas came.—
For life is Hugh of Larbert lame;
Scarce better John of Alloa's fare,
Whom senseless home his comrades bare.
Prize of the wrestling match, the King
To Douglas gave a golden ring,
While coldly glanced his eye of blue,
As frozen drop of wintry dew.
Douglas would speak, but in his breast

His struggling soul his words suppressed;
Indignant then he turned him where
Their arms the brawny yeomen bare,
To hurl the massive bar in air.
When each his utmost strength had shown,
The Douglas rent an earth-fast stone
From its deep bed, then heaved it high,
And sent the fragment through the sky
A rood beyond the farthest mark;
And still in Stirling's royal park,
The gray-haired sires, who know the past,
To strangers point the Douglas cast,
And moralize on the decay
Of Scottish strength in modern day.

XXIV.

The vale with loud applauses rang,
The Ladies' Rock sent back the clang.
The King, with look unmoved, bestowed
A purse well filled with pieces broad.
Indignant smiled the Douglas proud,
And threw the gold among the crowd,
Who now with anxious wonder scan,
And sharper glance, the dark gray man;
Till whispers rose among the throng,
That heart so free, and hand so strong,
Must to the Douglas blood belong.
The old men marked and shook the head,
To see his hair with silver spread,
And winked aside, and told each son
Of feats upon the English done,
Ere Douglas of the stalwart hand
Was exiled from his native land.
The women praised his stately form,
Though wrecked by many a winter's storm;
The youth with awe and wonder saw
His strength surpassing Nature's law.
Thus judged, as is their wont, the crowd
Till murmurs rose to clamours loud.
But not a glance from that proud ring
Of peers who circled round the King
With Douglas held communion kind,
Or called the banished man to mind;
No, not from those who at the chase
Once held his side the honoured place,

Begirt his board, and in the field
Found safety underneath his shield;
For he whom royal eyes disown,
When was his form to courtiers known!

XXV.

The Monarch saw the gambols flag
And bade let loose a gallant stag,
Whose pride, the holiday to crown,
Two favorite greyhounds should pull down,
That venison free and Bourdeaux wine
Might serve the archery to dine.
But Lufra,—whom from Douglas' side
Nor bribe nor threat could e'er divide,
The fleetest hound in all the North,—
Brave Lufra saw, and darted forth.
She left the royal hounds midway,
And dashing on the antlered prey,
Sunk her sharp muzzle in his flank,
And deep the flowing life-blood drank.
The King's stout huntsman saw the sport
By strange intruder broken short,
Came up, and with his leash unbound
In anger struck the noble hound.
The Douglas had endured, that morn,
The King's cold look, the nobles' scorn,
And last, and worst to spirit proud,
Had borne the pity of the crowd;
But Lufra had been fondly bred,
To share his board, to watch his bed,
And oft would Ellen Lufra's neck
In maiden glee with garlands deck;
They were such playmates that with name
Of Lufra Ellen's image came.
His stifled wrath is brimming high,
In darkened brow and flashing eye;
As waves before the bark divide,
The crowd gave way before his stride;
Needs but a buffet and no more,
The groom lies senseless in his gore.
Such blow no other hand could deal,
Though gauntleted in glove of steel.

XXVI.

Then clamored loud the royal train,
And brandished swords and staves amain,
But stern the Baron's warning:
'Back! Back, on your lives, ye menial pack!
Beware the Douglas.—Yes! behold,
King James! The Douglas, doomed of old,
And vainly sought for near and far,
A victim to atone the war,
A willing victim, now attends,
Nor craves thy grace but for his friends.—'
'Thus is my clemency repaid?
Presumptuous Lord!' the Monarch said:
'Of thy misproud ambitious clan,
Thou, James of Bothwell, wert the man,
The only man, in whom a foe
My woman-mercy would not know;
But shall a Monarch's presence brook
Injurious blow and haughty look?—
What ho! the Captain of our Guard!
Give the offender fitting ward.—
Break off the sports!'—for tumult rose,
And yeomen 'gan to bend their bows,
'Break off the sports!' he said and frowned,
'And bid our horsemen clear the ground.'

XXVII.

Then uproar wild and misarray
Marred the fair form of festal day.
The horsemen pricked among the crowd,
Repelled by threats and insult loud;
To earth are borne the old and weak,
The timorous fly, the women shriek;
With flint, with shaft, with staff, with bar,
The hardier urge tumultuous war.
At once round Douglas darkly sweep
The royal spears in circle deep,
And slowly scale the pathway steep,
While on the rear in thunder pour
The rabble with disordered roar
With grief the noble Douglas saw
The Commons rise against the law,
And to the leading soldier said:
'Sir John of Hyndford, 'twas my blade
That knighthood on thy shoulder laid;
For that good deed permit me then

A word with these misguided men.—

XXVIII.

'Hear, gentle friends, ere yet for me
Ye break the bands of fealty.
My life, my honour, and my cause,
I tender free to Scotland's laws.
Are these so weak as must require
'Fine aid of your misguided ire?
Or if I suffer causeless wrong,
Is then my selfish rage so strong,
My sense of public weal so low,
That, for mean vengeance on a foe,
Those cords of love I should unbind
Which knit my country and my kind?
O no! Believe, in yonder tower
It will not soothe my captive hour,
To know those spears our foes should dread
For me in kindred gore are red:
'To know, in fruitless brawl begun,
For me that mother wails her son,
For me that widow's mate expires,
For me that orphans weep their sires,
That patriots mourn insulted laws,
And curse the Douglas for the cause.
O let your patience ward such ill,
And keep your right to love me still!'

XXIX.

The crowd's wild fury sunk again
In tears, as tempests melt in rain.
With lifted hands and eyes, they prayed
For blessings on his generous head
Who for his country felt alone,
And prized her blood beyond his own.
Old men upon the verge of life
Blessed him who stayed the civil strife;
And mothers held their babes on high,
The self-devoted Chief to spy,
Triumphant over wrongs and ire,
To whom the prattlers owed a sire.
Even the rough soldier's heart was moved;
As if behind some bier beloved,
With trailing arms and drooping head,

The Douglas up the hill he led,
And at the Castle's battled verge,
With sighs resigned his honoured charge.

XXX.

The offended Monarch rode apart,
With bitter thought and swelling heart,
And would not now vouchsafe again
Through Stirling streets to lead his train.
'O Lennox, who would wish to rule
This changeling crowd, this common fool?
Hear'st thou,' he said, 'the loud acclaim
With which they shout the Douglas name?
With like acclaim the vulgar throat
Strained for King James their morning note;
With like acclaim they hailed the day
When first I broke the Douglas sway;
And like acclaim would Douglas greet
If he could hurl me from my seat.
Who o'er the herd would wish to reign,
Fantastic, fickle, fierce, and vain?
Vain as the leaf upon the stream,
And fickle as a changeful dream;
Fantastic as a woman's mood,
And fierce as Frenzy's fevered blood.
Thou many-headed monster-thing,
O who would wish to be thy king?—

XXXI.

'But soft! what messenger of speed
Spurs hitherward his panting steed?
I guess his cognizance afar—
What from our cousin, John of Mar?'
'He prays, my liege, your sports keep bound
Within the safe and guarded ground;
For some foul purpose yet unknown,—
Most sure for evil to the throne,—
The outlawed Chieftain, Roderick Dhu,
Has summoned his rebellious crew;
'Tis said, in James of Bothwell's aid
These loose banditti stand arrayed.
The Earl of Mar this morn from Doune
To break their muster marched, and soon
Your Grace will hear of battle fought;

But earnestly the Earl besought,
Till for such danger he provide,
With scanty train you will not ride.'

XXXII.

'Thou warn'st me I have done amiss,—
I should have earlier looked to this;
I lost it in this bustling day.—
Retrace with speed thy former way;
Spare not for spoiling of thy steed,
The best of mine shall be thy meed.
Say to our faithful Lord of Mar,
We do forbid the intended war;
Roderick this morn in single fight
Was made our prisoner by a knight,
And Douglas hath himself and cause
Submitted to our kingdom's laws.
The tidings of their leaders lost
Will soon dissolve the mountain host,
Nor would we that the vulgar feel,
For their Chief's crimes, avenging steel.
Bear Mar our message, Braco, fly!'
He turned his steed,—'My liege, I hie,
Yet ere I cross this lily lawn
I fear the broadswords will be drawn.'
The turf the flying courser spurned,
And to his towers the King returned.

XXXIII.

Ill with King James's mood that day
Suited gay feast and minstrel lay;
Soon were dismissed the courtly throng,
And soon cut short the festal song.
Nor less upon the saddened town
The evening sunk in sorrow down.
The burghers spoke of civil jar,
Of rumoured feuds and mountain war,
Of Moray, Mar, and Roderick Dhu,
All up in arms;—the Douglas too,
They mourned him pent within the hold,
'Where stout Earl William was of old.'—
And there his word the speaker stayed,
And finger on his lip he laid,
Or pointed to his dagger blade.

THE LADY OF THE LAKE

But jaded horsemen from the west
At evening to the Castle pressed,
And busy talkers said they bore
Tidings of fight on Katrine's shore;
At noon the deadly fray begun,
And lasted till the set of sun.
Thus giddy rumor shook the town,
Till closed the Night her pennons brown.

CANTO SIXTH. THE GUARD-ROOM.

I.

The sun, awakening, through the smoky air
Of the dark city casts a sullen glance,
Rousing each caitiff to his task of care,
Of sinful man the sad inheritance;
Summoning revellers from the lagging dance,
Scaring the prowling robber to his den;
Gilding on battled tower the warder's lance,
And warning student pale to leave his pen,
And yield his drowsy eyes to the kind nurse of men.

What various scenes, and O, what scenes of woe,
Are witnessed by that red and struggling beam!
The fevered patient, from his pallet low,
Through crowded hospital beholds it stream;
The ruined maiden trembles at its gleam,
The debtor wakes to thought of gyve and jail,
'The love-lore wretch starts from tormenting dream:
The wakeful mother, by the glimmering pale,
Trims her sick infant's couch, and soothes his feeble wail.

II.

At dawn the towers of Stirling rang
With soldier-step and weapon-clang,
While drums with rolling note foretell
Relief to weary sentinel.
Through narrow loop and casement barred,
The sunbeams sought the Court of Guard,
And, struggling with the smoky air,
Deadened the torches' yellow glare.
In comfortless alliance shone
The lights through arch of blackened stone,

And showed wild shapes in garb of war,
Faces deformed with beard and scar,
All haggard from the midnight watch,
And fevered with the stern debauch;
For the oak table's massive board,
Flooded with wine, with fragments stored,
And beakers drained, and cups o'erthrown,
Showed in what sport the night had flown.
Some, weary, snored on floor and bench;
Some labored still their thirst to quench;
Some, chilled with watching, spread their hands
O'er the huge chimney's dying brands,
While round them, or beside them flung,
At every step their harness rung.

III.

These drew not for their fields the sword,
Like tenants of a feudal lord,
Nor owned the patriarchal claim
Of Chieftain in their leader's name;
Adventurers they, from far who roved,
To live by battle which they loved.
There the Italian's clouded face,
The swarthy Spaniard's there you trace;
The mountain-loving Switzer there
More freely breathed in mountain-air;
The Fleming there despised the soil
That paid so ill the labourer's toil;
Their rolls showed French and German name;
And merry England's exiles came,
To share, with ill-concealed disdain,
Of Scotland's pay the scanty gain.
All brave in arms, well trained to wield
The heavy halberd, brand, and shield;
In camps licentious, wild, and bold;
In pillage fierce and uncontrolled;
And now, by holytide and feast,
From rules of discipline released.

IV.

'They held debate of bloody fray,
Fought 'twixt Loch Katrine and Achray.
Fierce was their speech, and mid their words
'Their hands oft grappled to their swords;

THE LADY OF THE LAKE

Nor sunk their tone to spare the ear
Of wounded comrades groaning near,
Whose mangled limbs and bodies gored
Bore token of the mountain sword,
Though, neighbouring to the Court of Guard,
Their prayers and feverish wails were heard,—
Sad burden to the ruffian joke,
And savage oath by fury spoke!—
At length up started John of Brent,
A yeoman from the banks of Trent;
A stranger to respect or fear,
In peace a chaser of the deer,
In host a hardy mutineer,
But still the boldest of the crew
When deed of danger was to do.
He grieved that day their games cut short,
And marred the dicer's brawling sport,
And shouted loud, 'Renew the bowl!
And, while a merry catch I troll,
Let each the buxom chorus bear,
Like brethren of the brand and spear.'

V.

Soldier's Song.

Our vicar still preaches that Peter and Poule
Laid a swinging long curse on the bonny brown bowl,
That there's wrath and despair in the jolly black-jack,
And the seven deadly sins in a flagon of sack;
Yet whoop, Barnaby! off with thy liquor,
Drink upsees out, and a fig for the vicar!

Our vicar he calls it damnation to sip
The ripe ruddy dew of a woman's dear lip,
Says that Beelzebub lurks in her kerchief so sly,
And Apollyon shoots darts from her merry black eye;
Yet whoop, Jack! kiss Gillian the quicker,
Till she bloom like a rose, and a fig for the vicar!

Our vicar thus preaches,—and why should he not?
For the dues of his cure are the placket and pot;
And 'tis right of his office poor laymen to lurch
Who infringe the domains of our good Mother Church.
Yet whoop, bully-boys! off with your liquor,
Sweet Marjorie's the word and a fig for the vicar!

VI.

The warder's challenge, heard without,
Stayed in mid-roar the merry shout.
A soldier to the portal went,—
'Here is old Bertram, sirs, of Ghent;
And—beat for jubilee the drum!—
A maid and minstrel with him come.'
Bertram, a Fleming, gray and scarred,
Was entering now the Court of Guard,
A harper with him, and, in plaid
All muffled close, a mountain maid,
Who backward shrunk to 'scape the view
Of the loose scene and boisterous crew.
'What news?' they roared:—'I only know,
From noon till eve we fought with foe,
As wild and as untamable
As the rude mountains where they dwell;
On both sides store of blood is lost,
Nor much success can either boast.'—
'But whence thy captives, friend? such spoil
As theirs must needs reward thy toil.
Old dost thou wax, and wars grow sharp;
Thou now hast glee-maiden and harp!
Get thee an ape, and trudge the land,
The leader of a juggler band.'

VII.

'No, comrade;—no such fortune mine.
After the fight these sought our line,
That aged harper and the girl,
And, having audience of the Earl,
Mar bade I should purvey them steed,
And bring them hitherward with speed.
Forbear your mirth and rude alarm,
For none shall do them shame or harm.—
'Hear ye his boast?' cried John of Brent,
Ever to strife and jangling bent;
'Shall he strike doe beside our lodge,
And yet the jealous niggard grudge
To pay the forester his fee?
I'll have my share howe'er it be,
Despite of Moray, Mar, or thee.'
Bertram his forward step withstood;
And, burning in his vengeful mood,

Old Allan, though unfit for strife,
Laid hand upon his dagger-knife;
But Ellen boldly stepped between,
And dropped at once the tartan screen:—
So, from his morning cloud, appears
The sun of May through summer tears.
The savage soldiery, amazed,
As on descended angel gazed;
Even hardy Brent, abashed and tamed,
Stood half admiring, half ashamed.

VIII.

Boldly she spoke: 'Soldiers, attend!
My father was the soldier's friend,
Cheered him in camps, in marches led,
And with him in the battle bled.
Not from the valiant or the strong
Should exile's daughter suffer wrong.'
Answered De Brent, most forward still
In every feat or good or ill:
'I shame me of the part I played;
And thou an outlaw's child, poor maid!
An outlaw I by forest laws,
And merry Needwood knows the cause.
Poor Rose,—if Rose be living now,'—
He wiped his iron eye and brow,—
'Must bear such age, I think, as thou.—
Hear ye, my mates! I go to call
The Captain of our watch to hall:
There lies my halberd on the floor;
And he that steps my halberd o'er,
To do the maid injurious part,
My shaft shall quiver in his heart!
Beware loose speech, or jesting rough;
Ye all know John de Brent. Enough.'

IX.

Their Captain came, a gallant young,—
Of Tullibardine's house he sprung,—
Nor wore he yet the spurs of knight;
Gay was his mien, his humor light
And, though by courtesy controlled,
Forward his speech, his bearing bold.
The high-born maiden ill could brook

The scanning of his curious look
And dauntless eye:—and yet, in sooth
Young Lewis was a generous youth;
But Ellen's lovely face and mien
Ill suited to the garb and scene,
Might lightly bear construction strange,
And give loose fancy scope to range.
'Welcome to Stirling towers, fair maid!
Come ye to seek a champion's aid,
On palfrey white, with harper hoar,
Like errant damosel of yore?
Does thy high quest a knight require,
Or may the venture suit a squire?'
Her dark eye flashed;—she paused and sighed:—
'O what have I to do with pride!—
Through scenes of sorrow, shame, and strife,
A suppliant for a father's life,
I crave an audience of the King.
Behold, to back my suit, a ring,
The royal pledge of grateful claims,
Given by the Monarch to Fitz-James.'

X.

The signet-ring young Lewis took
With deep respect and altered look,
And said: 'This ring our duties own;
And pardon, if to worth unknown,
In semblance mean obscurely veiled,
Lady, in aught my folly failed.
Soon as the day flings wide his gates,
The King shall know what suitor waits.
Please you meanwhile in fitting bower
Repose you till his waking hour.
Female attendance shall obey
Your hest, for service or array.
Permit I marshal you the way.'
But, ere she followed, with the grace
And open bounty of her race,
She bade her slender purse be shared
Among the soldiers of the guard.
The rest with thanks their guerdon took,
But Brent, with shy and awkward look,
On the reluctant maiden's hold
Forced bluntly back the proffered gold:—
'Forgive a haughty English heart,

And O, forget its ruder part!

The vacant purse shall be my share,
Which in my barrel-cap I'll bear,
Perchance, in jeopardy of war,
Where gayer crests may keep afar.'
With thanks— 'twas all she could—the maid
His rugged courtesy repaid.

XI.

When Ellen forth with Lewis went,
Allan made suit to John of Brent:—
'My lady safe, O let your grace
Give me to see my master's face!
His minstrel I,—to share his doom
Bound from the cradle to the tomb.
Tenth in descent, since first my sires
Waked for his noble house their lyres,
Nor one of all the race was known
But prized its weal above their own.
With the Chief's birth begins our care;
Our harp must soothe the infant heir,
Teach the youth tales of fight, and grace
His earliest feat of field or chase;
In peace, in war, our rank we keep,
We cheer his board, we soothe his sleep,
Nor leave him till we pour our verse—
A doleful tribute!—o'er his hearse.
Then let me share his captive lot;
It is my right,—deny it not!'
'Little we reck,' said John of Brent,
'We Southern men, of long descent;
Nor wot we how a name—a word—
Makes clansmen vassals to a lord:
Yet kind my noble landlord's part,—
God bless the house of Beaudesert!
And, but I loved to drive the deer
More than to guide the labouring steer,
I had not dwelt an outcast here.
Come, good old Minstrel, follow me;
Thy Lord and Chieftain shalt thou see.'

XII.

Then, from a rusted iron hook,

A bunch of ponderous keys he took,
Lighted a torch, and Allan led
Through grated arch and passage dread.
Portals they passed, where, deep within,
Spoke prisoner's moan and fetters' din;
Through rugged vaults, where, loosely stored,
Lay wheel, and axe, and headsmen's sword,
And many a hideous engine grim,
For wrenching joint and crushing limb,
By artists formed who deemed it shame
And sin to give their work a name.
They halted at a low-browed porch,
And Brent to Allan gave the torch,
While bolt and chain he backward rolled,
And made the bar unhasp its hold.
They entered:— 'twas a prison-room
Of stern security and gloom,
Yet not a dungeon; for the day
Through lofty gratings found its way,
And rude and antique garniture
Decked the sad walls and oaken floor,
Such as the rugged days of old
Deemed fit for captive noble's hold.
'Here,' said De Brent, 'thou mayst remain
Till the Leech visit him again.
Strict is his charge, the warders tell,
To tend the noble prisoner well.'
Retiring then the bolt he drew,
And the lock's murmurs growled anew.
Roused at the sound, from lowly bed
A captive feebly raised his head.
The wondering Minstrel looked, and knew—
Not his dear lord, but Roderick Dhu!
For, come from where Clan-Alpine fought,
They, erring, deemed the Chief he sought.

XIII.

As the tall ship, whose lofty prore
Shall never stem the billows more,
Deserted by her gallant band,
Amid the breakers lies astrand,—
So on his couch lay Roderick Dhu!
And oft his fevered limbs he threw
In toss abrupt, as when her sides
Lie rocking in the advancing tides,

THE LADY OF THE LAKE

That shake her frame with ceaseless beat,
Yet cannot heave her from her seat;—
O, how unlike her course at sea!
Or his free step on hill and lea!—
Soon as the Minstrel he could scan,—
'What of thy lady?—of my clan?—
My mother?—Douglas?—tell me all!
Have they been ruined in my fall?
Ah, yes! or wherefore art thou here?
Yet speak,—speak boldly,—do not fear.'—
For Allan, who his mood well knew,
Was choked with grief and terror too.—
'Who fought?—who fled?—Old man, be brief;—
Some might,—for they had lost their Chief.
Who basely live?—who bravely died?'
'O, calm thee, Chief!' the Minstrel cried,
'Ellen is safe!' 'For that thank Heaven!'
'And hopes are for the Douglas given;—
The Lady Margaret, too, is well;
And, for thy clan,—on field or fell,
Has never harp of minstrel told
Of combat fought so true and bold.
Thy stately Pine is yet unbent,
Though many a goodly bough is rent.'

XIV.

The Chieftain reared his form on high,
And fever's fire was in his eye;
But ghastly, pale, and livid streaks
Checkered his swarthy brow and cheeks.
'Hark, Minstrel! I have heard thee play,
With measure bold on festal day,
In yon lone isle,—again where ne'er
Shall harper play or warrior hear!—
That stirring air that peals on high,
O'er Dermid's race our victory.—
Strike it!—and then,—for well thou canst,—
Free from thy minstrel-spirit glanced,
Fling me the picture of the fight,
When met my clan the Saxon might.
I'll listen, till my fancy hears
The clang of swords' the crash of spears!
These grates, these walls, shall vanish then
For the fair field of fighting men,
And my free spirit burst away,

As if it soared from battle fray.'
The trembling Bard with awe obeyed,—
Slow on the harp his hand he laid;
But soon remembrance of the sight
He witnessed from the mountain's height,
With what old Bertram told at night,
Awakened the full power of song,
And bore him in career along;—
As shallop launched on river's tide,
'That slow and fearful leaves the side,
But, when it feels the middle stream,
Drives downward swift as lightning's beam.

XV.

Battle of Beal An Duine.

'The Minstrel came once more to view
The eastern ridge of Benvenue,
For ere he parted he would say
Farewell to lovely loch Achray
Where shall he find, in foreign land,
So lone a lake, so sweet a strand!—
There is no breeze upon the fern,
    No ripple on the lake,
Upon her eyry nods the erne,
    The deer has sought the brake;
The small birds will not sing aloud,
    The springing trout lies still,
So darkly glooms yon thunder-cloud,
That swathes, as with a purple shroud,
    Benledi's distant hill.
Is it the thunder's solemn sound
    That mutters deep and dread,
Or echoes from the groaning ground
    The warrior's measured tread?
Is it the lightning's quivering glance
    That on the thicket streams,
Or do they flash on spear and lance
    The sun's retiring beams?—
I see the dagger-crest of Mar,
I see the Moray's silver star,
Wave o'er the cloud of Saxon war,
That up the lake comes winding far!

    To hero boune for battle-strife,

Or bard of martial lay,
'Twere worth ten years of peaceful life,
One glance at their array!

XVI.

'Their light-armed archers far and near
   Surveyed the tangled ground,
Their centre ranks, with pike and spear,
   A twilight forest frowned,
Their barded horsemen in the rear
   The stern battalia crowned.
No cymbal clashed, no clarion rang,
   Still were the pipe and drum;
Save heavy tread, and armor's clang,
   The sullen march was dumb.
There breathed no wind their crests to shake,
   Or wave their flags abroad;
Scarce the frail aspen seemed to quake
   That shadowed o'er their road.
Their vaward scouts no tidings bring,
   Can rouse no lurking foe,
Nor spy a trace of living thing,
   Save when they stirred the roe;
The host moves like a deep-sea wave,
Where rise no rocks its pride to brave
   High-swelling, dark, and slow.
The lake is passed, and now they gain
A narrow and a broken plain,
Before the Trosachs' rugged jaws;
And here the horse and spearmen pause
While, to explore the dangerous glen
Dive through the pass the archer-men.

XVII.

'At once there rose so wild a yell
Within that dark and narrow dell,
As all the fiends from heaven that fell
Had pealed the banner-cry of hell!
   Forth from the pass in tumult driven,
   Like chaff before the wind of heaven,
      The archery appear:
   For life! for life! their flight they ply—
   And shriek, and shout, and battle-cry,
   And plaids and bonnets waving high,

And broadswords flashing to the sky,
Are maddening in the rear.
Onward they drive in dreadful race,
Pursuers and pursued;
Before that tide of flight and chase,
How shall it keep its rooted place,
The spearmen's twilight wood?—"
"Down, down," cried Mar, "your lances down'
Bear back both friend and foe! "—
Like reeds before the tempest's frown,
That serried grove of lances brown
At once lay levelled low;
And closely shouldering side to side,
The bristling ranks the onset bide.—"
"We'll quell the savage mountaineer,
As their Tinchel cows the game!
They come as fleet as forest deer,
We'll drive them back as tame."

XVIII.

'Bearing before them in their course
The relics of the archer force,
Like wave with crest of sparkling foam,
Right onward did Clan-Alpine come.
    Above the tide, each broadsword bright
    Was brandishing like beam of light,
    Each targe was dark below;
    And with the ocean's mighty swing,
    When heaving to the tempest's wing,
    They hurled them on the foe.
I heard the lance's shivering crash,
As when the whirlwind rends the ash;
I heard the broadsword's deadly clang,
As if a hundred anvils rang!
But Moray wheeled his rearward rank
Of horsemen on Clan-Alpine's flank,—
    "My banner-man, advance!
    I see," he cried, "their column shake.
    Now, gallants! for your ladies' sake,
    Upon them with the lance!"—
The horsemen dashed among the rout,
    As deer break through the broom;

Their steeds are stout, their swords are out,
    They soon make lightsome room.

Clan-Alpine's best are backward borne—
    Where, where was Roderick then!
One blast upon his bugle-horn
    Were worth a thousand men.
And refluent through the pass of fear
    The battle's tide was poured;
Vanished the Saxon's struggling spear,
    Vanished the mountain-sword.
As Bracklinn's chasm, so black and steep,
    Receives her roaring linn
As the dark caverns of the deep
    Suck the wild whirlpool in,
So did the deep and darksome pass
Devour the battle's mingled mass;
None linger now upon the plain
Save those who ne'er shall fight again.

XIX.

'Now westward rolls the battle's din,
That deep and doubling pass within.—
Minstrel, away! the work of fate
Is bearing on; its issue wait,
Where the rude Trosachs' dread defile
Opens on Katrine's lake and isle.
Gray Benvenue I soon repassed,
Loch Katrine lay beneath me cast.
    The sun is set;—the clouds are met,
    The lowering scowl of heaven
    An inky hue of livid blue
    To the deep lake has given;
Strange gusts of wind from mountain glen
Swept o'er the lake, then sunk again.
I heeded not the eddying surge,
Mine eye but saw the Trosachs' gorge,
Mine ear but heard that sullen sound,
Which like an earthquake shook the ground,
And spoke the stern and desperate strife
That parts not but with parting life,
Seeming, to minstrel ear, to toll
The dirge of many a passing soul.
    Nearer it comes—the dim-wood glen
    The martial flood disgorged again,
    But not in mingled tide;
    The plaided warriors of the North
    High on the mountain thunder forth

And overhang its side,
While by the lake below appears
The darkening cloud of Saxon spears.
At weary bay each shattered band,
Eying their foemen, sternly stand;
Their banners stream like tattered sail,
That flings its fragments to the gale,
And broken arms and disarray
Marked the fell havoc of the day.

XX.

'Viewing the mountain's ridge askance,
The Saxons stood in sullen trance,
Till Moray pointed with his lance,
    And cried: "Behold yon isle!—
See! none are left to guard its strand
But women weak, that wring the hand:
'Tis there of yore the robber band
    Their booty wont to pile;—
My purse, with bonnet-pieces store,
To him will swim a bow-shot o'er,
And loose a shallop from the shore.
Lightly we'll tame the war-wolf then,
Lords of his mate, and brood, and den."
Forth from the ranks a spearman sprung,
On earth his casque and corselet rung,
    He plunged him in the wave:—
All saw the deed,—the purpose knew,
And to their clamors Benvenue
    A mingled echo gave;
The Saxons shout, their mate to cheer,
The helpless females scream for fear
And yells for rage the mountaineer.
'T was then, as by the outcry riven,
Poured down at once the lowering heaven:
A whirlwind swept Loch Katrine's breast,
Her billows reared their snowy crest.
Well for the swimmer swelled they high,
To mar the Highland marksman's eye;
For round him showered, mid rain and hail,
The vengeful arrows of the Gael.
In vain.—He nears the isle—and lo!
His hand is on a shallop's bow.
Just then a flash of lightning came,
It tinged the waves and strand with flame;

I marked Duncraggan's widowed dame,
Behind an oak I saw her stand,
A naked dirk gleamed in her hand:—
It darkened,—but amid the moan
Of waves I heard a dying groan;—
Another flash!—the spearman floats
A weltering corse beside the boats,
And the stern matron o'er him stood,
Her hand and dagger streaming blood.

XXI.

"'Revenge! revenge!" the Saxons cried,
The Gaels' exulting shout replied.
Despite the elemental rage,
Again they hurried to engage;
But, ere they closed in desperate fight,
Bloody with spurring came a knight,
Sprung from his horse, and from a crag
Waved 'twixt the hosts a milk-white flag.
Clarion and trumpet by his side
Rung forth a truce-note high and wide,
While, in the Monarch's name, afar
A herald's voice forbade the war,
For Bothwell's lord and Roderick bold
Were both, he said, in captive hold.'—
But here the lay made sudden stand,
The harp escaped the Minstrel's hand!
Oft had he stolen a glance, to spy
How Roderick brooked his minstrelsy:
At first, the Chieftain, to the chime,
With lifted hand kept feeble time;
That motion ceased,—yet feeling strong
Varied his look as changed the song;
At length, no more his deafened ear
The minstrel melody can hear;
His face grows sharp,—his hands are clenched'
As if some pang his heart-strings wrenched;
Set are his teeth, his fading eye
Is sternly fixed on vacancy;
Thus, motionless and moanless, drew
His parting breath stout Roderick Dhu!—
Old Allan-bane looked on aghast,
While grim and still his spirit passed;
But when he saw that life was fled,
He poured his wailing o'er the dead.

XXII.

Lament.

'And art thou cold and lowly laid,
Thy foeman's dread, thy people's aid,
Breadalbane's boast, Clan-Alpine's shade!
For thee shall none a requiem say?—
For thee, who loved the minstrel's lay,
For thee, of Bothwell's house the stay,
The shelter of her exiled line,
E'en in this prison-house of thine,
I'll wail for Alpine's honored Pine!

'What groans shall yonder valleys fill!
What shrieks of grief shall rend yon hill!
What tears of burning rage shall thrill,
When mourns thy tribe thy battles done,
Thy fall before the race was won,
Thy sword ungirt ere set of sun!
There breathes not clansman of thy line,
But would have given his life for thine.
O, woe for Alpine's honoured Pine!

'Sad was thy lot on mortal stage!—
The captive thrush may brook the cage,
The prisoned eagle dies for rage.
Brave spirit, do Dot scorn my strain!
And, when its notes awake again,
Even she, so long beloved in vain,
Shall with my harp her voice combine,
And mix her woe and tears with mine,
To wail Clan-Alpine's honoured Pine.'

XXIII.

Ellen the while, with bursting heart,
Remained in lordly bower apart,
Where played, with many-coloured gleams,
Through storied pane the rising beams.
In vain on gilded roof they fall,
And lightened up a tapestried wall,
And for her use a menial train
A rich collation spread in vain.
The banquet proud, the chamber gay,
Scarce drew one curious glance astray;

Or if she looked, 't was but to say,
With better omen dawned the day
In that lone isle, where waved on high
The dun-deer's hide for canopy;
Where oft her noble father shared
The simple meal her care prepared,
While Lufra, crouching by her side,
Her station claimed with jealous pride,
And Douglas, bent on woodland game,
Spoke of the chase to Malcolm Graeme,
Whose answer, oft at random made,
The wandering of his thoughts betrayed.
Those who such simple joys have known
Are taught to prize them when they 're gone.
But sudden, see, she lifts her head;
The window seeks with cautious tread.
What distant music has the power
To win her in this woful hour?
'T was from a turret that o'erhung
Her latticed bower, the strain was sung.

XXIV.

Lay of the Imprisoned Huntsman.

'My hawk is tired of perch and hood,
My idle greyhound loathes his food,
My horse is weary of his stall,
And I am sick of captive thrall.
I wish I were as I have been,
Hunting the hart in forest green,
With bended bow and bloodhound free,
For that's the life is meet for me.

I hate to learn the ebb of time
From yon dull steeple's drowsy chime,
Or mark it as the sunbeams crawl,
Inch after inch, along the wall.
The lark was wont my matins ring,
The sable rook my vespers sing;
These towers, although a king's they be,
Have not a hall of joy for me.

No more at dawning morn I rise,
And sun myself in Ellen's eyes,
Drive the fleet deer the forest through,

And homeward wend with evening dew;
A blithesome welcome blithely meet,
And lay my trophies at her feet,
While fled the eve on wing of glee,—
That life is lost to love and me!'

XXV.

The heart-sick lay was hardly said,
The listener had not turned her head,
It trickled still, the starting tear,
When light a footstep struck her ear,
And Snowdoun's graceful Knight was near.
She turned the hastier, lest again
The prisoner should renew his strain.
'O welcome, brave Fitz-James!' she said;
'How may an almost orphan maid
Pay the deep debt—' 'O say not so!
To me no gratitude you owe.
Not mine, alas! the boon to give,
And bid thy noble father live;
I can but be thy guide, sweet maid,
With Scotland's King thy suit to aid.
No tyrant he, though ire and pride
May lay his better mood aside.
Come, Ellen, come! 'tis more than time,
He holds his court at morning prime.'
With heating heart, and bosom wrung,
As to a brother's arm she clung.
Gently he dried the falling tear,
And gently whispered hope and cheer;
Her faltering steps half led, half stayed,
Through gallery fair and high arcade,
Till at his touch its wings of pride
A portal arch unfolded wide.

XXVI.

Within 't was brilliant all and light,
A thronging scene of figures bright;
It glowed on Ellen's dazzled sight,
As when the setting sun has given
Ten thousand hues to summer even,
And from their tissue fancy frames
Aerial knights and fairy dames.
Still by Fitz-James her footing staid;

THE LADY OF THE LAKE

A few faint steps she forward made,
Then slow her drooping head she raised,
And fearful round the presence gazed;
For him she sought who owned this state,
The dreaded Prince whose will was fate!—
She gazed on many a princely port
Might well have ruled a royal court;
On many a splendid garb she gazed,—
Then turned bewildered and amazed,
For all stood bare; and in the room
Fitz-James alone wore cap and plume.
To him each lady's look was lent,
On him each courtier's eye was bent;
Midst furs and silks and jewels sheen,
He stood, in simple Lincoln green,
The centre of the glittering ring,—
And Snowdoun's Knight is Scotland's King!

XXVII.

As wreath of snow on mountain-breast
Slides from the rock that gave it rest,
Poor Ellen glided from her stay,
And at the Monarch's feet she lay;
No word her choking voice commands,—
She showed the ring,—she clasped her hands.
O, not a moment could he brook,
The generous Prince, that suppliant look!
Gently he raised her,—and, the while,
Checked with a glance the circle's smile;
Graceful, but grave, her brow he kissed,
And bade her terrors be dismissed:—
'Yes, fair; the wandering poor
Fitz-James The fealty of Scotland claims.
To him thy woes, thy wishes, bring;
He will redeem his signet ring.
Ask naught for Douglas;—yester even,
His Prince and he have much forgiven;
Wrong hath he had from slanderous tongue,
I, from his rebel kinsmen, wrong.
We would not, to the vulgar crowd,
Yield what they craved with clamor loud;
Calmly we heard and judged his cause,
Our council aided and our laws.
I stanched thy father's death-feud stern
With stout De Vaux and gray Glencairn;

And Bothwell's Lord henceforth we own
The friend and bulwark of our throne.—
But, lovely infidel, how now?
What clouds thy misbelieving brow?
Lord James of Douglas, lend thine aid;
Thou must confirm this doubting maid.'

XXVIII.

Then forth the noble Douglas sprung,
And on his neck his daughter hung.
The Monarch drank, that happy hour,
The sweetest, holiest draught of Power,—
When it can say with godlike voice,
Arise, sad Virtue, and rejoice!
Yet would not James the general eye
On nature's raptures long should pry;
He stepped between—'Nay, Douglas, nay,
Steal not my proselyte away!
The riddle 'tis my right to read,
That brought this happy chance to speed.
Yes, Ellen, when disguised I stray
In life's more low but happier way,
'Tis under name which veils my power
Nor falsely veils,—for Stirling's tower
Of yore the name of Snowdoun claims,
And Normans call me James Fitz-James.
Thus watch I o'er insulted laws,
Thus learn to right the injured cause.'
Then, in a tone apart and low,—
'Ah, little traitress! none must know
What idle dream, what lighter thought
What vanity full dearly bought,
Joined to thine eye's dark witchcraft, drew
My spell-bound steps to Benvenue
In dangerous hour, and all but gave
Thy Monarch's life to mountain glaive!'
Aloud he spoke: 'Thou still dost hold
That little talisman of gold,
Pledge of my faith, Fitz-James's ring,—
What seeks fair Ellen of the King?'

XXIX.

Full well the conscious maiden guessed
He probed the weakness of her breast;

THE LADY OF THE LAKE

But with that consciousness there came
A lightening of her fears for Graeme,
And more she deemed the Monarch's ire
Kindled 'gainst him who for her sire
Rebellious broadsword boldly drew;
And, to her generous feeling true,
She craved the grace of Roderick Dhu.
'Forbear thy suit;—the King of kings
Alone can stay life's parting wings.
I know his heart, I know his hand,
Have shared his cheer, and proved his brand;
My fairest earldom would I give
To bid Clan-Alpine's Chieftain live!—
Hast thou no other boon to crave?
No other captive friend to save?'
Blushing, she turned her from the King,
And to the Douglas gave the ring,
As if she wished her sire to speak
The suit that stained her glowing cheek.
'Nay, then, my pledge has lost its force,
And stubborn justice holds her course.
Malcolm, come forth!'—and, at the word,
Down kneeled the Graeme to Scotland's Lord.
'For thee, rash youth, no suppliant sues,
From thee may Vengeance claim her dues,
Who, nurtured underneath our smile,
Hast paid our care by treacherous wile,
And sought amid thy faithful clan
A refuge for an outlawed man,
Dishonoring thus thy loyal name.—
Fetters and warder for the Graeme!'
His chain of gold the King unstrung,
The links o'er Malcolm's neck he flung,
Then gently drew the glittering band,
And laid the clasp on Ellen's hand.

Harp of the North, farewell! The hills grow dark,
   On purple peaks a deeper shade descending;
In twilight copse the glow-worm lights her spark,
   The deer, half seen, are to the covert wending.
Resume thy wizard elm! the fountain lending,
   And the wild breeze, thy wilder minstrelsy;
Thy numbers sweet with nature's vespers blending,
   With distant echo from the fold and lea,
And herd-boy's evening pipe, and hum of housing bee.

Yet, once again, farewell, thou Minstrel Harp!
    Yet, once again, forgive my feeble sway,
And little reck I of the censure sharp
    May idly cavil at an idle lay.
Much have I owed thy strains on life's long way,
    Through secret woes the world has never known,
When on the weary night dawned wearier day,
    And bitterer was the grief devoured alone.—
That I o'erlive such woes, Enchantress! is thine own.

Hark! as my lingering footsteps slow retire,
    Some Spirit of the Air has waked thy string!
'Tis now a seraph bold, with touch of fire,
    'Tis now the brush of Fairy's frolic wing.
Receding now, the dying numbers ring
    Fainter and fainter down the rugged dell;
And now the mountain breezes scarcely bring
    A wandering witch-note of the distant spell—
And now, 'tis silent all!—Enchantress, fare thee well!

ROB ROY

VOLUME ONE

For why? Because the good old rule
   Sufficeth them; the simple plan,
  That they should take who have the power,
    And they should keep who can.

— ROB ROY'S GRAVE—WORDSWORTH

AUTHOR'S INTRODUCTION (1829)

When the author projected this further encroachment on the patience of an indulgent public, he was at some loss for a title; a good name being very nearly of as much consequence in literature as in life. The title of *Rob Roy* was suggested by the late Mr. Constable, whose sagacity and experience foresaw the germ of popularity which it included.

No introduction can be more appropriate to the work than some account of the singular character whose name is given to the title-page, and who, through good report and bad report, has maintained a wonderful degree of importance in popular recollection. This cannot be ascribed to the distinction of his birth, which, though that of a gentleman, had in it nothing of high destination, and gave him little right to command in his clan. Neither, though he lived a busy, restless, and enterprising life, were his feats equal to those of other freebooters, who have been less distinguished. He owed his fame in a great measure to his residing on the very verge of the Highlands, and playing such pranks in the beginning of the 18th century, as are usually ascribed to Robin Hood in the middle ages,—and that within forty miles of Glasgow, a great commercial city, the seat of a learned university. Thus a character like his, blending the wild virtues, the subtle policy, and unrestrained license of an American Indian, was flourishing in Scotland during the Augustan age of Queen Anne and

George I. Addison, it is probable, or Pope, would have been considerably surprised if they had known that there existed in the same island with them a personage of Rob Roy's peculiar habits and profession. It is this strong contrast betwixt the civilised and cultivated mode of life on the one side of the Highland line, and the wild and lawless adventures which were habitually undertaken and achieved by one who dwelt on the opposite side of that ideal boundary, which creates the interest attached to his name. Hence it is that even yet,

> Far and near, through vale and hill,
> Are faces that attest the same,
> And kindle like a fire new stirr'd,
> At sound of Rob Roy's name.

There were several advantages which Rob Roy enjoyed for sustaining to advantage the character which he assumed.

The most prominent of these was his descent from, and connection with, the clan MacGregor, so famous for their misfortunes, and the indomitable spirit with which they maintained themselves as a clan, linked and banded together in spite of the most severe laws, executed with unheard-of rigour against those who bore this forbidden surname. Their history was that of several others of the original Highland clans, who were suppressed by more powerful neighbours, and either extirpated, or forced to secure themselves by renouncing their own family appellation, and assuming that of the conquerors. The peculiarity in the story of the MacGregors, is their retaining, with such tenacity, their separate existence and union as a clan under circumstances of the utmost urgency. The history of the tribe is briefly as follows—But we must premise that the tale depends in some degree on tradition; therefore, excepting when written documents are, quoted, it must be considered as in some degree dubious.

The sept of MacGregor claimed a descent from Gregor, or Gregorius, third son, it is said, of Alpin King of Scots, who flourished about 787. Hence their original patronymic is MacAlpine, and they are usually termed the Clan Alpine. An individual tribe of them retains the same name. They are accounted one of the most ancient clans in the Highlands, and it is certain they were a people of original Celtic descent, and occupied at one period very extensive possessions in Perthshire and Argyleshire, which they imprudently continued to hold by the *coir a glaive,* that is, the right of the sword. Their neighbours, the Earls of Argyle and Breadalbane, in the meanwhile, managed to leave the lands occupied by the MacGregors engrossed in those charters which they easily obtained from the Crown; and thus constituted a legal right in their own favour, without much regard to its justice. As opportunity occurred of annoying or extirpating their neighbours, they gradually extended their own domains, by usurping, under the pretext of such royal grants, those of their more uncivilised neighbours. A Sir Duncan Campbell of Lochow, known in the Highlands by the name of *Donacha Dhu nan Churraichd,* that is, Black Duncan with the Cowl, it being his pleasure to wear such a head-gear, is said to have been peculiarly successful in those acts of spoliation upon the clan MacGregor.

The devoted sept, ever finding themselves iniquitously driven from their possessions, defended themselves by force, and occasionally gained advantages, which they used cruelly enough. This conduct, though natural, considering the country and time, was studiously represented at the capital as arising from an untameable and innate ferocity, which nothing, it was said, could remedy, save cutting off the tribe of MacGregor root and branch.

In an act of Privy Council at Stirling, 22d September 1563, in the reign of Queen Mary, commission is granted to the most powerful nobles, and chiefs of the clans, to pursue the clan Gregor with fire and sword. A similar warrant in 1563, not only grants the like powers to Sir John Campbell of Glenorchy, the descendant of Duncan with the Cowl, but discharges the lieges to receive or assist any of the clan Gregor, or afford them, under any colour whatever, meat, drink, or clothes.

An atrocity which the clan Gregor committed in 1589, by the murder of John Drummond of Drummond-ernoch, a forester of the royal forest of Glenartney, is elsewhere given, with all its horrid circumstances. The clan swore upon the severed head of the murdered man, that they would make common cause in avowing the deed. This led to an act of the Privy Council, directing another crusade against the "wicked clan Gregor, so long continuing in blood, slaughter, theft, and robbery," in which letters of fire and sword are denounced against them for the space of three years. The reader will find this particular fact illustrated in the Introduction to the Legend of Montrose in the present edition of these Novels.

Other occasions frequently occurred, in which the MacGregors testified contempt for the laws, from which they had often experienced severity, but never protection. Though they were gradually deprived of their possessions, and of all ordinary means of procuring subsistence, they could not, nevertheless, be supposed likely to starve for famine, while they had the means of taking from strangers what they considered as rightfully their own. Hence they became versed in predatory forays, and accustomed to bloodshed. Their passions were eager, and, with a little management on the part of some of their most powerful neighbours, they could easily be *hounded out*, to use an expressive Scottish phrase, to commit violence, of which the wily instigators took the advantage, and left the ignorant MacGregors an undivided portion of blame and punishment. This policy of pushing on the fierce clans of the Highlands and Borders to break the peace of the country, is accounted by the historian one of the most dangerous practices of his own period, in which the MacGregors were considered as ready agents.

Notwithstanding these severe denunciations,—which were acted upon in the same spirit in which they were conceived, some of the clan still possessed property, and the chief of the name in 1592 is designed Allaster MacGregor of Glenstrae. He is said to have been a brave and active man; but, from the tenor of his confession at his death, appears to have been engaged in many and desperate feuds, one of which finally proved fatal to himself and many of his followers. This was the celebrated conflict at Glenfruin, near the southwestern extremity of Loch Lomond, in the vicinity of which the MacGregors continued to exercise much authority by the *coir a glaive,* or right of the strongest, which we have already mentioned.

There had been a long and bloody feud betwixt the MacGregors and the Laird of Luss, head of the family of Colquhoun, a powerful race on the lower part of Loch Lomond. The MacGregors' tradition affirms that the quarrel began on a very trifling subject. Two of the MacGregors being benighted, asked shelter in a house belonging to a dependant of the Colquhouns, and were refused. They then retreated to an outhouse, took a wedder from the fold, killed it, and supped off the carcass, for which (it is said) they offered payment to the proprietor. The Laird of Luss seized on the offenders, and, by the summary process which feudal barons had at their command, had them both condemned and executed. The MacGregors verify this account of the feud by appealing to a proverb current amongst them, execrating the hour *(Mult dhu an Carbail ghil)* that the black wedder with the white tail was ever lambed. To avenge this quarrel, the Laird of MacGregor assembled his clan, to the number of three or four hundred men, and marched towards Luss from the banks of Loch Long, by a pass called *Raid na Gael,* or the Highlandman's Pass.

Sir Humphrey Colquhoun received early notice of this incursion, and collected a strong force, more than twice the number of that of the invaders. He had with him the gentlemen of the name of Buchanan, with the Grahams, and other gentry of the Lennox, and a party of the citizens of Dumbarton, under command of Tobias Smollett, a magistrate, or bailie, of that town, and ancestor of the celebrated author.

The parties met in the valley of Glenfruin, which signifies the Glen of Sorrow—a name that seemed to anticipate the event of the day, which, fatal to the conquered party, was at least equally so to the victors, the "babe unborn" of Clan Alpine having reason to repent it. The MacGregors, somewhat discouraged by the appearance of a force much superior to their own, were cheered on to the attack by a Seer, or second-sighted person, who professed that he saw the shrouds of the dead wrapt around their principal opponents. The clan charged with great fury on the front of the enemy, while John MacGregor, with a strong party, made an unexpected attack on the flank. A great part of the Colquhouns' force consisted in cavalry, which could not act in the boggy ground. They were said to have disputed the field manfully, but were at length completely routed, and a merciless slaughter was exercised on the fugitives, of whom betwixt two and three hundred fell on the field and in the pursuit. If the MacGregors lost, as is averred, only two men slain in the action, they had slight provocation for an indiscriminate massacre. It is said that their fury extended itself to a party of students for clerical orders, who had imprudently come to see the battle. Some doubt is thrown on this fact, from the indictment against the chief of the clan Gregor being silent on the subject, as is the historian Johnston, and a Professor Ross, who wrote an account of the battle twenty-nine years after it was fought. It is, however, constantly averred by the tradition of the country, and a stone where the deed was done is called *Leck-a-Mhinisteir,* the Minister or Clerk's Flagstone. The MacGregors, by a tradition which is now found to be inaccurate, impute this cruel action to the ferocity of a single man of their tribe, renowned for size and strength, called Dugald, *Ciar Mhor,* or the great Mouse-coloured Man. He was MacGregor's foster-brother, and the chief committed the youths to his charge, with directions to keep them safely till the affray was over. Whether fearful of their escape, or incensed by some sarcasms which they threw on his tribe, or whether out of mere thirst of blood, this savage, while the other MacGregors were engaged in the pursuit, poniarded his helpless and defenceless prisoners. When the chieftain, on his return, demanded where the youths were, the *Ciar* (pronounced Kiar) *Mhor* drew out his bloody dirk, saying in Gaelic, "Ask that, and God save me!" The latter words allude to the exclamation which his victims used when he was murdering them. It would seem, therefore, that this horrible part of the story is founded on fact, though the number of the youths so slain is probably exaggerated in the Lowland accounts. The common people say that the blood of the Ciar Mhor's victims can never be washed off the stone. When MacGregor learnt their fate, he expressed the utmost horror at the deed, and upbraided his foster-brother with having done that which would occasion the destruction of him and his clan. This supposed homicide was the ancestor of Rob Roy, and the tribe from which he was descended. He lies buried at the church of Fortingal, where his sepulchre, covered with a large stone,[1] is still shown, and where his great strength and courage are the theme of many traditions.[2]

MacGregor's brother was one of the very few of the tribe who was slain. He was buried near the field of battle, and the place is marked by a rude stone, called the Grey Stone of MacGregor.

Sir Humphrey Colquhoun, being well mounted, escaped for the time to the castle of Banochar, or Benechra. It proved no sure defence, however, for he was shortly after murdered in a vault of the castle,—the family annals say by the MacGregors, though other accounts charge the deed upon the MacFarlanes.

This battle of Glenfruin, and the severity which the victors exercised in the pursuit, was reported to King James VI. in a manner the most unfavourable to the clan Gregor, whose general character, being that of lawless though brave men, could not much avail them in such a case. That James might fully understand the extent of the slaughter, the widows of the slain, to the number of eleven score, in deep mourning, riding upon white palfreys, and each bearing her husband's bloody shirt on a spear, appeared at Stirling, in presence of a monarch peculiarly accessible to such sights of fear and sorrow, to demand vengeance for the death of their husbands, upon those by whom they had been made desolate.

The remedy resorted to was at least as severe as the cruelties which it was designed to punish. By an Act of the Privy Council, dated 3d April 1603, the name of MacGregor was expressly abolished, and those who had hitherto borne it were commanded to change it for other surnames, the pain of death being denounced against those who should call themselves Gregor or MacGregor, the names of their fathers. Under the same penalty, all who had been at the conflict of Glenfruin, or accessory to other marauding parties charged in the act, were prohibited from carrying weapons, except a pointless knife to eat their victuals. By a subsequent act of Council, 24th June 1613, death was denounced against any persons of the tribe formerly called MacGregor, who should presume to assemble in greater numbers than four. Again, by an Act of Parliament, 1617, chap. 26, these laws were continued, and extended to the rising generation, in respect that great numbers of the children of those against whom the acts of Privy Council had been directed, were stated to be then approaching to maturity, who, if permitted to resume the name of their parents, would render the clan as strong as it was before.

The execution of those severe acts was chiefly intrusted in the west to the Earl of Argyle and the powerful clan of Campbell, and to the Earl of Athole and his followers in the more eastern Highlands of Perthshire. The MacGregors failed not to resist with the most determined courage; and many a valley in the West and North Highlands retains memory of the severe conflicts, in which the proscribed clan sometimes obtained transient advantages, and always sold their lives dearly. At length the pride of Allaster MacGregor, the chief of the clan, was so much lowered by the sufferings of his people, that he resolved to surrender himself to the Earl of Argyle, with his principal followers, on condition that they should be sent out of Scotland. If the unfortunate chief's own account be true, he had more reasons than one for expecting some favour from the Earl, who had in secret advised and encouraged him to many of the desperate actions for which he was now called to so severe a reckoning. But Argyle, as old Birrell expresses himself, kept a Highlandman's promise with them, fulfilling it to the ear, and breaking it to the sense. MacGregor was sent under a strong guard to the frontier of England, and being thus, in the literal sense, sent out of Scotland, Argyle was judged to have kept faith with him, though the same party which took him there brought him back to Edinburgh in custody.

MacGregor of Glenstrae was tried before the Court of Justiciary, 20th January 1604, and found guilty. He appears to have been instantly conveyed from the bar to the gallows; for Birrell, of the same date, reports that he was hanged at the Cross, and, for distinction sake, was suspended higher by his own height than two of his kindred and friends.

On the 18th of February following, more men of the MacGregors were executed, after a long imprisonment, and several others in the beginning of March.

The Earl of Argyle's service, in conducting to the surrender of the insolent and wicked race and name of MacGregor, notorious common malefactors, and in the inbringing of MacGregor, with a great many of the leading men of the clan, worthily executed to death for their offences, is thankfully acknowledged by an Act of Parliament, 1607, chap. 16, and rewarded with a grant of twenty chalders of victual out of the lands of Kintire.

The MacGregors, notwithstanding the letters of fire and sword, and orders for military execution repeatedly directed against them by the Scottish legislature, who apparently lost all the calmness of conscious dignity and security, and could not even name the outlawed clan without vituperation, showed no inclination to be blotted out of the roll of clanship. They submitted to the law, indeed, so far as to take the names of the neighbouring families amongst whom they happened to live, nominally becoming, as the case might render it most convenient, Drummonds, Campbells, Grahams, Buchanans, Stewarts, and the like; but to all intents and purposes of combination and mutual attachment, they remained the clan Gregor, united together for right or wrong, and menacing with the general vengeance of their race, all who committed aggressions against any individual of their number.

They continued to take and give offence with as little hesitation as before the legislative dispersion which had been attempted, as appears from the preamble to statute 1633, chapter 30, setting forth, that the clan Gregor, which had been suppressed and reduced to quietness by the great care of the late King James of eternal memory, had nevertheless broken out again, in the counties of Perth, Stirling, Clackmannan, Monteith, Lennox, Angus, and Mearns; for which reason the statute re-establishes the disabilities attached to the clan, and, grants a new commission for enforcing the laws against that wicked and rebellious race.

Notwithstanding the extreme severities of King James I. and Charles I. against this unfortunate people, who were rendered furious by proscription, and then punished for yielding to the passions which had been wilfully irritated, the MacGregors to a man attached themselves during the civil war to the cause of the latter monarch. Their bards have ascribed this to the native respect of the MacGregors for the crown of Scotland, which their ancestors once wore, and have appealed to their armorial bearings, which display a pine-tree crossed saltire wise with a naked sword, the point of which supports a royal crown. But, without denying that such motives may have had their weight, we are disposed to think, that a war which opened the low country to the raids of the clan Gregor would have more charms for them than any inducement to espouse the cause of the Covenanters, which would have brought them into contact with Highlanders as fierce as themselves, and having as little to lose. Patrick MacGregor, their leader, was the son of a distinguished chief, named Duncan Abbarach, to whom Montrose wrote letters as to his trusty and special friend, expressing his reliance on his devoted loyalty, with an assurance, that when once his Majesty's affairs were placed upon a permanent footing, the grievances of the clan MacGregor should be redressed.

At a subsequent period of these melancholy times, we find the clan Gregor claiming the immunities of other tribes, when summoned by the Scottish Parliament to resist the invasion of the Commonwealth's army, in 1651. On the last day of March in that year, a supplication to the King and Parliament, from Calum MacCondachie Vich Euen, and Euen MacCondachie Euen, in their own name, and that of the whole name of MacGregor, set forth, that while, in obedience to the orders of Parliament, enjoining all clans to come out in the present service under their chieftains, for the defence of religion, king, and kingdoms, the petitioners were drawing their men to guard the passes at the head of the river Forth, they were interfered with by the Earl of Athole and the Laird of Buchanan, who had required the attendance of many of the clan Gregor upon their arrays. This interference was, doubtless, owing to the change of name, which seems to have given rise to the claim of the Earl of Athole and the Laird of Buchanan to muster the MacGregors under their banners, as Murrays or Buchanans. It does not appear that the petition of the MacGregors, to be permitted to come out in a body, as other clans, received any answer. But upon the Restoration, King Charles, in the first Scottish Parliament of his reign (statute 1661, chap. 195), annulled the various acts against the clan Gregor, and restored them to the full use of their family name, and the other privileges of liege subjects, setting forth, as a reason for this lenity, that those who were formerly designed MacGregors had, during the late troubles, conducted themselves with such loyalty and affection to his Majesty, as might justly wipe off all memory of former miscarriages, and take away all marks of reproach for the same.

It is singular enough, that it seems to have aggravated the feelings of the nonconforming Presbyterians, when the penalties which were most unjustly imposed upon themselves were relaxed towards the poor MacGregors;—so little are the best men, any more than the worst, able to judge with impartiality of the same measures, as applied to themselves, or to others. Upon the Restoration, an influence inimical to this unfortunate clan, said to be the same with that which afterwards dictated the massacre of Glencoe, occasioned the re-enaction of the penal statutes against the MacGregors. There are no reasons given why these highly penal acts should have been renewed; nor is it alleged that the clan had been guilty of late irregularities. Indeed, there is some reason to think that the clause was formed of set purpose, in a shape which should elude observation; for, though containing conclusions fatal to the rights of so many Scottish subjects, it is neither mentioned in the title nor the rubric of the Act of Parliament in which it occurs, and is thrown briefly in at the close of the statute 1693, chap. 61, entitled, an Act for the Justiciary in the Highlands.

It does not, however, appear that after the Revolution the acts against the clan were severely enforced; and in the latter half of the eighteenth century, they were not enforced at all. Commissioners of supply were named in Parliament by the proscribed title of MacGregor, and decrees of courts of justice were pronounced, and legal deeds entered into, under the same appellative. The MacGregors, however, while the laws continued in the statute-book, still suffered under the deprivation of the name which was their birthright, and some attempts were made for the purpose of adopting another, MacAlpine or Grant being proposed as the title of the whole clan in future. No agreement, however, could be entered into; and the evil was submitted to as a matter of necessity, until full redress was obtained from the British Parliament, by an act abolishing for ever the penal statutes which had been so long imposed upon this ancient race. This statute, well merited by the services of many a gentleman of the clan in behalf of their King and country, was passed, and the clan proceeded to act upon it with the same spirit of ancient times, which had made them suffer severely under a deprivation that would have been deemed of little consequence by a great part of their fellow-subjects.

They entered into a deed recognising John Murray of Lanrick, Esq. (afterwards Sir John MacGregor, Baronet), representative of the family of Glencarnock, as lawfully descended from the ancient stock and blood of the Lairds and Lords of MacGregor, and therefore acknowledged him as their chief on all lawful occasions and causes whatsoever. The deed was subscribed by eight hundred and twenty-six persons of the name of MacGregor, capable of bearing arms. A great many of the clan during the last war formed themselves into what was called the Clan Alpine Regiment, raised in 1799, under the command of their Chief and his brother Colonel MacGregor.

Having briefly noticed the history of this clan, which presents a rare and interesting example of the indelible character of the patriarchal system, the author must now offer some notices of the individual who gives name to these volumes.

In giving an account of a Highlander, his pedigree is first to be considered. That of Rob Roy was deduced from Ciar Mhor, the great mouse-coloured man, who is accused by tradition of having slain the young students at the battle of Glenfruin.

Without puzzling ourselves and our readers with the intricacies of Highland genealogy, it is enough to say, that after the death of Allaster MacGregor of Glenstrae, the clan, discouraged by the unremitting persecution of their enemies, seem not to have had the means of placing themselves under the command of a single chief. According to their places of residence and immediate descent, the several families were led and directed by *Chieftains*, which, in the Highland acceptation, signifies the head of a particular branch of a tribe, in opposition to *Chief*, who is the leader and commander of the whole name.

The family and descendants of Dugald Ciar Mhor lived chiefly in the mountains between Loch Lomond and Loch Katrine, and occupied a good deal of property there —whether by sufferance, by the right of the sword, which it was never safe to dispute with them, or by legal titles of various kinds, it would be useless to inquire and unnecessary to detail. Enough;—there they certainly were—a people whom their most powerful neighbours were desirous to conciliate, their friendship in peace being very necessary to the quiet of the vicinage, and their assistance in war equally prompt and effectual.

Rob Roy MacGregor Campbell, which last name he bore in consequence of the Acts of Parliament abolishing his own, was the younger son of Donald MacGregor of Glengyle, said to have been a Lieutenant-Colonel (probably in the service of James II.), by his wife, a daughter of Campbell of Glenfalloch. Rob's own designation was of Inversnaid; but he appears to have acquired a right of some kind or other to the property or possession of Craig Royston, a domain of rock and forest, lying on the east side of Loch Lomond, where that beautiful lake stretches into the dusky mountains of Glenfalloch.

The time of his birth is uncertain. But he is said to have been active in the scenes of war and plunder which succeeded the Revolution; and tradition affirms him to have been the leader in a predatory incursion into the parish of Kippen, in the Lennox, which took place in the year 1691. It was of almost a bloodless character, only one person losing his life; but from the extent of the depredation, it was long distinguished by the name of the Her'-ship, or devastation, of Kippen.[3] The time of his death is also uncertain, but as he is said to have survived the year 1733, and died an aged man, it is probable he may have been twenty-five about the time of the Her'-ship of Kippen, which would assign his birth to the middle of the 17th century.

In the more quiet times which succeeded the Revolution, Rob Roy, or Red Robert, seems to have exerted his active talents, which were of no mean order, as a drover, or trader in cattle, to a great extent. It may well be supposed that in those days no Lowland, much less English drovers, ventured to enter the Highlands. The cattle, which were the staple commodity of the mountains, were escorted down to fairs, on the borders of the Lowlands, by a party of Highlanders, with their arms rattling around them; and who dealt, however, in all honour and good faith with their Southern customers. A fray, indeed, would sometimes arise, when the Lowlandmen, chiefly Borderers, who had to supply the English market, used to dip their bonnets in the next brook, and wrapping them round their hands, oppose their cudgels to the naked broadswords, which had not always the superiority. I have heard from aged persons who had been engaged in such affrays, that the Highlanders used remarkably fair play, never using the point of the sword, far less their pistols or daggers; so that

> With many a stiff thwack and many a bang,
> Hard crabtree and cold iron rang.

A slash or two, or a broken head, was easily accommodated, and as the trade was of benefit to both parties, trifling skirmishes were not allowed to interrupt its harmony. Indeed it was of vital interest to the Highlanders, whose income, so far as derived from their estates, depended entirely on the sale of black cattle; and a sagacious and experienced dealer benefited not only himself, but his friends and neighbours, by his speculations. Those of Rob Roy were for several years so successful as to inspire general confidence, and raise him in the estimation of the country in which he resided.

His importance was increased by the death of his father, in consequence of which he succeeded to the management of his nephew Gregor MacGregor of Glengyle's property, and, as his tutor, to such influence with the clan and following as was due to the representative of Dugald Ciar. Such influence was the more uncontrolled, that this family of the MacGregors seemed to have refused adherence to MacGregor of Glencarnock, the ancestor of the present Sir Ewan MacGregor, and asserted a kind of independence.

It was at this time that Rob Roy acquired an interest by purchase, wadset, or otherwise, to the property of Craig Royston already mentioned. He was in particular favour, during this prosperous period of his life, with his nearest and most powerful neighbour, James, first Duke of Montrose, from whom he received many marks of regard. His Grace consented to give his nephew and himself a right of property on the estates of Glengyle and Inversnaid, which they had till then only held as kindly tenants. The Duke also, with a view to the interest of the country and his own estate, supported our adventurer by loans of money to a considerable amount, to enable him to carry on his speculations in the cattle trade.

Unfortunately that species of commerce was and is liable to sudden fluctuations; and Rob Roy was, by a sudden depression of markets, and, as a friendly tradition adds, by the bad faith of a partner named MacDonald, whom he had imprudently received into his confidence, and intrusted with a considerable sum of money, rendered totally insolvent. He absconded, of course—not empty-handed, if it be true, as stated in an advertisement for his apprehension, that he had in his possession sums to the amount of L1000 sterling, obtained from several noblemen and gentlemen under pretence of purchasing cows for them in the Highlands. This advertisement appeared in June 1712, and was several times repeated. It fixes the period when Rob Roy exchanged his commercial adventures for speculations of a very different complexion.[4]

He appears at this period first to have removed from his ordinary dwelling at Inversnaid, ten or twelve Scots miles (which is double the number of English) farther into the Highlands, and commenced the lawless sort of life which he afterwards followed. The Duke of Montrose, who conceived himself deceived and cheated by MacGregor's conduct, employed legal means to recover the money lent to him. Rob Roy's landed property was attached by the regular form of legal procedure, and his stock and furniture made the subject of arrest and sale.

It is said that this diligence of the law, as it is called in Scotland, which the English more bluntly term distress, was used in this case with uncommon severity, and that the legal satellites, not usually the gentlest persons in the world, had insulted MacGregor's wife, in a manner which would have aroused a milder man than he to thoughts of unbounded vengeance. She was a woman of fierce and haughty temper, and is not unlikely to have disturbed the officers in the execution of their duty, and thus to have incurred ill treatment, though, for the sake of humanity, it is to be hoped that the story sometimes told is a popular exaggeration. It is certain that she felt extreme anguish at being expelled from the banks of Loch Lomond, and gave vent to her feelings in a fine piece of pipe-music, still well known to amateurs by the name of "Rob Roy's Lament."

The fugitive is thought to have found his first place of refuge in Glen Dochart, under the Earl of Breadalbane's protection; for, though that family had been active agents in the destruction of the MacGregors in former times, they had of late years sheltered a great many of the name in their old possessions. The Duke of Argyle was also one of Rob Roy's protectors, so far as to afford him, according to the Highland phrase, wood and water—the shelter, namely, that is afforded by the forests and lakes of an inaccessible country.

The great men of the Highlands in that time, besides being anxiously ambitious to keep up what was called their Following, or military retainers, were also desirous to have at their disposal men of resolute character, to whom the world and the world's law were no friends, and who might at times ravage the lands or destroy the tenants of a feudal enemy, without bringing responsibility on their patrons. The strife between the names of Campbell and Graham, during the civil wars of the seventeenth century, had been stamped with mutual loss and inveterate enmity. The death of the great Marquis of Montrose on the one side, the defeat at Inverlochy, and cruel plundering of Lorn, on the other, were reciprocal injuries not likely to be forgotten. Rob Roy was, therefore, sure of refuge in the country of the Campbells, both as having assumed their name, as connected by his mother with the family of Glenfalloch, and as an enemy to the rival house of Montrose. The extent of Argyle's possessions, and the power of retreating thither in any emergency, gave great encouragement to the bold schemes of revenge which he had adopted.

This was nothing short of the maintenance of a predatory war against the Duke of Montrose, whom he considered as the author of his exclusion from civil society, and of the outlawry to which he had been sentenced by letters of horning and caption (legal writs so called), as well as the seizure of his goods, and adjudication of his landed property. Against his Grace, therefore, his tenants, friends, allies, and relatives, he disposed himself to employ every means of annoyance in his power; and though this was a circle sufficiently extensive for active depredation, Rob, who professed himself a Jacobite, took the liberty of extending his sphere of operations against all whom he chose to consider as friendly to the revolutionary government, or to that most obnoxious of measures—the Union of the Kingdoms. Under one or other of these pretexts, all his neighbours of the Lowlands who had anything to lose, or were unwilling to compound for security by paying him an annual sum for protection or forbearance, were exposed to his ravages.

The country in which this private warfare, or system of depredation, was to be carried on, was, until opened up by roads, in the highest degree favourable for his purpose. It was broken up into narrow valleys, the habitable part of which bore no proportion to the huge wildernesses of forest, rocks, and precipices by which they were encircled, and which was, moreover, full of inextricable passes, morasses, and natural strengths, unknown to any but the inhabitants themselves, where a few men acquainted with the ground were capable, with ordinary address, of baffling the pursuit of numbers.

The opinions and habits of the nearest neighbours to the Highland line were also highly favourable to Rob Roy's purpose. A large proportion of them were of his own clan of MacGregor, who claimed the property of Balquhidder, and other Highland districts, as having been part of the ancient possessions of their tribe; though the harsh laws, under the severity of which they had suffered so deeply, had assigned the ownership to other families. The civil wars of the seventeenth century had accustomed these men to the use of arms, and they were peculiarly brave and fierce from remembrance of their sufferings. The vicinity of a comparatively rich Lowland district gave also great temptations to incursion. Many belonging to other clans, habituated to contempt of industry, and to the use of arms, drew towards an unprotected frontier which promised facility of plunder; and the state of the country, now so peaceable and quiet, verified at that time the opinion which Dr. Johnson heard with doubt and suspicion, that the most disorderly and lawless districts of the Highlands were those which lay nearest to the Lowland line. There was, therefore, no difficulty in Rob Roy, descended of a tribe which was widely dispersed in the country we have described, collecting any number of followers whom he might be able to keep in action, and to maintain by his proposed operations.

He himself appears to have been singularly adapted for the profession which he proposed to exercise. His stature was not of the tallest, but his person was uncommonly strong and compact. The greatest peculiarities of his frame were the breadth of his shoulders, and the great and almost disproportionate length of his arms; so remarkable, indeed, that it was said he could, without stooping, tie the garters of his Highland hose, which are placed two inches below the knee. His countenance was open, manly, stern at periods of danger, but frank and cheerful in his hours of festivity. His hair was dark red, thick, and frizzled, and curled short around the face. His fashion of dress showed, of course, the knees and upper part of the leg, which was described to me, as resembling that of a Highland bull, hirsute, with red hair, and evincing muscular strength similar to that animal. To these personal qualifications must be added a masterly use of the Highland sword, in which his length of arm gave him great advantage—and a perfect and intimate knowledge of all the recesses of the wild country in which he harboured, and the character of the various individuals, whether friendly or hostile, with whom he might come in contact.

His mental qualities seem to have been no less adapted to the circumstances in which he was placed. Though the descendant of the blood-thirsty Ciar Mhor, he inherited none of his ancestor's ferocity. On the contrary, Rob Roy avoided every appearance of cruelty, and it is not averred that he was ever the means of unnecessary bloodshed, or the actor in any deed which could lead the way to it. His schemes of plunder were contrived and executed with equal boldness and sagacity, and were almost universally successful, from the skill with which they were laid, and the secrecy and rapidity with which they were executed. Like Robin Hood of England, he was a kind and gentle robber,—and, while he took from the rich, was liberal in relieving the poor. This might in part be policy; but the universal tradition of the country speaks it to have arisen from a better motive. All whom I have conversed with, and I have in my youth seen some who knew Rob Roy personally, give him the character of a benevolent and humane man "in his way."

His ideas of morality were those of an Arab chief, being such as naturally arose out of his wild education. Supposing Rob Roy to have argued on the tendency of the life which he pursued, whether from choice or from necessity, he would doubtless have assumed to himself the character of a brave man, who, deprived of his natural rights by the partiality of laws, endeavoured to assert them by the strong hand of natural power; and he is most felicitously described as reasoning thus, in the high-toned poetry of my gifted friend Wordsworth:

> Say, then, that he was wise as brave,
> As wise in thought as bold in deed;
> For in the principles of things
> He sought his moral creed.
>
> Said generous Rob, "What need of Books?
> Burn all the statutes and their shelves!
> They stir us up against our kind,
> And worse, against ourselves.
>
> "We have a passion, make a law,
> Too false to guide us or control;
> And for the law itself we fight
> In bitterness of soul.
>
> "And puzzled, blinded, then we lose
> Distinctions that are plain and few;
> These find I graven on my heart,
> That tells me what to do.
>
> "The creatures see of flood and field,
> And those that travel on the wind
> With them no strife can last; they live
> In peace, and peace of mind.
>
> "For why? Because the good old rule
> Sufficeth them; the simple plan,
> That they should take who have the power,
> And they should keep who can.
>
> "A lesson which is quickly learn'd,
> A signal through which all can see;
> Thus, nothing here provokes the strong
> To wanton cruelty.
>
> "And freakishness of mind is check'd,
> He tamed who foolishly aspires,
> While to the measure of his might
> Each fashions his desires.
>
> "All kinds and creatures stand and fall

By strength of prowess or of wit;
'Tis God's appointment who must sway,
And who is to submit.

"Since then," said Robin, "right is plain,
And longest life is but a day,
To have my ends, maintain my rights,
I'll take the shortest way."

And thus among these rocks he lived,
Through summer's heat and winter's snow

The eagle, he was lord above,
And Rob was lord below.

We are not, however, to suppose the character of this distinguished outlaw to be that of an actual hero, acting uniformly and consistently on such moral principles as the illustrious bard who, standing by his grave, has vindicated his fame. On the contrary, as is common with barbarous chiefs, Rob Roy appears to have mixed his professions of principle with a large alloy of craft and dissimulation, of which his conduct during the civil war is sufficient proof. It is also said, and truly, that although his courtesy was one of his strongest characteristics, yet sometimes he assumed an arrogance of manner which was not easily endured by the high-spirited men to whom it was addressed, and drew the daring outlaw into frequent disputes, from which he did not always come off with credit. From this it has been inferred, that Rob Roy was more of a bully than a hero, or at least that he had, according to the common phrase, his fighting days. Some aged men who knew him well, have described him also as better at a *taich-tulzie,* or scuffle within doors, than in mortal combat. The tenor of his life may be quoted to repel this charge; while, at the same time, it must be allowed, that the situation in which he was placed rendered him prudently averse to maintaining quarrels, where nothing was to be had save blows, and where success would have raised up against him new and powerful enemies, in a country where revenge was still considered as a duty rather than a crime. The power of commanding his passions on such occasions, far from being inconsistent with the part which MacGregor had to perform, was essentially necessary, at the period when he lived, to prevent his career from being cut short.

I may here mention one or two occasions on which Rob Roy appears to have given way in the manner alluded to. My late venerable friend, John Ramsay of Ochtertyre, alike eminent as a classical scholar and as an authentic register of the ancient history and manners of Scotland, informed me, that on occasion of a public meeting at a bonfire in the town of Doune, Rob Roy gave some offence to James Edmondstone of Newton, the same gentleman who was unfortunately concerned in the slaughter of Lord Rollo (see Maclaurin's Criminal Trials, No. IX.), when Edmondstone compelled MacGregor to quit the town on pain of being thrown by him into the bonfire. "I broke one off your ribs on a former occasion," said he, "and now, Rob, if you provoke me farther, I will break your neck." But it must be remembered that Edmondstone was a man of consequence in the Jacobite party, as he carried the royal standard of James VII. at the battle of Sheriffmuir, and also, that he was near the door of his own mansion-house, and probably surrounded by his friends and adherents. Rob Roy, however, suffered in reputation for retiring under such a threat.

Another well-vouched case is that of Cunningham of Boquhan.

Henry Cunningham, Esq. of Boquhan, was a gentleman of Stirlingshire, who, like many *exquisites* of our own time, united a natural high spirit and daring character with an affectation of delicacy of address and manners amounting to foppery.[5]

He chanced to be in company with Rob Roy, who, either in contempt of Boquhan's supposed effeminacy, or because he thought him a safe person to fix a quarrel on (a point which Rob's enemies alleged he was wont to consider), insulted him so grossly that a challenge passed between them. The goodwife of the clachan had hidden Cunningham's sword, and while he rummaged the house in quest of his own or some other, Rob Roy went to the Shieling Hill, the appointed place of combat, and paraded there with great majesty, waiting for his antagonist. In the meantime, Cunningham had rummaged out an old sword, and, entering the ground of contest in all haste, rushed on the outlaw with such unexpected fury that he fairly drove him off the field, nor did he show himself in the village again for some time. Mr. MacGregor Stirling has a softened account of this anecdote in his new edition of Nimmo's Stirlingshire; still he records Rob Roy's discomfiture.

Occasionally Rob Roy suffered disasters, and incurred great personal danger. On one remarkable occasion he was saved by the coolness of his lieutenant, Macanaleister or Fletcher, the *Little John* of his band—a fine active fellow, of course, and celebrated as a marksman. It happened that MacGregor and his party had been surprised and dispersed by a superior force of horse and foot, and the word was given to "split and squander." Each shifted for himself, but a bold dragoon attached himself to pursuit of Rob, and overtaking him, struck at him with his broadsword. A plate of iron in his bonnet saved the MacGregor from being cut down to the teeth; but the blow was heavy enough to bear him to the ground, crying as he fell, "Oh, Macanaleister, is there naething in her?" (*i.e.* in the gun). The trooper, at the same time, exclaiming, "D—n ye, your mother never wrought your night-cap!" had his arm raised for a second blow, when Macanaleister fired, and the ball pierced the dragoon's heart.

Such as he was, Rob Roy's progress in his occupation is thus described by a gentleman of sense and talent, who resided within the circle of his predatory wars, had probably felt their effects, and speaks of them, as might be expected, with little of the forbearance with which, from their peculiar and romantic character, they are now regarded.

"This man (Rob Roy MacGregor) was a person of sagacity, and neither wanted stratagem nor address; and having abandoned himself to all licentiousness, set himself at the head of all the loose, vagrant, and desperate people of that clan, in the west end of Perth and Stirling shires, and infested those whole countries with thefts, robberies, and depredations. Very few who lived within his reach (that is, within the distance of a nocturnal expedition) could promise to themselves security, either for their persons or effects, without subjecting themselves to pay him a heavy and shameful tax of *black-mail*. He at last proceeded to such a degree of audaciousness that he committed robberies, raised contributions, and resented quarrels, at the head of a very considerable body of armed men, in open day, and in the face of the government."[6]

The extent and success of these depredations cannot be surprising, when we consider that the scene of them was laid in a country where the general law was neither enforced nor respected.

Having recorded that the general habit of cattle-stealing had blinded even those of the better classes to the infamy of the practice, and that as men's property consisted entirely in herds, it was rendered in the highest degree precarious, Mr. Grahame adds—

"On these accounts there is no culture of ground, no improvement of pastures, and from the same reasons, no manufactures, no trade; in short, no industry. The people are extremely prolific, and therefore so numerous, that there is not business in that country, according to its present order and economy, for the one-half of them. Every place is full of idle people, accustomed to arms, and lazy in everything but rapines and depredations. As *buddel* or *aquavitae* houses are to be found everywhere through the country, so in these they saunter away their time, and frequently consume there the returns of their illegal purchases. Here the laws have never been executed, nor the authority of the magistrate ever established. Here the officer of the law neither dare nor can execute his duty, and several places are about thirty miles from lawful persons. In short, here is no order, no authority, no government."

The period of the rebellion, 1715, approached soon after Rob Roy had attained celebrity. His Jacobite partialities were now placed in opposition to his sense of the obligations which he owed to the indirect protection of the Duke of Argyle. But the desire of "drowning his sounding steps amid the din of general war" induced him to join the forces of the Earl of Mar, although his patron the Duke of Argyle was at the head of the army opposed to the Highland insurgents.

The MacGregors, a large sept of them at least, that of Ciar Mhor, on this occasion were not commanded by Rob Roy, but by his nephew already mentioned, Gregor MacGregor, otherwise called James Grahame of Glengyle, and still better remembered by the Gaelic epithet of *Ghlune Dhu, i.e.* Black Knee, from a black spot on one of his knees, which his Highland garb rendered visible. There can be no question, however, that being then very young, Glengyle must have acted on most occasions by the advice and direction of so experienced a leader as his uncle.

The MacGregors assembled in numbers at that period, and began even to threaten the Lowlands towards the lower extremity of Loch Lomond. They suddenly seized all the boats which were upon the lake, and, probably with a view to some enterprise of their own, drew them overland to Inversnaid, in order to intercept the progress of a large body of west-country whigs who were in arms for the government, and moving in that direction.

The whigs made an excursion for the recovery of the boats. Their forces consisted of volunteers from Paisley, Kilpatrick, and elsewhere, who, with the assistance of a body of seamen, were towed up the river Leven in long-boats belonging to the ships of war then lying in the Clyde. At Luss they were joined by the forces of Sir Humphrey Colquhoun, and James Grant, his son-in-law, with their followers, attired in the Highland dress of the period, which is picturesquely described.[7] The whole party crossed to Craig-Royston, but the MacGregors did not offer combat.

If we are to believe the account of the expedition given by the historian Rae, they leapt on shore at Craig-Royston with the utmost intrepidity, no enemy appearing to oppose them, and by the noise of their drums, which they beat incessantly, and the discharge of their artillery and small arms, terrified the MacGregors, whom they appear never to have seen, out of their fastnesses, and caused them to fly in a panic to the general camp of the Highlanders at Strath-Fillan.[8] The low-country men succeeded in getting possession of the boats at a great expenditure of noise and courage, and little risk of danger.

After this temporary removal from his old haunts, Rob Roy was sent by the Earl of Mar to Aberdeen, to raise, it is believed, a part of the clan Gregor, which is settled in that country. These men were of his own family (the race of the Ciar Mhor). They were the descendants of about three hundred MacGregors whom the Earl of Murray, about the year 1624, transported from his estates in Menteith to oppose against his enemies the MacIntoshes, a race as hardy and restless as they were themselves.

But while in the city of Aberdeen, Rob Roy met a relation of a very different class and character from those whom he was sent to summon to arms. This was Dr. James Gregory (by descent a MacGregor), the patriarch of a dynasty of professors distinguished for literary and scientific talent, and the grandfather of the late eminent physician and accomplished scholar, Professor Gregory of Edinburgh. This gentleman was at the time Professor of Medicine in King's College, Aberdeen, and son of Dr. James Gregory, distinguished in science as the inventor of the reflecting telescope. With such a family it may seem our friend Rob could have had little communion. But civil war is a species of misery which introduces men to strange bed-fellows. Dr. Gregory thought it a point of prudence to claim kindred, at so critical a period, with a man so formidable and influential. He invited Rob Roy to his house, and treated him with so much kindness, that he produced in his generous bosom a degree of gratitude which seemed likely to occasion very inconvenient effects.

The Professor had a son about eight or nine years old,—a lively, stout boy of his age,—with whose appearance our Highland Robin Hood was much taken. On the day before his departure from the house of his learned relative, Rob Roy, who had pondered deeply how he might requite his cousin's kindness, took Dr. Gregory aside, and addressed him to this purport:—"My dear kinsman, I have been thinking what I could do to show my sense of your hospitality. Now, here you have a fine spirited boy of a son, whom you are ruining by cramming him with your useless book-learning, and I am determined, by way of manifesting my great good-will to you and yours, to take him with me and make a man of him." The learned Professor was utterly overwhelmed when his warlike kinsman announced his kind purpose in language which implied no doubt of its being a proposal which, would be, and ought to be, accepted with the utmost gratitude. The task of apology or explanation was of a most delicate description; and there might have been considerable danger in suffering Rob Roy to perceive that the promotion with which he threatened the son was, in the father's eyes, the ready road to the gallows. Indeed, every excuse which he could at first think of—such as regret for putting his friend to trouble with a youth who had been educated in the Lowlands, and so on—only strengthened the chieftain's inclination to patronise his young kinsman, as he supposed they arose entirely from the modesty of the father. He would for a long time take no apology, and even spoke of carrying off the youth by a certain degree of kindly violence, whether his father consented, or not. At length the perplexed Professor pleaded that his son was very young, and in an infirm state of health, and not yet able to endure the hardships of a mountain life; but that in another year or two he hoped his health would be firmly established, and he would be in a fitting condition to attend on his brave kinsman, and follow out the splendid destinies to which he opened the way. This agreement being made, the cousins parted,—Rob Roy pledging his honour to carry his young relation to the hills with him on his next return to Aberdeenshire, and Dr. Gregory, doubtless, praying in his secret soul that he might never see Rob's Highland face again.

James Gregory, who thus escaped being his kinsman's recruit, and in all probability his henchman, was afterwards Professor of Medicine in the College, and, like most of his family, distinguished by his scientific acquirements. He was rather of an irritable and pertinacious disposition; and his friends were wont to remark, when he showed any symptom of these foibles, "Ah! this comes of not having been educated by Rob Roy."

The connection between Rob Roy and his classical kinsman did not end with the period of Rob's transient power. At a period considerably subsequent to the year 1715, he was walking in the Castle Street of Aberdeen, arm in arm with his host, Dr. James Gregory, when the drums in the barracks suddenly beat to arms, and soldiers were seen issuing from the barracks. "If these lads are turning out," said Rob, taking leave of his cousin with great composure, "it is time for me to look after my safety." So saying, he dived down a close, and, as John Bunyan says, "went upon his way and was seen no more."[9]

We have already stated that Rob Roy's conduct during the insurrection of 1715 was very equivocal. His person and followers were in the Highland army, but his heart seems to have been with the Duke of Argyle's. Yet the insurgents were constrained to trust to him as their only guide, when they marched from Perth towards Dunblane, with the view of crossing the Forth at what are called the Fords of Frew, and when they themselves said he could not be relied upon.

This movement to the westward, on the part of the insurgents, brought on the battle of Sheriffmuir—indecisive, indeed, in its immediate results, but of which the Duke of Argyle reaped the whole advantage. In this action, it will be recollected that the right wing of the Highlanders broke and cut to pieces Argyle's left wing, while the clans on the left of Mar's army, though consisting of Stewarts, Mackenzies, and Camerons, were completely routed. During this medley of flight and pursuit, Rob Roy retained his station on a hill in the centre of the Highland position; and though it is said his attack might have decided the day, he could not be prevailed upon to charge. This was the more unfortunate for the insurgents, as the leading of a party of the Macphersons had been committed to MacGregor. This, it is said, was owing to the age and infirmity of the chief of that name, who, unable to lead his clan in person, objected to his heir-apparent, Macpherson of Nord, discharging his duty on that occasion; so that the tribe, or a part of them, were brigaded with their allies the MacGregors. While the favourable moment for action was gliding away unemployed, Mar's positive orders reached Rob Roy that he should presently attack. To which he coolly replied, "No, no! if they cannot do it without me, they cannot do it with me." One of the Macphersons, named Alexander, one of Rob's original profession, *videlicet*, a drover, but a man of great strength and spirit, was so incensed at the inactivity of this temporary leader, that he threw off his plaid, drew his sword, and called out to his clansmen, "Let us endure this no longer! if he will not lead you I will." Rob Roy replied, with great coolness, "Were the question about driving Highland stots or kyloes, Sandie, I would yield to your superior skill; but as it respects the leading of men, I must be allowed to be the better judge."—"Did the matter respect driving Glen-Eigas stots," answered the Macpherson, "the question with Rob would not be, which was to be last, but which was to be foremost." Incensed at this sarcasm, MacGregor drew his sword, and they would have fought upon the spot if their friends on both sides had not interfered. But the moment of attack was completely lost. Rob did not, however, neglect his own private interest on the occasion. In the confusion of an undecided field of battle, he enriched his followers by plundering the baggage and the dead on both sides.

The fine old satirical ballad on the battle of Sheriffmuir does not forget to stigmatise our hero's conduct on this memorable occasion—

Rob Roy he stood watch
On a hill for to catch
The booty for aught that I saw, man;
For he ne'er advanced
From the place where he stanced,
Till nae mair was to do there at a', man.

Notwithstanding the sort of neutrality which Rob Roy had continued to observe during the progress of the Rebellion, he did not escape some of its penalties. He was included in the act of attainder, and the house in Breadalbane, which was his place of retreat, was burned by General Lord Cadogan, when, after the conclusion of the insurrection, he marched through the Highlands to disarm and punish the offending clans. But upon going to Inverary with about forty or fifty of his followers, Rob obtained favour, by an apparent surrender of their arms to Colonel Patrick Campbell of Finnah, who furnished them and their leader with protections under his hand. Being thus in a great measure secured from the resentment of government, Rob Roy established his residence at Craig-Royston, near Loch Lomond, in the midst of his own kinsmen, and lost no time in resuming his private quarrel with the Duke of Montrose. For this purpose he soon got on foot as many men, and well armed too, as he had yet commanded. He never stirred without a body-guard of ten or twelve picked followers, and without much effort could increase them to fifty or sixty.

The Duke was not wanting in efforts to destroy this troublesome adversary. His Grace applied to General Carpenter, commanding the forces in Scotland, and by his orders three parties of soldiers were directed from the three different points of Glasgow, Stirling, and Finlarig near Killin. Mr. Graham of Killearn, the Duke of Montrose's relation and factor, Sheriff-depute also of Dumbartonshire, accompanied the troops, that they might act under the civil authority, and have the assistance of a trusty guide well acquainted with the hills. It was the object of these several columns to arrive about the same time in the neighbourhood of Rob Roy's residence, and surprise him and his followers. But heavy rains, the difficulties of the country, and the good intelligence which the Outlaw was always supplied with, disappointed their well-concerted combination. The troops, finding the birds were flown, avenged themselves by destroying the nest. They burned Rob Roy's house,—though not with impunity; for the MacGregors, concealed among the thickets and cliffs, fired on them, and killed a grenadier.

Rob Roy avenged himself for the loss which he sustained on this occasion by an act of singular audacity. About the middle of November 1716, John Graham of Killearn, already mentioned as factor of the Montrose family, went to a place called Chapel Errock, where the tenants of the Duke were summoned to appear with their termly rents. They appeared accordingly, and the factor had received ready money to the amount of about L300, when Rob Roy entered the room at the head of an armed party. The Steward endeavoured to protect the Duke's property by throwing the books of accounts and money into a garret, trusting they might escape notice. But the experienced freebooter was not to be baffled where such a prize was at stake. He recovered the books and cash, placed himself calmly in the receipt of custom, examined the accounts, pocketed the money, and gave receipts on the Duke's part, saying he would hold reckoning with the Duke of Montrose out of the damages which he had sustained by his Grace's means, in which he included the losses he had suffered, as well by the burning of his house by General Cadogan, as by the later expedition against Craig-Royston. He then requested Mr. Graham to attend him; nor does it appear that he treated him with any personal violence, or even rudeness, although he informed him he regarded him as a hostage, and menaced rough usage in case he should be pursued, or in danger of being overtaken. Few more audacious feats have been performed. After some rapid changes of place (the fatigue attending which was the only annoyance that Mr. Graham seems to have complained of), he carried his prisoner to an island on Loch Katrine, and caused him to write to the Duke, to state that his ransom was fixed at L3400 merks, being the balance which MacGregor pretended remained due to him, after deducting all that he owed to the Duke of Montrose.

However, after detaining Mr. Graham five or six days in custody on the island, which is still called Rob Roy's Prison, and could be no comfortable dwelling for November nights, the Outlaw seems to have despaired of attaining further advantage from his bold attempt, and suffered his prisoner to depart uninjured, with the account-books, and bills granted by the tenants, taking especial care to retain the cash.[10]

About 1717, our Chieftain had the dangerous adventure of falling into the hands of the Duke of Athole, almost as much his enemy as the Duke of Montrose himself; but his cunning and dexterity again freed him from certain death. See a contemporary account of this curious affair in the Appendix, No. V.

Other pranks are told of Rob, which argue the same boldness and sagacity as the seizure of Killearn. The Duke of Montrose, weary of his insolence, procured a quantity of arms, and distributed them among his tenantry, in order that they might defend themselves against future violences. But they fell into different hands from those they were intended for. The MacGregors made separate attacks on the houses of the tenants, and disarmed them all one after another, not, as was supposed, without the consent of many of the persons so disarmed.

As a great part of the Duke's rents were payable in kind, there were girnels (granaries) established for storing up the corn at Moulin, and elsewhere on the Buchanan estate. To these storehouses Rob Roy used to repair with a sufficient force, and of course when he was least expected, and insist upon the delivery of quantities of grain —sometimes for his own use, and sometimes for the assistance of the country people; always giving regular receipts in his own name, and pretending to reckon with the Duke for what sums he received.

In the meanwhile a garrison was established by Government, the ruins of which may be still seen about half-way betwixt Loch Lomond and Loch Katrine, upon Rob Roy's original property of Inversnaid. Even this military establishment could not bridle the restless MacGregor. He contrived to surprise the little fort, disarm the soldiers, and destroy the fortification. It was afterwards re-established, and again taken by the MacGregors under Rob Roy's nephew Ghlune Dhu, previous to the insurrection of 1745-6. Finally, the fort of Inversnaid was a third time repaired after the extinction of civil discord; and when we find the celebrated General Wolfe commanding in it, the imagination is strongly affected by the variety of time and events which the circumstance brings simultaneously to recollection. It is now totally dismantled.[11]

It was not, strictly speaking, as a professed depredator that Rob Roy now conducted his operations, but as a sort of contractor for the police; in Scottish phrase, a lifter of black-mail. The nature of this contract has been described in the Novel of Waverley, and in the notes on that work. Mr. Grahame of Gartmore's description of the character may be here transcribed:—

"The confusion and disorders of the country were so great, and the Government go absolutely neglected it, that the sober people were obliged to purchase some security to their effects by shameful and ignominious contracts of *black-mail*. A person who had the greatest correspondence with the thieves was agreed with to preserve the lands contracted for from thefts, for certain sums to be paid yearly. Upon this fund he employed one half of the thieves to recover stolen cattle, and the other half of them to steal, in order to make this agreement and black-mail contract necessary. The estates of those gentlemen who refused to contract, or give countenance to that pernicious practice, are plundered by the thieving part of the watch, in order to force them to purchase their protection. Their leader calls himself the *Captain* of the *Watch*, and his banditti go by that name. And as this gives them a kind of authority to traverse the country, so it makes them capable of doing any mischief. These corps through the Highlands make altogether a very considerable body of men, inured from their infancy to the greatest fatigues, and very capable, to act in a military way when occasion offers.

"People who are ignorant and enthusiastic, who are in absolute dependence upon their chief or landlord, who are directed in their consciences by Roman Catholic priests, or nonjuring clergymen, and who are not masters of any property, may easily be formed into any mould. They fear no dangers, as they have nothing to lose, and so can with ease be induced to attempt anything. Nothing can make their condition worse: confusions and troubles do commonly indulge them in such licentiousness, that by these they better it."[12]

As the practice of contracting for black-mail was an obvious encouragement to rapine, and a great obstacle to the course of justice, it was, by the statute 1567, chap. 21, declared a capital crime both on the part of him who levied and him who paid this sort of tax. But the necessity of the case prevented the execution of this severe law, I believe, in any one instance; and men went on submitting to a certain unlawful imposition rather than run the risk of utter ruin—just as it is now found difficult or impossible to prevent those who have lost a very large sum of money by robbery, from compounding with the felons for restoration of a part of their booty.

At what rate Rob Roy levied black-mail I never heard stated; but there is a formal contract by which his nephew, in 1741, agreed with various landholders of estates in the counties of Perth, Stirling, and Dumbarton, to recover cattle stolen from them, or to pay the value within six months of the loss being intimated, if such intimation were made to him with sufficient despatch, in consideration of a payment of L5 on each L100 of valued rent, which was not a very heavy insurance. Petty thefts were not included in the contract; but the theft of one horse, or one head of black cattle, or of sheep exceeding the number of six, fell under the agreement.

Rob Roy's profits upon such contracts brought him in a considerable revenue in money or cattle, of which he made a popular use; for he was publicly liberal as well as privately beneficent. The minister of the parish of Balquhidder, whose name was Robertson, was at one time threatening to pursue the parish for an augmentation of his stipend. Rob Roy took an opportunity to assure him that he would do well to abstain from this new exaction—a hint which the minister did not fail to understand. But to make him some indemnification, MacGregor presented him every year with a cow and a fat sheep; and no scruples as to the mode in which the donor came by them are said to have affected the reverend gentleman's conscience.

The following amount of the proceedings of Rob Roy, on an application to him from one of his contractors, had in it something very interesting to me, as told by an old countryman in the Lennox who was present on the expedition. But as there is no point or marked incident in the story, and as it must necessarily be without the half-frightened, half-bewildered look with which the narrator accompanied his recollections, it may possibly lose, its effect when transferred to paper.

My informant stated himself to have been a lad of fifteen, living with his father on the estate of a gentleman in the Lennox, whose name I have forgotten, in the capacity of herd. On a fine morning in the end of October, the period when such calamities were almost always to be apprehended, they found the Highland thieves had been down upon them, and swept away ten or twelve head of cattle. Rob Roy was sent for, and came with a party of seven or eight armed men. He heard with great gravity all that could be told him of the circumstances of the *creagh*, and expressed his confidence that the *herd-widdiefows*[13] could not have carried their booty far, and that he should be able to recover them.

He desired that two Lowlanders should be sent on the party, as it was not to be expected that any of his gentlemen would take the trouble of driving the cattle when he should recover possession of them. My informant and his father were despatched on the expedition. They had no good will to the journey; nevertheless, provided with a little food, and with a dog to help them to manage the cattle, they set off with MacGregor. They travelled a long day's journey in the direction of the mountain Benvoirlich, and slept for the night in a ruinous hut or bothy. The next morning they resumed their journey among the hills, Rob Roy directing their course by signs and marks on the heath which my informant did not understand.

About noon Rob commanded the armed party to halt, and to lie couched in the heather where it was thickest. "Do you and your son," he said to the oldest Lowlander, "go boldly over the hill;—you will see beneath you, in a glen on the other side, your master's cattle, feeding, it may be, with others; gather your own together, taking care to disturb no one else, and drive them to this place. If any one speak to or threaten you, tell them that I am here, at the head of twenty men."—"But what if they abuse us, or kill us?" said the Lowland, peasant, by no means delighted at finding the embassy imposed on him and his son. "If they do you any wrong," said Rob, "I will never forgive them as long as I live." The Lowlander was by no means content with this security, but did not think it safe to dispute Rob's injunctions.

He and his son climbed the hill therefore, found a deep valley, where there grazed, as Rob had predicted, a large herd of cattle. They cautiously selected those which their master had lost, and took measures to drive them over the hill. As soon as they began to remove them, they were surprised by hearing cries and screams; and looking around in fear and trembling they saw a woman seeming to have started out of the earth, who *flyted* at them, that is, scolded them, in Gaelic. When they contrived, however, in the best Gaelic they could muster, to deliver the message Rob Roy told them, she became silent, and disappeared without offering them any further annoyance. The chief heard their story on their return, and spoke with great complacency of the art which he possessed of putting such things to rights without any unpleasant bustle. The party were now on their road home, and the danger, though not the fatigue, of the expedition was at an end.

They drove on the cattle with little repose until it was nearly dark, when Rob proposed to halt for the night upon a wide moor, across which a cold north-east wind, with frost on its wing, was whistling to the tune of the Pipers of Strath-Dearn.[14]

The Highlanders, sheltered by their plaids, lay down on the heath comfortably enough, but the Lowlanders had no protection whatever. Rob Roy observing this, directed one of his followers to afford the old man a portion of his plaid; "for the callant (boy), he may," said the freebooter, "keep himself warm by walking about and watching the cattle." My informant heard this sentence with no small distress; and as the frost wind grew more and more cutting, it seemed to freeze the very blood in his young veins. He had been exposed to weather all his life, he said, but never could forget the cold of that night; insomuch that, in the bitterness of his heart, he cursed the bright moon for giving no heat with so much light. At length the sense of cold and weariness became so intolerable that he resolved to desert his watch to seek some repose and shelter. With that purpose he couched himself down behind one of the most bulky of the Highlanders, who acted as lieutenant to the party. Not satisfied with having secured the shelter of the man's large person, he coveted a share of his plaid, and by imperceptible degrees drew a corner of it round him. He was now comparatively in paradise, and slept sound till daybreak, when he awoke, and was terribly afraid on observing that his nocturnal operations had altogether uncovered the dhuiniewassell's neck and shoulders, which, lacking the plaid which should have protected them, were covered with *cranreuch* (*i.e.* hoar frost). The lad rose in great dread of a beating, at least, when it should be found how luxuriously he had been accommodated at the expense of a principal person of the party. Good Mr. Lieutenant, however, got up and shook himself, rubbing off the hoar frost with his plaid, and muttering something of a *cauld neight*. They then drove on the cattle, which were restored to their owner without farther adventure—The above can hardly be termed a tale, but yet it contains materials both for the poet and artist.

It was perhaps about the same time that, by a rapid march into the Balquhidder hills at the head of a body of his own tenantry, the Duke of Montrose actually surprised Rob Roy, and made him prisoner. He was mounted behind one of the Duke's followers, named James Stewart, and made fast to him by a horse-girth. The person who had him thus in charge was grandfather of the intelligent man of the same name, now deceased, who lately kept the inn in the vicinity of Loch Katrine, and acted as a guide to visitors through that beautiful scenery. From him I learned the story many years before he was either a publican, or a guide, except to moorfowl shooters.—It was evening (to resume the story), and the Duke was pressing on to lodge his prisoner, so long sought after in vain, in some place of security, when, in crossing the Teith or Forth, I forget which, MacGregor took an opportunity to conjure Stewart, by all the ties of old acquaintance and good neighbourhood, to give him some chance of an escape from an assured doom. Stewart was moved with compassion, perhaps with fear. He slipt the girth-buckle, and Rob, dropping down from behind the horse's croupe, dived, swam, and escaped, pretty much as described in the Novel. When James Stewart came on shore, the Duke hastily demanded where his prisoner was; and as no distinct answer was returned, instantly suspected Stewart's connivance at the escape of the Outlaw; and, drawing a steel pistol from his belt, struck him down with a blow on the head, from the effects of which, his descendant said, he never completely recovered.

In the success of his repeated escapes from the pursuit of his powerful enemy, Rob Roy at length became wanton and facetious. He wrote a mock challenge to the Duke, which he circulated among his friends to amuse them over a bottle. The reader will find this document in the Appendix.[15] It is written in a good hand, and not particularly deficient in grammar or spelling.

Our Southern readers must be given to understand that it was a piece of humour, —a *quiz,* in short,—on the part of the Outlaw, who was too sagacious to propose such a rencontre in reality. This letter was written in the year 1719.

In the following year Rob Roy composed another epistle, very little to his own reputation, as he therein confesses having played booty during the civil war of 1715. It is addressed to General Wade, at that time engaged in disarming the Highland clans, and making military roads through the country. The letter is a singular composition. It sets out the writer's real and unfeigned desire to have offered his service to King George, but for his liability to be thrown into jail for a civil debt, at the instance of the Duke of Montrose. Being thus debarred from taking the right side, he acknowledged he embraced the wrong one, upon Falstaff's principle, that since the King wanted men and the rebels soldiers, it were worse shame to be idle in such a stirring world, than to embrace the worst side, were it as black as rebellion could make it. The impossibility of his being neutral in such a debate, Rob seems to lay down as an undeniable proposition. At the same time, while he acknowledges having been forced into an unnatural rebellion against King George, he pleads that he not only avoided acting offensively against his Majesty's forces on all occasions, but, on the contrary, sent to them what intelligence he could collect from time to time; for the truth of which he refers to his Grace the Duke of Argyle. What influence this plea had on General Wade, we have no means of knowing.

Rob Roy appears to have continued to live very much as usual. His fame, in the meanwhile, passed beyond the narrow limits of the country in which he resided. A pretended history of him appeared in London during his lifetime, under the title of the Highland Rogue. It is a catch-penny publication, bearing in front the effigy of a species of ogre, with a beard of a foot in length; and his actions are as much exaggerated as his personal appearance. Some few of the best known adventures of the hero are told, though with little accuracy; but the greater part of the pamphlet is entirely fictitious. It is great pity so excellent a theme for a narrative of the kind had not fallen into the hands of De Foe, who was engaged at the time on subjects somewhat similar, though inferior in dignity and interest.

As Rob Roy advanced in years, he became more peaceable in his habits, and his nephew Ghlune Dhu, with most of his tribe, renounced those peculiar quarrels with the Duke of Montrose, by which his uncle had been distinguished. The policy of that great family had latterly been rather to attach this wild tribe by kindness than to follow the mode of violence which had been hitherto ineffectually resorted to. Leases at a low rent were granted to many of the MacGregors, who had heretofore held possessions in the Duke's Highland property merely by occupancy; and Glengyle (or Black-knee), who continued to act as collector of black-mail, managed his police, as a commander of the Highland watch arrayed at the charge of Government. He is said to have strictly abstained from the open and lawless depredations which his kinsman had practised.

It was probably after this state of temporary quiet had been obtained, that Rob Roy began to think of the concerns of his future state. He had been bred, and long professed himself, a Protestant; but in his later years he embraced the Roman Catholic faith,—perhaps on Mrs. Cole's principle, that it was a comfortable religion for one of his calling. He is said to have alleged as the cause of his conversion, a desire to gratify the noble family of Perth, who were then strict Catholics. Having, as he observed, assumed the name of the Duke of Argyle, his first protector, he could pay no compliment worth the Earl of Perth's acceptance save complying with his mode of religion. Rob did not pretend, when pressed closely on the subject, to justify all the tenets of Catholicism, and acknowledged that extreme unction always appeared to him a great waste of *ulzie*, or oil.[16]

In the last years of Rob Roy's life, his clan was involved in a dispute with one more powerful than themselves. Stewart of Appin, a chief of the tribe so named, was proprietor of a hill-farm in the Braes of Balquhidder, called Invernenty. The MacGregors of Rob Roy's tribe claimed a right to it by ancient occupancy, and declared they would oppose to the uttermost the settlement of any person upon the farm not being of their own name. The Stewarts came down with two hundred men, well armed, to do themselves justice by main force. The MacGregors took the field, but were unable to muster an equal strength. Rob Roy, fending himself the weaker party, asked a parley, in which he represented that both clans were friends to the *King*, and, that he was unwilling they should be weakened by mutual conflict, and thus made a merit of surrendering to Appin the disputed territory of Invernenty. Appin, accordingly, settled as tenants there, at an easy quit-rent, the MacLarens, a family dependent on the Stewarts, and from whose character for strength and bravery, it was expected that they would make their right good if annoyed by the MacGregors. When all this had been amicably adjusted, in presence of the two clans drawn up in arms near the Kirk of Balquhidder, Rob Roy, apparently fearing his tribe might be thought to have conceded too much upon the occasion, stepped forward and said, that where so many gallant men were met in arms, it would be shameful to part without it trial of skill, and therefore he took the freedom to invite any gentleman of the Stewarts present to exchange a few blows with him for the honour of their respective clans. The brother-in-law of Appin, and second chieftain of the clan, Alaster Stewart of Invernahyle, accepted the challenge, and they encountered with broadsword and target before their respective kinsmen.[17]

The combat lasted till Rob received a slight wound in the arm, which was the usual termination of such a combat when fought for honour only, and not with a mortal purpose. Rob Roy dropped his point, and congratulated his adversary on having been the first man who ever drew blood from him. The victor generously acknowledged, that without the advantage of youth, and the agility accompanying it, he probably could not have come off with advantage.

This was probably one of Rob Roy's last exploits in arms. The time of his death is not known with certainty, but he is generally said to have survived 1738, and to have died an aged man. When he found himself approaching his final change, he expressed some contrition for particular parts of his life. His wife laughed at these scruples of conscience, and exhorted him to die like a man, as he had lived. In reply, he rebuked her for her violent passions, and the counsels she had given him. "You have put strife," he said, "betwixt me and the best men of the country, and now you would place enmity between me and my God."

There is a tradition, no way inconsistent with the former, if the character of Rob Roy be justly considered, that while on his deathbed, he learned that a person with whom he was at enmity proposed to visit him. "Raise me from my bed," said the invalid; "throw my plaid around me, and bring me my claymore, dirk, and pistols—it shall never be said that a foeman saw Rob Roy MacGregor defenceless and unarmed." His foeman, conjectured to be one of the MacLarens before and after mentioned, entered and paid his compliments, inquiring after the health of his formidable neighbour. Rob Roy maintained a cold haughty civility during their short conference, and so soon as he had left the house. "Now," he said, "all is over—let the piper play, *Ha til mi tulidh*" (we return no more); and he is said to have expired before the dirge was finished.

This singular man died in bed in his own house, in the parish of Balquhidder. He was buried in the churchyard of the same parish, where his tombstone is only distinguished by a rude attempt at the figure of a broadsword.

The character of Rob Roy is, of course, a mixed one. His sagacity, boldness, and prudence, qualities so highly necessary to success in war, became in some degree vices, from the manner in which they were employed. The circumstances of his education, however, must be admitted as some extenuation of his habitual transgressions against the law; and for his political tergiversations, he might in that distracted period plead the example of men far more powerful, and less excusable in becoming the sport of circumstances, than the poor and desperate outlaw. On the other hand, he was in the constant exercise of virtues, the more meritorious as they seem inconsistent with his general character. Pursuing the occupation of a predatory chieftain,—in modern phrase a captain of banditti,—Rob Roy was moderate in his revenge, and humane in his successes. No charge of cruelty or bloodshed, unless in battle, is brought against his memory. In like manner, the formidable outlaw was the friend of the poor, and, to the utmost of his ability, the support of the widow and the orphan—kept his word when pledged—and died lamented in his own wild country, where there were hearts grateful for his beneficence, though their minds were not sufficiently instructed to appreciate his errors.

The author perhaps ought to stop here; but the fate of a part of Rob Roy's family was so extraordinary, as to call for a continuation of this somewhat prolix account, as affording an interesting chapter, not on Highland manners alone, but on every stage of society in which the people of a primitive and half-civilised tribe are brought into close contact with a nation, in which civilisation and polity have attained a complete superiority.

Rob had five sons,—Coll, Ronald, James, Duncan, and Robert. Nothing occurs worth notice concerning three of them; but James, who was a very handsome man, seems to have had a good deal of his father's spirit, and the mantle of Dougal Ciar Mhor had apparently descended on the shoulders of Robin Oig, that is, young Robin. Shortly after Rob Roy's death, the ill-will which the MacGregors entertained against the MacLarens again broke out, at the instigation, it was said, of Rob's widow, who seems thus far to have deserved the character given to her by her husband, as an Ate' stirring up to blood and strife. Robin Oig, under her instigation, swore that as soon as he could get back a certain gun which had belonged to his father, and had been lately at Doune to be repaired, he would shoot MacLaren, for having presumed to settle on his mother's land.[18]

He was as good as his word, and shot MacLaren when between the stilts of his plough, wounding him mortally.

The aid of a Highland leech was procured, who probed the wound with a probe made out of a castock; *i.e.*, the stalk of a colewort or cabbage. This learned gentleman declared he would not venture to prescribe, not knowing with what shot the patient had been wounded. MacLaren died, and about the same time his cattle were houghed, and his live stock destroyed in a barbarous manner.

Robin Oig, after this feat—which one of his biographers represents as the unhappy discharge of a gun—retired to his mother's house, to boast that he had drawn the first blood in the quarrel aforesaid. On the approach of troops, and a body of the Stewarts, who were bound to take up the cause of their tenant, Robin Oig absconded, and escaped all search.

The doctor already mentioned, by name Callam MacInleister, with James and Ronald, brothers to the actual perpetrator of the murder, were brought to trial. But as they contrived to represent the action as a rash deed committed by "the daft callant

Rob," to which they were not accessory, the jury found their accession to the crime was Not Proven. The alleged acts of spoil and violence on the MacLarens' cattle, were also found to be unsupported by evidence. As it was proved, however, that the two brothers, Ronald and James, were held and reputed thieves, they were appointed to find caution to the extent of L200, for their good behaviour for seven years.[19]

The spirit of clanship was at that time, so strong—to which must be added the wish to secure the adherence of stout, able-bodied, and, as the Scotch phrase then went, *pretty* men—that the representative of the noble family of Perth condescended to act openly as patron of the MacGregors, and appeared as such upon their trial. So at least the author was informed by the late Robert MacIntosh, Esq., advocate. The circumstance may, however, have occurred later than 1736—the year in which this first trial took place.

Robin Oig served for a time in the 42d regiment, and was present at the battle of Fontenoy, where he was made prisoner and wounded. He was exchanged, returned to Scotland, and obtained his discharge. He afterwards appeared openly in the MacGregor's country; and, notwithstanding his outlawry, married a daughter of Graham of Drunkie, a gentleman of some property. His wife died a few years afterwards.

The insurrection of 1745 soon afterwards called the MacGregors to arms. Robert MacGregor of Glencarnoch, generally regarded as the chief of the whole name, and grandfather of Sir John, whom the clan received in that character, raised a MacGregor regiment, with which he joined the standard of the Chevalier. The race of Ciar Mhor, however, affecting independence, and commanded by Glengyle and his cousin James Roy MacGregor, did not join this kindred corps, but united themselves to the levies of the titular Duke of Perth, until William MacGregor Drummond of Bolhaldie, whom they regarded as head of their branch, of Clan Alpine, should come over from France. To cement the union after the Highland fashion, James laid down the name of Campbell, and assumed that of Drummond, in compliment to Lord Perth. He was also called James Roy, after his father, and James Mhor, or Big James, from his height. His corps, the relics of his father Rob's band, behaved with great activity; with only twelve men he succeeded in surprising and burning, for the second time, the fort at Inversnaid, constructed for the express purpose of bridling the country of the MacGregors.

What rank or command James MacGregor had, is uncertain. He calls himself Major; and Chevalier Johnstone calls him Captain. He must have held rank under Ghlune Dhu, his kinsman, but his active and audacious character placed him above the rest of his brethren. Many of his followers were unarmed; he supplied the want of guns and swords with scythe-blades set straight upon their handles.

At the battle of Prestonpans, James Roy distinguished himself. "His company," says Chevalier Johnstone, "did great execution with their scythes." They cut the legs of the horses in two—the riders through the middle of their bodies. MacGregor was brave and intrepid, but at the same time, somewhat whimsical and singular. When advancing to the charge with his company, he received five wounds, two of them from balls that pierced his body through and through. Stretched on the ground, with his head resting on his hand, he called out loudly to the Highlanders of his company,

"My lads, I am not dead. By G—, I shall see if any of you does not do his duty." The victory, as is well known, was instantly obtained.

In some curious letters of James Roy,[20] it appears that his thigh-bone was broken on this occasion, and that he, nevertheless, rejoined the army with six companies, and was present at the battle of Culloden.

After that defeat, the clan MacGregor kept together in a body, and did not disperse till they had returned into their own country. They brought James Roy with them in a litter; and, without being particularly molested, he was permitted to reside in the MacGregor's country along with his brothers.

James MacGregor Drummond was attainted for high treason with persons of more importance. But it appears he had entered into some communication with Government, as, in the letters quoted, he mentions having obtained a pass from the Lord Justice-Clerk in 1747, which was a sufficient protection to him from the military. The circumstance is obscurely stated in one of the letters already quoted, but may perhaps, joined to subsequent incidents, authorise the suspicion that James, like his father, could look at both sides of the cards. As the confusion of the country subsided, the MacGregors, like foxes which had baffled the hounds, drew back to their old haunts, and lived unmolested. But an atrocious outrage, in which the sons of Rob Roy were concerned, brought at length on the family the full vengeance of the law.

James Roy was a married man, and had fourteen children. But his brother, Robin Oig, was now a widower; and it was resolved, if possible, that he should make his fortune by carrying off and marrying, by force if necessary, some woman of fortune from the Lowlands.

The imagination of the half-civilised Highlanders was less shocked at the idea of this particular species of violence, than might be expected from their general kindness to the weaker sex when they make part of their own families. But all their views were tinged with the idea that they lived in a state of war; and in such a state, from the time of the siege of Troy to "the moment when Previsa fell,"[21] the female captives are, to uncivilised victors, the most valuable part of the booty—

"The wealthy are slaughtered, the lovely are spared."

We need not refer to the rape of the Sabines, or to a similar instance in the Book of Judges, for evidence that such deeds of violence have been committed upon a large scale. Indeed, this sort of enterprise was so common along the Highland line as to give rise to a variety of songs and ballads.[22]

The annals of Ireland, as well as those of Scotland, prove the crime to have been common in the more lawless parts of both countries; and any woman who happened to please a man of spirit who came of a good house, and possessed a few chosen friends, and a retreat in the mountains, was not permitted the alternative of saying him nay. What is more, it would seem that the women themselves, most interested in the immunities of their sex, were, among the lower classes, accustomed to regard such marriages as that which is presently to be detailed as "pretty Fanny's way," or rather, the way of Donald with pretty Fanny. It is not a great many years since a respectable woman, above the lower rank of life, expressed herself very warmly to the author on his taking the freedom to censure the behaviour of the MacGregors on the occasion in question. She said "that there was no use in giving a bride too much choice upon such occasions; that the marriages were the happiest long syne which had been done offhand." Finally, she averred that her "own mother had never seen her father till the night he brought her up from the Lennox, with ten head of black cattle, and there had not been a happier couple in the country."

James Drummond and his brethren having similar opinions with the author's old acquaintance, and debating how they might raise the fallen fortunes of their clan, formed a resolution to settle their brother's fortune by striking up an advantageous marriage betwixt Robin Oig and one Jean Key, or Wright, a young woman scarce twenty years old, and who had been left about two months a widow by the death of her husband. Her property was estimated at only from 16,000 to 18,000 merks, but it seems to have been sufficient temptation to these men to join in the commission of a great crime.

This poor young victim lived with her mother in her own house at Edinbilly, in the parish of Balfron and shire of Stirling. At this place, in the night of 3d December 1750, the sons of Rob Roy, and particularly James Mhor and Robin Oig, rushed into the house where the object of their attack was resident, presented guns, swords, and pistols to the males of the family, and terrified the women by threatening to break open the doors if Jean Key was not surrendered, as, said James Roy, "his brother was a young fellow determined to make his fortune." Having, at length, dragged the object of their lawless purpose from her place of concealment, they tore her from her mother's arms, mounted her on a horse before one of the gang, and carried her off in spite, of her screams and cries, which were long heard after the terrified spectators of the outrage could no longer see the party retreat through the darkness. In her attempts to escape, the poor young woman threw herself from the horse on which they had placed her, and in so doing wrenched her side. They then laid her double over the pummel of the saddle, and transported her through the mosses and moors till the pain of the injury she had suffered in her side, augmented by the uneasiness of her posture, made her consent to sit upright. In the execution of this crime they stopped at more houses than one, but none of the inhabitants dared interrupt their proceedings. Amongst others who saw them was that classical and accomplished scholar the late Professor William Richardson of Glasgow, who used to describe as a terrible dream their violent and noisy entrance into the house where he was then residing. The Highlanders filled the little kitchen, brandishing their arms, demanding what they pleased, and receiving whatever they demanded. James Mhor, he said, was a tall, stern, and soldier-like man. Robin Oig looked more gentle; dark, but yet ruddy in complexion—a good-looking young savage. Their victim was so dishevelled in her dress, and forlorn in her appearance and demeanour, that he could hardly tell whether she was alive or dead.

The gang carried the unfortunate woman to Rowardennan, where they had a priest unscrupulous enough to read the marriage service, while James Mhor forcibly held the bride up before him; and the priest declared the couple man and wife, even while she protested against the infamy of his conduct. Under the same threats of violence, which had been all along used to enforce their scheme, the poor victim was compelled to reside with the pretended husband who was thus forced upon her. They even dared to carry her to the public church of Balquhidder, where the officiating clergyman (the same who had been Rob Roy's pensioner) only asked them if they were married persons. Robert MacGregor answered in the affirmative; the terrified female was silent.

The country was now too effectually subjected to the law for this vile outrage to be followed by the advantages proposed by the actors, Military parties were sent out in every direction to seize the MacGregors, who were for two or three weeks compelled to shift from one place to another in the mountains, bearing the unfortunate Jean Key along with them. In the meanwhile, the Supreme Civil Court issued a warrant, sequestrating the property of Jean Key, or Wright, which removed out of the reach of the actors in the violence the prize which they expected. They had, however, adopted a belief of the poor woman's spirit being so far broken that she would prefer submitting to her condition, and adhering to Robin Oig as her husband, rather than incur the disgrace, of appearing in such a cause in an open court. It was, indeed, a delicate experiment; but their kinsman Glengyle, chief of their immediate family, was of a temper averse to lawless proceedings;[23] and the captive's friends having had recourse to his advice, they feared that he would withdraw his protection if they refused to place the prisoner at liberty.

The brethren resolved, therefore, to liberate the unhappy woman, but previously had recourse to every measure which should oblige her, either from fear or otherwise, to own her marriage with Robin Oig. The cailliachs (old Highland hags) administered drugs, which were designed to have the effect of philtres, but were probably deleterious. James Mhor at one time threatened, that if she did not acquiesce in the match she would find that there were enough of men in the Highlands to bring the heads of two of her uncles who were pursuing the civil lawsuit. At another time he fell down on his knees, and confessed he had been accessory to wronging her, but begged she would not ruin his innocent wife and large family. She was made to swear she would not prosecute the brethren for the offence they had committed; and she was obliged by threats to subscribe papers which were tendered to her, intimating that she was carried off in consequence of her own previous request.

James Mhor Drummond accordingly brought his pretended sister-in-law to Edinburgh, where, for some little time, she was carried about from one house to another, watched by those with whom she was lodged, and never permitted to go out alone, or even to approach the window. The Court of Session, considering the peculiarity of the case, and regarding Jean Key as being still under some forcible restraint, took her person under their own special charge, and appointed her to reside in the family of Mr. Wightman of Mauldsley, a gentleman of respectability, who was married to one of her near relatives. Two sentinels kept guard on the house day and night—a precaution not deemed superfluous when the MacGregors were in question. She was allowed to go out whenever she chose, and to see whomsoever she had a mind, as well as the men of law employed in the civil suit on either side. When she first came to Mr. Wightman's house she seemed broken down with affright and suffering, so changed in features that her mother hardly knew her, and so shaken in mind that she scarce could recognise her parent. It was long before she could be assured that she was in perfect safety. But when she at length received confidence in her situation, she made a judicial declaration, or affidavit, telling the full history of her wrongs, imputing to fear her former silence on the subject, and expressing her resolution not to prosecute those who had injured her, in respect of the oath she had been compelled to take. From the possible breach of such an oath, though a compulsory one, she was relieved by the forms of Scottish jurisprudence, in that respect more equitable than those of England, prosecutions for crimes being always conducted at the expense and charge of the King, without inconvenience or cost to the private party who has sustained the wrong. But the unhappy sufferer did not live to be either accuser or witness against those who had so deeply injured her.

James Mhor Drummond had left Edinburgh so soon as his half-dead prey had been taken from his clutches. Mrs. Key, or Wright, was released from her species of confinement there, and removed to Glasgow, under the escort of Mr. Wightman. As they passed the Hill of Shotts, her escort chanced to say, "this is a very wild spot; what if the MacGregors should come upon us?"—"God forbid!" was her immediate answer, "the very sight of them would kill me." She continued to reside at Glasgow, without venturing to return to her own house at Edinbilly. Her pretended husband made some attempts to obtain an interview with her, which she steadily rejected. She died on the 4th October 1751. The information for the Crown hints that her decease might be the consequence of the usage she received. But there is a general report that she died of the small-pox. In the meantime, James Mhor, or Drummond, fell into the hands of justice. He was considered as the instigator of the whole affair. Nay, the deceased had informed her friends that on the night of her being carried off, Robin Oig, moved by her cries and tears, had partly consented to let her return, when James came up with a pistol in his hand, and, asking whether he was such a coward as to relinquish an enterprise in which he had risked everything to procure him a fortune, in a manner compelled his brother to persevere. James's trial took place on 13th July 1752, and was conducted with the utmost fairness and impartiality. Several witnesses, all of the MacGregor family, swore that the marriage was performed with every appearance of acquiescence on the woman's part; and three or four witnesses, one of them sheriff-substitute of the county, swore she might have made her escape if she wished, and the magistrate stated that he offered her assistance if she felt desirous to do so. But when asked why he, in his official capacity, did not arrest the MacGregors, he could only answer, that he had not force sufficient to make the attempt.

The judicial declarations of Jean Key, or Wright, stated the violent manner in which she had been carried off, and they were confirmed by many of her friends, from her private communications with them, which the event of her death rendered good evidence. Indeed, the fact of her abduction (to use a Scottish law term) was completely proved by impartial witnesses. The unhappy woman admitted that she had pretended acquiescence in her fate on several occasions, because she dared not trust such as offered to assist her to escape, not even the sheriff-substitute.

The jury brought in a special verdict, finding that Jean Key, or Wright, had been forcibly carried off from her house, as charged in the indictment, and that the accused had failed to show that she was herself privy and consenting to this act of outrage. But they found the forcible marriage, and subsequent violence, was not proved; and also found, in alleviation of the panel's guilt in the premises, that Jean Key did afterwards acquiesce in her condition. Eleven of the jury, using the names of other four who were absent, subscribed a letter to the Court, stating it was their purpose and desire, by such special verdict, to take the panel's case out of the class of capital crimes.

Learned informations (written arguments) on the import of the verdict, which must be allowed a very mild one in the circumstances, were laid before the High Court of Justiciary. This point is very learnedly debated in these pleadings by Mr. Grant, Solicitor for the Crown, and the celebrated Mr. Lockhart, on the part of the prisoner; but James Mhor did not wait the event of the Court's decision.

He had been committed to the Castle of Edinburgh on some reports that an escape would be attempted. Yet he contrived to achieve his liberty even from that fortress. His daughter had the address to enter the prison, disguised as a cobbler, bringing home work, as she pretended. In this cobbler's dress her father quickly arrayed himself. The wife and daughter of the prisoner were heard by the sentinels scolding the supposed cobbler for having done his work ill, and the man came out with his hat slouched over his eyes, and grumbling, as if at the manner in which they had treated him. In this way the prisoner passed all the guards without suspicion, and made his escape to France. He was afterwards outlawed by the Court of Justiciary, which proceeded to the trial of Duncan MacGregor, or Drummond, his brother, 15th January 1753. The accused had unquestionably been with the party which carried off Jean Key; but no evidence being brought which applied to him individually and directly, the jury found him not guilty—and nothing more is known of his fate.

That of James MacGregor, who, from talent and activity, if not by seniority, may be considered as head of the family, has been long misrepresented; as it has been generally averred in Law Reports, as well as elsewhere, that his outlawry was reversed, and that he returned and died in Scotland. But the curious letters published in Blackwood's Magazine for December 1817, show this to be an error. The first of these documents is a petition to Charles Edward. It is dated 20th September 1753, and pleads his service to the cause of the Stuarts, ascribing his exile to the persecution of the Hanoverian Government, without any allusion to the affair of Jean Key, or the Court of Justiciary. It is stated to be forwarded by MacGregor Drummond of Bohaldie, whom, as before mentioned, James Mhor acknowledged as his chief.

The effect which this petition produced does not appear. Some temporary relief was perhaps obtained. But, soon after, this daring adventurer was engaged in a very dark intrigue against an exile of his own country, and placed pretty nearly in his own circumstances. A remarkable Highland story must be here briefly alluded to. Mr. Campbell of Glenure, who had been named factor for Government on the forfeited estates of Stewart of Ardshiel, was shot dead by an assassin as he passed through the wood of Lettermore, after crossing the ferry of Ballachulish. A gentleman, named James Stewart, a natural brother of Ardshiel, the forfeited person, was tried as being accessory to the murder, and condemned and executed upon very doubtful evidence; the heaviest part of which only amounted to the accused person having assisted a nephew of his own, called Allan Breck Stewart, with money to escape after the deed was done. Not satisfied with this vengeance, which was obtained in a manner little to the honour of the dispensation of justice at the time, the friends of the deceased Glenure were equally desirous to obtain possession of the person of Allan Breck Stewart, supposed to be the actual homicide. James Mhor Drummond was secretly applied to to trepan Stewart to the sea-coast, and bring him over to Britain, to almost certain death. Drummond MacGregor had kindred connections with the slain Glenure; and, besides, the MacGregors and Campbells had been friends of late, while the former clan and the Stewarts had, as we have seen, been recently at feud; lastly, Robert Oig was now in custody at Edinburgh, and James was desirous to do some service by which his brother might be saved. The joint force of these motives may, in James's estimation of right and wrong, have been some vindication for engaging in such an enterprise, although, as must be necessarily supposed, it could only be executed by treachery of a gross description. MacGregor stipulated for a license to return to England, promising to bring Allan Breck thither along with him. But the intended victim was put upon his guard by two countrymen, who suspected James's intentions towards him. He escaped from his kidnapper, after, as MacGregor alleged, robbing his portmanteau of some clothes and four snuff-boxes. Such a charge, it may be observed, could scarce have been made unless the parties had been living on a footing of intimacy, and had access to each other's baggage.

Although James Drummond had thus missed his blow in the matter of Allan Breck Stewart, he used his license to make a journey to London, and had an interview, as he avers, with Lord Holdernesse. His Lordship, and the Under-Secretary, put many puzzling questions to him; and, as he says, offered him a situation, which would bring him bread, in the Government's service. This office was advantageous as to emolument; but in the opinion of James Drummond, his acceptance of it would have been a disgrace to his birth, and have rendered him a scourge to his country. If such a tempting offer and sturdy rejection had any foundation in fact, it probably relates to some plan of espionage on the Jacobites, which the Government might hope to carry on by means of a man who, in the matter of Allan Breck Stewart, had shown no great nicety of feeling. Drummond MacGregor was so far accommodating as to intimate his willingness to act in any station in which other gentlemen of honour served, but not otherwise;—an answer which, compared with some passages of his past life, may remind the reader of Ancient Pistol standing upon his reputation.

Having thus proved intractable, as he tells the story, to the proposals of Lord Holdernesse, James Drummond was ordered instantly to quit England.

On his return to France, his condition seems to have been utterly disastrous. He was seized with fever and gravel—ill, consequently, in body, and weakened and dispirited in mind. Allan Breck Stewart threatened to put him to death in revenge of the designs he had harboured against him.[24]

The Stewart clan were in the highest degree unfriendly to him: and his late expedition to London had been attended with many suspicious circumstances, amongst which it was not the slightest that he had kept his purpose secret from his chief Bohaldie. His intercourse with Lord Holdernesse was suspicious. The Jacobites were probably, like Don Bernard de Castel Blaze, in Gil Blas, little disposed to like those who kept company with Alguazils. Mac-Donnell of Lochgarry, a man of unquestioned honour, lodged an information against James Drummond before the High Bailie of Dunkirk, accusing him of being a spy, so that he found himself obliged to leave that town and come to Paris, with only the sum of thirteen livres for his immediate subsistence, and with absolute beggary staring him in the face.

We do not offer the convicted common thief, the accomplice in MacLaren's assassination, or the manager of the outrage against Jean Key, as an object of sympathy; but it is melancholy to look on the dying struggles even of a wolf or a tiger, creatures of a species directly hostile to our own; and, in like manner, the utter distress of this man, whose faults may have sprung from a wild system of education, working on a haughty temper, will not be perused without some pity. In his last letter to Bohaldie, dated Paris, 25th September 1754, he describes his state of destitution as absolute, and expresses himself willing to exercise his talents in breaking or breeding horses, or as a hunter or fowler, if he could only procure employment in such an inferior capacity till something better should occur. An Englishman may smile, but a Scotchman will sigh at the postscript, in which the poor starving exile asks the loan of his patron's bagpipes that he might play over some of the melancholy tunes of his own land. But the effect of music arises, in a great degree, from association; and sounds which might jar the nerves of a Londoner or Parisian, bring back to the Highlander his lofty mountain, wild lake, and the deeds of his fathers of the glen. To prove MacGregor's claim to our reader's compassion, we here insert the last part of the letter alluded to.

"By all appearance I am born to suffer crosses, and it seems they're not at an end; for such is my wretched case at present, that I do not know earthly where to go or what to do, as I have no subsistence to keep body and soul together. All that I have carried here is about 13 livres, and have taken a room at my old quarters in Hotel St. Pierre, Rue de Cordier. I send you the bearer, begging of you to let me know if you are to be in town soon, that I may have the pleasure of seeing you, for I have none to make application to but you alone; and all I want is, if it was possible you could contrive where I could be employed without going to entire beggary. This probably is a difficult point, yet unless it's attended with some difficulty, you might think nothing of it, as your long head can bring about matters of much more difficulty and consequence than this. If you'd disclose this matter to your friend Mr. Butler, it's possible he might have some employ wherein I could be of use, as I pretend to know as much of breeding and riding of horse as any in France, besides that I am a good hunter either on horseback or by footing. You may judge my reduction, as I propose the meanest things to lend a turn till better cast up. I am sorry that I am obliged to give you so much trouble, but I hope you are very well assured that I am grateful for what you have done for me, and I leave you to judge of my present wretched case. I am, and shall for ever continue, dear Chief, your own to command, Jas. MacGregor.

"P. S.—If you'd send your pipes by the bearer, and all the other little trinkims belonging to it, I would put them in order, and play some melancholy tunes, which I may now with safety, and in real truth. Forgive my not going directly to you, for if I could have borne the seeing of yourself, I could not choose to be seen by my friends in my wretchedness, nor by any of my acquaintance."

While MacGregor wrote in this disconsolate manner, Death, the sad but sure remedy for mortal evils, and decider of all doubts and uncertainties, was hovering near him. A memorandum on the back of the letter says the writer died about a week after, in October 1754.

It now remains to mention the fate of Robin Oig—for the other sons of Rob Roy seem to have been no way distinguished. Robin was apprehended by a party of military from the fort of Inversnaid, at the foot of Gartmore, and was conveyed to Edinburgh 26th May 1753. After a delay, which may have been protracted by the negotiations of James for delivering up Allan Breck Stewart upon promise of his brother's life, Robin Oig, on the 24th of December 1753, was brought to the bar of the High Court of Justiciary, and indicted by the name of Robert MacGregor, alias Campbell, alias Drummond, alias Robert Oig; and the evidence led against him resembled exactly that which was brought by the Crown on the former trial. Robert's case was in some degree more favourable than his brother's;—for, though the principal in the forcible marriage, he had yet to plead that he had shown symptoms of relenting while they were carrying Jean Key off, which were silenced by the remonstrances and threats of his harder natured brother James. A considerable space of time had also elapsed since the poor woman died, which is always a strong circumstance in favour of the accused; for there is a sort of perspective in guilt, and crimes of an old date seem less odious than those of recent occurrence. But notwithstanding these considerations, the jury, in Robert's case, did not express any solicitude to save his life as they had done that of James. They found him guilty of being art and part in the forcible abduction of Jean Key from her own dwelling.[25]

Robin Oig was condemned to death, and executed on the 14th February 1754. At the place of execution he behaved with great decency; and professing himself a Catholic, imputed all his misfortunes to his swerving from the true church two or three years before. He confessed the violent methods he had used to gain Mrs. Key, or Wright, and hoped his fate would stop further proceedings against his brother James.[26]

The newspapers observed that his body, after hanging the usual time, was delivered to his friends to be carried to the Highlands. To this the recollection of a venerable friend, recently taken from us in the fulness of years, then a schoolboy at Linlithgow, enables the author to add, that a much larger body of MacGregors than had cared to advance to Edinburgh received the corpse at that place with the coronach and other wild emblems of Highland mourning, and so escorted it to Balquhidder. Thus we may conclude this long account of Rob Roy and his family with the classic phrase,

Ite. Conclamatum est.

I have only to add, that I have selected the above from many anecdotes of Rob Roy which were, and may still be, current among the mountains where he flourished; but I am far from warranting their exact authenticity. Clannish partialities were very apt to guide the tongue and pen, as well as the pistol and claymore, and the features of an anecdote are wonderfully softened or exaggerated as the story is told by a MacGregor or a Campbell.

APPENDIX TO INTRODUCTION.

No. I.—ADVERTISEMENT FOR THE APPREHENSION OF ROB ROY.

(From the Edinburgh Evening Courant, June 18 to June 21, A.D. 1732. No. 1058.)
"That Robert Campbell, commonly known by the name of Rob Roy MacGregor, being lately intrusted by several noblemen and gentlemen with considerable sums for

buying cows for them in the Highlands, has treacherously gone off with the money, to the value of L1000 sterling, which he carries along with him. All Magistrates and Officers of his Majesty's forces are intreated to seize upon the said Rob Roy, and the money which he carries with him, until the persons concerned in the money be heard against him; and that notice be given, when he is apprehended, to the keepers of the Exchange Coffee-house at Edinburgh, and the keeper of the Coffee-house at Glasgow, where the parties concerned will be advertised, and the seizers shall be very reasonably rewarded for their pains."

It is unfortunate that this Hue and Cry, which is afterwards repeated in the same paper, contains no description of Rob Roy's person, which, of course, we must suppose to have been pretty generally known. As it is directed against Rob Roy personally, it would seem to exclude the idea of the cattle being carried off by his partner, MacDonald, who would certainly have been mentioned in the advertisement, if the creditors concerned had supposed him to be in possession of the money.

No. II.—LETTERS

FROM AND TO THE DUKE OF MONTROSE RESPECTING ROB ROY'S ARREST OF MR. GRAHAME OF KILLEARN.

The Duke of Montrose to—[27]
"Glasgow, the 21st November, 1716.

"My Lord,—I was surprised last night with the account of a very remarkable instance of the insolence of that very notorious rogue Rob Roy, whom your lordship has often heard named. The honour of his Majesty's Government being concerned in it, I thought it my duty to acquaint your lordship of the particulars by an express.

"Mr. Grahame of Killearn (whom I have had occasion to mention frequently to you, for the good service he did last winter during the rebellion) having the charge of my Highland estate, went to Monteath, which is a part of it, on Monday last, to bring in my rents, it being usual for him to be there for two or three nights together at this time of the year, in a country house, for the conveniency of meeting the tenants, upon that account. The same night, about 9 of the clock, Rob Roy, with a party of those ruffians whom he has still kept about him since the late rebellion, surrounded the house where Mr. Grahame was with some of my tenants doing his business, ordered his men to present their guns in att the windows of the room where he was sitting, while he himself at the same time with others entered at the door, with cocked pistols, and made Mr. Grahame prisoner, carrying him away to the hills with the money he had got, his books and papers, and my tenants' bonds for their fines, amounting to above a thousand pounds sterling, whereof the one-half had been paid last year, and the other was to have been paid now; and att the same time had the insolence to cause him to write a letter to me (the copy of which is enclosed) offering me terms of a treaty.

"That your Lordship may have the better view of this matter, it will be necessary that I should inform you, that this fellow has now, of a long time, put himself at the head of the Clan M'Gregor, a race of people who in all ages have distinguished themselves beyond others, by robberies, depredations, and murders, and have been the constant harbourers and entertainers of vagabonds and loose people. From the time of the Revolution he has taken every opportunity to appear against the Government, acting rather as a robber than doing any real service to those whom he pretended to appear for, and has really done more mischief to the countrie than all the other Highlanders have done.

"Some three or four years before the last rebellion broke out, being overburdened with debts, he quitted his ordinary residence, and removed some twelve or sixteen miles farther into the Highlands, putting himself under the protection of the Earl of Bredalbin. When my Lord Cadogan was in the Highlands, he ordered his house att this place to be burnt, which your Lordship sees he now places to my account.

"This obliges him to return to the same countrie he went from, being a most rugged inaccessible place, where he took up his residence anew amongst his own friends and relations; but well judging that it was possible to surprise him, he, with about forty-five of his followers, went to Inverary, and made a sham surrender of their arms to Coll. Campbell of Finab, Commander of one of the Independent Companies, and returned home with his men, each of them having the Coll.'s protection. This happened in the beginning of summer last; yet not long after he appeared with his men twice in arms, in opposition to the King's troops: and one of those times attackt them, rescued a prisoner from them, and all this while sent abroad his party through the countrie, plundering the countrie people, and amongst the rest some of my tenants.

"Being informed of these disorders after I came to Scotland, I applied to Lieut.-Genll. Carpenter, who ordered three parties from Glasgow, Stirling, and Finlarig, to march in the night by different routes, in order to surprise him and his men in their houses, which would have its effect certainly, if the great rains that happened to fall that verie night had not retarded the march of the troops, so as some of the parties came too late to the stations that they were ordered for. All that could be done upon the occasion was to burn a countrie house, where Rob Roy then resided, after some of his clan had, from the rocks, fired upon the king's troops, by which a grenadier was killed.

"Mr. Grahame of Killearn, being my deputy-sheriff in that countrie, went along with the party that marched from Stirling; and doubtless will now meet with the worse treatment from that barbarous people on that account. Besides, that he is my relation, and that they know how active he has been in the service of the Government —all which, your Lordship may believe, puts me under very great concern for the gentleman, while, at the same time, I can foresee no manner of way how to relieve him, other than to leave him to chance and his own management.

"I had my thoughts before of proposing to Government the building of some barracks as the only expedient for suppressing these rebels, and securing the peace of the countrie; and in that view I spoke to Genll. Carpenter, who has now a scheme of it in his hands; and I am persuaded that will be the true method for restraining them effectually; but, in the meantime, it will be necessary to lodge some of the troops in those places, upon which I intend to write to the Generall.

"I am sensible I have troubled your Lordship with a very long letter, which I should be ashamed of, were I myself singly concerned; but where the honour of the

King's Government is touched, I need make no apologie, and I shall only beg leave to add, that I am, with great respect, and truth,

"My Lord, "yr. Lord's most humble and obedient servant, "MONTROSE"

COPY OF GRAHAME OF KILLEARN'S LETTER, ENCLOSED IN THE PRECEDING.

"Chappellarroch, Nov. 19th, 1716.

"May it please your Grace,—I am obliged to give your Grace the trouble of this, by Robert Roy's commands, being so unfortunate at present as to be his prisoner. I refer the way and manner I was apprehended, to the bearer, and shall only, in short, acquaint your Grace with the demands, which are, that your Grace shall discharge him of all soumes he owes your Grace, and give him the soume of 3400 merks for his loss and damages sustained by him, both at Craigrostown and at his house, Auchinchisallen; and that your Grace shall give your word not to trouble or prosecute him afterwards; till which time he carries me, all the money I received this day, my books and bonds for entress, not yet paid, along with him, with assurance of hard usage, if any party are sent after him. The soume I received this day, conform to the nearest computation I can make before several of the gentlemen, is 3227L. 2sh. 8d. Scots, of which I gave them notes. I shall wait your Grace's return, and ever am,

"Your Grace's most obedient, faithful, "humble servant, *Sic subscribitur,* "John Grahame."

The Duke of Montrose to — —
28th Nov. 1716—Killearn's Release.
"Glasgow, 28th Nov. 1716.

"Sir,—Having acquainted you by my last, of the 21st instant, of what had happened to my friend, Mr. Grahame of Killearn, I'm very glad now to tell you, that last night I was very agreeably surprised with Mr. Grahame's coming here himself, and giving me the first account I had had of him from the time of his being carried away. It seems Rob Roy, when he came to consider a little better of it, found that, he could not mend his matters by retaining Killearn his prisoner, which could only expose him still the more to the justice of the Government; and therefore thought fit to dismiss him on Sunday evening last, having kept him from the Monday night before, under a very uneasy kind of restraint, being obliged to change continually from place to place. He gave him back the books, papers, and bonds, but kept the money.

"I am, with great truth, Sir, "your most humble servant, "MONTROSE."

[Some papers connected with Rob Roy Macgregor, signed "Ro. Campbell," in 1711, were lately presented to the Society of Antiquaries. One of these is a kind of contract between the Duke of Montrose and Rob Roy, by which the latter undertakes to deliver within a given time "Sixtie good and sufficient Kintaill highland Cowes, betwixt the age of five and nine years, at fourtene pounds Scotts per peice, with ane bull to the bargane, and that at the head dykes of Buchanan upon the twenty-eight day of May next."—Dated December 1711.—See *Proceedings*, vol. vii. p. 253.]

No. III.—CHALLENGE BY ROB ROY.

"ROB ROY TO *ain hie and mighty Prince*, James Duke of Montrose.

"In charity to your Grace's couradge and conduct, please know, the only way to retrive both is to treat Rob Roy like himself, in appointing tyme, place, and choice of arms, that at once you may extirpate your inveterate enemy, or put a period to your punny (puny?) life in falling gloriously by his hands. That impertinent criticks or flatterers may not brand me for challenging a man that's repute of a poor dastardly soul, let such know that I admit of the two great supporters of his character and the captain of his bands to joyne with him in the combat. Then sure your Grace wont have the impudence to clamour att court for multitudes to hunt me like a fox, under pretence that I am not to be found above ground. This saves your Grace and the troops any further trouble of searching; that is, if your ambition of glory press you to embrace this unequald venture offerd of Rob's head. But if your Grace's piety, prudence, and cowardice, forbids hazarding this gentlemanly expedient, then let your desire of peace restore what you have robed from me by the tyranny of your present cituation, otherwise your overthrow as a man is determined; and advertise your friends never more to look for the frequent civility payed them, of sending them home without their arms only. Even their former cravings wont purchase that favour; so your Grace by this has peace in your offer, if the sound of wax be frightful, and chuse you whilk, your good friend or mortal enemy."

This singular rhodomontade is enclosed in a letter to a friend of Rob Roy, probably a retainer of the Duke of Argyle in Isle, which is in these words:—

"Sir,—Receive the enclosd paper, qn you are takeing yor Botle it will divert yorself and comrad's. I gote noe news since I seed you, only qt wee had before about the Spainyard's is like to continue. If I'll get any further account about them I'll be sure to let you know of it, and till then I will not write any more till I'll have more sure account, and I am

"Sir, your most affectionate Cn [cousin], "and most humble servant, "Ro: Roy."

"*Apryle* 16*th*, 1719.

"To Mr. Patrick Anderson, at Hay—These.'

The seal, *a stag*—no bad emblem of a wild cateran.

It appears from the envelope that Rob Roy still continued to act as Intelligencer to the Duke of Argyle, and his agents. The war he alludes to is probably some vague report of invasion from Spain. Such rumours were likely enough to be afloat, in consequence of the disembarkation of the troops who were taken at Glensheal in the preceding year, 1718.

No. IV.—LETTER

FROM ROBERT CAMPBELL, alias M'Gregor, commonly called Rob Roy, to Field-Marshal Wade,

Then receiving the submission of disaffected Chieftains and Clans.[28]

Sir,—The great humanity with which you have constantly acted in the discharge of the trust reposed in you, and your ever having made use of the great powers with which you were vested as the means of doing good and charitable offices to such as ye found proper objects of compassion, will, I hope, excuse my importunity in endeavouring to approve myself not absolutely unworthy of that mercy and favour which your Excellency has so generously procured from his Majesty for others in my unfortunate circumstances. I am very sensible nothing can be alledged sufficient to excuse so great a crime as I have been guilty of it, that of Rebellion. But I humbly beg leave to lay before your Excellency some particulars in the circumstance of my guilt, which, I hope, will extenuate it in some measure. It was my misfortune, at the time the Rebellion broke out, to be liable to legal diligence and caption, at the Duke of Montrose's instance, for debt alledged due to him. To avoid being flung into prison, as I must certainly have been, had I followed my real inclinations in joining the King's troops at Stirling, I was forced to take party with the adherents of the Pretender; for the country being all in arms, it was neither safe nor indeed possible for me to stand neuter. I should not, however, plead my being forced into that unnatural rebellion against his Majesty, King George, if I could not at the same time assure your Excellency, that I not only avoided acting offensively against his Majesty's forces upon all occasions, but on the contrary, sent his Grace the Duke of Argyle all the intelligence I could from time to time, of the strength and situation of the rebels; which I hope his Grace will do me the justice to acknowledge. As to the debt to the Duke of Montrose, I have discharged it to the utmost farthing. I beg your Excellency would be persuaded that, had it been in my power, as it was in my inclination, I should always have acted for the service of his Majesty King George, and that one reason of my begging the favour of your intercession with his Majesty for the pardon of my life, is the earnest desire I have to employ it in his service, whose goodness, justice, and humanity, are so conspicuous to all mankind.—I am, with all duty and respect, your Excellency's most, &c.,

"Robert Campbell."

No. IVa.—LETTER.

ESCAPE OF ROB ROY FROM THE DUKE OF ATHOLE.

THE FOLLOWING copy of a letter which passed from one clergyman of the Church of Scotland to another, was communicated to me by John Gregorson, Esq. of Ardtornish. The escape of Rob Roy is mentioned, like other interesting news of the time with which it is intermingled. The disagreement between the Dukes of Athole and Argyle seems to have animated the former against Rob Roy, as one of Argyle's partisans.

"Rev. and dear Brother,

Yrs of the 28th Jun I had by the bearer. Im pleased yo have got back again yr Delinquent which may probably safe you of the trouble of her child. I'm sory I've yet very little of certain news to give you from Court tho' I've seen all the last weekes prints, only I find in them a pasage which is all the account I can give you of the

Indemnity yt when the estates of forfaulted Rebells Comes to be sold all Just debts Documented are to be preferred to Officers of the Court of enquiry. The Bill in favours of that Court against the Lords of Session in Scotland in past the house of Commons and Come before the Lords which is thought to be considerably more ample yn formerly wt respect to the Disposeing of estates Canvassing and paying of Debts. It's said yt the examinations of Cadugans accounts is droped but it wants Confirmations here as yet. Oxford's tryals should be entered upon Saturday last. We hear that the Duchess of Argyle is wt child. I doe not hear yt the Divisions at Court are any thing abated or of any appearance of the Dukes having any thing of his Maj: favour. I heartily wish the present humours at Court may not prove an encouragmt to watch-full and restles enemies.

My accounts of Rob Roy his escape are yt after severall Embassies between his Grace (who I hear did Correspond wt some at Court about it) and Rob he at length upon promise of protectione Came to waite upon the Duke & being presently secured his Grace sent post to Edr to acquent the Court of his being aprehended & call his friends at Edr and to desire a party from Gen Carpinter to receive and bring him to Edr which party came the length of Kenross in Fife, he was to be delivered to them by a party his Grace had demanded from the Governour at Perth, who when upon their march towards Dunkell to receive him, were mete wt and returned by his Grace having resolved to deliver him by a party of his own men and left Rob at Logierate under a strong guard till yt party should be ready to receive him. This space of time Rob had Imployed in taking the other dram heartily wt the Guard & qn all were pretty hearty, Rob is delivering a letter for his wife to a servant to whom he most needs deliver some private instructions at the Door (for his wife) where he's attended wt on the Guard. When serious in this privat Conversations he is making some few steps carelessly from the Door about the house till he comes close by this horse which he soon mounted and made off. This is no small mortifican to the guard because of the delay it give to there hopes of a Considerable additionall charge agt John Roy.[29] my wife was upon Thursday last delivered of a Son after sore travell of which she still continues very weak.

I give yl Lady hearty thanks for the Highland plaid. It's good cloath but it does not answer the sett I sent some time agae wt McArthur & tho it had I told in my last yt my wife was obliged to provid herself to finish her bed before she was lighted but I know yt letr came not timely to yr hand—I'm sory I had not mony to send by the bearer having no thought of it & being exposed to some little expenses last week but I expect some sure occasion when order by a letter to receive it excuse this freedom from &c.

"*Manse of Comrie, July 2d*, 1717. "I salute yr lady I wish my .... her Daughter much Joy."

No. V.—HIGHLAND WOOING.

THERE ARE many productions of the Scottish Ballad Poets upon the lion-like mode of wooing practised by the ancient Highlanders when they had a fancy for the person (or property) of a Lowland damsel. One example is found in Mr. Robert Jamieson's Popular Scottish Songs:—

Bonny Babby Livingstone
Gaed out to see the kye,
And she has met with Glenlyon,
Who has stolen her away.

He took free her her sattin coat,
But an her silken gown,
Syne roud her in his tartan plaid,
And happd her round and roun'.

In another ballad we are told how—

Four-and-twenty Hieland men,
Came doun by Fiddoch Bide,
And they have sworn a deadly aith,
Jean Muir suld be a bride:

And they have sworn a deadly aith,
Ilke man upon his durke,
That she should wed with Duncan Ger,
Or they'd make bloody works.

This last we have from tradition, but there are many others in the collections of Scottish Ballads to the same purpose.

The achievement of Robert Oig, or young Rob Roy, as the Lowlanders called him, was celebrated in a ballad, of which there are twenty different and various editions. The tune is lively and wild, and we select the following words from memory:—

Rob Roy is frae the Hielands come,
Down to the Lowland border;
And he has stolen that lady away,
To haud his house in order.

He set her on a milk-white steed,
Of none he stood in awe;
Untill they reached the Hieland hills,
Aboon the Balmaha'![30]

Saying, Be content, be content,
Be content with me, lady;
Where will ye find in Lennox land,
Sae braw a man as me, lady?

Rob Roy he was my father called,
MacGregor was his name, lady;
A' the country, far and near,
Have heard MacGregor's fame, lady.

He was a hedge about his friends,
A heckle to his foes, lady;
If any man did him gainsay,
He felt his deadly blows, lady.

I am as bold, I am as bold,
I am as bold and more, lady;
Any man that doubts my word,
May try my gude claymore, lady.

Then be content, be content.
Be content with me, lady;
For now you are my wedded wife,
Until the day you die, lady.

No. VI—GHLUNE DHU.

THE FOLLOWING notices concerning this Chief fell under the Author's eye while the sheets were in the act of going through the press. They occur in manuscript memoirs, written by a person intimately acquainted with the incidents of 1745.

This Chief had the important task intrusted to him of defending the Castle of Doune, in which the Chevalier placed a garrison to protect his communication with the Highlands, and to repel any sallies which might be made from Stirling Castle—Ghlune Dhu distinguished himself by his good conduct in this charge.

Ghlune Dhu is thus described:—"Glengyle is, in person, a tall handsome man, and has more of the mien of the ancient heroes than our modern fine gentlemen are possessed of. He is honest and disinterested to a proverb—extremely modest—brave and intrepid—and born one of the best partisans in Europe. In short, the whole people of that country declared that never did men live under so mild a government as Glengyle's, not a man having so much as lost a chicken while he continued there."

It would appear from this curious passage, that Glengyle—not Stewart of Balloch, as averred in a note on Waverley—commanded the garrison of Doune. Balloch might, no doubt, succeed MacGregor in the situation.

CHAPTER FIRST

How have I sinn'd, that this affliction
Should light so heavy on me? I have no more sons,

> And this no more mine own.—My grand curse
> Hang o'er his head that thus transformed thee!—
> Travel? I'll send my horse to travel next.
>
> — MONSIEUR THOMAS.

You have requested me, my dear friend, to bestow some of that leisure, with which Providence has blessed the decline of my life, in registering the hazards and difficulties which attended its commencement. The recollection of those adventures, as you are pleased to term them, has indeed left upon my mind a chequered and varied feeling of pleasure and of pain, mingled, I trust, with no slight gratitude and veneration to the Disposer of human events, who guided my early course through much risk and labour, that the ease with which he has blessed my prolonged life might seem softer from remembrance and contrast. Neither is it possible for me to doubt, what you have often affirmed, that the incidents which befell me among a people singularly primitive in their government and manners, have something interesting and attractive for those who love to hear an old man's stories of a past age.

Still, however, you must remember, that the tale told by one friend, and listened to by another, loses half its charms when committed to paper; and that the narratives to which you have attended with interest, as heard from the voice of him to whom they occurred, will appear less deserving of attention when perused in the seclusion of your study. But your greener age and robust constitution promise longer life than will, in all human probability, be the lot of your friend. Throw, then, these sheets into some secret drawer of your escritoire till we are separated from each other's society by an event which may happen at any moment, and which must happen within the course of a few—a very few years. When we are parted in this world, to meet, I hope, in a better, you will, I am well aware, cherish more than it deserves the memory of your departed friend, and will find in those details which I am now to commit to paper, matter for melancholy, but not unpleasing reflection. Others bequeath to the confidants of their bosom portraits of their external features—I put into your hands a faithful transcript of my thoughts and feelings, of my virtues and of my failings, with the assured hope, that the follies and headstrong impetuosity of my youth will meet the same kind construction and forgiveness which have so often attended the faults of my matured age.

One advantage, among the many, of addressing my Memoirs (if I may give these sheets a name so imposing) to a dear and intimate friend, is, that I may spare some of the details, in this case unnecessary, with which I must needs have detained a stranger from what I have to say of greater interest. Why should I bestow all my tediousness upon you, because I have you in my power, and have ink, paper, and time before me? At the same time, I dare not promise that I may not abuse the opportunity so temptingly offered me, to treat of myself and my own concerns, even though I speak of circumstances as well known to you as to myself. The seductive love of narrative, when we ourselves are the heroes of the events which we tell, often disregards the attention due to the time and patience of the audience, and the best and wisest have yielded to its fascination. I need only remind you of the singular instance evinced by the form of that rare and original edition of Sully's Memoirs, which you (with the fond vanity of a book-collector) insist upon preferring to that which is reduced to the useful and ordinary form of Memoirs, but which I think curious, solely as illustrating how far so great a man as the author was accessible to the foible of self-importance. If I recollect rightly, that venerable peer and great statesman had appointed no fewer than four gentlemen of his household to draw up the events of his life, under the title of Memorials of the Sage and Royal Affairs of State, Domestic, Political, and Military, transacted by Henry IV., and so forth. These grave recorders, having made their compilation, reduced the Memoirs containing all the remarkable events of their master's life into a narrative, addressed to himself in *propria persona*. And thus, instead of telling his own story, in the third person, like Julius Caesar, or in the first person, like most who, in the hall, or the study, undertake to be the heroes of their own tale, Sully enjoyed the refined, though whimsical pleasure, of having the events of his life told over to him by his secretaries, being himself the auditor, as he was also the hero, and probably the author, of the whole book. It must have been a great sight to have seen the ex-minister, as bolt upright as a starched ruff and laced cassock could make him, seated in state beneath his canopy, and listening to the recitation of his compilers, while, standing bare in his presence, they informed him gravely, "Thus said the duke—so did the duke infer—such were your grace's sentiments upon this important point—such were your secret counsels to the king on that other emergency,"—circumstances, all of which must have been much better known to their hearer than to themselves, and most of which could only be derived from his own special communication.

My situation is not quite so ludicrous as that of the great Sully, and yet there would be something whimsical in Frank Osbaldistone giving Will Tresham a formal account of his birth, education, and connections in the world. I will, therefore, wrestle with the tempting spirit of P. P., Clerk of our Parish, as I best may, and endeavour to tell you nothing that is familiar to you already. Some things, however, I must recall to your memory, because, though formerly well known to you, they may have been forgotten through lapse of time, and they afford the ground-work of my destiny.

You must remember my father well; for, as your own was a member of the mercantile house, you knew him from infancy. Yet you hardly saw him in his best days, before age and infirmity had quenched his ardent spirit of enterprise and speculation. He would have been a poorer man, indeed, but perhaps as happy, had he devoted to the extension of science those active energies, and acute powers of observation, for which commercial pursuits found occupation. Yet, in the fluctuations of mercantile speculation, there is something captivating to the adventurer, even independent of the hope of gain. He who embarks on that fickle sea, requires to possess the skill of the pilot and the fortitude of the navigator, and after all may be wrecked and lost, unless the gales of fortune breathe in his favour. This mixture of necessary attention and inevitable hazard,—the frequent and awful uncertainty whether prudence shall overcome fortune, or fortune baffle the schemes of prudence, affords full occupation for the powers, as well as for the feelings of the mind, and trade has all the fascination of gambling without its moral guilt.

Early in the 18th century, when I (Heaven help me) was a youth of some twenty years old, I was summoned suddenly from Bourdeaux to attend my father on business of importance. I shall never forget our first interview. You recollect the brief, abrupt, and somewhat stern mode in which he was wont to communicate his pleasure to those around him. Methinks I see him even now in my mind's eye;—the firm and upright figure,—the step, quick and determined,—the eye, which shot so keen and so penetrating a glance,—the features, on which care had already planted wrinkles,—and hear his language, in which he never wasted word in vain, expressed in a voice which had sometimes an occasional harshness, far from the intention of the speaker.

When I dismounted from my post-horse, I hastened to my father's apartment. He was traversing it with an air of composed and steady deliberation, which even my arrival, although an only son unseen for four years, was unable to discompose. I threw myself into his arms. He was a kind, though not a fond father, and the tear twinkled in his dark eye, but it was only for a moment.

"Dubourg writes to me that he is satisfied with you, Frank."

"I am happy, sir"—

"But I have less reason to be so" he added, sitting down at his bureau.

"I am sorry, sir"—

"Sorry and happy, Frank, are words that, on most occasions, signify little or nothing—Here is your last letter."

He took it out from a number of others tied up in a parcel of red tape, and curiously labelled and filed. There lay my poor epistle, written on the subject the nearest to my heart at the time, and couched in words which I had thought would work compassion if not conviction,—there, I say, it lay, squeezed up among the letters on miscellaneous business in which my father's daily affairs had engaged him. I cannot help smiling internally when I recollect the mixture of hurt vanity, and wounded feeling, with which I regarded my remonstrance, to the penning of which there had gone, I promise you, some trouble, as I beheld it extracted from amongst letters of advice, of credit, and all the commonplace lumber, as I then thought them, of a merchant's correspondence. Surely, thought I, a letter of such importance (I dared not say, even to myself, so well written) deserved a separate place, as well as more anxious consideration, than those on the ordinary business of the counting-house.

But my father did not observe my dissatisfaction, and would not have minded it if he had. He proceeded, with the letter in his hand. "This, Frank, is yours of the 21st ultimo, in which you advise me (reading from my letter), that in the most important business of forming a plan, and adopting a profession for life, you trust my paternal goodness will hold you entitled to at least a negative voice; that you have insuperable —ay, insuperable is the word—I wish, by the way, you would write a more distinct current hand—draw a score through the tops of your t's, and open the loops of your l's—insuperable objections to the arrangements which I have proposed to you. There is much more to the same effect, occupying four good pages of paper, which a little attention to perspicuity and distinctness of expression might have comprised within as many lines. For, after all, Frank, it amounts but to this, that you will not do as I would have you."

"That I cannot, sir, in the present instance, not that I will not."

"Words avail very little with me, young man," said my father, whose inflexibility always possessed the air of the most perfect calmness of self-possession. "*Can not* may be a more civil phrase than *will not*, but the expressions are synonymous where there is no moral impossibility. But I am not a friend to doing business hastily; we will talk this matter over after dinner.—Owen!"

Owen appeared, not with the silver locks which you were used to venerate, for he was then little more than fifty; but he had the same, or an exactly similar uniform suit of light-brown clothes,—the same pearl-grey silk stockings,—the same stock, with its silver buckle,—the same plaited cambric ruffles, drawn down over his knuckles in the parlour, but in the counting-house carefully folded back under the sleeves, that they might remain unstained by the ink which he daily consumed;—in a word, the same grave, formal, yet benevolent cast of features, which continued to his death to distinguish the head clerk of the great house of Osbaldistone and Tresham.

"Owen," said my father, as the kind old man shook me affectionately by the hand, "you must dine with us to-day, and hear the news Frank has brought us from our friends in Bourdeaux."

Owen made one of his stiff bows of respectful gratitude; for, in those days, when the distance between superiors and inferiors was enforced in a manner to which the present times are strangers, such an invitation was a favour of some little consequence.

I shall long remember that dinner-party. Deeply affected by feelings of anxiety, not unmingled with displeasure, I was unable to take that active share in the conversation which my father seemed to expect from me; and I too frequently gave unsatisfactory answers to the questions with which he assailed me. Owen, hovering betwixt his respect for his patron, and his love for the youth he had dandled on his knee in childhood, like the timorous, yet anxious ally of an invaded nation, endeavoured at every blunder I made to explain my no-meaning, and to cover my retreat; manoeuvres which added to my father's pettish displeasure, and brought a share of it upon my kind advocate, instead of protecting me. I had not, while residing in the house of Dubourg, absolutely conducted myself like

A clerk condemn'd his father's soul to cross,
Who penn'd a stanza when he should engross;—

but, to say truth, I had frequented the counting-house no more than I had thought absolutely necessary to secure the good report of the Frenchman, long a correspondent of our firm, to whom my father had trusted for initiating me into the mysteries of commerce. In fact, my principal attention had been dedicated to literature and manly exercises. My father did not altogether discourage such acquirements, whether mental or personal. He had too much good sense not to perceive, that they sate gracefully upon every man, and he was sensible that they relieved and dignified the character to which he wished me to aspire. But his chief ambition was, that I should succeed not merely to his fortune, but to the views and plans by which he imagined he could extend and perpetuate the wealthy inheritance which he designed for me.

Love of his profession was the motive which he chose should be most ostensible, when he urged me to tread the same path; but he had others with which I only became acquainted at a later period. Impetuous in his schemes, as well as skilful and daring, each new adventure, when successful, became at once the incentive, and furnished the means, for farther speculation. It seemed to be necessary to him, as to an ambitious conqueror, to push on from achievement to achievement, without stopping to secure, far less to enjoy, the acquisitions which he made. Accustomed to see his whole fortune trembling in the scales of chance, and dexterous at adopting expedients for casting the balance in his favour, his health and spirits and activity seemed ever to increase with the animating hazards on which he staked his wealth; and he resembled a sailor, accustomed to brave the billows and the foe, whose confidence rises on the eve of tempest or of battle. He was not, however, insensible to the changes which increasing age or supervening malady might make in his own constitution; and was anxious in good time to secure in me an assistant, who might take the helm when his hand grew weary, and keep the vessel's way according to his counsel and instruction. Paternal affection, as well as the furtherance of his own plans, determined him to the same conclusion. Your father, though his fortune was vested in the house, was only a sleeping partner, as the commercial phrase goes; and Owen, whose probity and skill in the details of arithmetic rendered his services invaluable as a head clerk, was not possessed either of information or talents sufficient to conduct the mysteries of the principal management. If my father were suddenly summoned from life, what would become of the world of schemes which he had formed, unless his son were moulded into a commercial Hercules, fit to sustain the weight when relinquished by the falling Atlas? and what would become of that son himself, if, a stranger to business of this description, he found himself at once involved in the labyrinth of mercantile concerns, without the clew of knowledge necessary for his extraction? For all these reasons, avowed and secret, my father was determined I should embrace his profession; and when he was determined, the resolution of no man was more immovable. I, however, was also a party to be consulted, and, with something of his own pertinacity, I had formed a determination precisely contrary. It may, I hope, be some palliative for the resistance which, on this occasion, I offered to my father's wishes, that I did not fully understand upon what they were founded, or how deeply his happiness was involved in them. Imagining myself certain of a large succession in future, and ample maintenance in the meanwhile, it never occurred to me that it might be necessary, in order to secure these blessings, to submit to labour and limitations unpleasant to my taste and temper. I only saw in my father's proposal for my engaging in business, a desire that I should add to those heaps of wealth which he had himself acquired; and imagining myself the best judge of the path to my own happiness, I did not conceive that I should increase that happiness by augmenting a fortune which I believed was already sufficient, and more than sufficient, for every use, comfort, and elegant enjoyment.

Accordingly, I am compelled to repeat, that my time at Bourdeaux had not been spent as my father had proposed to himself. What he considered as the chief end of my residence in that city, I had postponed for every other, and would (had I dared) have neglected altogether. Dubourg, a favoured and benefited correspondent of our mercantile house, was too much of a shrewd politician to make such reports to the head of the firm concerning his only child, as would excite the displeasure of both; and he might also, as you will presently hear, have views of selfish advantage in suffering me to neglect the purposes for which I was placed under his charge. My conduct was regulated by the bounds of decency and good order, and thus far he had no evil report to make, supposing him so disposed; but, perhaps, the crafty

Frenchman would have been equally complaisant, had I been in the habit of indulging worse feelings than those of indolence and aversion to mercantile business. As it was, while I gave a decent portion of my time to the commercial studies he recommended, he was by no means envious of the hours which I dedicated to other and more classical attainments, nor did he ever find fault with me for dwelling upon Corneille and Boileau, in preference to Postlethwayte (supposing his folio to have then existed, and Monsieur Dubourg able to have pronounced his name), or Savary, or any other writer on commercial economy. He had picked up somewhere a convenient expression, with which he rounded off every letter to his correspondent,—"I was all," he said, "that a father could wish."

My father never quarrelled with a phrase, however frequently repeated, provided it seemed to him distinct and expressive; and Addison himself could not have found expressions so satisfactory to him as, "Yours received, and duly honoured the bills enclosed, as per margin."

Knowing, therefore, very well what he desired me to, be, Mr. Osbaldistone made no doubt, from the frequent repetition of Dubourg's favourite phrase, that I was the very thing he wished to see me; when, in an evil hour, he received my letter, containing my eloquent and detailed apology for declining a place in the firm, and a desk and stool in the corner of the dark counting-house in Crane Alley, surmounting in height those of Owen, and the other clerks, and only inferior to the tripod of my father himself. All was wrong from that moment. Dubourg's reports became as suspicious as if his bills had been noted for dishonour. I was summoned home in all haste, and received in the manner I have already communicated to you.

CHAPTER SECOND

> I begin shrewdly to suspect the young man of a terrible
> taint—Poetry; with which idle disease if he be infected,
> there's no hope of him in astate course. Actum est of him
> for a commonwealth's man, if he goto't in rhyme once.
>
> — BEN JONSON'S BARTHOLOMEW FAIR.

My father had, generally speaking, his temper under complete self-command, and his anger rarely indicated itself by words, except in a sort of dry testy manner, to those who had displeased him. He never used threats, or expressions of loud resentment. All was arranged with him on system, and it was his practice to do "the needful" on every occasion, without wasting words about it. It was, therefore, with a bitter smile that he listened to my imperfect answers concerning the state of commerce in France, and unmercifully permitted me to involve myself deeper and deeper in the mysteries of agio, tariffs, tare and tret; nor can I charge my memory with his having looked positively angry, until he found me unable to explain the exact effect which the depreciation of the louis d'or had produced on the negotiation of bills of exchange. "The most remarkable national occurrence in my time," said my father (who nevertheless had seen the Revolution)—"and he knows no more of it than a post on the quay!"

"Mr. Francis," suggested Owen, in his timid and conciliatory manner, "cannot have forgotten, that by an *arret* of the King of France, dated 1st May 1700, it was provided that the *porteur*, within ten days after due, must make demand"—

"Mr. Francis," said my father, interrupting him, "will, I dare say, recollect for the moment anything you are so kind as hint to him. But, body o' me! how Dubourg could permit him! Hark ye, Owen, what sort of a youth is Clement Dubourg, his nephew there, in the office, the black-haired lad?"

"One of the cleverest clerks, sir, in the house; a prodigious young man for his time," answered Owen; for the gaiety and civility of the young Frenchman had won his heart.

"Ay, ay, I suppose *he* knows something of the nature of exchange. Dubourg was determined I should have one youngster at least about my hand who understood business. But I see his drift, and he shall find that I do so when he looks at the balance-sheet. Owen, let Clement's salary be paid up to next quarter-day, and let him ship himself back to Bourdeaux in his father's ship, which is clearing out yonder."

"Dismiss Clement Dubourg, sir?" said Owen, with a faltering voice.

"Yes, sir, dismiss him instantly; it is enough to have a stupid Englishman in the counting-house to make blunders, without keeping a sharp Frenchman there to profit by them."

I had lived long enough in the territories of the *Grand Monarque* to contract a hearty aversion to arbitrary exertion of authority, even if it had not been instilled into me with my earliest breeding; and I could not refrain from interposing, to prevent an innocent and meritorious young man from paying the penalty of having acquired that proficiency which my father had desired for me.

"I beg pardon, sir," when Mr. Osbaldistone had done speaking; "but I think it but just, that if I have been negligent of my studies, I should pay the forfeit myself. I have no reason to charge Monsieur Dubourg with having neglected to give me opportunities of improvement, however little I may have profited by them; and with respect to Monsieur Clement Dubourg"—

"With respect to him, and to you, I shall take the measures which I see needful," replied my father; "but it is fair in you, Frank, to take your own blame on your own shoulders—very fair, that cannot be denied.—I cannot acquit old Dubourg," he said, looking to Owen, "for having merely afforded Frank the means of useful knowledge, without either seeing that he took advantage of them or reporting to me if he did not. You see, Owen, he has natural notions of equity becoming a British merchant."

"Mr. Francis," said the head-clerk, with his usual formal inclination of the head, and a slight elevation of his right hand, which he had acquired by a habit of sticking his pen behind his ear before he spoke—"Mr. Francis seems to understand the fundamental principle of all moral accounting, the great ethic rule of three. Let A do to B, as he would have B do to him; the product will give the rule of conduct required."

My father smiled at this reduction of the golden rule to arithmetical form, but instantly proceeded.

"All this signifies nothing, Frank; you have been throwing away your time like a boy, and in future you must learn to live like a man. I shall put you under Owen's care for a few months, to recover the lost ground."

I was about to reply, but Owen looked at me with such a supplicatory and warning gesture, that I was involuntarily silent.

"We will then," continued my father, "resume the subject of mine of the 1st ultimo, to which you sent me an answer which was unadvised and unsatisfactory. So now, fill your glass, and push the bottle to Owen."

Want of courage—of audacity if you will—was never my failing. I answered firmly, "I was sorry that my letter was unsatisfactory, unadvised it was not; for I had given the proposal his goodness had made me, my instant and anxious attention, and it was with no small pain that I found myself obliged to decline it."

My father bent his keen eye for a moment on me, and instantly withdrew it. As he made no answer, I thought myself obliged to proceed, though with some hesitation, and he only interrupted me by monosyllables.—"It is impossible, sir, for me to have higher respect for any character than I have for the commercial, even were it not yours."

"Indeed!"

"It connects nation with nation, relieves the wants, and contributes to the wealth of all; and is to the general commonwealth of the civilised world what the daily intercourse of ordinary life is to private society, or rather, what air and food are to our bodies."

"Well, sir?"

"And yet, sir, I find myself compelled to persist in declining to adopt a character which I am so ill qualified to support."

"I will take care that you acquire the qualifications necessary. You are no longer the guest and pupil of Dubourg."

"But, my dear sir, it is no defect of teaching which I plead, but my own inability to profit by instruction."

"Nonsense.—Have you kept your journal in the terms I desired?"

"Yes, sir."

"Be pleased to bring it here."

The volume thus required was a sort of commonplace book, kept by my father's recommendation, in which I had been directed to enter notes of the miscellaneous information which I had acquired in the course of my studies. Foreseeing that he would demand inspection of this record, I had been attentive to transcribe such particulars of information as he would most likely be pleased with, but too often the pen had discharged the task without much correspondence with the head. And it had also happened, that, the book being the receptacle nearest to my hand, I had occasionally jotted down memoranda which had little regard to traffic. I now put it into my father's hand, devoutly hoping he might light on nothing that would increase his displeasure against me. Owen's face, which had looked something blank when the question was put, cleared up at my ready answer, and wore a smile of hope, when I brought from my apartment, and placed before my father, a commercial-looking volume, rather broader than it was long, having brazen clasps and a binding of rough calf. This looked business-like, and was encouraging to my benevolent well-wisher. But he actually smiled with pleasure as he heard my father run over some part of the contents, muttering his critical remarks as he went on.

"—*Brandies*—*Barils and barricants, also tonneaux.*—*At Nantz* 29—*Velles to the barique at Cognac and Rochelle 27—At Bourdeaux 32*—Very right, Frank—*Duties on tonnage and custom-house, see Saxby's Tables*—That's not well; you should have transcribed the passage; it fixes the thing in the memory—*Reports outward and inward—Corn debentures—Over-sea Cockets—Linens—Isingham—Gentish—Stock-fish—Titling—Cropling—Lub-fish.* You should have noted that they are all, nevertheless to be entered as titlings. —How many inches long is a titling?"

Owen, seeing me at fault, hazarded a whisper, of which I fortunately caught the import.

"Eighteen inches, sir."—

"And a lub-fish is twenty-four—very right. It is important to remember this, on account of the Portuguese trade—But what have we here?—*Bourdeaux founded in the year—Castle of the Trompette—Palace of Gallienus*—Well, well, that's very right too.—This is a kind of waste-book, Owen, in which all the transactions of the day,—emptions, orders, payments, receipts, acceptances, draughts, commissions, and advices,—are entered miscellaneously."

"That they may be regularly transferred to the day-book and ledger," answered Owen: "I am glad Mr. Francis is so methodical."

I perceived myself getting so fast into favour, that I began to fear the consequence would be my father's more obstinate perseverance in his resolution that I must become a merchant; and as I was determined on the contrary, I began to wish I had not, to use my friend Mr. Owen's phrase, been so methodical. But I had no reason for apprehension on that score; for a blotted piece of paper dropped out of the book, and, being taken up by my father, he interrupted a hint from Owen, on the propriety of securing loose memoranda with a little paste, by exclaiming, "To the memory of Edward the Black Prince—What's all this?—verses!—By Heaven, Frank, you are a greater blockhead than I supposed you!"

My father, you must recollect, as a man of business, looked upon the labour of poets with contempt; and as a religious man, and of the dissenting persuasion, he considered all such pursuits as equally trivial and profane. Before you condemn him, you must recall to remembrance how too many of the poets in the end of the seventeenth century had led their lives and employed their talents. The sect also to which my father belonged, felt, or perhaps affected, a puritanical aversion to the lighter exertions of literature. So that many causes contributed to augment the unpleasant surprise occasioned by the ill-timed discovery of this unfortunate copy of verses. As for poor Owen, could the bob-wig which he then wore have uncurled itself, and stood on end with horror, I am convinced the morning's labour of the friseur would have been undone, merely by the excess of his astonishment at this enormity. An inroad on the strong-box, or an erasure in the ledger, or a mis-summation in a fitted account, could hardly have surprised him more disagreeably. My father read the lines sometimes with an affectation of not being able to understand the sense—sometimes in a mouthing tone of mock heroic—always with an emphasis of the most bitter irony, most irritating to the nerves of an author.

"O for the voice of that wild horn,
On Fontarabian echoes borne,
The dying hero's call,

That told imperial Charlemagne,
How Paynim sons of swarthy Spain
Had wrought his champion's fall.

"*Fontarabian echoes!*" continued my father, interrupting himself; "the Fontarabian Fair would have been more to the purpose—*Paynim!*—What's Paynim?—Could you not say Pagan as well, and write English at least, if you must needs write nonsense?—

"Sad over earth and ocean sounding.
And England's distant cliffs astounding.
Such are the notes should say
How Britain's hope, and France's fear,
Victor of Cressy and Poitier,
In Bordeaux dying lay."

"Poitiers, by the way, is always spelt with an *s*, and I know no reason why orthography should give place to rhyme.—

"'Raise my faint head, my squires,' he said,
'And let the casement be display'd,
That I may see once more
The splendour of the setting sun
Gleam on thy mirrored wave, Garonne,
And Blaye's empurpled shore.

"*Garonne* and *sun* is a bad rhyme. Why, Frank, you do not even understand the beggarly trade you have chosen.

"'Like me, he sinks to Glory's sleep,
His fall the dews of evening steep,
As if in sorrow shed,
So soft shall fall the trickling tear,
When England's maids and matrons hear
Of their Black Edward dead.

"'And though my sun of glory set,
Nor France, nor England, shall forget
The terror of my name;
And oft shall Britain's heroes rise,
New planets in these southern skies,
Through clouds of blood and flame.'

"A cloud of flame is something new—Good-morrow, my masters all, and a merry Christmas to you!—Why, the bellman writes better lines." He then tossed the paper from him with an air of superlative contempt, and concluded—"Upon my credit, Frank, you are a greater blockhead than I took you for."

What could I say, my dear Tresham? There I stood, swelling with indignant mortification, while my father regarded me with a calm but stern look of scorn and pity; and poor Owen, with uplifted hands and eyes, looked as striking a picture of horror as if he had just read his patron's name in the Gazette. At length I took courage to speak, endeavouring that my tone of voice should betray my feelings as little as possible.

"I am quite aware, sir, how ill qualified I am to play the conspicuous part in society you have destined for me; and, luckily, I am not ambitious of the wealth I might acquire. Mr. Owen would be a much more effective assistant." I said this in some malice, for I considered Owen as having deserted my cause a little too soon.

"Owen!" said my father—"The boy is mad—actually insane. And, pray, sir, if I may presume to inquire, having coolly turned me over to Mr. Owen (although I may expect more attention from any one than from my son), what may your own sage projects be?"

"I should wish, sir," I replied, summoning up my courage, "to travel for two or three years, should that consist with your pleasure; otherwise, although late, I would willingly spend the same time at Oxford or Cambridge."

"In the name of common sense! was the like ever heard?—to put yourself to school among pedants and Jacobites, when you might be pushing your fortune in the world! Why not go to Westminster or Eton at once, man, and take to Lilly's Grammar and Accidence, and to the birch, too, if you like it?"

"Then, sir, if you think my plan of improvement too late, I would willingly return to the Continent."

"You have already spent too much time there to little purpose, Mr. Francis."

"Then I would choose the army, sir, in preference to any other active line of life."

"Choose the d—l!" answered my father, hastily, and then checking himself—"I profess you make me as great a fool as you are yourself. Is he not enough to drive one mad, Owen?"—Poor Owen shook his head, and looked down. "Hark ye, Frank," continued my father, "I will cut all this matter very short. I was at your age when my father turned me out of doors, and settled my legal inheritance on my younger brother. I left Osbaldistone Hall on the back of a broken-down hunter, with ten guineas in my purse. I have never crossed the threshold again, and I never will. I know not, and I care not, if my fox-hunting brother is alive, or has broken his neck; but he has children, Frank, and one of them shall be my son if you cross me farther in this matter."

"You will do your pleasure," I answered—rather, I fear, with more sullen indifference than respect, "with what is your own."

"Yes, Frank, what I have *is* my own, if labour in getting, and care in augmenting, can make a right of property; and no drone shall feed on my honeycomb. Think on it well: what I have said is not without reflection, and what I resolve upon I will execute."

"Honoured sir!—dear sir!" exclaimed Owen, tears rushing into his eyes, "you are not wont to be in such a hurry in transacting business of importance. Let Mr. Francis run up the balance before you shut the account; he loves you, I am sure; and when he puts down his filial obedience to the *per contra,* I am sure his objections will disappear."

"Do you think I will ask him twice," said my father, sternly, "to be my friend, my assistant, and my confidant?—to be a partner of my cares and of my fortune?—Owen, I thought you had known me better."

He looked at me as if he meant to add something more, but turned instantly away, and left the room abruptly. I was, I own, affected by this view of the case, which had not occurred to me; and my father would probably have had little reason to complain of me, had he commenced the discussion with this argument.

But it was too late. I had much of his own obduracy of resolution, and Heaven had decreed that my sin should be my punishment, though not to the extent which my transgression merited. Owen, when we were left alone, continued to look at me with eyes which tears from time to time moistened, as if to discover, before attempting the task of intercessor, upon what point my obstinacy was most assailable. At length he began, with broken and disconcerted accents,—"O L—d, Mr. Francis!—Good Heavens, sir!—My stars, Mr. Osbaldistone!—that I should ever have seen this day—and you so young a gentleman, sir!—For the love of Heaven! look at both sides of the account—think what you are going to lose—a noble fortune, sir—one of the finest houses in the City, even under the old firm of Tresham and Trent, and now Osbaldistone and Tresham—You might roll in gold, Mr. Francis—And, my dear young Mr. Frank, if there was any particular thing in the business of the house which you disliked, I would" (sinking his voice to a whisper) "put it in order for you termly, or weekly, or daily, if you will—Do, my dear Mr. Francis, think of the honour due to your father, that your days may be long in the land."

"I am much obliged to you, Mr. Owen," said I—"very much obliged indeed; but my father is best judge how to bestow his money. He talks of one of my cousins: let him dispose of his wealth as he pleases—I will never sell my liberty for gold."

"Gold, sir?—I wish you saw the balance-sheet of profits at last term—It was in five figures—five figures to each partner's sum total, Mr. Frank—And all this is to go to a Papist, and a north-country booby, and a disaffected person besides—It will break my heart, Mr. Francis, that have been toiling more like a dog than a man, and all for love of the firm. Think how it will sound, Osbaldistone, Tresham, and Osbaldistone—or perhaps, who knows" (again lowering his voice), "Osbaldistone, Osbaldistone, and Tresham, for our Mr. Osbaldistone can buy them all out."

"But, Mr. Owen, my cousin's name being also Osbaldistone, the name of the company will sound every bit as well in your ears."

"O fie upon you, Mr. Francis, when you know how well I love you—Your cousin, indeed!—a Papist, no doubt, like his father, and a disaffected person to the Protestant succession—that's another item, doubtless."

"There are many very good men Catholics, Mr. Owen," rejoined I.

As Owen was about to answer with unusual animation, my father re-entered the apartment.

"You were right," he said, "Owen, and I was wrong; we will take more time to think over this matter.—Young man, you will prepare to give me an answer on this important subject this day month."

I bowed in silence, sufficiently glad of a reprieve, and trusting it might indicate some relaxation in my father's determination.

The time of probation passed slowly, unmarked by any accident whatever. I went and came, and disposed of my time as I pleased, without question or criticism on the part of my father. Indeed, I rarely saw him, save at meal-times, when he studiously avoided a discussion which you may well suppose I was in no hurry to press onward. Our conversation was of the news of the day, or on such general topics as strangers discourse upon to each other; nor could any one have guessed, from its tenor, that there remained undecided betwixt us a dispute of such importance. It haunted me, however, more than once, like the nightmare. Was it possible he would keep his word, and disinherit his only son in favour of a nephew whose very existence he was not perhaps quite certain of? My grandfather's conduct, in similar circumstances, boded me no good, had I considered the matter rightly. But I had formed an erroneous idea of my father's character, from the importance which I recollected I maintained with him and his whole family before I went to France. I was not aware that there are men who indulge their children at an early age, because to do so interests and amuses them, and who can yet be sufficiently severe when the same children cross their expectations at a more advanced period. On the contrary, I persuaded myself, that all I had to apprehend was some temporary alienation of affection—perhaps a rustication of a few weeks, which I thought would rather please me than otherwise, since it would give me an opportunity of setting about my unfinished version of Orlando Furioso, a poem which I longed to render into English verse. I suffered this belief to get such absolute possession of my mind, that I had resumed my blotted papers, and was busy in meditation on the oft-recurring rhymes of the Spenserian stanza, when I heard a low and cautious tap at the door of my apartment. "Come in," I said, and Mr. Owen entered. So regular were the motions and habits of this worthy man, that in all probability this was the first time he had ever been in the second story of his patron's house, however conversant with the first; and I am still at a loss to know in what manner he discovered my apartment.

"Mr. Francis," he said, interrupting my expression of surprise and pleasure at seeing, him, "I do not know if I am doing well in what I am about to say—it is not right to speak of what passes in the compting-house out of doors—one should not tell, as they say, to the post in the warehouse, how many lines there are in the ledger. But young Twineall has been absent from the house for a fortnight and more, until two days since."

"Very well, my dear sir, and how does that concern us?"

"Stay, Mr. Francis;—your father gave him a private commission; and I am sure he did not go down to Falmouth about the pilchard affair; and the Exeter business with Blackwell and Company has been settled; and the mining people in Cornwall, Trevanion and Treguilliam, have paid all they are likely to pay; and any other matter of business must have been put through my books:—in short, it's my faithful belief that Twineall has been down in the north."

"Do you really suppose?" so said I, somewhat startled.

"He has spoken about nothing, sir, since he returned, but his new boots, and his Ripon spurs, and a cockfight at York—it's as true as the multiplication-table. Do, Heaven bless you, my dear child, make up your mind to please your father, and to be a man and a merchant at once."

I felt at that instant a strong inclination to submit, and to make Owen happy by requesting him to tell my father that I resigned myself to his disposal. But pride—

pride, the source of so much that is good and so much that is evil in our course of life, prevented me. My acquiescence stuck in my throat; and while I was coughing to get it up, my father's voice summoned Owen. He hastily left the room, and the opportunity was lost.

My father was methodical in everything. At the very same time of the day, in the same apartment, and with the same tone and manner which he had employed an exact month before, he recapitulated the proposal he had made for taking me into partnership, and assigning me a department in the counting-house, and requested to have my final decision. I thought at the time there was something unkind in this; and I still think that my father's conduct was injudicious. A more conciliatory treatment would, in all probability, have gained his purpose. As it was, I stood fast, and, as respectfully as I could, declined the proposal he made to me. Perhaps—for who can judge of their own heart?—I felt it unmanly to yield on the first summons, and expected farther solicitation, as at least a pretext for changing my mind. If so, I was disappointed; for my father turned coolly to Owen, and only said, "You see it is as I told you.—Well, Frank" (addressing me), "you are nearly of age, and as well qualified to judge of what will constitute your own happiness as you ever are like to be; therefore, I say no more. But as I am not bound to give in to your plans, any more than you are compelled to submit to mine, may I ask to know if you have formed any which depend on my assistance?"

I answered, not a little abashed, "That being bred to no profession, and having no funds of my own, it was obviously impossible for me to subsist without some allowance from my father; that my wishes were very moderate; and that I hoped my aversion for the profession to which he had designed me, would not occasion his altogether withdrawing his paternal support and protection."

"That is to say, you wish to lean on my arm, and yet to walk your own way? That can hardly be, Frank;—however, I suppose you mean to obey my directions, so far as they do not cross your own humour?"

I was about to speak—"Silence, if you please," he continued. "Supposing this to be the case, you will instantly set out for the north of England, to pay your uncle a visit, and see the state of his family. I have chosen from among his sons (he has six, I believe) one who, I understand, is most worthy to fill the place I intended for you in the counting-house. But some farther arrangements may be necessary, and for these your presence may be requisite. You shall have farther instructions at Osbaldistone Hall, where you will please to remain until you hear from me. Everything will be ready for your departure to-morrow morning."

With these words my father left the apartment.

"What does all this mean, Mr. Owen?" said I to my sympathetic friend, whose countenance wore a cast of the deepest dejection.

"You have ruined yourself, Mr. Frank, that's all. When your father talks in that quiet determined manner, there will be no more change in him than in a fitted account."

And so it proved; for the next morning, at five o'clock, I found myself on the road to York, mounted on a reasonably good horse, and with fifty guineas in my pocket; travelling, as it would seem, for the purpose of assisting in the adoption of a successor to myself in my father's house and favour, and, for aught I knew, eventually in his fortune also.

CHAPTER THIRD

> The slack sail shifts from side to side,
> The boat, untrimm'd, admits the tide,
> Borne down, adrift, at random tost,
> The oar breaks short, the rudder's lost.
>
> — GAY'S FABLES.

I have tagged with rhyme and blank verse the subdivisions of this important narrative, in order to seduce your continued attention by powers of composition of stronger attraction than my own. The preceding lines refer to an unfortunate navigator, who daringly unloosed from its moorings a boat, which he was unable to manage, and thrust it off into the full tide of a navigable river. No schoolboy, who, betwixt frolic and defiance, has executed a similar rash attempt, could feel himself, when adrift in a strong current, in a situation more awkward than mine, when I found myself driving, without a compass, on the ocean of human life. There had been such unexpected ease in the manner in which my father slipt a knot, usually esteemed the strongest which binds society together, and suffered me to depart as a sort of outcast from his family, that it strangely lessened the confidence in my own personal accomplishments, which had hitherto sustained me. Prince Prettyman, now a prince, and now a fisher's son, had not a more awkward sense of his degradation. We are so apt, in our engrossing egotism, to consider all those accessories which are drawn around us by prosperity, as pertaining and belonging to our own persons, that the discovery of our unimportance, when left to our own proper resources, becomes inexpressibly mortifying. As the hum of London died away on my ear, the distant peal of her steeples more than once sounded to my ears the admonitory "Turn again," erst heard by her future Lord Mayor; and when I looked back from Highgate on her dusky magnificence, I felt as if I were leaving behind me comfort, opulence, the charms of society, and all the pleasures of cultivated life.

But the die was cast. It was, indeed, by no means probable that a late and ungracious compliance with my father's wishes would have reinstated me in the situation which I had lost. On the contrary, firm and strong of purpose as he himself was, he might rather have been disgusted than conciliated by my tardy and compulsory acquiescence in his desire that I should engage in commerce. My constitutional obstinacy came also to my aid, and pride whispered how poor a figure I should make, when an airing of four miles from London had blown away resolutions formed during a month's serious deliberation. Hope, too, that never forsakes the young and hardy, lent her lustre to my future prospects. My father could not be serious in the sentence of foris-familiation, which he had so unhesitatingly pronounced. It must be but a trial of my disposition, which, endured with patience and steadiness on my part, would raise me in his estimation, and lead to an amicable accommodation of the point in dispute between us. I even settled in my own mind how far I would concede to him, and on what articles of our supposed treaty I would make a firm stand; and the result was, according to my computation, that I was to be reinstated in my full rights of filiation, paying the easy penalty of some ostensible compliances to atone for my past rebellion.

In the meanwhile, I was lord of my person, and experienced that feeling of independence which the youthful bosom receives with a thrilling mixture of pleasure and apprehension. My purse, though by no means amply replenished, was in a situation to supply all the wants and wishes of a traveller. I had been accustomed, while at Bourdeaux, to act as my own valet; my horse was fresh, young, and active, and the buoyancy of my spirits soon surmounted the melancholy reflections with which my journey commenced.

I should have been glad to have journeyed upon a line of road better calculated to afford reasonable objects of curiosity, or a more interesting country, to the traveller. But the north road was then, and perhaps still is, singularly deficient in these respects; nor do I believe you can travel so far through Britain in any other direction without meeting more of what is worthy to engage the attention. My mental ruminations, notwithstanding my assumed confidence, were not always of an unchequered nature. The Muse too,—the very coquette who had led me into this wilderness,—like others of her sex, deserted me in my utmost need, and I should have been reduced to rather an uncomfortable state of dulness, had it not been for the occasional conversation of strangers who chanced to pass the same way. But the characters whom I met with were of a uniform and uninteresting description. Country parsons, jogging homewards after a visitation; farmers, or graziers, returning from a distant market; clerks of traders, travelling to collect what was due to their masters, in provincial towns; with now and then an officer going down into the country upon the recruiting service, were, at this period, the persons by whom the turnpikes and tapsters were kept in exercise. Our speech, therefore, was of tithes and creeds, of beeves and grain, of commodities wet and dry, and the solvency of the retail dealers, occasionally varied by the description of a siege, or battle, in Flanders, which, perhaps, the narrator only gave me at second hand. Robbers, a fertile and alarming theme, filled up every vacancy; and the names of the Golden Farmer, the Flying Highwayman, Jack Needham, and other Beggars' Opera heroes, were familiar in our mouths as household words. At such tales, like children closing their circle round the fire when the ghost story draws to its climax, the riders drew near to each other, looked before and behind them, examined the priming of their pistols, and vowed to stand by each other in case of danger; an engagement which, like other offensive and defensive alliances, sometimes glided out of remembrance when there was an appearance of actual peril.

Of all the fellows whom I ever saw haunted by terrors of this nature, one poor man, with whom I travelled a day and a half, afforded me most amusement. He had upon his pillion a very small, but apparently a very weighty portmanteau, about the safety of which he seemed particularly solicitous; never trusting it out of his own immediate care, and uniformly repressing the officious zeal of the waiters and ostlers, who offered their services to carry it into the house. With the same precaution he laboured to conceal, not only the purpose of his journey, and his ultimate place of destination, but even the direction of each day's route. Nothing embarrassed him more than to be asked by any one, whether he was travelling upwards or downwards, or at what stage he intended to bait. His place of rest for the night he scrutinised with the most anxious care, alike avoiding solitude, and what he considered as bad neighbourhood; and at Grantham, I believe, he sate up all night to avoid sleeping in the next room to a thick-set squinting fellow, in a black wig, and a tarnished gold-laced waistcoat. With all these cares on his mind, my fellow traveller, to judge by his thews and sinews, was a man who might have set danger at defiance with as much impunity as most men. He was strong and well built; and, judging from his gold-laced hat and cockade, seemed to have served in the army, or, at least, to belong to the military profession in one capacity or other. His conversation also, though always sufficiently vulgar, was that of a man of sense, when the terrible bugbears which haunted his imagination for a moment ceased to occupy his attention. But every accidental association recalled them. An open heath, a close plantation, were alike subjects of apprehension; and the whistle of a shepherd lad was instantly converted into the signal of a depredator. Even the sight of a gibbet, if it assured him that one robber was safely disposed of by justice, never failed to remind him how many remained still unhanged.

I should have wearied of this fellow's company, had I not been still more tired of my own thoughts. Some of the marvellous stories, however, which he related, had in themselves a cast of interest, and another whimsical point of his peculiarities afforded me the occasional opportunity of amusing myself at his expense. Among his tales, several of the unfortunate travellers who fell among thieves, incurred that calamity from associating themselves on the road with a well-dressed and entertaining stranger, in whose company they trusted to find protection as well as amusement; who cheered their journey with tale and song, protected them against the evils of over-charges and false reckonings, until at length, under pretext of showing a near path over a desolate common, he seduced his unsuspicious victims from the public road into some dismal glen, where, suddenly blowing his whistle, he assembled his comrades from their lurking-place, and displayed himself in his true colours—the captain, namely, of the band of robbers to whom his unwary fellow-travellers had forfeited their purses, and perhaps their lives. Towards the conclusion of such a tale, and when my companion had wrought himself into a fever of apprehension by the progress of his own narrative, I observed that he usually eyed me with a glance of doubt and suspicion, as if the possibility occurred to him, that he might, at that very moment, be in company with a character as dangerous as that which his tale described. And ever and anon, when such suggestions pressed themselves on the mind of this ingenious self-tormentor, he drew off from me to the opposite side of the high-road, looked before, behind, and around him, examined his arms, and seemed to prepare himself for flight or defence, as circumstances might require.

The suspicion implied on such occasions seemed to me only momentary, and too ludicrous to be offensive. There was, in fact, no particular reflection on my dress or address, although I was thus mistaken for a robber. A man in those days might have all the external appearance of a gentleman, and yet turn out to be a highwayman. For the division of labour in every department not having then taken place so fully as since that period, the profession of the polite and accomplished adventurer, who nicked you out of your money at White's, or bowled you out of it at Marylebone, was often united with that of the professed ruffian, who on Bagshot Heath, or Finchley Common, commanded his brother beau to stand and deliver. There was also a touch of coarseness and hardness about the manners of the times, which has since, in a great degree, been softened and shaded away. It seems to me, on recollection, as if desperate men had less reluctance then than now to embrace the most desperate means of retrieving their fortune. The times were indeed past, when Anthony-a-Wood mourned over the execution of two men, goodly in person, and of undisputed courage and honour, who were hanged without mercy at Oxford, merely because their distress had driven them to raise contributions on the highway. We were still farther removed from the days of "the mad Prince and Poins." And yet, from the number of unenclosed and extensive heaths in the vicinity of the metropolis, and from the less populous state of remote districts, both were frequented by that species of mounted highwaymen, that may possibly become one day unknown, who carried on their trade with something like courtesy; and, like Gibbet in the Beaux Stratagem, piqued themselves on being the best behaved men on the road, and on conducting themselves with all appropriate civility in the exercise of their vocation. A young man, therefore, in my circumstances was not entitled to be highly indignant at the mistake which confounded him with this worshipful class of depredators.

Neither was I offended. On the contrary, I found amusement in alternately exciting, and lulling to sleep, the suspicions of my timorous companion, and in purposely so acting as still farther to puzzle a brain which nature and apprehension had combined to render none of the clearest. When my free conversation had lulled him into complete security, it required only a passing inquiry concerning the direction of his journey, or the nature of the business which occasioned it, to put his suspicions once more in arms. For example, a conversation on the comparative strength and activity of our horses, took such a turn as follows:—

"O sir," said my companion, "for the gallop I grant you; but allow me to say, your horse (although he is a very handsome gelding—that must be owned,) has too little bone to be a good roadster. The trot, sir" (striking his Bucephalus with his spurs),—"the trot is the true pace for a hackney; and, were we near a town, I should like to try that daisy-cutter of yours upon a piece of level road (barring canter) for a quart of claret at the next inn."

"Content, sir," replied I; "and here is a stretch of ground very favourable."

"Hem, ahem," answered my friend with hesitation; "I make it a rule of travelling never to blow my horse between stages; one never knows what occasion he may have to put him to his mettle: and besides, sir, when I said I would match you, I meant with even weight; you ride four stone lighter than I."

"Very well; but I am content to carry weight. Pray, what may that portmanteau of yours weigh?"

"My p-p-portmanteau?" replied he, hesitating—"O very little—a feather—just a few shirts and stockings."

"I should think it heavier, from its appearance. I'll hold you the quart of claret it makes the odds betwixt our weight."

"You're mistaken, sir, I assure you—quite mistaken," replied my friend, edging off to the side of the road, as was his wont on these alarming occasions.

"Well, I am willing to venture the wine; or, I will bet you ten pieces to five, that I carry your portmanteau on my croupe, and out-trot you into the bargain."

This proposal raised my friend's alarm to the uttermost. His nose changed from the natural copper hue which it had acquired from many a comfortable cup of claret or sack, into a palish brassy tint, and his teeth chattered with apprehension at the unveiled audacity of my proposal, which seemed to place the barefaced plunderer before him in full atrocity. As he faltered for an answer, I relieved him in some degree by a question concerning a steeple, which now became visible, and an observation that we were now so near the village as to run no risk from interruption on the road. At this his countenance cleared up: but I easily perceived that it was long ere he forgot a proposal which seemed to him so fraught with suspicion as that which I had now hazarded. I trouble you with this detail of the man's disposition, and the manner in which I practised upon it, because, however trivial in themselves, these particulars were attended by an important influence on future incidents which will occur in this narrative. At the time, this person's conduct only inspired me with contempt, and confirmed me in an opinion which I already entertained, that of all the propensities which teach mankind to torment themselves, that of causeless fear is the most irritating, busy, painful, and pitiable.

CHAPTER FOURTH

> The Scots are poor, cries surly English pride.
> True is the charge; nor by themselves denied.
> Are they not, then, in strictest reason clear,
> Who wisely come to mend their fortunes here?

> — CHURCHILL

There was, in the days of which I write, an old-fashioned custom on the English road, which I suspect is now obsolete, or practised only by the vulgar. Journeys of length being made on horseback, and, of course, by brief stages, it was usual always to make a halt on the Sunday in some town where the traveller might attend divine service, and his horse have the benefit of the day of rest, the institution of which is as humane to our brute labourers as profitable to ourselves. A counterpart to this decent practice, and a remnant of old English hospitality, was, that the landlord of a principal inn laid aside his character of a publican on the seventh day, and invited the guests who chanced to be within his walls to take a part of his family beef and pudding. This invitation was usually complied with by all whose distinguished rank did not induce them to think compliance a derogation; and the proposal of a bottle of wine after dinner, to drink the landlord's health, was the only recompense ever offered or accepted.

I was born a citizen of the world, and my inclination led me into all scenes where my knowledge of mankind could be enlarged; I had, besides, no pretensions to sequester myself on the score of superior dignity, and therefore seldom failed to accept of the Sunday's hospitality of mine host, whether of the Garter, Lion, or Bear.

The honest publican, dilated into additional consequence by a sense of his own importance, while presiding among the guests on whom it was his ordinary duty to attend, was in himself an entertaining, spectacle; and around his genial orbit, other planets of inferior consequence performed their revolutions. The wits and humorists, the distinguished worthies of the town or village, the apothecary, the attorney, even the curate himself, did not disdain to partake of this hebdomadal festivity. The guests, assembled from different quarters, and following different professions, formed, in language, manners, and sentiments, a curious contrast to each other, not indifferent to those who desired to possess a knowledge of mankind in its varieties.

It was on such a day, and such an occasion, that my timorous acquaintance and I were about to grace the board of the ruddy-faced host of the Black Bear, in the town of Darlington, and bishopric of Durham, when our landlord informed us, with a sort of apologetic tone, that there was a Scotch gentleman to dine with us.

"A gentleman!—what sort of a gentleman?" said my companion somewhat hastily—his mind, I suppose, running on gentlemen of the pad, as they were then termed.

"Why, a Scotch sort of a gentleman, as I said before," returned mine host; "they are all gentle, ye mun know, though they ha' narra shirt to back; but this is a decentish hallion—a canny North Briton as e'er cross'd Berwick Bridge—I trow he's a dealer in cattle."

"Let us have his company, by all means," answered my companion; and then, turning to me, he gave vent to the tenor of his own reflections. "I respect the Scotch, sir; I love and honour the nation for their sense of morality. Men talk of their filth and their poverty: but commend me to sterling honesty, though clad in rags, as the poet saith. I have been credibly assured, sir, by men on whom I can depend, that there was never known such a thing in Scotland as a highway robbery."

"That's because they have nothing to lose," said mine host, with the chuckle of a self-applauding wit.

"No, no, landlord," answered a strong deep voice behind him, "it's e'en because your English gaugers and supervisors,[31] that you have sent down benorth the Tweed, have taen up the trade of thievery over the heads of the native professors."

"Well said, Mr. Campbell," answered the landlord; "I did not think thoud'st been sae near us, mon. But thou kens I'm an outspoken Yorkshire tyke. And how go markets in the south?"

"Even in the ordinar," replied Mr. Campbell; "wise folks buy and sell, and fools are bought and sold."

"But wise men and fools both eat their dinner," answered our jolly entertainer; "and here a comes—as prime a buttock of beef as e'er hungry men stuck fork in."

So saying, he eagerly whetted his knife, assumed his seat of empire at the head of the board, and loaded the plates of his sundry guests with his good cheer.

This was the first time I had heard the Scottish accent, or, indeed, that I had familiarly met with an individual of the ancient nation by whom it was spoken. Yet, from an early period, they had occupied and interested my imagination. My father, as is well known to you, was of an ancient family in Northumberland, from whose seat I was, while eating the aforesaid dinner, not very many miles distant. The quarrel betwixt him and his relatives was such, that he scarcely ever mentioned the race from which he sprung, and held as the most contemptible species of vanity, the weakness which is commonly termed family pride. His ambition was only to be distinguished as William Osbaldistone, the first, at least one of the first, merchants on Change; and to have proved him the lineal representative of William the Conqueror would have far less flattered his vanity than the hum and bustle which his approach was wont to produce among the bulls, bears, and brokers of Stock-alley. He wished, no doubt, that I should remain in such ignorance of my relatives and descent as might insure a correspondence between my feelings and his own on this subject. But his designs, as will happen occasionally to the wisest, were, in some degree at least, counteracted by a being whom his pride would never have supposed of importance adequate to influence them in any way. His nurse, an old Northumbrian woman, attached to him from his infancy, was the only person connected with his native province for whom he retained any regard; and when fortune dawned upon him, one of the first uses which he made of her favours, was to give Mabel Rickets a place of residence within his household. After the death of my mother, the care of nursing me during my childish illnesses, and of rendering all those tender attentions which infancy exacts from female affection, devolved on old Mabel. Interdicted by her master from speaking to him on the subject of the heaths, glades, and dales of her beloved Northumberland, she poured herself forth to my infant ear in descriptions of the scenes of her youth, and long narratives of the events which tradition declared to have passed amongst them. To these I inclined my ear much more seriously than to graver, but less animated instructors. Even yet, methinks I see old Mabel, her head slightly agitated by the palsy of age, and shaded by a close cap, as white as the driven snow,—her face wrinkled, but still retaining the healthy tinge which it had acquired in rural labour—I think I see her look around on the brick walls and narrow street which presented themselves before our windows, as she concluded with a sigh the favourite old ditty, which I then preferred, and—why should I not tell the truth?—which I still prefer to all the opera airs ever minted by the capricious brain of an Italian Mus. D.—

Oh, the oak, the ash, and the bonny ivy tree,
They flourish best at home in the North Countrie!

Now, in the legends of Mabel, the Scottish nation was ever freshly remembered, with all the embittered declamation of which the narrator was capable. The inhabitants of the opposite frontier served in her narratives to fill up the parts which ogres and giants with seven-leagued boots occupy in the ordinary nursery tales. And how could it be otherwise? Was it not the Black Douglas who slew with his own hand the heir of the Osbaldistone family the day after he took possession of his estate, surprising him and his vassals while solemnizing a feast suited to the occasion? Was it not Wat the Devil, who drove all the year-old hogs off the braes of Lanthorn-side, in the very recent days of my grandfather's father? And had we not many a trophy, but, according to old Mabel's version of history, far more honourably gained, to mark our revenge of these wrongs? Did not Sir Henry Osbaldistone, fifth baron of the name, carry off the fair maid of Fairnington, as Achilles did his Chryseis and Briseis of old, and detain her in his fortress against all the power of her friends, supported by the most mighty Scottish chiefs of warlike fame? And had not our swords shone foremost at most of those fields in which England was victorious over her rival? All our family renown was acquired—all our family misfortunes were occasioned—by the northern wars.

Warmed by such tales, I looked upon the Scottish people during my childhood, as a race hostile by nature to the more southern inhabitants of this realm; and this view of the matter was not much corrected by the language which my father sometimes held with respect to them. He had engaged in some large speculations concerning oak-woods, the property of Highland proprietors, and alleged, that he found them much more ready to make bargains, and extort earnest of the purchase-money, than punctual in complying on their side with the terms of the engagements. The Scottish mercantile men, whom he was under the necessity of employing as a sort of middle-men on these occasions, were also suspected by my father of having secured, by one means or other, more than their own share of the profit which ought to have accrued. In short, if Mabel complained of the Scottish arms in ancient times, Mr. Osbaldistone inveighed no less against the arts of these modern Sinons; and between them, though without any fixed purpose of doing so, they impressed my youthful mind with a sincere aversion to the northern inhabitants of Britain, as a people bloodthirsty in time of war, treacherous during truce, interested, selfish, avaricious, and tricky in the business of peaceful life, and having few good qualities, unless there should be accounted such, a ferocity which resembled courage in martial affairs, and a sort of wily craft which supplied the place of wisdom in the ordinary commerce of mankind. In justification, or apology, for those who entertained such prejudices, I must remark, that the Scotch of that period were guilty of similar injustice to the English, whom they branded universally as a race of purse-proud arrogant epicures. Such seeds of national dislike remained between the two countries, the natural consequences of their existence as separate and rival states. We have seen recently the breath of a demagogue blow these sparks into a temporary flame, which I sincerely hope is now extinguished in its own ashes.[32]

It was, then, with an impression of dislike, that I contemplated the first Scotchman I chanced to meet in society. There was much about him that coincided with my previous conceptions. He had the hard features and athletic form said to be peculiar to his country, together with the national intonation and slow pedantic mode of expression, arising from a desire to avoid peculiarities of idiom or dialect. I could also observe the caution and shrewdness of his country in many of the observations which he made, and the answers which he returned. But I was not prepared for the air of easy self-possession and superiority with which he seemed to predominate over the company into which he was thrown, as it were by accident. His dress was as coarse as it could be, being still decent; and, at a time when great expense was lavished upon the wardrobe, even of the lowest who pretended to the character of gentleman, this indicated mediocrity of circumstances, if not poverty. His conversation intimated that he was engaged in the cattle trade, no very dignified professional pursuit. And yet, under these disadvantages, he seemed, as a matter of course, to treat the rest of the company with the cool and condescending politeness which implies a real, or imagined, superiority over those towards whom it is used. When he gave his opinion on any point, it was with that easy tone of confidence used by those superior to their society in rank or information, as if what he said could not be doubted, and was not to be questioned. Mine host and his Sunday guests, after an effort or two to support their consequence by noise and bold averment, sunk gradually under the authority of Mr. Campbell, who thus fairly possessed himself of the lead in the conversation. I was tempted, from curiosity, to dispute the ground with him myself, confiding in my knowledge of the world, extended as it was by my residence abroad, and in the stores with which a tolerable education had possessed my mind. In the latter respect he offered no competition, and it was easy to see that his natural powers had never been cultivated by education. But I found him much better acquainted than I was myself with the present state of France, the character of the Duke of Orleans, who had just succeeded to the regency of that kingdom, and that of the statesmen by whom he was surrounded; and his shrewd, caustic, and somewhat satirical remarks, were those of a man who had been a close observer of the affairs of that country.

On the subject of politics, Campbell observed a silence and moderation which might arise from caution. The divisions of Whig and Tory then shook England to her very centre, and a powerful party, engaged in the Jacobite interest, menaced the dynasty of Hanover, which had been just established on the throne. Every alehouse resounded with the brawls of contending politicians, and as mine host's politics were of that liberal description which quarrelled with no good customer, his hebdomadal visitants were often divided in their opinion as irreconcilably as if he had feasted the Common Council. The curate and the apothecary, with a little man, who made no boast of his vocation, but who, from the flourish and snap of his fingers, I believe to have been the barber, strongly espoused the cause of high church and the Stuart line. The excise-man, as in duty bound, and the attorney, who looked to some petty office under the Crown, together with my fellow-traveller, who seemed to enter keenly into the contest, staunchly supported the cause of King George and the Protestant succession. Dire was the screaming—deep the oaths! Each party appealed to Mr. Campbell, anxious, it seemed, to elicit his approbation.

"You are a Scotchman, sir; a gentleman of your country must stand up for hereditary right," cried one party.

"You are a Presbyterian," assumed the other class of disputants; "you cannot be a friend to arbitrary power."

"Gentlemen," said our Scotch oracle, after having gained, with some difficulty, a moment's pause, "I havena much dubitation that King George weel deserves the predilection of his friends; and if he can haud the grip he has gotten, why, doubtless, he may made the gauger, here, a commissioner of the revenue, and confer on our friend, Mr. Quitam, the preferment of solicitor-general; and he may also grant some good deed or reward to this honest gentleman who is sitting upon his portmanteau, which he prefers to a chair: And, questionless, King James is also a grateful person, and when he gets his hand in play, he may, if he be so minded, make this reverend gentleman archprelate of Canterbury, and Dr. Mixit chief physician to his household, and commit his royal beard to the care of my friend Latherum. But as I doubt mickle whether any of the competing sovereigns would give Rob Campbell a tass of aquavitae, if he lacked it, I give my vote and interest to Jonathan Brown, our landlord, to be the King and Prince of Skinkers, conditionally that he fetches us another bottle as good as the last."

This sally was received with general applause, in which the landlord cordially joined; and when he had given orders for fulfilling the condition on which his preferment was to depend, he failed not to acquaint them, "that, for as peaceable a gentleman as Mr. Campbell was, he was, moreover, as bold as a lion—seven highwaymen had he defeated with his single arm, that beset him as he came from Whitson-Tryste."

"Thou art deceived, friend Jonathan," said Campbell, interrupting him; "they were but barely two, and two cowardly loons as man could wish to meet withal."

"And did you, sir, really," said my fellow-traveller, edging his chair (I should have said his portmanteau) nearer to Mr. Campbell, "really and actually beat two highwaymen yourself alone?"

"In troth did I, sir," replied Campbell; "and I think it nae great thing to make a sang about."

"Upon my word, sir," replied my acquaintance, "I should be happy to have the pleasure of your company on my journey—I go northward, sir."

This piece of gratuitous information concerning the route he proposed to himself, the first I had heard my companion bestow upon any one, failed to excite the corresponding confidence of the Scotchman.

"We can scarce travel together," he replied, drily. "You, sir, doubtless, are well mounted, and I for the present travel on foot, or on a Highland shelty, that does not help me much faster forward."

So saying, he called for a reckoning for the wine, and throwing down the price of the additional bottle which he had himself introduced, rose as if to take leave of us. My companion made up to him, and taking him by the button, drew him aside into one of the windows. I could not help overhearing him pressing something—I supposed his company upon the journey, which Mr. Campbell seemed to decline.

"I will pay your charges, sir," said the traveller, in a tone as if he thought the argument should bear down all opposition.

"It is quite impossible," said Campbell, somewhat contemptuously; "I have business at Rothbury."

"But I am in no great hurry; I can ride out of the way, and never miss a day or so for good company."

"Upon my faith, sir," said Campbell, "I cannot render you the service you seem to desiderate. I am," he added, drawing himself up haughtily, "travelling on my own private affairs, and if ye will act by my advisement, sir, ye will neither unite yourself with an absolute stranger on the road, nor communicate your line of journey to those who are asking ye no questions about it." He then extricated his button, not very ceremoniously, from the hold which detained him, and coming up to me as the company were dispersing, observed, "Your friend, sir, is too communicative, considering the nature of his trust."

"That gentleman," I replied, looking towards the traveller, "is no friend of mine, but an acquaintance whom I picked up on the road. I know neither his name nor business, and you seem to be deeper in his confidence than I am."

"I only meant," he replied hastily, "that he seems a thought rash in conferring the honour of his company on those who desire it not."

"The gentleman," replied I, "knows his own affairs best, and I should be sorry to constitute myself a judge of them in any respect."

Mr. Campbell made no farther observation, but merely wished me a good journey, and the party dispersed for the evening.

Next day I parted company with my timid companion, as I left the great northern road to turn more westerly in the direction of Osbaldistone Manor, my uncle's seat. I cannot tell whether he felt relieved or embarrassed by my departure, considering the dubious light in which he seemed to regard me. For my own part, his tremors ceased to amuse me, and, to say the truth, I was heartily glad to get rid of him.

CHAPTER FIFTH

> How melts my beating heart as I behold
> Each lovely nymph, our island's boast and pride,
> Push on the generous steed, that sweeps along
> O'er rough, o'er smooth, nor heeds the steepy hill,
> Nor falters in the extended vale below!
>
> — THE CHASE.

I approached my native north, for such I esteemed it, with that enthusiasm which romantic and wild scenery inspires in the lovers of nature. No longer interrupted by the babble of my companion, I could now remark the difference which the country exhibited from that through which I had hitherto travelled. The streams now more properly deserved the name, for, instead of slumbering stagnant among reeds and willows, they brawled along beneath the shade of natural copsewood; were now hurried down declivities, and now purled more leisurely, but still in active motion, through little lonely valleys, which, opening on the road from time to time, seemed to invite the traveller to explore their recesses. The Cheviots rose before me in frowning majesty; not, indeed, with the sublime variety of rock and cliff which characterizes mountains of the primary class but huge, round-headed, and clothed with a dark robe of russet, gaining, by their extent and desolate appearance, an influence upon the imagination, as a desert district possessing a character of its own.

The abode of my fathers, which I was now approaching, was situated in a glen, or narrow valley, which ran up among those hills. Extensive estates, which once belonged to the family of Osbaldistone, had been long dissipated by the misfortunes or misconduct of my ancestors; but enough was still attached to the old mansion, to give my uncle the title of a man of large property. This he employed (as I was given to understand by some inquiries which I made on the road) in maintaining the prodigal hospitality of a northern squire of the period, which he deemed essential to his family dignity.

From the summit of an eminence I had already had a distant view of Osbaldistone Hall, a large and antiquated edifice, peeping out from a Druidical grove of huge oaks; and I was directing my course towards it, as straightly and as speedily as the windings of a very indifferent road would permit, when my horse, tired as he was, pricked up his ears at the enlivening notes of a pack of hounds in full cry, cheered by the occasional bursts of a French horn, which in those days was a constant accompaniment to the chase. I made no doubt that the pack was my uncle's, and drew up my horse with the purpose of suffering the hunters to pass without notice, aware that a hunting-field was not the proper scene to introduce myself to a keen sportsman, and determined when they had passed on, to proceed to the mansion-house at my own pace, and there to await the return of the proprietor from his sport. I paused, therefore, on a rising ground, and, not unmoved by the sense of interest which that species of silvan sport is so much calculated to inspire (although my mind was not at the moment very accessible to impressions of this nature), I expected with some eagerness the appearance of the huntsmen.

The fox, hard run, and nearly spent, first made his appearance from the copse which clothed the right-hand side of the valley. His drooping brush, his soiled appearance, and jaded trot, proclaimed his fate impending; and the carrion crow, which hovered over him, already considered poor Reynard as soon to be his prey. He crossed the stream which divides the little valley, and was dragging himself up a ravine on the other side of its wild banks, when the headmost hounds, followed by the rest of the pack in full cry, burst from the coppice, followed by the huntsman and three or four riders. The dogs pursued the trace of Reynard with unerring instinct; and the hunters followed with reckless haste, regardless of the broken and difficult nature of the ground. They were tall, stout young men, well mounted, and dressed in green and red, the uniform of a sporting association, formed under the auspices of old Sir Hildebrand Osbaldistone.—"My cousins!" thought I, as they swept past me. The next reflection was, what is my reception likely to be among these worthy successors of Nimrod? and how improbable is it that I, knowing little or nothing of rural sports, shall find myself at ease, or happy, in my uncle's family. A vision that passed me interrupted these reflections.

It was a young lady, the loveliness of whose very striking features was enhanced by the animation of the chase and the glow of the exercise, mounted on a beautiful horse, jet black, unless where he was flecked by spots of the snow-white foam which embossed his bridle. She wore, what was then somewhat unusual, a coat, vest, and hat, resembling those of a man, which fashion has since called a riding habit. The mode had been introduced while I was in France, and was perfectly new to me. Her long black hair streamed on the breeze, having in the hurry of the chase escaped from the ribbon which bound it. Some very broken ground, through which she guided her horse with the most admirable address and presence of mind, retarded her course, and brought her closer to me than any of the other riders had passed. I had, therefore, a full view of her uncommonly fine face and person, to which an inexpressible charm was added by the wild gaiety of the scene, and the romance of her singular dress and unexpected appearance. As she passed me, her horse made, in his impetuosity, an irregular movement, just while, coming once more upon open ground, she was again putting him to his speed. It served as an apology for me to ride close up to her, as if to her assistance. There was, however, no cause for alarm; it was not a stumble, nor a false step; and, if it had, the fair Amazon had too much self-possession to have been deranged by it. She thanked my good intentions, however, by a smile, and I felt encouraged to put my horse to the same pace, and to keep in her immediate neighbourhood. The clamour of "Whoop! dead! dead!"—and the corresponding flourish of the French horn, soon announced to us that there was no more occasion for haste, since the chase was at a close. One of the young men whom we had seen approached us, waving the brush of the fox in triumph, as if to upbraid my fair companion,

"I see," she replied,—"I see; but make no noise about it: if Phoebe," she said, patting the neck of the beautiful animal on which she rode, "had not got among the cliffs, you would have had little cause for boasting."

They met as she spoke, and I observed them both look at me, and converse a moment in an under-tone, the young lady apparently pressing the sportsman to do something which he declined shyly, and with a sort of sheepish sullenness. She instantly turned her horse's head towards me, saying,—"Well, well, Thornie, if you won't, I must, that's all.—Sir," she continued, addressing me, "I have been endeavouring to persuade this cultivated young gentleman to make inquiry of you whether, in the course of your travels in these parts, you have heard anything of a friend of ours, one Mr. Francis Osbaldistone, who has been for some days expected at Osbaldistone Hall?"

I was too happy to acknowledge myself to be the party inquired after, and to express my thanks for the obliging inquiries of the young lady.

"In that case, sir," she rejoined, "as my kinsman's politeness seems to be still slumbering, you will permit me (though I suppose it is highly improper) to stand mistress of ceremonies, and to present to you young Squire Thorncliff Osbaldistone, your cousin, and Die Vernon, who has also the honour to be your accomplished cousin's poor kinswoman."

There was a mixture of boldness, satire, and simplicity in the manner in which Miss Vernon pronounced these words. My knowledge of life was sufficient to enable me to take up a corresponding tone as I expressed my gratitude to her for her condescension, and my extreme pleasure at having met with them. To say the truth, the compliment was so expressed, that the lady might easily appropriate the greater share of it, for Thorncliff seemed an arrant country bumpkin, awkward, shy, and somewhat sulky withal. He shook hands with me, however, and then intimated his intention of leaving me that he might help the huntsman and his brothers to couple up the hounds,—a purpose which he rather communicated by way of information to Miss Vernon than as apology to me.

"There he goes," said the young lady, following him with eyes in which disdain was admirably painted—"the prince of grooms and cock-fighters, and blackguard horse-coursers. But there is not one of them to mend another.—Have you read Markham?" said Miss Vernon.

"Read whom, ma'am?—I do not even remember the author's name."

"O lud! on what a strand are you wrecked!" replied the young lady. "A poor forlorn and ignorant stranger, unacquainted with the very Alcoran of the savage tribe whom you are come to reside among—Never to have heard of Markham, the most celebrated author on farriery! then I fear you are equally a stranger to the more modern names of Gibson and Bartlett?"

"I am, indeed, Miss Vernon."

"And do you not blush to own it?" said Miss Vernon. "Why, we must forswear your alliance. Then, I suppose, you can neither give a ball, nor a mash, nor a horn!"

"I confess I trust all these matters to an ostler, or to my groom."

"Incredible carelessness!—And you cannot shoe a horse, or cut his mane and tail;

or worm a dog, or crop his ears, or cut his dew-claws; or reclaim a hawk, or give him his casting-stones, or direct his diet when he is sealed; or"—

"To sum up my insignificance in one word," replied I, "I am profoundly ignorant in all these rural accomplishments."

"Then, in the name of Heaven, Mr. Francis Osbaldistone, what *can* you do?"

"Very little to the purpose, Miss Vernon; something, however, I can pretend to—When my groom has dressed my horse I can ride him, and when my hawk is in the field, I can fly him."

"Can you do this?" said the young lady, putting her horse to a canter.

There was a sort of rude overgrown fence crossed the path before us, with a gate composed of pieces of wood rough from the forest; I was about to move forward to open it, when Miss Vernon cleared the obstruction at a flying leap. I was bound in point of honour to follow, and was in a moment again at her side. "There are hopes of you yet," she said. "I was afraid you had been a very degenerate Osbaldistone. But what on earth brings you to Cub-Castle?—for so the neighbours have christened this hunting-hall of ours. You might have stayed away, I suppose, if you would?"

I felt I was by this time on a very intimate footing with my beautiful apparition, and therefore replied, in a confidential under-tone—"Indeed, my dear Miss Vernon, I might have considered it as a sacrifice to be a temporary resident in Osbaldistone Hall, the inmates being such as you describe them; but I am convinced there is one exception that will make amends for all deficiencies."

"O, you mean Rashleigh?" said Miss Vernon.

"Indeed I do not; I was thinking—forgive me—of some person much nearer me."

"I suppose it would be proper not to understand your civility?—But that is not my way—I don't make a courtesy for it because I am sitting on horseback. But, seriously, I deserve your exception, for I am the only conversable being about the Hall, except the old priest and Rashleigh."

"And who is Rashleigh, for Heaven's sake?"

"Rashleigh is one who would fain have every one like him for his own sake. He is Sir Hildebrand's youngest son—about your own age, but not so—not well looking, in short. But nature has given him a mouthful of common sense, and the priest has added a bushelful of learning; he is what we call a very clever man in this country, where clever men are scarce. Bred to the church, but in no hurry to take orders."

"To the Catholic Church?"

"The Catholic Church? what Church else?" said the young lady. "But I forgot—they told me you are a heretic. Is that true, Mr. Osbaldistone?"

"I must not deny the charge."

"And yet you have been abroad, and in Catholic countries?"

"For nearly four years."

"You have seen convents?"

"Often; but I have not seen much in them which recommended the Catholic religion."

"Are not the inhabitants happy?"

"Some are unquestionably so, whom either a profound sense of devotion, or an experience of the persecutions and misfortunes of the world, or a natural apathy of temper, has led into retirement. Those who have adopted a life of seclusion from sudden and overstrained enthusiasm, or in hasty resentment of some disappointment or mortification, are very miserable. The quickness of sensation soon returns, and like the wilder animals in a menagerie, they are restless under confinement, while others muse or fatten in cells of no larger dimensions than theirs."

"And what," continued Miss Vernon, "becomes of those victims who are condemned to a convent by the will of others? what do they resemble? especially, what do they resemble, if they are born to enjoy life, and feel its blessings?"

"They are like imprisoned singing-birds," replied I, "condemned to wear out their lives in confinement, which they try to beguile by the exercise of accomplishments which would have adorned society had they been left at large."

"I shall be," returned Miss Vernon—"that is," said she, correcting herself—"I should be rather like the wild hawk, who, barred the free exercise of his soar through heaven, will dash himself to pieces against the bars of his cage. But to return to Rashleigh," said she, in a more lively tone, "you will think him the pleasantest man you ever saw in your life, Mr. Osbaldistone,—that is, for a week at least. If he could find out a blind mistress, never man would be so secure of conquest; but the eye breaks the spell that enchants the ear.—But here we are in the court of the old hall, which looks as wild and old-fashioned as any of its inmates. There is no great toilette kept at Osbaldistone Hall, you must know; but I must take off these things, they are so unpleasantly warm,—and the hat hurts my forehead, too," continued the lively girl, taking it off, and shaking down a profusion of sable ringlets, which, half laughing, half blushing, she separated with her white slender fingers, in order to clear them away from her beautiful face and piercing hazel eyes. If there was any coquetry in the action, it was well disguised by the careless indifference of her manner. I could not help saying, "that, judging of the family from what I saw, I should suppose the toilette a very unnecessary care."

"That's very politely said—though, perhaps, I ought not to understand in what sense it was meant," replied Miss Vernon; "but you will see a better apology for a little negligence when you meet the Orsons you are to live amongst, whose forms no toilette could improve. But, as I said before, the old dinner-bell will clang, or rather clank, in a few minutes—it cracked of its own accord on the day of the landing of King Willie, and my uncle, respecting its prophetic talent, would never permit it to be mended. So do you hold my palfrey, like a duteous knight, until I send some more humble squire to relieve you of the charge."

She threw me the rein as if we had been acquainted from our childhood, jumped from her saddle, tripped across the courtyard, and entered at a side-door, leaving me in admiration of her beauty, and astonished with the over-frankness of her manners, which seemed the more extraordinary at a time when the dictates of politeness, flowing from the court of the Grand Monarque Louis XIV., prescribed to the fair sex an unusual severity of decorum. I was left awkwardly enough stationed in the centre of the court of the old hall, mounted on one horse, and holding another in my hand.

The building afforded little to interest a stranger, had I been disposed to consider it attentively; the sides of the quadrangle were of various architecture, and with their stone-shafted latticed windows, projecting turrets, and massive architraves, resembled the inside of a convent, or of one of the older and less splendid colleges of Oxford. I called for a domestic, but was for some time totally unattended to; which was the more provoking, as I could perceive I was the object of curiosity to several servants, both male and female, from different parts of the building, who popped out their heads and withdrew them, like rabbits in a warren, before I could make a direct appeal to the attention of any individual. The return of the huntsmen and hounds relieved me from my embarrassment, and with some difficulty I got one down to relieve me of the charge of the horses, and another stupid boor to guide me to the presence of Sir Hildebrand. This service he performed with much such grace and good-will, as a peasant who is compelled to act as guide to a hostile patrol; and in the same manner I was obliged to guard against his deserting me in the labyrinth of low vaulted passages which conducted to "Stun Hall," as he called it, where I was to be introduced to the gracious presence of my uncle.

We did, however, at length reach a long vaulted room, floored with stone, where a range of oaken tables, of a weight and size too massive ever to be moved aside, were already covered for dinner. This venerable apartment, which had witnessed the feasts of several generations of the Osbaldistone family, bore also evidence of their success in field sports. Huge antlers of deer, which might have been trophies of the hunting of Chevy Chace, were ranged around the walls, interspersed with the stuffed skins of badgers, otters, martins, and other animals of the chase. Amidst some remnants of old armour, which had, perhaps, served against the Scotch, hung the more valued weapons of silvan war, cross-bows, guns of various device and construction, nets, fishing-rods, otter-spears, hunting-poles, with many other singular devices, and engines for taking or killing game. A few old pictures, dimmed with smoke, and stained with March beer, hung on the walls, representing knights and ladies, honoured, doubtless, and renowned in their day; those frowning fearfully from huge bushes of wig and of beard; and these looking delightfully with all their might at the roses which they brandished in their hands.

I had just time to give a glance at these matters, when about twelve blue-coated servants burst into the hall with much tumult and talk, each rather employed in directing his comrades than in discharging his own duty. Some brought blocks and billets to the fire, which roared, blazed, and ascended, half in smoke, half in flame, up a huge tunnel, with an opening wide enough to accommodate a stone seat within its ample vault, and which was fronted, by way of chimney-piece, with a huge piece of heavy architecture, where the monsters of heraldry, embodied by the art of some Northumbrian chisel, grinned and ramped in red free-stone, now japanned by the smoke of centuries. Others of these old-fashioned serving-men bore huge smoking dishes, loaded with substantial fare; others brought in cups, flagons, bottles, yea barrels of liquor. All tramped, kicked, plunged, shouldered, and jostled, doing as little service with as much tumult as could well be imagined. At length, while the dinner was, after various efforts, in the act of being arranged upon the board, "the clamour much of men and dogs," the cracking of whips, calculated for the intimidation of the latter, voices loud and high, steps which, impressed by the heavy-heeled boots of the period, clattered like those in the statue of the *Festin de Pierre*,[33] announced the arrival of those for whose benefit the preparations were made.

The hubbub among the servants rather increased than diminished as this crisis approached. Some called to make haste,—others to take time,—some exhorted to stand out of the way, and make room for Sir Hildebrand and the young squires,—

some to close round the table and be *in* the way,—some bawled to open, some to shut, a pair of folding-doors which divided the hall from a sort of gallery, as I afterwards learned, or withdrawing-room, fitted up with black wainscot. Opened the doors were at length, and in rushed curs and men,—eight dogs, the domestic chaplain, the village doctor, my six cousins, and my uncle.

CHAPTER SIXTH

> The rude hall rocks—they come, they come,—
> The din of voices shakes the dome;—
> In stalk the various forms, and, drest
> In varying morion, varying vest,
> All march with haughty step—all proudly shake the crest.
>
> — PENROSE.

If Sir Hildebrand Osbaldistone was in no hurry to greet his nephew, of whose arrival he must have been informed for some time, he had important avocations to allege in excuse. "Had seen thee sooner, lad," he exclaimed, after a rough shake of the hand, and a hearty welcome to Osbaldistone Hall, "but had to see the hounds kennelled first. Thou art welcome to the Hall, lad—here is thy cousin Percie, thy cousin Thornie, and thy cousin John—your cousin Dick, your cousin Wilfred, and—stay, where's Rashleigh?—ay, here's Rashleigh—take thy long body aside Thornie, and let's see thy brother a bit—your cousin Rashleigh. So, thy father has thought on the old Hall, and old Sir Hildebrand at last—better late than never—Thou art welcome, lad, and there's enough. Where's my little Die?—ay, here she comes—this is my niece Die, my wife's brother's daughter—the prettiest girl in our dales, be the other who she may—and so now let's to the sirloin."—

To gain some idea of the person who held this language, you must suppose, my dear Tresham, a man aged about sixty, in a hunting suit which had once been richly laced, but whose splendour had been tarnished by many a November and December storm. Sir Hildebrand, notwithstanding the abruptness of his present manner, had, at one period of his life, known courts and camps; had held a commission in the army which encamped on Hounslow Heath previous to the Revolution—and, recommended perhaps by his religion, had been knighted about the same period by the unfortunate and ill-advised James II. But the Knight's dreams of further preferment, if he ever entertained any, had died away at the crisis which drove his patron from the throne, and since that period he had spent a sequestered life upon his native domains. Notwithstanding his rusticity, however, Sir Hildebrand retained much of the exterior of a gentleman, and appeared among his sons as the remains of a Corinthian pillar, defaced and overgrown with moss and lichen, might have looked, if contrasted with the rough unhewn masses of upright stones in Stonhenge, or any other Druidical temple. The sons were, indeed, heavy unadorned blocks as the eye would desire to look upon. Tall, stout, and comely, all and each of the five eldest seemed to want alike the Promethean fire of intellect, and the exterior grace and manner, which, in the polished world, sometimes supply mental deficiency. Their most valuable moral quality seemed to be the good-humour and content which was expressed in their heavy features, and their only pretence to accomplishment was their dexterity in field sports, for which alone they lived. The strong Gyas, and the strong Cloanthus, are not less distinguished by the poet, than the strong Percival, the strong Thorncliff, the strong John, Richard, and Wilfred Osbaldistones, were by outward appearance.

But, as if to indemnify herself for a uniformity so uncommon in her productions, Dame Nature had rendered Rashleigh Osbaldistone a striking contrast in person and manner, and, as I afterwards learned, in temper and talents, not only to his brothers, but to most men whom I had hitherto met with. When Percie, Thornie, and Co. had respectively nodded, grinned, and presented their shoulder rather than their hand, as their father named them to their new kinsman, Rashleigh stepped forward, and welcomed me to Osbaldistone Hall, with the air and manner of a man of the world. His appearance was not in itself prepossessing. He was of low stature, whereas all his brethren seemed to be descendants of Anak; and while they were handsomely formed, Rashleigh, though strong in person, was bull-necked and cross-made, and from some early injury in his youth had an imperfection in his gait, so much resembling an absolute halt, that many alleged that it formed the obstacle to his taking orders; the Church of Rome, as is well known, admitting none to the clerical profession who labours under any personal deformity. Others, however, ascribed this unsightly defect to a mere awkward habit, and contended that it did not amount to a personal disqualification from holy orders.

The features of Rashleigh were such, as, having looked upon, we in vain wish to banish from our memory, to which they recur as objects of painful curiosity, although we dwell upon them with a feeling of dislike, and even of disgust. It was not the actual plainness of his face, taken separately from the meaning, which made this strong impression. His features were, indeed, irregular, but they were by no means vulgar; and his keen dark eyes, and shaggy eyebrows, redeemed his face from the charge of commonplace ugliness. But there was in these eyes an expression of art and design, and, on provocation, a ferocity tempered by caution, which nature had made obvious to the most ordinary physiognomist, perhaps with the same intention that she has given the rattle to the poisonous snake. As if to compensate him for these disadvantages of exterior, Rashleigh Osbaldistone was possessed of a voice the most soft, mellow, and rich in its tones that I ever heard, and was at no loss for language of every sort suited to so fine an organ. His first sentence of welcome was hardly ended, ere I internally agreed with Miss Vernon, that my new kinsman would make an instant conquest of a mistress whose ears alone were to judge his cause. He was about to place himself beside me at dinner, but Miss Vernon, who, as the only female in the family, arranged all such matters according to her own pleasure, contrived that I should sit betwixt Thorncliff and herself; and it can scarce be doubted that I favoured this more advantageous arrangement.

"I want to speak with you," she said, "and I have placed honest Thornie betwixt Rashleigh and you on purpose. He will be like—

Feather-bed 'twixt castle wall
And heavy brunt of cannon ball,

while I, your earliest acquaintance in this intellectual family, ask of you how you like us all?"

"A very comprehensive question, Miss Vernon, considering how short while I have been at Osbaldistone Hall."

"Oh, the philosophy of our family lies on the surface—there are minute shades distinguishing the individuals, which require the eye of an intelligent observer; but the species, as naturalists I believe call it, may be distinguished and characterized at once."

"My five elder cousins, then, are I presume of pretty nearly the same character."

"Yes, they form a happy compound of sot, gamekeeper, bully, horse-jockey, and fool; but as they say there cannot be found two leaves on the same tree exactly alike, so these happy ingredients, being mingled in somewhat various proportions in each individual, make an agreeable variety for those who like to study character."

"Give me a sketch, if you please, Miss Vernon."

"You shall have them all in a family-piece, at full length—the favour is too easily granted to be refused. Percie, the son and heir, has more of the sot than of the gamekeeper, bully, horse-jockey, or fool—My precious Thornie is more of the bully than the sot, gamekeeper, jockey, or fool—John, who sleeps whole weeks amongst the hills, has most of the gamekeeper—The jockey is powerful with Dickon, who rides two hundred miles by day and night to be bought and sold at a horse-race—And the fool predominates so much over Wilfred's other qualities, that he may be termed a fool positive."

"A goodly collection, Miss Vernon, and the individual varieties belong to a most interesting species. But is there no room on the canvas for Sir Hildebrand?"

"I love my uncle," was her reply: "I owe him some kindness (such it was meant for at least), and I will leave you to draw his picture yourself, when you know him better."

"Come," thought I to myself, "I am glad there is some forbearance. After all, who would have looked for such bitter satire from a creature so young, and so exquisitely beautiful?"

"You are thinking of me," she said, bending her dark eyes on me, as if she meant to pierce through my very soul.

"I certainly was," I replied, with some embarrassment at the determined suddenness of the question, and then, endeavouring to give a complimentary turn to my frank avowal—"How is it possible I should think of anything else, seated as I have the happiness to be?"

She smiled with such an expression of concentrated haughtiness as she alone could have thrown into her countenance. "I must inform you at once, Mr. Osbaldistone, that compliments are entirely lost upon me; do not, therefore, throw away your pretty sayings—they serve fine gentlemen who travel in the country, instead of the toys, beads, and bracelets, which navigators carry to propitiate the savage inhabitants of newly-discovered lands. Do not exhaust your stock in trade;—you will find natives in Northumberland to whom your fine things will recommend you—on me they would be utterly thrown away, for I happen to know their real value."

I was silenced and confounded.

"You remind me at this moment," said the young lady, resuming her lively and indifferent manner, "of the fairy tale, where the man finds all the money which he had carried to market suddenly changed into pieces of slate. I have cried down and ruined your whole stock of complimentary discourse by one unlucky observation. But come, never mind it—You are belied, Mr. Osbaldistone, unless you have much better conversation than these *fadeurs*, which every gentleman with a toupet thinks himself obliged to recite to an unfortunate girl, merely because she is dressed in silk and gauze, while he wears superfine cloth with embroidery. Your natural paces, as any of my five cousins might say, are far preferable to your complimentary amble. Endeavour to forget my unlucky sex; call me Tom Vernon, if you have a mind, but speak to me as you would to a friend and companion; you have no idea how much I shall like you."

"That would be a bribe indeed," returned I.

"Again!" replied Miss Vernon, holding up her finger; "I told you I would not bear the shadow of a compliment. And now, when you have pledged my uncle, who threatens you with what he calls a brimmer, I will tell you what you think of me."

The bumper being pledged by me, as a dutiful nephew, and some other general intercourse of the table having taken place, the continued and business-like clang of knives and forks, and the devotion of cousin Thorncliff on my right hand, and cousin Dickon, who sate on Miss Vernon's left, to the huge quantities of meat with which they heaped their plates, made them serve as two occasional partitions, separating us from the rest of the company, and leaving us to our *tete-a-tete*. "And now," said I, "give me leave to ask you frankly, Miss Vernon, what you suppose I am thinking of you!—I could tell you what I really *do* think, but you have interdicted praise."

"I do not want your assistance. I am conjuror enough to tell your thoughts without it. You need not open the casement of your bosom; I see through it. You think me a strange bold girl, half coquette, half romp; desirous of attracting attention by the freedom of her manners and loudness of her conversation, because she is ignorant of what the Spectator calls the softer graces of the sex; and perhaps you think I have some particular plan of storming you into admiration. I should be sorry to shock your self-opinion, but you were never more mistaken. All the confidence I have reposed in you, I would have given as readily to your father, if I thought he could have understood me. I am in this happy family as much secluded from intelligent listeners as Sancho in the Sierra Morena, and when opportunity offers, I must speak or die. I assure you I would not have told you a word of all this curious intelligence, had I cared a pin who knew it or knew it not."

"It is very cruel in you, Miss Vernon, to take away all particular marks of favour from your communications, but I must receive them on your own terms.—You have not included Mr. Rashleigh Osbaldistone in your domestic sketches."

She shrunk, I thought, at this remark, and hastily answered, in a much lower tone, "Not a word of Rashleigh! His ears are so acute when his selfishness is interested, that the sounds would reach him even through the mass of Thorncliff's person, stuffed as it is with beef, venison-pasty, and pudding."

"Yes," I replied; "but peeping past the living screen which divides us, before I put the question, I perceived that Mr. Rashleigh's chair was empty—he has left the table."

"I would not have you be too sure of that," Miss Vernon replied. "Take my advice, and when you speak of Rashleigh, get up to the top of Otterscope-hill, where you can see for twenty miles round you in every direction—stand on the very peak, and speak in whispers; and, after all, don't be too sure that the bird of the air will not carry the matter, Rashleigh has been my tutor for four years; we are mutually tired of each other, and we shall heartily rejoice at our approaching separation."

"Mr. Rashleigh leaves Osbaldistone Hall, then?"

"Yes, in a few days;—did you not know that?—your father must keep his resolutions much more secret than Sir Hildebrand. Why, when my uncle was informed that you were to be his guest for some time, and that your father desired to have one of his hopeful sons to fill up the lucrative situation in his counting-house which was vacant by your obstinacy, Mr. Francis, the good knight held a *cour ple'nie're* of all his family, including the butler, housekeeper, and gamekeeper. This reverend assembly of the peers and household officers of Osbaldistone Hall was not convoked, as you may suppose, to elect your substitute, because, as Rashleigh alone possessed more arithmetic than was necessary to calculate the odds on a fighting cock, none but he could be supposed qualified for the situation. But some solemn sanction was necessary for transforming Rashleigh's destination from starving as a Catholic priest to thriving as a wealthy banker; and it was not without some reluctance that the acquiescence of the assembly was obtained to such an act of degradation."

"I can conceive the scruples—but how were they got over?"

"By the general wish, I believe, to get Rashleigh out of the house," replied Miss Vernon. "Although youngest of the family, he has somehow or other got the entire management of all the others; and every one is sensible of the subjection, though they cannot shake it off. If any one opposes him, he is sure to rue having done so before the year goes about; and if you do him a very important service, you may rue it still more."

"At that rate," answered I, smiling, "I should look about me; for I have been the cause, however unintentionally, of his change of situation."

"Yes; and whether he regards it as an advantage or disadvantage, he will owe you a grudge for it—But here comes cheese, radishes, and a bumper to church and king, the hint for chaplains and ladies to disappear; and I, the sole representative of womanhood at Osbaldistone Hall, retreat, as in duty bound."

She vanished as she spoke, leaving me in astonishment at the mingled character of shrewdness, audacity, and frankness, which her conversation displayed. I despair conveying to you the least idea of her manner, although I have, as nearly as I can remember, imitated her language. In fact, there was a mixture of untaught simplicity, as well as native shrewdness and haughty boldness, in her manner, and all were modified and recommended by the play of the most beautiful features I had ever beheld. It is not to be thought that, however strange and uncommon I might think her liberal and unreserved communications, a young man of two-and-twenty was likely to be severely critical on a beautiful girl of eighteen, for not observing a proper distance towards him. On the contrary, I was equally diverted and flattered by Miss Vernon's confidence, and that notwithstanding her declaration of its being conferred on me solely because I was the first auditor who occurred, of intelligence enough to comprehend it. With the presumption of my age, certainly not diminished by my residence in France, I imagined that well-formed features, and a handsome person, both which I conceived myself to possess, were not unsuitable qualifications for the confidant of a young beauty. My vanity thus enlisted in Miss Vernon's behalf, I was far from judging her with severity, merely for a frankness which I supposed was in some degree justified by my own personal merit; and the feelings of partiality, which her beauty, and the singularity of her situation, were of themselves calculated to excite, were enhanced by my opinion of her penetration and judgment in her choice of a friend.

After Miss Vernon quitted the apartment, the bottle circulated, or rather flew, around the table in unceasing revolution. My foreign education had given me a distaste to intemperance, then and yet too common a vice among my countrymen. The conversation which seasoned such orgies was as little to my taste, and if anything could render it more disgusting, it was the relationship of the company. I therefore seized a lucky opportunity, and made my escape through a side door, leading I knew not whither, rather than endure any longer the sight of father and sons practising the same degrading intemperance, and holding the same coarse and disgusting conversation. I was pursued, of course, as I had expected, to be reclaimed by force, as a deserter from the shrine of Bacchus. When I heard the whoop and hollo, and the tramp of the heavy boots of my pursuers on the winding stair which I was descending, I plainly foresaw I should be overtaken unless I could get into the open air. I therefore threw open a casement in the staircase, which looked into an old-fashioned garden, and as the height did not exceed six feet, I jumped out without hesitation, and soon heard far behind the "hey whoop! stole away! stole away!" of my baffled pursuers. I ran down one alley, walked fast up another; and then, conceiving myself out of all danger of pursuit, I slackened my pace into a quiet stroll, enjoying the cool air which the heat of the wine I had been obliged to swallow, as well as that of my rapid retreat, rendered doubly grateful.

As I sauntered on, I found the gardener hard at his evening employment, and saluted him, as I paused to look at his work.

"Good even, my friend."

"Gude e'en—gude e'en t'ye," answered the man, without looking up, and in a tone which at once indicated his northern extraction.

"Fine weather for your work, my friend."

"It's no that muckle to be compleened o'," answered the man, with that limited degree of praise which gardeners and farmers usually bestow on the very best weather. Then raising his head, as if to see who spoke to him, he touched his Scotch bonnet with an air of respect, as he observed, "Eh, gude safe us!—it's a sight for sair een, to see a gold-laced jeistiecor in the Ha'garden sae late at e'en."

"A gold-laced what, my good friend?"

"Ou, a jeistiecor[34]—that's a jacket like your ain, there. They hae other things to do wi' them up yonder—unbuttoning them to make room for the beef and the bag-puddings, and the claret-wine, nae doubt—that's the ordinary for evening lecture on this side the border."

"There's no such plenty of good cheer in your country, my good friend," I replied, "as to tempt you to sit so late at it."

"Hout, sir, ye ken little about Scotland; it's no for want of gude vivers—the best of fish, flesh, and fowl hae we, by sybos, ingans, turneeps, and other garden fruit. But we hae mense and discretion, and are moderate of our mouths;—but here, frae the kitchen to the ha', it's fill and fetch mair, frae the tae end of the four-and-twenty till the tother. Even their fast days—they ca' it fasting when they hae the best o' sea-fish frae Hartlepool and Sunderland by land carriage, forbye trouts, grilses, salmon, and a' the lave o't, and so they make their very fasting a kind of luxury and abomination; and then the awfu' masses and matins of the puir deceived souls—But I shouldna speak about them, for your honour will be a Roman, I'se warrant, like the lave."

"Not I, my friend; I was bred an English presbyterian, or dissenter."

"The right hand of fellowship to your honour, then," quoth the gardener, with as much alacrity as his hard features were capable of expressing, and, as if to show that his good-will did not rest on words, he plucked forth a huge horn snuff-box, or mull, as he called it, and proffered a pinch with a most fraternal grin.

Having accepted his courtesy, I asked him if he had been long a domestic at Osbaldistone Hall.

"I have been fighting with wild beasts at Ephesus," said he, looking towards the building, "for the best part of these four-and-twenty years, as sure as my name's Andrew Fairservice."

"But, my excellent friend, Andrew Fairservice, if your religion and your temperance are so much offended by Roman rituals and southern hospitality, it seems to me that you must have been putting yourself to an unnecessary penance all this while, and that you might have found a service where they eat less, and are more orthodox in their worship. I dare say it cannot be want of skill which prevented your being placed more to your satisfaction."

"It disna become me to speak to the point of my qualifications," said Andrew, looking round him with great complacency; "but nae doubt I should understand my trade of horticulture, seeing I was bred in the parish of Dreepdaily, where they raise lang-kale under glass, and force the early nettles for their spring kale. And, to speak truth, I hae been flitting every term these four-and-twenty years; but when the time comes, there's aye something to saw that I would like to see sawn,—or something to maw that I would like to see mawn,—or something to ripe that I would like to see ripen,—and sae I e'en daiker on wi' the family frae year's end to year's end. And I wad say for certain, that I am gaun to quit at Cannlemas, only I was just as positive on it twenty years syne, and I find mysell still turning up the mouls here, for a' that. Forbye that, to tell your honour the evendown truth, there's nae better place ever offered to Andrew. But if your honour wad wush me to ony place where I wad hear pure doctrine, and hae a free cow's grass, and a cot, and a yard, and mair than ten punds of annual fee, and where there's nae leddy about the town to count the apples, I'se hold mysell muckle indebted t'ye."

"Bravo, Andrew! I perceive you'll lose no preferment for want of asking patronage."

"I canna see what for I should," replied Andrew; "it's no a generation to wait till ane's worth's discovered, I trow."

"But you are no friend, I observe, to the ladies."

"Na, by my troth, I keep up the first gardener's quarrel to them. They're fasheous bargains—aye crying for apricocks, pears, plums, and apples, summer and winter, without distinction o' seasons; but we hae nae slices o' the spare rib here, be praised for't! except auld Martha, and she's weel eneugh pleased wi' the freedom o' the berry-bushes to her sister's weans, when they come to drink tea in a holiday in the housekeeper's room, and wi' a wheen codlings now and then for her ain private supper."

"You forget your young mistress."

"What mistress do I forget?—whae's that?"

"Your young mistress, Miss Vernon."

"What! the lassie Vernon?—She's nae mistress o' mine, man. I wish she was her ain mistress; and I wish she mayna be some other body's mistress or it's lang—She's a wild slip that."

"Indeed!" said I, more interested than I cared to own to myself, or to show to the fellow—"why, Andrew, you know all the secrets of this family."

"If I ken them, I can keep them," said Andrew; "they winna work in my wame like harm in a barrel, I'se warrant ye. Miss Die is—but it's neither beef nor brose o' mine."

And he began to dig with a great semblance of assiduity.

"What is Miss Vernon, Andrew? I am a friend of the family, and should like to know."

"Other than a gude ane, I'm fearing," said Andrew, closing one eye hard, and shaking his head with a grave and mysterious look—"something glee'd—your honour understands me?"

"I cannot say I do," said I, "Andrew; but I should like to hear you explain yourself;" and therewithal I slipped a crown-piece into Andrew's horn-hard hand. The touch of the silver made him grin a ghastly smile, as he nodded slowly, and thrust it into his breeches pocket; and then, like a man who well understood that there was value to be returned, stood up, and rested his arms on his spade, with his features composed into the most important gravity, as for some serious communication.

"Ye maun ken, then, young gentleman, since it imports you to know, that Miss Vernon is"—

Here breaking off, he sucked in both his cheeks, till his lantern jaws and long chin assumed the appearance of a pair of nut-crackers; winked hard once more, frowned, shook his head, and seemed to think his physiognomy had completed the information which his tongue had not fully told.

"Good God!" said I—"so young, so beautiful, so early lost!"

"Troth ye may say sae—she's in a manner lost, body and saul; forby being a Papist, I'se uphaud her for"—and his northern caution prevailed, and he was again silent.

"For what, sir?" said I sternly. "I insist on knowing the plain meaning of all this."

"On, just for the bitterest Jacobite in the haill shire."

"Pshaw! a Jacobite?—is that all?"

Andrew looked at me with some astonishment, at hearing his information treated so lightly; and then muttering, "Aweel, it's the warst thing I ken aboot the lassie, howsoe'er," he resumed his spade, like the king of the Vandals, in Marmontel's late novel.

CHAPTER SEVENTH

Bardolph.—The sheriff, with a monstrous watch, is at the door.

— HENRY IV. FIRST PART.

I found out with some difficulty the apartment which was destined for my accommodation; and having secured myself the necessary good-will and attention from my uncle's domestics, by using the means they were most capable of comprehending, I secluded myself there for the remainder of the evening, conjecturing, from the fair way in which I had left my new relatives, as well as from the distant noise which continued to echo from the stone-hall (as their banqueting-room was called), that they were not likely to be fitting company for a sober man.

"What could my father mean by sending me to be an inmate in this strange family?" was my first and most natural reflection. My uncle, it was plain, received me as one who was to make some stay with him, and his rude hospitality rendered him as indifferent as King Hal to the number of those who fed at his cost. But it was plain my presence or absence would be of as little importance in his eyes as that of one of his blue-coated serving-men. My cousins were mere cubs, in whose company I might, if I liked it, unlearn whatever decent manners, or elegant accomplishments, I had acquired, but where I could attain no information beyond what regarded worming dogs, rowelling horses, and following foxes. I could only imagine one reason, which was probably the true one. My father considered the life which was led at Osbaldistone Hall as the natural and inevitable pursuits of all country gentlemen, and he was desirous, by giving me an opportunity of seeing that with which he knew I should be disgusted, to reconcile me, if possible, to take an active share in his own business. In the meantime, he would take Rashleigh Osbaldistone into the counting-house. But he had an hundred modes of providing for him, and that advantageously, whenever he chose to get rid of him. So that, although I did feel a certain qualm of conscience at having been the means of introducing Rashleigh, being such as he was described by Miss Vernon, into my father's business—perhaps into his confidence—I subdued it by the reflection that my father was complete master of his own affairs—a man not to be imposed upon, or influenced by any one—and that all I knew to the young gentleman's prejudice was through the medium of a singular and giddy girl, whose communications were made with an injudicious frankness, which might warrant me in supposing her conclusions had been hastily or inaccurately formed. Then my mind naturally turned to Miss Vernon herself; her extreme beauty; her very peculiar situation, relying solely upon her reflections, and her own spirit, for guidance and protection; and her whole character offering that variety and spirit which piques our curiosity, and engages our attention in spite of ourselves. I had sense enough to consider the neighbourhood of this singular young lady, and the chance of our being thrown into very close and frequent intercourse, as adding to the dangers, while it relieved the dulness, of Osbaldistone Hall; but I could not, with the fullest exertion of my prudence, prevail upon myself to regret excessively this new and particular hazard to which I was to be exposed. This scruple I also settled as young men settle most difficulties of the kind—I would be very cautious, always on my guard, consider Miss Vernon rather as a companion than an intimate; and all would do well enough. With these reflections I fell asleep, Miss Vernon, of course, forming the last subject of my contemplation.

Whether I dreamed of her or not, I cannot satisfy you, for I was tired and slept soundly. But she was the first person I thought of in the morning, when waked at dawn by the cheerful notes of the hunting horn. To start up, and direct my horse to be saddled, was my first movement; and in a few minutes I was in the court-yard, where men, dogs, and horses, were in full preparation. My uncle, who, perhaps, was not entitled to expect a very alert sportsman in his nephew, bred as he had been in foreign parts, seemed rather surprised to see me, and I thought his morning salutation wanted something of the hearty and hospitable tone which distinguished his first welcome. "Art there, lad?—ay, youth's aye rathe—but look to thysell—mind the old song, lad—

He that gallops his horse on Blackstone edge
May chance to catch a fall."

I believe there are few young men, and those very sturdy moralists, who would not rather be taxed with some moral peccadillo than with want of knowledge in horsemanship. As I was by no means deficient either in skill or courage, I resented my uncle's insinuation accordingly, and assured him he would find me up with the hounds.

"I doubtna, lad," was his reply; "thou'rt a rank rider, I'se warrant thee—but take heed. Thy father sent thee here to me to be bitted, and I doubt I must ride thee on the curb, or we'll hae some one to ride thee on the halter, if I takena the better heed."

As this speech was totally unintelligible to me—as, besides, it did not seem to be delivered for my use, or benefit, but was spoken as it were aside, and as if expressing aloud something which was passing through the mind of my much-honoured uncle, I concluded it must either refer to my desertion of the bottle on the preceding evening, or that my uncle's morning hours being a little discomposed by the revels of the night before, his temper had suffered in proportion. I only made the passing reflection, that if he played the ungracious landlord, I would remain the shorter while his guest, and then hastened to salute Miss Vernon, who advanced cordially to meet me. Some show of greeting also passed between my cousins and me; but as I saw them maliciously bent upon criticising my dress and accoutrements, from the cap to the stirrup-irons, and sneering at whatever had a new or foreign appearance, I exempted myself from the task of paying them much attention; and assuming, in requital of their grins and whispers, an air of the utmost indifference and contempt, I attached myself to Miss Vernon, as the only person in the party whom I could regard as a suitable companion. By her side, therefore, we sallied forth to the destined cover, which was a dingle or copse on the side of an extensive common. As we rode thither, I observed to Diana, "that I did not see my cousin Rashleigh in the field;" to which she replied,—"O no—he's a mighty hunter, but it's after the fashion of Nimrod, and his game is man."

The dogs now brushed into the cover, with the appropriate encouragement from the hunters—all was business, bustle, and activity. My cousins were soon too much interested in the business of the morning to take any further notice of me, unless that I overheard Dickon the horse-jockey whisper to Wilfred the fool—"Look thou, an our French cousin be nat off a' first burst."

To which Wilfred answered, "Like enow, for he has a queer outlandish binding on's castor."

Thorncliff, however, who in his rude way seemed not absolutely insensible to the beauty of his kinswoman, appeared determined to keep us company more closely than his brothers,—perhaps to watch what passed betwixt Miss Vernon and me—perhaps to enjoy my expected mishaps in the chase. In the last particular he was disappointed. After beating in vain for the greater part of the morning, a fox was at length found, who led us a chase of two hours, in the course of which, notwithstanding the ill-omened French binding upon my hat, I sustained my character as a horseman to the admiration of my uncle and Miss Vernon, and the secret disappointment of those who expected me to disgrace it. Reynard, however, proved too wily for his pursuers, and the hounds were at fault. I could at this time observe in Miss Vernon's manner an impatience of the close attendance which we received from Thorncliff Osbaldistone; and, as that active-spirited young lady never hesitated at taking the readiest means to gratify any wish of the moment, she said to him, in a tone of reproach—"I wonder, Thornie, what keeps you dangling at my horse's crupper all this morning, when you know the earths above Woolverton-mill are not stopt."

"I know no such an thing then, Miss Die, for the miller swore himself as black as night, that he stopt them at twelve o'clock midnight that was."

"O fie upon you, Thornie! would you trust to a miller's word?—and these earths, too, where we lost the fox three times this season! and you on your grey mare, that can gallop there and back in ten minutes!"

"Well, Miss Die, I'se go to Woolverton then, and if the earths are not stopt, I'se raddle Dick the miller's bones for him."

"Do, my dear Thornie; horsewhip the rascal to purpose—via—fly away, and about it;"—Thorncliff went off at the gallop—"or get horsewhipt yourself, which will serve my purpose just as well.—I must teach them all discipline and obedience to the word of command. I am raising a regiment, you must know. Thornie shall be my sergeant-major, Dickon my riding-master, and Wilfred, with his deep dub-a-dub tones, that speak but three syllables at a time, my kettle-drummer."

"And Rashleigh?"

"Rashleigh shall be my scout-master." "And will you find no employment for me, most lovely colonel?"

"You shall have the choice of being pay-master, or plunder-master, to the corps. But see how the dogs puzzle about there. Come, Mr. Frank, the scent's cold; they won't recover it there this while; follow me, I have a view to show you."

And in fact, she cantered up to the top of a gentle hill, commanding an extensive prospect. Casting her eyes around, to see that no one was near us, she drew up her horse beneath a few birch-trees, which screened us from the rest of the hunting-field —"Do you see yon peaked, brown, heathy hill, having something like a whitish speck upon the side?"

"Terminating that long ridge of broken moorish uplands?—I see it distinctly."

"That whitish speck is a rock called Hawkesmore-crag, and Hawkesmore-crag is in Scotland."

"Indeed! I did not think we had been so near Scotland."

"It is so, I assure you, and your horse will carry you there in two hours."

"I shall hardly give him the trouble; why, the distance must be eighteen miles as the crow flies."

"You may have my mare, if you think her less blown—I say, that in two hours you may be in Scotland."

"And I say, that I have so little desire to be there, that if my horse's head were over the Border, I would not give his tail the trouble of following. What should I do in Scotland?"

"Provide for your safety, if I must speak plainly. Do you understand me now, Mr. Frank?"

"Not a whit; you are more and more oracular."

"Then, on my word, you either mistrust me most unjustly, and are a better dissembler than Rashleigh Osbaldistone himself, or you know nothing of what is imputed to you; and then no wonder you stare at me in that grave manner, which I can scarce see without laughing."

"Upon my word of honour, Miss Vernon," said I, with an impatient feeling of her childish disposition to mirth, "I have not the most distant conception of what you mean. I am happy to afford you any subject of amusement, but I am quite ignorant in what it consists."

"Nay, there's no sound jest after all," said the young lady, composing herself; "only one looks so very ridiculous when he is fairly perplexed. But the matter is serious enough. Do you know one Moray, or Morris, or some such name?"

"Not that I can at present recollect."

"Think a moment. Did you not lately travel with somebody of such a name?"

"The only man with whom I travelled for any length of time was a fellow whose soul seemed to lie in his portmanteau."

"Then it was like the soul of the licentiate Pedro Garcias, which lay among the ducats in his leathern purse. That man has been robbed, and he has lodged an information against you, as connected with the violence done to him."

"You jest, Miss Vernon!"

"I do not, I assure you—the thing is an absolute fact."

"And do you," said I, with strong indignation, which I did not attempt to suppress, "do you suppose me capable of meriting such a charge?"

"You would call me out for it, I suppose, had I the advantage of being a man—You may do so as it is, if you like it—I can shoot flying, as well as leap a five-barred gate."

"And are colonel of a regiment of horse besides," replied I, reflecting how idle it was to be angry with her—"But do explain the present jest to me."

"There's no jest whatever," said Diana; "you are accused of robbing this man, and my uncle believes it as well as I did."

"Upon my honour, I am greatly obliged to my friends for their good opinion!"

"Now do not, if you can help it, snort, and stare, and snuff the wind, and look so exceedingly like a startled horse—There's no such offence as you suppose—you are not charged with any petty larceny or vulgar felony—by no means. This fellow was carrying money from Government, both specie and bills, to pay the troops in the north; and it is said he has been also robbed of some despatches of great consequence."

"And so it is high treason, then, and not simple robbery, of which I am accused!"

"Certainly—which, you know, has been in all ages accounted the crime of a gentleman. You will find plenty in this country, and one not far from your elbow, who think it a merit to distress the Hanoverian government by every means possible."

"Neither my politics nor my morals, Miss Vernon, are of a description so accommodating."

"I really begin to believe that you are a Presbyterian and Hanoverian in good earnest. But what do you propose to do?"

"Instantly to refute this atrocious calumny.—Before whom," I asked, "was this extraordinary accusation laid."

"Before old Squire Inglewood, who had sufficient unwillingness to receive it. He sent tidings to my uncle, I suppose, that he might smuggle you away into Scotland, out of reach of the warrant. But my uncle is sensible that his religion and old predilections render him obnoxious to Government, and that, were he caught playing booty, he would be disarmed, and probably dismounted (which would be the worse evil of the two), as a Jacobite, papist, and suspected person."[35]

"I can conceive that, sooner than lose his hunters, he would give up his nephew."

"His nephew, nieces, sons—daughters, if he had them, and whole generation," said Diana;—"therefore trust not to him, even for a single moment, but make the best of your way before they can serve the warrant."

"That I shall certainly do; but it shall be to the house of this Squire Inglewood—Which way does it lie?"

"About five miles off, in the low ground, behind yonder plantations—you may see the tower of the clock-house."

"I will be there in a few minutes," said I, putting my horse in motion.

"And I will go with you, and show you the way," said Diana, putting her palfrey also to the trot.

"Do not think of it, Miss Vernon," I replied. "It is not—permit me the freedom of a friend—it is not proper, scarcely even delicate, in you to go with me on such an errand as I am now upon."

"I understand your meaning," said Miss Vernon, a slight blush crossing her haughty brow;—"it is plainly spoken;" and after a moment's pause she added, "and I believe kindly meant."

"It is indeed, Miss Vernon. Can you think me insensible of the interest you show me, or ungrateful for it?" said I, with even more earnestness than I could have wished to express. "Yours is meant for true kindness, shown best at the hour of need. But I must not, for your own sake—for the chance of misconstruction—suffer you to pursue the dictates of your generosity; this is so public an occasion—it is almost like venturing into an open court of justice."

"And if it were not almost, but altogether entering into an open court of justice, do you think I would not go there if I thought it right, and wished to protect a friend? You have no one to stand by you—you are a stranger; and here, in the outskirts of the kingdom, country justices do odd things. My uncle has no desire to embroil himself in your affair; Rashleigh is absent, and were he here, there is no knowing which side he might take; the rest are all more stupid and brutal one than another. I will go with you, and I do not fear being able to serve you. I am no fine lady, to be terrified to death with law-books, hard words, or big wigs."

"But my dear Miss Vernon"—

"But my dear Mr. Francis, be patient and quiet, and let me take my own way; for when I take the bit between my teeth, there is no bridle will stop me."

Flattered with the interest so lovely a creature seemed to take in my fate, yet vexed at the ridiculous appearance I should make, by carrying a girl of eighteen along with me as an advocate, and seriously concerned for the misconstruction to which her motives might be exposed, I endeavoured to combat her resolution to accompany me to Squire Inglewood's. The self-willed girl told me roundly, that my dissuasions were absolutely in vain; that she was a true Vernon, whom no consideration, not even that of being able to do but little to assist him, should induce to abandon a friend in distress; and that all I could say on the subject might be very well for pretty, well-educated, well-behaved misses from a town boarding-school, but did not apply to her, who was accustomed to mind nobody's opinion but her own.

While she spoke thus, we were advancing hastily towards Inglewood Place, while, as if to divert me from the task of further remonstrance, she drew a ludicrous picture of the magistrate and his clerk.—Inglewood was—according to her description—a white-washed Jacobite; that is, one who, having been long a non-juror, like most of the other gentlemen of the country, had lately qualified himself to act as a justice, by taking the oaths to Government. "He had done so," she said, "in compliance with the urgent request of most of his brother squires, who saw, with regret, that the palladium of silvan sport, the game-laws, were likely to fall into disuse for want of a magistrate who would enforce them; the nearest acting justice being the Mayor of Newcastle, and he, as being rather inclined to the consumption of the game when properly dressed, than to its preservation when alive, was more partial, of course, to the cause of the poacher than of the sportsman. Resolving, therefore, that it was expedient some one of their number should sacrifice the scruples of Jacobitical loyalty to the good of the community, the Northumbrian country gentlemen imposed the duty on Inglewood, who, being very inert in most of his feelings and sentiments, might, they thought, comply with any political creed without much repugnance. Having thus procured the body of justice, they proceeded," continued Miss Vernon, "to attach to it a clerk, by way of soul, to direct and animate its movements. Accordingly they got a sharp Newcastle attorney, called Jobson, who, to vary my metaphor, finds it a good thing enough to retail justice at the sign of Squire Inglewood, and, as his own emoluments depend on the quantity of business which he transacts, he hooks in his principal for a great deal more employment in the justice line than the honest squire had ever bargained for; so that no apple-wife within the circuit of ten miles can settle her account with a costermonger without an audience of the reluctant Justice and his alert clerk, Mr. Joseph Jobson. But the most ridiculous scenes occur when affairs come before him, like our business of to-day, having any colouring of politics. Mr. Joseph Jobson (for which, no doubt, he has his own very sufficient reasons) is a prodigious zealot for the Protestant religion, and a great friend to the present establishment in church and state. Now, his principal, retaining a sort of instinctive attachment to the opinions which he professed openly until he relaxed his political creed with the patriotic view of enforcing the law against unauthorized destroyers of black-game, grouse, partridges, and hares, is peculiarly embarrassed when the zeal of his assistant involves him in judicial proceedings connected with his earlier faith; and, instead of seconding his zeal, he seldom fails to oppose to it a double dose of indolence and lack of exertion. And this inactivity does not by any means arise from actual stupidity. On the contrary, for one whose principal delight is in eating and drinking, he is an alert, joyous, and lively old soul, which makes his assumed dulness the more diverting. So you may see Jobson on such occasions, like a bit of a broken down blood-tit condemned to drag an overloaded cart, puffing, strutting, and spluttering, to get the Justice put in motion, while, though the wheels groan, creak, and revolve slowly, the great and preponderating weight of the vehicle fairly frustrates the efforts of the willing quadruped, and prevents its being brought into a state of actual progression. Nay more, the unfortunate pony, I understand, has been heard to complain that this same car of justice, which he finds it so hard to put in motion on some occasions, can on others run fast enough down hill of its own accord, dragging his reluctant self backwards along with it, when anything can be done of service to Squire Inglewood's quondam friends. And then Mr. Jobson talks big about reporting his principal to the Secretary of State for the Home Department, if it were not for his particular regard and friendship for Mr. Inglewood and his family."

As Miss Vernon concluded this whimsical description, we found ourselves in front of Inglewood Place, a handsome, though old-fashioned building, which showed the consequence of the family.

CHAPTER EIGHTH

"Sir," quoth the Lawyer, "not to flatter ye,
You have as good and fair a battery
As heart could wish, and need not shame
The proudest man alive to claim."

— BUTLER.

Our horses were taken by a servant in Sir Hildebrand's livery, whom we found in the court-yard, and we entered the house. In the entrance-hall I was somewhat surprised, and my fair companion still more so, when we met Rashleigh Osbaldistone, who could not help showing equal wonder at our rencontre.

"Rashleigh," said Miss Vernon, without giving him time to ask any question, "you have heard of Mr. Francis Osbaldistone's affair, and you have been talking to the Justice about it?"

"Certainly," said Rashleigh, composedly—"it has been my business here.— I have been endeavouring," he said, with a bow to me, "to render my cousin what service I can. But I am sorry to meet him here."

"As a friend and relation, Mr. Osbaldistone, you ought to have been sorry to have met me anywhere else, at a time when the charge of my reputation required me to be on this spot as soon as possible."

"True; but judging from what my father said, I should have supposed a short retreat into Scotland—just till matters should be smoothed over in a quiet way"—

I answered with warmth, "That I had no prudential measures to observe, and desired to have nothing smoothed over;—on the contrary, I was come to inquire into a rascally calumny, which I was determined to probe to the bottom."

"Mr. Francis Osbaldistone is an innocent man, Rashleigh," said Miss Vernon, "and he demands an investigation of the charge against him, and I intend to support him in it."

"You do, my pretty cousin?—I should think, now, Mr. Francis Osbaldistone was likely to be as effectually, and rather more delicately, supported by my presence than by yours."

"Oh, certainly; but two heads are better than one, you know."

"Especially such a head as yours, my pretty Die," advancing and taking her hand with a familiar fondness, which made me think him fifty times uglier than nature had made him. She led him, however, a few steps aside; they conversed in an under voice, and she appeared to insist upon some request which he was unwilling or unable to comply with. I never saw so strong a contrast betwixt the expression of two faces. Miss Vernon's, from being earnest, became angry; her eyes and cheeks became more animated, her colour mounted, she clenched her little hand, and stamping on the ground with her tiny foot, seemed to listen with a mixture of contempt and indignation to the apologies, which, from his look of civil deference, his composed and respectful smile, his body rather drawing back than advanced, and other signs of look and person, I concluded him to be pouring out at her feet. At length she flung away from him, with "I *will* have it so."

"It is not in my power—there is no possibility of it.—Would you think it, Mr. Osbaldistone?" said he, addressing me—

"You are not mad?" said she, interrupting him.

"Would you think it?" said he, without attending to her hint—"Miss Vernon insists, not only that I know your innocence (of which, indeed, it is impossible for any one to be more convinced), but that I must also be acquainted with the real perpetrators of the outrage on this fellow—if indeed such an outrage has been committed. Is this reasonable, Mr. Osbaldistone?"

"I will not allow any appeal to Mr. Osbaldistone, Rashleigh," said the young lady; "he does not know, as I do, the incredible extent and accuracy of your information on all points."

"As I am a gentleman, you do me more honour than I deserve."

"Justice, Rashleigh—only justice:—and it is only justice which I expect at your hands."

"You are a tyrant, Diana," he answered, with a sort of sigh—"a capricious tyrant, and rule your friends with a rod of iron. Still, however, it shall be as you desire. But you ought not to be here—you know you ought not;—you must return with me."

Then turning from Diana, who seemed to stand undecided, he came up to me in the most friendly manner, and said, "Do not doubt my interest in what regards you, Mr. Osbaldistone. If I leave you just at this moment, it is only to act for your advantage. But you must use your influence with your cousin to return; her presence cannot serve you, and must prejudice herself."

"I assure you, sir," I replied, "you cannot be more convinced of this than I; I have urged Miss Vernon's return as anxiously as she would permit me to do."

"I have thought on it," said Miss Vernon after a pause, "and I will not go till I see you safe out of the hands of the Philistines. Cousin Rashleigh, I dare say, means well; but he and I know each other well. Rashleigh, I will not go;—I know," she added, in a more soothing tone, "my being here will give you more motive for speed and exertion."

"Stay then, rash, obstinate girl," said Rashleigh; "you know but too well to whom you trust;" and hastening out of the hall, we heard his horse's feet a minute afterwards in rapid motion.

"Thank Heaven he is gone!" said Diana. "And now let us seek out the Justice."

"Had we not better call a servant?"

"Oh, by no means; I know the way to his den—we must burst on him suddenly —follow me."

I did follow her accordingly, as she tripped up a few gloomy steps, traversed a twilight passage, and entered a sort of ante-room, hung round with old maps, architectural elevations, and genealogical trees. A pair of folding-doors opened from this into Mr. Inglewood's sitting apartment, from which was heard the fag-end of an old ditty, chanted by a voice which had been in its day fit for a jolly bottle-song.

"O, in Skipton-in-Craven
Is never a haven,
But many a day foul weather;
And he that would say
A pretty girl nay,
I wish for his cravat a tether."

"Heyday!" said Miss Vernon, "the genial Justice must have dined already—I did not think it had been so late."

It was even so. Mr. Inglewood's appetite having been sharpened by his official investigations, he had antedated his meridian repast, having dined at twelve instead of one o'clock, then the general dining hour in England. The various occurrences of the morning occasioned our arriving some time after this hour, to the Justice the most important of the four-and-twenty, and he had not neglected the interval.

"Stay you here," said Diana. "I know the house, and I will call a servant; your sudden appearance might startle the old gentleman even to choking;" and she escaped from me, leaving me uncertain whether I ought to advance or retreat. It was impossible for me not to hear some part of what passed within the dinner apartment, and particularly several apologies for declining to sing, expressed in a dejected croaking voice, the tones of which, I conceived, were not entirely new to me.

"Not sing, sir? by our Lady! but you must—What! you have cracked my silver-mounted cocoa-nut of sack, and tell me that you cannot sing!—Sir, sack will make a cat sing, and speak too; so up with a merry stave, or trundle yourself out of my doors!

—Do you think you are to take up all my valuable time with your d-d declarations, and then tell me you cannot sing?"

"Your worship is perfectly in rule," said another voice, which, from its pert conceited accent, might be that of the cleric, "and the party must be conformable; he hath *canet* written on his face in court hand."

"Up with it then," said the Justice, "or by St. Christopher, you shall crack the cocoa-nut full of salt-and-water, according to the statute for such effect made and provided."

Thus exhorted and threatened, my quondam fellow-traveller, for I could no longer doubt that he was the recusant in question, uplifted, with a voice similar to that of a criminal singing his last psalm on the scaffold, a most doleful stave to the following effect:—

"Good people all, I pray give ear,
A woeful story you shall hear,
'Tis of a robber as stout as ever
Bade a true man stand and deliver.
With his foodle doo fa loodle loo.

"This knave, most worthy of a cord,
Being armed with pistol and with sword,
'Twixt Kensington and Brentford then
Did boldly stop six honest men.
With his foodle doo, etc.

"These honest men did at Brentford dine,
Having drank each man his pint of wine,
When this bold thief, with many curses,
Did say, You dogs, your lives or purses.
With his foodle doo," etc.

I question if the honest men, whose misfortune is commemorated in this pathetic ditty, were more startled at the appearance of the bold thief than the songster was at mine; for, tired of waiting for some one to announce me, and finding my situation as a listener rather awkward, I presented myself to the company just as my friend Mr. Morris, for such, it seems, was his name, was uplifting the fifth stave of his doleful ballad. The high tone with which the tune started died away in a quaver of consternation on finding himself so near one whose character he supposed to be little less suspicious than that of the hero of his madrigal, and he remained silent, with a mouth gaping as if I had brought the Gorgon's head in my hand.

The Justice, whose eyes had closed under the influence of the somniferous lullaby of the song, started up in his chair as it suddenly ceased, and stared with wonder at the unexpected addition which the company had received while his organs of sight were in abeyance. The clerk, as I conjectured him to be from his appearance, was also commoved; for, sitting opposite to Mr. Morris, that honest gentleman's terror communicated itself to him, though he wotted not why.

I broke the silence of surprise occasioned by my abrupt entrance.—"My name, Mr. Inglewood, is Francis Osbaldistone; I understand that some scoundrel has brought a complaint before you, charging me with being concerned in a loss which he says he has sustained."

"Sir," said the Justice, somewhat peevishly, "these are matters I never enter upon after dinner;—there is a time for everything, and a justice of peace must eat as well as other folks."

The goodly person of Mr. Inglewood, by the way, seemed by no means to have suffered by any fasts, whether in the service of the law or of religion.

"I beg pardon for an ill-timed visit, sir; but as my reputation is concerned, and as the dinner appears to be concluded"—

"It is not concluded, sir," replied the magistrate; "man requires digestion as well as food, and I protest I cannot have benefit from my victuals unless I am allowed two hours of quiet leisure, intermixed with harmless mirth, and a moderate circulation of the bottle."

"If your honour will forgive me," said Mr. Jobson, who had produced and arranged his writing implements in the brief space that our conversation afforded; "as this is a case of felony, and the gentleman seems something impatient, the charge is *contra pacem domini regis*"—

"D—n *dominie regis!*" said the impatient Justice—"I hope it's no treason to say so; but it's enough to made one mad to be worried in this way. Have I a moment of my life quiet for warrants, orders, directions, acts, bails, bonds, and recognisances?—I pronounce to you, Mr. Jobson, that I shall send you and the justiceship to the devil one of these days."

"Your honour will consider the dignity of the office one of the quorum and custos rotulorum, an office of which Sir Edward Coke wisely saith, The whole Christian world hath not the like of it, so it be duly executed."

"Well," said the Justice, partly reconciled by this eulogium on the dignity of his situation, and gulping down the rest of his dissatisfaction in a huge bumper of claret, "let us to this gear then, and get rid of it as fast as we can.—Here you, sir—you, Morris—you, knight of the sorrowful countenance—is this Mr. Francis Osbaldistone the gentleman whom you charge with being art and part of felony?"

"I, sir?" replied Morris, whose scattered wits had hardly yet reassembled themselves; "I charge nothing—I say nothing against the gentleman,"

"Then we dismiss your complaint, sir, that's all, and a good riddance— Push about the bottle—Mr. Osbaldistone, help yourself."

Jobson, however, was determined that Morris should not back out of the scrape so easily. "What do you mean, Mr. Morris?—Here is your own declaration—the ink scarce dried—and you would retract it in this scandalous manner!"

"How do I know," whispered the other in a tremulous tone, "how many rogues are in the house to back him? I have read of such things in Johnson's Lives of the Highwaymen. I protest the door opens"—

And it did open, and Diana Vernon entered—"You keep fine order here, Justice— not a servant to be seen or heard of."

"Ah!" said the Justice, starting up with an alacrity which showed that he was not so engrossed by his devotions to Themis or Comus, as to forget what was due to beauty—"Ah, ha! Die Vernon, the heath-bell of Cheviot, and the blossom of the Border, come to see how the old bachelor keeps house? Art welcome, girl, as flowers in May."

"A fine, open, hospitable house you do keep, Justice, that must be allowed—not a soul to answer a visitor."

"Ah, the knaves! they reckoned themselves secure of me for a couple of hours—But why did you not come earlier?—Your cousin Rashleigh dined here, and ran away like a poltroon after the first bottle was out—But you have not dined—we'll have something nice and ladylike—sweet and pretty like yourself, tossed up in a trice."

"I may eat a crust in the ante-room before I set out," answered Miss Vernon—"I have had a long ride this morning; but I can't stay long, Justice—I came with my cousin, Frank Osbaldistone, there, and I must show him the way back again to the Hall, or he'll lose himself in the wolds."

"Whew! sits the wind in that quarter?" inquired the Justice—

"She showed him the way, she showed him the way,
She showed him the way to woo.

What! no luck for old fellows, then, my sweet bud of the wilderness?"

"None whatever, Squire Inglewood; but if you will be a good kind Justice, and despatch young Frank's business, and let us canter home again, I'll bring my uncle to dine with you next week, and we'll expect merry doings."

"And you shall find them, my pearl of the Tyne—Zookers, lass, I never envy these young fellows their rides and scampers, unless when you come across me. But I must not keep you just now, I suppose?—I am quite satisfied with Mr. Francis Osbaldistone's explanation—here has been some mistake, which can be cleared at greater leisure."

"Pardon me, sir," said I; "but I have not heard the nature of the accusation yet."

"Yes, sir," said the clerk, who, at the appearance of Miss Vernon, had given up the matter in despair, but who picked up courage to press farther investigation on finding himself supported from a quarter whence assuredly he expected no backing—"Yes, sir, and Dalton saith, That he who is apprehended as a felon shall not be discharged upon any man's discretion, but shall be held either to bail or commitment, paying to the clerk of the peace the usual fees for recognisance or commitment."

The Justice, thus goaded on, gave me at length a few words of explanation.

It seems the tricks which I had played to this man Morris had made a strong impression on his imagination; for I found they had been arrayed against me in his evidence, with all the exaggerations which a timorous and heated imagination could suggest. It appeared also, that on the day he parted from me, he had been stopped on a solitary spot and eased of his beloved travelling-companion, the portmanteau, by two men, well mounted and armed, having their faces covered with vizards.

One of them, he conceived, had much of my shape and air, and in a whispering conversation which took place betwixt the freebooters, he heard the other apply to him the name of Osbaldistone. The declaration farther set forth, that upon inquiring into the principles of the family so named, he, the said declarant, was informed that they were of the worst description, the family, in all its members, having been Papists and Jacobites, as he was given to understand by the dissenting clergyman at whose house he stopped after his rencontre, since the days of William the Conqueror.

Upon all and each of these weighty reasons, he charged me with being accessory to the felony committed upon his person; he, the said declarant, then travelling in the special employment of Government, and having charge of certain important papers, and also a large sum in specie, to be paid over, according to his instructions, to certain persons of official trust and importance in Scotland.

Having heard this extraordinary accusation, I replied to it, that the circumstances on which it was founded were such as could warrant no justice, or magistrate, in any attempt on my personal liberty. I admitted that I had practised a little upon the terrors of Mr. Morris, while we travelled together, but in such trifling particulars as could have excited apprehension in no one who was one whit less timorous and jealous than himself. But I added, that I had never seen him since we parted, and if that which he feared had really come upon him, I was in nowise accessory to an action so unworthy of my character and station in life. That one of the robbers was called Osbaldistone, or that such a name was mentioned in the course of the conversation betwixt them, was a trifling circumstance, to which no weight was due. And concerning the disaffection alleged against me, I was willing to prove, to the satisfaction of the Justice, the clerk, and even the witness himself, that I was of the same persuasion as his friend the dissenting clergyman; had been educated as a good subject in the principles of the Revolution, and as such now demanded the personal protection of the laws which had been assured by that great event.

The Justice fidgeted, took snuff, and seemed considerably embarrassed, while Mr. Attorney Jobson, with all the volubility of his profession, ran over the statute of the 34 Edward III., by which justices of the peace are allowed to arrest all those whom they find by indictment or suspicion, and to put them into prison. The rogue even turned my own admissions against me, alleging, "that since I had confessedly, upon my own showing, assumed the bearing or deportment of a robber or malefactor, I had voluntarily subjected myself to the suspicions of which I complained, and brought myself within the compass of the act, having wilfully clothed my conduct with all the colour and livery of guilt."

I combated both his arguments and his jargon with much indignation and scorn, and observed, "That I should, if necessary, produce the bail of my relations, which I conceived could not be refused, without subjecting the magistrate in a misdemeanour."

"Pardon me, my good sir—pardon me," said the insatiable clerk; "this is a case in which neither bail nor mainprize can be received, the felon who is liable to be committed on heavy grounds of suspicion, not being replevisable under the statute of the 3d of King Edward, there being in that act an express exception of such as be charged of commandment, or force, and aid of felony done;" and he hinted that his worship would do well to remember that such were no way replevisable by common writ, nor without writ.

At this period of the conversation a servant entered, and delivered a letter to Mr. Jobson. He had no sooner run it hastily over, than he exclaimed, with the air of one who wished to appear much vexed at the interruption, and felt the consequence attached to a man of multifarious avocations—"Good God!—why, at this rate, I shall have neither time to attend to the public concerns nor my own—no rest—no quiet—I wish to Heaven another gentleman in our line would settle here!"

"God forbid!" said the Justice in a tone of *sotto-voce* deprecation; "some of us have enough of one of the tribe."

"This is a matter of life and death, if your worship pleases."

"In God's name! no more justice business, I hope," said the alarmed magistrate.

"No—no," replied Mr. Jobson, very consequentially; "old Gaffer Rutledge of Grime's-hill is subpoenaed for the next world; he has sent an express for Dr. Killdown to put in bail—another for me to arrange his worldly affairs."

"Away with you, then," said Mr. Inglewood, hastily; "his may not be a replevisable case under the statute, you know, or Mr. Justice Death may not like the doctor for a *main pernor*, or bailsman."

"And yet," said Jobson, lingering as he moved towards the door, "if my presence here be necessary—I could make out the warrant for committal in a moment, and the constable is below—And you have heard," he said, lowering his voice, "Mr. Rashleigh's opinion"—the rest was lost in a whisper.

The Justice replied aloud, "I tell thee no, man, no—we'll do nought till thou return, man; 'tis but a four-mile ride—Come, push the bottle, Mr. Morris—Don't be cast down, Mr. Osbaldistone—And you, my rose of the wilderness—one cup of claret to refresh the bloom of your cheeks."

Diana started, as if from a reverie, in which she appeared to have been plunged while we held this discussion. "No, Justice—I should be afraid of transferring the bloom to a part of my face where it would show to little advantage; but I will pledge you in a cooler beverage;" and filling a glass with water, she drank it hastily, while her hurried manner belied her assumed gaiety.

I had not much leisure to make remarks upon her demeanour, however, being full of vexation at the interference of fresh obstacles to an instant examination of the disgraceful and impertinent charge which was brought against me. But there was no moving the Justice to take the matter up in absence of his clerk, an incident which gave him apparently as much pleasure as a holiday to a schoolboy. He persisted in his endeavours to inspire jollity into a company, the individuals of which, whether considered with reference to each other, or to their respective situations, were by no means inclined to mirth. "Come, Master Morris, you're not the first man that's been robbed, I trow—grieving ne'er brought back loss, man. And you, Mr. Frank Osbaldistone, are not the first bully-boy that has said stand to a true man. There was Jack Winterfield, in my young days, kept the best company in the land—at horse-races and cock-fights who but he—hand and glove was I with Jack. Push the bottle, Mr. Morris, it's dry talking—Many quart bumpers have I cracked, and thrown many a merry main with poor Jack—good family—ready wit—quick eye—as honest a fellow, barring the deed he died for—we'll drink to his memory, gentlemen—Poor Jack Winterfield—And since we talk of him, and of those sort of things, and since that d— d clerk of mine has taken his gibberish elsewhere, and since we're snug among ourselves, Mr. Osbaldistone, if you will have my best advice, I would take up this matter—the law's hard—very severe—hanged poor Jack Winterfield at York, despite family connections and great interest, all for easing a fat west-country grazier of the price of a few beasts—Now, here is honest Mr. Morris, has been frightened, and so forth—D—n it, man, let the poor fellow have back his portmanteau, and end the frolic at once."

Morris's eyes brightened up at this suggestion, and he began to hesitate forth an assurance that he thirsted for no man's blood, when I cut the proposed accommodation short, by resenting the Justice's suggestion as an insult, that went directly to suppose me guilty of the very crime which I had come to his house with the express intention of disavowing. We were in this awkward predicament when a servant, opening the door, announced, "A strange gentleman to wait upon his honour;" and the party whom he thus described entered the room without farther ceremony.

CHAPTER NINTH

> One of the thieves come back again! I'll stand close,
> He dares not wrong me now, so near the house,
> And call in vain 'tis, till I see him offer it.
>
> — *THE WIDOW.*

"A stranger!" echoed the Justice—"not upon business, I trust, for I'll be"—

His protestation was cut short by the answer of the man himself. "My business is of a nature somewhat onerous and particular," said my acquaintance, Mr. Campbell—for it was he, the very Scotchman whom I had seen at Northallerton—"and I must solicit your honour to give instant and heedful consideration to it.—I believe, Mr. Morris," he added, fixing his eye on that person with a look of peculiar firmness and almost ferocity—"I believe ye ken brawly what I am—I believe ye cannot have forgotten what passed at our last meeting on the road?" Morris's jaw dropped—his countenance became the colour of tallow—his teeth chattered, and he gave visible signs of the utmost consternation. "Take heart of grace, man," said Campbell, "and dinna sit clattering your jaws there like a pair of castanets! I think there can be nae difficulty in your telling Mr. Justice, that ye have seen me of yore, and ken me to be a cavalier of fortune, and a man of honour. Ye ken fu' weel ye will be some time resident in my vicinity, when I may have the power, as I will possess the inclination, to do you as good a turn."

"Sir—sir—I believe you to be a man of honour, and, as you say, a man of fortune. Yes, Mr. Inglewood," he added, clearing his voice, "I really believe this gentleman to be so."

"And what are this gentleman's commands with me?" said the Justice, somewhat peevishly. "One man introduces another, like the rhymes in the 'house that Jack built,' and I get company without either peace or conversation!"

"Both shall be yours, sir," answered Campbell, "in a brief period of time. I come to release your mind from a piece of troublesome duty, not to make increment to it."

"Body o' me! then you are welcome as ever Scot was to England, and that's not saying much. But get on, man—let's hear what you have got to say at once."

"I presume, this gentleman," continued the North Briton, "told you there was a person of the name of Campbell with him, when he had the mischance to lose his valise?"

"He has not mentioned such a name, from beginning to end of the matter," said the Justice.

"Ah! I conceive—I conceive," replied Mr. Campbell;—"Mr. Morris was kindly afeared of committing a stranger into collision wi' the judicial forms of the country; but as I understand my evidence is necessary to the compurgation of one honest gentleman here, Mr. Francis Osbaldistone, wha has been most unjustly suspected, I will dispense with the precaution. Ye will therefore" (he added addressing Morris with the same determined look and accent) "please tell Mr. Justice Inglewood, whether we did not travel several miles together on the road, in consequence of your own anxious request and suggestion, reiterated ance and again, baith on the evening that we were at Northallerton, and there declined by me, but afterwards accepted, when I overtook ye on the road near Cloberry Allers, and was prevailed on by you to resign my ain intentions of proceeding to Rothbury; and, for my misfortune, to accompany you on your proposed route."

"It's a melancholy truth," answered Morris, holding down his head, as he gave this general assent to the long and leading question which Campbell put to him, and seemed to acquiesce in the statement it contained with rueful docility.

"And I presume you can also asseverate to his worship, that no man is better qualified than I am to bear testimony in this case, seeing that I was by you, and near you, constantly during the whole occurrence."

"No man better qualified, certainly," said Morris, with a deep and embarrassed sigh.

"And why the devil did you not assist him, then," said the Justice, "since, by Mr. Morris's account, there were but two robbers; so you were two to two, and you are both stout likely men?"

"Sir, if it please your worship," said Campbell, "I have been all my life a man of peace and quietness, noways given to broils or batteries. Mr. Morris, who belongs, as I understand, or hath belonged, to his Majesty's army, might have used his pleasure in resistance, he travelling, as I also understand, with a great charge of treasure; but, for me, who had but my own small peculiar to defend, and who am, moreover, a man of a pacific occupation, I was unwilling to commit myself to hazard in the matter."

I looked at Campbell as he muttered these words, and never recollect to have seen a more singular contrast than that between the strong daring sternness expressed in his harsh features, and the air of composed meekness and simplicity which his language assumed. There was even a slight ironical smile lurking about the corners of his mouth, which seemed, involuntarily as it were, to intimate his disdain of the quiet and peaceful character which he thought proper to assume, and which led me to entertain strange suspicions that his concern in the violence done to Morris had been something very different from that of a fellow-sufferer, or even of a mere spectator.

Perhaps some suspicious crossed the Justice's mind at the moment, for he exclaimed, as if by way of ejaculation, "Body o' me! but this is a strange story."

The North Briton seemed to guess at what was passing in his mind; for he went on, with a change of manner and tone, dismissing from his countenance some part of the hypocritical affectation of humility which had made him obnoxious to suspicion, and saying, with a more frank and unconstrained air, "To say the truth, I am just ane o' those canny folks wha care not to fight but when they hae gotten something to fight for, which did not chance to be my predicament when I fell in wi' these loons. But that your worship may know that I am a person of good fame and character, please to cast your eye over that billet."

Mr. Inglewood took the paper from his hand, and read, half aloud, "These are to certify, that the bearer, Robert Campbell of—of some place which I cannot pronounce," interjected the Justice—"is a person of good lineage, and peaceable demeanour, travelling towards England on his own proper affairs, &c. &c. &c. Given under our hand, at our Castle of Inver—Invera—rara—Argyle."

"A slight testimonial, sir, which I thought fit to impetrate from that worthy nobleman" (here he raised his hand to his head, as if to touch his hat), "MacCallum More."

"MacCallum who, sir?" said the Justice.

"Whom the Southern call the Duke of Argyle."

"I know the Duke of Argyle very well to be a nobleman of great worth and distinction, and a true lover of his country. I was one of those that stood by him in 1714, when he unhorsed the Duke of Marlborough out of his command. I wish we had more noblemen like him. He was an honest Tory in those days, and hand and glove with Ormond. And he has acceded to the present Government, as I have done myself, for the peace and quiet of his country; for I cannot presume that great man to have been actuated, as violent folks pretend, with the fear of losing his places and regiment. His testimonial, as you call it, Mr. Campbell, is perfectly satisfactory; and now, what have you got to say to this matter of the robbery?"

"Briefly this, if it please your worship,—that Mr. Morris might as weel charge it against the babe yet to be born, or against myself even, as against this young gentleman, Mr. Osbaldistone; for I am not only free to depone that the person whom he took for him was a shorter man, and a thicker man, but also, for I chanced to obtain a glisk of his visage, as his fause-face slipped aside, that he was a man of other features and complexion than those of this young gentleman, Mr. Osbaldistone. And I believe," he added, turning round with a natural, yet somewhat sterner air, to Mr. Morris, "that the gentleman will allow I had better opportunity to take cognisance wha were present on that occasion than he, being, I believe, much the cooler o' the twa."

"I agree to it, sir—I agree to it perfectly," said Morris, shrinking back as Campbell moved his chair towards him to fortify his appeal—"And I incline, sir," he added, addressing Mr. Inglewood, "to retract my information as to Mr. Osbaldistone; and I request, sir, you will permit him, sir, to go about his business, and me to go about mine also; your worship may have business to settle with Mr. Campbell, and I am rather in haste to be gone."

"Then, there go the declarations," said the Justice, throwing them into the fire—"And now you are at perfect liberty, Mr. Osbaldistone. And you, Mr. Morris, are set quite at your ease."

"Ay," said Campbell, eyeing Morris as he assented with a rueful grin to the Justice's observations, "much like the ease of a tod under a pair of harrows—But fear nothing, Mr. Morris; you and I maun leave the house thegither. I will see you safe—I hope you will not doubt my honour, when I say sae—to the next highway, and then we part company; and if we do not meet as friends in Scotland, it will be your ain fault."

With such a lingering look of terror as the condemned criminal throws, when he is informed that the cart awaits him, Morris arose; but when on his legs, appeared to hesitate. "I tell thee, man, fear nothing," reiterated Campbell; "I will keep my word with you—Why, thou sheep's heart, how do ye ken but we may can pick up some speerings of your valise, if ye will be amenable to gude counsel?—Our horses are ready. Bid the Justice fareweel, man, and show your Southern breeding."

Morris, thus exhorted and encouraged, took his leave, under the escort of Mr. Campbell; but, apparently, new scruples and terrors had struck him before they left the house, for I heard Campbell reiterating assurances of safety and protection as they left the ante-room—"By the soul of my body, man, thou'rt as safe as in thy father's kailyard—Zounds! that a chield wi' sic a black beard should hae nae mair heart than a hen-partridge!—Come on wi' ye, like a frank fallow, anes and for aye."

The voices died away, and the subsequent trampling of their horses announced to us that they had left the mansion of Justice Inglewood.

The joy which that worthy magistrate received at this easy conclusion of a matter which threatened him with some trouble in his judicial capacity, was somewhat damped by reflection on what his clerk's views of the transaction might be at his return. "Now, I shall have Jobson on my shoulders about these d—d papers—I doubt I should not have destroyed them, after all—But hang it! it is only paying his fees, and that will make all smooth—And now, Miss Die Vernon, though I have liberated all the others, I intend to sign a writ for committing you to the custody of Mother Blakes, my old housekeeper, for the evening, and we will send for my neighbour Mrs. Musgrave, and the Miss Dawkins, and your cousins, and have old Cobs the fiddler, and be as merry as the maids; and Frank Osbaldistone and I will have a carouse that will make us fit company for you in half-an-hour."

"Thanks, most worshipful," returned Miss Vernon; "but, as matters stand, we must return instantly to Osbaldistone Hall, where they do not know what has become of us, and relieve my uncle of his anxiety on my cousin's account, which is just the same as if one of his own sons were concerned."

"I believe it truly," said the Justice; "for when his eldest son, Archie, came to a bad end, in that unlucky affair of Sir John Fenwick's, old Hildebrand used to hollo out his name as readily as any of the remaining six, and then complain that he could not recollect which of his sons had been hanged. So, pray hasten home, and relieve his paternal solicitude, since go you must. But hark thee hither, heath-blossom," he said, pulling her towards him by the hand, and in a good-humoured tone of admonition, "another time let the law take its course, without putting your pretty finger into her old musty pie, all full of fragments of law gibberish—French and dog-Latin—And, Die, my beauty, let young fellows show each other the way through the moors, in case you should lose your own road, while you are pointing out theirs, my pretty Will o' the Wisp."

With this admonition, he saluted and dismissed Miss Vernon, and took an equally kind farewell of me.

"Thou seems to be a good tight lad, Mr. Frank, and I remember thy father too—he was my playfellow at school. Hark thee, lad,—ride early at night, and don't swagger with chance passengers on the king's highway. What, man! all the king's liege subjects are not bound to understand joking, and it's ill cracking jests on matters of felony. And here's poor Die Vernon too—in a manner alone and deserted on the face of this wide earth, and left to ride, and run, and scamper, at her own silly pleasure. Thou must be careful of Die, or, egad, I will turn a young fellow again on purpose, and fight thee myself, although I must own it would be a great deal of trouble. And now, get ye both gone, and leave me to my pipe of tobacco, and my meditations; for what says the song—

> The Indian leaf doth briefly burn;
> So doth man's strength to weakness turn
> The fire of youth extinguished quite,
> Comes age, like embers, dry and white.
> Think of this as you take tobacco."[36]

I was much pleased with the gleams of sense and feeling which escaped from the Justice through the vapours of sloth and self-indulgence, assured him of my respect to his admonitions, and took a friendly farewell of the honest magistrate and his hospitable mansion.

We found a repast prepared for us in the ante-room, which we partook of slightly, and rejoined the same servant of Sir Hildebrand who had taken our horses at our entrance, and who had been directed, as he informed Miss Vernon, by Mr. Rashleigh, to wait and attend upon us home. We rode a little way in silence, for, to say truth, my mind was too much bewildered with the events of the morning, to permit me to be the first to break it. At length Miss Vernon exclaimed, as if giving vent to her own reflections, "Well, Rashleigh is a man to be feared and wondered at, and all but loved; he does whatever he pleases, and makes all others his puppets—has a player ready to perform every part which he imagines, and an invention and readiness which supply expedients for every emergency."

"You think, then," said I, answering rather to her meaning, than to the express words she made use of, "that this Mr. Campbell, whose appearance was so opportune, and who trussed up and carried off my accuser as a falcon trusses a partridge, was an agent of Mr. Rashleigh Osbaldistone's?"

"I do guess as much," replied Diana; "and shrewdly suspect, moreover, that he would hardly have appeared so very much in the nick of time, if I had not happened to meet Rashleigh in the hall at the Justice's."

"In that case, my thanks are chiefly due to you, my fair preserver."

"To be sure they are," returned Diana; "and pray, suppose them paid, and accepted with a gracious smile, for I do not care to be troubled with hearing them in good earnest, and am much more likely to yawn than to behave becoming. In short, Mr. Frank, I wished to serve you, and I have fortunately been able to do so, and have only one favour to ask in return, and that is, that you will say no more about it.—But who comes here to meet us, 'bloody with spurring, fiery-red with haste?' It is the subordinate man of law, I think—no less than Mr. Joseph Jobson."

And Mr. Joseph Jobson it proved to be, in great haste, and, as it speedily appeared, in most extreme bad humour. He came up to us, and stopped his horse, as we were about to pass with a slight salutation.

"So, sir—so, Miss Vernon—ay, I see well enough how it is—bail put in during my absence, I suppose—I should like to know who drew the recognisance, that's all. If his worship uses this form of procedure often, I advise him to get another clerk, that's all, for I shall certainly demit."

"Or suppose he get this present clerk stitched to his sleeve, Mr. Jobson," said Diana; "would not that do as well? And pray, how does Farmer Rutledge, Mr. Jobson? I hope you found him able to sign, seal, and deliver?"

This question seemed greatly to increase the wrath of the man of law. He looked at Miss Vernon with such an air of spite and resentment, as laid me under a strong temptation to knock him off his horse with the butt-end of my whip, which I only suppressed in consideration of his insignificance.

"Farmer Rutledge, ma'am?" said the clerk, as soon as his indignation permitted him to articulate, "Farmer Rutledge is in as handsome enjoyment of his health as you are—it's all a bam, ma'am—all a bamboozle and a bite, that affair of his illness; and if you did not know as much before, you know it now, ma'am."

"La you there now!" replied Miss Vernon, with an affectation of extreme and simple wonder, "sure you don't say so, Mr. Jobson?"

"But I *do* say so, ma'am," rejoined the incensed scribe; "and moreover I say, that the old miserly clod-breaker called me pettifogger—pettifogger, ma'am—and said I came to hunt for a job, ma'am—which I have no more right to have said to me than any other gentleman of my profession, ma'am—especially as I am clerk to the peace, having and holding said office under *Trigesimo Septimo Henrici Octavi* and *Primo Gulielmi,* the first of King William, ma'am, of glorious and immortal memory—our immortal deliverer from papists and pretenders, and wooden shoes and warming pans, Miss Vernon."

"Sad things, these wooden shoes and warming pans," retorted the young lady, who seemed to take pleasure in augmenting his wrath;—"and it is a comfort you don't seem to want a warming pan at present, Mr. Jobson. I am afraid Gaffer Rutledge has not confined his incivility to language—Are you sure he did not give you a beating?"

"Beating, ma'am!—no"—(very shortly)—"no man alive shall beat me, I promise you, ma'am."

"That is according as you happen to merit, sir," said I: "for your mode of speaking to this young lady is so unbecoming, that, if you do not change your tone, I shall think it worth while to chastise you myself."

"Chastise, sir? and—me, sir?—Do you know whom you speak to, sir?"

"Yes, sir," I replied; "you say yourself you are clerk of peace to the county; and Gaffer Rutledge says you are a pettifogger; and in neither capacity are you entitled to be impertinent to a young lady of fashion."

Miss Vernon laid her hand on my arm, and exclaimed, "Come, Mr. Osbaldistone, I will have no assaults and battery on Mr. Jobson; I am not in sufficient charity with him to permit a single touch of your whip—why, he would live on it for a term at least. Besides, you have already hurt his feelings sufficiently—you have called him impertinent."

"I don't value his language, Miss," said the clerk, somewhat crestfallen: "besides, impertinent is not an actionable word; but pettifogger is slander in the highest degree, and that I will make Gaffer Rutledge know to his cost, and all who maliciously repeat the same, to the breach of the public peace, and the taking away of my private good name."

"Never mind that, Mr. Jobson," said Miss Vernon; "you know, where there is nothing, your own law allows that the king himself must lose his rights; and for the taking away of your good name, I pity the poor fellow who gets it, and wish you joy of losing it with all my heart."

"Very well, ma'am—good evening, ma'am—I have no more to say—only there are laws against papists, which it would be well for the land were they better executed. There's third and fourth Edward VI., of antiphoners, missals, grailes, professionals, manuals, legends, pies, portuasses, and those that have such trinkets in their possession, Miss Vernon—and there's summoning of papists to take the oaths—and there are popish recusant convicts under the first of his present Majesty—ay, and there are penalties for hearing mass—See twenty-third of Queen Elizabeth, and third James First, chapter twenty-fifth. And there are estates to be registered, and deeds and wills to be enrolled, and double taxes to be made, according to the acts in that case made and provided"—

"See the new edition of the Statutes at Large, published under the careful revision of Joseph Jobson, Gent., Clerk of the Peace," said Miss Vernon.

"Also, and above all," continued Jobson,—"for I speak to your warning—you, Diana Vernon, spinstress, not being a *femme couverte,* and being a convict popish recusant, are bound to repair to your own dwelling, and that by the nearest way, under penalty of being held felon to the king—and diligently to seek for passage at common ferries, and to tarry there but one ebb and flood; and unless you can have it in such places, to walk every day into the water up to the knees, assaying to pass over."

"A sort of Protestant penance for my Catholic errors, I suppose," said Miss Vernon, laughing.—"Well, I thank you for the information, Mr. Jobson, and will hie me home as fast as I can, and be a better housekeeper in time coming. Good-night, my dear Mr. Jobson, thou mirror of clerical courtesy."

"Good-night, ma'am, and remember the law is not to be trifled with."

And we rode on our separate ways.

"There he goes for a troublesome mischief-making tool," said Miss Vernon, as she gave a glance after him; "it is hard that persons of birth and rank and estate should be subjected to the official impertinence of such a paltry pickthank as that, merely for believing as the whole world believed not much above a hundred years ago—for certainly our Catholic Faith has the advantage of antiquity at least."

"I was much tempted to have broken the rascal's head," I replied.

"You would have acted very like a hasty young man," said Miss Vernon; "and yet, had my own hand been an ounce heavier than it is, I think I should have laid its weight upon him. Well, it does not signify complaining, but there are three things for which I am much to be pitied, if any one thought it worth while to waste any compassion upon me."

"And what are these three things, Miss Vernon, may I ask?"

"Will you promise me your deepest sympathy, if I tell you?"

"Certainly;—can you doubt it?" I replied, closing my horse nearer to hers as I spoke, with an expression of interest which I did not attempt to disguise.

"Well, it is very seducing to be pitied, after all; so here are my three grievances: In the first place, I am a girl, and not a young fellow, and would be shut up in a madhouse if I did half the things that I have a mind to;—and that, if I had your happy prerogative of acting as you list, would make all the world mad with imitating and applauding me."

"I can't quite afford you the sympathy you expect upon this score," I replied; "the misfortune is so general, that it belongs to one half of the species; and the other half"—

"Are so much better cared for, that they are jealous of their prerogatives," interrupted Miss Vernon—"I forgot you were a party interested. Nay," she said, as I was going to speak, "that soft smile is intended to be the preface of a very pretty compliment respecting the peculiar advantages which Die Vernon's friends and kinsmen enjoy, by her being born one of their Helots; but spare me the utterance, my good friend, and let us try whether we shall agree better on the second count of my indictment against fortune, as that quill-driving puppy would call it. I belong to an oppressed sect and antiquated religion, and, instead of getting credit for my devotion, as is due to all good girls beside, my kind friend, Justice Inglewood, may send me to the house of correction, merely for worshipping God in the way of my ancestors, and say, as old Pembroke did to the Abbess of Wilton,[37] when he usurped her convent and establishment, 'Go spin, you jade,—Go spin.'"

"This is not a cureless evil," said I gravely. "Consult some of our learned divines, or consult your own excellent understanding, Miss Vernon; and surely the particulars in which our religious creed differs from that in which you have been educated"—

"Hush!" said Diana, placing her fore-finger on her mouth,—"Hush! no more of that. Forsake the faith of my gallant fathers! I would as soon, were I a man, forsake their banner when the tide of battle pressed hardest against it, and turn, like a hireling recreant, to join the victorious enemy."

"I honour your spirit, Miss Vernon; and as to the inconveniences to which it exposes you, I can only say, that wounds sustained for the sake of conscience carry their own balsam with the blow."

"Ay; but they are fretful and irritating, for all that. But I see, hard of heart as you are, my chance of beating hemp, or drawing out flax into marvellous coarse thread, affects you as little as my condemnation to coif and pinners, instead of beaver and cockade; so I will spare myself the fruitless pains of telling my third cause of vexation."

"Nay, my dear Miss Vernon, do not withdraw your confidence, and I will promise you, that the threefold sympathy due to your very unusual causes of distress shall be all duly and truly paid to account of the third, providing you assure me, that it is one which you neither share with all womankind, nor even with every Catholic in England, who, God bless you, are still a sect more numerous than we Protestants, in our zeal for church and state, would desire them to be."

"It is indeed," said Diana, with a manner greatly altered, and more serious than I had yet seen her assume, "a misfortune that well merits compassion. I am by nature, as you may easily observe, of a frank and unreserved disposition—a plain true-hearted girl, who would willingly act openly and honestly by the whole world, and yet fate has involved me in such a series of nets and toils, and entanglements, that I dare hardly speak a word for fear of consequences—not to myself, but to others."

"That is indeed a misfortune, Miss Vernon, which I do most sincerely compassionate, but which I should hardly have anticipated."

"O, Mr. Osbaldistone, if you but knew—if any one knew, what difficulty I sometimes find in hiding an aching heart with a smooth brow, you would indeed pity me. I do wrong, perhaps, in speaking to you even thus far on my own situation; but you are a young man of sense and penetration—you cannot but long to ask me a hundred questions on the events of this day—on the share which Rashleigh has in your deliverance from this petty scrape—upon many other points which cannot but excite your attention; and I cannot bring myself to answer with the necessary falsehood and finesse—I should do it awkwardly, and lose your good opinion, if I have any share of it, as well as my own. It is best to say at once, Ask me no questions,—I have it not in my power to reply to them."

Miss Vernon spoke these words with a tone of feeling which could not but make a corresponding impression upon me. I assured her she had neither to fear my urging her with impertinent questions, nor my misconstruing her declining to answer those which might in themselves be reasonable, or at least natural.

"I was too much obliged," I said, "by the interest she had taken in my affairs, to misuse the opportunity her goodness had afforded me of prying into hers—I only trusted and entreated, that if my services could at any time be useful, she would command them without doubt or hesitation."

"Thank you—thank you," she replied; "your voice does not ring the cuckoo chime of compliment, but speaks like that of one who knows to what he pledges himself. If —but it is impossible—but yet, if an opportunity should occur, I will ask you if you remember this promise; and I assure you, I shall not be angry if I find you have forgotten it, for it is enough that you are sincere in your intentions just now—much may occur to alter them ere I call upon you, should that moment ever come, to assist Die Vernon, as if you were Die Vernon's brother."

"And if I were Die Vernon's brother," said I, "there could not be less chance that I should refuse my assistance—And now I am afraid I must not ask whether Rashleigh was willingly accessory to my deliverance?"

"Not of me; but you may ask it of himself, and depend upon it, he will say *yes;* for rather than any good action should walk through the world like an unappropriated adjective in an ill-arranged sentence, he is always willing to stand noun substantive to it himself."

"And I must not ask whether this Campbell be himself the party who eased Mr. Morris of his portmanteau,—or whether the letter, which our friend the attorney received, was not a finesse to withdraw him from the scene of action, lest he should have marred the happy event of my deliverance? And I must not ask"—

"You must ask nothing of me," said Miss Vernon; "so it is quite in vain to go on putting cases. You are to think just as well of me as if I had answered all these queries, and twenty others besides, as glibly as Rashleigh could have done; and observe, whenever I touch my chin just so, it is a sign that I cannot speak upon the topic which happens to occupy your attention. I must settle signals of correspondence with you, because you are to be my confidant and my counsellor, only you are to know nothing whatever of my affairs."

"Nothing can be more reasonable," I replied, laughing; "and the extent of your confidence will, you may rely upon it, only be equalled by the sagacity of my counsels."

This sort of conversation brought us, in the highest good-humour with each other, to Osbaldistone Hall, where we found the family far advanced in the revels of the evening.

"Get some dinner for Mr. Osbaldistone and me in the library," said Miss Vernon to a servant.—"I must have some compassion upon you," she added, turning to me, "and provide against your starving in this mansion of brutal abundance; otherwise I am not sure that I should show you my private haunts. This same library is my den—the only corner of the Hall-house where I am safe from the Ourang-Outangs, my cousins. They never venture there, I suppose for fear the folios should fall down and crack their skulls; for they will never affect their heads in any other way—So follow me."

And I followed through hall and bower, vaulted passage and winding stair, until we reached the room where she had ordered our refreshments.

CHAPTER TENTH

> In the wide pile, by others heeded not,
> Hers was one sacred solitary spot,
> Whose gloomy aisles and bending shelves contain
> For moral hunger food, and cures for moral pain.
>
> —ANONYMOUS.

The library at Osbaldistone Hall was a gloomy room, whose antique oaken shelves bent beneath the weight of the ponderous folios so dear to the seventeenth century, from which, under favour be it spoken, we have distilled matter for our quartos and octavos, and which, once more subjected to the alembic, may, should our sons be yet more frivolous than ourselves, be still farther reduced into duodecimos and pamphlets. The collection was chiefly of the classics, as well foreign as ancient history, and, above all, divinity. It was in wretched order. The priests, who in succession had acted as chaplains at the Hall, were, for many years, the only persons who entered its precincts, until Rashleigh's thirst for reading had led him to disturb the venerable spiders, who had muffled the fronts of the presses with their tapestry. His destination for the church rendered his conduct less absurd in his father's eyes, than if any of his other descendants had betrayed so strange a propensity, and Sir Hildebrand acquiesced in the library receiving some repairs, so as to fit it for a sitting-room. Still an air of dilapidation, as obvious as it was uncomfortable, pervaded the large apartment, and announced the neglect from which the knowledge which its walls contained had not been able to exempt it. The tattered tapestry, the worm-eaten shelves, the huge and clumsy, yet tottering, tables, desks, and chairs, the rusty grate, seldom gladdened by either sea-coal or faggots, intimated the contempt of the lords of Osbaldistone Hall for learning, and for the volumes which record its treasures.

"You think this place somewhat disconsolate, I suppose?" said Diana, as I glanced my eye round the forlorn apartment; "but to me it seems like a little paradise, for I call it my own, and fear no intrusion. Rashleigh was joint proprietor with me, while we were friends."

"And are you no longer so?" was my natural question. Her fore-finger immediately touched her dimpled chin, with an arch look of prohibition.

"We are still *allies*," she continued, "bound, like other confederate powers, by circumstances of mutual interest; but I am afraid, as will happen in other cases, the treaty of alliance has survived the amicable dispositions in which it had its origin. At any rate, we live less together; and when he comes through that door there, I vanish through this door here; and so, having made the discovery that we two were one too many for this apartment, as large as it seems, Rashleigh, whose occasions frequently call him elsewhere, has generously made a cession of his rights in my favour; so that I now endeavour to prosecute alone the studies in which he used formerly to be my guide."

"And what are those studies, if I may presume to ask?"

"Indeed you may, without the least fear of seeing my fore-finger raised to my chin. Science and history are my principal favourites; but I also study poetry and the classics."

"And the classics? Do you read them in the original?"

"Unquestionably. Rashleigh, who is no contemptible scholar, taught me Greek and Latin, as well as most of the languages of modern Europe. I assure you there has been some pains taken in my education, although I can neither sew a tucker, nor work cross-stitch, nor make a pudding, nor—as the vicar's fat wife, with as much truth as elegance, good-will, and politeness, was pleased to say in my behalf—do any other useful thing in the varsal world."

"And was this selection of studies Rashleigh's choice, or your own, Miss Vernon?" I asked.

"Um!" said she, as if hesitating to answer my question,—"It's not worth while lifting my finger about, after all. Why, partly his and partly mine. As I learned out of doors to ride a horse, and bridle and saddle him in cue of necessity, and to clear a five-barred gate, and fire a gun without winking, and all other of those masculine accomplishments that my brute cousins run mad after, I wanted, like my rational cousin, to read Greek and Latin within doors, and make my complete approach to the tree of knowledge, which you men-scholars would engross to yourselves, in revenge, I suppose, for our common mother's share in the great original transgression."

"And Rashleigh indulged your propensity to learning?"

"Why, he wished to have me for his scholar, and he could but teach me that which he knew himself—he was not likely to instruct me in the mysteries of washing lace-ruffles, or hemming cambric handkerchiefs, I suppose."

"I admit the temptation of getting such a scholar, and have no doubt that it made a weighty consideration on the tutor's part."

"Oh, if you begin to investigate Rashleigh's motives, my finger touches my chin once more. I can only be frank where my own are inquired into. But to resume—he has resigned the library in my favour, and never enters without leave had and obtained; and so I have taken the liberty to make it the place of deposit for some of my own goods and chattels, as you may see by looking round you."

"I beg pardon, Miss Vernon, but I really see nothing around these walls which I can distinguish as likely to claim you as mistress."

"That is, I suppose, because you neither see a shepherd or shepherdess wrought in worsted, and handsomely framed in black ebony, or a stuffed parrot,—or a breeding-cage, full of canary birds,—or a housewife-case, broidered with tarnished silver, —or a toilet-table with a nest of japanned boxes, with as many angles as Christmas minced-pies,—or a broken-backed spinet,—or a lute with three strings,—or rock-work,—or shell-work,—or needle-work, or work of any kind,—or a lap-dog with a litter of blind puppies—None of these treasures do I possess," she continued, after a pause, in order to recover the breath she had lost in enumerating them—"But there stands the sword of my ancestor Sir Richard Vernon, slain at Shrewsbury, and sorely slandered by a sad fellow called Will Shakspeare, whose Lancastrian partialities, and a certain knack at embodying them, has turned history upside down, or rather inside out;—and by that redoubted weapon hangs the mail of the still older Vernon, squire to the Black Prince, whose fate is the reverse of his descendant's, since he is more indebted to the bard who took the trouble to celebrate him, for good-will than for talents,—

> Amiddes the route you may discern one
> Brave knight, with pipes on shield, ycleped Vernon
> Like a borne fiend along the plain he thundered,
> Prest to be carving throtes, while others plundered.

"Then there is a model of a new martingale, which I invented myself—a great improvement on the Duke of Newcastle's; and there are the hood and bells of my falcon Cheviot, who spitted himself on a heron's bill at Horsely-moss—poor Cheviot, there is not a bird on the perches below, but are kites and riflers compared to him; and there is my own light fowling-piece, with an improved firelock; with twenty other treasures, each more valuable than another—And there, that speaks for itself."

She pointed to the carved oak frame of a full-length portrait by Vandyke, on which were inscribed, in Gothic letters, the words *Vernon semper viret*. I looked at her for explanation. "Do you not know," said she, with some surprise, "our motto—the Vernon motto, where,

> Like the solemn vice iniquity,
> We moralise two meanings in one word

And do you not know our cognisance, the pipes?" pointing to the armorial bearings sculptured on the oaken scutcheon, around which the legend was displayed.

"Pipes!—they look more like penny-whistles—But, pray, do not be angry with my ignorance," I continued, observing the colour mount to her cheeks, "I can mean no affront to your armorial bearings, for I do not even know my own."

"You an Osbaldistone, and confess so much!" she exclaimed. "Why, Percie,

Thornie, John, Dickon—Wilfred himself, might be your instructor. Even ignorance itself is a plummet over you."

"With shame I confess it, my dear Miss Vernon, the mysteries couched under the grim hieroglyphics of heraldry are to me as unintelligible as those of the pyramids of Egypt."

"What! is it possible?—Why, even my uncle reads Gwillym sometimes of a winter night—Not know the figures of heraldry!—of what could your father be thinking?"

"Of the figures of arithmetic," I answered; "the most insignificant unit of which he holds more highly than all the blazonry of chivalry. But, though I am ignorant to this inexpressible degree, I have knowledge and taste enough to admire that splendid picture, in which I think I can discover a family likeness to you. What ease and dignity in the attitude!—what richness of colouring—what breadth and depth of shade!"

"Is it really a fine painting?" she asked.

"I have seen many works of the renowned artist," I replied, "but never beheld one more to my liking!"

"Well, I know as little of pictures as you do of heraldry," replied Miss Vernon; "yet I have the advantage of you, because I have always admired the painting without understanding its value."

"While I have neglected pipes and tabors, and all the whimsical combinations of chivalry, still I am informed that they floated in the fields of ancient fame. But you will allow their exterior appearance is not so peculiarly interesting to the uninformed spectator as that of a fine painting.—Who is the person here represented?"

"My grandfather. He shared the misfortunes of Charles I., and, I am sorry to add, the excesses of his son. Our patrimonial estate was greatly impaired by his prodigality, and was altogether lost by his successor, my unfortunate father. But peace be with them who have got it!—it was lost in the cause of loyalty."

"Your father, I presume, suffered in the political dissensions of the period?"

"He did indeed;—he lost his all. And hence is his child a dependent orphan—eating the bread of others—subjected to their caprices, and compelled to study their inclinations; yet prouder of having had such a father, than if, playing a more prudent but less upright part, he had left me possessor of all the rich and fair baronies which his family once possessed."

As she thus spoke, the entrance of the servants with dinner cut off all conversation but that of a general nature.

When our hasty meal was concluded, and the wine placed on the table, the domestic informed us, "that Mr. Rashleigh had desired to be told when our dinner was removed."

"Tell him," said Miss Vernon, "we shall be happy to see him if he will step this way—place another wineglass and chair, and leave the room.— You must retire with him when he goes away," she continued, addressing herself to me; "even *my* liberality cannot spare a gentleman above eight hours out of the twenty-four; and I think we have been together for at least that length of time."

"The old scythe-man has moved so rapidly," I answered, "that I could not count his strides."

"Hush!" said Miss Vernon, "here comes Rashleigh;" and she drew off her chair, to which I had approached mine rather closely, so as to place a greater distance between us. A modest tap at the door,—a gentle manner of opening when invited to enter,—a studied softness and humility of step and deportment, announced that the education of Rashleigh Osbaldistone at the College of St. Omers accorded well with the ideas I entertained of the manners of an accomplished Jesuit. I need not add, that, as a sound Protestant, these ideas were not the most favourable. "Why should you use the ceremony of knocking," said Miss Vernon, "when you knew that I was not alone?"

This was spoken with a burst of impatience, as if she had felt that Rashleigh's air of caution and reserve covered some insinuation of impertinent suspicion. "You have taught me the form of knocking at this door so perfectly, my fair cousin," answered Rashleigh, without change of voice or manner, "that habit has become a second nature."

"I prize sincerity more than courtesy, sir, and you know I do," was Miss Vernon's reply.

"Courtesy is a gallant gay, a courtier by name and by profession," replied Rashleigh, "and therefore most fit for a lady's bower."

"But Sincerity is the true knight," retorted Miss Vernon, "and therefore much more welcome, cousin. But to end a debate not over amusing to your stranger kinsman, sit down, Rashleigh, and give Mr. Francis Osbaldistone your countenance to his glass of wine. I have done the honours of the dinner, for the credit of Osbaldistone Hall."

Rashleigh sate down, and filled his glass, glancing his eye from Diana to me, with an embarrassment which his utmost efforts could not entirely disguise. I thought he appeared to be uncertain concerning the extent of confidence she might have reposed in me, and hastened to lead the conversation into a channel which should sweep away his suspicion that Diana might have betrayed any secrets which rested between them. "Miss Vernon," I said, "Mr. Rashleigh, has recommended me to return my thanks to you for my speedy disengagement from the ridiculous accusation of Morris; and, unjustly fearing my gratitude might not be warm enough to remind me of this duty, she has put my curiosity on its side, by referring me to you for an account, or rather explanation, of the events of the day."

"Indeed?" answered Rashleigh; "I should have thought" (looking keenly at Miss Vernon) "that the lady herself might have stood interpreter;" and his eye, reverting from her face, sought mine, as if to search, from the expression of my features, whether Diana's communication had been as narrowly limited as my words had intimated. Miss Vernon retorted his inquisitorial glance with one of decided scorn; while I, uncertain whether to deprecate or resent his obvious suspicion, replied, "If it is your pleasure, Mr. Rashleigh, as it has been Miss Vernon's, to leave me in ignorance, I must necessarily submit; but, pray, do not withhold your information from me on the ground of imagining that I have already obtained any on the subject. For I tell you, as a man of honour, I am as ignorant as that picture of anything relating to the events I have witnessed to-day, excepting that I understand from Miss Vernon, that you have been kindly active in my favour."

"Miss Vernon has overrated my humble efforts," said Rashleigh, "though I claim full credit for my zeal. The truth is, that as I galloped back to get some one of our family to join me in becoming your bail, which was the most obvious, or, indeed, I may say, the only way of serving you which occurred to my stupidity, I met the man Cawmil—Colville—Campbell, or whatsoever they call him. I had understood from Morris that he was present when the robbery took place, and had the good fortune to prevail on him (with some difficulty, I confess) to tender his evidence in your exculpation—which I presume was the means of your being released from an unpleasant situation."

"Indeed?—I am much your debtor for procuring such a seasonable evidence in my behalf. But I cannot see why (having been, as he said, a fellow-sufferer with Morris) it should have required much trouble to persuade him to step forth and bear evidence, whether to convict the actual robber, or free an innocent person."

"You do not know the genius of that man's country, sir," answered Rashleigh;— "discretion, prudence, and foresight, are their leading qualities; these are only modified by a narrow-spirited, but yet ardent patriotism, which forms as it were the outmost of the concentric bulwarks with which a Scotchman fortifies himself against all the attacks of a generous philanthropical principle. Surmount this mound, you find an inner and still dearer barrier—the love of his province, his village, or, most probably, his clan; storm this second obstacle, you have a third—his attachment to his own family—his father, mother, sons, daughters, uncles, aunts, and cousins, to the ninth generation. It is within these limits that a Scotchman's social affection expands itself, never reaching those which are outermost, till all means of discharging itself in the interior circles have been exhausted. It is within these circles that his heart throbs, each pulsation being fainter and fainter, till, beyond the widest boundary, it is almost unfelt. And what is worst of all, could you surmount all these concentric outworks, you have an inner citadel, deeper, higher, and more efficient than them all—a Scotchman's love for himself."

"All this is extremely eloquent and metaphorical, Rashleigh," said Miss Vernon, who listened with unrepressed impatience; "there are only two objections to it: first, it is *not* true; secondly, if true, it is nothing to the purpose."

"It *is* true, my fairest Diana," returned Rashleigh; "and moreover, it is most instantly to the purpose. It is true, because you cannot deny that I know the country and people intimately, and the character is drawn from deep and accurate consideration—and it is to the purpose, because it answers Mr. Francis Osbaldistone's question, and shows why this same wary Scotchman, considering our kinsman to be neither his countryman, nor a Campbell, nor his cousin in any of the inextricable combinations by which they extend their pedigree; and, above all, seeing no prospect of personal advantage, but, on the contrary, much hazard of loss of time and delay of business"—

"With other inconveniences, perhaps, of a nature yet more formidable," interrupted Miss Vernon.

"Of which, doubtless, there might be many," said Rashleigh, continuing in the same tone—"In short, my theory shows why this man, hoping for no advantage, and afraid of some inconvenience, might require a degree of persuasion ere he could be prevailed on to give his testimony in favour of Mr. Osbaldistone."

"It seems surprising to me," I observed, "that during the glance I cast over the declaration, or whatever it is termed, of Mr. Morris, he should never have mentioned that Campbell was in his company when he met the marauders."

"I understood from Campbell, that he had taken his solemn promise not to mention that circumstance," replied Rashleigh: "his reason for exacting such an engagement you may guess from what I have hinted—he wished to get back to his own country, undelayed and unembarrassed by any of the judicial inquiries which he would have been under the necessity of attending, had the fact of his being present at the robbery taken air while he was on this side of the Border. But let him once be as distant as the Forth, Morris will, I warrant you, come forth with all he knows about him, and, it may be, a good deal more. Besides, Campbell is a very extensive dealer in cattle, and has often occasion to send great droves into Northumberland; and, when driving such a trade, he would be a great fool to embroil himself with our Northumbrian thieves, than whom no men who live are more vindictive."

"I dare be sworn of that," said Miss Vernon, with a tone which implied something more than a simple acquiescence in the proposition.

"Still," said I, resuming the subject, "allowing the force of the reasons which Campbell might have for desiring that Morris should be silent with regard to his promise when the robbery was committed, I cannot yet see how he could attain such an influence over the man, as to make him suppress his evidence in that particular, at the manifest risk of subjecting his story to discredit."

Rashleigh agreed with me, that it was very extraordinary, and seemed to regret that he had not questioned the Scotchman more closely on that subject, which he allowed looked extremely mysterious. "But," he asked, immediately after this acquiescence, "are you very sure the circumstance of Morris's being accompanied by Campbell is really not alluded to in his examination?"

"I read the paper over hastily," said I; "but it is my strong impression that no such circumstance is mentioned;—at least, it must have been touched on very slightly, since it failed to catch my attention."

"True, true," answered Rashleigh, forming his own inference while he adopted my words; "I incline to think with you, that the circumstance must in reality have been mentioned, but so slightly that it failed to attract your attention. And then, as to Campbell's interest with Morris, I incline to suppose that it must have been gained by playing upon his fears. This chicken-hearted fellow, Morris, is bound, I understand, for Scotland, destined for some little employment under Government; and, possessing the courage of the wrathful dove, or most magnanimous mouse, he may have been afraid to encounter the ill-will of such a kill-cow as Campbell, whose very appearance would be enough to fright him out of his little wits. You observed that Mr. Campbell has at times a keen and animated manner—something of a martial cast in his tone and bearing."

"I own," I replied, "that his expression struck me as being occasionally fierce and sinister, and little adapted to his peaceable professions. Has he served in the army?"

"Yes—no—not, strictly speaking, *served;* but he has been, I believe, like most of his countrymen, trained to arms. Indeed, among the hills, they carry them from boyhood to the grave. So, if you know anything of your fellow-traveller, you will easily judge, that, going to such a country, he will take cue to avoid a quarrel, if he can help it, with any of the natives. But, come, I see you decline your wine—and I too am a degenerate Osbaldistone, so far as respects the circulation of the bottle. If you will go to my room, I will hold you a hand at piquet."

We rose to take leave of Miss Vernon, who had from time to time suppressed, apparently with difficulty, a strong temptation to break in upon Rashleigh's details. As we were about to leave the room, the smothered fire broke forth.

"Mr. Osbaldistone," she said, "your own observation will enable you to verify the justice, or injustice, of Rashleigh's suggestions concerning such individuals as Mr. Campbell and Mr. Morris. But, in slandering Scotland, he has borne false witness against a whole country; and I request you will allow no weight to his evidence."

"Perhaps," I answered, "I may find it somewhat difficult to obey your injunction, Miss Vernon; for I must own I was bred up with no very favourable idea of our northern neighbours."

"Distrust that part of your education, sir," she replied, "and let the daughter of a Scotchwoman pray you to respect the land which gave her parent birth, until your own observation has proved them to be unworthy of your good opinion. Preserve your hatred and contempt for dissimulation, baseness, and falsehood, wheresoever they are to be met with. You will find enough of all without leaving England.—Adieu, gentlemen, I wish you good evening."

And she signed to the door, with the manner of a princess dismissing her train.

We retired to Rashleigh's apartment, where a servant brought us coffee and cards. I had formed my resolution to press Rashleigh no farther on the events of the day. A mystery, and, as I thought, not of a favourable complexion, appeared to hang over his conduct; but to ascertain if my suspicions were just, it was necessary to throw him off his guard. We cut for the deal, and were soon earnestly engaged in our play. I thought I perceived in this trifling for amusement (for the stake which Rashleigh proposed was a mere trifle) something of a fierce and ambitious temper. He seemed perfectly to understand the beautiful game at which he played, but preferred, as it were on principle, the risking bold and precarious strokes to the ordinary rules of play; and neglecting the minor and better-balanced chances of the game, he hazarded everything for the chance of piqueing, repiqueing, or capoting his adversary. So soon as the intervention of a game or two at piquet, like the music between the acts of a drama, had completely interrupted our previous course of conversation, Rashleigh appeared to tire of the game, and the cards were superseded by discourse, in which he assumed the lead.

More learned than soundly wise—better acquainted with men's minds than with the moral principles that ought to regulate them, he had still powers of conversation which I have rarely seen equalled, never excelled. Of this his manner implied some consciousness; at least, it appeared to me that he had studied hard to improve his natural advantages of a melodious voice, fluent and happy expression, apt language, and fervid imagination. He was never loud, never overbearing, never so much occupied with his own thoughts as to outrun either the patience or the comprehension of those he conversed with. His ideas succeeded each other with the gentle but unintermitting flow of a plentiful and bounteous spring; while I have heard those of others, who aimed at distinction in conversation, rush along like the turbid gush from the sluice of a mill-pond, as hurried, and as easily exhausted. It was late at night ere I could part from a companion so fascinating; and, when I gained my own apartment, it cost me no small effort to recall to my mind the character of Rashleigh, such as I had pictured him previous to this *tete-a-tete.*

So effectual, my dear Tresham, does the sense of being pleased and amused blunt our faculties of perception and discrimination of character, that I can only compare it to the taste of certain fruits, at once luscious and poignant, which renders our palate totally unfit for relishing or distinguishing the viands which are subsequently subjected to its criticism.

CHAPTER ELEVENTH

> What gars ye gaunt, my merrymen a'?
> What gars ye look sae dreary?
> What gars ye hing your head sae sair
> In the castle of Balwearie?
>
> — OLD SCOTCH BALLAD.

The next morning chanced to be Sunday, a day peculiarly hard to be got rid of at Osbaldistone Hall; for after the formal religious service of the morning had been performed, at which all the family regularly attended, it was hard to say upon which individual, Rashleigh and Miss Vernon excepted, the fiend of ennui descended with the most abundant outpouring of his spirit. To speak of my yesterday's embarrassment amused Sir Hildebrand for several minutes, and he congratulated me on my deliverance from Morpeth or Hexham jail, as he would have done if I had fallen in attempting to clear a five-barred gate, and got up without hurting myself.

"Hast had a lucky turn, lad; but do na be over venturous again. What, man! the king's road is free to all men, be they Whigs, be they Tories."

"On my word, sir, I am innocent of interrupting it; and it is the most provoking thing on earth, that every person will take it for granted that I am accessory to a crime which I despise and detest, and which would, moreover, deservedly forfeit my life to the laws of my country."

"Well, well, lad; even so be it; I ask no questions—no man bound to tell on himself —that's fair play, or the devil's in't."

Rashleigh here came to my assistance; but I could not help thinking that his arguments were calculated rather as hints to his father to put on a show of acquiescence in my declaration of innocence, than fully to establish it.

"In your own house, my dear sir—and your own nephew—you will not surely persist in hurting his feelings by seeming to discredit what he is so strongly interested in affirming. No doubt, you are fully deserving of all his confidence, and I am sure, were there anything you could do to assist him in this strange affair, he would have recourse to your goodness. But my cousin Frank has been dismissed as an innocent man, and no one is entitled to suppose him otherwise. For my part, I have not the least doubt of his innocence; and our family honour, I conceive, requires that we should maintain it with tongue and sword against the whole country."

"Rashleigh," said his father, looking fixedly at him, "thou art a sly loon—thou hast ever been too cunning for me, and too cunning for most folks. Have a care thou provena too cunning for thysell—two faces under one hood is no true heraldry. And since we talk of heraldry, I'll go and read Gwillym."

This resolution he intimated with a yawn, resistless as that of the Goddess in the Dunciad, which was responsively echoed by his giant sons, as they dispersed in quest of the pastimes to which their minds severally inclined them—Percie to discuss a pot of March beer with the steward in the buttery,—Thorncliff to cut a pair of cudgels, and fix them in their wicker hilts,—John to dress May-flies,—Dickon to play at pitch and toss by himself, his right hand against his left,—and Wilfred to bite his thumbs and hum himself into a slumber which should last till dinner-time, if possible. Miss Vernon had retired to the library.

Rashleigh and I were left alone in the old hall, from which the servants, with their usual bustle and awkwardness, had at length contrived to hurry the remains of our substantial breakfast. I took the opportunity to upbraid him with the manner in which he had spoken of my affair to his father, which I frankly stated was highly offensive to me, as it seemed rather to exhort Sir Hildebrand to conceal his suspicions, than to root them out.

"Why, what can I do, my dear friend?" replied Rashleigh "my father's disposition is so tenacious of suspicions of all kinds, when once they take root (which, to do him justice, does not easily happen), that I have always found it the best way to silence him upon such subjects, instead of arguing with him. Thus I get the better of the weeds which I cannot eradicate, by cutting them over as often as they appear, until at length they die away of themselves. There is neither wisdom nor profit in disputing with such a mind as Sir Hildebrand's, which hardens itself against conviction, and believes in its own inspirations as firmly as we good Catholics do in those of the Holy Father of Rome."

"It is very hard, though, that I should live in the house of a man, and he a near relation too, who will persist in believing me guilty of a highway robbery."

"My father's foolish opinion, if one may give that epithet to any opinion of a father's, does not affect your real innocence; and as to the disgrace of the fact, depend on it, that, considered in all its bearings, political as well as moral, Sir Hildebrand regards it as a meritorious action—a weakening of the enemy—a spoiling of the Amalekites; and you will stand the higher in his regard for your supposed accession to it."

"I desire no man's regard, Mr. Rashleigh, on such terms as must sink me in my own; and I think these injurious suspicions will afford a very good reason for quitting Osbaldistone Hall, which I shall do whenever I can communicate on the subject with my father."

The dark countenance of Rashleigh, though little accustomed to betray its master's feelings, exhibited a suppressed smile, which he instantly chastened by a sigh. "You are a happy man, Frank—you go and come, as the wind bloweth where it listeth. With your address, taste, and talents, you will soon find circles where they will be more valued, than amid the dull inmates of this mansion; while I—" he paused.

"And what is there in your lot that can make you or any one envy mine,—an outcast, as I may almost term myself, from my father's house and favour?"

"Ay, but," answered Rashleigh, "consider the gratified sense of independence which you must have attained by a very temporary sacrifice,—for such I am sure yours will prove to be; consider the power of acting as a free agent, of cultivating your own talents in the way to which your taste determines you, and in which you are well qualified to distinguish yourself. Fame and freedom are cheaply purchased by a few weeks' residence in the North, even though your place of exile be Osbaldistone Hall. A second Ovid in Thrace, you have not his reasons for writing Tristia."

"I do not know," said I, blushing as became a young scribbler, "how you should be so well acquainted with my truant studies."

"There was an emissary of your father's here some time since, a young coxcomb, one Twineall, who informed me concerning your secret sacrifices to the muses, and added, that some of your verses had been greatly admired by the best judges."

Tresham, I believe you are guiltless of having ever essayed to build the lofty rhyme; but you must have known in your day many an apprentice and fellow-craft, if not some of the master-masons, in the temple of Apollo. Vanity is their universal foible, from him who decorated the shades of Twickenham, to the veriest scribbler whom he has lashed in his Dunciad. I had my own share of this common failing, and without considering how little likely this young fellow Twineall was, by taste and habits, either to be acquainted with one or two little pieces of poetry, which I had at times insinuated into Button's coffee-house, or to report the opinion of the critics who frequented that resort of wit and literature, I almost instantly gorged the bait; which Rashleigh perceiving, improved his opportunity by a diffident, yet apparently very anxious request to be permitted to see some of my manuscript productions.

"You shall give me an evening in my own apartment," he continued; "for I must soon lose the charms of literary society for the drudgery of commerce, and the coarse every-day avocations of the world. I repeat it, that my compliance with my father's wishes for the advantage of my family, is indeed a sacrifice, especially considering the calm and peaceful profession to which my education destined me."

I was vain, but not a fool, and this hypocrisy was too strong for me to swallow. "You would not persuade me," I replied, "that you really regret to exchange the situation of an obscure Catholic priest, with all its privations, for wealth and society, and the pleasures of the world?"

Rashleigh saw that he had coloured his affectation of moderation too highly, and, after a second's pause, during which, I suppose, he calculated the degree of candour which it was necessary to use with me (that being a quality of which he was never needlessly profuse), he answered, with a smile—"At my age, to be condemned, as you say, to wealth and the world, does not, indeed, sound so alarming as perhaps it ought to do. But, with pardon be it spoken, you have mistaken my destination—a Catholic priest, if you will, but not an obscure one. No, sir,—Rashleigh Osbaldistone will be more obscure, should he rise to be the richest citizen in London, than he might have been as a member of a church, whose ministers, as some one says, 'set their sandall'd feet on princes.' My family interest at a certain exiled court is high, and the weight which that court ought to possess, and does possess, at Rome is yet higher—my talents not altogether inferior to the education I have received. In sober judgment, I might have looked forward to high eminence in the church—in the dream of fancy, to the very highest. Why might not"—(he added, laughing, for it was part of his manner to keep much of his discourse apparently betwixt jest and earnest)—"why might not Cardinal Osbaldistone have swayed the fortunes of empires, well-born and well-connected, as well as the low-born Mazarin, or Alberoni, the son of an Italian gardener?"

"Nay, I can give you no reason to the contrary; but in your place I should not much regret losing the chance of such precarious and invidious elevation."

"Neither would I," he replied, "were I sure that my present establishment was more certain; but that must depend upon circumstances which I can only learn by experience—the disposition of your father, for example."

"Confess the truth without finesse, Rashleigh; you would willingly know something of him from me?"

"Since, like Die Vernon, you make a point of following the banner of the good knight Sincerity, I reply—certainly."

"Well, then, you will find in my father a man who has followed the paths of thriving more for the exercise they afforded to his talents, than for the love of the gold with which they are strewed. His active mind would have been happy in any situation which gave it scope for exertion, though that exertion had been its sole reward. But his wealth has accumulated, because, moderate and frugal in his habits, no new sources of expense have occurred to dispose of his increasing income. He is a man who hates dissimulation in others; never practises it himself; and is peculiarly alert in discovering motives through the colouring of language. Himself silent by habit, he is readily disgusted by great talkers; the rather, that the circumstances by which he is most interested, afford no great scope for conversation. He is severely strict in the duties of religion; but you have no reason to fear his interference with yours, for he regards toleration as a sacred principle of political economy. But if you have any Jacobitical partialities, as is naturally to be supposed, you will do well to suppress them in his presence, as well as the least tendency to the highflying or Tory principles; for he holds both in utter detestation. For the rest, his word is his own bond, and must be the law of all who act under him. He will fail in his duty to no one, and will permit no one to fail towards him; to cultivate his favour, you must execute his commands, instead of echoing his sentiments. His greatest failings arise out of prejudices connected with his own profession, or rather his exclusive devotion to it, which makes him see little worthy of praise or attention, unless it be in some measure connected with commerce."

"O rare-painted portrait!" exclaimed Rashleigh, when I was silent—"Vandyke was a dauber to you, Frank. I see thy sire before me in all his strength and weakness; loving and honouring the King as a sort of lord mayor of the empire, or chief of the board of trade—venerating the Commons, for the acts regulating the export trade—and respecting the Peers, because the Lord Chancellor sits on a woolsack."

"Mine was a likeness, Rashleigh; yours is a caricature. But in return for the *carte du pays* which I have unfolded to you, give me some lights on the geography of the unknown lands"—

"On which you are wrecked," said Rashleigh. "It is not worth while; it is no Isle of Calypso, umbrageous with shade and intricate with silvan labyrinth—but a bare ragged Northumbrian moor, with as little to interest curiosity as to delight the eye; you may descry it in all its nakedness in half an hour's survey, as well as if I were to lay it down before you by line and compass."

"O, but something there is, worthy a more attentive survey—What say you to

Miss Vernon? Does not she form an interesting object in the landscape, were all round as rude as Iceland's coast?"

I could plainly perceive that Rashleigh disliked the topic now presented to him; but my frank communication had given me the advantageous title to make inquiries in my turn. Rashleigh felt this, and found himself obliged to follow my lead, however difficult he might find it to play his cards successfully. "I have known less of Miss Vernon," he said, "for some time, than I was wont to do formerly. In early age I was her tutor; but as she advanced towards womanhood, my various avocations,—the gravity of the profession to which I was destined,—the peculiar nature of her engagements,—our mutual situation, in short, rendered a close and constant intimacy dangerous and improper. I believe Miss Vernon might consider my reserve as unkindness, but it was my duty; I felt as much as she seemed to do, when compelled to give way to prudence. But where was the safety in cultivating an intimacy with a beautiful and susceptible girl, whose heart, you are aware, must be given either to the cloister or to a betrothed husband?"

"The cloister or a betrothed husband?" I echoed—"Is that the alternative destined for Miss Vernon?"

"It is indeed," said Rashleigh, with a sigh. "I need not, I suppose, caution you against the danger of cultivating too closely the friendship of Miss Vernon;—you are a man of the world, and know how far you can indulge yourself in her society with safety to yourself, and justice to her. But I warn you, that, considering her ardent temper, you must let your experience keep guard over her as well as yourself, for the specimen of yesterday may serve to show her extreme thoughtlessness and neglect of decorum."

There was something, I was sensible, of truth, as well as good sense, in all this; it seemed to be given as a friendly warning, and I had no right to take it amiss; yet I felt I could with pleasure have run Rashleigh Osbaldistone through the body all the time he was speaking.

"The deuce take his insolence!" was my internal meditation. "Would he wish me to infer that Miss Vernon had fallen in love with that hatchet-face of his, and become degraded so low as to require his shyness to cure her of an imprudent passion? I will have his meaning from him," was my resolution, "if I should drag it out with cart-ropes."

For this purpose, I placed my temper under as accurate a guard as I could, and observed, "That, for a lady of her good sense and acquired accomplishments, it was to be regretted that Miss Vernon's manners were rather blunt and rustic."

"Frank and unreserved, at least, to the extreme," replied Rashleigh: "yet, trust me, she has an excellent heart. To tell you the truth, should she continue her extreme aversion to the cloister, and to her destined husband, and should my own labours in the mine of Plutus promise to secure me a decent independence, I shall think of reviewing our acquaintance and sharing it with Miss Vernon."

"With all his fine voice, and well-turned periods," thought I, "this same Rashleigh Osbaldistone is the ugliest and most conceited coxcomb I ever met with!"

"But," continued Rashleigh, as if thinking aloud, "I should not like to supplant Thorncliff."

"Supplant Thorncliff!—Is your brother Thorncliff," I inquired, with great surprise, "the destined husband of Diana Vernon?"

"Why, ay, her father's commands, and a certain family-contract, destined her to marry one of Sir Hildebrand's sons. A dispensation has been obtained from Rome to Diana Vernon to marry *Blank* Osbaldistone, Esq., son of Sir Hildebrand Osbaldistone, of Osbaldistone Hall, Bart., and so forth; and it only remains to pitch upon the happy man whose name shall fill the gap in the manuscript. Now, as Percie is seldom sober, my father pitched on Thorncliff, as the second prop of the family, and therefore most proper to carry on the line of the Osbaldistones."

"The young lady," said I, forcing myself to assume an air of pleasantry, which, I believe, became me extremely ill, "would perhaps have been inclined to look a little lower on the family-tree, for the branch to which she was desirous of clinging."

"I cannot say," he replied. "There is room for little choice in our family; Dick is a gambler, John a boor, and Wilfred an ass. I believe my father really made the best selection for poor Die, after all."

"The present company," said I, "being always excepted."

"Oh, my destination to the church placed me out of the question; otherwise I will not affect to say, that, qualified by my education both to instruct and guide Miss Vernon, I might not have been a more creditable choice than any of my elders."

"And so thought the young lady, doubtless?"

"You are not to suppose so," answered Rashleigh, with an affectation of denial which was contrived to convey the strongest affirmation the case admitted of: "friendship—only friendship—formed the tie betwixt us, and the tender affection of an opening mind to its only instructor—Love came not near us—I told you I was wise in time."

I felt little inclination to pursue this conversation any farther, and shaking myself clear of Rashleigh, withdrew to my own apartment, which I recollect I traversed with much vehemence of agitation, repeating aloud the expressions which had most offended me.—"Susceptible—ardent—tender affection—Love—Diana Vernon, the most beautiful creature I ever beheld, in love with him, the bandy-legged, bull-necked, limping scoundrel! Richard the Third in all but his hump-back!—And yet the opportunities he must have had during his cursed course of lectures; and the fellow's flowing and easy strain of sentiment; and her extreme seclusion from every one who spoke and acted with common sense; ay, and her obvious pique at him, mixed with admiration of his talents, which looked as like the result of neglected attachment as anything else—Well, and what is it to me, that I should storm and rage at it? Is Diana Vernon the first pretty girl that has loved and married an ugly fellow? And if she were free of every Osbaldistone of them, what concern is it of mine?—a Catholic—a Jacobite—a termagant into the boot—for me to look that way were utter madness."

By throwing such reflections on the flame of my displeasure, I subdued it into a sort of smouldering heart-burning, and appeared at the dinner-table in as sulky a humour as could well be imagined.

CHAPTER TWELFTH

>Drunk?—and speak parrot?—and squabble?—swagger?—
>Swear?—and discourse fustian with one's own shadow?
>
>— OTHELLO

I have already told you, my dear Tresham, what probably was no news to you, that my principal fault was an unconquerable pitch of pride, which exposed me to frequent mortification. I had not even whispered to myself that I loved Diana Vernon; yet no sooner did I hear Rashleigh talk of her as a prize which he might stoop to carry off, or neglect, at his pleasure, than every step which the poor girl had taken, in the innocence and openness of her heart, to form a sort of friendship with me, seemed in my eyes the most insulting coquetry.—"Soh! she would secure me as a *pis aller,* I suppose, in case Mr. Rashleigh Osbaldistone should not take compassion upon her! But I will satisfy her that I am not a person to be trepanned in that manner—I will make her sensible that I see through her arts, and that I scorn them."

I did not reflect for a moment, that all this indignation, which I had no right whatever to entertain, proved that I was anything but indifferent to Miss Vernon's charms; and I sate down to table in high ill-humour with her and all the daughters of Eve.

Miss Vernon heard me, with surprise, return ungracious answers to one or two playful strokes of satire which she threw out with her usual freedom of speech; but, having no suspicion that offence was meant, she only replied to my rude repartees with jests somewhat similar, but polished by her good temper, though pointed by her wit. At length she perceived I was really out of humour, and answered one of my rude speeches thus:—

"They say, Mr. Frank, that one may gather sense from fools—I heard cousin Wilfred refuse to play any longer at cudgels the other day with cousin Thornie, because cousin Thornie got angry, and struck harder than the rules of amicable combat, it seems, permitted. 'Were I to break your head in good earnest,' quoth honest Wilfred, 'I care not how angry you are, for I should do it so much the more easily but it's hard I should get raps over the costard, and only pay you back in makebelieves'—Do you understand the moral of this, Frank?"

"I have never felt myself under the necessity, madam, of studying how to extract the slender portion of sense with which this family season their conversation."

"Necessity! and madam!—You surprise me, Mr. Osbaldistone."

"I am unfortunate in doing so."

"Am I to suppose that this capricious tone is serious? or is it only assumed, to make your good-humour more valuable?"

"You have a right to the attention of so many gentlemen in this family, Miss Vernon, that it cannot be worth your while to inquire into the cause of my stupidity and bad spirits."

"What!" she said, "am I to understand, then, that you have deserted my faction, and gone over to the enemy?"

Then, looking across the table, and observing that Rashleigh, who was seated opposite, was watching us with a singular expression of interest on his harsh features, she continued—

"Horrible thought!—Ay, now I see 'tis true,
For the grim-visaged Rashleigh smiles on me,
And points at thee for his!—

Well, thank Heaven, and the unprotected state which has taught me endurance, I do not take offence easily; and that I may not be forced to quarrel, whether I like it or no, I have the honour, earlier than usual, to wish you a happy digestion of your dinner and your bad humour."

And she left the table accordingly.

Upon Miss Vernon's departure, I found myself very little satisfied with my own conduct. I had hurled back offered kindness, of which circumstances had but lately pointed out the honest sincerity, and I had but just stopped short of insulting the beautiful, and, as she had said with some emphasis, the unprotected being by whom it was proffered. My conduct seemed brutal in my own eyes. To combat or drown these painful reflections, I applied myself more frequently than usual to the wine which circulated on the table.

The agitated state of my feelings combined with my habits of temperance to give rapid effect to the beverage. Habitual topers, I believe, acquire the power of soaking themselves with a quantity of liquor that does little more than muddy those intellects which in their sober state are none of the clearest; but men who are strangers to the vice of drunkenness as a habit, are more powerfully acted upon by intoxicating liquors. My spirits, once aroused, became extravagant; I talked a great deal, argued upon what I knew nothing of, told stories of which I forgot the point, then laughed immoderately at my own forgetfulness; I accepted several bets without having the least judgment; I challenged the giant John to wrestle with me, although he had kept the ring at Hexham for a year, and I never tried so much as a single fall.

My uncle had the goodness to interpose and prevent this consummation of drunken folly, which, I suppose, would have otherwise ended in my neck being broken.

It has even been reported by maligners, that I sung a song while under this vinous influence; but, as I remember nothing of it, and never attempted to turn a tune in all my life before or since, I would willingly hope there is no actual foundation for the calumny. I was absurd enough without this exaggeration. Without positively losing my senses, I speedily lost all command of my temper, and my impetuous passions whirled me onward at their pleasure. I had sate down sulky and discontented, and disposed to be silent—the wine rendered me loquacious, disputatious, and quarrelsome. I contradicted whatever was asserted, and attacked, without any respect to my uncle's table, both his politics and his religion. The affected moderation of Rashleigh, which he well knew how to qualify with irritating ingredients, was even more provoking to me than the noisy and bullying language of his obstreperous brothers. My uncle, to do him justice, endeavoured to bring us to order; but his authority was lost amidst the tumult of wine and passion. At length, frantic at some real or supposed injurious insinuation, I actually struck Rashleigh with my fist. No Stoic philosopher, superior to his own passion and that of others, could have received an insult with a higher degree of scorn. What he himself did not think it apparently worth while to resent, Thorncliff resented for him. Swords were drawn, and we exchanged one or two passes, when the other brothers separated us by main force; and I shall never forget the diabolical sneer which writhed Rashleigh's wayward features, as I was forced from the apartment by the main strength of two of these youthful Titans. They secured me in my apartment by locking the door, and I heard them, to my inexpressible rage, laugh heartily as they descended the stairs. I essayed in my fury to break out; but the window-grates, and the strength of a door clenched with iron, resisted my efforts. At length I threw myself on my bed, and fell asleep amidst vows of dire revenge to be taken in the ensuing day.

But with the morning cool repentance came. I felt, in the keenest manner, the violence and absurdity of my conduct, and was obliged to confess that wine and passion had lowered my intellects even below those of Wilfred Osbaldistone, whom I held in so much contempt. My uncomfortable reflections were by no means soothed by meditating the necessity of an apology for my improper behaviour, and recollecting that Miss Vernon must be a witness of my submission. The impropriety and unkindness of my conduct to her personally, added not a little to these galling considerations, and for this I could not even plead the miserable excuse of intoxication.

Under all these aggravating feelings of shame and degradation, I descended to the breakfast hall, like a criminal to receive sentence. It chanced that a hard frost had rendered it impossible to take out the hounds, so that I had the additional mortification to meet the family, excepting only Rashleigh and Miss Vernon, in full divan, surrounding the cold venison pasty and chine of beef. They were in high glee as I entered, and I could easily imagine that the jests were furnished at my expense. In fact, what I was disposed to consider with serious pain, was regarded as an excellent good joke by my uncle, and the greater part of my cousins. Sir Hildebrand, while he rallied me on the exploits of the preceding evening, swore he thought a young fellow had better be thrice drunk in one day, than sneak sober to bed like a Presbyterian, and leave a batch of honest fellows, and a double quart of claret. And to back this consolatory speech, he poured out a large bumper of brandy, exhorting me to swallow "a hair of the dog that had bit me."

"Never mind these lads laughing, nevoy," he continued; "they would have been all as great milksops as yourself, had I not nursed them, as one may say, on the toast and tankard."

Ill-nature was not the fault of my cousins in general; they saw I was vexed and hurt at the recollections of the preceding evening, and endeavoured, with clumsy kindness, to remove the painful impression they had made on me. Thorncliff alone looked sullen and unreconciled. This young man had never liked me from the beginning; and in the marks of attention occasionally shown me by his brothers, awkward as they were, he alone had never joined. If it was true, of which, however, I began to have my doubts, that he was considered by the family, or regarded himself, as the destined husband of Miss Vernon, a sentiment of jealousy might have sprung up in his mind from the marked predilection which it was that young lady's pleasure to show for one whom Thorncliff might, perhaps, think likely to become a dangerous rival.

Rashleigh at last entered, his visage as dark as mourning weed—brooding, I could not but doubt, over the unjustifiable and disgraceful insult I had offered to him. I had already settled in my own mind how I was to behave on the occasion, and had schooled myself to believe, that true honour consisted not in defending, but in apologising for, an injury so much disproportioned to any provocation I might have to allege.

I therefore hastened to meet Rashleigh, and to express myself in the highest degree sorry for the violence with which I had acted on the preceding evening. "No circumstances," I said, "could have wrung from me a single word of apology, save my own consciousness of the impropriety of my behaviour. I hoped my cousin would accept of my regrets so sincerely offered, and consider how much of my misconduct was owing to the excessive hospitality of Osbaldistone Hall."

"He shall be friends with thee, lad," cried the honest knight, in the full effusion of his heart; "or d—n me, if I call him son more!—Why, Rashie, dost stand there like a log? *Sorry for it* is all a gentleman can say, if he happens to do anything awry, especially over his claret. I served in Hounslow, and should know something, I think, of affairs of honour. Let me hear no more of this, and we'll go in a body and rummage out the badger in Birkenwood-bank."

Rashleigh's face resembled, as I have already noticed, no other countenance that I ever saw. But this singularity lay not only in the features, but in the mode of changing their expression. Other countenances, in altering from grief to joy, or from anger to satisfaction, pass through some brief interval, ere the expression of the predominant passion supersedes entirely that of its predecessor. There is a sort of twilight, like that between the clearing up of the darkness and the rising of the sun, while the swollen muscles subside, the dark eye clears, the forehead relaxes and expands itself, and the whole countenance loses its sterner shades, and becomes serene and placid. Rashleigh's face exhibited none of these gradations, but changed almost instantaneously from the expression of one passion to that of the contrary. I can compare it to nothing but the sudden shifting of a scene in the theatre, where, at the whistle of the prompter, a cavern disappears, and a grove arises.

My attention was strongly arrested by this peculiarity on the present occasion. At Rashleigh's first entrance, "black he stood as night!" With the same inflexible countenance he heard my excuse and his father's exhortation; and it was not until Sir Hildebrand had done speaking, that the cloud cleared away at once, and he expressed, in the kindest and most civil terms, his perfect satisfaction with the very handsome apology I had offered.

"Indeed," he said, "I have so poor a brain myself, when I impose on it the least burden beyond my usual three glasses, that I have only, like honest Cassio, a very vague recollection of the confusion of last night—remember a mass of things, but nothing distinctly—a quarrel, but nothing wherefore—So, my dear Cousin," he continued, shaking me kindly by the hand, "conceive how much I am relieved by finding that I have to receive an apology, instead of having to make one—I will not have a word said upon the subject more; I should be very foolish to institute any scrutiny into an account, when the balance, which I expected to be against me, has been so unexpectedly and agreeably struck in my favour. You see, Mr. Osbaldistone, I am practising the language of Lombard Street, and qualifying myself for my new calling."

As I was about to answer, and raised my eyes for the purpose, they encountered those of Miss Vernon, who, having entered the room unobserved during the conversation, had given it her close attention. Abashed and confounded, I fixed my eyes on the ground, and made my escape to the breakfast-table, where I herded among my busy cousins.

My uncle, that the events of the preceding day might not pass out of our memory without a practical moral lesson, took occasion to give Rashleigh and me his serious advice to correct our milksop habits, as he termed them, and gradually to inure our brains to bear a gentlemanlike quantity of liquor, without brawls or breaking of heads. He recommended that we should begin piddling with a regular quart of claret per day, which, with the aid of March beer and brandy, made a handsome competence for a beginner in the art of toping. And for our encouragement, he assured us that he had known many a man who had lived to our years without having drunk a pint of wine at a sitting, who yet, by falling into honest company, and following hearty example, had afterwards been numbered among the best good fellows of the time, and could carry off their six bottles under their belt quietly and comfortably, without brawling or babbling, and be neither sick nor sorry the next morning.

Sage as this advice was, and comfortable as was the prospect it held out to me, I profited but little by the exhortation—partly, perhaps, because, as often as I raised my eyes from the table, I observed Miss Vernon's looks fixed on me, in which I thought I could read grave compassion blended with regret and displeasure. I began to consider how I should seek a scene of explanation and apology with her also, when she gave me to understand she was determined to save me the trouble of soliciting an interview. "Cousin Francis," she said, addressing me by the same title she used to give to the other Osbaldistones, although I had, properly speaking, no title to be called her kinsman, "I have encountered this morning a difficult passage in the Divina Comme'dia of Dante; will you have the goodness to step to the library and give me your assistance? and when you have unearthed for me the meaning of the obscure Florentine, we will join the rest at Birkenwood-bank, and see their luck at unearthing the badger."

I signified, of course, my readiness to wait upon her. Rashleigh made an offer to accompany us. "I am something better skilled," he said, "at tracking the sense of Dante through the metaphors and elisions of his wild and gloomy poem, than at hunting the poor inoffensive hermit yonder out of his cave."

"Pardon me, Rashleigh," said Miss Vernon, "but as you are to occupy Mr. Francis's place in the counting-house, you must surrender to him the charge of your pupil's education at Osbaldistone Hall. We shall call you in, however, if there is any occasion; so pray do not look so grave upon it. Besides, it is a shame to you not to understand field-sports—What will you do should our uncle in Crane-Alley ask you the signs by which you track a badger?"

"Ay, true, Die,—true," said Sir Hildebrand, with a sigh, "I misdoubt Rashleigh will be found short at the leap when he is put to the trial. An he would ha' learned useful knowledge like his brothers, he was bred up where it grew, I wuss; but French antics, and book-learning, with the new turnips, and the rats, and the Hanoverians, ha' changed the world that I ha' known in Old England—But come along with us, Rashie, and carry my hunting-staff, man; thy cousin lacks none of thy company as now, and I wonna ha' Die crossed—It's ne'er be said there was but one woman in Osbaldistone Hall, and she died for lack of her will."

Rashleigh followed his father, as he commanded, not, however, ere he had whispered to Diana, "I suppose I must in discretion bring the courtier, Ceremony, in my company, and knock when I approach the door of the library?"

"No, no, Rashleigh," said Miss Vernon; "dismiss from your company the false archimage Dissimulation, and it will better ensure your free access to our classical consultations."

So saying, she led the way to the library, and I followed—like a criminal, I was going to say, to execution; but, as I bethink me, I have used the simile once, if not twice before. Without any simile at all, then, I followed, with a sense of awkward and conscious embarrassment, which I would have given a great deal to shake off. I thought it a degrading and unworthy feeling to attend one on such an occasion, having breathed the air of the Continent long enough to have imbibed the notion that lightness, gallantry, and something approaching to well-bred self-assurance, should distinguish the gentleman whom a fair lady selects for her companion in a *tete-a-tete*.

My English feelings, however, were too many for my French education, and I made, I believe, a very pitiful figure, when Miss Vernon, seating herself majestically in a huge elbow-chair in the library, like a judge about to hear a cause of importance, signed to me to take a chair opposite to her (which I did, much like the poor fellow who is going to be tried), and entered upon conversation in a tone of bitter irony.

CHAPTER THIRTEENTH

> Dire was his thought, who first in poison steeped
> The weapon formed for slaughter—direr his,
> And worthier of damnation, who instilled
> The mortal venom in the social cup,
> To fill the veins with death instead of life.
>
> — ANONYMOUS

"Upon my Word, Mr. Francis Osbaldistone," said Miss Vernon, with the air of one who thought herself fully entitled to assume the privilege of ironical reproach, which she was pleased to exert, "your character improves upon us, sir—I could not have thought that it was in you. Yesterday might be considered as your assay-piece, to prove yourself entitled to be free of the corporation of Osbaldistone Hall. But it was a masterpiece."

"I am quite sensible of my ill-breeding, Miss Vernon, and I can only say for myself that I had received some communications by which my spirits were unusually agitated. I am conscious I was impertinent and absurd."

"You do yourself great injustice," said the merciless monitor—"you have contrived, by what I saw and have since heard, to exhibit in the course of one evening a happy display of all the various masterly qualifications which distinguish your several cousins;—the gentle and generous temper of the benevolent Rashleigh,—the temperance of Percie,—the cool courage of Thorncliff,—John's skill in dog-breaking, —Dickon's aptitude to betting,—all exhibited by the single individual, Mr. Francis, and that with a selection of time, place, and circumstance, worthy the taste and sagacity of the sapient Wilfred."

"Have a little mercy, Miss Vernon," said I; for I confess I thought the schooling as severe as the case merited, especially considering from what quarter it came, "and forgive me if I suggest, as an excuse for follies I am not usually guilty of, the custom of this house and country. I am far from approving of it; but we have Shakspeare's authority for saying, that good wine is a good familiar creature, and that any man living may be overtaken at some time."

"Ay, Mr. Francis, but he places the panegyric and the apology in the mouth of the greatest villain his pencil has drawn. I will not, however, abuse the advantage your quotation has given me, by overwhelming you with the refutation with which the victim Cassio replies to the tempter Iago. I only wish you to know, that there is one person at least sorry to see a youth of talents and expectations sink into the slough in which the inhabitants of this house are nightly wallowing."

"I have but wet my shoe, I assure you, Miss Vernon, and am too sensible of the filth of the puddle to step farther in."

"If such be your resolution," she replied, "it is a wise one. But I was so much vexed at what I heard, that your concerns have pressed before my own,—You behaved to me yesterday, during dinner, as if something had been told you which lessened or lowered me in your opinion—I beg leave to ask you what it was?"

I was stupified. The direct bluntness of the demand was much in the style one gentleman uses to another, when requesting explanation of any part of his conduct in a good-humoured yet determined manner, and was totally devoid of the circumlocutions, shadings, softenings, and periphrasis, which usually accompany explanations betwixt persons of different sexes in the higher orders of society.

I remained completely embarrassed; for it pressed on my recollection, that Rashleigh's communications, supposing them to be correct, ought to have rendered Miss Vernon rather an object of my compassion than of my pettish resentment; and had they furnished the best apology possible for my own conduct, still I must have had the utmost difficulty in detailing what inferred such necessary and natural offence to Miss Vernon's feelings. She observed my hesitation, and proceeded, in a tone somewhat more peremptory, but still temperate and civil—"I hope Mr. Osbaldistone does not dispute my title to request this explanation. I have no relative who can protect me; it is, therefore, just that I be permitted to protect myself."

I endeavoured with hesitation to throw the blame of my rude behaviour upon indisposition—upon disagreeable letters from London. She suffered me to exhaust my apologies, and fairly to run myself aground, listening all the while with a smile of absolute incredulity.

"And now, Mr. Francis, having gone through your prologue of excuses, with the same bad grace with which all prologues are delivered, please to draw the curtain, and show me that which I desire to see. In a word, let me know what Rashleigh says of me; for he is the grand engineer and first mover of all the machinery of Osbaldistone Hall."

"But, supposing there was anything to tell, Miss Vernon, what does he deserve that betrays the secrets of one ally to another?—Rashleigh, you yourself told me, remained your ally, though no longer your friend."

"I have neither patience for evasion, nor inclination for jesting, on the present subject. Rashleigh cannot—ought not—dare not, hold any language respecting me, Diana Vernon, but what I may demand to hear repeated. That there are subjects of secrecy and confidence between us, is most certain; but to such, his communications to you could have no relation; and with such, I, as an individual, have no concern."

I had by this time recovered my presence of mind, and hastily determined to avoid making any disclosure of what Rashleigh had told me in a sort of confidence. There was something unworthy in retailing private conversation; it could, I thought, do no good, and must necessarily give Miss Vernon great pain. I therefore replied, gravely, "that nothing but frivolous talk had passed between Mr. Rashleigh Osbaldistone and me on the state of the family at the Hall; and I protested, that nothing had been said which left a serious impression to her disadvantage. As a gentleman," I said, "I could not be more explicit in reporting private conversation."

She started up with the animation of a Camilla about to advance into battle. "This shall not serve your turn, sir,—I must have another answer from you." Her features kindled—her brow became flushed—her eye glanced wild-fire as she proceeded—"I demand such an explanation, as a woman basely slandered has a right to demand from every man who calls himself a gentleman—as a creature, motherless, friendless, alone in the world, left to her own guidance and protection, has a right to require from every being having a happier lot, in the name of that God who sent *them* into the world to enjoy, and *her* to suffer. You shall not deny me—or," she added, looking solemnly upwards, "you will rue your denial, if there is justice for wrong either on earth or in heaven."

I was utterly astonished at her vehemence, but felt, thus conjured, that it became my duty to lay aside scrupulous delicacy, and gave her briefly, but distinctly, the heads of the information which Rashleigh had conveyed to me.

She sate down and resumed her composure, as soon as I entered upon the subject, and when I stopped to seek for the most delicate turn of expression, she repeatedly interrupted me with "Go on—pray, go on; the first word which occurs to you is the plainest, and must be the best. Do not think of my feelings, but speak as you would to an unconcerned third party."

Thus urged and encouraged, I stammered through all the account which Rashleigh had given of her early contract to marry an Osbaldistone, and of the uncertainty and difficulty of her choice; and there I would willingly have paused. But her penetration discovered that there was still something behind, and even guessed to what it related.

"Well, it was ill-natured of Rashleigh to tell this tale on me. I am like the poor girl in the fairy tale, who was betrothed in her cradle to the Black Bear of Norway, but complained chiefly of being called Bruin's bride by her companions at school. But besides all this, Rashleigh said something of himself with relation to me—Did he not?"

"He certainly hinted, that were it not for the idea of supplanting his brother, he would now, in consequence of his change of profession, be desirous that the word Rashleigh should fill up the blank in the dispensation, instead of the word Thorncliff."

"Ay? indeed?" she replied—"was he so very condescending?—Too much honour for his humble handmaid, Diana Vernon—And she, I suppose, was to be enraptured with joy could such a substitute be effected?"

"To confess the truth, he intimated as much, and even farther insinuated"—

"What?—Let me hear it all!" she exclaimed, hastily.

"That he had broken off your mutual intimacy, lest it should have given rise to an affection by which his destination to the church would not permit him to profit."

"I am obliged to him for his consideration," replied Miss Vernon, every feature of her fine countenance taxed to express the most supreme degree of scorn and contempt. She paused a moment, and then said, with her usual composure, "There is but little I have heard from you which I did not expect to hear, and which I ought not to have expected; because, bating one circumstance, it is all very true. But as there are some poisons so active, that a few drops, it is said, will infect a whole fountain, so there is one falsehood in Rashleigh's communication, powerful enough to corrupt the whole well in which Truth herself is said to have dwelt. It is the leading and foul falsehood, that, knowing Rashleigh as I have reason too well to know him, any circumstance on earth could make me think of sharing my lot with him. No," she continued with a sort of inward shuddering that seemed to express involuntary horror, "any lot rather than that—the sot, the gambler, the bully, the jockey, the insensate fool, were a thousand times preferable to Rashleigh:—the convent—the jail—the grave, shall be welcome before them all."

There was a sad and melancholy cadence in her voice, corresponding with the strange and interesting romance of her situation. So young, so beautiful, so untaught, so much abandoned to herself, and deprived of all the support which her sex derives from the countenance and protection of female friends, and even of that degree of defence which arises from the forms with which the sex are approached in civilised life,—it is scarce metaphorical to say, that my heart bled for her. Yet there was an expression of dignity in her contempt of ceremony—of upright feeling in her disdain of falsehood—of firm resolution in the manner in which she contemplated the dangers by which she was surrounded, which blended my pity with the warmest admiration. She seemed a princess deserted by her subjects, and deprived of her power, yet still scorning those formal regulations of society which are created for persons of an inferior rank; and, amid her difficulties, relying boldly and confidently on the justice of Heaven, and the unshaken constancy of her own mind.

I offered to express the mingled feelings of sympathy and admiration with which her unfortunate situation and her high spirit combined to impress me, but she imposed silence on me at once.

"I told you in jest," she said, "that I disliked compliments—I now tell you in earnest, that I do not ask sympathy, and that I despise consolation. What I have borne, I have borne—What I am to bear I will sustain as I may; no word of commiseration can make a burden feel one feather's weight lighter to the slave who must carry it. There is only one human being who could have assisted me, and that is he who has rather chosen to add to my embarrassment—Rashleigh Osbaldistone.—Yes! the time once was that I might have learned to love that man—But, great God! the purpose for which he insinuated himself into the confidence of one already so forlorn—the undeviating and continued assiduity with which he pursued that purpose from year to year, without one single momentary pause of remorse or compassion—the purpose for which he would have converted into poison the food he administered to my mind —Gracious Providence! what should I have been in this world, and the next, in body and soul, had I fallen under the arts of this accomplished villain!"

I was so much struck with the scene of perfidious treachery which these words disclosed, that I rose from my chair hardly knowing what I did, laid my hand on the hilt of my sword, and was about to leave the apartment in search of him on whom I might discharge my just indignation. Almost breathless, and with eyes and looks in which scorn and indignation had given way to the most lively alarm, Miss Vernon threw herself between me and the door of the apartment.

"Stay!" she said—"stay!—however just your resentment, you do not know half the secrets of this fearful prison-house." She then glanced her eyes anxiously round the room, and sunk her voice almost to a whisper—"He bears a charmed life; you cannot assail him without endangering other lives, and wider destruction. Had it been otherwise, in some hour of justice he had hardly been safe, even from this weak hand. I told you," she said, motioning me back to my seat, "that I needed no comforter. I now tell you I need no avenger."

I resumed my seat mechanically, musing on what she said, and recollecting also, what had escaped me in my first glow of resentment, that I had no title whatever to constitute myself Miss Vernon's champion. She paused to let her own emotions and mine subside, and then addressed me with more composure.

"I have already said that there is a mystery connected with Rashleigh, of a dangerous and fatal nature. Villain as he is, and as he knows he stands convicted in my eyes, I cannot—dare not, openly break with or defy him. You also, Mr. Osbaldistone, must bear with him with patience, foil his artifices by opposing to them prudence, not violence; and, above all, you must avoid such scenes as that of last night, which cannot but give him perilous advantages over you. This caution I designed to give you, and it was the object with which I desired this interview; but I have extended my confidence farther than I proposed."

I assured her it was not misplaced.

"I do not believe that it is," she replied. "You have that in your face and manners which authorises trust. Let us continue to be friends. You need not fear," she said, laughing, while she blushed a little, yet speaking with a free and unembarrassed voice, "that friendship with us should prove only a specious name, as the poet says, for another feeling. I belong, in habits of thinking and acting, rather to your sex, with which I have always been brought up, than to my own. Besides, the fatal veil was wrapt round me in my cradle; for you may easily believe I have never thought of the detestable condition under which I may remove it. The time," she added, "for expressing my final determination is not arrived, and I would fain have the freedom of wild heath and open air with the other commoners of nature, as long as I can be permitted to enjoy them. And now that the passage in Dante is made so clear, pray go and see what has become of the badger-baiters. My head aches so much that I cannot join the party."

I left the library, but not to join the hunters. I felt that a solitary walk was necessary to compose my spirits before I again trusted myself in Rashleigh's company, whose depth of calculating villany had been so strikingly exposed to me. In Dubourg's family (as he was of the reformed persuasion) I had heard many a tale of Romish priests who gratified, at the expense of friendship, hospitality, and the most sacred ties of social life, those passions, the blameless indulgence of which is denied by the rules of their order. But the deliberate system of undertaking the education of a deserted orphan of noble birth, and so intimately allied to his own family, with the perfidious purpose of ultimately seducing her, detailed as it was by the intended victim with all the glow of virtuous resentment, seemed more atrocious to me than the worst of the tales I had heard at Bourdeaux, and I felt it would be extremely difficult for me to meet Rashleigh, and yet to suppress the abhorrence with which he impressed me. Yet this was absolutely necessary, not only on account of the mysterious charge which Diana had given me, but because I had, in reality, no ostensible ground for quarrelling with him.

I therefore resolved, as far as possible, to meet Rashleigh's dissimulation with equal caution on my part during our residence in the same family; and when he should depart for London, I resolved to give Owen at least such a hint of his character as might keep him on his guard over my father's interests. Avarice or ambition, I thought, might have as great, or greater charms, for a mind constituted like Rashleigh's, than unlawful pleasure; the energy of his character, and his power of assuming all seeming good qualities, were likely to procure him a high degree of confidence, and it was not to be hoped that either good faith or gratitude would prevent him from abusing it. The task was somewhat difficult, especially in my circumstances, since the caution which I threw out might be imputed to jealousy of my rival, or rather my successor, in my father's favour. Yet I thought it absolutely necessary to frame such a letter, leaving it to Owen, who, in his own line, was wary, prudent, and circumspect, to make the necessary use of his knowledge of Rashleigh's true character. Such a letter, therefore, I indited, and despatched to the post-house by the first opportunity.

At my meeting with Rashleigh, he, as well as I, appeared to have taken up distant ground, and to be disposed to avoid all pretext for collision. He was probably conscious that Miss Vernon's communications had been unfavourable to him, though he could not know that they extended to discovering his meditated villany towards her. Our intercourse, therefore, was reserved on both sides, and turned on subjects of little interest. Indeed, his stay at Osbaldistone Hall did not exceed a few days after this period, during which I only remarked two circumstances respecting him. The first was the rapid and almost intuitive manner in which his powerful and active mind seized upon and arranged the elementary principles necessary to his new profession, which he now studied hard, and occasionally made parade of his progress, as if to show me how light it was for him to lift the burden which I had flung down from very weariness and inability to carry it. The other remarkable circumstance was, that, notwithstanding the injuries with which Miss Vernon charged Rashleigh, they had several private interviews together of considerable length, although their bearing towards each other in public did not seem more cordial than usual.

When the day of Rashleigh's departure arrived, his father bade him farewell with indifference; his brothers with the ill-concealed glee of school-boys who see their task-master depart for a season, and feel a joy which they dare not express; and I myself with cold politeness. When he approached Miss Vernon, and would have saluted her she drew back with a look of haughty disdain; but said, as she extended her hand to him, "Farewell, Rashleigh; God reward you for the good you have done, and forgive you for the evil you have meditated."

"Amen, my fair cousin," he replied, with an air of sanctity, which belonged, I thought, to the seminary of Saint Omers; "happy is he whose good intentions have borne fruit in deeds, and whose evil thoughts have perished in the blossom."

These were his parting words. "Accomplished hypocrite!" said Miss Vernon to me, as the door closed behind him—"how nearly can what we most despise and hate, approach in outward manner to that which we most venerate!"

I had written to my father by Rashleigh, and also a few lines to Owen, besides the confidential letter which I have already mentioned, and which I thought it more proper and prudent to despatch by another conveyance. In these epistles, it would have been natural for me to have pointed out to my father and my friend, that I was at present in a situation where I could improve myself in no respect, unless in the mysteries of hunting and hawking; and where I was not unlikely to forget, in the company of rude grooms and horse-boys, any useful knowledge or elegant accomplishments which I had hitherto acquired. It would also have been natural that I should have expressed the disgust and tedium which I was likely to feel among beings whose whole souls were centred in field-sports or more degrading pastimes—that I should have complained of the habitual intemperance of the family in which I was a guest, and the difficulty and almost resentment with which my uncle, Sir Hildebrand, received any apology for deserting the bottle. This last, indeed, was a topic on which my father, himself a man of severe temperance, was likely to be easily alarmed, and to have touched upon this spring would to a certainty have opened the doors of my prison-house, and would either have been the means of abridging my exile, or at least would have procured me a change of residence during my rustication.

I say, my dear Tresham, that, considering how very unpleasant a prolonged residence at Osbaldistone Hall must have been to a young man of my age, and with my habits, it might have seemed very natural that I should have pointed out all these disadvantages to my father, in order to obtain his consent for leaving my uncle's mansion. Nothing, however, is more certain, than that I did not say a single word to this purpose in my letters to my father and Owen. If Osbaldistone Hall had been Athens in all its pristine glory of learning, and inhabited by sages, heroes, and poets, I could not have expressed less inclination to leave it.

If thou hast any of the salt of youth left in thee, Tresham, thou wilt be at no loss to account for my silence on a topic seemingly so obvious. Miss Vernon's extreme beauty, of which she herself seemed so little conscious—her romantic and mysterious situation—the evils to which she was exposed—the courage with which she seemed to face them—her manners, more frank than belonged to her sex, yet, as it seemed to me, exceeding in frankness only from the dauntless consciousness of her innocence,—above all, the obvious and flattering distinction which she made in my favour over all other persons, were at once calculated to interest my best feelings, to excite my curiosity, awaken my imagination, and gratify my vanity. I dared not, indeed, confess to myself the depth of the interest with which Miss Vernon inspired me, or the large share which she occupied in my thoughts. We read together, walked together, rode together, and sate together. The studies which she had broken off upon her quarrel with Rashleigh, she now resumed, under the auspices of a tutor whose views were more sincere, though his capacity was far more limited.

In truth, I was by no means qualified to assist her in the prosecution of several profound studies which she had commenced with Rashleigh, and which appeared to me more fitted for a churchman than for a beautiful female. Neither can I conceive with what view he should have engaged Diana in the gloomy maze of casuistry which schoolmen called philosophy, or in the equally abstruse though more certain sciences of mathematics and astronomy; unless it were to break down and confound in her mind the difference and distinction between the sexes, and to habituate her to trains of subtle reasoning, by which he might at his own time invest that which is wrong with the colour of that which is right. It was in the same spirit, though in the latter case the evil purpose was more obvious, that the lessons of Rashleigh had encouraged Miss Vernon in setting at nought and despising the forms and ceremonial limits which are drawn round females in modern society. It is true, she was sequestrated from all female company, and could not learn the usual rules of decorum, either from example or precept; yet such was her innate modesty, and accurate sense of what was right and wrong, that she would not of herself have adopted the bold uncompromising manner which struck me with so much surprise on our first acquaintance, had she not been led to conceive that a contempt of ceremony indicated at once superiority of understanding and the confidence of conscious innocence. Her wily instructor had, no doubt, his own views in levelling those outworks which reserve and caution erect around virtue. But for these, and for his other crimes, he has long since answered at a higher tribunal.

Besides the progress which Miss Vernon, whose powerful mind readily adopted every means of information offered to it, had made in more abstract science, I found her no contemptible linguist, and well acquainted both with ancient and modern literature. Were it not that strong talents will often go farthest when they seem to have least assistance, it would be almost incredible to tell the rapidity of Miss Vernon's progress in knowledge; and it was still more extraordinary, when her stock of mental acquisitions from books was compared with her total ignorance of actual life. It seemed as if she saw and knew everything, except what passed in the world around her;—and I believe it was this very ignorance and simplicity of thinking upon ordinary subjects, so strikingly contrasted with her fund of general knowledge and information, which rendered her conversation so irresistibly fascinating, and rivetted the attention to whatever she said or did; since it was absolutely impossible to anticipate whether her next word or action was to display the most acute perception, or the most profound simplicity. The degree of danger which necessarily attended a youth of my age and keen feelings from remaining in close and constant intimacy with an object so amiable, and so peculiarly interesting, all who remember their own sentiments at my age may easily estimate.

CHAPTER FOURTEENTH

> Yon lamp its line of quivering light
> Shoots from my lady's bower;
> But why should Beauty's lamp be bright
> At midnight's lonely hour?
>
> — OLD BALLAD.

The mode of life at Osbaldistone Hall was too uniform to admit of description. Diana Vernon and I enjoyed much of our time in our mutual studies; the rest of the family killed theirs in such sports and pastimes as suited the seasons, in which we also took a share. My uncle was a man of habits, and by habit became so much accustomed to my presence and mode of life, that, upon the whole, he was rather fond of me than otherwise. I might probably have risen yet higher in his good graces, had I employed the same arts for that purpose which were used by Rashleigh, who, availing himself of his father's disinclination to business, had gradually insinuated himself into the management of his property. But although I readily gave my uncle the advantage of my pen and my arithmetic so often as he desired to correspond with a neighbour, or settle with a tenant, and was, in so far, a more useful inmate in his family than any of his sons, yet I was not willing to oblige Sir Hildebrand by relieving him entirely from the management of his own affairs; so that, while the good knight admitted that nevoy Frank was a steady, handy lad, he seldom failed to remark in the same breath, that he did not think he should ha' missed Rashleigh so much as he was like to do.

As it is particularly unpleasant to reside in a family where we are at variance with any part of it, I made some efforts to overcome the ill-will which my cousins entertained against me. I exchanged my laced hat for a jockey-cap, and made some progress in their opinion; I broke a young colt in a manner which carried me further into their good graces. A bet or two opportunely lost to Dickon, and an extra health pledged with Percie, placed me on an easy and familiar footing with all the young squires, except Thorncliff.

I have already noticed the dislike entertained against me by this young fellow, who, as he had rather more sense, had also a much worse temper, than any of his brethren. Sullen, dogged, and quarrelsome, he regarded my residence at Osbaldistone Hall as an intrusion, and viewed with envious and jealous eyes my intimacy with Diana Vernon, whom the effect proposed to be given to a certain family-compact assigned to him as an intended spouse. That he loved her, could scarcely be said, at least without much misapplication of the word; but he regarded her as something appropriated to himself, and resented internally the interference which he knew not how to prevent or interrupt. I attempted a tone of conciliation towards Thorncliff on several occasions; but he rejected my advances with a manner about as gracious as that of a growling mastiff, when the animal shuns and resents a stranger's attempts to caress him. I therefore abandoned him to his ill-humour, and gave myself no further trouble about the matter.

Such was the footing upon which I stood with the family at Osbaldistone Hall; but I ought to mention another of its inmates with whom I occasionally held some discourse. This was Andrew Fairservice, the gardener who (since he had discovered that I was a Protestant) rarely suffered me to pass him without proffering his Scotch mull for a social pinch. There were several advantages attending this courtesy. In the first place, it was made at no expense, for I never took snuff; and secondly, it afforded an excellent apology to Andrew (who was not particularly fond of hard labour) for laying aside his spade for several minutes. But, above all, these brief interviews gave Andrew an opportunity of venting the news he had collected, or the satirical remarks which his shrewd northern humour suggested.

"I am saying, sir," he said to me one evening, with a face obviously charged with intelligence, "I hae been down at the Trinlay-knowe."

"Well, Andrew, and I suppose you heard some news at the alehouse?"

"Na, sir; I never gang to the yillhouse—that is unless ony neighbour was to gie me a pint, or the like o' that; but to gang there on ane's ain coat-tail, is a waste o' precious time and hard-won siller.—But I was doun at the Trinlay-knowe, as I was saying, about a wee bit business o' my ain wi' Mattie Simpson, that wants a forpit or twa o' peers that will never be missed in the Ha'-house—and when we were at the thrangest o' our bargain, wha suld come in but Pate Macready the travelling merchant?"

"Pedlar, I suppose you mean?"

"E'en as your honour likes to ca' him; but it's a creditable calling and a gainfu', and has been lang in use wi' our folk. Pate's a far-awa cousin o' mine, and we were blythe to meet wi' ane anither."

"And you went and had a jug of ale together, I suppose, Andrew?—For Heaven's sake, cut short your story."

"Bide a wee—bide a wee; you southrons are aye in sic a hurry, and this is something concerns yourself, an ye wad tak patience to hear't—Yill?—deil a drap o' yill did Pate offer me; but Mattie gae us baith a drap skimmed milk, and ane o' her thick ait jannocks, that was as wat and raw as a divot. O for the bonnie girdle cakes o' the north!—and sae we sat doun and took out our clavers."

"I wish you would take them out just now. Pray, tell me the news, if you have got any worth telling, for I can't stop here all night."

"Than, if ye maun hae't, the folk in Lunnun are a' clean wud about this bit job in the north here."

"Clean wood! what's that?"

"Ou, just real daft—neither to haud nor to bind—a' hirdy-girdy—clean through ither—the deil's ower Jock Wabster."

"But what does all this mean? or what business have I with the devil or Jack Webster?"

"Umph!" said Andrew, looking extremely knowing, "it's just because—just that the dirdum's a' about yon man's pokmanty."

"Whose portmanteau? or what do you mean?"

"Ou, just the man Morris's, that he said he lost yonder: but if it's no your honour's affair, as little is it mine; and I mauna lose this gracious evening."

And, as if suddenly seized with a violent fit of industry, Andrew began to labour most diligently.

My attention, as the crafty knave had foreseen, was now arrested, and unwilling, at the same time, to acknowledge any particular interest in that affair, by asking direct questions, I stood waiting till the spirit of voluntary communication should again prompt him to resume his story. Andrew dug on manfully, and spoke at intervals, but nothing to the purpose of Mr. Macready's news; and I stood and listened, cursing him in my heart, and desirous at the same time to see how long his humour of contradiction would prevail over his desire of speaking upon the subject which was obviously uppermost in his mind.

"Am trenching up the sparry-grass, and am gaun to saw some Misegun beans; they winna want them to their swine's flesh, I'se warrant—muckle gude may it do them. And siclike dung as the grieve has gien me!—it should be wheat-strae, or aiten at the warst o't, and it's pease dirt, as fizzenless as chuckie-stanes. But the huntsman guides a' as he likes about the stable-yard, and he's selled the best o' the litter, I'se warrant. But, howsoever, we mauna lose a turn o' this Saturday at e'en, for the wather's sair broken, and if there's a fair day in seven, Sunday's sure to come and lick it up—Howsomever, I'm no denying that it may settle, if it be Heaven's will, till Monday morning,—and what's the use o' my breaking my back at this rate?—I think, I'll e'en awa' hame, for yon's the curfew, as they ca' their jowing-in bell."

Accordingly, applying both his hands to his spade, he pitched it upright in the trench which he had been digging and, looking at me with the air of superiority of one who knows himself possessed of important information, which he may communicate or refuse at his pleasure, pulled down the sleeves of his shirt, and walked slowly towards his coat, which lay carefully folded up upon a neighbouring garden-seat.

"I must pay the penalty of having interrupted the tiresome rascal," thought I to myself, "and even gratify Mr. Fairservice by taking his communication on his own terms." Then raising my voice, I addressed him,—"And after all, Andrew, what are these London news you had from your kinsman, the travelling merchant?"

"The pedlar, your honour means?" retorted Andrew—"but ca' him what ye wull, they're a great convenience in a country-side that's scant o' borough-towns like this Northumberland—That's no the case, now, in Scotland;—there's the kingdom of Fife, frae Culross to the East Nuik, it's just like a great combined city—sae mony royal boroughs yoked on end to end, like ropes of ingans, with their hie-streets and their booths, nae doubt, and their kraemes, and houses of stane and lime and fore-stairs—Kirkcaldy, the sell o't, is langer than ony town in England."

"I daresay it is all very splendid and very fine—but you were talking of the London news a little while ago, Andrew."

"Ay," replied Andrew; "but I dinna think your honour cared to hear about them—Howsoever" (he continued, grinning a ghastly smile), "Pate Macready does say, that they are sair mistrysted yonder in their Parliament House about this rubbery o' Mr. Morris, or whatever they ca' the chiel."

"In the House of Parliament, Andrew!—how came they to mention it there?"

"Ou, that's just what I said to Pate; if it like your honour, I'll tell you the very words; it's no worth making a lie for the matter—'Pate,' said I, 'what ado had the lords and lairds and gentles at Lunnun wi' the carle and his walise?—When we had a Scotch Parliament, Pate,' says I (and deil rax their thrapples that reft us o't!) 'they sate dousely down and made laws for a haill country and kinrick, and never fashed their beards about things that were competent to the judge ordinar o' the bounds; but I think,' said I, 'that if ae kailwife pou'd aff her neighbour's mutch they wad hae the twasome o' them into the Parliament House o' Lunnun. It's just,' said I, 'amaist as silly as our auld daft laird here and his gomerils o' sons, wi' his huntsmen and his hounds, and his hunting cattle and horns, riding haill days after a bit beast that winna weigh sax punds when they hae catched it.'"

"You argued most admirably, Andrew," said I, willing to encourage him to get into the marrow of his intelligence; "and what said Pate?"

"Ou," he said, "what better could be expected of a wheen pock-pudding English folk?—But as to the robbery, it's like that when they're a' at the thrang o' their Whig and Tory wark, and ca'ing ane anither, like unhanged blackguards—up gets ae lang-tongued chield, and he says, that a' the north of England were rank Jacobites (and, quietly, he wasna far wrang maybe), and that they had levied amaist open war, and a king's messenger had been stoppit and rubbit on the highway, and that the best bluid o' Northumberland had been at the doing o't—and mickle gowd ta'en aff him, and mony valuable papers; and that there was nae redress to be gotten by remeed of law for the first justice o' the peace that the rubbit man gaed to, he had fund the twa loons that did the deed birling and drinking wi' him, wha but they; and the justice took the word o' the tane for the compearance o' the tither; and that they e'en gae him leg-bail, and the honest man that had lost his siller was fain to leave the country for fear that waur had come of it."

"Can this be really true?" said I.

"Pate swears it's as true as that his ellwand is a yard lang—(and so it is, just bating an inch, that it may meet the English measure)—And when the chield had said his warst, there was a terrible cry for names, and out comes he wi' this man Morris's name, and your uncle's, and Squire Inglewood's, and other folk's beside" (looking sly at me)—"And then another dragon o' a chield got up on the other side, and said, wad they accuse the best gentleman in the land on the oath of a broken coward?—for it's like that Morris had been drummed out o' the army for rinning awa in Flanders; and he said, it was like the story had been made up between the minister and him or ever he had left Lunnun; and that, if there was to be a search-warrant granted, he thought the siller wad be fund some gate near to St. James's Palace. Aweel, they trailed up Morris to their bar, as they ca't, to see what he could say to the job; but the folk that were again him, gae him sic an awfu' throughgaun about his rinnin' awa, and about a' the ill he had ever dune or said for a' the forepart o' his life, that Patie says he looked mair like ane dead than living; and they cou'dna get a word o' sense out o' him, for downright fright at their growling and routing. He maun be a saft sap, wi' a head nae better than a fozy frosted turnip—it wad hae ta'en a hantle o' them to scaur Andrew Fairservice out o' his tale."

"And how did it all end, Andrew? did your friend happen to learn?"

"Ou, ay; for as his walk is in this country, Pate put aff his journey for the space of a week or thereby, because it wad be acceptable to his customers to bring down the news. It's just a' gaed aft like moonshine in water. The fallow that began it drew in his horns, and said, that though he believed the man had been rubbit, yet he acknowledged he might hae been mista'en about the particulars. And then the other child got up, and said, he caredna whether Morris was rubbed or no, provided it wasna to become a stain on ony gentleman's honour and reputation, especially in the north of England; for, said he before them, I come frae the north mysell, and I carena a boddle wha kens it. And this is what they ca' explaining—the tane gies up a bit, and the tither gies up a bit, and a' friends again. Aweel, after the Commons' Parliament had tuggit, and rived, and rugged at Morris and his rubbery till they were tired o't, the Lords' Parliament they behoved to hae their spell o't. In puir auld Scotland's Parliament they a' sate thegither, cheek by choul, and than they didna need to hae the same blethers twice ower again. But till't their lordships went wi' as muckle teeth and gude-will, as if the matter had been a' speck and span new. Forbye, there was something said about ane Campbell, that suld hae been concerned in the rubbery, mair or less, and that he suld hae had a warrant frae the Duke of Argyle, as a testimonial o' his character. And this put MacCallum More's beard in a bleize, as gude reason there was; and he gat up wi' an unco bang, and garr'd them a' look about them, and wad ram it even doun their throats, there was never ane o' the Campbells but was as wight, wise, warlike, and worthy trust, as auld Sir John the Graeme. Now, if your honour's sure ye arena a drap's bluid a-kin to a Campbell, as I am nane mysell, sae far as I can count my kin, or hae had it counted to me, I'll gie ye my mind on that matter."

"You may be assured I have no connection whatever with any gentleman of the name."

"Ou, than we may speak it quietly amang oursells. There's baith gude and bad o' the Campbells, like other names, But this MacCallum More has an unco sway and say baith, amang the grit folk at Lunnun even now; for he canna preceesely be said to belang to ony o' the twa sides o' them, sae deil any o' them likes to quarrel wi' him; sae they e'en voted Morris's tale a fause calumnious libel, as they ca't, and if he hadna gien them leg-bail, he was likely to hae ta'en the air on the pillory for leasing-making."

So speaking, honest Andrew collected his dibbles, spades, and hoes, and threw them into a wheel-barrow,—leisurely, however, and allowing me full time to put any further questions which might occur to me before he trundled them off to the tool-house, there to repose during the ensuing day. I thought it best to speak out at once, lest this meddling fellow should suppose there were more weighty reasons for my silence than actually existed.

"I should like to see this countryman of yours, Andrew and to hear his news from himself directly. You have probably heard that I had some trouble from the impertinent folly of this man Morris" (Andrew grinned a most significant grin), "and I should wish to see your cousin the merchant, to ask him the particulars of what he heard in London, if it could be done without much trouble."

"Naething mair easy," Andrew observed; "he had but to hint to his cousin that I wanted a pair or twa o' hose, and he wad be wi' me as fast as he could lay leg to the grund."

"O yes, assure him I shall be a customer; and as the night is, as you say, settled and fair, I shall walk in the garden until he comes; the moon will soon rise over the fells. You may bring him to the little back-gate; and I shall have pleasure, in the meanwhile, in looking on the bushes and evergreens by the bright frosty moonlight."

"Vara right, vara right—that's what I hae aften said; a kail-blade, or a collifiour, glances sae glegly by moonlight, it's like a leddy in her diamonds."

So saying, off went Andrew Fairservice with great glee. He had to walk about two miles, a labour he undertook with the greatest pleasure, in order to secure to his kinsman the sale of some articles of his trade, though it is probable he would not have given him sixpence to treat him to a quart of ale. "The good will of an Englishman would have displayed itself in a manner exactly the reverse of Andrew's," thought I, as I paced along the smooth-cut velvet walks, which, embowered with high, hedges of yew and of holly, intersected the ancient garden of Osbaldistone Hall.

As I turned to retrace my steps, it was natural that I should lift up my eyes to the windows of the old library; which, small in size, but several in number, stretched along the second story of that side of the house which now faced me. Light glanced from their casements. I was not surprised at this, for I knew Miss Vernon often sat there of an evening, though from motives of delicacy I put a strong restraint upon myself, and never sought to join her at a time when I knew, all the rest of the family being engaged for the evening, our interviews must necessarily have been strictly *tete-a'-tete*. In the mornings we usually read together in the same room; but then it often happened that one or other of our cousins entered to seek some parchment duodecimo that could be converted into a fishing-book, despite its gildings and illumination, or to tell us of some "sport toward," or from mere want of knowing where else to dispose of themselves. In short, in the mornings the library was a sort of public room, where man and woman might meet as on neutral ground. In the evening it was very different and bred in a country where much attention is paid, or was at least then paid, to *biense'ance*, I was desirous to think for Miss Vernon concerning those points of propriety where her experience did not afford her the means of thinking for herself. I made her therefore comprehend, as delicately as I could, that when we had evening lessons, the presence of a third party was proper.

Miss Vernon first laughed, then blushed, and was disposed to be displeased; and then, suddenly checking herself, said, "I believe you are very right; and when I feel inclined to be a very busy scholar, I will bribe old Martha with a cup of tea to sit by me and be my screen."

Martha, the old housekeeper, partook of the taste of the family at the Hall. A toast and tankard would have pleased her better than all the tea in China. However, as the use of this beverage was then confined to the higher ranks, Martha felt some vanity in being asked to partake of it; and by dint of a great deal of sugar, many words scarce less sweet, and abundance of toast and butter, she was sometimes prevailed upon to give us her countenance. On other occasions, the servants almost unanimously shunned the library after nightfall, because it was their foolish pleasure to believe that it lay on the haunted side of the house. The more timorous had seen sights and heard sounds there when all the rest of the house was quiet; and even the young squires were far from having any wish to enter these formidable precincts after nightfall without necessity.

That the library had at one time been a favourite resource of Rashleigh—that a private door out of one side of it communicated with the sequestered and remote apartment which he chose for himself, rather increased than disarmed the terrors which the household had for the dreaded library of Osbaldistone Hall. His extensive information as to what passed in the world—his profound knowledge of science of every kind—a few physical experiments which he occasionally showed off, were, in a house of so much ignorance and bigotry, esteemed good reasons for supposing him endowed with powers over the spiritual world. He understood Greek, Latin, and Hebrew; and, therefore, according to the apprehension, and in the phrase of his brother Wilfred, needed not to care "for ghaist or bar-ghaist, devil or dobbie." Yea, the servants persisted that they had heard him hold conversations in the library, when every varsal soul in the family were gone to bed; and that he spent the night in watching for bogles, and the morning in sleeping in his bed, when he should have been heading the hounds like a true Osbaldistone.

All these absurd rumours I had heard in broken hints and imperfect sentences, from which I was left to draw the inference; and, as easily may be supposed, I laughed them to scorn. But the extreme solitude to which this chamber of evil fame was committed every night after curfew time, was an additional reason why I should not intrude on Miss Vernon when she chose to sit there in the evening.

To resume what I was saying,—I was not surprised to see a glimmering of light from the library windows: but I was a little struck when I distinctly perceived the shadows of two persons pass along and intercept the light from the first of the windows, throwing the casement for a moment into shade. "It must be old Martha," thought I, "whom Diana has engaged to be her companion for the evening; or I must have been mistaken, and taken Diana's shadow for a second person. No, by Heaven! it appears on the second window,—two figures distinctly traced; and now it is lost again—it is seen on the third—on the fourth—the darkened forms of two persons distinctly seen in each window as they pass along the room, betwixt the windows and the lights. Whom can Diana have got for a companion?"—The passage of the shadows between the lights and the casements was twice repeated, as if to satisfy me that my observation served me truly; after which the lights were extinguished, and the shades, of course, were seen no more.

Trifling as this circumstance was, it occupied my mind for a considerable time. I did not allow myself to suppose that my friendship for Miss Vernon had any directly selfish view; yet it is incredible the displeasure I felt at the idea of her admitting any one to private interviews, at a time, and in a place, where, for her own sake, I had been at some trouble to show her that it was improper for me to meet with her.

"Silly, romping, incorrigible girl!" said I to myself, "on whom all good advice and delicacy are thrown away! I have been cheated by the simplicity of her manner, which I suppose she can assume just as she could a straw bonnet, were it the fashion, for the mere sake of celebrity. I suppose, notwithstanding the excellence of her understanding, the society of half a dozen of clowns to play at whisk and swabbers would give her more pleasure than if Ariosto himself were to awake from the dead."

This reflection came the more powerfully across my mind, because, having mustered up courage to show to Diana my version of the first books of Ariosto, I had requested her to invite Martha to a tea-party in the library that evening, to which arrangement Miss Vernon had refused her consent, alleging some apology which I thought frivolous at the time. I had not long speculated on this disagreeable subject, when the back garden-door opened, and the figures of Andrew and his country-man —bending under his pack—crossed the moonlight alley, and called my attention elsewhere.

I found Mr. Macready, as I expected, a tough, sagacious, long-headed Scotchman, and a collector of news both from choice and profession. He was able to give me a distinct account of what had passed in the House of Commons and House of Lords on the affair of Morris, which, it appears, had been made by both parties a touchstone to ascertain the temper of the Parliament. It appeared also, that, as I had learned from Andrew, by second hand, the ministry had proved too weak to support a story involving the character of men of rank and importance, and resting upon the credit of a person of such indifferent fame as Morris, who was, moreover, confused and contradictory in his mode of telling the story. Macready was even able to supply me with a copy of a printed journal, or News-Letter, seldom extending beyond the capital, in which the substance of the debate was mentioned; and with a copy of the Duke of Argyle's speech, printed upon a broadside, of which he had purchased several from the hawkers, because, he said, it would be a saleable article on the north of the Tweed. The first was a meagre statement, full of blanks and asterisks, and which added little or nothing to the information I had from the Scotchman; and the Duke's speech, though spirited and eloquent, contained chiefly a panegyric on his country, his family, and his clan, with a few compliments, equally sincere, perhaps, though less glowing, which he took so favourable an opportunity of paying to himself. I could not learn whether my own reputation had been directly implicated, although I perceived that the honour of my uncle's family had been impeached, and that this person Campbell, stated by Morris to have been the most active robber of the two by whom he was assailed, was said by him to have appeared in the behalf of a Mr. Osbaldistone, and by the connivance of the Justice procured his liberation. In this particular, Morris's story jumped with my own suspicions, which had attached to Campbell from the moment I saw him appear at Justice Inglewood's. Vexed upon the whole, as well as perplexed, with this extraordinary story, I dismissed the two Scotchmen, after making some purchases from Macready, and a small compliment to Fairservice, and retired to my own apartment to consider what I ought to do in defence of my character thus publicly attacked.

CHAPTER FIFTEENTH

Whence, and what art you?

— MILTON

After exhausting a sleepless night in meditating on the intelligence I had received, I was at first inclined to think that I ought, as speedily as possible, to return to London, and by my open appearance repel the calumny which had been spread against me. But I hesitated to take this course on recollection of my father's disposition, singularly absolute in his decisions as to all that concerned his family. He was most able, certainly, from experience, to direct what I ought to do, and from his acquaintance with the most distinguished Whigs then in power, had influence enough to obtain a hearing for my cause. So, upon the whole, I judged it most safe to state my whole story in the shape of a narrative, addressed to my father; and as the ordinary opportunities of intercourse between the Hall and the post-town recurred rarely, I determined to ride to the town, which was about ten miles' distance, and deposit my letter in the post-office with my own hands.

Indeed I began to think it strange that though several weeks had elapsed since my departure from home, I had received no letter, either from my father or Owen, although Rashleigh had written to Sir Hildebrand of his safe arrival in London, and of the kind reception he had met with from his uncle. Admitting that I might have been to blame, I did not deserve, in my own opinion at least, to be so totally forgotten by my father; and I thought my present excursion might have the effect of bringing a letter from him to hand more early than it would otherwise have reached me. But before concluding my letter concerning the affair of Morris, I failed not to express my earnest hope and wish that my father would honour me with a few lines, were it but to express his advice and commands in an affair of some difficulty, and where my knowledge of life could not be supposed adequate to my own guidance. I found it impossible to prevail on myself to urge my actual return to London as a place of residence, and I disguised my unwillingness to do so under apparent submission to my father's will, which, as I imposed it on myself as a sufficient reason for not urging my final departure from Osbaldistone Hall, would, I doubted not, be received as such by my parent. But I begged permission to come to London, for a short time at least, to meet and refute the infamous calumnies which had been circulated concerning me in so public a manner. Having made up my packet, in which my earnest desire to vindicate my character was strangely blended with reluctance to quit my present place of residence, I rode over to the post-town, and deposited my letter in the office. By doing so, I obtained possession, somewhat earlier than I should otherwise have done, of the following letter from my friend Mr. Owen:—

"Dear Mr. Francis,

"Yours received per favour of Mr. R. Osbaldistone, and note the contents. Shall do Mr. R. O. such civilities as are in my power, and have taken him to see the Bank and Custom-house. He seems a sober, steady young gentleman, and takes to business; so will be of service to the firm. Could have wished another person had turned his mind that way; but God's will be done. As cash may be scarce in those parts, have to trust you will excuse my enclosing a goldsmith's bill at six days' sight, on Messrs. Hooper and Girder of Newcastle, for L100, which I doubt not will be duly honoured.—I remain, as in duty bound, dear Mr. Frank, your very respectful and obedient servant,

"Joseph Owen.

"*Postscriptum.*—Hope you will advise the above coming safe to hand. Am sorry we have so few of yours. Your father says he is as usual, but looks poorly."

From this epistle, written in old Owen's formal style, I was rather surprised to observe that he made no acknowledgment of that private letter which I had written to him, with a view to possess him of Rashleigh's real character, although, from the course of post, it seemed certain that he ought to have received it. Yet I had sent it by the usual conveyance from the Hall, and had no reason to suspect that it could miscarry upon the road. As it comprised matters of great importance both to my father and to myself, I sat down in the post-office and again wrote to Owen, recapitulating the heads of my former letter, and requesting to know, in course of post, if it had reached him in safety. I also acknowledged the receipt of the bill, and promised to make use of the contents if I should have any occasion for money. I thought, indeed, it was odd that my father should leave the care of supplying my necessities to his clerk; but I concluded it was a matter arranged between them. At any rate, Owen was a bachelor, rich in his way, and passionately attached to me, so that I had no hesitation in being obliged to him for a small sum, which I resolved to consider as a loan, to be returned with my earliest ability, in case it was not previously repaid by my father; and I expressed myself to this purpose to Mr. Owen. A shopkeeper in a little town, to whom the post-master directed me, readily gave me in gold the amount of my bill on Messrs. Hooper and Girder, so that I returned to Osbaldistone Hall a good deal richer than I had set forth. This recruit to my finances was not a matter of indifference to me, as I was necessarily involved in some expenses at Osbaldistone Hall; and I had seen, with some uneasy impatience, that the sum which my travelling expenses had left unexhausted at my arrival there was imperceptibly diminishing. This source of anxiety was for the present removed. On my arrival at the Hall I found that Sir Hildebrand and all his offspring had gone down to the little hamlet, called Trinlay-knowes, "to see," as Andrew Fairservice expressed it, "a wheen midden cocks pike ilk ither's barns out."

"It is indeed a brutal amusement, Andrew; I suppose you have none such in Scotland?"

"Na, na," answered Andrew boldly; then shaded away his negative with, "unless it be on Fastern's-e'en, or the like o' that—But indeed it's no muckle matter what the folk do to the midden pootry, for they had siccan a skarting and scraping in the yard, that there's nae getting a bean or pea keepit for them.—But I am wondering what it is that leaves that turret-door open;—now that Mr. Rashleigh's away, it canna be him, I trow."

The turret-door to which he alluded opened to the garden at the bottom of a winding stair, leading down from Mr. Rashleigh's apartment. This, as I have already mentioned, was situated in a sequestered part of the house, communicating with the library by a private entrance, and by another intricate and dark vaulted passage with the rest of the house. A long narrow turf walk led, between two high holly hedges, from the turret-door to a little postern in the wall of the garden. By means of these communications Rashleigh, whose movements were very independent of those of the rest of his family, could leave the Hall or return to it at pleasure, without his absence or presence attracting any observation. But during his absence the stair and the turret-door were entirely disused, and this made Andrew's observation somewhat remarkable.

"Have you often observed that door open?" was my question.

"No just that often neither; but I hae noticed it ance or twice. I'm thinking it maun hae been the priest, Father Vaughan, as they ca' him. Ye'll no catch ane o' the servants gauging up that stair, puir frightened heathens that they are, for fear of bogles and brownies, and lang-nebbit things frae the neist warld. But Father Vaughan thinks himself a privileged person—set him up and lay him down!—I'se be caution the warst stibbler that ever stickit a sermon out ower the Tweed yonder, wad lay a ghaist twice as fast as him, wi' his holy water and his idolatrous trinkets. I dinna believe he speaks gude Latin neither; at least he disna take me up when I tell him the learned names o' the plants."

Of Father Vaughan, who divided his time and his ghostly care between Osbaldistone Hall and about half a dozen mansions of Catholic gentlemen in the neighbourhood, I have as yet said nothing, for I had seen but little. He was aged about sixty—of a good family, as I was given to understand, in the north—of a striking and imposing presence, grave in his exterior, and much respected among the Catholics of Northumberland as a worthy and upright man. Yet Father Vaughan did not altogether lack those peculiarities which distinguish his order. There hung about him an air of mystery, which, in Protestant eyes, savoured of priestcraft. The natives (such they might be well termed) of Osbaldistone Hall looked up to him with much more fear, or at least more awe, than affection. His condemnation of their revels was evident, from their being discontinued in some measure when the priest was a resident at the Hall. Even Sir Hildebrand himself put some restraint upon his conduct at such times, which, perhaps, rendered Father Vaughan's presence rather irksome than otherwise. He had the well-bred, insinuating, and almost flattering address peculiar to the clergy of his persuasion, especially in England, where the lay Catholic, hemmed in by penal laws, and by the restrictions of his sect and recommendation of his pastor, often exhibits a reserved, and almost a timid manner in the society of Protestants; while the priest, privileged by his order to mingle with persons of all creeds, is open, alert, and liberal in his intercourse with them, desirous of popularity, and usually skilful in the mode of obtaining it.

Father Vaughan was a particular acquaintance of Rashleigh's, otherwise, in all probability, he would scarce have been able to maintain his footing at Osbaldistone Hall. This gave me no desire to cultivate his intimacy, nor did he seem to make any advances towards mine; so our occasional intercourse was confined to the exchange of mere civility. I considered it as extremely probable that Mr. Vaughan might occupy Rashleigh's apartment during his occasional residence at the Hall; and his profession rendered it likely that he should occasionally be a tenant of the library. Nothing was more probable than that it might have been his candle which had excited my attention on a preceding evening. This led me involuntarily to recollect that the intercourse between Miss Vernon and the priest was marked with something like the same mystery which characterised her communications with Rashleigh. I had never heard her mention Vaughan's name, or even allude to him, excepting on the occasion of our first meeting, when she mentioned the old priest and Rashleigh as the only conversable beings, besides herself, in Osbaldistone Hall. Yet although silent with respect to Father Vaughan, his arrival at the Hall never failed to impress Miss Vernon with an anxious and fluttering tremor, which lasted until they had exchanged one or two significant glances.

Whatever the mystery might be which overclouded the destinies of this beautiful and interesting female, it was clear that Father Vaughan was implicated in it; unless, indeed, I could suppose that he was the agent employed to procure her settlement in the cloister, in the event of her rejecting a union with either of my cousins,—an office which would sufficiently account for her obvious emotion at his appearance. As to the rest, they did not seem to converse much together, or even to seek each other's society. Their league, if any subsisted between them, was of a tacit and understood nature, operating on their actions without any necessity of speech. I recollected, however, on reflection, that I had once or twice discovered signs pass betwixt them, which I had at the time supposed to bear reference to some hint concerning Miss Vernon's religious observances, knowing how artfully the Catholic clergy maintain, at all times and seasons, their influence over the minds of their followers. But now I was disposed to assign to these communications a deeper and more mysterious import. Did he hold private meetings with Miss Vernon in the library? was a question which occupied my thoughts; and if so, for what purpose? And why should she have admitted an intimate of the deceitful Rashleigh to such close confidence?

These questions and difficulties pressed on my mind with an interest which was greatly increased by the impossibility of resolving them. I had already begun to suspect that my friendship for Diana Vernon was not altogether so disinterested as in wisdom it ought to have been. I had already felt myself becoming jealous of the contemptible lout Thorncliff, and taking more notice, than in prudence or dignity of feeling I ought to have done, of his silly attempts to provoke me. And now I was scrutinising the conduct of Miss Vernon with the most close and eager observation, which I in vain endeavoured to palm on myself as the offspring of idle curiosity. All these, like Benedick's brushing his hat of a morning, were signs that the sweet youth was in love; and while my judgment still denied that I had been guilty of forming an attachment so imprudent, she resembled those ignorant guides, who, when they have led the traveller and themselves into irretrievable error, persist in obstinately affirming it to be impossible that they can have missed the way.

CHAPTER SIXTEENTH

> It happened one day about noon, going to my boat, I was exceedingly
> surprised with the print of a man's naked foot on the shore, which
> was very plain to be seen on the sand.
>
> — ROBINSON CRUSOE.

With the blended feelings of interest and jealousy which were engendered by Miss Vernon's singular situation, my observations of her looks and actions became acutely sharpened, and that to a degree which, notwithstanding my efforts to conceal it, could not escape her penetration. The sense that she was observed, or, more properly speaking, that she was watched by my looks, seemed to give Diana a mixture of embarrassment, pain, and pettishness. At times it seemed that she sought an opportunity of resenting a conduct which she could not but feel as offensive, considering the frankness with which she had mentioned the difficulties that surrounded her. At other times she seemed prepared to expostulate upon the subject. But either her courage failed, or some other sentiment impeded her seeking an *e'claircissement*. Her displeasure evaporated in repartee, and her expostulations died on her lips. We stood in a singular relation to each other,—spending, and by mutual choice, much of our time in close society with each other, yet disguising our mutual sentiments, and jealous of, or offended by, each other's actions. There was betwixt us intimacy without confidence;—on one side, love without hope or purpose, and curiosity without any rational or justifiable motive; and on the other, embarrassment and doubt, occasionally mingled with displeasure. Yet I believe that this agitation of the passions (such is the nature of the human bosom), as it continued by a thousand irritating and interesting, though petty circumstances, to render Miss Vernon and me the constant objects of each other's thoughts, tended, upon the whole, to increase the attachment with which we were naturally disposed to regard each other. But although my vanity early discovered that my presence at Osbaldistone Hall had given Diana some additional reason for disliking the cloister, I could by no means confide in an affection which seemed completely subordinate to the mysteries of her singular situation. Miss Vernon was of a character far too formed and determined, to permit her love for me to overpower either her sense of duty or of prudence, and she gave me a proof of this in a conversation which we had together about this period.

We were sitting together in the library. Miss Vernon, in turning over a copy of the Orlando Furioso, which belonged to me, shook a piece of writing paper from between the leaves. I hastened to lift it, but she prevented me.—"It is verse," she said, on glancing at the paper; and then unfolding it, but as if to wait my answer before proceeding—"May I take the liberty?—Nay, nay, if you blush and stammer, I must do violence to your modesty, and suppose that permission is granted."

"It is not worthy your perusal—a scrap of a translation—My dear Miss Vernon, it would be too severe a trial, that you, who understand the original so well, should sit in judgment."

"Mine honest friend," replied Diana, "do not, if you will be guided by my advice, bait your hook with too much humility; for, ten to one, it will not catch a single compliment. You know I belong to the unpopular family of Tell-truths, and would not flatter Apollo for his lyre."

She proceeded to read the first stanza, which was nearly to the following purpose:

"Ladies, and knights, and arms, and love's fair flame,
Deeds of emprize and courtesy, I sing;
What time the Moors from sultry Africk came,
Led on by Agramant, their youthful king—
He whom revenge and hasty ire did bring
O'er the broad wave, in France to waste and war;
Such ills from old Trojano's death did spring,
Which to avenge he came from realms afar,
And menaced Christian Charles, the Roman Emperor.
Of dauntless Roland, too, my strain shall sound,
In import never known in prose or rhyme,
How He, the chief, of judgment deemed profound,
For luckless love was crazed upon a time"—

"There is a great deal of it," said she, glancing along the paper, and interrupting the sweetest sounds which mortal ears can drink in,—those of a youthful poet's verses, namely, read by the lips which are dearest to him.

"Much more than ought to engage your attention, Miss Vernon," I replied, something mortified; and I took the verses from her unreluctant hand— "And yet," I continued, "shut up as I am in this retired situation, I have felt sometimes I could not amuse myself better than by carrying on—merely for my own amusement, you will of course understand—the version of this fascinating author, which I began some months since when I was on the banks of the Garonne."

"The question would only be," said Diana, gravely, "whether you could not spend your time to better purpose?"

"You mean in original composition?" said I, greatly flattered—"But, to say truth, my genius rather lies in finding words and rhymes than ideas; and therefore I am happy to use those which Ariosto has prepared to my hand. However, Miss Vernon, with the encouragement you give"—

"Pardon me, Frank—it is encouragement not of my giving, but of your taking. I meant neither original composition nor translation, since I think you might employ your time to far better purpose than in either. You are mortified," she continued, "and I am sorry to be the cause."

"Not mortified,—certainly not mortified," said I, with the best grace I could muster, and it was but indifferently assumed; "I am too much obliged by the interest you take in me."

"Nay, but," resumed the relentless Diana, "there is both mortification and a little grain of anger in that constrained tone of voice; do not be angry if I probe your feelings to the bottom—perhaps what I am about to say will affect them still more."

I felt the childishness of my own conduct, and the superior manliness of Miss Vernon's, and assured her, that she need not fear my wincing under criticism which I knew to be kindly meant.

"That was honestly meant and said," she replied; "I knew full well that the fiend of poetical irritability flew away with the little preluding cough which ushered in the declaration. And now I must be serious—Have you heard from your father lately?"

"Not a word," I replied; "he has not honoured me with a single line during the several months of my residence here."

"That is strange!—you are a singular race, you bold Osbaldistones. Then you are not aware that he has gone to Holland, to arrange some pressing affairs which required his own immediate presence?"

"I never heard a word of it until this moment."

"And farther, it must be news to you, and I presume scarcely the most agreeable, that he has left Rashleigh in the almost uncontrolled management of his affairs until his return."

I started, and could not suppress my surprise and apprehension.

"You have reason for alarm," said Miss Vernon, very gravely; "and were I you, I would endeavour to meet and obviate the dangers which arise from so undesirable an arrangement."

"And how is it possible for me to do so?"

"Everything is possible for him who possesses courage and activity," she said, with a look resembling one of those heroines of the age of chivalry, whose encouragement was wont to give champions double valour at the hour of need; "and to the timid and hesitating, everything is impossible, because it seems so."

"And what would you advise, Miss Vernon?" I replied, wishing, yet dreading, to hear her answer.

She paused a moment, then answered firmly—"That you instantly leave Osbaldistone Hall, and return to London. You have perhaps already," she continued, in a softer tone, "been here too long; that fault was not yours. Every succeeding moment you waste here will be a crime. Yes, a crime: for I tell you plainly, that if Rashleigh long manages your father's affairs, you may consider his ruin as consummated."

"How is this possible?"

"Ask no questions," she said; "but believe me, Rashleigh's views extend far beyond the possession or increase of commercial wealth: he will only make the command of Mr. Osbaldistone's revenues and property the means of putting in motion his own ambitious and extensive schemes. While your father was in Britain this was impossible; during his absence, Rashleigh will possess many opportunities, and he will not neglect to use them."

"But how can I, in disgrace with my father, and divested of all control over his affairs, prevent this danger by my mere presence in London?"

"That presence alone will do much. Your claim to interfere is a part of your birthright, and it is inalienable. You will have the countenance, doubtless, of your father's head-clerk, and confidential friends and partners. Above all, Rashleigh's schemes are of a nature that"—(she stopped abruptly, as if fearful of saying too much)—"are, in short," she resumed, "of the nature of all selfish and unconscientious plans, which are speedily abandoned as soon as those who frame them perceive their arts are discovered and watched. Therefore, in the language of your favourite poet—

To horse! to horse! Urge doubts to those that fear."

A feeling, irresistible in its impulse, induced me to reply—"Ah! Diana, can *you* give me advice to leave Osbaldistone Hall?—then indeed I have already been a resident here too long!"

Miss Vernon coloured, but proceeded with great firmness—"Indeed, I do give you this advice—not only to quit Osbaldistone Hall, but never to return to it more. You have only one friend to regret here," she continued, forcing a smile, "and she has been long accustomed to sacrifice her friendships and her comforts to the welfare of others. In the world you will meet a hundred whose friendship will be as disinterested—more useful—less encumbered by untoward circumstances—less influenced by evil tongues and evil times."

"Never!" I exclaimed, "never!—the world can afford me nothing to repay what I must leave behind me." Here I took her hand, and pressed it to my lips.

"This is folly!" she exclaimed—"this is madness!" and she struggled to withdraw her hand from my grasp, but not so stubbornly as actually to succeed until I had held it for nearly a minute. "Hear me, sir!" she said, "and curb this unmanly burst of passion. I am, by a solemn contract, the bride of Heaven, unless I could prefer being wedded to villany in the person of Rashleigh Osbaldistone, or brutality in that of his brother. I am, therefore, the bride of Heaven,—betrothed to the convent from the cradle. To me, therefore, these raptures are misapplied—they only serve to prove a farther necessity for your departure, and that without delay." At these words she broke suddenly off, and said, but in a suppressed tone of voice, "Leave me instantly—we will meet here again, but it must be for the last time."

My eyes followed the direction of hers as she spoke, and I thought I saw the tapestry shake, which covered the door of the secret passage from Rashleigh's room to the library. I conceived we were observed, and turned an inquiring glance on Miss Vernon.

"It is nothing," said she, faintly; "a rat behind the arras."

"Dead for a ducat," would have been my reply, had I dared to give way to the feelings which rose indignant at the idea of being subjected to an eaves-dropper on such an occasion. Prudence, and the necessity of suppressing my passion, and obeying Diana's reiterated command of "Leave me! leave me!" came in time to prevent my rash action. I left the apartment in a wild whirl and giddiness of mind, which I in vain attempted to compose when I returned to my own.

A chaos of thoughts intruded themselves on me at once, passing hastily through my brain, intercepting and overshadowing each other, and resembling those fogs which in mountainous countries are wont to descend in obscure volumes, and disfigure or obliterate the usual marks by which the traveller steers his course through the wilds. The dark and undefined idea of danger arising to my father from the machinations of such a man as Rashleigh Osbaldistone—the half declaration of love that I had offered to Miss Vernon's acceptance—the acknowledged difficulties of her situation, bound by a previous contract to sacrifice herself to a cloister or to an ill-assorted marriage,—all pressed themselves at once upon my recollection, while my judgment was unable deliberately to consider any of them in their just light and bearings. But chiefly and above all the rest, I was perplexed by the manner in which Miss Vernon had received my tender of affection, and by her manner, which, fluctuating betwixt sympathy and firmness, seemed to intimate that I possessed an interest in her bosom, but not of force sufficient to counterbalance the obstacles to her avowing a mutual affection. The glance of fear, rather than surprise, with which she had watched the motion of the tapestry over the concealed door, implied an apprehension of danger which I could not but suppose well grounded; for Diana Vernon was little subject to the nervous emotions of her sex, and totally unapt to fear without actual and rational cause. Of what nature could those mysteries be, with which she was surrounded as with an enchanter's spell, and which seemed continually to exert an active influence over her thoughts and actions, though their agents were never visible? On this subject of doubt my mind finally rested, as if glad to shake itself free from investigating the propriety or prudence of my own conduct, by transferring the inquiry to what concerned Miss Vernon. I will be resolved, I concluded, ere I leave Osbaldistone Hall, concerning the light in which I must in future regard this fascinating being, over whose life frankness and mystery seem to have divided their reign,—the former inspiring her words and sentiments—the latter spreading in misty influence over all her actions.

Joined to the obvious interests which arose from curiosity and anxious passion, there mingled in my feelings a strong, though unavowed and undefined, infusion of jealousy. This sentiment, which springs up with love as naturally as the tares with the wheat, was excited by the degree of influence which Diana appeared to concede to those unseen beings by whom her actions were limited. The more I reflected upon her character, the more I was internally though unwillingly convinced, that she was formed to set at defiance all control, excepting that which arose from affection; and I felt a strong, bitter, and gnawing suspicion, that such was the foundation of that influence by which she was overawed.

These tormenting doubts strengthened my desire to penetrate into the secret of Miss Vernon's conduct, and in the prosecution of this sage adventure, I formed a resolution, of which, if you are not weary of these details, you will find the result in the next chapter.

CHAPTER SEVENTEENTH

> I hear a voice you cannot hear,
> Which says, I must not stay;
> I see a hand you cannot see,
> Which beckons me awry.
>
> — TICKELL.

I have already told you, Tresham, if you deign to bear it in remembrance, that my evening visits to the library had seldom been made except by appointment, and under the sanction of old Dame Martha's presence. This, however, was entirely a tacit conventional arrangement of my own instituting. Of late, as the embarrassments of our relative situation had increased, Miss Vernon and I had never met in the evening at all. She had therefore no reason to suppose that I was likely to seek a renewal of these interviews, and especially without some previous notice or appointment betwixt us, that Martha might, as usual, be placed upon duty; but, on the other hand, this cautionary provision was a matter of understanding, not of express enactment. The library was open to me, as to the other members of the family, at all hours of the day and night, and I could not be accused of intrusion, however suddenly and unexpectedly I might made my appearance in it. My belief was strong, that in this apartment Miss Vernon occasionally received Vaughan, or some other person, by whose opinion she was accustomed to regulate her conduct, and that at the times when she could do so with least chance of interruption. The lights which gleamed in the library at unusual hours—the passing shadows which I had myself remarked—the footsteps which might be traced in the morning-dew from the turret-door to the postern-gate in the garden—sounds and sights which some of the servants, and Andrew Fairservice in particular, had observed, and accounted for in their own way,—all tended to show that the place was visited by some one different from the ordinary inmates of the hall. Connected as this visitant probably must be with the fates of Diana Vernon, I did not hesitate to form a plan of discovering who or what he was,—how far his influence was likely to produce good or evil consequences to her on whom he acted;—above all, though I endeavoured to persuade myself that this was a mere subordinate consideration, I desired to know by what means this person had acquired or maintained his influence over Diana, and whether he ruled over her by fear or by affection. The proof that this jealous curiosity was uppermost in my mind, arose from my imagination always ascribing Miss Vernon's conduct to the influence of some one individual agent, although, for aught I knew about the matter, her advisers might be as numerous am Legion. I remarked this over and over to myself; but I found that my mind still settled back in my original conviction, that one single individual, of the masculine sex, and in all probability young and handsome, was at the bottom of Miss Vernon's conduct; and it was with a burning desire of discovering, or rather of detecting, such a rival, that I stationed myself in the garden to watch the moment when the lights should appear in the library windows.

So eager, however, was my impatience, that I commenced my watch for a phenomenon, which could not appear until darkness, a full hour before the daylight disappeared, on a July evening. It was Sabbath, and all the walks were still and solitary. I walked up and down for some time, enjoying the refreshing coolness of a summer evening, and meditating on the probable consequences of my enterprise. The fresh and balmy air of the garden, impregnated with fragrance, produced its usual sedative effects on my over-heated and feverish blood. As these took place, the turmoil of my mind began proportionally to abate, and I was led to question the right I had to interfere with Miss Vernon's secrets, or with those of my uncle's family. What was it to me whom my uncle might choose to conceal in his house, where I was myself a guest only by tolerance? And what title had I to pry into the affairs of Miss Vernon, fraught, as she had avowed them to be, with mystery, into which she desired no scrutiny?

Passion and self-will were ready with their answers to these questions. In detecting this secret, I was in all probability about to do service to Sir Hildebrand, who was probably ignorant of the intrigues carried on in his family—and a still more important service to Miss Vernon, whose frank simplicity of character exposed her to so many risks in maintaining a private correspondence, perhaps with a person of doubtful or dangerous character. If I seemed to intrude myself on her confidence, it was with the generous and disinterested (yes, I even ventured to call it the *disinterested*) intention of guiding, defending, and protecting her against craft—against malice,—above all, against the secret counsellor whom she had chosen for her confidant. Such were the arguments which my will boldly preferred to my conscience, as coin which ought to be current, and which conscience, like a grumbling shopkeeper, was contented to accept, rather than come to an open breach with a customer, though more than doubting that the tender was spurious.

While I paced the green alleys, debating these things *pro* and *con*, I suddenly alighted upon Andrew Fairservice, perched up like a statue by a range of bee-hives, in an attitude of devout contemplation—one eye, however, watching the motions of the little irritable citizens, who were settling in their straw-thatched mansion for the evening, and the other fixed on a book of devotion, which much attrition had deprived of its corners, and worn into an oval shape; a circumstance which, with the close print and dingy colour of the volume in question, gave it an air of most respectable antiquity.

"I was e'en taking a spell o' worthy Mess John Quackleben's Flower of a Sweet Savour sawn on the Middenstead of this World," said Andrew, closing his book at my appearance, and putting his horn spectacles, by way of mark, at the place where he had been reading.

"And the bees, I observe, were dividing your attention, Andrew, with the learned author?"

"They are a contumacious generation," replied the gardener; "they hae sax days in the week to hive on, and yet it's a common observe that they will aye swarm on the Sabbath-day, and keep folk at hame frae hearing the word—But there's nae preaching at Graneagain chapel the e'en—that's aye ae mercy."

"You might have gone to the parish church as I did, Andrew, and heard an excellent discourse."

"Clauts o' cauld parritch—clauts o' cauld parritch," replied Andrew, with a most supercilious sneer,—"gude aneueh for dogs, begging your honour's pardon—Ay! I might nae doubt hae heard the curate linking awa at it in his white sark yonder, and the musicians playing on whistles, mair like a penny-wedding than a sermon—and to the boot of that, I might hae gaen to even-song, and heard Daddie Docharty mumbling his mass—muckle the better I wad hae been o' that!"

"Docharty!" said I (this was the name of an old priest, an Irishman, I think, who sometimes officiated at Osbaldistone Hall)—"I thought Father Vaughan had been at the Hall. He was here yesterday."

"Ay," replied Andrew; "but he left it yestreen, to gang to Greystock, or some o' thae west-country haulds. There's an unco stir among them a' e'enow. They are as busy as my bees are—God sain them! that I suld even the puir things to the like o' papists. Ye see this is the second swarm, and whiles they will swarm off in the afternoon. The first swarm set off sune in the morning.—But I am thinking they are settled in their skeps for the night; sae I wuss your honour good-night, and grace, and muckle o't."

So saying, Andrew retreated, but often cast a parting glance upon the *skeps*, as he called the bee-hives.

I had indirectly gained from him an important piece of information, that Father Vaughan, namely, was not supposed to be at the Hall. If, therefore, there appeared light in the windows of the library this evening, it either could not be his, or he was observing a very secret and suspicious line of conduct. I waited with impatience the time of sunset and of twilight. It had hardly arrived, ere a gleam from the windows of the library was seen, dimly distinguishable amidst the still enduring light of the evening. I marked its first glimpse, however, as speedily as the benighted sailor descries the first distant twinkle of the lighthouse which marks his course. The feelings of doubt and propriety, which had hitherto contended with my curiosity and jealousy, vanished when an opportunity of gratifying the former was presented to me. I re-entered the house, and avoiding the more frequented apartments with the consciousness of one who wishes to keep his purpose secret, I reached the door of the library—hesitated for a moment as my hand was upon the latch—heard a suppressed step within—opened the door—and found Miss Vernon alone.

Diana appeared surprised,—whether at my sudden entrance, or from some other cause, I could not guess; but there was in her appearance a degree of flutter, which I had never before remarked, and which I knew could only be produced by unusual emotion. Yet she was calm in a moment; and such is the force of conscience, that I, who studied to surprise her, seemed myself the surprised, and was certainly the embarrassed person.

"Has anything happened?" said Miss Vernon—"has any one arrived at the Hall?"

"No one that I know of," I answered, in some confusion; "I only sought the Orlando."

"It lies there," said Miss Vernon, pointing to the table. In removing one or two books to get at that which I pretended to seek, I was, in truth, meditating to make a handsome retreat from an investigation to which I felt my assurance inadequate, when I perceived a man's glove lying upon the table. My eyes encountered those of Miss Vernon, who blushed deeply.

"It is one of my relics," she said with hesitation, replying not to my words but to my looks; "it is one of the gloves of my grandfather, the original of the superb Vandyke which you admire."

As if she thought something more than her bare assertion was necessary to prove her statement true, she opened a drawer of the large oaken table, and taking out another glove, threw it towards me.—When a temper naturally ingenuous stoops to equivocate, or to dissemble, the anxious pain with which the unwonted task is laboured, often induces the hearer to doubt the authenticity of the tale. I cast a hasty glance on both gloves, and then replied gravely—"The gloves resemble each other, doubtless, in form and embroidery; but they cannot form a pair, since they both belong to the right hand."

She bit her lip with anger, and again coloured deeply.

"You do right to expose me," she replied, with bitterness: "some friends would have only judged from what I said, that I chose to give no particular explanation of a circumstance which calls for none—at least to a stranger. You have judged better, and have made me feel, not only the meanness of duplicity, but my own inadequacy to sustain the task of a dissembler. I now tell you distinctly, that that glove is not the fellow, as you have acutely discerned, to the one which I just now produced;—it belongs to a friend yet dearer to me than the original of Vandyke's picture—a friend by whose counsels I have been, and will be, guided—whom I honour—whom I"— she paused.

I was irritated at her manner, and filled up the blank in my own way— "Whom she *loves*, Miss Vernon would say."

"And if I do say so," she replied haughtily, "by whom shall my affection be called to account?"

"Not by me, Miss Vernon, assuredly—I entreat you to hold me acquitted of such presumption.—*But*," I continued, with some emphasis, for I was now piqued in return, "I hope Miss Vernon will pardon a friend, from whom she seems disposed to withdraw the title, for observing"—

"Observe nothing, sir," she interrupted with some vehemence, "except that I will neither be doubted nor questioned. There does not exist one by whom I will be either interrogated or judged; and if you sought this unusual time of presenting yourself in order to spy upon my privacy, the friendship or interest with which you pretend to regard me, is a poor excuse for your uncivil curiosity."

"I relieve you of my presence," said I, with pride equal to her own; for my temper has ever been a stranger to stooping, even in cases where my feelings were most deeply interested—"I relieve you of my presence. I awake from a pleasant, but a most delusive dream; and—but we understand each other."

I had reached the door of the apartment, when Miss Vernon, whose movements were sometimes so rapid as to seem almost instinctive, overtook me, and, catching hold of my arm, stopped me with that air of authority which she could so whimsically assume, and which, from the *naivete* and simplicity of her manner, had an effect so peculiarly interesting.

"Stop, Mr. Frank," she said, "you are not to leave me in that way neither; I am not so amply provided with friends, that I can afford to throw away even the ungrateful and the selfish. Mark what I say, Mr. Francis Osbaldistone. You shall know nothing of this mysterious glove," and she held it up as she spoke—"nothing—no, not a single iota more than you know already; and yet I will not permit it to be a gauntlet of strife and defiance betwixt us. My time here," she said, sinking into a tone somewhat softer, "must necessarily be very short; yours must be still shorter: we are soon to part never to meet again; do not let us quarrel, or make any mysterious miseries the pretext for farther embittering the few hours we shall ever pass together on this side of eternity."

I do not know, Tresham, by what witchery this fascinating creature obtained such complete management over a temper which I cannot at all times manage myself. I had determined on entering the library, to seek a complete explanation with Miss Vernon. I had found that she refused it with indignant defiance, and avowed to my face the preference of a rival; for what other construction could I put on her declared preference of her mysterious confidant? And yet, while I was on the point of leaving the apartment, and breaking with her for ever, it cost her but a change of look and tone, from that of real and haughty resentment to that of kind and playful despotism, again shaded off into melancholy and serious feeling, to lead me back to my seat, her willing subject, on her own hard terms.

"What does this avail?" said I, as I sate down. "What can this avail, Miss Vernon? Why should I witness embarrassments which I cannot relieve, and mysteries which I offend you even by attempting to penetrate? Inexperienced as you are in the world, you must still be aware that a beautiful young woman can have but one male friend. Even in a male friend I will be jealous of a confidence shared with a third party unknown and concealed; but with *you*, Miss Vernon"—

"You are, of course, jealous, in all the tenses and moods of that amiable passion? But, my good friend, you have all this time spoke nothing but the paltry gossip which simpletons repeat from play-books and romances, till they give mere cant a real and powerful influence over their minds. Boys and girls prate themselves into love; and when their love is like to fall asleep, they prate and tease themselves into jealousy. But you and I, Frank, are rational beings, and neither silly nor idle enough to talk ourselves into any other relation than that of plain honest disinterested friendship. Any other union is as far out of our reach as if I were man, or you woman—To speak truth," she added, after a moment's hesitation, "even though I am so complaisant to the decorum of my sex as to blush a little at my own plain dealing, we cannot marry if we would; and we ought not if we could."

And certainly, Tresham, she did blush most angelically, as she made this cruel declaration. I was about to attack both her positions, entirely forgetting those very suspicions which had been confirmed in the course of the evening, but she proceeded with a cold firmness which approached to severity—"What I say is sober and indisputable truth, on which I will neither hear question nor explanation. We are therefore friends, Mr. Osbaldistone—are we not?" She held out her hand, and taking mine, added—"And nothing to each other now, or henceforward, except as friends."

She let go my hand. I sunk it and my head at once, fairly *overcrowed*, as Spenser would have termed it, by the mingled kindness and firmness of her manner. She hastened to change the subject.

"Here is a letter," she said, "directed for you, Mr. Osbaldistone, very duly and distinctly; but which, notwithstanding the caution of the person who wrote and addressed it, might perhaps never have reached your hands, had it not fallen into the possession of a certain Pacolet, or enchanted dwarf of mine, whom, like all distressed damsels of romance, I retain in my secret service."

I opened the letter and glanced over the contents. The unfolded sheet of paper dropped from my hands, with the involuntary exclamation of "Gracious Heaven! my folly and disobedience have ruined my father!"

Miss Vernon rose with looks of real and affectionate alarm—"You grow pale—you are ill—shall I bring you a glass of water? Be a man, Mr. Osbaldistone, and a firm one. Is your father—is he no more?"

"He lives," said I, "thank God! but to what distress and difficulty"—

"If that be all, despair not. May I read this letter?" she said, taking it up.

I assented, hardly knowing what I said. She read it with great attention.

"Who is this Mr. Tresham, who signs the letter?"

"My father's partner"—(your own good father, Will)—"but he is little in the habit of acting personally in the business of the house."

"He writes here," said Miss Vernon, "of various letters sent to you previously."

"I have received none of them," I replied.

"And it appears," she continued, "that Rashleigh, who has taken the full management of affairs during your father's absence in Holland, has some time since left London for Scotland, with effects and remittances to take up large bills granted by your father to persons in that country, and that he has not since been heard of."

"It is but too true."

"And here has been," she added, looking at the letter, "a head-clerk, or some such person,—Owenson—Owen—despatched to Glasgow, to find out Rashleigh, if possible, and you are entreated to repair to the same place, and assist him in his researches."

"It is even so, and I must depart instantly."

"Stay but one moment," said Miss Vernon. "It seems to me that the worst which can come of this matter, will be the loss of a certain sum of money;—and can that bring tears into your eyes? For shame, Mr. Osbaldistone!"

"You do me injustice, Miss Vernon," I answered. "I grieve not for the loss of the money, but for the effect which I know it will produce on the spirits and health of my father, to whom mercantile credit is as honour; and who, if declared insolvent, would sink into the grave, oppressed by a sense of grief, remorse, and despair, like that of a soldier convicted of cowardice or a man of honour who had lost his rank and character in society. All this I might have prevented by a trifling sacrifice of the foolish pride and indolence which recoiled from sharing the labours of his honourable and useful profession. Good Heaven! how shall I redeem the consequences of my error?"

"By instantly repairing to Glasgow, as you are conjured to do by the friend who writes this letter."

"But if Rashleigh," said I, "has really formed this base and unconscientious scheme of plundering his benefactor, what prospect is there that I can find means of frustrating a plan so deeply laid?'

"The prospect," she replied, "indeed, may be uncertain; but, on the other hand, there is no possibility of your doing any service to your father by remaining here. Remember, had you been on the post destined for you, this disaster could not have happened: hasten to that which is now pointed out, and it may possibly be retrieved. —Yet stay—do not leave this room until I return."

She left me in confusion and amazement; amid which, however, I could find a lucid interval to admire the firmness, composure, and presence of mind which Miss Vernon seemed to possess on every crisis, however sudden.

In a few minutes she returned with a sheet of paper in her hand, folded and sealed like a letter, but without address. "I trust you," she said, "with this proof of my friendship, because I have the most perfect confidence in your honour. If I understand the nature of your distress rightly, the funds in Rashleigh's possession must be recovered by a certain day—the 12th of September, I think is named—in order that they may be applied to pay the bills in question; and, consequently, that if adequate funds be provided before that period, your father's credit is safe from the apprehended calamity."

"Certainly—I so understand Mr. Tresham"—I looked at your father's letter again, and added, "There cannot be a doubt of it."

"Well," said Diana, "in that case my little Pacolet may be of use to you. You have heard of a spell contained in a letter. Take this packet; do not open it until other and ordinary means have failed. If you succeed by your own exertions, I trust to your honour for destroying it without opening or suffering it to be opened;—but if not, you may break the seal within ten days of the fated day, and you will find directions which may possibly be of service to you. Adieu, Frank; we never meet more—but sometimes think of your friend Die Vernon."

She extended her hand, but I clasped her to my bosom. She sighed as she extricated herself from the embrace which she permitted—escaped to the door which led to her own apartment—and I saw her no more.

VOLUME TWO

CHAPTER FIRST

> And hurry, hurry, off they rode,
> As fast as fast might be;
> Hurra, hurra, the dead can ride,
> Dost fear to ride with me?
>
> — BURGER

There is one advantage in an accumulation of evils, differing in cause and character, that the distraction which they afford by their contradictory operation prevents the patient from being overwhelmed under either. I was deeply grieved at my separation from Miss Vernon, yet not so much so as I should have been, had not my father's apprehended distresses forced themselves on my attention; and I was distressed by the news of Mr. Tresham, yet less so than if they had fully occupied my mind. I was neither a false lover nor an unfeeling son; but man can give but a certain portion of distressful emotions to the causes which demand them; and if two operate at once, our sympathy, like the funds of a compounding bankrupt, can only be divided between them. Such were my reflections when I gained my apartment—it seems, from the illustration, they already began to have a twang of commerce in them.

I set myself seriously to consider your father's letter. It was not very distinct, and referred for several particulars to Owen, whom I was entreated to meet with as soon as possible at a Scotch town called Glasgow; being informed, moreover, that my old friend was to be heard of at Messrs. MacVittie, MacFin, and Company, merchants in the Gallowgate of the said town. It likewise alluded to several letters,—which, as it appeared to me, must have miscarried or have been intercepted, and complained of my obdurate silence, in terms which would have, been highly unjust, had my letters reached their purposed destination. I was amazed as I read. That the spirit of Rashleigh walked around me, and conjured up these doubts and difficulties by which I was surrounded, I could not doubt for one instant; yet it was frightful to conceive the extent of combined villany and power which he must have employed in the perpetration of his designs. Let me do myself justice in one respect. The evil of parting from Miss Vernon, however distressing it might in other respects and at another time have appeared to me, sunk into a subordinate consideration when I thought of the dangers impending over my father. I did not myself set a high estimation on wealth, and had the affectation of most young men of lively imagination, who suppose that they can better dispense with the possession of money, than resign their time and faculties to the labour necessary to acquire it. But in my father's case, I knew that bankruptcy would be considered as an utter and irretrievable disgrace, to which life would afford no comfort, and death the speediest and sole relief.

My mind, therefore, was bent on averting this catastrophe, with an intensity which the interest could not have produced had it referred to my own fortunes; and the result of my deliberation was a firm resolution to depart from Osbaldistone Hall the next day and wend my way without loss of time to meet Owen at Glasgow. I did not hold it expedient to intimate my departure to my uncle, otherwise than by leaving a letter of thanks for his hospitality, assuring him that sudden and important business prevented my offering them in person. I knew the blunt old knight would readily excuse ceremony; and I had such a belief in the extent and decided character of Rashleigh's machinations, that I had some apprehension of his having provided means to intercept a journey which was undertaken with a view to disconcert them, if my departure were publicly announced at Osbaldistone Hall.

I therefore determined to set off on my journey with daylight on the ensuing morning, and to gain the neighbouring kingdom of Scotland before any idea of my departure was entertained at the Hall. But one impediment of consequence was likely to prevent that speed which was the soul of my expedition. I did not know the shortest, nor indeed any road to Glasgow; and as, in the circumstances in which I stood, despatch was of the greatest consequence, I determined to consult Andrew Fairservice on the subject, as the nearest and most authentic authority within my reach. Late as it was, I set off with the intention of ascertaining this important point, and after a few minutes' walk reached the dwelling of the gardener.

Andrew's dwelling was situated at no great distance from the exterior wall of the garden—a snug comfortable Northumbrian cottage, built of stones roughly dressed with the hammer, and having the windows and doors decorated with huge heavy architraves, or lintels, as they are called, of hewn stone, and its roof covered with broad grey flags, instead of slates, thatch, or tiles. A jargonelle pear-tree at one end of the cottage, a rivulet and flower-plot of a rood in extent in front, and a kitchen-garden behind; a paddock for a cow, and a small field, cultivated with several crops of grain, rather for the benefit of the cottager than for sale, announced the warm and cordial comforts which Old England, even at her most northern extremity, extends to her meanest inhabitants.

As I approached the mansion of the sapient Andrew, I heard a noise, which, being of a nature peculiarly solemn, nasal, and prolonged, led me to think that

Andrew, according to the decent and meritorious custom of his countrymen, had assembled some of his neighbours to join in family exercise, as he called evening devotion. Andrew had indeed neither wife, child, nor female inmate in his family. "The first of his trade," he said, "had had eneugh o'thae cattle." But, notwithstanding, he sometimes contrived to form an audience for himself out of the neighbouring Papists and Church-of-Englandmen—brands, as he expressed it, snatched out of the burning, on whom he used to exercise his spiritual gifts, in defiance alike of Father Vaughan, Father Docharty, Rashleigh, and all the world of Catholics around him, who deemed his interference on such occasions an act of heretical interloping. I conceived it likely, therefore, that the well-disposed neighbours might have assembled to hold some chapel of ease of this nature. The noise, however, when I listened to it more accurately, seemed to proceed entirely from the lungs of the said Andrew; and when I interrupted it by entering the house, I found Fairservice alone, combating as he best could, with long words and hard names, and reading aloud, for the purpose of his own edification, a volume of controversial divinity.

"I was just taking a spell," said he, laying aside the huge folio volume as I entered, "of the worthy Doctor Lightfoot."

"Lightfoot!" I replied, looking at the ponderous volume with some surprise; "surely your author was unhappily named."

"Lightfoot was his name, sir; a divine he was, and another kind of a divine than they hae now-adays. Always, I crave your pardon for keeping ye standing at the door, but having been mistrysted (gude preserve us!) with ae bogle the night already, I was dubious o' opening the yett till I had gaen through the e'ening worship; and I had just finished the fifth chapter of Nehemiah—if that winna gar them keep their distance, I wotna what will."

"Trysted with a bogle!" said I; "what do you mean by that, Andrew?"

"I said mistrysted," replied Andrew; "that is as muckle as to say, fley'd wi' a ghaist—Gude preserve us, I say again!"

"Flay'd by a ghost, Andrew! how am I to understand that?"

"I did not say flay'd," replied Andrew, "but *fley'd*,—that is, I got a fleg, and was ready to jump out o' my skin, though naebody offered to whirl it aff my body as a man wad bark a tree."

"I beg a truce to your terrors in the present case, Andrew, and I wish to know whether you can direct me the nearest way to a town in your country of Scotland, called Glasgow?"

"A town ca'd Glasgow!" echoed Andrew Fairservice. "Glasgow's a ceety, man.—And is't the way to Glasgow ye were speering if I ken'd?—What suld ail me to ken it? —it's no that dooms far frae my ain parish of Dreepdaily, that lies a bittock farther to the west. But what may your honour be gaun to Glasgow for?"

"Particular business," replied I.

"That's as muckle as to say, Speer nae questions, and I'll tell ye nae lees.—To Glasgow?"—he made a short pause—"I am thinking ye wad be the better o' some ane to show you the road."

"Certainly, if I could meet with any person going that way."

"And your honour, doubtless, wad consider the time and trouble?"

"Unquestionably—my business is pressing, and if you can find any guide to accompany me, I'll pay him handsomely."

"This is no a day to speak o' carnal matters," said Andrew, casting his eyes upwards; "but if it werena Sabbath at e'en, I wad speer what ye wad be content to gie to ane that wad bear ye pleasant company on the road, and tell ye the names of the gentlemen's and noblemen's seats and castles, and count their kin to ye?"

"I tell you, all I want to know is the road I must travel; I will pay the fellow to his satisfaction—I will give him anything in reason."

"Onything," replied Andrew, "is naething; and this lad that I am speaking o' kens a' the short cuts and queer by-paths through the hills, and"—

"I have no time to talk about it, Andrew; do you make the bargain for me your own way."

"Aha! that's speaking to the purpose," answered Andrew.—"I am thinking, since sae be that sae it is, I'll be the lad that will guide you mysell."

"You, Andrew?—how will you get away from your employment?"

"I tell'd your honour a while syne, that it was lang that I hae been thinking o' flitting, maybe as lang as frae the first year I came to Osbaldistone Hall; and now I am o' the mind to gang in gude earnest—better soon as syne—better a finger aff as aye wagging."

"You leave your service, then?—but will you not lose your wages?"

"Nae doubt there will be a certain loss; but then I hae siller o' the laird's in my hands that I took for the apples in the auld orchyard—and a sair bargain the folk had that bought them—a wheen green trash—and yet Sir Hildebrand's as keen to hae the siller (that is, the steward is as pressing about it) as if they had been a' gowden pippins—and then there's the siller for the seeds—I'm thinking the wage will be in a manner decently made up.—But doubtless your honour will consider my risk of loss when we win to Glasgow—and ye'll be for setting out forthwith?"

"By day-break in the morning," I answered.

"That's something o' the suddenest—whare am I to find a naig?—Stay—I ken just the beast that will answer me."

"At five in the morning, then, Andrew, you will meet me at the head of the avenue."

"Deil a fear o' me (that I suld say sae) missing my tryste," replied Andrew, very briskly; "and if I might advise, we wad be aff twa hours earlier. I ken the way, dark or light, as weel as blind Ralph Ronaldson, that's travelled ower every moor in the country-side, and disna ken the colour of a heather-cowe when a's dune."

I highly approved of Andrew's amendment on my original proposal, and we agreed to meet at the place appointed at three in the morning. At once, however, a reflection came across the mind of my intended travelling companion.

"The bogle! the bogle! what if it should come out upon us?—I downa forgather wi' thae things twice in the four-and-twenty hours."

"Pooh! pooh!" I exclaimed, breaking away from him, "fear nothing from the next world—the earth contains living fiends, who can act for themselves without assistance, were the whole host that fell with Lucifer to return to aid and abet them."

With these words, the import of which was suggested by my own situation, I left Andrew's habitation, and returned to the Hall.

I made the few preparations which were necessary for my proposed journey, examined and loaded my pistols, and then threw myself on my bed, to obtain, if possible, a brief sleep before the fatigue of a long and anxious journey. Nature, exhausted by the tumultuous agitations of the day, was kinder to me than I expected, and I stink into a deep and profound slumber, from which, however, I started as the old clock struck two from a turret adjoining to my bedchamber. I instantly arose, struck a light, wrote the letter I proposed to leave for my uncle, and leaving behind me such articles of dress as were cumbrous in carriage, I deposited the rest of my wardrobe in my valise, glided down stairs, and gained the stable without impediment. Without being quite such a groom as any of my cousins, I had learned at Osbaldistone Hall to dress and saddle my own horse, and in a few minutes I was mounted and ready for my sally.

As I paced up the old avenue, on which the waning moon threw its light with a pale and whitish tinge, I looked back with a deep and boding sigh towards the walls which contained Diana Vernon, under the despondent impression that we had probably parted to meet no more. It was impossible, among the long and irregular lines of Gothic casements, which now looked ghastly white in the moonlight, to distinguish that of the apartment which she inhabited. "She is lost to me already," thought I, as my eye wandered over the dim and indistinguishable intricacies of architecture offered by the moonlight view of Osbaldistone Hall—"She is lost to me already, ere I have left the place which she inhabits! What hope is there of my maintaining any correspondence with her, when leagues shall lie between?"

While I paused in a reverie of no very pleasing nature, the "iron tongue of time told three upon the drowsy ear of night," and reminded me of the necessity of keeping my appointment with a person of a less interesting description and appearance—Andrew Fairservice.

At the gate of the avenue I found a horseman stationed in the shadow of the wall, but it was not until I had coughed twice, and then called "Andrew," that the horticulturist replied, "I'se warrant it's Andrew."

"Lead the way, then," said I, "and be silent if you can, till we are past the hamlet in the valley."

Andrew led the way accordingly, and at a much brisker pace than I would have recommended.—and so well did he obey my injunctions of keeping silence, that he would return no answer to my repeated inquiries into the cause of such unnecessary haste. Extricating ourselves by short cuts, known to Andrew, from the numerous stony lanes and by-paths which intersected each other in the vicinity of the Hall, we reached the open heath and riding swiftly across it, took our course among the barren hills which divide England from Scotland on what are called the Middle Marches. The way, or rather the broken track which we occupied, was a happy interchange of bog and shingles; nevertheless, Andrew relented nothing of his speed, but trotted manfully forward at the rate of eight or ten miles an hour. I was both surprised and provoked at the fellow's obstinate persistence, for we made abrupt ascents and descents over ground of a very break-neck character, and traversed the edge of precipices, where a slip of the horse's feet would have consigned the rider to certain death. The moon, at best, afforded a dubious and imperfect light; but in some places we were so much under the shade of the mountain as to be in total darkness, and then I could only trace Andrew by the clatter of his horse's feet, and the fire which they struck from the flints. At first, this rapid motion, and the attention which, for the sake of personal safety, I was compelled to give to the conduct of my horse, was of service, by forcibly diverting my thoughts from the various painful reflections which must otherwise have pressed on my mind. But at length, after hallooing repeatedly to Andrew to ride slower, I became seriously incensed at his impudent perseverance in refusing either to obey or to reply to me. My anger was, however, quite impotent. I attempted once or twice to get up alongside of my self-willed guide, with the purpose of knocking him off his horse with the butt-end of my whip; but Andrew was better mounted than I, and either the spirit of the animal which he bestrode, or more probably some presentiment of my kind intentions towards him, induced him to quicken his pace whenever I attempted to make up to him. On the other hand, I was compelled to exert my spurs to keep him in sight, for without his guidance I was too well aware that I should never find my way through the howling wilderness which we now traversed at such an unwonted pace. I was so angry at length, that I threatened to have recourse to my pistols, and send a bullet after the Hotspur Andrew, which should stop his fiery-footed career, if he did not abate it of his own accord. Apparently this threat made some impression on the tympanum of his ear, however deaf to all my milder entreaties; for he relaxed his pace upon hearing it, and, suffering me to close up to him, observed, "There wasna muckle sense in riding at sic a daft-like gate."

"And what did you mean by doing so at all, you self-willed scoundrel?" replied I; for I was in a towering passion,—to which, by the way, nothing contributes more than the having recently undergone a spice of personal fear, which, like a few drops of water flung on a glowing fire, is sure to inflame the ardour which it is insufficient to quench.

"What's your honour's wull?" replied Andrew, with impenetrable gravity.

"My will, you rascal?—I have been roaring to you this hour to ride slower, and you have never so much as answered me—Are you drunk or mad to behave so?"

"An it like your honour, I am something dull o' hearing; and I'll no deny but I might have maybe taen a stirrup-cup at parting frae the auld bigging whare I hae dwelt sae lang; and having naebody to pledge, nae doubt I was obliged to do mysell reason, or else leave the end o' the brandy stoup to thae papists—and that wad be a waste, as your honour kens."

This might be all very true,—and my circumstances required that I should be on good terms with my guide; I therefore satisfied myself with requiring of him to take his directions from me in future concerning the rate of travelling.

Andrew, emboldened by the mildness of my tone, elevated his own into the pedantic, conceited octave, which was familiar to him on most occasions.

"Your honour winna persuade me, and naebody shall persuade me, that it's either halesome or prudent to tak the night air on thae moors without a cordial o' clow-gilliflower water, or a tass of brandy or aquavitae, or sic-like creature-comfort. I hae taen the bent ower the Otterscrape-rigg a hundred times, day and night, and never could find the way unless I had taen my morning; mair by token that I had whiles twa bits o' ankers o' brandy on ilk side o' me."—

"In other words, Andrew," said I, "you were a smuggler—how does a man of your strict principles reconcile yourself to cheat the revenue?"

"It's a mere spoiling o' the Egyptians," replied Andrew; "puir auld Scotland suffers eneugh by thae blackguard loons o' excisemen and gaugers, that hae come down on her like locusts since the sad and sorrowfu' Union; it's the part of a kind son to bring her a soup o' something that will keep up her auld heart,—and that will they nill they, the ill-fa'ard thieves!"

Upon more particular inquiry, I found Andrew had frequently travelled these mountain-paths as a smuggler, both before and after his establishment at Osbaldistone Hall—a circumstance which was so far of importance to me, as it proved his capacity as a guide, notwithstanding the escapade of which he had been guilty at his outset. Even now, though travelling at a more moderate pace, the stirrup-cup, or whatever else had such an effect in stimulating Andrew's motions, seemed not totally to have lost its influence. He often cast a nervous and startled look behind him; and whenever the road seemed at all practicable, showed symptoms of a desire to accelerate his pace, as if he feared some pursuit from the rear. These appearances of alarm gradually diminished as we reached the top of a high bleak ridge, which ran nearly east and west for about a mile, with a very steep descent on either side. The pale beams of the morning were now enlightening the horizon, when Andrew cast a look behind him, and not seeing the appearance of a living being on the moors which he had travelled, his hard features gradually unbent, as he first whistled, then sung, with much glee and little melody, the end of one of his native songs—

"Jenny, lass! I think I hae her
Ower the muir amang the heather,
All their clan shall never get her."

He patted at the same time the neck of the horse which had carried him so gallantly; and my attention being directed by that action to the animal, I instantly recognised a favourite mare of Thorncliff Osbaldistone. "How is this, sir?" said I sternly; "that is Mr. Thorncliff's mare!"

"I'll no say but she may aiblins hae been his honour's Squire Thorncliff's in her day—but she's mine now."

"You have stolen her, you rascal."

"Na, na, sir—nae man can wyte me wi' theft. The thing stands this gate, ye see. Squire Thorncliff borrowed ten punds o' me to gang to York Races—deil a boddle wad he pay me back again, and spake o' raddling my banes, as he ca'd it, when I asked him but for my ain back again;—now I think it will riddle him or he gets his horse ower the Border again—unless he pays me plack and bawbee, he sall never see a hair o' her tail. I ken a canny child at Loughmaben, a bit writer lad, that will put me in the way to sort him. Steal the mear! na, na, far be the sin o' theft frae Andrew Fairservice—I have just arrested her *jurisdictionis fandandy causey*. Thae are bonny writer words—amaist like the language o' huz gardeners and other learned men—it's a pity they're sae dear;—thae three words were a' that Andrew got for a lang law-plea and four ankers o' as gude brandy as was e'er coupit ower craig—Hech, sirs! but law's a dear thing."

"You are likely to find it much dearer than you suppose, Andrew, if you proceed in this mode of paying yourself, without legal authority."

"Hout tout, we're in Scotland now (be praised for't!) and I can find baith friends and lawyers, and judges too, as weel as ony Osbaldistone o' them a'. My mither's mither's third cousin was cousin to the Provost o' Dumfries, and he winna see a drap o' her blude wranged. Hout awa! the laws are indifferently administered here to a' men alike; it's no like on yon side, when a chield may be whuppit awa' wi' ane o' Clerk Jobson's warrants, afore he kens where he is. But they will hae little enough law amang them by and by, and that is ae grand reason that I hae gi'en them gude-day."

I was highly provoked at the achievement of Andrew, and considered it as a hard fate, which a second time threw me into collision with a person of such irregular practices. I determined, however, to buy the mare of him, when he should reach the end of our journey, and send her back to my cousin at Osbaldistone Hall; and with this purpose of reparation I resolved to make my uncle acquainted from the next post-town. It was needless, I thought, to quarrel with Andrew in the meantime, who had, after all, acted not very unnaturally for a person in his circumstances. I therefore smothered my resentment, and asked him what he meant by his last expressions, that there would be little law in Northumberland by and by?

"Law!" said Andrew, "hout, ay—there will be club-law eneugh. The priests and the Irish officers, and thae papist cattle that hae been sodgering abroad, because they durstna bide at hame, are a' fleeing thick in Northumberland e'enow; and thae corbies dinna gather without they smell carrion. As sure as ye live, his honour Sir Hildebrand is gaun to stick his horn in the bog—there's naething but gun and pistol, sword and dagger, amang them—and they'll be laying on, I'se warrant; for they're fearless fules the young Osbaldistone squires, aye craving your honour's pardon."

This speech recalled to my memory some suspicions that I myself had entertained, that the Jacobites were on the eve of some desperate enterprise. But, conscious it did not become me to be a spy on my uncle's words and actions, I had rather avoided than availed myself of any opportunity which occurred of remarking upon the signs of the times.— Andrew Fairservice felt no such restraint, and doubtless spoke very truly in stating his conviction that some desperate plots were in agitation, as a reason which determined his resolution to leave the Hall.

"The servants," he stated, "with the tenantry and others, had been all regularly enrolled and mustered, and they wanted me to take arms also. But I'll ride in nae siccan troop—they little ken'd Andrew that asked him. I'll fight when I like mysell, but it sall neither be for the hure o' Babylon, nor any hure in England."

CHAPTER SECOND

> Where longs to fall yon rifted spire,
> As weary of the insulting air,—
> The poet's thoughts, the warrior's fire,
> The lover's sighs, are sleeping there.
>
> — LANGHORNE.

At the first Scotch town which we reached, my guide sought out his friend and counsellor, to consult upon the proper and legal means of converting into his own lawful property the "bonny creature," which was at present his own only by one of those sleight-of-hand arrangements which still sometimes took place in that once lawless district. I was somewhat diverted with the dejection of his looks on his return. He had, it seems, been rather too communicative to his confidential friend, the attorney; and learned with great dismay, in return for his unsuspecting frankness, that Mr. Touthope had, during his absence, been appointed clerk to the peace of the county, and was bound to communicate to justice all such achievements as that of his friend Mr. Andrew Fairservice. There was a necessity, this alert member of the police stated, for arresting the horse, and placing him in Bailie Trumbull's stable, therein to remain at livery, at the rate of twelve shillings (Scotch) per diem, until the question of property was duly tried and debated. He even talked as if, in strict and rigorous execution of his duty, he ought to detain honest Andrew himself; but on my guide's most piteously entreating his forbearance, he not only desisted from this proposal, but made a present to Andrew of a broken-winded and spavined pony, in order to enable him to pursue his journey. It is true, he qualified this act of generosity by exacting from poor Andrew an absolute cession of his right and interest in the gallant palfrey of Thorncliff Osbaldistone—a transference which Mr. Touthope represented as of very little consequence, since his unfortunate friend, as he facetiously observed, was likely to get nothing of the mare excepting the halter.

Andrew seemed woeful and disconcerted, as I screwed out of him these particulars; for his northern pride was cruelly pinched by being compelled to admit that attorneys were attorneys on both sides of the Tweed; and that Mr. Clerk Touthope was not a farthing more sterling coin than Mr. Clerk Jobson.

"It wadna hae vexed him half sae muckle to hae been cheated out o' what might amaist be said to be won with the peril o' his craig, had it happened amang the Inglishers; but it was an unco thing to see hawks pike out hawks' e'en, or ae kindly Scot cheat anither. But nae doubt things were strangely changed in his country sin' the sad and sorrowfu' Union;" an event to which Andrew referred every symptom of depravity or degeneracy which he remarked among his countrymen, more especially the inflammation of reckonings, the diminished size of pint-stoups, and other grievances, which he pointed out to me during our journey.

For my own part, I held myself, as things had turned out, acquitted of all charge of the mare, and wrote to my uncle the circumstances under which she was carried into Scotland, concluding with informing him that she was in the hands of justice, and her worthy representatives, Bailie Trumbull and Mr. Clerk Touthope, to whom I referred him for farther particulars. Whether the property returned to the Northumbrian fox-hunter, or continued to bear the person of the Scottish attorney, it is unnecessary for me at present to say.

We now pursued our journey to the north-westward, at a rate much slower than that at which we had achieved our nocturnal retreat from England. One chain of barren and uninteresting hills succeeded another, until the more fertile vale of Clyde opened upon us; and, with such despatch as we might, we gained the town, or, as my guide pertinaciously termed it, the city, of Glasgow. Of late years, I understand, it has fully deserved the name, which, by a sort of political second sight, my guide assigned to it. An extensive and increasing trade with the West Indies and American colonies, has, if I am rightly informed, laid the foundation of wealth and prosperity, which, if carefully strengthened and built upon, may one day support an immense fabric of commercial prosperity; but in the earlier time of which I speak, the dawn of this splendour had not arisen. The Union had, indeed, opened to Scotland the trade of the English colonies; but, betwixt want of capital, and the national jealousy of the English, the merchants of Scotland were as yet excluded, in a great measure, from the exercise of the privileges which that memorable treaty conferred on them. Glasgow lay on the wrong side of the island for participating in the east country or continental trade, by which the trifling commerce as yet possessed by Scotland chiefly supported itself. Yet, though she then gave small promise of the commercial eminence to which, I am informed, she seems now likely one day to attain, Glasgow, as the principal central town of the western district of Scotland, was a place of considerable rank and importance. The broad and brimming Clyde, which flows so near its walls, gave the means of an inland navigation of some importance. Not only the fertile plains in its immediate neighbourhood, but the districts of Ayr and Dumfries regarded Glasgow as their capital, to which they transmitted their produce, and received in return such necessaries and luxuries as their consumption required.

The dusky mountains of the western Highlands often sent forth wilder tribes to frequent the marts of St. Mungo's favourite city. Hordes of wild shaggy, dwarfish cattle and ponies, conducted by Highlanders, as wild, as shaggy, and sometimes as dwarfish, as the animals they had in charge, often traversed the streets of Glasgow. Strangers gazed with surprise on the antique and fantastic dress, and listened to the unknown and dissonant sounds of their language, while the mountaineers, armed, even while engaged in this peaceful occupation, with musket and pistol, sword, dagger, and target, stared with astonishment on the articles of luxury of which they knew not the use, and with an avidity which seemed somewhat alarming on the articles which they knew and valued. It is always with unwillingness that the Highlander quits his deserts, and at this early period it was like tearing a pine from its rock, to plant him elsewhere. Yet even then the mountain glens were over-peopled, although thinned occasionally by famine or by the sword, and many of their inhabitants strayed down to Glasgow—there formed settlements—there sought and found employment, although different, indeed, from that of their native hills. This supply of a hardy and useful population was of consequence to the prosperity of the place, furnished the means of carrying on the few manufactures which the town already boasted, and laid the foundation of its future prosperity.

The exterior of the city corresponded with these promising circumstances. The principal street was broad and important, decorated with public buildings, of an architecture rather striking than correct in point of taste, and running between rows of tall houses, built of stone, the fronts of which were occasionally richly ornamented with mason-work—a circumstance which gave the street an imposing air of dignity and grandeur, of which most English towns are in some measure deprived, by the slight, insubstantial, and perishable quality and appearance of the bricks with which they are constructed.

In the western metropolis of Scotland, my guide and I arrived on a Saturday evening, too late to entertain thoughts of business of any kind. We alighted at the door of a jolly hostler-wife, as Andrew called her,—the Ostelere of old father Chaucer, —by whom we were civilly received.

On the following morning the bells pealed from every steeple, announcing the sanctity of the day. Notwithstanding, however, what I had heard of the severity with which the Sabbath is observed in Scotland, my first impulse, not unnaturally, was to seek out Owen; but on inquiry I found that my attempt would be in vain, "until kirk time was ower." Not only did my landlady and guide jointly assure me that "there wadna be a living soul either in the counting-house or dwelling-house of Messrs. MacVittie, MacFin, and Company," to which Owen's letter referred me, but, moreover, "far less would I find any of the partners there. They were serious men, and wad be where a' gude Christians ought to be at sic a time, and that was in the Barony Laigh Kirk."[1]

Andrew Fairservice, whose disgust at the law of his country had fortunately not extended itself to the other learned professions of his native land, now sung forth the praises of the preacher who was to perform the duty, to which my hostess replied with many loud amens. The result was, that I determined to go to this popular place of worship, as much with the purpose of learning, if possible, whether Owen had arrived in Glasgow, as with any great expectation of edification. My hopes were exalted by the assurance, that if Mr. Ephraim MacVittie (worthy man) were in the land of life, he would surely honour the Barony Kirk that day with his presence; and if he chanced to have a stranger within his gates, doubtless he would bring him to the duty along with him. This probability determined my motions, and under the escort of my faithful Andrew, I set forth for the Barony Kirk.

On this occasion, however, I had little need of his guidance; for the crowd, which forced its way up a steep and rough-paved street, to hear the most popular preacher in the west of Scotland, would of itself have swept me along with it. On attaining the summit of the hill, we turned to the left, and a large pair of folding doors admitted us, amongst others, into the open and extensive burying-place which surrounds the Minster or Cathedral Church of Glasgow. The pile is of a gloomy and massive, rather than of an elegant, style of Gothic architecture; but its peculiar character is so strongly preserved, and so well suited with the accompaniments that surround it, that the impression of the first view was awful and solemn in the extreme. I was indeed so much struck, that I resisted for a few minutes all Andrew's efforts to drag me into the interior of the building, so deeply was I engaged in surveying its outward character.

Situated in a populous and considerable town, this ancient and massive pile has the appearance of the most sequestered solitude. High walls divide it from the buildings of the city on one side; on the other it is bounded by a ravine, at the bottom of which, and invisible to the eye, murmurs a wandering rivulet, adding, by its gentle noise, to the imposing solemnity of the scene. On the opposite side of the ravine rises a steep bank, covered with fir-trees closely planted, whose dusky shade extends itself over the cemetery with an appropriate and gloomy effect. The churchyard itself had a peculiar character; for though in reality extensive, it is small in proportion to the number of respectable inhabitants who are interred within it, and whose graves are almost all covered with tombstones. There is therefore no room for the long rank grass, which, in most cases, partially clothes the surface of those retreats where the wicked cease from troubling, and the weary are at rest. The broad flat monumental stones are placed so close to each other, that the precincts appear to be flagged with them, and, though roofed only by the heavens, resemble the floor of one of our old English churches, where the pavement is covered with sepulchral inscriptions. The contents of these sad records of mortality, the vain sorrows which they preserve, the stern lesson which they teach of the nothingness of humanity, the extent of ground which they so closely cover, and their uniform and melancholy tenor, reminded me of the roll of the prophet, which was "written within and without, and there was written therein lamentations and mourning and woe."

The Cathedral itself corresponds in impressive majesty with these accompaniments. We feel that its appearance is heavy, yet that the effect produced would be destroyed were it lighter or more ornamental. It is the only metropolitan church in Scotland, excepting, as I am informed, the Cathedral of Kirkwall, in the Orkneys, which remained uninjured at the Reformation; and Andrew Fairservice, who saw with great pride the effect which it produced upon my mind, thus accounted for its preservation—"Ah! it's a brave kirk—nane o' yere whig-maleeries and curliewurlies and opensteek hems about it—a' solid, weel-jointed mason-wark, that will stand as lang as the warld, keep hands and gunpowther aff it. It had amaist a douncome lang syne at the Reformation, when they pu'd doun the kirks of St. Andrews and Perth, and thereawa', to cleanse them o' Papery, and idolatry, and image worship, and surplices, and sic like rags o' the muckle hure that sitteth on seven hills, as if ane wasna braid eneugh for her auld hinder end. Sae the commons o' Renfrew, and o' the Barony, and the Gorbals and a' about, they behoved to come into Glasgow no fair morning, to try their hand on purging the High Kirk o' Popish nick-nackets. But the townsmen o' Glasgow, they were feared their auld edifice might slip the girths in gaun through siccan rough physic, sae they rang the common bell, and assembled the train-bands wi' took o' drum. By good luck, the worthy James Rabat was Dean o' Guild that year—(and a gude mason he was himself, made him the keener to keep up the auld bigging)—and the trades assembled, and offered downright battle to the commons, rather than their kirk should coup the crans as others had done elsewhere. It wasna for luve o' Paperie—na, na!—nane could ever say that o' the trades o' Glasgow—Sae they sune came to an agreement to take a' the idolatrous statues of sants (sorrow be on them) out o' their neuks—and sae the bits o' stane idols were broken in pieces by Scripture warrant, and flung into the Molendinar burn, and the auld kirk stood as crouse as a cat when the flaes are kaimed aff her, and a' body was alike pleased. And I hae heard wise folk say, that if the same had been done in ilka kirk in Scotland, the Reform wad just hae been as pure as it is e'en now, and we wad hae mair Christian-like kirks; for I hae been sae lang in England, that naething will drived out o' my head, that the dog-kennel at Osbaldistone Hall is better than mony a house o' God in Scotland."

Thus saying, Andrew led the way into the place of worship.

CHAPTER THIRD

—It strikes an awe
And terror on my aching sight; the tombs

WALTER SCOTT

And monumental caves of death look cold,
And shoot a chillness to the trembling heart.

— MOURNING BRIDE

Notwithstanding the impatience of my conductor, I could not forbear to pause and gaze for some minutes on the exterior of the building, rendered more impressively dignified by the solitude which ensued when its hitherto open gates were closed, after having, as it were, devoured the multitude which had lately crowded the churchyard, but now, enclosed within the building, were engaged, as the choral swell of voices from within announced to us, in the solemn exercises of devotion. The sound of so many voices united by the distance into one harmony, and freed from those harsh discordances which jar the ear when heard more near, combining with the murmuring brook, and the wind which sung among the old firs, affected me with a sense of sublimity. All nature, as invoked by the Psalmist whose verses they chanted, seemed united in offering that solemn praise in which trembling is mixed with joy as she addressed her Maker. I had heard the service of high mass in France, celebrated with all the e'clat which the choicest music, the richest dresses, the most imposing ceremonies, could confer on it; yet it fell short in effect of the simplicity of the Presbyterian worship. The devotion in which every one took a share seemed so superior to that which was recited by musicians as a lesson which they had learned by rote, that it gave the Scottish worship all the advantage of reality over acting.

As I lingered to catch more of the solemn sound, Andrew, whose impatience became ungovernable, pulled me by the sleeve—"Come awa', sir—come awa'; we maunna be late o' gaun in to disturb the worship; if we bide here the searchers will be on us, and carry us to the guard-house for being idlers in kirk-time."

Thus admonished, I followed my guide, but not, as I had supposed, into the body of the cathedral. "This gate—this gate, sir," he exclaimed, dragging me off as I made towards the main entrance of the building—"There's but cauldrife law-work gaun on yonder—carnal morality, as dow'd and as fusionless as rue leaves at Yule—Here's the real savour of doctrine."

So saying, we entered a small low-arched door, secured by a wicket, which a grave-looking person seemed on the point of closing, and descended several steps as if into the funeral vaults beneath the church. It was even so; for in these subterranean precincts,—why chosen for such a purpose I knew not,—was established a very singular place of worship.

Conceive, Tresham, an extensive range of low-browed, dark, and twilight vaults, such as are used for sepulchres in other countries, and had long been dedicated to the same purpose in this, a portion of which was seated with pews, and used as a church. The part of the vaults thus occupied, though capable of containing a congregation of many hundreds, bore a small proportion to the darker and more extensive caverns which yawned around what may be termed the inhabited space. In those waste regions of oblivion, dusky banners and tattered escutcheons indicated the graves of those who were once, doubtless, "princes in Israel." Inscriptions, which could only be read by the painful antiquary, in language as obsolete as the act of devotional charity which they employed, invited the passengers to pray for the souls of those whose bodies rested beneath. Surrounded by these receptacles of the last remains of mortality, I found a numerous congregation engaged in the act of prayer. The Scotch perform this duty in a standing instead of a kneeling posture—more, perhaps, to take as broad a distinction as possible from the ritual of Rome than for any better reason; since I have observed, that in their family worship, as doubtless in their private devotions, they adopt, in their immediate address to the Deity, that posture which other Christians use as the humblest and most reverential. Standing, therefore, the men being uncovered, a crowd of several hundreds of both sexes, and all ages, listened with great reverence and attention to the extempore, at least the unwritten, prayer of an aged clergyman,[2] who was very popular in the city.

Educated in the same religious persuasion, I seriously bent my mind to join in the devotion of the day; and it was not till the congregation resumed their seats, that my attention was diverted to the consideration of the appearance of all around me.

At the conclusion of the prayer, most of the men put on their hats or bonnets, and all who had the happiness to have seats sate down. Andrew and I were not of this number, having been too late of entering the church to secure such accommodation. We stood among a number of other persons in the same situation, forming a sort of ring around the seated part of the congregation. Behind and around us were the vaults I have already described; before us the devout audience, dimly shown by the light which streamed on their faces through one or two low Gothic windows, such as give air and light to charnel-houses. By this were seen the usual variety of countenances which are generally turned towards a Scotch pastor on such occasions, almost all composed to attention, unless where a father or mother here and there recalls the wandering eyes of a lively child, or disturbs the slumbers of a dull one. The highboned and harsh countenance of the nation, with the expression of intelligence and shrewdness which it frequently exhibits, is seen to more advantage in the act of devotion, or in the ranks of war, than on lighter and more cheerful occasions of assemblage. The discourse of the preacher was well qualified to call forth the various feelings and faculties of his audience.

Age and infirmities had impaired the powers of a voice originally strong and sonorous. He read his text with a pronunciation somewhat inarticulate; but when he closed the Bible, and commenced his sermon, his tones gradually strengthened, as he entered with vehemence into the arguments which he maintained. They related chiefly to the abstract points of the Christian faith,—subjects grave, deep, and fathomless by mere human reason, but for which, with equal ingenuity and propriety, he sought a key in liberal quotations from the inspired writings. My mind was unprepared to coincide in all his reasoning, nor was I sure that in some instances I rightly comprehended his positions. But nothing could be more impressive than the eager enthusiastic manner of the good old man, and nothing more ingenious than his mode of reasoning. The Scotch, it is well known, are more remarkable for the exercise of their intellectual powers, than for the keenness of their feelings; they are, therefore, more moved by logic than by rhetoric, and more attracted by acute and argumentative reasoning on doctrinal points, than influenced by the enthusiastic appeals to the heart and to the passions, by which popular preachers in other countries win the favour of their hearers.

Among the attentive group which I now saw, might be distinguished various expressions similar to those of the audience in the famous cartoon of Paul preaching at Athens. Here sat a zealous and intelligent Calvinist, with brows bent just as much as to indicate profound attention; lips slightly compressed; eyes fixed on the minister with an expression of decent pride, as if sharing the triumph of his argument; the forefinger of the right hand touching successively those of the left, as the preacher, from argument to argument, ascended towards his conclusion. Another, with fiercer and sterner look, intimated at once his contempt of all who doubted the creed of his pastor, and his joy at the appropriate punishment denounced against them. A third, perhaps belonging to a different congregation, and present only by accident or curiosity, had the appearance of internally impeaching some link of the reasoning; and you might plainly read, in the slight motion of his head, his doubts as to the soundness of the preacher's argument. The greater part listened with a calm, satisfied countenance, expressive of a conscious merit in being present, and in listening to such an ingenious discourse, although perhaps unable entirely to comprehend it. The women in general belonged to this last division of the audience; the old, however, seeming more grimly intent upon the abstract doctrines laid before them; while the younger females permitted their eyes occasionally to make a modest circuit around the congregation; and some of them, Tresham (if my vanity did not greatly deceive me), contrived to distinguish your friend and servant, as a handsome young stranger and an Englishman. As to the rest of the congregation, the stupid gaped, yawned, or slept, till awakened by the application of their more zealous neighbours' heels to their shins; and the idle indicated their inattention by the wandering of their eyes, but dared give no more decided token of weariness. Amid the Lowland costume of coat and cloak, I could here and there discern a Highland plaid, the wearer of which, resting on his basket-hilt, sent his eyes among the audience with the unrestrained curiosity of savage wonder; and who, in all probability, was inattentive to the sermon for a very pardonable reason—because he did not understand the language in which it was delivered. The martial and wild look, however, of these stragglers, added a kind of character which the congregation could not have exhibited without them. They were more numerous, Andrew afterwards observed, owing to some cattle-fair in the neighbourhood.

Such was the group of countenances, rising tier on tier, discovered to my critical inspection by such sunbeams as forced their way through the narrow Gothic lattices of the Laigh Kirk of Glasgow; and, having illuminated the attentive congregation, lost themselves in the vacuity of the vaults behind, giving to the nearer part of their labyrinth a sort of imperfect twilight, and leaving their recesses in an utter darkness, which gave them the appearance of being interminable.

I have already said that I stood with others in the exterior circle, with my face to the preacher, and my back to those vaults which I have so often mentioned. My position rendered me particularly obnoxious to any interruption which arose from any slight noise occurring amongst these retiring arches, where the least sound was multiplied by a thousand echoes. The occasional sound of rain-drops, which, admitted through some cranny in the ruined roof, fell successively, and splashed upon the pavement beneath, caused me to turn my head more than once to the place from whence it seemed to proceed, and when my eyes took that direction, I found it difficult to withdraw them; such is the pleasure our imagination receives from the attempt to penetrate as far as possible into an intricate labyrinth, imperfectly lighted, and exhibiting objects which irritate our curiosity, only because they acquire a mysterious interest from being undefined and dubious. My eyes became habituated to the gloomy atmosphere to which I directed them, and insensibly my mind became more interested in their discoveries than in the metaphysical subtleties which the preacher was enforcing.

My father had often checked me for this wandering mood of mind, arising perhaps from an excitability of imagination to which he was a stranger; and the finding myself at present solicited by these temptations to inattention, recalled the time when I used to walk, led by his hand, to Mr. Shower's chapel, and the earnest injunctions which he then laid on me to redeem the time, because the days were evil. At present, the picture which my thoughts suggested, far from fixing my attention, destroyed the portion I had yet left, by conjuring up to my recollection the peril in which his affairs now stood. I endeavoured, in the lowest whisper I could frame, to request Andrew to obtain information, whether any of the gentlemen of the firm of MacVittie & Co. were at present in the congregation. But Andrew, wrapped in profound attention to the sermon, only replied to my suggestion by hard punches with his elbow, as signals to me to remain silent. I next strained my eyes, with equally bad success, to see if, among the sea of up-turned faces which bent their eyes on the pulpit as a common centre, I could discover the sober and business-like physiognomy of Owen. But not among the broad beavers of the Glasgow citizens, or the yet broader brimmed Lowland bonnets of the peasants of Lanarkshire, could I see anything resembling the decent periwig, starched ruffles, or the uniform suit of light-brown garments appertaining to the head-clerk of the establishment of Osbaldistone and Tresham. My anxiety now returned on me with such violence as to overpower not only the novelty of the scene around me, by which it had hitherto been diverted, but moreover my sense of decorum. I pulled Andrew hard by the sleeve, and intimated my wish to leave the church, and pursue my investigation as I could. Andrew, obdurate in the Laigh Kirk of Glasgow as on the mountains of Cheviot, for some time deigned me no answer; and it was only when he found I could not otherwise be kept quiet, that he condescended to inform me, that, being once in the church, we could not leave it till service was over, because the doors were locked so soon as the prayers began. Having thus spoken in a brief and peevish whisper, Andrew again assumed the air of intelligent and critical importance, and attention to the preacher's discourse.

While I endeavoured to make a virtue of necessity, and recall my attention to the sermon, I was again disturbed by a singular interruption. A voice from behind whispered distinctly in my ear, "You are in danger in this city."—I turned round, as if mechanically.

One or two starched and ordinary-looking mechanics stood beside and behind me,—stragglers, who, like ourselves, had been too late in obtaining entrance. But a glance at their faces satisfied me, though I could hardly say why, that none of these was the person who had spoken to me. Their countenances seemed all composed to attention to the sermon, and not one of them returned any glance of intelligence to the inquisitive and startled look with which I surveyed them. A massive round pillar, which was close behind us, might have concealed the speaker the instant he uttered his mysterious caution; but wherefore it was given in such a place, or to what species of danger it directed my attention, or by whom the warning was uttered, were points on which my imagination lost itself in conjecture. It would, however, I concluded, be repeated, and I resolved to keep my countenance turned towards the clergyman, that the whisperer might be tempted to renew his communication under the idea that the first had passed unobserved.

My plan succeeded. I had not resumed the appearance of attention to the preacher for five minutes, when the same voice whispered, "Listen, but do not look back." I kept my face in the same direction. "You are in danger in this place," the voice proceeded; "so am I—meet me to-night on the Brigg, at twelve preceesely—keep at home till the gloaming, and avoid observation."

Here the voice ceased, and I instantly turned my head. But the speaker had, with still greater promptitude, glided behind the pillar, and escaped my observation. I was determined to catch a sight of him, if possible, and extricating myself from the outer circle of hearers, I also stepped behind the column. All there was empty; and I could only see a figure wrapped in a mantle, whether a Lowland cloak, or Highland plaid, I could not distinguish, which traversed, like a phantom, the dreary vacuity of vaults which I have described.

I made a mechanical attempt to pursue the mysterious form, which glided away and vanished in the vaulted cemetery, like the spectre of one of the numerous dead who rested within its precincts. I had little chance of arresting the course of one obviously determined not to be spoken with; but that little chance was lost by my stumbling and falling before I had made three steps from the column. The obscurity which occasioned my misfortune, covered my disgrace; which I accounted rather lucky, for the preacher, with that stern authority which the Scottish ministers assume for the purpose of keeping order in their congregations, interrupted his discourse, to desire the "proper officer" to take into custody the causer of this disturbance in the place of worship. As the noise, however, was not repeated, the beadle, or whatever else he was called, did not think it necessary to be rigorous in searching out the offender, so that I was enabled, without attracting farther observation, to place myself by Andrew's side in my original position. The service proceeded, and closed without the occurrence of anything else worthy of notice.

As the congregation departed and dispersed, my friend Andrew exclaimed, "See, yonder is worthy Mr. MacVittie, and Mrs. MacVittie, and Miss Alison MacVittie, and Mr. Thamas MacFin, that they say is to marry Miss Alison, if a' bowls row right—she'll hae a hantle siller, if she's no that bonny."

My eyes took the direction he pointed out. Mr. MacVittie was a tall, thin, elderly man, with hard features, thick grey eyebrows, light eyes, and, as I imagined, a sinister expression of countenance, from which my heart recoiled. I remembered the warning I had received in the church, and hesitated to address this person, though I could not allege to myself any rational ground of dislike or suspicion.

I was yet in suspense, when Andrew, who mistook my hesitation for bashfulness, proceeded to exhort me to lay it aside. "Speak till him—speak till him, Mr. Francis—he's no provost yet, though they say he'll be my lord neist year. Speak till him, then—he'll gie ye a decent answer for as rich as he is, unless ye were wanting siller frae him —they say he's dour to draw his purse."

It immediately occurred to me, that if this merchant were really of the churlish and avaricious disposition which Andrew intimated, there might be some caution necessary in making myself known, as I could not tell how accounts might stand between my father and him. This consideration came in aid of the mysterious hint which I had received, and the dislike which I had conceived at the man's countenance. Instead of addressing myself directly to him, as I had designed to have done, I contented myself with desiring Andrew to inquire at Mr. MacVittie's house the address of Mr. Owen, an English gentleman; and I charged him not to mention the person from whom he received the commission, but to bring me the result to the small inn where we lodged. This Andrew promised to do. He said something of the duty of my attending the evening service; but added with a causticity natural to him, that "in troth, if folk couldna keep their legs still, but wad needs be couping the creels ower through-stanes, as if they wad raise the very dead folk wi' the clatter, a kirk wi' a chimley in't was fittest for them."

CHAPTER FOURTH

On the Rialto, every night at twelve,
I take my evening's walk of meditation:
There we two will meet.

— VENICE PRESERVED.

Full of sinister augury, for which, however, I could assign no satisfactory cause, I shut myself up in my apartment at the inn, and having dismissed Andrew, after resisting his importunity to accompany him to St. Enoch's Kirk,[3] where, he said, "a soul-searching divine was to haud forth," I set myself seriously to consider what were best to be done.

I never was what is properly called superstitious; but I suppose that all men, in situations of peculiar doubt and difficulty, when they have exercised their reason to little purpose, are apt, in a sort of despair, to abandon the reins to their imagination, and be guided altogether by chance, or by those whimsical impressions which take possession of the mind, and to which we give way as if to involuntary impulses. There was something so singularly repulsive in the hard features of the Scotch trader, that I could not resolve to put myself into his hands without transgressing every caution which could be derived from the rules of physiognomy; while, at the same time, the warning voice, the form which flitted away like a vanishing shadow through those vaults, which might be termed "the valley of the shadow of death," had something captivating for the imagination of a young man, who, you will farther please to remember, was also a young poet.

If danger was around me, as the mysterious communication intimated, how could I learn its nature, or the means of averting it, but by meeting my unknown counsellor, to whom I could see no reason for imputing any other than kind intentions. Rashleigh and his machinations occurred more than once to my remembrance;—but so rapid had my journey been, that I could not suppose him apprised of my arrival in Glasgow, much less prepared to play off any stratagem against my person. In my temper also I was bold and confident, strong and active in person, and in some measure accustomed to the use of arms, in which the French youth of all kinds were then initiated. I did not fear any single opponent; assassination was neither the vice of the age nor of the country; the place selected for our meeting was too public to admit any suspicion of meditated violence. In a word, I resolved to meet my mysterious counsellor on the bridge, as he had requested, and to be afterwards guided by circumstances. Let me not conceal from you, Tresham, what at the time I endeavoured to conceal from myself—the subdued, yet secretly-cherished hope, that Diana Vernon might—by what chance I knew not—through what means I could not guess—have some connection with this strange and dubious intimation conveyed at a time and place, and in a manner so surprising. She alone—whispered this insidious thought—she alone knew of my journey; from her own account, she possessed friends and influence in Scotland; she had furnished me with a talisman, whose power I was to invoke when all other aid failed me; who then but Diana Vernon possessed either means, knowledge, or inclination, for averting the dangers, by which, as it seemed, my steps were surrounded? This flattering view of my very doubtful case pressed itself upon me again and again. It insinuated itself into my thoughts, though very bashfully, before the hour of dinner; it displayed its attractions more boldly during the course of my frugal meal, and became so courageously intrusive during the succeeding half-hour (aided perhaps by the flavour of a few glasses of most excellent claret), that, with a sort of desperate attempt to escape from a delusive seduction, to which I felt the danger of yielding, I pushed my glass from me, threw aside my dinner, seized my hat, and rushed into the open air with the feeling of one who would fly from his own thoughts. Yet perhaps I yielded to the very feelings from which I seemed to fly, since my steps insensibly led me to the bridge over the Clyde, the place assigned for the rendezvous by my mysterious monitor.

Although I had not partaken of my repast until the hours of evening church-service were over,—in which, by the way, I complied with the religious scruples of my landlady, who hesitated to dress a hot dinner between sermons, and also with the admonition of my unknown friend, to keep my apartment till twilight,—several hours had still to pass away betwixt the time of my appointment and that at which I reached the assigned place of meeting. The interval, as you will readily credit, was wearisome enough; and I can hardly explain to you how it passed away. Various groups of persons, all of whom, young and old, seemed impressed with a reverential feeling of the sanctity of the day, passed along the large open meadow which lies on the northern bank of the Clyde, and serves at once as a bleaching-field and pleasure-walk for the inhabitants, or paced with slow steps the long bridge which communicates with the southern district of the county. All that I remember of them was the general, yet not unpleasing, intimation of a devotional character impressed on each little party—formally assumed perhaps by some, but sincerely characterising the greater number—which hushed the petulant gaiety of the young into a tone of more quiet, yet more interesting, interchange of sentiments, and suppressed the vehement argument and protracted disputes of those of more advanced age. Notwithstanding the numbers who passed me, no general sound of the human voice was heard; few turned again to take some minutes' voluntary exercise, to which the leisure of the evening, and the beauty of the surrounding scenery, seemed to invite them: all hurried to their homes and resting-places. To one accustomed to the mode of spending Sunday evenings abroad, even among the French Calvinists, there seemed something Judaical, yet, at the same time striking and affecting, in this mode of keeping the Sabbath holy. Insensibly I felt my mode of sauntering by the side of the river, and crossing successively the various persons who were passing homeward, and without tarrying or delay, must expose me to observation at least, if not to censure; and I slunk out of the frequented path, and found a trivial occupation for my mind in marshalling my revolving walk in such a manner as should least render me obnoxious to observation. The different alleys lined out through this extensive meadow, and which are planted with trees, like the Park of St. James's in London, gave me facilities for carrying into effect these childish manoeuvres.

As I walked down one of these avenues, I heard, to my surprise, the sharp and conceited voice of Andrew Fairservice, raised by a sense of self-consequence to a pitch somewhat higher than others seemed to think consistent with the solemnity of the day. To slip behind the row of trees under which I walked was perhaps no very dignified proceeding; but it was the easiest mode of escaping his observation, and perhaps his impertinent assiduity, and still more intrusive curiosity. As he passed, I heard him communicate to a grave-looking man, in a black coat, a slouched hat, and Geneva cloak, the following sketch of a character, which my self-love, while revolting against it as a caricature, could not, nevertheless, refuse to recognise as a likeness.

"Ay, ay, Mr. Hammorgaw, it's e'en as I tell ye. He's no a'thegither sae void o' sense neither; he has a gloaming sight o' what's reasonable—that is anes and awa'—a glisk and nae mair; but he's crack-brained and cockle-headed about his nipperty-tipperty poetry nonsense—He'll glowr at an auld-warld barkit aik-snag as if it were a queez-maddam in full bearing; and a naked craig, wi' a bum jawing ower't, is unto him as a garden garnisht with flowering knots and choice pot-herbs. Then he wad rather claver wi' a daft quean they ca' Diana Vernon (weel I wet they might ca' her Diana of the Ephesians, for she's little better than a heathen—better? she's waur—a Roman, a mere Roman)—he'll claver wi' her, or any ither idle slut, rather than hear what might do him gude a' the days of his life, frae you or me, Mr. Hammorgaw, or ony ither sober and sponsible person. Reason, sir, is what he canna endure—he's a' for your vanities and volubilities; and he ance tell'd me (puir blinded creature!) that the Psalms of David were excellent poetry! as if the holy Psalmist thought o' rattling rhymes in a blether, like his ain silly clinkum-clankum things that he ca's verse. Gude help him!—twa lines o' Davie Lindsay would ding a' he ever clerkit."

While listening to this perverted account of my temper and studies, you will not be surprised if I meditated for Mr. Fairservice the unpleasant surprise of a broken pate on the first decent opportunity. His friend only intimated his attention by "Ay, ay!" and "Is't e'en sae?" and suchlike expressions of interest, at the proper breaks in Mr. Fairservice's harangue, until at length, in answer to some observation of greater length, the import of which I only collected from my trusty guide's reply, honest Andrew answered, "Tell him a bit o'my mind, quoth ye? Wha wad be fule then but Andrew? He's a red-wad deevil, man—He's like Giles Heathertap's auld boar;—ye need but shake a clout at him to make him turn and gore. Bide wi' him, say ye?—Troth, I kenna what for I bide wi' him mysell. But the lad's no a bad lad after a'; and he needs some carefu' body to look after him. He hasna the right grip o' his hand—

the gowd slips through't like water, man; and it's no that ill a thing to be near him when his purse is in his hand, and it's seldom out o't. And then he's come o' guid kith and kin—My heart warms to the poor thoughtless callant, Mr. Hammorgaw—and then the penny fee"—

In the latter part of this instructive communication, Mr. Fairservice lowered his voice to a tone better beseeming the conversation in a place of public resort on a Sabbath evening, and his companion and he were soon beyond my hearing. My feelings of hasty resentment soon subsided, under the conviction that, as Andrew himself might have said, "A harkener always hears a bad tale of himself," and that whoever should happen to overhear their character discussed in their own servants'-hall, must prepare to undergo the scalpel of some such anatomist as Mr. Fairservice. The incident was so far useful, as, including the feelings to which it gave rise, it sped away a part of the time which hung so heavily on my hand.

Evening had now closed, and the growing darkness gave to the broad, still, and deep expanse of the brimful river, first a hue sombre and uniform—then a dismal and turbid appearance, partially lighted by a waning and pallid moon. The massive and ancient bridge which stretches across the Clyde was now but dimly visible, and resembled that which Mirza, in his unequalled vision, has described as traversing the valley of Bagdad. The low-browed arches, seen as imperfectly as the dusky current which they bestrode, seemed rather caverns which swallowed up the gloomy waters of the river, than apertures contrived for their passage. With the advancing night the stillness of the scene increased. There was yet a twinkling light occasionally seen to glide along by the stream, which conducted home one or two of the small parties, who, after the abstinence and religious duties of the day, had partaken of a social supper—the only meal at which the rigid Presbyterians made some advance to sociality on the Sabbath. Occasionally, also, the hoofs of a horse were heard, whose rider, after spending the Sunday in Glasgow, was directing his steps towards his residence in the country. These sounds and sights became gradually of more rare occurrence; at length they altogether ceased, and I was left to enjoy my solitary walk on the shores of the Clyde in solemn silence, broken only by the tolling of the successive hours from the steeples of the churches.

But as the night advanced my impatience at the uncertainty of the situation in which I was placed increased every moment, and became nearly ungovernable. I began to question whether I had been imposed upon by the trick of a fool, the raving of a madman, or the studied machinations of a villain, and paced the little quay or pier adjoining the entrance to the bridge, in a state of incredible anxiety and vexation. At length the hour of twelve o'clock swung its summons over the city from the belfry of the metropolitan church of St. Mungo, and was answered and vouched by all the others like dutiful diocesans. The echoes had scarcely ceased to repeat the last sound, when a human form—the first I had seen for two hours—appeared passing along the bridge from the southern shore of the river. I advanced to meet him with a feeling as if my fate depended on the result of the interview, so much had my anxiety been wound up by protracted expectation. All that I could remark of the passenger as we advanced towards each other, was that his frame was rather beneath than above the middle size, but apparently strong, thick-set, and muscular; his dress a horseman's wrapping coat. I slackened my pace, and almost paused as I advanced in expectation that he would address me. But to my inexpressible disappointment he passed without speaking, and I had no pretence for being the first to address one who, notwithstanding his appearance at the very hour of appointment, might nevertheless be an absolute stranger. I stopped when he had passed me, and looked after him, uncertain whether I ought not to follow him. The stranger walked on till near the northern end of the bridge, then paused, looked back, and turning round, again advanced towards me. I resolved that this time he should not have the apology for silence proper to apparitions, who, it is vulgarly supposed, cannot speak until they are spoken to. "You walk late, sir," said I, as we met a second time.

"I bide tryste," was the reply; "and so I think do you, Mr. Osbaldistone."

"You are then the person who requested to meet me here at this unusual hour?"

"I am," he replied. "Follow me, and you shall know my reasons."

"Before following you, I must know your name and purpose," I answered.

"I am a man," was the reply; "and my purpose is friendly to you."

"A man!" I repeated;—"that is a very brief description."

"It will serve for one who has no other to give," said the stranger. "He that is without name, without friends, without coin, without country, is still at least a man; and he that has all these is no more."

"Yet this is still too general an account of yourself, to say the least of it, to establish your credit with a stranger."

"It is all I mean to give, howsoe'er; you may choose to follow me, or to remain without the information I desire to afford you."

"Can you not give me that information here?" I demanded.

"You must receive it from your eyes, not from my tongue—you must follow me, or remain in ignorance of the information which I have to give you."

There was something short, determined, and even stern, in the man's manner, not certainly well calculated to conciliate undoubting confidence.

"What is it you fear?" he said impatiently. "To whom, think ye, is your life of such consequence, that they should seek to bereave ye of it?"

"I fear nothing," I replied firmly, though somewhat hastily. "Walk on—I attend you."

We proceeded, contrary to my expectation, to re-enter the town, and glided like mute spectres, side by side, up its empty and silent streets. The high and gloomy stone fronts, with the variegated ornaments and pediments of the windows, looked yet taller and more sable by the imperfect moonshine. Our walk was for some minutes in perfect silence. At length my conductor spoke.

"Are you afraid?"

"I retort your own words," I replied: "wherefore should I fear?"

"Because you are with a stranger—perhaps an enemy, in a place where you have no friends and many enemies."

"I neither fear you nor them; I am young, active, and armed."

"I am not armed," replied my conductor: "but no matter, a willing hand never lacked weapon. You say you fear nothing; but if you knew who was by your side, perhaps you might underlie a tremor."

"And why should I?" replied I. "I again repeat, I fear nought that you can do."

"Nought that I can do?—Be it so. But do you not fear the consequences of being found with one whose very name whispered in this lonely street would make the stones themselves rise up to apprehend him—on whose head half the men in Glasgow would build their fortune as on a found treasure, had they the luck to grip him by the collar—the sound of whose apprehension were as welcome at the Cross of Edinburgh as ever the news of a field stricken and won in Flanders?"

"And who then are you, whose name should create so deep a feeling of terror?" I replied.

"No enemy of yours, since I am conveying you to a place, where, were I myself recognised and identified, iron to the heels and hemp to the craig would be my brief dooming."

I paused and stood still on the pavement, drawing back so as to have the most perfect view of my companion which the light afforded me, and which was sufficient to guard against any sudden motion of assault.

"You have said," I answered, "either too much or too little—too much to induce me to confide in you as a mere stranger, since you avow yourself a person amenable to the laws of the country in which we are—and too little, unless you could show that you are unjustly subjected to their rigour."

As I ceased to speak, he made a step towards me. I drew back instinctively, and laid my hand on the hilt of my sword.

"What!" said he—"on an unarmed man, and your friend?"

"I am yet ignorant if you are either the one or the other," I replied; "and to say the truth, your language and manner might well entitle me to doubt both."

"It is manfully spoken," replied my conductor; "and I respect him whose hand can keep his head.—I will be frank and free with you—I am conveying you to prison."

"To prison!" I exclaimed—"by what warrant or for what offence?—You shall have my life sooner than my liberty—I defy you, and I will not follow you a step farther."

"I do not," he said, "carry you there as a prisoner; I am," he added, drawing himself haughtily up, "neither a messenger nor sheriff's officer. I carry you to see a prisoner from whose lips you will learn the risk in which you presently stand. Your liberty is little risked by the visit; mine is in some peril; but that I readily encounter on your account, for I care not for risk, and I love a free young blood, that kens no protector but the cross o' the sword."

While he spoke thus, we had reached the principal street, and were pausing before a large building of hewn stone, garnished, as I thought I could perceive, with gratings of iron before the windows.

"Muckle," said the stranger, whose language became more broadly national as he assumed a tone of colloquial freedom—"Muckle wad the provost and bailies o' Glasgow gie to hae him sitting with iron garters to his hose within their tolbooth that now stands wi' his legs as free as the red-deer's on the outside on't. And little wad it avail them; for an if they had me there wi' a stane's weight o' iron at every ankle, I would show them a toom room and a lost lodger before to-morrow—But come on, what stint ye for?"

As he spoke thus, he tapped at a low wicket, and was answered by a sharp voice, as of one awakened from a dream or reverie,—"Fa's tat?—Wha's that, I wad say?—

and fat a deil want ye at this hour at e'en?—Clean again rules—clean again rules, as they ca' them."

The protracted tone in which the last words were uttered, betokened that the speaker was again composing himself to slumber. But my guide spoke in a loud whisper—"Dougal, man! hae ye forgotten Ha nun Gregarach?"

"Deil a bit, deil a bit," was the ready and lively response, and I heard the internal guardian of the prison-gate bustle up with great alacrity. A few words were exchanged between my conductor and the turnkey in a language to which I was an absolute stranger. The bolts revolved, but with a caution which marked the apprehension that the noise might be overheard, and we stood within the vestibule of the prison of Glasgow,—a small, but strong guard-room, from which a narrow staircase led upwards, and one or two low entrances conducted to apartments on the same level with the outward gate, all secured with the jealous strength of wickets, bolts, and bars. The walls, otherwise naked, were not unsuitably garnished with iron fetters, and other uncouth implements, which might be designed for purposes still more inhuman, interspersed with partisans, guns, pistols of antique manufacture, and other weapons of defence and offence.

At finding myself so unexpectedly, fortuitously, and, as it were, by stealth, introduced within one of the legal fortresses of Scotland, I could not help recollecting my adventure in Northumberland, and fretting at the strange incidents which again, without any demerits of my own, threatened to place me in a dangerous and disagreeable collision with the laws of a country which I visited only in the capacity of a stranger.

CHAPTER FIFTH

> Look round thee, young Astolpho: Here's the place
> Which men (for being poor) are sent to starve in;
> Rude remedy, I trow, for sore disease.
> Within these walls, stifled by damp and stench,
> Doth Hope's fair torch expire; and at the snuff,
> Ere yet 'tis quite extinct, rude, wild, and way-ward,
> The desperate revelries of wild despair,
> Kindling their hell-born cressets, light to deeds
> That the poor captive would have died ere practised,
> Till bondage sunk his soul to his condition.
>
> — THE PRISON, SCENE III. ACT I.

At my first entrance I turned an eager glance towards my conductor; but the lamp in the vestibule was too low in flame to give my curiosity any satisfaction by affording a distinct perusal of his features. As the turnkey held the light in his hand, the beams fell more full on his own scarce less interesting figure. He was a wild shock-headed looking animal, whose profusion of red hair covered and obscured his features, which were otherwise only characterised by the extravagant joy that affected him at the sight of my guide. In my experience I have met nothing so absolutely resembling my idea of a very uncouth, wild, and ugly savage, adoring the idol of his tribe. He grinned, he shivered, he laughed, he was near crying, if he did not actually cry. He had a "Where shall I go?—What can I do for you?" expression of face; the complete, surrendered, and anxious subservience and devotion of which it is difficult to describe, otherwise than by the awkward combination which I have attempted. The fellow's voice seemed choking in his ecstasy, and only could express itself in such interjections as "Oigh! oigh!—Ay! ay!—it's lang since she's seen ye!" and other exclamations equally brief, expressed in the same unknown tongue in which he had communicated with my conductor while we were on the outside of the jail door. My guide received all this excess of joyful gratulation much like a prince too early accustomed to the homage of those around him to be much moved by it, yet willing to requite it by the usual forms of royal courtesy. He extended his hand graciously towards the turnkey, with a civil inquiry of "How's a' wi' you, Dougal?"

"Oigh! oigh!" exclaimed Dougal, softening the sharp exclamations of his surprise as he looked around with an eye of watchful alarm—"Oigh! to see you here—to see you here!—Oigh!—what will come o' ye gin the bailies suld come to get witting—ta filthy, gutty hallions, tat they are?"

My guide placed his finger on his lip, and said, "Fear nothing, Dougal; your hands shall never draw a bolt on me."

"Tat sall they no," said Dougal; "she suld—she wad—that is, she wishes them hacked aff by the elbows first—But when are ye gaun yonder again? and ye'll no forget to let her ken—she's your puir cousin, God kens, only seven times removed."

"I will let you ken, Dougal, as soon as my plans are settled."

"And, by her sooth, when you do, an it were twal o' the Sunday at e'en, she'll fling her keys at the provost's head or she gie them anither turn, and that or ever Monday morning begins—see if she winna."

My mysterious stranger cut his acquaintance's ecstasies short by again addressing him, in what I afterwards understood to be the Irish, Earse, or Gaelic, explaining, probably, the services which he required at his hand. The answer, "Wi' a' her heart—wi' a' her soul," with a good deal of indistinct muttering in a similar tone, intimated the turnkey's acquiescence in what he proposed. The fellow trimmed his dying lamp, and made a sign to me to follow him.

"Do you not go with us?" said I, looking to my conductor.

"It is unnecessary," he replied; "my company may be inconvenient for you, and I had better remain to secure our retreat."

"I do not suppose you mean to betray me to danger," said I.

"To none but what I partake in doubly," answered the stranger, with a voice of assurance which it was impossible to mistrust.

I followed the turnkey, who, leaving the inner wicket unlocked behind him, led me up a *turnpike* (so the Scotch call a winding stair), then along a narrow gallery—then opening one of several doors which led into the passage, he ushered me into a small apartment, and casting his eye on the pallet-bed which occupied one corner, said with an under voice, as he placed the lamp on a little deal table, "She's sleeping."

"She!—who?—can it be Diana Vernon in this abode of misery?"

I turned my eye to the bed, and it was with a mixture of disappointment oddly mingled with pleasure, that I saw my first suspicion had deceived me. I saw a head neither young nor beautiful, garnished with a grey beard of two days' growth, and accommodated with a red nightcap. The first glance put me at ease on the score of Diana Vernon; the second, as the slumberer awoke from a heavy sleep, yawned, and rubbed his eyes, presented me with features very different indeed—even those of my poor friend Owen. I drew back out of view an instant, that he might have time to recover himself; fortunately recollecting that I was but an intruder on these cells of sorrow, and that any alarm might be attended with unhappy consequences.

Meantime, the unfortunate formalist, raising himself from the pallet-bed with the assistance of one hand, and scratching his cap with the other, exclaimed in a voice in which as much peevishness as he was capable of feeling, contended with drowsiness, "I'll tell you what, Mr. Dug-well, or whatever your name may be, the sum-total of the matter is, that if my natural rest is to be broken in this manner, I must complain to the lord mayor."

"Shentlemans to speak wi' her," replied Dougal, resuming the true dogged sullen tone of a turnkey, in exchange for the shrill clang of Highland congratulation with which he had welcomed my mysterious guide; and, turning on his heel, he left the apartment.

It was some time before I could prevail upon the unfortunate sleeper awakening to recognise me; and when he did so, the distress of the worthy creature was extreme, at supposing, which he naturally did, that I had been sent thither as a partner of his captivity.

"O, Mr. Frank, what have you brought yourself and the house to?—I think nothing of myself, that am a mere cipher, so to speak; but you, that was your father's sum-total—his omnium,—you that might have been the first man in the first house in the first city, to be shut up in a nasty Scotch jail, where one cannot even get the dirt brushed off their clothes!"

He rubbed, with an air of peevish irritation, the once stainless brown coat, which had now shared some of the impurities of the floor of his prison-house,—his habits of extreme punctilious neatness acting mechanically to increase his distress.—"O Heaven be gracious to us!" he continued. "What news this will be on 'Change! There has not the like come there since the battle of Almanza, where the total of the British loss was summed up to five thousand men killed and wounded, besides a floating balance of missing—but what will that be to the news that Osbaldistone and Tresham have stopped!"

I broke in on his lamentations to acquaint him that I was no prisoner, though scarce able to account for my being in that place at such an hour. I could only silence his inquiries by persisting in those which his own situation suggested; and at length obtained from him such information as he was able to give me. It was none of the most distinct; for, however clear-headed in his own routine of commercial business, Owen, you are well aware, was not very acute in comprehending what lay beyond that sphere.

The sum of his information was, that of two correspondents of my father's firm at Glasgow, where, owing to engagements in Scotland formerly alluded to, he transacted a great deal of business, both my father and Owen had found the house of MacVittie, MacFin, and Company, the most obliging and accommodating. They had deferred to the great English house on every possible occasion; and in their bargains and transactions acted, without repining, the part of the jackall, who only claims what the lion is pleased to leave him. However small the share of profit allotted to them, it was always, as they expressed it, "enough for the like of them;" however large the portion of trouble, "they were sensible they could not do too much to deserve the continued patronage and good opinion of their honoured friends in Crane Alley."

The dictates of my father were to MacVittie and MacFin the laws of the Medes and Persians, not to be altered, innovated, or even discussed; and the punctilios exacted by Owen in their business transactions, for he was a great lover of form, more especially when he could dictate it *ex cathedra,* seemed scarce less sanctimonious in their eyes. This tone of deep and respectful observance went all currently down with Owen; but my father looked a little closer into men's bosoms, and whether suspicious of this excess of deference, or, as a lover of brevity and simplicity in business, tired with these gentlemen's long-winded professions of regard, he had uniformly resisted their desire to become his sole agents in Scotland. On the contrary, he transacted many affairs through a correspondent of a character perfectly different—a man whose good opinion of himself amounted to self-conceit, and who, disliking the English in general as much as my father did the Scotch, would hold no communication but on a footing of absolute equality; jealous, moreover; captious occasionally; as tenacious of his own opinions in point of form as Owen could be of his; and totally indifferent though the authority of all Lombard Street had stood against his own private opinion.

As these peculiarities of temper rendered it difficult to transact business with Mr. Nicol Jarvie,—as they occasioned at times disputes and coldness between the English house and their correspondent, which were only got over by a sense of mutual interest,—as, moreover, Owen's personal vanity sometimes suffered a little in the discussions to which they gave rise, you cannot be surprised, Tresham, that our old friend threw at all times the weight of his influence in favour of the civil, discreet, accommodating concern of MacVittie and MacFin, and spoke of Jarvie as a petulant, conceited Scotch pedlar, with whom there was no dealing.

It was also not surprising, that in these circumstances, which I only learned in detail some time afterwards, Owen, in the difficulties to which the house was reduced by the absence of my father, and the disappearance of Rashleigh, should, on his arrival in Scotland, which took place two days before mine, have recourse to the friendship of those correspondents, who had always professed themselves obliged, gratified, and devoted to the service of his principal. He was received at Messrs. MacVittie and MacFin's counting-house in the Gallowgate, with something like the devotion a Catholic would pay to his tutelar saint. But, alas! this sunshine was soon overclouded, when, encouraged by the fair hopes which it inspired, he opened the difficulties of the house to his friendly correspondents, and requested their counsel and assistance. MacVittie was almost stunned by the communication; and MacFin, ere it was completed, was already at the ledger of their firm, and deeply engaged in the very bowels of the multitudinous accounts between their house and that of Osbaldistone and Tresham, for the purpose of discovering on which side the balance lay. Alas! the scale depressed considerably against the English firm; and the faces of MacVittie and MacFin, hitherto only blank and doubtful, became now ominous, grim, and lowering. They met Mr. Owen's request of countenance and assistance with a counter-demand of instant security against imminent hazard of eventual loss; and at length, speaking more plainly, required that a deposit of assets, destined for other purposes, should be placed in their hands for that purpose. Owen repelled this demand with great indignation, as dishonourable to his constituents, unjust to the other creditors of Osbaldistone and Tresham, and very ungrateful on the part of those by whom it was made.

The Scotch partners gained, in the course of this controversy, what is very convenient to persons who are in the wrong, an opportunity and pretext for putting themselves in a violent passion, and for taking, under the pretext of the provocation they had received, measures to which some sense of decency, if not of conscience, might otherwise have deterred them from resorting.

Owen had a small share, as I believe is usual, in the house to which he acted as head-clerk, and was therefore personally liable for all its obligations. This was known to Messrs. MacVittie and MacFin; and, with a view of making him feel their power, or rather in order to force him, at this emergency, into those measures in their favour, to which he had expressed himself so repugnant, they had recourse to a summary process of arrest and imprisonment,—which it seems the law of Scotland (therein surely liable to much abuse) allows to a creditor, who finds his conscience at liberty to make oath that the debtor meditates departing from the realm. Under such a warrant had poor Owen been confined to durance on the day preceding that when I was so strangely guided to his prison-house.

Thus possessed of the alarming outline of facts, the question remained, what was to be done and it was not of easy determination. I plainly perceived the perils with which we were surrounded, but it was more difficult to suggest any remedy. The warning which I had already received seemed to intimate, that my own personal liberty might be endangered by an open appearance in Owen's behalf. Owen entertained the same apprehension, and, in the exaggeration of his terror, assured me that a Scotchman, rather than run the risk of losing a farthing by an Englishman, would find law for arresting his wife, children, man-servant, maidservant, and stranger within his household. The laws concerning debt, in most countries, are so unmercifully severe, that I could not altogether disbelieve his statement; and my arrest, in the present circumstances, would have been a *coup-de-grace* to my father's affairs. In this dilemma, I asked Owen if he had not thought of having recourse to my father's other correspondent in Glasgow, Mr. Nicol Jarvie?

"He had sent him a letter," he replied, "that morning; but if the smooth-tongued and civil house in the Gallowgate[4] had used him thus, what was to be expected from the cross-grained crab-stock in the Salt-Market?

You might as well ask a broker to give up his percentage, as expect a favour from him without the *per contra*. He had not even," Owen said, "answered his letter though it was put into his hand that morning as he went to church." And here the despairing man-of-figures threw himself down on his pallet, exclaiming,—"My poor dear master! My poor dear master! O Mr. Frank, Mr. Frank, this is all your obstinacy!—But God forgive me for saying so to you in your distress! It's God's disposing, and man must submit."

My philosophy, Tresham, could not prevent my sharing in the honest creature's distress, and we mingled our tears,—the more bitter on my part, as the perverse opposition to my father's will, with which the kind-hearted Owen forbore to upbraid me, rose up to my conscience as the cause of all this affliction.

In the midst of our mingled sorrow, we were disturbed and surprised by a loud knocking at the outward door of the prison. I ran to the top of the staircase to listen, but could only hear the voice of the turnkey, alternately in a high tone, answering to some person without, and in a whisper, addressed to the person who had guided me hither—"She's coming—she's coming," aloud; then in a low key, "O hon-a-ri! O hon-a-ri! what'll she do now?—Gang up ta stair, and hide yourself ahint ta Sassenach shentleman's ped.—She's coming as fast as she can.—Ahellanay! it's my lord provosts, and ta pailies, and ta guard—and ta captain's coming toon stairs too—Got press her! gang up or he meets her.—She's coming—she's coming—ta lock's sair roosted."

While Dougal, unwillingly, and with as much delay as possible, undid the various fastenings to give admittance to those without, whose impatience became clamorous, my guide ascended the winding stair, and sprang into Owen's apartment, into which I followed him. He cast his eyes hastily round, as if looking for a place of concealment; then said to me, "Lend me your pistols—yet it's no matter, I can do without them—Whatever you see, take no heed, and do not mix your hand in another man's feud—This gear's mine, and I must manage it as I dow; but I have been as hard bested, and worse, than I am even now."

As the stranger spoke these words, he stripped from his person the cumbrous upper coat in which he was wrapt, confronted the door of the apartment, on which he fixed a keen and determined glance, drawing his person a little back to concentrate his force, like a fine horse brought up to the leaping-bar. I had not a moment's doubt that he meant to extricate himself from his embarrassment, whatever might be the cause of it, by springing full upon those who should appear when the doors opened, and forcing his way through all opposition into the street;—and such was the appearance of strength and agility displayed in his frame, and of determination in his look and manner, that I did not doubt a moment but that he might get clear through his opponents, unless they employed fatal means to stop his purpose. It was a period of awful suspense betwixt the opening of the outward gate and that of the door of the apartment, when there appeared—no guard with bayonets fixed, or watch with clubs, bills, or partisans, but a good-looking young woman, with grogram petticoats, tucked up for trudging through the streets, and holding a lantern in her hand. This female ushered in a more important personage, in form, stout, short, and somewhat corpulent; and by dignity, as it soon appeared, a magistrate, bob-wigged, bustling, and breathless with peevish impatience. My conductor, at his appearance, drew back as if to escape observation; but he could not elude the penetrating twinkle with which this dignitary reconnoitered the whole apartment.

"A bonny thing it is, and a beseeming, that I should be kept at the door half an hour, Captain Stanchells," said he, addressing the principal jailor, who now showed himself at the door as if in attendance on the great man, "knocking as hard to get into the tolbooth as onybody else wad to get out of it, could that avail them, poor fallen creatures!—And how's this?—how's this?—strangers in the jail after lock-up hours, and on the Sabbath evening!—I shall look after this, Stanchells, you may depend on't —Keep the door locked, and I'll speak to these gentlemen in a gliffing—But first I maun hae a crack wi' an auld acquaintance here.— Mr. Owen, Mr. Owen, how's a' wi' ye, man?"

"Pretty well in body, I thank you, Mr. Jarvie," drawled out poor Owen, "but sore afflicted in spirit."

"Nae doubt, nae doubt—ay, ay—it's an awfu' whummle—and for ane that held his head sae high too—human nature, human nature—Ay ay, we're a' subject to a downcome. Mr. Osbaldistone is a gude honest gentleman; but I aye said he was ane o' them wad make a spune or spoil a horn, as my father the worthy deacon used to say. The deacon used to say to me, 'Nick—young Nick' (his name was Nicol as weel as mine; sae folk ca'd us in their daffin', young Nick and auld Nick)—'Nick,' said he, 'never put out your arm farther than ye can draw it easily back again.' I hae said sae to Mr. Osbaldistone, and he didna seem to take it a'thegither sae kind as I wished—but it was weel meant—weel meant."

This discourse, delivered with prodigious volubility, and a great appearance of self-complacency, as he recollected his own advice and predictions, gave little promise of assistance at the hands of Mr. Jarvie. Yet it soon appeared rather to proceed from a total want of delicacy than any deficiency of real kindness; for when Owen expressed himself somewhat hurt that these things should be recalled to memory in his present situation, the Glaswegian took him by the hand, and bade him "Cheer up a gliff! D'ye think I wad hae comed out at twal o'clock at night, and amaist broken the Lord's day, just to tell a fa'en man o' his backslidings? Na, na, that's no Bailie Jarvie's gate, nor was't his worthy father's the deacon afore him. Why, man! it's my rule never to think on warldly business on the Sabbath, and though I did a' I could to keep your note that I gat this morning out o' my head, yet I thought mair on it a' day, than on the preaching—And it's my rule to gang to my bed wi' the yellow curtains preceesely at ten o'clock—unless I were eating a haddock wi' a neighbour, or a neighbour wi' me—ask the lass-quean there, if it isna a fundamental rule in my household; and here hae I sitten up reading gude books, and gaping as if I wad swallow St. Enox Kirk, till it chappit twal, whilk was a lawfu' hour to gie a look at my ledger, just to see how things stood between us; and then, as time and tide wait for no man, I made the lass get the lantern, and came slipping my ways here to see what can be dune anent your affairs. Bailie Jarvie can command entrance into the tolbooth at ony hour, day or night;—sae could my father the deacon in his time, honest man, praise to his memory."

Although Owen groaned at the mention of the ledger, leading me grievously to fear that here also the balance stood in the wrong column; and although the worthy magistrate's speech expressed much self-complacency, and some ominous triumph in his own superior judgment, yet it was blended with a sort of frank and blunt good-nature, from which I could not help deriving some hopes. He requested to see some papers he mentioned, snatched them hastily from Owen's hand, and sitting on the bed, to "rest his shanks," as he was pleased to express the accommodation which that posture afforded him, his servant girl held up the lantern to him, while, pshawing, muttering, and sputtering, now at the imperfect light, now at the contents of the packet, he ran over the writings it contained.

Seeing him fairly engaged in this course of study, the guide who had brought me hither seemed disposed to take an unceremonious leave. He made a sign to me to say nothing, and intimated, by his change of posture, an intention to glide towards the door in such a manner as to attract the least possible observation. But the alert magistrate (very different from my old acquaintance, Mr. Justice Inglewood) instantly detected and interrupted his purposes. "I say, look to the door, Stanchells—shut and lock it, and keep watch on the outside."

The stranger's brow darkened, and he seemed for an instant again to meditate the effecting his retreat by violence; but ere he had determined, the door closed, and the ponderous bolt revolved. He muttered an exclamation in Gaelic, strode across the floor, and then, with an air of dogged resolution, as if fixed and prepared to see the scene to an end, sate himself down on the oak table, and whistled a strathspey.

Mr. Jarvie, who seemed very alert and expeditious in going through business, soon showed himself master of that which he had been considering, and addressed himself to Mr. Owen in the following strain:— "Weel, Mr. Owen, weel—your house are awin' certain sums to Messrs. MacVittie and MacFin (shame fa' their souple snouts! they made that and mair out o' a bargain about the aik-woods at Glen-Cailziechat, that they took out atween my teeth—wi' help o' your gude word, I maun needs say, Mr. Owen—but that makes nae odds now)—Weel, sir, your house awes them this siller; and for this, and relief of other engagements they stand in for you, they hae putten a double turn o' Stanchells' muckle key on ye.— Weel, sir, ye awe this siller—and maybe ye awe some mair to some other body too—maybe ye awe some to myself, Bailie Nicol Jarvie."

"I cannot deny, sir, but the balance may of this date be brought out against us, Mr. Jarvie," said Owen; "but you'll please to consider"—

"I hae nae time to consider e'enow, Mr. Owen—Sae near Sabbath at e'en, and out o' ane's warm bed at this time o' night, and a sort o' drow in the air besides—there's nae time for considering—But, sir, as I was saying, ye awe me money—it winna deny —ye awe me money, less or mair, I'll stand by it. But then, Mr. Owen, I canna see how you, an active man that understands business, can redd out the business ye're come down about, and clear us a' aff—as I have gritt hope ye will—if ye're keepit lying here in the tolbooth of Glasgow. Now, sir, if you can find caution *judicio sisti*,—that is, that ye winna flee the country, but appear and relieve your caution when ca'd for in our legal courts, ye may be set at liberty this very morning."

"Mr. Jarvie," said Owen, "if any friend would become surety for me to that effect, my liberty might be usefully employed, doubtless, both for the house and all connected with it."

"Aweel, sir," continued Jarvie, "and doubtless such a friend wad expect ye to appear when ca'd on, and relieve him o' his engagement."

"And I should do so as certainly, bating sickness or death, as that two and two make four."

"Aweel, Mr. Owen," resumed the citizen of Glasgow, "I dinna misdoubt ye, and I'll prove it, sir—I'll prove it. I am a carefu' man, as is weel ken'd, and industrious, as the hale town can testify; and I can win my crowns, and keep my crowns, and count my crowns, wi' onybody in the Saut Market, or it may be in the Gallowgate. And I'm a prudent man, as my father the deacon was before me;—but rather than an honest civil gentleman, that understands business, and is willing to do justice to all men, should lie by the heels this gate, unable to help himself or onybody else—

why, conscience, man! I'll be your bail myself—But ye'll mind it's a bail *judicio sisti*, as our town-clerk says, not *judicatum solvi;* ye'll mind that, for there's muckle difference."

Mr. Owen assured him, that as matters then stood, he could not expect any one to become surety for the actual payment of the debt, but that there was not the most distant cause for apprehending loss from his failing to present himself when lawfully called upon.

"I believe ye—I believe ye. Eneugh said—eneugh said. We'se hae your legs loose by breakfast-time.—And now let's hear what thir chamber chiels o' yours hae to say for themselves, or how, in the name of unrule, they got here at this time o' night."

CHAPTER SIXTH

> Hame came our gudeman at e'en,
> And hame came he,
> And there he saw a man
> Where a man suldna be.
> "How's this now, kimmer?
> How's this?" quo he,—
> "How came this carle here
> Without the leave o' me?"
>
> — OLD SONG.

The magistrate took the light out of the servant-maid's hand, and advanced to his scrutiny, like Diogenes in the street of Athens, lantern-in-hand, and probably with as little expectation as that of the cynic, that he was likely to encounter any especial treasure in the course of his researches. The first whom he approached was my mysterious guide, who, seated on a table as I have already described him, with his eyes firmly fixed on the wall, his features arranged into the utmost inflexibility of expression, his hands folded on his breast with an air betwixt carelessness and defiance, his heel patting against the foot of the table, to keep time with the tune which he continued to whistle, submitted to Mr. Jarvie's investigation with an air of absolute confidence and assurance which, for a moment, placed at fault the memory and sagacity of the acute investigator.

"Ah!—Eh!—Oh!" exclaimed the Bailie. "My conscience!—it's impossible!—and yet—no!—Conscience!—it canna be!—and yet again—Deil hae me, that I suld say sae! —Ye robber—ye cateran—ye born deevil that ye are, to a' bad ends and nae gude ane! —can this be you?"

"E'en as ye see, Bailie," was the laconic answer.

"Conscience! if I am na clean bumbaized—*you*, ye cheat-the-wuddy rogue —*you* here on your venture in the tolbooth o' Glasgow?—What d'ye think's the value o' your head?"

"Umph!—why, fairly weighed, and Dutch weight, it might weigh down one provost's, four bailies', a town-clerk's, six deacons', besides stent-masters'"—

"Ah, ye reiving villain!" interrupted Mr. Jarvie. "But tell ower your sins, and prepare ye, for if I say the word"—

"True, Bailie," said he who was thus addressed, folding his hands behind him with the utmost *nonchalance*, "but ye will never say that word."

"And why suld I not, sir?" exclaimed the magistrate—"Why suld I not? Answer me that—why suld I not?"

"For three sufficient reasons, Bailie Jarvie.—First, for auld langsyne; second, for the sake of the auld wife ayont the fire at Stuckavrallachan, that made some mixture of our bluids, to my own proper shame be it spoken! that has a cousin wi' accounts, and yarn winnles, and looms and shuttles, like a mere mechanical person; and lastly, Bailie, because if I saw a sign o' your betraying me, I would plaster that wa' with your harns ere the hand of man could rescue you!"

"Ye're a bauld desperate villain, sir," retorted the undaunted Bailie; "and ye ken that I ken ye to be sae, and that I wadna stand a moment for my ain risk."

"I ken weel," said the other, "ye hae gentle bluid in your veins, and I wad be laith to hurt my ain kinsman. But I'll gang out here as free as I came in, or the very wa's o' Glasgow tolbooth shall tell o't these ten years to come."

"Weel, weel," said Mr. Jarvie, "bluid's thicker than water; and it liesna in kith, kin, and ally, to see motes in ilka other's een if other een see them no. It wad be sair news to the auld wife below the Ben of Stuckavrallachan, that you, ye Hieland limmer, had knockit out my harns, or that I had kilted you up in a tow. But ye'll own, ye dour deevil, that were it no your very sell, I wad hae grippit the best man in the Hielands."

"Ye wad hae tried, cousin," answered my guide, "that I wot weel; but I doubt ye wad hae come aff wi' the short measure; for we gang-there-out Hieland bodies are an unchancy generation when you speak to us o' bondage. We downa bide the coercion of gude braid-claith about our hinderlans, let a be breeks o' free-stone, and garters o' iron."

"Ye'll find the stane breeks and the airn garters—ay, and the hemp cravat, for a' that, neighbour," replied the Bailie.

"Nae man in a civilised country ever played the pliskies ye hae done—but e'en pickle in your ain pock-neuk—I hae gi'en ye wanting."

"Well, cousin," said the other, "ye'll wear black at my burial."

"Deil a black cloak will be there, Robin, but the corbies and the hoodie-craws, I'se gie ye my hand on that. But whar's the gude thousand pund Scots that I lent ye, man, and when am I to see it again?"

"Where it is," replied my guide, after the affectation of considering for a moment, "I cannot justly tell—probably where last year's snaw is."

"And that's on the tap of Schehallion, ye Hieland dog," said Mr. Jarvie; "and I look for payment frae you where ye stand."

"Ay," replied the Highlander, "but I keep neither snaw nor dollars in my sporran. And as to when you'll see it—why, just when the king enjoys his ain again, as the auld sang says."

"Warst of a', Robin," retorted the Glaswegian,—"I mean, ye disloyal traitor—Warst of a'!—Wad ye bring popery in on us, and arbitrary power, and a foist and a warming-pan, and the set forms, and the curates, and the auld enormities o' surplices and cerements? Ye had better stick to your auld trade o' theft-boot, black-mail, spreaghs, and gillravaging—better stealing nowte than ruining nations."

"Hout, man—whisht wi' your whiggery," answered the Celt; "we hae ken'd ane anither mony a lang day. I'se take care your counting-room is no cleaned out when the Gillon-a-naillie[5] come to redd up the Glasgow buiths, and clear them o' their auld shop-wares.

And, unless it just fa' in the preceese way o' your duty, ye maunna see me oftener, Nicol, than I am disposed to be seen."

"Ye are a dauring villain, Rob," answered the Bailie; "and ye will be hanged, that will be seen and heard tell o'; but I'se ne'er be the ill bird and foul my nest, set apart strong necessity and the skreigh of duty, which no man should hear and be inobedient. And wha the deevil's this?" he continued, turning to me—"Some gillravager that ye hae listed, I daur say. He looks as if he had a bauld heart to the highway, and a lang craig for the gibbet."

"This, good Mr. Jarvie," said Owen, who, like myself, had been struck dumb during this strange recognition, and no less strange dialogue, which took place betwixt these extraordinary kinsmen—"This, good Mr. Jarvie, is young Mr. Frank Osbaldistone, only child of the head of our house, who should have been taken into our firm at the time Mr. Rashleigh Osbaldistone, his cousin, had the luck to be taken into it"—(Here Owen could not suppress a groan)—"But howsoever"—

"Oh, I have heard of that smaik," said the Scotch merchant, interrupting him; "it is he whom your principal, like an obstinate auld fule, wad make a merchant o', wad he or wad he no,—and the lad turned a strolling stage-player, in pure dislike to the labour an honest man should live by. Weel, sir, what say you to your handiwork? Will Hamlet the Dane, or Hamlet's ghost, be good security for Mr. Owen, sir?"

"I don't deserve your taunt," I replied, "though I respect your motive, and am too grateful for the assistance you have afforded Mr. Owen, to resent it. My only business here was to do what I could (it is perhaps very little) to aid Mr. Owen in the management of my father's affairs. My dislike of the commercial profession is a feeling of which I am the best and sole judge."

"I protest," said the Highlander, "I had some respect for this callant even before I ken'd what was in him; but now I honour him for his contempt of weavers and spinners, and sic-like mechanical persons and their pursuits."

"Ye're mad, Rob," said the Bailie—"mad as a March hare—though wherefore a hare suld be mad at March mair than at Martinmas, is mair than I can weel say. Weavers! Deil shake ye out o' the web the weaver craft made. Spinners! ye'll spin and wind yourself a bonny pirn. And this young birkie here, that ye're hoying and hounding on the shortest road to the gallows and the deevil, will his stage-plays and his poetries help him here, dye think, ony mair than your deep oaths and drawn dirks, ye reprobate that ye are?—Will *Tityre tu patulae,* as they ca' it, tell him where Rashleigh Osbaldistone is? or Macbeth, and all his kernes and galla-glasses, and your awn to boot, Rob, procure him five thousand pounds to answer the bills which fall due ten days hence, were they a' rouped at the Cross,—basket-hilts, Andra-Ferraras, leather targets, brogues, brochan, and sporrans?"

"Ten days," I answered, and instinctively drew out Diana Vernon's packet; and the time being elapsed during which I was to keep the seal sacred, I hastily broke it open.

A sealed letter fell from a blank enclosure, owing to the trepidation with which I opened the parcel. A slight current of wind, which found its way through a broken pane of the window, wafted the letter to Mr. Jarvie's feet, who lifted it, examined the address with unceremonious curiosity, and, to my astonishment, handed it to his Highland kinsman, saying, "Here's a wind has blown a letter to its right owner, though there were ten thousand chances against its coming to hand."

The Highlander, having examined the address, broke the letter open without the least ceremony. I endeavoured to interrupt his proceeding.

"You must satisfy me, sir," said I, "that the letter is intended for you before I can permit you to peruse it."

"Make yourself quite easy, Mr. Osbaldistone," replied the mountaineer with great composure.—"remember Justice Inglewood, Clerk Jobson, Mr. Morris—above all, remember your vera humble servant, Robert Cawmil, and the beautiful Diana Vernon. Remember all this, and doubt no longer that the letter is for me."

I remained astonished at my own stupidity.—Through the whole night, the voice, and even the features of this man, though imperfectly seen, haunted me with recollections to which I could assign no exact local or personal associations. But now the light dawned on me at once; this man was Campbell himself. His whole peculiarities flashed on me at once,—the deep strong voice—the inflexible, stern, yet considerate cast of features—the Scottish brogue, with its corresponding dialect and imagery, which, although he possessed the power at times of laying them aside, recurred at every moment of emotion, and gave pith to his sarcasm, or vehemence to his expostulation. Rather beneath the middle size than above it, his limbs were formed upon the very strongest model that is consistent with agility, while from the remarkable ease and freedom of his movements, you could not doubt his possessing the latter quality in a high degree of perfection. Two points in his person interfered with the rules of symmetry; his shoulders were so broad in proportion to his height, as, notwithstanding the lean and lathy appearance of his frame, gave him something the air of being too square in respect to his stature; and his arms, though round, sinewy, and strong, were so very long as to be rather a deformity. I afterwards heard that this length of arm was a circumstance on which he prided himself; that when he wore his native Highland garb, he could tie the garters of his hose without stooping; and that it gave him great advantage in the use of the broad-sword, at which he was very dexterous. But certainly this want of symmetry destroyed the claim he might otherwise have set up, to be accounted a very handsome man; it gave something wild, irregular, and, as it were, unearthly, to his appearance, and reminded me involuntarily of the tales which Mabel used to tell of the old Picts who ravaged Northumberland in ancient times, who, according to her tradition, were a sort of half-goblin half-human beings, distinguished, like this man, for courage, cunning, ferocity, the length of their arms, and the squareness of their shoulders.

When, however, I recollected the circumstances in which we formerly met, I could not doubt that the billet was most probably designed for him. He had made a marked figure among those mysterious personages over whom Diana seemed to exercise an influence, and from whom she experienced an influence in her turn. It was painful to think that the fate of a being so amiable was involved in that of desperadoes of this man's description;—yet it seemed impossible to doubt it. Of what use, however, could this person be to my father's affairs?—I could think only of one. Rashleigh Osbaldistone had, at the instigation of Miss Vernon, certainly found means to produce Mr. Campbell when his presence was necessary to exculpate me from Morris's accusation—Was it not possible that her influence, in like manner, might prevail on Campbell to produce Rashleigh? Speaking on this supposition, I requested to know where my dangerous kinsman was, and when Mr. Campbell had seen him. The answer was indirect.

"It's a kittle cast she has gien me to play; but yet it's fair play, and I winna baulk her. Mr. Osbaldistone, I dwell not very far from hence—my kinsman can show you the way—Leave Mr. Owen to do the best he can in Glasgow—do you come and see me in the glens, and it's like I may pleasure you, and stead your father in his extremity. I am but a poor man; but wit's better than wealth—and, cousin" (turning from me to address Mr. Jarvie), "if ye daur venture sae muckle as to eat a dish of Scotch collops, and a leg o' red-deer venison wi' me, come ye wi' this Sassenach gentleman as far as Drymen or Bucklivie,—or the Clachan of Aberfoil will be better than ony o' them,—and I'll hae somebody waiting to weise ye the gate to the place where I may be for the time—What say ye, man? There's my thumb, I'll ne'er beguile thee."

"Na, na, Robin," said the cautious burgher, "I seldom like to leave the Gorbals;[6] I have nae freedom to gang among your wild hills, Robin, and your kilted red-shanks —it disna become my place, man."

"The devil damn your place and you baith!" reiterated Campbell. "The only drap o' gentle bluid that's in your body was our great-grand-uncle's that was justified[7] at Dumbarton, and you set yourself up to say ye wad derogate frae your place to visit me!

Hark thee, man—I owe thee a day in harst—I'll pay up your thousan pund Scots, plack and bawbee, gin ye'll be an honest fallow for anes, and just daiker up the gate wi' this Sassenach."

"Hout awa' wi' your gentility," replied the Bailie; "carry your gentle bluid to the Cross, and see what ye'll buy wi't. But, if I *were* to come, wad ye really and soothfastly pay me the siller?"

"I swear to ye," said the Highlander, "upon the halidome of him that sleeps beneath the grey stane at Inch-Cailleach."[8]

"Say nae mair, Robin—say nae mair—We'll see what may be dune. But ye maunna expect me to gang ower the Highland line—I'll gae beyond the line at no rate. Ye maun meet me about Bucklivie or the Clachan of Aberfoil,—and dinna forget the needful."

"Nae fear—nae fear," said Campbell; "I'll be as true as the steel blade that never failed its master. But I must be budging, cousin, for the air o' Glasgow tolbooth is no that ower salutary to a Highlander's constitution."

"Troth," replied the merchant, "and if my duty were to be dune, ye couldna change your atmosphere, as the minister ca's it, this ae wee while.—Ochon, that I sud ever be concerned in aiding and abetting an escape frae justice! it will be a shame and disgrace to me and mine, and my very father's memory, for ever."

"Hout tout, man! let that flee stick in the wa'," answered his kinsman; "when the dirt's dry it will rub out—Your father, honest man, could look ower a friend's fault as weel as anither."

"Ye may be right, Robin," replied the Bailie, after a moment's reflection; "he was a considerate man the deacon; he ken'd we had a' our frailties, and he lo'ed his friends—Ye'll no hae forgotten him, Robin?" This question he put in a softened tone, conveying as much at least of the ludicrous as the pathetic.

"Forgotten him!" replied his kinsman—"what suld ail me to forget him?—a wapping weaver he was, and wrought my first pair o' hose.—But come awa', kinsman,

> Come fill up my cap, come fill up my cann,
> Come saddle my horses, and call up my man;
> Come open your gates, and let me gae free,
> I daurna stay langer in bonny Dundee."

"Whisht, sir!" said the magistrate, in an authoritative tone—"lilting and singing sae near the latter end o' the Sabbath! This house may hear ye sing anither tune yet—Aweel, we hae a' backslidings to answer for—Stanchells, open the door."

The jailor obeyed, and we all sallied forth. Stanchells looked with some surprise at the two strangers, wondering, doubtless, how they came into these premises without his knowledge; but Mr. Jarvie's "Friends o' mine, Stanchells—friends o' mine," silenced all disposition to inquiries. We now descended into the lower vestibule, and hallooed more than once for Dougal, to which summons no answer was returned; when Campbell observed with a sardonic smile, "That if Dougal was the lad he kent him, he would scarce wait to get thanks for his ain share of the night's wark, but was in all probability on the full trot to the pass of Ballamaha"—

"And left us—and, abune a', me, mysell, locked up in the tolbooth a' night!" exclaimed the Bailie, in ire and perturbation. "Ca' for forehammers, sledge-hammers, pinches, and coulters; send for Deacon Yettlin, the smith, an let him ken that Bailie Jarvie's shut up in the tolbooth by a Highland blackguard, whom he'll hang up as high as Haman"—

"When ye catch him," said Campbell, gravely; "but stay—the door is surely not locked."

Indeed, on examination, we found that the door was not only left open, but that Dougal in his retreat had, by carrying off the keys along with him, taken care that no one should exercise his office of porter in a hurry.

"He has glimmerings o' common sense now, that creature Dougal," said Campbell.—"he ken'd an open door might hae served me at a pinch."

We were by this time in the street.

"I tell you, Robin," said the magistrate, "in my puir mind, if ye live the life ye do, ye suld hae ane o' your gillies door-keeper in every jail in Scotland, in case o' the warst."

"Ane o' my kinsmen a bailie in ilka burgh will just do as weel, cousin Nicol—So, gude-night or gude-morning to ye; and forget not the Clachan of Aberfoil."

And without waiting for an answer, he sprung to the other side of the street, and was lost in darkness. Immediately on his disappearance, we heard him give a low whistle of peculiar modulation, which was instantly replied to.

"Hear to the Hieland deevils," said Mr. Jarvie; "they think themselves on the skirts of Benlomond already, where they may gang whewingand whistling about without minding Sunday or Saturday." Here he was interrupted by something which fell with a heavy clash on the street before us—"Gude guide us what's this mair o't?—Mattie, haud up the lantern—Conscience if it isna the keys!—Weel, that's just as weel—they cost the burgh siller, and there might hae been some clavers about the loss o' them. O, an Bailie Grahame were to get word o' this night's job, it would be a sair hair in my neck!"

As we were still but a few steps from the tolbooth door, we carried back these implements of office, and consigned them to the head jailor, who, in lieu of the usual mode of making good his post by turning the keys, was keeping sentry in the vestibule till the arrival of some assistant, whom he had summoned in order to replace the Celtic fugitive Dougal.

Having discharged this piece of duty to the burgh, and my road lying the same way with the honest magistrate's, I profited by the light of his lantern, and he by my arm, to find our way through the streets, which, whatever they may now be, were then dark, uneven, and ill-paved. Age is easily propitiated by attentions from the young. The Bailie expressed himself interested in me, and added, "That since I was nane o' that play-acting and play-ganging generation, whom his saul hated, he wad be glad if I wad eat a reisted haddock or a fresh herring, at breakfast wi' him the morn, and meet my friend, Mr. Owen, whom, by that time, he would place at liberty."

"My dear sir," said I, when I had accepted of the invitation with thanks, "how could you possibly connect me with the stage?"

"I watna," replied Mr. Jarvie;—"it was a bletherin' phrasin' chield they ca' Fairservice, that cam at e'en to get an order to send the crier through the toun for ye at skreigh o' day the morn. He tell't me whae ye were, and how ye were sent frae your father's house because ye wadna be a dealer, and that ye mightna disgrace your family wi' ganging on the stage. Ane Hammorgaw, our precentor, brought him here, and said he was an auld acquaintance; but I sent them both away wi' a flae in their lug for bringing me sic an errand, on sic a night. But I see he's a fule-creature a'thegither, and clean mistaen about ye. I like ye, man," he continued; "I like a lad that will stand by his friends in trouble—I aye did it mysell, and sae did the deacon my father, rest and bless him! But ye suldna keep ower muckle company wi' Hielandmen and thae wild cattle. Can a man touch pitch and no be defiled?—aye mind that. Nae doubt, the best and wisest may err—Once, twice, and thrice have I backslidden, man, and dune three things this night—my father wadna hae believed his een if he could hae looked up and seen me do them."

He was by this time arrived at the door of his own dwelling. He paused, however, on the threshold, and went on in a solemn tone of deep contrition,—"Firstly, I hae thought my ain thoughts on the Sabbath—secondly, I hae gi'en security for an Englishman—and, in the third and last place, well-a-day! I hae let an ill-doer escape from the place of imprisonment—But there's balm in Gilead, Mr. Osbaldistone—Mattie, I can let mysell in—see Mr. Osbaldistone to Luckie Flyter's, at the corner o' the wynd.—Mr. Osbaldistone"—in a whisper—"ye'll offer nae incivility to Mattie—she's an honest man's daughter, and a near cousin o' the Laird o' Limmerfield's."

CHAPTER SEVENTH

"Will it please your worship to accept of my poor service? I beseech
that I may feed upon your bread, though it be the brownest, and
drink of your drink, though it be of the smallest; for I will do
your Worship as much service for forty shillings as another man
shall for three pounds."

— GREENE'S TU QUOQUE.

I remembered the honest Bailie's parting charge, but did not conceive there was any incivility in adding a kiss to the half-crown with which I remunerated Mattie's attendance;—nor did her "Fie for shame, sir!" express any very deadly resentment of the affront. Repeated knocking at Mrs. Flyter's gate awakened in due order, first, one or two stray dogs, who began to bark with all their might; next two or three night-capped heads, which were thrust out of the neighbouring windows to reprehend me for disturbing the solemnity of the Sunday night by that untimely noise. While I trembled lest the thunders of their wrath might dissolve in showers like that of Xantippe, Mrs. Flyter herself awoke, and began, in a tone of objurgation not unbecoming the philosophical spouse of Socrates, to scold one or two loiterers in her kitchen, for not hastening to the door to prevent a repetition of my noisy summons.

These worthies were, indeed, nearly concerned in the fracas which their laziness occasioned, being no other than the faithful Mr. Fairservice, with his friend Mr. Hammorgaw, and another person, whom I afterwards found to be the town-crier, who were sitting over a cog of ale, as they called it (at my expense, as my bill afterwards informed me), in order to devise the terms and style of a proclamation to be made through the streets the next day, in order that "the unfortunate young gentleman," as they had the impudence to qualify me, might be restored to his friends without farther delay. It may be supposed that I did not suppress my displeasure at this impertinent interference with my affairs; but Andrew set up such ejaculations of transport at my arrival, as fairly drowned my expressions of resentment. His raptures, perchance, were partly political; and the tears of joy which he shed had certainly their source in that noble fountain of emotion, the tankard. However, the tumultuous glee which he felt, or pretended to feel, at my return, saved Andrew the broken head which I had twice destined him;—first, on account of the colloquy he had held with the precentor on my affairs; and secondly, for the impertinent history he had thought proper to give of me to Mr. Jarvie. I however contented myself with slapping the door of my bedroom in his face as he followed me, praising Heaven for my safe return, and mixing his joy with admonitions to me to take care how I walked my own ways in future. I then went to bed, resolving my first business in the morning should be to discharge this troublesome, pedantic, self-conceited coxcomb, who seemed so much disposed to constitute himself rather a preceptor than a domestic.

Accordingly in the morning I resumed my purpose, and calling Andrew into my apartment, requested to know his charge for guiding and attending me as far as Glasgow. Mr. Fairservice looked very blank at this demand, justly considering it as a presage to approaching dismission.

"Your honour," he said, after some hesitation, "wunna think—wunna think"—

"Speak out, you rascal, or I'll break your head," said I, as Andrew, between the double risk of losing all by asking too much, or a part, by stating his demand lower than what I might be willing to pay, stood gasping in the agony of doubt and calculation.

Out it came with a bolt, however, at my threat; as the kind violence of a blow on the back sometimes delivers the windpipe from an intrusive morsel.—"Aughteen pennies sterling per diem—that is, by the day—your honour wadna think unconscionable."

"It is double what is usual, and treble what you merit, Andrew; but there's a guinea for you, and get about your business."

"The Lord forgi'e us! Is your honour mad?" exclaimed Andrew.

"No; but I think you mean to make me so—I give you a third above your demand, and you stand staring and expostulating there as if I were cheating you. Take your money, and go about your business."

"Gude safe us!" continued Andrew, "in what can I hae offended your honour? Certainly a' flesh is but as the flowers of the field; but if a bed of camomile hath value in medicine, of a surety the use of Andrew Fairservice to your honour is nothing less evident—it's as muckle as your life's worth to part wi' me."

"Upon my honour," replied I, "it is difficult to say whether you are more knave or fool. So you intend then to remain with me whether I like it or no?"

"Troth, I was e'en thinking sae," replied Andrew, dogmatically; "for if your honour disna ken when ye hae a gude servant, I ken when I hae a gude master, and the deil be in my feet gin I leave ye—and there's the brief and the lang o't besides I hae received nae regular warning to quit my place."

"Your place, sir!" said I;—"why, you are no hired servant of mine,—you are merely a guide, whose knowledge of the country I availed myself of on my road."

"I am no just a common servant, I admit, sir," remonstrated Mr. Fairservice; "but your honour kens I quitted a gude place at an hour's notice, to comply wi' your honour's solicitations. A man might make honestly, and wi' a clear conscience, twenty sterling pounds per annum, weel counted siller, o' the garden at Osbaldistone Hall, and I wasna likely to gi'e up a' that for a guinea, I trow—I reckoned on staying wi' your honour to the term's end at the least o't; and I account my wage, board-wage, fee and bountith,—ay, to that length o't at the least."

"Come, come, sir," replied I, "these impudent pretensions won't serve your turn; and if I hear any more of them, I shall convince you that Squire Thorncliff is not the only one of my name that can use his fingers."

While I spoke thus, the whole matter struck me as so ridiculous, that, though really angry, I had some difficulty to forbear laughing at the gravity with which Andrew supported a plea so utterly extravagant. The rascal, aware of the impression he had made on my muscles, was encouraged to perseverance. He judged it safer, however, to take his pretensions a peg lower, in case of overstraining at the same time both his plea and my patience.

"Admitting that my honour could part with a faithful servant, that had served me and mine by day and night for twenty years, in a strange place, and at a moment's warning, he was weel assured," he said, "it wasna in my heart, nor in no true gentleman's, to pit a puir lad like himself, that had come forty or fifty, or say a hundred miles out o' his road purely to bear my honour company, and that had nae handing but his penny-fee, to sic a hardship as this comes to."

I think it was you, Will, who once told me, that, to be an obstinate man, I am in certain things the most gullable and malleable of mortals. The fact is, that it is only contradiction which makes me peremptory, and when I do not feel myself called on to give battle to any proposition, I am always willing to grant it, rather than give myself much trouble. I knew this fellow to be a greedy, tiresome, meddling coxcomb; still, however, I must have some one about me in the quality of guide and domestic, and I was so much used to Andrew's humour, that on some occasions it was rather amusing. In the state of indecision to which these reflections led me, I asked Fairservice if he knew the roads, towns, etc., in the north of Scotland, to which my father's concerns with the proprietors of Highland forests were likely to lead me. I believe if I had asked him the road to the terrestrial paradise, he would have at that moment undertaken to guide me to it; so that I had reason afterwards to think myself fortunate in finding that his actual knowledge did not fall very much short of that which he asserted himself to possess. I fixed the amount of his wages, and reserved to myself the privilege of dismissing him when I chose, on paying him a week in advance. I gave him finally a severe lecture on his conduct of the preceding day, and then dismissed him rejoicing at heart, though somewhat crestfallen in countenance, to rehearse to his friend the precentor, who was taking his morning draught in the kitchen, the mode in which he had "cuitled up the daft young English squire."

Agreeable to appointment, I went next to Bailie Nicol Jarvie's, where a comfortable morning's repast was arranged in the parlour, which served as an apartment of all hours, and almost all work, to that honest gentleman. The bustling and benevolent magistrate had been as good as his word. I found my friend Owen at liberty, and, conscious of the refreshments and purification of brush and basin, was of course a very different person from Owen a prisoner, squalid, heart-broken, and hopeless. Yet the sense of pecuniary difficulties arising behind, before, and around him, had depressed his spirit, and the almost paternal embrace which the good man gave me, was embittered by a sigh of the deepest anxiety. And when he sate down, the heaviness in his eye and manner, so different from the quiet composed satisfaction which they usually exhibited, indicated that he was employing his arithmetic in mentally numbering up the days, the hours, the minutes, which yet remained as an interval between the dishonour of bills and the downfall of the great commercial establishment of Osbaldistone and Tresham. It was left to me, therefore, to do honour to our landlord's hospitable cheer—to his tea, right from China, which he got in a present from some eminent ship's-husband at Wapping—to his coffee, from a snug plantation of his own, as he informed us with a wink, called Saltmarket Grove, in the island of Jamaica—to his English toast and ale, his Scotch dried salmon, his Lochfine herrings, and even to the double-damask table-cloth, "wrought by no hand, as you may guess," save that of his deceased father the worthy Deacon Jarvie.

Having conciliated our good-humoured host by those little attentions which are great to most men, I endeavoured in my turn to gain from him some information which might be useful for my guidance, as well as for the satisfaction of my curiosity. We had not hitherto made the least allusion to the transactions of the preceding night, a circumstance which made my question sound somewhat abrupt, when, without any previous introduction of the subject, I took advantage of a pause when the history of the table-cloth ended, and that of the napkins was about to commence, to inquire, "Pray, by the by, Mr. Jarvie, who may this Mr. Robert Campbell be, whom we met with last night?"

The interrogatory seemed to strike the honest magistrate, to use the vulgar phrase, "all of a heap," and instead of answering, he returned the question—"Whae's Mr. Robert Campbell?—ahem! ahay! Whae's Mr. Robert Campbell, quo' he?"

"Yes," said I, "I mean who and what is he?"

"Why, he's—ahay!—he's—ahem!—Where did ye meet with Mr. Robert Campbell, as ye ca' him?"

"I met him by chance," I replied, "some months ago in the north of England."

"Ou then, Mr. Osbaldistone," said the Bailie, doggedly, "ye'll ken as muckle about him as I do."

"I should suppose not, Mr. Jarvie," I replied;—"you are his relation, it seems, and his friend."

"There is some cousin-red between us, doubtless," said the Bailie reluctantly; "but we hae seen little o' ilk other since Rob gae tip the cattle-line o' dealing, poor fallow! he was hardly guided by them might hae used him better—and they haena made their plack a bawbee o't neither. There's mony ane this day wad rather they had never chased puir Robin frae the Cross o' Glasgow—there's mony ane wad rather see him again at the tale o' three hundred kyloes, than at the head o' thirty waur cattle."

"All this explains nothing to me, Mr. Jarvie, of Mr. Campbell's rank, habits of life, and means of subsistence," I replied.

"Rank?" said Mr. Jarvie; "he's a Hieland gentleman, nae doubt—better rank need nane to be;—and for habit, I judge he wears the Hieland habit amang the hills, though he has breeks on when he comes to Glasgow;—and as for his subsistence, what needs we care about his subsistence, sae lang as he asks naething frae us, ye ken? But I hae nae time for clavering about him e'en now, because we maun look into your father's concerns wi' all speed."

So saying, he put on his spectacles, and sate down to examine Mr. Owen's states, which the other thought it most prudent to communicate to him without reserve. I knew enough of business to be aware that nothing could be more acute and sagacious than the views which Mr. Jarvie entertained of the matters submitted to his examination; and, to do him justice, it was marked by much fairness, and even liberality. He scratched his ear indeed repeatedly on observing the balance which stood at the debit of Osbaldistone and Tresham in account with himself personally.

"It may be a dead loss," he observed; "and, conscience! whate'er ane o' your Lombard Street goldsmiths may say to it, it's a snell ane in the Saut-Market[9] o' Glasgow. It will be a heavy deficit—a staff out o' my bicker, I trow.

But what then?—I trust the house wunna coup the crane for a' that's come and gane yet; and if it does, I'll never bear sae base a mind as thae corbies in the Gallowgate—an I am to lose by ye, I'se ne'er deny I hae won by ye mony a fair pund sterling

—Sae, an it come to the warst, I'se een lay the head o' the sow to the tail o' the grice."[10]

I did not altogether understand the proverbial arrangement with which Mr. Jarvie consoled himself, but I could easily see that he took a kind and friendly interest in the arrangement of my father's affairs, suggested several expedients, approved several plans proposed by Owen, and by his countenance and counsel greatly abated the gloom upon the brow of that afflicted delegate of my father's establishment.

As I was an idle spectator on this occasion, and, perhaps, as I showed some inclination more than once to return to the prohibited, and apparently the puzzling subject of Mr. Campbell, Mr. Jarvie dismissed me with little formality, with an advice to "gang up the gate to the college, where I wad find some chields could speak Greek and Latin weel—at least they got plenty o' siller for doing deil haet else, if they didna do that; and where I might read a spell o' the worthy Mr. Zachary Boyd's translation o' the Scriptures—better poetry need nane to be, as he had been tell'd by them that ken'd or suld hae ken'd about sic things." But he seasoned this dismission with a kind and hospitable invitation "to come back and take part o' his family-chack at ane preceesely—there wad be a leg o' mutton, and, it might be, a tup's head, for they were in season;" but above all, I was to return at "ane o'clock preceesely—it was the hour he and the deacon his father aye dined at—they pat it off for naething nor for naebody."

CHAPTER EIGHTH

> So stands the Thracian herdsman with his spear
> Full in the gap, and hopes the hunted bear;
> And hears him in the rustling wood, and sees
> His course at distance by the bending trees,
> And thinks—Here comes my mortal enemy,
> And either he must fall in fight, or I.
>
> — PALAMON AND ARCITE

I took the route towards the college, as recommended by Mr. Jarvie, less with the intention of seeking for any object of interest or amusement, than to arrange my own ideas, and meditate on my future conduct. I wandered from one quadrangle of old-fashioned buildings to another, and from thence to the College-yards, or walking ground, where, pleased with the solitude of the place, most of the students being engaged in their classes, I took several turns, pondering on the waywardness of my own destiny.

I could not doubt, from the circumstances attending my first meeting with this person Campbell, that he was engaged in some strangely desperate courses; and the reluctance with which Mr. Jarvie alluded to his person or pursuits, as well as all the scene of the preceding night, tended to confirm these suspicions. Yet to this man Diana Vernon had not, it would seem, hesitated to address herself in my behalf; and the conduct of the magistrate himself towards him showed an odd mixture of kindness, and even respect, with pity and censure. Something there must be uncommon in Campbell's situation and character; and what was still more extraordinary, it seemed that his fate was doomed to have influence over, and connection with, my own. I resolved to bring Mr. Jarvie to close quarters on the first proper opportunity, and learn as much as was possible on the subject of this mysterious person, in order that I might judge whether it was possible for me, without prejudice to my reputation, to hold that degree of farther correspondence with him to which he seemed to invite.

While I was musing on these subjects, my attention was attracted by three persons who appeared at the upper end of the walk through which I was sauntering, seemingly engaged in very earnest conversation. That intuitive impression which announces to us the approach of whomsoever we love or hate with intense vehemence, long before a more indifferent eye can recognise their persons, flashed upon my mind the sure conviction that the midmost of these three men was Rashleigh Osbaldistone. To address him was my first impulse;—my second was, to watch him until he was alone, or at least to reconnoitre his companions before confronting him. The party was still at such distance, and engaged in such deep discourse, that I had time to step unobserved to the other side of a small hedge, which imperfectly screened the alley in which I was walking. It was at this period the fashion of the young and gay to wear, in their morning walks, a scarlet cloak, often laced and embroidered, above their other dress, and it was the trick of the time for gallants occasionally to dispose it so as to muffle a part of the face. The imitating this fashion, with the degree of shelter which I received from the hedge, enabled me to meet my cousin, unobserved by him or the others, except perhaps as a passing stranger. I was not a little startled at recognising in his companions that very Morris on whose account I had been summoned before Justice Inglewood, and Mr. MacVittie the merchant, from whose starched and severe aspect I had recoiled on the preceding day.

A more ominous conjunction to my own affairs, and those of my father, could scarce have been formed. I remembered Morris's false accusation against me, which he might be as easily induced to renew as he had been intimidated to withdraw; I recollected the inauspicious influence of MacVittie over my father's affairs, testified by the imprisonment of Owen;—and I now saw both these men combined with one, whose talent for mischief I deemed little inferior to those of the great author of all ill, and my abhorrence of whom almost amounted to dread.

When they had passed me for some paces, I turned and followed them unobserved. At the end of the walk they separated, Morris and MacVittie leaving the gardens, and Rashleigh returning alone through the walks. I was now determined to confront him, and demand reparation for the injuries he had done my father, though in what form redress was likely to be rendered remained to be known. This, however, I trusted to chance; and flinging back the cloak in which I was muffled, I passed through a gap of the low hedge, and presented myself before Rashleigh, as, in a deep reverie, he paced down the avenue.

Rashleigh was no man to be surprised or thrown off his guard by sudden occurrences. Yet he did not find me thus close to him, wearing undoubtedly in my face the marks of that indignation which was glowing in my bosom, without visibly starting at an apparition so sudden and menacing.

"You are well met, sir," was my commencement; "I was about to take a long and doubtful journey in quest of you."

"You know little of him you sought then," replied Rashleigh, with his usual undaunted composure. "I am easily found by my friends—still more easily by my foes;—your manner compels me to ask in which class I must rank Mr. Francis Osbaldistone?"

"In that of your foes, sir," I answered—"in that of your mortal foes, unless you instantly do justice to your benefactor, my father, by accounting for his property."

"And to whom, Mr. Osbaldistone," answered Rashleigh, "am I, a member of your father's commercial establishment, to be compelled to give any account of my proceedings in those concerns, which are in every respect identified with my own?—Surely not to a young gentleman whose exquisite taste for literature would render such discussions disgusting and unintelligible."

"Your sneer, sir, is no answer; I will not part with you until I have full satisfaction concerning the fraud you meditate—you shall go with me before a magistrate."

"Be it so," said Rashleigh, and made a step or two as if to accompany me; then pausing, proceeded—"Were I inclined to do so as you would have me, you should soon feel which of us had most reason to dread the presence of a magistrate. But I have no wish to accelerate your fate. Go, young man! amuse yourself in your world of poetical imaginations, and leave the business of life to those who understand and can conduct it."

His intention, I believe, was to provoke me, and he succeeded. "Mr. Osbaldistone," I said, "this tone of calm insolence shall not avail you. You ought to be aware that the name we both bear never submitted to insult, and shall not in my person be exposed to it."

"You remind me," said Rashleigh, with one of his blackest looks, "that it was dishonoured in my person!—and you remind me also by whom! Do you think I have forgotten the evening at Osbaldistone Hall when you cheaply and with impunity played the bully at my expense? For that insult—never to be washed out but by blood!—for the various times you have crossed my path, and always to my prejudice—for the persevering folly with which you seek to traverse schemes, the importance of which you neither know nor are capable of estimating,—for all these, sir, you owe me a long account, for which there shall come an early day of reckoning."

"Let it come when it will," I replied, "I shall be willing and ready to meet it. Yet you seem to have forgotten the heaviest article—that I had the pleasure to aid Miss Vernon's good sense and virtuous feeling in extricating her from your infamous toils."

I think his dark eyes flashed actual fire at this home-taunt, and yet his voice retained the same calm expressive tone with which he had hitherto conducted the conversation.

"I had other views with respect to you, young man," was his answer: "less hazardous for you, and more suitable to my present character and former education. But I see you will draw on yourself the personal chastisement your boyish insolence so well merits. Follow me to a more remote spot, where we are less likely to be interrupted."

I followed him accordingly, keeping a strict eye on his motions, for I believed him capable of the very worst actions. We reached an open spot in a sort of wilderness, laid out in the Dutch taste, with clipped hedges, and one or two statues. I was on my guard, and it was well with me that I was so; for Rashleigh's sword was out and at my breast ere I could throw down my cloak, or get my weapon unsheathed, so that I only saved my life by springing a pace or two backwards. He had some advantage in the difference of our weapons; for his sword, as I recollect, was longer than mine, and had one of those bayonet or three-cornered blades which are now generally worn; whereas mine was what we then called a Saxon blade—narrow, flat, and two-edged, and scarcely so manageable as that of my enemy. In other respects we were pretty equally matched: for what advantage I might possess in superior address and agility, was fully counterbalanced by Rashleigh's great strength and coolness. He fought, indeed, more like a fiend than a man—with concentrated spite and desire of blood, only allayed by that cool consideration which made his worst actions appear yet worse from the air of deliberate premeditation which seemed to accompany them. His obvious malignity of purpose never for a moment threw him off his guard, and he exhausted every feint and stratagem proper to the science of defence; while, at the same time, he meditated the most desperate catastrophe to our rencounter.

On my part, the combat was at first sustained with more moderation. My passions, though hasty, were not malevolent; and the walk of two or three minutes' space gave me time to reflect that Rashleigh was my father's nephew, the son of an uncle, who after his fashion had been kind to me, and that his falling by my hand could not but occasion much family distress. My first resolution, therefore, was to attempt to disarm my antagonist—a manoeuvre in which, confiding in my superiority of skill and practice, I anticipated little difficulty. I found, however, I had met my match; and one or two foils which I received, and from the consequences of which I narrowly escaped, obliged me to observe more caution in my mode of fighting. By degrees I became exasperated at the rancour with which Rashleigh sought my life, and returned his passes with an inveteracy resembling in some degree his own; so that the combat had all the appearance of being destined to have a tragic issue. That issue had nearly taken place at my expense. My foot slipped in a full lounge which I made at my adversary, and I could not so far recover myself as completely to parry the thrust with which my pass was repaid. Yet it took but partial effect, running through my waistcoat, grazing my ribs, and passing through my coat behind. The hilt of Rashleigh's sword, so great was the vigour of his thrust, struck against my breast with such force as to give me great pain, and confirm me in the momentary belief that I was mortally wounded. Eager for revenge, I grappled with my enemy, seizing with my left hand the hilt of his sword, and shortening my own with the purpose of running him through the body. Our death-grapple was interrupted by a man who forcibly threw himself between us, and pushing us separate from each other, exclaimed, in a loud and commanding voice, "What! the sons of those fathers who sucked the same breast shedding each others bluid as it were strangers'!—By the hand of my father, I will cleave to the brisket the first man that mints another stroke!"

I looked up in astonishment. The speaker was no other than Campbell. He had a basket-hilted broadsword drawn in his hand, which he made to whistle around his head as he spoke, as if for the purpose of enforcing his mediation. Rashleigh and I stared in silence at this unexpected intruder, who proceeded to exhort us alternately:

—"Do you, Maister Francis, opine that ye will re-establish your father's credit by cutting your kinsman's thrapple, or getting your ain sneckit instead thereof in the College-yards of Glasgow?—Or do you, Mr. Rashleigh, think men will trust their lives and fortunes wi' ane, that, when in point of trust and in point of confidence wi' a great political interest, gangs about brawling like a drunken gillie?—Nay, never look gash or grim at me, man—if ye're angry, ye ken how to turn the buckle o' your belt behind you."

"You presume on my present situation," replied Rashleigh, "or you would have hardly dared to interfere where my honour is concerned."

"Hout! tout! tout!—Presume? And what for should it be presuming?—Ye may be the richer man, Mr. Osbaldistone, as is maist likely; and ye may be the mair learned man, whilk I dispute not: but I reckon ye are neither a prettier man nor a better gentleman than mysell—and it will be news to me when I hear ye are as gude. And *dare* too? Muckle daring there's about it—I trow, here I stand, that hae slashed as het a haggis as ony o' the twa o' ye, and thought nae muckle o' my morning's wark when it was dune. If my foot were on the heather as it's on the causeway, or this pickle gravel, that's little better, I hae been waur mistrysted than if I were set to gie ye baith your ser'ing o't."

Rashleigh had by this time recovered his temper completely. "My kinsman," he said, "will acknowledge he forced this quarrel on me. It was none of my seeking. I am glad we are interrupted before I chastised his forwardness more severely."

"Are ye hurt, lad?" inquired Campbell of me, with some appearance of interest.

"A very slight scratch," I answered, "which my kind cousin would not long have boasted of had not you come between us."

"In troth, and that's true, Maister Rashleigh," said Campbell; "for the cauld iron and your best bluid were like to hae become acquaint when I mastered Mr. Frank's right hand. But never look like a sow playing upon a trump for the luve of that, man—come and walk wi' me. I hae news to tell ye, and ye'll cool and come to yourself, like MacGibbon's crowdy, when he set it out at the window-bole."

"Pardon me, sir," said I. "Your intentions have seemed friendly to me on more occasions than one; but I must not, and will not, quit sight of this person until he yields up to me those means of doing justice to my father's engagements, of which he has treacherously possessed himself."

"Ye're daft, man," replied Campbell; "it will serve ye naething to follow us e'enow; ye hae just enow o' ae man—wad ye bring twa on your head, and might bide quiet?"

"Twenty," I replied, "if it be necessary."

I laid my hand on Rashleigh's collar, who made no resistance, but said, with a sort of scornful smile, "You hear him, MacGregor! he rushes on his fate—will it be my fault if he falls into it?—The warrants are by this time ready, and all is prepared."

The Scotchman was obviously embarrassed. He looked around, and before, and behind him, and then said—"The ne'er a bit will I yield my consent to his being ill-guided for standing up for the father that got him—and I gie God's malison and mine to a' sort o' magistrates, justices, bailies., sheriffs, sheriff-officers, constables, and sic-like black cattle, that hae been the plagues o' puir auld Scotland this hunder year.—it was a merry warld when every man held his ain gear wi' his ain grip, and when the country side wasna fashed wi' warrants and poindings and apprizings, and a' that cheatry craft. And ance mair I say it, my conscience winna see this puir thoughtless lad ill-guided, and especially wi' that sort o' trade. I wad rather ye fell till't again, and fought it out like douce honest men."

"Your conscience, MacGregor!" said Rashleigh; "you forget how long you and I have known each other."

"Yes, my conscience," reiterated Campbell, or MacGregor, or whatever was his name; "I hae such a thing about me, Maister Osbaldistone; and therein it may weel chance that I hae the better o' you. As to our knowledge of each other,—if ye ken what I am, ye ken what usage it was made me what I am; and, whatever you may think, I would not change states with the proudest of the oppressors that hae driven me to tak the heather-bush for a beild. What *you* are, Maister Rashleigh, and what excuse ye hae for being *what* you are, is between your ain heart and the lang day.—And now, Maister Francis, let go his collar; for he says truly, that ye are in mair danger from a magistrate than he is, and were your cause as straight as an arrow, he wad find a way to put you wrang—So let go his craig, as I was saying."

He seconded his words with an effort so sudden and unexpected, that he freed Rashleigh from my hold, and securing me, notwithstanding my struggles, in his own Herculean gripe, he called out—"Take the bent, Mr. Rashleigh—Make ae pair o' legs worth twa pair o' hands; ye hae dune that before now."

"You may thank this gentleman, kinsman," said Rashleigh, "if I leave any part of my debt to you unpaid; and if I quit you now, it is only in the hope we shall soon meet again without the possibility of interruption."

He took up his sword, wiped it, sheathed it, and was lost among the bushes.

The Scotchman, partly by force, partly by remonstrance, prevented my following him; indeed I began to be of opinion my doing so would be to little purpose.

"As I live by bread," said Campbell, when, after one or two struggles in which he used much forbearance towards me, he perceived me inclined to stand quiet, "I never saw sae daft a callant! I wad hae gien the best man in the country the breadth o' his back gin he had gien me sic a kemping as ye hae dune. What wad ye do?—Wad ye follow the wolf to his den? I tell ye, man, he has the auld trap set for ye—He has got the collector-creature Morris to bring up a' the auld story again, and ye maun look for nae help frae me here, as ye got at Justice Inglewood's;—it isna good for my health to come in the gate o' the whigamore bailie bodies. Now gang your ways hame, like a gude bairn—jouk and let the jaw gae by—Keep out o' sight o' Rashleigh, and Morris, and that MacVittie animal—Mind the Clachan of Aberfoil, as I said before, and by the word of a gentleman, I wunna see ye wranged. But keep a calm sough till we meet again—I maun gae and get Rashleigh out o' the town afore waur comes o't, for the neb o' him's never out o' mischief—Mind the Clachan of Aberfoil."

He turned upon his heel, and left me to meditate on the singular events which had befallen me. My first care was to adjust my dress and reassume my cloak, disposing it so as to conceal the blood which flowed down my right side. I had scarcely accomplished this, when, the classes of the college being dismissed, the gardens began to be filled with parties of the students. I therefore left them as soon as possible; and in my way towards Mr. Jarvie's, whose dinner hour was now approaching, I stopped at a small unpretending shop, the sign of which intimated the indweller to be Christopher

Neilson, surgeon and apothecary. I requested of a little boy who was pounding some stuff in a mortar, that he would procure me an audience of this learned pharmacopolist. He opened the door of the back shop, where I found a lively elderly man, who shook his head incredulously at some idle account I gave him of having been wounded accidentally by the button breaking off my antagonist's foil while I was engaged in a fencing match. When he had applied some lint and somewhat else he thought proper to the trifling wound I had received, he observed—"There never was button on the foil that made this hurt. Ah! young blood! young blood!—But we surgeons are a secret generation—If it werena for hot blood and ill blood, what wad become of the twa learned faculties?"

With which moral reflection he dismissed me; and I experienced very little pain or inconvenience afterwards from the scratch I had received.

CHAPTER NINTH

> An iron race the mountain-cliffs maintain,
> Foes to the gentler genius of the plain.
> ...
> Who while their rocky ramparts round they see,
> The rough abode of want and liberty,
> As lawless force from confidence will grow,
> Insult the plenty of the vales below.
>
> — GRAY.

"What made ye sae late?" said Mr. Jarvie, as I entered the dining-parlour of that honest gentleman; "it is chappit ane the best feek o' five minutes by-gane. Mattie has been twice at the door wi' the dinner, and weel for you it was a tup's head, for that canna suffer by delay. A sheep's head ower muckle boiled is rank poison, as my worthy father used to say—he likit the lug o' ane weel, honest man."

I made a suitable apology for my breach of punctuality, and was soon seated at table, where Mr. Jarvie presided with great glee and hospitality, compelling, however, Owen and myself to do rather more justice to the Scottish dainties with which his board was charged, than was quite agreeable to our southern palates. I escaped pretty well, from having those habits of society which enable one to elude this species of well-meant persecution. But it was ridiculous enough to see Owen, whose ideas of politeness were more rigorous and formal, and who was willing, in all acts of lawful compliance, to evince his respect for the friend of the firm, eating with rueful complaisance mouthful after mouthful of singed wool, and pronouncing it excellent, in a tone in which disgust almost overpowered civility.

When the cloth was removed, Mr. Jarvie compounded with his own hands a very small bowl of brandy-punch, the first which I had ever the fortune to see.

"The limes," he assured us, "were from his own little farm yonder-awa" (indicating the West Indies with a knowing shrug of his shoulders), "and he had learned the art of composing the liquor from auld Captain Coffinkey, who acquired it," he added in a whisper, "'as maist folk thought, among the Buccaniers. But it's excellent liquor," said he, helping us round; "and good ware has aften come frae a wicked market. And as for Captain Coffinkey, he was a decent man when I kent him, only he used to swear awfully—But he's dead, and gaen to his account, and I trust he's accepted—I trust he's accepted."

We found the liquor exceedingly palatable, and it led to a long conversation between Owen and our host on the opening which the Union had afforded to trade between Glasgow and the British Colonies in America and the West Indies, and on the facilities which Glasgow possessed of making up sortable cargoes for that market. Mr. Jarvie answered some objection which Owen made on the difficulty of sorting a cargo for America, without buying from England, with vehemence and volubility.

"Na, na, sir, we stand on our ain bottom—we pickle in our ain pock-neuk—We hae our Stirling serges, Musselburgh stuffs, Aberdeen hose, Edinburgh shalloons, and the like, for our woollen or worsted goods—and we hae linens of a' kinds better and cheaper than you hae in Lunnon itsell—and we can buy your north o' England wares, as Manchester wares, Sheffield wares, and Newcastle earthenware, as cheap as you can at Liverpool—And we are making a fair spell at cottons and muslins—Na, na! let every herring hing by its ain head, and every sheep by its ain shank, and ye'll find, sir, us Glasgow folk no sae far ahint but what we may follow.—This is but poor entertainment for you, Mr. Osbaldistone" (observing that I had been for some time silent); "but ye ken cadgers maun aye be speaking about cart-saddles."

I apologised, alleging the painful circumstances of my own situation, and the singular adventures of the morning, as the causes of my abstraction and absence of mind. In this manner I gained what I sought—an opportunity of telling my story distinctly and without interruption. I only omitted mentioning the wound I had received, which I did not think worthy of notice. Mr. Jarvie listened with great attention and apparent interest, twinkling his little grey eyes, taking snuff, and only interrupting me by brief interjections. When I came to the account of the rencounter, at which Owen folded his hands and cast up his eyes to Heaven, the very image of woeful surprise, Mr. Jarvie broke in upon the narration with "Wrang now—clean wrang—to draw a sword on your kinsman is inhibited by the laws o' God and man; and to draw a sword on the streets of a royal burgh is punishable by fine and imprisonment—and the College-yards are nae better privileged—they should be a place of peace and quietness, I trow. The College didna get gude L600 a year out o' bishops' rents (sorrow fa' the brood o' bishops and their rents too!), nor yet a lease o' the archbishopric o' Glasgow the sell o't, that they suld let folk tuilzie in their yards, or the wild callants bicker there wi' snaw-ba's as they whiles do, that when Mattie and I gae through, we are fain to make a baik and a bow, or run the risk o' our harns being knocked out—it suld be looked to.[11]—But come awa' wi' your tale—what fell neist?"

On my mentioning the appearance of Mr. Campbell, Jarvie arose in great surprise, and paced the room, exclaiming, "Robin again!—Robert's mad—clean wud, and waur—Rob will be hanged, and disgrace a' his kindred, and that will be seen and heard tell o'. My father the deacon wrought him his first hose—Od, I am thinking Deacon Threeplie, the rape-spinner, will be twisting his last cravat. Ay, ay, puir Robin is in a fair way o' being hanged—But come awa', come awa'—let's hear the lave o't."

I told the whole story as pointedly as I could; but Mr. Jarvie still found something lacking to make it clear, until I went back, though with considerable reluctance, on the whole story of Morris, and of my meeting with Campbell at the house of Justice Inglewood. Mr. Jarvie inclined a serious ear to all this, and remained silent for some time after I had finished my narrative.

"Upon all these matters I am now to ask your advice, Mr. Jarvie, which, I have no doubt, will point out the best way to act for my father's advantage and my own honour."

"Ye're right, young man—ye're right," said the Bailie. "Aye take the counsel of those who are aulder and wiser than yourself, and binna like the godless Rehoboam, who took the advice o' a wheen beardless callants, neglecting the auld counsellors who had sate at the feet o' his father Solomon, and, as it was weel put by Mr. Meiklejohn, in his lecture on the chapter, were doubtless partakers of his sapience. But I maun hear naething about honour—we ken naething here but about credit. Honour is a homicide and a bloodspiller, that gangs about making frays in the street; but Credit is a decent honest man, that sits at hame and makes the pat play."

"Assuredly, Mr. Jarvie," said our friend Owen, "credit is the sum total; and if we can but save that, at whatever discount"—

"Ye are right, Mr. Owen—ye are right; ye speak weel and wisely; and I trust bowls will row right, though they are a wee ajee e'enow. But touching Robin, I am of opinion he will befriend this young man if it is in his power. He has a gude heart, puir Robin; and though I lost a matter o' twa hundred punds wi' his former engagements, and haena muckle expectation ever to see back my thousand punds Scots that he promises me e'enow, yet I will never say but what Robin means fair by men."

"I am then to consider him," I replied, "as an honest man?"

"Umph!" replied Jarvie, with a precautionary sort of cough—"Ay, he has a kind o' Hieland honesty—he's honest after a sort, as they say. My father the deacon used aye to laugh when he tauld me how that by-word came up. Ane Captain Costlett was cracking crouse about his loyalty to King Charles, and Clerk Pettigrew (ye'll hae heard mony a tale about him) asked him after what manner he served the king, when he was fighting again him at Wor'ster in Cromwell's army; and Captain Costlett was a ready body, and said that he served him *after a sort*. My honest father used to laugh weel at that sport—and sae the by-word came up."

"But do you think," I said, "that this man will be able to serve me after a sort, or should I trust myself to this place of rendezvous which he has given me?"

"Frankly and fairly, it's worth trying. Ye see yourself there's some risk in your staying here. This bit body Morris has gotten a custom-house place doun at Greenock—that's a port on the Firth doun by here; and tho' a' the world kens him to be but a twa-leggit creature, wi' a goose's head and a hen's heart, that goes about on the quay plaguing folk about permits, and cockits, and dockits, and a' that vexatious trade, yet if he lodge an information—ou, nae doubt a man in magisterial duty maun attend to it, and ye might come to be clapped up between four wa's, whilk wad be ill-convenient to your father's affairs."

"True," I observed; "yet what service am I likely to render him by leaving Glasgow, which, it is probable, will be the principal scene of Rashleigh's machinations, and committing myself to the doubtful faith of a man of whom I know little but that he fears justice, and has doubtless good reasons for doing so; and that, for some secret, and probably dangerous purpose, he is in close league and alliance with the very person who is like to be the author of our ruin?"

"Ah, but ye judge Rob hardly," said the Bailie, "ye judge him hardly, puir chield; and the truth is, that ye ken naething about our hill country, or Hielands, as we ca' them. They are clean anither set frae the like o' huz;—there's nae bailie-courts amang them—nae magistrates that dinna bear the sword in vain, like the worthy deacon that's awa', and, I may say't, like mysell and other present magistrates in this city— But it's just the laird's command, and the loon maun loup; and the never another law hae they but the length o' their dirks—the broadsword's pursuer, or plaintiff, as you Englishers ca' it, and the target is defender; the stoutest head bears langest out;—and there's a Hieland plea for ye."

Owen groaned deeply; and I allow that the description did not greatly increase my desire to trust myself in a country so lawless as he described these Scottish mountains.

"Now, sir," said Jarvie, "we speak little o' thae things, because they are familiar to oursells; and where's the use o' vilifying ane's country, and bringing a discredit on ane's kin, before southrons and strangers? It's an ill bird that files its ain nest."

"Well, sir, but as it is no impertinent curiosity of mine, but real necessity, that obliges me to make these inquiries, I hope you will not be offended at my pressing for a little farther information. I have to deal, on my father's account, with several gentlemen of these wild countries, and I must trust your good sense and experience for the requisite lights upon the subject."

This little morsel of flattery was not thrown out in vain. "Experience!" said the Bailie—"I hae had experience, nae doubt, and I hae made some calculations—Ay, and to speak quietly amang oursells, I hae made some perquisitions through Andrew Wylie, my auld clerk; he's wi' MacVittie & Co. now—but he whiles drinks a gill on the Saturday afternoons wi' his auld master. And since ye say ye are willing to be guided by the Glasgow weaver-body's advice, I am no the man that will refuse it to the son of an auld correspondent, and my father the deacon was nane sic afore me. I have whiles thought o' letting my lights burn before the Duke of Argyle, or his brother Lord Ilay (for wherefore should they be hidden under a bushel?), but the like o' thae grit men wadna mind the like o' me, a puir wabster body—they think mair o' wha says a thing, than o' what the thing is that's said. The mair's the pity—mair's the pity. Not that I wad speak ony ill of this MacCallum More—'Curse not the rich in your bedchamber,' saith the son of Sirach, 'for a bird of the air shall carry the clatter, and pint-stoups hae lang lugs.'"

I interrupted these prolegomena, in which Mr. Jarvie was apt to be somewhat diffuse, by praying him to rely upon Mr. Owen and myself as perfectly secret and safe confidants.

"It's no for that," he replied, "for I fear nae man—what for suld I?—I speak nae treason—Only thae Hielandmen hae lang grips, and I whiles gang a wee bit up the glens to see some auld kinsfolks, and I wadna willingly be in bad blude wi' ony o' their clans. Howsumever, to proceed—ye maun understand I found my remarks on figures, whilk as Mr. Owen here weel kens, is the only true demonstrable root of human knowledge."

Owen readily assented to a proposition so much in his own way, and our orator proceeded.

"These Hielands of ours, as we ca' them, gentlemen, are but a wild kind of warld by themsells, full of heights and howes, woods, caverns, lochs, rivers, and mountains, that it wad tire the very deevil's wings to flee to the tap o' them. And in this country, and in the isles, whilk are little better, or, to speak the truth, rather waur than the mainland, there are about twa hunder and thirty parochines, including the Orkneys, where, whether they speak Gaelic or no I wotna, but they are an uncivilised people. Now, sirs, I sall haud ilk parochine at the moderate estimate of eight hunder examinable persons, deducting children under nine years of age, and then adding one-fifth to stand for bairns of nine years auld, and under, the whole population will reach to the sum of—let us add one-fifth to 800 to be the multiplier, and 230 being the multiplicand"—

"The product," said Mr. Owen, who entered delightedly into these statistics of Mr. Jarvie, "will be 230,000."

"Right, sir—perfectly right; and the military array of this Hieland country, were a' the men-folk between aughteen and fifty-six brought out that could bear arms, couldna come weel short of fifty-seven thousand five hundred men. Now, sir, it's a sad and awfu' truth, that there is neither wark, nor the very fashion nor appearance of wark, for the tae half of thae puir creatures; that is to say, that the agriculture, the pasturage, the fisheries, and every species of honest industry about the country, cannot employ the one moiety of the population, let them work as lazily as they like, and they do work as if a pleugh or a spade burnt their fingers. Aweel, sir, this moiety of unemployed bodies, amounting to"—

"To one hundred and fifteen thousand souls," said Owen, "being the half of the above product."

"Ye hae't, Mr. Owen—ye hae't—whereof there may be twenty-eight thousand seven hundred able-bodied gillies fit to bear arms, and that do bear arms, and will touch or look at nae honest means of livelihood even if they could get it—which, lack-a-day! they cannot."

"But is it possible," said I, "Mr. Jarvie, that this can be a just picture of so large a portion of the island of Britain?"

"Sir, I'll make it as plain as Peter Pasley's pike-staff. I will allow that ilk parochine, on an average, employs fifty pleughs, whilk is a great proportion in sic miserable soil as thae creatures hae to labour, and that there may be pasture enough for pleugh-horses, and owsen, and forty or fifty cows; now, to take care o' the pleughs and cattle, we'se allow seventy-five families of six lives in ilk family, and we'se add fifty mair to make even numbers, and ye hae five hundred souls, the tae half o' the population, employed and maintained in a sort o' fashion, wi' some chance of sour-milk and crowdie; but I wad be glad to ken what the other five hunder are to do?"

"In the name of God!" said I, "what *do* they do, Mr. Jarvie? It makes me shudder to think of their situation."

"Sir," replied the Bailie, "ye wad maybe shudder mair if ye were living near hand them. For, admitting that the tae half of them may make some little thing for themsells honestly in the Lowlands by shearing in harst, droving, hay-making, and the like; ye hae still mony hundreds and thousands o' lang-legged Hieland gillies that will neither work nor want, and maun gang thigging and sorning[12] about on their acquaintance, or live by doing the laird's bidding, be't right or be't wrang.

And mair especially, mony hundreds o' them come down to the borders of the low country, where there's gear to grip, and live by stealing, reiving, lifting cows, and the like depredations—a thing deplorable in ony Christian country!—the mair especially, that they take pride in it, and reckon driving a spreagh (whilk is, in plain Scotch, stealing a herd of nowte) a gallant, manly action, and mair befitting of pretty[13] men (as sic reivers will ca' themselves), than to win a day's wage by ony honest thrift.

And the lairds are as bad as the loons; for if they dinna bid them gae reive and harry, the deil a bit they forbid them; and they shelter them, or let them shelter themselves, in their woods and mountains, and strongholds, whenever the thing's dune. And every ane o' them will maintain as mony o' his ane name, or his clan, as we say, as he can rap and rend means for; or, whilk's the same thing, as many as can in ony fashion, fair or foul, mainteen themsells. And there they are wi' gun and pistol, dirk and dourlach, ready to disturb the peace o' the country whenever the laird likes; and that's the grievance of the Hielands, whilk are, and hae been for this thousand years by-past, a bike o' the maist lawless unchristian limmers that ever disturbed a douce, quiet, God-fearing neighbourhood, like this o' ours in the west here."

"And this kinsman of yours, and friend of mine, is he one of those great proprietors who maintain the household troops you speak of?" I inquired.

"Na, na," said Bailie Jarvie; "he's nane o' your great grandees o' chiefs, as they ca' them, neither. Though he is weel born, and lineally descended frae auld Glenstrae—I ken his lineage—indeed he is a near kinsman, and, as I said, of gude gentle Hieland blude, though ye may think weel that I care little about that nonsense—it's a' moonshine in water—waste threads and thrums, as we say—But I could show ye letters frae his father, that was the third aff Glenstrae, to my father Deacon Jarvie (peace be wi' his memory!) beginning, Dear Deacon, and ending, your loving kinsman to command,—they are amaist a' about borrowed siller, sae the gude deacon, that's dead and gane, keepit them as documents and evidents—He was a carefu' man."

"But if he is not," I resumed, "one of their chiefs or patriarchal leaders, whom I have heard my father talk of, this kinsman of yours has, at least, much to say in the Highlands, I presume?"

"Ye may say that—nae name better ken'd between the Lennox and Breadalbane. Robin was ance a weel-doing, painstaking drover, as ye wad see amang ten thousand —It was a pleasure to see him in his belted plaid and brogues, wi' his target at his back, and claymore and dirk at his belt, following a hundred Highland stots, and a dozen o' the gillies, as rough and ragged as the beasts they drave. And he was baith civil and just in his dealings; and if he thought his chapman had made a hard bargain, he wad gie him a luck-penny to the mends. I hae ken'd him gie back five shillings out o' the pund sterling."

"Twenty-five per cent," said Owen—"a heavy discount."

"He wad gie it though, sir, as I tell ye; mair especially if he thought the buyer was a puir man, and couldna stand by a loss. But the times cam hard, and Rob was venturesome. It wasna my faut—it wasna my faut; he canna wyte me—I aye tauld him o't—And the creditors, mair especially some grit neighbours o' his, gripped to his living and land; and they say his wife was turned out o' the house to the hill-side, and sair misguided to the boot. Shamefu'! shamefu'!—I am a peacefu' man and a magistrate, but if ony ane had guided sae muckle as my servant quean, Mattie, as it's like they guided Rob's wife, I think it suld hae set the shabble[14] that my father the deacon had at Bothwell brig a-walking again.

Weel, Rob cam hame, and fand desolation, God pity us! where he left plenty; he looked east, west, south, north, and saw neither hauld nor hope—neither beild nor shelter; sae he e'en pu'd the bonnet ower his brow, belted the broadsword to his side, took to the brae-side, and became a broken man."[15]

The voice of the good citizen was broken by his contending feelings. He obviously, while he professed to contemn the pedigree of his Highland kinsman, attached a secret feeling of consequence to the connection, and he spoke of his friend in his prosperity with an overflow of affection, which deepened his sympathy for his misfortunes, and his regret for their consequences.

"Thus tempted and urged by despair," said I, seeing Mr. Jarvie did not proceed in his narrative, "I suppose your kinsman became one of those depredators you have described to us?"

"No sae bad as that," said the Glaswegian,—"no a'thegither and outright sae bad as that; but he became a levier of black-mail, wider and farther than ever it was raised in our day, a through the Lennox and Menteith, and up to the gates o' Stirling Castle."

"Black-mail?—I do not understand the phrase," I remarked.

"Ou, ye see, Rob soon gathered an unco band o' blue-bonnets at his back, for he comes o' a rough name when he's kent by his ain, and a name that's held its ain for mony a lang year, baith again king and parliament, and kirk too, for aught I ken—an auld and honourable name, for as sair as it has been worried and hadden down and oppressed. My mother was a MacGregor—I carena wha kens it—And Rob had soon a gallant band; and as it grieved him (he said) to see sic *hership* and waste and depredation to the south o' the Hieland line, why, if ony heritor or farmer wad pay him four punds Scots out of each hundred punds of valued rent, whilk was doubtless a moderate consideration, Rob engaged to keep them scaithless;—let them send to him if they lost sae muckle as a single cloot by thieving, and Rob engaged to get them again, or pay the value—and he aye keepit his word—I canna deny but he keepit his word—a' men allow Rob keeps his word."

"This is a very singular contract of assurance," said Mr. Owen.

"It's clean again our statute law, that must be owned," said Jarvie, "clean again law; the levying and the paying black-mail are baith punishable: but if the law canna protect my barn and byre, whatfor suld I no engage wi' a Hieland gentleman that can?—answer me that."

"But," said I, "Mr. Jarvie, is this contract of black-mail, as you call it, completely voluntary on the part of the landlord or farmer who pays the insurance? or what usually happens, in case any one refuses payment of this tribute?"

"Aha, lad!" said the Bailie, laughing, and putting his finger to his nose, "ye think ye hae me there. Troth, I wad advise ony friends o' mine to gree wi' Rob; for, watch as they like, and do what they like, they are sair apt to be harried[16] when the lang nights come on.

Some o' the Grahame and Cohoon gentry stood out; but what then?—they lost their haill stock the first winter; sae maist folks now think it best to come into Rob's terms. He's easy wi' a' body that will be easy wi' him; but if ye thraw him, ye had better thraw the deevil."

"And by his exploits in these vocations," I continued, "I suppose he has rendered himself amenable to the laws of the country?"

"Amenable?—ye may say that; his craig wad ken the weight o' his hurdies if they could get haud o' Rob. But he has gude friends amang the grit folks; and I could tell ye o' ae grit family that keeps him up as far as they decently can, to be a them in the side of another. And then he's sic an auld-farran lang-headed chield as never took up the trade o' cateran in our time; mony a daft reik he has played—mair than wad fill a book, and a queer ane it wad be—as gude as Robin Hood, or William Wallace—a' fu' o' venturesome deeds and escapes, sic as folk tell ower at a winter ingle in the daft days. It's a queer thing o' me, gentlemen, that am a man o' peace mysell, and a peacefu man's son—for the deacon my father quarrelled wi' nane out o the town-council—it's a queer thing, I say, but I think the Hieland blude o' me warms at thae daft tales, and whiles I like better to hear them than a word o' profit, gude forgie me! But they are vanities—sinfu' vanities—and, moreover, again the statute law—again the statute and gospel law."

I now followed up my investigation, by inquiring what means of influence this Mr. Robert Campbell could possibly possess over my affairs, or those of my father.

"Why, ye are to understand," said Mr. Jarvie in a very subdued tone—"I speak amang friends, and under the rose—Ye are to understand, that the Hielands hae been keepit quiet since the year aughty-nine—that was Killiecrankie year. But how hae they been keepit quiet, think ye? By siller, Mr. Owen—by siller, Mr. Osbaldistone. King William caused Breadalbane distribute twenty thousand oude punds sterling amang them, and it's said the auld Hieland Earl keepit a lang lug o't in his ain sporran. And then Queen Anne, that's dead, gae the chiefs bits o' pensions, sae they had wherewith to support their gillies and caterans that work nae wark, as I said afore; and they lay by quiet eneugh, saying some spreagherie on the Lowlands, whilk is their use and wont, and some cutting o' thrapples amang themsells, that nae civilised body kens or cares onything anent.—Weel, but there's a new warld come up wi' this King George (I say, God bless him, for ane)—there's neither like to be siller nor pensions gaun amang them; they haena the means o' mainteening the clans that eat them up, as ye may guess frae what I said before; their credit's gane in the Lowlands; and a man that can whistle ye up a thousand or feifteen hundred linking lads to do his will, wad hardly get fifty punds on his band at the Cross o' Glasgow—This canna stand lang—there will be an outbreak for the Stuarts—there will be an outbreak—they will come down on the low country like a flood, as they did in the waefu' wars o' Montrose, and that will be seen and heard tell o' ere a twalmonth gangs round."

"Yet still," I said, "I do not see how this concerns Mr. Campbell, much less my father's affairs."

"Rob can levy five hundred men, sir, and therefore war suld concern him as muckle as maist folk," replied the Bailie; "for it is a faculty that is far less profitable in time o' peace. Then, to tell ye the truth, I doubt he has been the prime agent between some o' our Hieland chiefs and the gentlemen in the north o' England. We a' heard o' the public money that was taen frae the chield Morris somewhere about the fit o'

Cheviot by Rob and ane o' the Osbaldistone lads; and, to tell ye the truth, word gaed that it was yoursell Mr. Francis,—and sorry was I that your father's son suld hae taen to sic practices—Na, ye needna say a word about it—I see weel I was mistaen; but I wad believe onything o' a stage-player, whilk I concluded ye to be. But now, I doubtna, it has been Rashleigh himself or some other o' your cousins—they are a' tarred wi' the same stick—rank Jacobites and papists, and wad think the government siller and government papers lawfu' prize. And the creature Morris is sic a cowardly caitiff, that to this hour he daurna say that it was Rob took the portmanteau aff him; and troth he's right, for your custom-house and excise cattle are ill liket on a' sides, and Rob might get a back-handed lick at him, before the Board, as they ca't, could help him."

"I have long suspected this, Mr. Jarvie," said I, "and perfectly agree with you. But as to my father's affairs"—

"Suspected it?—it's certain—it's certain—I ken them that saw some of the papers that were taen aff Morris—it's needless to say where. But to your father's affairs—Ye maun think that in thae twenty years by-gane, some o' the Hieland lairds and chiefs hae come to some sma' sense o' their ain interest—your father and others hae bought the woods of Glen-Disseries, Glen Kissoch, Tober-na-Kippoch, and mony mair besides, and your father's house has granted large bills in payment, —and as the credit o' Osbaldistone and Tresham was gude—for I'll say before Mr. Owen's face, as I wad behind his back, that, bating misfortunes o' the Lord's sending, nae men could be mair honourable in business—the Hieland gentlemen, holders o' thae bills, hae found credit in Glasgow and Edinburgh—(I might amaist say in Glasgow wholly, for it's little the pridefu' Edinburgh folk do in real business) —for all, or the greater part of the contents o' thae bills. So that—Aha! d'ye see me now?"

I confessed I could not quite follow his drift.

"Why," said he, "if these bills are not paid, the Glasgow merchant comes on the Hieland lairds, whae hae deil a boddle o' siller, and will like ill to spew up what is item a' spent—They will turn desperate—five hundred will rise that might hae sitten at hame—the deil will gae ower Jock Wabster—and the stopping of your father's house will hasten the outbreak that's been sae lang biding us."

"You think, then," said I, surprised at this singular view of the case, "that Rashleigh Osbaldistone has done this injury to my father, merely to accelerate a rising in the Highlands, by distressing the gentlemen to whom these bills were originally granted?"

"Doubtless—doubtless—it has been one main reason, Mr. Osbaldistone. I doubtna but what the ready money he carried off wi' him might be another. But that makes comparatively but a sma' part o' your father's loss, though it might make the maist part o' Rashleigh's direct gain. The assets he carried off are of nae mair use to him than if he were to light his pipe wi' them. He tried if MacVittie & Co. wad gie him siller on them—that I ken by Andro Wylie—but they were ower auld cats to draw that strae afore them—they keepit aff, and gae fair words. Rashleigh Osbaldistone is better ken'd than trusted in Glasgow, for he was here about some jacobitical papistical troking in seventeen hundred and seven, and left debt ahint him. Na, na—he canna pit aff the paper here; folk will misdoubt him how he came by it. Na, na—he'll hae the stuff safe at some o' their haulds in the Hielands, and I daur say my cousin Rob could get at it gin he liked."

"But would he be disposed to serve us in this pinch, Mr. Jarvie?" said I. "You have described him as an agent of the Jacobite party, and deeply connected in their intrigues: will he be disposed for my sake, or, if you please, for the sake of justice, to make an act of restitution, which, supposing it in his power, would, according to your view of the case, materially interfere with their plans?"

"I canna preceesely speak to that: the grandees among them are doubtfu' o' Rob, and he's doubtfu' o' them.—And he's been weel friended wi' the Argyle family, wha stand for the present model of government. If he was freed o' his hornings and captions, he would rather be on Argyle's side than he wad be on Breadalbane's, for there's auld ill-will between the Breadalbane family and his kin and name. The truth is, that Rob is for his ain hand, as Henry Wynd feught[17]—he'll take the side that suits him best; if the deil was laird, Rob wad be for being tenant; and ye canna blame him, puir fallow, considering his circumstances.

But there's ae thing sair again ye—Rob has a grey mear in his stable at hame."

"A grey mare?" said I. "What is that to the purpose?"

"The wife, man—the wife,—an awfu' wife she is. She downa bide the sight o' a kindly Scot, if he come frae the Lowlands, far less of an Inglisher, and she'll be keen for a' that can set up King James, and ding down King George."

"It is very singular," I replied, "that the mercantile transactions of London citizens should become involved with revolutions and rebellions."

"Not at a', man—not at a'," returned Mr. Jarvie; "that's a' your silly prejudications. I read whiles in the lang dark nights, and I hae read in Baker's Chronicle[18] that the merchants o'London could gar the Bank of Genoa break their promise to advance a mighty sum to the King o' Spain, whereby the sailing of the Grand Spanish Armada was put aff for a haill year—What think you of that, sir?"

"That the merchants did their country golden service, which ought to be honourably remembered in our histories."

"I think sae too; and they wad do weel, and deserve weal baith o' the state and o' humanity, that wad save three or four honest Hieland gentlemen frae louping heads ower heels into destruction, wi' a' their puir sackless[19] followers, just because they canna pay back the siller they had reason to count upon as their ain—and save your father's credit—and my ain gude siller that Osbaldistone and Tresham awes me into the bargain.

I say, if ane could manage a' this, I think it suld be done and said unto him, even if he were a puir ca'-the-shuttle body, as unto one whom the king delighteth to honour."

"I cannot pretend to estimate the extent of public gratitude," I replied; "but our own thankfulness, Mr. Jarvie, would be commensurate with the extent of the obligation."

"Which," added Mr. Owen, "we would endeavour to balance with a *per contra*, the instant our Mr. Osbaldistone returns from Holland."

"I doubtna—I doubtna—he is a very worthy gentleman, and a sponsible, and wi' some o' my lights might do muckle business in Scotland—Weel, sir, if these assets could be redeemed out o' the hands o' the Philistines, they are gude paper—they are the right stuff when they are in the right hands, and that's yours, Mr. Owen. And I'se find ye three men in Glasgow, for as little as ye may think o' us, Mr. Owen—that's Sandie Steenson in the Trade's-Land, and John Pirie in Candleriggs, and another that sall be nameless at this present, sall advance what soums are sufficient to secure the credit of your house, and seek nae better security."

Owen's eyes sparkled at this prospect of extrication; but his countenance instantly fell on recollecting how improbable it was that the recovery of the assets, as he technically called them, should be successfully achieved.

"Dinna despair, sir—dinna despair," said Mr. Jarvie; "I hae taen sae muckle concern wi' your affairs already, that it maun een be ower shoon ower boots wi' me now. I am just like my father the deacon (praise be wi' him!) I canna meddle wi' a friend's business, but I aye end wi' making it my ain—Sae, I'll e'en pit on my boots the morn, and be jogging ower Drymen Muir wi' Mr. Frank here; and if I canna mak Rob hear reason, and his wife too, I dinna ken wha can—I hae been a kind freend to them afore now, to say naething o' ower-looking him last night, when naming his name wad hae cost him his life—I'll be hearing o' this in the council maybe frae Bailie Grahame and MacVittie, and some o' them. They hae coost up my kindred to Rob to me already—set up their nashgabs! I tauld them I wad vindicate nae man's faults; but set apart what he had done again the law o' the country, and the hership o' the Lennox, and the misfortune o' some folk losing life by him, he was an honester man than stood on ony o' their shanks—And whatfor suld I mind their clavers? If Rob is an outlaw, to himsell be it said—there is nae laws now about reset of inter-communed persons, as there was in the ill times o' the last Stuarts—I trow I hae a Scotch tongue in my head—if they speak, I'se answer."

It was with great pleasure that I saw the Bailie gradually surmount the barriers of caution, under the united influence of public spirit and good-natured interest in our affairs, together with his natural wish to avoid loss and acquire gain, and not a little harmless vanity. Through the combined operation of these motives, he at length arrived at the doughty resolution of taking the field in person, to aid in the recovery of my father's property. His whole information led me to believe, that if the papers were in possession of this Highland adventurer, it might be possible to induce him to surrender what he could not keep with any prospect of personal advantage; and I was conscious that the presence of his kinsman was likely to have considerable weight with him. I therefore cheerfully acquiesced in Mr. Jarvie's proposal that we should set out early next morning.

That honest gentleman was indeed as vivacious and alert in preparing to carry his purpose into execution, as he had been slow and cautious in forming it. He roared to Mattie to "air his trot-cosey, to have his jack-boots greased and set before the kitchen-fire all night, and to see that his beast be corned, and a' his riding gear in order." Having agreed to meet him at five o'clock next morning, and having settled that Owen, whose presence could be of no use to us upon this expedition, should await our return at Glasgow, we took a kind farewell of this unexpectedly zealous friend. I installed Owen in an apartment in my lodgings, contiguous to my own, and, giving orders to Andrew Fairservice to attend me next morning at the hour appointed, I retired to rest with better hopes than it had lately been my fortune to entertain.

CHAPTER TENTH

> Far as the eye could reach no tree was seen,
> Earth, clad in russet, scorned the lively green;
> No birds, except as birds of passage flew;
> No bee was heard to hum, no dove to coo;
> No streams, as amber smooth-as amber clear,
> Were seen to glide, or heard to warble here.
>
> — PROPHECY OF FAMINE.

It was in the bracing atmosphere of a harvest morning, that I met by appointment Fairservice, with the horses, at the door of Mr. Jarvie's house, which was but little space distant from Mrs. Flyter's hotel. The first matter which caught my attention was, that whatever were the deficiencies of the pony which Mr. Fairservice's legal adviser, Clerk Touthope, generously bestowed upon him in exchange for Thorncliff's mare, he had contrived to part with it, and procure in its stead an animal with so curious and complete a lameness, that it seemed only to make use of three legs for the purpose of progression, while the fourth appeared as if meant to be flourished in the air by way of accompaniment. "What do you mean by bringing such a creature as that here, sir? and where is the pony you rode to Glasgow upon?" were my very natural and impatient inquiries.

"I sell't it, sir. It was a slink beast, and wad hae eaten its head aff, standing at Luckie Flyter's at livery. And I hae bought this on your honour's account. It's a grand bargain—cost but a pund sterling the foot—that's four a'thegither. The stringhalt will gae aff when it's gaen a mile; it's a weel-ken'd ganger; they call it Souple Tam."

"On my soul, sir," said I, "you will never rest till my supple-jack and your shoulders become acquainted. If you do not go instantly and procure the other brute, you shall pay the penalty of your ingenuity."

Andrew, notwithstanding my threats, continued to battle the point, as he said it would cost him a guinea of rue-bargain to the man who had bought his pony, before he could get it back again. Like a true Englishman, though sensible I was duped by the rascal, I was about to pay his exaction rather than lose time, when forth sallied Mr. Jarvie, cloaked, mantled, hooded, and booted, as if for a Siberian winter, while two apprentices, under the immediate direction of Mattie, led forth the decent ambling steed which had the honour on such occasions to support the person of the Glasgow magistrate. Ere he "clombe to the saddle," an expression more descriptive of the Bailie's mode of mounting than that of the knights-errant to whom Spenser applies it, he inquired the cause of the dispute betwixt my servant and me. Having learned the nature of honest Andrew's manoeuvre he instantly cut short all debate, by pronouncing, that if Fairservice did not forthwith return the three-legged palfrey, and produce the more useful quadruped which he had discarded, he would send him to prison, and amerce him in half his wages. "Mr. Osbaldistone," said he, "contracted for the service of both your horse and you—twa brutes at ance—ye unconscionable rascal!—but I'se look weel after you during this journey."

"It will be nonsense fining me," said Andrew, doughtily, "that hasna a grey groat to pay a fine wi'—it's ill taking the breeks aff a Hielandman."

"If ye hae nae purse to fine, ye hae flesh to pine," replied the Bailie, "and I will look weel to ye getting your deserts the tae way or the tither."

To the commands of Mr. Jarvie, therefore, Andrew was compelled to submit, only muttering between his teeth, "Ower many maisters,—ower many maisters, as the paddock said to the harrow, when every tooth gae her a tig."

Apparently he found no difficulty in getting rid of Supple Tam, and recovering possession of his former Bucephalus, for he accomplished the exchange without being many minutes absent; nor did I hear further of his having paid any smart-money for breach of bargain.

We now set forward, but had not reached the top of the street in which Mr. Jarvie dwelt, when a loud hallooing and breathless call of "Stop, stop!" was heard behind us. We stopped accordingly, and were overtaken by Mr. Jarvie's two lads, who bore two parting tokens of Mattie's care for her master. The first was conveyed in the form of a voluminous silk handkerchief, like the mainsail of one of his own West-Indiamen, which Mrs. Mattie particularly desired he would put about his neck, and which, thus entreated, he added to his other integuments. The second youngster brought only a verbal charge (I thought I saw the rogue disposed to laugh as he delivered it) on the part of the housekeeper, that her master would take care of the waters. "Pooh! pooh! silly hussy," answered Mr. Jarvie; but added, turning to me, "it shows a kind heart though—it shows a kind heart in sae young a quean—Mattie's a carefu' lass." So speaking, he pricked the sides of his palfrey, and we left the town without farther interruption.

While we paced easily forward, by a road which conducted us north-eastward from the town, I had an opportunity to estimate and admire the good qualities of my new friend. Although, like my father, he considered commercial transactions the most important objects of human life, he was not wedded to them so as to undervalue more general knowledge. On the contrary, with much oddity and vulgarity of manner,—with a vanity which he made much more ridiculous by disguising it now and then under a thin veil of humility, and devoid as he was of all the advantages of a learned education, Mr. Jarvie's conversation showed tokens of a shrewd, observing, liberal, and, to the extent of its opportunities, a well-improved mind. He was a good local antiquary, and entertained me, as we passed along, with an account of remarkable events which had formerly taken place in the scenes through which we passed. And as he was well acquainted with the ancient history of his district, he saw with the prospective eye of an enlightened patriot, the buds of many of those future advantages which have only blossomed and ripened within these few years. I remarked also, and with great pleasure, that although a keen Scotchman, and abundantly zealous for the honour of his country, he was disposed to think liberally of the sister kingdom. When Andrew Fairservice (whom, by the way, the Bailie could not abide) chose to impute the accident of one of the horses casting his shoe to the deteriorating influence of the Union, he incurred a severe rebuke from Mr. Jarvie.

"Whisht, sir!—whisht! it's ill-scraped tongues like yours, that make mischief atween neighbourhoods and nations. There's naething sae gude on this side o' time but it might hae been better, and that may be said o' the Union. Nane were keener against it than the Glasgow folk, wi' their rabblings and their risings, and their mobs, as they ca' them now-a-days. But it's an ill wind blaws naebody gude—Let ilka ane roose the ford as they find it—I say let Glasgow flourish! whilk is judiciously and elegantly putten round the town's arms, by way of by-word.—Now, since St. Mungo catched herrings in the Clyde, what was ever like to gar us flourish like the sugar and tobacco trade? Will onybody tell me that, and grumble at the treaty that opened us a road west-awa' yonder?"

Andrew Fairservice was far from acquiescing in these arguments of expedience, and even ventured to enter a grumbling protest, "That it was an unco change to hae Scotland's laws made in England; and that, for his share, he wadna for a' the herring-barrels in Glasgow, and a' the tobacco-casks to boot, hae gien up the riding o' the Scots Parliament, or sent awa' our crown, and our sword, and our sceptre, and Mons Meg,[20] to be keepit by thae English pock-puddings in the Tower o' Lunnon.

What wad Sir William Wallace, or auld Davie Lindsay, hae said to the Union, or them that made it?"

The road which we travelled, while diverting the way with these discussions, had become wild and open, as soon as we had left Glasgow a mile or two behind us, and was growing more dreary as we advanced. Huge continuous heaths spread before, behind, and around us, in hopeless barrenness—now level and interspersed with swamps, green with treacherous verdure, or sable with turf, or, as they call them in Scotland, peat-bogs,—and now swelling into huge heavy ascents, which wanted the dignity and form of hills, while they were still more toilsome to the passenger. There were neither trees nor bushes to relieve the eye from the russet livery of absolute sterility. The very heath was of that stinted imperfect kind which has little or no flower, and affords the coarsest and meanest covering, which, as far as my experience enables me to judge, mother Earth is ever arrayed in. Living thing we saw none, except occasionally a few straggling sheep of a strange diversity of colours, as black, bluish, and orange. The sable hue predominated, however, in their faces and legs. The very birds seemed to shun these wastes, and no wonder, since they had an easy method of escaping from them;—at least I only heard the monotonous and plaintive cries of the lapwing and curlew, which my companions denominated the peasweep and whaup.

At dinner, however, which we took about noon, at a most miserable alehouse, we had the good fortune to find that these tiresome screamers of the morass were not the only inhabitants of the moors. The goodwife told us, that "the gudeman had been at the hill;" and well for us that he had been so, for we enjoyed the produce of his *chasse* in the shape of some broiled moor-game,—a dish which gallantly eked out the ewe-milk cheese, dried salmon, and oaten bread, being all besides that the house afforded. Some very indifferent two-penny ale, and a glass of excellent brandy, crowned our repast; and as our horses had, in the meantime, discussed their corn, we resumed our journey with renovated vigour.

I had need of all the spirits a good dinner could give, to resist the dejection which crept insensibly on my mind, when I combined the strange uncertainty of my errand with the disconsolate aspect of the country through which it was leading me. Our road continued to be, if possible, more waste and wild than that we had travelled in the forenoon. The few miserable hovels that showed some marks of human habitation, were now of still rarer occurrence; and at length, as we began to ascend an uninterrupted swell of moorland, they totally disappeared. The only exercise which my imagination received was, when some particular turn of the road gave us a partial view, to the left, of a large assemblage of dark-blue mountains stretching to the north and north-west, which promised to include within their recesses a country as wild perhaps, but certainly differing greatly in point of interest, from that which we now travelled. The peaks of this screen of mountains were as wildly varied and distinguished, as the hills which we had seen on the right were tame and lumpish; and while I gazed on this Alpine region, I felt a longing to explore its recesses, though accompanied with toil and danger, similar to that which a sailor feels when he wishes for the risks and animation of a battle or a gale, in exchange for the insupportable monotony of a protracted calm. I made various inquiries of my friend Mr. Jarvie respecting the names and positions of these remarkable mountains; but it was a subject on which he had no information, or did not choose to be communicative. "They're the Hieland hills—the Hieland hills—Ye'll see and hear eneugh about them before ye see Glasgow Cross again—I downa look at them—I never see them but they gar me grew. It's no for fear—no for fear, but just for grief, for the puir blinded half-starved creatures that inhabit them—but say nae mair about it—it's ill speaking o' Hielandmen sae near the line. I hae ken'd mony an honest man wadna hae ventured this length without he had made his last will and testament—Mattie had ill-will to see me set awa' on this ride, and grat awee, the sillie tawpie; but it's nae mair ferlie to see a woman greet than to see a goose gang barefit."

I next attempted to lead the discourse on the character and history of the person whom we were going to visit; but on this topic Mr. Jarvie was totally inaccessible, owing perhaps in part to the attendance of Mr. Andrew Fairservice, who chose to keep so close in our rear that his ears could not fail to catch every word which was spoken, while his tongue assumed the freedom of mingling in our conversation as often as he saw an opportunity. For this he occasionally incurred Mr. Jarvie's reproof.

"Keep back, sir, as best sets ye," said the Bailie, as Andrew pressed forward to catch the answer to some question I had asked about Campbell. —"ye wad fain ride the fore-horse, an ye wist how.—That chield's aye for being out o' the cheese-fat he was moulded in.—Now, as for your questions, Mr. Osbaldistone, now that chield's out of ear-shot, I'll just tell you it's free to you to speer, and it's free to me to answer, or no—Gude I canna say muckle o' Rob, puir chield; ill I winna say o' him, for, forby that he's my cousin, we're coming near his ain country, and there may be ane o' his gillies ahint every whin-bush, for what I ken—And if ye'll be guided by my advice, the less ye speak about him, or where we are gaun, or what we are gaun to do, we'll be the mair likely to speed us in our errand. For it's like we may fa' in wi' some o' his unfreends—there are e'en ower mony o' them about—and his bonnet sits even on his brow yet for a' that; but I doubt they'll be upsides wi' Rob at the last—air day or late day, the fox's hide finds aye the flaying knife."

"I will certainly," I replied, "be entirely guided by your experience."

"Right, Mr. Osbaldistone—right. But I maun speak to this gabbling skyte too, for bairns and fules speak at the Cross what they hear at the ingle-side.—D'ye hear, you, Andrew—what's your name?—Fairservice!"

Andrew, who at the last rebuff had fallen a good way behind, did not choose to acknowledge the summons.

"Andrew, ye scoundrel!" repeated Mr. Jarvie; "here, sir here!"

"Here is for the dog." said Andrew, coming up sulkily.

"I'll gie you dog's wages, ye rascal, if ye dinna attend to what I say t'ye—We are gaun into the Hielands a bit"—

"I judged as muckle," said Andrew.

"Haud your peace, ye knave, and hear what I have to say till ye—We are gaun a bit into the Hielands"—

"Ye tauld me sae already," replied the incorrigible Andrew.

"I'll break your head," said the Bailie, rising in wrath, "if ye dinna haud your tongue."

"A hadden tongue," replied Andrew, "makes a slabbered mouth."

It was now necessary I should interfere, which I did by commanding Andrew, with an authoritative tone, to be silent at his peril.

"I am silent," said Andrew. "I'se do a' your lawfu' bidding without a nay-say. My puir mother used aye to tell me,

Be it better, be it worse,
Be ruled by him that has the purse.

Sae ye may e'en speak as lang as ye like, baith the tane and the tither o' you, for Andrew."

Mr. Jarvie took the advantage of his stopping after quoting the above proverb, to give him the requisite instructions. "Now, sir, it's as muckle as your life's worth—that wad be dear o' little siller, to be sure—but it is as muckle as a' our lives are worth, if ye dinna mind what I sae to ye. In this public whar we are gaun to, and whar it is like we may hae to stay a' night, men o' a' clans and kindred—Hieland and Lawland—tak up their quarters—And whiles there are mair drawn dirks than open Bibles amang them, when the usquebaugh gets uppermost. See ye neither meddle nor mak, nor gie nae offence wi' that clavering tongue o' yours, but keep a calm sough, and let ilka cock fight his ain battle."

"Muckle needs to tell me that," said Andrew, contemptuously, "as if I had never seen a Hielandman before, and ken'd nae how to manage them. Nae man alive can cuitle up Donald better than mysell—I hae bought wi' them, sauld wi' them, eaten wi' them, drucken wi' them"—

"Did ye ever fight wi' them?" said Mr. Jarvie.

"Na, na," answered Andrew, "I took care o' that: it wad ill hae set me, that am an artist and half a scholar to my trade, to be fighting amang a wheen kilted loons that dinna ken the name o' a single herb or flower in braid Scots, let abee in the Latin tongue."

"Then," said Mr. Jarvie, "as ye wad keep either your tongue in your mouth, or your lugs in your head (and ye might miss them, for as saucy members as they are), I charge ye to say nae word, gude or bad, that ye can weel get by, to onybody that may be in the Clachan. And ye'll specially understand that ye're no to be bleezing and blasting about your master's name and mine, or saying that this is Mr. Bailie Nicol

Jarvie o' the Saut Market, son o' the worthy Deacon Nicol Jarvie, that a' body has heard about; and this is Mr. Frank Osbaldistone, son of the managing partner of the great house of Osbaldistone and Tresham, in the City."

"Eneueh said," answered Andrew—"eneueh said. What need ye think I wad be speaking about your names for?—I hae many things o' mair importance to speak about, I trow."

"It's thae very things of importance that I am feared for, ye blethering goose; ye maunna speak ony thing, gude or bad, that ye can by any possibility help."

"If ye dinna think me fit," replied Andrew, in a huff, "to speak like ither folk, gie me my wages and my board-wages, and I'se gae back to Glasgow—There's sma' sorrow at our parting, as the auld mear said to the broken cart."

Finding Andrew's perverseness again rising to a point which threatened to occasion me inconvenience, I was under the necessity of explaining to him, that he might return if he thought proper, but that in that case I would not pay him a single farthing for his past services. The argument *ad crumenam,* as it has been called by jocular logicians, has weight with the greater part of mankind, and Andrew was in that particular far from affecting any trick of singularity. He "drew in his horns," to use the Bailie's phrase, on the instant, professed no intention whatever to disoblige, and a resolution to be guided by my commands, whatever they might be.

Concord being thus happily restored to our small party, we continued to pursue our journey. The road, which had ascended for six or seven English miles, began now to descend for about the same space, through a country which neither in fertility nor interest could boast any advantage over that which we had passed already, and which afforded no variety, unless when some tremendous peak of a Highland mountain appeared at a distance. We continued, however, to ride on without pause and even when night fell and overshadowed the desolate wilds which we traversed, we were, as I understood from Mr. Jarvie, still three miles and a bittock distant from the place where we were to spend the night.

CHAPTER ELEVENTH

> Baron of Bucklivie,
> May the foul fiend drive ye,
> And a' to pieces rive ye,
> For building sic a town,
> Where there's neither horse meat,
> Nor man's meat,
> Nor a chair to sit down.
>
> — SCOTTISH POPULAR RHYMES ON A BAD INN.

The night was pleasant, and the moon afforded us good light for our journey. Under her rays, the ground over which we passed assumed a more interesting appearance than during the broad daylight, which discovered the extent of its wasteness. The mingled light and shadows gave it an interest which naturally did not belong to it;

and, like the effect of a veil flung over a plain woman, irritated our curiosity on a subject which had in itself nothing gratifying.

The descent, however, still continued, turned, winded, left the more open heaths, and got into steeper ravines, which promised soon to lead us to the banks of some brook or river, and ultimately made good their presage. We found ourselves at length on the bank of a stream, which rather resembled one of my native English rivers than those I had hitherto seen in Scotland. It was narrow, deep, still, and silent; although the imperfect light, as it gleamed on its placid waters, showed also that we were now among the lofty mountains which formed its cradle. "That's the Forth," said the Bailie, with an air of reverence, which I have observed the Scotch usually pay to their distinguished rivers. The Clyde, the Tweed, the Forth, the Spey, are usually named by those who dwell on their banks with a sort of respect and pride, and I have known duels occasioned by any word of disparagement. I cannot say I have the least quarrel with this sort of harmless enthusiasm. I received my friend's communication with the importance which he seemed to think appertained to it. In fact, I was not a little pleased, after so long and dull a journey, to approach a region which promised to engage the imagination. My faithful squire, Andrew, did not seem to be quite of the same opinion, for he received the solemn information, "That is the Forth," with a "Umph!—an he had said that's the public-house, it wad hae been mair to the purpose."

The Forth, however, as far as the imperfect light permitted me to judge, seemed to merit the admiration of those who claimed an interest in its stream. A beautiful eminence of the most regular round shape, and clothed with copsewood of hazels, mountain-ash, and dwarf-oak, intermixed with a few magnificent old trees, which, rising above the underwood, exposed their forked and bared branches to the silver moonshine, seemed to protect the sources from which the river sprung. If I could trust the tale of my companion, which, while professing to disbelieve every word of it, he told under his breath, and with an air of something like intimidation, this hill, so regularly formed, so richly verdant, and garlanded with such a beautiful variety of ancient trees and thriving copsewood, was held by the neighbourhood to contain, within its unseen caverns, the palaces of the fairies—a race of airy beings, who formed an intermediate class between men and demons, and who, if not positively malignant to humanity, were yet to be avoided and feared, on account of their capricious, vindictive, and irritable disposition.[21]

"They ca' them," said Mr. Jarvie, in a whisper, "*Daoine Schie*,—whilk signifies, as I understand, men of peace; meaning thereby to make their gudewill. And we may e'en as weel ca' them that too, Mr. Osbaldistone, for there's nae gude in speaking ill o' the laird within his ain bounds." But he added presently after, on seeing one or two lights which twinkled before us, "It's deceits o' Satan, after a', and I fearna to say it—for we are near the manse now, and yonder are the lights in the Clachan of Aberfoil."

I own I was well pleased at the circumstance to which Mr. Jarvie alluded; not so much that it set his tongue at liberty, in his opinion, with all safety to declare his real sentiments with respect to the *Daoine Schie*, or fairies, as that it promised some hours' repose to ourselves and our horses, of which, after a ride of fifty miles and upwards, both stood in some need.

We crossed the infant Forth by an old-fashioned stone bridge, very high and very narrow. My conductor, however, informed me, that to get through this deep and important stream, and to clear all its tributary dependencies, the general pass from the Highlands to the southward lay by what was called the Fords of Frew, at all times deep and difficult of passage, and often altogether unfordable. Beneath these fords, there was no pass of general resort until so far east as the bridge of Stirling; so that the river of Forth forms a defensible line between the Highlands and Lowlands of Scotland, from its source nearly to the Firth, or inlet of the ocean, in which it terminates. The subsequent events which we witnessed led me to recall with attention what the shrewdness of Bailie Jarvie suggested in his proverbial expression, that "Forth bridles the wild Highlandman."

About half a mile's riding, after we crossed the bridge, placed us at the door of the public-house where we were to pass the evening. It was a hovel rather worse than better than that in which we had dined; but its little windows were lighted up, voices were heard from within, and all intimated a prospect of food and shelter, to which we were by no means indifferent. Andrew was the first to observe that there was a peeled willow-wand placed across the half-open door of the little inn. He hung back and advised us not to enter. "For," said Andrew, "some of their chiefs and grit men are birling at the usquebaugh in by there, and dinna want to be disturbed; and the least we'll get, if we gang ramstam in on them, will be a broken head, to learn us better havings, if we dinna come by the length of a cauld dirk in our wame, whilk is just as likely."

I looked at the Bailie, who acknowledged, in a whisper, "that the gowk had some reason for singing, ance in the year."

Meantime a staring half-clad wench or two came out of the inn and the neighbouring cottages, on hearing the sound of our horses' feet. No one bade us welcome, nor did any one offer to take our horses, from which we had alighted; and to our various inquiries, the hopeless response of "Ha niel Sassenach," was the only answer we could extract. The Bailie, however, found (in his experience) a way to make them speak English. "If I gie ye a bawbee," said he to an urchin of about ten years old, with a fragment of a tattered plaid about him, "will you understand Sassenach?"

"Ay, ay, that will I," replied the brat, in very decent English. "Then gang and tell your mammy, my man, there's twa Sassenach gentlemen come to speak wi' her."

The landlady presently appeared, with a lighted piece of split fir blazing in her hand. The turpentine in this species of torch (which is generally dug from out the turf-bogs) makes it blaze and sparkle readily, so that it is often used in the Highlands in lieu of candles. On this occasion such a torch illuminated the wild and anxious features of a female, pale, thin, and rather above the usual size, whose soiled and ragged dress, though aided by a plaid or tartan screen, barely served the purposes of decency, and certainly not those of comfort. Her black hair, which escaped in uncombed elf-locks from under her coif, as well as the strange and embarrassed look with which she regarded us, gave me the idea of a witch disturbed in the midst of her unlawful rites. She plainly refused to admit us into the house. We remonstrated anxiously, and pleaded the length of our journey, the state of our horses, and the certainty that there was not another place where we could be received nearer than Callander, which the Bailie stated to be seven Scots miles distant. How many these may exactly amount to in English measurement, I have never been able to ascertain, but I think the double *ratio* may be pretty safely taken as a medium computation. The obdurate hostess treated our expostulation with contempt. "Better gang farther than fare waur," she said, speaking the Scottish Lowland dialect, and being indeed a native of the Lennox district—"Her house was taen up wi' them wadna like to be intruded on wi' strangers. She didna ken wha mair might be there—red-coats, it might be, frae the garrison." (These last words she spoke under her breath, and with very strong emphasis.) "The night," she said, "was fair abune head—a night amang the heather wad caller our bloods—we might sleep in our claes, as mony a gude blade does in the scabbard—there wasna muckle flowmoss in the shaw, if we took up our quarters right, and we might pit up our horses to the hill, naebody wad say naething against it."

"But, my good woman," said I, while the Bailie groaned and remained undecided, "it is six hours since we dined, and we have not taken a morsel since. I am positively dying with hunger, and I have no taste for taking up my abode supperless among these mountains of yours. I positively must enter; and make the best apology you can to your guests for adding a stranger or two to their number. Andrew, you will see the horses put up."

The Hecate looked at me with surprise, and then ejaculated—"A wilfu' man will hae his way—them that will to Cupar maun to Cupar!—To see thae English belly-gods! he has had ae fu' meal the day already, and he'll venture life and liberty, rather than he'll want a het supper! Set roasted beef and pudding on the opposite side o' the pit o' Tophet, and an Englishman will mak a spang at it—But I wash my hands o't—Follow me sir" (to Andrew), "and I'se show ye where to pit the beasts."

I own I was somewhat dismayed at my landlady's expressions, which seemed to be ominous of some approaching danger. I did not, however, choose to shrink back after having declared my resolution, and accordingly I boldly entered the house; and after narrowly escaping breaking my shins over a turf back and a salting tub, which stood on either side of the narrow exterior passage, I opened a crazy half-decayed door, constructed not of plank, but of wicker, and, followed by the Bailie, entered into the principal apartment of this Scottish caravansary.

The interior presented a view which seemed singular enough to southern eyes. The fire, fed with blazing turf and branches of dried wood, blazed merrily in the centre; but the smoke, having no means to escape but through a hole in the roof, eddied round the rafters of the cottage, and hung in sable folds at the height of about five feet from the floor. The space beneath was kept pretty clear by innumerable currents of air which rushed towards the fire from the broken panel of basket-work which served as a door—from two square holes, designed as ostensible windows, through one of which was thrust a plaid, and through the other a tattered great-coat—and moreover, through various less distinguishable apertures in the walls of the tenement, which, being built of round stones and turf, cemented by mud, let in the atmosphere at innumerable crevices.

At an old oaken table, adjoining to the fire, sat three men, guests apparently, whom it was impossible to regard with indifference. Two were in the Highland dress; the one, a little dark-complexioned man, with a lively, quick, and irritable expression of features, wore the trews, or close pantaloons wove out of a sort of chequered stocking stuff. The Bailie whispered me, that "he behoved to be a man of some consequence, for that naebody but their Duinhe'wassels wore the trews—they were ill to weave exactly to their Highland pleasure."

The other mountaineer was a very tall, strong man, with a quantity of reddish hair, freckled face, high cheek-bones, and long chin—a sort of caricature of the national features of Scotland. The tartan which he wore differed from that of his companion, as it had much more scarlet in it, whereas the shades of black and dark-green predominated in the chequers of the other. The third, who sate at the same table, was in the Lowland dress,—a bold, stout-looking man, with a cast of military daring in his eye and manner, his riding-dress showily and profusely laced, and his cocked hat of formidable dimensions. His hanger and a pair of pistols lay on the table before him. Each of the Highlanders had their naked dirks stuck upright in the board beside him,—an emblem, I was afterwards informed, but surely a strange one, that their computation was not to be interrupted by any brawl. A mighty pewter measure, containing about an English quart of usquebaugh, a liquor nearly as strong as brandy, which the Highlanders distil from malt, and drink undiluted in excessive quantities, was placed before these worthies. A broken glass, with a wooden foot, served as a drinking cup to the whole party, and circulated with a rapidity, which, considering the potency of the liquor, seemed absolutely marvellous. These men spoke loudly and eagerly together, sometimes in Gaelic, at other times in English. Another Highlander, wrapt in his plaid, reclined on the floor, his head resting on a stone, from which it was only separated by a wisp of straw, and slept or seemed to sleep, without attending to what was going on around him. He also was probably a stranger, for he lay in full dress, and accoutred with the sword and target, the usual arms of his countrymen when on a journey. Cribs there were of different dimensions beside the walls, formed, some of fractured boards, some of shattered wicker-work or plaited boughs, in which slumbered the family of the house, men, women, and children, their places of repose only concealed by the dusky wreaths of vapour which arose above, below, and around them.

Our entrance was made so quietly, and the carousers I have described were so eagerly engaged in their discussions, that we escaped their notice for a minute or two. But I observed the Highlander who lay beside the fire raise himself on his elbow as we entered, and, drawing his plaid over the lower part of his face, fix his look on us for a few seconds, after which he resumed his recumbent posture, and seemed again to betake himself to the repose which our entrance had interrupted,

We advanced to the fire, which was an agreeable spectacle after our late ride, during the chillness of an autumn evening among the mountains, and first attracted the attention of the guests who had preceded us, by calling for the landlady. She approached, looking doubtfully and timidly, now at us, now at the other party, and returned a hesitating and doubtful answer to our request to have something to eat.

"She didna ken," she said, "she wasna sure there was onything in the house," and then modified her refusal with the qualification—"that is, onything fit for the like of us."

I assured her we were indifferent to the quality of our supper; and looking round for the means of accommodation, which were not easily to be found, I arranged an old hen-coop as a seat for Mr. Jarvie, and turned down a broken tub to serve for my own. Andrew Fairservice entered presently afterwards, and took a place in silence behind our backs. The natives, as I may call them, continued staring at us with an air as if confounded by our assurance, and we, at least I myself, disguised as well as we could, under an appearance of indifference, any secret anxiety we might feel concerning the mode in which we were to be received by those whose privacy we had disturbed.

At length, the lesser Highlander, addressing himself to me said, in very good English, and in a tone of great haughtiness, "Ye make yourself at home, sir, I see."

"I usually do so," I replied, "when I come into a house of public entertainment."

"And did she na see," said the taller man, "by the white wand at the door, that gentlemans had taken up the public-house on their ain business?"

"I do not pretend to understand the customs of this country but I am yet to learn," I replied, "how three persons should be entitled to exclude all other travellers from the only place of shelter and refreshment for miles round."

"There's nae reason for't, gentlemen," said the Bailie; "we mean nae offence—but there's neither law nor reason for't; but as far as a stoup o' gude brandy wad make up the quarrel, we, being peaceable folk, wad be willing."

"Damn your brandy, sir!" said the Lowlander, adjusting his cocked hat fiercely upon his head; "we desire neither your brandy nor your company," and up he rose from his seat. His companions also arose, muttering to each other, drawing up their plaids, and snorting and snuffing the air after the mariner of their countrymen when working themselves into a passion.

"I tauld ye what wad come, gentlemen," said the landlady, "an ye wad hae been tauld:—get awa' wi' ye out o' my house, and make nae disturbance here—there's nae gentleman be disturbed at Jeanie MacAlpine's an she can hinder. A wheen idle English loons, gaun about the country under cloud o' night, and disturbing honest peaceable gentlemen that are drinking their drap drink at the fireside!"

At another time I should have thought of the old Latin adage,

"Dat veniam corvis, vexat censure columbas"—

But I had not any time for classical quotation, for there was obviously a fray about to ensue, at which, feeling myself indignant at the inhospitable insolence with which I was treated, I was totally indifferent, unless on the Bailie's account, whose person and qualities were ill qualified for such an adventure. I started up, however, on seeing the others rise, and dropped my cloak from my shoulders, that I might be ready to stand on the defensive.

"We are three to three," said the lesser Highlander, glancing his eyes at our party: "if ye be pretty men, draw!" and unsheathing his broadsword, he advanced on me. I put myself in a posture of defence, and aware of the superiority of my weapon, a rapier or small-sword, was little afraid of the issue of the contest. The Bailie behaved with unexpected mettle. As he saw the gigantic Highlander confront him with his weapon drawn, he tugged for a second or two at the hilt of his *shabble,* as he called it; but finding it loth to quit the sheath, to which it had long been secured by rust and disuse, he seized, as a substitute, on the red-hot coulter of a plough which had been employed in arranging the fire by way of a poker, and brandished it with such effect, that at the first pass he set the Highlander's plaid on fire, and compelled him to keep a respectful distance till he could get it extinguished. Andrew, on the contrary, who ought to have faced the Lowland champion, had, I grieve to say it, vanished at the very commencement of the fray. But his antagonist, crying "Fair play, fair play!" seemed courteously disposed to take no share in the scuffle. Thus we commenced our rencontre on fair terms as to numbers. My own aim was, to possess myself, if possible, of my antagonist's weapon; but I was deterred from closing, for fear of the dirk which he held in his left hand, and used in parrying the thrusts of my rapier. Meantime the Bailie, notwithstanding the success of his first onset, was sorely bested. The weight of his weapon, the corpulence of his person, the very effervescence of his own passions, were rapidly exhausting both his strength and his breath, and he was almost at the mercy of his antagonist, when up started the sleeping Highlander from the floor on which he reclined, with his naked sword and target in his hand, and threw himself between the discomfited magistrate and his assailant, exclaiming, "Her nainsell has eaten the town pread at the Cross o' Glasgow, and py her troth she'll fight for Bailie Sharvie at the Clachan of Aberfoil—tat will she e'en!" And seconding his words with deeds, this unexpected auxiliary made his sword whistle about the ears of his tall countryman, who, nothing abashed, returned his blows with interest. But being both accoutred with round targets made of wood, studded with brass, and covered with leather, with which they readily parried each other's strokes, their combat was attended with much more noise and clatter than serious risk of damage. It appeared, indeed, that there was more of bravado than of serious attempt to do us any injury; for the Lowland gentleman, who, as I mentioned, had stood aside for want of an antagonist when the brawl commenced, was now pleased to act the part of moderator and peacemaker.

"Hand your hands! haud your hands!—eneugh done!—eneugh done! the quarrel's no mortal. The strange gentlemen have shown themselves men of honour, and gien reasonable satisfaction. I'll stand on mine honour as kittle as ony man, but I hate unnecessary bloodshed."

It was not, of course, my wish to protract the fray—my adversary seemed equally disposed to sheathe his sword—the Bailie, gasping for breath, might be considered as *hors de combat*, and our two sword-and-buckler men gave up their contest with as much indifference as they had entered into it.

"And now," said the worthy gentleman who acted as umpire, "let us drink and gree like honest fellows—The house will haud us a'. I propose that this good little gentleman, that seems sair forfoughen, as I may say, in this tuilzie, shall send for a tass o' brandy and I'll pay for another, by way of archilowe,[22] and then we'll birl our bawbees a' round about, like brethren."

"And fa's to pay my new ponnie plaid," said the larger Highlander, "wi' a hole burnt in't ane might put a kail-pat through? Saw ever onybody a decent gentleman fight wi' a firebrand before?"

"Let that be nae hinderance," said the Bailie, who had now recovered his breath, and was at once disposed to enjoy the triumph of having behaved with spirit, and avoid the necessity of again resorting to such hard and doubtful arbitrament—"Gin I hae broken the head," he said, "I sall find the plaister. A new plaid sall ye hae, and o' the best—your ain clan-colours, man,—an ye will tell me where it can be sent t'ye frae Glasco."

"I needna name my clan—I am of a king's clan, as is weel ken'd," said the Highlander; "but ye may tak a bit o' the plaid—figh! she smells like a singit sheep's head!

—and that'll learn ye the sett—and a gentleman, that's a cousin o' my ain, that carries eggs doun frae Glencroe, will ca' for't about Martimas, an ye will tell her where ye bide. But, honest gentleman, neist time ye fight, an ye hae ony respect for your athversary, let it be wi' your sword, man, since ye wear ane, and no wi' thae het culters and fireprands, like a wild Indian."

"Conscience!" replied the Bailie, "every man maun do as he dow. My sword hasna seen the light since Bothwell Brigg, when my father that's dead and gane, ware it; and I kenna weel if it was forthcoming then either, for the battle was o' the briefest—At ony rate, it's glued to the scabbard now beyond my power to part them; and, finding that, I e'en grippit at the first thing I could make a fend wi'. I trow my fighting days is done, though I like ill to take the scorn, for a' that.—But where's the honest lad that tuik my quarrel on himself sae frankly?—I'se bestow a gill o' aquavitae on him, an I suld never ca' for anither."

The champion for whom he looked around was, however, no longer to be seen. He had escaped unobserved by the Bailie, immediately when the brawl was ended, yet not before I had recognised, in his wild features and shaggy red hair, our acquaintance Dougal, the fugitive turnkey of the Glasgow jail. I communicated this observation in a whisper to the Bailie, who answered in the same tone, "Weel, weel,—I see that him that ye ken o' said very right; there *is* some glimmering o' common sense about that creature Dougal; I maun see and think o' something will do him some gude."

Thus saying, he sat down, and fetching one or two deep aspirations, by way of recovering his breath, called to the landlady—"I think, Luckie, now that I find that there's nae hole in my wame, whilk I had muckle reason to doubt frae the doings o' your house, I wad be the better o' something to pit intill't."

The dame, who was all officiousness so soon as the storm had blown over, immediately undertook to broil something comfortable for our supper. Indeed, nothing surprised me more, in the course of the whole matter, than the extreme calmness with which she and her household seemed to regard the martial tumult that had taken place. The good woman was only heard to call to some of her assistants—"Steek the door! steek the door! kill or be killed, let naebody pass out till they hae paid the lawin." And as for the slumberers in those lairs by the wall, which served the family for beds, they only raised their shirtless bodies to look at the fray, ejaculated, "Oigh! oigh!" in the tone suitable to their respective sex and ages, and were, I believe, fast asleep again, ere our swords were well returned to their scabbards.

Our landlady, however, now made a great bustle to get some victuals ready, and, to my surprise, very soon began to prepare for us in the frying-pan a savoury mess of venison collops, which she dressed in a manner that might well satisfy hungry men, if not epicures. In the meantime the brandy was placed on the table, to which the Highlanders, however partial to their native strong waters, showed no objection, but much the contrary; and the Lowland gentleman, after the first cup had passed round, became desirous to know our profession, and the object of our journey.

"We are bits o' Glasgow bodies, if it please your honour," said the Bailie, with an affectation of great humility, "travelling to Stirling to get in some siller that is awing us."

I was so silly as to feel a little disconcerted at the unassuming account which he chose to give of us; but I recollected my promise to be silent, and allow the Bailie to manage the matter his own way. And really, when I recollected, Will, that I had not only brought the honest man a long journey from home, which even in itself had been some inconvenience (if I were to judge from the obvious pain and reluctance with which he took his seat, or arose from it), but had also put him within a hair's-breadth of the loss of his life, I could hardly refuse him such a compliment. The spokesman of the other party, snuffing up his breath through his nose, repeated the words with a sort of sneer;—"You Glasgow tradesfolks hae naething to do but to gang frae the tae end o' the west o' Scotland to the ither, to plague honest folks that may chance to be awee ahint the hand, like me."

"If our debtors were a' sic honest gentlemen as I believe you to be, Garschatachin," replied the Bailie, "conscience! we might save ourselves a labour, for they wad come to seek us."

"Eh! what! how!" exclaimed the person whom he had addressed,—"as I shall live by bread (not forgetting beef and brandy), it's my auld friend Nicol Jarvie, the best man that ever counted doun merks on a band till a distressed gentleman. Were ye na coming up my way?—were ye na coming up the Endrick to Garschattachin?"

"Troth no, Maister Galbraith," replied the Bailie, "I had other eggs on the spit—and I thought ye wad be saying I cam to look about the annual rent that's due on the bit heritable band that's between us."

"Damn the annual rent!" said the laird, with an appearance of great heartiness—"Deil a word o' business will you or I speak, now that ye're so near my country. To see how a trot-cosey and a joseph can disguise a man—that I suldna ken my auld feal friend the deacon!"

"The Bailie, if ye please," resumed my companion; "but I ken what gars ye mistak —the band was granted to my father that's happy, and he was deacon; but his name was Nicol as weel as mine. I dinna mind that there's been a payment of principal sum or annual rent on it in my day, and doubtless that has made the mistake."

"Weel, the devil take the mistake and all that occasioned it!" replied Mr. Galbraith. "But I am glad ye are a bailie. Gentlemen, fill a brimmer—this is my excellent friend, Bailie Nicol Jarvie's health—I ken'd him and his father these twenty years. Are ye a' cleared kelty aff?—Fill anither. Here's to his being sune provost—I say provost—Lord Provost Nicol Jarvie!—and them that affirms there's a man walks the Hie-street o' Glasgow that's fitter for the office, they will do weel not to let me, Duncan Galbraith of Garschattachin, hear them say sae—that's all." And therewith Duncan Galbraith martially cocked his hat, and placed it on one side of his head with an air of defiance.

The brandy was probably the best recommendation of there complimentary toasts to the two Highlanders, who drank them without appearing anxious to comprehend their purport. They commenced a conversation with Mr. Galbraith in Gaelic, which he talked with perfect fluency, being, as I afterwards learned, a near neighbour to the Highlands.

"I ken'd that Scant-o'-grace weel eneugh frae the very outset," said the Bailie, in a whisper to me; "but when blude was warm, and swords were out at ony rate, wha kens what way he might hae thought o' paying his debts? it will be lang or he does it in common form. But he's an honest lad, and has a warm heart too; he disna come often to the Cross o' Glasgow, but mony a buck and blackcock he sends us doun frae the hills. And I can want my siller weel eneugh. My father the deacon had a great regard for the family of Garschattachin."

Supper being now nearly ready, I looked round for Andrew Fairservice; but that trusty follower had not been seen by any one since the beginning of the rencontre. The hostess, however, said that she believed our servant had gone into the stable, and offered to light me to the place, saying that "no entreaties of the bairns or hers could make him give any answer; and that truly she caredna to gang into the stable herself at this hour. She was a lone woman, and it was weel ken'd how the Brownie of Ben-ye-gask guided the gudewife of Ardnagowan; and it was aye judged there was a Brownie in our stable, which was just what garr'd me gie ower keeping an hostler."

As, however, she lighted me towards the miserable hovel into which they had crammed our unlucky steeds, to regale themselves on hay, every fibre of which was as thick as an ordinary goose-quill, she plainly showed me that she had another reason for drawing me aside from the company than that which her words implied. "Read that," she said, slipping a piece of paper into my hand, as we arrived at the door of the shed; "I bless God I am rid o't. Between sogers and Saxons, and caterans and cattle-lifters, and hership and bluidshed, an honest woman wad live quieter in hell than on the Hieland line."

So saying, she put the pine-torch into my hand, and returned into the house,

CHAPTER TWELFTH

> Bagpipes, not lyres, the Highland hills adorn,
> MacLean's loud hollo, and MacGregor's horn.
>
> — JOHN COOPER'S REPLY TO ALLAN RAMSAY.

I stopped in the entrance of the stable, if indeed a place be entitled to that name where horses were stowed away along with goats, poultry, pigs, and cows, under the same roof with the mansion-house; although, by a degree of refinement unknown to the rest of the hamlet, and which I afterwards heard was imputed to an overpride on the part of Jeanie MacAlpine, our landlady, the apartment was accommodated with an entrance different from that used by her biped customers. By the light of my torch, I deciphered the following billet, written on a wet, crumpled, and dirty piece of paper, and addressed—"For the honoured hands of Mr. F. O., a Saxon young gentleman—These." The contents were as follows:—

"Sir,

"There are night-hawks abroad, so that I cannot give you and my respected kinsman, B. N. J., the meeting at the Clachan of Aberfoil, whilk was my purpose. I pray you to avoid unnecessary communication with those you may find there, as it may give future trouble. The person who gives you this is faithful and may be trusted, and will guide you to a place where, God willing, I may safely give you the meeting, when I trust my kinsman and you will visit my poor house, where, in despite of my enemies, I can still promise sic cheer as ane Hielandman may gie his friends, and where we will drink a solemn health to a certain D. V., and look to certain affairs whilk I hope to be your aidance in; and I rest, as is wont among gentlemen,

your servant to command, R. M. C."

I was a good deal mortified at the purport of this letter, which seemed to adjourn to a more distant place and date the service which I had hoped to receive from this man Campbell. Still, however, it was some comfort to know that he continued to be in my interest, since without him I could have no hope of recovering my father's papers. I resolved, therefore, to obey his instructions; and, observing all caution before the guests, to take the first good opportunity I could find to procure from the landlady directions how I was to obtain a meeting with this mysterious person.

My next business was to seek out Andrew Fairservice, whom I called several times by name, without receiving any answer, surveying the stable all round, at the same time, not without risk of setting the premises on fire, had not the quantity of wet litter and mud so greatly counterbalanced two or three bunches of straw and hay. At length my repeated cries of "Andrew Fairservice! Andrew! fool!—ass! where are you?" produced a doleful "Here," in a groaning tone, which might have been that of the Brownie itself. Guided by this sound, I advanced to the corner of a shed, where, ensconced in the angle of the wall, behind a barrel full of the feathers of all the fowls which had died in the cause of the public for a month past, I found the manful Andrew; and partly by force, partly by command and exhortation, compelled him forth into the open air. The first words he spoke were, "I am an honest lad, sir."

"Who the devil questions your honesty?" said I, "or what have we to do with it at present? I desire you to come and attend us at supper."

"Yes," reiterated Andrew, without apparently understanding what I said to him, "I am an honest lad, whatever the Bailie may say to the contrary. I grant the warld and the warld's gear sits ower near my heart whiles, as it does to mony a ane—But I am an honest lad; and, though I spak o' leaving ye in the muir, yet God knows it was far frae my purpose, but just like idle things folk says when they're driving a bargain, to get it as far to their ain side as they can—And I like your honour weel for sae young a lad, and I wadna part wi' ye lightly."

"What the deuce are you driving at now?" I replied. "Has not everything been settled again and again to your satisfaction? And are you to talk of leaving me every hour, without either rhyme or reason?"

"Ay,—but I was only making fashion before," replied Andrew; "but it's come on me in sair earnest now—Lose or win, I daur gae nae farther wi' your honour; and if ye'll tak my foolish advice, ye'll bide by a broken tryste, rather than gang forward yoursell. I hae a sincere regard for ye, and I'm sure ye'll be a credit to your friends if ye live to saw out your wild aits, and get some mair sense and steadiness—But I can follow ye nae farther, even if ye suld founder and perish from the way for lack of guidance and counsel. To gang into Rob Roy's country is a mere tempting o' Providence."

"Rob Roy?" said I, in some surprise; "I know no such person. What new trick is this, Andrew?"

"It's hard," said Andrew—"very hard, that a man canna be believed when he speaks Heaven's truth, just because he's whiles owercome, and tells lees a little when there is necessary occasion. Ye needna ask whae Rob Roy is, the reiving lifter that he is—God forgie me! I hope naebody hears us—when ye hae a letter frae him in your pouch. I heard ane o' his gillies bid that auld rudas jaud of a gudewife gie ye that. They thought I didna understand their gibberish; but, though I canna speak it muckle, I can gie a gude guess at what I hear them say—I never thought to hae tauld ye that, but in a fright a' things come out that suld be keepit in. O, Maister Frank! a' your uncle's follies, and a' your cousin's pliskies, were naething to this! Drink clean cap out, like Sir Hildebrand; begin the blessed morning with brandy sops, like Squire Percy; swagger, like Squire Thorncliff; rin wud amang the lasses, like Squire John; gamble, like Richard; win souls to the Pope and the deevil, like Rashleigh; rive, rant, break the Sabbath, and do the Pope's bidding, like them a' put thegither—But, merciful Providence! take care o' your young bluid, and gang nae near Rob Roy!"

Andrew's alarm was too sincere to permit me to suppose he counterfeited. I contented myself, however, with telling him, that I meant to remain in the alehouse that night, and desired to have the horses well looked after. As to the rest, I charged him to observe the strictest silence upon the subject of his alarm, and he might rely upon it I would not incur any serious danger without due precaution. He followed me with a dejected air into the house, observing between his teeth, "Man suld be served afore beast—I haena had a morsel in my mouth, but the rough legs o' that auld muircock, this haill blessed day."

The harmony of the company seemed to have suffered some interruption since my departure, for I found Mr. Galbraith and my friend the Bailie high in dispute.

"I'll hear nae sic language," said Mr. Jarvie, as I entered, "respecting the Duke o' Argyle and the name o' Campbell. He's a worthy public-spirited nobleman, and a credit to the country, and a friend and benefactor to the trade o' Glasgow."

"I'll sae naething against MacCallum More and the Slioch-nan-Diarmid," said the lesser Highlander, laughing. "I live on the wrang side of Glencroe to quarrel with Inverara."

"Our loch ne'er saw the Cawmil lymphads,"[23] said the bigger Highlander.

"She'll speak her mind and fear naebody—She doesna value a Cawmil mair as a Cowan, and ye may tell MacCallum More that Allan Iverach said sae— It's a far cry to Lochow."[24]

Mr. Galbraith, on whom the repeated pledges which he had quaffed had produced some influence, slapped his hand on the table with great force, and said, in a stern voice, "There's a bloody debt due by that family, and they will pay it one day—The banes of a loyal and a gallant Grahame hae lang rattled in their coffin for vengeance on thae Dukes of Guile and Lords for Lorn. There ne'er was treason in Scotland but a Cawmil was at the bottom o't; and now that the wrang side's uppermost, wha but the Cawmils for keeping down the right? But this warld winna last lang, and it will be time to sharp the maiden[25] for shearing o' craigs and thrapples. I hope to see the auld rusty lass linking at a bluidy harst again."

"For shame, Garschattachin!" exclaimed the Bailie; "fy for shame, sir! Wad ye say sic things before a magistrate, and bring yoursell into trouble?—How d'ye think to mainteen your family and satisfy your creditors (mysell and others), if ye gang on in that wild way, which cannot but bring you under the law, to the prejudice of a' that's connected wi' ye?"

"D—n my creditors!" retorted the gallant Galbraith, "and you if ye be ane o' them!

I say there will be a new warld sune—And we shall hae nae Cawmils cocking their bonnet sae hie, and hounding their dogs where they daurna come themsells, nor protecting thieves, nor murderers, and oppressors, to harry and spoil better men and mair loyal clans than themsells."

The Bailie had a great mind to have continued the dispute, when the savoury vapour of the broiled venison, which our landlady now placed before us, proved so powerful a mediator, that he betook himself to his trencher with great eagerness, leaving the strangers to carry on the dispute among themselves.

"And tat's true," said the taller Highlander—whose name I found was Stewart— "for we suldna be plagued and worried here wi' meetings to pit down Rob Roy, if the Cawmils didna gie him refutch. I was ane o' thirty o' my ain name—part Glenfinlas, and part men that came down frae Appine. We shased the MacGregors as ye wad shase rae-deer, till we came into Glenfalloch's country, and the Cawmils raise, and wadna let us pursue nae farder, and sae we lost our labour; but her wad gie twa and a plack to be as near Rob as she was tat day."

It seemed to happen very unfortunately, that in every topic of discourse which these warlike gentlemen introduced, my friend the Bailie found some matter of offence. "Ye'll forgie me speaking my mind, sir; but ye wad maybe hae gien the best bowl in your bonnet to hae been as far awae frae Rob as ye are e'en now—Od! my het pleugh-culter wad hae been naething to his claymore."

"She had better speak nae mair about her culter, or, by G—! her will gar her eat her words, and twa handfuls o' cauld steel to drive them ower wi'!" And, with a most inauspicious and menacing look, the mountaineer laid his hand on his dagger.

"We'll hae nae quarrelling, Allan," said his shorter companion; "and if the Glasgow gentleman has ony regard for Rob Roy, he'll maybe see him in cauld irons the night, and playing tricks on a tow the morn; for this country has been owre lang plagued wi' him, and his race is near-hand run—And it's time, Allan, we were ganging to our lads."

"Hout awa, Inverashalloch," said Galbraith;—"Mind the auld saw, man— It's a bauld moon, quoth Bennygask—another pint, quoth Lesley;—we'll no start for another chappin."

"I hae had chappins eneugh," said Inverashalloch; "I'll drink my quart of usquebaugh or brandy wi' ony honest fellow, but the deil a drap mair when I hae wark to do in the morning. And, in my puir thinking, Garschattachin, ye had better be thinking to bring up your horsemen to the Clachan before day, that we may ay start fair."

"What the deevil are ye in sic a hurry for?" said Garschattachin; "meat and mass never hindered wark. An it had been my directing, deil a bit o' me wad hae fashed ye to come down the glens to help us. The garrison and our ain horse could hae taen Rob Roy easily enough. There's the hand," he said, holding up his own, "should lay him on the green, and never ask a Hielandman o' ye a' for his help."

"Ye might hae loot us bide still where we were, then," said Inverashalloch. "I didna come sixty miles without being sent for. But an ye'll hae my opinion, I redd ye keep your mouth better steekit, if ye hope to speed. Shored folk live lang, and sae may him ye ken o'. The way to catch a bird is no to fling your bannet at her. And also thae gentlemen hae heard some things they suldna hae heard, an the brandy hadna been ower bauld for your brain, Major Galbraith. Ye needna cock your hat and bully wi' me, man, for I will not bear it."

"I hae said it," said Galbraith, with a solemn air of drunken gravity, "that I will quarrel no more this night either with broadcloth or tartan. When I am off duty I'll quarrel with you or ony man in the Hielands or Lowlands, but not on duty—no—no. I wish we heard o' these red-coats. If it had been to do onything against King James, we wad hae seen them lang syne—but when it's to keep the peace o' the country they can lie as lound as their neighbours."

As he spoke we heard the measured footsteps of a body of infantry on the march; and an officer, followed by two or three files of soldiers, entered the apartment. He spoke in an English accent, which was very pleasant to my ears, now so long accustomed to the varying brogue of the Highland and Lowland Scotch.—"You are, I suppose, Major Galbraith, of the squadron of Lennox Militia, and these are the two Highland gentlemen with whom I was appointed to meet in this place?"

They assented, and invited the officer to take some refreshments, which he declined.—"I have been too late, gentlemen, and am desirous to make up time. I have orders to search for and arrest two persons guilty of treasonable practices."

"We'll wash our hands o' that," said Inverashalloch. "I came here wi' my men to fight against the red MacGregor that killed my cousin, seven times removed, Duncan MacLaren, in Invernenty;[26] but I will hae nothing to do touching honest gentlemen that may be gaun through the country on their ain business."

"Nor I neither," said Iverach.

Major Galbraith took up the matter more solemnly, and, premising his oration with a hiccup, spoke to the following purpose:—

"I shall say nothing against King George, Captain, because, as it happens, my commission may rin in his name—But one commission being good, sir, does not make another bad; and some think that James may be just as good a name as George. There's the king that is—and there's the king that suld of right be—I say, an honest man may and suld be loyal to them both, Captain. But I am of the Lord Lieutenant's opinion for the time, as it becomes a militia officer and a depute-lieutenant—and about treason and all that, it's lost time to speak of it—least said is sunest mended."

"I am sorry to see how you have been employing your time, sir," replied the English officer—as indeed the honest gentleman's reasoning had a strong relish of the liquor he had been drinking—"and I could wish, sir, it had been otherwise on an occasion of this consequence. I would recommend to you to try to sleep for an hour.—Do these gentlemen belong to your party?"—looking at the Bailie and me, who, engaged in eating our supper, had paid little attention to the officer on his entrance.

"Travellers, sir," said Galbraith—"lawful travellers by sea and land, as the prayer-book hath it."

"My instructions." said the Captain, taking a light to survey us closer, "are to place under arrest an elderly and a young person—and I think these gentlemen answer nearly the description."

"Take care what you say, sir," said Mr. Jarvie; "it shall not be your red coat nor your laced hat shall protect you, if you put any affront on me. I'se convene ye baith in an action of scandal and false imprisonment—I am a free burgess and a magistrate o'

Glasgow; Nicol Jarvie is my name, sae was my father's afore me—I am a bailie, be praised for the honour, and my father was a deacon."

"He was a prick-eared cur," said Major Galbraith, "and fought agane the King at Bothwell Brigg."

"He paid what he ought and what he bought, Mr. Galbraith," said the Bailie, "and was an honester man than ever stude on your shanks."

"I have no time to attend to all this," said the officer; "I must positively detain you, gentlemen, unless you can produce some respectable security that you are loyal subjects."

"I desire to be carried before some civil magistrate," said the Bailie—"the sherra or the judge of the bounds;—I am not obliged to answer every red-coat that speers questions at me."

"Well, sir, I shall know how to manage you if you are silent—And you, sir" (to me), "what may your name be?"

"Francis Osbaldistone, sir."

"What, a son of Sir Hildebrand Osbaldistone of Northumberland?"

"No, sir," interrupted the Bailie; "a son of the great William Osbaldistone of the House of Osbaldistone and Tresham, Crane-Alley, London."

"I am afraid, sir," said the officer, "your name only increases the suspicions against you, and lays me under the necessity of requesting that you will give up what papers you have in charge."

I observed the Highlanders look anxiously at each other when this proposal was made.

"I had none," I replied, "to surrender."

The officer commanded me to be disarmed and searched. To have resisted would have been madness. I accordingly gave up my arms, and submitted to a search, which was conducted as civilly as an operation of the kind well could. They found nothing except the note which I had received that night through the hand of the landlady.

"This is different from what I expected," said the officer; "but it affords us good grounds for detaining you. Here I find you in written communication with the outlawed robber, Robert MacGregor Campbell, who has been so long the plague of this district—How do you account for that?"

"Spies of Rob!" said Inverashalloch. "We wad serve them right to strap them up till the neist tree."

"We are gaun to see after some gear o' our ain, gentlemen," said the Bailie, "that's fa'en into his hands by accident—there's nae law agane a man looking after his ain, I hope?"

"How did you come by this letter?" said the officer, addressing himself to me.

I could not think of betraying the poor woman who had given it to me, and remained silent.

"Do you know anything of it, fellow?" said the officer, looking at Andrew, whose jaws were chattering like a pair of castanets at the threats thrown out by the Highlander.

"O ay, I ken a' about it—it was a Hieland loon gied the letter to that lang-tongued jaud the gudewife there; I'll be sworn my maister ken'd naething about it. But he's wilfu' to gang up the hills and speak wi' Rob; and oh, sir, it wad be a charity just to send a wheen o' your red-coats to see him safe back to Glasgow again whether he will or no—And ye can keep Mr. Jarvie as lang as ye like—He's responsible enough for ony fine ye may lay on him—and so's my master for that matter; for me, I'm just a puir gardener lad, and no worth your steering."

"I believe," said the officer, "the best thing I can do is to send these persons to the garrison under an escort. They seem to be in immediate correspondence with the enemy, and I shall be in no respect answerable for suffering them to be at liberty. Gentlemen, you will consider yourselves as my prisoners. So soon as dawn approaches, I will send you to a place of security. If you be the persons you describe yourselves, it will soon appear, and you will sustain no great inconvenience from being detained a day or two. I can hear no remonstrances," he continued, turning away from the Bailie, whose mouth was open to address him; "the service I am on gives me no time for idle discussions."

"Aweel, aweel, sir," said the Bailie, "you're welcome to a tune on your ain fiddle; but see if I dinna gar ye dance till't afore a's dune."

An anxious consultation now took place between the officer and the Highlanders, but carried on in so low a tone, that it was impossible to catch the sense. So soon as it was concluded they all left the house. At their departure, the Bailie thus expressed himself:—"Thae Hielandmen are o' the westland clans, and just as light-handed as their neighbours, an a' tales be true, and yet ye see they hae brought them frae the head o' Argyleshire to make war wi' puir Rob for some auld ill-will that they hae at him and his sirname. And there's the Grahames, and the Buchanans, and the Lennox gentry, a' mounted and in order—It's weel ken'd their quarrel; and I dinna blame them—naebody likes to lose his kye. And then there's sodgers, puir things, hoyed out frae the garrison at a' body's bidding—Puir Rob will hae his hands fu' by the time the sun comes ower the hill. Weel—it's wrang for a magistrate to be wishing onything agane the course o' justice, but deil o' me an I wad break my heart to hear that Rob had gien them a' their paiks!"

CHAPTER THIRTEENTH

>   —General,
>   Hear me, and mark me well, and look upon me
>   Directly in my face—my woman's face—
>   See if one fear, one shadow of a terror,
>   One paleness dare appear, but from my anger,
>   To lay hold on your mercies.
>
>   — BONDUCA

We were permitted to slumber out the remainder of the night in the best manner that the miserable accommodations of the alehouse permitted. The Bailie, fatigued with his journey and the subsequent scenes—less interested also in the event of our arrest, which to him could only be a matter of temporary inconvenience—perhaps less nice than habit had rendered me about the cleanliness or decency of his couch,—tumbled himself into one of the cribs which I have already described, and soon was heard to snore soundly. A broken sleep, snatched by intervals, while I rested my head upon the table, was my only refreshment. In the course of the night I had occasion to observe that there seemed to be some doubt and hesitation in the motions of the soldiery. Men were sent out, as if to obtain intelligence, and returned apparently without bringing any satisfactory information to their commanding officer. He was obviously eager and anxious, and again despatched small parties of two or three men, some of whom, as I could understand from what the others whispered to each other, did not return again to the Clachan.

The morning had broken, when a corporal and two men rushed into the hut, dragging after them, in a sort of triumph, a Highlander, whom I immediately recognised as my acquaintance the ex-turnkey. The Bailie, who started up at the noise with which they entered, immediately made the same discovery, and exclaimed—"Mercy on us! they hae grippit the puir creature Dougal.—Captain, I will put in bail—sufficient bail, for that Dougal creature."

To this offer, dictated undoubtedly by a grateful recollection of the late interference of the Highlander in his behalf, the Captain only answered by requesting Mr. Jarvie to "mind his own affairs, and remember that he was himself for the present a prisoner."

"I take you to witness, Mr. Osbaldistone," said the Bailie, who was probably better acquainted with the process in civil than in military cases, "that he has refused sufficient bail. It's my opinion that the creature Dougal will have a good action of wrongous imprisonment and damages agane him, under the Act seventeen hundred and one, and I'll see the creature righted."

The officer, whose name I understood was Thornton, paying no attention to the Bailie's threats or expostulations, instituted a very close inquiry into Dougal's life and conversation, and compelled him to admit, though with apparent reluctance, the successive facts,—that he knew Rob Roy MacGregor—that he had seen him within these twelve months—within these six months—within this month—within this week; in fine, that he had parted from him only an hour ago. All this detail came like drops of blood from the prisoner, and was, to all appearance, only extorted by the threat of a halter and the next tree, which Captain Thornton assured him should be his doom, if he did not give direct and special information.

"And now, my friend," said the officer, "you will please inform me how many men your master has with him at present."

Dougal looked in every direction except at the querist, and began to answer, "She canna just be sure about that."

"Look at me, you Highland dog," said the officer, "and remember your life depends on your answer. How many rogues had that outlawed scoundrel with him when you left him?"

"Ou, no aboon sax rogues when I was gane."

"And where are the rest of his banditti?"

"Gane wi' the Lieutenant agane ta westland carles."

"Against the westland clans?" said the Captain. "Umph—that is likely enough; and what rogue's errand were you despatched upon?"

"Just to see what your honour and ta gentlemen red-coats were doing doun here at ta Clachan."

"The creature will prove fause-hearted, after a'," said the Bailie, who by this time had planted himself close behind me; "it's lucky I didna pit mysell to expenses anent him."

"And now, my friend," said the Captain, "let us understand each other. You have confessed yourself a spy, and should string up to the next tree—But come, if you will do me one good turn, I will do you another. You, Donald—you shall just, in the way of kindness, carry me and a small party to the place where you left your master, as I wish to speak a few words with him on serious affairs; and I'll let you go about your business, and give you five guineas to boot."

"Oigh! oigh!" exclaimed Dougal, in the extremity of distress and perplexity; "she canna do tat—she canna do tat; she'll rather be hanged."

"Hanged, then, you shall be, my friend" said the officer; "and your blood be upon your own head. Corporal Cramp, do you play Provost-Marshal—away with him!"

The corporal had confronted poor Dougal for some time, ostentatiously twisting a piece of cord which he had found in the house into the form of a halter. He now threw it about the culprit's neck, and, with the assistance of two soldiers, had dragged Dougal as far as the door, when, overcome with the terror of immediate death, he exclaimed, "Shentlemans, stops—stops! She'll do his honour's bidding—stops!"

"Awa' wi' the creature!" said the Bailie, "he deserves hanging mair now than ever; awa' wi' him, corporal. Why dinna ye tak him awa'?"

"It's my belief and opinion, honest gentleman," said the corporal, "that if you were going to be hanged yourself, you would be in no such d—d hurry."

This by-dialogue prevented my hearing what passed between the prisoner and Captain Thornton; but I heard the former snivel out, in a very subdued tone, "And ye'll ask her to gang nae farther than just to show ye where the MacGregor is?—Ohon! ohon!"

"Silence your howling, you rascal—No; I give you my word I will ask you to go no farther.—Corporal, make the men fall in, in front of the houses. Get out these gentlemen's horses; we must carry them with us. I cannot spare any men to guard them here. Come, my lads, get under arms."

The soldiers bustled about, and were ready to move. We were led out, along with Dougal, in the capacity of prisoners. As we left the hut, I heard our companion in captivity remind the Captain of "ta foive kuineas."

"Here they are for you," said the officer, putting gold into his hand; "but observe, that if you attempt to mislead me, I will blow your brains out with my own hand."

"The creature," said the Bailie, "is waur than I judged him—it is a warldly and a perfidious creature. O the filthy lucre of gain that men gies themsells up to! My father the deacon used to say, the penny siller slew mair souls than the naked sword slew bodies."

The landlady now approached, and demanded payment of her reckoning, including all that had been quaffed by Major Galbraith and his Highland friends. The English officer remonstrated, but Mrs. MacAlpine declared, if "she hadna trusted to his honour's name being used in their company, she wad never hae drawn them a stoup o' liquor; for Mr. Galbraith, she might see him again, or she might no, but weel did she wot she had sma' chance of seeing her siller—and she was a puir widow, had naething but her custom to rely on."

Captain Thornton put a stop to her remonstrances by paying the charge, which was only a few English shillings, though the amount sounded very formidable in Scottish denominations. The generous officer would have included Mr. Jarvie and me in this general acquittance; but the Bailie, disregarding an intimation from the landlady to "make as muckle of the Inglishers as we could, for they were sure to gie us plague eneugh," went into a formal accounting respecting our share of the reckoning, and paid it accordingly. The Captain took the opportunity to make us some slight apology for detaining us. "If we were loyal and peaceable subjects," he said, "we would not regret being stopt for a day, when it was essential to the king's service; if otherwise, he was acting according to his duty."

We were compelled to accept an apology which it would have served no purpose to refuse, and we sallied out to attend him on his march.

I shall never forget the delightful sensation with which I exchanged the dark, smoky, smothering atmosphere of the Highland hut, in which we had passed the night so uncomfortably, for the refreshing fragrance of the morning air, and the glorious beams of the rising sun, which, from a tabernacle of purple and golden clouds, were darted full on such a scene of natural romance and beauty as had never before greeted my eyes. To the left lay the valley, down which the Forth wandered on its easterly course, surrounding the beautiful detached hill, with all its garland of woods. On the right, amid a profusion of thickets, knolls, and crags, lay the bed of a broad mountain lake, lightly curled into tiny waves by the breath of the morning breeze, each glittering in its course under the influence of the sunbeams. High hills, rocks, and banks, waving with natural forests of birch and oak, formed the borders of this enchanting sheet of water; and, as their leaves rustled to the wind and twinkled in the sun, gave to the depth of solitude a sort of life and vivacity. Man alone seemed to be placed in a state of inferiority, in a scene where all the ordinary features of nature were raised and exalted. The miserable little *bourocks*, as the Bailie termed them, of which about a dozen formed the village called the Clachan of Aberfoil, were composed of loose stones, cemented by clay instead of mortar, and thatched by turfs, laid rudely upon rafters formed of native and unhewn birches and oaks from the woods around. The roofs approached the ground so nearly, that Andrew Fairservice observed we might have ridden over the village the night before, and never found out we were near it, unless our horses' feet had "gane through the riggin'."

From all we could see, Mrs. MacAlpine's house, miserable as were the quarters it afforded, was still by far the best in the hamlet; and I dare say (if my description gives you any curiosity to see it) you will hardly find it much improved at the present day, for the Scotch are not a people who speedily admit innovation, even when it comes in the shape of improvement.[27]

The inhabitants of these miserable dwellings were disturbed by the noise of our departure; and as our party of about twenty soldiers drew up in rank before marching off, we were reconnoitred by many a beldam from the half-opened door of her cottage. As these sibyls thrust forth their grey heads, imperfectly covered with close caps of flannel, and showed their shrivelled brows, and long skinny arms, with various gestures, shrugs, and muttered expressions in Gaelic addressed to each other, my imagination recurred to the witches of Macbeth, and I imagined I read in the features of these crones the malevolence of the weird sisters. The little children also, who began to crawl forth, some quite naked, and others very imperfectly covered with tatters of tartan stuff, clapped their tiny hands, and grinned at the English soldiers, with an expression of national hate and malignity which seemed beyond their years. I remarked particularly that there were no men, nor so much as a boy of ten or twelve years old, to be seen among the inhabitants of a village which seemed populous in proportion to its extent; and the idea certainly occurred to me, that we were likely to receive from them, in the course of our journey, more effectual tokens of ill-will than those which lowered on the visages, and dictated the murmurs, of the women and children. It was not until we commenced our march that the malignity of the elder persons of the community broke forth into expressions. The last file of men had left the village, to pursue a small broken track, formed by the sledges in which the natives transported their peats and turfs, and which led through the woods that fringed the lower end of the lake, when a shrilly sound of female exclamation broke forth, mixed with the screams of children, the whooping of boys, and the clapping of hands, with which the Highland dames enforce their notes, whether of rage or lamentation. I asked Andrew, who looked as pale as death, what all this meant.

"I doubt we'll ken that ower sune," said he. "Means? It means that the Highland wives are cursing and banning the red-coats, and wishing ill-luck to them, and ilka ane that ever spoke the Saxon tongue. I have heard wives flyte in England and Scotland—it's nae marvel to hear them flyte ony gate; but sic ill-scrapit tongues as thae Highland carlines'—and sic grewsome wishes, that men should be slaughtered like sheep—and that they may lapper their hands to the elbows in their heart's blude—and that they suld dee the death of Walter Cuming of Guiyock,[28] wha hadna as muckle o' him left thegither as would supper a messan-dog—sic awsome language as that I ne'er heard out o' a human thrapple;—and, unless the deil wad rise amang them to gie them a lesson, I thinkna that their talent at cursing could be amended. The warst o't is, they bid us aye gang up the loch, and see what we'll land in."

Adding Andrew's information to what I had myself observed, I could scarce doubt that some attack was meditated upon our party. The road, as we advanced, seemed to afford every facility for such an unpleasant interruption. At first it winded apart from the lake through marshy meadow ground, overgrown with copsewood, now traversing dark and close thickets which would have admitted an ambuscade to be sheltered within a few yards of our line of march, and frequently crossing rough mountain torrents, some of which took the soldiers up to the knees, and ran with such violence, that their force could only be stemmed by the strength of two or three men holding fast by each other's arms. It certainly appeared to me, though altogether unacquainted with military affairs, that a sort of half-savage warriors, as I had heard the Highlanders asserted to be, might, in such passes as these, attack a party of regular forces with great advantage. The Bailie's good sense and shrewd observation had led him to the same conclusion, as I understood from his requesting to speak with the captain, whom he addressed nearly in the following terms:— "Captain, it's no to fleech ony favour out o' ye, for I scorn it—and it's under protest that I reserve my action and pleas of oppression and wrongous imprisonment;—but, being a friend to King George and his army, I take the liberty to speer—Dinna ye think ye might tak a better time to gang up this glen? If ye are seeking Rob Roy, he's ken'd to be better than half a hunder men strong when he's at the fewest; an if he brings in the Glengyle folk, and the Glenfinlas and Balquhidder lads, he may come to gie you your kail through the reek; and it's my sincere advice, as a king's friend, ye had better tak back again to the Clachan, for thae women at Aberfoil are like the scarts and seamaws at the Cumries—there's aye foul weather follows their skirting."

"Make yourself easy, sir," replied Captain Thornton; "I am in the execution of my orders. And as you say you are a friend to King George, you will be glad to learn that it is impossible that this gang of ruffians, whose license has disturbed the country so long, can escape the measures now taken to suppress them. The horse squadron of militia, commanded by Major Galbraith, is already joined by two or more troops of cavalry, which will occupy all the lower passes of this wild country; three hundred Highlanders, under the two gentlemen you saw at the inn, are in possession of the upper part, and various strong parties from the garrison are securing the hills and glens in different directions. Our last accounts of Rob Roy correspond with what this fellow has confessed, that, finding himself surrounded on all sides, he had dismissed the greater part of his followers, with the purpose either of lying concealed, or of making his escape through his superior knowledge of the passes."

"I dinna ken," said the Bailie; "there's mair brandy than brains in Garschattachin's head this morning—And I wadna, an I were you, Captain, rest my main dependence on the Hielandmen—hawks winna pike out hawks' een. They may quarrel among themsells, and gie ilk ither ill names, and maybe a slash wi' a claymore; but they are sure to join in the lang run, against a' civilised folk, that wear breeks on their hinder ends, and hae purses in their pouches."

Apparently these admonitions were not altogether thrown away on Captain Thornton. He reformed his line of march, commanded his soldiers to unsling their firelocks and fix their bayonets, and formed an advanced and rear-guard, each consisting of a non-commissioned officer and two soldiers, who received strict orders to keep an alert look-out. Dougal underwent another and very close examination, in which he steadfastly asserted the truth of what he had before affirmed; and being rebuked on account of the suspicious and dangerous appearance of the route by which he was guiding them, he answered with a sort of testiness that seemed very natural, "Her nainsell didna mak ta road; an shentlemans likit grand roads, she suld hae pided at Glasco."

All this passed off well enough, and we resumed our progress.

Our route, though leading towards the lake, had hitherto been so much shaded by wood, that we only from time to time obtained a glimpse of that beautiful sheet of water. But the road now suddenly emerged from the forest ground, and, winding close by the margin of the loch, afforded us a full view of its spacious mirror, which now, the breeze having totally subsided, reflected in still magnificence the high dark heathy mountains, huge grey rocks, and shaggy banks, by which it is encircled. The hills now sunk on its margin so closely, and were so broken and precipitous, as to afford no passage except just upon the narrow line of the track which we occupied, and which was overhung with rocks, from which we might have been destroyed merely by rolling down stones, without much possibility of offering resistance. Add to this, that, as the road winded round every promontory and bay which indented the lake, there was rarely a possibility of seeing a hundred yards before us. Our commander appeared to take some alarm at the nature of the pass in which he was engaged, which displayed itself in repeated orders to his soldiers to be on the alert, and in many threats of instant death to Dougal, if he should be found to have led them into danger. Dougal received these threats with an air of stupid impenetrability, which might arise either from conscious innocence, or from dogged resolution.

"If shentlemans were seeking ta Red Gregarach," he said, "to be sure they couldna expect to find her without some wee danger."

Just as the Highlander uttered these words, a halt was made by the corporal commanding the advance, who sent back one of the file who formed it, to tell the Captain that the path in front was occupied by Highlanders, stationed on a commanding point of particular difficulty. Almost at the same instant a soldier from the rear came to say, that they heard the sound of a bagpipe in the woods through which we had just passed. Captain Thornton, a man of conduct as well as courage, instantly resolved to force the pass in front, without waiting till he was assailed from the rear; and, assuring his soldiers that the bagpipes which they heard were those of the friendly Highlanders who were advancing to their assistance, he stated to them the importance of advancing and securing Rob Roy, if possible, before these auxiliaries should come up to divide with them the honour, as well as the reward which was placed on the head of this celebrated freebooter. He therefore ordered the rear-guard to join the centre, and both to close up to the advance, doubling his files so as to occupy with his column the whole practicable part of the road, and to present such a front as its breadth admitted. Dougal, to whom he said in a whisper, "You dog, if you have deceived me, you shall die for it!" was placed in the centre, between two grenadiers, with positive orders to shoot him if he attempted an escape. The same situation was assigned to us, as being the safest, and Captain Thornton, taking his half-pike from the soldier who carried it, placed himself at the head of his little detachment, and gave the word to march forward.

The party advanced with the firmness of English soldiers. Not so Andrew Fairservice, who was frightened out of his wits; and not so, if truth must be told, either the Bailie or I myself, who, without feeling the same degree of trepidation, could not with stoical indifference see our lives exposed to hazard in a quarrel with which we had no concern. But there was neither time for remonstrance nor remedy.

We approached within about twenty yards of the spot where the advanced guard had seen some appearance of an enemy. It was one of those promontories which run into the lake, and round the base of which the road had hitherto winded in the manner I have described. In the present case, however, the path, instead of keeping the water's edge, sealed the promontory by one or two rapid zigzags, carried in a broken track along the precipitous face of a slaty grey rock, which would otherwise have been absolutely inaccessible. On the top of this rock, only to be approached by a road so broken, so narrow, and so precarious, the corporal declared he had seen the bonnets and long-barrelled guns of several mountaineers, apparently couched among the long heath and brushwood which crested the eminence. Captain Thornton ordered him to move forward with three files, to dislodge the supposed ambuscade, while, at a more slow but steady pace, he advanced to his support with the rest of his party.

The attack which he meditated was prevented by the unexpected apparition of a female upon the summit of the rock.

"Stand!" she said, with a commanding tone, "and tell me what ye seek in MacGregor's country?"

I have seldom seen a finer or more commanding form than this woman. She might be between the term of forty and fifty years, and had a countenance which must once have been of a masculine cast of beauty; though now, imprinted with deep lines by exposure to rough weather, and perhaps by the wasting influence of grief and passion, its features were only strong, harsh, and expressive. She wore her plaid, not drawn around her head and shoulders, as is the fashion of the women in Scotland, but disposed around her body as the Highland soldiers wear theirs. She had a man's bonnet, with a feather in it, an unsheathed sword in her hand, and a pair of pistols at her girdle.

"It's Helen Campbell, Rob's wife," said the Bailie, in a whisper of considerable alarm; "and there will be broken heads amang us or it's lang."

"What seek ye here?" she asked again of Captain Thornton, who had himself advanced to reconnoitre.

"We seek the outlaw, Rob Roy MacGregor Campbell," answered the officer, "and make no war on women; therefore offer no vain opposition to the king's troops, and assure yourself of civil treatment."

"Ay," retorted the Amazon, "I am no stranger to your tender mercies. Ye have left me neither name nor fame—my mother's bones will shrink aside in their grave when mine are laid beside them—Ye have left me neither house nor hold, blanket nor bedding, cattle to feed us, or flocks to clothe us—Ye have taken from us all—all!—The very name of our ancestors have ye taken away, and now ye come for our lives."

"I seek no man's life," replied the Captain; "I only execute my orders. If you are alone, good woman, you have nought to fear—if there are any with you so rash as to offer useless resistance, their own blood be on their own heads. Move forward, sergeant."

"Forward! march!" said the non-commissioned officer. "Huzza, my boys, for Rob Roy's head and a purse of gold."

He quickened his pace into a run, followed by the six soldiers; but as they attained the first traverse of the ascent, the flash of a dozen of firelocks from various parts of the pass parted in quick succession and deliberate aim. The sergeant, shot through the body, still struggled to gain the ascent, raised himself by his hands to clamber up the face of the rock, but relaxed his grasp, after a desperate effort, and falling, rolled from the face of the cliff into the deep lake, where he perished. Of the soldiers, three fell, slain or disabled; the others retreated on their main body, all more or less wounded.

"Grenadiers, to the front!" said Captain Thornton.—You are to recollect, that in those days this description of soldiers actually carried that destructive species of firework from which they derive their name. The four grenadiers moved to the front accordingly. The officer commanded the rest of the party to be ready to support them, and only saying to us, "Look to your safety, gentlemen," gave, in rapid succession, the word to the grenadiers—"Open your pouches—handle your grenades—blow your matches—fall on."

The whole advanced with a shout, headed by Captain Thornton,—the grenadiers preparing to throw their grenades among the bushes where the ambuscade lay, and the musketeers to support them by an instant and close assault. Dougal, forgotten in the scuffle, wisely crept into the thicket which overhung that part of the road where we had first halted, which he ascended with the activity of a wild cat. I followed his example, instinctively recollecting that the fire of the Highlanders would sweep the open track. I clambered until out of breath; for a continued spattering fire, in which every shot was multiplied by a thousand echoes, the hissing of the kindled fusees of the grenades, and the successive explosion of those missiles, mingled with the huzzas of the soldiers, and the yells and cries of their Highland antagonists, formed a contrast which added—I do not shame to own it—wings to my desire to reach a place of safety. The difficulties of the ascent soon increased so much, that I despaired of reaching Dougal, who seemed to swing himself from rock to rock, and stump to stump, with the facility of a squirrel, and I turned down my eyes to see what had become of my other companions. Both were brought to a very awkward standstill.

The Bailie, to whom I suppose fear had given a temporary share of agility, had ascended about twenty feet from the path, when his foot slipping, as he straddled from one huge fragment of rock to another, he would have slumbered with his father the deacon, whose acts and words he was so fond of quoting, but for a projecting branch of a ragged thorn, which, catching hold of the skirts of his riding-coat, supported him in mid-air, where he dangled not unlike to the sign of the Golden Fleece over the door of a mercer in the Trongate of his native city.

As for Andrew Fairservice, he had advanced with better success, until he had attained the top of a bare cliff, which, rising above the wood, exposed him, at least in his own opinion, to all the dangers of the neighbouring skirmish, while, at the same time, it was of such a precipitous and impracticable nature, that he dared neither to advance nor retreat. Footing it up and down upon the narrow space which the top of the cliff afforded (very like a fellow at a country-fair dancing upon a trencher), he roared for mercy in Gaelic and English alternately, according to the side on which the scale of victory seemed to predominate, while his exclamations were only answered by the groans of the Bailie, who suffered much, not only from apprehension, but from the pendulous posture in which he hung suspended by the loins.

On perceiving the Bailie's precarious situation, my first idea was to attempt to render him assistance; but this was impossible without the concurrence of Andrew, whom neither sign, nor entreaty, nor command, nor expostulation, could inspire with courage to adventure the descent from his painful elevation, where, like an unskilful and obnoxious minister of state, unable to escape from the eminence to which he had presumptuously ascended, he continued to pour forth piteous prayers for mercy, which no one heard, and to skip to and fro, writhing his body into all possible antic shapes to avoid the balls which he conceived to be whistling around him.

In a few minutes this cause of terror ceased, for the fire, at first so well sustained, now sunk at once—a sure sign that the conflict was concluded. To gain some spot from which I could see how the day had gone was now my object, in order to appeal to the mercy of the victors, who, I trusted (whichever side might be gainers), would not suffer the honest Bailie to remain suspended, like the coffin of Mahomet, between heaven and earth, without lending a hand to disengage him. At length, by dint of scrambling, I found a spot which commanded a view of the field of battle. It was indeed ended; and, as my mind already augured, from the place and circumstances attending the contest, it had terminated in the defeat of Captain Thornton. I saw a party of Highlanders in the act of disarming that officer, and the scanty remainder of his party. They consisted of about twelve men most of whom were wounded, who, surrounded by treble their number, and without the power either to advance or retreat, exposed to a murderous and well-aimed fire, which they had no means of returning with effect, had at length laid down their arms by the order of their officer, when he saw that the road in his rear was occupied, and that protracted resistance would be only wasting the lives of his brave followers. By the Highlanders, who fought under cover, the victory was cheaply bought, at the expense of one man slain and two wounded by the grenades. All this I learned afterwards. At present I only comprehended the general result of the day, from seeing the English officer, whose face was covered with blood, stripped of his hat and arms, and his men, with sullen and dejected countenances which marked their deep regret, enduring, from the wild and martial figures who surrounded them, the severe measures to which the laws of war subject the vanquished for security of the victors.

CHAPTER FOURTEENTH

> "Woe to the vanquished!" was stern Brenno's word,
> When sunk proud Rome beneath the Gallic sword—
> "Woe to the vanquished!" when his massive blade
> Bore down the scale against her ransom weigh'd;
> And on the field of foughten battle still,
> Woe knows no limits save the victor's will.
>
> — THE GAULLIAD

I anxiously endeavoured to distinguish Dougal among the victors. I had little doubt that the part he had played was assumed, on purpose to lead the English officer into the defile, and I could not help admiring the address with which the ignorant, and apparently half-brutal savage, had veiled his purpose, and the affected reluctance with which he had suffered to be extracted from him the false information which it must have been his purpose from the beginning to communicate. I foresaw we should incur some danger on approaching the victors in the first flush of their success, which was not unstained with cruelty; for one or two of the soldiers, whose wounds prevented them from rising, were poniarded by the victors, or rather by some ragged Highland boys who had mingled with them. I concluded, therefore, it would be unsafe to present ourselves without some mediator; and as Campbell, whom I now could not but identify with the celebrated freebooter Rob Roy, was nowhere to be seen, I resolved to claim the protection of his emissary, Dougal.

After gazing everywhere in vain, I at length retraced my steps to see what assistance I could individually render to my unlucky friend, when, to my great joy, I saw Mr. Jarvie delivered from his state of suspense; and though very black in the face, and much deranged in the garments, safely seated beneath the rock, in front of which he had been so lately suspended. I hastened to join him and offer my congratulations, which he was at first far from receiving in the spirit of cordiality with which they were offered. A heavy fit of coughing scarce permitted him breath enough to express the broken hints which he threw out against my sincerity.

"Uh! uh! uh! uh!—they say a friend—uh! uh!—a friend sticketh closer than a brither—uh! uh! uh! When I came up here, Maister Osbaldistone, to this country, cursed of God and man—uh! uh—Heaven forgie me for swearing—on nae man's errand but yours, d'ye think it was fair—uh! uh! uh!—to leave me, first, to be shot or drowned atween red-wad Highlanders and red-coats; and next to be hung up between heaven and earth, like an auld potato-bogle, without sae muckle as trying—uh! uh!—sae muckle as trying to relieve me?"

I made a thousand apologies, and laboured so hard to represent the impossibility of my affording him relief by my own unassisted exertions, that at length I succeeded, and the Bailie, who was as placable as hasty in his temper, extended his favour to me once more. I next took the liberty of asking him how he had contrived to extricate himself.

"Me extricate! I might hae hung there till the day of judgment or I could hae helped mysell, wi' my head hinging down on the tae side, and my heels on the tother, like the yarn-scales in the weigh-house. It was the creature Dougal that extricated me, as he did yestreen; he cuttit aff the tails o' my coat wi' his durk, and another gillie and him set me on my legs as cleverly as if I had never been aff them. But to see what a thing gude braid claith is! Had I been in ony o' your rotten French camlets now, or your drab-de-berries, it would hae screeded like an auld rag wi' sic a weight as mine. But fair fa' the weaver that wrought the weft o't—I swung and bobbit yonder as safe as a gabbart[29] that's moored by a three-ply cable at the Broomielaw."

I now inquired what had become of his preserver.

"The creature," so he continued to call the Highlandman, "contrived to let me ken there wad be danger in gaun near the leddy till he came back, and bade me stay here. I am o' the mind," he continued, "that he's seeking after you—it's a considerate creature—and troth, I wad swear he was right about the leddy, as he ca's her, too—Helen Campbell was nane o' the maist douce maidens, nor meekest wives neither, and folk say that Rob himsell stands in awe o' her. I doubt she winna ken me, for it's mony years since we met—I am clear for waiting for the Dougal creature or we gang near her."

I signified my acquiescence in this reasoning; but it was not the will of fate that day that the Bailie's prudence should profit himself or any one else.

Andrew Fairservice, though he had ceased to caper on the pinnacle upon the cessation of the firing, which had given occasion for his whimsical exercise, continued, as perched on the top of an exposed cliff, too conspicuous an object to escape the sharp eyes of the Highlanders, when they had time to look a little around them. We were apprized he was discovered, by a wild and loud halloo set up among the assembled victors, three or four of whom instantly plunged into the copsewood, and ascended the rocky side of the hill in different directions towards the place where they had discovered this whimsical apparition.

Those who arrived first within gunshot of poor Andrew, did not trouble themselves to offer him any assistance in the ticklish posture of his affairs, but levelling their long Spanish-barrelled guns, gave him to understand, by signs which admitted of no misconstruction, that he must contrive to come down and submit himself to their mercy, or to be marked at from beneath, like a regimental target set up for ball-practice. With such a formidable hint for venturous exertion, Andrew Fairservice could no longer hesitate; the more imminent peril overcame his sense of that which seemed less inevitable, and he began to descend the cliff at all risks, clutching to the ivy and oak stumps, and projecting fragments of rock, with an almost feverish anxiety, and never failing, as circumstances left him a hand at liberty, to extend it to the plaided gentry below in an attitude of supplication, as if to deprecate the discharge of their levelled firearms. In a word, the fellow, under the influence of a counteracting motive for terror, achieved a safe descent from his perilous eminence, which, I verily believe, nothing but the fear of instant death could have moved him to attempt. The awkward mode of Andrew's descent greatly amused the Highlanders below, who fired a shot or two while he was engaged in it, without the purpose of injuring him, as I believe, but merely to enhance the amusement they derived from his extreme terror, and the superlative exertions of agility to which it excited him.

At length he attained firm and comparatively level ground—or rather, to speak more correctly, his foot slipping at the last point of descent, he fell on the earth at his full length, and was raised by the assistance of the Highlanders, who stood to receive him, and who, ere he gained his legs, stripped him not only of the whole contents of his pockets, but of periwig, hat, coat, doublet, stockings, and shoes, performing the feat with such admirable celerity, that, although he fell on his back a well-clothed and decent burgher-seeming serving-man, he arose a forked, uncased, bald-pated, beggarly-looking scarecrow. Without respect to the pain which his undefended toes experienced from the sharp encounter of the rocks over which they hurried him, those who had detected Andrew proceeded to drag him downward towards the road through all the intervening obstacles.

In the course of their descent, Mr. Jarvie and I became exposed to their lynx-eyed observation, and instantly half-a-dozen of armed Highlanders thronged around us, with drawn dirks and swords pointed at our faces and throats, and cocked pistols presented against our bodies. To have offered resistance would have been madness, especially as we had no weapons capable of supporting such a demonstration. We therefore submitted to our fate; and with great roughness on the part of those who assisted at our toilette, were in the act of being reduced to as unsophisticated a state (to use King Lear's phrase) as the plume-less biped Andrew Fairservice, who stood shivering between fear and cold at a few yards' distance. Good chance, however, saved us from this extremity of wretchedness; for, just as I had yielded up my cravat (a smart Steinkirk, by the way, and richly laced), and the Bailie had been disrobed of the fragments of his riding-coat—enter Dougal, and the scene was changed. By a high tone of expostulation, mixed with oaths and threats, as far as I could conjecture the tenor of his language from the violence of his gestures, he compelled the plunderers, however reluctant, not only to give up their further depredations on our property, but to restore the spoil they had already appropriated. He snatched my cravat from the fellow who had seized it, and twisted it (in the zeal of his restitution) around my neck with such suffocating energy as made me think that he had not only been, during his residence at Glasgow, a substitute of the jailor, but must moreover have taken lessons as an apprentice of the hangman. He flung the tattered remnants of Mr. Jarvie's coat around his shoulders, and as more Highlanders began to flock towards us from the high road, he led the way downwards, directing and commanding the others to afford us, but particularly the Bailie, the assistance necessary to our descending with comparative ease and safety. It was, however, in vain that Andrew Fairservice employed his lungs in obsecrating a share of Dougal's protection, or at least his interference to procure restoration of his shoes.

"Na, na," said Dougal in reply, "she's nae gentle pody, I trow; her petters hae ganged parefoot, or she's muckle mista'en." And, leaving Andrew to follow at his leisure, or rather at such leisure as the surrounding crowd were pleased to indulge him with, he hurried us down to the pathway in which the skirmish had been fought, and hastened to present us as additional captives to the female leader of his band.

We were dragged before her accordingly, Dougal fighting, struggling, screaming, as if he were the party most apprehensive of hurt, and repulsing, by threats and efforts, all those who attempted to take a nearer interest in our capture than he seemed to do himself. At length we were placed before the heroine of the day, whose appearance, as well as those of the savage, uncouth, yet martial figures who surrounded us, struck me, to own the truth, with considerable apprehension. I do not know if Helen MacGregor had personally mingled in the fray, and indeed I was afterwards given to understand the contrary; but the specks of blood on her brow, her hands and naked arms, as well as on the blade of her sword which she continued to hold in her hand—her flushed countenance, and the disordered state of the raven locks which escaped from under the red bonnet and plume that formed her head-dress, seemed all to intimate that she had taken an immediate share in the conflict. Her keen black eyes and features expressed an imagination inflamed by the pride of gratified revenge, and the triumph of victory. Yet there was nothing positively sanguinary, or cruel, in her deportment; and she reminded me, when the immediate alarm of the interview was over, of some of the paintings I had seen of the inspired heroines in the Catholic churches of France. She was not, indeed, sufficiently beautiful for a Judith, nor had she the inspired expression of features which painters have given to Deborah, or to the wife of Heber the Kenite, at whose feet the strong oppressor of Israel, who dwelled in Harosheth of the Gentiles, bowed down, fell, and lay a dead man. Nevertheless, the enthusiasm by which she was agitated gave her countenance and deportment, wildly dignified in themselves, an air which made her approach nearly to the ideas of those wonderful artists who gave to the eye the heroines of Scripture history.

I was uncertain in what terms to accost a personage so uncommon, when Mr. Jarvie, breaking the ice with a preparatory cough (for the speed with which he had been brought into her presence had again impeded his respiration), addressed her as follows:—"Uh! uh! &c. &c. I am very happy to have this *joyful* opportunity" (a quaver in his voice strongly belied the emphasis which he studiously laid on the word joyful) —"this joyful occasion," he resumed, trying to give the adjective a more suitable accentuation, "to wish my kinsman Robin's wife a very good morning—Uh! uh!— How's a' wi' ye?" (by this time he had talked himself into his usual jog-trot manner, which exhibited a mixture of familiarity and self-importance)—"How's a' wi' ye this lang time? Ye'll hae forgotten me, Mrs. MacGregor Campbell, as your cousin—uh! uh!

—but ye'll mind my father, Deacon Nicol Jarvie, in the Saut Market o' Glasgow?—an honest man he was, and a sponsible, and respectit you and yours. Sae, as I said before, I am right glad to see you, Mrs. MacGregor Campbell, as my kinsman's wife. I wad crave the liberty of a kinsman to salute you, but that your gillies keep such a dolefu' fast haud o' my arms, and, to speak Heaven's truth and a magistrate's, ye wadna be the waur of a cogfu' o' water before ye welcomed your friends."

There was something in the familiarity of this introduction which ill suited the exalted state of temper of the person to whom it was addressed, then busied with distributing dooms of death, and warm from conquest in a perilous encounter.

"What fellow are you," she said, "that dare to claim kindred with the MacGregor, and neither wear his dress nor speak his language?—What are you, that have the tongue and the habit of the hound, and yet seek to lie down with the deer?"

"I dinna ken," said the undaunted Bailie, "if the kindred has ever been weel redd out to you yet, cousin—but it's ken'd, and can be prov'd. My mother, Elspeth MacFarlane, was the wife of my father, Deacon Nicol Jarvie—peace be wi' them baith!—and Elspeth was the daughter of Parlane MacFarlane, at the Sheeling o' Loch Sloy. Now, this Parlane MacFarlane, as his surviving daughter Maggy MacFarlane, *alias* MacNab, wha married Duncan MacNab o' Stuckavrallachan, can testify, stood as near to your gudeman, Robert MacGregor, as in the fourth degree of kindred, for"—

The virago lopped the genealogical tree, by demanding haughtily, "If a stream of rushing water acknowledged any relation with the portion withdrawn from it for the mean domestic uses of those who dwelt on its banks?"

"Vera true, kinswoman," said the Bailie; "but for a' that, the burn wad be glad to hae the milldam back again in simmer, when the chuckie-stanes are white in the sun. I ken weel eneugh you Hieland folk haud us Glasgow people light and cheap for our language and our claes;—but everybody speaks their native tongue that they learned in infancy; and it would be a daft-like thing to see me wi' my fat wame in a short Hieland coat, and my puir short houghs gartered below the knee, like ane o' your lang-legged gillies. Mair by token, kinswoman," he continued, in defiance of various intimations by which Dougal seemed to recommend silence, as well as of the marks of impatience which the Amazon evinced at his loquacity, "I wad hae ye to mind that the king's errand whiles comes in the cadger's gate, and that, for as high as ye may think o' the gudeman, as it's right every wife should honour her husband—there's Scripture warrant for that—yet as high as ye haud him, as I was saying, I hae been serviceable to Rob ere now;—forbye a set o' pearlins I sent yourself when ye was gaun to be married, and when Rob was an honest weel-doing drover, and nane o' this unlawfu' wark, wi' fighting, and flashes, and fluff-gibs, disturbing the king's peace and disarming his soldiers."

He had apparently touched on a key which his kinswoman could not brook. She drew herself up to her full height, and betrayed the acuteness of her feelings by a laugh of mingled scorn and bitterness.

"Yes," she said, "you, and such as you, might claim a relation to us, when we stooped to be the paltry wretches fit to exist under your dominion, as your hewers of wood and drawers of water—to find cattle for your banquets, and subjects for your laws to oppress and trample on. But now we are free—free by the very act which left us neither house nor hearth, food nor covering—which bereaved me of all—of all—

and makes me groan when I think I must still cumber the earth for other purposes than those of vengeance. And I will carry on the work, this day has so well commenced, by a deed that shall break all bands between MacGregor and the Lowland churls. Here Allan—Dougal—bind these Sassenachs neck and heel together, and throw them into the Highland Loch to seek for their Highland kinsfolk."

The Bailie, alarmed at this mandate, was commencing an expostulation, which probably would have only inflamed the violent passions of the person whom he addressed, when Dougal threw himself between them, and in his own language, which he spoke with a fluency and rapidity strongly contrasted by the slow, imperfect, and idiot-like manner in which he expressed himself in English, poured forth what I doubt not was a very animated pleading in our behalf.

His mistress replied to him, or rather cut short his harangue, by exclaiming in English (as if determined to make us taste in anticipation the full bitterness of death) —"Base dog, and son of a dog, do you dispute my commands? Should I tell ye to cut out their tongues and put them into each other's throats, to try which would there best knap Southron, or to tear out their hearts and put them into each other's breasts, to see which would there best plot treason against the MacGregor—and such things have been done of old in the day of revenge, when our fathers had wrongs to redress —Should I command you to do this, would it be your part to dispute my orders?"

"To be sure, to be sure," Dougal replied, with accents of profound submission; "her pleasure suld be done—tat's but reason; but an it were—tat is, an it could be thought the same to her to coup the ill-faured loon of ta red-coat Captain, and hims corporal Cramp, and twa three o' the red-coats, into the loch, herself wad do't wi' muckle mair great satisfaction than to hurt ta honest civil shentlemans as were friends to the Gregarach, and came up on the Chiefs assurance, and not to do no treason, as herself could testify."

The lady was about to reply, when a few wild strains of a pibroch were heard advancing up the road from Aberfoil, the same probably which had reached the ears of Captain Thornton's rear-guard, and determined him to force his way onward rather than return to the village, on finding the pass occupied. The skirmish being of very short duration, the armed men who followed this martial melody, had not, although quickening their march when they heard the firing, been able to arrive in time sufficient to take any share in the rencontre. The victory, therefore, was complete without them, and they now arrived only to share in the triumph of their countrymen.

There was a marked difference betwixt the appearance of these new comers and that of the party by which our escort had been defeated—and it was greatly in favour of the former. Among the Highlanders who surrounded the Chieftainess, if I may presume to call her so without offence to grammar, were men in the extremity of age, boys scarce able to bear a sword, and even women—all, in short, whom the last necessity urges to take up arms; and it added a shade of bitter shame to the defection which clouded Thornton's manly countenance, when he found that the numbers and position of a foe, otherwise so despicable, had enabled them to conquer his brave veterans. But the thirty or forty Highlanders who now joined the others, were all men in the prime of youth or manhood, active clean-made fellows, whose short hose and belted plaids set out their sinewy limbs to the best advantage. Their arms were as superior to those of the first party as their dress and appearance. The followers of the female Chief had axes, scythes, and other antique weapons, in aid of their guns; and some had only clubs, daggers, and long knives. But of the second party, most had pistols at the belt, and almost all had dirks hanging at the pouches which they wore in front. Each had a good gun in his hand, and a broadsword by his side, besides a stout round target, made of light wood, covered with leather, and curiously studded with brass, and having a steel spike screwed into the centre. These hung on their left shoulder during a march, or while they were engaged in exchanging fire with the enemy, and were worn on their left arm when they charged with sword in hand.

But it was easy to see that this chosen band had not arrived from a victory such as they found their ill-appointed companions possessed of. The pibroch sent forth occasionally a few wailing notes expressive of a very different sentiment from triumph; and when they appeared before the wife of their Chieftain, it was in silence, and with downcast and melancholy looks. They paused when they approached her, and the pipes again sent forth the same wild and melancholy strain.

Helen rushed towards them with a countenance in which anger was mingled with apprehension.—"What means this, Alaster?" she said to the minstrel—"why a lament in the moment of victory?—Robert—Hamish—where's the MacGregor?—where's your father?"

Her sons, who led the band, advanced with slow and irresolute steps towards her, and murmured a few words in Gaelic, at hearing which she set up a shriek that made the rocks ring again, in which all the women and boys joined, clapping their hands and yelling as if their lives had been expiring in the sound. The mountain echoes, silent since the military sounds of battle had ceased, had now to answer these frantic and discordant shrieks of sorrow, which drove the very night-birds from their haunts in the rocks, as if they were startled to hear orgies more hideous and ill-omened than their own, performed in the face of open day.

"Taken!" repeated Helen, when the clamour had subsided—"Taken!— captive!— and you live to say so?—Coward dogs! did I nurse you for this, that you should spare your blood on your father's enemies? or see him prisoner, and come back to tell it?"

The sons of MacGregor, to whom this expostulation was addressed, were youths, of whom the eldest had hardly attained his twentieth year. *Hamish*, or James, the elder of these youths, was the tallest by a head, and much handsomer than his brother; his light-blue eyes, with a profusion of fair hair, which streamed from under his smart blue bonnet, made his whole appearance a most favourable specimen of the Highland youth. The younger was called Robert; but, to distinguish him from his father, the Highlanders added the epithet *Oig,* or the young. Dark hair, and dark features, with a ruddy glow of health and animation, and a form strong and well-set beyond his years, completed the sketch of the young mountaineer.

Both now stood before their mother with countenances clouded with grief and shame, and listened, with the most respectful submission, to the reproaches with which she loaded them. At length when her resentment appeared in some degree to subside, the eldest, speaking in English, probably that he might not be understood by their followers, endeavoured respectfully to vindicate himself and his brother from his mother's reproaches. I was so near him as to comprehend much of what he said;

and, as it was of great consequence to me to be possessed of information in this strange crisis, I failed not to listen as attentively as I could.

"The MacGregor," his son stated, "had been called out upon a trysting with a Lowland hallion, who came with a token from"—he muttered the name very low, but I thought it sounded like my own. "The MacGregor," he said, "accepted of the invitation, but commanded the Saxon who brought the message to be detained, as a hostage that good faith should be observed to him. Accordingly he went to the place of appointment" (which had some wild Highland name that I cannot remember), "attended only by Angus Breck and Little Rory, commanding no one to follow him. Within half an hour Angus Breck came back with the doleful tidings that the MacGregor had been surprised and made prisoner by a party of Lennox militia, under Galbraith of Garschattachin." He added, "that Galbraith, on being threatened by MacGregor, who upon his capture menaced him with retaliation on the person of the hostage, had treated the threat with great contempt, replying, 'Let each side hang his man; we'll hang the thief, and your catherans may hang the gauger, Rob, and the country will be rid of two damned things at once, a wild Highlander and a revenue officer.' Angus Breck, less carefully looked to than his master, contrived to escape from the hands of the captors, after having been in their custody long enough to hear this discussion, and to bring off the news."

"And did you learn this, you false-hearted traitor," said the wife of MacGregor, "and not instantly rush to your father's rescue, to bring him off, or leave your body on the place?"

The young MacGregor modestly replied, by representing the very superior force of the enemy, and stated, that as they made no preparation for leaving the country, he had fallen back up the glen with the purpose of collecting a band sufficient to attempt a rescue with some tolerable chance of success. At length he said, "the militiamen would quarter, he understood, in the neighbouring house of Gartartan, or the old castle in the port of Monteith, or some other stronghold, which, although strong and defensible, was nevertheless capable of being surprised, could they but get enough of men assembled for the purpose."

I understood afterwards that the rest of the freebooter's followers were divided into two strong bands, one destined to watch the remaining garrison of Inversnaid, a party of which, under Captain Thornton, had been defeated; and another to show front to the Highland clans who had united with the regular troops and Lowlanders in this hostile and combined invasion of that mountainous and desolate territory, which lying between the lakes of Loch Lomond, Loch Katrine, and Loch Ard, was at this time currently called Rob Roy's, or the MacGregor country. Messengers were despatched in great haste, to concentrate, as I supposed, their forces, with a view to the purposed attack on the Lowlanders; and the dejection and despair, at first visible on each countenance, gave place to the hope of rescuing their leader, and to the thirst of vengeance. It was under the burning influence of the latter passion that the wife of MacGregor commanded that the hostage exchanged for his safety should be brought into her presence. I believe her sons had kept this unfortunate wretch out of her sight, for fear of the consequences; but if it was so, their humane precaution only postponed his fate. They dragged forward at her summons a wretch already half dead with terror, in whose agonised features I recognised, to my horror and astonishment, my old acquaintance Morris.

He fell prostrate before the female Chief with an effort to clasp her knees, from which she drew back, as if his touch had been pollution, so that all he could do in token of the extremity of his humiliation, was to kiss the hem of her plaid. I never heard entreaties for life poured forth with such agony of spirit. The ecstasy of fear was such, that instead of paralysing his tongue, as on ordinary occasions, it even rendered him eloquent; and, with cheeks pale as ashes, hands compressed in agony, eyes that seemed to be taking their last look of all mortal objects, he protested, with the deepest oaths, his total ignorance of any design on the person of Rob Roy, whom he swore he loved and honoured as his own soul. In the inconsistency of his terror, he said he was but the agent of others, and he muttered the name of Rashleigh. He prayed but for life—for life he would give all he had in the world: it was but life he asked—life, if it were to be prolonged under tortures and privations: he asked only breath, though it should be drawn in the damps of the lowest caverns of their hills.

It is impossible to describe the scorn, the loathing, and contempt, with which the wife of MacGregor regarded this wretched petitioner for the poor boon of existence.

"I could have bid ye live," she said, "had life been to you the same weary and wasting burden that it is to me—that it is to every noble and generous mind. But you —wretch! you could creep through the world unaffected by its various disgraces, its ineffable miseries, its constantly accumulating masses of crime and sorrow: you could live and enjoy yourself, while the noble-minded are betrayed—while nameless and birthless villains tread on the neck of the brave and the long-descended: you could enjoy yourself, like a butcher's dog in the shambles, battening on garbage, while the slaughter of the oldest and best went on around you! This enjoyment you shall not live to partake of!—you shall die, base dog! and that before yon cloud has passed over the sun."

She gave a brief command in Gaelic to her attendants, two of whom seized upon the prostrate suppliant, and hurried him to the brink of a cliff which overhung the flood. He set up the most piercing and dreadful cries that fear ever uttered—I may well term them dreadful, for they haunted my sleep for years afterwards. As the murderers, or executioners, call them as you will, dragged him along, he recognised me even in that moment of horror, and exclaimed, in the last articulate words I ever heard him utter, "Oh, Mr. Osbaldistone, save me!—save me!"

I was so much moved by this horrid spectacle, that, although in momentary expectation of sharing his fate, I did attempt to speak in his behalf, but, as might have been expected, my interference was sternly disregarded. The victim was held fast by some, while others, binding a large heavy stone in a plaid, tied it round his neck, and others again eagerly stripped him of some part of his dress. Half-naked, and thus manacled, they hurled him into the lake, there about twelve feet deep, with a loud halloo of vindictive triumph,—above which, however, his last death-shriek, the yell of mortal agony, was distinctly heard. The heavy burden splashed in the dark-blue waters, and the Highlanders, with their pole-axes and swords, watched an instant to guard, lest, extricating himself from the load to which he was attached, the victim might have struggled to regain the shore. But the knot had been securely bound—the wretched man sunk without effort; the waters, which his fall had disturbed, settled calmly over him, and the unit of that life for which he had pleaded so strongly, was for ever withdrawn from the sum of human existence.

CHAPTER FIFTEENTH

> And be he safe restored ere evening set,
> Or, if there's vengeance in an injured heart,
> And power to wreak it in an armed hand,
> Your land shall ache for't.
>
> — OLD PLAY

I know not why it is that a single deed of violence and cruelty affects our nerves more than when these are exercised on a more extended scale. I had seen that day several of my brave countrymen fall in battle: it seemed to me that they met a lot appropriate to humanity, and my bosom, though thrilling with interest, was affected with nothing of that sickening horror with which I beheld the unfortunate Morris put to death without resistance, and in cold blood. I looked at my companion, Mr. Jarvie, whose face reflected the feelings which were painted in mine. Indeed he could not so suppress his horror, but that the words escaped him in a low and broken whisper,—

"I take up my protest against this deed, as a bloody and cruel murder—it is a cursed deed, and God will avenge it in his due way and time."

"Then you do not fear to follow?" said the virago, bending on him a look of death, such as that with which a hawk looks at his prey ere he pounces.

"Kinswoman," said the Bailie, "nae man willingly wad cut short his thread of life before the end o' his pirn was fairly measured off on the yarn-winles—And I hae muckle to do, an I be spared, in this warld—public and private business, as weel that belonging to the magistracy as to my ain particular; and nae doubt I hae some to depend on me, as puir Mattie, wha is an orphan—She's a far-awa' cousin o' the Laird o' Limmerfield. Sae that, laying a' this thegither—skin for skin, yea all that a man hath, will he give for his life."

"And were I to set you at liberty," said the imperious dame, "what name could you give to the drowning of that Saxon dog?"

"Uh! uh!—hem! hem!" said the Bailie, clearing his throat as well as he could, "I suld study to say as little on that score as might be—least said is sunest mended."

"But if you were called on by the courts, as you term them, of justice," she again demanded, "what then would be your answer?"

The Bailie looked this way and that way, like a person who meditates an escape, and then answered in the tone of one who, seeing no means of accomplishing a retreat, determines to stand the brunt of battle—"I see what you are driving me to the wa' about. But I'll tell you't plain, kinswoman,—I behoved just to speak according to my ain conscience; and though your ain gudeman, that I wish had been here for his ain sake and mine, as wool as the puir Hieland creature Dougal, can tell ye that Nicol Jarvie can wink as hard at a friend's failings as onybody, yet I'se tell ye, kinswoman, mine's ne'er be the tongue to belie my thought; and sooner than say that yonder puir wretch was lawfully slaughtered, I wad consent to be laid beside him—though I think ye are the first Hieland woman wad mint sic a doom to her husband's kinsman but four times removed."

It is probable that the tone and firmness assumed by the Bailie in his last speech was better suited to make an impression on the hard heart of his kinswoman than the tone of supplication he had hitherto assumed, as gems can be cut with steel, though they resist softer metals. She commanded us both to be placed before her. "Your name," she said to me, "is Osbaldistone?—the dead dog, whose death you have witnessed, called you so."

"My name *is* Osbaldistone," was my answer.

"Rashleigh, then, I suppose, is your Christian name?" she pursued.

"No,—my name is Francis."

"But you know Rashleigh Osbaldistone," she continued. "He is your brother, if I mistake not,—at least your kinsman and near friend."

"He is my kinsman," I replied, "but not my friend. We were lately engaged together in a rencontre, when we were separated by a person whom I understand to be your husband. My blood is hardly yet dried on his sword, and the wound on my side is yet green. I have little reason to acknowledge him as a friend."

"Then," she replied, "if a stranger to his intrigues, you can go in safety to Garschattachin and his party without fear of being detained, and carry them a message from the wife of the MacGregor?"

I answered that I knew no reasonable cause why the militia gentlemen should detain me; that I had no reason, on my own account, to fear being in their hands; and that if my going on her embassy would act as a protection to my friend and servant, who were here prisoners, "I was ready to set out directly." I took the opportunity to say, "That I had come into this country on her husband's invitation, and his assurance that he would aid me in some important matters in which I was interested; that my companion, Mr. Jarvie, had accompanied me on the same errand."

"And I wish Mr. Jarvie's boots had been fu' o' boiling water when he drew them on for sic a purpose," interrupted the Bailie.

"You may read your father," said Helen MacGregor, turning to her sons, "in what this young Saxon tells us—Wise only when the bonnet is on his head, and the sword is in his hand, he never exchanges the tartan for the broad-cloth, but he runs himself into the miserable intrigues of the Lowlanders, and becomes again, after all he has suffered, their agent—their tool—their slave."

"Add, madam," said I, "and their benefactor."

"Be it so," she said; "for it is the most empty title of them all, since he has uniformly sown benefits to reap a harvest of the most foul ingratitude.—But enough of this. I shall cause you to be guided to the enemy's outposts. Ask for their commander, and deliver him this message from me, Helen MacGregor;—that if they injure a hair of MacGregor's head, and if they do not set him at liberty within the space of twelve hours, there is not a lady in the Lennox but shall before Christmas cry the coronach for them she will be loath to lose,—there is not a farmer but shall sing well-a-wa over a burnt barnyard and an empty byre,—there is not a laird nor heritor shall lay his head on the pillow at night with the assurance of being a live man in the morning,—and, to begin as we are to end, so soon as the term is expired, I will send them this Glasgow Bailie, and this Saxon Captain, and all the rest of my prisoners, each bundled in a plaid, and chopped into as many pieces as there are checks in the tartan."

As she paused in her denunciation, Captain Thornton, who was within hearing, added, with great coolness, "Present my compliments—Captain Thornton's of the Royals, compliments—to the commanding officer, and tell him to do his duty and secure his prisoner, and not waste a thought upon me. If I have been fool enough to have been led into an ambuscade by these artful savages, I am wise enough to know how to die for it without disgracing the service. I am only sorry for my poor fellows," he said, "that have fallen into such butcherly hands."

"Whist! whist!" exclaimed the Bailie; "are ye weary o' your life?—Ye'll gie *my* service to the commanding officer, Mr. Osbaldistone—Bailie Nicol Jarvie's service, a magistrate o' Glasgow, as his father the deacon was before him—and tell him, here are a wheen honest men in great trouble, and like to come to mair; and the best thing he can do for the common good, will be just to let Rob come his wa's up the glen, and nae mair about it. There's been some ill dune here already; but as it has lighted chiefly on the gauger, it winna be muckle worth making a stir about."

With these very opposite injunctions from the parties chiefly interested in the success of my embassy, and with the reiterated charge of the wife of MacGregor to remember and detail every word of her injunctions, I was at length suffered to depart; and Andrew Fairservice, chiefly, I believe, to get rid of his clamorous supplications, was permitted to attend me. Doubtful, however, that I might use my horse as a means of escape from my guides, or desirous to retain a prize of some value, I was given to understand that I was to perform my journey on foot, escorted by Hamish MacGregor, the elder brother, who, with two followers, attended, as well to show me the way, as to reconnoitre the strength and position of the enemy. Dougal had been at first ordered on this party, but he contrived to elude the service, with the purpose, as we afterwards understood, of watching over Mr. Jarvie, whom, according to his wild principles of fidelity, he considered as entitled to his good offices, from having once acted in some measure as his patron or master.

After walking with great rapidity about an hour, we arrived at an eminence covered with brushwood, which gave us a commanding prospect down the valley, and a full view of the post which the militia occupied. Being chiefly cavalry, they had judiciously avoided any attempt to penetrate the pass which had been so unsuccessfully essayed by Captain Thornton. They had taken up their situation with some military skill, on a rising ground in the centre of the little valley of Aberfoil, through which the river Forth winds its earliest course, and which is formed by two ridges of hills, faced with barricades of limestone rock, intermixed with huge masses of breecia, or pebbles imbedded in some softer substance which has hardened around them like mortar; and surrounded by the more lofty mountains in the distance. These ridges, however, left the valley of breadth enough to secure the cavalry from any sudden surprise by the mountaineers and they had stationed sentinels and outposts at proper distances from this main body, in every direction, so that they might secure full time to mount and get under arms upon the least alarm. It was not, indeed, expected at that time, that Highlanders would attack cavalry in an open plain, though late events have shown that they may do so with success.[30]

When I first knew the Highlanders, they had almost a superstitious dread of a mounted trooper, the horse being so much more fierce and imposing in his appearance than the little shelties of their own hills, and moreover being trained, as the more ignorant mountaineers believed, to fight with his feet and his teeth. The appearance of the piequeted horses, feeding in this little vale—the forms of the soldiers, as they sate, stood, or walked, in various groups in the vicinity of the beautiful river, and of the bare yet romantic ranges of rock which hedge in the landscape on either side,—formed a noble foreground; while far to the eastward the eye caught a glance of the lake of Menteith; and Stirling Castle, dimly seen along with the blue and distant line of the Ochil Mountains, closed the scene.

After gazing on this landscape with great earnestness, young MacGregor intimated to me that I was to descend to the station of the militia and execute my errand to their commander,—enjoining me at the same time, with a menacing gesture, neither to inform them who had guided me to that place, nor where I had parted from my escort. Thus tutored, I descended towards the military post, followed by Andrew, who, only retaining his breeches and stockings of the English costume, without a hat, bare-legged, with brogues on his feet, which Dougal had given him out of compassion, and having a tattered plaid to supply the want of all upper garments, looked as if he had been playing the part of a Highland Tom-of-Bedlam. We had not proceeded far before we became visible to one of the videttes, who, riding towards us, presented his carabine and commanded me to stand. I obeyed, and when the soldier came up, desired to be conducted to his commanding-officer. I was immediately brought where a circle of officers, sitting upon the grass, seemed in attendance upon one of superior rank. He wore a cuirass of polished steel, over which were drawn the insignia of the ancient Order of the Thistle. My friend Garschattachin, and many other gentlemen, some in uniform, others in their ordinary dress, but all armed and well attended, seemed to receive their orders from this person of distinction. Many servants in rich liveries, apparently a part of his household, were also in waiting.

Having paid to this nobleman the respect which his rank appeared to demand, I acquainted him that I had been an involuntary witness to the king's soldiers having suffered a defeat from the Highlanders at the pass of Loch-Ard (such I had learned was the name of the place where Mr. Thornton was made prisoner), and that the victors threatened every species of extremity to those who had fallen into their power, as well as to the Low Country in general, unless their Chief, who had that morning been made prisoner, were returned to them uninjured. The Duke (for he whom I addressed was of no lower rank) listened to me with great composure, and then replied, that he should be extremely sorry to expose the unfortunate gentlemen who had been made prisoners to the cruelty of the barbarians into whose hands they had fallen, but that it was folly to suppose that he would deliver up the very author of all these disorders and offences, and so encourage his followers in their license. "You may return to those who sent you," he proceeded, "and inform them, that I shall certainly cause Rob Roy Campbell, whom they call MacGregor, to be executed, by break of day, as an outlaw taken in arms, and deserving death by a thousand acts of violence; that I should be most justly held unworthy of my situation and commission did I act otherwise; that I shall know how to protect the country against their insolent threats of violence; and that if they injure a hair of the head of any of the unfortunate gentlemen whom an unlucky accident has thrown into their power, I will take such ample vengeance, that the very stones of their glens shall sing woe for it this hundred years to come!"

I humbly begged leave to remonstrate respecting the honourable mission imposed on me, and touched upon the obvious danger attending it, when the noble commander replied, "that such being the case, I might send my servant."

"The deil be in my feet," said Andrew, without either having respect to the presence in which he stood, or waiting till I replied—"the deil be in my feet, if I gang my tae's length. Do the folk think I hae another thrapple in my pouch after John Highlandman's sneeked this ane wi' his joctaleg? or that I can dive doun at the tae side of a Highland loch and rise at the tother, like a shell-drake? Na, na—ilk ane for himsell, and God for us a'. Folk may just make a page o' their ain age, and serve themsells till their bairns grow up, and gang their ain errands for Andrew. Rob Roy never came near the parish of Dreepdaily, to steal either pippin or pear frae me or mine."

Silencing my follower with some difficulty, I represented to the Duke the great danger Captain Thornton and Mr. Jarvie would certainly be exposed to, and entreated he would make me the bearer of such modified terms as might be the means of saving their lives. I assured him I should decline no danger if I could be of service; but from what I had heard and seen, I had little doubt they would be instantly murdered should the chief of the outlaws suffer death.

The Duke was obviously much affected. "It was a hard case," he said, "and he felt it as such; but he had a paramount duty to perform to the country—Rob Roy must die!"

I own it was not without emotion that I heard this threat of instant death to my acquaintance Campbell, who had so often testified his good-will towards me. Nor was I singular in the feeling, for many of those around the Duke ventured to express themselves in his favour. "It would be more advisable," they said, "to send him to Stirling Castle, and there detain him a close prisoner, as a pledge for the submission and dispersion of his gang. It were a great pity to expose the country to be plundered, which, now that the long nights approached, it would be found very difficult to prevent, since it was impossible to guard every point, and the Highlanders were sure to select those that were left exposed." They added, that there was great hardship in leaving the unfortunate prisoners to the almost certain doom of massacre denounced against them, which no one doubted would be executed in the first burst of revenge.

Garschattachin ventured yet farther, confiding in the honour of the nobleman whom he addressed, although he knew he had particular reasons for disliking their prisoner. "Rob Roy," he said, "though a kittle neighbour to the Low Country, and particularly obnoxious to his Grace, and though he maybe carried the catheran trade farther than ony man o' his day, was an auld-farrand carle, and there might be some means of making him hear reason; whereas his wife and sons were reckless fiends, without either fear or mercy about them, and, at the head of a' his limmer loons, would be a worse plague to the country than ever he had been."

"Pooh! pooh!" replied his Grace, "it is the very sense and cunning of this fellow which has so long maintained his reign—a mere Highland robber would have been put down in as many weeks as he has flourished years. His gang, without him, is no more to be dreaded as a permanent annoyance—it will no longer exist—than a wasp without its head, which may sting once perhaps, but is instantly crushed into annihilation."

Garschattachin was not so easily silenced. "I am sure, my Lord Duke," he replied, "I have no favour for Rob, and he as little for me, seeing he has twice cleaned out my ain byres, beside skaith amang my tenants; but, however"—

"But, however, Garschattachin," said the Duke, with a smile of peculiar expression, "I fancy you think such a freedom may be pardoned in a friend's friend, and Rob's supposed to be no enemy to Major Galbraith's friends over the water."

"If it be so, my lord," said Garschattachin, in the same tone of jocularity, "it's no the warst thing I have heard of him. But I wish we heard some news from the clans, that we have waited for sae lang. I vow to God they'll keep a Hielandman's word wi' us—I never ken'd them better—it's ill drawing boots upon trews."

"I cannot believe it," said the Duke. "These gentlemen are known to be men of honour, and I must necessarily suppose they are to keep their appointment. Send out two more horse-men to look for our friends. We cannot, till their arrival, pretend to attack the pass where Captain Thornton has suffered himself to be surprised, and which, to my knowledge, ten men on foot might make good against a regiment of the best horse in Europe—Meanwhile let refreshments be given to the men."

I had the benefit of this last order, the more necessary and acceptable, as I had tasted nothing since our hasty meal at Aberfoil the evening before. The videttes who had been despatched returned without tidings of the expected auxiliaries, and sunset was approaching, when a Highlander belonging to the clans whose co-operation was expected, appeared as the bearer of a letter, which he delivered to the Duke with a most profound conge'.

"Now will I wad a hogshead of claret," said Garschattachin, "that this is a message to tell us that these cursed Highlandmen, whom we have fetched here at the expense of so much plague and vexation, are going to draw off, and leave us to do our own business if we can."

"It is even so, gentlemen," said the Duke, reddening with indignation, after having perused the letter, which was written upon a very dirty scrap of paper, but most punctiliously addressed, "For the much-honoured hands of Ane High and Mighty Prince, the Duke," &c. &c. &c. "Our allies," continued the Duke, "have deserted us, gentlemen, and have made a separate peace with the enemy."

"It's just the fate of all alliances," said Garschattachin, "the Dutch were gaun to serve us the same gate, if we had not got the start of them at Utrecht."

"You are facetious, air," said the Duke, with a frown which showed how little he liked the pleasantry; "but our business is rather of a grave cut just now.—I suppose no gentleman would advise our attempting to penetrate farther into the country, unsupported either by friendly Highlanders, or by infantry from Inversnaid?"

A general answer announced that the attempt would be perfect madness.

"Nor would there be great wisdom," the Duke added, "in remaining exposed to a night-attack in this place. I therefore propose that we should retreat to the house of Duchray and that of Gartartan, and keep safe and sure watch and ward until morning. But before we separate, I will examine Rob Roy before you all, and make you sensible, by your own eyes and ears, of the extreme unfitness of leaving him space for farther outrage." He gave orders accordingly, and the prisoner was brought before him, his arms belted down above the elbow, and secured to his body by a horse-girth buckled tight behind him. Two non-commissioned officers had hold of him, one on each side, and two file of men with carabines and fixed bayonets attended for additional security.

I had never seen this man in the dress of his country, which set in a striking point of view the peculiarities of his form. A shock-head of red hair, which the hat and periwig of the Lowland costume had in a great measure concealed, was seen beneath the Highland bonnet, and verified the epithet of *Roy*, or Red, by which he was much better known in the Low Country than by any other, and is still, I suppose, best remembered. The justice of the appellation was also vindicated by the appearance of that part of his limbs, from the bottom of his kilt to the top of his short hose, which the fashion of his country dress left bare, and which was covered with a fell of thick, short, red hair, especially around his knees, which resembled in this respect, as well as from their sinewy appearance of extreme strength, the limbs of a red-coloured Highland bull. Upon the whole, betwixt the effect produced by the change of dress, and by my having become acquainted with his real and formidable character, his appearance had acquired to my eyes something so much wilder and more striking than it before presented, that I could scarce recognise him to be the same person.

His manner was bold, unconstrained unless by the actual bonds, haughty, and even dignified. He bowed to the Duke, nodded to Garschattachin and others, and showed some surprise at seeing me among the party.

"It is long since we have met, Mr. Campbell," said the Duke.

"It is so, my Lord Duke; I could have wished it had been" (looking at the fastening on his arms) "when I could have better paid the compliments I owe to your Grace;—but there's a gude time coming."

"No time like the time present, Mr. Campbell," answered the Duke, "for the hours are fast flying that must settle your last account with all mortal affairs. I do not say this to insult your distress; but you must be aware yourself that you draw near the end of your career. I do not deny that you may sometimes have done less harm than others of your unhappy trade, and that you may occasionally have exhibited marks of talent, and even of a disposition which promised better things. But you are aware how long you have been the terror and the oppressor of a peaceful neighbourhood, and by what acts of violence you have maintained and extended your usurped authority. You know, in short, that you have deserved death, and that you must prepare for it."

"My Lord," said Rob Roy, "although I may well lay my misfortunes at your Grace's door, yet I will never say that you yourself have been the wilful and witting author of them. My Lord, if I had thought sae, your Grace would not this day have been sitting in judgment on me; for you have been three times within good rifle distance of me when you were thinking but of the red deer, and few people have ken'd me miss my aim. But as for them that have abused your Grace's ear, and set you up against a man that was ance as peacefu' a man as ony in the land, and made your name the warrant for driving me to utter extremity,—I have had some amends of them, and, for a' that your Grace now says, I expect to live to hae mair."

"I know," said the Duke, in rising anger, "that you are a determined and impudent villain, who will keep his oath if he swears to mischief; but it shall be my care to prevent you. You have no enemies but your own wicked actions."

"Had I called myself Grahame, instead of Campbell, I might have heard less about them," answered Rob Roy, with dogged resolution.

"You will do well, sir," said the Duke, "to warn your wife and family and followers, to beware how they use the gentlemen now in their hands, as I will requite tenfold on them, and their kin and allies, the slightest injury done to any of his Majesty's liege subjects."

"My Lord," said Roy in answer, "none of my enemies will allege that I have been a bloodthirsty man, and were I now wi' my folk, I could rule four or five hundred wild Hielanders as easy as your Grace those eight or ten lackeys and foot-boys—But if your Grace is bent to take the head away from a house, ye may lay your account there will be misrule amang the members.—However, come o't what like, there's an honest man, a kinsman o' my ain, maun come by nae skaith. Is there ony body here wad do a gude deed for MacGregor?—he may repay it, though his hands be now tied."

The Highlander who had delivered the letter to the Duke replied, "I'll do your will for you, MacGregor; and I'll gang back up the glen on purpose."

He advanced, and received from the prisoner a message to his wife, which, being in Gaelic, I did not understand, but I had little doubt it related to some measures to be taken for the safety of Mr. Jarvie.

"Do you hear the fellow's impudence?" said the Duke; "he confides in his character of a messenger. His conduct is of a piece with his master's, who invited us to make common cause against these freebooters, and have deserted us so soon as the MacGregors have agreed to surrender the Balquhidder lands they were squabbling about.

No truth in plaids, no faith in tartan trews!
Chameleon-like, they change a thousand hues."

"YOUR GREAT ANCESTOR never said so, my Lord," answered Major Galbraith;—"and, with submission, neither would your Grace have occasion to say it, wad ye but be for beginning justice at the well-head—Gie the honest man his mear again—Let every head wear it's ane bannet, and the distractions o' the Lennox wad be mended wi' them o'the land."

"Hush! hush! Garschattachin," said the Duke; "this is language dangerous for you to talk to any one, and especially to me; but I presume you reckon yourself a privileged person. Please to draw off your party towards Gartartan; I shall myself see the prisoner escorted to Duchray, and send you orders tomorrow. You will please grant no leave of absence to any of your troopers."

"Here's auld ordering and counter-ordering," muttered Garschattachin between his teeth. "But patience! patience!—we may ae day play at change seats, the king's coming."

The two troops of cavalry now formed, and prepared to march off the ground, that they might avail themselves of the remainder of daylight to get to their evening quarters. I received an intimation, rather than an invitation, to attend the party; and I perceived, that, though no longer considered as a prisoner, I was yet under some sort of suspicion. The times were indeed so dangerous,—the great party questions of Jacobite and Hanoverian divided the country so effectually,—and the constant disputes and jealousies between the Highlanders and Lowlanders, besides a number of inexplicable causes of feud which separated the great leading families in Scotland from each other, occasioned such general suspicion, that a solitary and unprotected stranger was almost sure to meet with something disagreeable in the course of his travels.

I acquiesced, however, in my destination with the best grace I could, consoling myself with the hope that I might obtain from the captive freebooter some information concerning Rashleigh and his machinations. I should do myself injustice did I not add, that my views were not merely selfish. I was too much interested in my singular acquaintance not to be desirous of rendering him such services as his unfortunate situation might demand, or admit of his receiving.

CHAPTER SIXTEENTH

> And when he came to broken brigg,
> He bent his bow and swam;
> And when he came to grass growing,
> Set down his feet and ran.
>
> — GIL MORRICE

The echoes of the rocks and ravines, on either side, now rang to the trumpets of the cavalry, which, forming themselves into two distinct bodies, began to move down the valley at a slow trot. That commanded by Major Galbraith soon took to the right hand, and crossed the Forth, for the purpose of taking up the quarters assigned them for the night, when they were to occupy, as I understood, an old castle in the vicinity. They formed a lively object while crossing the stream, but were soon lost in winding up the bank on the opposite side, which was clothed with wood.

We continued our march with considerable good order. To ensure the safe custody of the prisoner, the Duke had caused him to be placed on horseback behind one of his retainers, called, as I was informed, Ewan of Brigglands, one of the largest and strongest men who were present. A horse-belt, passed round the bodies of both, and buckled before the yeoman's breast, rendered it impossible for Rob Roy to free himself from his keeper. I was directed to keep close beside them, and accommodated for the purpose with a troop-horse. We were as closely surrounded by the soldiers as the width of the road would permit, and had always at least one, if not two, on each side, with pistol in hand. Andrew Fairservice, furnished with a Highland pony, of which they had made prey somewhere or other, was permitted to ride among the other domestics, of whom a great number attended the line of march, though without falling into the ranks of the more regularly trained troopers.

In this manner we travelled for a certain distance, until we arrived at a place where we also were to cross the river. The Forth, as being the outlet of a lake, is of considerable depth, even where less important in point of width, and the descent to the ford was by a broken precipitous ravine, which only permitted one horseman to descend at once. The rear and centre of our small body halting on the bank while the front files passed down in succession, produced a considerable delay, as is usual on such occasions, and even some confusion; for a number of those riders, who made no proper part of the squadron, crowded to the ford without regularity, and made the militia cavalry, although tolerably well drilled, partake in some degree of their own disorder.

It was while we were thus huddled together on the bank that I heard Rob Roy whisper to the man behind whom he was placed on horseback, "Your father, Ewan, wadna hae carried an auld friend to the shambles, like a calf, for a' the Dukes in Christendom."

Ewan returned no answer, but shrugged, as one who would express by that sign that what he was doing was none of his own choice.

"And when the MacGregors come down the glen, and ye see toom faulds, a bluidy hearthstone, and the fire flashing out between the rafters o' your house, ye may be thinking then, Ewan, that were your friend Rob to the fore, you would have had that safe which it will make your heart sair to lose."

Ewan of Brigglands again shrugged and groaned, but remained silent.

"It's a sair thing," continued Rob, sliding his insinuations so gently into Ewan's ear that they reached no other but mine, who certainly saw myself in no shape called upon to destroy his prospects of escape—"It's a sair thing, that Ewan of Brigglands, whom Roy MacGregor has helped with hand, sword, and purse, suld mind a gloom from a great man mair than a friend's life."

Ewan seemed sorely agitated, but was silent.—We heard the Duke's voice from the opposite bank call, "Bring over the prisoner."

Ewan put his horse in motion, and just as I heard Roy say, "Never weigh a MacGregor's bluid against a broken whang o' leather, for there will be another accounting to gie for it baith here and hereafter," they passed me hastily, and dashing forward rather precipitately, entered the water.

"Not yet, sir—not yet," said some of the troopers to me, as I was about to follow, while others pressed forward into the stream.

I saw the Duke on the other side, by the waning light, engaged in commanding his people to get into order, as they landed dispersedly, some higher, some lower. Many had crossed, some were in the water, and the rest were preparing to follow, when a sudden splash warned me that MacGregor's eloquence had prevailed on Ewan to give him freedom and a chance for life. The Duke also heard the sound, and instantly guessed its meaning. "Dog!" he exclaimed to Ewan as he landed, "where is your prisoner?" and, without waiting to hear the apology which the terrified vassal began to falter forth, he fired a pistol at his head, whether fatally I know not, and exclaimed, "Gentlemen, disperse and pursue the villain—An hundred guineas for him that secures Rob Roy!"

All became an instant scene of the most lively confusion. Rob Roy, disengaged from his bonds, doubtless by Ewan's slipping the buckle of his belt, had dropped off at the horse's tail, and instantly dived, passing under the belly of the troop-horse which was on his left hand. But as he was obliged to come to the surface an instant for air, the glimpse of his tartan plaid drew the attention of the troopers, some of whom plunged into the river, with a total disregard to their own safety, rushing, according to the expression of their country, through pool and stream, sometimes swimming their horses, sometimes losing them and struggling for their own lives. Others, less zealous or more prudent, broke off in different directions, and galloped up and down the banks, to watch the places at which the fugitive might possibly land. The hollowing, the whooping, the calls for aid at different points, where they saw, or conceived they saw, some vestige of him they were seeking,—the frequent report of pistols and carabines, fired at every object which excited the least suspicion,—the sight of so many horsemen riding about, in and out of the river, and striking with their long broadswords at whatever excited their attention, joined to the vain exertions used by their officers to restore order and regularity,—and all this in so wild a scene, and visible only by the imperfect twilight of an autumn evening, made the most extraordinary hubbub I had hitherto witnessed. I was indeed left alone to observe it, for our whole cavalcade had dispersed in pursuit, or at least to see the event of the search. Indeed, as I partly suspected at the time, and afterwards learned with certainty, many of those who seemed most active in their attempts to waylay and recover the fugitive, were, in actual truth, least desirous that he should be taken, and only joined in the cry to increase the general confusion, and to give Rob Roy a better opportunity of escaping.

Escape, indeed, was not difficult for a swimmer so expert as the freebooter, as soon as he had eluded the first burst of pursuit. At one time he was closely pressed, and several blows were made which flashed in the water around him; the scene much resembling one of the otter-hunts which I had seen at Osbaldistone Hall, where the animal is detected by the hounds from his being necessitated to put his nose above the stream to vent or breathe, while he is enabled to elude them by getting under water again so soon as he has refreshed himself by respiration. MacGregor, however, had a trick beyond the otter; for he contrived, when very closely pursued, to disengage himself unobserved from his plaid, and suffer it to float down the stream, where in its progress it quickly attracted general attention; many of the horsemen were thus put upon a false scent, and several shots or stabs were averted from the party for whom they were designed.

Once fairly out of view, the recovery of the prisoner became almost impossible, since, in so many places, the river was rendered inaccessible by the steepness of its banks, or the thickets of alders, poplars, and birch, which, overhanging its banks, prevented the approach of horsemen. Errors and accidents had also happened among the pursuers, whose task the approaching night rendered every moment more hopeless. Some got themselves involved in the eddies of the stream, and required the assistance of their companions to save them from drowning. Others, hurt by shots or blows in the confused mele'e, implored help or threatened vengeance, and in one or two instances such accidents led to actual strife. The trumpets, therefore, sounded the retreat, announcing that the commanding officer, with whatsoever unwillingness, had for the present relinquished hopes of the important prize which had thus unexpectedly escaped his grasp, and the troopers began slowly, reluctantly, and brawling with each other as they returned, again to assume their ranks. I could see them darkening, as they formed on the southern bank of the river,—whose murmurs, long drowned by the louder cries of vengeful pursuit, were now heard hoarsely mingling with the deep, discontented, and reproachful voices of the disappointed horsemen.

Hitherto I had been as it were a mere spectator, though far from an uninterested one, of the singular scene which had passed. But now I heard a voice suddenly exclaim, "Where is the English stranger?—It was he gave Rob Roy the knife to cut the belt."

"Cleeve the pock-pudding to the chafts!" cried one voice.

"Weize a brace of balls through his harn-pan!" said a second.

"Drive three inches of cauld airn into his brisket!" shouted a third.

And I heard several horses galloping to and fro, with the kind purpose, doubtless, of executing these denunciations. I was immediately awakened to the sense of my situation, and to the certainty that armed men, having no restraint whatever on their irritated and inflamed passions, would probably begin by shooting or cutting me down, and afterwards investigate the justice of the action. Impressed by this belief, I leaped from my horse, and turning him loose, plunged into a bush of alder-trees, where, considering the advancing obscurity of the night, I thought there was little chance of my being discovered. Had I been near enough to the Duke to have invoked his personal protection, I would have done so; but he had already commenced his retreat, and I saw no officer on the left bank of the river, of authority sufficient to have afforded protection, in case of my surrendering myself. I thought there was no point of honour which could require, in such circumstances, an unnecessary exposure of my life. My first idea, when the tumult began to be appeased, and the clatter of the horses' feet was heard less frequently in the immediate vicinity of my hiding-place, was to seek out the Duke's quarters when all should be quiet, and give myself up to him, as a liege subject, who had nothing to fear from his justice, and a stranger, who had every right to expect protection and hospitality. With this purpose I crept out of my hiding-place, and looked around me.

The twilight had now melted nearly into darkness; a few or none of the troopers were left on my side of the Forth, and of those who were already across it, I only heard the distant trample of the horses' feet, and the wailing and prolonged sound of their trumpets, which rung through the woods to recall stragglers. Here, therefore, I was left in a situation of considerable difficulty. I had no horse, and the deep and wheeling stream of the river, rendered turbid by the late tumult of which its channel had been the scene, and seeming yet more so under the doubtful influence of an imperfect moonlight, had no inviting influence for a pedestrian by no means accustomed to wade rivers, and who had lately seen horsemen weltering, in this dangerous passage, up to the very saddle-laps. At the same time, my prospect, if I remained on the side of the river on which I then stood, could be no other than of concluding the various fatigues of this day and the preceding night, by passing that which was now closing in, *al fresco* on the side of a Highland hill.

After a moment's reflection, I began to consider that Fairservice, who had doubtless crossed the river with the other domestics, according to his forward and impertinent custom of putting himself always among the foremost, could not fail to satisfy the Duke, or the competent authorities, respecting my rank and situation; and that, therefore, my character did not require my immediate appearance, at the risk of being drowned in the river—of being unable to trace the march of the squadron in case of my reaching the other side in safety—or, finally, of being cut down, right or wrong, by some straggler, who might think such a piece of good service a convenient excuse for not sooner rejoining his ranks. I therefore resolved to measure my steps back to the little inn, where I had passed the preceding night. I had nothing to apprehend from Rob Roy. He was now at liberty, and I was certain, in case of my falling in with any of his people, the news of his escape would ensure me protection. I might thus also show, that I had no intention to desert Mr. Jarvie in the delicate situation in which he had engaged himself chiefly on my account. And lastly, it was only in this quarter that I could hope to learn tidings concerning Rashleigh and my father's papers, which had been the original cause of an expedition so fraught with perilous adventure. I therefore abandoned all thoughts of crossing the Forth that evening; and, turning my back on the Fords of Frew, began to retrace my steps towards the little village of Aberfoil.

A sharp frost-wind, which made itself heard and felt from time to time, removed the clouds of mist which might otherwise have slumbered till morning on the valley; and, though it could not totally disperse the clouds of vapour, yet threw them in confused and changeful masses, now hovering round the heads of the mountains, now filling, as with a dense and voluminous stream of smoke, the various deep gullies where masses of the composite rock, or breccia, tumbling in fragments from the cliffs, have rushed to the valley, leaving each behind its course a rent and torn ravine resembling a deserted water-course. The moon, which was now high, and twinkled with all the vivacity of a frosty atmosphere, silvered the windings of the river and the peaks and precipices which the mist left visible, while her beams seemed as it were absorbed by the fleecy whiteness of the mist, where it lay thick and condensed; and gave to the more light and vapoury specks, which were elsewhere visible, a sort of filmy transparency resembling the lightest veil of silver gauze. Despite the uncertainty of my situation, a view so romantic, joined to the active and inspiring influence of the frosty atmosphere, elevated my spirits while it braced my nerves. I felt an inclination to cast care away, and bid defiance to danger, and involuntarily whistled, by way of cadence to my steps, which my feeling of the cold led me to accelerate, and I felt the pulse of existence beat prouder and higher in proportion as I felt confidence in my own strength, courage, and resources. I was so much lost in these thoughts, and in the feelings which they excited, that two horsemen came up behind me without my hearing their approach, until one was on each side of me, when the left-hand rider, pulling up his horse, addressed me in the English tongue—"So ho, friend! whither so late?"

"To my supper and bed at Aberfoil," I replied.

"Are the passes open?" he inquired, with the same commanding tone of voice.

"I do not know," I replied; "I shall learn when I get there. But," I added, the fate of Morris recurring to my recollection, "if you are an English stranger, I advise you to turn back till daylight; there has been some disturbance in this neighbourhood, and I should hesitate to say it is perfectly safe for strangers."

"The soldiers had the worst?—had they not?" was the reply.

"They had indeed; and an officer's party were destroyed or made prisoners."

"Are you sure of that?" replied the horseman.

"As sure as that I hear you speak," I replied. "I was an unwilling spectator of the skirmish."

"Unwilling!" continued the interrogator. "Were you not engaged in it then?"

"Certainly no," I replied; "I was detained by the king's officer."

"On what suspicion? and who are you? or what is your name?" he continued.

"I really do not know, sir," said I, "why I should answer so many questions to an unknown stranger. I have told you enough to convince you that you are going into a dangerous and distracted country. If you choose to proceed, it is your own affair; but as I ask you no questions respecting your name and business, you will oblige me by making no inquiries after mine."

"Mr. Francis Osbaldistone," said the other rider, in a voice the tones of which thrilled through every nerve of my body, "should not whistle his favourite airs when he wishes to remain undiscovered."

And Diana Vernon—for she, wrapped in a horseman's cloak, was the last speaker—whistled in playful mimicry the second part of the tune which was on my lips when they came up.

"Good God!" I exclaimed, like one thunderstruck, "can it be you, Miss Vernon, on such a spot—at such an hour—in such a lawless country—in such"—

"In such a masculine dress, you would say.—But what would you have? The philosophy of the excellent Corporal Nym is the best after all; things must be as they may—*pauca verba*."

While she was thus speaking, I eagerly took advantage of an unusually bright gleam of moonshine, to study the appearance of her companion; for it may be easily supposed, that finding Miss Vernon in a place so solitary, engaged in a journey so dangerous, and under the protection of one gentleman only, were circumstances to excite every feeling of jealousy, as well as surprise. The rider did not speak with the deep melody of Rashleigh's voice; his tones were more high and commanding; he was taller, moreover, as he sate on horseback, than that first-rate object of my hate and suspicion. Neither did the stranger's address resemble that of any of my other cousins; it had that indescribable tone and manner by which we recognise a man of sense and breeding, even in the first few sentences he speaks.

The object of my anxiety seemed desirous to get rid of my investigation.

"Diana," he said, in a tone of mingled kindness and authority, "give your cousin his property, and let us not spend time here."

Miss Vernon had in the meantime taken out a small case, and leaning down from her horse towards me, she said, in a tone in which an effort at her usual quaint lightness of expression contended with a deeper and more grave tone of sentiment, "You see, my dear coz, I was born to be your better angel. Rashleigh has been compelled to yield up his spoil, and had we reached this same village of Aberfoil last night, as we purposed, I should have found some Highland sylph to have wafted to you all these representatives of commercial wealth. But there were giants and dragons in the way; and errant-knights and damsels of modern times, bold though they be, must not, as of yore, run into useless danger—Do not you do so either, my dear coz."

"Diana," said her companion, "let me once more warn you that the evening waxes late, and we are still distant from our home."

"I am coming, sir, I am coming—Consider," she added, with a sigh, "how lately I have been subjected to control—besides, I have not yet given my cousin the packet, and bid him fare-well—for ever. Yes, Frank," she said, "for ever!—there is a gulf between us—a gulf of absolute perdition;—where we go, you must not follow—what we do, you must not share in—Farewell—be happy!"

IN THE ATTITUDE in which she bent from her horse, which was a Highland pony, her face, not perhaps altogether unwillingly, touched mine. She pressed my hand, while the tear that trembled in her eye found its way to my cheek instead of her own. It was a moment never to be forgotten—inexpressibly bitter, yet mixed with a sensation of pleasure so deeply soothing and affecting, as at once to unlock all the flood-gates of the heart. It was *but* a moment, however; for, instantly recovering from the feeling to which she had involuntarily given way, she intimated to her companion she was ready to attend him, and putting their horses to a brisk pace, they were soon far distant from the place where I stood.

Heaven knows, it was not apathy which loaded my frame and my tongue so much, that I could neither return Miss Vernon's half embrace, nor even answer her farewell. The word, though it rose to my tongue, seemed to choke in my throat like the fatal *guilty,* which the delinquent who makes it his plea, knows must be followed by the doom of death. The surprise—the sorrow, almost stupified me. I remained motionless with the packet in my hand, gazing after them, as if endeavouring to count the sparkles which flew from the horses' hoofs. I continued to look after even these had ceased to be visible, and to listen for their footsteps long after the last distant trampling had died in my ears. At length, tears rushed to my eyes, glazed as they were by the exertion of straining after what was no longer to be seen. I wiped them mechanically, and almost without being aware that they were flowing—but they came thicker and thicker; I felt the tightening of the throat and breast—the *hysterica passio* of poor Lear; and sitting down by the wayside, I shed a flood of the first and most bitter tears which had flowed from my eyes since childhood.

CHAPTER SEVENTEENTH

Dangle.—Egad, I think the interpreter is the harder to be understood of the two.

— CRITIC.

I had scarce given vent to my feelings in this paroxysm, ere was ashamed of my weakness. I remembered that I had been for some time endeavouring to regard Diana Vernon, when her idea intruded itself on my remembrance, as a friend, for whose welfare I should indeed always be anxious, but with whom I could have little further communication. But the almost unrepressed tenderness of her manner, joined to the romance of our sudden meeting where it was so little to have been expected, were circumstances which threw me entirely off my guard. I recovered, however, sooner than might have been expected, and without giving myself time accurately to examine my motives. I resumed the path on which I had been travelling when overtaken by this strange and unexpected apparition.

"I am not," was my reflection, "transgressing her injunction so pathetically given, since I am but pursuing my own journey by the only open route.—If I have succeeded in recovering my father's property, it still remains incumbent on me to see my Glasgow friend delivered from the situation in which he has involved himself on my account; besides, what other place of rest can I obtain for the night excepting at the little inn of Aberfoil? They also must stop there, since it is impossible for travellers on horseback to go farther—Well, then, we shall meet again—meet for the last time perhaps—But I shall see and hear her—I shall learn who this happy man is who exercises over her the authority of a husband—I shall learn if there remains, in the difficult course in which she seems engaged, any difficulty which my efforts may remove, or aught that I can do to express my gratitude for her generosity—for her disinterested friendship."

As I reasoned thus with myself, colouring with every plausible pretext which occurred to my ingenuity my passionate desire once more to see and converse with my cousin, I was suddenly hailed by a touch on the shoulder; and the deep voice of a Highlander, who, walking still faster than I, though I was proceeding at a smart pace, accosted me with, "A braw night, Maister Osbaldistone—we have met at the mirk hour before now."

There was no mistaking the tone of MacGregor; he had escaped the pursuit of his enemies, and was in full retreat to his own wilds and to his adherents. He had also contrived to arm himself, probably at the house of some secret adherent, for he had a musket on his shoulder, and the usual Highland weapons by his side. To have found myself alone with such a character in such a situation, and at this late hour in the evening, might not have been pleasant to me in any ordinary mood of mind; for, though habituated to think of Rob Roy in rather a friendly point of view, I will confess frankly that I never heard him speak but that it seemed to thrill my blood. The intonation of the mountaineers gives a habitual depth and hollowness to the sound of their words, owing to the guttural expression so common in their native language, and they usually speak with a good deal of emphasis. To these national peculiarities Rob Roy added a sort of hard indifference of accent and manner, expressive of a mind neither to be daunted, nor surprised, nor affected by what passed before him, however dreadful, however sudden, however afflicting. Habitual danger, with unbounded confidence in his own strength and sagacity, had rendered him indifferent to fear, and the lawless and precarious life he led had blunted, though its dangers and errors had not destroyed, his feelings for others. And it was to be remembered that I had very lately seen the followers of this man commit a cruel slaughter on an unarmed and suppliant individual.

Yet such was the state of my mind, that I welcomed the company of the outlaw leader as a relief to my own overstrained and painful thoughts; and was not without hopes that through his means I might obtain some clew of guidance through the maze in which my fate had involved me. I therefore answered his greeting cordially, and congratulated him on his late escape in circumstances when escape seemed impossible.

"Ay," he replied, "there is as much between the craig and the woodie[31] as there is between the cup and the lip. But my peril was less than you may think, being a stranger to this country.

Of those that were summoned to take me, and to keep me, and to retake me again, there was a moiety, as cousin Nicol Jarvie calls it, that had nae will that I suld be either taen, or keepit fast, or retaen; and of tother moiety, there was as half was feared to stir me; and so I had only like the fourth part of fifty or sixty men to deal withal."

"And enough, too, I should think," replied I.

"I dinna ken that," said he; "but I ken, that turn every ill-willer that I had amang them out upon the green before the Clachan of Aberfoil, I wad find them play with broadsword and target, one down and another come on."

He now inquired into my adventures since we entered his country, and laughed heartily at my account of the battle we had in the inn, and at the exploits of the Bailie with the red-hot poker.

"Let Glasgow Flourish!" he exclaimed. "The curse of Cromwell on me, if I wad hae wished better sport than to see cousin Nicol Jarvie singe Iverach's plaid, like a sheep's head between a pair of tongs. But my cousin Jarvie," he added, more gravely, "has some gentleman's bluid in his veins, although he has been unhappily bred up to a peaceful and mechanical craft, which could not but blunt any pretty man's spirit.— Ye may estimate the reason why I could not receive you at the Clachan of Aberfoil as I purposed. They had made a fine hosenet for me when I was absent twa or three days at Glasgow, upon the king's business—But I think I broke up the league about their lugs—they'll no be able to hound one clan against another as they hae dune. I hope soon to see the day when a' Hielandmen will stand shouther to shouther. But what chanced next?"

I gave him an account of the arrival of Captain Thornton and his party, and the arrest of the Bailie and myself under pretext of our being suspicious persons; and upon his more special inquiry, I recollected the officer had mentioned that, besides my name sounding suspicious in his ears, he had orders to secure an old and young person, resembling our description. This again moved the outlaw's risibility.

"As man lives by bread," he said, "the buzzards have mistaen my friend the Bailie for his Excellency, and you for Diana Vernon—O, the most egregious night-howlets!"

"Miss Vernon?" said I, with hesitation, and trembling for the answer—"Does she still bear that name? She passed but now, along with a gentleman who seemed to use a style of authority."

"Ay, ay," answered Rob, "she's under lawfu' authority now; and full time, for she was a daft hempie—But she's a mettle quean. It's a pity his Excellency is a thought eldern. The like o' yourself, or my son Hamish, wad be mair sortable in point of years."

Here, then, was a complete downfall of those castles of cards which my fancy had, in despite of my reason, so often amused herself with building. Although in truth I had scarcely anything else to expect, since I could not suppose that Diana could be travelling in such a country, at such an hour, with any but one who had a legal title to protect her, I did not feel the blow less severely when it came; and MacGregor's voice, urging me to pursue my story, sounded in my ears without conveying any exact import to my mind.

"You are ill," he said at length, after he had spoken twice without receiving an answer; "this day's wark has been ower muckle for ane doubtless unused to sic things."

The tone of kindness in which this was spoken, recalling me to myself, and to the necessities of my situation, I continued my narrative as well as I could. Rob Roy expressed great exultation at the successful skirmish in the pass.

"They say," he observed, "that king's chaff is better than other folk's corn; but I think that canna be said o' king's soldiers, if they let themselves be beaten wi' a wheen auld carles that are past fighting, and bairns that are no come till't, and wives wi' their rocks and distaffs, the very wally-draigles o' the countryside. And Dougal Gregor, too—wha wad hae thought there had been as muckle sense in his tatty-pow, that ne'er had a better covering than his ain shaggy hassock of hair!—But say away—though I dread what's to come neist—for my Helen's an incarnate devil when her bluid's up—puir thing, she has ower muckle reason."

I observed as much delicacy as I could in communicating to him the usage we had received, but I obviously saw the detail gave him great pain.

"I wad rather than a thousand merks," he said, "that I had been at hame! To misguide strangers, and forbye a', my ain natural cousin, that had showed me sic kindness—I wad rather they had burned half the Lennox in their folly! But this comes o' trusting women and their bairns, that have neither measure nor reason in their dealings. However, it's a' owing to that dog of a gauger, wha betrayed me by pretending a message from your cousin Rashleigh, to meet him on the king's affairs, whilk I thought was very like to be anent Garschattachin and a party of the Lennox declaring themselves for King James. Faith! but I ken'd I was clean beguiled when I heard the Duke was there; and when they strapped the horse-girth ower my arms, I might hae judged what was biding me; for I ken'd your kinsman, being, wi' pardon, a slippery loon himself, is prone to employ those of his ain kidney—I wish he mayna hae been at the bottom o' the ploy himsell—I thought the chield Morris looked devilish queer when I determined he should remain a wad, or hostage, for my safe back-coming. But I *am* come back, nae thanks to him, or them that employed him; and the question is, how the collector loon is to win back himself—I promise him it will not be without a ransom."

"Morris," said I, "has already paid the last ransom which mortal man can owe."

"Eh! What?" exclaimed my companion hastily; "what d'ye say? I trust it was in the skirmish he was killed?"

"He was slain in cold blood after the fight was over, Mr. Campbell."

"Cold blood?—Damnation!" he said, muttering betwixt his teeth—"How fell that, sir? Speak out, sir, and do not Maister or Campbell me—my foot is on my native heath, and my name is MacGregor!"

His passions were obviously irritated; but without noticing the rudeness of his tone, I gave him a short and distinct account of the death of Morris. He struck the butt of his gun with great vehemence against the ground, and broke out—"I vow to God, such a deed might make one forswear kin, clan, country, wife, and bairns! And yet the villain wrought long for it. And what is the difference between warsling below the water wi' a stane about your neck, and wavering in the wind wi' a tether round it?—it's but choking after a', and he drees the doom he ettled for me. I could have wished, though, they had rather putten a ball through him, or a dirk; for the fashion of removing him will give rise to mony idle clavers—But every wight has his weird, and we maun a' dee when our day comes—And naebody will deny that Helen MacGregor has deep wrongs to avenge."

So saying, he seemed to dismiss the theme altogether from his mind, and proceeded to inquire how I got free from the party in whose hands he had seen me.

My story was soon told; and I added the episode of my having recovered the papers of my father, though I dared not trust my voice to name the name of Diana.

"I was sure ye wad get them," said MacGregor;—"the letter ye brought me contained his Excellency's pleasure to that effect and nae doubt it was my will to have aided in it. And I asked ye up into this glen on the very errand. But it's like his Excellency has foregathered wi' Rashleigh sooner than I expected."

The first part of this answer was what most forcibly struck me.

"Was the letter I brought you, then, from this person you call his Excellency? Who is he? and what is his rank and proper name?"

"I am thinking," said MacGregor, "that since ye dinna ken them already they canna be o' muckle consequence to you, and sae I shall say naething on that score. But weel I wot the letter was frae his ain hand, or, having a sort of business of my ain on my hands, being, as ye weel may see, just as much as I can fairly manage, I canna say I would hae fashed mysell sae muckle about the matter."

I now recollected the lights seen in the library—the various circumstances which had excited my jealousy—the glove—the agitation of the tapestry which covered the secret passage from Rashleigh's apartment; and, above all, I recollected that Diana retired in order to write, as I then thought, the billet to which I was to have recourse in case of the last necessity. Her hours, then, were not spent in solitude, but in listening to the addresses of some desperate agent of Jacobitical treason, who was a secret resident within the mansion of her uncle! Other young women have sold themselves for gold, or suffered themselves to be seduced from their first love from vanity; but Diana had sacrificed my affections and her own to partake the fortunes of some desperate adventurer—to seek the haunts of freebooters through midnight deserts, with no better hopes of rank or fortune than that mimicry of both which the mock court of the Stuarts at St. Germains had in their power to bestow.

"I will see her," I said internally, "if it be possible, once more. I will argue with her as a friend—as a kinsman—on the risk she is incurring, and I will facilitate her retreat to France, where she may, with more comfort and propriety, as well as safety, abide the issue of the turmoils which the political trepanner, to whom she has united her fate, is doubtless busied in putting into motion."

"I conclude, then," I said to MacGregor, after about five minutes' silence on both sides, "that his Excellency, since you give me no other name for him, was residing in Osbaldistone Hall at the same time with myself?"

"To be sure—to be sure—and in the young lady's apartment, as best reason was." This gratuitous information was adding gall to bitterness. "But few," added MacGregor, "ken'd he was derned there, save Rashleigh and Sir Hildebrand; for you were out o' the question; and the young lads haena wit eneugh to ca' the cat frae the cream—But it's a bra' auld-fashioned house, and what I specially admire is the abundance o' holes and bores and concealments—ye could put twenty or thirty men in ae corner, and a family might live a week without finding them out—whilk, nae doubt, may on occasion be a special convenience. I wish we had the like o' Osbaldistone Hall on the braes o' Craig-Royston—But we maun gar woods and caves serve the like o' us puir Hieland bodies."

"I suppose his Excellency," said I, "was privy to the first accident which befell"—I could not help hesitating a moment.

"Ye were going to say Morris," said Rob Roy coolly, for he was too much accustomed to deeds of violence for the agitation he had at first expressed to be of long continuance. "I used to laugh heartily at that reik; but I'll hardly hae the heart to do't again, since the ill-far'd accident at the Loch. Na, na—his Excellency ken'd nought o' that ploy—it was a' managed atween Rashleigh and mysell. But the sport that came after—and Rashleigh's shift o' turning the suspicion aff himself upon you, that he had nae grit favour to frae the beginning—and then Miss Die, she maun hae us sweep up a' our spiders' webs again, and set you out o' the Justice's claws—and then the frightened craven Morris, that was scared out o' his seven senses by seeing the real man when he was charging the innocent stranger—and the gowk of a clerk—and the drunken carle of a justice—Ohon! ohon!—mony a laugh that job's gien me—and now, a' that I can do for the puir devil is to get some messes said for his soul."

"May I ask," said I, "how Miss Vernon came to have so much influence over Rashleigh and his accomplices as to derange your projected plan?"

"Mine! it was none of mine. No man can say I ever laid my burden on other folk's shoulders—it was a' Rashleigh's doings. But, undoubtedly, she had great influence wi' us baith on account of his Excellency's affection, as weel as that she ken'd far ower mony secrets to be lightlied in a matter o' that kind.—Deil tak him," he ejaculated, by way of summing up, "that gies women either secret to keep or power to abuse—fules shouldna hae chapping-sticks."

We were now within a quarter of a mile from the village, when three Highlanders, springing upon us with presented arms, commanded us to stand and tell our business. The single word *Gregaragh,* in the deep and commanding voice of my companion, was answered by a shout, or rather yell, of joyful recognition. One, throwing down his firelock, clasped his leader so fast round the knees, that he was unable to extricate himself, muttering, at the same time, a torrent of Gaelic gratulation, which every now and then rose into a sort of scream of gladness. The two others, after the first howling was over, set off literally with the speed of deers, contending which should first carry to the village, which a strong party of the MacGregors now occupied, the joyful news of Rob Roy's escape and return. The intelligence excited such shouts of jubilation, that the very hills rung again, and young and old, men, women, and children, without distinction of sex or age, came running down the vale to meet us, with all the tumultuous speed and clamour of a mountain torrent. When I heard the rushing noise and yells of this joyful multitude approach us, I thought it a fitting precaution to remind MacGregor that I was a stranger, and under his protection. He accordingly held me fast by the hand, while the assemblage crowded around him with such shouts of devoted attachment, and joy at his return, as were really affecting; nor did he extend to his followers what all eagerly sought, the grasp, namely, of his hand, until he had made them understand that I was to be kindly and carefully used.

The mandate of the Sultan of Delhi could not have been more promptly obeyed.

Indeed, I now sustained nearly as much inconvenience from their well-meant attentions as formerly from their rudeness. They would hardly allow the friend of their leader to walk upon his own legs, so earnest were they in affording me support and assistance upon the way; and at length, taking advantage of a slight stumble which I made over a stone, which the press did not permit me to avoid, they fairly seized upon me, and bore me in their arms in triumph towards Mrs. MacAlpine's.

On arrival before her hospitable wigwam, I found power and popularity had its inconveniences in the Highlands, as everywhere else; for, before MacGregor could be permitted to enter the house where he was to obtain rest and refreshment, he was obliged to relate the story of his escape at least a dozen times over, as I was told by an officious old man, who chose to translate it at least as often for my edification, and to whom I was in policy obliged to seem to pay a decent degree of attention. The audience being at length satisfied, group after group departed to take their bed upon the heath, or in the neighbouring huts, some cursing the Duke and Garschattachin, some lamenting the probable danger of Ewan of Brigglands, incurred by his friendship to MacGregor, but all agreeing that the escape of Rob Roy himself lost nothing in comparison with the exploit of any one of their chiefs since the days of Dougal Ciar, the founder of his line.

The friendly outlaw, now taking me by the arm, conducted me into the interior of the hut. My eyes roved round its smoky recesses in quest of Diana and her companion; but they were nowhere to be seen, and I felt as if to make inquiries might betray some secret motives, which were best concealed. The only known countenance upon which my eyes rested was that of the Bailie, who, seated on a stool by the fireside, received with a sort of reserved dignity, the welcomes of Rob Roy, the apologies which he made for his indifferent accommodation, and his inquiries after his health.

"I am pretty weel, kinsman," said the Bailie—"indifferent weel, I thank ye; and for accommodations, ane canna expect to carry about the Saut Market at his tail, as a snail does his caup;—and I am blythe that ye hae gotten out o' the hands o' your unfreends."

"Weel, weel, then," answered Roy, "what is't ails ye, man—a's weel that ends weel!—the warld will last our day—Come, take a cup o' brandy—your father the deacon could take ane at an orra time."

"It might be he might do sae, Robin, after fatigue—whilk has been my lot mair ways than ane this day. But," he continued, slowly filling up a little wooden stoup which might hold about three glasses, "he was a moderate man of his bicker, as I am mysell—Here's wussing health to ye, Robin" (a sip), "and your weelfare here and hereafter" (another taste), "and also to my cousin Helen—and to your twa hopefu' lads, of whom mair anon."

So saying, he drank up the contents of the cup with great gravity and deliberation, while MacGregor winked aside to me, as if in ridicule of the air of wisdom and superior authority which the Bailie assumed towards him in their intercourse, and which he exercised when Rob was at the head of his armed clan, in full as great, or a greater degree, than when he was at the Bailie's mercy in the Tolbooth of Glasgow. It seemed to me, that MacGregor wished me, as a stranger, to understand, that if he submitted to the tone which his kinsman assumed, it was partly out of deference to the rights of hospitality, but still more for the jest's sake.

As the Bailie set down his cup he recognised me, and giving me a cordial welcome on my return, he waived farther communication with me for the present.—"I will speak to your matters anon; I maun begin, as in reason, wi' those of my kinsman.—I presume, Robin, there's naebody here will carry aught o' what I am gaun to say, to the town-council or elsewhere, to my prejudice or to yours?"

"Make yourself easy on that head, cousin Nicol," answered MacGregor; "the tae half o' the gillies winna ken what ye say, and the tother winna care—besides that, I wad stow the tongue out o' the head o' any o' them that suld presume to say ower again ony speech held wi' me in their presence."

"Aweel, cousin, sic being the case, and Mr. Osbaldistone here being a prudent youth, and a safe friend—I'se plainly tell ye, ye are breeding up your family to gang an ill gate." Then, clearing his voice with a preliminary hem, he addressed his kinsman, checking, as Malvolio proposed to do when seated in his state, his familiar smile with an austere regard of control.—"Ye ken yourself ye haud light by the law—and for my cousin Helen, forbye that her reception o' me this blessed day—whilk I excuse on account of perturbation of mind, was muckle on the north side o' *friendly,* I say (outputting this personal reason of complaint) I hae that to say o' your wife"—

"Say *nothing* of her, kinsman," said Rob, in a grave and stern tone, "but what is befitting a friend to say, and her husband to hear. Of me you are welcome to say your full pleasure."

"Aweel, aweel," said the Bailie, somewhat disconcerted, "we'se let that be a passover—I dinna approve of making mischief in families. But here are your twa sons, Hamish and Robin, whilk signifies, as I'm gien to understand, James and Robert—I trust ye will call them sae in future—there comes nae gude o' Hamishes, and Eachines, and Angusses, except that they're the names ane aye chances to see in the indictments at the Western Circuits for cow-lifting, at the instance of his majesty's advocate for his majesty's interest. Aweel, but the twa lads, as I was saying, they haena sae muckle as the ordinar grunds, man, of liberal education—they dinna ken the very multiplication table itself, whilk is the root of a' usefu' knowledge, and they did naething but laugh and fleer at me when I tauld them my mind on their ignorance—It's my belief they can neither read, write, nor cipher, if sic a thing could be believed o' ane's ain connections in a Christian land."

"If they could, kinsman," said MacGregor, with great indifference, "their learning must have come o' free will, for whar the deil was I to get them a teacher?—wad ye hae had me put on the gate o' your Divinity Hall at Glasgow College, 'Wanted, a tutor for Rob Roy's bairns?'"

"Na, kinsman," replied Mr. Jarvie, "but ye might hae sent the lads whar they could hae learned the fear o' God, and the usages of civilised creatures. They are as ignorant as the kyloes ye used to drive to market, or the very English churls that ye sauld them to, and can do naething whatever to purpose."

"Umph!" answered Rob; "Hamish can bring doun a black-cock when he's on the wing wi' a single bullet, and Rob can drive a dirk through a twa-inch board."

"Sae muckle the waur for them, cousin!—sae muckle the waur for them baith!" answered the Glasgow merchant in a tone of great decision; "an they ken naething better than that, they had better no ken that neither. Tell me yourself, Rob, what has a' this cutting, and stabbing, and shooting, and driving of dirks, whether through human flesh or fir deals, dune for yourself?—and werena ye a happier man at the tail o' your nowte-bestial, when ye were in an honest calling, than ever ye hae been since, at the head o' your Hieland kernes and gally-glasses?"

I observed that MacGregor, while his well-meaning kinsman spoke to him in this manner, turned and writhed his body like a man who indeed suffers pain, but is determined no groan shall escape his lips; and I longed for an opportunity to interrupt the well-meant, but, as it was obvious to me, quite mistaken strain, in which Jarvie addressed this extraordinary person. The dialogue, however, came to an end without my interference.

"And sae," said the Bailie, "I hae been thinking, Rob, that as it may be ye are ower deep in the black book to win a pardon, and ower auld to mend yourself, that it wad be a pity to bring up twa hopefu' lads to sic a godless trade as your ain, and I wad blythely tak them for prentices at the loom, as I began mysell, and my father the deacon afore me, though, praise to the Giver, I only trade now as wholesale dealer— And—and"—

He saw a storm gathering on Rob's brow, which probably induced him to throw in, as a sweetener of an obnoxious proposition, what he had reserved to crown his own generosity, had it been embraced as an acceptable one;—"and Robin, lad, ye needna look sae glum, for I'll pay the prentice-fee, and never plague ye for the thousand merks neither."

"*Ceade millia diaoul,* hundred thousand devils!" exclaimed Rob, rising and striding through the hut, "My sons weavers!—*Millia molligheart!*—but I wad see every loom in Glasgow, beam, traddles, and shuttles, burnt in hell-fire sooner!"

With some difficulty I made the Bailie, who was preparing a reply, comprehend the risk and impropriety of pressing our host on this topic, and in a minute he recovered, or reassumed, his serenity of temper.

"But ye mean weel—ye mean weel," said he; "so gie me your hand, Nicol, and if ever I put my sons apprentice, I will gie you the refusal o' them. And, as you say, there's the thousand merks to be settled between us.— Here, Eachin MacAnaleister, bring me my sporran."

The person he addressed, a tall, strong mountaineer, who seemed to act as MacGregor's lieutenant, brought from some place of safety a large leathern pouch, such as Highlanders of rank wear before them when in full dress, made of the skin of the sea-otter, richly garnished with silver ornaments and studs.

"I advise no man to attempt opening this sporran till he has my secret," said Rob Roy; and then twisting one button in one direction, and another in another, pulling one stud upward, and pressing another downward, the mouth of the purse, which was bound with massive silver plate, opened and gave admittance to his hand. He made me remark, as if to break short the subject on which Bailie Jarvie had spoken, that a small steel pistol was concealed within the purse, the trigger of which was connected with the mounting, and made part of the machinery, so that the weapon would certainly be discharged, and in all probability its contents lodged in the person of any one, who, being unacquainted with the secret, should tamper with the lock which secured his treasure. "This," said he touching the pistol—"this is the keeper of my privy purse."

The simplicity of the contrivance to secure a furred pouch, which could have been ripped open without any attempt on the spring, reminded me of the verses in the Odyssey, where Ulysses, in a yet ruder age, is content to secure his property by casting a curious and involved complication of cordage around the sea-chest in which it was deposited.

The Bailie put on his spectacles to examine the mechanism, and when he had done, returned it with a smile and a sigh, observing—"Ah! Rob, had ither folk's purses been as weel guarded, I doubt if your sporran wad hae been as weel filled as it kythes to be by the weight."

"Never mind, kinsman," said Rob, laughing; "it will aye open for a friend's necessity, or to pay a just due—and here," he added, pulling out a rouleau of gold, "here is your ten hundred merks—count them, and see that you are full and justly paid."

Mr. Jarvie took the money in silence, and weighing it in his hand for an instant, laid it on the table, and replied, "Rob, I canna tak it—I downa intromit with it—there can nae gude come o't—I hae seen ower weel the day what sort of a gate your gowd is made in—ill-got gear ne'er prospered; and, to be plain wi' you, I winna meddle wi't—it looks as there might be bluid on't."

"Troutsho!" said the outlaw, affecting an indifference which perhaps he did not altogether feel; "it's gude French gowd, and ne'er was in Scotchman's pouch before mine. Look at them, man—they are a' louis-d'ors, bright and bonnie as the day they were coined."

"The waur, the waur—just sae muckle the waur, Robin," replied the Bailie, averting his eyes from the money, though, like Caesar on the Lupercal, his fingers seemed to itch for it—"Rebellion is waur than witchcraft, or robbery either; there's gospel warrant for't."

"Never mind the warrant, kinsman," said the freebooter; "you come by the gowd honestly, and in payment of a just debt—it came from the one king, you may gie it to the other, if ye like; and it will just serve for a weakening of the enemy, and in the point where puir King James is weakest too, for, God knows, he has hands and hearts eneugh, but I doubt he wants the siller."

"He'll no get mony Hielanders then, Robin," said Mr. Jarvie, as, again replacing his spectacles on his nose, he undid the rouleau, and began to count its contents.

"Nor Lowlanders neither," said MacGregor, arching his eyebrow, and, as he looked at me, directing a glance towards Mr. Jarvie, who, all unconscious of the ridicule, weighed each piece with habitual scrupulosity; and having told twice over the sum, which amounted to the discharge of his debt, principal and interest, he returned three pieces to buy his kinswoman a gown, as he expressed himself, and a brace more for the twa bairns, as he called them, requesting they might buy anything they liked with them except gunpowder. The Highlander stared at his kinsman's unexpected generosity, but courteously accepted his gift, which he deposited for the time in his well-secured pouch.

The Bailie next produced the original bond for the debt, on the back of which he had written a formal discharge, which, having subscribed himself, he requested me to sign as a witness. I did so, and Bailie Jarvie was looking anxiously around for another, the Scottish law requiring the subscription of two witnesses to validate either a bond or acquittance. "You will hardly find a man that can write save ourselves within these three miles," said Rob, "but I'll settle the matter as easily;" and, taking the paper from before his kinsman, he threw it in the fire. Bailie Jarvie stared in his turn, but his kinsman continued, "That's a Hieland settlement of accounts. The time might come, cousin, were I to keep a' these charges and discharges, that friends might be brought into trouble for having dealt with me."

The Bailie attempted no reply to this argument, and our supper now appeared in a style of abundance, and even delicacy, which, for the place, might be considered as extraordinary. The greater part of the provisions were cold, intimating they had been prepared at some distance; and there were some bottles of good French wine to relish pasties of various sorts of game, as well as other dishes. I remarked that MacGregor, while doing the honours of the table with great and anxious hospitality, prayed us to excuse the circumstance that some particular dish or pasty had been infringed on before it was presented to us. "You must know," said he to Mr. Jarvie, but without looking towards me, "you are not the only guests this night in the MacGregor's country, whilk, doubtless, ye will believe, since my wife and the twa lads would otherwise have been maist ready to attend you, as weel beseems them."

Bailie Jarvie looked as if he felt glad at any circumstance which occasioned their absence; and I should have been entirely of his opinion, had it not been that the outlaw's apology seemed to imply they were in attendance on Diana and her companion, whom even in my thoughts I could not bear to designate as her husband.

While the unpleasant ideas arising from this suggestion counteracted the good effects of appetite, welcome, and good cheer, I remarked that Rob Roy's attention had extended itself to providing us better bedding than we had enjoyed the night before. Two of the least fragile of the bedsteads, which stood by the wall of the hut, had been stuffed with heath, then in full flower, so artificially arranged, that, the flowers being uppermost, afforded a mattress at once elastic and fragrant. Cloaks, and such bedding as could be collected, stretched over this vegetable couch, made it both soft and warm. The Bailie seemed exhausted by fatigue. I resolved to adjourn my communication to him until next morning; and therefore suffered him to betake himself to bed so soon as he had finished a plentiful supper. Though tired and harassed, I did not myself feel the same disposition to sleep, but rather a restless and feverish anxiety, which led to some farther discourse betwixt me and MacGregor.

CHAPTER EIGHTEENTH

> A hopeless darkness settles o'er my fate;
> I've seen the last look of her heavenly eyes,—
> I've heard the last sound of her blessed voice,—
> I've seen her fair form from my sight depart;
> My doom is closed.
>
> — COUNT BASIL

"I ken not what to make of you, Mr. Osbaldistone," said MacGregor, as he pushed the flask towards me. "You eat not, you show no wish for rest; and yet you drink not, though that flask of Bourdeaux might have come out of Sir Hildebrand's ain cellar.

Had you been always as abstinent, you would have escaped the deadly hatred of your cousin Rashleigh."

"Had I been always prudent," said I, blushing at the scene he recalled to my recollection, "I should have escaped a worse evil—the reproach of my own conscience."

MacGregor cast a keen and somewhat fierce glance on me, as if to read whether the reproof, which he evidently felt, had been intentionally conveyed. He saw that I was thinking of myself, not of him, and turned his face towards the fire with a deep sigh. I followed his example, and each remained for a few minutes wrapt in his own painful reverie. All in the hut were now asleep, or at least silent, excepting ourselves.

MacGregor first broke silence, in the tone of one who takes up his determination to enter on a painful subject. "My cousin Nicol Jarvie means well," he said, "but he presses ower hard on the temper and situation of a man like me, considering what I have been—what I have been forced to become—and, above all, that which has forced me to become what I am."

He paused; and, though feeling the delicate nature of the discussion in which the conversation was likely to engage me, I could not help replying, that I did not doubt his present situation had much which must be most unpleasant to his feelings.

"I should be happy to learn," I added, "that there is an honourable chance of your escaping from it."

"You speak like a boy," returned MacGregor, in a low tone that growled like distant thunder—"like a boy, who thinks the auld gnarled oak can be twisted as easily as the young sapling. Can I forget that I have been branded as an outlaw—stigmatised as a traitor—a price set on my head as if I had been a wolf—my family treated as the dam and cubs of the hill-fox, whom all may torment, vilify, degrade, and insult—the very name which came to me from a long and noble line of martial ancestors, denounced, as if it were a spell to conjure up the devil with?"

As he went on in this manner, I could plainly see, that, by the enumeration of his wrongs, he was lashing himself up into a rage, in order to justify in his own eyes the errors they had led him into. In this he perfectly succeeded; his light grey eyes contracting alternately and dilating their pupils, until they seemed actually to flash with flame, while he thrust forward and drew back his foot, grasped the hilt of his dirk, extended his arm, clenched his fist, and finally rose from his seat.

"And they *shall* find," he said, in the same muttered but deep tone of stifled passion, "that the name they have dared to proscribe—that the name of MacGregor —*is* a spell to raise the wild devil withal. *They* shall hear of my vengeance, that would scorn to listen to the story of my wrongs—The miserable Highland drover, bankrupt, barefooted,—stripped of all, dishonoured and hunted down, because the avarice of others grasped at more than that poor all could pay, shall burst on them in an awful change. They that scoffed at the grovelling worm, and trode upon him, may cry and howl when they see the stoop of the flying and fiery-mouthed dragon.—But why do I speak of all this?" he said, sitting down again, and in a calmer tone—"Only ye may opine it frets my patience, Mr. Osbaldistone, to be hunted like an otter, or a sealgh, or a salmon upon the shallows, and that by my very friends and neighbours; and to have as many sword-cuts made, and pistols flashed at me, as I had this day in the ford of Avondow, would try a saint's temper, much more a Highlander's, who are not famous for that gude gift, as ye may hae heard, Mr. Osbaldistone.—But as thing bides wi' me o' what Nicol said;—I'm vexed for the bairns—I'm vexed when I think o' Hamish and Robert living their father's life." And yielding to despondence on account of his sons, which he felt not upon his own, the father rested his head upon his hand.

I was much affected, Will. All my life long I have been more melted by the distress under which a strong, proud, and powerful mind is compelled to give way, than by the more easily excited sorrows of softer dispositions. The desire of aiding him rushed strongly on my mind, notwithstanding the apparent difficulty, and even impossibility, of the task.

"We have extensive connections abroad," said I: "might not your sons, with some assistance—and they are well entitled to what my father's house can give—find an honourable resource in foreign service?"

I believe my countenance showed signs of sincere emotion; but my companion, taking me by the hand, as I was going to speak farther, said—"I thank—I thank ye—but let us say nae mair o' this. I did not think the eye of man would again have seen a tear on MacGregor's eye-lash." He dashed the moisture from his long gray eye-lash and shaggy red eye-brow with the back of his hand. "To-morrow morning," he said, "we'll talk of this, and we will talk, too, of your affairs—for we are early starters in the dawn, even when we have the luck to have good beds to sleep in. Will ye not pledge me in a grace cup?" I declined the invitation.

"Then, by the soul of St. Maronoch! I must pledge myself," and he poured out and swallowed at least half-a-quart of wine.

I laid myself down to repose, resolving to delay my own inquiries until his mind should be in a more composed state. Indeed, so much had this singular man possessed himself of my imagination, that I felt it impossible to avoid watching him for some minutes after I had flung myself on my heath mattress to seeming rest. He walked up and down the hut, crossed himself from time to time, muttering over some Latin prayer of the Catholic church; then wrapped himself in his plaid, with his naked sword on one side, and his pistol on the other, so disposing the folds of his mantle that he could start up at a moment's warning, with a weapon in either hand, ready for instant combat. In a few minutes his heavy breathing announced that he was fast asleep. Overpowered by fatigue, and stunned by the various unexpected and extraordinary scenes of the day, I, in my turn, was soon overpowered by a slumber deep and overwhelming, from which, notwithstanding every cause for watchfulness, I did not awake until the next morning.

When I opened my eyes, and recollected my situation, I found that MacGregor had already left the hut. I awakened the Bailie, who, after many a snort and groan, and some heavy complaints of the soreness of his bones, in consequence of the unwonted exertions of the preceding day, was at length able to comprehend the joyful intelligence, that the assets carried off by Rashleigh Osbaldistone had been safely recovered. The instant he understood my meaning, he forgot all his grievances, and, bustling up in a great hurry, proceeded to compare the contents of the packet which I put into his hands, with Mr. Owen's memorandums, muttering, as he went on, "Right, right—the real thing—Bailie and Whittington—where's Bailie and Whittington?—seven hundred, six, and eight—exact to a fraction—Pollock and Peelman—twenty-eight, seven—exact—Praise be blest!—Grub and Grinder—better men cannot be—three hundred and seventy—Gliblad—twenty; I doubt Gliblad's ganging—Slipprytongue; Slipprytongue's gaen—but they are sma'sums—sma'sums—the rest's a'right—Praise be blest! we have got the stuff, and may leave this doleful country. I shall never think on Loch-Ard but the thought will gar me grew again."

"I am sorry, cousin," said MacGregor, who entered the hut during the last observation, "I have not been altogether in the circumstances to make your reception sic as I could have desired—natheless, if you would condescend to visit my puir dwelling"—

"Muckle obliged, muckle obliged," answered Mr. Jarvie, very hastily—"But we maun be ganging—we maun be jogging, Mr. Osbaldistone and me—business canna wait."

"Aweel, kinsman," replied the Highlander, "ye ken our fashion—foster the guest that comes—further him that maun gang. But ye cannot return by Drymen—I must set you on Loch Lomond, and boat ye down to the Ferry o' Balloch, and send your nags round to meet ye there. It's a maxim of a wise man never to return by the same road he came, providing another's free to him."

"Ay, ay, Rob," said the Bailie, "that's ane o' the maxims ye learned when ye were a drover;—ye caredna to face the tenants where your beasts had been taking a rug of their moorland grass in the by-ganging, and I doubt your road's waur marked now than it was then."

"The mair need not to travel it ower often, kinsman," replied Rob; "but I'se send round your nags to the ferry wi' Dougal Gregor, wha is converted for that purpose into the Bailie's man, coming—not, as ye may believe, from Aberfoil or Rob Roy's country, but on a quiet jaunt from Stirling. See, here he is."

"I wadna hae ken'd the creature," said Mr. Jarvie; nor indeed was it easy to recognise the wild Highlander, when he appeared before the door of the cottage, attired in a hat, periwig, and riding-coat, which had once called Andrew Fairservice master, and mounted on the Bailie's horse, and leading mine. He received his last orders from his master to avoid certain places where he might be exposed to suspicion—to collect what intelligence he could in the course of his journey, and to await our coming at an appointed place, near the Ferry of Balloch.

At the same time, MacGregor invited us to accompany him upon our own road, assuring us that we must necessarily march a few miles before breakfast, and recommending a dram of brandy as a proper introduction to the journey, in which he was pledged by the Bailie, who pronounced it "an unlawful and perilous habit to begin the day wi' spirituous liquors, except to defend the stomach (whilk was a tender part) against the morning mist; in whilk case his father the deacon had recommended a dram, by precept and example."

"Very true, kinsman," replied Rob, "for which reason we, who are Children of the Mist, have a right to drink brandy from morning till night."

The Bailie, thus refreshed, was mounted on a small Highland pony; another was offered for my use, which, however, I declined; and we resumed, under very different guidance and auspices, our journey of the preceding day.

Our escort consisted of MacGregor, and five or six of the handsomest, best armed, and most athletic mountaineers of his band, and whom he had generally in immediate attendance upon his own person.

When we approached the pass, the scene of the skirmish of the preceding day, and of the still more direful deed which followed it, MacGregor hastened to speak, as if it were rather to what he knew must be necessarily passing in my mind, than to any thing I had said—he spoke, in short, to my thoughts, and not to my words.

"You must think hardly of us, Mr. Osbaldistone, and it is not natural that it should be otherwise. But remember, at least, we have not been unprovoked. We are a rude and an ignorant, and it may be a violent and passionate, but we are not a cruel people. The land might be at peace and in law for us, did they allow us to enjoy the blessings of peaceful law. But we have been a persecuted generation."

"And persecution," said the Bailie, "maketh wise men mad."

"What must it do then to men like us, living as our fathers did a thousand years since, and possessing scarce more lights than they did? Can we view their bluidy edicts against us—their hanging, heading, hounding, and hunting down an ancient and honourable name—as deserving better treatment than that which enemies give to enemies?—Here I stand, have been in twenty frays, and never hurt man but when I was in het bluid; and yet they wad betray me and hang me like a masterless dog, at the gate of ony great man that has an ill will at me."

I replied, "that the proscription of his name and family sounded in English ears as a very cruel and arbitrary law;" and having thus far soothed him, I resumed my propositions of obtaining military employment for himself, if he chose it, and his sons, in foreign parts. MacGregor shook me very cordially by the hand, and detaining me, so as to permit Mr. Jarvie to precede us, a manoeuvre for which the narrowness of the road served as an excuse, he said to me—"You are a kind-hearted and an honourable youth, and understand, doubtless, that which is due to the feelings of a man of honour. But the heather that I have trode upon when living, must bloom ower me when I am dead—my heart would sink, and my arm would shrink and wither like fern in the frost, were I to lose sight of my native hills; nor has the world a scene that would console me for the loss of the rocks and cairns, wild as they are, that you see around us.—And Helen—what could become of her, were I to leave her the subject of new insult and atrocity?—or how could she bear to be removed from these scenes, where the remembrance of her wrongs is aye sweetened by the recollection of her revenge?—I was once so hard put at by my Great enemy, as I may well ca' him, that I was forced e'en to gie way to the tide, and removed myself and my people and family from our dwellings in our native land, and to withdraw for a time into MacCallum More's country—and Helen made a Lament on our departure, as weel as MacRimmon[32] himsell could hae framed it—and so piteously sad and waesome, that our hearts amaist broke as we sate and listened to her—it was like the wailing of one that mourns for the mother that bore him—the tears came down the rough faces of our gillies as they hearkened; and I wad not have the same touch of heartbreak again, no, not to have all the lands that ever were owned by MacGregor."

"But your sons," I said—"they are at the age when your countrymen have usually no objection to see the world?"

"And I should be content," he replied, "that they pushed their fortune in the French or Spanish service, as is the wont of Scottish cavaliers of honour; and last night your plan seemed feasible eneugh—But I hae seen his Excellency this morning before ye were up."

"Did he then quarter so near us?" said I, my bosom throbbing with anxiety.

"Nearer than ye thought," was MacGregor's reply; "but he seemed rather in some shape to jalouse your speaking to the young leddy; and so you see"—

"There was no occasion for jealousy," I answered, with some haughtiness; —"I should not have intruded on his privacy."

"But ye must not be offended, or look out from amang your curls then, like a wildcat out of an ivy-tod, for ye are to understand that he wishes most sincere weel to you, and has proved it. And it's partly that whilk has set the heather on fire e'en now."

"Heather on fire?" said I. "I do not understand you."

"Why," resumed MacGregor, "ye ken weel eneugh that women and gear are at the bottom of a' the mischief in this warld. I hae been misdoubting your cousin Rashleigh since ever he saw that he wasna to get Die Vernon for his marrow, and I think he took grudge at his Excellency mainly on that account. But then came the splore about the surrendering your papers—and we hae now gude evidence, that, sae soon as he was compelled to yield them up, he rade post to Stirling, and tauld the Government all and mair than all, that was gaun doucely on amang us hill-folk; and, doubtless, that was the way that the country was laid to take his Excellency and the leddy, and to make sic an unexpected raid on me. And I hae as little doubt that the poor deevil Morris, whom he could gar believe onything, was egged on by him, and some of the Lowland gentry, to trepan me in the gate he tried to do. But if Rashleigh Osbaldistone were baith the last and best of his name, and granting that he and I ever forgather again, the fiend go down my weasand with a bare blade at his belt, if we part before my dirk and his best blude are weel acquainted thegither!"

He pronounced the last threat with an ominous frown, and the appropriate gesture of his hand upon his dagger.

"I should almost rejoice at what has happened," said I, "could I hope that Rashleigh's treachery might prove the means of preventing the explosion of the rash and desperate intrigues in which I have long suspected him to be a prime agent."

"Trow ye na that," said Rob Roy; "traitor's word never yet hurt honest cause. He was ower deep in our secrets, that's true; and had it not been so, Stirling and Edinburgh Castles would have been baith in our hands by this time, or briefly hereafter, whilk is now scarce to be hoped for. But there are ower mony engaged, and far ower gude a cause to be gien up for the breath of a traitor's tale, and that will be seen and heard of ere it be lang. And so, as I was about to say, the best of my thanks to you for your offer anent my sons, whilk last night I had some thoughts to have embraced in their behalf. But I see that this villain's treason will convince our great folks that they must instantly draw to a head, and make a blow for it, or be taen in their houses, coupled up like hounds, and driven up to London like the honest noblemen and gentlemen in the year seventeen hundred and seven. Civil war is like a cockatrice;— we have sitten hatching the egg that held it for ten years, and might hae sitten on for ten years mair, when in comes Rashleigh, and chips the shell, and out bangs the wonder amang us, and cries to fire and sword. Now in sic a matter I'll hae need o' a' the hands I can mak; and, nae disparagement to the Kings of France and Spain, whom I wish very weel to, King James is as gude a man as ony o' them, and has the best right to Hamish and Rob, being his natural-born subjects."

I easily comprehended that these words boded a general national convulsion; and, as it would have been alike useless and dangerous to have combated the political opinions of my guide, at such a place and moment, I contented myself with regretting the promiscuous scene of confusion and distress likely to arise from any general exertion in favour of the exiled royal family.

"Let it come, man—let it come," answered MacGregor; "ye never saw dull weather clear without a shower; and if the world is turned upside down, why, honest men have the better chance to cut bread out of it."

I again attempted to bring him back to the subject of Diana; but although on most occasions and subjects he used a freedom of speech which I had no great delight in listening to, yet upon that alone which was most interesting to me, he kept a degree of scrupulous reserve, and contented himself with intimating, "that he hoped the leddy would be soon in a quieter country than this was like to be for one while." I was obliged to be content with this answer, and to proceed in the hope that accident might, as on a former occasion, stand my friend, and allow me at least the sad gratification of bidding farewell to the object which had occupied such a share of my affections, so much beyond even what I had supposed, till I was about to be separated from her for ever.

We pursued the margin of the lake for about six English miles, through a devious and beautifully variegated path, until we attained a sort of Highland farm, or assembly of hamlets, near the head of that fine sheet of water, called, if I mistake not, Lediart, or some such name. Here a numerous party of MacGregor's men were stationed in order to receive us. The taste as well as the eloquence of tribes in a savage, or, to speak more properly, in a rude state, is usually just, because it is unfettered by system and affectation; and of this I had an example in the choice these mountaineers had made of a place to receive their guests. It has been said that a British monarch would judge well to receive the embassy of a rival power in the cabin of a man-of-war; and a Highland leader acted with some propriety in choosing a situation where the natural objects of grandeur proper to his country might have their full effect on the minds of his guests.

We ascended about two hundred yards from the shores of the lake, guided by a brawling brook, and left on the right hand four or five Highland huts, with patches of arable land around them, so small as to show that they must have been worked with the spade rather than the plough, cut as it were out of the surrounding copsewood, and waving with crops of barley and oats. Above this limited space the hill became more steep; and on its edge we descried the glittering arms and waving drapery of about fifty of MacGregor's followers. They were stationed on a spot, the recollection of which yet strikes me with admiration. The brook, hurling its waters downwards from the mountain, had in this spot encountered a barrier rock, over which it had made its way by two distinct leaps. The first fall, across which a magnificent old oak, slanting out from the farther bank, partly extended itself as if to shroud the dusky stream of the cascade, might be about twelve feet high; the broken waters were received in a beautiful stone basin, almost as regular as if hewn by a sculptor; and after wheeling around its flinty margin, they made a second precipitous dash, through a dark and narrow chasm, at least fifty feet in depth, and from thence, in a hurried, but comparatively a more gentle course, escaped to join the lake.

With the natural taste which belongs to mountaineers, and especially to the Scottish Highlanders, whose feelings, I have observed, are often allied with the romantic and poetical, Rob Roy's wife and followers had prepared our morning repast in a scene well calculated to impress strangers with some feelings of awe. They are also naturally a grave and proud people, and, however rude in our estimation, carry their ideas of form and politeness to an excess that would appear overstrained, except from the demonstration of superior force which accompanies the display of it; for it must be granted that the air of punctilious deference and rigid etiquette which would seem ridiculous in an ordinary peasant, has, like the salute of a *corps-de-garde,* a propriety when tendered by a Highlander completely armed. There was, accordingly, a good deal of formality in our approach and reception.

The Highlanders, who had been dispersed on the side of the hill, drew themselves together when we came in view, and, standing firm and motionless, appeared in close column behind three figures, whom I soon recognised to be Helen MacGregor and her two sons. MacGregor himself arranged his attendants in the rear, and, requesting Mr. Jarvie to dismount where the ascent became steep, advanced slowly, marshalling us forward at the head of the troop. As we advanced, we heard the wild notes of the bagpipes, which lost their natural discord from being mingled with the dashing sound of the cascade. When we came close, the wife of MacGregor came forward to meet us. Her dress was studiously arranged in a more feminine taste than it had been on the preceding day, but her features wore the same lofty, unbending, and resolute character; and as she folded my friend the Bailie in an unexpected and apparently unwelcome embrace, I could perceive by the agitation of his wig, his back, and the calves of his legs, that he felt much like to one who feels himself suddenly in the gripe of a she-bear, without being able to distinguish whether the animal is in kindness or in wrath.

"Kinsman," she said, "you are welcome—and you, too, stranger," she added, releasing my alarmed companion, who instinctively drew back and settled his wig, and addressing herself to me—"you also are welcome. You came," she added, "to our unhappy country, when our bloods were chafed, and our hands were red. Excuse the rudeness that gave you a rough welcome, and lay it upon the evil times, and not upon us." All this was said with the manners of a princess, and in the tone and style of a court. Nor was there the least tincture of that vulgarity, which we naturally attach to the Lowland Scottish. There was a strong provincial accentuation, but, otherwise, the language rendered by Helen MacGregor, out of the native and poetical Gaelic, into English, which she had acquired as we do learned tongues, but had probably never heard applied to the mean purposes of ordinary life, was graceful, flowing, and declamatory. Her husband, who had in his time played many parts, used a much less elevated and emphatic dialect;—but even *his* language rose in purity of expression, as you may have remarked, if I have been accurate in recording it, when the affairs which he discussed were of an agitating and important nature; and it appears to me in his case, and in that of some other Highlanders whom I have known, that, when familiar and facetious, they used the Lowland Scottish dialect,—when serious and impassioned, their thoughts arranged themselves in the idiom of their native language; and in the latter case, as they uttered the corresponding ideas in English, the expressions sounded wild, elevated, and poetical. In fact, the language of passion is almost always pure as well as vehement, and it is no uncommon thing to hear a Scotchman, when overwhelmed by a countryman with a tone of bitter and fluent upbraiding, reply by way of taunt to his adversary, "You have gotten to your English."

Be this as it may, the wife of MacGregor invited us to a refreshment spread out on the grass, which abounded with all the good things their mountains could offer, but was clouded by the dark and undisturbed gravity which sat on the brow of our hostess, as well as by our deep and anxious recollection of what had taken place on the preceding day. It was in vain that the leader exerted himself to excite mirth;—a chill hung over our minds, as if the feast had been funereal; and every bosom felt light when it was ended.

"Adieu, cousin," she said to Mr. Jarvie, as we rose from the entertainment; "the best wish Helen MacGregor can give to a friend is, that he may see her no more."

The Bailie struggled to answer, probably with some commonplace maxim of morality;—but the calm and melancholy sternness of her countenance bore down and disconcerted the mechanical and formal importance of the magistrate. He coughed,—hemmed,—bowed,—and was silent.

"For you, stranger," she said, "I have a token, from one whom you can never"—

"Helen!" interrupted MacGregor, in a loud and stern voice, "what means this?—have you forgotten the charge?"

"MacGregor," she replied, "I have forgotten nought that is fitting for me to remember. It is not such hands as these," and she stretched forth her long, sinewy, and bare arm, "that are fitting to convey love-tokens, were the gift connected with aught but misery. Young man," she said, presenting me with a ring, which I well remembered as one of the few ornaments that Miss Vernon sometimes wore, "this comes from one whom you will never see more. If it is a joyless token, it is well fitted to pass through the hands of one to whom joy can never be known. Her last words were—Let him forget me for ever."

"And can she," I said, almost without being conscious that I spoke, "suppose that is possible?"

"All may be forgotten," said the extraordinary female who addressed me,—"all—but the sense of dishonour, and the desire of vengeance."

"*Seid suas!*"[33] cried the MacGregor, stamping with impatience.

The bagpipes sounded, and with their thrilling and jarring tones cut short our conference. Our leave of our hostess was taken by silent gestures; and we resumed our journey with an additional proof on my part, that I was beloved by Diana, and was separated from her for ever.

CHAPTER NINETEENTH

> Farewell to the land where the clouds love to rest,
> Like the shroud of the dead, on the mountain's cold breast
> To the cataract's roar where the eagles reply,
> And the lake her lone bosom expands to the sky.

Our route lay through a dreary, yet romantic country, which the distress of my own mind prevented me from remarking particularly, and which, therefore, I will not attempt to describe. The lofty peak of Ben Lomond, here the predominant monarch of the mountains, lay on our right hand, and served as a striking landmark. I was not awakened from my apathy, until, after a long and toilsome walk, we emerged through a pass in the hills, and Loch Lomond opened before us. I will spare you the attempt to describe what you would hardly comprehend without going to see it. But certainly this noble lake, boasting innumerable beautiful islands, of every varying form and outline which fancy can frame,—its northern extremity narrowing until it is lost among dusky and retreating mountains,—while, gradually widening as it extends to the southward, it spreads its base around the indentures and promontories of a fair and fertile land, affords one of the most surprising, beautiful, and sublime spectacles in nature. The eastern side, peculiarly rough and rugged, was at this time the chief seat of MacGregor and his clan,—to curb whom, a small garrison had been stationed in a central position betwixt Loch Lomond and another lake. The extreme strength of the country, however, with the numerous passes, marshes, caverns, and other places of concealment or defence, made the establishment of this little fort seem rather an acknowledgment of the danger, than an effectual means of securing against it.

On more than one occasion, as well as on that which I witnessed, the garrison suffered from the adventurous spirit of the outlaw and his followers. These advantages were never sullied by ferocity when he himself was in command; for, equally good-tempered and sagacious, he understood well the danger of incurring unnecessary odium. I learned with pleasure that he had caused the captives of the preceding day to be liberated in safety; and many traits of mercy, and even of generosity, are recorded of this remarkable man on similar occasions.

A boat waited for us in a creek beneath a huge rock, manned by four lusty Highland rowers; and our host took leave of us with great cordiality, and even affection. Betwixt him and Mr. Jarvie, indeed, there seemed to exist a degree of mutual regard, which formed a strong contrast to their different occupations and habits. After kissing each other very lovingly, and when they were just in the act of parting, the Bailie, in the fulness of his heart, and with a faltering voice, assured his kinsman, "that if ever an hundred pund, or even twa hundred, would put him or his family in a settled way, he need but just send a line to the Saut-Market;" and Rob, grasping his basket-hilt with one hand, and shaking Mr. Jarvie's heartily with the other, protested, "that if ever anybody should affront his kinsman, an he would but let him ken, he would stow his lugs out of his head, were he the best man in Glasgow."

With these assurances of mutual aid and continued good-will, we bore away from the shore, and took our course for the south-western angle of the lake, where it gives birth to the river Leven. Rob Roy remained for some time standing on the rock from beneath which we had departed, conspicuous by his long gun, waving tartans, and the single plume in his cap, which in those days denoted the Highland gentleman and soldier; although I observe that the present military taste has decorated the Highland bonnet with a quantity of black plumage resembling that which is borne before funerals. At length, as the distance increased between us, we saw him turn and go slowly up the side of the hill, followed by his immediate attendants or bodyguard.

We performed our voyage for a long time in silence, interrupted only by the Gaelic chant which one of the rowers sung in low irregular measure, rising occasionally into a wild chorus, in which the others joined.

My own thoughts were sad enough;—yet I felt something soothing in the magnificent scenery with which I was surrounded; and thought, in the enthusiasm of the moment, that had my faith been that of Rome, I could have consented to live and die a lonely hermit in one of the romantic and beautiful islands amongst which our boat glided.

The Bailie had also his speculations, but they were of somewhat a different complexion; as I found when, after about an hour's silence, during which he had been mentally engaged in the calculations necessary, he undertook to prove the possibility of draining the lake, and "giving to plough and harrow many hundred, ay, many a thousand acres, from whilk no man could get earthly gude e'enow, unless it were a gedd,[34] or a dish of perch now and then."

Amidst a long discussion, which he "crammed into mine ear against the stomach of my sense," I only remember, that it was part of his project to preserve a portion of the lake just deep enough and broad enough for the purposes of water-carriage, so that coal-barges and gabbards should pass as easily between Dumbarton and Glenfalloch as between Glasgow and Greenock.

At length we neared our distant place of landing, adjoining to the ruins of an ancient castle, and just where the lake discharges its superfluous waters into the Leven. There we found Dougal with the horses. The Bailie had formed a plan with respect to "the creature," as well as upon the draining of the lake; and, perhaps in both cases, with more regard to the utility than to the practical possibility of his scheme. "Dougal," he said, "ye are a kindly creature, and hae the sense and feeling o' what is due to your betters—and I'm e'en wae for you, Dougal, for it canna be but that in the life ye lead you suld get a Jeddart cast[35] ae day suner or later. I trust, considering my services as a magistrate, and my father the deacon's afore me, I hae interest eneugh in the council to gar them wink a wee at a waur faut than yours.

Sae I hae been thinking, that if ye will gang back to Glasgow wi' us, being a strong-backit creature, ye might be employed in the warehouse till something better suld cast up."

"Her nainsell muckle obliged till the Bailie's honour," replied Dougal; "but teil be in her shanks fan she gangs on a cause-way'd street, unless she be drawn up the Gallowgate wi' tows, as she was before."

In fact, I afterwards learned that Dougal had originally come to Glasgow as a prisoner, from being concerned in some depredation, but had somehow found such favour in the eyes of the jailor, that, with rather overweening confidence, he had retained him in his service as one of the turnkeys; a task which Dougal had discharged with sufficient fidelity, so far as was known, until overcome by his clannish prejudices on the unexpected appearance of his old leader.

Astonished at receiving so round a refusal to so favourable an offer, the Bailie, turning to me, observed, that the "creature was a natural-born idiot." I testified my own gratitude in a way which Dougal much better relished, by slipping a couple of guineas into his hand. He no sooner felt the touch of the gold, than he sprung twice or thrice from the earth with the agility of a wild buck, flinging out first one heel and then another, in a manner which would have astonished a French dancing-master. He ran to the boatmen to show them the prize, and a small gratuity made them take part in his raptures. He then, to use a favourite expression of the dramatic John Bunyan, "went on his way, and I saw him no more."

The Bailie and I mounted our horses, and proceeded on the road to Glasgow. When we had lost the view of the lake, and its superb amphitheatre of mountains, I could not help expressing with enthusiasm, my sense of its natural beauties, although I was conscious that Mr. Jarvie was a very uncongenial spirit to communicate with on such a subject.

"Ye are a young gentleman," he replied, "and an Englishman, and a' this may be very fine to you; but for me, wha am a plain man, and ken something o' the different values of land, I wadna gie the finest sight we hae seen in the Hielands, for the first keek o' the Gorbals o' Glasgow; and if I were ance there, it suldna be every fule's errand, begging your pardon, Mr. Francis, that suld take me out o' sight o' Saint Mungo's steeple again!"

The honest man had his wish; for, by dint of travelling very late, we arrived at his own house that night, or rather on the succeeding morning. Having seen my worthy fellow-traveller safely consigned to the charge of the considerate and officious Mattie, I proceeded to Mrs. Flyter's, in whose house, even at this unwonted hour, light was still burning. The door was opened by no less a person than Andrew Fairservice himself, who, upon the first sound of my voice, set up a loud shout of joyful recognition, and, without uttering a syllable, ran up stairs towards a parlour on the second floor, from the windows of which the light proceeded. Justly conceiving that he went to announce my return to the anxious Owen, I followed him upon the foot. Owen was not alone, there was another in the apartment—it was my father.

The first impulse was to preserve the dignity of his usual equanimity,—"Francis, I am glad to see you." The next was to embrace me tenderly,—"My dear—dear son!"— Owen secured one of my hands, and wetted it with his tears, while he joined in gratulating my return. These are scenes which address themselves to the eye and to the heart rather than to the ear—My old eye-lids still moisten at the recollection of our meeting; but your kind and affectionate feelings can well imagine what I should find it impossible to describe.

When the tumult of our joy was over, I learnt that my father had arrived from Holland shortly after Owen had set off for Scotland. Determined and rapid in all his movements, he only stopped to provide the means of discharging the obligations incumbent on his house. By his extensive resources, with funds enlarged, and credit fortified, by eminent success in his continental speculation, he easily accomplished what perhaps his absence alone rendered difficult, and set out for Scotland to exact justice from Rashleigh Osbaldistone, as well as to put order to his affairs in that country. My father's arrival in full credit, and with the ample means of supporting his engagements honourably, as well as benefiting his correspondents in future, was a stunning blow to MacVittie and Company, who had conceived his star set for ever. Highly incensed at the usage his confidential clerk and agent had received at their hands, Mr. Osbaldistone refused every tender of apology and accommodation; and having settled the balance of their account, announced to them that, with all its numerous contingent advantages, that leaf of their ledger was closed for ever.

While he enjoyed this triumph over false friends, he was not a little alarmed on my account. Owen, good man, had not supposed it possible that a journey of fifty or sixty miles, which may be made with so much ease and safety in any direction from London, could be attended with any particular danger. But he caught alarm, by sympathy, from my father, to whom the country, and the lawless character of its inhabitants, were better known.

These apprehensions were raised to agony, when, a few hours before I arrived, Andrew Fairservice made his appearance, with a dismal and exaggerated account of the uncertain state in which he had left me. The nobleman with whose troops he had been a sort of prisoner, had, after examination, not only dismissed him, but furnished him with the means of returning rapidly to Glasgow, in order to announce to my friends my precarious and unpleasant situation.

Andrew was one of those persons who have no objection to the sort of temporary attention and woeful importance which attaches itself to the bearer of bad tidings, and had therefore by no means smoothed down his tale in the telling, especially as the rich London merchant himself proved unexpectedly one of the auditors. He went at great length into an account of the dangers I had escaped, chiefly, as he insinuated, by means of his own experience, exertion, and sagacity.

"What was to come of me now, when my better angel, in his (Andrew's) person, was removed from my side, it was," he said, "sad and sair to conjecture; that the Bailie was nae better than just naebody at a pinch, or something waur, for he was a conceited body—and Andrew hated conceit—but certainly, atween the pistols and the carabines of the troopers, that rappit aff the tane after the tother as fast as hail, and the dirks and claymores o' the Hielanders, and the deep waters and weils o' the Avondow, it was to be thought there wad be a puir account of the young gentleman."

This statement would have driven Owen to despair, had he been alone and unsupported; but my father's perfect knowledge of mankind enabled him easily to appreciate the character of Andrew, and the real amount of his intelligence. Stripped of all exaggeration, however, it was alarming enough to a parent. He determined to set out in person to obtain my liberty by ransom or negotiation, and was busied with Owen till a late hour, in order to get through some necessary correspondence, and devolve on the latter some business which should be transacted during his absence; and thus it chanced that I found them watchers.

It was late ere we separated to rest, and, too impatient long to endure repose, I was stirring early the next morning. Andrew gave his attendance at my levee, as in duty bound, and, instead of the scarecrow figure to which he had been reduced at Aberfoil, now appeared in the attire of an undertaker, a goodly suit, namely, of the deepest mourning. It was not till after one or two queries, which the rascal affected as long as he could to misunderstand, that I found out he "had thought it but decent to put on mourning, on account of my inexpressible loss; and as the broker at whose shop he had equipped himself, declined to receive the goods again, and as his own garments had been destroyed or carried off in my honour's service, doubtless I and my honourable father, whom Providence had blessed wi' the means, wadna suffer a puir lad to sit down wi' the loss; a stand o' claes was nae great matter to an Osbaldistone (be praised for't!), especially to an old and attached servant o' the house."

As there was something of justice in Andrew's plea of loss in my service, his finesse succeeded; and he came by a good suit of mourning, with a beaver and all things conforming, as the exterior signs of woe for a master who was alive and merry.

My father's first care, when he arose, was to visit Mr. Jarvie, for whose kindness he entertained the most grateful sentiments, which he expressed in very few, but manly and nervous terms. He explained the altered state of his affairs, and offered the Bailie, on such terms as could not but be both advantageous and acceptable, that part in his concerns which had been hitherto managed by MacVittie and Company. The Bailie heartily congratulated my father and Owen on the changed posture of their affairs, and, without affecting to disclaim that he had done his best to serve them, when matters looked otherwise, he said, "He had only just acted as he wad be done by—that, as to the extension of their correspondence, he frankly accepted it with thanks. Had MacVittie's folk behaved like honest men," he said, "he wad hae liked ill to hae come in ahint them, and out afore them this gate. But it's otherwise, and they maun e'en stand the loss."

The Bailie then pulled me by the sleeve into a corner, and, after again cordially wishing me joy, proceeded, in rather an embarrassed tone—"I wad heartily wish, Maister Francis, there suld be as little said as possible about the queer things we saw up yonder awa. There's nae gude, unless ane were judicially examinate, to say onything about that awfu' job o' Morris—and the members o' the council wadna think it creditable in ane of their body to be fighting wi' a wheen Hielandmen, and singeing their plaidens—And abune a', though I am a decent sponsible man, when I am on my right end, I canna but think I maun hae made a queer figure without my hat and my periwig, hinging by the middle like bawdrons, or a cloak flung ower a cloak-pin. Bailie Grahame wad hae an unco hair in my neck an he got that tale by the end."

I could not suppress a smile when I recollected the Bailie's situation, although I certainly thought it no laughing matter at the time. The good-natured merchant was a little confused, but smiled also when he shook his head—"I see how it is—I see how it is. But say naething about it—there's a gude callant; and charge that lang-tongued, conceited, upsetting serving man o' yours, to sae naething neither. I wadna for ever sae muckle that even the lassock Mattie ken'd onything about it. I wad never hear an end o't."

He was obviously relieved from his impending fears of ridicule, when I told him it was my father's intention to leave Glasgow almost immediately. Indeed he had now no motive for remaining, since the most valuable part of the papers carried off by Rashleigh had been recovered. For that portion which he had converted into cash and expended in his own or on political intrigues, there was no mode of recovering it but by a suit at law, which was forthwith commenced, and proceeded, as our law-agents assured us, with all deliberate speed.

We spent, accordingly, one hospitable day with the Bailie, and took leave of him, as this narrative now does. He continued to grow in wealth, honour, and credit, and actually rose to the highest civic honours in his native city. About two years after the period I have mentioned, he tired of his bachelor life, and promoted Mattie from her wheel by the kitchen fire to the upper end of his table, in the character of Mrs. Jarvie. Bailie Grahame, the MacVitties, and others (for all men have their enemies, especially in the council of a royal burgh), ridiculed this transformation. "But," said Mr. Jarvie, "let them say their say. I'll ne'er fash mysell, nor lose my liking for sae feckless a matter as a nine days' clash. My honest father the deacon had a byword,

> Brent brow and lily skin,
> A loving heart, and a leal within,
> Is better than gowd or gentle kin.

Besides," as he always concluded, "Mattie was nae ordinary lassock-quean; she was akin to the Laird o' Limmerfield."

Whether it was owing to her descent or her good gifts, I do not presume to decide; but Mattie behaved excellently in her exaltation, and relieved the apprehensions of some of the Bailie's friends, who had deemed his experiment somewhat hazardous. I do not know that there was any other incident of his quiet and useful life worthy of being particularly recorded.

CHAPTER TWENTIETH

> "Come ye hither my 'six' good sons,
> Gallant men I trow ye be,
> How many of you, my children dear,
> Will stand by that good Earl and me?"
>
> "Five" of them did answer make—
> "Five" of them spoke hastily,
> "O father, till the day we die,
> We'll stand by that good Earl and thee."
>
> — THE RISING IN THE NORTH.

On the morning when we were to depart from Glasgow, Andrew Fairservice bounced into my apartment like a madman, jumping up and down, and singing, with more vehemence than tune,

> The kiln's on fire—the kiln's on fire—
> The kiln's on fire—she's a' in a lowe.

With some difficulty I prevailed on him to cease his confounded clamour, and explain to me what the matter was. He was pleased to inform me, as if he had been bringing the finest news imaginable, "that the Hielands were clean broken out, every man o' them, and that Rob Roy, and a' his breekless bands, wad be down upon Glasgow or twenty-four hours o' the clock gaed round."

"Hold your tongue," said I, "you rascal! You must be drunk or mad; and if there is any truth in your news, is it a singing matter, you scoundrel?"

"Drunk or mad? nae doubt," replied Andrew, dauntlessly; "ane's aye drunk or mad if he tells what grit folks dinna like to hear—Sing? Od, the clans will make us sing on the wrang side o' our mouth, if we are sae drunk or mad as to bide their coming."

I rose in great haste, and found my father and Owen also on foot, and in considerable alarm.

Andrew's news proved but too true in the main. The great rebellion which agitated Britain in the year 1715 had already broken out, by the unfortunate Earl of Mar's setting up the standard of the Stuart family in an ill-omened hour, to the ruin of many honourable families, both in England and Scotland. The treachery of some of the Jacobite agents (Rashleigh among the rest), and the arrest of others, had made George the First's Government acquainted with the extensive ramifications of a conspiracy long prepared, and which at last exploded prematurely, and in a part of the kingdom too distant to have any vital effect upon the country, which, however, was plunged into much confusion.

This great public event served to confirm and elucidate the obscure explanations I had received from MacGregor; and I could easily see why the westland clans, who were brought against him, should have waived their private quarrel, in consideration that they were all shortly to be engaged in the same public cause. It was a more melancholy reflection to my mind, that Diana Vernon was the wife of one of those who were most active in turning the world upside down, and that she was herself exposed to all the privations and perils of her husband's hazardous trade.

We held an immediate consultation on the measures we were to adopt in this crisis, and acquiesced in my father's plan, that we should instantly get the necessary passports, and make the best of our way to London. I acquainted my father with my wish to offer my personal service to the Government in any volunteer corps, several being already spoken of. He readily acquiesced in my proposal; for though he disliked war as a profession, yet, upon principle, no man would have exposed his life more willingly in defence of civil and religious liberty.

We travelled in haste and in peril through Dumfriesshire and the neighbouring counties of England. In this quarter, gentlemen of the Tory interest were already in motion, mustering men and horses, while the Whigs assembled themselves in the principal towns, armed the inhabitants, and prepared for civil war. We narrowly escaped being stopped on more occasions than one, and were often compelled to take circuitous routes to avoid the points where forces were assembling.

When we reached London, we immediately associated with those bankers and eminent merchants who agreed to support the credit of Government, and to meet that run upon the funds, on which the conspirators had greatly founded their hopes of furthering their undertaking, by rendering the Government, as it were, bankrupt. My father was chosen one of the members of this formidable body of the monied interest, as all had the greatest confidence in his zeal, skill, and activity. He was also the organ by which they communicated with Government, and contrived, from funds belonging to his own house, or over which he had command, to find purchasers for a quantity of the national stock, which was suddenly flung into the market at a depreciated price when the rebellion broke out. I was not idle myself, but obtained a commission, and levied, at my father's expense, about two hundred men, with whom I joined General Carpenter's army.

The rebellion, in the meantime, had extended itself to England. The unfortunate

Earl of Derwentwater had taken arms in the cause, along with General Foster. My poor uncle, Sir Hildebrand, whose estate was reduced to almost nothing by his own carelessness and the expense and debauchery of his sons and household, was easily persuaded to join that unfortunate standard. Before doing so, however, he exhibited a degree of precaution of which no one could have suspected him—he made his will!

By this document he devised his estates at Osbaldistone Hall, and so forth, to his sons successively, and their male heirs, until he came to Rashleigh, whom, on account of the turn he had lately taken in politics, he detested with all his might,—he cut him off with a shilling, and settled the estate on me as his next heir. I had always been rather a favourite of the old gentleman; but it is probable that, confident in the number of gigantic youths who now armed around him, he considered the destination as likely to remain a dead letter, which he inserted chiefly to show his displeasure at Rashleigh's treachery, both public and domestic. There was an article, by which he, bequeathed to the niece of his late wife, Diana Vernon, now Lady Diana Vernon Beauchamp, some diamonds belonging to her late aunt, and a great silver ewer, having the arms of Vernon and Osbaldistone quarterly engraven upon it.

But Heaven had decreed a more speedy extinction of his numerous and healthy lineage, than, most probably, he himself had reckoned on. In the very first muster of the conspirators, at a place called Green-Rigg, Thorncliff Osbaldistone quarrelled about precedence with a gentleman of the Northumbrian border, to the full as fierce and intractable as himself. In spite of all remonstrances, they gave their commander a specimen of how far their discipline might be relied upon, by fighting it out with their rapiers, and my kinsman was killed on the spot. His death was a great loss to Sir Hildebrand, for, notwithstanding his infernal temper, he had a grain or two of more sense than belonged to the rest of the brotherhood, Rashleigh always excepted.

Perceval, the sot, died also in his calling. He had a wager with another gentleman (who, from his exploits in that line, had acquired the formidable epithet of Brandy Swalewell), which should drink the largest cup of strong liquor when King James was proclaimed by the insurgents at Morpeth. The exploit was something enormous. I forget the exact quantity of brandy which Percie swallowed, but it occasioned a fever, of which he expired at the end of three days, with the word, *water, water,* perpetually on his tongue.

Dickon broke his neck near Warrington Bridge, in an attempt to show off a foundered blood-mare which he wished to palm upon a Manchester merchant who had joined the insurgents. He pushed the animal at a five-barred gate; she fell in the leap, and the unfortunate jockey lost his life.

Wilfred the fool, as sometimes befalls, had the best fortune of the family. He was slain at Proud Preston, in Lancashire, on the day that General Carpenter attacked the barricades, fighting with great bravery, though I have heard he was never able exactly to comprehend the cause of quarrel, and did not uniformly remember on which king's side he was engaged. John also behaved very boldly in the same engagement, and received several wounds, of which he was not happy enough to die on the spot.

Old Sir Hildebrand, entirely brokenhearted by these successive losses, became, by the next day's surrender, one of the unhappy prisoners, and was lodged in Newgate with his wounded son John.

I was now released from my military duty, and lost no time, therefore, in endeavouring to relieve the distresses of these new relations. My father's interest with Government, and the general compassion excited by a parent who had sustained the successive loss of so many sons within so short a time, would have prevented my uncle and cousin from being brought to trial for high treason. But their doom was given forth from a greater tribunal. John died of his wounds in Newgate, recommending to me in his last breath, a cast of hawks which he had at the Hall, and a black spaniel bitch called Lucy.

My poor uncle seemed beaten down to the very earth by his family calamities, and the circumstances in which he unexpectedly found himself. He said little, but seemed grateful for such attentions as circumstances permitted me to show him. I did not witness his meeting with my father for the first time for so many years, and under circumstances so melancholy; but, judging from my father's extreme depression of spirits, it must have been melancholy in the last degree. Sir Hildebrand spoke with great bitterness against Rashleigh, now his only surviving child; laid upon him the ruin of his house, and the deaths of all his brethren, and declared, that neither he nor they would have plunged into political intrigue, but for that very member of his family, who had been the first to desert them. He once or twice mentioned Diana, always with great affection; and once he said, while I sate by his bedside—"Nevoy, since Thorncliff and all of them are dead, I am sorry you cannot have her."

The expression affected me much at the time; for it was a usual custom of the poor old baronet's, when joyously setting forth upon the morning's chase, to distinguish Thorncliff, who was a favourite, while he summoned the rest more generally; and the loud jolly tone in which he used to hollo, "Call Thornie—call all of them," contrasted sadly with the woebegone and self-abandoning note in which he uttered the disconsolate words which I have above quoted. He mentioned the contents of his will, and supplied me with an authenticated copy;—the original he had deposited with my old acquaintance Mr. Justice Inglewood, who, dreaded by no one, and confided in by all as a kind of neutral person, had become, for aught I know, the depositary of half the wills of the fighting men of both factions in the county of Northumberland.

The greater part of my uncle's last hours were spent in the discharge of the religious duties of his church, in which he was directed by the chaplain of the Sardinian ambassador, for whom, with some difficulty, we obtained permission to visit him. I could not ascertain by my own observation, or through the medical attendants, that Sir Hildebrand Osbaldistone died of any formed complaint bearing a name in the science of medicine. He seemed to me completely worn out and broken down by fatigue of body and distress of mind, and rather ceased to exist, than died of any positive struggle,—just as a vessel, buffeted and tossed by a succession of tempestuous gales, her timbers overstrained, and her joints loosened, will sometimes spring a leak and founder, when there are no apparent causes for her destruction.

It was a remarkable circumstance that my father, after the last duties were performed to his brother, appeared suddenly to imbibe a strong anxiety that I should act upon the will, and represent his father's house, which had hitherto seemed to be the thing in the world which had least charms for him. But formerly, he had been like the fox in the fable, contemning what was beyond his reach; and, moreover, I doubt not that the excessive dislike which he entertained against Rashleigh (now Sir Rashleigh) Osbaldistone, who loudly threatened to attack his father Sir Hildebrand's will and settlement, corroborated my father's desire to maintain it.

"He had been most unjustly disinherited," he said, "by his own father—his brother's will had repaired the disgrace, if not the injury, by leaving the wreck of his property to Frank, the natural heir, and he was determined the bequest should take effect."

In the meantime, Rashleigh was not altogether a contemptible personage as an opponent. The information he had given to Government was critically well-timed, and his extreme plausibility, with the extent of his intelligence, and the artful manner in which he contrived to assume both merit and influence, had, to a certain extent, procured him patrons among Ministers. We were already in the full tide of litigation with him on the subject of his pillaging the firm of Osbaldistone and Tresham; and, judging from the progress we made in that comparatively simple lawsuit, there was a chance that this second course of litigation might be drawn out beyond the period of all our natural lives.

To avert these delays as much as possible, my father, by the advice of his counsel learned in the law, paid off and vested in my person the rights to certain large mortgages affecting Osbaldistone Hall. Perhaps, however, the opportunity to convert a great share of the large profits which accrued from the rapid rise of the funds upon the suppression of the rebellion, and the experience he had so lately had of the perils of commerce, encouraged him to realise, in this manner, a considerable part of his property. At any rate, it so chanced, that, instead of commanding me to the desk, as I fully expected, having intimated my willingness to comply with his wishes, however they might destine me, I received his directions to go down to Osbaldistone Hall, and take possession of it as the heir and representative of the family. I was directed to apply to Squire Inglewood for the copy of my uncle's will deposited with him, and take all necessary measures to secure that possession which sages say makes nine points of the law.

At another time I should have been delighted with this change of destination. But now Osbaldistone Hall was accompanied with many painful recollections. Still, however, I thought, that in that neighbourhood only I was likely to acquire some information respecting the fate of Diana Vernon. I had every reason to fear it must be far different from what I could have wished it. But I could obtain no precise information on the subject.

It was in vain that I endeavoured, by such acts of kindness as their situation admitted, to conciliate the confidence of some distant relations who were among the prisoners in Newgate. A pride which I could not condemn, and a natural suspicion of the Whig Frank Osbaldistone, cousin to the double-distilled traitor Rashleigh, closed every heart and tongue, and I only received thanks, cold and extorted, in exchange for such benefits as I had power to offer. The arm of the law was also gradually abridging the numbers of those whom I endeavoured to serve, and the hearts of the survivors became gradually more contracted towards all whom they conceived to be concerned with the existing Government. As they were led gradually, and by detachments, to execution, those who survived lost interest in mankind, and the desire of communicating with them. I shall long remember what one of them, Ned Shafton by name, replied to my anxious inquiry, whether there was any indulgence I could procure him? "Mr. Frank Osbaldistone, I must suppose you mean me kindly, and therefore I thank you. But, by G—, men cannot be fattened like poultry, when they see their neighbours carried off day by day to the place of execution, and know that their own necks are to be twisted round in their turn."

Upon the whole, therefore, I was glad to escape from London, from Newgate, and from the scenes which both exhibited, to breathe the free air of Northumberland. Andrew Fairservice had continued in my service more from my father's pleasure than my own. At present there seemed a prospect that his local acquaintance with Osbaldistone Hall and its vicinity might be useful; and, of course, he accompanied me on my journey, and I enjoyed the prospect of getting rid of him, by establishing him in his old quarters. I cannot conceive how he could prevail upon my father to interest himself in him, unless it were by the art, which he possessed in no inconsiderable degree, of affecting an extreme attachment to his master; which theoretical attachment he made compatible in practice with playing all manner of tricks without scruple, providing only against his master being cheated by any one but himself.

We performed our journey to the North without any remarkable adventure, and we found the country, so lately agitated by rebellion, now peaceful and in good order. The nearer we approached to Osbaldistone Hall, the more did my heart sink at the thought of entering that deserted mansion; so that, in order to postpone the evil day, I resolved first to make my visit at Mr. Justice Inglewood's.

That venerable person had been much disturbed with thoughts of what he had been, and what he now was; and natural recollections of the past had interfered considerably with the active duty which in his present situation might have been expected from him. He was fortunate, however, in one respect; he had got rid of his clerk Jobson, who had finally left him in dudgeon at his inactivity, and become legal assistant to a certain Squire Standish, who had lately commenced operations in those parts as a justice, with a zeal for King George and the Protestant succession, which, very different from the feelings of his old patron, Mr. Jobson had more occasion to restrain within the bounds of the law, than to stimulate to exertion.

Old Justice Inglewood received me with great courtesy, and readily exhibited my uncle's will, which seemed to be without a flaw. He was for some time in obvious distress, how he should speak and act in my presence; but when he found, that though a supporter of the present Government upon principle, I was disposed to think with pity on those who had opposed it on a mistaken feeling of loyalty and duty, his discourse became a very diverting medley of what he had done, and what he had left undone,—the pains he had taken to prevent some squires from joining, and to wink at the escape of others, who had been so unlucky as to engage in the affair.

We were *tete-a'-tete*, and several bumpers had been quaffed by the Justice's special desire, when, on a sudden, he requested me to fill a *bona fide* brimmer to the health of poor dear Die Vernon, the rose of the wilderness, the heath-bell of Cheviot, and the blossom that's transplanted to an infernal convent.

"Is not Miss Vernon married, then?" I exclaimed, in great astonishment. "I thought his Excellency"—

"Pooh! pooh! his Excellency and his Lordship's all a humbug now, you know— mere St. Germains titles—Earl of Beauchamp, and ambassador plenipotentiary from France, when the Duke Regent of Orleans scarce knew that he lived, I dare say. But you must have seen old Sir Frederick Vernon at the Hall, when he played the part of Father Vaughan?"

"Good Heavens! then Vaughan was Miss Vernon's father?"

"To be sure he was," said the Justice coolly;—"there's no use in keeping the secret now, for he must be out of the country by this time—otherwise, no doubt, it would be my duty to apprehend him.—Come, off with your bumper to my dear lost Die!

> And let her health go round, around, around,
> And let her health go round;
> For though your stocking be of silk,
> Your knees near kiss the ground, aground, aground."[36]

I was unable, as the reader may easily conceive, to join in the Justice's jollity. My head swam with the shock I had received. "I never heard," I said, "that Miss Vernon's father was living."

"It was not our Government's fault that he is," replied Inglewood, "for the devil a man there is whose head would have brought more money. He was condemned to death for Fenwick's plot, and was thought to have had some hand in the Knightsbridge affair, in King William's time; and as he had married in Scotland a relation of the house of Breadalbane, he possessed great influence with all their chiefs. There was a talk of his being demanded to be given up at the peace of Ryswick, but he shammed ill, and his death was given publicly out in the French papers. But when he came back here on the old score, we old cavaliers knew him well,—that is to say, I knew him, not as being a cavalier myself, but no information being lodged against the poor gentleman, and my memory being shortened by frequent attacks of the gout, I could not have sworn to him, you know."

"Was he, then, not known at Osbaldistone Hall?" I inquired.

"To none but to his daughter, the old knight, and Rashleigh, who had got at that secret as he did at every one else, and held it like a twisted cord about poor Die's neck. I have seen her one hundred times she would have spit at him, if it had not been fear for her father, whose life would not have been worth five minutes' purchase if he had been discovered to the Government.—But don't mistake me, Mr. Osbaldistone; I say the Government is a good, a gracious, and a just Government; and if it has hanged one-half of the rebels, poor things, all will acknowledge they would not have been touched had they staid peaceably at home."

Waiving the discussion of these political questions, I brought back Mr. Inglewood to his subject, and I found that Diana, having positively refused to marry any of the Osbaldistone family, and expressed her particular detestation of Rashleigh, he had from that time begun to cool in zeal for the cause of the Pretender; to which, as the youngest of six brethren, and bold, artful, and able, he had hitherto looked forward as the means of making his fortune. Probably the compulsion with which he had been forced to render up the spoils which he had abstracted from my father's counting-house by the united authority of Sir Frederick Vernon and the Scottish Chiefs, had determined his resolution to advance his progress by changing his opinions and betraying his trust. Perhaps also—for few men were better judges where his interest was concerned—he considered their means and talents to be, as they afterwards proved, greatly inadequate to the important task of overthrowing an established Government. Sir Frederick Vernon, or, as he was called among the Jacobites, his Excellency Viscount Beauchamp, had, with his daughter, some difficulty in escaping the consequences of Rashleigh's information. Here Mr. Inglewood's information was at fault; but he did not doubt, since we had not heard of Sir Frederick being in the hands of the Government, he must be by this time abroad, where, agreeably to the cruel bond he had entered into with his brother-in-law, Diana, since she had declined to select a husband out of the Osbaldistone family, must be confined to a convent. The original cause of this singular agreement Mr. Inglewood could not perfectly explain; but he understood it was a family compact, entered into for the purpose of securing to Sir Frederick the rents of the remnant of his large estates, which had been vested in the Osbaldistone family by some legal manoeuvre; in short, a family compact, in which, like many of those undertaken at that time of day, the feelings of the principal parties interested were no more regarded than if they had been a part of the live-stock upon the lands.

I cannot tell,—such is the waywardness of the human heart,—whether this intelligence gave me joy or sorrow. It seemed to me, that, in the knowledge that Miss Vernon was eternally divided from me, not by marriage with another, but by seclusion in a convent, in order to fulfil an absurd bargain of this kind, my regret for her loss was aggravated rather than diminished. I became dull, low-spirited, absent, and unable to support the task of conversing with Justice Inglewood, who in his turn yawned, and proposed to retire early. I took leave of him overnight, determining the next day, before breakfast, to ride over to Osbaldistone Hall.

Mr. Inglewood acquiesced in my proposal. "It would be well," he said, "that I made my appearance there before I was known to be in the country, the more especially as Sir Rashleigh Osbaldistone was now, he understood, at Mr. Jobson's house, hatching some mischief, doubtless. They were fit company," he added, "for each other, Sir Rashleigh having lost all right to mingle in the society of men of honour; but it was hardly possible two such d—d rascals should collogue together without mischief to honest people."

He concluded, by earnestly recommending a toast and tankard, and an attack upon his venison pasty, before I set out in the morning, just to break the cold air on the words.

CHAPTER TWENTY-FIRST

His master's gone, and no one now
Dwells in the halls of Ivor;
Men, dogs, and horses, all are dead,
He is the sole survivor.

— WORDSWORTH

There are few more melancholy sensations than those with which we regard scenes of past pleasure when altered and deserted. In my ride to Osbaldistone Hall, I passed the same objects which I had seen in company with Miss Vernon on the day of our memorable ride from Inglewood Place. Her spirit seemed to keep me company on the way; and when I approached the spot where I had first seen her, I almost listened for the cry of the hounds and the notes of the horn, and strained my eye on the vacant space, as if to descry the fair huntress again descend like an apparition from the hill. But all was silent, and all was solitary. When I reached the Hall, the closed doors and windows, the grass-grown pavement, the courts, which were now so silent, presented a strong contrast to the gay and bustling scene I had so often seen them exhibit, when the merry hunters were going forth to their morning sport, or returning to the daily festival. The joyous bark of the fox-hounds as they were uncoupled, the cries of the huntsmen, the clang of the horses' hoofs, the loud laugh of the old knight at the head of his strong and numerous descendants, were all silenced now and for ever.

While I gazed round the scene of solitude and emptiness, I was inexpressibly affected, even by recollecting those whom, when alive, I had no reason to regard with affection. But the thought that so many youths of goodly presence, warm with life, health, and confidence, were within so short a time cold in the grave, by various, yet all violent and unexpected modes of death, afforded a picture of mortality at which the mind trembled. It was little consolation to me, that I returned a proprietor to the halls which I had left almost like a fugitive. My mind was not habituated to regard the scenes around as my property, and I felt myself an usurper, at least an intruding stranger, and could hardly divest myself of the idea, that some of the bulky forms of my deceased kinsmen were, like the gigantic spectres of a romance, to appear in the gateway, and dispute my entrance.

While I was engaged in these sad thoughts, my follower Andrew, whose feelings were of a very different nature, exerted himself in thundering alternately on every door in the building, calling, at the same time, for admittance, in a tone so loud as to intimate, that *he*, at least, was fully sensible of his newly acquired importance, as squire of the body to the new lord of the manor. At length, timidly and reluctantly, Anthony Syddall, my uncle's aged butler and major-domo, presented himself at a lower window, well fenced with iron bars, and inquired our business.

"We are come to tak your charge aff your hand, my auld friend," said Andrew Fairservice; "ye may gie up your keys as sune as ye like—ilka dog has his day. I'll tak the plate and napery aff your hand. Ye hae had your ain time o't, Mr. Syddall; but ilka bean has its black, and ilka path has its puddle; and it will just set you henceforth to sit at the board-end, as weel as it did Andrew lang syne."

Checking with some difficulty the forwardness of my follower, I explained to Syddall the nature of my right, and the title I had to demand admittance into the Hall, as into my own property. The old man seemed much agitated and distressed, and testified manifest reluctance to give me entrance, although it was couched in a humble and submissive tone. I allowed for the agitation of natural feelings, which really did the old man honour; but continued peremptory in my demand of admittance, explaining to him that his refusal would oblige me to apply for Mr. Inglewood's warrant, and a constable.

"We are come from Mr. Justice Inglewood's this morning," said Andrew, to enforce the menace;—"and I saw Archie Rutledge, the constable, as I came up by;—

the country's no to be lawless as it has been, Mr. Syddall, letting rebels and papists gang on as they best listed."

The threat of the law sounded dreadful in the old man's ears, conscious as he was of the suspicion under which he himself lay, from his religion and his devotion to Sir Hildebrand and his sons. He undid, with fear and trembling, one of the postern entrances, which was secured with many a bolt and bar, and humbly hoped that I would excuse him for fidelity in the discharge of his duty.—I reassured him, and told him I had the better opinion of him for his caution.

"Sae have not I," said Andrew; "Syddall is an auld sneck-drawer; he wadna be looking as white as a sheet, and his knees knocking thegither, unless it were for something mair than he's like to tell us."

"Lord forgive you, Mr. Fairservice," replied the butler, "to say such things of an old friend and fellow-servant!—Where"—following me humbly along the passage—"where would it be your honour's pleasure to have a fire lighted? I fear me you will find the house very dull and dreary—But perhaps you mean to ride back to Inglewood Place to dinner?"

"Light a fire in the library," I replied.

"In the library!" answered the old man;—"nobody has sat there this many a day, and the room smokes, for the daws have built in the chimney this spring, and there were no young men about the Hall to pull them down."

"Our ain reekes better than other folk's fire," said Andrew. "His honour likes the library;—he's nane o' your Papishers, that delight in blinded ignorance, Mr. Syddall."

Very reluctantly as it appeared to me, the butler led the way to the library, and, contrary to what he had given me to expect, the interior of the apartment looked as if it had been lately arranged, and made more comfortable than usual. There was a fire in the grate, which burned clearly, notwithstanding what Syddall had reported of the vent. Taking up the tongs, as if to arrange the wood, but rather perhaps to conceal his own confusion, the butler observed, "it was burning clear now, but had smoked woundily in the morning."

Wishing to be alone, till I recovered myself from the first painful sensations which everything around me recalled, I desired old Syddall to call the land-steward, who lived at about a quarter of a mile from the Hall. He departed with obvious reluctance. I next ordered Andrew to procure the attendance of a couple of stout fellows upon whom he could rely, the population around being Papists, and Sir Rashleigh, who was capable of any desperate enterprise, being in the neighbourhood. Andrew Fairservice undertook this task with great cheerfulness, and promised to bring me up from Trinlay-Knowe, "twa true-blue Presbyterians like himself, that would face and out-face baith the Pope, the Devil, and the Pretender—and blythe will I be o' their company mysell, for the very last night that I was at Osbaldistone Hall, the blight be on ilka blossom in my bit yard, if I didna see that very picture" (pointing to the full-length portrait of Miss Vernon's grandfather) "walking by moonlight in the garden! I tauld your honour I was fleyed wi' a bogle that night, but ye wadna listen to me—I aye thought there was witchcraft and deevilry amang the Papishers, but I ne'er saw't wi' bodily een till that awfu' night."

"Get along, sir," said I, "and bring the fellows you talk of; and see they have more sense than yourself, and are not frightened at their own shadow."

"I hae been counted as gude a man as my neighbours ere now," said Andrew, petulantly; "but I dinna pretend to deal wi' evil spirits." And so he made his exit, as Wardlaw the land-steward made his appearance.

He was a man of sense and honesty, without whose careful management my uncle would have found it difficult to have maintained himself a housekeeper so long as he did. He examined the nature of my right of possession carefully, and admitted it candidly. To any one else the succession would have been a poor one, so much was the land encumbered with debt and mortgage. Most of these, however, were already vested in my father's person, and he was in a train of acquiring the rest; his large gains by the recent rise of the funds having made it a matter of ease and convenience for him to pay off the debt which affected his patrimony.

I transacted much necessary business with Mr. Wardlaw, and detained him to dine with me. We preferred taking our repast in the library, although Syddall strongly recommended our removing to the stone-hall, which he had put in order for the occasion. Meantime Andrew made his appearance with his true-blue recruits, whom he recommended in the highest terms, as "sober decent men, weel founded in doctrinal points, and, above all, as bold as lions." I ordered them something to drink, and they left the room. I observed old Syddall shake his head as they went out, and insisted upon knowing the reason.

"I maybe cannot expect," he said, "that your honour should put confidence in what I say, but it is Heaven's truth for all that—Ambrose Wingfield is as honest a man as lives, but if there is a false knave in the country, it is his brother Lancie;—the whole country knows him to be a spy for Clerk Jobson on the poor gentlemen that have been in trouble—But he's a dissenter, and I suppose that's enough now-a-days."

Having thus far given vent to his feelings,—to which, however, I was little disposed to pay attention,—and having placed the wine on the table, the old butler left the apartment.

Mr. Wardlaw having remained with me until the evening was somewhat advanced, at length bundled up his papers, and removed himself to his own habitation, leaving me in that confused state of mind in which we can hardly say whether we desire company or solitude. I had not, however, the choice betwixt them; for I was left alone in the room of all others most calculated to inspire me with melancholy reflections.

As twilight was darkening the apartment, Andrew had the sagacity to advance his head at the door,—not to ask if I wished for lights, but to recommend them as a measure of precaution against the bogles which still haunted his imagination. I rejected his proffer somewhat peevishly, trimmed the wood-fire, and placing myself in one of the large leathern chairs which flanked the old Gothic chimney, I watched unconsciously the bickering of the blaze which I had fostered. "And this," said I alone, "is the progress and the issue of human wishes! Nursed by the merest trifles, they are first kindled by fancy—nay, are fed upon the vapour of hope, till they consume the substance which they inflame; and man, and his hopes, passions, and desires, sink into a worthless heap of embers and ashes!"

There was a deep sigh from the opposite side of the room, which seemed to reply to my reflections. I started up in amazement—Diana Vernon stood before me, resting on the arm of a figure so strongly resembling that of the portrait so often mentioned, that I looked hastily at the frame, expecting to see it empty. My first idea was, either that I had gone suddenly distracted, or that the spirits of the dead had arisen and been placed before me. A second glance convinced me of my being in my senses, and that the forms which stood before me were real and substantial. It was Diana herself, though paler and thinner than her former self; and it was no tenant of the grave who stood beside her, but Vaughan, or rather Sir Frederick Vernon, in a dress made to imitate that of his ancestor, to whose picture his countenance possessed a family resemblance. He was the first that spoke, for Diana kept her eyes fast fixed on the ground, and astonishment actually riveted my tongue to the roof of my mouth.

"We are your suppliants, Mr. Osbaldistone," he said, "and we claim the refuge and protection of your roof till we can pursue a journey where dungeons and death gape for me at every step."

"Surely," I articulated with great difficulty—"Miss Vernon cannot suppose—you, sir, cannot believe, that I have forgot your interference in my difficulties, or that I am capable of betraying any one, much less you?"

"I know it," said Sir Frederick; "yet it is with the most inexpressible reluctance that I impose on you a confidence, disagreeable perhaps—certainly dangerous—and which I would have specially wished to have conferred on some one else. But my fate, which has chased me through a life of perils and escapes, is now pressing me hard, and I have no alternative."

At this moment the door opened, and the voice of the officious Andrew was heard —"A'm bringin' in the caunles—Ye can light them gin ye like—Can do is easy carried about wi' ane."

I ran to the door, which, as I hoped, I reached in time to prevent his observing who were in the apartment, I turned him out with hasty violence, shut the door after him, and locked it—then instantly remembering his two companions below, knowing his talkative humour, and recollecting Syddall's remark, that one of them was supposed to be a spy, I followed him as fast as I could to the servants' hall, in which they were assembled. Andrew's tongue was loud as I opened the door, but my unexpected appearance silenced him.

"What is the matter with you, you fool?" said I; "you stare and look wild, as if you had seen a ghost."

"N—n—no—nothing," said Andrew.—"but your worship was pleased to be hasty."

"Because you disturbed me out of a sound sleep, you fool. Syddall tells me he cannot find beds for these good fellows tonight, and Mr. Wardlaw thinks there will be no occasion to detain them. Here is a crown-piece for them to drink my health, and thanks for their good-will. You will leave the Hall immediately, my good lads."

The men thanked me for my bounty, took the silver, and withdrew, apparently unsuspicious and contented. I watched their departure until I was sure they could have no further intercourse that night with honest Andrew. And so instantly had I followed on his heels, that I thought he could not have had time to speak two words with them before I interrupted him. But it is wonderful what mischief may be done by only two words. On this occasion they cost two lives.

Having made these arrangements, the best which occurred to me upon the pressure of the moment, to secure privacy for my guests, I returned to report my proceedings, and added, that I had desired Syddall to answer every summons, concluding that it was by his connivance they had been secreted in the Hall. Diana raised her eyes to thank me for the caution.

"You now understand my mystery," she said;—"you know, doubtless, how near and dear that relative is, who has so often found shelter here; and will be no longer surprised that Rashleigh, having such a secret at his command, should rule me with a rod of iron."

Her father added, "that it was their intention to trouble me with their presence as short a time as was possible."

I entreated the fugitives to waive every consideration but what affected their safety, and to rely on my utmost exertions to promote it. This led to an explanation of the circumstances under which they stood.

"I always suspected Rashleigh Osbaldistone," said Sir Frederick; "but his conduct towards my unprotected child, which with difficulty I wrung from her, and his treachery in your father's affairs, made me hate and despise him. In our last interview I concealed not my sentiments, as I should in prudence have attempted to do; and in resentment of the scorn with which I treated him, he added treachery and apostasy to his catalogue of crimes. I at that time fondly hoped that his defection would be of little consequence. The Earl of Mar had a gallant army in Scotland, and Lord Derwentwater, with Forster, Kenmure, Winterton, and others, were assembling forces on the Border. As my connections with these English nobility and gentry were extensive, it was judged proper that I should accompany a detachment of Highlanders, who, under Brigadier MacIntosh of Borlum, crossed the Firth of Forth, traversed the low country of Scotland, and united themselves on the Borders with the English insurgents. My daughter accompanied me through the perils and fatigues of a march so long and difficult."

"And she will never leave her dear father!" exclaimed Miss Vernon, clinging fondly to his arm.

"I had hardly joined our English friends, when I became sensible that our cause was lost. Our numbers diminished instead of increasing, nor were we joined by any except of our own persuasion. The Tories of the High Church remained in general undecided, and at length we were cooped up by a superior force in the little town of Preston. We defended ourselves resolutely for one day. On the next, the hearts of our leaders failed, and they resolved to surrender at discretion. To yield myself up on such terms, were to have laid my head on the block. About twenty or thirty gentlemen were of my mind: we mounted our horses, and placed my daughter, who insisted on sharing my fate, in the centre of our little party. My companions, struck with her courage and filial piety, declared that they would die rather than leave her behind. We rode in a body down a street called Fishergate, which leads to a marshy ground or meadow, extending to the river Ribble, through which one of our party promised to show us a good ford. This marsh had not been strongly invested by the enemy, so that we had only an affair with a patrol of Honeywood's dragoons, whom we dispersed and cut to pieces. We crossed the river, gained the high road to Liverpool, and then dispersed to seek several places of concealment and safety. My fortune led me to Wales, where there are many gentlemen of my religious and political opinions. I could not, however, find a safe opportunity of escaping by sea, and found myself obliged again to draw towards the North. A well-tried friend has appointed to meet me in this neighbourhood, and guide me to a seaport on the Solway, where a sloop is prepared to carry me from my native country for ever. As Osbaldistone Hall was for the present uninhabited, and under the charge of old Syddall, who had been our confidant on former occasions, we drew to it as to a place of known and secure refuge. I resumed a dress which had been used with good effect to scare the superstitious rustics, or domestics, who chanced at any time to see me; and we expected from time to time to hear by Syddall of the arrival of our friendly guide, when your sudden coming hither, and occupying this apartment, laid us under the necessity of submitting to your mercy."

Thus ended Sir Fredericks story, whose tale sounded to me like one told in a vision; and I could hardly bring myself to believe that I saw his daughter's form once more before me in flesh and blood, though with diminished beauty and sunk spirits. The buoyant vivacity with which she had resisted every touch of adversity, had now assumed the air of composed and submissive, but dauntless resolution and constancy. Her father, though aware and jealous of the effect of her praises on my mind, could not forbear expatiating upon them.

"She has endured trials," he said, "which might have dignified the history of a martyr;—she has faced danger and death in various shapes;—she has undergone toil and privation, from which men of the strongest frame would have shrunk;—she has spent the day in darkness, and the night in vigil, and has never breathed a murmur of weakness or complaint. In a word, Mr. Osbaldistone," he concluded, "she is a worthy offering to that God, to whom" (crossing himself) "I shall dedicate her, as all that is left dear or precious to Frederick Vernon."

There was a silence after these words, of which I well understood the mournful import. The father of Diana was still as anxious to destroy my hopes of being united to her now as he had shown himself during our brief meeting in Scotland.

"We will now," said he to his daughter, "intrude no farther on Mr. Osbaldistone's time, since we have acquainted him with the circumstances of the miserable guests who claim his protection."

I requested them to stay, and offered myself to leave the apartment. Sir Frederick observed, that my doing so could not but excite my attendant's suspicion; and that the place of their retreat was in every respect commodious, and furnished by Syddall with all they could possibly want. "We might perhaps have even contrived to remain there, concealed from your observation; but it would have been unjust to decline the most absolute reliance on your honour."

"You have done me but justice," I replied.—"To you, Sir Frederick, I am but little known; but Miss Vernon, I am sure, will bear me witness that"—

"I do not want my daughter's evidence," he said, politely, but yet with an air calculated to prevent my addressing myself to Diana, "since I am prepared to believe all that is worthy of Mr. Francis Osbaldistone. Permit us now to retire; we must take repose when we can, since we are absolutely uncertain when we may be called upon to renew our perilous journey."

He drew his daughter's arm within his, and with a profound reverence, disappeared with her behind the tapestry.

CHAPTER TWENTY-SECOND

> But now the hand of fate is on the curtain,
> And gives the scene to light.
>
> — DON SEBASTIAN

I felt stunned and chilled as they retired. Imagination, dwelling on an absent object of affection, paints her not only in the fairest light, but in that in which we most desire to behold her. I had thought of Diana as she was, when her parting tear dropped on my cheek—when her parting token, received from the wife of MacGregor, augured her wish to convey into exile and conventual seclusion the remembrance of my affection. I saw her; and her cold passive manner, expressive of little except composed melancholy, disappointed, and, in some degree, almost offended me.

In the egotism of my feelings, I accused her of indifference—of insensibility. I upbraided her father with pride—with cruelty—with fanaticism,—forgetting that both were sacrificing their interest, and Diana her inclination, to the discharge of what they regarded as their duty.

Sir Frederick Vernon was a rigid Catholic, who thought the path of salvation too narrow to be trodden by an heretic; and Diana, to whom her father's safety had been for many years the principal and moving spring of thoughts, hopes, and actions, felt that she had discharged her duty in resigning to his will, not alone her property in the world, but the dearest affections of her heart. But it was not surprising that I could not, at such a moment, fully appreciate these honourable motives; yet my spleen sought no ignoble means of discharging itself.

"I am contemned, then," I said, when left to run over the tenor of Sir Frederick's communications—"I am contemned, and thought unworthy even to exchange words with her. Be it so; they shall not at least prevent me from watching over her safety. Here will I remain as an outpost, and, while under my roof at least, no danger shall threaten her, if it be such as the arm of one determined man can avert."

I summoned Syddall to the library. He came, but came attended by the eternal Andrew, who, dreaming of great things in consequence of my taking possession of the Hall and the annexed estates, was resolved to lose nothing for want of keeping himself in view; and, as often happens to men who entertain selfish objects, overshot his mark, and rendered his attentions tedious and inconvenient.

His unrequired presence prevented me from speaking freely to Syddall, and I dared not send him away for fear of increasing such suspicions as he might entertain from his former abrupt dismissal from the library. "I shall sleep here, sir," I said, giving them directions to wheel nearer to the fire an old-fashioned day-bed, or settee. "I have much to do, and shall go late to bed."

Syddall, who seemed to understand my look, offered to procure me the accommodation of a mattress and some bedding. I accepted his offer, dismissed my attendant, lighted a pair of candles, and desired that I might not be disturbed till seven in the ensuing morning.

The domestics retired, leaving me to my painful and ill-arranged reflections, until nature, worn out, should require some repose.

I endeavoured forcibly to abstract my mind from the singular circumstances in which I found myself placed. Feelings which I had gallantly combated while the exciting object was remote, were now exasperated by my immediate neighbourhood to her whom I was so soon to part with for ever. Her name was written in every book which I attempted to peruse; and her image forced itself on me in whatever train of thought I strove to engage myself. It was like the officious slave of Prior's Solomon,—

Abra was ready ere I named her name,
And when I called another, Abra came.

I alternately gave way to these thoughts, and struggled against them, sometimes yielding to a mood of melting tenderness of sorrow which was scarce natural to me, sometimes arming myself with the hurt pride of one who had experienced what he esteemed unmerited rejection. I paced the library until I had chafed myself into a temporary fever. I then threw myself on the couch, and endeavoured to dispose myself to sleep;—but it was in vain that I used every effort to compose myself—that I lay without movement of finger or of muscle, as still as if I had been already a corpse —that I endeavoured to divert or banish disquieting thoughts, by fixing my mind on some act of repetition or arithmetical process. My blood throbbed, to my feverish apprehension, in pulsations which resembled the deep and regular strokes of a distant fulling-mill, and tingled in my veins like streams of liquid fire.

At length I arose, opened the window, and stood by it for some time in the clear moonlight, receiving, in part at least, that refreshment and dissipation of ideas from the clear and calm scene, without which they had become beyond the command of my own volition. I resumed my place on the couch—with a heart, Heaven knows, not lighter but firmer, and more resolved for endurance. In a short time a slumber crept over my senses; still, however, though my senses slumbered, my soul was awake to the painful feelings of my situation, and my dreams were of mental anguish and external objects of terror.

I remember a strange agony, under which I conceived myself and Diana in the power of MacGregor's wife, and about to be precipitated from a rock into the lake; the signal was to be the discharge of a cannon, fired by Sir Frederick Vernon, who, in the dress of a Cardinal, officiated at the ceremony. Nothing could be more lively than the impression which I received of this imaginary scene. I could paint, even at this moment, the mute and courageous submission expressed in Diana's features—the wild and distorted faces of the executioners, who crowded around us with "mopping and mowing;" grimaces ever changing, and each more hideous than that which preceded. I saw the rigid and inflexible fanaticism painted in the face of the father—I saw him lift the fatal match—the deadly signal exploded—It was repeated again and again and again, in rival thunders, by the echoes of the surrounding cliffs, and I awoke from fancied horror to real apprehension.

The sounds in my dream were not ideal. They reverberated on my waking ears, but it was two or three minutes ere I could collect myself so as distinctly to understand that they proceeded from a violent knocking at the gate. I leaped from my couch in great apprehension, took my sword under my arm, and hastened to forbid the admission of any one. But my route was necessarily circuitous, because the library looked not upon the quadrangle, but into the gardens. When I had reached a staircase, the windows of which opened upon the entrance court, I heard the feeble and intimidated tones of Syddall expostulating with rough voices, which demanded admittance, by the warrant of Justice Standish, and in the King's name, and threatened the old domestic with the heaviest penal consequences if he refused instant obedience. Ere they had ceased, I heard, to my unspeakable provocation, the voice of Andrew bidding Syddall stand aside, and let him open the door.

"If they come in King George's name, we have naething to fear—we hae spent baith bluid and gowd for him—We dinna need to darn ourselves like some folks, Mr. Syddall—we are neither Papists nor Jacobites, I trow."

It was in vain I accelerated my pace down stairs; I heard bolt after bolt withdrawn by the officious scoundrel, while all the time he was boasting his own and his master's loyalty to King George; and I could easily calculate that the party must enter before I could arrive at the door to replace the bars. Devoting the back of Andrew Fairservice to the cudgel so soon as I should have time to pay him his deserts, I ran back to the library, barricaded the door as I best could, and hastened to that by which Diana and her father entered, and begged for instant admittance. Diana herself undid the door. She was ready dressed, and betrayed neither perturbation nor fear.

"Danger is so familiar to us," she said, "that we are always prepared to meet it. My father is already up—he is in Rashleigh's apartment. We will escape into the garden, and thence by the postern-gate (I have the key from Syddall in case of need.) into the wood—I know its dingles better than any one now alive. Keep them a few minutes in play. And, dear, dear Frank, once more fare-thee-well!"

She vanished like a meteor to join her father, and the intruders were rapping violently, and attempting to force the library door by the time I had returned into it.

"You robber dogs!" I exclaimed, wilfully mistaking the purpose of their disturbance, "if you do not instantly quit the house I will fire my blunderbuss through the door."

"Fire a fule's bauble!" said Andrew Fairservice; "it's Mr. Clerk Jobson, with a legal warrant"—

"To search for, take, and apprehend," said the voice of that execrable pettifogger, "the bodies of certain persons in my warrant named, charged of high treason under the 13th of King William, chapter third."

And the violence on the door was renewed. "I am rising, gentlemen," said I, desirous to gain as much time as possible—"commit no violence—give me leave to look at your warrant, and, if it is formal and legal, I shall not oppose it."

"God save great George our King!" ejaculated Andrew. "I tauld ye that ye would find nae Jacobites here."

Spinning out the time as much as possible, I was at length compelled to open the door, which they would otherwise have forced.

Mr. Jobson entered, with several assistants, among whom I discovered the younger Wingfield, to whom, doubtless, he was obliged for his information, and exhibited his warrant, directed not only against Frederick Vernon, an attainted traitor, but also against Diana Vernon, spinster, and Francis Osbaldistone, gentleman, accused of misprision of treason. It was a case in which resistance would have been madness; I therefore, after capitulating for a few minutes' delay, surrendered myself a prisoner.

I had next the mortification to see Jobson go straight to the chamber of Miss Vernon, and I learned that from thence, without hesitation or difficulty, he went to the room where Sir Frederick had slept. "The hare has stolen away," said the brute, "but her form is warm—the greyhounds will have her by the haunches yet."

A scream from the garden announced that he prophesied too truly. In the course of five minutes, Rashleigh entered the library with Sir Frederick Vernon and his daughter as prisoners.

"The fox," he said, "knew his old earth, but he forgot it could be stopped by a careful huntsman.—I had not forgot the garden-gate, Sir Frederick—or, if that title suits you better, most noble Lord Beauchamp."

"Rashleigh," said Sir Frederick, "thou art a detestable villain!"

"I better deserved the name, Sir Knight, or my Lord, when, under the direction of an able tutor, I sought to introduce civil war into the bosom of a peaceful country. But I have done my best," said he, looking upwards, "to atone for my errors."

I could hold no longer. I had designed to watch their proceedings in silence, but I felt that I must speak or die. "If hell," I said, "has one complexion more hideous than another, it is where villany is masked by hypocrisy."

"Ha! my gentle cousin," said Rashleigh, holding a candle towards me, and surveying me from head to foot; "right welcome to Osbaldistone Hall!—I can forgive your spleen—It is hard to lose an estate and a mistress in one night; for we shall take possession of this poor manor-house in the name of the lawful heir, Sir Rashleigh Osbaldistone."

While Rashleigh braved it out in this manner, I could see that he put a strong force upon his feelings, both of anger and shame. But his state of mind was more obvious when Diana Vernon addressed him. "Rashleigh," she said, "I pity you—for, deep as the evil is which you have laboured to do me, and the evil you have actually done, I cannot hate you so much as I scorn and pity you. What you have now done may be the work of an hour, but will furnish you with reflection for your life—of what nature I leave to your own conscience, which will not slumber for ever."

Rashleigh strode once or twice through the room, came up to the side-table, on which wine was still standing, and poured out a large glass with a trembling hand; but when he saw that we observed his tremor, he suppressed it by a strong effort, and, looking at us with fixed and daring composure, carried the bumper to his head without spilling a drop. "It is my father's old burgundy," he said, looking to Jobson; "I am glad there is some of it left.—You will get proper persons to take care of old butler, and that foolish Scotch rascal. Meanwhile we will convey these persons to a more proper place of custody. I have provided the old family coach for your convenience," he said, "though I am not ignorant that even the lady could brave the night-air on foot or on horseback, were the errand more to her mind."

Andrew wrung his hands.—"I only said that my master was surely speaking to a ghaist in the library—and the villain Lancie to betray an auld friend, that sang aff the same Psalm-book wi' him every Sabbath for twenty years!"

He was turned out of the house, together with Syddall, without being allowed to conclude his lamentation. His expulsion, however, led to some singular consequences. Resolving, according to his own story, to go down for the night where Mother Simpson would give him a lodging for old acquaintance' sake, he had just got clear of the avenue, and into the old wood, as it was called, though it was now used as a pasture-ground rather than woodland, when he suddenly lighted on a drove of Scotch cattle, which were lying there to repose themselves after the day's journey. At this Andrew was in no way surprised, it being the well-known custom of his countrymen, who take care of those droves, to quarter themselves after night upon the best unenclosed grass-ground they can find, and depart before day-break to escape paying for their night's lodgings. But he was both surprised and startled, when a Highlander, springing up, accused him of disturbing the cattle, and refused him to pass forward till he had spoken to his master. The mountaineer conducted Andrew into a thicket, where he found three or four more of his countrymen. "And," said Andrew, "I saw sune they were ower mony men for the drove; and from the questions they put to me, I judged they had other tow on their rock."

They questioned him closely about all that had passed at Osbaldistone Hall, and seemed surprised and concerned at the report he made to them.

"And troth," said Andrew, "I tauld them a' I ken'd; for dirks and pistols were what I could never refuse information to in a' my life."

They talked in whispers among themselves, and at length collected their cattle together, and drove them close up to the entrance of the avenue, which might be half a mile distant from the house. They proceeded to drag together some felled trees which lay in the vicinity, so as to make a temporary barricade across the road, about fifteen yards beyond the avenue. It was now near daybreak, and there was a pale eastern gleam mingled with the fading moonlight, so that objects could be discovered with some distinctness. The lumbering sound of a coach drawn by four horses, and escorted by six men on horseback, was heard coming up the avenue. The Highlanders listened attentively. The carriage contained Mr. Jobson and his unfortunate prisoners. The escort consisted of Rashleigh, and of several horsemen, peace-officers and their assistants. So soon as we had passed the gate at the head of the avenue, it was shut behind the cavalcade by a Highland-man, stationed there for that purpose. At the same time the carriage was impeded in its farther progress by the cattle, amongst which we were involved, and by the barricade in front. Two of the escort dismounted to remove the felled trees, which they might think were left there by accident or carelessness. The others began with their whips to drive the cattle from the road.

"Who dare abuse our cattle?" said a rough voice.—"Shoot him, Angus!"

Rashleigh instantly called out—"A rescue! a rescue!" and, firing a pistol, wounded the man who spoke.

"*Claymore!*" cried the leader of the Highlanders, and a scuffle instantly commenced. The officers of the law, surprised at so sudden an attack, and not usually possessing the most desperate bravery, made but an imperfect defence, considering the superiority of their numbers. Some attempted to ride back to the Hall, but on a pistol being fired from behind the gate, they conceived themselves surrounded, and at length galloped of in different directions. Rashleigh, meanwhile, had dismounted, and on foot had maintained a desperate and single-handed conflict with the leader of the band. The window of the carriage, on my side, permitted me to witness it. At length Rashleigh dropped.

"Will you ask forgiveness for the sake of God, King James, and auld friendship?" said a voice which I knew right well.

"No, never!" said Rashleigh, firmly.

"Then, traitor, die in your treason!" retorted MacGregor, and plunged his sword in his prostrate antagonist.

In the next moment he was at the carriage door—handed out Miss Vernon, assisted her father and me to alight, and dragging out the attorney, head foremost, threw him under the wheel.

"Mr. Osbaldistone," he said, in a whisper, "you have nothing to fear—I must look after those who have—Your friends will soon be in safety—Farewell, and forget not the MacGregor."

He whistled—his band gathered round him, and, hurrying Diana and her father along with him, they were almost instantly lost in the glades of the forest. The coachman and postilion had abandoned their horses, and fled at the first discharge of firearms; but the animals, stopped by the barricade, remained perfectly still; and well for Jobson that they did so, for the slightest motion would have dragged the wheel over his body. My first object was to relieve him, for such was the rascal's terror that he never could have risen by his own exertions. I next commanded him to observe, that I had neither taken part in the rescue, nor availed myself of it to make my escape, and enjoined him to go down to the Hall, and call some of his party, who had been left there, to assist the wounded.— But Jobson's fears had so mastered and controlled every faculty of his mind, that he was totally incapable of moving. I now resolved to go myself, but in my way I stumbled over the body of a man, as I thought, dead or dying. It was, however, Andrew Fairservice, as well and whole as ever he was in his life, who had only taken this recumbent posture to avoid the slashes, stabs, and pistol-balls, which for a moment or two were flying in various directions. I was so glad to find him, that I did not inquire how he came thither, but instantly commanded his assistance.

Rashleigh was our first object. He groaned when I approached him, as much through spite as through pain, and shut his eyes, as if determined, like Iago, to speak no word more. We lifted him into the carriage, and performed the same good office to another wounded man of his party, who had been left on the field. I then with difficulty made Jobson understand that he must enter the coach also, and support Sir Rashleigh upon the seat. He obeyed, but with an air as if he but half comprehended my meaning. Andrew and I turned the horses' heads round, and opening the gate of the avenue, led them slowly back to Osbaldistone Hall.

Some fugitives had already reached the Hall by circuitous routes, and alarmed its garrison by the news that Sir Rashleigh, Clerk Jobson, and all their escort, save they who escaped to tell the tale, had been cut to pieces at the head of the avenue by a whole regiment of wild Highlanders. When we reached the mansion, therefore, we heard such a buzz as arises when bees are alarmed, and mustering in their hives. Mr. Jobson, however, who had now in some measure come to his senses, found voice enough to make himself known. He was the more anxious to be released from the carriage, as one of his companions (the peace-officer) had, to his inexpressible terror, expired by his side with a hideous groan.

Sir Rashleigh Osbaldistone was still alive, but so dreadfully wounded that the bottom of the coach was filled with his blood, and long traces of it left from the entrance-door into the stone-hall, where he was placed in a chair, some attempting to stop the bleeding with cloths, while others called for a surgeon, and no one seemed willing to go to fetch one. "Torment me not," said the wounded man—"I know no assistance can avail me—I am a dying man." He raised himself in his chair, though the damps and chill of death were already on his brow, and spoke with a firmness which seemed beyond his strength. "Cousin Francis," he said, "draw near to me." I approached him as he requested.—"I wish you only to know that the pangs of death do not alter I one iota of my feelings towards you. I hate you!" he said, the expression of rage throwing a hideous glare into the eyes which were soon to be closed for ever —"I hate you with a hatred as intense, now while I lie bleeding and dying before you, as if my foot trode on your neck."

"I have given you no cause, sir," I replied,—"and for your own sake I could wish your mind in a better temper."

"You *have* given me cause," he rejoined. "In love, in ambition, in the paths of interest, you have crossed and blighted me at every turn. I was born to be the honour of my father's house—I have been its disgrace—and all owing to you. My very patrimony has become yours—Take it," he said, "and may the curse of a dying man cleave to it!"

In a moment after he had uttered this frightful wish, he fell back in the chair; his eyes became glazed, his limbs stiffened, but the grin and glare of mortal hatred survived even the last gasp of life. I will dwell no longer on so painful a picture, nor say any more of the death of Rashleigh, than that it gave me access to my rights of inheritance without farther challenge, and that Jobson found himself compelled to allow, that the ridiculous charge of misprision of high treason was got up on an affidavit which he made with the sole purpose of favouring Rashleigh's views, and removing me from Osbaldistone Hall. The rascal's name was struck off the list of attorneys, and he was reduced to poverty and contempt.

I returned to London when I had put my affairs in order at Osbaldistone Hall, and felt happy to escape from a place which suggested so many painful recollections. My anxiety was now acute to learn the fate of Diana and her father. A French gentleman who came to London on commercial business, was intrusted with a letter to me from Miss Vernon, which put my mind at rest respecting their safety.

It gave me to understand that the opportune appearance of MacGregor and his party was not fortuitous. The Scottish nobles and gentry engaged in the insurrection, as well as those of England, were particularly anxious to further the escape of Sir Frederick Vernon, who, as an old and trusted agent of the house of Stuart, was possessed of matter enough to have ruined half Scotland. Rob Roy, of whose sagacity and courage they had known so many proofs, was the person whom they pitched upon to assist his escape, and the place of meeting was fixed at Osbaldistone Hall. You have already heard how nearly the plan had been disconcerted by the unhappy Rashleigh. It succeeded, however, perfectly; for when once Sir Frederick and his daughter were again at large, they found horses prepared for them, and, by MacGregor's knowledge of the country—for every part of Scotland, and of the north of England, was familiar to him—were conducted to the western sea-coast, and safely embarked for France. The same gentleman told me that Sir Frederick was not expected to survive for many months a lingering disease, the consequence of late hardships and privations. His daughter was placed in a convent, and although it was her father's wish she should take the veil, he was understood to refer the matter entirely to her own inclinations.

When these news reached me, I frankly told the state of my affections to my father, who was not a little startled at the idea of my marrying a Roman Catholic. But he was very desirous to see me "settled in life," as he called it; and he was sensible that, in joining him with heart and hand in his commercial labours, I had sacrificed my own inclinations. After a brief hesitation, and several questions asked and answered to his satisfaction, he broke out with—"I little thought a son of mine should have been Lord of Osbaldistone Manor, and far less that he should go to a French convent for a spouse. But so dutiful a daughter cannot but prove a good wife. You have worked at the desk to please me, Frank; it is but fair you should wive to please yourself."

How I sped in my wooing, Will Tresham, I need not tell you. You know, too, how long and happily I lived with Diana. You know how I lamented her; but you do not—cannot know, how much she deserved her husband's sorrow.

I have no more of romantic adventure to tell, nor, indeed, anything to communicate farther, since the latter incidents of my life are so well known to one who has shared, with the most friendly sympathy, the joys, as well as the sorrows, by which its scenes have been chequered. I often visited Scotland, but never again saw the bold Highlander who had such an influence on the early events of my life. I learned, however, from time to time, that he continued to maintain his ground among the mountains of Loch Lomond, in despite of his powerful enemies, and that he even obtained, to a certain degree, the connivance of Government to his self-elected office of protector of the Lennox, in virtue of which he levied black-mail with as much regularity as the proprietors did their ordinary rents. It seemed impossible that his life should have concluded without a violent end. Nevertheless he died in old age and by a peaceful death, some time about the year 1733, and is still remembered in his country as the Robin Hood of Scotland—the dread of the wealthy, but the friend of the poor—and possessed of many qualities, both of head and heart, which would have graced a less equivocal profession than that to which his fate condemned him.

Old Andrew Fairservice used to say, that "There were many things ower bad for blessing, and ower gude for banning, like Rob Roy."

Here the original manuscript ends somewhat abruptly. I have reason to think that what followed related to private affairs.

POSTSCRIPT

The second article of the Appendix to the Introduction to Rob Roy contains two curious letters respecting the arrest of Mr. Grahame of Killearn by that daring freebooter, while levying the Duke of Montrose's rents. These were taken from scroll copies in the possession of his Grace the present Duke, who kindly permitted the use of them in the present publication.—The Novel had but just passed through the press, when the Right Honourable Mr. Peel—whose important state avocations do not avert his attention from the interests of literature—transmitted to the author copies of the original letters and enclosure, of which he possessed only the rough draught. The originals were discovered in the State Paper Office, by the indefatigable researches of Mr. Lemon, who is daily throwing more light on that valuable collection of records. From the documents with which the Author has been thus kindly favoured, he is enabled to fill up the addresses which were wanting in the scrolls. That of the 21st Nov. 1716 is addressed to Lord Viscount Townshend, and is accompanied by one of the same date to Robert Pringle, Esquire, Under-Secretary of State, which is here inserted as relative to so curious an incident:—

Letter from the Duke of Montrose, to Robert Pringle, Esq., Under-Secretary to Lord Viscount Townshend.

"Sr, *Glasgow,* 21 *Nov.* 1716.

"Haveing had so many dispatches to make this night, I hope ye'l excuse me that I make use of another hand to give yow a short account of the occasion of this express, by which I have written to my Ld. Duke of Roxburgh, and my Lord Townshend, which I hope ye'l gett carefully deleivered.

"Mr. Graham, younger of Killearn, being on Munday last in Menteith att a country house, collecting my rents, was about nine o'clock that same night surprised by Rob Roy with a party of his men in arms, who haveing surrounded the house and secured the avenues, presented their guns in at the windows, while he himself entered the room with some others with cokt pistolls, and seased Killearn with all his money, books, papers, and bonds, and carryed all away with him to the hills, at the same time ordering Killearn to write a letter to me (of which ye have the copy inclosed), proposeing a very honourable treaty to me. I must say this story was as surprising to me as it was insolent; and it must bring a very great concern upon me, that this gentleman, my near relation, should be brought to suffer all the barbaritys and crueltys, which revenge and mallice may suggest to these miscreants, for his haveing acted a faithfull part in the service of the Government, and his affection to me in my concerns.

"I need not be more particular to you, since I know that my Letter to my Lord Townshend will come into your hands, so shall only now give you the assurances of my being, with great sincerity,

"Sr, yr most humble servant, (Signed) "Montrose."

"I long exceedingly for a return of my former dispatches to the Secretary's about Methven and Colll Urquhart, and my wife's cousins, Balnamoon and Phinaven.

"I must beg yow'll give my humble service to Mr. Secretary Methven, and tell him that I must refer him to what I have written to My Lord Townshend in this affair of Rob Roy, believing it was needless to trouble both with letters."

Examined, Robt. Lemon, *Deputy Keeper of State Papers*
State Paper Office,
Nov. 4, 1829

Note.—The enclosure referred to in the preceding letter is another copy of the letter which Mr. Grahame of Killearn was compelled by Rob Roy to write to the Duke of Montrose, and is exactly the same as the one enclosed in his Grace's letter to Lord Townshend, dated November 21st, 1716. R. L.

The last letter in the Appendix No. II. (28th November), acquainting the Government with Killearn's being set at liberty, is also addressed to the Under-Secretary of State, Mr. Pringle.

The Author may also here remark, that immediately previous to the insurrection of 1715, he perceives, from some notes of information given to Government, that Rob Roy appears to have been much employed and trusted by the Jacobite party, even in the very delicate task of transporting specie to the Earl of Breadalbane, though it might have somewhat resembled trusting Don Raphael and Ambrose de Lamela with the church treasure.

NOTES

VOLUME ONE

1. The Grey Stone of MacGregor.
    I have been informed that, at no very remote period, it was proposed to take this large stone, which marks the grave of Dugald Ciar Mhor, and convert it to the purpose of the lintel of a window, the threshold of a door, or some such mean use. A man of the clan MacGregor, who was somewhat deranged, took fire at this insult; and when the workmen came to remove the stone, planted himself upon it, with a broad axe in his hand, swearing he would dash out the brains of any one who should disturb the monument. Athletic in person, and insane enough to be totally regardless of consequences, it was thought best to give way to his humour; and the poor madman kept sentinel on the stone day and night, till the proposal of removing it was entirely dropped.
2. Dugald Ciar Mhor.
    The above is the account which I find in a manuscript history of the clan MacGregor, of which I was indulged with a perusal by Donald MacGregor, Esq., late Major of the 33d regiment, where great pains have been taken to collect traditions and written documents concerning the family. But an ancient and constant tradition, preserved among the inhabitants of the country, and particularly those of the clan MacFarlane, relieves Dugald Ciar Mhor of the guilt of murdering the youths, and lays the blame on a certain Donald or Duncan Lean, who performed the act of cruelty, with the assistance of a gillie who attended him, named Charlioch, or Charlie. They say that the homicides dared not again join their clan, but that they resided in a wild and solitary state as outlaws, in an unfrequented part of the MacFarlanes' territory. Here they lived for some time undisturbed, till they committed an act of brutal violence on two defenceless women, a mother and daughter of the MacFarlane clan. In revenge of this atrocity, the MacFarlanes hunted them down, and shot them. It is said that the younger ruffian, Charlioch, might have escaped, being remarkably swift of foot. But his crime became his punishment, for the female whom he had outraged had defended herself desperately, and had stabbed him with his own dirk in the thigh. He was lame from the wound, and was the more easily overtaken and killed.
    I always inclined to think this last the true edition of the story, and that the guilt was transferred to Dugald Ciar Mhor, as a man of higher name, but I have learned that Dugald was in truth dead several years before the battle—my authority being his representative, Mr. Gregorson of Ardtornish.
3. See *Statistcal Account of Scotland*, 1st edition, vol. xviii. p. 332. Parish of Kippen.
4. See Appendix, No. I.
5. His courage and affectation of foppery were united, which is less frequently the case, with a spirit of innate modesty. He is thus described in Lord Binning's satirical verses, entitled "Argyle's Levee:"

    "*Six times had Harry bowed unseen,*
    Before he dared advance;
    The Duke then, turning round well pleased,
    Said, 'Sure you've been in France!
    A more polite and jaunty man
    I never saw before:'
    Then Harry bowed, and blushed, and bowed,
    And strutted to the door."

    See a Collection of original Poems, by Scotch Gentlemen, vol. ii. p. 125.
6. Mr. Grahame of Gartmore's Causes of the Disturbances in the Highlands. See Jamieson's edition of Burt's Letters from the North of Scotland, Appendix, vol. ii. p. 348.
7. "At night they arrived at Luss, where they were joined by Sir Humphrey Colquhoun of Luss, and James Grant of Plascander, his son-in-law, followed by forty or fifty stately fellows in their short hose and belted plaids, armed each of them with a well-fixed gun on his shoulder, a strong handsome target, with a sharp-pointed steel of above half an ell in length screwed into the navel of it, on his left arm, a sturdy claymore by his side, and a pistol or two, with a dirk and knife, in his belt."—*Rae's History of the Rebellion*, 4to, p. 287.
8. The Loch Lomond Expedition.
    The Loch Lomond expedition was judged worthy to form a separate pamphlet, which I have not seen; but, as quoted by the historian Rae, it must be delectable.
    "On the morrow, being Thursday the 13th, they went on their expedition, and about noon came to Inversnaid, the place of danger, where the Paisley men and those of Dumbarton, and several of the other companies, to the number of an hundred men, with the greatest intrepidity leapt on shore, got up to the top of the mountains, and stood a considerable time, beating their drums all the while; but no enemy

NOTES

appearing, they went in quest of their boats, which the rebels had seized, and having casually lighted on some ropes and oars hid among the shrubs, at length they found the boats drawn up a good way on the land, which they hurled down to the loch. Such of them as were not damaged they carried off with them, and such as were, they sank and hewed to pieces. That same night they returned to Luss, and thence next day to Dumbarton, from whence they had at first set out, bringing along with them the whole boats they found in their way on either side of the loch, and in the creeks of the isles, and mooring them under the cannon of the castle. During this expedition, the pinnaces discharging their patararoes, and the men their small-arms, made such a thundering noise, through the multiplied rebounding echoes of the vast mountains on both sides of the loch, that the MacGregors were cowed and frighted away to the rest of the rebels who were encamped at Strath Fillan."—*Rae's History of the Rebellion*, 4to, p. 287.

9. The first of these anecdotes, which brings the highest pitch of civilisation so closely in contact with the half-savage state of society, I have heard told by the late distinguished Dr. Gregory; and the members of his family have had the kindness to collate the story with their recollections and family documents, and furnish the authentic particulars. The second rests on the recollection of an old man, who was present when Rob took French leave of his literary cousin on hearing the drums beat, and communicated the circumstance to Mr. Alexander Forbes, a connection of Dr. Gregory by marriage, who is still alive.
10. The reader will find two original letters of the Duke of Montrose, with that which Mr. Graham of Killearn despatched from his prison-house by the Outlaw's command, in the Appendix, No. II.
11. About 1792, when the author chanced to pass that way while on a tour through the Highlands, a garrison, consisting of a single veteran, was still maintained at Inversnaid. The venerable warder was reaping his barley croft in all peace and tranquillity and when we asked admittance to repose ourselves, he told us we would find the key of the Fort under the door.
12. *Letters from the North of Scotland*, vol. ii. pp. 344, 345.
13. Mad herdsmen—a name given to cattle-stealers [properly one who deserves to fill a *widdie*, or halter].
14. The winds which sweep a wild glen in Badenoch are so called.
15. Appendix, No. III.
16. Such an admission is ascribed to the robber Donald Bean Lean in Waverley, chap. lxii.
17. Some accounts state that Appin himself was Rob Roy's antagonist on this occasion. My recollection, from the account of Invernahyle himself, was as stated in the text. But the period when I received the information is now so distant, that it is possible I may be mistaken. Invernahyle was rather of low stature, but very well made, athletic, and an excellent swordsman.
18. This fatal piece was taken from Robin Oig, when he was seized many years afterwards. It remained in possession of the magistrates before whom he was brought for examination, and now makes part of a small collection of arms belonging to the Author. It is a Spanish-barrelled gun, marked with the letters R. M. C., for Robert MacGregor Campbell.
19. Author's expedition against the MacLarens.

The Author is uncertain whether it is worth while to mention, that he had a personal opportunity of observing, even in his own time, that the king's writ did not pass quite current in the Brass of Balquhidder. There were very considerable debts due by Stewart of Appin (chiefly to the author's family), which were likely to be lost to the creditors, if they could not be made available out of this same farm of Invernenty, the scene of the murder done upon MacLaren.

His family, consisting of several strapping deer-stalkers, still possessed the farm, by virtue of a long lease, for a trifling rent. There was no chance of any one buying it with such an encumbrance, and a transaction was entered into by the MacLarens, who, being desirous to emigrate to America, agreed to sell their lease to the creditors for L500, and to remove at the next term of Whitsunday. But whether they repented their bargain, or desired to make a better, or whether from a mere point of honour, the MacLarens declared they would not permit a summons of removal to be executed against them, which was necessary for the legal completion of the bargain. And such was the general impression that they were men capable of resisting the legal execution of warning by very effectual means, no king's messenger would execute the summons without the support of a military force. An escort of a sergeant and six men was obtained from a Highland regiment lying in Stirling; and the Author, then a writer's apprentice, equivalent to the honourable situation of an attorney's clerk, was invested with the superintendence of the expedition, with directions to see that the messenger discharged his duty fully, and that the gallant sergeant did not exceed his part by committing violence or plunder. And thus it happened, oddly enough, that the Author first entered the romantic scenery of Loch Katrine, of which he may perhaps say he has somewhat extended the reputation, riding in all the dignity of danger, with a front and rear guard, and loaded arms. The sergeant was absolutely a Highland Sergeant Kite, full of stories of Rob Roy and of himself, and a very good companion. We experienced no interruption whatever, and when we came to Invernenty, found the house deserted. We took up our quarters for the night, and used some of the victuals which we found there. On the morning we returned as unmolested as we came.

The MacLarens, who probably never thought of any serious opposition, received their money and went to America, where, having had some slight share in removing them from their *paupera regna*, I sincerely hope they prospered.

The rent of Invernenty instantly rose from L10 to L70 or L80; and when sold, the farm was purchased (I think by the late Laird of MacNab) at a price higher in proportion than what even the modern rent authorised the parties interested to hope for.

NOTES

20. Published in Blackwood's Magazine, vol. ii. p. 228.
21. Childe Harold's Pilgrimage, Canto II.
22. See Appendix, No. VI.
23. Such, at least, was his general character; for when James Mhor, while perpetrating the violence at Edinbilly, called out, in order to overawe opposition, that Glengyle was lying in the moor with a hundred men to patronise his enterprise, Jean Key told him he lied, since she was confident Glengyle would never countenance so scoundrelly a business.
24. Allan Breck Stewart.

    Allan Breck Stewart was a man likely in such a matter to keep his word. James Drummond MacGregor and he, like Katherine and Petruchio, were well matched "for a couple of quiet ones." Allan Breck lived till the beginning of the French Revolution. About 1789, a friend of mine, then residing at Paris, was invited to see some procession which was supposed likely to interest him, from the windows of an apartment occupied by a Scottish Benedictine priest. He found, sitting by the fire, a tall, thin, rawboned, grim-looking, old man, with the petit croix of St. Louis. His visage was strongly marked by the irregular projections of the cheek-bones and chin. His eyes were grey. His grizzled hair exhibited marks of having been red, and his complexion was weather-beaten, and remarkably freckled. Some civilities in French passed between the old man and my friend, in the course of which they talked of the streets and squares of Paris, till at length the old soldier, for such he seemed, and such he was, said with a sigh, in a sharp Highland accent, "Deil ane o' them a' is worth the Hie Street of Edinburgh!" On inquiry, this admirer of Auld Reekie, which he was never to see again, proved to be Allan Breck Stewart. He lived decently on his little pension, and had, in no subsequent period of his life, shown anything of the savage mood in which he is generally believed to have assassinated the enemy and oppressor, as he supposed him, of his family and clan.
25.
26. James died near three months before, but his family might easily remain a long time without the news of that event.
27. It does not appear to whom this letter was addressed. Certainly, from its style and tenor, It was designed for some person high in rank and office—perhaps the King's Advocate for the time.
28. This curious epistle is copied from an authentic narrative of Marshal Wade's proceedings in the Highlands, communicated by the late eminent antiquary, George Chalmers, Esq., to Mr. Robert Jamieson, of the Register House, Edinburgh, and published in the Appendix to an Edition of Burt's Letters from the North of Scotland, 2 vols. 8vo, Edinburgh, 1818.
29. *i.e.* John the Red—John Duke of Argyle, so called from his complexion, more commonly styled "Red John the Warriour."
30. A pass on the eastern margin of Loch Lomond, and an entrance to the Highlands.
31. The introduction of gaugers, supervisors, and examiners, was one of the great complaints of the Scottish nation, though a natural consequence of the Union.
32. This seems to have been written about the time of Wilkes and Liberty.
33. Now called Don Juan.
34. Perhaps from the French *Juste-au-corps*.
35. On occasions of public alarm, in the beginning of the eighteenth century, the horses of the Catholics were often seized upon, as they were always supposed to be on the eve of rising in rebellion.
36. The lines here quoted belong to or were altered from a set of verses at one time very popular in England, beginning, *Tobacco that is withered quite*. In Scotland, the celebrated Ralph Erskine, author of the *Gospel Sonnets*, published what he called "*Smoking Spiritualized*, in two parts. The first part being an Old Meditation upon Smoking Tobacco." It begins—

    This Indian weed now withered quite,
    Tho' green at noon, cut down at night,
    Shows thy decay;
    All flesh is hay.
    Thus thank, and smoke tobacco.

37. The Abbess of Wilton.

    The nunnery of Wilton was granted to the Earl of Pembroke upon its dissolution, by the magisterial authority of Henry VIII., or his son Edward VI. On the accession of Queen Mary, of Catholic memory, the Earl found it necessary to reinstate the Abbess and her fair recluses, which he did with many expressions of his remorse, kneeling humbly to the vestals, and inducting them into the convent and possessions from which he had expelled them. With the accession of Elizabeth, the accommodating Earl again resumed his Protestant faith, and a second time drove the nuns from their sanctuary. The remonstrances of the Abbess, who reminded him of his penitent expressions on the former occasion, could wring from him no other answer than that in the text—"Go spin, you jade!—Go spin!"

NOTES

VOLUME TWO

1. The Laigh Kirk or Crypt of the Cathedral of Glasgow served for more than two centuries as the church of the Barony Parish, and, for a time, was converted into a burial-place. In the restorations of this grand building the crypt was cleared out, and is now admired as one of the richest specimens of Early English architecture existing in Scotland.
2. I have in vain laboured to discover this gentleman's name, and the period of his incumbency. I do not, however, despair to see these points, with some others which may elude my sagacity, satisfactorily elucidated by one or other of the periodical publications which have devoted their pages to explanatory commentaries on my former volumes; and whose research and ingenuity claim my peculiar gratitude, for having discovered many persons and circumstances connected with my narratives, of which I myself never so much as dreamed.
3. This I believe to be an anachronism, as Saint Enoch's Church was not built at the date of the story. [It was founded in 1780, and has since been rebuilt.]
4. A street in the old town of Glasgow.
5. The lads with the kilts or petticoats.
6. The *Gorbals* or "suburbs" are situate on the south side of the River.
7. Executed for treason.
8. Inch-Cailleach is an island in Lochlomond, where the clan of MacGregor were wont to be interred, and where their sepulchres may still be seen. It formerly contained a nunnery: hence the name of Inch-Cailleach, or the island of Old Women.
9. The Saltmarket. This ancient street, situate in the heart of Glasgow, has of late been almost entirely renovated.
10. *Anglice,* the head of the sow to the tail of the pig.
11. The boys in Scotland used formerly to make a sort of Saturnalia in a snow-storm, by pelting passengers with snowballs. But those exposed to that annoyance were excused from it on the easy penalty of a baik (courtesy) from a female, or a bow from a man. It was only the refractory who underwent the storm.
12. *Thigging* and *sorning* was a kind of genteel begging, or rather something between begging and robbing, by which the needy in Scotland used to extort cattle, or the means of subsistence, from those who had any to give.
13. The word *pretty* is or was used in Scotch, in the sense of the German *prachtig,* and meant a gallant, alert fellow, prompt and ready at his weapons.
14. Cutlass.
15. An outlaw.
16. Plundered.
17. Two great clans fought out a quarrel with thirty men of a side, in presence of the king, on the North Inch of Perth, on or about the year 1392; a man was amissing on one side, whose room was filled by a little bandy-legged citizen of Perth. This substitute, Henry Wynd—or, as the Highlanders called him, *Gow Chrom,* that is, the bandy-legged smith—fought well, and contributed greatly to the fate of the battle, without knowing which side he fought on;—so, "To fight for your own hand, like Henry Wynd," passed into a proverb. This incident forms a conspicuous part of the subsequent novel, "The Fair Maid of Perth."
18. *The Chronicle of the Kings of England,* by Sir Richard Baker, with continuations, passed through several editions between 1641 and 1733. Whether any of them contain the passage alluded to is doubtful.
19. Sackless, that is, innocent.
20. Mons Meg.

    Mons Meg was a large old-fashioned piece of ordnance, a great favourite with the Scottish common people; she was fabricated at Mons, in Flanders, in the reign of James IV. or V. of Scotland. This gun figures frequently in the public accounts of the time, where we find charges for grease, to grease Meg's mouth withal (to increase, as every schoolboy knows, the loudness of the report), ribands to deck her carriage, and pipes to play before her when she was brought from the Castle to accompany the Scottish army on any distant expedition. After the Union, there was much popular apprehension that the Regalia of Scotland, and the subordinate Palladium, Mons Meg, would be carried to England to complete the odious surrender of national independence. The Regalia, sequestered from the sight of the public, were generally supposed to have been abstracted in this manner. As for Mons Meg, she remained in the Castle of Edinburgh, till, by order of the Board of Ordnance, she was actually removed to Woolwich about 1757. The Regalia, by his Majesty's special command, have been brought forth from their place of concealment in 1818, and exposed to the view of the people, by whom they must be looked upon with deep associations; and, in this very winter of 1828-9, Mons Meg has been restored to the country, where that, which in every other place or situation was a mere mass of rusty iron, becomes once more a curious monument of antiquity.
21. Fairy Superstition.

    The lakes and precipices amidst which the Avon-Dhu, or River Forth, has its birth, are still, according to popular tradition, haunted by the Elfin people, the most peculiar, but most pleasing, of the creations of Celtic superstitions. The opinions entertained about these beings are much the same with those of the Irish, so exquisitely well narrated by Mr. Crofton Croker. An eminently beautiful little conical hill, near

NOTES

the eastern extremity of the valley of Aberfoil, is supposed to be one of their peculiar haunts, and is the scene which awakens, in Andrew Fairservice, the terror of their power. It is remarkable, that two successive clergymen of this parish of Aberfoil have employed themselves in writing about this fairy superstition. The eldest of these was Robert Kirke, a man of some talents, who translated the Psalms into Gaelic verse. He had formerly been minister at the neighbouring parish of Balquhidder, and died at Aberfoil in 1688, at the early age of forty-two.

He was author of the Secret Commonwealth, which was printed after his death in 1691—(an edition which I have never seen)—and was reprinted in Edinburgh, 1815. This is a work concerning the fairy people, in whose existence Mr. Kirke appears to have been a devout believer. He describes them with the usual powers and qualities ascribed to such beings in Highland tradition.

But what is sufficiently singular, the Rev. Robert Kirke, author of the said treatise, is believed himself to have been taken away by the fairies,—in revenge, perhaps, for having let in too much light upon the secrets of their commonwealth. We learn this catastrophe from the information of his successor, the late amiable and learned Dr. Patrick Grahame, also minister at Aberfoil, who, in his Sketches of Perthshire, has not forgotten to touch upon the *Daoine Schie*, or men of peace.

The Rev. Robert Kirke was, it seems, walking upon a little eminence to the west of the present manse, which is still held a *Dun Shie*, or fairy mound, when he sunk down, in what seemed to mortals a fit, and was supposed to be dead. This, however, was not his real fate.

"Mr. Kirke was the near relation of Graham of Duchray, the ancestor of the present General Graham Stirling. Shortly after his funeral, he appeared, in the dress in which he had sunk down, to a medical relation of his own, and of Duchray. 'Go,' said he to him, 'to my cousin Duchray, and tell him that I am not dead. I fell down in a swoon, and was carried into Fairyland, where I now am. Tell him, that when he and my friends are assembled at the baptism of my child (for he had left his wife pregnant), I will appear in the room, and that if he throws the knife which he holds in his hand over my head, I will be released and restored to human society.' The man, it seems, neglected, for some time, to deliver the message. Mr. Kirke appeared to him a second time, threatening to haunt him night and day till he executed his commission, which at length he did. The time of the baptism arrived. They were seated at table; the figure of Mr. Kirke entered, but the Laird of Duchray, by some unaccountable fatality, neglected to perform the prescribed ceremony. Mr. Kirke retired by another door, and was seen no more. It is firmly believed that he is, at this day, in Fairyland."—(*Sketches of Perthshire*, p. 254.)

[The treatise by Robert Kirke, here mentioned, was written in the year 1691, but not printed till 1815.]

22. Archilowe, of unknown derivation, signifies a peace-offering.
23. *Lymphads*. The galley which the family of Argyle and others of the Clan Campbell carry in their arms.
24. Lochow and the adjacent districts formed the original seat of the Campbells. The expression of a "far cry to Lochow" was proverbial.
25. A rude kind of guillotine formerly used in Scotland.
26. This, as appears from the introductory matter to this Tale, is an anachronism. The slaughter of MacLaren, a retainer of the chief of Appine, by the MacGregors, did not take place till after Rob Roy's death, since it happened in 1736.
27. Clachan of Aberfoil.
    I do not know how this might stand in Mr. Osbaldistone's day, but I can assure the reader, whose curiosity may lead him to visit the scenes of these romantic adventures, that the Clachan of Aberfoil now affords a very comfortable little inn. If he chances to be a Scottish antiquary, it will be an additional recommendation to him, that he will find himself in the vicinity of the Rev. Dr. Patrick Grahame, minister of the gospel at Aberfoil, whose urbanity in communicating information on the subject of national antiquities, is scarce exceeded even by the stores of legendary lore which he has accumulated.—*Original Note.* The respectable clergyman alluded to has been dead for some years.
28. A great feudal oppressor, who, riding on some cruel purpose through the forest of Guiyock, was thrown from his horse, and his foot being caught in the stirrup, was dragged along by the frightened animal till he was torn to pieces. The expression, "Walter of Guiyock's curse," is proverbial.
29. A kind of lighter used in the river Clyde,—probably from the French *abare*.
30. The affairs of Prestonpans and Falkirk are probably alluded to, which marks the time of writing the Memoirs as subsequent to 1745.
31. *i.e.* The throat and the withy. Twigs of willow, such as bind faggots, were often used for halters in Scotland and Ireland, being a sage economy of hemp.
32. The MacRimmons or MacCrimonds were hereditary pipers to the chiefs of MacLeod, and celebrated for their talents. The pibroch said to have been composed by Helen MacGregor is still in existence. See the Introduction to this Novel.
33. "Strike up."
34. A pike.
35. "The memory of Dunbar's legal (?) proceedings at Jedburgh is preserved in the proverbial phrase *Jeddart Justice*, which signifies trial *after* execution."—*Minstrelsy of the Border*, Preface, p. lvi.
36. This pithy verse occurs, it is believed, in Shadwell's play of Bury Fair.

Printed in Great Britain
by Amazon